The crackhead sulks in the middle of the rehab's lobby, his arms crossed, facing us. He's bitching at me and my coworker. The flaking paint and busted chairs lining the wall behind the crackhead amplify his complaints of neglect. Under the baggy tent of his wife-beater you can see guy's ribs. I could improvise a xylophone recital on them, and his arms are about as thick around as my dick.

(*not* a compliment to either of us)

He rocks back and forth, heels to toes. There's no rhythm to the crackhead's movements, just an angry urgency. After running for so long on coke and baking powder he just can't relax. He just can't shut up. The crackhead grits his teeth between sentences and glares, like he wants to show how much the communication is costing him. How it's *my* fault he's nailed to the cross of his own drug-wrecked body.

The crackhead is the epitome of decades of proud Black defiance whittled down into a sickly, whining form. The sullen archetype of a people brought low. Think *Malcolm X*, if Mr. Little had professionally stuck with dealing drugs and just used the preaching as an outlet for his persecution complex.

Twitching in the ruins of the lobby, the crackhead's like the Ghost of Drug Epidemics Past, Present, and Future. Generations of chemical coping, all rolled into one repulsive package. His words whistle from the space where his front teeth should be. The vowels dribble out like a pervert drooling over little girls. I have to actively decipher his gruntings before he sounds like something other than Charlie Brown's teachers.

The crackhead's speaking to me and my coworker. Haranguing us as we slouch behind the front desk. A target is needed for his anger. In rough translation, he says something like: "If y'all so great, what *y'all* fuckers do all day? 'Sides just sittin' around on your asses?"

Well, there's the rampant sadism and pill-popping, but…"We sit around some more," I answer. "It takes a well-trained ass to handle this job."

The voices in my head agree that crackheads all resemble Muppets. *Angry* Muppets.

I think of Kermit smoking rock and start giggling. It's tough to stop.

"Us Techs run this place," my coworker clarifies. The crackhead isn't satisfied with the answer, so Jack gives a broken smile to show that he's been there, too. "We in charge of emergency counseling and stuff. We deal with y'all clients after the counselors spend the day getting y'all all riled up. Talk and listen to ya."

Actually, me and Jack talk *at* the clients and *pretend* to listen to them. We give them abuse and neglect and call it healthcare. Shit, that's good enough, in my opinion.

But, it's not like anyone's going to care what you think when you're as stoned as I am...

SO THIS BABY SEAL WALKS INTO A CLUB . . .

DRUNKEN THEODICIES AND HALFWAY STORIES

ABOUT SELFISHNESS AND SCHADENFREUDE

BY

Your Mother

R.E. Woock, 2022, Colorado Springs, CO:
Anjuli\Kapoor Publishing.

Book Jacket Redesign: Rachael Binford, 2022.

The Passing Years Only Taught Me How to Hate:
An Update for 2022, Just Because No One Asked

You shouldn't need to be told this at your age, but the P.O.V character of a narrative doesn't have to be that narrative's hero. The protagonist isn't naturally equivalent to a story's moral center. Just because someone is telling you a story, it doesn't follow that you need to agree with them, want to grow up to be like them, encourage your own offspring to mingle seed with them, or even want to let them into your home. Protagonist-centered morality is for teevee-watching yokels.

This book's narrator is not a hero. He's not the one running an organization designed to help the discarded members of our merciless society. He's not a mouthpiece for the author's deeply held beliefs. I gave him my cracker-average looks. I gave him my piss-poor education and work ethic and inability to maintain a healthy relationship. Also, I gave him the white-bread, American delusion of '*I'm not racist, but…*' so prevalent then and now. That doesn't make this book an autobiography.

Ezra Pound once wrote that if your work has a structure, you should let the reader know about it. *So…*I tried to write an examination of an idea—in this case, human suffering: what, why, and how funny—made concrete by a place. Something along the lines of Moore's Utopia, Huxley's Island, or DeSade's 120 Days of Sodom. Promise that I've read at least one of those books…

I probably failed in the attempt. Okay, I *grievously* failed in this, but at least that makes it consistent with the rest of my life. And hey, even if you don't pick up on all that, there's still plenty of dick jokes scattered throughout. You're welcome.

Christ, and that excuse-making doesn't even scratch the proverbial surface of the 'unreliable narrator' trope. Smart consumer of media culture that you are, I'm sure you're instantly doubtful when hearing things that you don't agree with, or that sound different from whatever the authority figures shouted when they took the hickory stick to your vulnerable little backside. But, what about when it's shit you want to believe? Are you checking references after you receive a compliment? When your current *Dildo-ATM-Combo* or your favorite *Overly-Emotional-Fleshlight* tells you that you're the best fuck that they've every had? Are you questioning sources and logical fallacies when you hear that *Those People* are the reason that we, as a society, can't have nice things?

Really? Honestly?

Sure. Whatever. Just keep telling yourself that.

Self-justifications aside, let's get back to the main point: narrator ≠ hero.

Maybe there are heroic people out there in the real world. Maybe. According to the folks who own everything and tell you what to think, those heroes are wielders of state-sponsored violence, bravely protecting the status quo and the petroleum companies' profit margins. Back the blue, support the troops, enlist and serve today, *you disposable, peasant fuck.*

(healthcare workers are occasionally given this label during pandemics and other public health crises, but it's temporary and they better not ask for raises)

Heroes? *Seriously*? Most people are just trying to get through another shitty day in a life they never asked for, five minutes late to everything, and hoping that no one can tell how barely they're holding it all together. People may have opportunities for heroic or selfless acts during the day—but, let's be honest: any such 'opportunity' arises and most of us will avert our gaze to wait for the moment to pass. Hey, me too!

This doesn't make us bad people, though we're certainly not deserving of any label more positive. It just identifies us as beaten down, maladjusted to a society not worth adjusting to.

And villains are about as likely in our crappy world as heroes. I say this as someone who'd elbow pregnant teenagers out of the way if it meant getting to the front of the line to lynch a previous head of my state's banking association. He knows what he did. And yes, I flaunt my little-known grudges like I'm trying to impress other '90s hipsters with local obscurities in my CD collection. That's the style of my own irrational *hate-foci*, but you probably have your own.

Maybe the hate-triggers look like single mothers using an EBT card in front of you at Kroger's. I get it. The world presented to us through our newsfeeds and propaganda channels are populated by two-dimensional caricatures with all the moral complexity of a Golden Age comic book. And that may repeatedly convince our dumb asses to vote against own economic interests, just because somebody smarter waived the right flags and religious symbols in our general direction.

And, I get it. Personally, I hate having to share a society with ignorant chucklefucks that cheer on every war, and who will cut their own throats on command just so their neighbors can't have anything nice, either…but, *I get it.*

At heart, we're all just talking monkeys designed to bend at the knee to anyone with the right badge/flag/god. We all spend the majority of each month in a state of low-grade panic about affording rent/food/medical expenses. We're slowly killing ourselves with the stress of underpaid jobs from which we could be fired at a moment's notice. And our owners are helping to kill us faster by outsourcing the pollution and miseries that make their fortunes at the rest of our expense.

Because, hey, Freedom. <waives flag>

None of this is conducive to our individual happiness, to our collective flourishing as human beings. Nothing about the shit state of U.S. society in the 21st Century is designed to promote our peasant asses doing anything beyond going to work, coming home, buying crap, and generally causing as little trouble for our owners as possible. Stay quiet, hate whoever the teevee points you at, and keep your messy little life out of the view of your betters. When they need you to rubberstamp the latest authoritarian strongman or neo-liberal austerities every few years, then you can come out of your caves and shanties to vote. Maybe. Within reason. As long as you look right.

(I spent the first 1.5 years of the coronavirus pandemic hiding inside, alone, doom-scrolling through social media. Pretty sure it broke my brain…and whatever might have been left of my heart after a decade of marriage.)

This book was originally written during the early years of the Bush-Cheney Junta's fascist onslaught. The good ol' U.S. of A. has always been a neo-liberal craphole with patriotic lies paved so shallowly over the bones of the exploited and dispossessed that you heard crunching sounds with every policed step you took. Still, it was impressive how quickly in the 'Post 9/11' era that our society rotted into an omni-surveillance state, one at war with the rest of the world and its own citizenry. The Fourth Amendment was gutted; air travel got a million times worse; the military budget exploded like a moneyshot all over the face of any hopes for our tax dollars ever being spent on us. We're all spied on now, all the time, for everything.

The amount of veterans in my classes the second time I attended college, compared to the first, showed that my generation failed its biggest intelligence test. It was a shock seeing uniformed amputees on television during Bush II's first term. In contrast to the crippled Vietnam War vets of my parents' generation, these folks were my age. That makes a much more visceral impact than, say, watching old actors in Hollywood movies pretend to feel conflicted about napalming Third World villagers. And then, by the end of the Bush II administration, all those below-knee amputees I kept encountering in public were kids younger than me.

Good job, America. Good Fucking Job.

I'm not saying that things weren't bad before the start of this lousy century: I grew up watching the Clinton-era feds barbecue dozens of my fellow Texans while the rest of the country cheered on the slaughter. Our parents hated the homos and mud people enough to vote for Reagan (*twice!*) to shit all over the very concept of a civil society, and each president since that hateful prick cemented every Ruling Class win. In less than a decade, we went from global bloodshed with an inbred, scripture-mouthing puppet like Bush II (*twice!*), to electing a fucking senile, racist, gameshow host because enough of the country had seen saw him *all actin' like a Big Man* on the teevee.

So hey, thanks for being such a reliable voting block for incompetent fascism, *assholes*.

And, of course, after the corpses-in-the-street clusterfuck of his first term, Americans voted for that grifter, again, in even greater numbers. All because the most pagan of U.S. presidents gave you hateful shitbags what you'd always wanted for your Jesus Fan Club in the public sphere: to use your religion as a police truncheon on the rest of us.

Seriously, and from the bottom of my three-sizes-too-small heart: Fuck y'all and the cross you rode in on.

Everything's bad all over, and it's only going to get worse. The Ruling Class is currently prying the gold fillings from the corpse of the American Empire. It's only a matter of time before our owners decide that another splendid little world war would be a great way to decrease the surplus population while tweaking those Q3 profit margins. Your neighbors are stockpiling an arsenal in preparation for hunting season on all you commies they didn't see in church last week. It's going to cost another kidney to pay the medical debt on the small pharmacy of pills that drag your ass through each miserable day. All our water is poisoned, and the skies are on fire.

So anyways, here's a new goddamn edition of something that probably shouldn't have been created in the first place. In that, it's not so different from everything else cheating you out of your meager wages in this shitty grift of a society. I was scrubbing toilets in a western Oregon nuthouse when I had a bachelor's degree. I weighed the same as I did in Sixth Grade and could count my ribs in the mirror. At 40, I was living in yet-another basement apartment to afford my medical debt and student loans. The first year I ever had a viable income was the same one I started noticing all those gray hairs on my ballsack.

I wanted to share that sense of '*you gotta be fuckin' kidding me*' with the rest of y'all. Then, I realized that most of you probably also wake up with that same burning feeling in your gut, of having been cheated of a decent life in a world that doesn't have to suck anywhere near as bad or constantly as it does. But, it does. It really fucking does.

Because, hey, Freedom. <waives cross>

Robert Anton Wilson once remarked that literature without hope was a crime against the younger generations. This work, I suppose, is guilty as charged. I mean, not like I'm running an organized kiddie-fuck-pyramid-scheme like the Catholic Church, and it's not like I'm cutting SNAP funding for impoverished children like our elected representatives, but *still.* Sorry, kids.

Shit really is terrible all over. I don't know how to make it better. But I do know that enough of you stupid cocksuckers will cheer as everything goes up in flames around us, just so long as no one can force you to share a lunch counter with *Those People*. Or, say, make you follow simple public health regulations in order to avoid killing your fellow citizens.

So yeah, I suck, but it's not like you grew up as anything to be proud of, either.

Hope you enjoy this new edition of So This Baby Seal Walks Into A Club… If you don't, I hope you've realized it a day too late to ask for a refund.

I vaguely recall, years ago, hearing Kimya Dawson sing something about, '*Take all that pain, and turn it into love*.' I obviously didn't—you have the proof in your hands—and now it's way too late to ever learn how. For me. For all of us.

Hey, whatever. *Fukkit*. See you all in Hell, which is apparently just a page-turn away…

Yeah, so…

This is about a bunch of stuff that happened when I worked at a rehab back in the early 2000s.

Some of it's funny.

Some of it's not.

Some of it's horrific.

Some of it's not.

This is a book about crackheads and bums. About junkies and losers. About what it's like to spend all your time around sick people.

This book is a 100% true work of fiction. And that's all it is. Promise.

It is not an extended allegory for the futility of human existence. Segments of it don't correspond to the cantos of *Dante's Inferno* or *The Tibetan Book of the Dead*. There are no secret allegories or cabbalistic correspondences hidden within it. I'm not a writer. I don't have an English degree. This book was not written to impress the other no-talent jack-offs in my Creative Writing class.

It's not even a novel. There is no building action, no plot, no first, second, or third act, no climax, no dénouement. This book is just an account of a year at a rehab/halfway house for recovering addicts, told in the form of random vignettes.

It's all set up non-chronologically, you should be warned. Characters reminisce about events that occur later in the book, and they anticipate things that you, the reader, have already encountered. Events that take place in December are followed by a chapter from the previous March. Think of it as a jumbled slideshow from a vacation you'd never want to take. Keeping things straight shouldn't be any trouble for a literate and *seriously sexy* individual like yourself, but giving a friendly warning seemed like the nice thing to do.

You're fucking welcome.

The people you meet in this book are all real people with real problems. Only the names have been changed to protect the guilty. No one is imaginary or a composite. There are no tidy morals here. No warm feelings that will tickle your heart. No one in this book learns a lesson by the end of it and neither will you. This isn't fucking *Sesame Street*. If you still need moral guidance at your age, there was something seriously wrong with your upbringing.

Everyone in this book ruined their lives because they have a disease, or because they are weak, unlucky, or stupid. One excuse is just as good as the next.

The fault for these ruined lives lay squarely at the feet of the people living those lives. No one forced them. No one else could stop them. That they also frequently destroyed the lives of those who loved them is just part of the tragedy of addiction.

Part of the tragedy…and maybe part of the comedy, as well.

Hope you like your humor black.

Wait, One More Thing

Always remember: "*New Start Rule #1*: Never Trust a Junkie."

MORNING SHIFT
(8am-4pm)

7:47am
PROLOGUE:
THAT'S ALL WELL AND GOOD FOR SHEEP, BUT WHAT ARE WE TO DO?

My name is Ray, and I'm a Substance Abuse Technician.

The sun is failing to break through the petrochemical clouds of downtown Pasadena, leaving the world hazy and grey. I push my bike through the front door of *A New Start,* the local drug rehab/halfway house. It's an Ozone Warning day, and the Terror Alert level is at Orange. This means the young and elderly are to stay inside, and the rest of us should remain scared.

The door closes behind me as I transition from one toxic environment to another. The vomit on my tires rolls itself onto the linoleum of the lobby floor. It's drippy and brown, like rotten syrup. The ink for the world's most disgusting notary stamp comes from a puddle of stomach juices blocking the front door.

Maybe the acidic broth I'm trailing is the fault of one of the three bums slumped against the outside wall. Maybe it had been a collaborative effort on all their parts. Maybe not. All that matters to me is that Lake Puke represents the moat separating my work from the rest of the world. The helplessly sick isolated from those who can hide it. This lets the human wastes here know that they're in their element. It's as much of a calling card as that big-ass cross we've got out front. And a lot more honest.

That's right: *Symbolism.*

I'm a psychology major, but I did sleep through English 201 last semester. Picked up a few things by osmosis. This is one honky whose college education won't go to waste.

The front lobby's small and cramped, lined with rotting chairs and a cracked leather couch. A smell that drifts between burnt garbage and a sewage martini sulks in the air. Somewhere a radio talks about dead children and U.S. bombing raids. There's a busted telephone on a table by the door and a bookshelf stacked with spotty encyclopedia collections. An L-shaped desk cordons off the back-right corner of the lobby. Behind it stand two filing cabinets and a scrawny, middle-aged black guy.

"Ray!" My coworker cheers at the sight of me. Weasley little man. Huge forehead and small body. He looks like the sole survivor of an traffic incident between a short bus and a mobile neutering station. Bastard's ratted me out for misconduct twice before, but I don't hold it against him. He's just another person whose open coffin I'll piss in one of these days.

I nod in his direction. "Hey Regg," is called back with less enthusiasm. My bike leaves a slime trail as it's maneuvered through the lobby and into the side hallway. The tires print a pattern of indigestion as they roll, like they're laying the red carpet for a bulimics' convention.

Someone else will clean it up.

My backpack is shed behind the front desk. I stretch out one shoulder, then the other. It's a short ride here from my girlfriend's place, but I'm so out of shape that any exertion takes a toll. Having a job that consists of sitting on your ass for eight-to-sixteen hours will do that. Had I arrived only an hour later, I'd also be drenched in sweat from the subtropical East Texas climate.

So, it could be worse. It could always be worse. It's remembering those little things that help with maintaining an attitude of gratitude.

"Anything to report?" I ask.

Reginald shakes his head. That means none of our clients got fucked up on crack, huffed Scotch Guard, attacked another client or any of the usual things that make working here so amusing. "Quiet as can be," he says.

"That's the way I like it," I say back to him. It's the same verbal exchange every time I show up for work. Our little ritual.

Reginald finishes packing his things and heads to where his car's parked in the back lot. He calls out a final, "*Take it easy!*" as he departs.

I wait till he's out of range before shouting, "That's what your mom says when we do anal!"

Immature, but satisfying. And also a part of our little ritual.

There's no one else in the lobby. I settle behind the desk, slap a Pixies album on the CD player and pump up the volume.

"*Wanna grow up to be…!*" Frank Black screams at me, "*Be a Debaser!*"

My feet thump on the desk as I adjust myself through my shorts. In a little while I'll go raid the facility's fridge to see what's left over from breakfast.

My name is Ray, and I'm a 23-year-old cracker plugging his way through college. I work as a Substance Abuse Technician at the rehab since I'm too lazy to have a real job. Being a Tech just means that I babysit a bunch of grown-up failures. Drug addicts stay at *A New Start* after they've gone through detox. The junkies, the alkies, the pill-poppers, and crackheads all live in this dreary little place and spend their days attending 12-Step meetings at outside locations. It's an all-male establishment, which at least keeps the sexual harassment charges against me to a minimum.

The rehab is also an expensive place, about three grand a month. You'd be right to suspect that the average addict doesn't have piles of cash just lying around, so most of them are funded by a state program. Most of *New Start*'s income is derived from government handouts. Money is taken straight from your paychecks to be used on sorry-assed junkies. It's one of the last remaining examples of our society helping the less fortunate.

That, or just another way the government funnels your tax dollars to private businesses.

There's a banging on the front door. I lean over the desk to scope it out. The lobby's got a glass front, and through it I can see some bum with his face busted to hell and back, like he got tag-teamed by a hammer and ginsu knife. He hits the door again. Blood's caked on his face and down the front of his jacket. Apparently under the impression that our secret knock involves punching the glass as hard as possible, I watch him smack the door a few more times. Then he notices me watching and gives it an extra kick.

Somebody wants in.

Somebody is shit-out-of-luck.

I give him a slow shake of my head, and he responds by smashing his face against the door and smearing a bloody streak across the glass. Then the guy turns and stalks off.

He'll be back.

My employers share a building and its lobby with a Methodist Homeless Assistance Ministry. It's called *Christ in the Gutter*. Cute name, though vaguely unflattering. As if having a bunch of junkies and crackheads here wasn't bad enough, for half the day the downstairs is packed with piss-soaked bums and crazed transients. There's nothing so bad in this world that we can't find some way to make it worse.

This is probably the most educational job I've ever had. Pushing T-shirts made by Indonesian slave-labor at The Gap might pay more and (*maybe…?*) offer health insurance, but at least working here guarantees me something interesting to say when I'm at parties and somebody asks me: *So, what do you do?*

Well...I tell them:

I catch people using dirty needles to inject urine into their bladders to cheat a piss test. I hang around homeless families where the parents use their kids to stub out cigarettes. I see alcoholics chug vodka and drive their trucks off the side of elevated highways. I watch hookers get thrown from moving automobiles.

I tell them: My name is Ray, and I get to see the worst that humanity has to offer. I watch people go 10 hard rounds with life and, trust me, *life always wins*. I see where the American Dream said '*fukkit*' and decided to go back to blowing its dealer for a fix. I witness despair, pain, insanity, and the human spirit getting its spine broken in half, only to drag itself back to standing for one more shot at survival. I spend hours each day around people whose biggest accomplishment is not slitting their throat and the throats of everyone around them.

I catch the shit and the filth and the shame. Every horrible thing we try to hide from each other gets broadcast in fucking Technicolor right in front of my face. I meet all the monsters you double-bolt your doors against, and it's funny how they're just as frightened as the rest of us.

My name is Ray, and I love my job.

7:52am
SIMPLE MACHINES

Solomon waddled into the lobby and shouted a hello at me. In addition to being fat and AIDS-ridden, Solly was also stuck talking at several-dozen decibels louder than needed. The headphones permanently attached to his ears probably had something to do with this.

Solomon shouted at me, "WHATCHA KNOW, BOSS MAN?" as he wrote his name in the sign-out sheet on my desk.

"I know a lot," I said. Such are the useless benefits of higher education. "Especially about *your* crazy ass."

And I did:

I knew that Solly was in here for his crack addiction. I knew that it took a small pharmacy of pills to keep his liver, heart and immune system from imploding. I knew that he stored his own urine in cranberry juice bottles. I knew that he had two felony counts of statutory rape and one for the sexual assault of a child. I also knew that he'd spent fourteen years in jail and that he wasn't the first multiple rapist I'd met at work.

I was in charge of filing the medical records and legal papers for the clients. There was no way I could resist reading the stuff. Having grown up around nothing but middle-class white folk, the job was really expanding my horizons. It was as educational as it was horrifying.

What I *didn't* know about Solomon was to how many of those little girls he had spread his disease. It was a small detail, but I couldn't help but be curious.

Solly hummed to himself as he wrote, tossing his head from one side to the other. Back and forth while I watched the fat rolls on his neck bunch up on the right side, then the left. He looked like the world's most harmless black man. Pudgy and content, like a harem eunuch. Nothing about his appearance suggested the guy was a crackheaded kiddie-fucker.

Solly coughed once, and I instinctively held my breath. Irrational AIDS fear.

It's so easy to be judgmental towards people. It's also against company policy. As if any of us limited little robots have much control over the fucked-up shit we all do. I'm sure that we'd like to think otherwise, especially when other people do stuff we disapprove of. But, most of us seem to be little more than the unwitting combination of our genetics, imprinting, and early conditioning.

Solomon squinted up at the clock on the wall behind me, pondering what the hell the big and little hands were trying to say.

I had to wonder: are we all helpless, or just weak and lazy?

Does it matter either way?

“Did you like it when they screamed?” I asked him. “Or was it the pre-teen tightness that did it for ya, Solly? Maybe you’re scared of body hair?”

Solomon looked up from the sign-out sheet and blessed me with a gap-toothed smile. “THAT’S GREAT, BOSS MAN.” Guy hadn’t heard a word I’d said. “GOIN’ TO THE STO’. YOU NEED ANYTHING?”

I thought for a second before suggesting, “Something young and unable to fight back?”

“*Huh*?” Solomon reached up and lifted a headphone away from his left ear. Could have *sworn* I heard Tchaikovsky’s Fourth blasting at a distorted volume, but, *nah*....

I shook my head and smiled back at him. “Fine, thanks.”

He lowered the headphones back over his ears. “YOU ALRIGHT FOR A CRACKER, RAY.”

Sol gave me another smile to go with the compliment and turned to leave. I waved at him as he walked out the door.

Friendly motherfucker.

7:56am
FORGET IT WITH PEOPLE

I sat at the front desk and picked at the powdered eggs and sausage on my plate. It's what was left over from the clients' breakfast. It's what was *always* left over from the clients' breakfast. A fourth of my bodyweight was probably comprised of this shit.

Horrid stuff. As one of the clients had told me: '*It like prison food, but ain't nobody gonna shank you while ya eatin' it.*'

I wouldn't have been too surprised to find out that a steady diet of the stuff caused cancer in lab rats. It seemed like everything else did. Hell, maybe those furry little bastards were just naturally prone to cancer. Why should humans be the only species weighted towards destruction?

The doorbell rang. I clicked the unlock switch under the desk without first checking to see who wanted in. Wouldn't have been too difficult; the door was about fifteen feet in front of me and made of glass. And, in case I was incredibly near-sighted, a security camera pointed at the door, broadcasting its image onto the small monitor on my desk.

The *Christ in the Gutter* signs taped to the door (like the one stating that free handouts don't start till 9am) obscured the face of the person seeking entrance. Made it damn tough to see who was banging on the door unless you were willing to go to the trouble of lifting your fat ass from your seat for a look. So, like most of us, the security camera was both extraneous *and* useless.

The sound of feet shuffling on linoleum announced the entrance of two people into the lobby. I glanced up to see a tall, scruffy, black man and a fat old bum in a tattered overcoat. Their size differences made for a nicely mismatched pair. The stereotypical odd couple. Hell, in a better world they could've been a classic comedy duo. Imagine the matinee title: *It's Laurel and Hardy in: 'Will Knife You for Food!'*

The two homeless men were shaking from the cold. East Texas winters might not have the low numbers that make for impressive viewing on The Weather Channel, but the cold has a way of seeping right into you. The guys, shivering in unison, looked at me expectantly.

I sighed. It was time to deal with the homeless. Time to take care of stuff that wasn't even my problem. Time to let these people know that they were going to have to go wanting for just a little while longer.

I put on my patient/friendly face. "Can I help y'all?"

The tall one was the more in-charge of the two. He lacked that submissive crouch that most of the homeless acquired after a short while of living on charity. "We hungry," he stated, looking first at me, then down at my sumptuous meal.

Christ in the Gutter typically gave out free crap like hand-me-down clothes and toothbrushes. The occasional bus passes, maybe. Free food for the homeless was a rare thing around here. Sometimes restaurants donated their nearly spoiled excess, but not often.

I looked up at the guy. He stared back. "Too bad this isn't a *Luby's*," I said.

My sarcasm didn't go over well. I mean, why would it? "*Whatchu* say?" He glared down at me. Hands planted firmly on my desk. His compatriot hung a few feet back, satisfied with letting him do the heavy work.

I leaned back in my seat and let out another sigh. *Jesus*. As if aggression was required to get the handouts they were after. I guess that living too long in a capitalist society makes us feel like we always have to stomp on somebody to get what we want.

"You heard me," I said. "They don't start giving out the free shit till Nine. Right now this is an entirely different business."

The homeless always had the hardest time understanding that I didn't have a damn thing to do with free socks or sandwiches or whatever. I was just an innocent bystander, unlucky enough to be in the same vicinity as their deprivation.

"Think you can talk to us like that?" The tall guy was getting angry. Well, he'd actually started out kind of angry, and was now rapidly moving towards *pissed*. Someone would have to work on their panhandling technique if they were going to keep from starving. '*Friendly and passive*' tends to be a lot more effective. It lets the people helping you feel powerfully magnanimous.

"*Look*," I said. "The only food we've got is what's right here on my plate."

The fat bum jumped to attention. "I take it!"

It hadn't really been an offer, but…

I shrugged and handed over the food. He rushed up to the desk, grabbed the plate, then hauled ass out the door. Me and Captain Pissed were left alone.

I looked back up at him. "You might wanna go tackle your pal if you're expecting him to share."

What was this guy still hanging around for? Waiting to see if I whipped an emergency breakfast stash from my pants?

He leaned across the desk. "You keep talkin' to me like that, and there gonna be consequences." We exchanged stares, angry energy in his eyes, boredom in mine. "You do know what *consequences* means, don't you?"

"Why?" I asked. "That your vocabulary word for the day?"

You're always on top of a situation as long as you can still make smart-ass remarks.

Never ceasing to stare at me (guess it was supposed to be intimidating), he growled, “I just got outta jail, and I ain’t goin’ back for you.”

I rolled my eyes. Why did I have to put up with these people when it wasn’t part of *my* job? So the rehab shared the building with a bunch of religious do-gooders; so fuckin’ what? It would be like the employees at the Cookie Bouquet having to fold towels just because they shared the same mall with Bed Bath and Beyond.

Where were the goddamn Christers? *Their* charity organization, *their* religious compulsion to not leave the helpless to the oblivion our society had consigned ‘em, so let *them* deal with all this!

“No one’s making you go back to jail…”

He reached into his back pocket. Out came a knife.

“I just sayin’ there be *consequences*.” On the last word he flicked out the blade. My heart revved up several gears. “I slit you open before I go back.”

My mouth went dry. My balls tried to hide in my stomach. I could feel the pulse thrumming in my ears. It was too early in the morning to have my life threatened.

A definite word would be had with those Methodist motherfuckers about me having to put up with this kind of shit.

“*Y-you* need to leave,” I said, looking around the desk for something heavy to hit him with. Hopefully something with a decent reach, so I could crack his skull open before he had the chance to carve his initials in my face. The facility’s key ring was attached to a large hunk of solid oak, but it was nowhere in sight. Had I left it in the kitchen? Panic was beginning to seem like a viable alternative. “*Please?*”

He smiled. They may not teach too much about social rehabilitation in prison, but apparently you do learn the finer points of submission and dominance. Mr. Switchblade saw that he had the upper hand on an uppity white boy, so he wasn't going anywhere. "*Consequences*," he said again.

His verbal needle was stuck, and from the look in his eyes, I might get stuck, too.

I tried to speak. Tried to tell him to take a fucking hike, to go play in traffic, but my tongue picked that moment to freeze in my mouth. The rest of my body thought that seemed like a great idea, and I was riveted to the spot. I wasn't going anywhere, and neither was he.

"*Consequences.*"

Not until my boss rounded the corner. At the sight of Gim, my new playmate folded his blade and headed for the door.

"*Consequences*!" he called back to me.

"*…fuck you…*" was all I could think to say. My legs started shaking and wouldn't stop.

8:01am
WE ALMOST HAD THE COURAGE TO CHANGE THE THINGS WE CAN

My boss was a monster. Not morally, like Hitler or myself, but physically. The man was around seven feet tall and used to play for the NFL. Biggest mammal I'd ever seen outside of a zoo. Two steps were all it took to carry him from the edge of the lobby to the side of my desk. His handshake smothered mine like an envelope.

Gim was the director for the rehab/halfway house. Bigger and blacker than anyone I've ever met. Friendlier, too. He had the body of a linebacker and the personality of a PR Agent, all smiles and warmth. And since faking respectability was half the battle in today's world, Gim had a wardrobe that consisted of nothing but plaid golf shirts and slacks large enough to house a Cub Scout troop. The Big and Tall store apparently had a pretty limited selection. Not that I'd really know: I'm so all-over average that you could lose me in any decent-sized crowd of honkies.

Gim's job was to oversee all the clients, counselors, and—beneath the counselors—the Substance Abuse Techs like me. It wasn't the easiest job in the world to manage a bunch of intellectual lightweights and slackers like me and my coworkers. There's only so much idiocy and sloth that one man can try to compensate for. But, Gim was a pretty likeable chap, so no one held it against him when shit went wrong. Someone as big as Gim, you're just glad the man didn't feel like stepping on you. He totally could, if the urge ever struck.

"How're you doing, Ray?" Gim stepped around the side of the desk to give me a hug (my boss *hugs* me; how many people can say that? and not just during sexual harassment hearings?). I zoned out while he engaged me in the sort of small talk that's all a part of his outgoing personality and such a big hit with potential clients. *Chat chat chat, smile smile smile.* How am I doing, how's school, how's my cold, how's life in general? And all the while, a look of '*genuine*' interest on his face. Still haven't figured out how he fakes it so well.

With most folks I wouldn't have even pretended to care, but since Gim's my boss (and signs my paychecks), I reciprocated the pleasantries. How's his life, how's the family, how're the old football injuries, *etc.*

Gim told me about his recent trip to Rome, a vacation the rest of us employees could never hope to afford. He saw the sights, acted like a typical tourist, and endured a guide that never stopped talking about himself the entire time. According to Gim (while I could pay attention), the guy ignored anything of historical interest and just blabbed about shit that had happened to his own Italian ass: getting arrested for disorderly conduct in the Trajan Market, taking acid at the Vatican, how he nailed his cousin in the Coliseum, *etc.*

Personally, I can identify with that sorta egocentrism. My reaction to stuff is always more important than what's going on around me, but Gim was the opposite. He actually seemed interested in other people.

It made him stand out around here almost as much as his height.

A nice perk of being so huge was that Gim never needed to form all the defensive complexes that make the rest of us so edgy, uncomfortable, and introverted. Nothing could hurt him, so he could be as open as he wanted. It's like being physically imposing gave Gim the ultimate '*Get Out Of Your Self-Imposed Jail Free'* card. The only thing that could lay the man low was himself, and that's probably why he used to be such a huge cokehead and drunk.

"Did you see that sunrise?" Gim asked. "We came out of our morning meeting, and I don't think anyone had ever seen such a shade of russet in the clouds!"

"That's the pollution," I said.

Nobody, and I mean *nobody*, sneaks into this place through the back door. Every employee here was a resident at one time or another ('cept for me, of course). Every one of my coworkers used to be an alcoholic or crackhead or junkie or just huff way too much glue. They're all the walking wounded, but I guess that's what makes them interesting.

Even Reginald, the pud-whacker that I relieve on Thursday mornings and a couple different nights. *Christ*, I've heard the craziest shit about that guy stealing cars while cracked out of his skull. Heard about it taking four cops to beat him into submission. To look at the guy now, you'd never believe that he was capable of anything beyond stamp collecting and sniffing bicycle seats.

Or, I don't know, maybe he's full of shit.

New Start Rule #1: Never Trust a Junkie.

Done hugging and talking to me, my boss walked back to his office. Once he was out of sight, I patted my back pocket. The wallet was still there.

8:13am
BALLAD OF A COMEBACK KID

The lobby's CD player skipped and stuttered over the latest Locust Ghost recording. There was enough time for the band to get a decent jam going, and then the disk would start tripping over itself again. I was cursing a sincere "*Goddamnit!*" when one of the clients shuffled in. They all lived on the second level of the building. It's a narrow hallway lined by dormitory closets, all crammed full of clients. We pack them in four or five to a 'room'.

The medication room is up there, too. Filled with the legal drugs that the clients now used to get through the day in lieu of their preferred pharmaceuticals. The money made from this socially-approved form of chemical coping flowed into the righteous coffers of Big Pharm companies, instead of the smaller pockets of local businessmen. The well-connected families peddling percocets across the nation might earn enough from sky-rocketing OD rates to plaster their names on all those art galleries and concert halls that wouldn't let your skuzzy ass in the door, but god help the poor bastard that tries to push a few dime bags to help make rent.

Purely the Invisible Hand of the free market, I assure you, plus all those other fancy, economic concepts that we know you don't understand.

Across from the med room was our other narcotic dispenser, our ultimate in addict pacification technology: the TV lounge. Seventy-six channels and twenty-four hours of mindless distraction. The junkies spent hours basking in its benevolent rays, starring slack-jawed and vacant like all good Americans should. That's what we in the healthcare industry call Progress.

The Methodists used to house the bums up on the second floor. This was before the rehab moved in, and before they had two murders and one overdose during a single week.

I was hitting the CD player when, "Hey *nigga*!" was shouted at me from across the lobby.

"Hey *honky*!" I called back. Strolling toward my desk was Robert. He'd survived a five-year addiction to crack-cocaine, four marriages, and six years in prison only to come down with throat cancer last Christmas.

If there is a God, I think He hates us.

"*Whaddup*, Ray!" Robert reached across the desk to give me a real *brutha*-style handshake. Our fingers made a snapping sound as we pulled our palms away. After a few months of working here, I'd become something of an expert at eleven varieties of exotic handshaking. All I needed now was to join the Masons, and I'd have a full set.

Robert asked how I was doing, how was my Tuesday (or whatever day it was), same as he did every time he saw me working here. When he talks I can see the gap where his front teeth used to be. Just about all the crackheads have this. I used to think that part of crackheadedness was that you were too high to care about proper dental hygiene, but then someone told me that the smoke rots your teeth.

Sexy.

When Robert shifted his head, the lights changed their refractive pattern on his skull. The chemo had left him an utter cue ball. This was actually something of an improvement for the guy. He used to have a wild, Jheri Curl-style *do* like Samuel Jackson's in *Pulp Fiction*. Looked cool on Samuel Jackson, but that's why he's a millionaire and Robert's dying in a halfway house.

"I tell you I goin' to the VA today?" Robert asked. He had, but I said nothing. "Doc gonna check me out; see how my cancer doin'."

Utterly Terminal was how his cancer had been doing, but Robert was one of those oddly irrepressible souls. Always smiling, or willing to fake it, at least. That's a rare trait in the world, and an even rarer one around here. Most of the people between these walls were Officially Crushed by Life and seemed to have grown to accept it. As far as attitudes go, that's a pretty contagious one.

Even so, Robert's glaring exception wasn't all that inspiring. Saintly cancer patients are hoary clichés, thanks to network television. So, besides thinking of Robert as anyone to learn a valuable lesson from, he just made me feel like my work was a crappy Made for TV movie. I'd seen the plot a million times before: Robert would die horribly, but, in those brief flashes of programming between all the car ads and beer commercials, the story would give us viewers a warm glow about the resiliency of the human spirit or some such crap.

If Robert weren't such a nice guy, I'd almost resent him for it.

"I know I be all right," Robert said. I slid low in my seat to adjust myself once, then again for the fun of it. "Had a dream 'bout my *momma* last night. She tell me I gonna be fine."

A few other clients came up to my desk to sign out from the building while Robert and I were yapping. We keep track of these guys' comings and goings like overprotective mothers. All clients used the sign-out sheet to exit or enter the building. They have to log the date, where they're going, what they're going to be doing there, expected time back and then the actual time when they return.

Pike, an alcoholic and compulsive philanderer from New Orleans, signed out first. James, a crackhead resembling a black version of Sloth from *The Goonies,* was next. Then Paul, a lanky, twitchy pill head with a drooling problem. Those broad strokes were all I knew about any of them, and all I cared to know. Statistics said they'd be gone and relapsed soon, so why bother with details?

Upon signing out, all three reached across the desk to slap palms with me. A mental note was made to wash my hands.

James asked, "Wassup, uhhh...*Einstein*?"

I answered, "Hey, uhhhh...*James*."

Wiping the drool from his chin with the back of his hand, Paul said he'd see me when he got back from hauling freight to Louisiana. Yeah, our program lets some of the clients keep working their jobs while they're in here. No lengthy sabbaticals from the outside world required. I mean, Allah forbid that any programs of self-change affect too much of your life.

I dug around in my backpack and tossed Paul a handmade card. "Happy belated birthday, man."

He'd told me yesterday about turning 50, and so I'd spent five minutes making Paul a card celebrating how half a century had seen him manage not dying of an overdose. Someone pretending to give a shit about your existence is just one of the many perks offered by *A New Start.*

Paul looked embarrassingly grateful for this small gesture that had been nothing more than a product of my boredom, so I turned back to Robert. "Couldn't your mom have used the phone?" I asked. "Or does nothin' say lovin' like showing up in someone's dream?"

Occasionally my sarcasm gets the best of me, but the clients seemed so used to life shitting on them that a little more abuse didn't make a difference.

The smile expired on Robert's face. "My momma *dead*, Ray."

"Oh, *fuck*," I said. *Open mouth, insert foot*. "Sorry to hear that, man."

"That's okay," he said, leaning on the front edge of the desk. "I ever tell you 'bout my momma?"

"Don't think so." I made myself comfortable. My *faux paus* obliged me to listen to him ramble for a bit.

"My momma had a special power," Robert said (*What*, I thought, *bitch could fly?*). "She do that healin' thing, ya know? Heal people with 'er hands."

"Your mom was a *faith healer*?" This was a little more interesting than expected.

Robert could tell that he had my attention. "She always say that she didn't do it. She say that *God* do it through her. She just lay her hands on somebody and start praying and then they get better."

Interesting.

Curious for first-hand details, I asked, "She say what it was like?" As a psychology student, I'd gotten used to unscientific mumbo-jumbo. And hell, it wasn't like the 12-Step programs the clients used were built on a firm foundation of double-blind laboratory testing.

"She just always say that she start prayin', then step aside and God takes over. That's all. She say she don't do nothin'. It all from God. She ain't even there while it's happening." Then he nodded at me, like that was all the explanation needed to scientifically duplicate the experience.

Translating Robert's none-too-helpful description from *ignorant-old-lady-ese*, it sounded like his mom went into a sort of healing trance, using prayer as a trance-inducing mantra. Textbook case, basically.

"Think your mom could get rid of my jock-itch?" I asked.

Robert laughed. "I don't think I want my momma goin' anywhere near yo dreams or yo dick!"

"Let ya borrow my sisters for yours," I offered.

He cackled. "For my *what*?"

"Your call," I said. "But they're related to me, so *caveat emptor*, man!"

I laughed alone.

Robert tugged his ear. "*What*?"

8:27am
BEWARE THE RELIGIOUS: THEIR GOD WILL FORGIVE THEM FOR ANYTHING

There was an uproar among the Methodists at the Homeless Assistance Ministry. Apparently, some miscreant had defaced property of theirs. Defaced it in a highly disrespectful manner. Actually, make that disrespectful *and* amusing.

The property in question was a large headshot photo of the current American president, eyes raised to heaven, looking properly pious. The Head Puppet-in-Chief was posed for the photo as if he had just concluded his bedtime prayers by asking Jesus—in his best Shirley Temple voice—to '*...bless all the little kittens and puppies and the bunny rabbits, too!*'

Taped next to the photo on the chapel door was a written statement circulated by the Methodist hierarchy. It reminded all their minions of the great necessity to pray for our Good and Christian leader in *his* time of need. The prez, at the time the picture was posted, was busy trying to rally support for the slaughter of yet more dark-skinned folks halfway around the world.

(In the fucker's defense, it's not like there wasn't precedent for that sort of thing.)

Apparently someone, tired of seeing that glaring example of religious hypocrisy every time they came to work, had added something to the photo late one night. It was a word balloon, like the kind you see in comics. It was pointing to the president and bearing the words, "`Thou Shalt Not` *`What?`*"

In what I thought was a cool, artistic touch, the words dripped red highlighter blood.

The seriously religious are even less tolerant than your average moron when it comes to having the contradictions in their belief system pointed out. So, the Christers were pretty pissed when the affront was discovered the next morning. Threats were issued every which way. Heads were promised to roll, and it would have surprised no one had they started crucifying people at random until somebody broke down and confessed.

Since I had been on duty the night it happened, I was called in and confronted.

Chatting with the Head Christer seemed unavoidable. I steeled myself for the meeting. "If you don't hear back from me," I told my girlfriend over the office phone, "I want to know that I've loved you more than anyone else I've ever just used for sex."

Christ in the Gutter had their offices in a separate hallway from the one *A New Start* used. More towards the back of the building. I usually tried to avoid that area since the sewage smell was stronger around there. Reminded me of Ezra Pound's great line: "*shit and religion always stinking in concord.*"

I was stopped on the way back there by a client. The guy's tall, blonde, handsome, and looks so out of place here. JDZ pointed at me and laughed. "Heard you're in trouble with the Methodists," he said.

"Apparently, someone killed their god," I said. "And you know I get blamed for everything around here…"

JDZ pulled a switchblade out of his back pocket, flicking it open with a smile. I took an involuntary step back. Bad memories. "Want me to knife that fuckin' cunt for you?"

He might have resembled the average junior executive, but JDZ was just a thieving, scheming, and dangerous junkie like the rest of the clients. The guy was polite to me, though, and that's all I really cared about.

"I'll shove this right up her and twist." He held the blade out for my inspection. "You like it? I got it off some crackhead for real cheap."

JDZ was his own social blight, no doubt, but it's best to keep all of your options open. "I'll let ya know how it goes," I told him. "And don't go waving that thing around in here."

In her cross-covered office was Selma, the whale of a minister in charge of *Christ in the Gutter*. The majority of the people working at *C.i.t.G.* were homeless volunteers. They did all the dirty work. The people who actually got paid were mouthy white folks in charge of…well, not too much besides ordering the volunteers around. Sounded like a pretty cushy gig.

Considering that she didn't employ me, since we only worked in the same building and were at-best neighbors, I wondered if the Good Reverend really had the power to call me on the carpet. Bitch wasn't my boss, after all, and there's only so much I would take from *him*. Did she let Gim know that she would be interrogating me?

Maybe. Since the Christers owned the building (and *A New Start* was just renting space), Gim had probably given her *carte blanche* to do whatever she felt. Us bottom-rung Techs were easily thrown to the lions.

I popped my head around the door into her office. "Hey! How's it hangin'?"

Selma was wearing a purple sweat suit with the customary minister's collar somehow attached. Sitting behind her desk and overflowing the sides of her chair, she had her scowl in its usual place. Curly, gray hair framed her angry face. I wondered how long it had been since the last time she had smiled. During church, perhaps? Or maybe then she just turned her frown in the direction of the nearest cross.

She glared at me and I did my best not to glance back at her for too long. Selma looked like the result of a liposuction gone horribly wrong, like during the operation someone had kicked the machine in reverse. She was puffiness stretched to the limit. So, I stared instead at the crosses that covered her office like a dead forest.

Pretty fucking morbid to plaster your workspace in ancient torture devices. It'd be like decorating a nursery with guillotine wallpaper. Still, they were easier on the eyes than Selma.

I wasn't avoiding the sight of her just for aesthetic reasons. Whenever my gaze flickered in Selma's direction, I got a horrible mental image of her wearing nothing but her minister's collar while working the Tijuana donkey show. Christ knows where that thought came from, but it made me feel bad for the donkey.

She pointed at the chair in front of her desk, but I chose to stand. Thankfully, Selma was pretty quick to get to the point with me. Did my heathen ass have something to do with the desecration, she wanted to know.

Did I?

DID I?

"Course not," I lied. And she never said '*heathen*,' though I picked up on the subtext. "But, ya gotta admit; it *does* make a pretty good point."

9:33am OMNISCIENT, OMNIPOTENT, OMNIBENEVOLENT

A shriek cut through the general murmur of the lobby.

"My stepfather's outside!" Mary screamed. She tore through the lobby, pigtails flapping in the air. "Call the police!" Her face was tattooed with the boundless fear of a child. "My stepfather's outside!" She pushed her way through the hordes of homeless waiting for handouts.

"Call the police! He's gonna get me!"

It's hypothesized that Dissociate Identity Disorder can be caused by extreme childhood sexual abuse. Mary was such an obvious D.I.D. case that whoever did the abusing in her long-ago childhood must've stuck it to her good and hard.

"My stepfather's outside! He's gonna get me! *Please!* He's gonna get me!"

Dressed in pink overalls like a four-year-old (but actually closer in age to forty), Mary and her hysteria were starting to excite the herd. Waves of agitation swept the room. Feet shuffled faster. Tongues ran over chapped lips in quicker and quicker repetition. Nervous twitches multiplied, and a few additional shrieks answered Mary's like the response to a particularly unhinged mating call.

A worker for *Christ in the Gutter* led Mary into a back room before she started a stampede of homeless hysteria.

"*My stepfather's right out-*" Mary was cut off mid-shriek by the slamming of a door. The entire lobby was still turned in her direction. I held the office phone loosely to my ear. On the other end my girlfriend asked what the screaming was all about. The momentary excitement Mary provided had dragged us all from our own problems, and we returned to them grudgingly.

Mary was a common fixture at *Christ in the Gutter*. She even volunteered sometimes. That got her preferential treatment of a sort. Like being taken into the women's bathroom to be calmed down instead of getting tossed out onto the street.

I had watched Mary's freak-out from behind the front desk. Just another nutcase in a job full of them, as far as I was concerned—or, as Mother Teresa had phrased it, *Christ in His most wretched of guises*. Hanging around the needy and pathetic had been a divinely mandated hobby for ol' Teresa. To us less-charitable types it was an unfortunate part of an otherwise easy job.

"Yeah, the crazy-o-meter just hit 11," I said into the phone. "I'll call ya back later."

I lit another scented candle—the homeless fucking reek—and stepped out from behind the desk for a look. Figured I'd catch a glimpse of Mary's demonic stepfather.

Hiding behind my protective shield of potpourri and scented candles was bad enough; venturing out into the mass of vagrants was like swimming through a garbage dump. Your average middle-class citizen, living in their perfumed world of colognes and deodorants *cannot* imagine the noxious fumes the human body can produce. Scents that ooze their way into your defenseless nostrils, cling to your sinuses and repeatedly rape your basal ganglia. The human wrecks surrounding me radiated vile bouquets containing weeks of sweat, piss, vomit, and recycled booze.

And if that wasn't your dollar's worth of gagging, there was also the building's pervasive scent of sewage mixed with rotten eggs. It's a real classy joint they run here. After months of exposure you'd think the nose would develop some kind of immunity, but each day was still an extended exercise in suppressing the gag reflex.

I picked my way through the living sea of the desolate that clogged the lobby. Stepped over trash bags full of aluminum cans that never left their owner's grasp. Dodged dirty children that ran underfoot while their mothers sat slumped, unconscious, and drooling against the walls. Elbowed my way through drunks too slow to move aside. Strode past the young mulatto girl with a swollen belly and frightened eyes.

Every Monday through Friday, from nine till four, *Christ in the Gutter* opened its doors to the homeless, the crazy, and the dispossessed of downtown Pasadena. *C.i.t.G.* wasn't a homeless shelter, merely what they called an Assistance Ministry. This meant that handouts were plentiful, nothing besides tax write-offs were asked in return, and the homeless came in droves. Wouldn't you? What else is there?

Richest society in the goddamn world, and this was the best any of us cared to do.

I told myself, as I shouldered through the crowd, that I only had to put up with them and their stench and crazed ramblings for a few hours a day. After that I had nothing to do but sit on my ass, feet propped on the desk, and collect an hourly wage for the simple act of existing. Just a few short hours. Chill with the '*homelies'* for a bit before my company was upgraded to nothing but junkies, alcoholics, and crackheads.

I finally made it out the door and peered down the street in one direction, then another, scanning for Mary's step-bogeyman.

The street, of course, was deserted.

9:54am
LEVENDIS

"*1. We admitted we were powerless over alcohol—that our lives had become unmanageable.*"

I was browsing through *The Big Book*, which serves as the AA bible. They call it *The Big Book* to distinguish the thing from *The Good Book*, a.k.a. the Christian bible. That they took such care not to impugn the Bible's space kind of put the lie to the AA line about not being a Christian organization. Not to mention how most of the meetings ended with the Lord's Prayer.

I'd occasionally call my girlfriend and read her some of the more amusing case studies from the book. She didn't find them as funny as I did. Guess you had to be there. Or here.

"*3. Made a decision to turn our will and our lives over to the care of God as we understood Him.*"

Nicely submissive stuff. Good and weak. Exactly what I'd expect from an organization started by a couple Protestant drunks. Of course, in official AA terminology, the term '*God*' is replaced by the more ambiguous phrase, '*Higher Power*.' It keeps the organization open to people with more brain cells than the terminally religious. Guess it's also a concession to 21st century social reality. These days, it's best to keep nice and vague about delusional terminology: once you're off the drugs, you no longer have an excuse for thinking that invisible monsters watch your every move.

(Unless you live in America, where a vast majority of the population believes they have an all-powerful imaginary friend. Every time they cut federal funding to schools, I'm reminded of that.)

I flipped though a few more pages, tried to read, got bored. My original plan had been to finish all of *The Big Book*. I figured that it'd help out on the job; give me some insight into the stumbling wrecks around me. Besides, there's not much else to do around here on the weekend. It'd be more entertaining than just sitting and scratching myself for the entire shift (left nut for the first four hours, then start with the right). The reading was turning out to be a lot more difficult than I figured. The Big Book was about as thrilling as sitting through church, was full of embarrassing stereotypes and probably about as helpful as suntan lotion in a burn ward.

If I couldn't get through the damn thing, how'd they expect a bunch of semi-literate crackheads to manage?

"Hey, Ray!" Robert limped into the lobby, a huge smile on his face.

"Thought ya could smell the evil coming down the hallway," I teased. Leaning forward in my seat so he didn't have to reach too far, we slapped palms.

"*Naw*," said Robert, "That's just the cancer."

We both threw our heads back and howled with laughter. Robert laughed because that's how he was dealing with his impending death, me because I hadn't a clue how else to react to something so morbid.

Robert pointed at the blue hardback in my hands. "You reading the Big Book?" he asked. "You ain't an addict like the rest of us, is ya?"

I shook my head, stifling a yawn. The girl from *Christ in the Gutter* had been over way too late the previous night. It'd been pretty tough getting rid of her. Guess I should've known that someone with nowhere else to sleep would be reluctant to take a hint and leave.

“Just too lazy to have a real job.” I said. “Thought it couldn’t hurt to get familiar with the thing.”

It was tossed onto the desk. “Boring as fuck, though.”

Robert nodded. “Never could get more than a chapter or two in,” he said. “Guess I should keep trying.”

I hadn’t worked at the rehab long, but the Big Book already struck me as extraneous to one’s sobriety. Either you were going to do it, or you weren’t. If books really made that much difference in peoples’ lives, everyone who owned a Bible would be canonized.

“If you wanna,” I shrugged.

Robert walked over to the sign-out sheet. “I gonna go hit me a meetin’,” he said, “But I wanted to let ya know that I goin’ in for more chemo tomorrow, so I ain’t gonna be here.”

I wasn’t going to be here the next day either, and Robert knew my schedule. There was also a listing of his chemo treatments in Gim’s office, so the reminder was doubly unnecessary. But if Robert wanted to share about his life, who was I to stop him?

“Good luck with it, man.”

“Thanks, Ray,” he said. “They got some real pretty nurses there, so I gonna be fine.”

We both laughed. “Bring me back one,” I requested.

“I get you a skinny one,” Robert said. “You white boys like that. Just don’t forget to pray for me!”

Now *there* was something to request from the local atheist. My hands folded in mock prayer before me, I asked, “But, who am I to interfere with the divine plan…?”

Robert laughed. “White guy. Y’all think you’re in charge of everything.”

10:01am
LIVING WITH SICK PEOPLE MAKES ME FEEL SO STRONG

The lobby was crowded with homelies, and two bums fought over an old flannel jacket. Their struggle danced from one side of the room to the other. Grunting and cursing, one hand fought for a better hold on the jacket, and the other struggled for a tighter grip on their opponent's throat.

The entire lobby watched, enraptured. Now *this* was entertainment. I watched, the homelies watched, and the black guy writing his name in *A New Start*'s sign-out sheet stopped to watch the spectacle. Two people had their hands on each other's throats over a faded piece of cloth, and the rest of us couldn't have been more entertained.

The bums would careen into a chair-lined wall, and the chairs' occupants would shout and push them away, leading the opponents to stumble into another group of on-lookers. The *New Start* client wedged himself into the corner where the desk met the wall, his hands out protectively.

"Left hook!" I shouted encouragement to no one in particular. The clothing given away by the Christers didn't strike me as anything worth paying for, let alone hurting another human being over, but the homelies were welcome to their own value system. When staying warm each night was a struggle, one's appraisal of the relative worth of clothing probably underwent drastic revision. Hell, under the right circumstances, it'd probably make sense to kill for a hoodie.

The bums kept shouting a '*muthafucka*' this and '*gah-damn*' that as they tore at the flannel between them. "I fuckin' kill you!" one screamed before a left hook caught him upside the head.

He staggered, but never let go of the flannel.

"Now go for the right!" I shouted. Instead of manifesting as a follow-up, this advice was taken by the bum who'd just been struck. He let go of his opponent's throat long enough to switch hands on the flannel, then lashed out with a right hook. Spit and blood flew from the other bum's mouth.

"*Oooh*!" said the crowd.

I was apparently coaching both sides of the fight and doing a decent job of it. "Now kick!" I shrieked. "*Kick*!"

Both bums tried this move at the same time. One kick went wild, the other landed firmly in the nearest crotch.

The room went silent like the voice of God.

The recipient of the crotch-busting slowly bent in half, still gripping the flannel. He gasped twice, each louder than the other, then let out a long groan. This was followed by an even louder moan that seemed to drag on forever as he waited for his balls to drop back into place.

I waited for another kick to land, a punch at the very least. This would seem to be the ideal time for some additional violence, now that one party was unable to resist, but none was forthcoming. The winner was just as intrigued to see what further course the reaction would take.

Would the bum start to cry? Would he vomit blood? Would he scream '*Eloi, Eloi, lema sabachthani!*' and breathe his last?

Then, as if to spite us, the loser just fell over backwards, his grip on the flannel finally loosening. He lay on the floor, on his back. He didn't move.

It was pretty anticlimactic. I could swear I heard a disappointed sigh escape the audience. TV and movies had accustomed us to things ending with a bang. Violence that didn't conclude in explosions always fell short of expectation.

It was then we all noticed dark stain spreading from his crotch. It started small, then quickly consumed the front of this pants. As if to make up for the low level of violence we'd just tolerated, nature rewarded us with some degradation as the bum submissively pissed his own pants.

There was a collective "*Ewww*!" from the crowd, despite how many of them reeked of their own fluids. It's funny how our tolerance levels tend to stop with our own squalor.

I watched the winner of the bum brawl take a running start to deliver a game-winning kick into his opponent's side. This elicited another "*Ooh*!" from the crowd and still more urine into the loser's pants. Then, clutching the torn flannel, the victor rushed out the door.

"Man, I been there," said the *New Start* client standing in front of the desk. He shook his head. "Been there and worse."

I looked at the client. Glanced over his gut and bald spot. Imagined him piss-stained on the dirty carpet of some crackhouse. Wondered if he'd looked as pathetic as the bum on the lobby floor.

"Not me," I said. "But I'm still young. Give me time."

10:39am
JUNKIE DRAMA

When I arrived at work Saturday morning one of the clients was missing. JDZ had relapsed. He'd disappeared, robbed his family and friends, and—we assumed—had taken to the needle with a vengeance.

Junkie-relapse S.O.P. Nothing too original.

Other clients were informing me of this when JDZ walked in. He looked like shit. He smelled like shit. He had the same scruffy five o'clock shadow that all the guys here seem to acquire when they relapse. It was like their drug of choice stimulated hair growth. His pale face and long, scabby fingers looked greasy, as if he'd wiped them on the bottom of a bucket of fried chicken.

"Speak of the devil," said one of the clients.

(I've stopped expecting anything clever from these guys.)

JDZ had come for his clothes, which were stuffed upstairs in the med room along with the personal items of other junkies who'd relapsed or simply left with nowhere else to put it all. We usually kept their crap for a month before donating it to the Methodists.

Walking up the stairs with him, making friendly small talk (*how's life on the needle treatin' you, price of the stuff fluctuate much since the last time you did it?, etc.*) I couldn't get over his stench. "*Good Christ*, you fuckin' reek!"

"Really?" he asked, like the possibility had never occurred to him.

I assured JDZ of his smell, comparing it unfavorably with that of the combined homeless odors that filled the lobby on crowded days. He shrugged it off. Who cares about body odor when you got an armful, right? It took a little prodding (I made it a condition of him getting his stuff), but eventually he came to see bathing as his civic duty.

JDZ took about twenty minutes to gather his things and shower. I was never more than ten feet away the entire time. Not like I suddenly felt the need for proximity to someone who had an even harder time being human than myself. Nor was I hoping for a glimpse of him toweling off. It just would have been a *bad* idea to leave JDZ alone upstairs with everybody else's stuff. Like that famous line from *Sid & Nancy* (and *New Start Rule #1*): Never Trust a Junkie.

Especially one who'd spent the past week ripping off everyone he knew.

Walking back downstairs, JDZ enlightened me on the panhandling technique that—along with petty theft—was earning his daily smack. Apparently, aggressiveness and dogged persistence play a big role in successful begging. Looking vaguely threatening doesn't hurt, either, and I bet the knife I'd seen him with played the occasional part.

This went against all the ideas I'd ever had about using a submissive air when you're trying to convince people to give money they'd worked for to some skuzzy stranger…but, JDZ had practical experience to my mere theorizing.

I couldn't explain why I had always liked JDZ, besides how he was such an unrepentant degenerate. The guy seemed to recognize that his purpose in life was to make the world an uglier place, and he was cool with that. If people crossed to the other side of the street when they saw him coming, if he blew every job he ever had, if all he knew how to do was steal and get fucked up, if he couldn't stay sober for more than a month at a time, if he always destroyed his life and the lives of those around him, then So Be It. That seemed to be his attitude. Hard not to admire such a perverse sense of self-acceptance.

When we got back to the lobby his old girlfriend was waiting outside the front door for him. You'd think she'd have learned her lesson about JDZ by now, but who was I to argue with somebody else's co-dependence?

This was the same lady whose credit cards he'd ran off with last week, and similar acts had been performed at least twice before. She was apparently the forgiving type (and *absolutely perfect* for that special someone on your Xmas list who wants not a companion, but a talking doormat they can hump). I waved *adios* and closed the door behind them, leaving the two lovebirds alone on the front steps.

I figured, now that JDZ had stopped wearing his alluring *Scent of a Junkie* All-Natural Cologne, that their dysfunctional asses would go reenact their American version of *Trainspotting* somewhere else.

Admittedly, it wasn't like they were affecting the property value by being in front of the building. Now that JDZ had showered and changed clothes, the pair of them could have been mistaken for any other urbanite couple in their early thirties.

Still, I wanted them gone. Illusions that profound never last long, and I wanted JDZ and his woman to get lost before the mirage faded.

Yeah, them leaving and taking their sickness with them would have been nice, but first they felt a need to indulge in that pastime shared by couples everywhere: fighting.

I had gone back to the desk to call my girlfriend. I'd figured on telling her JDZ's story as a reminder that she could do a hell of a lot worse than me. Then the plan was aborted like a prom-night pregnancy when I heard angry voices coming in from outside.

It was JDZ and his woman. Her hysterical shrieking and the bass of JDZ's counter-screams made a charming fugue of our basic inability to all get along.

Jesus, I thought. *Time to go play the authority figure.*

I went outside to tell them to take their bullshit elsewhere. Not only because it looks jank to have people scream at each other in front of your establishment (even in a part of town with a large bum population), but because I hated listening to couples fight. It made me feel like a little kid again, watching my parents trying to draw blood in front of me and my siblings. I couldn't force my folks to stop it at the time, but I could sure as hell get rid of the human wastes shouting in front of my workplace.

"*Hey*!" I shoved the door open between them. "Go be trash somewhere else!"

Having been told to fuck off and do it promptly, JDZ started leaving. But, his girlfriend stood where she was, faced me (she had been pretty at one time, possibly still was from a distance, but life—or life with JDZ—had worn her down around the eyes) and stated that she needed to speak with one of the other junkies.

"I need to talk with Jamie," she said.

The name didn't ring a bell. Like I'd waste time memorizing over fifty constantly changing names. I was about to say so when a greasy white kid pushed up from behind me. He looked to be late teens, early twenties; heavily tattooed and with a posture like he was constantly cringing. The kid was taken by the girlfriend around to the side of the building. JDZ followed behind them, shouting.

"Hope they don't kill each other on my shift," I said to the other clients watching the drama with me. "Fuck knows there'd be lots of paperwork to fill out."

We all laughed at this, and of course we made a few more jokes at the expense of whatever the hell was going on outside. I thought about what a great anecdote this would make to tell my girlfriend.

The door shook. *BANG!BANG!BANG!BANG!BANG!*

I jumped at the noise. It was a quick, frantic pounding on the glass, mixed with a desperate ringing of the bell. It felt frightened, as if ignoring the banging and ringing ensured that blood would start seeping in under the door.

I turned around. There was the kid. Jamie's head swiveled back and forth, looking through the door, then back at the far side of the building. His eyes pleaded for entrance.

I contemplated leaving him there, just to see what would happen if his fears—whatever had him so shaken—were allowed to come true.

The small part of me that still feels compassion won out, and I opened the door. Jamie scurried in like a Ritalin baby chased by an alcoholic father.

"He tried to hit me!" the kid said, chest fluttering with adrenaline rapidity.

"*Shit*!" We all cheered, our combined maleness excited at the prospect of a fight.

Jamie was shaking like a freezing epileptic. "He tried to hit me, but decked his girlfriend instead!"

There was a pause while we decided how exactly to respond to this news. Actions require more contemplation than usual if they fall outside our usual *stimulus-response* repertoire.

We all decided on explosive laughter.

But once we got the rest of the story out of the greasy little chap, it turned out to be no laughing matter.

(Well, nothing to laugh about in front of the people it affected, at least.)

JDZ and Jamie had known each other for a while. They used to shoot up together, share needles and all sorts of other healthy behaviors. This would be uncool enough on its own, even without the kid having recently discovered that he's got…Hepatitis C (*dum Dum DUM*!).

Apparently, JDZ didn't want his girlfriend to find this out. As all of us disease-literate types know, not only is Hepatitis C currently considered terminal, it's also communicable in all the same ways as AIDS. That includes blood transfusions, sharing needles, and sex. So many different ways to transfer it, so many different ways to pass along the love.

Ripped off by a loved one, fed a right hook, infected with a terminal disease...*goddamn* if somebody's girlfriend didn't just have the worst week imaginable.

It's tough, but junkie dramas rarely come with happy endings.

10:58am
ALWAYS MORE BOTTOM TO BE SCRAPED IN YOUR BARREL

Sitting on my desk, Cassandra handed me a post-it note with the number to the assisted-living apartment she shared with her dad. Her old man was also on federal assistance. Counting the baby on her chest covered by a nursing blanket, that made three generations suckling on the welfare teat.

The thought of that may outrage some hard-working folks in the heartland. But, if the government just *had* to steal my money, I'd prefer the taxes go to help people rather than hurt them. The way the politicians and press had been howling for foreign blood these past few months, I knew that it wouldn't be long before we were all paying to kill dark-skinned babies instead of feeding the little bastards.

"Give me a call," she said over the rumble and shrieks of the homeless. The downstairs of the facility was filled with just about every variety of hard-luck story imaginable. It was like a discount emporium of human suffering. In my imagination, I caused all of their heads to explode.

"Any time before nine is okay."

It's so easy to hate the helpless. The loathing's in our blood. There's a million years of social biology behind the repugnance you feel when you pass a bum on the street. It's instinctual to abhor the weak and the failed. Primates and other mammals loathe vulnerability to the point of attacking any group member that becomes disabled, that can't take care of itself. Birds do it, too. Why would people be any different?

It's so easy, so natural to hate the helpless. Any excuse will do, and it's not like they're capable of stopping you.

"*Okay?*"

Temporary vulnerability is one thing. We'll all help somebody change a flat tire or walk a little old lady across the street. But when you're permanently and consistently unable to care for yourself, most people just want you to stop being such a burden and crawl off somewhere to die. Some folks can admit to these feelings. Some can't.

Don't think I always felt this way. Did I? It was tough to recall when my thinking changed on the subject of charity. Probably sometime after I started working here.

"Okay," I said to Cassandra, having no intention of doing what I just agreed to. Sure, she might have been a volunteer rather than a recipient of *C.i.t.G.* charity. Sure, she might've been looking rather nice in her tight blue jeans and the tan shirt that matched her skin tone. But, it wasn't too long ago that Cassandra had been big and pregnant and sitting in the lobby with the rest of the homelies.

Making a Homeless Assistance Ministry into my own sexual hunting ground was something that I'd have to be a fuck of a lot more desperate to even consider. Maybe if I broke up with my current girlfriend, or if I found myself on the other side of the desk, or if I just got bored, or *whatever*.

But, even then, I couldn't imagine hooking up with a welfare mother. From a mile off, my paranoid ass can smell a plot to make me the surrogate daddy to someone's ugly little baby.

"This where I sign in?" interrupted a bum, about to write his name down on the *New Start*'s sign-out sheet. The bum, in the increasingly filthy jogging suit he wore every day, never failed to ask this question.

“On the pink paper.” I pointed to the glaringly obvious sheet of hot pink paper on the adjacent side of the desk. “Write your name down there and they’ll call it eventually. *Then* you can go get your free shit.”

“Right here?” he asked, starting to write in the same place.

“Pink paper!” I repeated, pointing with more emphasis.

“You got change?” He kept scribbling in the same spot.

I slapped my palm on the correct sign-in sheet. “*Here*!”

“*Oh…*” the bum shuffled on over. Just like he had the day before and the day before that.

“*Oooh…*” Cassandra carefully slid down from where she had been sitting on top of my desk. Suckling sounds drifted from under her nursing blanket. “You gettin’ a little upset? I thought you were more laid-back than that.”

She gave me a smile that I guess was supposed to be flirtatious. Seeing her in full-on maternal mode didn’t quite do it for me, though. Cassandra was an ex-stripper, hiding down in Pasadena from her abusive baby-daddy. She was on welfare thanks to having quit dancing out of fear that she’d be killed if the guy ever found her.

Love’s a pretty fucked up thing, isn’t it? I can’t ever imagine hitting my own girlfriends, but maybe that just shows my lack of commitment.

I returned Cassandra’s smile with a faked one of my own. She beamed at this, showing that she was just as starved for attention as the rest of us. “Just feelin’ a little thirsty,” I said, nodding towards her mammary glands. “You weren’t planning on letting that other one go to waste, were ya?”

Cassandra ducked behind her hair and smiled. If her skin was lighter she might’ve blushed.

(Yeah, I flirt back. It passes the time.)

“You racist!” someone yelled. I turned to look into what had once been a woman’s face. Now it was distorted, angry, and unnaturally sallow to the point of caricature. Her lips were ruined with herpetic sores and heat blisters.

(I swear; the first crackhead to invent a pipe with an insulated mouthpiece would make a fortune. Of course, you know they’d just blow that fortune on more crack.)

“Racist!” The woman’s look of triumphant outrage said that she’d just found an outlet for some of the shit life had been dumping on her. “I wanna file a complaint. You a goddamn racist!”

While the woman shouted variations on that theme, all four of her kids were scampering around the lobby. They fought and screamed and got underfoot while Mommy busied herself with more important matters. The entire scene was a living advertisement for those involuntary sterilizations the government used to conduct.

I sighed. *God*, I was tired. Too tired for anyone’s persecution complex. I was on the third leg of a 24-hour shift. There was probably some kind of labor law against making workers do such things, but it’s not like that shit ever gets enforced. Companies do what they like in America, and the rest of us can play along or starve.

“Racist honky motherfucker!” Calling me several kinds of bigot was something of a hobby with the homeless. Just something to say when they were pissed off in my general direction. Even the white ones did it. Accusing me of racial bias apparently passed the time better than reading the donated magazines they had lying around here. *And* it wouldn’t rot the brain like TV does.

I was tempted to ask the woman: ‘*Don’t you see me flirting with this mulatto girl? Isn’t it proof of what an open-minded chap I am if I’m almost considering shagging someone who’s halfway like you?*’

Hated to give Cassandra false hope, though.

“They don’t pay me enough to discriminate,” I assured the woman. I wondered what had set her off. We hadn’t exchanged a single word before her accusation. Maybe I had a bigoted aura. “You can be sure you’re getting the same crappy treatment as everyone else.”

She started yelling again as Toni showed back up. I had been covering at the front desk for the guy while he grabbed a smoke in the back lot. Toni was a swishy little ex-crackhead (of the Caucasian variety) who worked for *Christ in the Gutter*.

“Customer for you,” I told him, and Toni got busy ignoring the woman’s complaints.

It was actually *his* job to sit at the front desk and deal with the transients. I was just there to hang out and make sure that the junkies didn’t need anything. They usually didn’t. Not during the 8-4 shift on weekdays. Or, if they did need something, they usually couldn’t be bothered to come downstairs to ask me for it.

As long as I hung out in the lobby, I was safe from responsibility. Probably had something to do with all the homeless down here. The junkies were scared of them. They tended to see the homelies as Ghosts of Xmas Future, *This Could Be You!* warning signs.

Personally, I was beginning to see them as proof that maybe euthanasia shouldn’t be limited to the elderly. But that’s just the kind-hearted sort of fucker that I’m finding myself to be these days. If I start voting against my own economic interests to spite the rest of you assholes—and justifying it—I just hope someone’s waiting with a decent hug and a handjob to welcome me to the Dark Side.

I glanced over at Cassandra, adjusting her nursing blanket on one of the lobby’s busted couches. She caught my gaze and smiled.

On the second thought, save the hugs. I’m a busy guy.

11:23am
TECH TAX

"Ya can't have fuckin' nothin' in this fuckin' place without some fuckin' addict stealing it!"

Curtis was on a nice little bender of outrage. The fists at the end of his skinny white arms were waving like antennae towards the heavens, and his patchy hair stood up straight from either indignation or static electricity.

I didn't really care about whatever of his got lifted. Jesus was boning Mary Magdalene in the book I was reading, and that was a hell of a lot more arousing than anything Curtis had to say. Toni wasn't busy with anything, but he ignored Curtis, too.

Curtis repeated his gripe a few more times, talking into the air and/or indirectly at me. A few of the homelies stared at him, then they also lost interest. Curtis was obviously just waiting to hear the magic question, so after making him wait a few more seconds, I asked.

"My fuckin' dinner's gone!" With a faded iron-cross tattooed on his arm, he was now the white-trash version of Job. "*Ah* ate at *Pappadeaux's* last night, took most of it back here and stuck it in the fridge, put my *gah*-damn name on it, and this mornin' it was gone!"

Oh. I went back to my book. "Life is indeed suffering," I said, after searching for an appropriate phrase of commiseration. "If ya wanna make sure no one's gonna munch your stuff, just ask me and I'll stick it in the back freezer, the one with locks on it."

"Can I put my lunch in there?" Toni asked.

"Sorry," I told him. "Can't risk your Christian food infecting the rest of the grub, turning the sandwich bread into dead carpenter or whatever. For all I know, you people said grace over the stuff."

Toni folded his arms in a dramatized pout. "*Bitch*."

I had considered the matter with Curtis closed, but he apparently didn't. "And I had twenty bucks that disappeared outta my wallet! *Motherfuckers*! No one respects anything 'round here!"

My interest in Curtis and his grievance had expired about two seconds after it'd started. Still, I managed to mumble, "What'd you expect from a bunch of addicts?"

"Not too much," he said. And that's our species for you; we're all covered in shit and complaining about everyone else's smell. "*Ah* wonder who the hell took it? One of them niggers, *Ah* bet!"

Apparently, it takes one piss-poor example of a race to know another. "*Watch* that word," I told him, while Toni said "*Oooh*!"

Curtis was lucky that no one else seemed to have heard him. A bunch of ignorant white and black guys (not sure where all the Hispanics are) living in relative peace under the same roof in the Deep South was one of the few real miracles about this place. It'd be a pity for the delicate balance maintained here to be toppled by something as stupid as an angry hick saying the wrong word.

"*Ah'm* not racist," Curtis protested, like they always do, "But *Ah* bet that—"

I glared. "Zip it, *honky*!"

Conversation over.

Curtis did have a legitimate complaint, even if I hadn't felt like listening to him voice it. Stuff here does do a good job of walking off on its own. The theft rate's high enough that, if I was unlucky enough to ever live in this shit hole (*please god no*), everything I owned would be under lock and key. Christ knows I don't leave any of my own stuff just lying out on the desk. Not unless I'm sitting behind it.

Still, it's probably asking a bit much to live in a building full of people who used to steal from everyone they knew, and not expect a few of them to slip back into their old ways. That theft was only *common* and not *epidemic*—considering the client population—was yet another of this place's mundane miracles.

I guess that's just the optimist in me talking. Work here long enough and the sunshine can't help but pour out of your ass.

But, all that was beside the point. Not a clue about his money, but I knew exactly who had stolen Curtis' dinner. I knew who had snuck into the fridge in the middle of the night and microwaved then munched his shrimp etouffee, hush puppies, and 'slaw, but I'd be goddamned if I was gonna turn them in.

I'm no snitch. And besides, those all-night shifts make a man hungry.

11:35am
SETTLING FOR HALF THE TEA IN CHINA

The woman was hunched over like a gorilla, ratty orange hair in her face. "I'm tired of you assholes stealing my money!" she screamed at me and Toni.

The rest of the lobby watched intently. Sometimes I suspected that the homeless took turns flipping out to keep each other entertained.

"*Yeah*," I said to Toni from my usual seat on the filing cabinets behind the desk. "Give her back the money, you fuckin' thief!"

"Give me back my money!" the woman echoed. Every time she opened her mouth to screech I could see the blackened ruins of her teeth.

"Shut up," Toni warned me. "Don't encourage her."

This was the third time the woman had flipped out about her money this month. No one had stolen it. She was just nuts. The aggressive sort of crazy that likes to share its fucked-upness with the rest of the world. Whatever had set her off in our general direction was a mystery to everyone but her. Toni spoke in a gentle tone, "*Dearie*, you're going to have to calm down or leave."

The woman had a better idea. "I oughtta kick the shit outta both you faggot asslicks!"

"*Faggot*?" I played shocked to Toni. "Have you been telling everyone about our Friday nights?"

"Ray, shut up!" He spoke more firmly to the woman. "You're going to have to leave now, before I call the cops."

"Fuck you!" she screamed, making the only possible response to a world that had given her a damaged brain and bad temper. "I want my fuckin' money! I'm not retarded!"

"Nope," I agreed. "You're just crazy."

Work brought out my compassionate side. Earlier in the shift I had to chase several of the homelies out of *New Start*'s kitchen, where they had been trying to eat the clients' lunches. They screamed and fussed, called me a racist, and I was left there to reflect on how I earned eight bucks an hour denying food to starving people.

It's pretty apparent why some professions don't attract groupies.

"Faggot asslicks!" the woman screamed.

"How do I keep getting lumped in with you people?" I asked Toni. "It's 'cause I'm such a snappy dresser, isn't it?" Old t-shirts with shorts and sandals were due to come back into fashion any day now. I could feel it.

"We're calling the cops," Toni informed the woman when she showed no sign of ceasing her newfound hobby of calling us *faggot asslicks*. I couldn't blame her. Not only was she a few carbs short of a water pipe, but *faggot asslicks* was actually pretty fun to say.

"*Faggot asslicks*," I repeated to myself and chuckled.

Toni picked up the phone, and the woman shouted, "You go ahead and call the cops!" She rushed to the desk, grabbed the phone base unit, and heaved it at us. Toni shrieked and jumped back. I had no time to duck. The phone flew straight at me. My eyes closed.

It stopped a foot short, jerked back by its cord.

"That does it!" Toni shouted. "Get the hell out now!"

The woman screamed, "*Faggot asslicks*!" one last time before running out the door. I gave her a cheerful wave goodbye.

"Ray?" Tony put a piece of the phone back on the desk and continued fishing for the rest of the broken bits. They were scattered all over the floor. "Ray? You mind giving me a hand with this?"

"Do it yourself," I said, then had to add, "*Faggot asslick*."

11:55pm
...MONKEY IS THE GATE. MONKEY IS THE KEY AND GUARDIAN OF THE

GATE. PAST, PRESENT AND FUTURE, ALL IS ONE IN MONKEY...

I came to the realization that, during the few times when I was actually called upon to do my job in the morning, the task usually involved little more than the opening or closing of doors at the behest of clients.

Open door. Shut door. Open med room door. Unlock TV room door. Lock med room door. Unlock offices. Open back gate with remote. Close back gate with remote. Talk to junkie. Ignore junkie. My college education was really coming in handy.

(The whole Open/Close binary did get a little confusing at times, but I tried my goddamnedest to keep it all straight.)

My job therefore got a failing grade for the R.M. Test. This means that it officially could've been done—and possibly done better—by a Retarded Monkey. Possibly one that was drunk, as well. Maybe even crippled.

Of course, I'm convinced that a neurologically challenged, disabled primate with a drinking problem wouldn't appreciate the Selbyan nuances of the job like I did (or like I enjoyed pretending that I did). Nor would it have figured just which pill combination to take from the med room in order to have as interesting a shift as possible.

It was going on the fourth hour of a midweek workday, and my big accomplishments of the shift were flirting with homeless girls, arranging a post-work meeting with my girlfriend, and then heading back to the kitchen for that second bowl of Lucky Charms.

I love my job.

12:03am
BABY-BUTT ASHTRAY

When one member of the homeless couple would leave the lobby to smoke outside, the other would get stuck holding their infant offspring. The second the smoke break was over, the kid was passed off, and the previous holder would be free to go outside and smoke. I watched this process recur for over seventy minutes.

The couple, a weatherworn man and woman here for the handouts, took turns holding their baby during the other's nicotine breaks. The kid, a skinny little thing dressed in what was probably its father's white T-shirt, was traded off with all the tenderness typically reserved for a frozen turkey.

During one of the pass-offs, as the baby was plopped from one lap to the other, the kid's shirt/gown slipped up to reveal its little ass. The Anne Geddes potential of the moment was somewhat ruined by the circular burn marks that pocked the baby's butt. No one was going to make a sunblock ad out of something like that.

Then the parental hand came and pulled the shirt back down. Not in haste or worry. There was nothing in the action that could have been construed as: '*gosh, sure hope someone doesn't notice that I often mistake my offspring for an ashtray!*' Just the typically languid motion of a parent straightening out their child's ruffled apparel.

The thought of calling Child Protective Services never crossed my mind. Growing up homeless would fuck up the baby enough as it was. The kid was already a lost cause. Worrying about the other stuff its parents might be doing was like worrying about wetting the ocean by pissing on it.

Look at it this way, kid, I thought as I watched it being passed from one unhappy parent to the other, *Your folks putting out cigarettes on your ass could one day make some pretty decent fodder for your public defender.*

The shirt slipped up again and I caught a second glimpse of the baby's scarred backside. I quickly averted my eyes. *I'm sorry, kid.*

Jesus, I'm sorry.

12:21pm
THE WINNER AT CANDYLAND GETS A FREE LOLLIPOP ENEMA

There was a weird bacteria covering my hands. They were peeling in discrete flakes that came off only when ripped by a firm application of front teeth. Looked like a light version of leprosy. Hopefully temporary.

I had probably picked it up here. Fuck knows that this place was crawling with germs and bacteria. A terminally toxic environment. It's filled with homelies who wash themselves on a monthly basis. Who pick their meals out of dumpsters. Who consider sink-baths to be adequate hygiene. They're joined by all the junkies and crackheads who have the luxury of hand washing but no inclination to use it.

Filthy, *filthy* fucking place. From now on I'd use a shirttail over my hand to touch anything.

After work I'd go home and masturbate with latex gloves.

I made a mental note to steal some from the supply room, and that was when Toni handed me the pills. Five Vicodin for sixteen bucks. Not a great deal, but not a bad one, either. There was nobody else in the lobby besides a few homelies staring at the floor, but Toni passed them off to me using that totally obvious druggie handshake.

I laughed at him. "You hokey motherfucker." Christ knows where that bacteria on my hands had come from, but now Toni had it, too.

Drool lurked at the edge of his mouth. "Ray-*baaaaby*," he sighed, "They are *gooood.*"

I believed him. Toni was having trouble keeping his eyes open, and even more trouble keeping his words from slurring. He looked fucked up in a way that you really shouldn't look in a rehab.

Everyone who worked here was trained to catch people trying to hide just how high they were. I would've detected Toni blindfolded at a hundred paces. The guy was going to get himself busted, but it wouldn't be the first time. And I'm sure it wouldn't be as bad as the time he got caught dealing coke. That little infraction had landed him in prison from the time he was seventeen till his mid-thirties. Just another casualty of the American War on Some Drugs.

"*You should try one*," Toni urged in an exaggerated whisper. He seemed ready to kiss linoleum at any moment. I crossed my fingers for something interesting.

"Try one…"

"I'll wait, thanks." Work wasn't too intolerable, yet. Not quite enough to warrant being fucked up during it. Maybe someday, but not right now. The pills would keep until I figured out something to do with them. Maybe slip one into my girlfriend's drink the next time I felt like trying anal. Lord knows it took a lot of talking to get her into that strap-on, otherwise.

Our hands had just parted contact when the phone rang. I picked it up, and a solicitor on the other end asked for Mr. Lou Reed. About once a week here we got a call for "*a Mr. Lou Reed*." I was pretty sure that we don't have any client here by that name. Celebrity monikers tend to stick in the mind like any other form of advertising. And none of my co-workers could recall anyone by that name from the past five years. Somehow the name and this phone number got stuck on a phone solicitor's list, and now—sure as death, taxes, and dysfunctional relationships—I could always count on fielding the weekly call for Mr. Reed.

Since my main goal in life is to amuse myself, I always told the solicitors, "Sorry, but Mr. Reed is currently touring in support of his new album while nailing a groupie, mainlining heroin, and feasting upon the remains of his former band mates. He's old but spry."

That, or I'd offer to go fetch him, and Toni would burst on the phone a few minutes later with his own rendition of *Heroin*.

That's not humor at its sophisticated finest, but we always enjoyed it.

1:11pm
COMES IN TWO NEW SCENTS: WINTERGREEN AND CRACKHEAD

Said one of the junkies, "I feel like I about to go crazy, living here with all these guys. Need me some titty."

There was a general round of agreement from the other junkies. We were all shooting the shit in the front lobby. The day was crawling by. Anything to pass the time.

My work is a place of inaction, a place where people cease to do things and focus on *not* doing them. My English teacher last semester said that F. Scott Fitzgerald claimed action to be character. We are what we do, right? At the time, I didn't get what the asshole meant, but here at the rehab the maxim designates our clients to be even bigger nobodies than before. Their presence is based upon a cessation of previous actions, quitting the things that used to define their days. Their personalities seem to fade into generalities without the drugs to back them up. Their individual identities couldn't be asserted without the framework of the things from which they were fleeing.

That let me feel fine about not remembering the clients' identities, and so, they mostly just become *junkies* to me. What the hell, it beat having to memorize all those names.

"I fuckin' bet," I said. "I don't see how y'all live in such a purely dick-filled environment."

"We jack off constantly," one said, and the others laughed and shouted agreements.

I shrugged. "Hell, I do that anyways." I do at home, at least, when the girlfriend isn't around. Still haven't sunk to the level of masturbating at work.

Someone asked, "Ever do it in the *downstairs bathroom*?" and there was another round of shouts and laughter, like someone had just named the secret word on *PeeWee's Playhouse*. "Go in there, lock the door, *bambambam*, tug one out real quick?"

"Here?" I asked, thinking that *bambambam* as a masturbatory sound effect reminded me how the Victorians used to call it *self-abuse*. "Not while I'm on the clock, thanks." Which doesn't mean that I've never been tempted to, but... "I mean, I piss in it, but isn't that the *ladies'* bathroom?"

Big smiles and nods of acknowledgement all around. "Yep," said one of the guys. "Jes' somethin' about that sweet potpourri smell…"

1:56pm
THE UNKINDNESS OF STRANGERS

The buzz of a poverty-filled lobby surrounded us while Toni shared prison stories with me. I sat on the filing cabinets above him, scanning the lobby in hopes that I'd recognize someone from high school. Anything was better than looking Toni in the face. Not from close up. Toni had a mug like he shaved with a sand-belt. Like he'd hit a second puberty and started developing into a reptile. Like every year spent in prison had counted for double on his face.

One horribly wrinkled motherfucker. And all of thirty-six years old.

Which isn't *too* young, but *Jeeezus…*

"I just munched Xanax and Valium every day," he said, and I nodded like I actually gave a shit. "And by the time my seventeen years was up, I was all, *what, finished already?*"

Toni had a voice like a Southern Belle. High-pitched, twanged with Dixie inflections, and terminally infected with camp. He sounded like Blanche Dubois's effeminate male twin.

It's tough ridding your mind of stereotypes when you're surrounded by them.

Everyone starts getting to me by the middle of a shift. Even the people I can usually tolerate. Toni's stories about being a prison bitch were wearing thin. If he said the phrase, '*all the meat I could handle*,' one more time, I was going to tump the filing cabinet over on him. Just get it rocking back and forth before hopping off at the last minute. Watch it fall forward and flatten him against the desk.

It was probably the annoyance of being stuck in a single location for so long. I liked to be able to move around. Having to stay in the same place for hours on end started to wear on me, especially considering the fine specimens of human potential with whom I was stuck.

"I heard about your guys' parties getting busted." Now that Toni had something bad to say about other people, he could finally stop talking about himself.

Some of the clients had been throwing coke parties upstairs at night. They'd do huge lines off the tables in the TV room and chug beer till the early hours.

The people I'm supposed to be watching during nightshifts? That's what they do while I'm asleep.

"Too bad about Sam and Pike," Toni said. "They were cute."

I shrugged in reply. Not my types, really. He followed up his evaluation with a stage whisper that I heard just fine over the noise of the lobby. "*Had them both*."

"At the same time?"

Toni waved me off. "Oh, don't I wish!"

Scott shuffled up to the desk. He kept his eyes mostly on the floor, but threw occasional side-glances at the homeless. Looked like a shy man at a freak show. Entranced and horrified by what he saw, but not wanting to admit to his car-crash fascination. Scott looked someone had forced an accountant to mate with a cashmere sweater. "Is my counselor in today?" he asked in a quiet voice.

I made Scott repeat himself twice before answering with a shrug. That's service the *New Start* style!

He spit out an exasperated huff. "I've been here two weeks!" Scott said, like it was my fault he couldn't handle the outside world.

"And?"

"Two weeks, and I've only seen them once!"

I shrugged again. It's the expression I've found most useful in my job. Eight in the morning to four in the afternoon *was* the time when the entire staff was supposed to be available for the clients.

Office doors *were* supposed to be open and inviting. That's what the brochures claimed, at least. But, the counselors never told me how to do my job, and I was determined to reciprocate.

"State law says your counselor's only gotta see ya twice a month." Although, considering how many times Scott had been here, and in every other treatment facility in Pasadena and neighboring Houston, he should've moved his bed into his counselor's office. And then maybe chained himself to the headboard.

"That's *bullshit*," he whined, and I was about to agree with him when Toni cut in.

"Hey, Mr. Grumpy," Toni said. "Somebody's *awfully* cranky! I bet you just need a little reciprocation, huh?"

Scott blushed like a klieg light and mumbled something about checking on his counselor himself. Toni smiled and gave a fingers-only wave as Scott hurried off into the side hallway. Then Toni turned to me and said, "Don't even bother asking, 'cause I'm not going to tell."

He didn't need to. It was already old news to me. Last week I'd been upstairs grabbing something from the med room when I'd heard a weird sound coming from the community bathroom. Not the usual theatrical grunting. Something else. More like a loud sigh. Loud and happy. I'd stopped and listened for it again. Heard it a second time. Curiosity piqued, I tiptoed in to investigate. Crouched to peer down the line of stalls.

What I saw were two occupants in one stall. A pair of legs with pants crumpled around the ankles, and a second pair kneeling before the first. More happy sighing. And then even more happy sighing. Didn't take a genius to figure out what was going on. Or going down. We all had different ways of relieving the tedium of this place. I'm sure there were plenty worse than getting sucked off in the men's bathroom.

Toni and Scott had walked out from the bathroom a whole five seconds apart, as if that was going to fool anybody. I smiled at them both and admired the dirty knees on Scott's pants. It was tempting to ask him if Toni had mentioned his Hepatitis, but I decided to keep that question to myself.

2:22pm
SOMETIMES MEANING WELL JUST ISN'T ENOUGH

Knowledge isn't exactly power, and ignorance isn't always bliss. But on some occasions they're close enough.

Troubled by the number of clients I'd seen relapse in my first few months at work, I did a little research on Alcoholics Anonymous and the 12-Step programs that went along with it. Researched the history, used the databases at school to search medical journals for studies and turned up an interesting fact or two.

Now I just had to figure out whether to tell the clients.

The first controlled study on AA took place in San Diego in the '60s. A group of "chronic drunk offenders" was used, and no statistically significant differences were found between the ones who went through AA, the ones who had clinical treatment and the guys who had no treatment at all.

How about that? Listening to how the clients and the counselors blather about "The Program" (as they called it) and the importance of going to meetings, you'd almost think AA was the only thing standing between human decency and a world of crazed drunks.

The second controlled study was in Kentucky in the '70s. They slapped the chronic alcoholics in the study into five different treatment groups. The AA subjects had the highest relapse rate, about a third more than any of the other treatment groups. Things like Rational Behavior therapy and even Freudian therapy whipped the crap out of it. Hell, the AA folks had an even higher binging relapse rate than the fucking control group.

Pretty goddamn sad, in my opinion.

Made me wonder why anyone would base a recovery establishment on a program that obviously didn't work for shit. Did they want people constantly coming back, or what? And, like most things in our ruthlessly capitalist society, was money involved? A revolving-door clientele would definitely put more cash in the coffers.

I thought about this possibility for a while. I hoped that plain ol' human stupidity was more to blame than avarice, but with our species it's usually something of a toss-up between the two.

Herman interrupted my pondering as he waddled into the lobby, slow and arthritic. I set the Xeroxed articles down and gave him a half-assed salute.

"How ya doin', old man?"

He looked up from the sign out sheet to squint at the clock on the back wall. "Jes' blessed," he said to me. "Jes' blessed, boy. Off to a meetin'!"

Herman gave another squint at the articles spread over the desk. "You readin', boy?"

"Yep," I said. "If you're nice, I'll teach you how some day."

"Fuck you," he said. Chances are Herman was probably either borderline illiterate or totally so. A lot of the old guys here were. Modern schools in Texas are bad enough. I can't imagine what the old ones were like. "What you readin' about?"

I stared at his withered face and considered spilling the beans for a second. Just to see how he'd react to the revelation that he was placing all his hope for improvement in something that was ineffective at best.

Would he soldier on, regardless? Would he relapse? Would he tell the other guys and there'd be a keg party upstairs before the day was over? Would they care that, thanks to the program's worthlessness, all their hopes had been conceived stillborn? How would everybody react if they knew how useless were all their dreams of a better life?

I swept the papers off the desk. "It's nothing," I said.

Herman gave a smug nod. "That's why I never bother with that shit."

3:11pm
PEOPLE LIKE US WERE PUT HERE TO MAKE THINGS WORSE

"Y'all do realize," I said to the other guys sitting on the sidewalk, "That our gawking and jeering's probably ruinin' what's supposed to be a very beautiful day."

One of the junkies bothered raising his fist at me to extend the middle finger. "Shut up and get me some popcorn," he said.

Across the street from the rehab/halfway house stands a large colonial mansion. The bleach-white facade and thick, Doric columns made it stick out in this part of town like a Matisse painting in a field of broken syringes. Inside the mansion was a bridal boutique, and on the left side was a lush garden and flower-covered gazebo.

They held a wedding reception there today.

The valet parking covered both sides of the street in either direction with SUVs, sports cars, and limousines. The only empty space for fifty yards was where we all dangled our feet in the gutter, refusing to move and lose our front row seats.

Or maybe *front row* was too complementary of a term. The wedding was not only across the street and behind a wrought-iron fence, but also guarded by three large men with blue suits and guns. The cops, off-duty or not, are always there to protect money and/or its possessors. They were a clear message that the riff-raff so prevalent in this area should stay the hell out.

The junkies hooted, hollered, and pointed freely at the wedding guests, especially those of the young and female variety. We watched a family walk through the front gate. "Whenever I see a hot-ass bitch with a baby," said Frankie, "I always think to myself, *Damn, somebody done had the same idea as me!*"

Everyone laughed, and the woman's husband glared back at us. We weren't more than thirty yards away. It was myself, Robert, Pike, Frankie, Warren, Solomon of the Eternal Headphones, and a host of other characters that would have most people keeping an eye on their wallets. With the rehab's door propped open, we sat and cooked in the East Texas heat, our profuse sweating a small price to pay for the entertainment.

Everyone was *just chillin'*. Just enjoying the show. It couldn't have been too difficult for the wedding guests to hear us; the idea of yapping at less than full-blast was an alien concept to most of the junkies.

"She *is* attractive," I agreed; studying the woman's retreating figure in its tight, gray dress. "But I could do without the marriage or the kid."

"You ain't married, is ya?" Frankie asked me.

"*Jesus Fuck, no!*" I cried in horror, prompting laughter from the junkies. My folks had three kids and a twenty-year mortgage by my age; I'm determined to learn from the mistakes of others. "Can't imagine being dumb enough for something like that."

"What's so dumb about marriage?" he asked. Frankie was a huge, 'fro-ridden bastard. Like somebody had forgotten to inform him that the '70s were over and his side lost.

"*Muthafuka*." Robert said. "Ask a stupid question like that, I know yo' ass ain't never been married."

I asked Robert, "You've been married, haven't ya?" He'd told me before, but my listening skills could do with some improvement. I decided that the amount I listened attentively to people should be directly proportional to how close they were to death. Robert, being cancer-ridden, deserved an open ear. Then again, Solomon had AIDS, and there was no way he was going to say anything worthwhile.

It had been well intentioned, but another policy quickly bit the dust.

"*Shit*," Robert said. "I been married fo' fuckin' times, and each time I like, *nigga, what was you thinkin'*?"

Pike chimed in with, "I bet they asked themselves the same fuckin' thing!" and we all cracked up.

Each time we laughed, a few wedding guests would look over in our direction, certain that their sacred event was being mocked by the collection of white trash and street niggers across the road.

"*Fuck 'dat*," Robert said. "I always marry fat bitches. They just grateful to have a man."

Well, he was half-right, at least. Robert had shown me pictures of his ex-wives once, and sure enough, none of them could even make it through the entrance of a *5-7-9* store.

How *they* had felt about having a husband who was first a crack dealer, then an addict of the product he once sold, all the while in and out of one jail after another…well, Pike's remark probably summed it up nicely.

"*Man*," said Frankie, "My wife got a restraining order 'gainst me last week. Can't go within a hundred yards of the bitch."

Maybe he was expecting consolation. No one offered any.

"Wait till you're paying alimony," Pike said. "Costs me seven-hundred a month to my ex."

The other junkies chimed in with their respective sums: *three-fifty, two-hundred, five-twenty-five…*

"Reason two-billion-and-thirty-seven why marriage is retarded," I said. "Can't imagine giving money to my ex-girlfriends. Once you're off my dick, you're also the hell outta my wallet."

"Goddamn right," said Pike. "Judge at my hearing called alimony, *the fucking you get for the fucking you got*."

We all found this hilarious. Even Solomon started laughing, though I doubt he could hear anything through his headphones. Made me wonder what he was chuckling about. Probably some fantasy involving the little kids across the street.

The garden next to the mansion was slowly filling up with wedding attendants. Resplendent in their formal wear, the guests laughed softly and socialized among themselves. Proud parents balanced spotless children on their hips. Everyone smiled, everyone was polite, everyone had sizable bank accounts. It was a priceless scene of White Protestant America as brought to you by *Reader's Digest*, *Nick at Nite* and the Klu Klux Klan.

"Why the restraining order?" I asked Frankie. Not like those were rare around my work. Addicts have a lovely habit of dragging everyone down with them, and sometimes their spouses found sacrificing the family to one member's sickness to be an unacceptable option. Couldn't say I blamed them.

"Ah, I used to get a bit rough with 'er," he said with a shrug. "Ain't touched the bitch in months, though."

A pair of binoculars circulated among the guys. They were passed from one sweaty pair of hands to another for a closer examination of all things feminine across the street. The off-duty cops watching us from in front of the fence were obviously displeased by this. So were the members of the wedding party standing further up the driveway, but nobody wanted to draw more attention to what we were doing.

Solomon boomed, "HURRY UP WITH THEM GLASSES!" and I bypassed my turn to speed the binoculars to him before boredom led the guy to start molesting people at random.

The binoculars had passed to Solomon, still jamming on his headphones, when the bride and groom emerged from the mansion's front door. They stood arm in arm, framed in the doorway. The wedding guests all stood at attention. A reverent hush fell over the crowd.

"*GODDAMN*, THAT MOTHERFUCKER OLD!" Solomon shouted. "SHE YOUNG ENOUGH TO BE HIS GRANDDAUGHTER! YOU JUST KNOW THAT FUCKER RICH AS HELL!"

Sound travels. The entire wedding turned around to gape at us as one shocked and outraged entity.

Shit! All the guys ran inside the rehab, leaving me and Solly alone on the curb.

Solomon watched the guys bolt inside. "THE FUCK'S THEY PROBLEM?"

A quick look across the street explained things. The crowd stared pure anger. A hundred or so eyes were still on us, the wedding utterly forgotten in light of the tremendous *faux-paus*. Murmurs swept back and forth through the crowd. They all stared at us. Stared and probably wondered; who *were* these sad little creatures daring to desecrate their magical day?

All those eyes belonging to the happily wed and comfortably loved, now focused on an AIDS-ridden child molester and a minimum-wage white boy. We'd never be welcome at their parties. We'd never be that comfortable or loved or happy.

Being on display got old quick. I stood up and raised my arms at the crowd.

"Fuckin' *WHAT*?" I screamed. This didn't cause a single person to turn away, but it did make the cops decide to cross the street to pay us a visit.

Solly and I scampered inside. The pigs rang the buzzer repeatedly, but on my orders no one answered the door.

3:25pm
GOD IS PUNISHING YOU ...OR WOULD BE, IF HE THOUGHT YOU WORTH THE EFFORT

"...and then my dad jumped on my back and my sister grabbed my arm, and gosh, I don't like to be touched, so..."

Warren was telling me and Old Herman about beating up his family. Apparently, they had tried to stop him from going out and buying more crack. Warren gave his dad a concussion and knocked out four of his sister's front teeth.

The lesson here is to *never* get between a man and his rock.

Warren was the kind of guy you'd expect to get picked on by cripples. He'd have to bulk up to be a ninety-seven pound weakling. It was hard to imagine him beating up anyone. He looked too timid to even throw a punch. You'd expect him to shit himself at the very thought of violence. Maybe I could see Warren roughing up a few prostitutes. It's always the impotent types who get caught doing that shit.

Warren sighed. "I paid for their medical bills, for my sister's dental surgery, but they still won't talk to me." He seemed genuinely confused by their obstinacy. It's always a shock to realize that there isn't such a thing as unconditional love.

Herman, sitting on the lobby's couch next to Warren, shook his head sadly. I propped my feet up on the desk. This was definitely a story I'd be sharing with my girlfriend. Christ knows if a constant supply of disturbing anecdotes were enough to keep someone's love, but it wasn't like I had too much else going for me.

"I'm sure they'll come around eventually," I said. "Just give 'em a few years or maybe a death in the family or somethin' else to make this not seem like such a big deal. Or, for twenty bucks, I'll set ya on fire."

"What?" Warren took off his glasses and squinted at me. Why he thought that'd help his hearing is one hell of a mystery.

"Deal of a lifetime," I said with a straight face. I had seventeen copies of a newspaper clipping that I had just taken from the Xerox machine. Per Gim's orders, I was supposed to tape one to every door upstairs. "You give me twenty bucks—fifteen 'cause I like ya—and I'll set you on fire. Family's sure to visit you in the hospital."

"Forget that shit." Sensing an opportunity to make light of another's suffering, Herman joined in. "I'll do it for twelve dollars, boy."

I wadded up one of the newspaper clippings and threw it at Herman. I said, "Stop underselling me, you old bastard!" and we both laughed.

Warren put his glasses back on and squinted again at both of us. Then he coughed a few times, and Herman started coughing, and I resisted the urge to do the same. We were all sick, of course. Hard not to catch the occasional cold in this place, but it was a great excuse for coming to work wrecked on Nyquil.

"If they don't visit," I said generously, "I'll give ya half your money back."

Herman laughed. "It's double your money with me, boy." I laughed, too. It seemed like Herman and I had finally found something we could bond over. Maybe next we'd team up to go mug cripples together.

Unsettled by our mocking of his trauma, Warren just said, "Let me think about it," and got up to leave.

I held one of the clippings out to him. "Tape this up on the fridge if you're headed to the kitchen." He took the clipping from me and looked it over as he walked off.

"Where does Highway 288 connect to Highway 59?" Warren asked. I pointed in a vaguely southeastern direction towards the elevated on-ramp. "Is that a long drop?"

"Oh yeah," I said. "It's *way* up in the air. Go over the side there, and you've got plenty of time for a decent scream. I used to live by there, and I always wondered what that would be like."

Warren gave a slow shudder. "Guess Gerry found out the hard way." Herman slowly shook his head.

My response was a wave of dismissal. "Fucker was probably too drunk to even appreciate it."

We all laughed, but only Warren and Herman looked guilty about it afterwards.

3:33pm
QUALITY TIME

A blur of a little kid ran from the back hallway into the women's bathroom. I caught it as a flash of movement out of the corner of my eye. Thought it was just my imagination. I used to get that back in the days when I did a lot of acid. Some dark movement in the peripheral vision that vanished when the head was turned for a better look. We called them the *Black Acid Cats*.

I thought this was just another long-delayed manifestation of the BACs, so I went back to scanning the newspaper. Then a second little blur repeated the feat.

A New Start is an 18-and-Up establishment. *Ergo*, I couldn't have just witnessed two little kids running around in here.

"Did you see that, too?" I asked Frankie as he bent over the sign-out sheet.

He shook his head. "Ain't payin' attention to nothin' but my recovery," Frankie said. "Gotta look after me, now. Caring 'bout other people's problems what got me here."

He earned a disgusted look. Nothing made me want to retch more than self-pity. Fuck knows it flowed in rather copious amounts around here. It was just another reason why every shift was an exercise in the suppression of my gag reflex.

"You poor, wounded soul," I said.

My peripheral vision caught the two small blurs racing from the women's bathroom to the back hallway. I turned to catch a better look, but they were already gone. We either had an infestation of children or an under-aged pair of apparitions on the loose.

Poltergeists wouldn't have been so bad. Our building's already filled with addicts, the homeless and a pervasive smell of sewage. It'd be hard for things to get much worse, but I'm sure we'd manage to find some way.

I heard the back door swing shut with its usual squealing protest and went to investigate.

Out in the back lot, where everyone congregates to smoke inside a barbwire fence, Curtis sat on a plastic chair. Surrounding him like a solar system of impoverished planets were his wife and five children. Two boys, two girls and a baby.

His buck-toothed kids were all dressed in ragged clothes. The wife might have been pretty in the days before Curtis turned her into a walking incubator. Now, she was a skinny mess of worry lines and moved with an irritated slowness. Just a little extra stress was probably needed before shotgun swallowing became a viable option.

"Are *all* these yours?" I asked. Someone had snuck an entire family past me. It just went to show how much attention was paid to my job.

I glanced over the rotten fruit of Curtis's loins. The thought that anyone would have so many offspring baffled me. The oldest one looked to be about twelve and had done the usual overblown, adolescent job of painting her face. The baby was being carried by the second oldest girl. Two boys chased each other around the back lot. The baby and both of the boys were barefoot.

I meet way too many stereotypes at my job.

"Got another at home," Curtis said. His mustache rippled as he talked. It was so large I almost didn't notice that he was one of the few crackheads I'd met with all his teeth. Considering how popular it was in the hinterlands, it surprised me that someone as rural as Curtis wasn't more into methamphetamines than crack. Guess we all like to think that we're different. "They've come on down to visit me for the weekend...that okay?" He waved his boys on over towards us. They stopped tempting tetanus and shuffled over to join the rest of the brood.

I looked over Curtis's spawn again. Portrait of the American family as misery machine. They all stood by or around their dad. No one actually sat *with* dad, or *on* dad's lap, and no one looked particularly thrilled to be there.

Couldn't blame them.

"So, where y'all from?" I was so surprised by my feelings of pity for Curtis's brood that I was making small talk. Poor fucking kids. As if being so obviously shit-poor and numerous wasn't bad enough. Now they were spending their Saturday watching Daddy detox in a trash-strewn back lot. The theological theory of God's omnibenevolence wears really thin around here. "Anywhere close?"

None of the kids responded to the question. They just stared at the ground. I seemed to be making them as uncomfortable as they were making me. They stared at the ground, kept quiet, and I could feel them wishing me gone. Probably didn't want me witnessing their embarrassment of a family life.

That was fine. I didn't really care what pocket of rural poverty they spent the rest of their week infesting.

A childless front desk was beckoning to me when Curtis's wife answered for her unresponsive litter. Said they were from a small town (name unimportant) about five hours west of here, and did I have any coffee?

The question sounded like such a desperate plea that I volunteered to go fetch her some (getting away from the palpable misery of the Trailer Park Posse comprised the real motive). She insisted on coming with me. Apparently, someone felt the same way about being around her family as I did.

The oldest daughter asked if she could have some coffee, too. When her mom said no, she muttered that common reply of childhood desire thwarted by maternal authority: "...*bitch*."

Her mother spun around and backhanded her face. Her head whipped to the side. I jumped. "*Jesus Christ!*"

The mother strolled right on inside. Kept going, like she hadn't just assaulted a child in front of me. I didn't follow her. My gaze was locked onto her daughter, who hadn't given much of a response to the recent meeting of cheek and knuckles. Blood seeped from the corner of her mouth.

The girl didn't make a noise. Didn't cry, didn't do anything but stare in the direction of her mother with a hatred that could have burned holes through steel.

"You okay?" I asked the girl.

Curtis chuckled. "Sure she is."

3:45pm
FORGIVE YOUR OWN TRESPASSES AND LEAVE MINE THE HELL ALONE

I watched in fascination as the fat old bum puked blood all over the desktop. One retch, two retches, three retches worth of stuff meant to stay on the inside.

"*Jesus Christ*!" Toni shrieked as the blood splashed and started spreading. It soaked the sign-up sheet and began dribbling over the edges.

“*Oooh g-g-god*,” the bum moaned before collapsing onto his own fluids. His head bonked on the desk and blood splashed again as his upper body collapsed into it. Then he was dragged off the desk by his own weight, wiping a clean swath in the middle of the blood pool.

Everyone just stared. Myself, Toni, the other homelies, all transfixed and silent. No one moved to help. The homelies stared at their compatriot on the floor. I stared at the blood flowing back into the space wiped by the bum’s torso and face. Toni stared at the splotches of blood on his shirt. We could’ve stayed that way forever if the human blood dispenser hadn’t given a quiet moan from the floor.

Everyone snapped back to life.

The homeless started shouting. Toni screamed for someone to call *9-1-1*. I went back to reading the paper’s Help Wanted section, commenting, “*There’s* somethin’ you don’t see every day.”

It had been a slow morning, so something interesting was long overdue. If that ‘*something interesting*’ ended up costing some bum his life, *well*…plenty more where that came from.

“*Jesus Jesus Jesus*, he got blood on me,” Toni whined. “He got blood on me. There’s blood on me.”

There sure was. Toni’s shirt was pretty ruined, unless bloodstained button-downs were back in fashion. I ignored his wardrobe complaints and pointed at the desk phone.

“You gonna call *9-1-1* or what?”

The homelies crowded around the dying bum like their favorite TV show was playing on his chest. Wouldn’t have surprised me if they poked him with a stick. ‘*Give him air! Back up!*’ a few shouted, but of course no one did.

“What?” Toni asked.

I pointed at the phone again. "That *9-1-1* shit you were yellin' about. Looks like you're the only one able to do something about it." I was just getting over case of strep, so me talking on the phone would have been rough on my vocal cords. *Priorities*.

He gave a slow nod and picked up the phone. It was halfway to his ear before he shrieked again and dropped it. "There's blood on it!"

Big surprise. There was blood everywhere on the desk, spreading across the top and dripping over the sides. Toni made a few aborted grabs for the phone, dangling by its cord. Blood flowed down the curly-q path to drip from the earpiece. "Ray, give me your shirt!" Toni said.

"Use your own damn shirt," I countered. "It's already ruined."

Toni was frozen by disgust and a desire to not further sully his clothes. One hand reached towards the phone, the other held his shirt away from his skin. Figuring that this distraction had used up its novelty after only thirty seconds (my attention span sucks), I slipped off the filing cabinets and headed for the door.

My boss stuck his head out from his office. Gim asked what was going on. I answered with an exaggerated shrug as I edged between the mob and the lobby's Xmas tree. The homelies were giving their fallen comrade as little breathing room as possible. Not that he would've been able to use the air, anyways. Not with the gurgling sounds he was making.

I caught a glimpse of curly gray hair poking out from the back hallway where the Christers kept their offices. It was a rare appearance by the infamous Reverend Selma. She apparently wasn't going to expose more of her massive bulk until the situation was safely under control.

"TELL ME WHAT'S GOING ON!" she demanded.

"Y'all just got one less tax write-off," was the only decent response to make. Not that religious institutions even pay taxes, but hell, it sounded good at the time.

I went and sat outside in the smog and autumn heat, fending off demands for spare change or free cigarettes. Cars drove past on their way to someplace nicer. Bums watched the cars and provided incentive for them to keep driving. The front of the building always swarmed with the homeless during *C.i.t.G.'s* regular business hours. I thought about how the bum had face-planted into his own blood. There had been a look of realization in his eyes before he hit that said, '*Well, that's me fucked.*'

I chuckled at the image. There's so much suffering in the world that we'd be stupid *not* to find it funny. I hoped my own demise would be equally amusing.

At the end of the street another victim of modern life stood screaming at no one in particular. He wore two different army jackets in spite of the heat and emphasized each word by jabbing his finger at the sky. His dreadlocks jerked with each stab of his finger. The flecks of blue paint on his face meant that he'd recently been maced.

"OUR FATHER," he screamed hoarsely, "HALLOWED BE THY NAME!"

This was the guy's seventh go at the Lord's Prayer since I had been outside. Each time he got more incoherent and louder. Maybe he was worried that his god wouldn't be able to hear him over the traffic. "GIVE US THIS DAY OUR DAILY BREAD!"

Religion and the mentally ill: like they were made for each other.

"He's not listening!" I shouted at the street preacher. An ambulance pulled in front of the building. The lights and sirens were off. There was no hurry. It was too little, too late, and we all knew it

3:59pm
DEAR CATASTROPHE BABYSITTER

"The party in yo mouth, *bitch*, and everyone's coming!"

Julian's belly shook as he laughed at his own joke. Despite his threats, he hadn't killed himself after being booted from the rehab a few days back. It was by far the most disappointing thing to have happened to me all week.

How the kid had managed to talk his way back in here was beyond me. I'd busted Julian and thrown him out, myself. For most folks, failing a piss test meant that we evicted you and kept your money. But, here was this smarmy little bastard still giving me crap after I'd already sent him packing. I bet his parents had talked Gim into it.

Well, if they could talk to Gim, so could I. A serious word was going to be had with my boss about this crap. This job was for sitting on my ass and laughing in the face of other people's suffering. Not for playing babysitter to fat Hispanic kids.

Julian was eighteen, though. A legal adult. He just acted like a brain-damaged child, a side effect of his mom's reproductive system not picking the right fetuses to spontaneously abort.

Just about the entire shift had been spent stopping him from doing one thing or another. I'd caught him at property damage and starting fights with the older clients and hustling stolen goods.

It was apparent which of us was enjoying this more.

"Look, kid," I said, and felt uncomfortably old for having said it, "You can't go around acting like a stupid-ass motherfucker for the rest of your life."

Hearing myself talk in crude, but slightly paternal tones was another reason to get my hackles up. Made me sound too much like my old man. And calling a client '*stupid-ass motherfucker*' was probably one of those things they had talked about in that training seminar I'd slept through.

Calm the fuck down, I told myself. *You're not really letting some fat kid get your goat, are ya?*

I took a deep breath. Don't strangle the little shit. Don't play those games. Grow up. Be mature.

Julian smiled from across the lobby. He winked and grabbed his balls at me. Sorry little bastard. In his mind I'm sure he was the cool and rebellious Thugg defying The Man (as portrayed by the uptight cracker sitting behind that eternal symbol of authority, a desk).

He's not a goddamn kid, I told myself. *Fat little fuck's 18-years old, and when you were that goddamn age you were…well, doing a lot of drugs and being obnoxious. Still, you weren't in a goddamn rehab, and you sure as hell weren't fat or Hispanic. The hell with this little shit playing Vato Without A Cause with you in the role of the joyless authority figure.*

"I got fifty G's in the bank," Julian said. "How much you got?"

Bastard was a Trust Fund baby. His family was loaded enough to buy him his own rehab. Try as he might to pretend that he was one *hard-livin' gangsta* from the Mean Streets, Julian was just another punk-ass rich kid. The young ones at the rehab always were.

"Bet I own yo bitch ass."

The pudgy little fucker wasn't the first client to try an economic pissing contest with me. Usually the clients who did were middle-aged business owners who had built their own companies only to drink it all away (never '*smoke it all away*;' alcoholics seemed to have the best luck climbing the corporate ladder; crackheads never made it beyond assistant manager). Having them flash their old bank statements at me was an obvious ego-defense reaction caused by being in the rehab, by having fallen so far. Julian, on the other hand, hadn't done shit in his life besides chose the wrong male archetype to emulate and then failed at everything accordingly.

High school dropout. Claimed to have done every drug under the sun, but his file only read marijuana and alcohol. He'd call the front desk from the upstairs phone and play some crank call that ended with the phrase, *'deez nuts.'* Then he'd hang up and call back thirty seconds later, asking to speak to himself as if anyone was going be fooled.

I took another deep breath and reminded myself that the biggest challenge in life was to love the unlovable.

This crap thought was replaced two seconds later by the decision that I'd trade all the self-righteous sanctimony in my body for the chance to throttle the mouthy little fuck while bashing his head into the linoleum.

The desire to keep my job wrestled with my urge for temporary satisfaction.

"How much you got, *bitch*?" He threw his chubby arms up while saying that. Fucking retard.

"What you got?"

All this flashed through my head the next day when I arrived at work to find an ambulance and several cop cars in front of the building. They had blocked off three lanes of traffic, and in the middle of the mess were five cops and Julian. They all knelt with their full weight on him, knees jammed into sensitive parts of his body while a paramedic strapped him down to a gurney. He writhed and screamed an incomprehensible mix of fear and pain.

Somebody had smoked some bad shit. Or huffed it.

I stood on the edge of the gawking crowd and watched him being loaded into the ambulance—still struggling, still screaming—and found myself filled with the sort of gleeful satisfaction to which we're not supposed to admit in polite society. There went my biggest work-related headache. Today's shift would be much quieter.

Julian kept lifting his head and smashing it back into the gurney. "*Heeeeelp!*" he screamed.

I gave into temptation and waved a heartfelt goodbye as the ambulance doors closed. Good fucking riddance. A silent prayer was offered up that someone in the mental ward had a thing for fat boys.

Whistling a happy tune as best I could, the door to the rehab was knocked on. Still trying to whistle through an irrepressible smile, I opened the door when it clicked unlocked. Yeah, I might have been too atheist to think that Somebody Up There liked me, but at least They seemed to hate the same people I did.

SWING SHIFT
(4PM-MIDNIGHT)

4:04pm
MORE THAN YOU CAN CHEW

All the homeless were supposed to be cleared out of the building by four. That's when *Christ in the Gutter* closed its doors for the day and the place became 100% rehab/halfway house. Goodbye bums, hello addicts. It was *something* of a step up, or close enough that it was hard to complain.

Personally, my uncharitable ass didn't see why they let the homeless hang around after they finished giving out free shit at noon. All the homelies did was pass out around the lobby, beg for change, and stink up the place. Maybe Selma owned stock in a potpourri company, I dunno.

It was a few minutes past four and, as usual, some of the homeless were still loitering around the building. When I worked the swing shift on the weekdays, it was up to me to send them on their way. That kind of sucked, since I wasn't the one who invited them here in the first place. It was hard enough to clean up my own messes, let alone problems created by other people.

Hunched over the lobby's phone, and smelling strong enough for me to get a whiff of him from behind the desk, was a thick black guy in a poncho. Just a poncho, no undershirt. He kept his bag of flattened beer cans tucked between his legs, he and thumbed through the complimentary phone book on the table next to the phone. He'd flip to a random page, run his finger down the list of names without even looking at the page, then punch a couple numbers into the phone. The guy would mumble a few incoherencies into the receiver before hanging up and repeating the process. It was like a bizarre pantomime of a hard-working secretary, the kind who probably phoned the cops when this guy wandered into their office.

I watched for a little while, amused, then called to him, "Time to pack it in and head on out!"

He looked up at me and barked, "I busy!" then went back to his routine.

Great, I thought, *Semi-retarded AND surly*.

Figuring that he might get tired of his little game after awhile, I went back to reading. A few pages later I looked back up and, seeing that he was still there, called out, "Hey, *Christ of the Crap* is closed, man! Time for you to head out."

He put his hand over the receiver and growled, "I said *I busy*!" then went back to his mummery.

I was pulling an 8-to-12 double shift. After having already spent a few hours around the homeless, my daily allotment of 'tolerating-the-eccentricities-of-the-less-fortunate' was at a low point.

You can mouth all the pious, compassionate bullshit you want when you're speaking it from the freshly scented comfort of your own home. But, spend enough time around the folks that you're supposed to feel so enlightened about, and your feelings change a bit. You start out feeling bad for them, then you get sick of your own pity and start despising the folks who make you feel that way.

Compassion fatigue, I think it's called. How Mother Teresa tolerated those fucking lepers for so long, I'll never know.

Personally, at this point I would've given my left nut to work a job that didn't involve humanity's rejects. Then again, I'd give my left nut for a lot of things. Most of them nowhere near what you'd expect a testicle to go for in an open market economy.

Still...even though I was miffed at being saddled with problems created by the Christers' charity hard-on, I thought I'd stay on the polite side of things:

"No, *really*. Get the hell out."

The bum slammed down the phone and turned, mouth agape that anyone would speak to him like that. Eyes wide with disbelief, he shook his head like I had just made the biggest, most incredibly stupid mistake in the world.

Then he stood up.

Mr. Bum was One Huge Motherfucker. Nearly seven-feet tall and stocky as hell.

Oh...Jesus, something squeaked in the back of my brain. He hadn't looked half this big sitting down.

"Somebody need to kick yo ass!" he thundered.

Oh, shit.

"Somebody need to," he repeated, "But I ain't gonna...not today." Then the Amazing Colossal Bum grabbed his sack of flattened cans and marched out the door.

Except that he missed the handle, and the door failed to open. The entire door shook as the bum walked face-first into it, bumping his forehead against the frame.

Usually not a fan of slapstick, I found this hilarious.

"Really fucked up your exit, huh?"

The bum turned, face red with hate. "THAT DOES IT!" he roared and came for me.

Panicking, I reached back for the solid oak cudgel attached to the building's key ring. I'd always suspected it'd be needed for something like this. Hopefully I could get in a few good whacks at his skull while he slowly crushed the life from me. I reached back and—

Nothing.

I was grabbing for the cudgel but there was a big fucking *Nothing* where my salvation should have been. Spinning around I scanned the desk for it. Where was the goddamn thing? I kept it right behind my chair in case of emergencies. *Dear fucking Christ*, where did it go?

He lunged across the desk. I shot my chair back and almost fell out sideways.

My eyes scanned the desk: nothing, nothing, Nothing!

Shit!

Where did it fucking go?

I backed up against the filing cabinets. Contemplated climbing on top of them. The bum headed around the desk to pulp me up close and personal.

Was this how it was going to end? I wasn't going to die of cancer? A traffic accident? Nor a horrible sexual mishap involving cocoa butter and capuchin monkeys, but from a bum-induced mangling? Shit! Where the fuck was everybody when I was about to get killed? The clients? My ex-NFL boss?

Where had the cudgel gone?

A voice in my head whimpered, *My only regret is to die without ever having 'shroomed with the Pope*. The bum rounded the desk and reached for me.

"That's enough!" shouted a squeaky voice. "That's *quite* enough!"

A small, skinny body wedged itself between me and certain death. "*You* need to leave," Toni instructed the bum. "Time to go. Time to get out. *Shoo! Shoo!"*

The bum was herded out of the building by my favorite *C.i.t.G.* employee. Still flattened against the filing cabinets, I watched in relief as the door shut behind him.

Toni came back to inspect me. "Don't you worry," he said, taking the opportunity to pat me repeatedly on the chest and help me back into my chair. "Don't you worry; he won't hurt you."

Toni patted and fussed over me for a short while longer (a little groping was better than the previous option). Then he grabbed his bags, took a cigarette from its pack, and headed home for the day. The cigarette was lit as he walked out the front door. Despite having just finished an end-of-shift cigarette break, touching me apparently called for a celebratory smoke.

"*Fuck...me*," I sighed. A poncho-wearing minority from a lower tax bracket had almost killed me. It was exactly what all those conservative pundits had always warned would happen. But where the fucking hell had the cudgel gone? Where was my one means of defense when I had needed it?

The question was answered when my boss strolled past the desk, carrying a plate of food that he had just liberated from the kitchen fridge...the *locked* kitchen fridge.

Gim smiled at me as he passed. "Keep up the good work, Ray!" Then he tossed the cudgel-mounted keys onto the desk.

I stared after him in disbelief. I had almost gotten killed because someone's oversized ass couldn't wait to hit a drive-thru on the way home from work? Thanks to him I'd had to suffer the agony of expecting my life to flash before my eyes while only getting reruns of *Friends*?

Bastard!

I made a plan to wait till my boss was gone and then piss in one of the potted plants he kept in his office. It wouldn't threaten Gim's life in a similar manner, no. But the week or so he'd spend wondering where *that smell* was coming from would go a ways toward evening the score.

4:08PM
JOE HILL DIED IN VAIN

Gim was hanging around longer than usual. Most days he'd be already gone, but at a little past four he walked out of his office and handed questionnaires to myself and Jack.

As head Tech and my immediate supervisor, Jack was manning the front desk (and thus stuck answering the phone and clicking the door unlocked) while I lay on the lobby's leather couch.

State law dictated that two Techs always be on duty whenever the client population exceeded thirty-five persons. We had fifty-plus clients at any one time. My employers broke the law every morning, night, and weekend by only having one Tech on duty (and thus, only one on the payroll). To make up for this, on weekday afternoons there were two people sitting around for a job that barely required one of us.

Gim towered over me, tall enough to block out the lobby's florescent lighting. He handed a sheet of paper first to Jack, then myself.

"It's from the head office," Gim explained as I hurriedly sat up on the couch. Reclining like I was discussing my Oedipal tendencies was all well and good when Gim was gone, but otherwise I did try to *look* busy. Awake, at the very least.

I examined the paper. "The hell's this?"

It read:

FROM THE DESK OF GEORGE FRIST, CEO:

LET'S WORK TOGETHER TO MAKE OUR COMPANY BETTER!

Our company, huh? So why didn't I ever get an invite when the board of directors convened for a meeting?

ONLY BY WORKING TOGETHER CAN WE MAKE THIS THE BEST CHEMICAL DEPENDENCY REHABILITATION SERVICE IN TEXAS! ANSWER THE SIMPLE QUESTIONS BELOW AND SHARE WITH US WHAT YOU CAN DO TO IMPROVE A NEW START, INC.!

As far as I was concerned, I was doing my part for the company by working for shit wages with no medical benefits. What more did the guy want from us plebeians? Effort?

1. WHAT CAN YOU DO TO HELP OUR COMPANY CUT DOWN ON EXTRANEOUS COSTS?

For starters, I could probably stop stealing office supplies. It wouldn't be easy to kick my monthly stapler habit cold turkey. Maybe if I switched to something less addictive, like paper clips.

2. HOW CAN YOU INCREASE OUR COMPANY'S BUSINESS LEVELS?

What the fuck? When did I get drafted to work in the advertising department? Did they want me to suggest installing a giant-sized Junkie Magnet outside our building?

It began to dawn on me that our cheap-ass CEO just hadn't felt like springing for a consulting firm. He'd apparently hoped that canvassing his employees for ideas would save a few thousand bucks. Considering how most of my coworkers could barely alphabetize (sad, really, but it gave an accurate view of the American education system), I'd have to say that the fucker was majorly shit out of luck.

Served him right.

I took my pen and wrote under the second question: '*I'm going to get all my friends hooked on crack.*'

Gim cleared his throat. "By the way, guys, George's birthday is coming up, and everybody's pitching in five bucks for a present."

Our boss looked at me and then Jack, expectantly. I stared right back.

"Is this the asshole that gives us ten-cent raises? Or is it the prick that refuses to pay us for overtime?" Two purely rhetorical questions.

Gim shrugged and turned to my coworker. "Jack?"

"Fuck him," said Jack. "I had a birthday, too."

4:13pm
BLACK HISTORY MONTH: ABRIDGED

February was Black History Month. I was surrounded by living Black History. There were guys here old enough to tell me what it was like to live in Pasadena during segregation. They could give me a first-hand appreciation of what it felt like to be legally recognized as a second-class citizen.

Fuck knows why I cared. Possibly it was intellectual curiosity, but the smart money would've been on boredom. Time passed damn slow around here, just like it does at any braindead job.

I decided to ask Jack about it. He was my coworker for the four-to-midnight shift. An ex-crackhead like Toni. He looked like an aged version of the actor, Danny Glover, if only Mr. Glover had shot Mel Gibson in the back midway through the first *Lethal Weapon* movie and then stolen his wallet.

Jack was the shiftiest fucker I'd met in my life. And I admired the hell out of him for it. Whenever something went wrong during our shift he'd blame me like it was a natural reflex.

Tap the knee. "*Ray done it*!"

And yeah, I'd shrug and take the blame. What the fuck; like I was going to make a career out of this shit? Jack, on the other hand, was in his 70s, already retired, and worked the rehab as a way of augmenting his social security or something. Maybe they paid him under the table, I don't know.

Jack had lived in Pasadena all his life. He'd remember what it was like to drink from '*Colored*' fountains. How it felt to address every white man with a polite '*Sir*' and downcast eyes. Jack would be able to tell me what it was like to spend his youth in the back of the bus.

If all those years of smoking crack hadn't eaten up that part of his brain.

(the hippocampus, isn't it?)

"What was it like back then?" I asked him as he sat at the front desk making up the chore list. I was on the couch, thumbing through the *Help Wanted* section of the newspaper. "What was it like living in Texas back during segregation?"

"What was *what*?" Jack's old, but not *that* hard of hearing.

"What was it like to live here in Pasadena back during segregation? The water fountains and separate dining areas and shit. What was it like?"

Jack kept staring down at the chore list. I thought he wasn't going to answer, but then he said, "It sucked."

I waited for elaboration.

None was forthcoming.

"Yeah, I figured that much," I said. "But what was it like? What was the sucking like?"

Jack just shrugged. "It sucked."

Obviously, this was as informative as the guy was going to get. I guess as a white boy I didn't have the proper security clearance to hear about it. Or maybe he didn't want painful memories to be used as entertainment fodder by someone who could never understand what it had been like to be born on society's bottom rung.

Or was I just indulging in the sort of liberal bullshit that I usually despised?

A strong dose of cheap cologne hit my nose, and then Corey walked into the lobby. He was done up in a purple dress suit with a striped yellow tie. The word '*natty'* came to mind, for some reason. The suit made him look even smaller than usual, and Corey couldn't have been more than a few inches over five feet. No wonder his wife wouldn't talk with him anymore. How could you take someone so diminutive seriously in the sack?

Corey and I had gotten off to a rough start earlier that week, so I decided to be extra nice with the guy. "Off to church?" I asked.

"Sure am," he smiled broadly as he signed himself out. "Gonna go give some praise to the Lord with my brothers and sisters."

"You got brothers and sisters?" Jack asked. "Figure yo' parents woulda known to stop after you."

Corey stiffened for a second, then said as sweetly as possible, "I'm ignorin' you today, Jack."

"Lucky me."

"You ain't gonna get my goat, today," Corey said.

Jack loved giving Corey shit. *Reverend Leroy*, Jack called him. It was the same name he gave to every client with only a few days' sobriety and a mouthful of Jesus. '*Yo' mouth the first thing to heal*,' Jack would always say. '*Yo brain may still be sick as shit, but that don't stop yo' mouth from flappin*'.'

Corey was the third Reverend Leroy I'd known here. They never lasted long. I had no idea what the nickname referenced, but the clients seemed to hate it enough.

“Don’t want yo’ goats,” Jack said. “Just you *gone*.”

Picking on the junkies was a hobby of Jack’s. Fuck knows how he got away with it, but nobody had fired him yet. Corey looked like he was about to lose his cool—and right before church, to boot—so I changed the subject.

I asked, “*You* live down here during segregation and around then-abouts?” He nodded.

“*Hell yeah*,” Corey said, then made an obvious display of crossing himself for having cursed. “Course, I wasn’t born till fifty-eight, and by that time the Good Lord was already leading our people from the Valley of Shadows into the Prom—”

“*Reverend* Leroy!” Jack slapped the desk. “Shut the *hell* up!”

For a second it looked like Corey was actually going to say something back. “*Jack*, I don’t…”

Jack stared him down. “You don’t *what*?”

Corey gave up and stormed out the front door.

Jack went back to the chore list. “Stupid *muthafucka*,” he said. “Let’s see how full of God he be when I put his ass scrubbin’ pots and pans.”

4:16pm
THANKS FOR THE CONTEMPT

Late getting out the door, my boss passed by the couch to give me a small plastic box. Another was placed on the desk next to Jack. It was transparent, wrapped in pink ribbon and filled with confetti. An envelope was nestled inside.

“The head office thought morale was getting low among you Techs,” he explained with a *not-my-fault* shrug.

“There better be a raise in here,” I said. I’d just learned about the scam the management at American Airlines had pulled on its employees while giving a humongous bonus to its CEO, so I wasn’t in the mood to get jerked around by ours. “Or some health insurance.”

Gim never stopped walking as he passed, just handed the package off like we were playing Hot Potato. “It’s a $10 gift certificate to *Einstein’s Bagels*,” he explained.

“That’s perfect!” I shouted at his retreating form. “Since I can’t *fucking* afford groceries!”

Not receiving shit for a salary meant that even on my days off I’d sneak back up to work and eat dinner with the junkies. The food got shoveled down my throat fast enough to give me indigestion. Not even free grub made me want to spend time around here without getting paid for it.

There’s a theory that if you hang around *anything* long enough you’ll start to emulate it, and I’d hate to ever find myself blowing strangers for a fix.

(Oddly enough, even though I can’t afford groceries, I *can* afford to go out and hit the clubs on my days off. Prioritizing can be a bitch.)

I would have yelled something else, but Gim’s enormous stride had him out the back door before my brain could devise anything angry enough to express my displeasure, yet safe to yell at someone twice my size.

“Can you believe this shit?” I asked Jack, who answered with a shrug. “I haven’t had health insurance in almost a year, our CEO lives in a River Oaks estate, and their thanks for us working on starvation wages is a fuckin’ *bagel certificate*?” I got up to slam my gilded piece of class warfare into the trash, then plopped back down on the couch in a sulk.

I realized that my not getting paid for shit at work was possibly related to my not *doing* shit at work, but why should I be penalized for the inherent laziness of my job?

We sat in silence for a while, me stewing in my own self-righteous juices and Jack listening to smooth jazz on the radio. “I'll show ’em,” I said finally. “Just for that, I'm gonna work *half* as hard!”

Jack started chuckling and I joined in, both of us laughing at the thought of putting any sort of effort into our jobs. Then I sat around and fantasized about violating our CEO with a bowie knife strap-on.

“If somebody can get away with doing somethin’ to your ass, they gonna do it,” Jack said. “Ain’t nothin’ personal, just how people are.”

“Whatever,” I said.

At the end of the shift, when no one was looking, I fished the certificate out of the trash. I knew I’d probably need it.

4:20pm
WATCHING OTHER MEN URINATE: FOR FUN AND PROFIT

There was a long list of names in my work mailbox, and I knew what that meant: Mass U.A.s Urinary Analyses.

Piss tests, in the common vernacular.

It was time once again for my favorite part of the job: watching other men urinate.

Joy.

Rapture.

Yee-*fuckin'*-haw.

Time to observe the junkies as they dribbled their wastes into plastic containers. Time to seal those plastic containers and ship them off to laboratories to be searched for those naughty chemical compounds that shouldn't be there. Time to argue with the clients about who was more degraded by the whole procedure.

Fucking piss tests. I had to take one to work here. Drank six cups of water and took that crucial, seal-breaker of a first piss before the test. The result was a 'diluted specimen,' but Gim was cool enough to let me bullshit my way past that. His trusting nature was the first hint that here was the nicest boss I'd ever had. What else could I do but take advantage of it?

The waiting list to get into the facility must've been getting long. Whenever there were large amounts of people waiting to get in here, the word came down from on high to pick about twenty of the clients to test. Broad sweeps like this would always turn up a few guys whose claims to sobriety were as big of a sham as my own. The offending parties would get the boot, the facility would keep the money they'd already shelled out for the month, and someone new would move into their bed and cough up even more dough. Twice the money for half the junkies.

So, like most things in America, these episodes of mass testing were basically moneymaking scams. Fuck this entire place, top to bottom: micro and macro levels and all stops in-between.

This mercenary bit of bullshit wasn't Gim's fault. I think my boss was actually interested in helping addicts, having once been in their shoes, himself. The fault for this crap, and for all client/employee-screwing schemes that occurred at our facility, was squarely on the shoulders of our Beloved CEO and Leader. I think his name is 'George' or whatever. *Fukkit*, not like he remembers mine.

I mean, that's where I put the blame for all this, at least. It had to go somewhere, right?

I attended a speech the guy gave once, and all he did was ramble on about money for twenty minutes. Money. Money. Money. At three-grand a month each, with more than fifty guys here, this place was lucrative as all fucking hell. And Georgie-boy happened to own about six or seven of these facilities.

Yeah, *A New Start* is basically a franchise. We're the McDonald's of rehabilitation: '*Billions and billions failed*.'

I remembered listening in horror to our CEO's lack of subtlety during his speech. Apparently, pretending like he was at least *somewhat* interested in helping people was too much effort for the asshole. It was all about the money. And then there were the ten-cent raises the guy gave. Needless to say, I wouldn't piss up his ass if his guts were on fire.

I made a large sign and taped it to the front of the desk. It read: "`PEOPLE LUCKY ENOUGH TO PISS IN FRONT OF ME`," and under that the names were listed. The guys could then come up to me and say: '*My name on that list*'. It kept me from having to put names I didn't know with faces I couldn't be bothered to recognize.

"Hey!" A knock on the desk wrenched me from my book. A gangly pill-head, all flailing limbs and desperation, Paul danced an urgent shuffle in front of me. "My name's on the list, big guy. Let's do this 'cause I gotta piss like hell."

"All right." I set the book aside and whipped out the complicated form that gets shipped off to the lab along with the sample. Wiping drool off his lips with the back of his hand, Paul stared at in it horror.

Sign here, sign here, initial here, birthday here, today's date here, evening phone number here, initial here, bequeath us the rights to your first-born son here, and finally, sign right here.

"*Jesus*," Paul moaned, saliva dripping from his chin. "You're gonna have a hell of a mess if this doesn't start going any faster!"

"Suits me fine." I pointed out the appropriate locations for his signature. "Dunno if whoever's in charge of moppin' downstairs this week would appreciate it, though."

"That's me." Paul was hunched over, crossing his skinny white legs.

"Oh…have at, then."

"Don't tempt me."

I walked Paul to the ladies' bathroom. It's the one I always use since it's about ten times cleaner and less disgusting than the men's. A pair of oversized pants was lying in a heap on the floor. Homeless fodder. I kicked them out of the way.

Paul stood over the toilet and aimed himself into the plastic sample cup. I slouched in the corner and gazed everywhere except at him. "Gonna hold it for me?" Paul asked over his shoulder.

"Nope," I said. "But for an extra five bucks I'll give it a final shake or two."

He laughed and called me a sick bastard. It was the nicest compliment I'd gotten all day.

4:31pm
ACUTE MALE SYNDROME

Being possessed of a fine pair of working eardrums, I'd already eavesdropped on Pike's conversation. He was talking with his wife on the lobby telephone. I heard the pleading, heard the apologizing, heard the angry words exchanged before the phone was slammed into the receiver. When he plopped down across from my desk with an exaggerated sigh, I realized that I was going to hear the story all over again.

Pike, like most males capable of it, was a compulsive philanderer. In the two months that he'd been here Pike had shagged his way through an impressive number of young ladies. They were all met through AA functions and other 12-Step meetings. As the more predatory among us know, nobody is easier to screw than the emotionally vulnerable, and few places have more emotionally vulnerable women than 12-Step meetings.

It's not a pretty strategy. Not one you'd brag about to your friends. But it works, and that's all most guys ask.

The slang term for picking up the other human wrecks you met at recovery meetings is *13th Stepping*.

Pike was king of the 13th Step.

I'm not sure how he pulled it off so well. Pike wasn't unattractive, but he wasn't about to model for Calvin Klein in his underwear, either. The guy was just your average-looking, dark-haired cracker. Vaguely Mediterranean face. The kind you could walk past on the street (or in his case, step over in the gutter) and never look at twice. Generic with a capital *G*.

The only thing surprising about Pike was his age. Pike was 38 years old. I originally took him for about 25. Considering all the poisons that had traveled through his system, I'd have to grant the guy a super-human constitution.

Pike got back up from the couch to look down the surrounding hallways, making sure they were as empty as the rest of the lobby. Everything was clear, so Pike felt safe to tell me, "I'm in trouble."

"That's why you're here." I smiled at him without getting one in return.

Pike needed someone to talk at, and like most clients, he was willing to put up with a bit of sarcasm if it meant that he could indulge in some gut-spilling. The desperate human need for disclosure can be exploited by those of us with an equally desperate need to make snide remarks at the expense of others.

"There's this girl I've been seeing..." Pike began. I slapped on my listening-attentively face, waiting for the next opportunity to amuse myself at his expense. He was about to continue the story, but a horrible coughing jag cut him short. Pike was sick, of course, just like everybody else in this goddamn place. I had the start of a cold, myself. Hopefully it'd go away on its own. Being one of the millions of American without health insurance meant that I had to use community clinics. At those places I sat right next to the same stinking homeless people I saw here in the mornings. It sucked.

Having hacked his contagion all over his hand, which he then wiped on the couch, Pike gave me the clincher: "And it turns out the girl's pregnant."

"Demand a blood test," I suggested. "And if that fails, there's always the next Greyhound outta town."

He just looked down at his hands. "It's probably mine," Pike said. "We haven't been using protection."

"Withdraw, at least?"

He shook his head.

Jesus. Now, I can understand not wanting to use condoms, but *for fuck sakes...*

"Just got off the phone with my wife about it," he said.

I know the details, I thought to myself. *Your pain is nothin' but cheap entertainment to me.*

"And," Pike sighed, "She wants me to never see the girl again."

I nodded, waiting for him to hurry up and get to the juicy parts.

"That's no problem," Pike continued. "I've hurt my wife enough, as is." The guy's got four—make that five—kids. There's three with his wife, one from a previous indiscretion, and now this little bundle of trouble.

"But then, she wanted me to promise that I'd never see the kid." He was aghast at the suggestion. "*Problem*. I grew up without a dad, myself. And look at me now!" I looked at him and saw a guy with womanizing skills I'd kill for. "No goddamn kid of mine is gonna do the same!"

His righteous declaration made, Pike stood up to leave. "Don't tell anyone, okay?"

There was no real need for him to make the request. Everyone here already knew or would know soon enough. Word travels so fast around this place, it's like the grapevine's wired with fiber optics.

"*Hey*," I said, doing my best to look offended. "Don't know why I'd tell anyone, and I don't know why anyone would care." Obviously, guys enjoy gossip just as much as the alternate sex. I was already looking forward to spreading around this little tidbit.

Pike tried to smile. "Thanks, Ray," he said. "Appreciate it." His spirits seemed to have lifted slightly. The burden a little less heavy on his brow. There's nothing like hearing a comforting lie to make things better.

Telling them helps, too. As Pike left the lobby, he called back, "No more girls, man! I'm sticking by my wife, and she's sticking by me!"

"Good luck!" I called after him. It was hard to suppress a disbelieving smirk, but what counts is that I tried.

Pike tried, too. He lasted four days. It was a personal record.

4:39pm
THERE'S NO RISING FROM THE GRAVE OF STUPIDITY

In order to fund the slaughter of Latin Americans back in the 1980s, the CIA helped flood inner-city America with coke. This created such a surplus of the product that crack cocaine came into popular being. Money was made by all the right folks, and only brown people were harmed. It was Keynesian capitalism at its finest.

A New Start's crackheads, fresh off the pipe, now went around discussing their simpleton's version of religion: the god of the 12-Step and his Lowest Common Denominator theology. They had jumped straight from one White Man's Dope to another.

Easter was next Sunday, so the miracle of the resurrection was the main topic of discussion in the lobby. Today, they argued fairy tales. Sunday, they would go to church and listen to the preacher tell how Jesus hit rock bottom and made his subsequent recovery. It was just the sort of act the junkies were all hoping to emulate.

In a reversal of our usual seating arrangement, Jack sat on the lobby's couch while I manned the desk. He was moderating the discussion with a few of the clients. And by 'moderating,' I mean that he reserved for himself the right to interrupt whenever the urge hit.

"Okay, so Jesus go and descend into hell…" Frankie said.

"I *know* what yo' ass about to say." Jack had apparently turned psychic sometime during the shift. "Jesus choose to die, right? But that ain't no suicide like if me or you do it. And even though he came back to life, that still don't take back that dyin' for our sins thing."

I tuned them out. Stupid-ass, Sunday school motherfuckers. Listening to the guys nitpick about their favorite fairy tales, I decided that AA hadn't picked Christianity as its religious model for reasons of intellectual complexity. Most of the crackheads could barely read, let alone tell poetic allegories from a factual assertion. And so here they were, discussing a metaphor for personal growth like they'd heard it on yesterday's evening news.

Looking for a distraction, I called my girlfriend's number. Her voice mail picked up. Busting out my best Barry White impression, I breathed, "This is Christ thy Lord, baby. I died for your sins, sugar, so the least you can do is call me back." I was about to return the phone to its cradle, but then inspiration struck and I screamed into the receiver, "*You owe me, bitch!*"

The phone was hung up. I chuckled to myself, always amused by my own jokes. Then I looked around me. The phone line might have been dead, but now so were any nearby theological discussions. There was utter silence in the lobby. I must've interrupted things with my high-volume profanity. A dozen black faces stared at me. Robert spoke for all of them. "The fuck…?"

A smile was beamed at everyone. "That's right," I said. "*Never* turn your back on a messiah."

Look, it's not that I'm trying to talk shit about Easter. I'm not even trying to mock the overall myth of Jesus. Actually, I'm rather fond of it. I've grown to like what it says about our species. What hardcore bad-asses it makes us out to be.

To illustrate:

God shows up on our planet, tries to tell us how to live, and what do we do?

We *lynch* the Bastard!

Humans: 1

Loving God: 0

4:44pm
FAVORS AND (IN)GRATITUDE

There was an envelope in my mail slot. Scrawled on it in a crude and sloppy print was my name. The handwriting looked female, but with the sharp edges and lack of grace usually associated with male scribblings.

My paycheck was the only envelope I was used to getting at work. I tore this new discovery open with all the hurry and excitement that novelty deserves. Inside was a photograph.

The front of our building formed the background of the shot, and the focus was a lone subject, Cassandra. She was the single mom whom volunteered at the homeless ministry. Whom had herself recently been homeless. And whom I had shagged the other week.

No fuckin' way, I thought, not sure whether to be amused, revolted, or a mixture of the two.

The picture was a close-up shot of a blue-jean covered butt. Plump and wide in that down-home Southern style. Cassandra's smiling face peeked out from behind the mound of blue that occupied most of the shot. She had bent over and grabbed her ass at the camera. Her hands squeezed the cheeks.

Never thought I'd write this about a butt-shot, but the overall effect was monstrous. Cassandra's ass swelled to gigantic proportions and loomed almost threateningly. The grin on her face looked like it was stolen off a homicidal circus clown.

Historically speaking, this was The Scariest Picture I Had Ever Seen.

Was she mooning me? Was this supposed to be sensuous? Was her ass really bigger than I recalled? And, most importantly, whom did she convince to stick that camera in her butt and snap a picture?

Hell, the answer to the last question could have been: *anybody*. All the dirty old men in the building drooled a river whenever Cassandra walked in the door. True, they tended to overreact to any female on the premises, but Cassandra's frequent presence and cute young face guaranteed her a constant male following. And undoubtedly, a starring role in the private games of pocket-pool played in the late hours upstairs.

She probably got Toni to take the picture. Who better than a middle-aged gay man to attempt heterosexual erotica with a welfare mother? It all made sense, in its own cracked-out way.

Man, what's the opposite of arousal? I wondered. And, if my girlfriend ever found this, would she be pissed at me for cheating, or laugh at me for what I had cheated on her with?

I looked again at the picture, just to make sure that there wasn't something subtle I was missing. Maybe there was some hidden pictorial key that could reassure me that I wasn't really supposed to take it seriously. This just *couldn't* have been meant to arouse me. I checked the envelope for a "*just kidding!*" note in her jagged scrawl, but there was nothing in it apart from good intentions and failed results.

Just remember, I told myself, *Nobody forced you to sleep with the girl.*

No, no one had. I saw Cassandra occasionally when I worked the 8-4 shift. She would hang around making small talk and complaining about how long it had been since she'd gotten laid (before her kid was conceived about *13 months* ago—yikes!). I always made the usual polite and commiserative noises until I realized that she wasn't just making idle conversation.

Nor was she coming on to me. Not really. Basically, Cassandra had a problem and wanted my help taking care of it.

Why the hell not? I remember thinking. *How often are people going to ask for favors like this?* If someone needing sex wasn't an obvious chance for charity, I didn't know what was.

Cassandra was friendly enough, so my lack of physical attraction to her could be placed aside as unimportant. If she needed a favor, I might as well lend a hand. Or some other appendage. Consider it a labor of…well, not love. Not at all. *Jesus*, no. Maybe lust, at the very most. As an emotion it's way more common and inconsequential than love, and therefore infinitely more trustworthy.

"It's the one corporeal work of mercy that Thomas Aquinas's celibate ass missed out on," I explained later to Robert. "He had Feeding the Hungry and Burying the Dead, but forgot all about Shaggin' the Hard-Up."

Robert just said, "Who?"

I had met Cassandra one Sunday for drinks. She'd insisted on the alcohol, being more than a little nervous. We boozed, we chatted, and we avoided talking about the purpose for our meeting. I mentioned the Lamarckian heresy of acquired traits as an explanation for hereditary alcoholism; Cassandra told me about having worn pasties as a stripper to protect the Good and Christian people of Oklahoma from her nipples. Then we headed back to my place for that thing we all love to do.

It all felt very formal and business-like. The fucking, I mean. Like each thrust counted for an extra tally on the pay-meter. As if we should've given each other a handshake afterwards, instead of that awkward kiss. She was the first mulatto I'd ever slept with, but nothing too memorable besides that.

'*Not bad for a white boy,*' was Cassandra's evaluation (to my face, at least).

And I had figured that to be that. Patted myself on the back, scrubbed my genitals with antibiotic soap and considered our interactions complete. Cassandra tried to phone me a few times at work, but I always managed to dodge the call.

I did, however, learn a very important lesson about shagging the recently pregnant. A lesson aside from how cool stretch marks look when they spider-web a melanin-tanned belly. It had to do with me thinking, as I lifted her legs over my shoulders: *Jesus Christ! Maybe I should just reach up in there and jack myself off*!

It wasn't that I regretted fucking Cassandra. Not really. A shag's a shag, after all, and it had been kind of flattering to be picked for stud-service out of an entire building of willing males. Most of them weren't what I'd consider serious competition, but the ego takes what it can get.

The photograph was looked at one more time. The blue mountain of a butt still erupted at me. Cassandra's expression looked no less frightening. I guess we're all grotesques when seen from the right angle.

I stuffed the photo back in its envelope. Maybe I could sell it to one of the guys.

4:55pm
LIKE AN ALCOHOLIC ST. FRANCIS

"I'd get up all early in the mornin', have a loaf of stale bread and a bottle of Thunderbird with me, and I'd go sit in my momma's backyard. All morning I'd drink and be feedin' the squirrels and birds."

Technically, you're not supposed to look back on any part of your addiction fondly. It's one of the innumerable AA rules. But I could have sworn that while he rambled at me from the one of the chairs lining the lobby's wall, there was something like a peaceful smile on Herman's ugly mug.

From my place on the couch, I pointed and laughed. "Who the fuck are you, the alcoholic St. Francis of Assisi?"

A puzzled look. "Who's that, boy?"

Lecture time. Professor Ray on Special Ed duty. "Catholic saint. Preached to the birds and animals when no one else would listen to his ass. Personally, I think his legend's a comp from some of the pagan nature gods, just like a bunch of the other saints. With Francis it was probably either—"

He rolled his eyes. Herman couldn't have given two shits about a lecture on comparative mythology. It figured. Most of the guys here were allergic to anything more than monosyllabic grunting.

As if that set them apart from the rest of the country.

"*The fuck* you talking about?" he asked me. "*Boy*, you either stupid or crazy!"

Herman grew up here in Texas. Until he was almost thirty, anyone a few shades paler could address him with a condescending '*Boy*.' The guy had to be enjoying his turn to use the label right back on white folk without fear of reciprocation. Herman probably adopted the term right after the passage of the Civil Rights Act in '64 and hadn't stopped since.

"You gotta talk real loud and real slow, Ray." Jack strolled back into the lobby. "He gettin' deaf *and* senile."

Jack sometimes even came here on his days off to torment the clients. We've all got our hobbies.

Herman wasn't going to play along, though. "You better watch how you talk to me, old man." Jack's got five years on Herman, though it looks the other way around and doubled. "I'd hate to have to take you out front and whup yo ass in front of all them bums."

You can get thrown out for threatening the staff, but Jack just sat down behind the front desk and made a fist with his left hand. "You see this?" he held it up to Herman. "Registered as a lethal weapon. And this," he held up his right hand, "I'm scared of this one, myself."

I reclined on the couch to leave the two of them to their shit-talking. A broken marionette that someone had dressed in a blue-jean jacket and cowboy boots strolled into the lobby. Flashing me a smile through a beard that probably outweighed the rest of him, Terry came and sat on the other side of the couch. I moved my feet for him, but not much.

Terry indicated Jack and Herman with a nod of his head. "What's going on here?"

"They're taking turns threatening each other."

"Old black men love to talk shit." Terry stated this authoritatively, like it was a factoid he'd gotten off The Discovery Channel. "Go to the AA meetings and it's the same thing; get two of them together and they can't shut up about how they're still bad-asses." A look of mild disgust crossed his face and decided to stay there.

"Must be the Viagra," I suggested. Jack was on the stuff, or something like it. He had shown me a handful of little blue pills. Refused to share any, though.

"And I'm pretty sick of *that one*," Terry pointed at Herman, "Calling me a fucking '*boy*.'"

Tired of sparring with Jack, Herman turned to walk from the lobby. He pointed at the duffel bag he had brought with him. "Grab my bags, Ray."

I took a deep breath, counted to five, exhaled. People giving me orders drives me ape shit. Worthless old alcoholics thinking that my title was *Addicts' Bitch* were an especially sore spot with me.

He's old, I told myself in an attempt to keep calm. *He's old and going to be dead soon. He's old and going to be dead soon.*

"*Ray*! I said grab—"

"Get the fuck outta here," I growled. "And next time, stop and think before you piss off someone with keys to your insulin supply."

Herman found this hilarious. "You all right, Ray," he laughed. "You all right…no matter *what* shit Jack says behind your back."

5:02pm
DON'T WRENCH YOUR ARM OUT OF SOCKET…

In addition to sharing a building with the *Christ in the Gutter*, my work also shares a phone number with them. That means, after the Methodists have gone home, there's always people stopping by for free handouts or calling me on the phone to ask about the free handouts or anything to do with the idea of getting something for nothing.

Despite my quickness in telling about the lack of free shit to be found at the time, some of them hang around past the telling. The homelies who come wandering in want to use the facilities and/or see if it's possible to bum food or money off me. They ask for spare change or spare sandwiches, whatever's available.

Unfortunately for them, assisting the perpetually helpless and stinky was no longer part of *my* ethical code. It might've been at one time, but now I figured that they could die in the street for all my uncharitable ass cared.

One of the homelies, a skinny black guy in a worn tracksuit and purple jacket (obvious charity cast-offs) took offense when I wouldn't open my wallet to him. "You hang around here?" he asked, as if I'd come to this part of town without being paid for it.

"Maybe."

He narrowed his eyes at me. "Then I'll be waitin' for your white ass. Watch yo'self."

I shot him the bird as he walked out the door. That had been my fifth threat of the day, but it'd been a slow shift.

A mental note was made to vote Republican in the next election. Fuck these people. Then I remembered that the poor are generally left to fend for themselves in this country, no matter which branch of the ruling class held office.

I think it was British wit Samuel Johnson who said that the true worth of a man is how he treats someone who can do him no good in return. This probably meant that I was getting nothing but coal in my stocking for Christmas. If I followed Johnson's maxim, I'd be going out of my way to lavish all the free crap I could on the homelies. Hell, I'd happily give them money from my wallet, the literal shirt off my own back. I'd steal them food from the kitchen.

But, maybe it wasn't Samuel Johnson who said that. Scholars are divided on the attribution.

Almost as annoying as the homelies were the folks who called for the Methodists. These potential donors always felt the need—after I'd done the Methodists' work and recited the basic info about how the donations are handled—to continue to ramble on to me about what Great and Caring People they are. How they do the Good Lord's work and help out the street folk.

And they tell me.

And they tell me some more.

And then some more.

All the Great and Beautiful things that they do in selfless service to what Mother Teresa called, '*Christ in his Most Wretched of Guises*.'

And I'm like: '*Hey, great! Spiffy for you! Just why the fuck are you telling me this? Hoping, maybe, that through me it'll get back to Jesus?*'

'*Am I in charge of redeeming the 'GoodWorks' tickets for those brownie points you're obviously expecting in heaven?*'

'*Is altruism like martyrdom; there's no point bothering with it if you don't have an audience?*'

"Them donations do help a lot of people," Robert pointed out to me.

"Maybe," I said, "But don't mistake it for altruism. Those fucks are hoping for one hell of a reward. Like, the ultimate retirement package. A post-mortem pay-off!"

Robert rolled his eyes. "Alright, Ray; I get it."

"Hell," I said, "Those folks are expecting eternal bliss in their paychecks. I'm just doing this for eight bucks an hour." And then the phone rang again with another Good Samaritan wanting to know where he could get rid of his old sweatshirts.

Yes, God bless the big-hearted folk who take care of those less fortunate. Theirs is the kingdom *blah blah blah*...

It's just that...*well*...if you're really doing that much good in the world, I figure other people will do your bragging for you. There's no need to go tell it on the mountain. No need to bother me with it. If you're really the second fucking coming of Momma T., then other people (or your god with his hard-on for volunteerism) will notice those good deeds and reward you with the accolades that you crave. Either in this world or the one that you're so goddamn sure is yet to come.

5:18pm
LIVE AND DON'T LEARN

Jack's smile pushed the wrinkles on his face into turbulent ripples of dark brown. Switching the front desk's unit to 'speaker phone,' he keyed in the number for his voice mail, then selected his saved messages and turned up the volume.

This was to be our entertainment.

Sharing the lobby's couch were myself, Robert, and Frankie. A couple other crackheads also lounged around the lobby, either gathered by the desk or slouched in the chairs lining the lobby. Jack was the center of our attention, and he knew it. This wasn't the first time Jack had amused us with phone messages from his ex-girlfriends. Considering the promiscuous life he led, it probably wouldn't be the last.

Still grinning, Jack gave a little shrug as the message blared from the speaker.

It was a woman's voice. Vaguely unhappy. "*You fuckin' slime-ass nigger piece of shit!! Pick yo goddamn phone up! I know yo stupid nigger ass be there! I know you there! Pick up the motherfuckin' phone befo' I fuckin' kill—*"

From the second the voice split the lobby's air, we were all hooting loud enough to almost drown out the message.

"*Ah haw haw hoo*!" Jack cackled along with the rest of us. It seemed that by the time you reached his age, you were comfortable enough to flaunt your failures. Most of us tried to hide how lousy we were at relationships. Not Jack. His M.O. seemed to be something along the lines of: '*Hey! Come check this out! Think y'all can't keep somebody's love for shit? Look how crazy I drove this bitch! And in record time, too*!'

Jack had been on the pipe for nine years, sober now for eight. Not only had he smoked his weight in crack, he'd also gotten his ex-wife doing it. I had asked him whatever happened to her, but he just changed the subject.

Jack also used to deal the stuff, and he'd told me a few tricks of the trade. I now knew how to make a roll of one-dollar bills look like a roll of twenties, and how to mix baking soda, water and a little bit of Carmex to make fake crack. I knew that you only sold a few on the corner before you got the hell out of there, since nothing's more dangerous than an addict who just gave you his last twenty bucks for something that won't get him high.

What I didn't know was how the hell Jack survived nine years of all that. There had to be plenty of people smarter and luckier who ended up dead on the floor of some filthy crackhouse.

"The *Good Load* lookin' out for me," Jack had said once.

"You really think so?"

He took off his cap to scratch at the mesh of hair underneath. "Fuck if I know or care."

5:30pm
FAITH

Back when Gim was in the depths of his addiction, he had decided that enough was enough. His marriage was ruined. His sports career was over. He was estranged from his children. He'd blown his fortune on booze and coke.

Gim's solution to this was to kill himself. He took a handful of sleeping pills, climbed into his sports car and started it in his garage with the door still down.

Asphyxiation is a pretty gentle way to die, as far as those things go. You just go to sleep, never wake up and all your problems are foisted off onto your loved ones.

Gim had drifted off to sleepy land as his garage filled with exhaust, convinced that he was closing his eyes for the last time, and was damn confused when he actually woke back up. Seems his car had run out of gas.

That bit of good fortune must have blown Gim's store of luck with automobiles. He'd had three accidents in the past two weeks, exacerbating some old football injuries. It was pretty sad to see him limping around the facility, so I was almost relieved when he took off work for a while. The rehab was left under the control of us lower-level employees.

The rest of the slackers and goofballs comprising the staff had to be graced with a few guidelines before he left. A special meeting was called, and Gim gave us the sort of pep talk that he'd probably heard in countless locker rooms back in his glory days.

"You Techs need to remember," he said, giving us an earnest look, "You're the first and biggest example of the power of sobriety that the clients get to see. Remember that they look up to you guys."

I started to laugh until I noticed that no one else was. Laugh, and the world laughs with you. If they *don't* laugh with you, you're in danger of someone realizing just how fucking high you are.

Looking around the room at my coworkers made me wonder how low someone would have to be to look up to people like us. Reginald was semi-literate with an old conviction for exposing himself to elderly women at a traffic stop. Jack received disability payments for his mental problems (called it his 'crazy check'). And as for myself…*shit*, I was so stoned I could barely hold my head up. The beginnings of Gim's sentences were forgotten by the time he got to the end of them.

None of us were in any danger of canonization.

"Just keep setting that same great example that you all have been, and I'm sure things will be fine." Gim smiled at us. I almost laughed again but brought myself under control. *Never* had I seen a bigger case of misplaced confidence.

Reginald started fidgeting in his seat. This meant that he was warming up his brain to talk. "We'll…*uhhh*…we'll do…*ummm*…our…our best, Gim," he said.

Five words in five times that number of seconds. Jack rolled his eyes, and I started giggling and couldn't stop.

5:35pm THE PITY LINE

Sometimes you have to wonder at times if anyone could really miss putting up with your shit.

Corey:

"Baby! Just pick up the phone! I know you there! I just wanna say two words to you! I wanna let you know I'm *Okay in Christ*! Baby! C'mon! I wanna talk to you. That's all! I miss you! Please pick up the phone! *Baaaabyyyy...*"

The lobby phone was slammed down.

"*GODDAMNIT!*"

I didn't even bother to look up from re-reading my copy of *Hocus Pocus*. "Don't break the phone, man. Everybody else has to use it, too." *And it's not the phone's fault you're such a fuck-up.*

He walked over to the desk. "Lord, what do I do?" His eyes were raised and hands held out beseechingly. "How can I make her see the light?"

"You talkin' to me or your god?" I asked.

"Ray, I just don't know what to do." Corey adjusted his gaze. He apparently hadn't gotten much of a response from the ceiling he'd been looking up at. "She *still* won't talk to me. I wanna tell her that she my wife, that we one flesh in Christ, that *nothin'* gonna change that!"

Nothing except her apparently getting sick and tired of his crackhead bullshit.

I just shrugged at Corey. "Don't ask me about relationships, man. I can never make the fuckin' things work, either."

Zack:

He looked vaguely Italian, vaguely everything else that someone could look and still be considered white. Zack was probably a little older than me, mid-to-late 20s. All I knew was that he came from a rich family and loved crack. Trust fund junkies tended to be more into the heroin scene, but I guess we all need to feel different somehow. There are probably better ways to assert your individuality than being a crackhead, but I had to give Zack credit for at least trying.

His whining drifted to my desk from where he huddled over the phone.

"Dad…look, Dad…I'm all out…no…*Dad!* Look, I can't find…I *can't* find a job…there's nothing around here...Dad…*c'mon*…just two-…Dad…just two hundred…I'll go out looking tomorrow…I'll find one tomorrow…no…to-*morrow*…okay, I'll go to the labor hall …*Jesus*…why do you have to be so difficult…*fine*, I'll go slave with the nig—"

Remembering where he was, Zack cut himself off with a look in my direction. I gave a slow shake of the head: *No*.

"*Jesus*, Dad," he resumed, "Do you really want me working around those people? 'Cause that's exactly what I'll go do...that's the only other people there at the labor hall…well, hurry up, then…I need it soon as possible…Tuesday's too late…"

Curtis:

I tried reading aloud to drown out Curtis' half of the phone conversation. Mumbling passages from *The Lucifer Principle*—out loud, but not loud enough for anyone else to hear Howard Bloom's anti-Muslim sentiments in case one of the crackheads had converted in jail—was hopefully all the shield needed to keep from hearing about Curtis' life. If the book wasn't so thick, it would've been torn in half then stuffed in both ears. I was too wrapped up in my own problems (stuff with the girlfriend, *blah blah blah*) to want the complication of knowing about anyone else's.

The nasal whine of his Texas twang cut through my distractions.

"Well, *Ah* was really kinda hopin' that y'all would be able to…no, but…*Ah* know how much it costs…*Ah* can 'preciate that…*Ah* underst—…*Ah* said *Ah understand*…that's why *Ah'm* here…*Ah'm* tryin' to get better so *Ah can* be there for the kids…*Ah* realize it ain't easy for ya…shit…they ain't…they ain't gonna file charges, are they?…are they?…put 'er on the phone…"

I listened to Curtis speak to one of his daughters. He gave her '*a good talkin' to*,' as they say down here in Texas. I counted three physical threats, one couched in a physiological impossibility, and still the rant ended with, "Sure, Daddy loves you, too."

Getting off the phone, he wandered by my desk. Curtis was obviously desperate to tell me what his family had the audacity to burden him with while he was living several hours away, trying to concentrate on his recovery.

Curtis stalked across the lobby like a man tormented. No, make that: *like a man trying to imitate the same act he had seen various actors do as they portrayed tormented characters in movies*. He ran his hands through his thinning hair, grimaced aloud a few times, licked his lips as loudly as possible, paced quickly, *etc.*

I didn't take the bait. I refused to say, '*Gosh, what's troubling you, old chum?*' to such a hackneyed attempt to grab my interest. Having already worked here for six months, I was well versed in all the ways the desperate and pathetic tried to suck you into their dramas. I had learned the hard way how difficult it was to get them to shut up once they had the limelight.

Curtis kept mugging for the camera. Compared to all the drama-queens I had already encountered, Curtis's need for gut spilling was strictly amateur shit. It was going to take a better display than that to drag me from my book.

Realizing that his act was failing to hook me, Curtis upped the ante. "*Ah* know what she said. They wouldn't tell me, but *Ah* know what she said."

Like '*Ah*' gave a crap what somebody said that involved the guy. Curtis had not only proven himself incapable of doing anything right around here—from making curfew to mopping a floor—but had also committed the sin of passing on his Fuck-Up genes to way too many offspring.

"*Ah* can't believe she said that."

I concentrated harder on the book. My attention would be warranted only if this anonymous '*she*' had ordered Curtis's retroactive vasectomy. Then my response would be to applaud her civic-minded decision-making.

"*Ah* know what she said," Curtis repeated. "My little girl was on the bus, and she got in a fight with another girl." There you had it; the guts got spilled whether anyone asked or not. *Jesus*, our species is desperate for attention.

But…as long as child-on-child violence was involved, I decided to fake interest.

"Your kid bite the other one?" Biting had been long considered a traditional fighting technique of lower-class kids here in the Deep South.

"*Naw*," Curtis smiled once he realized that he had his audience. "Just shoved 'er on the bus."

"Oh." How disappointing.

"But they still called the cops on 'er. Took 'er to the station and everything."

"For a kid-on-kid shoving match?" *Shit*, I was glad they didn't do that back when I was in junior high.

"Yeah," Curtis made an obvious production out of clenching then unclenching his fists. "And they wouldn't tell me what the girl said. They wouldn't tell me what the girl said!" I wondered if Curtis realized that he had just repeated himself. Probably not. The guy had obviously fried a few too many synapses during his partying days.

"*Ah* know what she said," Curtis spoke through gritted teeth (he was getting unbearably cheesy). "She probably said: '*Your daddy's a crackhead!*'"

Curtis paused, waiting for my reaction.

"Well," I said, "You are."

"What?"

"I said you *are* a fuckin' crackhead. That's why you're here!"

Curtis put on an air of offense. "I'm here to take care of my family!"

He had come to the wrong person for pity. "You're takin' care of your kids from five hours away?" I asked. "Neat trick."

He shot back what he thought was an irrefutable retort. "*You* don't know how hard it is to raise a family."

I returned the volley. "Then next time don't breed so much."

A real from-the-heart sentiment. From my heart straight into his.

Curtis was knocked temporarily speechless.

It would have been nice if it was longer, but no, only temporary.

"*Ah…Ah* can't believe you just said somethin' so cold."

Did he want me to repeat it? Because proliferate breeding by poor drug addicts really burned me up.

Stupid, *selfish* motherfuckers! Too goddamn stupid to use birth control, and too selfish to think beyond how happy they were to have another little clone of themselves. It would be real fucking cute in five-to-ten years when Curtis' neglected brood were out mugging the other kids.

Hell, it's not just children raised in poverty by drug addicts that the world could do with less of. It's children, period. No one's ever convinced me that people were such a great idea that there should be more of us. We as a species can be amusing at times, but any animal that came up with shit like nuclear weapons, religion, and the forty-hour workweek needed a pretty good lawyer to argue that its pros outweighed the cons.

"Every one of those kids was a gift from God!" Curtis said.

"They were a gift from your inability to use birth control," I countered.

Curtis opened then closed his mouth several times like he was going to say something, but—cursed with a burnt raisin for a brain—nothing happened. Frustrated by his own lack of verbal acuity, Curtis stormed off.

"Try not to spread any more of your seed while you're down here!" was called after him.

It was meant in the best way possible, but I don't think he heard me.

5:49pm
NO PLACE FOR THE SENSITIVE

Undercooked chicken was on the menu for dinner again. The last batch of it had resulted in a rather traumatic experience, but the clients weren't the types to learn from past experience. They just dug right in, hopefully developing their first useful cases of tolerance.

"It taste a little better this time," Robert told me, licking sauce from his fingers. "Probably just more barbecue on it."

Wanting to avoid another case of salmonella poisoning, I gave the meal a pass and decided to do a little scavenging in the kitchen.

Our high level of cuisine had resulted in three cases of mass food poisoning in the past month. Around half the clients had woken up at two in the morning last Sunday, spewing from both ends. Twenty-seven sick men in a facility with only six toilets upstairs and two down is a recipe for a particularly nasty brand of trouble.

Luckily, I'd been working at the rehab for a while, and had developed something of a cast-iron gut. I could feast on bat guano, chug pure aspartame, and almost tolerate the food served here. Instead of the killer combo that had felled most of the clients, all I had was a vicious case of the shits.

Work was the last place I'd wanted to be stranded in the bathroom. For a solid hour-and-a half I rocked back and forth in bowel-churning agony in the downstairs bathroom. I alternated between worrying that whatever butt-bacteria the homeless brought in could eat through the layers of toilet paper on the seat, and then screaming "*Occupied, Motherfucker!*" at the desperate souls who wandered downstairs in search of an empty stall.

For this little bit of unpleasantness, I earned 12 dollars (before taxes).

The cook wasn't reprimanded for that case of mass poisoning. It wasn't the first time that sort of thing had happened. It wouldn't be the last, unless one of the clients cracked and beat the guy to death with a saltshaker. The cook was something of a pro at cutting corners in the kitchen. He ordered prison-grade food, then cooked and served and reheated and served and reheated and served the food long after it had gone bad.

Meat starting to smell? Nothing that a little more barbeque sauce won't fix! Why waste money on proper storage containers or luxuries like Saran Wrap when you could just leave the food sitting out on the counter overnight? Bring on the curdled milk! Pass the rotting vegetables! Have some seconds on that chicken from last Tuesday!

The cook was part of the giant client-fucking machine that took the three-grand a month paid to stay here and gave them as little as possible in return. That was his job security. Three grand would score you a month's stay in a hotel room that you didn't have to share with four or five other addicts. For three grand you could find a residence that wasn't filled with bums and vagrants for half the day. And, most importantly, for three grand you could afford to eat somewhere without the fear that your meals would be considered illegal by most biological weapon treaties.

But hey, who really gives a shit how a bunch of junkies and crackheads got treated, right? Fucking scumbags. People who ripped off their own families for an armful deserved to get ripped off in return, right?

Sure seemed to be company policy.

In the back of the kitchen, I picked through crates of fruit. Figured that making a dinner out of apples would do in lieu of the poultry that I recognized from a few days back.

The apples were all picked up and turned over. There was a naive hope in my head that at least one of them would be edible.

Three minutes of inspecting produce and not an unspoiled one in the bunch.

Thinking that maybe the cook had something edible stashed back in his office, I worked the chain off the door and flicked on the lights. The office was a narrow room, barely bigger than a closet, but still larger than the so-called 'Tech Office' upstairs.

Roaches scattered with the light, then realized that they outnumbered me and went about their business. I scanned the shelves, hoping for a spare box of cereal, when my eyes settled on a delicious surprise. A large hunk of roast beef, already cooked and resting in a pan of grease, was sitting on the shelf.

Just sitting there. Just chillin'.

Roaches scaled the thing, reached the summit, used their antennae to flick me off and then scurried down the other side. Unless I missed my guess, I was looking at tomorrow's dinner. A mental note was made to bring a sack lunch to work the next day. And, unless I kept missing guesses, that was the cook lying on the office floor. At least he'd managed to serve dinner that day…

He was an old black man, curled up in the fetal position, and still wearing his apron and hair net. The guy might've been unconscious, but, credit where credit was due, he was still obeying a few health regulations.

"Hey, man." I nudged him with my shoe. "You okay?"

He moaned slightly and vomited. Nice.

It was at this point that I noticed the heavy reek of booze in the air. Worried, I gave myself a discreet sniff. Surprisingly, it seemed come from somewhere else.

I looked down at the cook as he managed to roll himself over onto his stomach. "Is that you?" I asked.

Not one for verbal communication, he vomited again in reply.

At a loss for anything else to do, I went and rounded up the clients. Figured I'd bring them in for a look at their food, the roaches and the guy who let one eat the other.

They were all pretty pissed off and swore justice. Management was contacted and complained to, but shit was never done about it.

Why should there be, when there was money to be saved?

6:07pm
ANOTHER ONE OF GOD'S LITTLE TRICKS

I called him *Sloth*, after the character from *The Goonies*. He looked like someone had tried to bring Frankenstein's monster to life by using crack instead of lightning. The left side of his face looked like it had started to run a bit like candle wax.

I never used James's nickname to his face. Not just because he was a giant of a man who could've crushed my head using only three fingers. I just figured that he'd probably heard similar remarks a million times before. It may be tough to trust people with things like your money or affections, but you can always count on them finding your weak spots with laser-sighted accuracy.

He called me '*Einstein*' because our rehab makes a pretty decent setting for the kingdom of the blind. "I like givin' people names," Sloth explained. I decided that as long as it wasn't followed by a punch to the groin, he was welcome to call me whatever he wanted (and it had to beat Jack's nickname of '*Asshole*'). The only thing standing in his way was the challenge of remembering it.

Each time we saw each other Sloth would call out, "Hey, wassup...uh...uh...*Einstein*!"

"Yo...uh...uh... *James*!" I'd reply. Not sure if the crack had rotted his brain or if he was born sub-intelligent (or if, like most of the clients, it was a mixture of the two). One thing for certain, though, motherfucker could play the piano like somebody had shoved Chopin's ghost up his ass. He had a wide-ranging repertoire, and his execution was nearly flawless.

"What you wanna hear?" he'd bellow at me from the piano in the chapel off the main lobby.

I'd call back, "Gimme some Beethoven, bitch!" And Sloth would pound out something totally unrelated, like a Billy Joel song. He couldn't match compositions and composers any better than most crackheads. Asking for Bach might get you Tchaikovsky, a request for Brahms might score Philip Glass's oeuvre. Like your average philistine, Sloth didn't have a clue when it came to the labels of classical music. Or any music, really. I could've asked for *Rock the Casbah* and he would play the *Moonlight Sonata*. I don't think he even knew what he was doing. Or how he did it.

Sloth couldn't read music. The guy only knew pieces he'd heard before, which he could then play back perfectly. He was like a big, dumb, black jukebox that ate your quarters and then spat out songs at random.

It took me a while to realize how clueless Sloth was about what he was doing. It first occurred to me when I noticed how he answered every question about the song just played with a shrug and a "*Dunno*."

Sloth was an Idiot Savant in the purest sense of the word. He was thick as a fucking brick, quasi-literate at best, couldn't even speak Ebonics that well and had the social skills that God gave a crippled amoeba. But *Jesus*, that guy could play the piano better than most of us play with ourselves.

Not sure if that made up for his being short-changed in every other aspect, but it's not like life really gives you a choice in these matters.

6:16pm
RAPE THE HORSES AND RIDE OFF ON THE WOMEN

There was a bloodstain on the sidewalk in front of the rehab. It hadn't fully dried when I showed up over two hours late for my shift. "Man, you went and missed all the fun," they told me.

The blood belonged to Corey. He spilled it there by winning the nose-diving contest he'd held with himself. Number One in a field of one.

This was how the clients explained it to me: our latest Reverend Leroy (*Corey!*) had been rambling at his halfway housemates at the crack-appropriate speed of about two-hundred words per minute. Suddenly, his eyes rolled up into his head, and the stream of words petered out into a mumbled slur. Corey toppled forward, thankfully remembering to catch himself with his face.

He broke his nose, got a nice boo-boo on his forehead and scored a free ride in the ambulance for his troubles. He's probably fine, but no one's that concerned about it.

The puddle of blood Corey left behind, however, had garnered interest. It was pretty impressive. Myself and a few clients stood around the puddle, objectively discussing it's size, shape, and other properties like it was a piece of coffee table art.

Not bad, but seen better, was the general consensus.

Few things can gush blood with the sheer volume of a head wound. Severed limbs, maybe. Or two simultaneous head wounds. Whatever the case, Corey had relapsed in the manner most beloved by other clients and those of us on staff: *Entertainingly*.

There's no enjoyment to be gotten from someone who packs their bags and sneaks out of the facility, filled with shame at having succumbed to their addiction. Clients who phone in to slur out a lame excuse as to why they won't be returning that night are dull. Junkies who get busted by the bad luck of a random piss-test don't make for decent anecdotes. What we like to see here, what'll keep us chuckling for days, is when somebody fails and fails *big*.

I blessed Corey's unintentionally generous heart for giving everyone a topic of conversation for the night. Five different people did their Corey impressions for me, eyes rolling up into their heads and toppling forward. They all caught themselves in time, unlike the Crackhead of the Hour, who was probably still at the hospital.

I wondered if anyone had noticed that he was about to fall over. Maybe somebody saw that Corey was swaying dangerously, maybe the thought of catching him crossed their minds as he tipped over. Maybe not.

More likely, everyone sat on the front porch and watched as he got ready to kiss pavement. Why not? The closest anyone here comes to helping their fellow man is when they rat out another client for using. But, I doubt that squealing really counts as a good deed. Especially since it's usually done out of a strong sense of jealousy that the other guy is getting high and they're not.

6:22pm
SELF-ACCLIMATING SYSTEMS

I was regaling the clients gathered around my desk with the visit to my girlfriend's family the previous night.

"Motherfuckers poisoned me!" I said, and the clients laughed.

One of the crackheads replied, "I poison yo ass, too, you come near *my* daughter!" And they all laughed even harder.

It had been yet another installment of Ray's adventures in humility, guest-starring his girlfriend. I'd gotten violently ill at her parents' place in the suburbs north of Houston. It had to be food poisoning, since I didn't feel like I could paint the walls with my own vomit until after dinner.

In the interest of not being known as '*the guy who was violently sick that one Labor Day*,' I'd done my damnedest to ignore the pain and keep smiling. That's a tough thing to do when your food is fighting just as hard to come back up as you are to keep it down.

It was a pity, since the ribs and side dishes had to be some of the best goddamn food I had eaten all year. Well-seasoned, tender enough to fall apart in your mouth, it beat the living hell out of the cereal and prison food I'd been living off at work.

Then, about ten minutes after dining, I felt my stomach do a few spastic jolts, and had to clamp down on my throat to keep from ralphing everywhere. Projectile vomiting is typically frowned upon at family gatherings, and it would've seemed pretty ungrateful to spray my girlfriend's family with the food they had just fed me. I'm not the casual *puke-and-party* type, so I just breathed deep, kept my throat clenched, and refused to let myself be sick.

It was a real shitty way to spend the next two hours.

After a series of good-byes that seemed to last an eternity (as everything does when you're trying not to vomit on the person talking to you), we finally drove off. I made my girlfriend stop at the first gas station we saw. It was a putrid filth-hole, but you can ignore a lot of uncleanliness when you're disgorging an entire day's worth of food. Apparently, my system can't handle nice things anymore.

(I told my girlfriend it must have been a bug I picked up at work.)

The clients thought that me puking was the funniest goddamn thing they'd heard in months. Riotous, whooping laughter ensued. I had to keep repeating the story for each new person that walked by the desk and asked, '*Whuzzo funny?*'

We must've been on the fourth retelling when the phone rang. It was my girlfriend; she was in the area, and did I want her to bring me some dinner?

Well, *hell yes*, I did!

"*Pretty please, Beautiful,*" I said in my sappy, singsong voice. We said our cutesy goodbyes, and I hung up the phone.

The clients all stared at me with huge grin on their faces. "That was pussy," Robert declared. He was smiling so big you'd think that we had switched places, and I was going for his chemo treatments while Robert got blown after work.

"That *was* pussy," I confirmed, showing that I spoke fluent Male. "And I don't want any of you creepy bastards hanging around when it shows up."

6:29pm
BE THE CHANGE YOU WANT TO SEE IN THE WORLD

Sunday night is check-in time at the rehab. All the junkies, crackheads and alkies granted two-day passes came back from wherever they spent their weekend fighting temptation. Check-in officially occurred upstairs in the TV room at seven o'clock sharp. A minute late and your ass got locked out (of the TV room, that is).

Sunday was also the day we checked to see who relapsed over the weekend. See who fought their addiction and lost. See who got bent over and fucked by the monkey on their back. Sometimes the guys were polite enough to call ahead and let me know that they'd blown their sobriety ("*I jusht had...zhe one mardini...*"). Sometimes they tried to fake sobriety when they arrived.

And, if I'd learned one thing at this job (besides how to change a prescription for antibiotics into one for Xanax, or how to still shoot up if you're locked in a bathroom without your rig), it's that it was damn hard to act normal after smoking a fat rock. There was something about the twitching and bloodshot eyes that gave you away.

"Motherfucker been smokin' like Sittin' Bull," Jack would say. And then, of course, blame me when Gim asked who'd been calling the clients '*motherfuckers*.'

I had a client nod out on my desk once. Mid-sentence. One second Jamie was chatting with me as he signed back into the building—talking a little slow, but coherent—and the next he collapsed onto the desktop. Barely missed dialing the phone with his forehead.

I just pushed him off onto the floor and laughed. No condemnation or lectures from me. They're not my style. And besides, that day I had downed three Bloody Marys and the same number of bong rips before coming to work.

I was laughing about a lot of things that day.

6:43pm
TERTULLIAN PROMISED THE PLEASURES OF HEAVEN WOULD INCLUDE LAUGHING AT THOSE IN HELL

The bag of medication was set down on the desk next to the phone. I opened the bag and rooted through the vials. Serequel, Celexa, Trazadone, Risperdal, Adderal, and a few others. Thanks to Zack, some pharmaceutical executive was buying his kids a new yacht for Xmas.

Jack chuckled to himself as he strolled away from the desk, leaving me to count all the meds by myself. The last thing I heard as he escaped responsibility down the back hallway was a mumbled, "Motherfucker open his own pharmacy."

"Well, young man," I smiled up at Zack, "Hope you brought enough for everybody." Zack gave his ponytail a nervous tug and tried to smile. He failed. As usual, I had succeeded only in amusing myself.

Hell, good enough.

Zack obviously wasn't too happy to leave his family after the Thanksgiving holiday. Most of the junkies seemed unenthusiastic about abandoning their loved ones to come back to the rehab. But, hell, at least they had families to visit. Twenty-seven clients went absolutely nowhere over the holiday.

Most of America was eating turkey with their families, and our cook didn't even bother coming in on Thanksgivings to feed these guys. They just sat around the building, moping and feeling even more sorry for themselves than usual. One asked me if it was true that the suicide rate went up during the holidays.

I had replied with another question: '*That desperate for any kind of company?*'

(Yeah, I'd been there for Thanksgivings, too; no such thing as a holiday at this fucking company.)

This weekend had been depressing for them, but it wouldn't be as bad as spending Xmas in a rehab. The holidays lose their customary cheer when spent in our linoleum hallways, empty except for a few other people of the unloved variety. Bad enough to be a crackhead, but realizing that you're not even well liked in comparison to your fellow addicts has to be tough on what's left of the ol' self-esteem. The relapse quotient skyrockets.

The clients don't know any of this yet, but I remember it from when I'd just started here last Xmas.

The holidays produce enough melancholy on their own. Adding institutionalization into the mix was hardly going to turn those frowns upside down. Some of these bastards were in for one intensely miserable time. Xmas alone in rehab. They didn't see it coming, but I knew it was inevitable. The heavy stink of fatalism was in the air (along with that goddamn sewage smell).

Everything in this place had the weight of inevitability dragging it down. You knew what would happen, and you could see it coming a mile off.

Eventually, everyone here will leave. Eventually, everyone here will relapse. Eventually, I'll get caught looking at porn, or showing up intoxicated, or whatever, and get fired. Eventually, I'll end up in one of these places, myself. Eventually, Robert's cancer will come back. Eventually, we'll all get old and die. Eventually, the earth will fall into the sun.

Everything's falling apart, everything's turning to crap, and all our attempts to reverse or slow the process are just band-aids on a gushing stump wound. It's the second law of thermodynamics. Give anything enough time and it'll fall to shit. The colors fade on the Sistine Chapel. Wind and rain grind the mountains to dust. The American dollar plummets in value. *The Simpsons* stops being funny.

It happens.

What happens?

Shit happens.

So deal with it. Cope. Adjust like the sentient being you are. When you know that Rome's going to burn, there isn't a goddamn thing to do but strike up the fiddle and maybe dance the Cotton Eyed Joe while the tenements go up in flames.

And then laugh like hell when they feed the Christians to the lions for it.

Consider it like watching a historical movie. Sure, everything may be going tolerably okay-ish right now, but you *know* that's temporary. Things are guaranteed to get worse. Eventually the slaves *will* end up crucified along the Appian Way. Bambi's mother *will* get shot. Everything *will* end on one hell of a down-note.

It can be seen coming a mile off, but there isn't shit to be done about it except shutting your eyes and trying not to pay attention. Stick your head in that sand and wait for the badness to end.

But, if you've got that car-crash fascination going, if you can't help to watch it all crumble, then *do* try to see the funny side of things.

It occurred to me to send special Xmas cards to everyone stuck here over the coming holidays. It would be a little something to add holiday cheer to an otherwise dismal time. The tiniest bit of light to ward off the darkness of spending the holidays in this desolate place. It wouldn't be much at all, but it'd be nice. Maybe I'd bake some cookies for everyone, too.

Twenty seconds later the idea was abandoned in favor of a much simpler plan. I would just be grateful that, out of everyone who'd be spending the holidays alone here, one of them wouldn't be me.

Instantly, I felt better about everything. Nothing was solved. Nothing had been improved. Nothing had changed but my outlook.

Hell, *Mission Accomplished.*

6:57pm
SOMEONE ELSE MIGHT NEED THE WOOD

Corey's wife walked after him into the rehab. He had a dark look on his face, and not just because his skin was one of the deeper shades of black possible. I never really noticed the subtle color gradient on people before working around a bunch of black guys. God, they can be obsessive about it.

Corey reeked of guilt and fright. Like a child caught playing with himself. Like the priest had burst from the confessional and shouted, '*Holy Shit! You'll never guess what this pervert just told me!*'

Corey's nose and forehead were bandaged from his concrete pratfall of the previous day. His damaged appearance was the perfect match for his wife. She had an angry mouth, body like an overstuffed pillow, and a face that never had the chance, even in youth, to be beautiful. Tears dripped from her eyes.

"Baby, *please*," Corey whined quietly as possible.

"You *made* me do this!" she hissed loud enough to get everyone's attention. That, we soon found out, was the point. There were about eight us in the lobby: myself, Jack, Robert, Paul, Pike, and a few other junkies. We all stopped to tune into the living soap opera. Everyone digs drama, so long as they can sit back and watch without being dragged into it.

Voice raised and cracking, she said, "I want y'all to hear what I got to say to this man."

There was no way we would have missed it. This promised to be good. Nothing's more entertaining than public humiliation. "Corey," she said, as he tried to shrink into himself, "You have let me down for the last time. I have *tried* to stand by you. I have *tried* to do the right thing by you. The Lord knows I've tried."

This was her in a textbook feat of self-crucifixion. Nothing I hadn't seen my own mother do countless times, growing up. Just another variation on the endless theme of self-pity. Sometimes I think it's the only thing our species does well (except for making war, of course, and maybe french fries).

"*Baaay-beee*," he said, and the tears started seeping from his eyes.

"But you have *let me down* for the last time, Corey. I love you. Jesus knows I love you, but you too sick, and I can't stand to be with you no more. *No more*, you hear me?"

Well, the speech was crap. But, considering that she had stayed with Corey after he had fucked up three times previously, the lady was obviously no Rhodes scholar. Expecting Pulitzer-quality speechwriting from her was obviously asking a bit much. It made me think that there might be a decent business opportunity ghostwriting tell-off speeches for the terminally ineloquent.

"I can't be with you no more. You outta my life for good."

Corey was blubbering by this point, and some of the junkies started to look away. Even Jack ducked his head, hiding the scene behind the bill of his cap. Watching public humiliation was one thing, but emasculation was something that no man enjoys. We're all so sensitive about our own balls that we hate to see another man lose his. Unless, of course, we're the one taking them.

It reminded me of fights back in junior high. The inflicting of pain was all well and good until one party started crying, and then it was just embarrassing.

Still, sitting on the lobby's couch, I was riveted. Something good had to come of all this emotional trauma, even if it was only a moment's entertainment for my jaded ass.

"Goodbye," she said, starting to blubber herself, and pushed past Corey to rush out the door.

It was a decent exit, or it would've been had she hopped in her car and peeled out into traffic. Instead, Corey's wife sat in her car, parked right outside the door, and wept with her head on the steering wheel.

Corey, the focus of all this unhappiness, didn't even get that far. He didn't run from the lobby. Didn't slowly trudge upstairs. He just stood in place, crying and snuffling. Still on display, but now an exhibit that everyone wished would hurry and close down.

Nobody looked at him. As much as Corey may have wished earlier for the ground to open up and swallow him, we were all wishing twice as hard for it to happen now. His suffering had turned grotesque.

The more progressive parts of the modern world have caught on to how the notion that Boys Don't Cry is unhealthy bullshit. But still, there are quite a few of us who were raised with the notion. The sight of a weeping male makes a lot of people uncomfortable. The prejudices of youth can be tougher to toss than we'd like to admit.

I watched Corey weep for a while. Why he was still hanging around after his public emasculation was hard to say. Perhaps he was waiting for some consolation, some words of encouragement. Someone to say, '*Don't worry, man; it'll be okay.*'

If so, he was disappointed. Corey had made a leper of himself, an emotional pariah, and now no one wanted to get close. We all just wanted him to vanish. Sure, it's common to hear the complaint that guys don't share emotion, can't communicate about their feelings, won't *blah blah blah*...but, I've personally never noticed a goddamn bit of good to ever come of it.

If you're a guy, try it in your own fucking life and see if anyone is going put up with you having emotional states beyond (1) Happiness, or (2) Paying for Things.

Go ahead. I'll wait. I'll do it right here. *<gestures expansively at rehab lobby>*

I made a mental note of Corey's misery, and decided to schedule my next emotional breakdown for somewhere else. A place where traumatizing events would at least rate a hug. Wherever that might be.

7:07pm PAVLOV'S PEOPLE

Sloth rushed up to the front desk. It's the dark center that the junkies' sick little world revolved around. "Ray!" he pleaded. "You gotta loan me a buck, man!"

I was a little scared by his agitation. "Why do I *gotta*?"

"My girlfriend outside, man!" Sloth threw worried looks out the front door. "I swear I pay ya back, Ray! Just *quick*, man! I need a dollar!"

“*Okay*,” I said, thinking about how much my own girlfriends always cost me. “Long as you don’t gnaw through my neck or spend it on crack or—”

Sloth yanked the dollar from my hand and bolted through the door.

“There goes one excited mongoloid,” I said to Jack, who’d walked into the lobby in time to witness Sloth’s exit.

“He ain’t got no girlfriend,” Jack said. “There’s just some ho at the bus stop sucks ’im off for eight dollars.”

I shrugged. “Well, the economy being what it is…just didn’t realize it was affecting the Freelance Pleasure Industry, too.”

Jack sat down across from me. “Shit,” he said. “You imagine the kinda girl gonna give an eight-dollar blowjob?”

I shook my head. “Fuck, I can’t imagine *anyone* putting Sloth’s dick in their mouth, for a thousand dollars, let alone eight.” The thought of someone choking on Sloth’s donkey-dick was banished from my mind. At least, I hope the guy was well endowed. He needed some extra compensation for being himself, something besides the piano skills.

“People do funny shit for the rock,” Jack said. “Sometimes it works out to yo’ advantage.”

“Really?”

“Yeah. Used to know a girl who’d let ya fuck her, then give ’er a good beating, for thirty dollars.”

“By ‘*beating*,’ you mean, like, *kick her ass*?”

“*Mmm-hmmm*.”

I considered asking Jack if he’d ever made use of her services, but decided the question was pretty unnecessary.

Smiling, Jack reached down to adjust himself. I looked the other way. "Yep," he said. "That's what you call a night's entertainment."

7:10pm
CHILD-REARING IN MORIAH

Sam rolled the creaky leather chair up to my desk. He'd gotten tired of having to repeat himself, since he had a soft voice and my hearing was shit. Having just arrived at the rehab early Friday, it was his first weekend here.

Sam was a young guy with scruffy black hair. He was scrawny and goofy-looking in a way that told me that he had, at some time in his young life, probably skateboarded. Maybe listened to *The Misfits* or some other shitty middle school band. It's just a type that one learns to recognize. Sam was now sitting across from me due to a DWI acquired during a month he described as being, 'like *Leaving Las Vegas*, but without the attractive hookers.'

Sam had spent all day wandering the drab hallways of the facility before deciding that I was the best way to pass his time. For my part, I didn't mind the company. The guy seemed to be about my age and had some of the same interests. We discussed Broken Social Scene albums, the playing style of Austin drummer Dave Evans, and Hunter S. Thompson's connection to the East LA Chicano uprising in the early '70s. We did the CD swapping that seems to be the modern equivalent of mutual butt-sniffing.

Sam checked out fine so far.

"I always try to be up-front with girls about my bullshit," he said. By *'bullshit,'* Sam meant not only the continual alcoholism and drug abuse of the past 10 years, but also the traumatic upbringing caused by his old man going schizoid.

His dad's craziness had something of a religious bent to it. The old man became convinced that he was the biblical patriarch, Abraham, and his son was Isaac (with all the lethal cultural baggage this entailed). Also, that God wanted him to take his boy to First Grade orientation in his underwear. Years later, Sam still found the public humiliations more traumatic than his dad's attempts to kill him in private. That's what we get for being social creatures.

Luckily, Sam's dad was able to talk God out of modeling his BVDs at Sam's elementary. Being a shrewd bargainer, his dad compromised by amusing the other parents with screaming '*Jesus*!' for twenty minutes straight.

('*You mean like one long Jeeeezuuuuus*?' I asked. '*No*,' said Sam. '*Lots and lots of Jesus*.')

"Yeah," I said. "The less propaganda you spew when you first hook up with somebody, the less ya have to worry about letting 'em down when you get tired of keeping up the Perfect You facade."

Sam agreed.

I continued, "Like, I always tell somebody when we first hook up about my problems with fidelity."

Sam looked puzzled. "*Fidel-*?"

"Faithfulness. Not cheating."

"Right, right," he said. "I knew that."

Sam gave me a look like I had just announced my candidacy for the Second Coming. "You're kidding, *right*?" He settled back in his chair with a look of pure disbelief. The chair concurred with a long, drawn-out squeak of its own. "You don't...tell them...don't really...do that, really? *Do you?*"

"Well, *yeah*," I said. "Wouldn't want somebody dating me under false pretenses."

Made perfect sense to me. Might as well pick *something* in life to be honest about.

"Man…you just...that..."

"Seems a bit on the stupid side to you?"

"Well…" Sam ran a hand through his hair. He was obviously trying to think of a polite way to phrase this. "Well…yeah. Yeah, it really, really does. Honesty's one thing, but that…

"Really fuckin' stupid?"

He nodded at me like I was his retarded kid brother.

Something sank in my chest. Damn, was he right? Was it foolish to be that open with somebody? Was it really such a bad idea to share the truth about yourself? Was it preferable to have a relationship built on desirable lies? Should you misrepresent yourself to people so they wouldn't know that you weren't as great as advertised? I wouldn't think so, but...

'*Why do you know so many women? You're not sleeping with anybody else, are you? Pleeeeeze don't sleep with anybody while you're on vacation. You didn't sleep with anybody while you were gone, did you? You sure you didn't sleep with anybody there? You didn't pick anyone up when you went out last night? You'd tell me if you slept with someone else, wouldn't you? etc. Etc. ETC.*'

I thought about my current girlfriend's worried whining, and how the questions had started coming more and more frequently for some god-knows-why reason (it *couldn't* have anything to do with my sleeping around on her). But really, what else did I expect besides a whole lot of worried nagging after telling her that I had a habit of doing the one thing that people fear their partner doing above all else? I always figured that people would want to go into relationships with their eyes wide open, but what else could you expect from them once the initial buzz wore off? What else could they do when it became apparent that you would do nothing but let them down, time and time again?

What else?

"Maybe you're on to something," I told Sam. "I think my relationship S.O.P. just changed."

Sam brushed a strand of black hair from his eyes. "It's okay if I don't believe you on that, right?"

I laughed. "No, I meant that I'm gonna lie even more than usual."

"Oh," he said. "*That* I believe."

7:15pm
NON-APOCALYPTIC EVENTS AND LOOKING OUT FOR NUMBER ONE

The heater dying on a cold night apparently wasn't bad enough for the God of Shit Luck. Both of our microwaves decided that they'd toiled long enough in the service of hungry addicts and expired within minutes of each other. There was no other way to reheat the food that had been cooked in advance for the weekend. Cold junkies found themselves faced with the prospect of cold food and were understandably upset.

"*The fuck this shit?*" was the typically eloquent response.

I gave as non-committal a shrug as I could manage while shivering and pulling a blanket tighter around myself. "I just work here," was said in my best *don't-kill-the-honky* voice. "But if you guys are gonna revolt, I get to be that French chick in the dress with my right tit hangin' out."

Distributing extra blankets just seemed to worsen the prevailing mood. Nobody enjoys being in a cold, dirty building where other addicts wander around wrapped in multiple blankets. It's bad enough to live in a rehab/halfway house, but having it resemble a homeless shelter really does a number on everyone's morale.

I wasn't too happy with the state of affairs, either. Our stash of the one thing we have that didn't require heating, cereal, had dwindled to a few crumbs. I quickly polished them off to save the junkies from reducing themselves to desperate scavenging.

It looked like I would have to go down into the basement and break into the Christers' storage room. My grumbling stomach and sense of self-preservation told me it had to be done. It's bad enough having work as your primary food source. When that dries up, too, you start seeing visions of yourself on the cover of National Geographic, all swollen-bellied in the dirt with vultures lurking in the background.

The storage room downstairs was filled with pile upon pile of old clothes. It contained all the necessary supplies for looking unfashionable in any time period over the last fifty years. I picked a random spot and started rummaging. Tossed aside polyester suits and parachute pants, dug under tweed jackets and tie-dye shirts. Sure enough, stuck in a small freezer hidden under layers of unwanted crap and used footwear, the Methodists had a crapload of frozen sandwiches.

A food truck dropped off about a hundred pounds of donated sandwiches a week to the Methodists. I had always wondered why, when it came time to dole them out to the homelies, they seemed to run out so fast. Looked like the Christers were hoarding the sandwiches, and—from the expiration dates on some of them—had been doing so for some time.

What the hell? I had to wonder. Was this their anti-terrorist stash? Did they start hoarding food back during the Cold War and just couldn't break the habit? I had never known Methodists to be more weirdly apocalyptic than any other Christian sect, but, on the other hand, it's not like they had any greater claim to pragmatic rationality, either.

I grew up around a lot of Mormon kids. Sometimes we would play in their garage shelters, full of the canned goods and other non-perishables that their families kept in preparation for some upcoming apocalyptic event. Not sure what it was supposed to be, exactly. Nuclear war, perhaps? They never said, and I don't think that I had proper security clearance as a nonbeliever. All I ever found out was that after whatever big-shit event was coming, there was expected to be a year of famine and horror, during which time the faithful would get the pleasure of chillin' in their garage shelters, praising the goodness of the Lord while living off creamed corn and Spam.

I can't help but think that there'd also be plenty of chuckling at how emaciated the heretics were getting outside. After all, there's no point in being the Elect of God if no one's around to whom you can feel superior.

If memory serves me well (and it rarely does), said apocalyptic event was supposed to occur sometime in:

1997.

So, like most things in this modern world, I guess it's just a little behind schedule.

I fished out a sandwich whose expiration date didn't scare me too much. Then, I heated it up in an old microwave I found underneath a card table. A stylish leather jacket was also appropriated.

I looked good and felt good.

Properly satiated, my ass toddled back upstairs. Everyone there was still bitching about the lack of edibles. “The fuck we ’sposed to do ’bout eating?”

I settled back into my desk and picked at my teeth. Good question!

Scratching myself for the fun of it, I tried to recall the advice my old man always used to give me. What was it?

Oh yeah!

“If I was y’all,” I told them, “I’d start with cannibalizing the small and the weak."

7:19pm
MY GRANDPA COULDN’T GET IT UP IF HE TRIED

The girl, all slender 5′4″ of her, turned and gave a fingers-only wave to my co-worker as she stepped out the door. Jack pretended not to notice her exit. I raised an eyebrow at him, hoping the explanation would prove more interesting than the book on theodicies I’d been reading.

Jack grinned like the world’s naughtiest schoolboy as he sauntered over to the front desk, beaming that his old black ass could show up a young cracker like myself. He just stood there grinning, so I asked, “Well?”

Like I’d slipped a quarter into his coin slot, Jack came to life. He doubled over and slapped the edge of the desk.

“*Oooooh-weee*!” he squealed. “In a chapel! That’s *nasty*!” My fellow Tech was obviously on the verge of bursting with self-satisfaction.

I had been covering for Jack during the past half-hour while he and the mini-skirted girl absconded to the chapel. '*Covering*,' of course, meant sitting at the desk with my feet propped up, clicking the door-release button whenever someone tugged on the door handle. The usual.

For all I knew, Jack and his girl could've been in there saying their respective rosaries. The last thing I was going to trust were the insinuations of a seventy-something ex-crackhead. Working in a halfway house quickly taught you to not believe anything you were told. And junkies, whether practicing or recovering, told lies like bees made honey. Only faster and in greater quantities. It's just their nature.

One more time with *New Start Rule #1*: Never Trust a Junkie.

But, just because I had my personal reservations about whatever bullshit Jack was about to try on me, didn't mean I wouldn't play along. Everyone has their own little persona they try to present to the world. Being skilled with the alternate sex is a common facet of the male facade. So long as it's not annoying and you're in a generous mood, hey, what's the harm in playing along?

Besides, she wasn't the first young girl to come visit Joe.

"Not bad," I said. "She's cute, man. And she was on the clock, too."

"Ya know, you right!" Jack said. "I do believe George just paid me for a bit of fun!"

The thought of our miserly CEO coughing up money to get his employees a little play was way too funny for us. We both convulsed with laughter. Jack's high-pitched seesaw of a laugh dueled with my own impression of a rhino having seizures.

Once we finally stopped laughing, I asked, "Was she my age?"

"You twenty-two?" asked Jack.

Dear fucking Christ! "Twenty-three, actually." And here I was, single and miserably celibate. It almost made me wish there was a God, so I could introduce my foot to His crotch.

"Close enough," Jack said. The smile on his face got even bigger as he sat down on the couch across from me. He was the happiest black man I'd seen all month, but it's not like there was a lot of competition in this place.

Worried that Jack's good mood would interfere with everyone else's suffering, I decided to take him down a notch: "Any particular reason why your women always show up here on payday?"

7:22pm
GLASS HOUSES IN A WORLD WITHOUT WINDEX

Jack said he'd cover for me while I '*took care of important business*.' So, thanks to him, I was able to go to the movies on the company's dime. The first 45 minutes of watching *Lost in La Mancha* covered the ticket price, and every minute after that I was getting paid to stare at the screen by the kindly folks who employed me.

My Sunday shift lasted sixteen hours, from four in the afternoon Sunday to eight o'clock Monday morning. That's a long while to breathe the hopeless contagion of the rehab, so I figured everyone would understand if I took a two-hour break somewhere in the middle. And if they didn't understand, I knew they could at least be counted on not to care.

My ex showed up to grab me after Sunday check-in. She had finally given in to my requests to '*just hang out and chat*.'

Real kind of her. Especially since I was getting tired of my own pleading. And all the blatant bribery was threatening to turn expensive. Had she not been sending back all my presents unopened, there's no way I could ever have returned them. Not even for in-store credit.

At a bit past seven there was a commotion outside the front door. I knew that somebody had either dropped a two-pound crack-rock on the sidewalk or a female was in the immediate vicinity. A woman's presence is a disruptive element in a building full of hard-up males, many of whom were just beginning to feel their sex drives return after years of drug-induced dormancy. All unescorted women over the age of 11 and under the age of sixty got mobbed upon setting foot on the premises. My ex had the additional bad timing of showing up right as a group of junkies were pouring out the front door.

I called to Jack that my ride was here and hurried outside to snatch my ex from the mob of swinging dicks. "All right, back off, fuckers," I called as I elbowed my way through the crowd. "She's with me!"

The clients booed and jeered as I walked off with my ex. It was likely that I'd have to listen to them go on about her once I got back.

Crackhead: *Man, Ray, that yo girl?*

Ray: *Ex-girl, actually.*

Junkie: *Cool! Is she single?*

Ray: *Along with being too good for you, yes.*

(general uproar at being slandered by uppity white boy)

Crackhead: *Goddamn, the booty that girl got!*

Ray: *Hey fuckers, see previous response!*

Typically, I wouldn't mind that a couple dozen guys were going to be stroking themselves that night to my ex. Flattering for most of the parties involved, in its own little way. A lot of the clients tended to get excited whenever anyone came to see me, whether it was a girlfriend, my mom, or one of my sisters. I'd even pretended to give numbers out to a few of the more persistent ones (which would invariably connect them with the day care center for St. Jerome's Catholic Church).

Tonight I just wasn't in the mood for their desperation. It reminded me too much of my own.

Staring up at the screen next to my ex, I fought the urge to grab her hand. There's a thing or two to remember when hanging out with an ex. The most important of these to carve into the frontal lobe of your brain is to Maintain Personal Space.

Yes, yes, yes, it's obvious that '*personal space*' has to be the most horrible concept ever conceived by the human mind (next to genocide, lite beer, and regressive tax structures). The idea that we shouldn't come within three feet of each other goes a long way toward making our society the sick place that it is. In such a sterile environment, it's no wonder that so many people turn to drugs in order to just feel *something*.

Keeping this 'personal space' concept in mind, however, should prevent you from making the huge *faux paus* of acting like you did while dating. Basically, it'll keep your stupid ass from being absent-mindedly affectionate towards your ex. Maybe I'm the only fucker on the planet who has this problem, but I doubt it.

Lodged in your body's memory is how to physically respond to the presence of everyone you know. Around some people your body automatically remembers to cringe. Around others it knows to puff itself up. Around those it was used to rubbing all over, well…

At the movie I had to stop myself from trying to hold my ex's hand. Afterwards, I had to consciously keep from slipping my arm around her waist. Tell myself not to touch her hair. Not to kiss her cheek. Not to smash her head in from the sheer frustration of it all.

Having to reassert the concept of personal space after you'd finally overcome it with somebody was probably the lousiest part of a defunct relationship. Like playing *Risk* and only conquering Rhode Island, then having to give that up as well. Back to square one in that *You vs. The World* thing.

It bugs the crap out of me. I'm always like, '*goddamn, weren't you one of the few people in the world with whom I could dispense with that sick, keep-your-distance bullshit?'*

But *whatever*. I had blown it with my ex, just like the junkies had burned their own bridges with their loved ones. They proved time and again that they loved their drugs more than their mates. I was apparently just an asshole. Me and the junkies both had something else in our lives that we'd cared about more than the people we'd been with.

For some of us it was crack, for others it was our own selfish asses. Kind of understandable that our significant others would get sick of playing second fiddle to it. It looked like we'd all have to live with the consequences of our unsociable actions.

Movie over, my ex took me back to work. On the drive there she chain-smoked like hell. Cigarette after cigarette after cigarette. Sucking carcinogens like mother's milk. She didn't used to smoke. Not when we were together. But I guess that after dating me, lung cancer doesn't seem so bad.

We stopped in front of my work. The facility squatted on the side of the road, oversized cross on the exterior like a pungent mausoleum.

Steeling myself with a deep breath, halfway out of the car, I told my ex that I missed her. I was sorry for what an ass I'd been. Sorry that I hadn't appreciated her like I should have. Sorry that I wasn't a good boyfriend. Sorry that I wasn't even a decent one. Sorry that I sucked the big one and didn't deserve a precious jewel like her.

Sorry that I was sorry that I was sorry that I was sorry.

Silence. She stared straight ahead.

Was I, I prompted, missed in return? Just a little?

My ex stared straight ahead, now irritated at what she'd been dreading.

"*Get out*," she said.

7:26pm
IF SELLING PISS FOR PROFIT IS WRONG, WHO WANTS TO BE RIGHT?

I asked Scott if he wanted me to turn on the faucet to help his urinating.

"*Please*," he said, straining like his life depended on it.

His life didn't depend on his ability to piss quick and piss clean, but his place of residency sure did.

Scott had shown up for Sunday check-in in a funny mood. '*Funny*' meant that he was slurring his words, rambling incoherently, and generally making a relapsed spectacle out of himself. If Jack hadn't been around, if Scott's stupid ass hadn't been so obvious about his drugged-up state, I'd have let him get away with it.

So he was fucked up? So what? His life to ruin as he saw fit. What business was it of mine?

Right?

Isn't minding your own business part of the American way? Myself, I'm a non-interventionist at heart. M.Y.O.B. and all that. Had I been born Woodrow Wilson or FDR instead of the middle-class cracker that I was, I'd have been like, '*Eh, let the fuckin' Europeans kill each other. What else is new?*'

But I was working the Sunday evening shift with Jack, and Scott was rambling at the other clients about the Knights Templar and the International Jewish Banking Conspiracy and the healthy goodness of Quaker-brand oatmeal. So, my hand was forced in the matter. I had to get some Financial Consultant-flavored piss out of the guy. I did that, or I risked being too obvious about how little I had grown to care about my job.

Flaunting one's apathy *is* somewhat discouraged in most fields of employment.

Scott looked like a Cabbage Patch Kid grown up bad. He had a soft white face and easily tousled hair that would've rated a maternal hug, if only all the warmth hadn't been snuffed out of me months ago. Snuffed, buried, then dug back up to be raped and buried again.

What can I say, being around human suffering every day in this job did the same thing to your soul that cigarettes do to your lungs.

But...thankfully, I don't believe in the soul.

Standing over the toilet, Scott farted with the strain. He was really putting a lot more effort into this than was required.

"Ease up," I told him. "It's just the urine that I'm after."

He tried to laugh but only farted again. From where I slouched in the far corner of the bathroom, I could tell the guy was shaking. Somebody was going to be pissing a stream of pure narcotics, and we both knew it.

It wouldn't be the first time. Jack had told me about Scott's frequent visits to the facility over the last five years. He'd show up, try to get clean, and fail. Then he'd try again, and fail again. Try and fail, try and fail, *ad nauseum*.

Scott always paid in cash, though, so they always let him back in.

"You…you h-hear about Anderson?"

I didn't look up from cleaning my nails with the facility's key ring. Just stayed squatted in the bathroom's corner, looking at anything but Scott. "Anderson who?"

"Dave," he said. "Dave An-Anderson."

Oh. That guy.

Dave had been a client a few months back. He was an airline pilot and hopeless drunk all rolled into one affable package.

Nice guy.

Real friendly.

I liked him.

"He's dead," said Scott.

Ah well.

"It happens," I replied, and then had to know: "How'd it happen?"

Scott interrupted his grimacing for a second, "How'd what…"

Stupid fucking junkie. I pictured Dave standing next to my desk, telling me his horrible Polack jokes. I took a deep breath. It didn't help. "*Gee Scott*, I was wondering how the Ainu originally got to then northern Japan islands so many centuries before the Koreans? Did they build primitive floatation devices or just evolve there from snow monkeys or—*How Did Dave Fucking Die?*"

"Oh…" Scott looked like he understood the question for a second, then it was gone like an alcoholic's paycheck.

"Cirrhosis?" I prompted. "Cancer of the kidneys? Liver give up and chuck itself out his ass?"

"*Oh*!" The light went back on in his eyes. "Dave! Yeah…no. No, Dave died in a car wreck. Church bus ran a stop sign. Decapitated him."

"No shit?" I was mildly impressed.

"*MM-hmm.*"

"Wow," I said. "Gimme some of that old time religion, huh?"

Instead of devising an insensitive remark of his own, Scott stopped trying to strain fluids into the plastic cup he was holding. He turned his head to look at me.

"How much do you earn here?" Scott asked.

I knew where this was headed. They'd warned us about it in training. "Starvation wages," I answered.

"Did you have to take a urine test to work here?"

My evaluation of workers' rights in America came packaged in a defeated shrug. "Ya gotta piss in a cup to work anywhere in this fuckin' country."

I had cheated on my own urinary analysis, but that wasn't any of Scott's business. I could smell the scent of filthy lucre, and since Scott had his own financial consulting firm to go with his pill addiction, I knew he was good for a decent amount. Still, I figured I'd play a little coy. "Why ya asking?"

"One hundred dollars," Scott whispered, still holding himself over the toilet.

“For what?” I asked innocently.

“*You know*,” he hissed.

“Do I now?” Just couldn’t resist the opportunity to fuck with the guy.

Scott made a noise of exasperation. “Look—”

“Two hundred,” I interrupted him. What the fuck, why not?

“All I have is a hundred-sixty,” he whined.

Why not put my job on the line? This way, I could actually afford groceries for the month. Or a higher grade of pot. Booze that didn’t come in plastic bottles. If my employers wanted me to honestly execute my duties, they should pay me a living wage.

“*Two hundred*,” I repeated, glancing at the bathroom door to make sure it was locked. “You can give me the other forty later tonight.”

“Okay,” Scott said, looking even more nervous as he zipped himself up.

I took the cup from him and whipped my dick out over the toilet. All that water running from the faucet had me needing to piss like hell.

“Get me that money by the end of the shift,” I said, penis in hand, looking at Scott as sternly as I could. “Or you’re *fucked*. Breathe a *word* of this to any-fuckin’-body…”

‘*Didn’t you used to be a nice person?*’ asked a little voice in my head.

‘*Nope,*’ I told it. ‘*You must be thinking of someone else*.’

“Right,” said Scott. He was now far, far away from his white-collar office. His addiction had taken him into a shadowy land distant from those respectable cubicles. A world where he paid young men to urinate for him. A world where he was mesmerized by the shriveled organ I held in my hand.

His staring was interrupting my attempt at pissing.

"*What*?" I asked. "It hypnotic or something?"

Scott turned increasingly bright shades of red and looked away.

The piss then started to flow. I occupied myself with trying to remember all the shit I had done at those Halloween parties the previous night. I vaguely remembered adopting a bottle of Jack Daniels to drag from party to party, and somewhere in there, people kept shoving blunts in my mouth. After the first few of those it got kind of hazy. A fellow partygoer claimed to see me doing a line of coke or two, but damned if I recalled.

Busy pissing for Scott's money, I also wondered if the Percodan I'd munched earlier that day would show up on the test.

7:54pm
ON THE IMPORTANCE OF ASKING FOR IDENTIFICATION

There was a round-table bullshit session in the lobby while Todd played everyone an acoustic parody of *Beat It* on his guitar. The topic of discussion: prison stints and why.

It was Paul's turn at the imaginary microphone. Thanks to how my horror of my job had developed into a form of car-crash fascination, I appreciated Paul with a connoisseur's eye. Any physical imposition that his height could give was offset by his twitchy movements, all sharp and jerky like he was living claymation. Paul looked like someone had sucked all the color and life out of Gumby and gave him a drooling problem thanks to the painkiller addiction that landed him here.

This time.

Paul's visit last winter was for alcoholism.

Obviously, the treatment didn't take too well. That's pretty common. Anyone making it through their stay here sober still has a pretty good chance of relapsing after they leave. This speaks worlds about the effectiveness of the program.

Paul had spent six months in the LA County Jail. He denied ever being ass-raped while incarcerated, but hey, I'd lie about it, too.

"I got off the plane in LA in full black-out mode, so I remember none of this," he said, adding in the excuse about being on antibiotics at the time. "But I knew I was supposed to meet my girlfriend downstairs, so I apparently dropped my luggage in the middle of the terminal and walked on down to her car."

Drool was wiped off Paul's chin with the back of his hand.

"Me and Cindy get in a big argument about me being sober enough to drive, so I went back to get my bags. When I got back outside I staggered up to the car that was at the curb, stuck my head inside and shouted at the woman: '*Cindy, get out of the car before I beat yer ass!*' And she did and I hopped in the car and pulled off without her." He paused to wipe the drool off his chin again.

"Bitch call the cops on ya?" someone asked Paul, and there was a general shaking of heads. No matter what horrible shit the junkies put their loved ones through, they always regard the contacting of law enforcement as the ultimate betrayal.

"Got the cops called on me, all right," Paul resumed. "Big problem was: that wasn't my girlfriend's car and that *wasn't my girlfriend!*"

Six months in a cage.

8:25pm
GRAND SLAM JUNKIE

He spoke into the cell phone, voice dripping with self-pity and rage. "I'm just trying my best to love you!"

Hearing his weak-ass whining, I cackled like a hag.

For somebody who'd spent so much time on the front pages of newspapers, this Local Boy Made Good was one sorry motherfucker.

Bagger (obviously not his real name, but that's par for the course in this book) was a big-time sports star with a big-time drug problem. An MVP for three years running, he had blown it all through repeated drug arrests, relapses, and highly publicized jail time. Now he was here, sentenced by the courts as part of his parole (since the rich and famous don't stay long in jail) to spend a month at The Best Little Rehab/Halfway House in Texas.

Having a celebrity here wasn't entirely unusual. I mean, this isn't the Betty Ford Clinic, but I've seen my share of the famous here. Athletes, mostly. My boss, being ex-NFL himself, still had plenty of connections that netted the rehab some big-name clients. It was never anyone I gave a shit about, but it's hard for me to get excited about being around people who make millions from playing a fucking game. After all, we had dumb jocks back in high school, too. Meeting people who had gone professional with the act didn't exactly blow my little pink socks off.

A lot of the junkies, of course, were in awe of the athletes that ended up here. When Bagger first arrived he was bum-rushed for autographs. Everyone about shit themselves at how someone they had watched on TV was now slumming it in the same facility as them.

"Man, Curtis rushed up to the poor guy and asked him to autograph his fuckin' hacky-sack!"

Me and a few of the junkies were discussing Bagger's presence in their humble home while Bagger yelled into his cell phone further down the hallway. I was shaking my head at the stories about their housemates overreacting to a sports star.

"I didn't know they had professional hacky-sackers," I confessed. For all the attention I paid to pro sports, their existence was something of a possibility. Hell, ESPN could show 24-hour lawn dart competitions and I'd never know about it.

"They don't," Robert said. "Curtis just an idiot." The other guys nodded in agreement.

"No comment," I said, grimacing at the number of kids to whom the guy had passed on his idiocy genes.

Bagger bellowed into his phone, "*Why won't you let me love you?*" The other clients cringed with sympathetic embarrassment, but I just rolled my eyes in contempt.

Our current *Reverend Leroy*, Corey, had been walking through the lobby past our little group, but hearing that we were busy slandering other people, he decided to join in. "Y'all know that Johnson called his family to let them know Bagger was staying here."

A collective groan went up. So much for the facility's confidentiality clause!

'*Stupid motherfucker*,' was the term on everyone's lips.

"Surprised to hear you're not hero-worshipping the guy," I said to Corey. He was a pretty religious chap, so I figured the IQ necessary for admiring athletes was similar to the numbers required to have imaginary friends past the age of five.

"There's only one *supa-star* for me," Corey said, his eyes looking upward as he pointed towards the ceiling with reverence. "And that's *Jesus*."

Another collective groan. I glanced up at the ceiling. When somebody mentioned their god while pointing up, I always expected to see something clinging to the ceiling like Spider-man.

"Fuck y'all," Corey said, and stormed off.

"Is that what Jesus would say?" I called after him.

In the background, Bagger was still whining, "Why do you always have to bring that up, goddamnit? I *said* I was sorry!"

"Look," I said, "So long as *he's* here—" I motioned back at Bagger, "—Dude gets the same treatment as the rest of you scumbags. End of story." There was a general murmur of agreement, with only a single '*hey*!' when someone caught the *scumbag* part.

"*Fuck you*, then!" Bagger yelled into his phone. We went silent, straining to hear the next part of the drama. "*Baby?…Hello?*" No matter how many times you've graced the cover of *Sports Illustrated*, there's apparently still a limit to the amount of shit people will take from you.

"*Goddamnit*!" Bagger yelled. I could hear him stomp towards the back of the facility, and then up the stairway.

"Yeah," Robert said, "I 'member what it was like when I first got here, so everybody just treat him no different. He just like us."

Nods all around. It was unanimous.

A minute later Bagger came back through the lobby with Johnson in tow. I had always thought of Johnson as a muscular guy, but Bagger's bulk and height eclipsed him entirely. "Sign me out," he said to Johnson, who went to the front desk to do just that.

"*C'mon*, damnit," Bagger growled when Johnson took too long. Unable to wait another three seconds, Bagger stormed out the front door. Johnson ran after him.

We all watched the twin spectacles of submission and dominance as they got into the Hummer at the curb and sped off.

"*Wow*," said one of the guys said. "I want one of those."

"Not me," said Robert. "Already had me a puppy dog."

8:59pm TURNING THE OTHER CHEEK, IF ONLY TO MOON

Eddy loomed over my desk, big and wide with an excess of prison-honed muscles. He stuck out his hand. I flinched before realizing that he desired a mutual shaking of appendages. I looked at the proffered hand, then up at him. His face shown with self-congratulatory delight. He was proud of what he was doing, that much was clear.

I grasped Eddy's hand, twice the size of my own, and gave it a manly pump or two. His smile got even wider. He said, "You okay, man," as if bestowing a priestly benediction. "You all right."

Had I verbalized any sort of reciprocation it would have been a lie. So I just said, "*Thanks*,'' and left it at that.

Eddy had only been here a short while. In that time he'd already managed to lose his cool and toss a promise that he was going to '*beat yo white ass*' in the direction of *my* white ass. Eddy was under the impression that I was picking on him, and, *by god*, he wasn't going to take it anymore!

(This from somebody I've talked with only twice: once to ask how his weekend went, and once to remind him to do his assigned chore.)

It'd all gone a little something like this:

“I’m fuckin’ sick of it!” Eddy screamed at me. Eyes bugged out. Nostrils flared. Hands clenched into very large fists aimed in my direction. I took a step back. “No more shit from you, motherfucker!”

Why the violent reaction? Beats me. Everybody tries to fill the drug-shaped hole in their life somehow. I guess Eddy thought he could do it through the random assaulting of cracker-ass employees.

He took another step towards me. “Gonna beat yo white ass into the *ground*!” I took another two steps back. Hoped I didn’t look as scared as I felt.

His blow-up caught me by surprise. I wasn’t expecting to segue from my question of how his weekend went to him screaming in my face. One second, I was mentioning that his assigned chore needed to get done, then the next thing I knew he was bathing me in angry spittle. And the *breath* that fucker had…

“Show all you motherfuckers who you’re fuckin’ with!”

I mean, I’ve got enough practice at being a dick that I’m *very* aware when I'm doing it. I felt pretty sure that wasn’t one of those times. Eddy obviously disagreed. Fortunately, the large hunk of oak attached to our facility’s key ring kept homeboy in his place.

I held it up in front of me over my head. “You wanna try something?” I interrupted his screaming with my bluff. “Go right ahead.” We were out in the back lot, gnats swarming the light posts over our heads.

He almost raised his fist, but stopped short. “You thinkin’ of using that on me?” he asked, pointing at my cudgel. The fucker sounded almost offended, like I was violating the rules of etiquette established by centuries of more compliant weaklings.

An honest question deserved an honest response, so I said, “I know my defensive capabilities.”

Grade school was the last time I'd been in a fight, and my skills had never improved much beyond the biting that was so effective back then. Maybe I could have pulled Eddy's hair, if he wasn't shaved clean.

Eddy came closer. Instinct told me to keep backing up. "I pays cash money to be here!" he shouted. "Three thousand a month, and I don't gotta put up with nobody's shit!"

My heel bumped against the fence. He'd backed me up a good ten yards. "I could give a hemorrhaging *fuck*," I replied, voice calmer than I felt. "I get paid the same no matter where your stupid ass is."

"This 'cause I black, ain't it?"

Lovely. I had the expected amount of sympathy for that query that you could expect from someone so pale that their skin was almost translucent, especially when mine was the socially-favored hue.

Of course, I thought, everything in life has to do with one's melanin levels, *you criminal fuck*. Nice to know that if the crack hadn't made you paranoid enough, there was always the Black Persecution Complex.

"Sure it's because you're black," I told him. "All of us crackers have weekly meetings where we get together to watch NASCAR and discuss how to keep the brothers down."

Eddy reared back like he was going to swing at me. I reared back like I didn't want to get hit.

Jack picked that moment to break through the crowd that had formed around us—since there's always a crowd around two guys who might hit each other. Jack steered Eddy away, talking softly to him the whole time. Probably asking the guy to wait till the 4-12 shift was over (and Jack went home) before killing me.

"Don't worry, Ray," a few of the other addicts told me later (once they could no longer be of any help). "We wouldn't let him do shit to ya."

"Thanks," I said, a lot more relieved than I wanted to admit. I didn't know if Eddy would actually have tried to kill me, but I do know that everyone would have found it entertaining. Considering our size differences and my lack of fighting prowess, his pulping me wouldn't have been too difficult. At most, Eddy might've bruised one of his knuckles while giving my face a full-contact massage.

Or maybe the violence that had seemed so imminent wouldn't have happened. Maybe Eddy would have simply kept up the macho posturing till it deteriorated into him beating his chest and tearing up the surrounding foliage. Or, maybe he had been planning on making a few more threats and then walking off. Had he done so, *my* plan was to wait for his back to be turned before taking the cudgel and cracking him across the back of his skull.

I know, *I know.* It's never sporting to hit someone when their back's turned. But notions of fighting fair meant fuck-all to me when it would entail having to watch my own ass at work. I'd be damned if I was going to wait for some crackhead to decide that Today Was The Day he would take it no longer from his white oppressors...with Yours Truly as the franchise's local representative.

And besides, I find face-to-face confrontations pretty difficult when I'm stoned.

Despite our brief and acrimonious history, I wasn't too surprised to see Eddy later offer me a handshake. I especially wasn't surprised to see how full of self-righteous pleasure he was at doing it. I had walked past the chapel earlier and, glancing in, noticed him kneeling on the floor. His head had been resting on the seat of a chair, hands clasped tightly above it, whining to his god about all the persecutions and tribulations contained in a life that he'd managed to fuck up enough to find himself here.

Apparently, his god told him to forgive those persecuting him (like me, for example) and to be as smug as possible while doing so.

Fucking sklavmoralist, I thought as we squeezed hands. But hey, if both of the delusions born from the lack of crack in his life (my persecutions and the god of the 12-Step) canceled each other out, then no harm done.

Still, as Eddy was walking away, self-satisfied for having turned the other cheek, I had to wonder if I should still give the back of his skull a good whacking.

9:09pm
WILL WORK FOR CHANGE

It was past nine, and that meant it was time for the more industrious of the junkies to get started on their chores. Everyone living here had a chore. "Take Care of Your Community," as the signs posted on the walls read. It's odd to expect any form of civic pride out of people who used to rob and beat their neighbors for drug money, but changing old habits is what this place is supposedly all about.

Mops and brooms were taken from closets. Arms scarred with needle marks pushed them along the floor. Fingers that held red-hot crack pipes without feeling pain gripped the edges of toilet bowls and gave a half-assed scrub. Everyone had a chore to do, myself included.

My chore was to sit on my ass and watch the cleaning going on around me. It's tough, but I manage.

My chair was scooted out of the way to accommodate a mop being pushed by a client. He's a sweet guy, asking questions as he works around me: *How'm I doing? How's school? Did I get that flat fixed on my back tire? How'd my sister's birthday go?* I tended to forget that, like a lot of our guys, he's only been out of prison for the past month or two. He was in there for stabbing a guy to death in Vidor, TX for, let's say, an unfortunate misuse of racial terminology.

(someone in Vidor probably had it coming)

Or so he claimed. Junkies tell lies like Starbucks sells coffee. Hence, *New Start Rule #1*: Never Trust A Junkie.

Junkies also have a great propensity for shirking responsibility. I can identify with that, but it also meant that I was supposed to go check to see if each one of these grown men had completed their assigned chore. If this made them like a bunch of over-grown teenagers, then following that simile made me the sorriest excuse for an authority figure imaginable.

There was a chart on my desk that everybody was required to sign after completing their chore. I was supposed to make sure the junkies had actually done their job before letting them sign it, but that's easily avoided with a wave of my hand and a simple declaration. "*Eh*, I trust ya."

I didn't, of course—*New Start Rule #1*—not any further than I could shotput my weight in crack. But, my apathy and desire not to have my reading interrupted outweighed any responsibility that I might've felt. If these guys didn't want to clean up their temporary home, if they felt like living in a garbage dump, more power to them.

I didn't live here; what did I care?

“I used the crack to keep everybody at arm’s length,” said the client cleaning around my desk. I hadn’t even noticed that he was still talking at me. “It was like, my shield ’gainst the world.”

I nodded without bothering to look up from my book. “Whatever works, man.”

9:13pm
HIDING FROM YOU LIKE THE MOON IN A TREE

I wish I could say that I knew Gerry, but he was just another sullen, black face that I’d see wandering the hallways at work, dying for one more fix of whatever used to get him through the day. I’d grace him with the occasional ‘*hey*!’ or ‘*howdy*!’ but that’d be about it.

Gerry was pretty quiet and kept to himself. I didn’t know his name, didn’t know his problem, and most of all, I didn’t fucking care.

So, it caught me by surprise when he utterly lost it. Like most kids of the past few generations, I liked to pretend that my life could be arranged into something resembling an orderly movie or novel. Maybe a series of slightly amusing anecdotes, at the very least. This made it unsettling when one of the peripheral characters decided to grab the limelight of their own volition, foreshadowing be damned.

It upsets the balance of things. Takes a little while to get adjusted.

I didn’t think too much of it when client after client came in from their 8pm 12-step meetings. They walked through the front door, each one looking over their shoulders with frightened expressions. Frightened, and maybe even a little bit jealous.

I figured the cause of the disturbance was some bum smoking crack on the nearest street corner. This isn't the swankiest part of town, and public drug use occurs around here plenty. I find it amusing, but to the clients it's a temptation that they don't particularly need. It would be like munching on a seafood buffet in front of starving Somalians (or whoever the *en vogue* hungry are these days).

If one of the clients hadn't screamed the bum out of the neighborhood yet—which sometimes happens—then the task would fall to me. Far be it from my ass to interfere with a non-client's attempt to enjoy themselves. I wasn't even keen on getting involved in the clients' business; live and let live had become my policy after only a few months at work. But, if some crackhead bum was riling the herd, then it was probably best for me run him off.

Whatever kept my job as trouble-free as possible.

I was about to drag my lazy ass out the front door, but Robert met me halfway.

"Need to talk to—"

Wanting to spare myself the five feet to the door, I asked Robert, "What's goin' on out there?"

"Gerry out there," he said.

"Which one's he?"

"He tall, bald head, huge gut." A *slightly* useful description. It takes a bit of paying attention before you realize that the only time most people don't bother to mention ethnicity as a physical detail is when it matches their own.

Robert was black as they came; *ergo*, so was Gerry.

Another client rushed up while my Apple II processor of a brain was still working on this. "Gerry's outside chuggin' a fifth!" he cried.

Once it became apparent that snitching was now an acceptable option, another five clients came to tell me the same damn thing. Gerry was standing out in front of the building, pulling a non-stop chug-a-thon on a fifth of *something*. Vodka or gin or tequila or paint remover, depending on which hysterical recounting you believed.

I guess Gerry figured that if he was going to relapse, he might as well go public with the act. Fucking drama queen.

I was about to stop relying on second-hand information and actually look out the goddamn door myself when Jack hurried into the lobby. Some of the clients had by-passed me to squeal directly to Jack.

It was annoying to be reminded that a curmudgeon like Jack was Head Tech while I was *just* another grunt. I looked like being almost fifty-years younger than him would have to compensate me for our differences in job seniority. Knowing that I'd still be in the prime of my life while Jack was fertilizing a graveyard lawn made up for a lot of things.

We both moved towards the front door. "You hear?" I asked Jack.

"I hear 'bout it."

Jack swung the door outwards to almost hit a scruffy, bald black guy. The guy listed strongly to one side. His t-shirt was torn at the shoulder, and blood caked his chin. Someone had probably fallen down a few times getting here.

We can't all smell like concentrated rose powder, but *Jeeezus*, did that guy reek of booze! I took a step back, pushed by his alcoholic shield. My amazing deductive skills told me this was probably Gerry.

Holding the door open with one hand, he still had the bottle of *Night Train* in the other. Gerry swung it back and forth in erratic circles like a broken pendulum.

Ewww, I thought. *If you're gonna relapse, why not do it with a bit of style?*

I also wondered if I should mention that he'd missed the 9pm curfew.

Me and Jack stared at him for a few seconds, and him at us. Or, at least he tried to stare back. The emptiness of the bottle explained why Gerry was having trouble focusing. No doubt it hadn't been his first.

Gerry tossed the bottle out the door behind him. It shattered on the street with the sound of a million broken promises. The noise snapped us into action…or as close to action as lazy bastards like myself and Jack can manage.

"You know I can't let you in here like that," said Jack. I stood next to him, trying to look like an authority figure.

"*Thass* cool," Gerry slurred, almost flooring us with his breath. We stepped back even further to get out of range. "*Ah jus'…wan mah trug…*" A thin sliver of drool crept over his lips and sprinted down his chin to hang like a noose.

"His *what*?" I asked. African American Vernacular English (*ebonics, you racists!*) had been tough enough to master, but the drunken variety of AAVE was one dialect that I still hadn't gotten the hang of.

"Can't let you drive outta here like this," Jack said back to him. "Why don't you give us your keys?"

"C'mon, Gerry," I said. Dude was *fuuuucked up*! "Toss those puppies over this way, and we'll go make us some coffee and chill out some, huh?"

Actually, I planned to take Gerry's keys, then push him back out the door to sleep it off on a sewer grate, but he didn't need to know that.

Gerry paused for a second. Maybe considering my offer. Maybe waiting for his brain to cut through the booze that his body wasn't finished processing.

"*Fuck y'all*," he decided, and pushed past us towards the back of the building.

I looked with dismay at the handprint he'd left on my shirt, then exchanged a shrug with Jack. Gerry could go sit in his truck in the back lot all he wanted. No way he was getting far with the back gate being closed.

Still, me and Jack followed Gerry, making sure he stayed out of trouble. He stumbled into the back door, bounced off it, then wasted a few seconds pulling rather than pushing it open. I followed him ahead of Jack, who was having trouble keeping up with the pace. Through the door, into the back lot, was an unexpected sight:

The back gate was wide open.

"*Fuck*!" I shouted. "Jack, go get the fuckin' clicker!"

"The what?" Jack asked.

"The *clicker*! The *fuckin'* remote!" *This* was where my college-educated ass had communication issues with a 70-something recovering crackhead? *Really*? And *now*?

Should I have sprinted back to desk to grab it myself? "The gate's open! Grab the fuckin' clicker-remote-whatever!"

Jack could close the gate from the front desk by himself. I stayed shadowing Gerry.

For all the good it did.

He climbed into his truck. Gave me a disgusted look and slammed the door closed. A group of clients stood behind me, watching the show.

"C'mon, man," I pleaded with Gerry, my 'used car salesman' smile on my face. "Let's talk about this, huh?"

Gerry used his right hand to fish under his seat. And, since there was no accounting for the man's tastes, he came up with a plastic flask of *Stoli's*. A smile—or maybe a smirk—was flashed in my direction before Gerry twisted off the cap and, head tossed back, proceeded to down the entire goddamn bottle.

The.

Entire.

Goddamn.

Bottle.

I stood transfixed by something I'd only expect at a sideshow or family reunion. "*Jesus*," I managed to mutter, a sentiment echoed by the rest of the crowd.

Robert busted out the back door, distracting from the alcoholic marvel before us. "Jack can't find the clicker!" he yelled.

Fuck! The gate!

Finished with his display of alcohol tolerance, Gerry started up his truck. The engine growled, nearly stalled in an admirable show of foresight, then gave an angry roar before shifting into gear.

"*Dude*!" I shouted at him, out of words and giving as many universal signs for pleading as I could recall. Gerry just flipped me the bird again—using the wrong finger—and with an alarming squeal of his tires skidded out the back gate. He drove straight at the building across from ours, then busted a sharp right at last second. The truck bounced off the curb and tore off in a cloud of garbage scraps and bad choices.

The back gate hummed to life and creaked itself shut.

Surrounded by the other voyeurs, I stood staring after Gerry. I could hear his tires shrieking in the distance.

"*Fuck!*" I screamed after him. "*Fuuuuck!*"

Life-saving attempt over and officially failed, I stalked back inside.

The group of clients watched me go. One of them muttered, "That boy got a mouth on him."

9:18pm
THINK OF ENGLAND

Johnson reminded me of a young Arnold Schwarzenegger. Not that Johnson was a political tool of Californian energy conglomerates, it was more his muscles and height. Johnson had the sort of rugged charm that shouted at you from across the room. When he dipped his head slightly in a false '*aw, shucks*' display of humility, I realized that I'd be sopping wet if granted the proper equipment.

The only thing off was his eyes. One moved slightly independent of the other. It lagged behind by a half-second when looking about the room, and never seemed to settle on the same point of focus.

I was having a similar problem with my eyes, but more about keeping them open. Of course, the Vicodin I'd munched probably had more to do with this than any natural defect. The best method for preventing myself from nodding off seemed to be concentrating on maintaining eye contact with Johnson. I made a game of it. Picked one of his eyes and tried to follow its gaze.

I found this entrancing. So entrancing that I was having trouble paying attention to the gut-spilling Johnson was doing. He had started off by cornering me in Gim's office and, without warning, gave me the director's cut of his recovery/relapse history.

The junkies had a tendency to do shit like that. If there's one thing that no member of our species can resist, it's talking about themselves. '*How I'm dealing with this drug-shaped hole in my life'* is how this manifests in a rehab.

Way too many of the clients did this to me, the effusive spilling of guts. I was just somebody else for them to blather at and bore with details of their less-than-mediocre existence. I was a giant ear taking the place previously filled by their bartender, priest, or dealer.

"I really feel like I'm going to do it this time," he told me, and I nodded, slow and appreciative.

Jack picked that time to stroll past the open door. "And I really feel like you gonna relapse like you always do."

Johnson muttered a "*Fuck you*," at Jack's receding laughter. He then gave me an expectant look, like it was my responsibility to toss him a verbal lifesaver. Some phrase to keep his ass afloat in the hostile waters of Jack's well-earned doubt. Took me a while to think of anything, but I eventually managed to spit out, "Ya gotta do it…sometime. Why not…now?"

Johnson was a mere quarter-century old, and he'd already been in rehab and relapsed six times. He was an alcoholic and occasional sampler of crack. He had been sober now for five days, only three more to go and he'd beat his last time. As he rambled on, Johnson was probably dying for a drink.

Fuck, me too.

I wondered if the state of Johnson's eyes was a result of all his drug intake. Then I realized that the cause of other people's misfortunes wasn't half as important as the entertainment value.

Johnson kept talking, and I kept nodding and making the appropriate noises at random intervals, all the while watching his eyes. It's odd, but I was generally known around here as the

Tech to whom you could talk. That was why so many of the guys came to me when it was gut-spilling time, though I got the feeling that anyone, even a brick wall or water fountain, would do.

How I ever got a reputation as a good listener was beyond me. Like most of my generation, my attention span was screwed. I couldn't listen attentively if an anecdote was punctuated with free money and topless girls. So, I guess it's good that I never cared enough to pay attention in the first place.

When listening, like with most forms of human interaction, all you needed was to display a few simple mechanical responses and no one could tell the difference. Smile, nod on occasion, and try not to let your eyes wander too much. Whether you actually had any interest in what was being spewed at you was irrelevant.

It reminded me of a good friend from high school. She was a short blonde who—in addition to bearing the label of *school slut*—was also gifted with the reputation of being The Greatest Lay on Planet Earth. At our high school, at least, and maybe a neighboring one or two. Some of us just peak young. I asked her once what her secret was (and requested a demonstration, of course). She had said, '*I dunno; I just lie there and try to look interested.*'

Indeed.

There may be a lesson here for all of us, but goddamn if I know what it is.

9:31pm
BOX WINE IN A JEWELED CHALICE

"Toilets are all done, sir." His plastic gloves were stripped off and tossed into the wastebasket next to my desk.

I said, "Thanks for taking care of your shit," and didn't bother looking up from my homework. Just one more class and I'd graduate. I'd have a big, bad college degree and could go off and find myself a *real* job. Something that paid better than starvation wages. Something where I didn't have to watch people urinate through units that dwarfed my own.

"Did you want to check it before I signed the chore list, sir?"

I still didn't bother to look up, just waved my hand and said, "*Naw*, I trust ya."

"Thank you," he said, oblivious of my lie.

I considered the matter closed until he asked, "*Umm*...could I please borrow your pen, sir?"

I handed it over. "As long as you stop calling me, *sir*."

I looked up for the first time at the guy I'd been communicating with. He was paunchy and black, with a slight ring of graying hair around the back of his skull. A general vibe of harmlessness wafted off the guy like watered-down cologne. On sight, you'd trust him to babysit your kids.

He smiled at me as I handed my pen up to him. "Thanks...*Ray*." He was reading it off my nametag. This rapid-fire literacy put him a few steps ahead of most clients.

I smiled back. "No prob." Maybe I'd pay attention to my actual job for a while. Anything for a break from neurology homework. "What's your name, man?"

"Davis," he answered, and we shook hands firmly. "Sorry about the '*sir*' convention. It's just best to play it safe in these places and hard to go wrong with such a standardized form of address."

"I dig."

Davis motioned at my book. "I take it you're in school. There aren't too many people who read textbooks for fun."

I said, "Yep, studyin' psychology up at UH. This is my last semester."

My last semester, and I hadn't learned a goddamn thing. Seriously. My tuition money would've been better spent on twenty-grand worth of coke and hookers.

Davis gave a little smile. "Going to get your masters then, are you?"

"Yeah, eventually." I said. "Turns out there's not too goddamn much you can do with a bachelors in Psych. Wish I'd known that about three years ago."

He laughed politely. "I know, I know. Realizing that I was going to have to get my Ph.D. was something of a shock."

"Whatcha got a Ph.D. in?" An educated crackhead. Rare specimen. *Weird...*

He shrugged with what I could tell was false humility. "Oh, just aerospace engineering."

"*Goddamn...*" I tried to whistle to show how impressed I was, but whistling's never been a skill of mine. "So, whatcha do?"

Davis was unable to contain his smile. "I worked for NASA. Shuttle design."

That had to be one fat paycheck the guy used to drag in. And his job was probably what Davis used to assure himself that he was better than the other wrecks here. All the clients have some sort of ego-defense like that. It's human nature to try to defend ourselves from uncomfortable truths (such as: '*I've fucked up my life and am currently living with a bunch of other failures*') in any way we can.

The junkies used everything possible to distance themselves from the other failures around them. Everything and anything along the lines of: '*At least I only drank instead of shooting up, at least I ain't a nigger, at least I ain't poor white trash, at least I've got a job, at least I've never been to jail, at least I never sucked dick for my habit,'* etc., etc., etc.

I know this because they never fail to tell me, usually as a sort of disclaimer at the end of a story about ripping off their mom's jewelry or killing the guy who stiffed them on a rock. '*Yeah, I did some lousy shit, but at least I ain't as bad as some of these other scumbags.*'

It's right there on the bottom rung of Maslow's Hierarchy of Needs: food, clothing, shelter, and someone to whom you can feel superior. I wondered if everyone here was aware of the low regard in which everybody else held them.

Of course, a college boy like myself doesn't bother with such delusions.

I smiled up at Davis. He smiled back before giving a disgusted look around the lobby at the rest of his fellow addicts. He was probably telling himself how his multiple degrees from Yale and MIT (he made sure to name-drop those later), and the high-paying job he once held, made him not only better than his fellow addicts, but also higher and mightier than the lowly cracker from a state college earning eight bucks an hour to baby-sit him.

Davis was more than welcome to feel that way. I knew which sides of the desk we were on.

9:40pm
...IN ALL THE WRONG PLACES

Jack rolled his eyes as the phone kept squeaking. "Yeah. Yep. *Uh-huh.*" He was a man of few words and even fewer worth remembering. I watched from the corner of my eye as I lounged on the lobby's couch. The slacker sees all and acknowledges nothing.

"Yeah," Jack said into the phone, "I see yo Daddy earlier. Yeah, he right here about noon or so. Lookin' kinda bad."

We're not supposed to give any information about the clients over the phone, so I listened as attentively as possible while pretending to be engrossed in my book. *"...the EPR paradox does suggest that distant parts of the universe are connected in some peculiar way not yet understood..."*

"Yeah, I tell ya if I see him. *Uh-huh.*" He rolled his eyes again. "Yeah. Yeah. Sweet dreams to you, too."

He hung up the phone. "The hell was I thinkin'?"

"Homicidal ex, again?" I asked.

Jack gave a mischievous grin. "I don't want you thinkin' less of me, Ray, but..."

Yeah, like he gave a shit, or like it was possible for me to think less of an elderly ex-crackhead. Someone was obviously preparing to brag about something.

"That was Cassandra."

I looked at Jack's smile and understood everything. *Oh god.* The undercooked chicken we'd had for dinner begged to see the light again. *Oh...dear...fuck.*

Not her and Jack. I almost fell to my knees to plead with a god in whom I didn't believe.

Not Jack. Anyone but Jack.

He nodded at me: *Yeah, I done hit that.*

"Is it your goddamn fault that my crotch has been itching in three-week intervals?"

Jack smiled even wider at my joke and gave a little shrug. I couldn't believe that I might have stuck my dick in the same zip code as Jack's. Had we been sleeping with Cassandra around the same time? I felt like breaking into the nearest pharmacy and bathing myself in penicillin. Either that or I needed to rush home and scrub with a wire brush.

"Just tell me when," I requested.

His face beamed with the pride of senior virility. "Oh, you too?"

"We'll vote on who gets to be club president at the next meeting," I assured him. "But right now, I just need a time frame."

There was no way I had humped the same person with whom Jack had played human sewing machine. What sort of horrid, super-resilient crap can you get from a seventy-something ex-crackhead? Anything Jack had could've been picked up in the Korean War, brought back to the States, and then incubated for several decades, strengthening itself on crack and the carcasses of weaker STDs.

"Time frame?" Jack asked. "I figure I lasted 'bout twenty, twenty-five minutes." I laughed, 'cause he had me beat, and then remembered that my genital health was at stake here. "Bless that *Cialis*," Jack said, giving his pocket a pat. I heard the rattle of pills. They were apparently something he never left home without.

"Not what I meant." I've never been one of those hypocrites who advocated promiscuity for themselves and monogamy for the rest of the world. I just wanted some warning if my dick was in danger of rotting-off soon.

I seriously considered adding welfare mothers to my list of people to never trust. Did Jack's probably-diseased cock pull Cassandra's AM shift while I worked the PM? How long had the two of them been shagging?

"Oh, I get ya" Jack said. "Happened about a week or two ago. It okay for once, but nothin' I'd pay to ride twice." Then he laughed at his own little joke.

Thank fuck...

It had been months since my Corporal Work of Shagging with Cassandra. Damn good to know that I was in a no danger of having sampled Jack's sloppy seconds. My immune system breathed a huge sigh of relief.

I did kind of admire Jack for fucking someone a half-century younger than him. How could I not? But sharing in the viral downside of decades worth of questionable lays wasn't too appealing an option. Of course, I'd been tested since being balls-deep in Cassandra (*can't be too careful!*), so I guess the momentary panic was for nothing. This honky needs to switch to decaf.

Still smiling, Jack asked, "Gotcha some of that, huh?"

At this point in the conversation I realized that not once had we referred to Cassandra with anything resembling an acknowledgement of her humanity. Jack talked about her like an amusement-park ride, and I had thought of Cassandra as a potentially dangerous petri dish.

Charming.

"Long time ago," I answered. It never would have occurred to me that the two of us would share the same notch on our bedposts. I wondered if I should be insulted or impressed that someone who found me attractive also had space in their sense of sexual aesthetics for Jack's decrepit old ass. Or, likely, which of us she had charged more. "Who the hell goes cruisin' for guys at a fuckin' rehab?"

Jack shrugged. “The desperate kind,” he said. “The only kind of person you gonna meet around here.”

9:49pm
THE CRASH OF THE HINDENBURG CONSIDERED AS A MATTER OF ‘PRINCIPAL’
or
THE MEANEST NIGGER I KNOW

“You wanna fight? *C’mon*! I know you wanna fight! *Somebody* wants to fight!”

Something was wrong with Johnson’s medication level. Or maybe something hadn’t mixed with his anti-psychotics too well. I hear crack doesn’t go well with much else besides more crack. He was in the middle of a full-on violent rage, and he was looking for someone—anyone—to take it out on.

Portrait of the Junkie as a Young Psychopath: Johnson was one of those people for whom the phrase, ‘*like a brick shithouse*,’ was invented. He was wide enough to be almost a perfect square in shape, except for the muscles that erupted from his body like an anabolic nightmare. I swear the guy’s cheeks were buff.

He was also out of his head with self-righteous belligerence. This was worse than the time he tried to hang a Confederate flag in his room.

“Fight me, you fuckers!”

Johnson was slamming holes into the walls of the stairwell, each furious punch leaving a fist-sized crater. I was trying to calm Johnson down, using soothing tones and phrases that were as effective as trying to piss out the sun.

"It's a matter of fucking principle!" Johnson screamed. Then he threw himself into the wall. *BOOM!* He seemed to enjoy the experience, repeating it immediately. *BOOM!* And again. *BOOM!*

There was a hollow reverberation as the wall dented around Johnson's massive bulk. The '*matter of fucking principle*' referenced was his earlier refusal to take a piss test. That's grounds for instant dismissal from the rehab.

Johnson had shown up from a weekend pass in a state of complete disorientation. He didn't know what day it was; couldn't string together a coherent sentence; became increasingly hostile when questioned about his behavior. That's what we call *begging* for a U.A.

He had gone upstairs to grab his stuff and '*clear the fuck outta this fucking shit-hole with you fucking homos always wanting to look at my dick.*' Jack followed after him. I followed too, wanting to ensure Johnson didn't let his instability loose in the direction of other clients. With everybody housed upstairs, there were plenty of targets for his chemical rage.

I was halfway up the stairs when it occurred to me just how much Johnson's size dwarfed my own. I ran back downstairs and grabbed the cudgel. Better safe than sorry, especially with the mentally unstable.

I made it upstairs, grabbed Jack, and sent him back down. I had a feeling Johnson would be less likely to attack me. There were plenty of non-deranged clients who'd beat Jack into the ground, given half an excuse.

Not that I blamed them.

"You *wanna* fucking fight?"

I was trying to herd Johnson back down the stairs (in much the same way I'd herd a bus down the street) when we ran into another client on the way up. It was Sam, our resident ex-skater and probably the least likely combatant at the rehab. Johnson instantly locked onto this scrawny cracker as a potential release valve. He puffed himself up, bared his teeth, clenched his fists, and waved them about. Typical aggressive primate behavior. "I know you wanna fuckin' fight me!"

"We're all friends here," I said as I tried to move myself between the two (breaking a cardinal rule of dealing with the unstable by turning my back on Johnson). "We're all friends. Let's keep moving." I made '*get-the-fuck-outta-here*' motions at Sam, who was now frozen up against the wall.

He wasn't moving. Sam seemed scared enough to piss his acid-washed jeans, so I pushed him ahead of us—always staying between him and Johnson, who never stopped shouting threats. We made it out of the stairwell into the back hallway. Walking in front of Johnson was like riding a freight of nitroglycerin down a Nigerian highway. You knew at any second your rough ride could get rougher, and then *BOOM!*

Some of the clients followed at a distance. Johnson was a mad gorilla on display, and when he wheeled around and screamed "*C'mon!*" everyone jumped back ten feet. Then resumed following.

There was conflict in the air, and no one wanted to miss it. Violence is one thing; it's quick and frightening. The *anticipation* of violence is something else entirely. It has an allure all its own.

I shoved Sam off at the nearest cross-hall and hoped Johnson didn't follow him. "This way, Johnson." I motioned towards the lobby.

He followed, cursing and shouting. "It's about principle, you fucks! About princ—not *p-r-c-i-p-a-l*, but *p-r-i-n-goddamnit*!" Johnson kept waving his arms and shouting more examples of his lack of spelling skills.

We made it to the lobby. Jack was busy at the front desk, dialing the phone. I knew he was calling the cops. It's what we're supposed to do when one client becomes a threat to the others, but I don't like the cops. Not just because they're government-issued thugs charged with repressing the rest of the lower classes, but due to their lousy history of dealing with the deranged. They tend to kill them. Call in the pigs to handle somebody unstable, and you're basically signing their death warrant.

I motioned for Jack to hang up the phone as I walked Johnson to the door. Thankfully, he did. Johnson caught me motioning to Jack and started screaming even louder; angry, incoherent shit about the government, Mormons, and how Jack always picked on him.

I managed to get Johnson outside where he changed tunes and started screaming about how he needed his breathing machine. He had to have it. He'd '*fucking die*' without it. Apparently this great white beast of a man had asthma.

I ran upstairs to grab the machine, then raced back down to the lobby. Jack was no longer at the front desk. I looked about, and what I saw through the front door registered as a worst-case scenario. Jack was outside arguing with Johnson.

"*Jesus*!" I expected Jack get a hole punched through his sternum. This was why I had originally sent Jack downstairs. It's why I had wanted my coworker away from Johnson. Jack was guaranteed to set him off even more.

Johnson was screaming louder and louder. Arms swinging more and more wild. I swung open our front door to bring it between the two of them, then grabbed Jack by the arm.

I growled, "*C'mere*, goddamnit!" yanked him inside, and waved goodbye to Johnson.

The door locked behind us. I started to vent the stress of the last ten minutes at Jack. "The *hemorrhaging fuck* did I tell you about staying away from—" only to be distracted by Johnson tugging on the front door. A second yank and he ripped it open, locks and all.

Then other clients in the lobby all stepped back. Me and Jack were rooted to the spot. Within striking distance.

"I just wanna say…" he started, before lapsing into more incomprehensibility. Angry blather and nonsense showered us. Johnson took a step closer. Then another. I waited for him to take a swing. Waited for the violence. Johnson kept screaming before finishing with, "...and *fuck you*, Jack." He pointed at my coworker, seething with righteous fury so intense there were tears in his eyes. "You're the *meanest nigger* I know!"

With that—having broken the ultimate taboo at the rehab—Johnson stormed out the door.

We said nothing.

No one moved.

We all just stood and stared at each other. Shaking slightly. Myself, Jack, and all the guys who had watched the spectacle still held our breaths.

No one was dead. It was like seeing the A-bomb fall to the streets of Hiroshima and lay dented on the pavement, a total dud. No one was dead. We were all in shock.

"*Gah*-damn," Jack said finally, his legs giving out and depositing him in the closest seat. More silence. Despite Jack having given the *all-clear* signal, no one else moved. No one else spoke.

I sank to the floor next to Jack's chair. The silence extended.

Finally, I said, "Don't sweat it, Jack," loud enough for everyone to hear. "I know *plenty* of niggers meaner than you."

It wasn't funny, but we all started laughing and couldn't stop.

10:01pm
YOU GET MY VOTE FOR JESUS IN THE NEXT ELECTION

"I'm a good person!" Corey asserted as loud as possible.

His wife had finally agreed to talk with him over the phone, only to use the opportunity to tell him all the several kinds of bastard he was.

Corey was now apparently in need of the sort of reassurance that only he could provide for himself at top volume. He wandered around the lobby, repeating this affirmation.

Some people have trouble reading silently. Corey couldn't even *think* to himself. I was beginning to suspect that anyone who believed in egalitarianism had never set foot outside a college campus.

"I'm a good person!"

"Sure ya are," Jack said. "We all good people here. We just got real shitty decision-making skills."

"I *know* I'm a good person," Corey repeated with even more conviction.

It didn't seem worth it to bother replying. We're all Good People. Each and every one of us. It's always the rest of the fucking world that has a problem. We're all just a bunch of well-meaning shmoes who have the misfortune to be continually abused and confounded by the other paragons of evil that surround us.

So, we occasionally do stuff not condoned by our society's moral code…*hey*, these things happen! Nobody's perfect. So, I ripped off my parents; so, I cheated on my girlfriend; so, I sold some bad crack; so, I killed someone; so, I continually act in a selfish, shitty manner…*hey*, I'm only human!

I am a Good Person, *goddamnit*! Ignore all the evidence to the contrary!

As for myself, I had always thought of myself as a Good Person, too. Why not?

I always thought of myself as a Good Person until I started working here and heard junkies, rapists, and murderers referring to themselves in a similar manner.

I'm a good person!

I know I'm a good person!

I a damn good person!

I'm still a good person inside!

Fuck them! I'm a good person and I don't have to hear that shit from them assholes!

Hearing this, day after day, from people considered the scum of society gave me insight into the amazing powers of self-delusion. If the junkies and crackheads could have convinced themselves that they were only a half-step from canonization, then what kind of crap could I have been feeding myself? What sort of preposterous bullshit did I tell myself in order to avoid having to face some sort of horrible self-awareness?

Was I a Good Person?

Was I? In spite of how I steal food and clothing meant for the homeless? Even though I'll throw old men out onto the freezing streets in the middle of the night? Despite how the junkies come to me looking for sympathy and I respond with sarcasm and mockery? And what about my leaving porn on Gim's computer and making sure other employees caught the blame?

Was I still a Good Person?

Was I ever?

The answer came bubbling up from my forebrain. From the newest, most recently developed part of my goopy think-box came the instant reply: *Who fuckin' cares?*

It had a decent point.

Be concerned about shit like that and I risked becoming another 12-Step weakling like the junkies. It was a slippery slope from worrying about how well you're following some arbitrary moral code to spending your Sunday mornings kissing the ass of some middle-eastern slave god.

Boo-hoo-hoo, I'm powerless over my addictions and myself. *Boo-hoo-hoo*, help me god, help me somebody, help me *anybody*, because I'm too fucking weak to do it myself.

Piss on that.

I resolved to never waste my time wondering about shit like that again.

Thanks, I said to my forebrain.

No problem, it replied. *Now let's wait for Jack to leave and then go scope out some porn on Gim's computer. You can always blame one of your coworkers for it!*

I smiled to myself. Sounded like a plan.

10:31pm
'TIS BETTER TO HAVE LOVED AND STALKED

A lot of the clients destroyed their families through their addictions. As we all know, misery loves company, and most addicts are like giant toilets, sucking everyone down into the shit with them. That's the price we all pay for being social animals, I guess.

Some of the smarter spouses had restraining orders taken out on their addict husbands to prevent their families from being dragged down with them. I doubt it's an easy thing to do, filing a court order to ensure that a loved one stays the hell away.

Not an easy thing to do, and not much easier to have done to you.

Corey had just come back from his house—well, what *was* his house—where his wife not only refused to let him inside, but also reminded him through the screen door that he wasn't allowed within 100 yards of his family.

Corey screamed and banged on the door, then ran like hell when the police showed up. It took him a while to ditch the cops, but he eventually made his way back to the facility. A perpetual victim, Corey was now crying on his roommate's shoulder about it all.

"She-she say I can't come 'round no more," he sobbed, apparently surprised that people might get tired of you selling their possessions for crack after the third time. "She call the cops on me. She *really* called the cops on me!"

He was the saddest black man I'd seen all day, and considering my job, that's saying quite a bit.

Love that was once returned but no longer is? That can be a *real* bitch. Especially if you had once earned someone's love but then lost it.

Unless you're the one whose love has done the disappearing act, you just can't imagine how a person could just *stop loving* somebody. It's such a mystery. But, like most ways of hurting people, it makes perfect sense from the other side. After all, it's *your* prerogative to get sick of people. Always comes as a bit of a shock when someone does it to you first.

Some variation of *requited-then-unrequited* love has happened to everybody at some point. It had graced *my* life recently when my girlfriend told me to take a fucking flying leap. Thus, was I reminded me of the eternal lesson: suffering is only funny when it happens to other people.

You love, they love, and then one of you—but not the other—has a change of heart. Sometimes there's a reason, like you destroying the family through your selfish addiction, and sometimes that love just dies all on its own.

It happens.

The rejection of a previously-mutual love is simply another example of the old adage that Nothing Lasts Forever and Everything Changes. Few things teach this like a deflated relationship. The Buddha wasn't enlightened, just heartbroken. It's tragic that love tends to die in one person before the other, rather than occurring simultaneously in both parties, but *C'est la vie*, right?

If you want a perfect world, go live at Disneyland.

I considered telling Corey all this, but one look at him and I decided to keep the insight to myself.

10:34pm
NO MOVIE SCRIPT ENDING

Frankie set his pill bottles on the med room desk. "I takin' one each of these," he said. "And then two of this one." He held up his Trazodone bottle for me. A lot of the junkies do something along those lines: the pill bottle charades. It's simpler than trying to pronounce those big words on the label.

"Gotcha," I said. Before logging the information in the med book, I went and changed all the mathematical mistakes my coworker, Reginald, had made earlier during the complex and tricky process of subtracting one or two pills from the previous amounts.

"No IQ test to work at this fuckin' place," I commented to Frankie.

Bent over the med book, I watched out of the corner of my eye as he dumped more than the stated amount of pills into his hand. Tried to act sneaky about it. Frankie was probably desperate for a high, but all he'd get off Trazodone was the joy of sleeping for the next day or two. Or hell, maybe oblivion was exactly what he was after.

"Don't take no genius to end up here, neither," Frankie said. The man was living proof of his own theory, so I had to agree.

Frankie stood and watched me fudge a few numbers on another med sheet to hide how I had *borrowed* a few Adderall from the stash of a younger client. I could cover my tracks in clear view of most of the guys, confident that they didn't know what the hell was going on.

"That ain't my med sheet," Frankie pointed out. Apparently, his literacy extended to recognizing his own name. Good for him. "Whose med sheet that?"

"I'm correcting Reginald's mistakes," I said. "I have to do this every day." Half-truths are said to be whole lies, but they're good enough for most social situations.

"He a dumb motherfucker," Frankie said. A couple other guys popped their heads in the door while me and Frankie wasted oxygen. They asked for linens and towels and other supplies stashed in the med room. I motioned for them to grab the stuff themselves. My back being turned to all the supplies, medical and otherwise, could make it pretty easy for someone to raid the medicine cabinet without me noticing.

More power to them, if that's what they wanted.

"Can't believe Davis relapsed," Frankie said. I had personally given the boot to Davis' rocket scientist, Ivy League ass, and taken no small amount of pleasure in doing so. "He's just not one of the people I expected to do that."

"I expect all of you to," I said. Frankie looked offended. "Hey, I'm right more often than not!"

"You ain't got no faith in us," he accused me. "That's harsh, man. Even from a white guy. Ya gotta have faith."

"Got something better than faith," I said. "It's called *observation*."

If Frankie was more observant, himself, he could have pointed out that I spent most of my time ignoring the clients rather than observing them. Instead, he just said a hurt, "*Whatever*," and walked out, forgetting his pills on the desktop. I decided to let them sit there a while before I claimed scavenging rights.

10:42pm
BEGGARS, CHOOSERS, AND THOSE STRUNG-OUT IN-BETWEEN

I hadn't seen JDZ for a few months and had figured him for dead. No one lives on the street, shooting heroin, to increase their life expectancy. So, it was surprising when I came downstairs from rooting through the med-room to find him sitting in the lobby.

"Hey, remember me?" he asked. I did, but it took me a little while to decide if I had been wrong about that death supposition.

JDZ looked like he'd just scaled the fence at Auschwitz. He was a tall guy, over six feet, but it seemed like his clothes weighed more than the rest of him. His short, curly hair looked ready to abandon ship and drop right off his head. His face was so sunken that it wouldn't have been the least bit surprising to learn that somebody had just painted flesh tones on his skull.

Luckily for him it was a Saturday night, and most of the clients were off at some miserable AA dance. Had more of the guys been home, it wouldn't have been too long before he was recognized and chased off. It was popular opinion that JDZ was a thief, degenerate, and should probably be put down for the good of society.

We can't all be Nobel Prize winners.

"Can we talk?" JDZ motioned towards the door.

He's gonna ask for money, I thought. *Unless he's about to try to sell me something he boosted.* Someone asking if they can speak with you never bodes well. It's normally assumed that we all have an inherent right to communicate with each other. Anyone who prepares me for it sets off my alarms. Nobody has ever asked permission for a conversation and then given me a wad of hundreds or a free handjob.

JDZ opened the door and we both stepped out into the cold. "Don't worry," he said, "I'm not going to rob you." I hadn't expected him to, but, on the other hand, it wouldn't have surprised me. You don't survive four junk-sick months on the street simply through the generosity of others. Not with our species, you don't.

What JDZ wanted, of course, was money. No surprise there, but I didn't have any that I'd give to him. JDZ would just blow it on drugs, and that was already my plan.

Switching tactics, he tried small talk. "How's school?" he asked. I told JDZ that I had graduated in May.

"Then what're you still doing here?"

"What are *you* still doing on the streets?" I countered.

"It's *sooo* fucked up out here," JDZ said, telling me about eating out of dumpsters (*Subway* has the best, y'all). He talked about boosting stuff to trade for money, food, or drugs. He rambled about the people he thought were trying to kill him, the people he was *sure* were trying to kill him, and a whole bunch of other paranoid babblings in the classic junkie style I'd grown to know and love.

Looking down—since his sore-ridden face was unnerving as hell—I noticed he was wearing sandals. It had been cold as shit this autumn, and here was JDZ on the streets in *sandals*. No coat, either. He had owned shoes the last time I'd seen him, but they'd probably been traded for a fix or some food or *something* a long time ago.

I also wondered whatever happened to his old girlfriend. My last encounter with JDZ ended with him cold-cocking her. Hopefully she had grown some brains and hooked up with somebody whose life wasn't an express train to hell.

"Can you help me out?" he asked. The best response at that point would've been to whip out my sawed-off twelve-gauge and blow away the top of his head. But, unfortunately for JDZ, I'd left all the high-caliber firearms in my other pants. *Still...*

Though the facility's glass front wall, I pointed at the shelves full of donated books. "You oughtta be able to get a few bucks for 'em at *Half-Price Books.*" His eyes lit up, and I'm sure he was already dreaming of fixes to come.

It took less than three minutes to load JDZ with two shopping bags full of paperbacks and encyclopedias. I helped him pile in the books, wondering if it would be kosher to ask how many times he had whored himself for dope. JDZ hadn't been too bad-looking in his less strung-out days. One glance at the desperation that soaked his body told that he wasn't above gagging if it meant scoring his fix.

I didn't get the chance to ask him about it; he babbled endlessly about his need and inability to get clean. "I gotta do something soon," he said. "Before I either kill myself or somebody else again."

I pretended like I hadn't heard that last word.

The door was propped open for JDZ, and he waddled out like a penguin. Then, overwhelmed with either gratitude or the need to spread contagion, he set down a bag to shake my hand. '*Fuck,*' I grimaced. '*Wasn't he just telling me about dumpster diving? When was the last time this fucker washed up?*'

I waved good riddance as JDZ headed down the street, fast as possible. He was smart enough to not want to be in this part of town at night with an excess of material goods. His sandals slapped against the concrete as he shuffled through the cold and past the other bums huddled in their doorways. Quick clouds of breath puffed over his head as he continued his locomotion down the street. JDZ was the little junkie who could.

Sloth was waiting for me as I came back inside. He asked, "Whatchu give 'im all our books fo'?"

"Shut the fuck up," I explained.

Then I went into the bathroom and scrubbed my hands with scalding water.

When I was done with that, I scrubbed them again.

10:50pm
OLD SPICE AND REGRET

Todd sat across the lobby from me on the couch. Occasionally he would try to play a song on his guitar. Occasionally he'd try to make conversation.

Neither attempt was very successful.

Todd's playing was fine. The lack of connection was my fault. Recently, everything felt like my fault.

I kept going over, in Technicolor detail, the last conversation I'd had with my girlfriend. I was deep in the process of revising everything in my memory so that I had a perfect answer for everything she said at the moment she had said it. Snappy comebacks and merciless putdowns were delivered with skill and just the right touch of disinterested malice for maximum emotional effect.

It didn't make me feel any better, but I couldn't stop myself from doing it. This was much more funny when it happened to the junkies.

Readjusting the Rastafarian beanie he always wore, Todd said, "I bet you meet some pretty interesting people, working here." Usually, I didn't mind talking with Todd. He was close to my age, and we shared some similar interests. Of course, sharing interests just meant that the same marketing strategies had suckered us both.

It gave us something to talk about, at least. Todd mentioned music, movies, and toys we played with as kids. I made an affirmative grunt whenever I recognized a brand name. Since he was a similar age to myself and Todd, I had the same conversations with Sam the skater-boy.

What commercials you enjoyed were the American equivalent of personality tests. And liking the same products as another person was just as good as liking them, since in a materialist society like ours, you are what you consume.

Or, in the junkies' cases, what you couldn't stop consuming. What you thought you were consuming, but was actually consuming you.

There was a thought, addiction as nothing more than the typical consumer impulse taken to its gruesome and inevitable conclusion. It's what will eventually happen to all of us TV-watching, SUV-driving, latte-guzzling losers. We'll all be eaten alive by our need for the shiny new shit we see on TV, and then our possessions will take over our lives and inherit the earth.

I'd like to think of my job as proof that such a thing was possible. Sure, the pleasure the junkies derived from their drugs was incredibly short-lived, but it's not like that 42-inch digital television you've been saving up for will have you shitting rainbows for the rest of *your* life.

Todd plucked a few more strings. He sang, "*You can meet any freak you want, at A New Start Halfway House...*" It didn't rhyme, but so what?

"You'd think so," I said. "But it's a more dull than exotic job. I got a college degree to do shit that I could've done in grade school. Ninety-percent of the time here's spent sitting on my ass. And if ya seen one junkie, you've seen them all."

There is an old maxim about how it's good for your mental health to have a job that you feel makes a difference in the world. My job doesn't. I'm just part of a janitorial crew monitoring human wastes. And these guys weren't even the big-time losers. They were strictly bottom-rung mediocrities. The junkies had only ruined a couple lives. Maybe killed a few people. Some theft. A rape or two. They hadn't started wars for oil or poisoned anyone's water supply to make a few bucks.

They were bad news, but nothing worth a Made for TV movie.

"I had a girlfriend who loved meth," Todd said while he strummed. "And when she'd do it she'd just start freaking and shaking, and the only thing I could do would be put a dust rag in her hand. Give her somewhere to focus all that energy. I had a meth-head for a girlfriend and the world's cleanest apartment."

Todd had killed his girlfriend and her little brother while driving fucked up. Right into a concrete culvert at fifty miles an hour.

Todd, of course, was fine. The seriously drugged always are. The coroner's report said that everybody else had survived the initial impact, too. Maybe they'd have lived if Todd had gone for help instead of running away from their drug-filled car to save his own intoxicated ass.

Maybe not.

It's amazing, the shit people will tell you. They'll do it because they're convinced that all the horrible things they've done is the fault of their '*disease.*' Like they were just riding shotgun in their lives while the drugs swerved from lane to lane. Like you can admit to anything once you're given a ready-made excuse to grant your ass some absolution.

I decided that I would hate everyone in here, if it were worth the trouble. Hate them so goddamn hard, and cleanse this fucking place with fire, and me locked inside too, if only it was worth the effort.

Of course, it wasn't.

The lobby was empty except for the two of us. Todd kept picking at strings while I stared into space.

"Could you tell what that was?" Todd asked. He strummed a few chords again. I shook my head, admitting defeat. "*Floyd*, man! It's the start of *Wish You Were Here!*"

He played it again. "*Now* can you tell?"

"Kind of…"

I leaned back in my seat. "You know, ya never get a full view of the people you meet. Just little snippets of 'em as they paddle around in and *sometimes* try to climb out of their own self-created hells. We never get to know each other, and I don't think we really want to."

Todd gave me a funny look. "You're talking about here?"

I shrugged. "Sure."

"You got a girlfriend?" he asked.

"Did," I said. "Used to. Now I guess they can smell the failure on me."

Todd laughed. "So *that's* what failure smells like!"

"Yup," I said, "Like a mixture of Old Spice and regret."

He bent over his guitar. "*This'll* cheer your ass up." Todd strummed away for a few rapid minutes. "You know what *that* was?"

I shook my head. "No."

11:11pm
DARWIN WAS A HOPELESS OPTIMIST

Someone came and got me when Swanky wouldn't stop vomiting. Since I was working a double shift and doing the second half by myself, I'd let Jack leave early. Of course, everything had waited till then to happen.

Swanky was hunched over the toilet. He concentrated on spewing his stomach contents with as much effort and volume as possible. His entire body shook with the force of the regurgitations. In the small space between the fits of retching, Swanky found time to cry. His body shook with the sobs, then his body would shake with the vomiting. He almost had something of a rhythm going.

"You okay?" I asked. A rhetorical question, obviously, which was fine since I inquired more out of social protocol than compassion. After having a few of them die over the past year, there wasn't much the junkies could do to faze me. Hell, I'll admit that this entire place could burn up with everyone trapped inside, and all I would do is light a joint off the smoldering ruins and shrug, '*Eh, no big loss...*'

Used to feel the same way about my high school.

“I—I took my meds,” Swanky said, echoing into the toilet bowl. He might have been about to say more, but—right on schedule—violent shaking and retching interrupted his attempts at communicating. Well, at communicating anything other than a general lack of well-being.

I leaned back against the far wall of the bathroom, watching as his tiny body changed tempo and returned to shaking with sobs. Swanky was the kind of guy who gave crackheads a bad name. A frighteningly skinny wreck of a human being. He was small, bald, illiterate, and possessed of a manic nature that caused him to rocket around the building like he had trained his brain to manufacture its own crack so that being in a rehab wouldn’t kill his buzz.

Swanky was...well, to give you a decent idea of the guy, it’d be like if you took Corky from *Life Goes On* (remember that show?), made him short, black, and started off each of his days by replacing his Rice Krispies with a bowl of sugar-coated crack rocks.

And then stuck him in a building with me for eight-to-sixteen hours.

Swanky had been caught the other day fucking some fat old homeless woman behind a dumpster. *Sans* protection, of course. He had apparently bribed her with a plate of the pasta the junkies had for lunch. It was just another example of the weak taking advantage of the even weaker.

“I don’t recall giving you any meds,” I commented, already bored with Swanky and his suffering. The junkies were required to turn in all their medication to me. I gave them back in the specified doses at pre-arranged times.

Yeah, for some reason they didn’t trust the addicts in here with their own medications. Still scratching my head over that one.

“Dentist—” pause to retch, “Dentist give ’em to me today.”

It would've been pointless to stand there lecturing Swanky about facility rules while he did his damnedest to turn himself inside out. Instead, I counted Swanky's pills, handed to me by his roommate. They were some kind of antibiotic. The directions on them read: '*take with food...one pill two times daily.*'

Seven pills were missing.

"Did you take all these at once?" I asked him. Swanky tried to answer. It took me a while to discern his nodding from the usual convulsions. "Well, there's your problem," I said to his quivering form, still hunched over the toilet bowl. "Turns out you're a fuckin' idiot."

Diagnosis complete, I stuffed the rest of his meds in my pocket and headed back downstairs. Technically, Swanky's medicinal misadventure would be classified as an overdose. I was going to have to document this. Fill out the appropriate paperwork. And thoroughly. *Goddamnit.*

The sound of Swanky gagging followed me through the hallway. I called back over my shoulder, "Someone let me know if homeboy starts bringing up blood."

11:44pm
GRACIAS ESPIRITU SANTO, POR MI SALVADOR

Warren leaned over my desk. His hair looked like it had been viciously raped by a blow dryer, and the red circles around his bloodshot eyes meant something other than drugs. If I didn't know what a sin it was for men to show vulnerability, I'd almost think he'd been crying.

I had been amusing myself with my new bottle of pepper spray, wishing there was someone to try it on. Warren, unfortunately, was too harmless to be a serious candidate. I gave him a lazy smile. "What's up?"

"I need…" his voice came out fragile and dry, "I need to check into a mental hospital."

I gave Warren a quick once-over. He did indeed look like several kinds of refried shit. "Isn't this place bad enough?"

Warren didn't laugh. Didn't smile. He just pulled up the sleeves of his shirt. Fresh red fissures ran east to west on both his wrists. Done bleeding, thankfully.

A quiet "*Goodness*," was all I could think to say. How disappointing it must have been when it finally dawned on the guy that he hadn't cut deep enough. Slicing both wrists had probably shot his courage wad. No way could he bring himself to do it again. Not right away. The amount of despairing valor required to slash your wrists couldn't be easy to come by, or we all would've done it by now.

I was about to suggest slapping a bandage on his cuts—before they got infected—when the phone rang. And rang. I looked at Warren. I looked at the phone. I finally gave in and picked it up.

Poor Warren, his big moment had ended with him being upstaged by an appliance.

Staring at Warren's wrists, I forgot the professional phone greeting and just said, "*Yeah*?"

Gim's friendly bass sounded over the phone. Before my boss could get to past his initial greeting, I interrupted with, "There's somebody here you might wanna talk to," and handed the receiver to Warren. As a Tech, my $7.50/hr worth of client care only went so far.

"*It's Gim*," I said to Warren, like he was a mixture of stunted child and frightened rabbit. "Why don't you be a dear and tell him what you just showed me."

He took the phone. The waterworks started almost immediately. "I've got—" a huge sob wracked his body, "I've got nothing to live for."

Warren's ability to jump right to the heart of the matter impressed me immensely. None of that *beating-around-the-bush* crap for him. Unfortunately, the lack of introductions probably left Gim wondering whom the fuck had ambushed him with their suicidal longings.

"Warren told Gim that he had been drinkin' bleach," I reported later to Robert. Keeping secrets never was a strong point of mine. "Kinda makes me wonder what it tastes like."

"We got us some in the kitchen," Robert suggested. I shook my head.

"Not that curious, thanks." After Warren had talked to Gim he'd basically crumbled into a little ball against my desk. I had half-walked, half-dragged him into the chapel where he'd be out of the way, then went to find someone to drive Warren to the nearest funny farm. Hopefully they had thought to drop him off with a note about keeping the guy away from industrial-strength cleansers, especially if he looked thirsty.

"Why bleach?" I posed the eternal question. "Why not *Drano*? Probably be the most horrifically painful three minutes of your life, but at least it'd be pretty final."

Robert nodded. "I thought about endin' myself when I learn about my cancer, but I never woulda drank no bleach."

I had heard Warren do a decent amount of gut-spilling to Gim. "Your typical hard luck story," I said. "He's got a couple varieties of Hepatitis, basic death sentence right there, wife left him, unemployed, disowned by offspring, cognizant of his own vast failings in life, *blah blah blah...*"

Robert, who had survived 'terminal' throat cancer, four divorces, six years in jail, and two years on the street, just shook his head. "Pussy," he said.

Yeah, we're all heart. But, I really had to wonder how some people ended up with one misfortune after another in their lives. We've all known folks who had nothing but tragedy followed by tragedy followed by more tragedy with an economy-sized helping of tragedy bringing up the caboose. Their job moves to Mexico, they got hooked on crack, their kids are wiped out in a freak tornado, bad investments destroy them financially, they come home to find their house burglarized, their dog hanging from the ceiling fan…all the typical Job-like trials.

How does shit like that happen? Do some people just get on a roll with suffering? Does misery just attract more misery, like attracting like? Do we send our shit-luck vibes into the ether that, in turn, attract more shit-luck? Or would that just be blaming the victim? Was there some big roulette wheel up in the sky with all of our names on it that God liked to spin, asking Himself as He watched it: '*Hmmm, now who am I going to hate this week?*'

Or, was life just as capricious as it seemed, and if shit happened for no reason, then did shit also happened *repeatedly* for no reason, as well?

Maybe. Doubt too many of us talking monkeys were important enough to rate any sort of celestial enmity. Not that we needed the extra help fucking things up. Most of us handled that just fine on our own.

"You realize that was our third suicide attempt this month?" I asked Robert.

He nodded, causing the lobby lights to dance along the bumps of his skull. "None of us here much good at *anything*."

This place wasn't funny anymore. Everyone's suffering wasn't funny anymore.

I wanted out.

NIGHT SHIFT
(Midnight-8am)

12:30pm
GREEN SCREEN LIFE

I bumped into the doorframe on my way into the building. My attempts at hiding how drunk I was were gonna have to be a wee bit more strenuous. Yep, just a *wee* bit.

"*Wuzzup*?" I said to Reginald. He gave me a nod in return as he packed his things to leave.

"You're late."

I *thought* it was Reginald, at least. It tended to be that fucker that I relieved on these evening shifts. My vision was a smidgen too blurry to be sure. Could've been some other skinny little black fuck stuck behind the desk. Some other skinny little black fuck with a reedy voice like his balls were waiting till his late 50s to drop.

Closing one eye to cut down on the double vision seemed like a good idea. I squinted, then realized that sort of shit was exactly what those crafty motherfuckers would be looking for. That, and the swaying and the slurred speech and the stench and whatever else it was that they tried to tell us about in our training classes.

But not from me, they wouldn't. Not from a Tech. Nobody thinks to check a Tech for overt signs of intoxication, nobody watches the watchmen, and that's why I got away with it every time.

"*Howz it goin'*?" I kept myself to short, easily pronounced sentences as I marched my bike right past Reginald to the side hallway.

"Paul got kicked out today," Reginald said. "Said he'll come back and shoot everyone. If he really do show up, don't let him in."

"*Gotcha*."

I'd gotten it down to something of an art form over the past few months. Go out and drink like it was the cure to all of life's little problems until about 10:45pm. Rush home. Shower. Douse myself with near-toxic levels of cologne. Arrive at work around midnight, still buzzing like hell and ready to pass the fuck out for five or six hours.

And get paid for it.

God bless my job, and *God Bless America!*

I started to tip to the side, bike and all. Caught myself right before the tilt of no return.

Maintain, motherfucker. Maintain! I steadied myself as I pushed my bike down the hallway. It was taking all my concentration not to fall over the thing as I steered it.

I had belly-flopped twice on my way to work. Was probably bleeding under my jeans. Hadn't wiped out on a bike since grade school. Now here I was fifteen years later, a college grad trying not to trip over a bicycle as he showed up at work tanked enough to be flammable.

My mother would be so proud.

Arriving at work in a state of extreme intoxication ain't the smartest thing to do in any profession. Not only is your functioning impaired (only a problem if your job requires functioning), but if they catch you, your ass is good and fired. Obviously.

You'd think that more employers would understand. That they'd be keyed into the bleakness of working-class life. Living paycheck to paycheck. Every day a financial near-panic, at best. The dull routine that required chemical coping. The economy that went belly-up just in time for you to graduate. The useless degree wasted at the dead-end McJob…

But they're not. Fuckers just don't understand. Management's got no pity for the workers. Top dogs never care about the ones on the bottom. So, it's best that they don't catch you.

Too bad that drunk people are a lot more obvious than they think. Alcohol, from the smell to the effect, runs counter to any notion of subtlety. Someone's either going to notice that you're obnoxious, or that your speech is slurred, or your motor-functions are impaired, or that a strong bouquet of booze is seeping from your pores.

And that's just in normal jobs. Imagine if everyone in your place of employment was qualified, either by profession or lifestyle, to sniff out your symptoms. My fellow Techs are trained to look for any-and-all signs of altered functioning. And most of the clients—especially the alkies—can smell a drop of beer from fifty paces. Being here drunk, being here under the influence of *anything*, is pretty risky. Pretty stupid.

Pretty common on my part.

Screw it, though. If I got fired, what would I have to lose aside from a shit job with shit wages earned by watching shit people?

Right?

Distracted by the act of thinking, my motor skills abandoned me in the side hallway. Myself and the bike were in a heap. Being horizontal and in pain told me I must've fallen at some point. Wish I could've recalled when. Walking with bike, then laying on bike. Gravity's tricky like that.

I could guess what occurred in between, but damned if I noticed it happen.

"*Ouchie*," I said, and giggled before I could stop myself.

Took me a few seconds to realized that Reginald might get curious about a loud crash coming from the back hall. It could blow my cover. Get me caught. Kill my buzz.

I struggled to right the bike, and myself, as quickly as possible. It took a few tries. Damn tough to pull something upright when you're off-balance, too. Eventually I stumbled on the method of bracing myself against the wall with one hand while tugging on my handlebars with the other. The bike was pulled upright, and for a second I rejoiced.

It fell back over.

"*Oh*, the kickstand!" I drunkenly clapped my hand over my mouth. Had Reginald heard that? *Christ*, my voice sounded like I was gargling marbles! He'd know!

I pulled the bike upright a second time. Put down the kickstand. Psyched myself out to act normal. Reached into my pocket and popped another mint. Gave myself a reminder to be cool.

I strolled back into the lobby, prepared to sit on the couch and not speak until spoken to. Not give away the game. Fake my way through yet another drunken night of work.

The worry was unnecessary. The lobby was empty. Reginald was gone. *Thank Christ.*

I started to shout after him, "That's what your mom says when we… *fukkit.*"

The hell with our little routine. Considering how the job market had up and shat itself, I'd probably be shouting immature crap at Reginald till I was twice as old as he is now.

How utterly fucking depressing.

The dangerous part of the shift was over. I flopped into the chair behind the desk and concentrated on keeping the room from spinning.

12:38am
LAST MAN STANDING

The showers hadn't let up all night. I sat outside the rehab with a book and a cup of the second-rate kool-aid the junkies drank. A stolen copy of Blake's collected poetry was splattered with errant raindrops. I watched Pasadena get washed for the fifth day in a row. It's always raining in my memories of work. The water level's always rising on the street, and everyone walks through the door wet and miserable.

Paul was standing next to me on the front porch. He had recently relapsed for the third time this year. The current record is five times in the same month, but I'm still getting sick of seeing the guy.

He showed me his hands. There were large red blisters on both his palms.

"Ooh, *stigmata*!" I said. "Truly you are the Junkie Messiah!"

Paul just stared at me, so I asked for a cigarette to break the silence. He complied. Two puffs on the thing and I was reminded why I don't smoke. Paul was blathering about some sitcom he liked watching. Not giving a shit about the socially approved ways that he rotted his brain, I asked if he'd fucked up his hands while high.

"I was playin' with my kid!" Paul said, a little angry.

I reiterated the question.

"Yeah..." he said. "Yeah I was fucked up...but, I *was* playing with my kid."

And that makes everything better!

My skepticism wasn't hidden enough, so Paul stalked off to the second-floor rooms where we stack our junkies like cordwood. Back to the dormitory sleeping arrangements for him, and back to solitude for me. I was left alone.

Any and all urges to be sociable never really hit until the junkies go to bed. Then I get sloughed down in an overwhelming need for human interaction. Preferably with someone not fucked up or pathetic. By the time I'm halfway through my double shift, that's the only sort of person I've been interacting with for the past eight hours.

No luck, though. Everybody here crashed out early. Everyone I knew in the real world had to get up early for their own miserable jobs the next day. I still had eight hours to go. After all those months of employment here, I really should've been used to the solitude.

It was just me, my CDs, a computer, and a medication room that only I had the keys to. So, it wasn't all bad. Could've been worse. After keeping this place running *smoothly-ish* for eight hours, there was nobody I was responsible for beside myself (and those fifty-plus guys upstairs, I guess). I put a collection of Beethoven's late string quartets on the player and reclined on the couch.

Three different crackheads had asked me today about my ex-girlfriend. The most recent, I mean. They wanted to know, "What happen to that fine little girl usedta come bring ya food and y'all be all kissin' out in front and all?"

"She went the way of all flesh," I'd respond.

From two of them this earned blank looks, but the third asked in horror, "Shit, she dead?"

I'd shrugged. "Far as I'm concerned..."

For a while, it was a pretty frequent question: whatever happened to my ex. Or, as they liked to put it, that '*girl wit dat vicious booty*.' I'm not sure about how 'vicious' it was (or why this was any of their goddamn business), but she did used to have this utter ghetto-booty of an ass that jutted out like a shelf from her lower back. Surprisingly firm and high riding, too. Never seen anything like it on any Hispanic girl besides her. I dubbed it the Ninth Wonder of the World.

(King Kong was the Eighth, if you recall)

I couldn't say why my tastes in women had been running more and more along the same lines as the 'thick' type that the crackheads always picked up at their 12-Step meetings. Didn't think that was what I dug. Us dumb white boys, after all, are supposed to be well trained by years of *Playboy* and Hollywood to only lust after the *twig-with-tits* variety of the female form. My most-recent ex, plus Cassandra's *pregnant-minus-the-baby* figure, this past year would seem to suggest that my brainwashing was a bit faulty. Made me wonder if I should report for reprogramming.

Still, out of all the habits I could pick up from these guys, an appreciation for full-figured women was pretty harmless. If I ever found myself blowing my neighbors for some rock money, *then* I'd know it was past time to find another job.

12:48pm
TIME FOR US TO GIVE A LITTLE LOVE BACK TO GOD

Even at night in December the weather was warm enough for shorts, so that's what I wore. If this kept up, it'd be another Lawn Chair Xmas here in Pasadena.

It was probably due to the temperate weather (and neurological damage from Pasadena's petrochemical pollution) that my new coworker was wearing a Hawaiian shirt. It was covered with all the Warner Bros. cartoon characters dancing in hula skirts. Occasionally, you'll see someone for the first time and instantly go: '*Oh. That's all I could ever possibly want to know about you.*'

I saw Chris in his shirt created by a merchandising committee and instantly lost faith in the notion of human progress. Knowing that I belonged to a species committed to creating—and spending money on—soul-crushing banalities, I felt despair. There was an overwhelming temptation to go hang myself in the bathroom using a roll of double-ply, but suicide attempts weren't covered by Workman's Comp in Texas.

"Amazing," I said as we shook hands. "Your wardrobe manages to represent everything I loathe about our culture."

If I die alone and unloved, at least I'll have only myself to blame. Well, me and the alcohol.

"*What?*" he said. Chris turned out to be a little hard of hearing. He also had a few other quirks that would blow his chance for a seat on the last shuttle to safety if the earth ever fell into the sun. Nice guy, but nobody would ever consider using him for breeding stock to restart the human race.

Chris looked to be in his mid-thirties. His tiny, near-set eyes gave him a sort of Clueless and Inbred vibe. He had a lumpy body, and representing it to the world was one hellaciously puffy face, like Chris dipped his head in a beehive every morning before work. There was a resemblance to the Pillsbury Dough Boy, if Mr. Dough giggled when you poked him in the ass instead of his belly.

It was the first day at work for Chris, and Yours Truly was to show him the proverbial ropes.

No problem.

For his first lesson, I led Chris over to the front desk. Our rotting chair was pointed at. Making sure not to breathe margarita on the guy, I ordered, "Sit."

He looked at me and grinned a little, unsure.

"*Sit*!" I repeated. He did.

"Feet up," I said, pointing at the desktop. Chris got this on the first try. He was uickly improving.

"Just do that for eight hours," I told him. "That, and try to kill your sense of compassion before your next shift when you'll have to be around the homeless."

I didn't mention how much he'd grow to hate the clients, too. I was sure pissed at the bastards. One of them had told Gim that I'd left my post last week to hit a fraternity party. Actually, I don't attend *frat* parties. I'm graduated, and they always have such crap beer at those things. Besides, I'd totally had Sam covering the front desk for the hour I'd been at a friend's birthday celebration.

Lying sacks of shit. I couldn't believe my boss had even considered believing them. It seemed like Gim had yet to learn *New Start Rule #1*.

"Is this all there is to it?" Chris asked me.

"*Basically*."

"Do I have to be able to speak Spanish?"

I shook my head. "Nope. Just Ebonics, White Trash, and Self-Pity…"

"Oh." Chris just stared at me. I could tell he was going to be loads of fun. I wondered what made a harmless chap like him sign up to work with the burnouts and degenerates that comprised the rest of my coworkers. And me.

"...a few local dialects of Uneducated and maybe a bit of Crazy-Talk. If you can't understand what somebody's saying, it's a good bet they're talkin' shit to ya."

"How long have you worked here?" Chris asked.

"Just about a year."

"Do you *like* your job?"

"Love it," I lied. "But *careful*; it destroys the weak and gives an ice-cold moral enema to the rest of us."

Instruction over, I flopped down on the lobby's couch and commenced earning an hourly wage for searching through the Help Wanted section of the paper.

"You'll get the ass calluses in a month or so," I assured Chris. "Things'll get easier from there."

1:11am
ASK MASTER P

I was listening to *Master P* on the stereo (left my own CDs at home) and reading obituaries with some of the clients who couldn't sleep. Some months I was guaranteed enough company to keep me up all night. Other months I could get four to five hours of solitude.

One of the junkies, six days fresh off kicking the habit, was making a morbid experience even cheerier. "Lucky fuckers," he said at each obit read aloud. Sobriety was apparently not agreeing with the guy.

Everybody signs an agreement to refrain from self-harm while staying here, but I was keeping an eye on him just in case. *New Start Rule #1*, and all that jazz. Dead junkies mean plenty of paperwork for yours truly, so it was something I wouldn't mind avoiding. Learning his name could be a waste of time if he ended up relapsed or dead, but he told me it's *Jamie*.

Jamie was a scuzzy little bastard, his hair matted in clumps like he'd sworn off shampoo as a useless luxury years ago. I looked over his arms and noticed a nice, jagged scar on both wrists. They went well with the tattoos that circled his biceps, twin snakes that stopped just short of swallowing their own tails. Noticing the direction of my gaze, Jamie just shrugged. "I was young and stupid."

There's no standard social protocol for responding to something like that, so I said, "Yeah?"

"*Yeah*," he said. "Next time I'm cutting down, not across."

"This fella seems to have led a pretty full life," Curtis said. He read aloud the obit of some guy who'd worked on a refinery team for Exxon. He held the picture of the deceased up for everyone else to see. It seemed like Curtis was trying to score substitute Parenting Points by reading obituaries to junkies in lieu of bedtime stories to his own distant children.

I shook my head. "So, he did his part to help destroy the environment? That's a *great* legacy."

"What killed him?" It was the same question Jamie asked every time. He'd be real fun at parties.

"Doesn't say," Curtis shrugged. It never does, but the junkie always asked. I guess hope paradoxically springs eternal for the chronically morbid. Then Curtis' head jerked up to look at the stereo. "*What'd* he just say? *What* was that? The hell's wrong with music today? He just mentioned killin' nig—*fellas*…and for no damn reason."

Curtis wasn't going get a Rhodes Scholarship anytime soon, but he had eventually caught on that there are words you don't say around here without sufficient melanin levels.

"There ya go," I suggested to Jamie (it's his CD). "Maybe Master P killed that guy."

"He's killin' my ears." Curtis was set on sounding as old and white as possible. "And the dead guy was white. Feller on the stereo's only talkin' about killing black people."

"Master P's a *playah*," I told Curtis, "Not a bigot. I'm sure he'd kill some honkies, too."

Honky and *cracker* were the only racial slurs allowed in the rehab. This was likely due to my own inability to stop using them. They're just fun. Some of the crackheads (not all of whom are black, but it's an 80% thing), when they were doing chores, would refer to each other as '*house nigger*' or '*field nigger*.' I found this hilarious, but they were eventually told that such terminology was Old Behavior (a catchphrase for the sort of thinking that landed them in rehab in the first place), and that put an end to that.

"Who else we got?" Jamie asked, impatient for Curtis to keep reading.

"Umm, thirty-eight-year-old mother of...three," Curtis read, and the death toll rolled on.

1:23am
EURO-WHORES and *BARELY 18*

I listened to Eddy talk about his romantic strategies. About how he wooed the shattered women he encountered at 12-step meetings. Once he'd decided against his initial plan of killing me in the rehab's back lot, Eddy had leapt to the other side of the social spectrum and decided we were pals. I was his token white friend. He now came down to talk at me every damn night. Sometimes I was drunk enough to ramble back at him; sometimes I just pretended to listen.

It'd be a lie to claim that I cared about anything Eddy had to say. But, considering our past interactions, so long as he stayed non-violent, I was an attentive audience.

"…and I put the sparkling apple juice next to the bathtub," he said. "That goes at the head of the tub. And then there's the tape player at the foot. Close enough to make sure she don't miss a sound, but far enough to where you can do your own sweet talkin'."

I scratched my head. "People really fuck without booze?" Man, just when I thought this place couldn't get any weirder.

Eddie assured me that such marvels really occurred, and he promised to lay a few tips on me the next day. "I'll show ya how spot the *vulnerable* ones," he said. Then we knocked knuckles (causing me to flinch), and he headed upstairs for the night.

I was now alone to entertain myself.

A nice thing about working night shift was the opportunity it provided to snoop through the offices of the day workers. Sometimes I turned up interesting stuff. For example, my boss has a HUGE pornography collection. Nudie mag after nudie mag, just stuffed in the bottom filing cabinet in that man's office. No videos, unfortunately, just paper-based porn.

Don't know why, but finding this stuff in his drawers was so much cooler than just using his computer to snag it online.

I guessed that the administrative hassles, on top of having to deal with the junkies and crackheads, got way too stressful sometimes, and this is what Gim used in lieu of going back to the bottle. Still...couldn't help but wonder if—when it's time for a little *stress relief*—if the guy sneaks off to the bathroom with them, or if he just locks his door.

Hopefully the former, since his office door has a small window in it, and there'd be something funny about another employee walking past his door just in time to catch his orgasm face. And since he's about Seven Fucking Feet Tall, I ever caught sight of his dick, I'd probably be forced to kill myself before the inferiority complex could fully set in.

But on an odd note: some of the magazines with the younger girls had the titles cut off the front page. As far as typical shame-motivated behavior goes, this was a new one. I realize that lots of people would be embarrassed to be caught with a magazine full of stuff designed to <*gasp*> sexually arouse them, but why get rid of the titles?

What was Gim hoping for? That, if somebody saw a magazine cover featuring buxom teens squatting on mag-lites—but with no title—hopefully they'd figure he was into extreme performance art? How lurid can a title be to where you don't mind being caught jacking off to something, you just don't want to be caught jacking off to something called *that*?

I picked out two or three of my favorites from Gim's office, poked my head into the hallway to make sure the coast was clear, then fast-walked to the bathroom.

1:34am
WRONG PLACE, WRONG TIME, WRONG SPECIES

I was talking with one of the junkies about the latest U.S. military action. Curtis couldn't sleep, and I was trying to read the newspaper, so the guy just happened to be in the wrong place at the wrong time. We discussed and argued our personal feelings about it all.

Curtis was more patriotic and gung-ho than myself. He'd been a veteran for about a decade or so. Knowing that Curtis had fallen for the Army recruitment commercials on TV, my already-low opinion of his IQ sank to new depths.

I made my usual case about what a crock of shit the newest invasion was. While the U.S. Ruling Elite used the usual terms like 'liberation,' 'freedom,' and 'democracy,' I argued to Curtis, it all came down to killing shitloads of people who had as little say in their country's politics as I did in ours.

"Yeah," he concurred. "*Ah* was stationed in the Persian Gulf back in the nineties. That's basically what we did." I decided to pay attention for a change. Maybe this would be more interesting than the usual client-babble. "They told us, *kill everybody you find*, and we did…"

I nodded. A good nod can make up for a lot of things.

"We'd just walk into a building and shoot everybody in there," Curtis said. "Mostly women and kids. *Ah* dunno where all the men were."

Well, it wasn't like the guy was the first murderer I'd met in here. Although, since he killed foreigners on command, I guess the proper term would be 'Hero.' I'd read a study once that showed how Americans rarely won battles unless they outnumbered the enemy by at least two-to-one. Little surprise then that they tended to slaughter people in impoverished third world countries. Bullies always prefer easy targets.

"What part of Iraq were you in?" I asked. It was a bland follow-up to a hell of a revelation, but I decided to wait a little while before asking him what sound babies made when gut-shot.

Curtis shook his head. "We weren't in Iraq," he said. "*Ah* was stationed in Kuwait. Never made it to Iraq."

New Start Rule #1 was dancing in the back of my head, but I just asked, "No shit?"

It was all I could think to say.

"No shit," Curtis replied. It was all he could think to say, too.

We sat in silence for a minute. Me wondering what it took to slaughter a family with machine-gun fire. Him remembering what it took to slaughter a family with machine-gun fire.

Curtis finally spoke. "It really chops them up." Typically, my memory is such shit that I would've already forgotten what we'd been discussing. But not this time. "Bullets do. They really do a number on the little ones. The kids and the babies. It's like an eraser on them cartoon characters. One second they got a hand, next second it's gone."

I nodded again. It's part of being an attentive listener. "Fuckin' Arabs," Curtis said, as if it was *their* fault. He pronounced the word, *Ay-rabs*, like a good patriot should. "Fuckin' Arabs."

Then he started to cry. Quiet little mewlings that retained his country twang. Tears ran down the side of his nose to collect in his moustache.

I went back to the paper. People crying had ceased to interest me. I used Curtis's distraction to pop another Valium.

"*Yeah…*" I said to Curtis. "And just think how they felt about it."

1:57am
INEVITABLE LANDSCAPES

A heavy fog had settled over downtown Pasadena. I couldn't see more than forty yards up the street in either direction. There was a palpable thickness to the air, like always during an East Texas summer. Streetlights and security lamps gave the sky an eerie, pinkish glow, causing this section of town to resemble a post-industrial version of Hell. Bums walked out of the fog, stumbled past our building, and then disappeared further down the street. I half-expected to hear screams coming from that direction, some indication that the night felt weird and shitty for any reason other than because I did, but there was only the occasional and distant sound of car engines. Besides that, the entire world could have disappeared except for my own private, addict-filled island.

"FREE CRACK!" I screamed out the front door, desiring more signs of life. "Get your FREE CRACK right here!"

I waited a while before closing the door and heading back to my boss' office. I felt lonely. Maybe I should've tossed a toaster oven into the deal as well.

I might've stolen this practice from the Buddhists, but fuck them for oppressing the Tamils in Sri Lanka and the Rohingya in Burma. Also reminded that those codpieces used their religion to run a feudal empire in Tibet into the 20th Century.

Anyways, before I start each shift, and after showering-off the booze stench at home, I wipe the condensation from the bathroom mirror and repeat into it a simple affirmation: that I'm going to die, and that everyone I love will also die. On the bright side, so will all the people I hate.

I wish knowing that helped. I wish there was some deeper meaning to all this, something beyond the growing number of days that I'm unable to even meet my own gaze in the mirror.

But…there isn't. I know there isn't. I've stopped lying to myself about it.

2:03 am
WHAT I HATE ABOUT MY JOB, AND WHAT MY JOB HATES ABOUT ME

I heard the door to the chapel close and soft footfalls padding their way to the bathroom.

'*If he comes outta the chapel*,' Jack had told me, '*You send his ass along.*'

When the bathroom door opened up, I was waiting for him. My shoulders were straight and chest puffed out in my best *Pretend Authority* stance. Somebody had relapsed before my shift started, and Jack had left it for me to deal with. I molded a stern scowl on my face. You have to look hardened if you're going to throw someone out onto the freezing streets in the middle of the night.

He stepped out, and I finally saw whom it was that had shown up drunk tonight: Old Herman. About 65-years old, stooped with age, and wrinkled like he was twice what the calendar insisted. Addiction ages no one well.

I deflated. *Shit*. Now I knew why Jack hadn't been able to toss the guy out like we're supposed to. Now I understood why he had merely made Herman a pallet in the chapel and told him to sleep it off. Now it made sense why Jack had passed the buck to me. Who would want to throw an old man into the gutter?

Give it to the honky, he'll toss anyone.

Fucker.

"*Hey*, Ray!" Herman smiled wide at the sight of me. Damn, the guy could've been my grandpa...if, like, my grandpa was shorter, blacker, and more of a hopeless alcoholic.

"Time to get going," I said, maintaining distance between us so he couldn't smell my own booze reek, hoping he wouldn't fight me on this.

Herman did, of course. *Fuck you too, God.*

"But…*but...but...*" he started protesting. Herman insisted that he had been told that he could stay until morning. Insisted that it was way too cold outside. Insisted that we were in a horrible part of town. Insisted that there were still too many hours left in the night.

He looked so pathetic and helpless with his hunched frame and slow, arthritic movements. I imagined my own grandpa having to humiliate himself by begging some uppity white boy to not throw him out in the cold.

Very easily, I reached up inside my own head and shut off that little part that makes me human. It's a little trick I've picked up here. Nothing too difficult about it. I reckon cops and soldiers do it all the time.

My eyes got heavy-lidded and my face went slack like it always does when Nobody's Home. "Don't need to repeat myself, do I?"

It wasn't a question.

Herman left, gathering his things and whining the entire way. I didn't watch him walking out the door then down the street, easy prey for all the desperate types that wander this area. I just went back to my desk, tossed on another CD, and propped up my feet.

I was pissed that Old Herman's eviction had been left up to me. I was pissed that my coworkers had stuck me with the unpleasant job. I was pissed that I had let Jack get away with shouting vague instructions as he headed out the door, just so I didn't risk breathing my own wine-and-margarita bouquet on him.

The lobby's lights were switched off, and I sat in the dark. Some classical music bullshit warbled out of the stereo's cheap speakers. I was pissed at everyone involved in the past 20 minutes. Worst of all, I almost wish I could have felt pissed about how easy it had all been.

2:12am
COMMON AFFLICTIONS

Chris stared at me in horror. "That's...that's one of my addiction triggers."

I met my coworker's eyes from across the room. Chris was learning the nuances of the night shift from me. This meant the lobby's lights had to stay on, but it wasn't all bad.

"You're addicted…" I couldn't believe I'd heard him right, "To *masturbating*?" And then, God help my insensitive ass, I laughed. And laughed. And laughed until my stomach cramped around all the beer I'd drank earlier.

Tears were wiped from my eyes. "I know what you mean," I assured Chris. "And I understand where you're coming from, brother. With me, it started out as just a weekend thing. Seemed harmless enough. Everyone was doing it. Then the next thing I knew I was doing it twice a week. And then three times. Then it was every day."

I sank my head into my hands. "And then there was the wank before work, and then the wank *instead* of work, and I'll never forget the dark, shameful day they had to resuscitate me after my heart stopped from protein loss."

Too amused for my own good, I looked up at Chris. I was the only one smiling.

"You're serious," I said. My coworker gave a solemn nod. *Jesus Christ...* "You're addicted to masturbating?" He nodded again.

"Me, too," I assured him.

"Really?"

"Really."

His eyes lit up with the joy of comradery. "Do you go to the meeting down by—"

"No!" I shouted. "It's called I'm a *fucking human being* and so are you!"

Fucking loser. Slave. I had met a couple of people who claimed to be sexual addicts of one kind or another, and they all struck me as having healthy sex drives with an unhealthy amount of Judeo-Christian guilt. Figures they'd make some kind of 12-Step bullshit out of it.

"But I have to do it to Internet pornography," he said, as if that was supposed to shock me. I had half an urge to jump on the guy and flail away at him, screaming, '*You monster!*' in a voice of high patrician outrage.

Instead, I nodded in understanding. "Yeah, growing up with Fantasia and MTV killed my imagination, too."

Chris seemed really disappointed, so an assurance was in order. "Look," I said, "I'm not trying to rob you of your pathology. Be as sick as you want. I'm just having a hard time agreeing that there's something wrong with listening to what your body's telling ya. You eat if you're hungry, don't you?" Of course, that was a viewpoint that could be fatal in a place like this. Most bodies here were telling their owners to smoke crack and keep smoking it until their hearts exploded.

Maybe Chris was going for pity points, or maybe he was just trying to depress me, but the guy gave a sad little shrug and said, "I haven't had sex in over four years."

Ooooohhh...

That was officially The Worst Thing I'd Heard All Night. My own, current bout of celibacy paled in comparison.

Chris wasn't the most attractive of guys (never seen a face so damn *puffy*), but nobody deserved something like that.

I suppressed a chuckle at his expense.

Stretching for something consoling, something to help me fight down the giggles, I went on to say, "*Ummm*...well, it's been a damn long time since I…*uhhh*…I dunno…pretended to—what's the term?—make love?"

Chris shook his head. "That doesn't help at all."

2:23am
CLUB COMBO, HOLD THE GRADITUDE

I now regularly turned off the lobby's lights when I worked the night shift. This had a three-fold purpose:

1) It's easier to sleep with the lights off.

2) The clients were discouraged from bothering me with whatever little need they may have at 4am.

3) The homeless were less likely to try to get in the building in the middle of the night.

Reason 1 was the main focus of '*Operation: In the Dark*,' but when the clients asked, I always shared Reason 3 with them. None of their damn business, anyways.

There's a large cross on the front of our building. The homeless who wandered the streets of midtown had a tendency to identify cross-marked buildings with charities and shelters and the like. Equating Christianity with selfless kindness was just one of the many places where the bums and I differed.

I had an average of three after-hours visitors a night. Seven if I left the lobby lights on. Sometimes I just ignored their repeated knocking or ringing of the doorbell. Sometimes I stood in front of the door and mouthed—and gave the hand-signs for—'*We're Closed*' through the glass. Sometimes I opened the door and chatted with them. They usually wanted to sleep in the building, get free food, get my pocket change, or use the phone.

A few months working here, and I now filed the homeless under the heading: *Not My Fucking Problem*. And, despite all the rest of my social deviancies, I like to believe that single position makes me as 100% American as the rest of you selfish, pitiless assholes.

Maybe if all those state hospitals hadn't gotten their budgets slashed over the past twenty years, with so many of their inhabitants tossed to the curb. Maybe if social programs weren't so horribly under-funded in this country. Maybe if all our tax dollars didn't go the military or other forms of corporate welfare.

Let's just say that the homeless problem was something that a few free sandwiches weren't going to fix. Not that we'd even try the minimal effort of something like that. A starving man would never be fed at a banquet in this shit-hole excuse of a society.

And speaking of free sandwiches:

There was a desperate ringing of the doorbell, one quick ring after another. Worried that a client was being dismembered on the front porch while I wasted time tucking my erection back into my pants in the women's bathroom, I hurried out to the lobby. Latex gloves were stripped from hands and tossed into the trash before I glanced at the door. A tall, scraggly black man sought entrance. I almost flipped the switch to unlock the door and let him in, then gave a second look. He was maybe a shade *too* scraggly to be a client. Just a bit much on the seedy side.

We stared at each other in the dark, separated by a locked door and wall of glass. I peered at him with curiosity. He returned the look with frustration and annoyance. Then the guy tugged hard on the door: *Open up, motherfucker!*

Grabbing the cudgel for insurance, I stuck my head out the door.

"Yeah?"

"Gotta let me in," he said.

"No, I don't." His face turned angry. Sweat dripped down it. Cold as it was outside, this guy was perspiring like a hippo in a sauna. Had to be crack or some other stimulant.

Apparently a fan of rhetorical questions, the bum asked, "Why not?"

We played the '*if-you-have-to-ask-you'll-never-know*' game for a while before he demanded to use the phone. Angry bums were the last people I wanted to spend time with. Especially when the rest of the building was asleep. I imagined the junkies coming down in the morning to find my bludgeoned corpse behind the front desk.

'Ray make any coffee fo' he die?' they'd ask.

The bum continued to insist on his need for the phone. "I wan' call my momma," he said.

I was in the middle of informing the guy that the lobby phone opened for public use at nine (like the sign said on the door), when it hit me: *I knew this guy!*

Well, I *kind of* knew him. He had promised to kill me once, but besides that we weren't too close. It had been a few months since we'd seen each other. Mr. Switchblade wasn't looking too well.

It was dark, thanks to the lobby lights being off, so I doubted that he recognized me. Hell, maybe I was mistaken in thinking that I had recognized him. The *homelies* weren't much more than one-dimensional caricatures to me. That might be vapid on my part, but it's hard to appreciate someone's deeper qualities when all they do is beg for change or threaten bloody death.

I was in the process of closing the door on the guy when he asked for some food. Well, more like *demanded* it:

"*Jus' some food, goddamnit! Jus' a sammich! Jus' a gah-damn sammich!*"

His panhandling technique still needed some work.

Perhaps moved by how much skinnier he was than the last time I'd seen him, maybe wanting to surprise myself, I told the guy to wait while I went to fix him something. A minute later I was back with a ham sandwich and potato chips. Not the healthiest meal in the world, but it beat starving. Maybe.

I opened the door up just enough to hand the plate on through. Even though he hadn't recognized me as being on his '*To Kill*' list, I still felt like being careful. Just in case something jogged his memory. And in case he still had that knife.

The guy looked down at the plate, his face screwed up in confusion.

"Mustard, lettuce, onions and mayonnaise," I told him. "We're outta pickles."

He looked even angrier. "What, no salad?"

I slammed the door.

Fucker spent the next few minutes banging on the front walls. The sandwich was smeared against the glass, leaving a yellow and white slug-trail of ingratitude. I wondered if he would write messages on the glass with the rejected condiments. Maybe some empowering slogan like '*Fight the Real Enemy!*' next to a crude mustard caricature of the pope. But, life being the endless disappointment it is, he only smeared abstractions while the rest of his body shook in the universal language of impotence.

"I'll fucking *kill you*!" he screamed after I'd flicked him off through the glass. "Fuckin' kill you!"

Yeah, I'd heard *that* enough times with this job.

He kicked and punched at the glass. "Fuckin' kill yo white fuckin' ass!" It was like watching a rampage at the monkey house, except that I was the one inside the glass cage.

(and, yeah: choke on that simile unless your time is spent volunteering with the lower classes)

"*Kill you!*"

Charmingly repetitive bastard. And intensely quotable, too.

I flicked him off once more and then went to the kitchen to grab the biggest knife I could find. For protection. Just in case it occurred to him to scale the back fence.

2:30am
AT LEAST IT'S NOT *THE HARDY BOYS*

Todd ran down the back hallway, shouting my name. This gave me time to stop rifling through Gim's desk and saunter back out to the lobby. Todd's lanky white form was followed closely by Sam's smaller, whiter edition. Sam had just celebrated his 26th birthday in the confines of The Best Little Rehab in Texas. "If my dad was still alive," Sam had told me, "He'd shit himself with pride."

Todd shouted my name, again. My brain in its whiskey aquarium throbbed in response. Everyone else in the rehab was long-since asleep, but these two young'uns were bursting with energy. They slapped at the light fixtures and *literally* bounced off the walls as they ran down the hallway. It was impressive. I would've given them both piss-tests if I'd been in more of a mood to watch other men urinate.

Todd called my name for the fifth and loudest time before asking, "Will you read me *Sweet Valley High* books while I touch myself?"

It was an odd request, but not the weirdest one I've ever gotten. Definitely, however, the most unusual that didn't involve an offer of money.

Sam playfully slammed his shorter body into Todd's, sending them both into the lobby wall. "Fucking shut up, man!"

I shook my head at them. "I can't believe you kids are talking about filth like that? Sweet Valley High? *Jesus*!"

(This all references pre-teen literature. I'm too tired to spoon-food you trash culture beyond what you're already reading right now. Look it up, yourself, if you're not in the right age group.)

"How's about the Baby Sitter's Club?" Todd asked. "Or that sexy Nancy Drew bitch?" He dodged another slam-attempt from Sam. Seeing two young guys beating each other while discussing erotic stimulation to pre-teen literature might win a few points for novelty alone, but I wasn't really in the mood for it. My wholesome self just wanted them to bugger off so I could watch Afghan Muslim decapitation videos on my boss's computer.

"*Samuel*," I asked in my best what-I-thought-Austrian-Freudians-talked-like voice, "Do you have *somezing zhat you'd like to discuss with ze class*?"

Todd laughed. "Tell 'im, you pedophile!"

My male intuition told me that someone had spilled their guts during a bullshitting session. Apparently, the recipient of that info hadn't been too open-minded about it. As usual. Our tolerance for deviation tends to stop with our own perversions.

Sam blushed a stoplight shade of red. "Fuck you both," he said, ducking behind his hair. "I was sixteen years old!"

I asked, "Weren't the Sweet Valley Twins only fourteen?"

(Not like I really know; the only childhood lit that sticks in my mind are the Choose Your Own Adventure books…and damned if those things didn't always make me die in a volcano).

This started Todd jumping up and down again, pointing a condemning finger at Sam. "I knew it!" he crowed. "Fucking pedophile!"

I shouldn't let people know that I was aware of the distinction between such things, but…"Actually, when the target of your lust is post-adolescent, it makes ya an *ephebophile*."

But they weren't listening. Sam was chasing Todd again. They made a few circuits of the lobby, trying to slam into each other or place a kick in the other's backside. I was tempted to suggest that they strip on down and oil up for some genuine junkie-on-junkie action. If you're going to sublimate sexual frustration, you might as well make it interesting.

The grab-ass continued till Todd darted out the lobby, past the chapel, and down the back hallway. Sam followed him, shouting back over his shoulder at me, "At least I'm not a *pederast*, right?"

No, I suppose he wasn't.

Not that I would've cast down fire-and-brimstone on the guy if he were. The only useful thing I'd ever learned in my psych classes was that sexual orientation was nothing more than the result of accidental imprinting mixed with some genetics and a little conditioning. In other words: a bunch of shit that's beyond your control.

Being the simple machines that we are, can we do anything but follow our original programming? And why does knowing this not stop me from loathing everyone around here?

"*Homo*!" I heard Todd yell. There was the sound of something heavy hitting a wall.

I know that it's our duty as good Americans to hate, fear and generally abhor those whose sexuality differs from our own. Keeping focused on people who find different uses for their genitals is a great diversion. It makes sure our attention is elsewhere than on all the powerful people and interests who are *really* fucking us.

Like, if you're too concerned about why those guys over there are holding hands, you're nicely distracted from the important shit. You have a safe outlet for your proletarian rage and don't need to vent at things like the ever-widening income gap, your disappearing pension fund, or all those vanishing civil liberties that you weren't using anyways.

Your brother or sister or cousin or favorite work-pal that likes to kiss folks that look like them are okay. They're *exceptions*. But, all the faggots elsewhere are *definitely* organizing to undermine all the positive/Christian aspects of American society as intended by the Founding Fathers, Quaker slavers, Chinese manufacturers of U.S. flags, and the red/white/blue ejaculate gushed by Reagan across the face of Lenin's preserved corpse to signal Our Great Victory in what the U.S. armaments industry wants you to think of as the Cold War.

Few things play better in American politics than homophobia. Killing foreigners, maybe.

(And no, I'm *not* some bloody leftist. I've just got a real sensitive sphincter and can always tell whose dick is up my ass.)

Laughing, grunting and squealing, Sam and Todd's voices drifted back to me long after they had disappeared into the rear of the building. It must have been hard to live in a building filled only with males (for the hetero-types, at least). *Especially* when that building not only had a strict 'no booze or drugs' policy, but also shared space with a flock of self-righteous Methodists.

Denied every pleasure of the flesh while getting a daily dose of Jesus. As much as I've grown hardened to it all, I can't help but pity the clients sometimes.

2:37am
CELESTIALLY NUMB

In my own special, American way, I *liberated* some liquid codeine from the med room. Although not being a true-blooded patriot, I didn't kill anyone to do it. It helped with my strep throat. A tablespoon of the stuff every hour—when nobody's around—and I could start consuming relatively solid foods again. Two tablespoons of the stuff and I could chew brambles and gargle razor blades.

The codeine blankness was enough to make me eat in front of a mirror to ensure that I didn't bite off my tongue while chewing. A mental note was made to conserve the stuff, so I'd have plenty left to chug for fun once my case of strep throat was over.

The codeine belonged to Robert, who'd had throat cancer once upon a time. Things had been getting worse and worse until one night his dead mom showed up in his dreams and declared him cured. At his next doctor's appointment, sure enough, not a trace of cancer in his body.

It's about as likely, but a similar thing was claimed to happened to Magic Johnson and his HIV infection. Of course, Magic was a rich basketball player, compared to Robert being some broke-ass felon. So, Magic got his healing message delivered by Jesus *His-Own-Bad-Self*, instead of some dead black lady. Apparently, even the celestial realms work on an economic hierarchy.

And on a personal note, I used to know a girl who claimed a similar experience. She was dating a good friend of mine and, after a pregnancy scare, she turned Catholic. *Hysterically* Catholic. As in: no more sex, and she started planning on being a nun. I can't claim that everyone who's been naked around me has found it a 5-star experience, but I also never heard of anyone booking for a monastery, afterwards.

Anyways, this hysterical Catholicism went on for a few months until, once at a birthday party (after making sure that I'd left the room), the girl confided to everyone—tears in her eyes at the beauty of the experience—that she had been visited the previous night by an angel who restored unto the dear girl her long-lost virginity.

Seriously. In the 21st Century.

I was listening in on this touching story from the kitchen a room over—making double-whatevers with stolen booze that I was curious if I should take back to the rehab to thank Skater-boy Sam for watching the desk for me— and my first thought was, *did her hymen regrow?*

(and, yes, I know that's not the point, but our desire for cruelty can frequently overshadow our knowledge of biology)

So, I strolled back from the into the main room, unable to keep the grin off my face, and announced to everyone that I had been, for some time now, regretting my childhood circumcision, and did anyone know of a cost-effective method of reversing the process?

Having the greatest religious experience of your life mocked is something that few of us would take well. Realizing that's exactly what I was doing, the girl responded with a quick and savage kick to my genitals. I made a noise like a broken chew-toy and crumpled to the ground.

That night, after dragging myself back to work and passing out there, no celestial beings appeared in my dreams to heal my aching crotch. I don't think I've ever really forgiven them for the neglect.

2:42am
APOPTOSIS

It was raining and I couldn't sleep. I read a book. Worked on a cover letter for a new job I wanted. Felt my pre-work buzz subsiding. And when the junkies were all finally asleep, I turned off the downstairs lights and sat in the dark. Just me and that goddamn sewage stench.

The soft illumination of streetlights shone through the front glass. The overwhelming applause of the rain on the streets was accompanied by a string quartet on the radio. Groups of the homeless huddled under the roof of the covered bus stop down the street. I sat on my desk in the semi-darkness and watched the *Good Load* piss on the just on the unjust alike.

The air quality in Pasadena had to be the cleanest in months. The days and nights of rain piled upon more rain had finally washed some of the industrial pollutants from their normal place in the sky. I marveled at how, for the first time, maybe we weren't all killing ourselves with every breath we took.

Amazing.

If I had any cigarettes, I'd chain-smoke the pack.

The long day, plus the empty time alone, got me thinking about how stupid and pointless life could be. The endless failures, the boredom, the fact that radiation gives you cancer instead of superpowers, and how we spend our existence being herded from one cage to another. School during our youth, mind-numbing jobs throughout adulthood, and by the time that's all over there's not much else we're capable of besides soiling ourselves in some state-run nursing home. Having served our purpose to the machine, we're put out to pasture where everybody waits for us to die.

But, I have to say; the sponge baths you get in nursing homes strike me as the only positive aspect of aging. I'd soil myself every hour, on the hour, for those. Yeah, *that'd* make it worth waking up every day to pain.

"*Dude*," I said to myself. "Shut the hell up."

Existential whining was just the sort of mental habit I thought I'd kicked a long time ago. But in my teens there had been more despair behind the thoughts, rather than the current sense of resigned acceptance.

I scratched myself a few times, decided that I missed my ex-girlfriend, then decided that she could go fuck herself, then decided that I missed her, then decided that—

Screw it.

Being depressed is juvenile. By the time you're out of high school, you should have figured out an emotional strategy for dealing with life's little letdowns. We're all stupid and going to die, but that's no reason to mope. If all you saw around yourself was pain and suffering, wouldn't it be pretty maladaptive to be bothered by those kinds of things?

I decided that if life really was as Stupid and Pointless as my mind was telling me, then it had to be even more Stupid and Pointless to do something as lame as sitting around thinking about *how* Stupid and Pointless it all was.

Right?

God, I wished I believed that. But, it seemed like our society tolerated nothing beyond that. And you need to pay rent and buy food, right? So, capitulate and pretend, you weakling, peasant fuck.

Sitting in the rotting chairs of the rehab lobby, I shuddered, then closed down another part of my soul.

Relieved at how my idiocy, my obstinacy, and that useless desire for selfhood had all cancelled each other out, I decided to make myself a sandwich and then go catch some porn on Gim's computer. Nothing was better, nothing had been solved, but at least I no longer cared.

3:04am
SO LONG AS IT'S UNFAIR IN MY FAVOR

"Seriously, Michael Jackson does not *deserve* to own that man's skeleton!"

I never thought I'd hear the ownership of anyone's corpse discussed with such conviction, let alone the remains of that great Victorian grotesque, the Elephant Man.

The inanity of it all forced a laugh out of me.

"I didn't think you could buy people's remains," I said to the young junkie sitting across the lobby from me. "Did he bribe a cemetery owner, or what?"

Todd shook his head. "It was probably at a university. Some folks they just don't bury."

I nodded. The last assertion carried the weight of truth that only self-evident things can at three in the morning.

"Remember that part in the movie where he's in front of the mirror?" Todd asked. "Trying to make himself look all good for that girl he's got a date with?" I shook my head, but Todd didn't care. "God, it was horrible! That scene made me want to go hug my mom."

I laughed again. "Guess there could be worse deformities…"

"There could also be better ones than having your head so big that laying down makes you suffocate," he pointed out. "Like, I saw this kung-fu movie once that had this bad-ass guy with hands but no arms who could twirl a bo-stick like a fucking champ!"

Todd withdrew his long and skinny arms most of the way into his shirt and proceeded to pantomime this particular brand of crippled karate.

"Holy shit!" I cried, sitting upright in my chair. "They have Thalidomide Babies in kung-fu movies?"

Todd wrinkled his forehead for a second before lighting up with comprehension. "Oh! *That's* what those are called! We've got one of those in my Narcotics Anonymous group."

"I'll bet y'all do," I said. "And I bet he's the only one of y'all with a decent excuse to be there."

Addicts hate nothing worse than to be robbed of the excuse that they've ruined their lives due to some disease that they can't control, instead of their own personal weakness (a popular Victorian Age theory). So, Todd ignored my remark.

I'd caught the guy relapsed the other night. Stumbled into the women's bathroom downstairs and there was Todd: nodded out on the toilet seat, pants around his ankles, slumped half off the seat and against the wall. I would've busted him, but I was a bit too drunk at the time to bother. My motor functions too impaired for any finger-pointing.

Instead, I had just closed the door and staggered down the hall to throw up in the men's room.

Todd: "But this guy…this guy's got like…his arms stop about halfway down his forearms and just form these flipper things. Like, he's only got three fingers, like they're fused together with a huge finger nail on each one."

"Like the Penguin in the second Batman," I offered.

“Yeah!” said Todd. “And I was sitting next to him the other week and he starts sharing about his problems with lust, and I’m like: ‘*Oh God, I don’t wanna hear about how much money he spends on prostitutes*.”

I could imagine. The suffering of others is only amusing at a certain level before it descends into pathos or accelerates into farce.

“Imagine,” I said, determined to follow this train of thought no matter where it led, “Not only does he have to pay for sex, but the best he can hope for is that the girl doesn’t cringe when he touches her.”

Todd’s face dropped. I could barely hear him mumble, “*Jesus.*”

Todd got up to wander out of the lobby in a semi-daze. I watched him go, dragging with him the horrible knowledge that life could be even worse than you had imagined. “I need some fresh air,” Todd announced as he headed out back for a smoke.

The lobby was quiet after he left, so I gave a quick shrug at the basic unfairness of life and went back to scanning the newspaper’s Help Wanted section.

“Hey!” Todd poked his head back around the corner. “I gotta wonder…how the hell, with hands way up by his shoulders, how the hell does the guy masturbate?”

It was time for my own face to fall. “*Jesus*,” I muttered, before Todd stuffed his arms back up his sleeves and bent over, pretending to make desperate grabs for his own genitals. We both burst out laughing.

Why do bad things happen to people who did nothing to deserve it? Why is there such horribly unfair shit in the world?

Well, sometimes I almost believed Joe Orton’s classic response: ‘…because it’s *funnier* that way.’

3:10am
CORNROWS AND PINK TRIANGLES

Tennil's hair was in geometrically precise cornrows. Looking closely, I could see the beads of sweat starting on the top of his skull, zig-zagging down from row to row, gathering mass and moisture as they sped towards the abrupt slope of his forehead. Tennil didn't wipe them from his forehead so much as he intercepted each bead with a mighty slap like he was being assaulted by imaginary mosquitoes.

Maybe that would come later in the night. An assault by fantasized insects wouldn't be too surprising, seeing how he was speeding harder than a Ferrari on nitrous.

I decided to leave word to bust him with the morning shift. For now, though, Tennil's company was worth granting him a short reprieve. My own state of mind played an important role in the clemency, since I appreciated the presence of others so much more when I had a decent drunk going.

Tennil twitched and nervously twisted his football jersey between his fingers. He was in full-blown confession mode. It's easy to achieve this state with stimulants, but while the average cokehead can ramble on at Mach 5 about nothing at all, Tennil was kind enough to actually hold my interest. This was good for him, since it meant that when he came down he'd have somewhere to sleep before my coworkers threw him out.

I detest the empty verbosity of cokeheads enough that, were he less entertaining, I would piss-test the guy just to get rid of him. Tennil's rambling was amusing enough to distract me from the interracial midget porn I'd been watching online, so I let him sit across Gim's desk from me. He blathered on about his secret predilection for teenage boys.

"Don't nobody know," he told me, and I suspected that your average homophobe wouldn't identify Tennil in a police line-up of sodomites (if they held police line-ups for that, which I don't think they do anymore, except maybe in Wyoming). He didn't possess any of the stereotypical characteristics that TV and movies told us in the late 20th Century to expect in those frequently given to homoerotic acts. No earring in the right ear, no lisp, no 'screaming queen' behaviors, no impeccable fashion sense.

It was weird to meet someone here who didn't act like a bad stereotype.

Tennil looked slightly more attractive (strong chin and lean, muscular build) than most of the black youths seen on the average episode of *Cops*. He claimed to have been on the show a few years back, and when I voiced my doubts, promised to get the tape from his mom's house.

Tennil was also quite insistent that, despite his predilection for the backsides of Korean boys, he was *Not Gay*. Or, as he so eloquently—almost pleadingly—put it time and time again (in case I had missed the first fifteen assertions), "*…ain't no fuckin' faggot*."

At those moments, he sounded remarkably like the hicks I'd attended high school with back in the tiny town of Bullfuck, TX. If Tennil could restrain them from assaulting his regrettably darker-hued body, they'd probably all get along great.

And to support his '*Not Gay*' thesis, Tennil whipped out his wallet and showed me photos of his kids. All four of them. Some of the pictures were a bit old, but he hadn't seen a few of the kids in a while, since he only got along with two of the three mothers.

Yeah, nothing says 'die-hard heterosexual' like being a deadbeat dad.

The kids were pretty cute, though.

When Tennil managed to pause for breath after spilling his guts for over fifty minutes, I filled him in on the notion of sexuality as a verb, rather than a noun. That there are no such things are 'homosexual' or 'heterosexual' people, just people who sometimes perform 'homosexual' or 'heterosexual' acts.

By the same logic, there'd be no 'druggies,' just people who sometimes did drugs (in which case I'd be out of a job).

That's a decent theory of sexuality, as far as my understanding of those things go. It's consistent with post-Fullerian psychology, and it's what I told my cousin when she became interested in girls around the same time she was being inundated with the typical *God Hates Fags* propaganda at her Catholic school.

Tennil was more interested in the man behind the notion than the notion itself. "Where'd ya hear that?" he asked.

"Umm…book of essays," I said, slurring a little. "One of Gore Vidal's."

"He a fag?" Tennil asked. Somebody had apparently missed the point of the explanation.

"*Sure*," I sighed. "Totally."

Tennil sank his head into his hands, like he'd just lost his last friend in the world.

"*Shiiiiiiiit*," he said.

3:18am
YOU GOT TO HAVE FEAR IN YOUR HEART

Someone was howling outside of the rehab. One long wail was followed by a minute of silence, then another drawn-out howl. It was eerie. The wailing permeated the walls and oozed a sonic slime-trail across the lobby to the couch I was lying on. It seeped into my ears.

I listened to the wailing for a while and was able to make out words. Whoever felt the need to be extra loud at three in the morning was delivering an important message to the sleeping world.

They were saying: *MoooooOOOOOoooootheeerFuuuUUUUUckeeeeers!*

Male voice. Long and loud and slurred just enough to give the proper tone of resigned despair.

MoooooOOOOOoooootheeeerFuuuUUUUUckeeeeers!

Got kind of eerie after a while. There was no change in tone or pitch or speed or tempo. Just the same gutter-wail of profane sentiment over and again.

MoooooOOOOOoooootheeeerFuuuUUUUUckeeeeers!

Probably a drunk. Some street bum coping with street bum existence thanks to a few bottles of Night Train. Maybe a 40oz of Olde English. Whatever gets you through the night.

MoooooOOOOOoooootheeeerFuuuUUUUUckeeeeers!

It was really screwing with my ability to sleep on the job.

MoooooOOOOOoooootheeeerFuuuUUUUUckeeeeers!

I poked my head out the front door. Looked up the street one way and the other. No sign of the elusive Urban Howler Monkey. Still, just because I couldn't see the bastard, didn't mean that I couldn't hear him.

MoooooOOOOOoooootheeeerFuuuUUUUckeeeeers!

It seemed to echo off the surrounding buildings and drip its despair in stereo. Like having the landscape moan at you. This made sense. I mean, if there was a sentiment that this part of town, with its bums and slums and trash-strewn streets, would be trying to impart, it'd have to be:

MoooooOOOOOoooootheeeerFuuuUUUUckeeeeers!

Running through my head as I scanned for the source of the howling were all the lessons I'd learned as a kid about aiding people in need. About how when somebody was hurting you should comfort them. Be a Good Samaritan. Lend assistance. Help out.

"SHUT the FUCK UP!" I screamed into the night. It was a nice idea, but did no good.

MoooooOOOOOoooootheeeerFuuuUUUUckeeeeers!

We've all got something to bitch about, but unless you're being creative or amusing in the expressing of discomfort, keep it to yourself.

MoooooOOO—"SHUT UP Before I *FUCKING KILL YOU*!"

That did the trick. The howling ceased and I stumbled back to the lobby couch. My own physical tiredness was now tinged with the extra weight of disappointment. Twenty-four years of life had led to my participating in screaming contests with winos. I sighed and tried to fall back asleep.

3:24am
SELLING YOURSELF AN EGYPTIAN RIVER

Few things suck worse than waking up in the middle of the night with a hangover. One of those is waking up in the middle of the night with a hangover at work, especially when it felt like your body was about to find somewhere new for the contents of your stomach.

And that's why I was hovering over the toilet in the women's bathroom. Bent at the waist, my arms propped me against the wall as I retched and heaved, aiming at the water a few feet below. My mouth burned from the acidic wash of upchuck, and I shuddered to feel tiny drops splashing my legs. I'd puke, flush so I didn't have to endure the sight or smell, and then puke some more. No way in hell I'd touch the toilet. Not after homeless ass had been on it all day.

It'd been a mad dash to the bathroom from the lobby couch. Didn't think I'd make it.

Forgive me, Father, for if I knew not what I did, it'd show a real poor grasp of cause and effect. My initial guess centered on blaming the cheap margaritas from earlier in the night. Or maybe all the beer. The bong hits probably figured in there somewhere, as well.

And yeah, showing up for work in a state of intoxication is typically one of those signs that you've got 'a problem.' But, with myself, I was certain it was a sign that I had a useful job. It didn't interfere with me going out for the night—even if going out for the night occurred right before work.

That's what I was thinking about when I regained consciousness, and it put me in a bit of a funk. It almost ruined my mood as much as vomiting gallons into the downstairs toilet. It doesn't take a degree in psychology—even though I've got one—to recognize a classic case of denial. Was

I denying that I had a tendency to overindulge these days? Denying that my overindulgence occurred with increasing frequency? Was my willingness to show up for work in delightfully-altered states less of a good thing then I usually took it for? Did I need to start cutting back on my chemical in-take?

Maybe, but just a little bit. Total abstinence is for the over-reactive. I'd just switch it over to having fun every other night of the week. Cut my habits in half. Maybe drink less, toke more.

After Happy Hour tomorrow.

3:27am
JESUS LOVES YOU, BUT I'M ACTUALLY HIS FAVORITE

I figured the baggie of coke under one of the kitchen tables to be that '*God*' chap's last attempt at making things right between the two of us. It sat there, partly hidden behind a table leg, alone and sad like the discarded nut-sack from a midget albino. I found it while locking up the dining room for the night, scoping out all the crap on the floor that should've been swept at chore time.

"Worthless, lazy motherfuckers," I had been mumbling to myself. Then that vision of Contra-funding, Columbian joy caught my eye. I thought, '*Is that…?*' and leaned down for a closer look at the heavenly gift.

Tiny twenty-sack. Stuffed to the brim.

'*Here you go, Ray*,' I could hear The Non-Existent One say. '*Hope this makes up for you being stuck in a dead-end job and humping your own fist for the past few months.*'

'*We cool, right?*'

Quick look to the left, quick look to the right. All clear. I picked up the baggie and stuffed it in my pocket. "It's definitely a start."

The original plan was to save the stuff for the next time I went out clubbing. Do bumps off my apartment key in the bathroom. Being coked and drunk always makes for a better night than being merely drunk. Makes me feels powerfully stupid and beautiful. Like five-feet, ten-inches of pure erectile tissue. Like I could fuck the world and make it beg for seconds. Like all the shit techno, strobe lights, and desperate women in the club were actually appealing.

It makes for a great twenty minutes till I need to head back to the bathroom for another bump.

That had been the original plan. But, my brain switched to autopilot, and when the manual controls came back online I was in the bathroom, chopping up a line with a kitchen knife. Just a short line. Something to help with the nagging remains of my hangover from all those tequila shots before work.

And, what the hell, it would help with the tedium of the night shift.

The last dollar bill in my wallet was rolled into a cylinder. Maneuvered up my right nostril like a cannon of pure happiness aimed at my brain. Facing away from the counter and its frosted goodness, I exhaled thoroughly, then dove back in on the coke. I swept the line from right to left like I was reading Hebrew. Grain after grain of coke—and whatever the fuck it was cut with—lacerated my sinuses on their way to do more damage further up the canals.

I tilted my head back, dollar still jutting from my nose, and gave the makeshift straw a thump or two with a spare finger. Snorted each time I did. Finished off any coca survivors of the nostril holocaust.

And then waited.

Five seconds…four seconds…three...tw—

There was a familiar burst of light in my frontal lobes. Like someone hooked electrical wires to an ice pick, then shoved it through my forehead. Like John C. Holmes ejaculated uranium in my morning coffee and offered me a drink.

We're talking *total dirty goodness*.

There was a sudden driving sense of energy and purpose. I wanted to dance I wanted to fuck I wanted to twirl around the bathroom to the beat of water dripping from the faucet this was some good stuff dear Christ the average coke on the street's so adulterated that the only way to get the blast you're wanting is to mix the high with something else 'cause on its own it's cool but not quite enough being coked and drunk is what you need or being coked and stoned or mix the stuff with heroin which I've never tried doing or *BAMBAMBAM!*

"*Yo*, Ray!"

Jesus! I almost pissed myself. It sounded like the Big Black Voice of Death. My heart and colon fought over whom had the right to explode first.

BAM!

"You in there, Ray?"

Some asshole was banging on the bathroom door.

It's not the cops. Deep breath. It's not the cops.

BAM! "Who you talkin' to in there?" *BAM*!

Frankie. It was Frankie. Big fucking 'fro-boy Frankie. The guy who couldn't spell past a Third Grade level but could eyeball a rock to the nearest eighth of a gram. Motherfuckin' Frankie.

BAM! "Hey man!"

I finally responded. "WHAT?"

Outside the door I heard him chuckle. "Thought you was in there."

Yeah, me and a heart that was on the verge of erupting from my chest.

"Fuck do you want?" Goddamn needy fuckin' crackheads can't do shit for themselves always needing somebody else to take care of them like addicts are the ultimate in arrested development like they never matured past the age of four always selfish shit and immediate personal fulfillment like they—

"The kitchen locked, man. You gonna let me in?"

"*The fuck*?!" I screamed at Frankie, and it occurred to me that I'd always been screaming at him. "Of course it's fuckin' locked! It's always locked at night. It was locked yesterday! It'll be locked tomorrow! Why the fuck would tonight be any different; the hell were you expecting?"

There was a slight pause of silence, another slight pause, and for me it stretched out into a silence that went on and on as Frankie tried to starve me out on the other side of the bathroom door and I valiantly resisted his efforts and my veins pulsed in time with my heroic resolve to resist the evil crackhead resist his entreaties to leave the safety of the bathroom where he'd laid a trap that just had to consist of fifteen huge black men all hung like polar bears waiting quietly waiting for me to leave the bathroom so they could punish me for years of black oppression and how my middle class upbringing depended on centuries on black enslavement and how it was my fault that the ERA had failed in the eighties and how all the shows on BET were crap and my cousin called it Niggervision and that they knew how my—

"I need to get in there, Ray!"

Right! Frankie! Shit!

What to do what to do what to do what to do what to what to what to do?

"Fuck off!" I settled on shouting through the door. "The fuck do you think I'm doing in here?!"

Please don't say coke please don't say coke please don't say don't say don't say coke don't say coke *please* don't say coke.

Frankie adopted a more conciliatory tone. "I…I just need to get me somethin' when you done in there."

Aha!

Something like a little lost baggie of coke, perhaps?

"Whatcha need?" I asked with a certain relish in my voice. Ray was no longer on the defensive. The world's sexiest Tech now had the upper hand and was using it to punch other people in the ball-sack. "Gotta grab something?"

It took Frankie a long time to answer. 'Course, it always took Frankie a while to answer. Somebody stole his brain as a baby and replaced it with an Etch-a-Sketch.

He babbled something about a drink of water, as if there weren't water fountains upstairs, while I held a staring contest with my reflection on the faucet handles. I kept losing, but so did my image. Me versus the crazy man. Yours truly on one side, and some distorted, scruffy bastard on the other. He needed to shave. He needed a haircut. He looked like a Hitler Youth grown up apathetic. Blond-haired, blue-eyed decadence. His eyes blinked again and again like he was attempting flight with his lashes. Pupils huge enough to host a dinner party in—provided, as Hemmingway would've said, that it was a small dinner party and you wanted to host it there.

"Ray?"

"Ray!"

"FUCK OFF!" I screamed. "Fuck off before I reach in the toilet and smack you with the first thing I find!"

There was quiet on the other side of the door. Then, "What you say?"

"*Jesus Christ*!" I put my hand over my heart. It's a bad thing to do on stimulants, and that's why I can never resist. My ticker was two seconds away from exploding through my ribcage and showering the bathroom with blood and bone shards. I was going to die. I was going have a heart attack at the age of 24. The paramedics would bust me out of the bathroom and the body bag's zipper would get stuck on this throbbing erection I'd popped out of nowhere.

"Ray? C'mon and let me in the—"

I threw myself against the door. Kicked it twice. "Leave me the fuck alone!" My voice was cracking. "Go to fuckin' bed, or I'm gonna give myself a piss test and sign your fuckin' name to it!"

I was about to freak out. I *was* freaking out. I sat down in the sink. Calm down. Calm down. Deep breath. Deep breath. Calm down. Inhale, count to four. Exhale, count to four.

"Ray?"

Deep breath.

"Ray?"

Calm down.

"*C'mon* Ray."

I sat in the sink. Tried to calm the hell down. Tasted the coke dregs in the back of my throat. My butt was getting wet.

"Ray?"

I was trapped.

"I need in the kitchen, Ray!"

And worst of all, that fucker was totally killing my buzz.

3:33am
SUCH A LACK OF ACHIEVEMENT THAT IT'S AN ACHIEVEMENT IN ITSELF

After hanging around the rehab long enough, I'd come to the grim conclusion that it was far more likely for people to fail in life than succeed (or why would success be such a big deal?). I'd also come to the conclusion that life needed to come with some sort of consolation prize.

We needed an award for all those poor fuckers that try *so* hard but fall flat on their goddamn faces every time. Give them something to say, '*thanks for playing and better luck next time*.' We could enlist Ed McMahon's corpse to fly out with a camera crew to present the award to each hapless participant.

There would be awards for the starving Honduran farmers, whose crops and children get doused by U.S.-sponsored herbicides. We could give posthumous prizes to depressives and suicides the world over, who gave life their best shot but just couldn't take it anymore. One for single-parent households who fell short of making rent each month. Another award for my sorry little addicts relapsing over and over again. Awards to everyone who's tried to quit smoking more than once. Awards to all the blank, brutalized people who start every day with smiles and go home each night in tears.

The award itself could be a little statuette showing God, in his bearded-old-man guise, with His holy foot on the neck of some unidentified individual, who would represent the broken spirit in All of Us. It'd be kind of like a glorified version of those participation ribbons they'd to give to all the slow and fat kids on Field Day. We could call the awards *Hitlers*, after the biggest 20th Century example of a sad bastard who tried his damnedest but still failed miserably.

And if there were going to be awards for Trying-but-Failing, then in all fairness we needed awards for people who knew better than to even try in the first place. We could give out a little plaque with a stick figure on it, shrugging deeply. Not sure what we could call those, though I'm kind of tempted to name them after myself.

3:38am
THROB FOR THROB, POUND FOR POUND, LIGHT FOR LIGHT

There's a nifty little technique for dealing with headaches that I got out of Robert Anton Wilson's book, *The Earth Will Shake*. Just visualize and concentrate on a mental image of your brain, and then imagine a bright, white light surrounding and enveloping your brain. If you can concentrate well enough, your headache will fade from your consciousness while you're doing this.

POUNDPOUNDPOUNDPOUNDPOUNDPOUNDPOUNDPOUNDPOUNDPOUND

It's basically just a distraction, but especially handy for when you're hungover and waiting for the aspirin to kick in.

POUNDPOUNDPOUNDPOUNDPOUNDPOUNDPOUNDPOUNDPOUNDPOUND

And dear *fucking* Christ, if only I could find some of the stuff! But of course, aspirin wasn't allowed in the building. Couldn't have the junkies munching entire bottles of the stuff in sobriety-fueled fits of despair. Thanks to those fucking weaklings I was stuck with the pain. *God*, if only my head would just explode and get things over with.

POUNDPOUNDPOUNDPOUNDPOUNDPOUNDPOUNDPOUNDPOUNDPOUND

The lobby's lights were out and only a small glow was coming from the hallway. I was sitting hunched over on the couch. It was a filthy fucking thing. Cracked leather and discolored stains. I was probably absorbing countless little germs from the countless asses of the countless bums who sat on it during the day. God knows nothing in the building ever got cleaned except the floor and an occasional toilet. And hell, before it was donated to *Christ in the Gutter*, the couch had previous owners. Those fuckers probably took turns sneezing on the thing.

POUNDPOUNDPOUNDPOUNDPOUNDPOUNDPOUNDPOUNDPOUNDPOUND

Any relief would do. I sat upright, straight-backed, and took a deep, relaxing breath. The tension drained from my body in degrees. First my jaw, then neck, then shoulders, back, arms, hands, legs, toes. It was meditation time.

POUNDPOUNDPOUNDPOUNDPOUNDPOUNDPOUNDPOUNDPOUNDPOUND

I formed an image of my brain in my mind's eye. The picture-maker pictured itself. Focusing that electro-colloidal mess in my skull was difficult even under normal circumstances. Living in the modern world assured me an attention span that had been raped, killed, and then dug back up to have its corpse violated again by cheap entertainment and flashy images that blurred into one meaningless tableau after another. Flicker to one thing. Flicker to something else equally meaningless. Flickering back again. It becomes such a habit for the mind that it can't imagine needing an attention span exceeding three seconds. It's addicted to the flash and flash and flash and flash so much that its basic structure comes to mimic the empty quickness. Just like a junkie's metabolism restructures itself for heroin.

POUNDPOUNDPOUNDPOUNDPOUNDPOUNDPOUNDPOUNDPOUNDPOUND

But still, I strained to hold an image of my aching brain in my mind's eye. Just a bit of focus and a bit of relief. I pictured the lobes, the brain stem, the hemispheres. Hold the image. Hold the image.

Don't think about—

POUNDPOUNDPOUNDPOUNDPOUNDPOUNDPOUNDPOUNDPOUNDPOUND

Shit.

POUNDPOUNDPOUNDPOUNDPOUNDPOUNDPOUNDPOUNDPOUNDPOUND

Hold the image.

And then I imagined the hemispheres being—*shit*—hold the image. And then I imagined my brain being consumed in a blissful holocaust of white light. It was a million suns, a nuclear explosion of healing energy in my head, and as long as I stayed focused on the image—*shit*—as long as I focused on my brain being filled with and overpowered by—

Shit!

POUNDPOUNDPOUNDPOUNDPOUNDPOUNDPOUNDPOUNDPOUNDPOUND

As long as I stayed focused on my brain being consumed by this white light all the pain faded away. All the hurt in my head went somewhere else.

POUNDPOUNDPOUNDPOUNDPOUNDPOUNDPOUNDPOUNDPOUNDPOUND

Focus.

Focus.

Focus.

That's *better*—I mean, Focus….

Focus.

Focus.

The door to the stairwell banged open and footsteps headed in my direction. *Fuck*!

The pounding in my head picked up right where it let off.

POUNDPOUNDPOUNDPOUNDPOUNDPOUNDPOUNDPOUNDPOUNDPOUND

I made plans to kill and dismember whoever this turned out to be. Somebody had *better* be having a heart attack or gushing blood from a stump wound. If this was the usual, bullshit junkie desire to chat or get some ice from the kitchen, I was going to take the nearest copy of the Big Book and fucking *bludgeon* them with it.

POUNDPOUNDPOUNDPOUNDPOUNDPOUNDPOUNDPOUNDPOUNDPOUND

The footsteps got louder and closer, my head went back into my hands, and a little black head poked itself around the corner in my peripheral vision.

POUNDPOUNDPOUNDPOUNDPOUNDPOUNDPOUNDPOUNDPOUNDPOUND

"That you there, Ray?" Swanky asked.

POUNDPOUNDPOUNDPOUNDPOUNDPOUNDPOUNDPOUNDPOUNDPOUND

I sighed. "What's up, man?" *And it had better be real fuckin' good...*

POUNDPOUNDPOUNDPOUNDPOUNDPOUNDPOUNDPOUNDPOUNDPOUND

"Not much," he said, stepping around the corner to take a seat next to me on the couch. Swanky looked like the long-lost eighth dwarf. The black one that Disney would have to insert into the story for a multi-cultural remake. He was short, muscular, and had lupus scars on his face.

POUNDPOUNDPOUNDPOUNDPOUNDPOUNDPOUNDPOUNDPOUNDPOUND

"*Not much*," I echoed in despair. My path was now clear. Before the night was over, I would have the blood of a midget crackhead on my hands.

POUNDPOUNDPOUNDPOUNDPOUNDPOUNDPOUNDPOUNDPOUNDPOUND

We sat a while in silence, me rubbing at my temples.

POUNDPOUNDPOUNDPOUNDPOUNDPOUNDPOUNDPOUNDPOUNDPOUND

"Did…you *need*…something?" I asked.

POUNDPOUNDPOUNDPOUNDPOUNDPOUNDPOUNDPOUNDPOUNDPOUND

"Couldn't sleep."

POUNDPOUNDPOUNDPOUNDPOUNDPOUNDPOUNDPOUNDPOUNDPOUND

"You…couldn't sleep." That was it. The proverbial camel's proverbial back was proverbially broken. Swanky was a dead man. Or midget…however they classified these guys. I lifted my head from my hands to scan the darkened lobby for the key ring and its attached cudgel. Just a few good whacks and I could go back to meditating. A few good hits and it would be quiet again. Just claim it was self-defense.

POUNDPOUNDPOUNDPOUNDPOUNDPOUNDPOUNDPOUNDPOUNDPOUND

They'd believe me. I'm a college graduate. White boy. Swanky's a black ex-con. I know how the system works in this country.

POUNDPOUNDPOUNDPOUNDPOUNDPOUNDPOUNDPOUNDPOUNDPOUND

"Woke up and thought I was back in jail," Swanky said. "That been happening a lot recently."

POUNDPOUNDPOUNDPOUNDPOUNDPOUNDPOUNDPOUNDPOUNDPOUND

I rubbed at my temples. Looked around. Still no sign of the cudgel. "Think it might have something to do with sleepin' in a room with five other guys?" I'd get Swanky off-guard, make him feel safe, and then—*Crack*! "All that extra breathing and snoring in the room with ya could be doin' the trick. Maybe your subconscious is picking up on it while you're sleeping, so it's the first thing that crosses your mind when ya wake up."

POUNDPOUNDPOUNDPOUNDPOUNDPOUNDPOUNDPOUNDPOUNDPOUND

“Could be that.” Swanky nodded in the half-light. “Could be.”

POUNDPOUNDPOUNDPOUNDPOUNDPOUNDPOUNDPOUNDPOUNDPOUND

More silence. More dead air. More of my head trying to collapse in on itself.

POUNDPOUNDPOUNDPOUNDPOUNDPOUNDPOUNDPOUNDPOUNDPOUND

“It sure rainin’ hard,” Swanky said, finally. I looked out the glass front of the building. The world had turned to pounding water. Rain was coming down in wave after wave. Half a world away, American munitions were doing the same in foreign cities.

POUNDPOUNDPOUNDPOUNDPOUNDPOUNDPOUNDPOUNDPOUNDPOUND

This stupid, fucking planet.

POUNDPOUNDPOUNDPOUNDPOUNDPOUNDPOUNDPOUNDPOUNDPOUND

I hadn’t even noticed the rain. Too busy concentrating on my headache. Too wrapped up in my own misery. “So it is,” I said.

POUNDPOUNDPOUNDPOUNDPOUNDPOUNDPOUNDPOUNDPOUNDPOUND

“Couldn’t tell what the weather was like in prison,” Swanky said. “It just always cold. I was in there four years, and only one or two times I know it was raining.”

POUNDPOUNDPOUNDPOUNDPOUNDPOUNDPOUNDPOUNDPOUNDPOUND

“That sucks,” I said, for a lack of anything better to say. *My poor fucking head!* I had come into work utterly plastered. Had a few martinis at a vegan-feminist lecture—I was there to pick up chicks—and then a good bong-rip or two at home. Showered before work to take care of the smell. A heavy dose of crap cologne and I was ready to earn my daily bread.

POUNDPOUNDPOUNDPOUNDPOUNDPOUNDPOUNDPOUNDPOUNDPOUND

“In prison, we’d lay in bed and bullshit,” Swanky said. “Tell halfway stories.”

POUNDPOUNDPOUNDPOUNDPOUNDPOUNDPOUNDPOUNDPOUNDPOUND

"Hell, I'd probably just be getting ass-raped," I managed to joke.

POUNDPOUNDPOUNDPOUNDPOUNDPOUNDPOUNDPOUNDPOUNDPOUND

Swanky looked me up and down like he was appraising a particularly disappointing bull. "Yeah," he said. "You would."

POUNDPOUNDPOUNDPOUNDPOUNDPOUNDPOUNDPOUNDPOUNDPOUND

I needed to change the subject before Swanky decided a demonstration was in order. Felt so horrible that only being raped by a midget crackhead could possibly make things worse, and I didn't want to give Life the chance to test that theory. Where the hemorrhaging *fuck* was that cudgel? Would I actually have to haul myself off the couch to go look for it? "What's a halfway story?"

POUNDPOUNDPOUNDPOUNDPOUNDPOUNDPOUNDPOUNDPOUNDPOUND

Swanky thought about this for a while. "It quick," he said. "Real short. Just something that happen that don't take long to tell. The sorta shit you tell your friends about when somethin' cool happen. Like if you gettin' some pussy and somethin' funny happen like her momma walk in and complain that it's a school night. Quick story."

POUNDPOUNDPOUNDPOUNDPOUNDPOUNDPOUNDPOUNDPOUNDPOUND

Oh. "Like an anecdote," I said. "Or vignette."

POUNDPOUNDPOUNDPOUNDPOUNDPOUNDPOUNDPOUNDPOUNDPOUND

Swanky shook his head. "Don't know 'bout that," he said.

POUNDPOUNDPOUNDPOUNDPOUNDPOUNDPOUNDPOUNDPOUNDPOUND

"Same thing," I assured him. "Vignette's kind of like a written version of an anecdote or…what was the term?"

POUNDPOUNDPOUNDPOUNDPOUNDPOUNDPOUNDPOUNDPOUNDPOUND

"Halfway story," he said. "That the same thing?"

POUNDPOUNDPOUNDPOUNDPOUNDPOUNDPOUNDPOUNDPOUNDPOUND

I went to nod, but it just made me feel worse. "Same thing," I repeated. It was time for an explanation using phrases understandable to someone whose mother not only dropped him as a child, but also probably dribbled him up and down the court a few times. Maybe she'd tried a lay-up shot or two. "It's like, you never get the full story or complete picture from an anecdote. What came before, the long-term shit that led up to it all, and all sorts of background details get left out. That sound like what you were talkin' about?"

POUNDPOUNDPOUNDPOUNDPOUNDPOUNDPOUNDPOUNDPOUNDPOUND

He nodded. "Spiffy," I said. If there was one thing I had become something of an expert on while working here, it was anecdotes and vignettes. Heard shitloads of 'em from the junkies—everything from funny drug stories to not-so funny drug stories. From confessions of mugging their own grandmothers to the time someone's piss test turned up positive for pregnancy. Eventually, I could figure out what made a good anecdote or vignette or halfway story differ from one that I couldn't even bother pretending to listen to. They usually tell instead of show. Anecdotes and vignettes don't need a point, just a punch line. They lack a sense of completeness. They're like the drive-by version of storytelling. Just little Polaroid glimpses into people's lives, usually blurry, red-eyed, and underdeveloped. But hey, so long as the thing's amusing, who gives a fuck?

POUNDPOUNDPOUNDPOUNDPOUNDPOUNDPOUNDPOUNDPOUNDPOUND

"*Whassamatter*?" Swanky asked me. "Got a headache?"

POUNDPOUNDPOUNDPOUNDPOUNDPOUNDPOUNDPOUNDPOUNDPOUND

I almost nodded again but caught myself. "Yeah," I said, remembering my earlier desire to bash his head in. If he didn't leave soon…

POUNDPOUNDPOUNDPOUNDPOUNDPOUNDPOUNDPOUNDPOUNDPOUND

"Got some ibuprofen upstairs," he said. "You want some?"

POUNDPOUNDPOUNDPOUNDPOUNDPOUNDPOUNDPOUNDPOUNDPOUND

Possession of that stuff was against the rules, but I found myself willing to overlook it this time. "*Pretty please*!" I moaned, and he jumped up to fetch it.

POUNDPOUNDPOUNDPOUNDPOUNDPOUNDPOUNDPOUNDPOUNDPOUND

Sitting alone in the dark again, I found myself somewhat relieved that I'd let him live.

3:41am
ALL SUFFERING COMES FROM ATTACHMENT, EXCEPT FOR WHEN YOU STUB YOUR TOE

I'd never had a parent plead with me for their child's life before tonight. It's just something new here every day. Almost makes me glad to be alive. Almost.

Another bright young member of the Pasadena addict community sat across my boss' desk from me. Zack fidgeted in his seat, shifting his weight, scratching his head, tugging his ponytail, and covering his face with his hands.

And whining.

And whining some more.

By his own admission, he had smoked cracked around two-and-a-half hours ago. Judging by his current state, it was a move he rather regretted.

In his late twenties with strong Italian features, Zack oozed repentance from every pore. The past hour or so of my time had been spent listening to Zack beat himself up over his relapse. The fun was had, and now he was deep in the Magical Land of Comedown.

The psychic territory of Comedown Land was like driving through West Texas. It was bleak, harsh, there was nothing to do but wait for it to be over, and the end never came soon enough.

Shit, this entire place was one big comedown.

I had been in the process of breaking into the chef's office (paranoid bastard had chained the door shut again) when Zack showed up hours past curfew.

"Just wanted you to know I was back," he said. I hadn't even noticed Zack was gone, didn't have a clue how he'd made it back into the building, but now his late return had triggered my Amazing Psychic Tech Sense. Or maybe it wasn't my latent psychic powers so much as seeing Zack twitch like he'd just finished humping an electrical outlet.

I watched his muscles spasm for a while. "Any reason why you're geekin'?"

Well...first he told me a story about being real tired (this when he seemed energized enough to telekinetically cause both our heads to explode), and then it became the fault of all the coffee he drank, and then slowly it came out that he had been around some people who had started smoking crack.

"And you smoked it, too." Not a question. Zack shook his head so violently it seemed he'd give himself whiplash.

"*Bullshit*, man." If only Zack hadn't been so damn obvious about it. I could've sent him off to bed and let somebody else deal with it tomorrow. "You're geekin' so hard your heart's probably about to explode."

(For the record, that's a *horrible* thing to say to someone on any type of stimulant. I decided to sneak mentions of it into the rest of our conversation.)

"*No no no I didn't no I swear no I didn't man I…I smoked it*." It was then that the remorse started flowing out of his mouth like somebody busted a hole in the dam that held back the mighty waters of Lake Regret.

He said:

"*GodIcan'tbelieveIdidthatI'msuchafuckupIcan'tstaysoberformorethantwodayswhydidIdothatafterItookthatshitIwassosorryohgodwhydidIdothatIcan'thelpbutfuckupwhydoIalwaysfuckuptheguyjustlitupinfrontofmeandIhadabsolutelynodesiretosmokebutthenthenext—*" *etc. etc. etc. etc.*

I'd be lying if I claimed it made any sense.

Company policy was to throw homeboy out on his ass. In the street. In the middle of the night. I've done it before. Done it to people almost three times his age in the middle of winter.

*Buuuuuuuuuut…*I just couldn't bring myself to do it to Zack. Don't know why. Pity isn't a strong suit of mine. Shit, I agree with the Greek and Nietzschean analysis that pity's a spiritual poison. It's unhealthy. Makes you weak. Corrodes that *soul* thingy that I don't believe in.

Doubt it had anything to do with the fact that Zack's had one failure after another in his short life. So have most of the other guys here. They wouldn't be here if that wasn't the case. And it probably wasn't because Zack committed suicide back in February. He hung himself from one of the rafters in his parents' garage.

Amusingly enough, he succeeded at it, too. Suicide was probably the only thing in his life that he didn't fuck up. Other people ruined it for him. Zack was dead as the proverbial doorknob for over five minutes while his dad did CPR on him until the paramedics arrived. It wasn't knowing this that kept me from tossing his ass to the street. Hell, in my slightly unChrist-like opinion, suicide would be an improvement for the guy.

But, for some reason I just couldn't give Zack the boot. Go figure. It's nice to be able to still surprise yourself every now and then.

I told Zack he could stay with me till the sun came up. Our section of Pasadena wasn't the sort of area to be out in at this late hour.

"But you're not leaving my fuckin' sight," I told him, along with the caveat that he had to be out of the building before everyone else woke up. And that's how I came to enjoy the cheery company of a young crackhead as he woefully came down from the drug that had already ruined his life several times, was currently running his life, and would probably continue to ruin his life…for ever and ever and ever, self-degradation without end, amen.

Most addicts are nothing if not consistent.

We sat in my boss' office, Zack on the other side of the desk so he couldn't see my internet browsing habits. Finally he asked, "C-c-can I call my dad?" And while I may not have wanted to hear him whine to his old man about how he had fucked up yet again, I shrugged out a '*sure, why not?*'

I set Zack up on the phone in the lobby, then I went back to scoping out the usual porn sites on Gim's computer. More than anything, I wanted to be able to close the door, to shut out Zack's half of what was probably the most pathetic conversation occurring within a fifty-mile radius.

Voyeurism is all well and good, but the pathos of a boy doomed by his love for crack and a father doomed by his love for a fuck-up son wasn't anything I was interested in hearing that night.

Sure, it would be amusing up to a point, but you can only hear the same record so many times before a song's familiarity starts to grate on you. If my job was a jukebox, it wouldn't play too many other tunes.

"He's going to throw me out on the street, dad!" I heard Zack say. "You know what this part of town's like. He's just gonna…no, he says he has to. *Dad*! He says he has to throw me out!"

The fuck? I thought. How'd I end up the goddamn bad guy here? Sneaky fuckin' crackhead trying to switch the focus from his relapse to my heartless villainy! *Goddamnit*!

I found myself wishing that the little bastard had learned to tie better knots in Boy Scouts.

"My dad wants to talk to you," Zack called to me, a new note of smugness in his voice now that his high-priced lawyer of a daddy (*mucho* important, *mucho* wealthy, and head of the city council in their small Texas town, I'd been repeatedly told) was going to make everything okay.

"*Fucker*," I muttered before picking up my boss' phone. My eyes did a spectacular rolling tour of their sockets as I answered with my customary, "*Yello*?"

Zack's dad had a deep and commanding voice. Soaked in authority. I expected him to *order* my peasant ass to absolve his son of all wrongdoing. Then, I imagined, he'd force me to apologize for even considering the removal of such a fine young lad from this establishment, and before the end of the call I'd be agreeing to pay alimony to my ex-girlfriends (or something like that).

Instead, he immediately began to beg.

He asked me if I knew about Zack's suicide attempt (*I did*, I said nonchalantly), and then went on to say that he was afraid—so very, *very* afraid—that Zack would try it again if I threw him out in the middle of the night. That, or the '*niggers in that part of town*' (his phrase, I promise) might do horrible things to Zack.

I didn't bother informing him of my plan to let Zack stay till sun-up. What would be the point? Daddy wasn't listening to me, anyway, being too busy begging in what he doubtless thought to be the defense of his son's life.

The most important case I ever argued, I'm sure he'll call it in his memoirs.

I half-listened as he pleaded on and on that I not callously kick his boy out on the streets. I scoped out leather bondage sites online while Zack's dad whined into my left ear. He could be there in three hours, he begged; couldn't I *please* just let Zack stay till then?

"Look…" I tried to cut in, to no avail.

"Just give him his meds and send him to bed," his dad implored. "I can be there by six-thirty! *Please*!"

Six-thirty *was* around the time that I'd been planning on giving Zack the boot, anyway. What a waste of breath this had been for the guy!

"*Well…*" I said, as if I were carefully considering the matter. Zack's dad was finally quiet. I could almost hear someone's heart beating like a drum machine on overdrive. "*Okay*. But let me patch you on through to my boss' voicemail. You can explain things to him."

"Oh, *thank you*," he said. "Thank you thank you thank y—" I put him on hold as I tried to figure out how to transfer him to the voicemail of the phone I was already using.

Zack blathered happy words at me as I walked him upstairs to the med room, but I wasn't listening. My mind kept going over the tone of desperation in his dad's voice. For all his success, he was powerless before the love that bonded him to a crackhead son. And, for all his riches, everything he held dear in the world had been at the mercy of some jerk-off slacker earning eight bucks an hour.

I managed to keep myself under control until Zack was safely medicated and in bed. Then I went back downstairs, put a Bach concerto on the stereo, sat in the dark, and laughed myself sick.

3:54am
WEIGHING SUICIDE VERSUS KILLING THE REST OF THE WORLD

I clicked the window closed on the geriatric porn site and tucked myself back into my pants. A hook shot missed my boss's trashcan, and the tissue lay soiled on his carpet. I use Gim's computer solely for porn 'cause checking my email means seeing rejection letters from other jobs I'd applied to. Rejection after rejection for the sort of jobs that I sweated through college for. The sort that don't involve fighting bums or handling other people's piss.

They're not available. The economy was crap. I was shit out of luck. There were no decent jobs. The only growth sector was the military and prisons. The American Dream had left to build sweatshops overseas.

I was about to look up another porn site, make a marathon of it, before I was struck by my own lack of interest. Watching other poor people do unpleasant things for money no longer struck me as amusing.

This meant jerking off on the job had *Officially* ceased to be entertaining (usually takes around 5 minutes, so I figure I earned about 67-cents per climax). My most reliable method of diversion had just failed me. Not a fucking clue how I was going to pass the time now.

All the counselors' offices had been searched from top to bottom months ago. No clients were around for me to torment. The Christers had taken to locking up their storage bins. I was in serious danger of becoming bored.

Somebody stop me before I go looking for new ways to amuse myself…

4:11am PSEUDOSPECIATION

I was tossing on the lobby's couch, pissed that I was at work and unable to sleep. A painful burning sensation in my mouth kept me awake. '*Strep throat*,' the clinic physician had said, but to me the little white bumps all over the inside of my mouth had looked a hell of a lot like herpes.

Dear fuck, I had worried a few days back as I'd shifted my gaze—mouth open with tongue hanging out—back and forth from the mirror to the pictures on the computer monitor. *It's herpes, all right! That's what I get for licking welfare vagina. The WASP-ish God of Propriety is punishing me for shagging outside of my social class!*

The doctor's assurances later at the community clinic were soothing on the paranoia. However, they did nothing to change how the little white bumps inside my mouth seemed to exist for no purpose other than throbbing with fiery pain. Not only did this fuck with my sleeping ability, but it also made eating solid foods downright impossible. That's why I'd subsisted on milk and Nyquil for three days. The Nyquil was finally cut out when I started excreting a runny shade of pink.

Still, I suppose it beat having herpes.

So, I had wandered out to our back lot at work, half-crazed after three days of constant pain. The air was still, muggy and unbelievably hot for the middle of the night. It smelled like microwaved armpits. Pasadena's a hazardous environment, unfit for human occupancy, even without all the airborne pollution.

A shape moving along the fence's perimeter caught my eye. It was a bum, of course. Long, ragged hair, dreadlocks that probably owed more to hygiene neglect than Rastafarian devotion. He had two army-surplus jackets that came to his knees, a bushy beard, and an erratic gait that told he was passing the night with a foreign substance or two in his veins.

Right near the gate he stopped and bent over. It looked like he was fiddling with the chain. "Keep moving," I said, not feeling like his variety of company.

He jumped back at the sound of my voice, his hands balled into fists.

"*Whatchu* say?" he yelled.

"Said *keep moving.*" I hated to repeat myself. Even talking was painful, thanks to those charming bumps on my tongue. Here I was, hurting myself for the sake of some fucking bum. "Nothin' for ya here, man."

His eyes got huge. "The *fuck?*" he shrieked. "The *FUCK?* Think you tell me what to do? *Fuck You!*"

The rest of us often forget that street people have their own sense of dignity.

Or maybe we just don't care.

"Ya heard me," I said. "Now get outta here."

The bum was livid. His eyes bugged big and saucer-shaped like he'd escaped from an anime asylum. "I tie my shoes where I wanna! Don't need yo fuckin' permission, *honky*!"

Was that all he had been doing? Maybe I had been mistaken. The strep and its attendant misery making me edgy.

"Oh…well, in that case, my mist—"

"Fuck *YOU*!" he shrieked, slamming himself up against the chain-link fence like a rabid dog. "Come out here, and I fuckin' kill ya! Come on! Fuckin' honky! Come on out!"

I watched him throw his entire body into the fence again and again, screaming and practically foaming at the mouth. Now *this* was entertainment. "*Fuck you fuckin' honky fuckin' goddamn kill you…*" And so on…

Not much to brag about in the vocabulary department, but he knew how to get his point across. "*Fuckin' muthafuckin' fuckin' honky-ass fuckin' honky goddamn fucker…*" Unfortunately, he was doing it loud enough to make me worry that he'd wake the clients. I didn't want to have to deal with those guys, too.

"Wait here," I told him. "I'll be right back. Don't go anywhere."

Back inside, I reached behind the Xmas tree in the lobby and grabbed the pepper-spray from my backpack. I had a simple plan that seemed utterly rational. I was going to go back outside, hose the bum down with the spray, and then bring something heavy with me to accept his invitation for a (somewhat unfair at that point) fight.

You'd expect that spending lots of time amongst the Down and Out would make one more compassionate towards them. Not really. What it will do is make you treat them like you would any other human being. Whether that means poorly or not is up to you.

No special treatment. Nor do you ignore them or act like they're invisible. Just treat them normal. Like anybody else.

If I was walking down the street and a random person became violently belligerent towards me, most likely macing-then-beating them is exactly what I'd do. I'm all about quick and easy solutions, these days.

(This job killed the pacifist in me.)

When I returned to the back lot my new pal had calmed down. He still clung to the fence, but all the fight was gone. The outburst had drained off his hate and anger. He was calm. Subdued.

The bum looked up like he was seeing me for the first time. Probably didn't even remember what had happened only a half-minute before. "Hey," he said. "Hey buddy. Hey…you got some food in there? Got something to eat?"

I smiled and sprayed him in the face.

Screaming, he fell off the fence and writhed on the ground, clawing at his eyes. Pepper spray hurts like a motherfucker. Burns the eyes and closes off the throat. My particular brand also leaves blue paint on your face. The bum shrieked his lungs empty before fighting for the breath to start screaming again. His legs kicked at the gravel. I stood behind the fence and watched my newfound diversion. *Kick, kick, shriek. Kick, kick, shriek.*

Kick, shriek, kick. Like the world's most painful dance routine. Fascinating. I watched him claw at his eyes. He convulsed in the gravel and screamed himself hoarse. *Fascinating*. Even louder than before, but still fascinating.

Unfortunately, it wasn't long before my own eyes started watering from the backdraft. I sprayed him once more for good luck before hurrying back inside.

4:39am
MY DAD, MY DEALER

Robert was giving me his Unified Theory of Everything: what the world's like, why it's like that, and why anybody who sees it differently is full of shit. He also discussed his plans to attend chef school. "Got me a second chance," Robert said. "And I'm gonna use it."

He's a likeable guy, so I lounged on the couch and pretended to listen.

The lobby was dark, lit only by the filtered glow of the streetlights. Watching the lights reflect on Robert's head made me wish I had somebody to snuggle with, cliché as that emotion may be. All I wanted was another warm body to crawl up on this ratty leather couch with me. Someone to hide under a blanket with me and watch the lightshow on Robert's head for hours. Just one person to snuggle with for the simple, and long missed, sake of human contact.

I would've asked Robert, but I didn't know how close-up I wanted to experience his spare-toothed grin. So, I just sat, nodded on occasion, and appreciated the fact that, after working at the rehab for several months, I had finally found the light switch for the lobby.

"Yeah," Robert said, "I wouldn't mind havin' me a son." He had five daughters, all grown, with four different women.

"Haven't you bred enough?" I mumbled, thinking, *let the non-crackheads have a shot at it, now*.

"Just a son," he repeated. "I'm a good daddy. Just a son."

"Weren't you just telling me what a deadbeat dad you were?" I asked, having caught a few bits of his rambling. "And you want *more* kids?"

Not that it's any of *my* business, but I had a definite desire not to be car-jacked by any of his offspring once they were grown-up and I was too old to fight back.

"Was in jail some," Robert conceded, "But that don't count. I take care of my business. I'd be out there at the Crack Corner, doin' my sellin', and somebody be like, '*Ain't that yo kid?*'"

I nodded, wondering what Take Your Daughter to Work Day was like for his children.

"...and my kid be all '*Daddy, I need twenty-bucks*,' and I whip out one for 'em right there on the spot!" Robert smiled at the memory with a close approximation of paternal pride.

I was torn between honesty about how under whelmed I was by this, or just telling Robert that the black community thanked him for providing such an endearing role model for his offspring. Since neither sounded like much of an option, I turned back to watching the lights dance on his scalp. "Now *that's* parenting," I sighed.

It's always easier to criticize than to try something yourself. Don't know about everybody else, but that's why I do it so often.

5:29am
BURNS SO QUICK AND IT MUST BE AMERICA

The anti-carcinogens in coffee transform into carcinogens in just fifteen minutes. I learned this at school, so it must be true.

Occasionally I drank a cup out of the batch meant for the junkies. Mixed it about a third coffee and two-thirds milk. Just enough to get a little boost without having to taste the shit. I always hated the flavor, and I distrusted the hell out of anything that society shoved down our throats in mass quantities. Especially something that's an addictive stimulant.

Besides, screw that pansy stuff! Why does the American workforce run on such a weak-ass stimulant? No wonder the economy was in the shitter. They should give everyone a bump of meth on the way to the office. Bet your ass we'd see some work getting done then! Chronic nosebleeds and weight loss would become acceptable side effects of earning your daily bread, just like caffeine headaches and nervous tension are now.

If they gave it to office workers, I bet we'd get a classier level of client here. More junior executives and high-priced lawyers rather than all these truck drivers and the unemployed. It made me wonder if those other folks would have as much trouble switching from their favorite stimulants to America's legal ones.

And, if our rulers legalized stuff like meth for productivity's sake, would it fuck us up as badly as the current, legal stimulants had?

Or, as Grant Morrison once put it: "*...like almost everyone else in western culture you're hopelessly addicted to refined sugar and caffeine. Both these drugs are high-level stimulants and here are some of the clinical symptoms of speed psychoses: '...user feels depressed, extremely anxious, irritable, hostile, alienated, fearful, confused, and paranoid.'*"

Yeah, that sounds familiar.

5:41am
A GENUINE FACE, BRACED FOR SURVIVAL

Seeing some of the junkies off to work in the morning was the second-greatest part of pulling an all-nighter. Being paid to sleep for most of the shift was number one, of course.

I don't know why, but there's just *something* about seeing the guys put their best junk-sick faces forward to struggle through yet another day. I mean, those fuckers don't just have to cope with crappy jobs like most people. Every minute of the day they're fighting the urge to run back to their dealer for another armful or a crack-rock or to just head down to the Quik-Stop for a cold one.

If that's not an effective way to make life a million times more difficult, I couldn't say what is. Maybe being crippled.

Despite this, the junkies come downstairs bright and early (the few with jobs, at least). They get their socially-approved drugs from me, then head on their way. I've noticed that if I watch the junkies as they walk onto the morning streets of Pasadena, I can catch a little spasm of fear crossing their faces. Some hide it better than others, but it happens to all of them. That quick look of '*aw, shit*' as they brace for their daily ass-kicking by the world.

They can't cope with life. Wouldn't be here if they could. Existence proved too much for them. It was Them versus Life, and, for every one of them, Life won hands down.

Yet they headed back out every goddamn day to go another ten rounds with the world. And having seen them straggle back in at the end of the day, I can say that the world always comes out on top. Still, they brace themselves, swallow down their fears, and fight like hell to make it through the day. Each and every day.

If I weren't so cynical, I'd almost find it inspiring.

7:05pm
THE FEMALE TERM FOR 'BOSS'

My heart skipped a beat when the phone rang. It had been quiet for hours, so a shrill noise exploding by my ear caught me off guard. Recovering quickly, I grabbed the phone and said, in a soft and courteous voice that was supposed to sound like Sean Connery, "*Christ in the Gutter and A New Start for Men*, how can I be of help to you?"

"THIS IS SELMA!" was screeched into my ear. Such a powerful, hateful voice. Fuck knows how she thought I could mistake her for anyone else. "I JUST DROVE BY AND TWO WINDOWS ARE OPEN UPSTAIRS." I automatically held the phone an extra six inches from my head. "IT'S THE SECOND AND THE THIRD FROM THE LEFT. AIR-CONDITIONING COSTS MONEY, AND THIS IS THE SECOND TIME THIS WEEK THAT—" My ear drums felt violated, like they had ended up on the wrong side of John Holmes anal-raping choir boys.

I cut her off. "I'll see to it," and set the phone back in its cradle. I glared at it for a while. *I trusted you, you fucking appliance; how could you do this to me?*

"Fuckin' bitch," I said, shaking my head. The living skeleton dressed in '80s denim looked up from doing crossword puzzles on the couch. Terry was using a pen, which meant that the crossword was officially ruined for all of the facility's late-risers.

"Selma called, huh?"

I rubbed at my ear. "Could you sense the evil coming over the phone lines?"

"*Naw*," said Terry. "I could hear the bitch from over here."

What Selma actually did around here, besides yell at anyone who got in her path, I really couldn't say. I avoided her too much to study her habits and behaviors. I guess that would make me a pretty lousy anthropologist.

Not that I paid too much attention to the less obnoxious, non-clergy folks around here. People came, people went, people suffered around me, and their one-dimensional selves didn't really make much of an impression anymore. They all just blurred into one big smear of frustration and failure. I wasn't even sure that I had Terry's name right. He looked to me like a dozens of other prematurely-aged, half-dead crackers I'd met here, all of them one stiff drink from sepsis and total organ failure.

"I mean, strike one for being a total bitch," I said to Terry. "Strike two for being a member of the fuckin' clergy, which means that she's trained to prey on fear and gullibility." It's never too early for a spot of character assassination.

Chewing on the end of the pen I'd lent him, Terry suggested, "And strike three for being so goddamn fat."

I had to disagree with him there. "Being fat doesn't make you an intrinsically bad person."

"Sure it does," Terry said. "Means you're getting more than your fair share."

I laughed. "What, you want 'er to share the wealth? Pass some of that lard around for the rest of us? Should she shed some pounds to give to those less blessed by gravity? You're like some weird mix of Marxist and aerobics instructor."

Terry put down the paper to better make his point. "It's like this," he said, "By eating so much stuff, she's stealing *your* potential to be fat, too. Just in case that had ever been a dream of yours."

Matter of fact..."Never considered that. Bitch really is the worst sort of a parasite."

And at that choice moment the '*Bitch*' in question waddled in from the back hallway. Terry tried to fold his scarecrow frame behind the newspaper.

The hell was she doin' here on a Saturday?

"THOSE WINDOWS BETTER BE CLOSED," she said.

Selma had a mean, bitter face. She looked like someone had ordained Jabba the Hutt and draped him in a gray wig and priestly robes. Hatred for everything around her radiated off Selma in waves, but besides that we didn't have too much in common. Her voice was loud and booming, yet still managed to maintain a nasal quality. If someone dragged their broken nails over a chalkboard while broadcasting through a jerry-rigged amplifier, it might approximate the aural torture that poured from Selma's mouth.

Obviously, I wasn't the lady's biggest fan. *Fuckin' clergy*. Anyone who flips out over petty shit gets tossed off my Xmas card list. Especially when they flip in my direction. I mean, it wasn't like my window-watching negligence was giving anyone childhood leukemia. The government wasn't jacking up the terrorist-threat level another color or two because our facility wasn't airtight. Easter would still arrive on time.

Over-reactive bitch. Or maybe I just hated middle-aged women. They're too old to be sexually appealing, and too young to feel grandmotherly affection towards me. No sucking my dick, no baking me cookies. What was the point to them, then?

I gave the idea of age-dependent misogyny another thought before filing it in the *Reject* pile with my old plan to market dually-packaged vodka and sleeping pills as Home Euthanasia Kits.

I eyed Selma for a second. Watched her huff and puff like the big bad wolf with a thyroid problem. “They’re not closed,” I said.

“WHAT?” she screeched. *Somebody would dare to not run cowering to do her will? Off with their head!*

She waddled over to the desk as Terry tried to make himself invisible on the couch. “WHY AREN’T THOSE WINDOWS CLOSED? YOU’RE COSTING US MONEY! WE’RE LOSING ENERGY AND *BLAH BLAH BLAH BLAH…*”

Tough as it may have been, I tuned her out. I could still hear her harpy screeches, still see her bulk resting against my desk, but she was now no more comprehensible to me than someone yodeling Hebrew. It’s a neat trick I picked up from all those Sundays wasted in church as a kid.

Keep yappin’, bitch, I smiled to myself as the spittle flew from her mouth. *Soon as the revolution comes, you and all your clergy buddies are goin’ up against the wall with the politicians and CEOs.*

I got a mental image of Selma flopping dead over the president’s corpse, causing organs and bile to be squished out like someone biting into an éclair. Thoughts like that kept me warm at night.

She hadn’t stopped yelling at me, so I calmly picked up the local section from the newspaper and scanned the front page. *Hmmm*, looked like another high-ozone day. Nice to know that just living in Pasadena was killing me. I contemplated whether the air inside or outside the rehab was worse. It seemed like I just couldn’t escape toxic environments.

“HEY! I’M TALKING TO YOU!”

I didn’t look up from the paper. Another double homicide on the south side. Burglary and rape in the suburbs. Radio conglomerate staged a pro-war rally in Houston. “No,” I said, “You were screeching *at* me. Once you feel like being civil, let me know.”

I gave her a quick glance with a raised eyebrow that said, *'Not used to being spoken to like that, are ya, bitch?'* Then went back to perusing the paper.

Hit and run by the Galleria. Child abducted in the Second Ward. And through it all, Selma sputtered and fumed. I thought her fat fucking face would explode with disbelief. Lard and eyeballs flying in every direction. "I'LL…I'LL SEE WHAT GIM HAS TO SAY ABOUT THIS!"

Ooh, a sale at Mervyns! "Hopefully he'll tell you to leave his employees the fuck alone."

She leaned in on the desk, two of her stomach rolls smothering the sign-out sheet. Her breath came heavy and labored, air sucked-into then blown-out of her mouth with maximum force. Being angry was apparently quite the exertion for Selma. I wondered if she ever stopped to think why she had gotten so upset in the first place, and was it really worth it? People so rarely do. We're all such miserable bastards that any excuse to vent our frustrations will suffice.

"YOU CAN…KISS…YOUR JOB…GOODBYE." Then she gave me an angry stare. Guess it was supposed to be threatening.

I looked up at her. Then, never breaking eye contact, I leaned over and licked the top of the desk. "That work for ya?" *You clergy fuck*!

Selma realized that I wasn't going to be as easily cowed as her homeless volunteers. She stormed off in a huff of heavy breathing and self-righteousness.

Terry peeked out from where he'd buried himself in the newspaper. "Is it safe to come out?" he asked.

I nodded.

He jumped up from his seat and walked over to me. "I gotta shake your hand," he said.

"For standing up to some fat, old lady?" I asked as we shook. "What a brave young warrior I am!"

“More than I’ve seen anyone else around here do,” Terry said. “Even Gim tip-toes around her.”

“They *do* own the place,” I pointed out. “The Christers ever get tired of us, y’all are out on your asses.”

Terry laughed and scratched at his beard. “Be funny if you just broke the camel’s back, there. Like, *that-bitch-sat-on-it* level of broken.”

“*Eh*,” I shrugged. “Wouldn’t be the first time my big mouth’s fucked things up for everybody. The economy being what it is, I’ll just take my degree to some other dead-end McJob.”

“Yeah, I know what that’s like,” Terry said.

I smiled up at him. “Oh, you partied your way through college and blew all your potential, too?” I should have been in grad school by this point. I should have had a real job earning real money. I should have been doing something with my life besides hanging around the wretched of the earth.

Terry walked back over to the couch and picked up his crossword puzzles. “Sort of,” he said. “The last part, at least. What the hell else are we all doing here?”

7:12am
THE SERIAL PROCESSING OF THE KLEENEX PEOPLE

“See that girl over there?” Tennil pointed out the front door. I ignored him. “Hey, Ray! *Ray*!”

I looked up like I was doing him a favor by responding. “What?”

“Come look at this girl, man!” I dragged myself from behind the desk.

He pointed across the street at a young girl limping past the old colonial mansion. She had a hooded jacket and Sesame Street backpack. Looked to be late teens, early twenties. "And?"

Tennil grabbed at himself, probably without noticing. "Me and JDZ and Robert had her suck our dicks yesterday," he said. There was pride in Tennil's voice. "And then JDZ fucked her. He says it was up the ass, but I dunno."

The girl walked with a careful step. Maybe JDZ really had. "Y'all get a group rate?" I asked.

"Bought her dinner," Tennil said. "*Taco Cabana*."

I wondered what had happened to the American dollar if three blowjobs and anal sex didn't rate anything more than a Black Bean Burrito with picante sauce. Maybe they'd had a coupon.

"Think Robert gave 'er a few bucks, too. Always supposed to tip for good service, right?" And then he laughed.

The girl turned in our direction, like she could hear the slander from the other side of the street. She started limping across the road towards the rehab.

"Hey, she's headed this way!" Tennil smiled. Christmas had apparently come early this year. "Maybe we can do 'er again! You wanna turn?"

I shuddered. "I wash my hands after I touch the same doorknob as you fuckers. No way I'm sharing dick-space with y'all." The girl limped through lane after lane of traffic, eyes on the pavement, not watching to see what might be about to run her over. It was like watching a suicidal game of *Frogger*.

"Yo' loss," Tennil said. "Man, we did her behind the YMCA. I got to go first, throat-fucked that bitch, then I came all over her top. Bitch never stopped complaining 'bout that. She was all mumblin', '*my shirt...fuckin' cum on my fuckin' sweater…*' while JDZ's all doin' her from behind."

Tennil reached down to adjust himself. “Like, when she wasn't crying.”

Nice. That was *my* spiritual affirmation for the day. Every shift I worked here made me fall in love with humanity all over again.

Tennil's anecdote also meant that none of these guys were going to have their lives made into movies. Two crackheads and a skuzzy Caucasian junkie taking turns with a young, weeping white girl wouldn't play too well in theaters across Midwestern America. Not without some moral tacked on to the end. Something to excuse all accidental erections that may have occurred during the viewing.

Or, maybe it would set box office records. Never underestimate the public's hunger for degradation. Christ knows we all cheer like hell when it's time to slaughter foreigners.

The girl climbed up the front steps. Slowly. Carefully.

“I got to feel on her titties,” Tennil said. “Play with 'em while she was suckin' me. They kinda saggy, but not bad.”

“Go away,” I told him.

Tennil stepped outside to meet the girl, the beaded cornrows swinging off the back of his head. She looked up at him, not a hint of recognition in her eyes. He talked at her for few minutes, acting friendly and touching her shoulder. The girl didn't back away from his physical closeness, but she didn't respond, either. Just stood there, letting her head drop to stare at the ground.

Seeing the girl up close changed my earlier estimation of her age. Her being over twenty was pretty unlikely, despite the worn look on her face. Resting on the girl's chest was a large metal cross. It was the Catholic variety, a crucifix, with Jesus' half-naked body still nailed to the cross in all His sexy glory.

The cross Tennil wore on the outside of his shirts had no Jesus. I wondered if he had enjoyed hosing genetic material all over his professed messiah. It's not every day that a guy gets to cum on his god.

I opened the door for Tennil to come back inside. "She hungry," he said. "It cool if I go get her a plate from breakfast?" I looked at the girl through the glass door. She was just sitting there, scratching at her leg. It was a mindless, repetitive movement. Fuck knows what she was coming down from.

"Sure," I said. Tennil ran off to the kitchen, probably dreaming of soiled sweaters and blowjobs to come. I stayed and watched the girl. In my mind, she took on three guys behind the local Y. In my mind, she had her Sweet Sixteen party and first day of school. In my mind, she was too drugged to even notice she was crying while JDZ rammed her from behind. In my mind, I wondered if there was another species I could go join.

You could bet she never planned on growing up to whore herself for fast food and a little drug money. Who would? Hell, I thought I'd grow up to be a cross between Han Solo and Jesus. Guess nobody got their wish.

Tennil returned with the food. I took it from him and headed outside, closing the door behind me so he couldn't follow. The girl looked up briefly and reached for the plate. "Here ya go," I said as I squatted down to hand it over. Tennil had forgotten utensils, but the girl didn't care. She dug into the powdered eggs and sausage with her fingers.

I straightened back up. "Don't worry," I told her, "This stuff's free of charge."

As usual, it was the wrong thing to say. She never stopped shoveling food into her mouth, just raised her eyes to glare like it had been me taking advantage of her last night. Me ramming her behind the Y. Me spraying cum all over her shirt.

Total distilled hatred.

It was the first and only expression I'd seen her make, and it was plenty.

I rushed back inside mumbling apologies.

7:18am
THE HEARTBREAK IS INTENTIONAL THE DISGUST COMES AS A HAPPY BONUS

Once we got to the eighth page of Solomon's meds in the Medicine Log, I gave a low whistle. Or tried to, at least. There are just some things in life that I'm no good at.

Like:

Feeling bad for people who repeatedly fuck up their own lives,

Solving for the third variable in geometric equations, and

Whistling.

Despite the signs posted everywhere about the times that meds are distributed, Solomon always caught me in the medicine room by pure accident. He'd waddle on past the open door going back to his room from breakfast and would give a start when he saw me in the med room. Like it was always a surprise to find me there.

Every goddamn time. Every goddamn day.

This day, however, was the first I'd ever seen Solomon without his headphones. He probably figured they were broke when the batteries ran down. The poor guy would now have to find another way to block out the world. I shuddered at the thought of his vulnerability.

"You givin' out them meds?" he asked. Same question as always.

"Sure am!" I grinned at him like a carnivore, engines revving on caffeine and other stimulants. My fingers fidgeted nervously with the zipper on my jacket, dragging it up-then-down its track. Up then down, up then down, up then down. "We got Vicodin at three apiece or four for ten, but today's big special is Rohypnol. It comes pre-crushed so it's that much easier to slip into that unattainable someone's martini."

He just looked at me. Small brown eyes almost swallowed by his fat black face.

Nobody home. Nobody ever going to be home.

"They work just as well in a 40oz," I offered.

"I come back later," he said finally.

"*No No Nooo*," I cried. "I've been up here three minutes without anybody stoppin' by. Two minutes from now my ass is *Gone*. Get your meds now so I can get out of this cramped little room and go home."

At the end of every night shift I was supposed to sit in the med room from about seven-fifteen to seven-thirty, waiting for some of the junkies to stop by for their morning fix of socially approved drugs. Regulations do say that we're supposed to be med-fetchin' from seven to half-past, but fifteen minutes seemed like a big enough waste. So, I was usually in there about five minutes at most.

The med room (or Tech Office, as it was officially known for no other reason than to make us feel better about sitting in a goddamn closet) was filled with cleaning supplies, linens, and a two-door chest containing two locks and the clients' meds.

I handed Solomon the key ring and its cudgel attachment. Considering how much I'd grown to enjoy tormenting the clients, handing them my only form of defense might not have been the greatest idea in the world. But, it was either that or actually get down from the desk and take the two steps on over to the med cabinet to unlock the goddamn thing myself.

Taking the key ring by the proffered (and correct) key, Solomon fiddled with the lock for a while before managing to outsmart it. He then reached into the cabinet and pulled out a small garbage bag filled with his meds. Typically, the clients have small plastic trays for that sort of thing, but it was apparent that no regular tray would hold all of Solomon's massive med collection. The man needed the *Magnum* size.

"Takin' the usual?" I asked him. Each different med that a client took had its own sheet in the med book. On that sheet we recorded: the amount of that medicine they were taking; the amount of that med they had before taking any; and the amount of that med remaining now that they just took a dose.

Each different medication got its own sheet. Solomon had a total of sixteen sheets.

I made sure to take the key cudgel back from Solly. "Takes a lot to keep your ass alive," I commented.

Behind that observation, especially at the end of a double shift, is the uncharitable question of whether it was worth it. Pills, after all, cost money.

"You totally win the Walking Pharmacy award for this month," I told him. "Congrats."

Solomon didn't say anything for a while. Just kept fishing pill bottles out of his sack like some pharmaceutical Santa Claus. Then, "Just 'tween you and me, I got the AIDS."

Yeah, I already knew that. Solly had AIDS. Solly was going to die. He wasn't the first client we'd had here like that. Get enough intravenous drug users in one place and chances are that some of them will have something nicely lethal. Hepatitis C was way more popular, but I'd run across enough AIDS cases since I'd been here to no longer feel shocked for the guys with that particular death sentence.

And on the 8th Day, God said, *Let life be majorly fucking unfair*, and it was.

And it was good.

Good for those of us who could stand on the sidelines joking about it, at least.

Laugh, and the world laughs with you. Cry out in pain, and everyone's going to chuckle at your sorry ass. We, as a garbage species, get our yuks where we can.

"So…"

We cohabitated in silence for a while. Solomon unscrewed the top to one med bottle after another, and I perched on the desk documenting his med intake. Perhaps it was the last Adderall I'd munched to see me through to the end of the shift, perhaps it was my desire to—*naw*, it was the Adderall.

Had to be.

What else could have squeezed out my next line?

"So…" I said. "How's that *imminent death* thing treatin' ya?"

Solomon didn't even look up at me. Just kept poppin' pill after pill into his pudgy little mouth.

"How 'bout I didn't hear that," he said. "'Cause I don't take no shit off white boys."

I pretended to consider his offer for a while.

“*Deal,*” I said as cheerfully as possible, while a shrill voice in my head starting screaming. The voice sounded exactly like all the people I’d grown up around in the little town of Goatscrew, TX. It pops up these days whenever I’m at work and in desperate need of sleep. Or just at work. The voice screamed at me: ‘*You’re not takin’ that shit from some fat little nigger, are ya?*’

I’m shit-scared that one day the voice, and that word it uses, will spew right out of my mouth. Not only will this probably get me killed, but…but…hell, I’ll admit; it’s just the ensuing violence that I’d be worried about. Considering how frequently I get accused of racial bias here, actually saying ‘*nigger*’ would probably confirm the suspicions that I was just another white devil out to pick on people for being better tanned than me.

It was a pity for so many of the guys to waste their energy on persecution complexes. Still, I guess it was easier than the possibility that maybe the world really had followed Dr. King’s advice and judged them ‘*not by the color of their skin, but on the content of their character*’…and still decided that they sucked.

“Fuckin’ white folk,” Solomon said, slowly shaking his head at the pity of it all.

I nodded in agreement. “I hear ya.”

Solly gave a funny look like he wasn’t sure how to take me, then settled on shoving the rest of the pills into his mouth at once and waddling off.

‘*Nigger,*’ said the voice in my head.

Everything you’ve ever read about the South being full of bigots and race-baiters is true. Same goes for the North and the east and west coasts, too. They just don’t get as much publicity about it. Human beings seem to have an inborn need to hate someone or something *en masse.* If us Texas-brand honkies didn’t have the niggers and the spics to hate, and if the niggers and spics didn’t have us, we'd all pitch in to find somebody else. That's what happens in a society where most people's hobbies consist of watching TV and loathing anyone who's a little bit different.

Beats stamp collecting, I guess.

Down the hall I could hear Solomon slam the door to his room. He could block himself off from the rest of the world in there till he either got new batteries for his headphones or his immune system imploded.

I had the strangest urge to chase him down the hallway. The feeling erupted from nowhere. I wanted to burst into Solly's room and say that I was sorry. Just *sorry sorry sorry*. Not for my attempts at levity that used his impending death as fuel for the comedy fire, but sorry for the shit world that we both inhabited.

Not an apology, 'cause it wasn't my fault that we all suffered. Not my fault, not Solly's fault, probably not anyone's fault. It's time like this that'd it be real handy to have a god to blame.

I just had the need to tell Solly that I was sorry we lived in a world where people died horribly, died slowly. Sorry that even if Solly managed to stay off crack he'd still, at best, waste away in some AIDS hospice. Sorry that not only did people die horribly, die slowly, they also died horribly and slowly frequently enough that the survivors had to swallow their fears and give an uneasy chuckle while waiting for their own grisly demise. Sorry that we lived in a world bad enough for gallows humor to even be considered a coping option.

Then the urge passed, as quickly as it had come. I found myself staring at Solly's bag of meds, wondering where that little burst of compassion had come from. Maybe it was something I'd eaten, like all those uppers.

Walking Solly's meds back to the med locker, I gave a heavy sigh. The Adderall I'd munched was apparently wearing off. Goddamn legal pharmaceuticals. The high lasted too long for me to bother taking another. Not so close to the end of a shift. Crap. I was fixing to crash, and it wouldn't be pleasant.

God, I needed a drink.

7:22am
GOD LOVES HIS CHILDREN

When Robert's throat cancer came back, it took two months to kill him. One to realize just how bad he was feeling. One more to strain for his last breath in a community hospice. Scared and sharing a room with three other dying strangers, no one went to see him.

The last time I saw Robert was three months, one week, and four days ago. He had stopped by the facility on the way to his morning classes at cooking school. He was halfway through the semester.

You wouldn't believe the shit that go into a goddamn soup, he told me. Robert was keeping his head shaved, even though the hair had started to grow back once his chemo ended. He had decided it looked better that way. I agreed.

Once he was done with cooking school, Robert would go intern at a restaurant.

I gonna be pullin' down some big money, he'd said. *Good chef can make twenty or thirty bucks an hour.*

Not bad, I'd told him. *I'm gonna have to start coming to you for money.*

You know I give it to you, he had said.

I know, man.

"You know his cancer had to come back at some point," Todd told me. "That's what *remission* means."

"You're right," I said.

"Guess his momma changed her mind about healing 'im," Jack shrugged. "That's why they don't let dead bitches be doctors."

"You're right," I said.

"At least it was quick," Gim said. "It's not like he lingered in the hospital for months."

"You're right," I said.

I got three sisters and they all ministers, Robert told me one time. *Ya know, Ray, I the only fuck-up in my family.*

Got three sisters, too, I'd replied. *And I think you're okay.*

He had smiled his big, goofy smile, teeth missing in front. *Thanks, Ray,* he'd said. *That mean a lot to me.*

I had smiled right back.

I know, man.

7:27am
EVERYONE GETS THE LIFE THEY DESERVE
EVERYONE GETS THE LOVE THEY DESERVE

Almost halfway through the fifteenth hour of a sixteen-hour shift, and I was getting twitchy. Yours truly had been at the rehab since the previous afternoon. I saw the day turn into night, and then back into day, without leaving the diseased confines of my workplace.

I watched the junkies. Watched the crackheads. Watched the clock. Arrived drunk. Sobered up. Suffered though a hangover.

Not a happy camper.

It was in this miserable state that I had to turn away one homeless person after another. The past few hours had seen a large number of homelies seeking entrance to the building. Much more than usual, and probably because it was so goddamn cold outside. No one who came ringing the bell or banging on the door (which killed my poor head) asked for the usual things. No begging for spare change or sandwiches or to use the bathroom. They all just wanted in. Wanted to get the hell out of the cold.

I couldn't blame them. I was inside the building and still had my leather jacket zipped up tight. It had to be freezing as all hell outside. The wind was blowing knives down the street, and it rained off and on. No one would want to be out in weather like that. Not me. Not the bums. Not anybody without a radiator shoved down their pants.

So, they all wanted inside. Predictably, I wasn't as hot for the idea. For them, getting inside the building represented a temporary end to their suffering. For me, it represented nothing but hassles. They wouldn't have to worry about freezing or catching pneumonia. I'd have to worry about them going where they shouldn't, getting into things they shouldn't. The homeless aren't housebroken. So, I decided they could stay out in the cold.

I made the decision. They could live with the consequences.

My lack of charity got the usual angry responses. The last three bums I told this to all responded with a variation of the last guy's line. To quote: "I comin' back, and I killin' that white motherfucker!"

He shouted this to two other bums I had turned away at the door. They had also issued threats against my life when informed that they could work on their frostbite for all I cared. In response to the last guy's declaration, they shouted a unanimous agreement. Then, they went on to discuss killing me at some length. I could hear them all through the glass front of the building. They sat on the front steps, waiting for me to get off work, and discussed killing me.

Resolved: That the honky should die as painfully as possible.

For: 3

Against: 1 (*me*, of course)

Who says democracy doesn't work?

"We oughtta *kill* that white motherfucker," I could hear them saying.

On a normal day I would have laughed this off. I've had my life threatened at work so often that I barely noticed it anymore. Part of the job. No one had killed me yet, so no biggie.

I told myself that bums getting upset was an understandable thing. They had nothing, led dangerous and desperate lives, and were usually some combination of crazy and drugged. Being given another reminder of how little the rest of the world cared about their well-being wasn't going to make them any happier.

"We oughtta *kill* that white motherfucker."

Understandable.

"We oughtta *kill* that white motherfucker."

Well, *typically* understandable. It suddenly became the Breaking Point.

I was tired, miserable, wanted to go home, and was *livid* at being threatened by people associated with a business that I didn't even work for. I was pissed at the Christers for running a ministry that lured the homeless to where I had to deal with them. I was pissed at the bums for threatening my life day after day. I was pissed at humanity for not committing mass suicide after I blew out the candles on my last birthday cake.

I was pissed, and I was going to do something about it.

"We oughtta *kill* that white motherfucker!"

I stalked into the kitchen, grabbed the biggest knife I could find, walked back to the lobby, kicked open the front door, and screamed, "*WHO'S* GONNA KILL THE WHITE MOTHERFUCKER?"

This was me waving a butcher knife at three bums. This was me flipping out at work. This was me menacing the downtrodden and desperate. This was me hoping that somebody rushed me so I could hack them open. This was everything horrible about the job having finally eaten my soul.

This was why you shouldn't fuck with me when I'm hungover.

"*WHO'S* GONNA KILL THE WHITE MOTHERFUCKER?"

The bums screamed and bolted. All three put as much distance as possible, as quickly as possible, between themselves and the bully at the door.

I'd never thought it possible to run so fast wearing so many overcoats. The bums shoved and trampled each other. They scrambled like hell off the porch and down the sidewalk. If someone held a Street Olympics (like the Special Olympics, but not as depressing), these guys would be the ones with cereal endorsements. They ran and tripped and ran and stumbled and kept running. One tried to push his shopping cart with him, but when it tumped into the street he left it and kept running. All his worldly possessions, dumped in the gutter, soaking up rainwater.

I watched them haul ass around the corner and considered laughing for a second, but it passed.

7:28pm
THE GOD WHO FAILED BUT TRIED, TRIED AGAIN

I was adjusting my backpack for the ride home when the doorbell rang. Being on my way out, I clicked the door unlocked. I would be gone in seconds, so it didn't matter to me who got in here. They would very quickly become someone else's problem.

The door was pushed open. In walked the most destitute human being I had ever seen. That is, *if* the shambling wreck twitching his way towards me even qualified for the title. His hair was falling out in patches, he was barefoot, there were running sores on his arms and face, his left eye wouldn't stop blinking, and the torn t-shirt he wore was smeared with foreign substances.

The worst part was, I kind of recognized the guy.

No way his wife was going to take him back now.

"H-hey there, Ray. How you doin'?" He smiled at me. There's no way that a homeless crack addict can be anything but repulsive, so fuck knows why he was bothering to try.

I moved my backpack off the desk and lowered myself into the seat. My Sadist-sense was screaming like a boiled porpoise. This was going to be entertaining.

"*Reverend* Leroy!"

“Hi,” said Corey.

I smiled at him. “I’d ask how ya been, but it’s pretty apparent.”

“Yeah,” he said, ducking his head a little, “I been better, but—”

“But—*what*?” I interrupted. “Can’t imagine any modifier drastic enough to alter your situation. Like, you’re a homeless crack addict, *but* you finally got that online degree you’ve been after. Or maybe you’re looking like hell these days, *but* Universal Studios finally bought your first screenplay…”

Corey just stared at me. His eye never stopped blinking, but the rest of him went slack. “What?”

I sighed, then cut to the chase. “Well, it’s nice to see you went back to your real god,” I said. “That *Jesus* shit got really old, really quick.”

His face flashed anger, but it was quickly smoothed back down into a half-hearted smile. Guy even tried a little chuckle to brush over my viciousness.

Pathetic.

One hand scratching at his muck-smeared T-shirt, he whined, “Now, I dunno ’bout that. I’m still filled with the love of Christ. He never leave—”

I cut him off before he could spew any more self-denial. “*Bullshit*,” I said. “You were born a crack worshipper, and you’ll fucking die one. *That*…is your god.”

He looked down at the floor and mumbled something I couldn’t hear. The human spirit is never so broken that it can’t be stomped into a few more pieces.

“Now, what did you want?”

“What?” Corey looked back up.

“*You’re* the one who came *here*,” I said. “Unless it was to show off how well you’re doing, I’m guessin’ you want something.”

I had lost ten bucks on the guy. The obnoxiously religious never last too long before they're sucking the pipe again, but *this* Reverend Leroy had relapsed and disappeared two weeks quicker than I had bet my money on. Jack had called him almost to the day.

"I…" it seemed to get stuck in his throat.

"You…*what*?"

The Reverend wiped at his greasy face a few times in what could have been shame. "I need a few bucks, man. Just a few. I gotta have—just a few dollars."

I felt the need to make him spell it out. "And?"

He glared at me. "Could I…please have…you got just a buck or two, man?" He shifted from angry to pathetic at warp speed. "I'm *really* hurtin'."

I looked him up and down. "I believe ya."

"Can you help me, *please*?"

I glanced past him at the few other homelies wandering around the lobby. Reverend Leroy was worse off than all of them. No way in hell his wife was *ever* taking him back now.

"*Well*…" I glanced down the back hallway, making sure no one important would catch what I was about to pull. "Ya know that you're not supposed to come beggin' around here, but…" I reached into my pocket and pulled out my wallet. A dollar was extracted from it. "I just might have something for you."

His face lit up. "Oh, *bless ya*, Ray. Thank you. Bless you. Thank—"

"I got somethin' for ya…if *you* can do somethin' for me."

The Reverend looked unsure. "Uh…sure, Ray. Whatcha need?"

I had a need, all right. Not for anything material, though. I needed something that only The Reverend, that only *It*, could give me. Something that I never knew I needed till I worked here. Something that I never would've admitted to needing before I worked here.

"I just want you to say, and I want to hear it nice and clear," this was gonna be good, "…*Fuck Jesus*."

The Reverend's eyes bulged. It put its hands up like I had taken a swing at it. "*What*?"

"You heard me."

I think, in that moment, my own soul should have gone belly-up and cried uncle.

But, of course, I don't believe in the soul.

"C'mon," I said, "Mr. Dollar wants to hear you say it…*Fuck Jesus*."

"I can't…I…I can't do…you know I…*c'mon*, Ray! You kiddin', right?"

Not smiling, I slowly shook my head from side to side. The dollar was waved in the air.

The Reverend's gaze followed the dollar. "*Raaaay*, that ain't right, man! That ain't right! You can't do that to a brother!"

"I'm not," I said, still not smiling. "I'm doing it to *you*. And it's nothing worse than what you've done to yourself. I'm just making you chose, one more time, between your gods. Now who's it gonna be? C'mon, *Reverend*. Rock or the cross? Crack or the Christ? *Whoooo's* it gonna be?"

The Reverend squeezed its eyes shut. It grimaced. Then he opened them back up and said, "No thanks, Ray. You can keep your dollar. I'll keep my *Jesus*." His eyes were bright, probably for the first time in weeks, and he smiled with pride.

Still, Corey didn't leave. Just stood there in front of the desk. It's people's body language that gives them away every time.

"Fair enough," I shrugged, and laid the dollar on the desk. The Reverend's gaze never left it. "But what we have here is…" I reached into my wallet for a few more bills. "*Nine* more dollars to join up with the first."

I placed them on the desk with the other dollar. Not close enough for The Reverend to reach out and grab them. I knew it'd do that if given the chance. *New Start Rule #1*, and all. "You're halfway to a pretty fat rock with ten bucks."

"*C'mon*, Ray."

"Choice is yours, man."

"Ray, this ain't cool!" Its voice broke; its face scrunched up. Homeboy looked on the verge of crying.

"Ten dollars," I repeated. "Easiest thing in the world. If you're gonna self-destruct, ya might as well make it entertaining."

I fanned myself with the money. "C'mon, Rev.! *Fuck* that *Jesus*!"

"*C'mon!*"

I saw his eyes begin to mist. You never sink so low that there's not some new bottom to hit.

"So…what's it gonna be?"

"*Raaaaaay*!" The tears started to flow. "I'm hurtin' so bad, man!" The Reverend's entire body trembled, and the snot ran from its nose just as fast as the tears leaked from its eyes.

I rolled my eyes. "And I'm startin' to get bored here, *you junkie shit!*"

There is no depth that people won't sink to. Nothing that they won't do. No excuse that they won't make for their own failings. I'd seen it all and heard it all over the past year, and I was so sick of human weakness. So sick of our excuses. So *goddamn sick* of the disgusting, hopeless world we lived in.

"What's it gonna be, bitch?"

So sick of it.

"Come on, *Reverend*!"

So sick of it all, that what could I do but embrace it with open arms?

"What's it gonna be?"

Later, still enveloped in post-orgasmic bliss, I clicked the door button to let Toni into the building.

"Hey, Ray baby!" he called to me.

Feet up on the desk, I gave him a casual salute. "Hey, there."

Toni dropped his backpack behind the desk and gave me a friendly hug. I actually hugged him back. I felt horribly radiant.

He patted me on the feet, but I couldn't be bothered to take them off the desk. Not any more than I could take the smile from off my face.

"What are you so happy about?" Toni asked. "You're all Mr. Smiley over there."

I gave a little shrug. "It's a horrible world, man." I tossed a wink in his direction. "Proud to be a part of it."

7:33am
ANYONE WHO LETS LIFE BEAT THEM DOWN
DIDN'T DESERVE HAPPINESS IN THE FIRST PLACE

It was finally cold in Pasadena. Something like 30-ish degrees outside, or so the junkies told me. It was too bad that I hadn't thought to bring my jacket the previous night, but on the upside, all the mosquitoes would finally be dying off. I almost wished that the change in weather could do the same for the other parasites around here. But hell, why waste energy on spite?

There was still a little time left to the shift, but I was leaving anyways. My replacement hadn't shown up, Gim wasn't here, but that didn't matter. Enough was enough.

It was time to pack up my stuff and write the same bullshit as every day on the shift report:

'*Made rounds every hour*.'

'*Nothing to report*.'

A new sheet of paper for each shift report. Trees died for this.

Both written assertions were lies. Naturally. I had been upstairs a total of once the entire eight-hour shift, and plenty of stuff had happened—everything from bum fights to relapses—but I just didn't feel like taking the time to record it.

Todd asked if I was really going to bike home in the cold. East Texans are total pansies when it comes to low temperatures. "Wish I could just burrow on home," I said. "But I don't think that's going to happen."

Being about to leave work and its few responsibilities, I disabled the lock on the front door. A horde of homelies rushed into the building. Now that I wasn't going to have to deal with them, they were welcome to come in out of the cold. This would be great news to the ones who had been huddled up against the building all night.

Their noxious scent trailed after them and made itself comfortable in the lobby. The first familiar waft of stale sweat, piss, old beer and vomit smashed me in the nose. I packed quicker. The Methodists were going to be pissed that the homelies had gotten into the building so far ahead of schedule…and that was kind of the point.

The floodgates were opened, and in flowed the tides of human refuse. I instantly dubbed it the best idea I'd had all shift.

Fending off the usual demands for my spare change (*zakat* delays the inevitable), I slung my backpack over my shoulders and cinched the straps. The backpack was heavier than when I had arrived. About three rolls of toilet paper, a stapler, and a gallon of milk heavier. I fetched my bike and rolled it out to the lobby.

Todd was by the front desk, talking with a homeless women. She had a pointy nose, warty face, and long, bony fingers coupled with a shriek of a voice. The woman was tailor-made for children's nightmares. And if her looks weren't enough, the sharp, overpowering stench of rank cunt would do the trick.

Her: "My husband's in…my husband's in jail. You got a quarter?"

Todd: "Actually, I've got two dollars for you. You're going to use them to take care of yourself, right?"

Her: "My husband's in jail. I need some paper. He broke his ribs. Can you get me paper?"

Todd: "I'll see what I can do. Just make sure you stay warm out there, okay?"

Her: "Why don't you—my husband in...*you* can keep me warm."

Todd: "What?"

Her: "Why don't *you* keep me warm?"

Todd: "*Whoa*…ummm...hey, Ray…in the mood for an early birthday present?"

I shook my head as I wheeled past them towards the door.

"Sure I've done worse," was called back, "But not this sober."

The door was kicked open, and I escaped into the light.

7:47am
EPILOGUE:
THE REAL PAYCHECK AT THE END OF A SHIFT

I kick off my shoes and start stripping the moment I walk in my apartment. My shirt, shorts, boxers and socks are tossed to the floor. I'm so grateful there's a place on this madhouse of a planet where I don't have to drape myself in a bunch of ridiculous fabrics.

The rehab's stench still clings to me, but I've learned that not even bathing gets rid of it entirely. It's just something you adjust to.

Martini ingredients and a Valium wait for me in the kitchen pantry. They counteract the coffee on the days when I've had some. When I haven't, they just make me feel better.

I mix the drink, drop in the pill, and slam it while heading for the bedroom.

Then, an urge hits, and I go back for another drink. This, too, is downed quickly. Then I make myself a third, with half of a second pill, just to be on the safe side. With that polished off, I head back to the bedroom.

Feelin' tired, Ray? asks a little voice in my head.

Mmm-hmmm, I respond—in my head, of course; otherwise I'd be crazy.

My bedroom door is swung open. *Well then*, the voice says, *Everyday's your birthday, man. Here ya go*.

And curled up in the bed, beatific from the sunlight sneaking around the edge of the blinds, is my girlfriend. Short hair tousled like Medusa gone butch, stout and dark figure, clad only in a pair of large gray panties. She doesn't respond to my entrance, just lays there. Just keeps on breathing in and breathing out like there was nothing else in the world that would ever need to be done.

One of the more emotionally satisfying feelings is coming home to find somebody waiting for you in bed (as long as you know them and/or they're not armed). It's like being granted an official pardon for all the unpleasant shit you've done or had done to you throughout the day. Like God winked down from his gold-plated throne and let you into that special preview of heaven normally reserved for the faithful. Like all the suffering in life suddenly became extraneous and unimportant, and how can anyone really be pessimistic when the world has such wonderful gifts in it?

There's someone; they're in your bed; they're in some stage of undress; they're waiting for you.

Consider yourself forgiven and absolved.

I lift the edge of the sheets and slide in next to her, matching tabs and slots, recesses and protrusions, until we've got a perfect spoon going. She still isn't awake. People never look so immaculate as when they're asleep. Perhaps it says something about us as a species that we never shine with such beauty—all the hate, worry, and pettiness melted away—as when we're unconscious and drooling on ourselves, but *whatever*.

My girlfriend reaches over to pull my arm tight around her, presses her back against me. All this without waking up.

Let sleeping girlfriends lie, the saying goes, but I'm feeling selfish. I kiss a line down her back, from the shoulder in. This finally wakes her.

She turns her head to smile at me. "Hey, baby," I say gently.

"*Hey*," she breathes back at me. Her hair falls in her eyes and she wipes it away with the back of her hand. I interlace my fingers with hers and give them a light squeeze.

"Missed you at work," I say, kissing her hand.

"*Mumble, mumble* you, too," she says.

I prop myself up on an elbow and give her a quick kiss and as big of a hug as I can. "Sorry...morning breath," she says. Yeah, she's got one hellacious case of it (and I taste like martini), but at this point it's just another beautiful part of her that contributes to the beautiful whole.

Of course, anyone's attractive when you're about to shove yourself up 'em.

"I love you," I say, as I move myself into a straddling position. She smiles up at me, all adoration and trust. I reach for the bedside lube. It's a decent substitute for foreplay. "I really do."

She says she loves me back, and I can't stop smiling. Because I'm about to get laid, and because as much as I tell my girlfriend about my job, I've never told her about *New Start Rule #1*.

FINIS

(*bitches!*)

IF THIS WAS AT THE START OF THE BOOK, YOU COULD'VE SAVED YOURSELF A LOT OF READING

"It is not true that suffering ennobles the spirit; happiness does that sometimes, but suffering for the most part makes men mean and vindictive."
–Maugham, The Moon and Sixpence (*I think*; *you fucking look it up*!)

"A wretched soul bruised with adversity,
We bid be quiet when we hear it cry;
But were we ourselves burdened with like weight of pain,
As much, or more, would we ourselves complain."
--Shakespeare, *The Comedy of Errors* (2.1.35)

"There's so much suffering in the world that we'd be stupid *not* to find it funny."
--Ray, talking to himself, *again*

ACKNOWLEDGEMENTS

Despite the heavy atmosphere of misogyny in these halfway stories, this book wouldn't have been possible without the support and help of several wonderful women. Thanks go to Kiwi, Ariel, Marie, Sar, Rame, Karen, Ellen, Leeann. Thanks to Anjuli for bullying me into doing this stupid revision, then acting like it's my fault for being unable to say '*no*' to a beautiful woman.

Thanks also to Greg, who taught me the true meaning of Easter.

And I'd be a real shit if I didn't mention my folks (only half-female). They always went above and beyond their biological duties for me, so the complete fuck-up I am is entirely my fault and none of theirs.

<u>UNA DEDICATORIA</u>

Este libro es para mi familia, con gratitude y disculpas.

www.ingramcontent.com/pod-product-compliance
Lightning Source LLC
Chambersburg PA
CBHW081128020726
47505CB00010B/2274

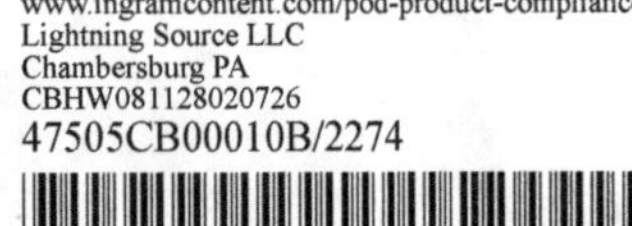

روایتی از ادبیات فارسی در تبعید

(۱۳۵۷ - ۱۳۹۲)

ملیحه تیره‌گُل

جلد اول

کیستیِ ما

نشر آفتاب

ناشر سانسور شده‌ها، نشر بی سانسور

info@aftab.pub

www.aftab.pub

برای همسفر زندگی‌ام
دکتر عزیز عطایی

There is no gate، no lock، no bolt that you can set upon the freedom of my mind.

(Virginia Woolf، A Room of One's Own)

در وُ دروازه وُ قفل وُ بندِ تو نمی‌تواند آزادی‌ی اندیشه‌ی مرا مهار کند.
در نهان‌گاهِ فرهنگی‌ی من، اما،
در وُ دروازه وُ قفل وُ بند،
آنی‌ست «که با چراغ می‌آید»

(ملیحه تیره‌گل)

[...] فقط می ترسم که فردا بمیرم
و هنوز خودم را نشناخته باشم.

(صادق هدایت، بوف کور)

شناسنامه‌ی کتاب

نام کتاب: **روایتی از ادبیات فارسی در تبعید (۱۳۹۲ - ۱۳۵۷)**
نوع ادبی: **پژوهش**
نویسنده: **ملیحه تیره‌گل**
جلد اول: **کیستیِ ما**
نوبت چاپ: **چاپ اول / ۱۳۹۸ / ۲۰۲۰**
صفحه‌آرایی: **عزیز عطایی / مهتاب محمدی**
طرح روی جلد: **عزیز عطایی**
اجرای طرح: **نادیا ویشنوسکا**
ناشر: **نشر آفتاب**
شابک: **۶-۹۲۴-۶۷۸۱۴-۱-۹۷۸**

Love read the name of this book before I had written a sentence.

(Ovid)[1]

در روزهای «نیمه ابری»ی این ساحلِ دور
در لحظه‌های خیزش یا فروکشِ خورشید
- که ابرها بُعد می‌گیرند-
شکل تو را می‌جویم
شکل تو را می‌بینم
بانوی فیروزه‌تاجِ فیروزه‌دامنِ من!
و هر بار، هر بار،
از خودم می‌پرسم:
این چشمه‌ی عشق
از کجای آن نقشه می‌خیزد؟
این جاری‌ی حرف
به کجای آن نقشه می‌ریزد؟

(ملیحه تیره گل)

---

۱ Publius Ovidius Naso متخلص به «Ovid»، شاعر رُمی (۴۳ پیش از میلاد تا ۱۸ بعد از میلاد).

فهرست جلد اول
کیستی‌ی ما

عنوان	صفحه
سپاسگزاری	۷
پیش گفتار مجموعه	۹
مقدمه	۱۹
فصل اول:	
سازه‌های بنیادین تاریخی- فرهنگی: مقدمه	۲۵
پیشینه‌ی کانون «ما» (ایران)	۲۸
فصل دوم:	
انقلاب‌های ناتمام ایران	۸۷
انقلاب مشروطه	۹۱
رضاشاه پهلوی	۱۲۰
محمدرضا شاه پهلوی	۱۳۵
جمع‌بندی	۳۲۱
نامنامه	۳۲۵

سپاس‌گزاری

در درجه‌ی نخست، مراتب سپاس‌گزاری‌ی خود را به ناشرانی که «فراخوان» مرا- در مورد گردآوری‌ی مأخذ- در نشریه‌ی خود منتشر کردند، تقدیم می‌دارم:

- مجید روشنگر، بنیادگذار و ویراستار نشریه‌ی «بررسی‌ی کتاب»، لس‌انجلس.
- حسن زرهی، مدیر، و نسرین الماسی، سردبیر نشریه‌ی «شهروند»، کانادا.
- میرزاآقا عسگری، سردبیر نشریه‌ی الکترونیکی‌ی «ادبیات و فرهنگ»، آلمان.
- فرهنگ فرهی، سردبیر بخش ادبی/ هنری در نشریه‌ی «جوانان»، لس‌انجلس.
- پرویز قلیچخانی، مدیر، و نجمه موسوی، سردبیر نشریه‌ی «آرش»، پاریس.
- تقی مختار، مدیر و سردبیر نشریه‌ی «ایرانیان»، واشنگتن دی.سی.
- مرتضا میرآفتابی، مدیر و ناشر نشریه‌ی «سیمرغ»، کالیفرنیای جنوبی.

فهرستِ نام نویسندگان و ناشرانی که در درازنای سه دهه‌ی گذشته، بی‌هیچ چشمداشتی، برای من کتاب و نشریه فرستاده‌اند، آن چنان درازدامن است که در این مختصر نمی‌گنجد؛ اما با کمال شرمندگی از غیبت نامشان، سپاس‌گزاری‌ی خود را به یک یک آن‌ها معروض می‌دارم. در مورد تازه‌های نشر فارسی، از ناصر پاکدامن، منصور خاکسار، پیرایه خلیلی، خسرو دوامی، لاله قهرمان، رضا گوهرزاد، ژیلا میرافشار، مهرنوش مزارعی، ن. ناجی، سهیلا ناجی، رباب محب، و شاداب وجدی تشکر می‌کنم. از نویسندگانی که با فرستادن «لینکِ» تارنماها مرا در جریان رویدادها، کتاب‌ها، و مقاله‌های مربوط به ایران گذاشته‌اند، از جمله، الهه امانی، گلرخ جهانگیری، خسرودوامی، منیره کاظمی، محمود صفریان، الهام قیطانچی، سهیلا ناجی، ن. ناجی، و شهلا بهاردوست سپاس‌گزاری می‌کنم. همچنین از باربارا هافکر Barbara Hufker، مدرس «روابط بین‌المللی» در دانشگاه وبستر در سنت‌لوئیس سپاسگزارم؛ او که از طریق گزاره‌های شفاهی، تا حدودی از بحث من درباره‌ی «مؤثرهای پیرامونی» در مجموعه‌ی حاضر خبر داشت، مآخذ معتبری را به من معرفی کرد؛ به ویژه در زمینه‌ی رابطه‌ی گفتمانِ «جهانی‌سازی» با گفتمان «پست مدرنیسم». از آلکس مِی Alex May حقوقدانِ عاشق ایران، به خاطر معرفی و ارسال کتاب‌ها و مقاله‌های انگلیسی‌زبانِ مربوط به ایران سپاس‌گزاری می‌کنم. در گردآوری‌ی مآخذ مربوط به اینترنت، وبلاگ، سایت، و دیگر اطلاعات مربوط به نشر الکترونیکی از یاری‌های کریستوفر نیمایر Chritopher Niemeyer و رالی منز Raleigh Muns ، دو کتابدار بخش «مرجع» در کتابخانه‌ی دانشگاه میزوری در شهر سنت لوئیس، برخوردار بوده‌ام. با تشکر، حق آنان را بر کتاب حاضر محترم و محفوظ می‌دارم. پَت تنزی Pat Tansey، تکنولوژیست کتابخانه‌ی دانشگاه میزوری در سنت لوئیس، و آذین رایت Azin Wright، آرشیتکتِ تکنولوژی‌ی اطلاعات، در طول تدوین این مجموعه، حل مشکلات مربوط به کامپیوترم را بارها با خوشرویی پذیرفتند. به

خاطر دقت علمی و حوصله و وقتی که برای این کار صرف کردند، از هر دو سپاس‌گزاری می‌کنم. تردید ندارم که در غیاب این یاری‌ها، کتاب حاضر- با همه‌ی کاستی‌هایش که در قلمرو مسئولیت من است- نمی‌شد آن چه که هست. و اما، وامی را که مجموعه‌ی حاضر به عزیز عطائی دارد، با هیچ تشکری نمی‌توانم بپردازم. او نه تنها در گردآوری منابع و مآخذ از تارنماها و کتابخانه‌های دور و نزدیک مرا یاری داد، بلکه پیاده کردن کلیه‌ی کارهای فنی‌ی این کتاب و طرحی که برای جلد آن داشتم، به عهده‌ی او بود؛ و در این رهگذر، وسواس‌ها و بدخلقی‌های مرا با بردباری تاب آورد.

در نشستی که روز ۵ نوامبر ۲۰۰۷ (آبان ۱۳۸۶)، با نُه تن از نویسندگان مقیم شهر لس‌انجلس داشتم، طرح خامِ «پیش‌گفتار» و نیز «فهرست» جلدهای مجموعه را به مشورت گذاشتم. در این جلسه، فریبا صدیقیم (شاعر و داستان‌نویس) با نثر پیچیده‌ی من مشکل داشت. منصور خاکسار (شاعر) و بیژن بیجاری (داستان‌نویس)، با نگرانی، مرا نسبت به وسعت کار هشدار دادند؛ و یادآوری کردند که تدوین متن‌های چنین فهرستی کار یک تیم است نه یک تن منفرد؛ به ویژه در بخش «ادبیات سیاسی». مهرنوش مزارعی (داستان‌نویس)، در طرح خام «پیش‌گفتار»، نوعی «خودکم‌بینی» دیده بود، و آن را ناشی از سرکوب هزاران ساله‌ی زن ایرانی تلقی کرد. مجید روشنگر (ناشر و منتقد ادبی)، مجید نفیسی (شاعر و منتقد ادبی)، و خسرو دوامی (داستان‌نویس)، متن پیش‌گفتار و ساختاری که همان فهرست‌ها نشان می‌دادند را با سنت «تاریخ‌نگاری»ی ما مغایر دیدند، و الگوی «تاریخ ادبیاتِ ذبیح‌الله صفا» و «از صبا تا نیمای یحیی آرین‌پور» را پیشنهاد کردند. ضمن تشکر از وقت، انرژی، و راهنمایی‌های این فرهیختگان، و ضمن احترام به نظر یک یک آن‌ها، انگار در ادامه‌ی کار، «پابلو نرودا» بود که در گوشم می‌خواند: «**مرگ تدریجی‌ی ما آغاز خواهد شد/ اگر حاشیه‌ی امنیت خود را برای آرزویی نامطمئن به خطر نیاندازیم/ اگر به خودمان اجازه ندهیم یک بار هم که شده، از پندی عاقلانه بگریزیم**». این بود که من گریختم؛ یعنی، نتوانستم از سرپیچی از پندهای عاقلانه‌ی یارانم سرپیچی کنم.

م. ت.

پیش‌گفتار مجموعه

و اگر کتاب دراز شود و خوانندگان را از خواندن ملالت افزاید، طمع دارم به فضل ایشان
که مرا از مبرمان نشمرند، که هیچ چیز نیست که به خواندن نیارزد،
که آخر هیچ حکایت از نکته‌ای که بِه کار آید خالی نباشد.
تاریخ بیهقی، نوشته‌ی ابوالفضل بیهقی
(۳۸۵ – ۴۷۰ ه. ق./ ۹۹۵- ۱۰۷۷ میلادی)

کارشناس تاریخ همه فن حریف نیست که از هر دری سخن راند.
به ناگزیر باید یک برهه‌ی معین از تاریخ گذشته را برگزیند و پیش روی نهد.
تاریخ نگار نمی‌تواند هم درباره‌ی ساسانیان قلم بزند، هم در دودمان صفوی، هم در دوره‌ی قاجار و هم در خاندان پهلوی. اگر جز این باشد یا کلی‌بافی است یا خودنمائی و یا ناآگاهی.
به مثل، نگارنده ۴۶ سال درباره‌ی دوران قاجار پژوهیده‌ام،
هنوز به دوران احمد شاه نرسیده‌ام.
(هما ناطق)

امریکائی‌ها ضرب‌المثلی دارند که می‌گوید:
«Who cares after a hundred years!»
و من با مجموعه‌ی حاضر پاسخ داده‌ام:
« especially after a hundred years.،I do»
(ملیحه تیره گل)

مجموعه‌ی حاضر، ادامه‌ی کتابی است با عنوان «مقدمه‌ای بر ادبیات فارسی در تبعید»، که در سال ۱۳۷۷/ ۱۹۹۸ منتشر کردم. منتها اکنون، نه من همانم که در زمان نوشتن آن کتاب بودم، و نه ویژگی‌های موضوع بررسی همان‌هائی هستند که آن زمان بودند. زمانی که نوشتن کتاب «مقدمه ...» را شروع کردم، هجده سال از انقلاب ۱۳۵۷، و دست کم، پانزده سال از اقامت ما و تولید نوشتار فارسی در زیستگاه‌های تازه می‌گذشت؛ هنوز نخستین لایه‌ی گریختگان از اسارت و اعدام، درصد بالایی از نویسندگان را رقم می‌زد، و لایه‌های بعدی نجات‌یافتگان و تشنگان آزادی، هنوز به گستردگی

امروز، به حجم آن لایه‌ی نخستین در تبعید نپیوسته بودند؛ هنوز «نسل دوم» ما به عرصه نرسیده بود، و ما، اکثر ما، نگران زبان فارسی و فرهنگ ایرانی‌ی نسل دوم بودیم؛ هنوز فریاد درد و خشمی مبهوت در متن‌های فارسی حرف اول را می‌زد؛ هنوز تبعیدیان و پناهندگان راهی‌ی کشور مادر نشده بودند؛ هنوز آثار تبعید در ایران منتشر نمی‌شد؛ هنوز گریز ناگزیر از ایران و خودتبعیدی، حتا برای اکثریت فرهیختگان درون‌مرزی ارزشی منفی تلقی می‌شد؛ و ارزیابی‌ی آنان از آثار ادبی‌ی ما با واژه‌ی «هیچ» برابر بود؛ یعنی، بیرونه‌ی این ادبیات هم، بدون هیچ اما و چرا و شاید، شناسه‌ی «تبعید» را تصویب می‌کرد؛ هنوز نهادهای فرهنگی و سیاسی و رسولان حکومت جمهوری‌ی اسلامی در میان تبعیدیان و مهاجران چندان گسترده، همه‌جانبه، و نیرومند نبودند؛ هنوز اینترنت به صورت کنونی همگانی نشده بود، و «کتاب» و نشریه‌ی چاپی، رسانه‌های رایج در انتقال کلام نوشتاری بودند؛ هنوز رسانه‌های دیداری/ شنیداری‌ی ما در سراسر دنیا، به تعداد انگشتان یک دست نمی‌رسید؛ و «هنوز»های بسیار دیگر هم هست.

اما مهمتر از دگرگونی‌های یادشده، دگرگونی‌های ذهنیتِ خودِ من است. مخاطب آن کتاب خودم بودم و نسل خودم، و به «دقیقه‌ی اکنون»؛ با خمیرمایه‌ی امیدی تعریف‌نشدنی، که در درازنای زمان گم شد. مخاطب مجموعه‌ی حاضر، اما الزاماً و فقط، خودم و نسل خودم و دقیقه‌ی اکنون نیست. این بار بر آنم که گوشه‌هایی از ذهنیت خود و نسل‌های اکنونی در تبعید/ مهاجرت را، و خبرهایی جسته و گریخته از امیدها، تلاش‌ها، کنش‌ها، و واکنش‌هامان در مصاف با رویدادهای ایران و جهان را بر بستر معرفت‌شناسی‌ی تبار خود بنشانم، و برآیند آن‌ها را- از دید خود- به نسل‌های آینده گزارش کنم. گزینش این راه نیز، نه به خاطر ثبت رویدادهای تاریخی در توالی‌ی یکدیگر و گنجاندن خود در زمره‌ی «تاریخ‌نگاران»، بلکه امید به نزدیک شدن به درک عقلانیت و خِردِ خودبنیادِ حاکم بر فرایندهای تاریخی در نوشته‌های هزاران نویسنده‌ی ایرانی در تبعید/ مهاجرت بوده است؛ تا آیندگان بدانند که «ما» هم بوده‌ایم، و «چه‌دانم»ها و «ندانم»ها و «می‌دانم»های ما چه بوده‌اند، از چه جنسی بوده‌اند، و در بستر چه شرایطی روان بوده‌اند. همین توجه به مخاطبِ دور، در چیستی‌ها و چه‌گونگی‌های بررسی‌ی حاضر- از جمله در گزینش قلمروهای آن، در ساختارهای عینی و ذهنی‌ی آن، در گزینش رویکرد روش‌شناختی، و در زبان کاربردی- نقشی تعیین‌کننده داشته است، که در همین پیش‌گفتار به کیفیت آن‌ها اشاره خواهم کرد.

انگیزه:

در زمان تألیف کتاب «مقدمه ...» می‌خواستم به یاری‌ی «شعر» و «داستان» و «نقد»های فارسی در تبعید بدانم: «ما» راندشدگان از وطن حالا چه می‌گوئیم؟ درد مشترکمان چیست؟ این درد مشترک، در آفرینش‌های ادبی و نقدهای ما با چه ابزار ذهنی و عینی‌ای تبیین شده است؟ جهان را چه‌گونه می‌بینیم؟ هویت فردی و جنسی و قومی‌ی خود را در متن جهان چه‌گونه تعریف می‌کنیم؟ چه پدیده‌هایی را به زیر سئوال برده‌ایم، و از چه زاویه‌ای به زیر سئوال برده‌ایم؟ تجربه‌ی انقلاب و تبعید در چه زمینه‌هایی از روان جمعی‌ی ما دست برده است؟ دریافت‌های تازه‌ی ما، تا چه حد به «شناخت» نزدیک شده، و تا چه حد در هاشوری از ایده‌ال/ شناخت شناور است؟

ناگفته پیداست که تلاش من در رسیدگی به این پرسش‌ها، دست بالا، من و مخاطب کتاب «مقدمه ...» را به درک بهتر از جوانب **پرسش‌ها** نزدیک کرد. اما رسیدن به «**پاسخ**» - اگر چنین چیزی اصولاً ممکن باشد- در قلمرو ادعای من نبود، و در مجموعه‌ی حاضر هم نیست. کما این که آن پرسش‌ها، هنوز که هنوز است به قوت خود باقی هستند، و به سبب دگرگونی‌های همه‌جانبه‌ی دهه‌ی اخیر، به حجم آن‌ها افزوده هم شده است؛ به ویژه اگر قلمرو نگاه را از ژانرهای «شعر» و «داستان» و «نقد»، تا گستره‌ی «متن فارسی در تبعید» بگشائیم؛ و به ویژه اگر داده‌های این آثار را در متن پیشینه‌ی

فرهنگی‌مان تبارشناسی کنیم. چنان که من در بررسی‌ی حاضر چنین کرده‌ام. دامان گسترده‌ی همان پرسش‌ها، خیزگاه پرسش‌های دیگری است که جولان‌گاه آن‌ها را کیفیت‌ها و کمیت‌های متن فارسی در تبعید رقم زده است. با خواندن و بررسی‌ی هر اثر ادبی و توجه به شناسنامه‌ی آن، و با ملاحظه‌ی اظهار نظرهای نویسندگان در نقدها و گفت‌وگوهای ادبی، فرهنگی، سیاسی، شمار و اعتبار این پرسش‌ها در ذهن من چنان فزونی گرفت که انجام جست‌وجوی حاضر را برای من به بایسته‌ای گریزناپذیر تبدیل کرد. گزینه‌ای از این پرسش‌ها را در این جا مطرح می‌کنم:

پس از گذران حدود سه دهه در کشورهای میزبان، و پس از آشنایی با فرهنگ این کشورها و آموختن زبان‌های دیگر، با این مخاطب کم حجمی که داریم، چرا هنوز به زبان فارسی می‌نویسیم؟ چرا، نه تنها در کتاب‌ها و جستارهای آزادمان، بلکه حتا در بسیاری از پایان‌نامه‌ها و جستارهای دانشگاهی‌مان «تاریخ ایران و زبان فارسی» را محور جست‌وجو قرار می‌دهیم؟ چرا اگر سرمایه‌ی اندکی را که داشته‌ایم یا گردآورده‌ایم، برای تأسیس مرکز انتشارات فارسی، نشریه و رسانه‌ی فارسی‌زبان، و کتاب فروشی‌ی فارسی هزینه کرده‌ایم، و در درازنای این سه دهه با چنگ و دندان آن‌ها را تداوم بخشیده‌ایم؟ چرا با برگزاری‌ی «کنفرانس» و «سمینار»، و با نوشتن «مقاله» و «اعلامیه» و «بیانیه»، یا با «جمع‌آوری‌ی امضاء» در برابر مسائل سیاسی/ اجتماعی/ فرهنگی/ هنری/ ادبی‌ی ایران، یا درباره‌ی ایران، هنوز چنین زنده و کوشنده واکنش نشان می‌دهیم؟ راه و روش کوشندگان ما برای حل مسائل از کانال چه ذهنیتی گذر می‌کند؟ در این پراکندگی‌ی جغرافیایی و با پایان عمر نسل اول و دوم تبعیدیان/ مهاجران، به سر این حجم انبوه از نوشتار فارسی چه خواهد آمد؟ این مجموعه‌ی عظیم، که بخش چشمگیر آن در دهه‌ی اخیر در فضاهای مجازی‌ی اینترنت منتشر شده است، در کجا ثبت و ضبط خواهد شد؟ دگرگونی‌های پرشتاب و فزاینده‌ی جهان- به عنوان «مؤثرهای پیرامونی»[۱]- و دگرگونی‌های سیاسی/ اجتماعی/ فرهنگی و ادبی‌ی ایران- به عنوان «مؤثرهای کانونی»- در درونه‌ی آفرینش‌های ادبی، نقد ادبی، متن‌های سیاسی، و نقدهای سیاسی/ اجتماعی/ فرهنگی‌ی دهه‌ی اخیر (در تبعید) چه دگرگونی‌هایی پدید آورده‌اند؟ این مؤثرها با چه ابزاری در متن فارسی ایفای نقش کرده‌اند؟ آیا می‌توان به جهت حرکت این نقش‌ها دست یافت، و پیامدهای عملی‌ی آن را در هر زمینه شناسایی کرد؟ از این‌ها فراتر، آیا دریافت‌های تازه در مورد «ذهنیت استبدادزده»- که **سخنِ** آن بسیاری از نوشته‌های فرهنگی‌ی ما را چراغانی کرده- به آن میزان در ادراک ما نهادینه شده است که در آفرینش‌های ادبی و **کنشِ** داوری‌های فرهنگی و سیاسی‌مان نمودی عینی بیابد؟ به بیانی دقیق‌تر، آیا در جامعه‌ی روشنفکران و اندیشه‌ورزان سیاسی/ اجتماعی/ فرهنگی/ ادبی/ هنری‌ی ما، «نظرِ» آزادی و آزادی‌خواهی، با «عملِ» تأیید می‌شود؟ و نهایتاً این پرسشِ بنیادین که: آیا می‌توان ادعا کرد که پس از این همه تجربه‌های همه تلخ، آرزوی رسیدن به «استقلال اندیشه» و فردیتِ خودبنیاد در جامعه‌ی فرهیختگانِ دست به قلم ما تحقق یافته است؟

اعتراف می‌کنم که از زمان گردآوری‌ی مطالب و طراحی‌ی فصل‌های این مجموعه، به روشنی می‌دانستم که پاسخِ سرراست و شسته/ رُفته‌ای به این پرسش‌ها نخواهم یافت. اما امیدم بر این بوده است که با تکیه بر ماهیت‌ها و سمت و سوی مؤثرهای «پیرامونی» و «کانونی»، و با غوطه خوردن در چند و چون متن‌های فارسی در تبعید، خود و خواننده‌ام را، دست کم، به شناسایی‌ی جوانبی از این پرسش‌ها برسانم، که می‌توانند پاسخ‌های احتمالی را گویا کنند. بنابراین امید، هدف من از این مطالعه به قرار زیر است:

---

[۱] با این که در بخش‌های بعدی‌ی این کتاب، درباره‌ی دو واژه‌ی قراردادی‌ی «پیرامون» و «کانون» توضیح داده‌ام. اما همین جا باید اشاره کنم که این دو واژه جنبه‌ی «مکانی» دارند، و نه ارزشی. منظورم از «پیرامون»، سرزمین‌ها و فرهنگ‌های غربی، یعنی، زیستگاه اکثریت تبعیدیان است، و منظورم از واژه‌ی «کانون»، سرزمین مادری‌ی نویسنده‌ی تبعیدی، یعنی ایران است.

هدف:

هدف این مطالعه دو گرانیـــگاه دارد: ۱) **ثبت گوشه‌هایی** از بینش‌ها و کنش‌های کوشندگان، فرهنگ‌پروران، هنرمندان، و نویسـندگان تبعیدی/ مهاجر در قلمرو متن‌های سیاسـی، فرهنگی، ادبی. ۲) **شـناسـاییِ** سـازه‌های ذهنی در بینش و کنش آن‌ها، و دگرگونی‌هایی که در تبعید در جهان‌بینیِ آن‌ها پدید آمده‌اند. بدیهی اسـت که دیدن و درک «دگرگونی»های ذهنی، ما را به تبارشـناسـیِ فرهنگی هدایت می‌کند؛ و این الزام به نوبه‌ی خود، هم شـناسـائیِ پیشـینه‌ی فرهنگیِ کانون ما (ایران) و پیرامون ما (غرب) را طلب می‌کند، و هم شناسائیِ مناسبات حاکم بر کانون و پیرامون ما در دوران کنونی را. در نتیجه، تا به «ادبیات تبعید» برسـم، حدود چهار جلد از این مجموعه‌ی حاضـر نوشـته شـده و به عنوان «مقدمه» به خوانندهام عرضه شده است.

۱) شناساییِ پیشینه‌ی فرهنگیِ «کانون» و «پیرامونِ» ما.
۲) شناساییِ مؤثرهای پیرامونی در زمان حال.
۳) شناساییِ مؤثرهای کانونی در زمان حال.
۴) شـــناســـاییِ برآیند ســـازه‌های «فرهنگ موروثی» و «مؤثرهای پیرامونی وکانونی» در بینش‌ها و کنش‌های نویسندگان متن‌های غیرتخیلی.
۵) شناساییِ برآیند سازه‌های «فرهنگ موروثی» و «مؤثرهای پیرامونی و کانونی» در آفرینش‌های ادبی.

با این توضیح که، هر یک از این مرحله‌ها نیز شامل زیرمجموعه‌های دیگری هستند، که عنوان و محتوای بندها، فصل‌ها، و بخش‌های مجموعه را رقم زده‌اند.

دیدگاه:

هدف کلیِ کتاب و مرحله‌های آن ، نشـان از پیوند جدایی‌ناپذیری دارند که بین «زندگی» و «نوشـتار» می‌بینم. به بیانی دیگر، هیچ ســخنی را از گوینده‌ی آن و از شــرایط خاص ابراز آن جدا نمی‌بینم. از این رو، در قلمروهای مختلف این مجموعه، هیچ یک از تئوری‌های اعلام‌شده را (که طبیعتاً فرآورده‌ی شرایط زمانی، زیستی، و اندیشگیِ خاصِ تئوریسین اسـت)، سـنجه‌ی بررسـی قرار نداده‌ام؛ گرچه به برخی از آن‌ها نزدیک شـده‌ام. زیرا، در عین حال که دانش تئوریک را به مثابه کلید درکِ زوایای متن، و راهگشـــای تحلیل، و گســترنده‌ی افق‌های دیدِ منتقد برآورد می‌کنم، و تسـلط بر آن را یک ضـرورت انکارناپذیر در نقد می‌دانم، گنجانیدن تمامیت هر پدیده‌ی انسـانی در یک تئوریِ خاص را (برای سـنجش)، نه فقط جزم‌گرایی، بلکه عین «جباریت» نسـبت به متن و نویسـنده‌ی آن می‌دانم. سـنجش متن در قالب یک تئوریِ معین، جباریت نسبت به خود منتقد هم هست؛ چرا که یک تئوریِ معین، مسیر عبور و ابزار کار را به او دیکته می‌کند، و راه جهش‌های ذهنی و کشف و خلاقیتِ او را می‌بندد؛ جباریت نسبت به «متن» هم هست؛ چرا که کاربرد یک چهارچوب از پیش سـاخته‌شـده برای سـنجـش و تحلیل داده‌های متن، برخوردی «پرُکراستی» است، و پدیده‌ی مورد سنجش را به نسبت ابعاد معیار (تخت) می‌سنجد: یعنی، یا بخشی از اثر را «می‌بُرد »، یا کل آن را «کِش می‌دهد». به بیانی دیگر، وجـــوهی از اثر را نادیـــــده می‌گیرد و وجوهی را از بیرونِ اثر به آن تحمیل می‌کند. سـنجش متن در قالب یک تئوریِ از پیش‌ســاخته‌شـده، افزون بر بریدن و کش دادن عناصـر متن، در ذات خود، دیدگاهی فرجام‌شـناختی دارد. چرا که، خودِ تئوری‌ها، چه در نگاه شـهودیِ افلاطون و ارسـطو، چه در نگاه «ایده‌آلیسـتی»ی هگل، چه در نگاه «ماتریالیسـتی»ی

مارکسیسمِ بعد از مارکس، به «سرنوشت مقدر» می‌انجامند.[۲] حتا تئوری‌های پست مدرنیستی که علیه سرنوشت مقدرِ مدرنیسم برخاستند، و کوشیدند تا از فرجام‌شناسی فاصله بگیرند، در ذات خود «فرجام» دیگری را پرورش دادند، که از مفهوم سرنوشت مقدر سربرکرده است. (خواهم گفت که چرا و چه‌گونه.)

بنا بر این دیدگاه، می‌توان گفت که کتاب حاضر در قلمرو کلی‌ی «نقد فرهنگی»، و در محدوده‌ی «شناخت‌شناسی» می‌گنجد؛ با رویکردی که، جهت حرکت و چه‌گونگی‌ی مقوله‌های هنری، ادبی، و فکری را - در رابطه با نظرگاه‌ها، ارزش‌ها، و زمینه‌های تاریخی‌ی تکوین آن‌ها- بررسی می‌کند؛ رویکردی که، بی‌پایانگی‌ی عبور، یعنی گذار مکرر علت‌ها از یکدیگر به یکدیگر را پی می‌گیرد. در نتیجه، تا جایی که به دیدگاه تئوریک من و به حیطه‌ی «جامعه‌شناسی‌ی معرفت» در این کتاب مربوط می‌شود، هیچ یک از پدیده‌ها (باشنده‌ای به نام «جامعه» و باشنده‌ای به نام «متن»)، در حضور و هستی و حرکت آن دیگری، حکم «علت غایی» را ندارد. بلکه این دو پدیده‌ی انسانی، و خرده‌پدیده‌های متحرکِ به هم پیوسته‌ای که آن‌ها را شکل داده‌اند، هر یک به طور هم‌زمان، هم محرک است و هم متحرک؛ هم تحریک است و هم پاسخ؛ هم «مؤثر» است و هم «تأثیرپذیر»؛ هم علت است و هم معلول. و با این تبادل بی‌وقفه، بر هر چه «فرجام» است خط بطلان می‌کشد. نکته‌ی دیگر در این زمینه، الگوهای شناخت‌شناسی‌ی کاربردی در این مجموعه است، که هیچ «پدیده»‌ی انسانی یا «متن»ی را، با معیارهای ضعف، قوت، ایدئولوژی، گرایش، و شهرت یا گمنامی‌ی نویسنده نمی‌سنجد. چرا که این متن‌ها، مستقل از من و مای نخبه‌گرا یا پوپولیست یا موافق یا مخالف، «هستی» دارند؛ و درست به همین سبب، از اعتبار انسانی برخوردارند؛ و درست به همین سبب باید فارغ از گرایش‌های زیبائی‌شناختی یا ایدئولوژیک در ثبت و شناخت آن‌ها کوشید. بی‌درنگ بگویم که البته کوشش من بر این حال وُ هوا بوده است؛ اما این که تا چه میزان در انجام آن موفق بوده‌ام، خودم نمی‌دانم.

روش:

از آن جا که سمت و سو و ماهیتِ هدفِ هر جستار، در گزینش رویکرد روش‌شناختی‌ی آن جستار نقش تعیین کننده دارد، و از آن جا که هدف مجموعه‌ی حاضر، عمدتاً، رسیدگی به کیفیت‌های ذهنی در نوشتار فارسی در تبعید است، رویکرد روش‌شناختی‌ی من در این مجموعه، به «رویکردهای پژوهش کیفی» (Qualitative Research Methods) نزدیک است. در این رویکردها، «تأویل‌گر متعهد است که از راه بررسی‌ی چشم‌اندازهای فردِ مورد مطالعه، و این که او جهان را چه‌گونه تجربه می‌کند، و واقعیت را چه‌گونه می‌بیند، به فهم و ادراک او دست یابد.»[۳] ابزار مادی در روش پژوهش کیفی، کلمات،

---

[۲] مبنای غایت شناسی (Teleology) ، اعتقاد به وجود «علت و قصد نهایی» در جهان است. در کیهان‌شناسی‌ی افلاطون و ارسطو، از دیدگاهی ذاتی و غیر عرَضی، «وجود خدا» علت غایی‌ی جهان برآورد می‌شود، و در تعبیر استالین از مارکسیسم، از دیدگاهی عرَضی و غیرذاتی، و طبیعی، «کشمکش طبقاتی» علت غایی‌ی حرکت تاریخ برآورد می‌شود. برای مطالعه‌ی بیش‌تر در این زمینه، البته باید به «فائدو» و «تیمائوس» نوشته‌ی افلاطون، و «سرچشمه‌ی حیوانات» نوشته‌ی ارسطو، و به «ماتریالیسم تاریخی»ی ساخته و پرداخته‌ی متفکران و روشنفکران روسی مراجعه کرد. اما در این جا برای روشن شدن موضوع شاید این یک توضیح مختصر لازم باشد که از دیدگاه افلاطون، هر«شونده» باید بر اثر علتی «بشود». زیرا ممکن نیست که چیزی بی‌علت به وجود آید. علت‌های افلاطون، به «علت‌های خدایی» و «علت‌های ضروری» تقسیم می‌شوند. از دیدگاه او، برای شناخت هر پدیده، باید بکوشیم که به علل خدایی‌ی آن پی ببریم. اما در عین حال، برای پی‌بردن به علل خدایی، باید به علل ناشی از ضرورت هم آگاه شویم. این دو نوع «علت» افلاطون، در ماتریالیسم تاریخی، به «ضرورت» و «تصادف» تبدیل می‌شوند که البته حامل نظرگاه طبیعت‌گرا در برابر نظرگاه متافیزیکی‌ی افلاطون و ارسطو است. اما علت غایی در این دستگاه نظری، همانا تضاد طبقاتی است که در مسیر حرکت خود، تصادف‌ها یا رویدادها تاریخی را شکل می‌دهد و تاریخ را می‌سازد. هر دو سیستم در نهایت امر، به سلب «اختیار» از انسان و به «سرنوشت مقدر» می‌انجامند.

[3] Steven J. Taylor & Robert Bogdan, ***Introduction to Qualitive Research Methods***, New York: John Wiley & Sons, Inc, 1998, p 3.

در زمینه‌ی روش تحقیق کیفی، هم‌چنین نگاه کنید به کتاب‌های زیر، که از جمله منابع مورد مطالعه‌ی من بوده‌اند:

- ❖ Charles C. Tagin, ***Constructing Social Research: The Unity and Diversity of Method***, New York: Pine Forge Press, 1994.

بافتارِ متن‌های نوشتاری، و مصاحبه‌های فردِ مورد مطالعه هستند. به بیانی دیگر، از طریق تحلیل این مواد است که جست‌وجوگر به نیروهای معنی‌داری دست می‌یابد که ایده‌های درونی، احساسات، عواطف، و کلاً، بینش و کنش فرد یا افراد مورد مطالعه را رقم زده‌اند. از آن جا که در علوم انسانی، هدف تحقیق با روش کیفی، همانا « درک عمیق رفتار انسان و شناخت دلایلی است که آن رفتار را پدید آورده‌اند»،[4] جست‌وجوگر، با مطالعه‌ی چه‌گونگی‌های هر نمونه، در آغاز به درک تک تکِ نمونه‌ها می‌رسد، و سپس، بسامد شباهت‌های موجود در نمونه‌های یک گروه اجتماعی را در شناسایی‌ی کل گروه دخالت می‌دهد؛ به طوری که، مجموعه‌ی نمونه‌ها، مهمترین ویژگی‌های تمامیت گروه را نمایندگی می‌کند. در نتیجه، وجه کاربردی این روش، بر اساس بازگشایی‌ی «نمونه»ها استوار است. استفاده از روش کیفی، البته بدان معنا نیست که کمیت‌ها را نادیده گرفته‌ام، بلکه در برخی از بزنگاه‌های استدلال، به آمار و ارقام نیز رجوع کرده‌ام.

نکته‌ی قابل یادآوری در زمینه‌ی روش، مسئله‌ی «زمان» است: در رویکردهای «پژوهش کمی» و «پژوهش کیفی»، جست‌وجوی علمی در چارچوبِ دوره‌ی معین و مکان معین صورت می‌گیرد؛ و من هم کوشیده‌ام تا در این چارچوب حرکت کنم. (پیرامون این موضوع در همین پیش‌گفتار توضیح داده‌ام.) اما پرش‌های ذهنی‌ی من در مجموعه‌ی حاضر تابع این محدودیت‌های روش‌شناختی نیستند. یعنی، تا تصویری که در هر زمینه‌ی سخن در ذهن دارم به تمامی ترسیم شود، در یک مبحث معین، از فراز یک زمان به زمانِ دیگری پریده‌ام: از فراز و نشیب‌های امروز، به فراز و نشیب‌های نقطه به نقطه‌ی گذشته‌های دور وُ نزدیک؛ وَ از گذشته‌ها، به نقطه نقطه‌ی فرداهاشان، که دیروز وُ امروز باشند. زیرا که، گوهر مورد بررسی‌ی من- با همه‌ی افت و خیزهایش- در درازنای زمان تپش داشته است. نه این که آن را «ازلی» و «ابدی» بپندارم، بلکه از آن رو که آغاز و پایانش در چشم‌انداز من پیدا نیستند؛ یعنی که خاستگاه آن گوهر، در چشم‌انداز من زمانمند نیست. کما این که، تا این خط شکسته/ پیوسته را در روند جست‌وجوهایم ندیدم، کارِ مجموعه‌ی حاضر- با همه‌ی بازنویسی‌های ساختاری- به جائی نرسید.

ساختارهای عینی و ذهنی‌ی مجموعه:

۱) در مجموعه‌ی حاضر، هر آن چه را که با نام «متن فارسی» شناسایی می‌شود، به قلمرو جست‌وجو راه داده‌ام، و در فرازی به عنوان «شناسنامه‌ی ما» و در «مقدمه»های متعددِ این مجموعه به چرائی‌های این کار پرداخته‌ام.

۲) همین جا باید به بزرگترین کاستی‌ی مجموعه‌ی حاضر اعتراف کنم، و اشاره کنم که زبان «فارسی»، تنها زبانی نیست که ایرانیان تبعیدی خود را با آن بیان کرده‌اند. از میانه‌های دهه‌ی دوم و با رواج اینترنت، صدها متن در زمینه‌های مختلف به زبان‌های آذری، کردی، و عربی در تارنماهای ایرانیان منتشر شده است، که من به سبب ندانستن این زبان‌ها، از خواندن آن‌ها محروم بوده‌ام. این غبن بزرگ، البته شامل متن‌هائی هم می‌شود که نویسندگان تبعیدی/ مهاجر به زبان‌های غیرایرانی- مانند فرانسوی و آلمانی و سوئدی- پدید آورده‌اند. گرچه «پوزش‌خواهی»، این کاستی را جبران نمی‌کند، اما جز این از من کاری ساخته نیست.

۳) درست است که دست‌مایه‌ی مجموعه‌ی حاضر، سی و پنج سال متن فارسی در تبعید/ مهاجرت است؛ اما، خواننده‌ی

❖ Karen Golden-Biddle and Karen Locke, ***Composing Qualitive Research***, second edition, Thousadn Oaks: Sage Publishers, 2007.

4 Steven J. Taylor & Robert Bogdan, ***Introduction to Qualitive Research Methods***, New York: John Wiley & Sons, Inc, 1998, p. 4; Karen Golen- Biddle and Karen Locke, ***Composing Qualitative Research***, Thousand Oaks, London, New Delhi: Sage Publisehers, 2007, pp. 9-24.

من باید به یاد داشته باشد که «سی و پنج سال متن فارسی»، تا آن جا که من خوانده‌ام؛ و به گونه‌ای که، این خوانده‌ها در ذهنیت من بازتابیده‌اند؛ و فارغ از دغدغه‌ی تکرارِ حرف‌های روز، استنباط خود را از حرف‌های روز بازگفته‌ام. من در جلدهای این مجموعه به بن‌مایه‌هایی پرداخته‌ام که در طول سده‌ی گذشته در متن‌های بسیاری توصیف و تحلیل شده‌اند، که گزارش‌های من از این گفتمان‌ها، در برابر آن‌ها می‌تواند یک «صـــفر» بزرگ جلوه کند. به ویژه که در روزگار کنونی، افزون بر کتاب‌ها و مقاله‌های چاپی، صدها گزارش و تحلیل پیرامون تک تک شخصیت‌ها و رویدادها و مناسبات سیاسی، اجتماعی، فرهنگی‌ی این دوره، و همه‌ی دوره‌های تاریخ ایران و جهان، در فضای مجازی‌ی اینترنت شناور است، و هر یک از آن‌ها با یک فشار انگشت در اختیار جست‌وجوگر قرار می‌گیرد. بنابراین، مرور سریع من بر این گفتمان‌ها، هر نوع ادعای «تاریخ‌نگاری» را از دوش ژانرشناسی‌ی مجموعه‌ی حاضر برمی‌گیرد.

۴) با این همه، به جرأت می‌توانم ادعا کنم که درصد بالایی از متن‌های تبعیدیان را خوانده‌ام، و انبوه سرسام‌آوری از آن‌ها (یا یادداشت‌هایی درباره‌ی آن‌ها) را در زمان تدوین مجموعه‌ی حاضر در اختیار داشته‌ام. اما به حکم روشی که برای جست‌وجو برگزیده‌ام، از بین انبوهی از متن‌های هر گفتمان، فقط یک یا چند نمونه را بررسیده‌ام. در نتیجه، نمونه‌هایی که در این مجموعه به تحلیل گذاشته‌ام، همه‌ی متن‌هایی نیستند که در سی و پنج ســـــال گذشته خوانده‌ام. اعتراف می‌کنم که گزینش نمونه‌ها، یکی از فرساینده‌ترین بخـــش‌های کار من در تدوین این مجموعه بوده اســـت. و همین جا، از صدها نویسنده‌ی تبعیدی/ مهاجر که اثری از آن‌ها خوانده‌ام، اما نام و اثرشان در این کتاب نیامده، پوزش می‌خواهم. همین کاستی، در عین حال، هر نوع ادعای «کتاب‌شناســی‌ی متن فارســی در تبعید» را نیز از دوش ژانرشناســی‌ی مجموعه‌ی حاضـر برمی‌دارد.

۵) این گفته‌ی بیهقی را در نظر داشته‌ام که: «احتیاط باید کردن نویسندگان را در هرچه نویسند، که از گفتار باز توان ایستاد و از نبشتن باز نتوان ایستاد و نبشته باز نتوان گردانید.» از این رو، در مجموعه‌ی حاضر، طول بازگفت‌ها را از حد متعارف بسیار فراتر برده‌ام. زیرا که فشرده کردن نظرات نویسنده، به ویژه در متن‌های انتقادی و تحلیلی، همواره این خطر را همراه دارد که ادراک تحلیل‌گر از متن، دقیقاً همانی نباشد که نویسنده‌ی متن در نظر داشته است. در نتیجه، با این هدف که خواننده‌ی کتاب- اگر به اصـل متن‌ها دســترســی نیابد- از بازگفت‌های بلند، هم نسـبت به زبان و دیدگاه و آراء نویسنده‌ی متن مجال داوری داشته باشد، و هم نسبت به داوری‌های من. و چنین شد که حجم فیزیکی‌ی مجموعه، نوشته‌ی من تنها نیست، و در همسرایی‌ی صدها نویسنده‌ی دیگر پیکر گرفته است.

۶) تا پیوند پارامترهای تشـــکیل دهنده‌ی شـــبکه‌ی یک گفتمان حفظ شـــود، کوشـــیده‌ام که در هر مبحث، یا دســـت کم در جمع‌بندی‌ی هر مبحث، محدوده‌ی هاشوری‌ی بین پارامترهای آن نادیده باقی نماند. این روش، هم به وســواس من در نشان دادن و تأکید کردن بر رابطه‌های متقابل و همایندِ «مؤثرها» و «تأثیرپذیری‌ها» پاســـــخ داده اســت، و هم، به برخی از بخش‌ها و فصـــل‌ها و حتا بندهای مجموعه هویتی مســـتقل بخشـــیده اســـت؛ به طوری که، هر یک از آن‌ها، جدا از متن سراسری‌ی مجموعه، قادر است با تمامیتی معنی‌دار، سخن مرا به خواننده منتقل کند. این وسواس، البته به تکرار برخی از مفاهیم نیز انجامیده، که ممکن است در نگاه نخست، انسجام ساختاری‌ی کتاب را به زیر سئوال ببرد. اما امیدوار بوده‌ام که این تکرارهای اشـــاره‌وار، در رابطه با «دیدگاه»ی که در این پیش‌گفتار ارائه می‌دهم، و نیز در رابطه با «هدف» کتاب، ضرورت وجودی‌ی خود را مستدل کنند.

۷) «دوره‌بندی»های این مجموعه نیز یکی از نکات قابل اشاره است. در هر دو رویکردهای «پژوهش کیفی» و «پژوهش کمّی»، دوره‌ی تاریخی‌ی موضـوع پژوهش، یکی از عناصـری اسـت که پژوهنده باید در نظر بگیرد؛ به ویژه اگر دامنه‌ی

موضوع جست‌وجو گسترده باشد. البته از دیدگاه جامعه‌شناسی‌ی شناخت، دوره‌های تاریخی را به نسبت تحولاتی که در مناسبات سیاسی، فرهنگی، اجتماعی، اقتصادی‌ی یک جامعه پدید می‌آید، تقسیم‌بندی می‌کنند. با این وصف، مرزبندی‌ی دوره‌های تبعید- به ویژه در درازای سی و پنج سال- اگر هم ممکن باشد، به دو علت، دقیق و عاری از چون و چرا نخواهد بود. نخست این که، «مجمع‌الجزایر نامتصل»[۵] تبعیدیان/ مهاجران ایرانی، به معنای دقیق کلمه، «جامعه» محسوب نمی‌شود. با این وصف، با توجه به کلی‌ترین مشخصاتِ مشترک، و البته باز هم با تسامح، برای نامیدنِ این پدیده‌ی ناپیوسته، واژه‌ی «جامعه» را به کار برده‌ام. علت دوم، این اصل جامعه‌شناختی است که ظهور و افول دوره‌های تاریخی، تابع یک نظام مرزبندی شده‌ی زمانی نیستند. چرا که همواره بخشی از دوره‌ی بعد، در دامان دوره‌ی در حال گذار ظهور می‌کند و بخشی از یک دوره‌ی سپری‌شده، در حاشیه‌ی دوره‌ی نوظهور تا مدت‌ها ادامه می‌یابد. مدت این بخش‌های هاشوری- با هیچ معیار علمی‌ای- قابل اندازه‌گیری‌ی دقیق نیستند. از این رو، من در زمینه‌های لازم، به فراخور موضوع مورد بحث، نوعی دوره‌بندی‌ی قراردادی را به خواننده‌ام معرفی کرده‌ام. این دوره‌بندی‌های قراردادی، در عین حال، پرش‌های ذهنی‌ی من (از نقطه‌ای در زمان به نقطه‌ی دیگر) را مهار نکرده‌اند.

۸) با این که در مجموعه‌ی حاضر بر «اندیشه»های کوشندگان سیاسی در تبعید درنگ‌های درازدامنی داشته‌ام، اما «تاریخ سازمان‌های سیاسی»، «گرایش سیاسی‌ی هر سازمان»، تفاوتِ گرایش‌های فلسفی/ سیاسی در «سازمان‌های سیاسی»، و «انشعاب‌های سازمانی» **در تبعید**، مطلقاً سوژه‌ی شناخت من در این کتاب نبوده‌اند. چرا که در این زمینه‌ها، نه از بضاعت علمی/ اطلاعاتی برخوردارم، و نه هدف کتابم درنگ طولانی بر چنین مقوله‌هایی را طلب می‌کند.

۹) بسیاری از تحلیل‌ها و جمع‌بندی‌های من در این مجموعه، گواهان گویایی هستند بر ناتوانی‌ی من در رسیدن به پاسخ معین و مشخص، و مخصوصاً بر پریشانی‌ی من در امر داوری‌های از پیش، «پیش‌بینی» شده. اما از آن جا که این کتاب، با مُرگّبی از **درد تاریخی** نوشته شده است، یک جست‌وجوی خنثا هم نیست. (بر عبارت «درد تاریخی» تأکید می‌کنم تا آن را از سوزِ «سوگواری» جدا کرده باشم. زیرا خودم چنین می‌اندیشم که آن مرحله را پشت سر نهاده‌ام.) در پژوهش‌های آکادمیک رسم جاری بر این است که آراء و باورهای شخصی‌ی پژوهشگر پشت بافتار اثر و پشت ذهنیتی سرد و خنثا پنهان بماند. اما من، در جای جای این مجموعه از بروز دردهای تاریخی‌ی خود- در قالب‌های پرسش، پاسخ‌های احتمالی، و داوری‌های موضعی- ابا نکرده‌ام. زیرا به نظر من، در زمانه‌ی شروری که ما آن را زیست می‌کنیم، نقد و تحلیل و جست‌وجو، در خلاء شور ُ تپش ُ تقلا برای شناخت، وَ در غیاب نبض تپنده‌ی داوری، و در حضور ترس از پرسیدن، و در غیاب جرأتِ ورود به قلمروهای ممنوعه‌ی فرهنگی، افسوس قلم است ُ بس. با این همه- از آن رو که به معنای واقعی «از هر طرف که رفتم جز وحشتم نیافزود»- در سراسر این جست‌وجوی بلند، نه پاسخی شسته‌ُرفته برای پرسش‌هایم یافته‌ام/ عرضه کرده‌ام، و نه «راه حلی» دیده‌ام و ارائه داده‌ام. البته این یادآوری را بدان نیاوردم که مسئولیت خود را در مورد نظرهائی که در این کتاب ارائه می‌دهم کمرنگ کرده باشم؛ یا، راه هرگونه نقد و سنجش را بر آن بسته باشم. در هر دو مورد برعکس است: من، در برابر تک تک داوری‌های خود، مسئول و پاسخگو هستم. و برای این که لغزش‌های احتمالی‌ی من در این مجموعه، در کنار خودِ مجموعه، به تاریخ گزارش شود، سنجش آن را از مسئولیت‌های «نقد» در زبان فارسی می‌دانم.

کاربرد زبان:

---

[۵] این اصطلاح را از منصور خاکسار به وام گرفته‌ام.

در نوشتار حاضر کوشیده‌ام که از «زبان آکادمیک»، از کاربرد واژگان تخصصی، و از بازگفتِ تئوری‌های نظریه‌پردازان (که معمولاً «غربی» هستند) تا حد ممکن خودداری کنم. در موارد اندکی که از این کار ناگزیر بوده‌ام، در خود متن، یا در زیرنویسِ وابسته، درباره‌ی هر یک از آن‌ها توضیح لازم را ارائه داده‌ام. و نیز، با هدف رسـیدن به طیف گسترده‌تری از مخاطبان، مسـئولیت انتقال معناها را مصرانه به عهده‌ی نثری گذاشته‌ام که در زمانه‌ی خودم، «نثر مُرسَل» برشمرده می‌شود. در نتیجه، در هنگام نوشتن این کتاب، فقط کافی بوده است که واژه/ مفهوم مورد نیازم، به پیکره‌ی زبان فارسی گره خورده باشد، و در قالب نحو جمله، رسالت معنا را از عهده برآید؛ خواه این واژه، فارسی‌ی «سره» باشد، خواه ریشه در زبان «عربی» داشته باشد، خواه در زبان‌های «غربی»، و خواه کلاً واژه‌ی غیرفارسی‌ای باشد که در زبان فارسی جا افتاده است. به عنوان مثال در مورد اخیر، به جای کاربرد واژه‌ی «پسا مدرنیسم» (واژه‌ای غیرفارسی با پیشوندی فارسی)، از اصطلاح «پُست مدرنیسم» استفاده کرده‌ام.

نکته‌ی دیگر در زمینه‌ی زبان، به «ترجمه»‌ی بازگفت‌ها مربوط می‌شود. گرچه کوشیده‌ام که تا حد ممکن از منابع فارسی استفاده کنم، اما مأخذ برخی از بازگفت‌های این نوشته، به زبان انگلیسی (اصیل یا ترجمه از زبان‌های دیگر) است، که شاید تاکنون بسیاری از آن‌ها به زبان فارسی ترجمه شده باشند. از آن‌جا که من این ترجمه‌ها را در اختیار نداشته‌ام- یا اگر داشته‌ام، تطبیق صفحات و پیدا کردن بازگفت‌هایی که در درازنای سالیان از کتاب‌های انگلیسی یادداشت کرده بودم، کاری بسیار وقت‌گیر بود- خود به ترجمه‌ی بازگفت‌ها پرداخته‌ام. بدیهی است که این نویسه‌گردانی، ضمن پذیرش مسئولیت در انتقال معنی، ظرافت‌های حرفه‌ای‌ی ترجمه را ادعا نمی‌کند.

ساختمان فیزیکی‌ی مجموعه:

۱) این مجموعه، ابتدا «سی سال» را در برمی‌گرفت، و در ۵ جلد تدوین شد؛ سپس- با وسواس‌های من از یک سو، و با وقوع رویدادهای مهم تاریخی از سوی دیگر- به ۷ جلد، و سپس‌ترها به ۱۴ جلد رسید؛ که هر بار، سازواره‌ی بخش‌بندی و فصل‌بندی‌ی مجموعه و هر جلد آن، آرایش تازه‌ای را طلب می‌کرد، و تا به انجام رسد، زندگی‌ی عینی و ذهنی‌ی مرا در خود می‌غلتاند؛ به ویژه که نگارش آن، به دلایل مختلفِ شخصی (مانند بیماری و عمل جراحی، نقل مکان از سنت لوئیس میزوری به تگزاس، و «نوه داری») با وقفه‌های متعدد انجام شد. از فراوردهای خطرناک این دربه‌دری همین بس که من در هنگام ویرایش نهائی‌ی این مجموعه، تفاوت خط (دبیره) خودم را در جای جای آن دیدم و فرصت یکنواخت کردنِ همه‌ی آن‌ها را نداشتم.

۲) چنان که بخش «یادداشت‌ها»‌ی هر جلد این مجموعه نشان می‌دهد، فهرستِ مأخذهای آن آکنده است از نشانی‌ی تارنماهائی که حتا خود من در مراجعه‌ی دوباره، به آن‌ها دست نیافتم؛ چه رسد به «مخاطب دور دست»‌ی که برای این کتاب در نظر دارم. در نتیجه- بنا بر پیشنهاد کتابخانه‌ی کنگره‌ی امریکا- کوشیده‌ام تا تاریخ انتشار هر متن در تارنما را- اگر در دسترس بوده- یا تاریخ بازدید آن را، در شناسنامه‌ی متن مورد استفاده‌ی خود بنویسم. همین مشکل سبب شد که از درج «کتاب‌شناسی»‌ی مراجع خود در این مجموعه خودداری کنم.

۳) بر پایه‌ی «هدف‌های مرحله‌ای»‌ی این مجموعه، آن را به چهارده جلد تقسیم کرده‌ام: جلد اول، پس از مروری در ذهنیت تبار ایرانی، به آراء روشنفکران دوران انقلاب مشروطه، رضا شاه پهلوی، و محمدرضا شاه پهلوی نگاه کرده‌ام. جلد دوم، انقلاب سال ۱۳۵۷ و دهه‌ی نخست جمهوری‌ی اسلامی را در برمی‌گیرد. در جلد سوم، جنگ ایران و عراق، کشتار زندانیان سیاسی، «عفو عمومی»، جنبش اصلاحات، گفت‌وگوی تمدن‌ها، جنبش‌های زنان، کارگران، دانشجویان و نسل بعد از انقلاب را، به عنوان سازه‌هائی که بر بینش و کنش تبعیدیان اثر می‌گذارند، بررسی کرده‌ام. در جلد چهارم، پس

از مروری در پیشـینه‌ی تاریخی/ فرهنگی «غرب»، گفتمان‌های «پسـت مدرنیسـم»، انگیزه‌های برآیش آن (بحران‌های «مدرنتیه»)، «کاپیتالیسم/ سوسیالیسم»، «فروریزی‌ی کمپ سوسیالیسم»، «جهانی‌سازی»، «تکنولوژی‌ی اطلاعات» را، باز به عنوان «مؤثر»هائی بر بینش و کنش تبعیدیان، بررسـیده‌ام. موضـوع محوری‌ی جلد پنجم، گفتمان «روشـنفکر و روشنفکری» است که مبحث «کانون نویسندگان ایران در تبعید» را نیز در برمی‌گیرد. جلد ششم را به «ادبیات سیاسی» اختصـاص داده‌ام، که به سـبب طول کلام، آن را به دو جلد جداگانه تقسـیم کرده‌ام. در بخش نخسـت، نهادهای مقاومت و جنبش‌های اپوزیسـیون در تبعید را بررسیده‌ام؛ و در بخش دوم، به نمونه‌هائی از «نقد و نظر»های کوشـندگان سیاسـی در تبعید پرداخته‌ام. جلد هفتم، با عنوان «ادبیات زندان»، «خاطرات زندان»، «نامه‌ها و وصیت‌نامه‌های اعدام‌شدگان»، «شعر و هنر زندان»، «نقد و نظرِ» تبعیدیان پیرامون «خاطراتِ» یکدیگر را در بر دارد. جلد هشتم، به یادمانِ «درگذشتگان در تبعید» اختصاص دارد. جلد نهم، شامل ژانرهای «داستان»، «نمایش‌نامه»، «فیلم‌نامه»، متن تبعیدیان «به زبان‌های دیگر»، و «گردآورده‌های ادبی» است. در جلد دهم، شاخه‌های «کهن‌سرائی»، «ترانه‌سرائی» و «طنزپردازی» در شعر فارسی در تبعید را بررسیده‌ام. جلد یازدهم، به شاخه‌ی «نوپردازی» در شعر تعلق دارد. جلد دوازدهم، یکسره به «نقد» تعلق دارد. اما به سـبب طول کلام آن را نیز به دو جلد تقسـیم کرده‌ام؛ که اولی، شـامل گزارش‌هائی اسـت پیرامون «نقد ادبی»، «نهادهای ادبی/ هنری»، «مراکز انتشـاراتی»، «نشـریه‌های ادواری»، «نمونه‌های نقد و پژوهش و نظریه‌ی ادبی» در تبعید. و در بخش دوم از جلد دوازدهم نیز «نقد پیرامون چهار گفتمان» را پی گرفته‌ام. این گفتمان‌ها عبارتند از: «هویت ملی»، «زبان و خط فارسی»، «دین»، و «جنسیت»؛ با همه متعلقاتِ مربوط به هر یک از این چهار گفتمان.

***

در پایان این پیش‌گفتار تأکید می‌کنم که در این جا، سخن بر سر چند قلمرو گسترده از دانش است، که ضمن استقلال، بر یکدیگر می‌لغزند، از یکدیگر برمی‌آیند و به یکدیگر نیرو می‌بخشـند. و در این تعامل مدام، خود مداوماً از درون دگرگون می‌شـوند. به ویژه در زمانه‌ی کنونی، که به قول آلوین تافلر، متفکر امریکایی، «بسـیاری از داوری‌ها و تصـمیم‌گیری‌های ما، بر اسـاس حقایقی اسـت که می‌تواند فردا تغییر کند و چه بسـا همین حالا منسـوخ شـده باشـد.»[۶] در نتیجه، شـناختن و شـناسـاندن تمام ابعاد هر یک از قلمروهای مورد بحث، اگر هم به طور کامل میسر باشـد، نه هدف نوشـته‌ی حاضر بوده اسـت، و نه در حیطه‌ی ادعای من. بنابراین، تصـویر فشـرده‌ای که از هر یک از این گفتمان‌ها ارائه داده‌ام، در محدوده‌ی تأثیری بوده است که ــ به استنباط من- این مقوله‌ها بر بینش و کنش کنشگران و فرهیختگان تبعیدی نهاده‌اند. با این توضیح که، استنباط‌ها نیز برخاسته از محدوده‌ی دانشی است که در آن قلمروها آموخته‌ام. منتها این آموزه‌ها، از صـافی‌ی ذهنیت **فرهنگی‌ی** من گذشـته‌اند؛ با عناصـر تجربه‌های **شـخصـی‌ی** من درآمیخته‌اند؛ باز سـازی شـده‌اند؛ شـاکله‌های ذهنی‌ی مرا ساخته‌اند؛ و به نام «ادراک»، در کیفیتِ «استنتاج»ها یا «استنباط»های من دخیل هستند. و من، با این که در حال حاضر، در نمایاندن نمودهای این ادراک (البته با پشتوانه‌ی استدلال) پافشـاری دارم، اما نه مدعی‌ی «حرف آخر» هستم و نه حق تجدید نظر را برای خود منتفی می‌دانم. چنان که قبلاً هم در همین پیش‌گفتار اشاره کردم، این مجموعه، با همه‌ی آن چه که هسـت و بی‌همه‌ی آن چه که باید می‌بود، خود، نمودی اسـت از بینش و کنش عضـوی از جامعه‌ی نویسـندگان ایرانی در تبعید، که من باشـم. اگر خواننده‌ی این مجموعه، مفاد این پیش‌گفتار را در خوانش سـراسـر مجموعه در نظر بگیرد، و با توجه به هدف اعلام شده، بر تحلیل گفتمان‌های آن نظر کند، این «نمود» را به روشنی می‌بیند.

م. ت

۲۰ مارس ۲۰۱۴

۲۹ اسفند ۱۳۹۲

---

[۶] ***گفت و گو با آلوین تافلر: نگاه تازه به آینده***، منتشر شده در تارنمای «digitalmpq»، ترجمه‌ی وحیدرضا نعمتی، منتشر شده در تارنمای «آینده نگر» در تاریخ ۶ اردی‌بهشت ۱۳۸۶ (۲۶ آوریل ۲۰۰۷):

www.ayandehnegar.org/page1.php?news_id=1991

مقدمه

پس از سال‌ها دربه‌دری/ عاقبت در این گوشه‌ی پرت‌افتاده/
خانه‌ی کوچک و سرسبزی/ با اقساط سی ساله خریدم/
که قطعاً به پای بهشت نمی‌رسد/
اما روزهایی که حوا شادمانه/ پنجره‌ها را باز می‌کند/
شباهت دوری/ به دنج‌ترین گوشه‌های بهشت/ پیدا می‌کند.
(عباس صفاری، «حکایت ما»)

همیشه چیزی ناچیز/ معنی‌ی گور را دور می‌کند:/
همان هیاهوی بسته‌ی گُلی کوچک/
- درست در انتهای دره‌ای بزرگ-/ که از خواب قله هیچ نمی‌داند،/
جهان را از مرگ حتمی می‌رهاند.
(محمود فلکی، «آخرین کتاب شعر»)

در درازنای سه دهه‌ی گذشته، نظریه‌پردازان و پژوهشگران تبعیدی پیرامون واژه‌ی «تبعید» و ابعاد متفاوتِ آن بسیار سخن گفته‌اند. مثلاً، در بُعد اسطوره‌ای، به تبعید آدم و حوا از بهشت، تبعید سیاووش اسطوره، و تبعید «جان از بدن» در عرفان، اشاره کرده‌اند؛ در بُعد روان‌شناختی، یعنی «تبعیدِ ذهنی»ی روشنفکرِ دگراندیش و به حاشیه رانده‌شده‌های فرهنگ ایران، از ناصرخسرو تا صادق هدایت یاد کرده‌اند؛ در بُعد جامعه‌شناختی/ سیاسی نیز، از «تبعید» در معنای قانون حکومتی و «نفی‌ی بلد»، و نیز در مورد «خودتبعیدی»های گریخته از زندان و شکنجه و اعدام، تعریف‌هائی بدست داده‌اند. پیوند مفهوم «تبعید» با «سیاست»، وجه مشترک این تعریف‌ها است، و مهم‌ترین شاخصه‌ی دو بُعدِ روان‌شناختی و جامعه‌شناختی‌ی آن نیز «اجبار» است.[۷] در مورد «مهاجرت» نیز، در این جا و آن‌جای متن‌ها به تعریف‌هایی برمی‌خوریم، که اکثراً با تکیه بر وجه «اختیار» در مفهوم مهاجرت، آن را از قلمرو مفهومی و کاربردی‌ی «تبعید» جدا

---

[۷] برای مثال پیرامون ابعاد مختلف مفهوم «تبعید» به منابع زیر مراجعه کنید:
- ❖ ملیحه تیره گل، ***مقدمه‌ای بر ادبیات فارسی در تبعید***، تکزاس: انتشارات یوتاچ، چاپ اول، ۱۳۷۷/ ۱۹۹۸.
- ❖ گفت و گوی پیمان وهاب زاده و یوسف علیخانی پیرامون ادبیات مهاجرت ایران: بخش اول: «***جزیره های سرگردان***»، تهران: روزنامه ی شرق سال سوم، شماره ی ۶۷۵، ۲۵ دی ماه ۱۳۸۴، ۱۵ ژانویه ی ۲۰۰۶. بخش دوم: با عنوان «***آینده به گذشته بدهکار نیست***»، همان، شماره ی ۶۷۶، ۲۶ دی ماه ۱۳۸۴، ۱۶ ژانویه ی ۲۰۰۶.
- ❖ گفت و گوی دکتر علیرضا زرین با شاهرخ تندرو صالح، ***پلی میان واژه‌ها و تنهایی***، تهران: روزنامه‌ی شرق، شماره‌ی ۸۸۷، ۲ تیر ۱۳۸۶.

کرده‌اند.[۸]

تاریخ «خودتبعیدی»، یا فرارهای ادواری‌ی ایرانیان در درازنای تاریخ نیز، در بسیاری از متن‌های ما دوره‌بندی شده است. اکثر پژوهندگان، دوره‌های تبعید ایرانی را از زمان اشغال ایران توسط تازیان تبارشناسی کرده‌اند. من نیز در بخش «پایانه» ی کتاب حاضر، با توجه به شاخصه‌های فرهنگی‌ی هر دوره، تاریخ تبعید ایرانی را دوره‌بندی کرده‌ام. اما تا خواننده‌ام به آن جا برسد، و در همین آغاز کار، یادآوری‌ی این نکته اهمیت دارد که «متن فارسی در تبعید»ی که من در این کتاب از آن سخن می‌گویم، در دامان **گسترده‌ترین** دوره‌ی فرار هنر و اندیشه‌ی ایرانی روییده و بالیده است؛ «گسترده‌ترین»، هم به لحاظ آماری و هم به اعتبار مغزها و قلم‌هائی که از ایران گریخته‌اند.

فرار از ایرانِ معاصر، عمدتاً، پس از شکست «فرقه‌ی دموکرات آذربایجان» (آذر ۱۳۲۵) آغاز شد؛ با کودتای ۲۸ مرداد ۱۳۳۲ اوجی دیگر گرفت؛ و با انقلاب سال ۱۳۵۷ ماهیت و چهره عوض کرد، و تا همین لحظه‌ی اکنون ادامه دارد. این بار، ابتدا طرفداران رژیم پادشاهی از یک سو، و «اقلیت‌های مذهبی» از سوی دیگر، به خودتبعیدی دست زدند. پس از استقرار جمهوری‌ی اسلامی، نوبت به گریزهای ناگزیر پیکارگران سیاسی و دانش‌آموختگان و کارشناسان رشته‌های مختلف هم رسید، که اکثراً در تحقق انقلاب و در استقرار جمهوری‌ی اسلامی سهم داشتند. بنا به گزارش وزارت فرهنگ و آموزش عالی در جمهوری‌ی اسلامی، پیش از «انقلاب فرهنگی»ی جمهوری‌ی اسلامی و تعطیل دانشگاه‌ها (در سال ۱۳۵۹)، تعداد ۱۶ هزار و ۲۲۲ استاد در مراکز آموزش عالی و دانشگاه‌های ایران حضور فعال داشتند. این رقم، پس از بازگشایی‌ی دانشگاه‌ها (در سال ۱۳۶۱)، به ۹ هزار و ۴۲ نفر کاهش یافته بود.[۹] یعنی در همان یورش نخستِ جمهوری‌ی اسلامی به سیستم آموزش عالی در ایران، بیش از ۷ هزار استاد در سراسر ایران از صحنه‌ی فعالیت زوده شدند. «پاکسازی»، اما به همین جا پایان نیافت. «انقلاب فرهنگی»، که هدفش حذف استادان و دانشجویان «غیراسلامی» و یا «نامعتقد به رژیم ولایت فقیه» بود،[۱۰] تا همین امروز ادامه دارد، و مدت‌هاست که شامل استادان و دانشجویان و کوشندگان «اسلامی» نیز شده است؛ چه رسد به استادان و دانشجویان ارمنی، آسوری، کلیمی، زرتشتی، و بهایی، یا آزاداندیشان مسلمانی که برای جدائی‌ی دین از دولت و رسیدن به حکومت سکولار فعالیت می‌کنند. سی و پنج سال پس از انقلاب، هنوز آمار نشان می‌دهد که از یک میلیون و نیم داوطلب برای شرکت در کنکور سالانه‌ی دانشگاه‌های ایران، فقط ۱۱ درصد پذیرفته می‌شوند؛[۱۱] و این در حالی است که هزاران تن از حزب‌اللهی‌ها- بدون داشتن مدرک و نمره‌های لازم- به سطح «دکترا» راه یافته‌اند و به عنوان عضوی از «هیئت علمی»ی دانشگاه‌های رژیم اسلامی، سرنوشت آموزش عالی در ایران را رقم زده‌اند. سی و پنج سال پس از انقلاب، هنوز آمار نشان می‌دهد که سالی ۱۵۰ تا ۱۸۰هزار تن از دانش‌آموختگان و جوانانی که اکثراً در همان دانشگاه‌های «اسلامی» تحصیل کرده‌اند، از ایران «مهاجرت» می‌کنند.[۱۲]

---

[۸] به عنوان مثال نگاه کنید به:

- اسماعیل نوری‌علا، ***شعر مهاجر فارسی، حال و آینده‌ی آن***، دفتر شناخت، کتاب پنجم- ویژه‌ی شعر مهاجرت، به کوشش منوچهر سلیمی و پیمان وهابزاده، کانادا: بهار ۱۳۷۷، صص ۳۳۳ تا ۳۴۲.

[9] Shirin Hakimzadeh, ***A Vast Diaspora and Millions of Refugees at Home***, in Migration Policy Institute (online), September 2006: www.migrationpolicy.org

[۱۰] نگاه کنید به تحلیل آرامش دوستدار در مورد بسته شدن دانشگاه‌ها و پاکسازی‌ی استادان در مأخذ زیر: مصاحبه‌ی سایت نیلگون با آرامش دوستدار، بخش اول: ***سپهر عمومی‌ی مباحثه میان روشنفکران ایرانی***، در تارنمای نیلگون، فوریه‌ی ۲۰۰۶، متن اصلاح شده در ۱۲ ژوئن ۲۰۰۶، به نشانی‌ی زیر:

www.nilgoon.org/articles/Dustdar_interview_Feb2006.html

[11] Shirin Hakimzadeh, ***A Vast Diaspora and Millions of Refugees at Home***, in Migration Policy Institute (online), September 2006: www.migrationpolicy.org

[12] Glonaz Esfandiari, ***Iran: Coping With The World's Highest Rate Of Brain Drain***, 8 May 2004, in:

گزارش دیگری می‌گوید: ۴ تن از هر ۵ تن دانشجویان یا فارغ‌التحصیلانی که برای شرکت در مسابقات علمی‌ی بین‌المللی از ایران خارج می‌شوند، هرگز به ایران بازنمی‌گردند.[13] گزارش دیگری می‌گوید: از سال ۱۹۸۵ تا ۲۰۰۸ تعداد دانشجویان ایرانی‌ی دانشگاه‌های کانادا ۲۴۰ در صد افزایش یافته است. در همان گزارش می‌خوانیم: بین سال‌های ۲۰۰۳ تا ۲۰۰۸، به تعداد دانشجویان ایرانی در دانشگاه‌های استرالیا ۱۵۰۰ تن افزوده شده است.[14] بنا به گزارش سازمان ملل، جمهوری‌ی اسلامی در فرار دادن مغزها، و به لحاظ تعداد پناهجویان ایرانی، در رأس فهرستِ جهانی قرار دارد.[15] و بنیادگذار جمهوری‌ی اسلامی- که به محض استقرار، همه‌ی سخنان آزادمنشانه‌ی خود در نوفل لوشاتو را معکوس کرده بود- گفت: «به جهنم که فرار می‌کنند»:

> منافقین هی می‌گویند مغزها دارند فرار می‌کنند. **به جهنم که فرار می‌کنند**. این دانشگاه رفته‌ها، این‌ها که همه‌اش دم از علم و تمدن غرب می‌زنند بگذارید بروند. ما این علم و دانش غرب را نمی‌خواهیم. اگر شما هم می‌دانید که این جا جای‌تان نیست فرار کنید. **راهتان باز است**. (سخنرانی در جماران، ۸ آبان ۱۳۵۸)[16]

البته، آیت‌الله خودش می‌دانست که «راه باز» نیست، نبود. اما گریز به شکل‌های مختلف و از راه‌های پنهانی اتفاق افتاد. دو دهه پس از این سخنان «رهبر انقلاب»، هم مقامات جمهوری‌ی اسلامی و هم نشریات وابسته به آن، تازه خطر را درمی‌یابند، و جسته و گریخته به ابعاد گسترده‌ی فرارها اشاره می‌کنند: بیژن نامدار زنگنه، وزیر نفت دولت سیدمحمد خاتمی می‌گوید: **«سالی ۵۰ میلیارد دلار از ثروت علمی‌ی کشور را فرار مغزها تباه می‌کند.»**[17] محمدتقی امان‌پور (که من مقام دولتی‌ی او را نمی‌دانم) می‌گوید: **«سالانه ۱۴۵ هزار نفر از کشور مهاجرت می‌کنند که ۱۰۵ هزار نفر آنان دارای تحصیلات دانشگاهی هستند.»**[18] نشریه‌ی «همشهری»، چاپ تهران، می‌نویسد: **«فقط در سال ۱۹۹۰ (۱۳۶۹) حدود ۱۵۰۵۰۶ نفر ایرانی به امریکا مهاجرت کردند.»**[19] روزنامه‌ی «صدای عدالت»، چاپ تهران، می‌نویسد: **«ایران سالانه ۳۸ میلیارد دلار مغز، و ۱۲ میلیارد دلار نفت صادر می‌کند.»**[20] خبرگزاری‌ی «ایسنا» گزارش می‌دهد: **«زیانی که در نتیجه‌ی فرار مغزها متوجه اقتصاد کلان ایران شده، معادل با درآمد ارزی‌ی ناشی از صد سال فروش نفت است.»**[21]

متأسفانه، از تعداد کل ایرانیانی که پس از انقلاب سال ۱۳۵۷ ترک وطن کرده‌اند، هنوز آمار دقیقی در دست نیست، یا دست کم من نتوانستم به آن دست یابم. اما اکثر پژوهش‌ها- تا پیش از انتخابات دور دهم ریاست جمهوری و کودتای بنیادگرایان (خرداد ۱۳۸۸)، که موج تازه‌ای از خودتبعیدی را سبب شد- در تخمین «سه تا چهار میلیون» اتفاق نظر

---

http://www.parstimes.com/news/archive/2004/rfe/brain_drain.html

13 Ibid.

14 Afshin Molavi, ***The Star Students of Islamic Republic***, in Newsweek, Aug. 18- 25, 2008 issue.

15 Glonaz Esfandiari, Ibid.

۱۶ برگرفته از پژوهش فرامرز خرد. من نمی‌دانم فرامرز خرد این نوشته را در رسانه‌ای منتشر کرده است یا نه. اما متن او توسط ای- میل به من رسیده است.

۱۷ نشریه‌ی ***چیستا***، تهران، مهرماه ۱۳۸۳.

۱۸ پیشین.

۱۹ پیشین.

۲۰ روزنامه‌ی صدای عدالت، تهران، ۹ مهر ۱۳۸۱. برگرفته از ***چیستا***، تهران، مهرماه ۱۳۸۳.

۲۱ برگرفته از ***چیستا***، تهران، مهرماه ۱۳۸۳.

داشتند؛[۲۲] که با سرکوب «جنبش سبز» مردم ایران، اکنون گسترده‌تر هم شده است. این «مغزها» بوده‌اند که ضمن دنبال کردنِ رویدادها و جنبش‌های فرهنگی و سیاسی‌ی مردم ایران، و حرکت در راستای آن‌ها، به مثابه سرمایه‌های انسانی، به ارتقاء دانش و تکنولوژی و اقتصاد و هنر کشورهای میزبان یاری داده‌اند. اطلاعات به دست آمده از «سرشماری» ی سال ۲۰۰۰ در ایالات متحده نشان داد که نسبت آماری‌ی ایرانیانِ بالای بیست و پنج سال و با تحصیلات دانشگاهی، به نسبت دانش‌آموختگان بالای بیست و پنج سال در کل جمعیت این کشور، از دو برابر بیش‌تر است (%۵۷/۲ به 24.4%).[۲۳] باید همین جا یادآور شوم که در سرشماری‌ی سال ۲۰۰۰، بسیاری از ایرانیان امریکائی، به دلایل مختلف از ثبت ملیت خود خودداری کرده بودند. البته جامعه‌ی ایرانی در امریکا برای پر کردن پرسش‌نامه‌ی سرشماری‌ی سال ۲۰۱۰، دستورالعملی را از راه رسانه‌های گروهی به ایرانیان آموزش داد، که اگر به آن عمل شده باشد، باید دست کم آمار نسبتاً دقیقی از جمعیت ایرانیان امریکا مشخص شده باشد. اما تا این لحظه این آمار منتشر نشده است.

ناگفته پیداست که نه همه‌ی این «سه/ چهار میلیون» ایرانی، «نویسنده» یا «هنرمند» هستند، و نه همه‌ی آن‌ها به معنای اختصاصی‌ی آن، «اندیشه‌ورز» یا «فرهنگ‌پرور» یا «کوشنده‌ی سیاسی» هستند، یا بوده‌اند. اما جمعیت انبوهی از اندیشه‌ورزان، فرهنگ‌پروران، نویسندگان و هنرمندان ایرانی، که هم اکنون در سراسر جهان پراکنده هستند نیز، در جنس ذهنی و راه‌های عینی و زمان فرار و تعلق «نسلی»، با هم تفاوت‌های چشمگیر دارند. در نتیجه، در سخن گفتن از «سی و پنج سال متن فارسی در تبعید»، باید تا جایی که هاشورها اجازه می‌دهند، و بر اساس خود «متن»ها، مرز این تفاوت‌ها را در هر زمینه‌ی سخن مشخص کنیم. اما وجه انکارناپذیر در زایش و رویش «متن فارسی در تبعید»، فرار بخش عظیمی از نخستین لایه‌ی تبعیدیان، از زندان، شکنجه، و اعدام است. گرچه این وجه در بسیاری از اجزاء لایه‌های بعدی‌ی تبعیدیان همسان و یکدست نیست، اما وجهی انکارپذیر هم نیست. به بیانی دیگر، اگر برخی افراد از گروه‌های اجتماعی‌ی مختلف برای دست‌یابی به زندگی‌ی بهتر، و امکانات بیش‌تر، زیستگاه تازه‌ی خود را آگاهانه برگزیدند و از ایران «مهاجرت» کردند، مطلقاً دلیل بر آن نمی‌شود که خروج همه‌ی برون‌مرزیانی که پس از لایه‌ی نخستین (ده سال نخست) از ایران خارج شدند را «اختیاری» برآورد کنیم. به عنوان مثال، با هیچ استدلالی نمی‌توان عنصر «اجبار» را در خروج «خودی»های «ناخودی» شده‌ی حکومت، مانند عبدالکریم سروش یا اکبر گنجی یا احمد باطبی را نادیده گرفت؛ یا خروج نویسندگانی مانند رضا براهنی، فرج سرکوهی، عباس معروفی، منصور کوشان، بیژن بیجاری، شیرین دقیقیان، مسعود بهنود، محمدرضا شفیعی کدکنی و ده‌ها تن مانند آن‌ها- که در دهه‌های دوم و سوم جمهوری‌ی اسلامی به «برون‌مرزیان» پیوستند- را نمی‌توان در قلمرو «مهاجرت» جا داد. (نمی‌دانم خبر خروج همیشگی‌ی شفیعی کدکنی از ایران دروغ بود، یا او به زودی پشیمان شد و به ایران بازگشت. اما من این خبر را در اینترنت خواندم. و متأسفانه مأخذ آن را یادداشت نکردم.) در هر حال، کوشندگان و نویسندگان و فرهنگ پرورانِ یادشده، به امید کارسازی‌های فرهنگی و بازکردن افق کور فرهنگ در جمهوری‌ی اسلامی، تا آخرین توان خود، و در دهان بازجویی و شلاق و زندان و حتا مرگ، با مناسباتِ سیاسی و فرهنگی‌ی جمهوری‌ی اسلامی جنگیدند. این «اجبار»، شامل بسیاری از جوانان و نوجوانانی نیز می‌شود که از همان دهه‌ی نخست این رژیم، از پر ریختن در میدان‌های «مین‌گذاری»شده در جنگ ایران و عراق، گریختند. این «اجبار»، البته، روزنامه‌نگاران و وبلاگ‌نویسان معترض، و کوشندگان حقوق بشر و حقوق زنان و دانشجویانِ رانده شده از دانشگاه‌ها و گریخته از بازجوئی‌های مکرر و شکنجه‌گاه‌های جمهوری‌ی اسلامی را هم شامل می‌شود.

---

22 Shirin Hakimzadeh, ***A Vast Diaspora and Millions of Refugees at Home***, in Migration Policy Institute (online), September 2006: www.migrationpolicy.org

23 Ali Mostashari and Ali Khodamhosseini, ***An Overview of Socioeconomic Characteristics of the Iranin-American Community based on the 2000 U.S. Census***, Iranian Studies Group at MIT, February 2004.

بنا بر این واقعیت‌های تاریخی، می‌توان گفت که غیر از لایه‌ی نخست تبعیدیان، «ما»، در درازنای سی و پنج سال گذشته، هم «مهاجر» داشته‌ایم و هم «تبعیدی». اما از آن رو که «نویسنده»، با «زبان» سر و کار دارد، و «نوشتن» را بخشی یا شاید بخش عظیمی از هویت خود شناسایی می‌کند، و از آن رو که تداوم این هویت را به وجود «مخاطب» وابسته می‌بیند، حتا اگر زیستگاه تازه‌ی خود را آگاهانه برگزیده باشد، خروج همیشگی‌ی او از زیستگاهِ زبان خود، امری صد در صد اجباری است، و دست کم به لحاظ این شاخصه‌ی بیرونی، می‌توان گفت که متن او، متنی تبعیدی است. بی‌درنگ باید اشاره کنم که این شاخصه البته به کسانی مربوط می‌شود که پیش از خروج از وطن، هم از سوی خود و هم از سوی جامعه‌ی خود به عنوان «نویسنده» شناسایی شده بودند. در حالی که گروه عظیمی از نویسندگان تبعیدی ، پیش از ترک ایران، «نویسنده» نبودند و چنین هویتی برای خود نمی‌شناختند. و تازه، افراد این گروه نیز از بسیاری جنبه‌ها زیر یک چتر نمی‌گنجند، چه رسد به نویسندگان و اندیشه‌ورزانی که ما آن‌ها را با عنوان نویسندگان «نسل دوم» شناسایی می‌کنیم. و باز تازه، در میان نویسندگان «نسل دوم»، گروه‌هایی هستند که شخصاً ایران را ترک کرده‌اند؛ و هم گروه‌هایی که، در کودکی همراه با خانواده‌ی خود از ایران خارج شده‌اند، و هم گروه‌هایی که، در زیستگاه تازه متولد شده‌اند. رسیدگی به این کیفیت‌ها، البته، محتوای کتاب حاضر را رقم زده است، اما این اشاره‌ی گذرا را از آن رو در این مقدمه لازم دیدم که خواننده‌ام را به تنوع پدیده‌ی مورد بررسی هشدار داده باشم؛ تنوعی که، همراه با گذشت زمان، و زیر تأثیر مؤثرهای گوناگون مداوماً دگرگون شده است، و برای شناسایی، مداوماً چون «ماهی» از دست شناسنده لیز می‌خورد.

«متن فارسی در تبعید»، با همه‌ی این گونه‌گونگی‌ها، اکنون از مرز سی و پنج سالگی گذشته است. سی و پنج سال؛ آن هم در عصری که یکی از مهم‌ترین شاخصه‌هایش شتاب است؛ شتابی چنان فزاینده، که به گفته‌ی «آرنولد توین‌بی»، مورخ امریکایی، «انسان از خود جا مانده است.»[۲۴]

ناگفته پیداست که در درازنای این زمان دراز، که هر ماه و سال آن، بارآور دگرگونی‌های تاریخ‌ساز بوده است، بسیاری از مناسبات سیاسی، اقتصادی، فرهنگی، ادبی و هنری در جامعه‌ی جهانی، در ایران، و در زندگی‌ی ایرانیان تبعیدی/ مهاجر، دستخوش دگرگونی‌های اساسی شده‌اند. و تردید نیست که برآیند نیروهای پدیدآمده از این دگرگونی‌ها، همراه با انبوه‌ترشدن و تنوع جمعیت تبعیدیان، همراه با پیامدهای طولانی شدن زندگی در زیستگاه تازه (برای گروه اول تبعیدیان) و جذب عناصر فرهنگ میزبان، و تعمق و بازاندیشی به خود و فرهنگ خودی، همه و همه، در بینش و کنش نویسندگان ایرانی در تبعید، مؤثر بوده و جلوه‌های خود را در درونه‌ی گفتار و نوشتار آن‌ها بر جا نهاده است.

از سوی دیگر، اگر بپذیریم که انسان غربی در شاهراه‌های اطلاعاتی، و در مسیر مناسباتی که تکنولوژی بر کلیه‌ی شئون زندگی‌ی او پیچانده، از «خود» جا مانده است، باید بپذیریم که ایرانی‌ی رانده‌شده از وطن، که فرهنگش پیش از تبعید یا مهاجرت از جهان جامانده بود، و اینک نیز از وطن و فرهنگِ خود جا مانده است، در برخورد با فرهنگ‌های تازه، قاعدتاً باید درگیر «جاماندگی»‌های مضاعف باشد.

می‌بینیم اگر در ده/ پانزده سال نخست تبعید می‌شد پیکر سراسری «ادبیات فارسی در تبعید» را در شعر و داستان و نقد ادبی خلاصه کرد، و آن را با یک یا چند کتابِ مقدمه‌وار پیمود، در سی سالگی‌ی این پدیده‌ی عظیم و پیچیده، کار- حتا مقدمه‌وار هم- به آن آسانی نیست. ده / پانزده سال پیش، گرچه پدیده‌ای به نام «خاطرات زندان» هم داشتیم. اما نه حجم آن

---

[۲۴] آرنولد توین بی حدود چهار دهه پیش، با تکیه بر سرعت دگرگونی ها و کثرت رویدادها و تنوع تفسیرها درباره ی هر رویداد جهانی، مسئله ی عدم توانایی ی مورخ و مفسر تاریخ در جمع بندی و رسیدن به یک نظر منسجم درباره ی هر رویداد را به صورت جدی مطرح کرده بود.

به میزانی بود که بتوان آن را «ادبیات زندان» نامید، و نه نمونه‌های گسترده‌ای از نامه‌ها و وصیت‌نامه‌ها و هنرهای زندان را در اختیار داشتیم. ده/ پانزده سال پیش، گرچه «کانون نویسندگان ایران در تبعید» را هم داشتیم، اما هنوز متن‌های مدونی، درباره‌ی تاریخ این کانون و تبارشناسی‌ی افت و خیز اندیشه‌ی آن در دست نداشتیم. ده/ پانزده سال پیش، گرچه «جنبش‌های سیاسی» هم داشتیم، اما بسیار بسیارانی از متن‌های تحلیلی و نقد و نظرهای سیاسی، آکنده از زخم پرتاب، عنصر شتابزدگی، تکرار و مرور ذهنیت‌های «گذشته» بود. و اگر متن‌هایی داشتیم که در بازخوانی‌ی گذشته متحول شده بود (که داشتیم)، تعداد آن‌ها بسیار اندک بود، و به دلیل پراکندگی‌ی جغرافیایی، امکان دسترسی به آن‌ها نیز اندک بود. اما در حال حاضر، آن «بسیار اندک‌ها» جای خود را به «بسیارها» داده‌اند. در حال حاضر، ما در نوشتار فارسی در تبعید پدیده‌ای داریم، که در کنار همان «اندک‌ها»ی دهه‌ی نخست، عنوان «ادبیات سیاسی» را برخود می‌پذیرند. به بیانی دیگر، در حال حاضر، «متن سی و سه ساله‌ی فارسی در تبعید» افزون بر آفرینش‌های ادبی، شامل رشته‌های مشخصی است که با نام‌های «ادبیات زندان»، «ادبیات سیاسی»، «نقد»، و «ادبیات پژوهشی» در زمینه‌های مختلف، قابل شناسایی هستند.

این است که سخن گفتن از «متن فارسی در تبعید» گذر از راه‌های پرپیچ و خمی را طلب می‌کند. اینک، رونده‌ی این راه پرپیچ و خم ناگزیر است، در حد توانایی‌ی علمی‌ی خود، تار و پود این شبکه را بگشاید، جنس آن را بشناسد، و داد و دهشِ متعاملِ هر یک را با دیگری بسنجد. بدیهی است که در این رهگذر، ناگزیر خواهد بود انگیزه‌ها، سازه‌ها، فرایندها، و جلوه‌های دگرگونی را قلمرو به قلمرو بررسی کند. و باز بدیهی است که تا در آغاز راه، «موثرهای» دگرگونی را شناسایی نکند، و تا جنس، نقطه‌ی عزیمت، و فرودگاه هر یک از آن‌ها را در ایجاد تحول یا ایستایی‌ی ذهنی به ملاحظه نگذارد، راه به جایی نخواهد برد، جز به داوری‌های بی‌پشتوانه.

می‌بینیم نقشه‌ی بالا، ما را قدم به قدم به عقب می‌راند، و رسیدگی به سرچشمه را به امری ناگزیر تبدیل می‌کند. یعنی، برای رسیدن به نمایی از بینش‌ها و کنش‌های تبعیدیان، و برای رسیدن به تحول یا ایستایی‌های ذهنی در «متن فارسی در تبعید»، باید مؤثرهای «پیرامونی» و «کانونی» را شناخت. اما برای آشنایی با هر یک از این «موثرها»، ابتدا باید زمینه و خیزگاه هر یک را در نظر گرفت. و برای شناخت زمینه‌های این‌زمانی، و برای این که بدانیم چرا از **این** «مؤثر» دگرگون شده‌ایم و نه از **آن**، باید نقبی زد بر پیشینه‌ی فرهنگ ایرانی و فرهنگ «غربی»، که میزبان اکثریت تبعیدیان این دوره از تاریخ ایران است.

من مجموعه‌ی حاضر را از همین نقطه آغاز می‌کنم. یعنی، در جلد اول، ابتدا درنگی خواهم داشت بر پیشینه‌ی فرهنگی‌ی «ایران» و «غرب»؛ سپس، مروری خواهم داشت بر تاریخ معاصر ایران، از انقلاب مشروطیت تا درگذشت آیت‌الله خمینی، بنیادگذار جمهوری‌ی اسلامی. این مرور سریع را با سه هدف انجام می‌دهم: ۱) شناسائی‌ی شاکله‌های ذهنی/ فرهنگی‌ی پیکارگران راه «آزدای، استقلال، آبادی، و سربلندی»ی ایران؛ ۲) شناسائی‌ی انگیزه‌های تبعید؛ ۳) به دست آوردن معیارهائی برای شناسائی‌ی «تحول» در شاکله‌های ذهنی/ فرهنگی‌ی پیکارگران کنونی در تبعید.

شاید پرداختن به پیشینه‌های دور و نزدیک، در رابطه با «متن فارسی در تبعید»، نقض غرض بشمار آید. اما با توجه به هدف نهائی‌ی مجموعه، امری کاملاً بایسته بوده است، و دلیل‌های بایستگی را نیز در مقدمه‌های کوتاه هر مبحث بدست داده‌ام. بدین ترتیب، نه تنها جلد نخست این مجموعه ظاهراً ربطی به «متن فارسی در تبعید» ندارد، بلکه جلد دوم نیز به شناسائی‌ی «مؤثرها»ئی اختصاص دارد، که در دگرگونی و تحول ذهنی‌ی تبعیدیان نقش داشته‌اند، بدون آن که ظاهراً به «متن فارسی در تبعید» مربوط باشند.

سازه‌های بنیادینِ تاریخی- فرهنگی

- «آی.../ پس آن کلام چیست/ که ما از آن زاده می‌شویم و در آن می‌میریم/
و در گذارَش، تنها گورستانی از صدف و ستاره باقی می‌ماند؟/ پس آن کلام چیست/
که موشک‌ها در آن رهسپار فلک‌اند/ و بمب‌ها از آن بار آتشناک برمی‌گیرند؟»
- «مادرِ دفترها و روزنامه‌ها و کتابخانه‌ها/ مادرِ هر آن چه می‌نویسد و نوشته می‌شود/
ذات بی‌کفایتِ دانستن/ و جوهر بلیغ ندانستن/
آن‌گاه که زمستان به کوچه‌ی ما می‌رسد و درختان را پیر می‌کند/ و فقط من می‌دانم/
که بهار در دانه‌های برف پنهان است و/ غفلت/ همیشه از جدی گرفتن زمستان آغاز می‌شود...»
(اسماعیل نوری علا، دفتر «موریانه‌ها و چشمه»)[۲۵]

ای خط !/ امتداد طولانی!/ همسایه‌ی زمان!/ عینیت حافظه- از سنگ، شمشیر، و دکمه!
مرا راه ببر در کوچه‌های پیچ پیچ وُ کور/ به دیروز دور/ به سال‌های بی‌عبور/
[...] مرا در خود راه ببر/
بگذار ببینم وقوع حادثه را، شروع فاصله را/
بگذار ببینم/ که چه‌گونه توان دست‌های تناورم/ این چنین باطل شد/
که ساختنم، برای ریختن بلندای خودم بر خاک است/
بگذار ببینم که چرا/ اعتلای خِرَدم را/ فقط در کتاب می‌نویسم. [...]
(ملیحه تیره گل، «با تاریخ»)

مقدمه: از آن جا که شناخت نسبی از سازه‌ها و الگوهای فرهنگی، ما را در فهم چرائی و چه‌گونگی‌ی دگرگونی‌های عینی و ذهنی در ادبیات سی و پنج سال اخیرمان هدایت می‌کند، پیش از هر سخنی در این مجموعه، تبارشناسی‌ی این سازه‌ها و الگوها را در دستور کار قرار می‌دهم. به بیانی دیگر، بررسی‌ی پیشینه‌ی شکل‌بندی‌ی سازه‌های فرهنگی و برایند آن‌ها در حیات اجتماعی‌ی «کانون» ما در طول زمان، ما را به دگرگونی‌ی این سازه‌ها در زمان حال، و کارکرد هر یک از آن‌ها در سازواره‌های ذهنی‌ی نوشتار فارسی در تبعید، نزدیک می‌کند، و ردیابی‌ی تحول و رشد را ممکن می‌سازد.

با این امید، بر آنم که، در چهارچوبی محدود، به کنش و واکنش شبکه‌واری که در طول تاریخ ما بین سیاست، دین، فلسفه، علم، و جامعه‌ی «کانونی»ی پدید آورندگان متن فارسی در تبعید وجود داشته، بپردازم. چرا که، بنا بر «دیدگاه»ی که در

---

[۲۵] اسماعیل نوری علا، ***موریانه‌ها و چشمه*** (شعر بلند)، دنور: انتشارات چاپار ۱۹۹۵، ص ۱۷.

پیش‌گفتار مجموعه اعلام کرده‌ام، ناگزیرم که حیات تاریخی‌ی جامعه‌ای را که نوشتار در آن آفریده شده، صورتی از بینش فلسفی و معرفت‌شناسی‌ی آن جامعه تلقی کنم. در مورد تأثیر متقابل پدیده‌های مورد بحث نیز، گفته‌ی «کارل مارکس» را پشتوانه می‌گیرم. کارل مارکس - نه در مقام یک «پیشوا»، نه به عنوان واضع «مارکسیسم»، بلکه - به عنوان فیلسوفی که شاهراه‌ها و کوره راه‌های فلسفه‌ی غرب را از سحرگاه آن تا زمان خودش مو به مو پیموده بود، در این زمینه می‌نویسد:

> هر فلسفه‌ی حقیقی، جوهر فکری‌ی زمان خودش است. فلسفه، نه تنها از درون با محتوای خود، بلکه از بیرون با شکل خود، با جهان واقعی‌ی زمان خود در تماس قرار دارد و با آن درگیرِ کنش و واکنش متقابل است. [...] این «کنش و واکنش متقابل، در تمام اعصار برقرار بوده است.[۲۶]

با پذیرش این گفته، که هر رهنورد تاریخ به آن می‌رسد، مسیر این تعامل را در تاریخ ایران به سرعت مرور می‌کنم. «یونان»، به عنوان مادر فرهنگ غربی، از آن رو در این بحث مطرح می‌شود، که اکثریت قریب به اتفاق کوشندگان سیاسی، نویسندگان و شاعران و منتقدان تبعیدی/ مهاجر ایرانی، در سراسر سرزمین‌هایی که ما با واژه‌ی «غرب» شناسایی می‌کنیم، پراکنده‌اند. از این گذشته، اندیشه‌ی غربی و وابسته‌های آن، نه تنها در تحول اندیشه در سده‌های نخستین ایران اسلامی مؤثر بوده، بلکه حدوداً از سده‌ی یازدهم هجری (هجدهم میلادی) تا همین امروز، در حیات سیاسی، فلسفی، علمی، و اجتماعی‌ی ایران، به طور فزاینده، نقشی تعیین‌کننده داشته است.

بدیهی است که بحث مربوط به تبارشناسی‌های فرهنگی در این فصل، یک مطالعه‌ی مرحله‌ای و ریزبینِ تاریخی نیست. منتها، برای آن که همین بازنگری‌ی سراسری، به تقلیل‌گرایی و کلی‌گویی متهم نشود، یادآوری‌ی چند نکته را بایسته می‌دانم:

* به سبب وجود بخش هاشوری‌ی دوره‌های تاریخی، تاریخ‌های **دقیقِ** خیزش و خروش و خاموشی‌ی روندهای فکری را به عنوان عنصری تعیین کننده در نظر نگرفته‌ام.

* زمانی که از تاریخ یک کشور یا ملت یا یک فرهنگ در یک دوره‌ی معین سخن می‌گوئیم، باید زمینه‌ی جغرافیائی‌ی تاریخ آن دوره‌ی معین را در نظر داشته باشیم. به قول ریچارد فرای (ایران‌شناس)، بدون دانستن جغرافیا و بدون شناخت بستر جغرافیائی‌ی تحولات تاریخی، تاریخ یکسره بی‌معنی جلوه می‌کند. کما این که خود این مورخ و محقق کم‌نظیر در کلیه‌ی کتاب‌هایش، از هر دوره‌ای که در مورد «ایران» سخن می‌گوید، نخست به جغرافیای ایران در آن دوره می‌پردازد. اما من در این فشرده، از بازشناسائی‌ی جغرافیائی‌ی تاریخ ایران در دوره‌های مورد سخنم معذورم. منظور من در این جا از «ایران باستان» و «ایران سده‌های نخستین اسلامی»، تمام سرزمین‌هائی است که بنا بر تشخیص ایران‌شناسان و باستان‌شناسانی چون ریچارد فرای، در درازنای این دوره‌ها به نام «ایران» شناسائی می‌شد.

* در سخن گفتن از «فرهنگ ایران باستان» نیز در درجه‌ی نخست به مشکل «دوره»ها، از جمله دوره‌های اساطیری و تاریخی برمی‌خوریم. چرا که افزون بر دوره‌بندی‌ی فردوسی در شاهنامه، و افزون بر گزاره‌های مورخان دوره‌ی اسلامی، در درازنای سی و پنج سال گذشته برخی از پژوهشگران تبعیدی، بر دوره‌های «فرهنگ سیمرغی»ی ایران و یا «فرهنگ دوره‌ی زنخدائی» در ایران تکیه کرده‌اند، که طبیعتاً به پیش از تشکیل نخستین دولت‌های تاریخی، به پیش از ظهور

---

[۲۶] مرتضی محیط، ***کارل مارکس: زندگی و دیدگاه‌های او***، (تهران: نشر اختران، ۱۳۸۲) صفحه‌ی ۸۹. مرجع مورد اشاره‌ی دکتر محیط: مجموعه‌ی آثار کارل مارکس، جلد اول، صفحه‌ی ۱۹۷.

زرتشت، و حتا به پیش از جدائیِ ایرانیان از فرهنگ «هند و ایرانی» مربوط می‌شوند.[۲۷] من در این جا، با حفظ احترام به این نوع پژوهش‌ها و یافته‌های گرانبهای آن‌ها، به این قلمروها وارد نمی‌شوم، و در این جا نیز امپراتوریِ هخامنشی را نقطه‌ی زمانیِ عزیمت قرار می‌دهم. گرچه به مناسبت بحث، گریزهائی نیز به فرهنگ دوران اساطیری خواهم زد.

* حکمت خسروانی، ابعاد عرفان اسلامی، تفاوت‌های آن با عرفان «گنوستیک»، شاخه‌های متعدد هر یک، تفاوتِ آن‌ها با یکدیگر، بحث‌های نظری درباره‌ی تفاوت «عرفان» با «تصوف»، و خاستگاه مکانی و زمانیِ هر یک از آن‌ها، کلاف بسیار پیچیده‌ای را تشکیل می‌دهد، که حتا اشاره‌وار، در این بررسیِ فشرده نمی‌گنجد. از این رو، می‌کوشم که با تکیه بر عام‌ترین ویژگی‌های عرفان ایرانی، به این پدیده نگاه کنم.

---

[۲۷] به عنوان مثال در این زمینه، خواننده‌ام را به کتاب‌های منوچهر کمالی، از جمله: «فرهنگ سیمرغیِ ایران»، «فرهنگ زن‌خدائیِ ایران»، «فرهنگ‌شهر: حکومت و جامعه بر شالوده‌ی فرهنگ ایران»، «جشن‌شهر»، «شهر بی‌شاه»، «از هومنی در فرهنگ ایران تا هومنیسم در باختر»، رجوع می‌دهم، و یادآور می‌شوم که شناسنامه‌ی انتشار بیشتر کتاب‌های این نویسنده، کامل نیست. اما دانش تاریخی و اساطیریِ گسترده‌ی او به همراه تسلط بی‌چون چرای او به زبان کردی (زبان اصیل و دست‌نخورده از دوران باستان ایران) و ریشه‌یابیِ واژگان آن، بسیاری از یافته‌ها و پیشنهادهای تازه را به نوشته‌های او ارمغان داده است.

پیشینه‌ی کانون «ما»
(ایران)

پارسیان به فرزندان خود تقوی و فضیلت می‌آموزند،
همان گونه که دیگران خواندن و نوشتن می‌آموزند.
(گزنفون)[۲۸]

پارسیان چه می‌گفتند: راست گو، و راست تیر بیانداز!
این است فضیلت پارسی. اکنون دریاب که از کی پس‌رَوی آغاز شد؛
هنگامی که راستی از زبان پارسی، و تیر و کمان از دست او بیافتاد!
(فردریک نیچه)[۲۹]

پارسیان، یونانی‌ها، رمی‌ها و تئوتون‌ها تنها سازندگان تاریخ
و تنها بانیان پیشرفت هستند.
(لرد آکتون، مورخ و سیاستمدار بریتانیائی)[۳۰]

ایران، خاستگاه یکی از کهن‌ترین تمدن‌های بشری،
تداوم شگفت فرهنگی پویا، که در هر برهه‌ای از انقطاع،
دوباره از خاکستر خویش جان گرفته و قد برافراشته است.
(رنه گروسه- ایران‌شناس فرانسوی)[۳۱]

---

[۲۸] برگرفته از: دکتر پرویز اذکائی، ***فهرست ماقبل الفهرست: آثار ایرانی‌ی پیش از اسلام***، مشهد: انتشارات بنیاد پژوهش‌های اسلامی‌ی آستان قدس، ۱۳۷۵.

[۲۹] فریدریش نیچه، ***اراده‌ی معطوف به قدرت***، ترجمه‌ی دکتر محمدباقر هوشیار، ویراسته‌ی جدید، تهران: نشر و پژوهش فرزان، ۱۳۷٦، ص ۲۹.

[30] John Dalberg- Acton, ***Mr. Goldwin Smith's Irish History***, in: The History of Freedom and Other Essays, edited by: J. N. Figgis and R. V. Laurence, London: Macmillian, 1907, chapter 8.
توضیح: بنا بر دانشنامه‌ی ویکی‌پدیا:«تئوتون‌ها»، قبایل ژرمن بودند که در فرایند جنگ‌های بی‌شمار از دو سده پیش از میلاد مسیح از زادگاه خود در اسکاندیناوی و دانمارک در سراسر اروپا پراکنده شده بودند.

[۳۱] گروهی از ایران‌شناسان مشهور، ***روح ایران***، با مقدمه‌ی داریوش شایگان، ترجمه به فارسی از محمود بهفروزی، تهران: نشر پندنامک، ۱۳۸۱. ص ٦٤.

اگر زمانی یک ملت واقعاً از خود شرمنده باشد،
مثل شیری در کنام برای طعمه دندان قروچه می‌کند.
(کارل مارکس)[۳۲]

صدای من/ صدای خلقم است/
من از عشق آنان/
غرور آنان/
و شرم پنهانشان/
می‌گویم.
(پریتیشناندی، شاعر انگلیسی‌زبانِ هند، ترجمه‌ی مهدی فلاحتی)[۳۳]

من، با فرهنگ ایرانی- با همه‌ی عظمت‌ها و خفّت‌هایش،
با همه‌ی سربلندی‌ها و شرمساری‌هایش- همگوهرم.
منتها، برای شناختِ انگیزه‌های این عظمت و خفت،
دستم را از آن چه که هست کوتاه‌تر نمی‌گیرم؛
گرچه هر قدر در این رهگذر پیش‌تر می‌روم،
به کوتاهی‌ی دستم بیش‌تر پی می‌برم.
(ملیحه تیره گل)

[...]
اینک نگاه کن از پشت پلک پنجره/
تکرار پُر تَرنّم باران را/
و گوش کن که در شب/
دیگر سکوت نیست/
بشنو سرود ریزش باران را/
که امشب به یاد تو می‌آرد/
گوئی صدای سُم سواران را
گوئی صدای سُم سواران را/
گوئی صدای سُم سواران را/
گوئی صدای سُم سواران را...
(از ترانه‌ی «بگذار تا ببارد باران»، با صدای حبیب محبیان)

---

[۳۲] شیرین دقیقیان، ***اندیشیدن ... هنوز: شناخت‌شناسی‌ی اصلاحات*** (گزیده‌ی مقالات اجتماعی/ فلسفی)، لس‌انجلس: انتشارات شرکت کتاب، ۱۳۸۷/ ۲۰۰۸، ص ٥٤.

[۳۳] پریتیش ناندی (Pritish Nandy)، ***پرسه در اقلیم حیرت‌آور زنبق‌ها***، ترجمه‌ی آزاد از مهدی فلاحتی (م. پیوند)، سوئد: نشر باران، ۱۹۹۵ (۱۳۷٤)، صفحه‌ی اول از «پیش درآمد یک»..

ایران باستان[۳۴]

حالا، ما در سحرگاه دمیدن تمدن ایرانی هستیم، پوشیده در مهی از اسطوره و افسانه و گزاره‌های پر از حدس و گمان و متناقض. اطلاعاتِ تاریخی‌ی ما، دست کم تا پایان ساسانیان، بیش‌تر از راه گزارش‌های دوردست و سینه به سینه‌ی نسل‌های هزار ساله، یا از کتاب‌های اکثراً تحریف‌شده‌ی مورخان یونان باستان به دست می‌آید، که اگر ناقض یکدیگر نباشند، یکدیگر را به طور کامل پشتیبانی نمی‌کنند. به عنوان مثال، «آرتور امانوئل کریستن‌سن» خاورشناس دانمارکی در مطالعه‌ی «سلطنت قباد و ظهور مزدک»، غیر از منابع سریانی و یونانی و رُمی و عربی، از حدود ۲۰ مأخذ ایرانی سود جسته، و با این که می‌گوید مأخذ همه‌ی آن‌ها «خواتاینامک» بوده است، هیچ دو روایتی را کاملاً مشابه نیافته است.[۳۵] نمونه‌های دیگر از گزاره‌های متناقض را در مجموعه‌ی پژوهش‌های ایران‌شناسان غربی می‌یابیم. مثلاً، در نوشته‌های بسیاری از این پژوهشگران، در مواردی چون تاریخ تولد زرتشت، زمان و مکان ظهور او، کیفیت آئین او، «گات‌ها»ئی که از او به جا مانده، چنان تناقضی به چشم می‌خورد، که نه تنها افراد «ناکارشناسی» مانند من، بلکه خود کارشناسان را به شگفتی واداشته است. به عنوان نمونه، هنریک سَموئل نی‌برگ، ایران‌شناس سوئدی، در کتاب «دین‌های ایران باستان»، عقیده‌ی عام ایران‌شناسان پیشین درباره‌ی زرتشت را چنین خلاصه می‌کند: «تصویر یک کشیش مترقی‌ی روستائی که به اصلاحات ارضی علاقمند بوده است.» او، زرتشت را «انسانی ماقبل تاریخ» و «جادوگری میگسار از قبایل وحشی‌ی آسیای مرکزی» شناسائی می‌کند، که پیرو نوعی «آئین شَمَنی» بود؛ گات‌های او، «اورادی بی‌معنی» بود که با استفاده از «بخور و بخار و بنگ و شاهدانه» بر زبان او جاری شده بود؛ علیه «یگانه‌پرستی» برخاست و در دستگاه نظری‌ی خود «اهریمن» را مستقل از «اهورامزدا»، و در برابر او گذاشت؛ و به این ترتیب، «دوگانه‌پرستی جازم شد.»[۳۶] ارنست امیل هرتسفلد، باستان‌شناس و ایران‌شناس آلمانی، در کتاب ۸۰۰ صفحه‌ای‌ی «زرتشت و جهان او»، نظرات نی‌برگ را یکسره مردود می‌داند، و خود، زرتشت را از خاندان درباری، و «سیاستمداری توطئه‌گر» معرفی می‌کند. هرتسفلد از یک سو، زرتشت را «توطئه‌گر»ی می‌داند که «قتل سرسخت‌ترین دشمنش، گئوماته‌ی مغ را تدارک دید»، و از سوی دیگر، می‌گوید: «زرتشت می‌خواست به جای زارعانِ برده، دهقانان آزاد و بیعت کرده را بنشاند، و در راه این هدف، با طبقات حاکم، و زمینداران کلان و اشراف و نجبا و روحانیان به کشمکش افتاد.»[۳۷] والتر برونو هنینگ، خاورشناس و ایران‌شناس آلمانی، در سلسله سخنرانی‌ها و نوشته‌های خود، گزاره‌های هر دو ایران‌شناس یادشده را مردود می‌داند، و در کمال شگفتی می‌پرسد:

> هر پژوهنده‌ای که به دو تصویر زرتشت، یکی اثر هرتسفلد و دیگری اثر نی‌برگ، بنگرد، و درباره‌ی آن‌ها اندیشه کند، بی‌گمان دچار **سرگیجه** می‌شود. چه‌گونه ممکن است که دو محقق طراز اول، که منابع تحقیق‌شان دقیقاً یکی است، به نتایجی برسند که درست نقطه‌ی مقابل هم باشد.[۳۸] (تأکید از من است.)

هنینگ پس از ابراز این شگفتی، و پیش از آن که به نقد خود بر فرضیه‌های نی‌برگ و هرتسفلد ادامه دهد، خود، درباره‌ی

---

[۳۴] با این که یافته‌های باستان‌شناسی، آغاز شکل‌گیری‌ی مدنیت در فلات ایران را به هزاره‌ی پنجم پیش از میلاد مسیح می‌رسانند، بدیهی است که منظور من از تاریخ «ایران باستان»، در این شرح مختصر، نمی‌تواند متکی به آن یافته‌ها باشد. بلکه، از زمانی آغاز می‌شود که پدیده‌ای با نام «دولت» در فلات ایران شکل گرفت.

[۳۵] آرتور امانوئل کریستن‌سن، ***سلطنت قباد و ظهور مزدک***، ترجمه‌ی احمد بیرشک، تهران: چاپ دوم، نام مرکز انتشارات ندارد، ۱۳۷۴.

[۳۶] والتر برونو هنینگ، ***زرتشت، سیاستمدار یا جادوگر!***، ترجمه‌ی کامران فانی، با مقدمه‌ای از فتح‌الله مجتبائی، تهران: انتشارات کتاب پرواز، چاپ سوم، ۱۳۷۹، صص ٤٤ تا ۵۰.

[۳۷] پیشین، صص ٤۰ تا ٤۳.

[۳۸] پیشین، ص۵۱ .

زرتشت می‌نویسد:

> زرتشت هر چه بود، به هر حال بنیانگذار یکی از بزرگترین ادیان عالم بود. ملتی بزرگ او را پیامبر خود می‌دانست و حرمتش می‌نهاد. قرن‌ها پس از آن که ایرانیان کوروش و داریوش و خدم و حشمشان را فراموش کردند، برای زرتشت همچنان مقامی آسمانی و الاهی قائل بودند. [...] **بهترین راه برای فهمیدن کیش زرتشت، همچون اغلب جنبش‌های دوگانه‌باوری آن است که مخالفت با یگانه‌پرستی را در آن می‌بینیم.**[۳۹] (تأکید از من است.)

از درستی یا نادرستیِ «بهترین راهِ» خودِ هنینگ که بگذریم، «سرگیجه» زمانی به «سرسام» تبدیل می‌شود که در جست‌وجوی یافتن رابطه بین گزاره‌های اسطوره‌ای و تاریخی باشیم. به عنوان مثال، حسن پیرنیا در کتاب ارجمند «عصر اساطیری‌ی تاریخ ایران» این پیشنهاد را مطرح می‌کند که چون کتاب‌های مرجع «شاهنامه‌ی ابومنصوری» و «شاهنامه»‌ی فردوسی و برخی از تاریخ‌های سده‌های نخستین اسلامی عمدتاً «خداینامک» بوده است، و چون «خداینامک» در اواخر دوره‌ی ساسانیان نوشته شده، شخصیت‌های تاریخی با شخصیت‌های اسطوره‌ای، به سبب بُعد زمانی و در غیاب سند نوشتاری، جایگزین یکدیگر شده‌اند. حسن پیرنیا با استدلال‌های علمی و آماری بر این پیشنهاد تأکید می‌کند که «کاووسِ» اسطوره‌ای همان «کمبوجیه‌ی هخامنشی»؛ و «کیخسرو» اسطوره‌ای، همان «کوروش هخامنشی» بوده است. او همچنین، ثابت می‌کند که در عصر اساطیری‌ی ایران، اصولاً ملت و قومی «تورانی‌نژاد»، یا از «نژاد اصفر» همسایه‌ی ایران نبوده است، و «تورانیان»، که در شاهنامه‌ها به عنوان دشمن «ایرانیان» قلمداد شده‌اند، گروه‌های دیگری از «اقوام آریائی» بوده‌اند.[۴۰] از «پیشدادیان» و دوره‌ی «اسطوره» که بگذریم و به «تاریخ» برسیم، باز به سبب کمبود مأخذهای اصیل نوشتاری، این «سرسام» همچنان ادامه می‌یابد. به عنوان نمونه، اگر در جست‌وجوی زمان و مکان تولد زرتشت، یا در جست‌وجوی مبنای ثنویتی که به تفکر او نسبت می‌دهند، به کتاب‌های ایران‌شناسان نگاه کنیم، در ابری از پیشنهادهای متناقض گم می‌شویم. مثلاً آرتور کریستن‌سن (Arthur Christensen) که ۳۰ صفحه از کتاب «مزداپرستی در ایران قدیم» را به بررسی‌ی زمان و مکان ظهور آئین زرتشتی اختصاص داده است، و تا به گمانه‌ی خود در مورد تاریخ و مکان زرتشت برسد، پیشنهادهای متضاد ده‌ها تن از ایران‌شناسان را بررسیده است، و با روش تطبیقی همه‌ی آن‌ها را بی‌پایه یافته است.[۴۱] یا ژاک دوشِن- گیمن (J.Duchesne-Guillemin)، ایران‌شناس فرانسوی، کتاب «اورمزد و اهریمن: ماجرای دوگانه‌باوری در عهد باستان» را با این جمله می‌گشاید که: « ایران کشور باستانی‌ی دوگانه‌باوری است. به نظر ارسطو و پلوتارک چنین بود. اما دوگانه‌باوری گونه‌های بسیار دارد.» و سپس در شرح «گونه‌ها»، از ده‌ها مورخ یونانی و ایران‌شناسان غربی نام می‌برد و درباره‌ی نظر هر یک از آن‌ها در زمینه‌ی دوگانه‌باوری‌ی ایران باستان بحث می‌کند. شگفتا که نظر و عقیده‌ی هیچ دو تنی از این افراد را در این کتاب یکسان نمی‌یابیم.[۴۲]

البته نباید فراموش کرد که پژوهش‌های ایران‌شناسان و باستان‌شناسان غربی، حق بزرگی بر آگاهی‌ی تاریخی‌ی ما ایرانیان دارند، اما هنوز نه آن‌ها و نه پژوهشگران و ایران‌شناسان ایرانی، در نشان دادن تصویری سراسری از تاریخ ایران باستان و حتا تاریخ پس از اسلام موفق نیستند. به عنوان مثال از این تلاش‌های ناتمام، باید به تفسیرهای آن‌ها از لوح‌های کشف

---

[۳۹] پیشین، ص ٥٦.

[۴۰] حسن پیرنیا، ***عصر اساطیری‌ی تاریخ ایران: خطوط برجسته‌ی داستان‌های ایران قدیم***، ویرایش سیروس ایزدی، تهران: انتشارات هیرمند، ۱۳۷۷، ص ۹۳ و صص ۱۱۷ تا ۱۲۰.

[۴۱] آرتور کریستن‌سن، ***مزداپرستی در ایران قدیم***، ترجمه‌ی دکتر ذبیح‌الله صفا، تهران: انتشارات هیرمند، چاپ چهارم، ۱۳۷٦.

[۴۲] ژاک دوشن گیمن، ***اورمزد و اهریمن: ماجرای دوگانه‌باوری در عهد باستان***، ترجمه‌ی دکتر عباس باقری، تهران: مرکز نشر و پژوهش فرزان روز، ۱۳۷۸.

شده در تخت جمشید مراجعه کرد. از اوایل سده‌ی بیستم میلادی که «لوحه‌های باروی تخت جمشید» و «لوحه‌های خزانه‌ی تخت جمشید» کشف شد،[۴۳] برخی از مورخان ما در قلمرو ایران باستان، با تطبیق یافته‌های تازه با گزاره‌های پیشین، کوشیده‌اند به واقعیت‌های تاریخی‌ی مربوط به گفتمان «زن در دوره‌ی هخامنشیان» نزدیک شوند، و به نتایج درخشانی هم رسیده‌اند. به عنوان نمونه، تورج دریائی، مورخ ایران باستان و استاد دانشگاه در امریکا، در کتاب‌ها و مقاله‌های خود، به این گزاره پافشاری دارد که زن دوران باستان ما، در سیاست مداخله داشته، در ارتش صاحبِ مقام بوده، از استقلال مالی برخوردار بوده است.[۴۴] من، نه تنها در گستردگی و ژرفای دانش تورج دریائی پیرامون تاریخ ایران باستان، کوچکترین تردیدی ندارم، بلکه از طریق مطالعه در متون تاریخی، به نمونه‌هائی برخورده‌ام که این گزاره‌های تورج دریائی را تأیید می‌کنند. اما متن لوحه‌های کشف‌شده، و سندهائی که مبنای این داوری هستند- ضمن روشن کردن برخی از مناسبات اقتصادی در زمینه‌ی «کار و کارفرما» در ایران دوره‌ی هخامنشی، و برخی از مناسبات جاری در دربارهای هخامنشی و در خاندان‌های اشرافی‌ی این دوره- به هیچ وجه روشنگر شرایط سیاسی، اقتصادی و فرهنگی‌ی حاکم بر زندگی‌ی توده‌های مردم ایران در زمان هخامنشیان نیستند. مثلاً روشن نیست که چندهمسری و داشتن «حرمسرا» یا ازدواج‌های درون‌خانوادگی- که بنا به مدارک و قرائن، وقوع آن در میان پادشاهان و اشراف و حکمرانان محلی در ایران هخامنشی ثابت شده- در میان تمام طبقات مردم رایج بوده است یا نه؛ همچنین، روشن نیست که استقلال مالی و «دخالت در سیاست و ارتش»، شامل حال زنان معمولی‌ی امپراتوری‌ی ایران می‌شده یا نه. در حالی که از دیدگاه بیش‌ترِ باستان‌گراهای ما، مفاد این «لوح»ها، به مثابه سند معتبری برای ادعای «آزادی و اعتبار زن در ایران باستان» تلقی می‌شود. اگر در اثبات «آزادی» و «اعتبارِ» زن (به معنای عام کلمه‌ی «زن») در دوره‌ی هخامنشی، عمدتاً به این لوح‌ها متوسل شویم، دست کم منابع بسیاری از دوره‌ی ساسانیان در دست داریم که به «انقیاد زن» در ایران باستان شهادت می‌دهند، که به لحاظ منطقی نمی‌تواند دنباله‌ی سنت‌های هخامنشی نباشد. این منابع شهادت می‌دهند که در عصر ساسانیان، در فرایند ازدواج (زنی پادخشای)، «قیمومیتِ» دختر، از پدر به شوهر منتقل می‌شد؛ و در فرایند نوعی ازدواج قرضی (چَگر)، مرد به دلایل مختلف، زن خود را به مرد دیگر وامی‌گذاشت. و «در این گونه ازدواج، رضایت زن شرط نبود».[۴۵]

پیرامون «کتاب» و «خواندن و نوشتن» و «سواد» در ایران باستان نیز از تفسیرهای ایران‌شناسان غربی (که برخی از آن‌ها هم‌اکنون به تحریف تاریخ ایران از سوی مورخان یونانی، و به تکرار همان تحریف‌ها از سوی برخی از ایران‌شناسانِ پیشین اعتراف می‌کنند[۴۶]) می‌گذریم، و به متن‌های دست اولی که در اختیار داریم نگاه می‌کنیم. می‌بینیم با مطالعه‌ی

---

[۴۳] در سال ۱۹۱۲ میلادی چند هزار لوح گلین در خرابه‌های تخت جمشید پیدا شد که خاورشناسان از آن‌ها با عنوان «الواح خزانه‌ی تخت جمشید» یاد می‌کنند. این لوح‌ها که اسناد دبیرخانه‌ی مرکزی‌ی حکومت هخامنشی بوده‌اند، بین ۴۹۲ و ۴۵۸ پیش از میلاد به خط عیلامی نوشته شده است. در سال ۱۹۳۳ نیز، تعداد ۴۷۰۶ لوحه، که با عنوان «الواح باروی تخت‌جمشید» شناسائی می‌شوند، هنگام کاوش‌های مؤسسه‌ی خاورشناسی‌ی شیکاگو، به سرپرستی‌ی ارنست هرتسفیلد، از خرابه‌های تخت جمشید به دست آمد. تا سال ۱۹۹۶ بیش از نیمی از این لوحه‌ها توسط ریچارد هالاک و جرج کمرون، باستان‌شناسان امریکائی، ترجمه و منتشر شده بود (بعد از آن را نمی‌دانم). تاریخ نگارش این لوحه‌ها، که به زبان عیلامی نوشته شده، بین ۵۰۹ و ۴۹۴ پیش از میلاد است، و شامل اسناد هزینه‌ی ساختمان کاخ‌های تخت جمشید است. بخش اعظم این لوح‌ها، به ویژه آن‌ها که ترجمه نشده‌اند، هنوز در مرکز خاورشناسی‌ی شهر شیکاگو نگهداری می‌شود. برای توضیح بیش‌تر در مورد این لوح‌ها به دو منبع زیر مراجعه کنید:

- ❖ ماریا بروسیوس، ***زنان هخامنشی***، ترجمه‌ی هایده مشایخ، تهران: انتشارات هرمس، ۱۳۸۱، ص ۱۶.
- ❖ مقاله‌ی مفصل ***مجموعه‌ی باستانی‌ی هخامنشی‌ی تخت جمشید***، «سایت جامع گردشگری‌ی ایران»، به نشانی‌ی زیر:

http://www.anobanini.ir/travel/fa/fars/1385/10/post_19.php

[۴۴] به عنوان نمونه‌ای از این نظرپردازی‌ی دکتر تورج دریائی، به متن زیر نگاه کنید:

- ❖ Touraj Daryaee, ***Go tell the Spartans: How "300" misrepresents Persians in history***, iranian.com, March 14, 2007: http://iranian.com/Daryaee/2007/March/300/index.html

[۴۵] تورج دریایی، ***شاهنشاهی‌ی ساسانی***، ترجمه‌ی مرتضی ثاقب‌فر. تهران: ققنوس، ۱۳۸۳، ص ۱۷۲ تا ۱۷۷.

[۴۶] با این که بسیاری از آگاهی‌های تاریخی‌ی ما در درجه‌ی نخست از منابع یونانی، و سپس از سوی خاورشناسان غربی به ما رسیده است، اما به اعتراف بسیاری از خاورشناسان متأخر، تحریف‌های بسیاری به این گزاره‌ها راه یافته است. به عنوان مثال، ریچارد فرای ایران‌شناس امریکائی، در کتاب‌ها و مقاله‌هایش بر شناخت و تلقی‌ی نادرست یونانیان از ایرانیان بارها تأکید کرده است. به تشخیص «ماریا بروسیوس Maria

سنگ‌نوشته‌ها و تطبیق آن‌ها با متن‌های ایرانی نیز گم‌گوشه‌های فراوانی وجود دارد. ما از سویی، با گزاره‌ی مرتباً تأکید شده‌ی سوزاندنِ «کتاب دینی‌ی ایرانیان» در خزانه‌ی فرهنگی‌ی هخامنشیان روبه‌رو هستیم، که به ادعای گردآورندگان بعدی‌ی اوستا (از جمله «تنسر»)، این کتاب دینی همانا «اوستا» بوده است،[۴۷] و از سوی دیگر، در کتیبه‌های هخامنشی از «زرتشت» نامی نیست. اگر «اوستا»ی زرتشت در خزانه‌ی هخامنشیان بوده، چرا نام زرتشت در کتیبه‌های شاهان هخامنشی غایب است؟ آیا می‌توان به گفته‌ی هرتسفلد اتکاء کرد که «از آن رو نام او در کتیبه‌ی داریوش [کتیبه‌ی مربوط به کشتن گئوماته‌ی مغ] نیامده که می‌خواسته در نهان و در تاریکی کار کند»؟ آیا حذف نام زرتشت را می‌توان به سیاست انحصار قدرت، توسط شاهان هخامنشی تعبیر کرد؟ یا باید – مانند برخی از پژوهشگران- به این نتیجه رسید که دین هخامنشیان اصلاً «زرتشتی» نبوده است،[۴۸] و «کتاب دینی‌ی سوخته شده» در حمله‌ی اسکندر، اوستای زرتشت نبوده است. در حالی که به گفته‌ی آله دال فک، پژوهشگر زرتشتی‌ی دوران ما (از گروه «پاسداران فرهنگ ایران»)، «خسانتوس Xantus، مورخ یونانی‌ی سده‌ی پنجم پیش از میلاد، که پیش از هرودوت می‌زیسته، زمان زرتشت را ۶۰۰ سال پیش از لشگرکشی‌ی خشایارشا به یونان، یعنی در سده‌ی ۱۱ پیش از میلاد مسیح) می‌داند.»[۴۹] این خبر را نیز در اختیار داریم که بلاش اشکانی، بخش‌هایی از اوستا را گردآوری کرد و به کتابت درآورد. اگر اوستای زرتشت در خزانه‌ی هخامنشیان نبوده، و هخامنشیان زرتشتی نبوده‌اند، پس چه مدارکی در حمله‌ی اسکندر در خزانه‌ی تخت جمشید سوخت؟ پیش از ساسانیان، دقیقاً در چه زمانی و در چه منطقه‌ای زرتشتیت دین رسمی‌ی ایرانیان بوده است؟ اخیراً نیز، عده‌ای از ایران‌شناسان ایرانی، از جمله جواد مشکور، قتل «گئوماته مغ» را ریشه‌ی عزاداری‌ی ایرانیان در محرم برآورد کرده است، و جواد مفرد، در تأیید اظهار نظر دکتر مشکور، با تکیه بر منابع ارمنی و آذری، «گئوماته مغ» را همان «زرتشت» شناسایی کرده است، که صورت تازه‌ای از ابهام، تناقض، پیچیدگی، و خلاء اطلاعاتی را مطرح می‌کند.[۵۰]

نمونه‌ی دیگر از ابهام، در مطالعه‌ی متن «اوستا» رخ می‌کند؛ به ویژه اگر بخواهیم مجموعه‌ی تفسیرها و پیشنهادهای متناقض ایران‌شناسان را دور بزنیم و از طریق مطالعه‌ی مستقیم متن اوستا، خود به شناخت و تفسیری دست یابیم. نکته‌ای که در این مطالعه ذهن جست‌وجوگر را مشغول می‌دارد، حضور نام «زرتشت» است هم در جایگاه «سوم شخص مفرد»، و هم در جایگاه «اول شخص مفرد» در سروده‌های منسوب به خود زرتشت؛[۵۱] مانند گات شماره‌ی ۲۸. ما نمی‌دانیم که آیا زرتشت، مانند ژولیوس سزار، قیصر رُم، خود را با ضمیر سوم شخص مفرد هم می‌نامیده، یا اصولاً، این صداهای

Brosius» این تحریف‌ها دو انگیزه‌ی مشخص داشته است: ۱) محدودیت شناخت و عدم آشنائی‌ی مستمر مورخان یونانی با فرهنگ ایران باستان؛ ۲) فرودست نشان دادن فرهنگ و تمدن ایران به سبب رقابت‌های سیاسی بین امپراتوری‌ی ایران و یونانیان. این پژوهشگر در مقدمه‌ی کتاب «زنان هخامنشی» خاطر نشان می‌کند که همین تحریف‌ها، در پیشداوری‌های خاورشناسان قرن نوزدهم و بیستم نیز تکرار شده و دامنه‌ی گسترده‌تری نیز یافته است. او، در صفحه‌ی ۱۵ همین کتاب می‌نویسد: «پژوهش‌های بریان (Brian) این نظر را تأیید و تقویت کرد. او به ویژه در مقاله‌اش به نام "تاریخ و مکتب فکری- a ۱۹۸۹" منابع یونانی، مخصوصاً آثار افلاطون، کتاب هفتم از کورش‌نامه‌ی گزنفون، نوشته‌های ایسقراط و آریان را به دقت بررسی کرده است. بریان اظهار کرد که گزارش‌های این نویسندگان از امور ایران، با هدف اثبات ضعف نظامی‌ی ایرانیان بوده است و بنابراین، باید این نوشته‌ها را نه تاریخ، بلکه تعابیر مکتب‌های فکری تلقی کرد.» نگاه کنید به: ماریا بروسیوس، ***زنان هخامنشی***، ترجمه‌ی هایده مشایخ، تهران: انتشارات هرمس، ۱۳۸۱.

[۴۷] در «***نامه‌ی تنسر***» که گزارشی مستقیم و بلاواسطه است، می‌خوانیم که اردشیر بابکان پاره‌های پراکنده‌ی اوستا را گردآورد، آن چه معتبر بود پذیرفت و بقیه را کنار گذاشت. نگاه کنید به:
احمد تفضلی، ***تاریخ ادبیات ایران باستان***، به کوشش ژاله آموزگار، تهران: انتشارات سخن، ۱۳۷٦، ص ٦٦.

[۴۸] بابک بامدادان، «***روشنفکری‌ی ایرانی و هنر نیندیشیدن***»، نشریه‌ی دبیره، فرانسه: شماره‌ی ٤، ۱۳٦۷، صص ۱۷ تا ٤۱.

[۴۹] برگرفته از مجموعه نامه‌های آله دال فک به دکتر احسان یارشاطر، منعکس در تارنمای «درفش کاویانی، بازدید ۲۲ ژانویه ۲۰۰۷:
http://derafsh-kaviyani.com

[50] http://www.akhbar-rooz.com/article.jsp?essayId=2564

[۵۱] به گزارش دکتر احمد تفضلی، از متون گاهانی که در اوستای کنونی زیر نام «یسن‌ها» تدوین شده، هفده گات نوشته‌ی خود زرتشت است: از گات ۲۸ تا ۳٤، از ۴۳ تا ۵۱، و گات ۵۳. نگاه کنید به:
❖ احمد تفضلی، ***تاریخ ادبیات ایران باستان***، به کوشش ژاله آموزگار، تهران: انتشارات سخن، ۱۳۷٦، ص ۳۷.

متفاوت در سرودهای منسوب به زرتشت، صدای سرودخوانان، شاعران، و نویسندگان مختلف را در دوره‌های مختلف نمایندگی می‌کنند. از این رو، ناگزیر هستیم که دست کم در این مرحله به تشخیص کارشناسان اوستا تکیه کنیم، که بنا به قدمت و همخوانی‌ی سبک و زبان، ۱۷ سرود گات‌ها را به خود زرتشت نسبت می‌دهند.

در خوانش من از تاریخ ایران باستان، سبب‌های این پوشیدگی‌ها، ابهام‌ها و تناقض‌ها عبارت‌اند از: سنت شفاهی‌ی پیش از اسلام؛ انحصار دانش، و ممنوعیتِ خواندن و نوشتن برای **همگان** در فرهنگ ایران باستان؛ تخریب آثار ادبی و فرهنگی‌ی خاندان‌های پیشین توسط خاندان‌های پسین پادشاهی؛[۵۲] خودسانسوری، یعنی همان که حافظ می‌گوید: «جریده رو که گذرگاه عافیت تنگ است»؛[۵۳] یا «چال کردنِ» کتاب یا عدم انتشار آن از ترس تکفیر شریعتمداران، و نابودی‌ی نسخه‌های کم‌شمار از متن‌های دست اول در جنگ‌ها و کتاب‌سوزانی‌ها و تاراج‌های خودی و بیگانه.

عامل دیگری که به سردرگمی‌ی پژوهشگر می‌افزاید، کاربردِ واژه/ مفهوم «فلسفه» است در مورد حیات فکری‌ی ایران باستان. حتا اگر این سخنِ «محمدرضا فشاهی» را نپذیریم که «فلسفه پدیده‌ای بود خاص یونان باستان، و در همان یونان نیز با ارسطو پایان یافت»، یعنی اگر بخواهیم به روال بسیاری از پژوهشگران تاریخ فرهنگ ایران، از حضور «فلسفه» در ایران باستان سخن بگوییم، ناگزیر هستیم که برای این واژه، تعریف تازه‌ای به دست دهیم. چرا که «فلسفه»، به مثابه علم شناخت و تفسیر جهان، سرشتی پُرسا دارد و در پرسایی‌ی خود جویا هم هست، و در جویایی‌ی خود، پویا و دگرشونده هم هست. در حالی که جهان‌شناسی‌ی ایرانی، از همان اسطوره‌ی «کیخسرو» یا دست کم از «اوستا»ی دوره‌ی ساسانیان، بر بنیادهای «سروشِ» عالم غیب و بر صبغه‌های پررنگ عرفانی/ باطنی- که یک سرش به رازوارگی و سر دیگرش به الاهیات می‌رسد- استوار است. و از آن جا که «سروش»، پاسخ تمامی‌ی پرسش‌ها را در اختیار می‌گذارد، و احکامش ابدی تلقی می‌شوند، و از آن جا که تمام جنبش‌های فکری در ایران باستان، یکی پس از دیگری، نسبت به این بنیادها وفادار مانده‌اند، برای شناسایی‌ی دقیق نحله‌های فکری، منطق درونی، و روند تکوین آن‌ها در ایران، به صورتی اجتناب‌ناپذیر از «اوستا» و کلاً از «ادیان ایران باستان» و عرفان «اپانیشادها»، یا بعداً از «حکمت خسروانی»، سر بر می‌کنیم، و در ابری از التقاط مفاهیم موجود در جهان‌شناسی‌های زروانیت، دین مغان، آیین مهر، زرتشیتِ آغازین، زرتشیت ساسانی، مانویت، آیین مزدک، عرفان بودایی، عرفان گنوستیک، و ... گم می‌شویم، و از «فلسفه» به معنای اخص آن فاصله می‌گیریم.

با این همه، ناگزبر هستیم که به همان هفده سرودی که همه‌ی ایران‌شناسان و اوستاشناسان در تعلق آن‌ها به زرتشت تردید ندارند، مراجعه کنیم، و، با پشتوانه‌ی تفسیرهایی که در دسترس داریم، بررسی‌ی سازه‌های اندیشگی در همین هفده سرود،

---

[۵۲] به عنوان مثال، مهرداد بهار از وجود ٦٠ کتاب در عصر اشکانیان خبر می‌دهد، که هیچ کدام به دست ما نرسیده است. و احمد تفضلی، در کتاب «تاریخ ادبیات ایران پیش از اسلام» ص. ۷۵، گزارش می‌دهد: «هیچ نوشته‌ی ادبی به زبان پارتی (= پهلوی‌ی اشکانی)، چه دینی و چه غیردینی، از دوران اشکانیان بر جای نمانده است.» آن چه که این پژوهشگر به عنوان ادبیات و نوشته‌های دوره‌ی اشکانی از آن‌ها یاد کرده، منحصر است به کتیبه، بنچاق، نامه، چرم‌نوشته، سفال نوشته، و فلز نوشته‌ها، که بسیاری از آن‌ها هم به خط یونانی نوشته شده است. البته، دکتر تفضلی از کتابی هم نام می‌برد، و می‌نویسد: «این کتاب احتمالاً از آثار دوره‌ی اشکانی بوده است.» از این‌ها گذشته، دستکاری‌ی ساسانیان در تقویم، و کوتاه کردن دوره‌ی پارتیان از ۵۰۰ سال به ۲۰۰ سال، و همچنین، از شاهنامه‌ی فردوسی، به یقین چنین برمی‌آید که ساسانیان همه‌ی آثار دوره‌ی پارتیان را نابود کرده بودند. کما این که فردوسی در کتاب عظیم شاهنامه، فقط ۱۸ بیت در مورد این دوره سروده است: چه کوتاه شد شاخ و هم بیخشان/ نگوید جهان‌دیده تاریخشان/ از ایشان جز او نام نشنیده‌ام/ نه در نامه‌ی خسروان دیده‌ام. حسن پیرنیا نیز در کتاب «عصر اساطیری‌ی تاریخ ایران» چند جا تکرار می‌کند که «جهت [این حذف]، بغض مغ‌ها و خصومت ساسانیان نسبت به اشکانیان بوده است.» از جمله، نگاه کنید به:

❖ حسن پیرنیا، ***عصر اساطیری‌ی تاریخ ایران: خطوط برجسته‌ی داستان‌های ایران قدیم***، ویرایش سیروس ایزدی، تهران: انتشارات هیرمند، ۱۳۷۷، ص ۱۱۱.

[۵۳] این تشبیه را از مقاله‌ی زیر برگرفته‌ام: نسیم خاکسار، ***پوشیده‌نویسی در ادبیات فارسی***، نشریه‌ی «باران»، سوئد، شماره‌ی ۱۷ و ۱۸، پائیز/ زمستان ۱۳۸٦، صص٦۷ تا ۷۱.

یا هفده «گات» را نقطه‌ی عزیمت قرار دهیم.

در نخستین گام این سفر فکری درمی‌یابیم که بُن‌ساخت جهان‌بینی در هیچ یک از این سرودها، خالی از صبغه‌های فلسفی نیست. به عنوان مثال، «گات ۴۴ از یسنه»ی اوستا، آکنده از پرسش‌های فلسفی است، که انگار تاریخ تفکر انسان، شکافتن و توضیح آن‌ها را از افلاطون می‌گیرد. زرتشت، ضمن این که در بند اول این «گات»، اهورامزدا را «خدا» می‌نامد، در میان پرسش‌های فراوان درباره‌ی هستی و چیستی‌ی انسان و جهان، بنیادی‌ترین پرسش فلسفی را مطرح می‌کند:

از تو پرسش می‌کنم ای اهورا: این آفرینش چه سان هستی یافت و چه کسی بر آن سروری دارد؟ (ترجمه‌ی هاشم رضی)

یا در «گات ۲۸ از یسنه»، می‌پرسد:

تو با «مینو»ی خود مرا بیاموز و به زبان خویش بازگوی که آفرینش در آغاز چه‌گونه پدید آمد؟ (ترجمه‌ی جلیل دوستخواه)

نگاه فلسفی‌ی زرتشت در «گات ۳۰» نیز- پیرامون گفتمان‌های فلسفی‌ی «آفرینش»، «وجود»، و «جبر» یا «اختیار»- دیده می‌شود. از این گات، سه ترجمه‌ی جلیل دوستخواه و هاشم رضی و حسین وحیدی را در دست دارم. ترجمه‌ی جلیل دوستخواه، با تفسیرهایی کوتاه‌تر همراه است؛ ترجمه‌ی هاشم رضی، ترجمه‌ی آزاد است و در قالب جمله‌بندی‌های زبان امروزی بیان شده است؛ و حسین وحیدی، ابتدا تلفظ کلمه‌ها را به فارسی نوشته و شماره گذاری کرده و سپس هر بند از این گات را در جمله نشانده است. به خاطر اهمیتی که این گات در بحث حاضر دارد، بخش‌های معینی از هر سه ترجمه را در این جا بازمی‌گویم. در این گات، زرتشت پس از اعلام این که هر «دو مینو آفریده‌ی مزداست»، و پس از ستایش اهورا و هومن، می‌گوید:

ترجمه‌ی جلیل دوستخواه:

ای هوشمندان!

بشنوید با گوش‌ها[ی خویش] بهترین [سخنان] را و ببینید با منش روشن و هر یک از شما – چه مرد، چه زن- پیش از آن که رویداد بزرگ به کام ما پایان گیرد، از میان دو راه، [یکی را] برای خویشتن برگزینید و این [پیام] را [به دیگران] بیاموزید. در آغاز آن دو «مینوی»ی همزاد و در اندیشه و گفتار و کردار [یکی] نیک و [دیگری] بد، با **یکدیگر سخن گفتند**. از آن دو، نیک‌آگاهان، راست را برگزیدند نه دُژآگاهان. آن گاه که آن دو «مینو» **به هم رسیدند**، نخست «زندگی» و «نازندگی» را [بنیاد] نهادند و چنین باشد تا **پایان هستی**: «بهترین منش»، پیروان «اشه» را و «بدترین زندگی»، هواداران «دروج» را خواهد بود. (همه‌ی قلاب‌ها از جلیل دوستخواه است.)[۵۴] (تأکیدها از من است.)

ترجمه‌ی هاشم رضی:

[...] و این است آموزش‌هایم: بشنوید اینک این سخنان را، با اندیشه‌ی روشن بنگرید. مرد و زن بایستی خود این چنین با رایزنی‌ی خود و اندیشه، راه خود را برگزینند. و این چنین است آموزش‌هایم. در دامان هستی، آن گاه که زمان مفهومی یافت، آن **دو گوهر همزاد نخستین** پیدا شدند؛ آن دو گوهری که یکی‌شان در اندیشه و گفتار و کردار نیک بود و دیگری زشت؛ از میان این دو، مردمان با داوری‌ی خرد، بایستی راه نیک را برگزینند، نه راه بد را. و چون این دو نیروی **قدیم** به

[۵۴] جلیل دوستخواه، ***اوستا: کهن‌ترین سرودهای ایرانیان،*** (گزارش و پژوهش)، چاپ نهم، تهران: انتشارات مروارید، ۱۳۸۴، جلد اول، ص ۱۴.

> هم رسیدند، **پدید آوردند زندگی را و مرگ را**؛ و این تضاد، همچنان پایدار باشد تا **واپسین و در انجام**، زندگی‌ی خوش و به کام در **دو جهان** از آنِ کسانی باشد که بهترین منش و راه راستی را برگزینند، و پویندگان راه دروغ، فرجامی خواهند داشت از بدترین چیزها.[٥٥] (تأکیدها از من است.)

ترجمه‌ی حسین وحیدی:

> [...] بهترین (پیام) را با گوش‌هایتان بشنوید، و با اندیشه‌ی روشن خود آن را دریابید، و پیش از آن که رویداد بزرگ در رسد، هر یک از شما برای خویش، یکی ار دو راه را برگزینید، به راستی بپاخیزید، و پیام را بگسترانید. در آغاز آفرینش دو **مینوی همزاد** پدیدار شدند، و **اینک آن دو مینو هستند که در اندیشه و گفتار و کردار به چهر نیکی و بدی نمایان می‌گردند**، و از این دو، آن که نیک می‌داند راستی را برمی‌گزیند، و آن گاه که آن دو مینو در آغاز آفرینش **به هم رسیدند**، یکی زندگی را بنیاد نهاد و آن دیگری نازندگی را، و هستی را تا پایان چنین (روندی) خواهد بود. و (در روند زندگی) بدترین جایگاه پیروان دروغ را خواهد بود و بهترین جایگاه، پیروان راستی را.[٥٦] (پرانتزها از حسین وحیدی است. تأکیدها از من است.)

از آن رو که موضوع «ترجمه»‌ی اوستا به بحث حاضر مربوط نیست، از تفاوت‌های معنی‌دار برخی از مفاهیم در این سه ترجمه می‌گذرم.[٥٧] اما تا جایی که به زیرساخت جهان‌بینی‌ی ایرانی مربوط می‌شود، به مفهوم‌هایی می‌پردازم که در قالب واژگان مختلف در هر سه ترجمه‌ی این گات مشترک هستند، و در گات‌های دیگر نیز تکرار شده‌اند. این مفهوم‌ها عبارت‌اند از: به هم رسیدن، سخن گفتن، اندیشیدن، کنشِ گزینش، منش، و البته در سرلوحه‌ی همه‌ی آن‌ها، «دو مینوی همزاد» در رابطه با «زندگی و نازندگی»:

مفهوم «**دو گوهر همزاد**» که یکی «**زندگی**» و دیگری «**نازندگی**» را نمایندگی می‌کند، ظاهراً ثنویتی عَرَضی را متبادر می‌کند. مدافعان این نظر، بنا به اصل «امتناع جمع دو ناسازه» در منطق ارسطوئی، قرن‌های متمادی استدلال کرده‌اند که این «دو مینوی همزاد»، هیچ یک در حضور دیگری هستی ندارد؛ یعنی، یا «زندگی» هست، یا «نازندگی»؛ پس تعارض بین این «دو مینو» تعارضی جوهری نیست، تا تقابل آن‌ها به دگرگونی و حرکت کل پدیده بیانجامد.[٥٨] مدافعان نظریه‌ی «ثنویتِ» ایرانی، این بینش را در برابر بینش یونانی قرار می‌دهند و استدلال می‌کنند که- مثلاً در اندیشه‌ی دموکریت یونانی- چون ناسازه‌های یک پدیده در حضور هم هستی دارند، طبیعتاً با یکدیگر در تعارضی مداوم به

---

[٥٥] هاشم رضی، ***اوستا: کهن‌ترین گنجینه‌ی مکتوب ایران باستان***، (ترجمه و پژوهش)، چاپ دوم، تهران: انتشارات بهجت، ۱۳۸۰، ص۱٥۹.

[٥٦] دکتر حسین وحیدی، ***همستاری (دیالکتیک) در گات‌ها و مثنوی‌ی مولوی***، محل انتشار؟، انتشارات اشا، خرداد ۱۳٦۰، صص ۸ تا ۱٤.

[٥٧] تفاوت مفاهیم در این سه ترجمه برای من که توانایی‌ی تطبیق با اصل آن را ندارم، بسیار گیج‌کننده و در عین حال بسیار شگفت‌انگیز است. هاشم رضی، مفهوم «قدیم» را که در فرهنگ مفاهیم اسلامی در تقابل با مفهوم «حادث» بودن جهان و قرآن است، معادل با چه واژه‌ای در متن اصلی به کار برده است، که جای آن در ترجمه‌ی جلیل دوستخواه و حسین وحیدی خالی است؟ بار معنایی‌ی «رویداد بزرگ» و «پایان هستی» در ترجمه‌ی جلیل دوستخواه کجا، و بار معنایی‌ی «واپسین و در انجام» در ترجمه‌ی هاشم رضی کجا؟ عبارت «دو جهان»، از کجا به ترجمه‌ی هاشم رضی راه یافته است، که در ترجمه‌ی آن دو دیگر غایب است؟ شگفتی در این است که، حتا حالا که دیگران خواندنِ «خط» ما را به ما آموخته‌اند، ما هنوز با میراث‌های فرهنگی‌ی خود (اگر نگوئیم «به نرخ روز»، و در خوش‌بینانه‌ترین داوری) چنبن سهل‌انگارانه برخورد می‌کنیم.

[٥٨] در واقع آن چه که از ارسطو در این تشخیص ملاک قرار گرفته، قانون تخطی‌ناپذیر «امتناع جمع اضداد» در دستگاه منطقی او است. در حالی که در فلسفه‌ی ارسطو ، «کُون» سه مبدأ دارد: ماده، هیئت، و عدم. یعنی، «کُون و فساد»، اجزائی غیرقابل تفکیک هستند. یعنی، نیستی یا «نازندگی»، با «هیولا و «صورت»»، تشکیل دهنده‌ی «کُون» یا هستی برشمرده شده است. نگاه کنید به: محمدعلی فروغی، ***سیر حکمت در اروپا***، تهران: نشر زوار، چاپ هشتم (جیبی)، ۱۳۸٥، زیرنویس شماره‌ی ۲ صفحه‌ی ٥۸۹.

سرمی‌برند، و کنش و واکنش آن‌ها نسبت به یکدیگر منشاء تغییر و حرکتِ پدیده است.[۵۹] اما به هگل که می‌رسیم، درزهای این استدلال از هم باز می‌شود. چرا که در دستگاه نظری‌ی هگل، «امتناع جمع دو ناسازه»، در سطح «فاهمه» ممکن است، و نه در مرتبه‌ی «عقل». پیش از باز کردن این بحث، به اطلاع خوانندهام می‌رسانم که مقایسه بین دستگاه نظری‌ی هگل و دستگاه نظری‌ی زرتشت، ابداع من نیست و پیش از این هم انجام شده است، و حتا به ضرب یک پیشداوری‌ی حیرت‌انگیز، مورد تمسخر برخی از ایران‌شناسان غربی نیز قرار گرفته است. مثلاً ژاک دوشن گیمنِ فرانسوی می‌نویسد:

> مدت‌ها بین دانشمندان رسم بود که «زروان‌باوری» را همچون وسیله‌ای بشناسند که گویا ایران، دیرهنگام و بی‌موقع، برای چیره شدن بر دوگانه‌باوری، به آن متوسل شده است. در واقع هم این راه حل مناسبی بود. زیرا «زروان» را پدر مشترک اورمزد و اهریمنِ همزاد می‌شناخت. به نظر من فراموش شده که **ایران از دوگانه‌باوری‌ی خود ناراحتی نداشت و مایل نبود که آن را با نوعی همنهادِ هگل‌مآبانه رفع و رجوع کند و لذا، ظاهراً به خوبی با آن سازگاری داشت.** (بی‌شک برای این که مثل یونانیان، چنان که پیش‌تر گفتیم، تصوری از مطلق نداشت.) یکی از شایستگی‌های نی‌برگ، در سخنرانی‌های پراحساسی که به سال ۱۹۲۹ در پاریس ایراد کرد و در کتابش به نام «ادیان ایران باستان» نیز آمده، در آن است که بطلان این نظریه‌ی خوش‌باورانه را ثابت کرده است.[۶۰] (تأکید از من است.)

من نمی‌دانم کسی از میان کارشناسان فن تاکنون از این ایران‌شناس محترم پرسیده است که او در کجا ثابت کرده است که «زروانیت» همانا «زرتشیت» است؛ از کجا می‌داند که «ایران از دوگانه‌باوری‌ی خود ناراحتی نداشت و مایل نبود که آن را با نوعی همنهادِ هگل‌مآبانه رفع و رجوع کند»؟ یا، اصلاً در این جمله از «ایرانِ» کدام دوره و زمانه سخن رفته است، که «فلسفه‌ی هگل» هم در آن دوره حضور داشته است؟ یا، «ایرانِ» کدام زمان با «دوگانه‌باوری به خوبی سازگاری داشت»، و پشتوانه‌ی این حکم چیست؟ اما این را می‌دانم که پیگیری‌ی آن چه که از دید این ایران‌شناس و همفکرانش «رفع و رجوع» تلقی شده (نه با هدف تخطئه‌ی نظر این ایران‌شناسان، بلکه برای درک بهتر از خودمان و تاریخ‌مان) برای ما امری بایسته است. و از آن رو که به قول خود این دانشمند محترم، «این راه حل مناسبی» برای نزدیک شدن به واقعیت است، من برای دیدن گات یادشده، با نگاهی گذرا به فلسفه‌ی هگل بحث را به پیش می‌برم.

هگل، از دو قلمرو «فهم» و «عقل» در ذهن انسان سخن می‌گوید، که جهان، در هر یک از آن‌ها تفسیرهای متفاوتی دارد. به پاس حقی که محمدعلی فروغی بر جوانه‌های فهم فلسفی‌ی من دارد، این مفهوم انتزاعی‌ی پیچیده را- از قلم توانای محمدعلی فروغی بازمی‌گویم. پیشاپیش بایسته است به این نکته اشاره کنم که جواد طباطبائی، مفسر فلسفه، در نخستین جلسه از سلسله «درس‌گفتار»های خود، می‌گوید که هگل‌شناسی، «راهی است» که در مسیر آن «سرها بریده بینی بی‌جرم و بی‌جنایت»؛ و با این توضیح، درک و فهم فلسفه‌ی هگل را عملاً تعلیق به محال می‌کند. البته، من که هگل‌شناس نیستم، تا جائی که خوانده‌ام، هیچ یک از توضیحات هگل‌شناسان، پیرامون رابطه بین دو مفهوم «فهم» و«عقل»، را از توضیح ساده‌ی فروغی رساتر ندیده‌ام. و باز، پیش از بازگفت از فروغی، به کسانی که کتاب «سیر حکمت در اروپا»ی او را نخوانده‌اند و در دسترس ندارند یادآور می‌شوم که موضوع بحث فروغی در این بازگفت هیچ ربطی به رد یا پذیرش ثنویت ایرانی ندارد. او در شرح فلسفه‌ی هگل می‌نویسد:

---

[۵۹] از سوی برخی از اوستاشناسان و پژوهندگان اوستا تلاش‌های بسیاری شده که روند دیالکتیکی‌ی ثنویت موجود در کیهان‌شناسی‌ی مزدایی را با دیدگاه ذره‌انگار «دموکریت» (دموکریتوس) یونانی مقایسه کنند و همجنسی‌ی آن‌ها را نشان دهند. به عنوان مثال، به کتاب زیر مراجعه کنید:

❖ شیوا کاویانی، ***روشنان سپهر اندیشه***، تهران: انتشارات کتاب خورشید، ۱۳۷۸، صص ۳۸ تا ۴۹.

[۶۰] ژاک دوشن گیمن، ***اورمزد و اهریمن: ماجرای دوگانه‌باوری در عهد باستان***، ترجمه‌ی دکتر عباس باقری، تهران: مرکز نشر و پژوهش فرزان روز، ۱۳۷۸، صص ۳ تا ٤.

> هگل نظرش به این است که ذهن انسان پس از فهم، تعقل می‌کند و به نکات دیگر برمی‌خورد؛ و عقل برتر از فهم است و مقولات را باید به سلوک عقلی کشف نمود. توضیح آن که «فهم» مقید به اصـــل این‌همانی و این‌نه‌آنی و امتنـــاع جمع متقـــلابلان اسـت. به این معنی که «فهم» می‌گوید یک چیز همان چیز اسـت و غیر آن چیز نیسـت. و چیز با ناچیز جمع نمی‌شود. به عبارت دیگر، هستی هست و نیستی نیست. هستی نیست نمی‌شود و نیستی هست نمی‌شود و هستی با نیستی جمع نمی‌آید. اما «عقل» می‌رسد به آن جا که درمی‌یابد که در هستی نیستی است و در نیستی هستی است و می‌توان گفت متقلابلان جمع می‌شوند. به این معنی که اموری که به تصور درمی‌آیند، همه اعتباری و اضافی و نسبی هستند و همه باهم **مناسباتی از مشابهت و مباینت و جز این دارند**، و **بدون منظور داشتن آن مناسبات، تصور آن معانی به درستی برای ذهن میسر نمی‌شود** و بی‌معنی خواهد بود. تا آن جا که همه‌ی مناسبات را از یک معنی سلب کنند، منتهی به نقیض‌اش، یعنی به عدم آن معنی می‌گردد. مثلاً وجود بحث بسیط و هستی‌ی صِرف، که او را با امر دیگر مرتبط و متناسب نیانگاریم، در عین این که وجود و هستی است، عدم و نیستی نیز هست. زیرا نه این چیز است و نه آن چیز. پس هیچ چیز نیست. چنان که اگر روشنائی‌ی مطلق باشد، چیزی دیده نمی‌شود، و در حکم تاریکی‌ی مطلق است، و بینائی وقتی دست می‌دهد که روشنی با سایه همراه شود. یعنی نور دارای رنگ باشد. پس هر مفهومی باید با نقیض خود جمع شود تا معنی‌ی تامی حاصل آید. و هر چیزی دو رو دارد. مانند پارچه که رویه و آستر [پشت و رو] دارد و از جمع آن دو رو، روی سوم درست می‌شود که حقیقت پارچه همان اسـت. [... هگل] برای رهائی از جمع دو متقابل، آن دو را با هم می‌نهد، و مقوله‌ی «**شـدن**» را از آن درمی‌آورد، که «شدن»، هم بودن اسـت و هم نبـودن؛ و جمـع دو متقـابـل، بـه این وجـه، هم متحقـق و هم معقـــول می‌گردد.[۶۱] (تأکیدها از من است.)

همان گونه که فروغی در دنباله‌ی سـخن یادآور شـده اسـت، منظور از پاراگراف بالا این نیسـت که بگوئیم «هگل جمع متقابلان را ممتنع نمی‌داند»، می‌داند. اما او با وارد کردن «مناسـباتی از مشـابهت و مباینت» بین دو مفهوم انتزاعی/ ذهنی (مثلاً «هستی و نیستی» یا «زندگی و نازندگی»)، به «شدن»، یعنی به سنتز این دو متضاد می‌رسد، که کانکریت و عینی است. و چون عینی است، خود به خود، چیستی و چه‌گونگی و زمان و مکان دارد.

با این مقـدمه‌ی فشرده، به سـراغ «دو مینوی همزاد»، یا «زندگی» و «نازندگی»‌ی زرتشت می‌روم و به مناسباتی که در همین گات بین این دو مفهوم انتزاعی برقرار شـده، و به «شدنِ» کانکریتی که روی داده نگاه می‌کنم. می‌بینم این دو گوهر همزاد در درون یک پدیده وجود دارند؛ «به هم می‌رسند»؛ رو در روی هم قرار می‌گیرند؛ و با یکدیگر «سخن می‌گویند». یعنی، درگیر دیالوگ و کشمکشی مداوم هستند. و تا زمانی که عنصر سومی در کار نیست، به عنوان دو پدیده‌ی ذهنی و انتزاعی، یا دو ضـدِ جمع‌ناشـدنی، در قلمرو «فاهمه» باقی می‌مانند. اما در مرتبه‌ی سـنجش عقلانی (به زبان زرتشـت: «خِرد»)[۶۲]، کنشِ «برگزیدن»، همانا «شدن» است، که تعیّن خارجی دارد. و طرفه این که زرتشت، چیستی و چه‌گونگی‌ی این متعیّن را، با «بهترین» و «بدترین» منش، یا به قول محمدعلی فروغی (در شـرح فلسـفه‌ی هگل) با «پشـت و روی پارچه»، شناسائی کرده است.

---

۶۱ محمدعلی فروغی، ***سیر حکمت در اروپا و رساله‌ی گفتار در روش راه بردن عقل از رنه دکارت***، تهران: انتشارات زوار، جلدهای اول تا سوم، چاپ هشتم، ۱۳۸۵، صص ۵۸۶ تا ۵۸۹.

۶۲ همین جا خاطر نشـان کنم که منوچهر کمالی، البته بدون هیچ اسـتدلالی، جانشـین کردن واژه‌ی «خرد» در زرتشـیت با واژه‌ی «عقل» را نادرست می‌داند. از آن رو که این بحث مستلزم زمان و فضائی گسترده است، در این جا به استدلال نمی‌پردازم. اما همین قدر می‌گویم که از منظر من، این دو واژه نسبتاً معادل هستند. و گرنه باید مفهوم «عقلانیت» را یکسره از دستگاه نظری‌ی زرتشت و آموزه‌های او زدود. برای خواندن نظر منوچهر کمالی به اثر زیر نگاه کنید:

*منوچهر کمالی، ***فرهنگ‌شهر: فرهنگ ایران، فرهنگ جهانیست***، لندن: انتشارات کورملی، تاریخ ندارد، ص ٦٤.

اگر من در رهگذر مطالعه‌ی فلسفه‌ی «هگل» و متن‌های متعددی که پیرامون آن نوشته شده، دیالکتیک هگل را درست فهمیده باشم، و اگر الگوی آن را با گات یادشده درست تطبیق کرده باشم، تز ثنویت عَرَضی‌ی ایرانی (نه در زروانیت، بلکه در زرتشیت) باطل می‌شود. چرا که به این تعبیر، از دیدگاه زرتشت، ذاتِ «باشندگی» (به عنوان عنصری بسیط)، مدام در حال «شدن» است.

از این چشم‌انداز است که به زعم من، تفکر زرتشت در مجموعه‌ی گات‌ها (نه در زرتشیت ساسانی)، ضمن این که در قالب مفاهیمی مانند «زندگی‌ی جاویدان» و متعلقات آن، پتانسیل پیوند با اندیشه‌های عرفانی را نیز دارا است، از نظر آموزه‌های عملی، تفکری دیالکتیکی، و البته، گیتیانه است؛ بهره‌وری‌ی انسان از عناصر طبیعت را تجویز می‌کند؛ بر زندگی‌ی فعال و مرفه و سرخوش انسان صحه می‌گذارد؛ اختیار و مسئولیت گزینش را به انسان می‌سپارد؛ و «رایزنی با خود»، با «خرد»، و با «اندیشه» را مبنای گزینش قرار می‌دهد. در این دستگاه نظری نه تنها بهای زندگی‌ی تنانه و گیتیانه به نفع «زندگی‌ی پسین» کاهش نمی‌یابد، بلکه «پیوستن به مینو» مشروط به خویشکاری، یعنی انتخابِ انسان در زندگی است. با توجه به ریشه‌ی واژه‌ی «مینو»- یعنی «منیدن»، که به معنای «اندیشیدن» بوده- «مینو»ی زرتشت، همانا «اندیشیدن» است. و با توجه به این که واژه‌ی «من» نیز از همین «مینو» مشتق شده، می‌توان گفت که در دستگاه هستی‌شناختی‌ی زرتشت، «من»- (یعنی یکان آدمی- بدون تمکین از قدرتی مافوق خود)، خود، ذاتِ اندیشیدن بوده است. بدین ترتیب انسان زرتشت، بر خود، بر هستی‌ی خود، و زمان و مکان خود اشراف دارد، یعنی، از تصور و آگاهی‌ی تاریخی برخوردار است. با این تفسیر، می‌توان گفت که انتقال «مینو» به «آسمان»، و مفهوم «زندگی‌ی پسین» که همانا «پل جینوت» (مادر پل صراط اسلامی) را آفرید، از برساخته‌های دوران پس از زندگی‌ی زرتشت، و به ویژه در عصر ساسانیان است.

منتها، زیرساختِ ذهنی‌ی ثنویت، نه به لحاظ هستی‌شناختی، بلکه به لحاظ معرفت‌شناختی- در سراسر همین هفده سرود زرتشت غیرقابل انکار است. به بیانی دیگر، آموزه‌های زرتشت، عنصر کنترل، تهدید، تنبیه، و اطاعت را مداوماً بر فراز سر این «من»، این «خویش»، این «خود»، نگه می‌دارد. واژه‌ی «دروج» در این گات، همانا سرپیچی از «فرمان» (دات) است که از منظر زرتشتیت، نخستین و بزرگترین گناهِ این «خود» برشمرده می‌شود.[۶۳] چیرگی‌ی بینش «تَک قدرتی»، در زبان و در تحول و تکوین اسطوره‌های ایرانی (تا به فردوسی برسند) نیز آشکارا دیده می‌شود، که وجه بارز این تأثیر را می‌توان در مفهوم «جام جهان‌نما»، یعنی «آینه‌ی نمادین» ایرانی دید.[۶۴]

به تشخیص دکتر محمد معین، از معنا و ریشه‌ی واژه‌ی «آینه» در زبان‌های باستانی‌ی ایران چنین برمی‌آید که کارکردهای آن، با «دیدن» یعنی با حسّ طبیعی و مهم‌ترین ابزار بی‌واسطه‌ی شناخت، در هم‌آمیختگی‌ی معنایی داشته است:

> واژه‌ی آینه در زبان پهلوی «آپنک» (ayenak) و «آدِنک» (adenak)؛ و در زبان پارتی «آدینگ» (ading) بوده است؛ مشتق از ریشه‌ی «دی» (di). در پارسی‌ی باستان didiy به معنای «ببین»، و در پارسی‌ی میانه معنای «دیدن» داشت.[۶۵]

در حالی که واژه‌ی «آینه» در کتاب «بندهشِ» دوره‌ی ساسانی، به ewenag، به معنای «رسم»، «شکل»، «گونه»، و

---

[۶۳] در این زمینه نگاه کنید به: کیوس باوند، ***تاریخ تطبیقی‌ی باستانی‌ی ایران***، تهران: گوتنبرگ، [بی تاریخ].

[۶۴] کل بخش مربوط به جام جهان نما را از مقاله‌ی زیر برگرفته‌ام: ملیحه تیره گل، ***«خود» در خط برکه در خط جام***، نشریه‌ی «سنجش» آلمان، شماره‌ی ۱، بهار ۱۳۷۶/ مه ۱۹۹۷، صص ۱۰۷ تا ۱۳۱.

[۶۵] از حواشی‌ی دکتر محمد معین بر برهان قاطع.

«قالب»، تبدیل شده است.[٦٦] از توضیح دکتر محمد معین، و معنایی که دکتر مهرداد بهار، صادق هدایت[٦٧]، و احمد تفضلی[٦٨] برای واژه‌ی ewenag ذکر کرده‌اند، چنین برمی‌آید که این تغییر، یعنی جدایی‌ی واژه‌ی «آینه» از ریشه‌ی «دیدن»، بعد از پارتیان (اشکانیان) صورت پذیرفته باشد.

در هر حال، «جام جهان‌نما» با تمام ویژگی‌های مادی و کارکرد زمینی‌اش در شاهنامه، کاربردی انحصاری دارد. به این معنی که صاحب «جام»، فقط «کیخسرو» است. و فقط اوست که می‌تواند در آن بنگرد و با خبری که از آن می‌گیرد، پیوند همیشگی‌ی عاشق و معشوق (بیژن و منیژه) را فعلیت بخشد. بنابراین، کیخسرو پادشاهی است با بینش گیتیانه، یار و یاور عشق زمینی، سیاستمداری برجسته، و جنگاوری پیروز، که حلال مشکل است، و دیگران، کارگزار حل مشکل. یعنی، وجه هستی‌شناختی‌ی «جام»، جهان‌بینی‌ی زمینی را نمایندگی می‌کند، و وجه معرفت‌شناختی‌ی آن، سیاست اجتماعی و مدنی را. سیاستی که، از یک سو «همه‌سونگر» و «فراگیرنده» و «برآورد کننده» است، و از سوی دیگر، نماد انحلال «همه» است در «یک». یعنی، یک نفر برای همه و به جای همه می‌بیند و می‌اندیشد و مشکل را شناسایی می‌کند و راه حل را نشان می‌دهد. از فرآورده‌های عملی‌ی این سیاستِ تک‌قدرتی و آن هستی‌شناسی‌ی زمینی، در طول زمان، از یک سو انحصار دانش و سواد، و میخکوب کردن یکان جامعه در «طبقه» است، و از سوی دیگر، رساندن ایران به عظمت نظامی، جغرافیایی، و تشکیلات مدنی، که کوشش برخی از ایران‌شناسان اروپامحور در نابوده جلوه دادن آن راه به جایی نبرده است، و باستان‌شناسی‌ی امروز، هنوز به کشف تمامی‌ی جلوه‌های آن نائل نشده است.[٦٩]

در تحلیل نهایی، اما، به وجه دیگری از «جام» برمی‌خوریم: «جام جهان‌نما»، همه چیز، همه کس، و همه جای جهان را بازمی‌تاباند، به جز «خودِ» نگاه‌کننده در آن را. یعنی، حتا فردی که در رأس هرم قدرت، جهان را در سیطره دارد و آن را برای دیگران معنی می‌کند، خودش در آینه پیدا نیست؛ خودش، هم «خود» را نمی‌بیند. با این ویژگی‌ی نهادین است که جام جهان‌نمای ایرانی، در برابر «برکه»، یعنی آینه‌ی نمادین یونانی، از «آینگی» تن می‌زند، و پتانسیل آن را دارد که در طول زمان به خدمت عرفان در آید، و در قالب ده‌ها لفظ عرفانی حلول کند؛ تا حمدالله مستوفی آن را به «درون صافی» تعبیر کند، تا صاحب اسرارالتوحید بیاید و بگوید: «**بنده را نرسد که گوید: من**»؛ تا، در لمیزرع صفویه، «خود» ایرانی را در اثیر «نقاش جهان» کاملاً منحل کند و از زبان صائب تبریزی ندا در دهد که: **صلح کردیم به یک نقش ز نقاش جهان/ محو یک نقش چو آیینه‌ی تصویر شدیم.** و جالب است بدانیم که «آینه‌ی تصویر» در جهان واقعی موجودیت داشته است، و آینه‌ای بوده که پیش از جیوه، تصویری بر شیشه می‌کشیدند، و به همین دلیل «تمثال در آن نفوذ نتوانست کرد».[٧٠]

هیمن جاست که شعور حافظ از تاریک‌ترین عصر تاریخ ایران می‌پرسد و پاسخ می‌دهد: **گفتم ای مسند جم جام جهان‌بینت کو؟/ گفت افسوس که آن دولت بیدار بخفت.** اما حافظ دیر آمده است، همان طور که فردوسی دیر آمده بود. درست است که تاریخ هجوم تازیان و اشغال ایران را می‌دانیم، اما به درستی پیدا نیست که کِی بود که «آن دولت بیدار بخفت»، پیش از اشغال، یا بعد از اشغال. و دقیقاً پیدا نیست که در چه زمانی و تحت تأثیر کدام مؤثرهای مشخص، «جام جهان‌نما»ی

---

[٦٦] ***بندهش***، ترجمه‌ی مهرداد بهار، تهران: انتشارات توس، ١٣٦٩، ص ٤٨، و یادداشت‌های همان کتاب، ص ١٦٦.

[٦٧] صادق هدایت در ترجمه‌ی ***زند و هومن‌یسن***، ترکیب «به یرآینه» را «به هر طریق» معنی کرده است.

[٦٨] احمد تفضلی، ***معرفی‌ی کتاب هیربدستان و نیرنگستان***، فصل‌نامه‌ی ایران‌شناسی، امریکا، سال هشتم، شماره‌ی ١، بهار ١٣٧٥، ص ١٧٧.

[٦٩] به عنوان مثال، خواننده‌ام را به نظر تیم باستان‌شناسان ایرانی و بریتانیایی درباره‌ی «مار سرخ»، یعنی دیوار عظیمی که در زمان ساسانیان به دور قلمرو امپراتوری‌ی ایران کشیده شده بود، و هنوز بخش‌هایی از آن سالم مانده است، رجوع می‌دهم. نگاه کنید به: الترانی اسمیت، ***قدمت دیوار بزرگ گرگان به دوره‌ی ساسانی می‌رسد***، تارنمای «بی.بی.سی»، ٢٢ فوریه‌ی ٢٠٠٨/ ٣ اسفند ١٣٨٦، به نشانی‌ی زیر:
http://www.bbc.co.uk/persian/science/story/2008/02/080221_si-gorgan-wall.shtml

[٧٠] احمد گلچین معانی، ***فرهنگ اشعار صائب*** (تنظیم و پردازش)، جلد اول، تهران: مؤسسه‌ی مطالعات و تحقیقات فرهنگی، ١٣٦٤، ص ٢٧.

ایرانی، همان وجه گیتیانه و عظمت‌خواهی را هم که داشت، فروگذاشت، و یکسره در مفاهیم عرفانی مستحیل شد. دکتر محمد معین و دکتر منوچهر مرتضوی با پژوهش در متن‌ها، زمان تغییر «جام گیتی‌نمای کیخسرو» به «جام جم» (به معنای جام شراب عرفانی) را از حدود سده‌ی ششم هجری به بعد برآورد کرده‌اند.[۷۱] اما به رغم تشخیص این دو پژوهشگر، واقعیت‌های تاریخی، زمینه‌های بروز و رشد این استحاله را تا آئین مهر و دست کم تا مانویت عقب می‌برند.

نکته‌ی مهم دیگری که در پژوهش‌های تاریخی دیده می‌شود، تغییر بار مفهومی‌ی «دیو» در اسطوره‌های ایرانی است. بنا به یافته‌های ایران‌شناسانی مانند «پورداود»، «بهرام فره‌وشی»، «بدیع‌الزمان فروزانفر»، «مهرداد بهار»، «احمد تفضلی» و «ژاله آموزگار»، «دیو»ها در اسطوره‌های کهنِ هند و ایرانی از زمره‌ی «ایزدان» برشمرده می‌شدند. همه‌ی این ایران‌شناسان، از زمان تغییر معنای «دیو» با بار منفی و اهریمنی، و چرائی‌ی این استحاله اظهار بی‌خبری می‌کنند. «شکوفه تقی»، پژوهشگر تبعیدی نیز می‌نویسد: «دیو در زبان سانسکریت، معادل کلمه‌ی خدا و به معنای روشنایی، و در فرهنگ هند و اروپایی معادل کلمه‌ی پدر و خدا است.» شکوفه تقی، با الهام از یافته‌های دانشمندان یادشده، با استناد به داستان «دیوها» و «تهمورث» در شاهنامه، «آموزش خط» را یکی از ویژگی‌های «دیو» در اسطوره‌های ایرانی شناسایی می‌کند:[۷۲]

نبشتن به خسرو بیاموختند/ دلش را به دانش برافروختند
نبشتن یکی نه که نزدیک سی/ چه رومی چه تازی و چه پارسی

«رکن‌الدین همایونفرخ»، پژوهشگر تاریخ و فرهنگ ایران باستان، در تبارشناسی‌ی خط فارسی، به معنای واژه‌ی «دیو» و رابطه‌ی آن با «خط» اشاره می‌کند. او بر اساس داده‌های «ابن ندیم» در «الفهرست»، و بر اساس شاهنامه، واژه‌ی «دیو» (به معنای «بزرگ») را لقب «بزرگان تپورستان- مازندران» می‌داند، و می‌نویسد:

> محققان بیگانه نظر داده‌اند که مقصود از «دیو»ها، «آرامی»ها هستند. و می‌گویند ایرانی‌ها بیگانگان را دیو می‌خوانده‌اند. لیکن با نکاتی که یادآور می‌شوم می‌توان نظر دیگری را پذیرفت. [...] ۱- در کتابخانه‌ای که- به نوشته‌ی ابن‌الندیم- در «سارویه جی» یافته شد، نوشته‌ای یافتند که بنیاد کتابخانه را به تهمورث منسوب می‌داشت. ۲- می‌دانیم که بزرگان تپورستان (مازندران) را دیو (بزرگ) می‌خواندند و به گفته‌ی فردوسی، مازندران جایگاه دیوان و مقر فرماندهی‌ی دیو سپید بوده است. ۳- نزدیکی‌ی واژه‌ی «دی پی» با «دیو»، که به معنی‌ی نوشته، در سنگ‌نبشته‌های داریوش آمده است. ۴- نزدیکی‌ی واژه‌ی «دی پی» با واژه‌ی «تی‌پورستان». ۵- کشف مهره‌های استوانه‌ای‌ی منقوش به خطوط ابتدائی و علائمی‌ی میخی در مارلیک (تپورستان). از مجموع نکاتی که یاد کردیم، این ظن بسیار قوت می‌گیرد که خط میخی پیدایش‌اش در مازندران بوده و به مرور راه تکامل پیموده است.[۷۳]

البته در این جا، تکیه‌ی من نه بر تاریخچه‌ی «خط»، بلکه بر مفهوم «دیو» و تغییر بار معنایی‌ی آن است. گرچه پیدا نیست در چه زمانی و تحت تأثیر کدام مؤثرهای اجتماعی/ سیاسی، این واژه‌ی هممعنا با «خدا» و «بزرگ»، در

---

[۷۱] الف) دکتر محمد معین، ***جام جهان نما***، در مجموعه‌ی مقالات، به کوشش دکتر مهدخت معین، جلد اول، چاپ دوم، تهران: مؤسسه‌ی انتشارات معین، ۱۳۶۸، صص ۳۴۵ تا ۳۶۶. ب) دکتر منوچهر مرتضوی، ***مکتب حافظ یا مقدمه‌ای بر حافظ شناسی***، تهران: انتشارات ابن سینا، ۱۳۴۷، ص ۱۴۸.

[۷۲] شکوفه تقی، ***دیو در فرهنگ شفاهی و مذهبی‌ی ایران***، سوئد، نشریه‌ی باران، شماره‌ی ۱۷ و ۱۸، پائیز/ زمستان ۱۳۸۶؛ ص ۵۸.

[۷۳] رکن‌الدین همایونفرخ، ***خط در ایران باستان***، برگرفته‌ی تارنمای «درفش کاویانی» از کتاب همایونفرخ با عنوان «تاریخچه‌ی کتاب و کتابخانه‌های شاهنشاهی‌ی ایران».

اسطوره‌ها و داستان‌های عامیانه‌ی ما بار منفی گرفته است. اما احتمال رابطه بین **انحصار** خواندن/ نوشتن/ دانش/ آگاهی در ایران باستان و این تغییر معنا را نمی‌توان نادیده گرفت. چرا که نبودِ دانش و آگاهی است که اطاعت بی‌چون و چرای شهروندان را تضمین می‌کند. و در این صورت است که آموزاننده‌ی خواندن و نوشتن (یا همان دیو)- که «اطاعت» را به «شورش» تبدیل می‌کند- از درگاه «نیک»های فرهنگ ایران رانده می‌شود.

مانی: اگر تجدید حیات میترابیسم در دوره‌ی اشکانی را - به خاطر تقدم زمانی‌ی این آیین بر آیین زرتشت- کنار بگذاریم، در روند تطور و تکوین معرفت‌شناسی‌ی ایرانی، از زرتشت به مانی‌ی دوره‌ی ساسانیان می‌رسیم. مانی، در مسیر اصلاح دین، با تأثیرپذیری از دین‌های بین‌النهرینی (عمدتاً فرقه‌های خزائی، مغتسله، و ماندائی)، سازمان‌بندی‌ی دین بودایی (تا رسیدن به تناسخ)، عرفان گنوستیک (خوارشمردن ماده و تن به عنوان زندان روشنائی)، «ده فرمان» در یهودیت، نظریه‌های «مکتب طب یونان»، و با برجسته کردن مفاهیم مجرد و عرفانی در آموزه‌های زرتشت، از نفی و نهی‌ی زندگی‌ی زمینی سر بر می‌کند. مانویت، نه تنها همان مسئولیت «خویش‌کاری» را هم از جامعه می‌گیرد، نه تنها از یکان جامعه بردگانی شخصی می‌سازد، بلکه با تقسیم قدرت بین نخبگانِ مانوی، مشروعیت همان تک‌قدرتِ آمیخته از «دین/ دولت» را به خطر می‌اندازد؛ «تک قدرت»ی که در عین تمکین طلبی و اطاعت‌خواهی از «پیروان» خود، امپراتوری‌ی بزرگ و قدرتمند ایران را ساخت و برپا نگه داشت. بازتاب عملی‌ی آموزه‌های مانی در زندگی‌ی روزمره‌ی پیروان بی‌شمار او این است که گروه انبوهی از آن‌ها («نغوشکان»، یا «شنوندگان»، یا به ترجمه‌ی عباس باقری: «نیوشندگان»)[۷۴]، در خدمت گروه کم‌شماری از نخبگانِ بیکاره‌ی این دین (یعنی «برگزیدگان») قرار گیرند.

> تنها برگزیدگان بودند که کلمه‌ی پارسا به آن‌ها اطلاق می‌شد. آن‌ها خود را وقف زندگی‌ای می‌کردند که به سوی نجات روحشان رهنمون می‌شد. آن‌ها برای به هم ریختن دوباره‌ی ذرات نور با دنیای نور، تلاش می‌کردند. از طرف دیگر، نغوشکان وظیفه داشتند کارهایی را که اجرای آن برای برگزیدگان ممنوع ولی برای ادامه‌ی حیات اجتناب‌ناپذیر بود، برایشان انجام دهند. بنا بر این، تهیه و تدارک اغذیه‌ی ضروری‌ی برگزیدگان به عهده‌ی نغوشکان بود. خوردن این غذاها همراه بود با اعلام بی‌تقصیری‌ی برگزیدگان. کتاب «آکتا آرخلای» [از آموزه‌های مانی] در فصل ده، صیغه‌ای را که برای خوردن نان به کار می‌رفته ذکر کرده است: «من تو را درو نکردم، آسیاب نکردم و همچنین خمیر ننمودم و تو را در تنور نگذاشتم./ بلکه دیگری این کار را کرد و تو را پیش من آورد/ من تو را بدون ارتکاب گناه می‌خورم.»[۷۵]

در دستگاه نظری‌ی این سلسله مراتبِ استثماری، گفتار نیک و کردار نیک و پندار نیکِ زرتشت، به «مُهر دهان»، «مُهر دست»، و «مُهر باطن» تبدیل می‌شود؛ «داوری و انتخاب خردمندانه»ی زرتشت، از قلمرو عینی («مرد و زن»)، به قلمرو ذهنی («نور مطلق») می‌گریزد، و «عصیانگری»، که البته، از دورترین سواد اسطوره و تاریخ ما (غیر از مورد فریدون و کاوه‌ی آهنگرش) «پلید» برشمرده می‌شد، با بارگیری از عرفان گنوستیک، به عنوان وجهی از «بدی» و «ظلمت»، نماد نیروهای شیطانی و دشمن نور برشمرده می‌شود. به باور من، همین جاست که فکرت «ثنویت» در فرهنگ ایران جا باز می‌کند. من متأسفانه هیچ نسخه‌ای از «ارژنگ» مانی را ندیده‌ام. اما با تکیه به شرح پژوهشگران، که: «مانی در ارژنگ، مفاهیم و کارکردهای نور و ظلمت را نمادینه کرده است»، می‌توانم بگویم که نقاشی‌های مانی هم مانند آموزه‌های کلامی‌ی او، جهان عینی را به ذهن منتقل می‌کند، و همان ذهنیتِ متباین با زندگی را، به عینیت (به زندگی) بازمی‌گرداند. اما در ورای این جهان‌بینی‌ی زندگی‌ستیز، تکیه‌ی مانی بر «نوشتار»، خط و نگارش را برای مدتی کوتاه از انحصار

---

[۷۴] فرانسوا دکره، ***مانی و سنت مانوی***، ترجمه‌ی دکتر عباس باقری، تهران: انتشارات نشر و پژوهش فرزان، چاپ دوم، ۱۳۸۳.

[۷۵] گئو ویدن‌گرن، ***مانی و تعلیمات او***، ترجمه‌ی نزهت صفای اصفهانی، تهران: نشر مرکز، ۱۳۷۶، صص ۱۲۸-۱۲۹.

طبقه‌ی نخبه و از محدوده‌ی «دژنبشت»های سلطنتی بیرون برد و همگانی کرد. منتها، پس از مرگ فجیع او در زندان، تمام آثارش نیز در ایران نابود شد؛ به طوری که اگر خودتبعیدیان مانوی آثارش را (عمدتاً ارژنگ، آکتا آرخلای، شاپورگان، و کفالایا) را از ایران خارج نمی‌کردند، اینک به جز گفته‌های ضد و نقیض مورخان پس از اسلام، هیچ ردپائی از اندیشه‌های مانی برجا نمانده بود. اما پرسشی که در این جا قد علم می‌کند، این است که با وجود سرشت سلسله مراتبی در مانویت، چرا مانی و پیروانش، در سیستم سلسله مراتبی‌ی ساسانی (و سپس در اروپای مسیحی و سپس‌تر در بغداد اسلامی)، قلع و قمع شدند؟ به باور من، افزون بر به خطر انداختن زرتشیت ساسانی و دین‌یاران آن (یا به خطر انداختن دین رسمی‌ی هر سرزمینی که مانویت را سرکوب کرد)، سبب عمده‌ی این ستیز مداوم، سرشت شورشی‌ی مانویت بر استبداد و اشرافیتِ حاکم بر دستگاه‌های سیاسی‌ی دین/ دولت بود؛ یعنی همان شورشی که چندی بعد، مزدک و مزدکیان را به قتلگاه ساسانی فرستاد.

مزدک[۷۶] ، مبنای نظری‌ی تقابل «نور» و «تاریکی»، و اصل عملی‌ی خوار شمردنِ تن و زندگی‌ی زمینی در مانویت را نگه می‌دارد. اما، چنان که پژوهشگران تشخیص داده‌اند، وجه تمایز عمده‌ی مزدک با مانی در این است که مزدک، گرایش انسان به «پلیدی» و «تاریکی» را امری اختیاری نمی‌داند. منتها از قراین چنین برمی‌آید که مزدک، مبدأ گرایش به «تاریکی» و «پلیدی» را در شرایط اجتماعی جست‌وجو می‌کند، نه مانند مانی در نهاد هستی. این استنباط، با کنار هم گذاشتن گزاره‌های تاریخی پشتیبانی می‌شود:

۱) به باور مانی و مزدک، «کشتن» و «خونریزی»، یاری دادن به «تاریکی» است و حضور نهایی‌ی «نور مطلق» را به تعویق می‌اندازد.

۲) بر خلاف مانی، مزدک بر این باور است که: «تاریکی، مانند روشنایی، از روی اراده کار نمی‌کند، بلکه رفتارش کورانه و از روی اتفاق است؛ بنا بر این، اختلاط نور و ظلمت، که نتیجه‌ی آن، این عالم مادی است، چنان که مانی پنداشته، از روی نقشه و اراده نبوده بلکه بی‌اختیار انجام یافته است.»[۷۷]

۳) در زمان ظهور مزدک، مردم ایران از نظر سیاسی و اقتصادی، یکی از سخت‌ترین دوره‌های تاریخی را می‌گذرانند: کشمکش‌های درازمدتی که بین خاندان‌های اشرافی و مدعیان تاج و تخت برقرار بود؛ تاخت و تاز «هپتالیان» و موفقیت کوتاه مدت آنان در تبدیل امپراتوری‌ی ایران به یک «خراج‌گذار»؛ خشکسالی‌ی دراز مدت؛ و مناسبات گسترده‌ی تیولداری و یکه‌تازی‌ی تیولداران بر مردم.[۷۸] در چنین شرایطی بود که مزدک، این رفرمیست دینی، به یاری‌ی فلسفه‌ی نظری‌ی خود، از تعدیل اقتصادی دم زد.

۴) به نظر مزدک، «آن چه از روشنایی ناراضی است و از تاریکی راضی، کینه‌ورزی و جنگ و نزاع است، و موجب جنگ و نزاع میان افراد بشر، همانا عدم تساوی در بهره‌وری از زن و خواسته‌ی این جهانی است.»[۷۹]

اگر نخواهیم داوری‌های مورخان اسلامی (ایرانی و تازی) را- که اکثراً در نفی‌ی مزدک و فلسفه‌ی او نوشته شده- ملاک

---

[۷۶] به نسبت منابعی که درباره‌ی مانی و از مانی در دست داریم، درباره‌ی مزدک، بسیار اندک می‌دانیم. اما همین ها هم که در دست است، یا اکثراً تفسیرهای متأخری هستند که صرفاً از دیدگاه ایدئولوژی‌های مارکسیستی نوشته شده‌اند، و در نتیجه، بنیادهای نظری‌ی او را به اندیشه‌ی «تعدیل اقتصادی» کاهش داده‌اند، و یا همان گزاره‌های افسانه‌وار و پر ابهامی که در منابع تاریخی‌ی سده‌های نخستین اسلامی نوشته شده‌اند، یا گزاره‌ی ابوالقاسم فردوسی، که مأخذ او هم «خداینامک» تدوین شده در عصر ساسانیان بوده است.

[۷۷] گئو ویدن‌گرن، ***مانی و تعلیمات او***، ص ۱۰۸

[۷۸] در زمینه‌ی بحران اجتماعی و اقتصادی‌ی زمان مزدک، به کتاب زیر مراجعه کنید:

فرهنگ رجایی، در کتاب ***تحول اندیشه‌ی سیاسی در شرق***، تهران: نشر قومس، ۱۳۷۲، صص ۱۱۰ تا ۱۱۵

[۷۹] گئو ویدن‌گرن، ***مانی و تعلیمات او***، ص ۹۶.

قرار دهیم، تا این جا می‌دانیم که مزدک مشکل عینی را شناسایی کرده، اما، به جز گزارش فشرده‌ی ابوالقاسم فردوسی، نمی‌دانیم (یا من نمی‌دانم) راه حل پیشنهادی‌ی او دقیقاً چه بوده است. حتا نمی‌دانیم که انگیزه‌ی پذیرش پادشاه (قباد) نسبت به آراء مزدک، چه بوده است. پرفسور نولدکه و پرفسور تورج دریائی معتقدند که قباد برای کاهش نفوذ موبدان دربارش از مزدک به عنوان ابزار سود جست؛ در حالی که پرفسور آرتور کریستن‌سن، با استفاده از نوشته‌های مورخی مانند طبری، حمزه اصفهانی، و ثعالبی، قباد را یک مزدکی‌ی تمام عیار می‌داند. در هر حال، با توجه به موافقت و همراهی‌ی درازمدتِ قباد ساسانی با مزدک، فقط می‌توانیم استنتاج کنیم که راه حل مزدک در توزیع عادلانه‌ی «زن و خواسته»، نمی‌توانسته با نظم طبقاتی‌ی جامعه‌ی جمشیدی در تضادی بنیادی بوده باشد. منتها اختلاف طبقاتی و تنگنای اقتصادی‌ی حاکم بر جامعه سبب شده که بنیادهای نظری‌ی آموزه‌های دینی‌ی مزدک از دید مردم محروم و فرودست پنهان بماند، اما بهره‌وری از «زن و خواسته»، که به قول فردوسی «در نهفتِ» فرادستان انبار شده بود، به مذاق آنان گوارا آید. این چنین است که «هرج و مرج»ی که تاریخ نویسان بعدی درباره‌ی اجرای تز مزدک گزارش کرده‌اند، سود ثروتمندان، از جمله خود قباد و روحانیان زمانه را تهدید می‌کرده است. از این روست که مزدک، در نگاه پاسداران نظم مقدس، ویژگی‌های ضحاک را می‌گیرد، و صرف نظر از آراء نظری/ دینی‌ی او، در نگاه مردم ایران به نمادی برای مبارزه علیه ستم اقتصادی تبدیل می‌شود و در حافظه‌ی جمعی باقی می‌ماند، تا یک بار دیگر در مبارزات مردم ایران علیه سلطه‌ی تازیان، در قامت «مازیار» و «جاویدان ابن سهل» و «بابک خرم دین» شکوفا شود.[۸۰]

در نگاه نخست به شباهت‌ها و اشتراک عناصر در جهان‌بینی‌های زرتشیت و زروانیت و متیرایسم و مانویت و آیین مزدک، چنین به نظر می‌رسد که جهان‌بینی‌های پس از زرتشت، محصول اجتناب‌ناپذیر بنیادهای مینوی و عرفانی‌ی جهان‌شناسی‌ی خود زرتشت بوده است. در آمیزش توحیدی‌ی این بنیادها با قدرت سیاسی، هم ابعاد گیتیانه و خردورزانه‌ی زرتشت (در همان هفده سرود) در درازنای زمان رنگ باخته و وجه عرفانی‌ی آن برجسته شده است، و هم، ابزار کلامی‌ی انقیاد هر چه بیش‌تر به آن تحمیل شده است. این پیوند نامبارک در چه زمانی و چه‌گونه صورت گرفته است، ما نمی‌دانیم. اما در رهگذر مطالعه‌ی متن‌های مربوط به ایران باستان (با همه‌ی تفاوت‌هائی که با هم دارند) به این نتیجه می‌رسیم که وحدت دین و دولت، پایه‌گزاری شده در جامعه‌ی جمشیدی،[۸۱] توسط زرتشت و مانی و مزدک نیز دنبال شده است. این است که هر سه تن آنان در پناه شاهان و قدرتمندان زمانه‌ی خود قرار می‌گیرند. زرتشت در گات ۴۶ (از سرودهای هفده‌گانه) می‌گوید:

> «به کدام خاک روی آورم، به کجا رفته و پناه جویم؟ شُرَفا و پیشوایان از من کناره می‌جویند و از برزیگران نیز خشنود نیستم و نه از پیروان دروغ که فرمانروایان شهر هستند. چه‌گونه تو را خشنود توانم ساخت ای مزدا؟» [۸۲]

متفکری که بنیاد معرفت‌شناسی‌ی او بر محور نیایش و ستایش خاک و آب و روشنایی، و کوشش برای رویاندن می‌گردد، و از نظر هستی‌شناسی، برای انسان اصل گیاهی قائل است،[۸۳] از «برزیگران» خشنود نیست. و چون «فرمانروایان شهرِ» خود را نیز از جمله «پیروان دروغ» می‌داند، در دربار فرمانروای دیگر، یعنی «ویشتاسب» شاه «پناه» می‌گیرد. مانی، این متفکر ضد ماده وُ مال وُ کار وُ رفاه وُ لذت، سال‌های سال در دربارهای مختلف می‌گردد، تا پس از مرگ

---

[۸۰] حمید حمید، ***نهضت خرمدینی در ایران***، انتشار الکترونیکی‌ی کتاب در تارنمای «مرز پرگهر»، به نشانی‌ی زیر: https://derafsh-kaviyani.com/books/khoramdin.pdf

[۸۱] به گزارش شاهنامه، جمشید در زمان تاجگذاری و پیش از اعلام چه‌گونگی و چرایی‌ی تقسیم طبقات اجتماعی، می‌گوید: «منم گفت با فره‌ی ایزدی/ همم شهریاری و هم موبدی.»

[۸۲] هاشم رضی، ***اوستا: کهن‌ترین گنجینه‌ی مکتوب ایران باستان***، تهران: انتشارات بهجت، ۱۳۷۸، ص ۳۳.

[۸۳] در فلسفه‌ی زرتشت، زن و مرد نخستین دو شاخه‌ی به هم پیوسته‌ی ریواس (ریباس) هستند که بعد از دمیدن «فره‌ی مینوی» به آن‌ها، از «گیاه‌پیکری» به «مردم‌پیکری» تبدیل می‌شوند و نام‌های مشی و مشیانه می‌گیرند.

اردشـیـر - «شاهنشاه/ مغ»- به دربار سـاسـانی می‌پیوندد، و از جمله تیولداران «شاپورشاه» ساسانی می‌شود، و در ماجرای تسلیم شدن «والرین» امپراتور رُم، به قول «عبدالحسین زرین‌کوب»، با «موکب شاهنشاه» همراه است. همچنین، «کرتیر»، سومین مؤلفِ فقه زرتشتی[۸۴]، که تازه ادعای سروشی هم نداشت، در دربار شاه ساسانی جا خوش کرد، و تا رسیدن به پیروزی در تدوین فقه زرتشتی، با هزار نیرنگ، از همان پایگاه با مانی مبارزه کرد. مزدکِ «عدالت‌خواه»، از سوی قباد ساسانی عنوان «موبدان موبد» گرفت و در دربار او «مجاور» شد. پیش از این نیز، تیرداد اول، پادشاه اشکانی‌ی ارمنستان، در مقام یک روحانی‌ی آیین مهر، و با عنوانِ «پسر خدا»، فاصله‌ی ارمنستان تا رم را در نُه ماه پیمود (۶۶ میلادی)، تا شخصاً به حضور امپراتور رم (نِرو) برسد، و به بهای «بنده»نامیدن خود و «خداوند»نامیدنِ امپراتوری که مداوماً با ایران در جنگ بود، او را به آیین مهر بگرواند.[۸۵] تلاش برای ایجاد این وحدت ترسناک، البته خاص پیامبران ایرانی نیست. تلاش برای به دست آوردن تأیید شاهان و قدرتمندان زمانه، در زندگی‌ی پیامبران دیگر نیز ثبت است. که البته نه پیامبر یهود تأیید فرعون را به دست آورد، نه پیامبر مسیحیت تأیید نماینده‌ی امپراتور رم را، و نه پیامبر اسلام تأیید حکمرانان مکه و شاه ساسانی را. شاید در غیاب همین وحدت شوم بوده است که دینِ هیچ یک از این پیامبران- تا پیش از تبدیل به یک مکتب سازمان‌یافته، با نمایندگی‌ی «معبد» و «کلیسا» و «مسجد»- مبنای سلسله مراتبی نداشت. یا شاید از آن رو مورد پذیرش دولتمداران زمانه واقع نشد، که مبنای سلسله مراتب نداشت، و با منافع تک قدرت سیاسی/ دینی‌ی زمان و مکان در تعارض بود. توسل دین‌کاران به قدرت سیاسی در عهد باستان، تا زمان بازگشت کاملِ شاه/ مغ در عهد صفویان، صدها مثال در تاریخ ایران دارد. به عنوان یک مثال، «قاضی نورالله» از «علمای شیعه»ی زمان هولاکوی مغول، ادعا کرد:

> تقرب خواجه نصیرالدین طوسی در حضرت ایلخان (هولاکوی مغول) به جایی رسید که [...] ایلخان و بیگم [همسر هولاکو] را، پنهان از اعیان لشگر به شرف اسلام فایز گردانید و چنان که مشهور است، ایشان را ختنه کرد.[۸۶]

در حالی که هولاکو بودایی بود و در قلمرو قدرت خود ده‌ها معبد بنا کرد و همسرش بیگم نیز مسیحی بود و ده‌ها کلیسا ساخت، «**و هر جا بود بر درگاهش ناقوس می‌زدند.**»[۸۷]

در هر حال، آمیزش دین‌کاران با قدرت سیاسی، در طول زمان توانست در جهان‌شناسی‌ی زرتشتیتِ آغازین دست ببرد، به تدریج، صبغه‌های فلسفی‌ی آن را به سود الاهیات بزداید، و در عوض، به وجه عرفانی‌ی آن پر و بال دهد. اما این روند، یک طرفه نبود. بلکه همین جهان‌شناسی نیز نیروی مؤثر خود را در دگرگون کردن قدرتِ سیاسی، به تماشای تاریخ گذاشت. به عنوان مثال، پادشاهان ماد و هخامنشی، با این که خود را «برگزیده‌ی» اهورا مزدا معرفی می‌کردند، از عنوان‌های «شاه شاهان»، یا «شاه این کشور بزرگ» فراتر نمی‌رفتند. اما شاهان اشکانی، عنوان «پسر خدا» را بر خود نهادند، و شاهان ساسانی، در زمره‌ی «ایزدان» جا گرفتند. «حسن پیرنیا»، این تغییر را برخاسته از رواج فرهنگ سلوکی در ایران و نشأت گرفته از ذهنیت اسطوره‌ای و قداست یونانی‌ی اسکندر برآورد می‌کند.[۸۸] البته این تشخیص می‌تواند به

---

[۸۴] پیش از «کرتیر»، فقه زرتشتی در دو نوبت نوشته شده بود، که نخستین آن به وسیله‌ی «تنسر»، در عهد اردشیر بابکان انجام شده بود.

[۸۵] مارتین ورمازِرن، ***آیین میترا***، ترجمه‌ی بزرگ نادرزاد، تهران: نشر چشمه، چاپ سوم، ۱۳۸۰، ص ۲۷.

[۸۶] دکتر ذبیح‌الله صفا، ***تاریخ ادبیات ایران: از اوایل قرن هفتم تا پایان قرن هشتم هجری***، جلد سوم- بخش اول، تهران: انتشارات فردوس، چاپ ششم، ۱۳۶۸، ص ۱۳۹.

[۸۷] دکتر ذبیح‌الله صفا، ***تاریخ ادبیات ایران: از اوایل قرن هفتم تا پایان قرن هشتم هجری***، جلد سوم- بخش اول، تهران: انتشارات فردوس، چاپ ششم، ۱۳۶۸، ص ۱۳۸.

[۸۸] حسن پیرنیا، تاریخ ایران از آغاز تا انقراض ساسانیان، در ***تاریخ ایران: از آغاز تا انقراض قاجاریه***، حسن پیرنیا و عباس اقبال، تهران: انتشارات خیام، چاپ نهم، ۱۳۸۰، ص ۱۳۷.

عنوان یک مؤثر شناسایی شود؛ اما تعامل جهان‌شناسیِ دینی و معرفت‌شناسیِ سیاسی/ مدنیِ ایرانی در هر دوره را نمی‌توان در این دگرگونی نادیده گرفت. مثلاً، نام بنیادگذار خاندان ساسانی، یعنی اردشیر بابکان، در اصل «ارتخشتره» بوده است، که از دو بخشِ «ارت» یعنی «مقدس»، و «خشتره»، یعنی «شهریار» تشکیل شده بود.[۸۹] و این «شهریار مقدس» یا «شهریار الاهی»، نسب خود را به هخامنشیان رسانده بود.

تا جایی که به جهان‌شناسی و مناسبات سیاسی/ اجتماعیِ دوره‌ی ساسانی مربوط می‌شود، بسیاری از پاسخ‌ها را می‌توان در کتاب‌های فقه زرتشتی و «اوستا»ی مدّون در همین دوره پیدا کرد، که از سوی موبدان زرتشتیِ آن روزگار، کتاب «قانون» نامیده می‌شد. اگر زرتشت نیایش می‌کرد که «ای اهورا مزدا! مرا بیاگاهان»، این کتاب قانون بر همه چیز آگاه است: حالا، در جهان مینو، «بهشت»ی هست و «دوزخ»ی، که تمام ریزه‌کاری‌های آن‌ها، به وسیله‌ی مغی به نام «ارداویرافِ» رفته به آن، و بازگشته از آن، ترسیم شده است؛ و دستورالعمل‌های ناشی از آن به صورت «شایست و ناشایست»، و به نام قانون، بر ذهن و زندگیِ روزمره‌ی مردم حکومت می‌کند. در این «قانون»، مردم طبقاتِ محروم از قدرت و آگاهی و دانش و آموزش، هم «فرومایه» تلقی می‌شوند، و هم باید تا پایان عمر و نسل بعد از نسل در همان سطح باقی بمانند. در خلاصه‌ای که دکتر احمد تفضلی (زبان‌شناس و پژوهشگر ایران باستان)، از کتاب «عهد اردشیر بابکان» به دست می‌دهد، می‌خوانیم:

> تأکید بر اتحاد دین و دولت، و هشدار در این مورد که فرومایگان نباید به کار دین و تحقیق در آن، و قوانین آن بپردازند. زیرا در این صورت، در خفا رهبرانی دینی از نوع همان مردم، که گرفتار ظلم و ستم و تحقیر فرمانروایان شده‌اند، پیدا خواهد شد. و این کار، به زیان پادشاهی است. [...] مردم با توسل به دین می‌توانند شاه را ساقط کنند.[۹۰]

در بند ۱۳ از کتاب «عهد اردشیر»، طبقات چهارگانه‌ی «رعیت» به شرح زیر ثبت شده است: ۱- جنگجویان، ۲- روحانیان، ۳- دبیران، منجمان، پزشکان، ۴- صنعتگران و بازرگانان و کشاورزان. و در بندهای ۱۲ و ۱۳ همین کتاب، بر «منع انتقال از یک طبقه‌ی اجتماعی به طبقه‌ی دیگر» تأکید شده است. شک نیست که در هر نظام سلسله مراتبی، هر یک از طبقه‌ها، خود دارای تشکیلاتی هِرمی شکل هستند، که فقط نخبگانِ هر طبقه در رأس آن جای دارند. در نتیجه، نه تنها بخش اعظم دامن هِرَم کلی را شهروندان طبقه‌ی چهارم، یعنی صنعتگران و بازرگانان و کشاورزان پر می‌کرده‌اند، بلکه از طبقه‌های سه‌گانه‌ی دیگر هم (به نسبت دوری از رأس هرم تشکیلاتی)، از هر نوع مشارکت در سیاست‌گذاری و از هر نوع نعمت معنوی محروم بوده‌اند. و همین شهروندان بوده‌اند که «فرومایه» تلقی می‌شدند، و برای حفظ این سلسله مراتب، باید همواره ناآگاه باقی می‌ماندند.

در این نظام دینی/ سیاسی، البته که قوانین «دین»، باید از اکثر شهروندان دریغ شود؛[۹۱] چرا که دین در خدمت حفظ قدرت است، و بنا بر سیاست روز، باید بتواند چهره عوض کند. خوانشِ نخستین، و رانشِ سپسینِ شاهپور نسبت به مانی، و قباد نسبت به مزدک، و نیز، نوسان رفتاریِ شاهان بعدیِ ساسانی در نشان دادن نرمش یا خشونت نسبت به نسطوریان،

---

[۸۹] صادق هدایت، ***زند و هومن یسن و کارنامه‌ی اردشیر پاپکان***، تهران: انتشارات آزادمهر، ۱۳۸٤، ص ۹.

[۹۰] احمد تفضلی، ***تاریخ ادبیات ایران باستان***، به کوشش ژاله آموزگار، تهران: انتشارات سخن، ۱۳۷٦، ص ۲۱٦.

[۹۱] فرهنگ رجایی، در کتاب ***تحول اندیشه‌ی سیاسی در شرق باستان***، تهران: نشر قومس، ۱۳۷۲، ص ۷٤. می‌نویسد:«خردک اوستا در دوره‌ی ساسانی، بالاخص در دوره‌ی شاهپور دوم، توسط «آذرپاد مهراسپندان» موبدان موبد آن دوران فراهم آمد، تا به سادگی در اختیار شهروندان قرار گیرد.» این نویسنده، در کتاب ارجمند خود مأخذ بخش پیرو این جمله را ثبت نکرده است. یعنی نگفته است که «تا به سادگی در اختیار شهروندان قرار گیرد» را با پشتوانه‌ی چه منبعی قید کرده است. اما از آن جا که «خرده اوستا» یک کتاب دعا و نماز است، بعید به نظر نمی‌آید که می‌بایست در «اختیار شهروندان» قرار می‌گرفت. منتها در این جا مسئله‌ی «سواد» خواندن مطرح است، که به عنوان یک واقعیت، می‌دانیم شهروندان طبقات پایین جامعه‌ی ایرانی، به آن دسترسی نداشته‌اند.

مسیحیان و یهودیان ایرانی، به نسبتِ جنگ یا صلحی که با امپراتوری‌ی رم داشتند، مثال‌های بارزی هستند که تغییر ماسک «دین / دولت» در مواقع ضروری، را توضیح می‌دهند.

منع مردم از خواندن، که همانا ترس از انتشار آگاهی است، نه به کتاب دینی منحصر می‌شد، و نه ابداع ساسانیان بود. افزون بر این که باستان‌شناسی، پیشینه‌ی کتابت در ایران را به هزاره‌ی چهارم پیش از میلاد می‌رساند، گزاره‌های تاریخی، از حضور ده‌ها کتاب اصیل و ترجمه در قلمروهای فلسفه، پزشکی، کشاورزی و تاریخ در دوره‌ی ساسانیان، و حتا در دوره‌ی هخامنشیان،[۹۲] خبر می‌دهند، که چون در «دژنبشت»ها، و در گنجینه‌ی شاهان، از چشم «عوام» پنهان می‌ماندند، نه تنها اثری از آن‌ها باقی نمانده، بلکه تبعاً، ردّ پایی از دانش و آگاهی‌های مطروحه در آن‌ها نیز، در روان توده‌ی شهروندان بر جا نمانده است. حتا از رویدادهای مهم تاریخی، مانند چرایی‌ها و چه‌گونگی‌های پیروزی یا شکست جنگ‌های ایران با یونان در دوره‌ی هخامنشی، جز کلیاتی که سنگ‌نوشته‌ها در اختیارمان گذاشته، هیچ خبری از نویسندگان و تاریخ‌نگاران ایرانی به ما نرسیده است؛ در حالی که هرودوت در چند جای کتاب «تاریخ‌ها»، از «تاریخ‌نگاران پارسی» و نظرهای آنان در قبال رویدادهای تاریخی یاد کرده است. اگر این گزاره را از هرودوت بپذیریم، باید بپذیریم که این کتاب‌ها، به سبب انحصاری بودنِ کتابت و توزیع دانش، احتمالاً در نسخه‌های معدود نوشته شده بود، و همان‌ها نیز پیچیده شده در «هفت لفاف»، در دژنبشت‌ها معلوم نیست منتظر چه زمانی باقی مانده بودند. به عنوان نمونه، شاپور سوم، در تاریخ ۸۰۴ سلوکی/ ۳۸۴ میلادی، در حاشیه‌ی «کارنامکِ» شاپور دوم ساسانی (موسوم به ذوالکتاف) نوشته است:

> [...] کارنامک پدرم، پس از برکناری‌ی و مرگ عمویم، در اختیار من قرار گرفت. آن را خواندم و برایم بسیار جالب و آموزنده بود. به خواسته‌ی پدرم، این کارنامک را در هفت لفاف و صندوق می‌گذارم و بر آن می‌نویسم و مُهر می‌زنم که تا هزار سال ناگشوده بماند و آن را در زیرزمین کتابخانه‌ی تیسفون در کنجی ایمن می‌نهم تا کی گشوده شود، و سرنوشتش چه‌باشد.[۹۳]

البته، سرنوشت این «کارنامک» از دسترس مهاجمانی که تیسفون را ویران کردند و کتابخانه‌اش را به آتش سپردند، در امان ماند. به گفته‌ی فریدون مجلسی، که این متن را به فارسی‌ی امروزی ترجمه کرده: «سرنوشت این صندوق آن بود که پس از شانزده قرن به دست باستان‌شناسان و با کمک یادداشت‌های تاریخی‌ی برجا مانده در ایران و ارمنستان رُم و [...] ترجمه و به دین صورت بازنگاری شود.» اما چرائی‌ی این رسم شگفت‌انگیز، پرسشی است که در تحلیل نهائی- و البته در خوانش من، هیچ پاسخی به جز «انحصار دانش»، از تاریخ ایران نمی‌گیرد. می‌توان استدلال کرد که تجربه‌ی آتش زدنِ پرسپولیس توسط اسکندر، چنین پنهان کردن‌هائی را سبب شده بود. اما این استدلال در صورتی پذیرفتنی بود که فقط یک نسخه از نسخه‌های منتشر شده، در نهان‌گاه‌ها، یا همان «دژنبشت‌ها»، نگه‌داری می‌شد.

گروهی از فرهیختگان ایرانی در حال حاضر پافشاری دارند که در ایران باستان و در زرتشتیتِ آن، نه تنها سوادآموزی، بلکه برابری‌ی زن و مرد قانونی بوده و رواج همگانی داشته است. به عنوان نمونه، جمشید سروشیان، نویسنده‌ی

---

[۹۲] فرهنگ رجایی، ***تحول اندیشه‌ی سیاسی در شرق***، تهران: نشر قومس، ۱۳۷۲، ص ۱۱۰. مهندس یونس کرامتی، در کتاب ***کارنامه‌ی ایرانیان: در زمینه‌ی نوآوری‌های ریاضیات، نجوم و گاه‌شماری***، تهران: مؤسسه‌ی فرهنگی‌ی اهل قلم، ۱۳۸۰، صص ۱۴ تا ۱۷. دکتر ذبیح‌الله صفا، ***تاریخ علوم عقلی در تمدن اسلامی، تا اواسط قرن پنجم***، جلد اول، تهران: انتشارات امیرکبیر، چاپ چهارم، ۲۵۳۵، ص ۱۷. همه‌ی این پژوهشگران از قول ابومعشر بلخی، یا حمزه‌ی اصفهانی، یا ابن ندیم، از گنجینه‌ی کتابی یاد می‌کند که بعد از هجوم تازیان در محلی به نام «دژ سارویه» در نزدیکی‌ی اصفهان کشف شد، که کتاب‌هایی از هزار سال پیش (به نسبت زمان زمخشری)، در آن گردآوری شده بود.

[۹۳] برگرفته از مجموعه نامه‌های آله دال فک به دکتر احسان یارشاطر، منعکس در تارنمای «درفش کاویانی، بازدید ۲۲ ژانویه ۲۰۰۷: http://derafsh-kaviyani.com

زرتشتی‌ی دوره‌ی ما، در کتاب «سوادآموزی و دبیری در دین زرتشت»، کوشیده است تا ثابت کند که در ایران باستان و بر اساس دستورات دین زرتشت، سوادآموزی، مخصوص طبقه‌ی ممتاز جامعه نبوده است و هر کس می‌توانست و می‌بایست که سواد بیاموزد. من این کتاب را ندیده‌ام. اما سیروس آموزگار، پس از این جمع‌بندی از کتاب یادشده، می‌نویسد:

> بر این سخن از سه جهت مختلف می‌توان نگریست: اول این که فارغ از دستورات مذهبی، مردم معمولاً در محدوده‌ی امکانات خود زندگی می‌کنند. تردید نیست که نگرانی‌ی وسائل زیست، در آن زمان نیز بسیاری را از همان کودکی به نبردگاه تهیه‌ی نان شب می‌راند و فرصتی که به سوادآموزی بپردازند برایشان باقی نمی‌گذاشت. به همین دلیل شواهدی که نویسنده در کتاب خود نقل می‌کند، همه، در محافل و مجالس شاهان و شاهزادگان می‌گذرد. دوم این که، قاعدتاً در ایران قدیم، [به نسبت امروز، واژه‌ی] «سواد»، می‌بایست دامنه‌ی وسیع‌تری می‌داشت و هر نوع آموزش صنعت و حرفه را در برمی‌گرفت. از این نظر، با توجه به جامعه‌ی «کاستی»ی ایران قدیم، تردید نیست که هر فرزندی، برای ادامه‌ی حرفه‌ی خانواده تربیت می‌شد. سوم این که حتا اینک و قرن‌ها بعد از بعثت زرتشت، در سال‌های پایانی‌ی قرن بیستم و با وجود این همه امکانات، که قطعاً از امکانات دوران قدیم بیش‌تر است، نیمی از ایرانیان فرصت و امکان رفتن به مدرسه را نمی‌یابند و جامعه‌ی ایران هنوز هم از نظر تعداد بی‌سواد، در رأس صورت‌ها قرار دارد. اگر واقعاً مدارکی موجود است که نشان دهد ایرانیان قدیم همه سوادآموخته بوده‌اند، لابد روش کاری بسیار هوشمندانه می‌داشته‌اند که باید آن را آموخت و به خاطر سعادت قوم ایرانی- زرتشتی یا غیرزرتشتی- به کار بست. افسوس که نویسنده، خصوصیات و نحوه‌ی عملکرد این روش را به دست نمی‌دهد. جمشید سروشیان، مرد دانشمندی است و بی‌شک سخن به گزاف نمی‌گوید. از وی بخواهیم که درباره‌ی ترتیب اِعمال این دستور مذهبی‌ی دین زرتشت، تحقیق کند و حاصل کار خود را در کتابی دیگر در دسترس علاقمندان بگذارد.[۹۴]

افزون بر انحصار دانش، تمرکز قدرت در دست «شاه/ موبد»، و عدم مشارکت اکثریت قریب به اتفاق یکان جامعه در تعیین سرنوشت خود، راه هر گونه تمرین و کسب هر گونه نگاه انتقادی و خرد سیاسی/ اجتماعی را بر روان جمعی سد کرده بود. گزنفون می‌نویسد: «ایرانیان به فرزندان خود تقوی و فضیلت می‌آموزند، همان گونه که دیگران خواندن و نوشتن می‌آموزند.»[۹۵] آموزش سینه به سینه‌ی همین تقوی و فضیلت بود که از سویی، فرهنگ موروثی را دست‌نخورده گذاشت، و حقانیت‌های آن، از جمله، حقانیت «شهریاری‌ی الاهی» را همراه با بارقه‌های بینش عرفانی در دورترین زوایای ذهن ایرانی حک کرد، و شگفتا که از سوی دیگر، ضامن قوام و دوام هویتی شد که تمدن ایرانی با آن رقم خورد. تمدنی که بسیاری از اصول سیاسی، جهان‌شناسی، علم، و حتا بن‌مایه‌های عرفانی‌ی آن، منبع الهام و کشف برخی از اندیشمندان و فیلسوفان یونان باستان- از جمله افلاتون- شد، اما در ایران، در غیاب مشارکت و جوشش اندیشه، نه تنها نتوانست از بارقه‌ی پرسش‌های فلسفی‌ی زرتشت فراتر رود، بلکه در طنین تک صدای مقدس، بار اندیشه‌ی فلسفی را نیز از زرتشتیت زدود. به عنوان مثال، تز پیشنهادی‌ی زرتشت در مورد «زندگی‌ی جاویدان» به تز «نامیرایی‌ی ماده و انرژی‌ی کیهانی» (چنان که در فلسفه‌ی یونان باستان رسید)، نیانجامید.

در روی دیگر سکه، تمدن ایرانی، ضمن این که در بدو پیدایش، حامل عناصری از فرهنگ‌های هند و آسیای میانه و بومیان فلات ایران بود، برای گیرش و گوارش از فرهنگ‌های دیگر نیز سرشتی گشوده و پذیرا داشت. این تمدن، در

---

[۹۴] سیروس آموزگار، ***نگاهی به پشت سر***، ماهنامه‌ی «روزگار نو»، چاپ پاریس، شماره‌ی ۱۱۲، دفتر چهارم، سال دهم، ۱۳۷۰، صص ۸۰-۸۱.

[۹۵] برگرفته از: دکتر پرویز آذکانی، ***فهرست ماقبل الفهرست: آثار ایرانی‌ی پیش از اسلام***، مشهد: انتشارات بنیاد پژوهش‌های اسلامی‌ی آستان قدس، ۱۳۷۵.

مسیر تشکیل و گسترش امپراتوری‌های هخامنشی، اشکانی، و ساسانی، از راه‌های متفاوتِ نظامی، مسالمت‌جویانه، داد وُ دهش علمی و نظری، و حتا به ضربِ «هزوارش»ها هم که شده، با جهان پیرامون خود رابطه برقرار کرد. خرد سیاسی و دانش پادشاهان و نخبگان ایرانی، ضمن این که بر فرهنگ کشورهای تحت سلطه اثر گذاشت، از آن فرهنگ‌ها نیز بسیار تأثیر پذیرفت. منتها، به صورت شگفت‌انگیزی، آموزه‌های تازه را در انبان همان جهان‌بینیِ «ایرانشهری» ریخت، و از آن، فرآورده‌ای پدید آورد وفادار به همان جهان‌بینی. چرا که در این جهان‌بینی، خرد و دانش، فرآورده‌ی جوشش درونیِ کل جامعه‌ی ایرانی نبود، و چه‌گونگی و پارامترهای آن از سوی رأس هرم قدرت (دین/ دولت) دیکته می‌شد، و نمودهای آن نیز از سوی همان هرم به عینیت درمی‌آمد، که همه در خدمت تحکیم قدرت قرار می‌گرفت؛ و آن چه که نصیب ذهنیت شهروندان معمولی می‌شد، چیزی نبود جز «ترس»؛ ترس از خدائی که در هیئت شهریار بر او حکم می‌راند.

مدارای شگفت‌انگیز و افتخارآفرین کوروش هخامنشی نسبت به شهروندان کشورهای مغلوب و پیروان دین‌های دیگر، از خرد سیاسی، نبوغ کشورگشائی، و از همه مهمتر، از عدم تعصب دینیِ این پادشاهِ پیروز حکایت می‌کند. در این جا مایلم سخنی حاکی از این نبوغ را از زبان رئیس موزه‌ی بریتانیا (در سخنرانیِ سال ۲۰۱۳) بازگو کنم:

> [...] کار خود را در ۵۳۰ قبل از میلاد آغاز کرد و وقتی زمانه‌ی حکومت داریوش فرارسید، تمام سرزمین‌های مدیترانه‌ی شرقی جزو این امپراتوری بود. به عبارت دیگر، خاورمیانه‌ای که امروز می‌شناسیم همان امپراتوریِ ایران است که تا آن زمان بزرگ‌ترین امپراتوریِ جهان محسوب می‌شد. اهمیت این واقعه در آن است که این امپراتوری اولین دولت چندفرهنگی و چندمذهبی محسوب می‌شود که در مقیاسی عظیم عمل می‌کرد و به ناچار باید به روشی کاملاً نوین اداره می‌شد. این واقعیت که مردم این امپراتوری به زبان‌های مختلف سخن می‌گفتند و باورها و عادات و ادیان گوناگونی داشتند، باید مورد توجه قرار می‌گرفتند. و کوروش به این همه تنوع احترام می‌گذاشت. کوروش در واقع سرنمونه‌ای از مدیریت یک سرزمین چند فرهنگی، چند زبانی، و چند مذهبی را به وجود آورد؛ و نتیجه‌ی آن، پیدایش سرزمین بزرگی بود که، همان گونه که بر نقشه‌ی روی پرده می‌بینید، گسترشی بزرگ داشت و چندین قرن پایدار باقی ماند. تا این که عاقبت اسکندر آن را فرو پاشاند. این رؤیای یک خاورمیانه‌ی بزرگ بود که در آن مردمانی با مذاهب گوناگون می‌توانستند در کنار هم زندگی کنند و حمله‌ی اسکندر به این رؤیا خاتمه داد؛ چرا که اسکندر قادر نبود چنین سرزمینی را اداره کند و به ناچار به تجزیه‌ی آن تن در داد. اما آن چه کوروش به نمایش گذاشت اهمیتی ویژه دارد. تاریخ نویسان یونانی همچون گزنفون، که کتاب پرورش کوروش را نوشته است، اذغان دارند که او حکمرانی بزرگ بود، و پس از او نیز به صورت سرنمونه‌ای اصلی در سراسر فرهنگ اروپائی به یادگار باقی مانده است. تصویری که می‌بینید به قرن شانزدهم تعلق دارد و نشان می‌دهد که نفوذ کوروش تا به کجاها کشیده است. کتاب گزنفون، در مورد کوروش و نحوه‌ی اداره‌ی یک امپراتوری، کتاب درسی مهمی است که الهام بخش آبای انقلاب امریکا نیز بوده است. جفرسون، تحسین‌گر بزرگ کوروش است، او در عین بیان عقاید قرن هجدهمیِ خود، در مورد ایجاد رواداری مذهبی در یک دولت جدید، از افکار کوروش تاثیر پذیرفته است. [...][۹۶]

و البته که «ما» حق داریم به چنین پیشینه‌ای ببالیم و بنازیم. اما در شناخت خود و ارزیابیِ ریشه‌های فرهنگیِ خود نمی‌توانیم این نکته را به فراموشی بسپاریم که همین پادشاه، هیچ نوع انتقادی را برنمی‌تابید، و منتقدان و دگراندیشان سیاسیِ بسیاری، از جمله برادر خود، را گردن می‌زد. همچنین، در منشور مداراگر او، جز احترام به دین و عقاید

---

[۹۶] نیل مک‌گرگو (رئیس موزه‌ی بریتانیا)، ***منشور کورش بزرگ هنوز قوی‌ترین و موثرترین صدا در خاورمیانه است***، ترجمه از سایت «جنبش سکولار دمکراسیِ ایران»، اکتبر ۲۰۱۳:
http://www.savepasargad.com/2013/2013-Oct/Cyrus%20the%20great%20day/ghavitarin-seda-Nilmacgroger.htm

دیگران- که از آن روزگاران تا اکنون سرشت انسانی و یگانه‌ی آن، به حق، مورد ستایش بوده است- از «**حقوق مدنی‌ی شهروندان**» و مشارکت آن‌ها در سیاست‌گذاری‌های مدنی خبری نیست؛ و هر چه هست، به سیاست خارجی و جهان‌گشائی‌های او مربوط می‌شود. یا، خشاریاشا را داریم، که از یک سو تاکتیک‌ها و استراتژی‌های او در روند کشورگشائی‌ها، از تدبیر خردمندانه‌ی این پادشاه در طراحی‌های نظامی حکایت می‌کند، و از سوی دیگر، کتیبه‌های او، از اطاعت طلبی‌ی این پادشاه، از کشتار استقلال‌طلبان و ویرانی‌ی سرزمین‌های اشغالی خبر می‌دهند.[۹۷] یا، کافی است پیش‌اندیشی‌ها و تدارکات سیاسی و نظامی‌ی نبوغ‌آمیز کمبوجیه را پیش از حمله به مصر، و کشتارهای او را پس از ورود به مصر، در «تاریخ‌ها»ی هرودوت بخوانیم، تا مانند نویسنده‌ی «تاریخ‌ها»، هم از خرد، آگاهی، و دوراندیشی‌ی سیاسی‌ی این پادشاه، و هم از خودکامگی و بی‌رحمی‌ی او، یک‌جا، دچار شگفتی شویم.[۹۸] طراحی و اجرای ایجاد کانال سوئز، پایه‌گذاری و نظارت بر دستگاه‌های راهداری، پست، فرمانداری (سیستم ساتراپی)، و حتا بنیادگذاری سازمان امنیت (چشم و گوش‌های شاه)، از نبوغ سیاسی‌ی داریوش بزرگ برای کسب و حفظ قدرت پادشاهی خبر می‌دهند، نه از رعایت «مصلحت عمومی»، با گوهری که در فلسفه‌ی سیاسی‌ی یونان مطرح بود. نمونه‌ی شوق به آموختن و استعداد فراگیری در مردم فرودست ایران، و نیز تفکر تک‌قدرتی (تا حد تجاوز به «نظم مقدس جمشیدی») را در خبر افسانه‌وار پیرمردی به نام «بیل» می‌بینیم: شاپور ساسانی در منطقه‌ای که بعداً شهر «گندی شاپور» را بر آن ساخت، به پیرمردی به نام «بیل» برمی‌خورد و از او می‌پرسد: آیا شایسته است که در این جا شهری ساخته شود؟ بیل می‌گوید: «اگر من در این سن پیری بتوانم نوشتن یاد بگیرم، ساختن شهری در این جا نیز شایسته است.» شاپور می‌گوید: «هر دو کار که تو نشدنی پنداشتی، خواهد شد.» و هر دو را نیز به تحقق می‌رساند: نه تنها یکی از مهم‌ترین شهرهای زمانه را در همان‌جا می‌رویاند، بلکه قانون ممنوعیت سوادآموزی در طبقات فرودست را استثنائاً درباره‌ی «بیل» نادیده می‌گیرد؛ پیرمرد را به آموزگار می‌سپارد؛ و پس از یک سال او را با قابلیت و ظرفیتی از آموزگار تحویل می‌گیرد، که می‌تواند شغل حسابداری‌ی ساختمان همان شهر را از عهده برآید.[۹۹] حتا اگر سخن تئودور نولدکه را بپذیریم که اشاره‌ی پیرمرد «به دشواری‌ی خط پهلوی بوده»، باز این داستان نمودی است از خواست مردم ایران در آموختن.

حتا اگر داستان «بیل» را یک «افسانه» بپنداریم، واقعیت‌های تاریخی‌ی بسیاری در اختیار داریم که از عشق ایرانیان به آموختن و فراگیری‌ی دانش- حتا به قیمت تغییر دین- خبر می‌دهند. نمونه‌ی این عشق و تلاش را در «دبستان ایرانیان»، که در سال ۳۶۳ میلادی در شهر «رها» تأسیس شد، می‌توان مشاهده کرد. شهر «رها»، واقع در شمال غربی‌ی الجزایر کنونی، متناوباً میان امپراتوری‌های ایران و رُم دست به دست می‌شد، و مردم آن با ادبیات و فلسفه‌ی یونان آشنا بودند. این شهر، ابتدا میدان نفوذ و انتشار آئین مسیح بود، اما با تأسیس «دبستان ایرانیان» در قرن چهارم میلادی، به لحاظ گسترش دانش‌های نجوم و جغرافیا و طبیعی و فن ترجمه و بحث و مناظره‌های فلسفی، در ردیف انطاکیه و اسکندریه‌ی آن زمان قرار گرفت. ذبیح‌الله صفا، پس از شرح نسبتاً جامعی از این فرایند، می‌نویسد:

> در علت تسمیه‌ی این دبستان به «دبستان ایرانیان» گفته‌اند یا بدان سبب است که غالب شاگردان آن ایرانی بوده، و یا

---

[۹۷] در کتیبه‌ی XPf متعلق به خشایارشا، ضمن ذکر نام سرزمین‌های زیر سلطه‌ی امپراتوری‌ی ایران، می‌خوانیم: «[...] هنگامی که من شاه شدم در میان این کشورها نافرمانانی بودند. پس اهورامزدا مرا یاری کرد. به خواست او، من آن کشور را درنوردیدم و [نافرمانان را] به جای خود نشاندم. در بین این کشورها، پیش از من جاهائی بود که دیوان را می‌پرستیدند. پس به فرمان اهورا مزدا، من آن پرستش‌خانه‌ی دیوان را برافکندم و فرمان دادم پرستش دیوان نکنند. [...]» نگاه کنید به: رضا مرادی غیاث‌آبادی، ***کتیبه‌های هخامنشی***، تهران: انتشارات نوید، ۱۳۷۹، صص ۲۱۹ تا ۲۲۰.

[۹۸] هرودوت، ***تواریخ***، ترجمه‌ی وحید مازندرانی، تهران: انتشارات افراسیاب، چاپ دوم، ۱۳۸۰، کتاب سوم، صص ۱۹۱ تا ۲۰۸.

[۹۹] تئودور نولدکه، ***تاریخ ایرانیان و عرب‌ها در زمان ساسانیان***، ترجمه‌ی عباس زریاب، تهران: پژوهشگاه علوم انسانی و مطالعات فرهنگی، چاپ دوم، ۱۳۷۸، ص ۷۰. یادآوری کنم که «تئودور نولدکه»، در زیرنویس این بخش می‌نویسد: «[پیرمرد] یادگرفتن خط را محال می‌داند. این داستان، دشواری‌های خط پهلوی را می‌رساند.»

> از آن جهت که بیش‌تر متخرجین [دانش‌آموختگان] آن قبول خدمت در کلیساهای ایرانی می‌کردند. از این دبستان بعد از ظهور نسطوریوس در قرن پنجم میلادی، عده‌ای پیرو مذهب نسطوری شدند و به همین سبب دچار مخالفت سخت مونوفیزیان گردیدند. چنان که در حدود سال ۴۸۳ گروه بزرگی از آنان به ایران پناه بردند، و مذهب نسطوری را در این کشور پراکندند.[۱۰۰]

ذبیح‌الله صفا، از دو تن مؤسسان ایرانی‌ی «مدرسه‌ی نصیبین» (شهری در شمال شرقی‌ی الجزایر کنونی) نیز یاد می‌کند. این مدرسه هم به لحاظ پرداختن به علوم عقلی، با اصول «دبستان ایرانیانِ» شهر رها اداره می‌شد. ذبیح‌الله صفا، تأکید می‌کند که «چون طرفداران مذهب نسطوری با امپراتوری رُم و کلیساهای رُمی دشمنی‌ی شدید داشتند، همواره مورد حمایت دولت ساسانی بودند.» (مأخذ پیشین، ص ۱۳)

مجموعه‌ی گزاره‌های تاریخی، ضمن این که از خودشیفتگی و خودکامگی‌ی شاهان ایران باستان خبر می‌دهد، گویای احاطه‌ی آن‌ها است بر سیاست و علم و دانش و فرهنگ زمانه‌ی خودشان، که البته با رنگ وُ بو وَ سمت وُ سوی «ایرانی» به عمل رسیده است. بی‌سبب نیست که گزنفون بارها شوق و توجه کوروش هخامنشی به آموختن را به خواننده‌اش خاطرنشان می‌کند؛ و بی‌سبب نیست که «آگاثیاس» مورخ یونانی‌ی هم‌عصر انوشیروان ساسانی، «**متحیر بود که چه‌گونه پادشاهی با آن همه اشتغالات سیاسی و نظامی می‌توانست به علوم یونانی توجه داشته باشد و آن‌ها را به زبان ابتدایی و خشن (مراد زبان پهلوی است) دریابد.**»[۱۰۱] و بی‌سبب نیست که اکثر مورخان ایرانی و غیرایرانی، به علاقه و توجه شاهان و نخبگان ایران باستان به دانش‌های نجوم، ریاضیات، موسیقی، و پزشکی اشاره کرده‌اند. به برکت مجموعه‌ی این گزارش‌ها درمی‌یابیم آن چه که ما به نام «عصر زرین فرهنگ اسلامی» (یا به قول شیرین‌دخت دقیقیان: «رنسانس صغیر») می‌شناسیم، پیش از اسلام و در دربارهای ساسانیان نطفه بسته شده است؛ و مهم‌ترین یاخته‌ی آن نیز «فن ترجمه» از متون یونانی و هندی و سریانی و رُمی بوده است. و در عین حال افسوس می‌خوریم که به خاطر انحصار دانش، این آثار نابود شده؛ و از این فراتر، افسوس می‌خوریم که دانش‌های فراآمده از این گردآوری‌ها و ترجمه‌ها در اختیار یکان مردم ایران نبوده است.

جمع‌بندی‌ی ایران باستان

تا جائی که به هستی‌شناسی مربوط می‌شود، از مجموعه‌ی متون باستانی‌ی ایران، ریگ‌ودا، مهابهاراته، و گزارش مورخان باستانی چنین برمی‌آید که اقوام آریائی- حتا پیش از مهاجرت به فلات ایران، و طبیعتا، پیش از ظهور زرتشت- به نیروئی آسمانی در حکمرانی بر انسان و سرنوشت او باور داشتند. امیرحسین خنجی، پژوهشگر تاریخ ایران باستان، این گزاره را به سادگی و زیبائی بیان کرده است. او می‌نویسد:

> آن چه قوم آریا را در هزاره‌ی دوم پیش از میلاد از دیگر اقوام جهان متمایز می‌سازد، آن است که این‌ها نه عقاید بت‌پرستانه داشتند و نه نیاپرستانه. [...] همه‌ی ایزدان قوم آریا، ذات‌هائی آسمانی بودند که در پدیده‌های طبیعی [مانند خورشید و ماه و اختران و آذرخش و باد] تجلی یافته بودند، تا جهان انسان‌ها را به نیروی خویش اداره کنند. [...] بر فراز این ایزدان، که جایگاهشان در زیر آسمان بود، [...] دو آفریدگار وجود داشتند که دو برادر بودند و جایگاهشان فراز آسمان

---

[۱۰۰] دکتر ذبیح‌الله صفا، ***تاریخ علوم عقلی در تمدن اسلامی تا اواسط قرن پنجم***، پیشین، ص ۱۲

[۱۰۱] دکتر ذبیح‌الله صفا، ***تاریخ علوم عقلی در تمدن اسلامی تا اواسط قرن پنجم***، پیشین، ص ۲۳.

بود. یکی از این دو، نامش اَهورَ بود و دیگری دَیوَ.[۱۰۲]

این درست است که در هستی‌شناسی‌ی یونانی نیز عناصر طبیعت در تشخّص خدایان نقش داشتند. اما خدایان یونان، جایگاه «آسمانی» نداشتند و به سبب برخورداری از سرشت نیمه‌انسانی/ نیمه خدائی، نه تنها در «اداره‌کردنِ جهان انسانی» ناتوان بودند، بلکه در کشمکش با یکدیگر آسیب‌پذیر و شکست‌پذیر بودند؛ به قول کاهنه‌ی معبد دلفی: «حتا خدایان هم تابع حکم قضا و قدر هستند.»[۱۰۳] در حالی که هزاره‌ها پیش از تشکیل «دولت» در ایران، در فرایند جدال بین «اهور» و «دیو» در هستی‌شناسی‌ی آریائی، «اهور» به تدریج خدای برتر شناخته شده بود؛ و جای تنها خدا را گرفته بود. به بیانی دیگر می‌توان گفت که عنصر ربوبیت از همان آغاز پیدایش تمدن ایرانی، با جهان‌بینی‌ی ایرانیان عجین بوده است. این تشخیصِ دکتر امیرحسین خنجی نیز که: اقوام آریائی «پیامبر شاه هم نداشتند»، برای من جای چون و چرا دارد. البته، هیچ یک از پادشاهان باستانی‌ی ایران (بر خلاف پادشاهان عبری) خود را «پیامبر» نخواندند. اما، مجموعه‌ی کتیبه‌های هخامنشیان آکنده است از حکایت برگزیده‌شدن شاهان از سوی اهورامزدا؛ و حتا برای هر کنش سیاسی از سوی اهورامزدا «فرمان» می‌یافتند؛ یا به «خواستِ» او عمل می‌کردند. به بیان نهائی، پادشاهان ایران باستان (به ویژه هخامنشیان)، خود را نماینده‌ی اهورامزدا بر زمین می‌دانستند.

فرآورده‌ی این هستی‌شناسی، بروز و تداوم «دین/ دولتِ» تک صدا بود؛ که برای حفظ قدرت خود و طبقه‌ی حاکم، نظم جمشیدی را پدید آورد و هزاران سال آن را محافظت کرد. مهمترین ویژگی‌ی نظم جمشیدی نیز، میخکوب‌کردن جامعه در «طبقاتِ» تعیین‌شده، به ویژه در لایه‌های پائین هرم اجتماعی بود. این که از قدرت و عظمت و ثروت افسانه‌ای‌ی امپراتوری‌های هخامنشی، اشکانی، و ساسانی (که هر یک به نوبه‌ی خود، هم پشت جهان شناخته‌شده‌ی روزگار خود را می‌لرزاند، و هم طمع تصاحب آن را برمی‌انگیخت) به توده‌های مردم ایران چه می‌رسید، یا نمی‌رسید، خبر چندانی در دست نیست. ما نمی‌دانیم گزارش هرودوت مبنی بر «پشمینه‌پوشی» و «قناعت ایرانیان»، و این که «در روز فقط دو نوبت غذا می‌خورند»، یا: «پارسیان از محل خاصی جنس و کالا نمی‌خرند و در واقع در تمامی‌ی سرزمین خود بازاری ندارند»،[۱۰۴] تا چه میزان درست است، و اگر درست است، تا چه میزان می‌تواند بازگوی وضع اقتصادی‌ی مردم باشد. اما به گزارش ابوالقاسم فردوسی می‌دانیم که «به یزدان که این کشور آباد بود»، و، «گدائی در این بوم و بر ننگ بود». همچنین، از مجموعه‌ی «الواح تخت جمشید» چنین برمی‌آید که- برخلاف یونان و سراسر جهان شناخته‌شده‌ی آن روزگار- پدیده‌ای به نام «بردگی» و «بیگاری»، دست کم در دربارهای هخامنشی، وجود نداشت، و کارگر و کارمند، از زن و مرد در برابر کار خود مزد دریافت می‌کردند. منتها یک نکته، که خارج از بُعدِ اقتصادی به «قناعت» مربوط می‌شود، پذیرش و بردباری‌ی مردم ایران است در برابر قوانین دینی/ دولتی‌ی تقسیم «طبقات»، که از چشم‌انداز آنان، قوانینی الهی و ازلی و ابدی تلقی می‌شد. کما این که تاریخ ما، تا پیش از تسلط تازیان، یعنی حدود هزار و پانصد سال تسلط بی‌چون و چرای تک‌صدایی، فقط از دو«شورش» مردمی خبر می‌دهد. اولی، به نام «گئوماته‌ی مغ» ثبت شده، و دومی به نام مزدک، که با تمام نیرو تلاش شد تا هر دو، در حافظه‌ی جمعی‌ی ایرانی به نماد پلیدی و گمراهی تبدیل شوند. افزون بر آن چه که داریوش بزرگ در کتیبه‌ی بیستون در سرزنش «شورشِ» «گئوماته‌ی مغ» نوشته‌است، کتیبه‌ی او در نقش رستم نیز، میزان حساسیت قدرت سیاسی را در برابر «شورش» نشان می‌دهد:

---

[۱۰۲] امیرحسین خُنجی، ***بازخوانی‌ی تاریخ ایران***، نشر الکترونیکی، بخش نخست، صص ۲۰ تا ۲۱:
http://xa.yimg.com/kq/groups/15752404/159730441/name/iranema1.pdf

[۱۰۳] هرودوت، ***تواریخ***، ترجمه‌ی وحید مازندرانی، تهران: انتشارات افراسیاب، ۱۳۸۰، ص ۵۵.

[۱۰۴] هرودوت، ***تواریخ***، پیشین، صص ۴۵، ۷۸.

> می‌گوید داریوش شاه، با اراده‌ی اهورامزدا، من آن گونه هستم که راستی را دوست هستم و بدی را دوست نیستم. نه مرا کام این است که به فقیر به خاطر غنی بدی کرده شود، و نه مرا میل است که به قوی به خاطر فقیر بدی کرده شود. آن چه را که راست است، همان مرا میل است، مرد دروغگو را دوست نیستم. تا آن جا که بدن من توانایی دارد، من یک جنگجو هستم، یک جنگجوی خوب، وقتی که با فهم خود در میدان جنگ می‌بینم کسی را که شورشی است و کسی را که می‌بینم شـــورشی نیست، با فـــهم و درک خود و با فرمان. بنا بر این جلوتر فکر می‌کنم، یا زمانی که می‌بینم یک شورشی را، و زمانی که می‌بینم کسی را که شورشی نیست. [...].[۱۰۵]

این تک صدا، که یک تنه «فکر می‌کند»، تشخیص می‌دهد و «فرمان» می‌دهد؛ و این نظم آهنین، که «غنی» و «فقیر» را در جایگاه تعیین شده مستقر می‌خواهد و هیچ «شورشی» را برای جابه‌جایی برنمی‌تابد؛ و در عین حال، ستم بر فقیر را روا نمی‌دارد، و شـگفتا که بارآور تمدن درخشـان و عظمت امپراتوری ایران هم هسـت؛ بی‌اختیار یادآور «اَبَرمرد» نیچه است. انگار نیچه، از فراسوی بیست و چهار سده، نظم اجتماعی‌ی داریوش هخامنشی را فرموله کرده است:

> اگر فرهنگ واقعاً بر خواسـت مردم متکی باشـد، اگر در این جا قدرت‌های بی‌چون و چرا- قدرت‌هایی که قانون‌اند و مانع فرد- حکم نرانند، آن گاه تحقیر فرهنگ، گرامیداشـت «حقارت روح»، نابودی‌ی بت‌شـکنانه‌ی ادعای هنری، چیزی بیش از قیام توده‌های سـتمدیده بر ضـد افراد انگل‌گونه خواهد بود؛ فریاد ترحمی خواهد بود که دیوارهای فرهنگ را فرو می‌ریزد؛ خواست عدالت، خواست برابری در رنج، تمام اندیشه‌های دیگر را در خود غرق خواهد کرد.[۱۰۶]

آن چه که این شباهت را در ذهن من تأیید می‌کند، این سخن نیچه است که: «**من می‌باید به یک ایرانی، به زرتشت، ادایِ احترام کنم. ایرانیان نخستین کسانی بودند که به تاریخ در تمامیّتِ آن اندیشیدند**»؟[۱۰۷] این شباهت، چه برخاسته از پندار من باشد و چه واقعاً منطبق بر الگوی فلسفه‌ی نیچه باشد، این واقعیت را منتفی نمی‌کند، که تاریخ دوران شکوه و عظمت ایران باستان به دست «ابرمردان»ی با تعریف نیچه‌ای ساخته و نوشته شد، که با «خواست قدرت» و «اراده‌ی آهنین»، با جهان روبه‌رو می‌شدند، و برای بنیان‌گذاری، استقرار، و حفظ وضع موجود، نیازمند کارگزارانی بودند، که در دستگاه نظری‌ی نیچه، با واژه‌ی «بردگان»، به معنای «اطاعت‌کننده»، نمایندگی می‌شوند.

صرف نظر از شرایط اقتصادی‌ی «طبقات»، و صرف نظر از عدم مشارکت شهروندان در امور مدنی و سیاسی، مفهوم و کارکرد غیرقابل تغییر «طبقات اجتماعی»، و به تبع آن، انحصـار دانش و سـوادآموزی در حقوق مدنی‌ی ایران، دست کم برای طبقات محروم از دانش و کتاب و کتابخانه و فرهنگ، محکومیتی ابدی را رقم می‌زد، و در نظم آهنین ابرمردان تاریخ باستان ایران، هر نوع سرپیچی از آن، همانا «شورش» تلقی می‌شد. محرومیت شهروندان فرودست از آموزش و فرهنگ، زمانی بیش‌تر به چشـم می‌آید- و شـگفتی و درد ما را فزونی می‌بخشـد- که مهره‌های به دسـت آمده از تپه‌ی «مارلیک» به ما می‌گویند، پیدایش خط در ایران دست کم به دو هزار سال قبل از میلاد مسیح می‌رسد؛ یا آن جا که «ابن ندیم» از قول «ابن مقفع»، از وجود «هفت نوع خط» در فرهنگ ایران باسـتان سـخن می‌گوید؛ یا آن جا که «کتزیاس»،

---

۱۰۵ هرمان بنگسون، ***یونانیان و پارسیان***، ترجمه‌ی دکتر تیمور قادری، تهران: انتشارات فکر روز، ۱۳۷۶، ص ۲۹.

۱۰۶ کیت آنسل- پی‌یرسُن، ***هیچ انگار تمام عیار***، ترجمه‌ی محسن حکیمی، تهران: انتشارات خجسته، ۱۳۷۵، ص ۱۱۳.

۱۰۷ داریوش آشوری، ***نیچه، زرتشت و ایران***، تارنمای «بی بی سی»، به نشانی‌ی زیر:
http://www.bbc.co.uk/persian/interactivity/debate/story/2004/04/040411_mj-ashouri-nietzsche-d.shtml
توضیح: همین جمله در ترجمه‌ی حسین مهری، به شکل زیر به فارسی برگردانده شده است: «ایرانیان نخستین کسانی بودند که از تاریخ، چشـم‌انداز گسـترده و همه‌سـویه‌ای برگرفتند.» نگاه کنید به: حسـین مهری، ***ایدئولوژی‌ی تبار*** (مجموعه مقالات)، تهران: انتشـارات توس، آبان ماه ۱۳۵۶، ص ۴۸.

مورخ یونان باستان، می‌نویسد که از دفترهای کتابخانه‌ی شاهی اردشیر در تدوین کتاب «پرسیکا» سود جسته است؛ یا آن جا که «ابومعشر بلخی» می‌نویسد که در ایران باستان کتابخانه‌هایی وجود داشته که تنها در اختیار بخردان و دانایان قرار می‌گرفته است؛ یا آن جا که ابن ندیم در «الفهرست»، از قول «ابوسهل نوبخت» (ستاره شناس ایرانی) به ما می‌گوید:

> اسکندر، از آن چه در دیوان‌ها و خزانه‌های استخر بود، رونوشتی برداشته و به زبان رومی و قبطی ترجمه کرد، و پس از نسخه‌برداری‌ها، آن چه که به خط گشتک در آن جا بود در آتش بسوخت. آن چه را از علم نجوم و طب و علم‌النفس می‌خواست از آن‌ها برگرفت و با دیگر چیزها، از علوم و اموال و گنجینه‌ها و دانشمندان تصاحب کرد و به مصر فرستاد.[۱۰۸]

محرومیت شهروندان فرودست ایرانی از آموزش، به ویژه زمانی بیش‌تر به چشم می‌آید، که در موزه‌ی واتیکان، زیر مجسمه‌ی «اوزاهاریس»- باز سازی‌کننده‌ی معبد «نیت» (در مصر باستان به دستور داریوش هخامنشی)- می‌خوانیم:

> شاهنشاه، پادشاه مصرِ بالا و پائین، داریوش شاه، به من فرمان داد که به مصر بازگردم. مأموریت من این بود که، ساختمان «پرآنخا» (بخشی از معبد نیت) را که ویران شده بود، بار دیگر بسازم. [...] به اراده‌ی شاهنشاه رفتار کردم. به کتابخانه‌ها کتاب دادم و جوانان را به آن‌ها داخل کردم، و آن‌ها را به مردان آزموده سپردم. و برای هر یک چیزی سودمند و ابزار کارهای لازم برابر با آن چه در کتاب‌هایشان آمده بود، ساختم و فراهم آوردم. این چنین بود فرمان شاهنشاه. زیرا او سود و بهره‌ی دانش پزشکی را می‌دانست و می‌خواست جان بیماران را از مرگ و بیماری رهایی بخشد. (ترجمه‌ی رکن‌الدین همایونفرخ)[۱۰۹]

در مورد وجود کتاب و کتابخانه و هنر و فرهنگ ایران باستان و توجه پادشاهانِ آن به دانش و دانش‌پروری، می‌توان صدها مثال از تاریخ‌ها و تفسیرها گرد آورد. اما در مورد انحصار دانش، مثال‌های چندان آشکاری در دست نیست. جز این که اکثر پژوهندگان تاریخ ایران باستان، ما را به کتابخانه‌های «شاهنشاهی» و به «دژنبشت»ها و به «گنجینه»های انحصاری رجوع می‌دهند، که می‌بایست در اختیار «بخردان و دانایان» قرار می‌گرفت. این بخردان و دانایان، چه کسانی بودند، اگر از طبقه‌ی اشراف و برگزیدگان «شاهنشاه» نبودند؟ یعنی «شاهنشاهان» نمی‌دانستند که نخوانده و نیاموخته نمی‌توان «بخرد» و «دانا» شد؟ گزارش‌های ابوالقاسم فردوسی در این جا و آن جای شاهنامه به ما می‌گویند که شاهنشاهان ایران باستان بر این معادله‌ی ساده به نیکی آگاه بودند، منتها، برای حفظ نظم موجود، همگانی‌شدنِ خرد و دانایی را برنمی‌تابیدند.

پرسش آزاردهنده این است که اگر این آرزو در مردم عادی وجود داشته، تسلط بی‌چون و چرای چه نیروهایی، حس طبیعیِ آزادی‌خواهی و برابری‌طلبی را این چنین پایدار، در مردم ایران خاموش نگه داشته بود؟ آیا می‌توان گفت که نیروی بازدارنده‌ی مردم برای حق‌طلبی، در هر دوره، فقط به ترس از قدرت سیاسی منحصر می‌شد؟ به دیگر سخن، آیا

---

[۱۰۸] ابن ندیم، الفهرست، مقاله‌ی هفتم. برگرفته از: رکن‌الدین همایونفرخ، ***تاریخچه‌ی کتاب و کتابخانه‌های شاهنشاهی ایران***، در تارنمای زیر:
http://www.ichodoc.ir/p-a/CHANGED/50/html/50-18.htm

[۱۰۹] برگرفته از: رکن‌الدین همایونفرخ، ***تاریخچه‌ی کتاب و کتابخانه‌های شاهنشاهی ایران***، در تارنمای زیر:
http://www.ichodoc.ir/p-a/CHANGED/50/html/50-18.htm

اطاعت محض، فقط ناشی از تسلط دستگاه‌های اجرایی، و ترس از مجازات‌های قانونی بود؟ یا عنصری ذهنی هم در آن سکوت و پذیرش دخالت داشته است؟

افزون بر این واقعیت که از همان دوران اساطیری، سلسله مراتب و طبقه‌بندی‌ی اجتماعی، به عنوان تحقق اراده‌ی پادشاه/ خدا، در حافظه‌ی جمعی‌ی ایرانی حک شده، باید به مفهوم «نافرمانی»، «شورش» و «طغیان‌گری» در دستگاه نظری‌ی میترائیسم، زرتشیت و مانوی نیز توجه کرد. این واژگان، هم در متون آئین مهر،هم در اوستا، و هم در نوشته‌های مانی، نمادی برای مفاهیم منفی، مانند اهریمن، دروغ، ناراستی، پلیدی، و تاریکی هستند. تردید نیست که آمیزش ناخجسته‌ی استبداد سیاسی با این بینش تلقینی (که مداوماً از یکدیگر برمی‌آیند و مداوماً یکدیگر را تأیید و توانا می‌کنند)، به ترس، اطاعت، و سکوت و باور مردم نسبت به سرنوشت مقدر یاری داده است.[۱۱۰] بی‌سبب نیست که یرواند آبراهامیان و فرهاد کاظمی، در متنی که هزار و چهار صد سال پس از اسلام نوشته‌اند، در مقایسه با شورش‌های دهقانی در سایر کشورهای جهان، از «فقدان غریب شورش‌های دهقانی» در ایران معاصر خود «دچار حیرت» می‌شوند، و می‌پرسند: «چرا در ایران هرگز خیزش دهقانی‌ی مهمی روی نداده است.» و می‌افزایند:

> نباید پنداشت که فقدان شورش‌های دهقانی از آن روست که دهقانان به خواست و اراده‌ی خود نظم موجود را پذیرفته‌اند؛ زیرا مردم‌شناسانی که جامعه‌ی روستائی‌ی ایران پیش از اصلاحات ارضی‌ی ۱۳۴۱/ ۱۹۶۲ را بررسی کرده‌اند، یادآور می‌شوند که رفتار ظاهری در روستاها به هیچ وجه بیانگر نگرش درونی‌ی روستائیان نیست. آنان در جمع مطیع‌اند، اما در خلوت، اقتدار مالکان را به زیر سئوال می‌برند. جواد صفی‌نژاد، یکی از مردم‌شناسان برجسته‌ی ایرانی و نویسنده‌ی رساله‌ی کلاسیک مربوط به روستای طالب آباد، می‌نویسد که اهالی‌ی روستا، از پیر و جوان، سهم‌بَر و روزمزد، همگی در خفا از مالکان با کینه سخن می‌گفتند (حتا از مالکانی که به نسبت، نرم‌خوتر بودند)، اما همین روستائیان در برابر عموم در اجرای دستورات ارباب درنگ نمی‌کردند، گوئی دستورات او فرمان‌های الاهی است.[۱۱۱]

تردید نیست که ترس از مقاومت در برابر ستم، فقط در قلمرو سیاسی/ مذهبی باقی نمی‌ماند، و بر هر نوع نوآوری در زمینه‌های مختلف اندیشه و تخیل خلاق نیز سایه می‌اندازد؛ و تردید نیست که به لحاظ روان‌شناسی، هویت انسانِ زیر سلطه‌ی مداوم، بدون آن که خود آگاه باشد، به بردگی‌ی اختیاری می‌انجامد. بازتاب عملی‌ی بردگی‌ی اختیاری، «سِپَر» شدن در دست فرادست است، و «شمشیر» شدن در برابر فرودست. تداوم فعال این مکانیسم در فرد، هم از تخریب و حذف «خود»، و هم از تخریب و حذف «دیگری» سربرمی‌کند. و ایرانی در این احوال است، که در سال ۱۵ هجری‌ی قمری، برابر با ۶۳۶ میلادی، تازیان و اسلام به ایران و تمدن ایرانی می‌تازند.

پس از اسلام

دکتر محمدرضا شفیعی کدکنی- پژوهشگرِ زمانِ ما- در پیش‌گفتار ترجمه‌ی جلد پنجم «آفرینش و تاریخ»، نوشته‌ی مطهربن طاهر مقدسی، ص ۱۹۱ می‌نویسد: «اگر نویسنده‌ای فکر کند که ایرانی‌ها با میل به اسلام تن دادند، ناشی از ناآگاهی‌ی

---

[۱۱۰] تورج دریائی، استاد تاریخ و پژوهشگر عصر ساسانی، در مقاله‌ی زیر از سیستم «به راه آوردن» مخالفان، یا «کیفر» آن‌ها، در دوره‌ی اردشیر بابکان به تفصیل سخن گفته است:

❖ تورج دریائی، ***نگاهی به بدعت‌گرائی در دوره‌ی ساسانی***، در فصل‌نامه‌ی «ایران نامه»، سال هفدهم، شماره‌ی ۲، بهار ۱۳۷۸، صص ۲۹۱-۲۹۵.

توضیح: تورج دریائی، پیرامون این دوره از تاریخ ایران کتاب‌های متعددی به زبان انگلیسی منتشر کرده است. من ترجمه‌ی فارسی‌ی یکی از آن‌ها را به شرح زیر دیده‌ام: تورج دریائی، ***شاهنشاهی‌ی ساسانی***، ترجمه‌ی مرتضی ثاقب‌فر، تهران: انتشارات ققنوس، ۱۳۸۳.

[۱۱۱] یرواند آبراهامیان، ***مقالاتی در جامعه‌شناسی‌ی ایران***، ترجمه‌ی سهیلا ترابی فارسانی، تهران: نشر شیرازه، ۱۳۷۶، صص ۵۶ تا ۵۸.

تاریخیِ اوست.» و شجاع‌الدین شفا- پژوهشگرِ دیگری در زمان ما- در یک مصاحبه می‌گوید: «بزرگترین دوروغ تاریخی این است که ایرانیان به علت نارضائی از حکومت، از مهاجمان عرب استقبال کردند.» پروانه پورشریعتی، استادیار دانشگاه ایالتیِ اُهایو، در پژوهش معتبر خود نشان می‌دهد که «تن دادن»ِی در کار نبوده، بلکه فتح سراسر ایران (به جز بخش‌هائی در شمال کشور) توسط تازیان، در درازنای بیست و شش سال، و طیِ سی و هشت نبرد ممکن شد.[۱۱۲] جلال متینی، در پژوهش گرامیِ خود به این نتیجه رسیده است که «ایرانیان نیز مانند دیگر اقوام مغلوب به مرور زمان مسلمان شدند» و «تصرفِ» کاملِ ایرانشهرِ دوران ساسانی توسط تازیان، حدود «دو قرن» به درازا کشیده است.[۱۱۳] تورج دریائی (پژوهشگر تاریخ ایران باستان، و کارشناس تاریخ ساسانی) از مطالعه‌ی تاریخ و سکه‌های سده‌ی نخست اشغال ایران، به این نتیجه رسیده است که در آن دوره، «بزرگان ایرانی، یا یک سری از نجبای ایرانی، همراه با امویان سکه ضرب می‌کردند؛ و در حقیقت قدرت را مابین خود تقسیم کرده بودند و بر فلات ایران حکومت می‌کردند. این نیست که اعراب آمدند و همه را ساقط کردند و فقط سر کار بودند. اوضاع خیلی پیچیده‌تر از آن است.»[۱۱۴] افزون بر این چند نمونه، می‌توان از منابع قدیم و جدید، ایرانی و عرب، فهرست بلندبالائی به دست داد که از تلاش خونبار ایرانیان در حفظ سرزمین و دین خود حکایت می‌کنند. در برابر، بوده‌اند و هستند پژوهشگرانی که بر استقبال ایرانیان از تازیان مهاجم، و بر تمایل ایرانیان نسبت به پذیرش دین اسلام تأیید کرده‌اند.[۱۱۵] هدف من در این سخن فشرده، اثبات یا نفیِ هیچ یک از این نظرها نیست. چرا که در درجه‌ی نخست، «پذیرش دین اسلام» و «استقبال از مهاجمان تازی» را به عنوان دو گفتمان جدا از هم برآورد می‌کنم. اما در برابرِ نظری که بر «پذیرش ایرانیان» قاطعانه تأکید می‌کند، این پرسش مطرح می‌شود که آیا گزارش‌های تاریخیِ نزدیک به زمانِ شکست، همه دروغ و تحریف بوده‌اند؟ زیرا تا جائی که این منابع گزارش می‌دهند، جنگ‌های پیاپیِ مهاجمان تازی در شهرها و مناطقِ قبلاً اشغال شده (مانند نیشابور و ری و بخش‌هائی از فارس و طبرستان)؛ از «کشته، پشته» ساختن و «جوی خون» روان کردنِ تازیان از مردم مقاوم شهرهای ایران زمین؛ کتاب‌سوزاندن‌های مکرر تازیان؛ انتقال کتابخانه‌های کشف‌شده به دارالخلافه و به دجله سپردنِ کتاب‌های ایرانی؛ و نیز، گماشتنِ مأمور تازی در خانه به خانه‌ی ایرانی (دست کم در شهرهای خراسان بزرگ)، شهادت می‌دهند که اکثریت مردم ایران، نه از مهاجمان عرب استقبال کردند و نه با میل خود به اسلام و فرهنگ آن تن دادند. به بیانی دیگر، زمانی که، مثلاً، دکتر محمدعلی معزی (اسلام‌شناس)، از «میل باطنی»ِی ایرانیان در پذیرش «معنویتِ اسلام» سخن می‌گوید،[۱۱۶] یا زمانی که دکتر حمید دباشی (استاد تاریخ و اسلام‌شناس)- به تأسی از نظرات مرتضی مطهری- گزاره‌ی «کتاب‌سوزانِ» تازیان در ایران یا اسکندریه را با اطمینان تمام رد می‌کند،[۱۱۷] خواه/ ناخواه، شهادتِ تاریخی در کتاب‌های تاریخ طبری، فارسنامه، تاریخ طبرستان، تاریخ بخارا، الفهرست و بسیاری از کتاب‌های مورخان عرب را نادیده گرفته، یا دروغ و تحریف برآورد کرده‌اند. همچنین، در برابر این نظرِ قطعی و فراگیر که: «ایرانیان به زور شمشیر اسلام آوردند»، عین

---

112 Parvaneh Pourshariati, ***Decline and Fall of the Sasanian Empire***, I. B. Tauris Publishers, 2008.

۱۱۳ جلال متینی، ***پس بد مطلق نباشد در جهان: درباره‌ی فقر فرهنگیِ مهاجمان و گسترش زبان فارسی***، در فصل‌نامه‌ی «ایران‌شناسی»، سال نهم، شماره‌ی ۱، بهار ۱۳۷۶ (۱۹۹۷)، ص ۲.

۱۱۴ ***معضل بررسیِ ایران باستان در غرب، تاریخ ایران، «تاریخ سیاست‌زده»***، (مصاحبه‌ی امیرمصدق کاتوزیان با تورج دریائی)، تارنمای «رادیو فردا»، ۲ خرداد ۱۳۹۰:
http://www.radiofarda.com/content/f2_iran_tooraj_daryayi_history_culture_heritage_interview_book/24183328.html

۱۱۵ علی شریعتی، در کتاب «علی و حیات بارورش پس از مرگ»، دین اسلام را «گمشده‌ای» می‌داند که ایرانیِ عصر ساسانی «به دنبالش می‌گشته است»؛ مرتضی مطهری، در کتاب «خدمات متقابل اسلام و ایران»، دین اسلام برای ایرانیان را به مثابه «غذای مطبوعی» برآورد کرده که «به حلق گرسنه‌ای فرو رود»؛ از جمله اسلام‌شناسانِ متأخری که با بیان‌های متفاوت، به «میل» ایرانیان در پذیرش اسلام اشاره کرده‌اند، می‌توان از دکتر حمید دباشی و دکتر محمدعلی معزی (در دانشنامه‌ی ایرانیکا) نام برد.

۱۱۶ مصاحبه‌ی رادیو فارسیِ فرانسه (ار. اف. ای) با دکتر محمدعلی معزی، به نمایندگیِ دانشنامه‌ی ایرانیکا، ۳ دی ماه ۱۳۷۹/ ۲۳ دسامبر ۲۰۰۰.

۱۱۷ مصاحبه‌ی رادیو فارسیِ فرانسه با دکتر حمید دباشی، به نمایندگیِ دانشنامه‌ی ایرانیکا، ۸ بهمن ماه ۱۳۷۹/ ۲۷ ژانویه ۲۰۰۱.

همین پرسش‌ها مطرح می‌شوند. به بیانی دیگر، زمانی که مثلاً پژوهشگر زرتشتی‌ی ما، آله دال فک، غیر این نظر را به «ایران‌ستیزی» تعبیر می‌کند، خواه/ ناخواه، شهادت مورخان- حتا شهادت ابوالقاسم فردوسی- را نادیده گرفته و دروغ و تحریف برآورد کرده است. آیا تمامی‌ی گزارش‌های مربوط به زراندوزی، پسرکشی و برادرکشی‌های پادشاهان واپسین ساسانی، و نابخردی‌ی آن‌ها در برخورد با نخبگان خاندان خود، و در برخورد با مرزداران و همسایگان عرب، و در فراز همه، حاکمیت فقه/ قانون زرتشتی‌ی برساخته‌ی مغان دوره‌ی ساسانی و قانون طبقاتی‌ی آن، که در کتاب‌های تاریخ آمده است، یکسره دروغ و تحریف است؟ آیا نباید بپرسیم که امپراتوری‌ی عظیمی که امپراتورِ تنها رقیب خود (رُم) را اسیر کرد و برگرده‌ی او بر اسب نشست، چرا به دست قومی، به قول ما «بدوی و بَدَوی» سقوط کرد؟ چرا گرانیگاه آثار مهم‌ترین و ماندگارترین اندیشه‌ورزان ایرانی (مانند ابن سینا و ...)، جان و روانِ اسلامی دارد؟ و چرا بیش‌تر این اندیشه‌ورزان- حتا زکریای رازی- آن هم زمانی که زبان دری انسجام یافته بود- اکثر کتاب‌های خود را به زبان عربی نوشتند؟ آیا می‌توان با برچسب «ایران‌سیتزی» با این پدیده‌ی پردامنه و پیچیده برخورد کرد و خوشحال بود که به «پاسخ» دست یافته‌ایم؟ حضور معتبر این پرسش‌هاست که گروهی دیگر از پژوهشگران را در چند دهه‌ی اخیر بر آن داشته که به جای تکیه‌ی مصرانه بر «استقبال» یا «عدم استقبال» ایرانیان از تازیان، و«تمایل» یا «عدم تمایل» ایرانیان به اسلام، پارامترهای سیاسی/ اجتماعی/ فرهنگی‌ی حاکم بر ایرانِ ساسانی را بسنجند، و مجموعه‌ی آن‌ها را به عنوان علت آن شکست تاریخ‌ساز پیشنهاد کنند.[۱۱۸]

اما در ورای این همهمه‌ی دوسویه، این پرسش اصولی سر برمی‌کند که اثبات قاطعانه‌ی یکی از این سویه‌ها و نفی‌ی قاطعانه‌ی دیگر سو، چه دردی از فرهنگِ کنونی‌ی ایران دوا می‌کند؟ درست است که ما بیش از هر چیز نیازمند «شناختِ» پیشینه‌ی خود هستیم. اما گرد و غباری که در رهگذر این تقابلِ اکثراً خصمانه برمی‌خیزد/ برخاسته، چه «شناخت»ی از ما به ما می‌دهد؛ جز زنده کردن همان فضای «حیدری/ نعمتی»؟

می‌دانیم مشابه همین شکست در تاریخ امپراتوری‌ی عظیم رُم هم واقع شد. رم غربی، با ارتشی عظیم، که حدود نیمی از جهان شناخته‌شده را در تصرف داشت، و برای حفظ دین‌ها و آئین‌های خود بیش از سه سده در برابر مسیحیت مقاومت کرده بود، پس از پذیرش مسیحیت، در زمانی بسیار کوتاه، به دست قبایل مهاجم بدوی و بَدَوی برای همیشه از صفحه‌ی جغرافیای جهان غایب شد. و من تاکنون هیچ پژوهشی از هیچ یک از پژوهشگرانِ تاریخ رم باستان نخوانده‌ام که در برآوردِ سقوط امپراتوری‌ی رم غربی، مانند ما، «تن دادن» یا «تن ندادنِ» رُمی‌ها به مهاجمان و به فرهنگ آن‌ها را عمده کرده باشد، و با این اطمینان، یکی را رد و دیگری را پذیرفته باشد.[۱۱۹] چرا که در خیزش و خاموشی‌ی یک تمدن، یک فرهنگ، و یک نظام سیاسی/ اجتماعی، تعاملِ همزمان و شبکه‌وارِ ده‌ها پارامتر دخالت دارد، که جدانگری به هر یک از آن‌ها، پیش از آن که ما را به جوانب پرسش یا به پاسخ‌های احتمالی برساند، بیش‌تر، جنبه‌ی ارضاء قومی/ دینی دارد؛

---

[۱۱۸] به عنوان مثال از کار این دسته از پژوهشگران، به مأخذ زیر نگاه کنید. با این توضیح که کاظم علمداری، با استفاده از منابع موجود و اظهارنظرهای مورخان و مفسران طیف‌های مختلف (از جمله احمد کسروی، ذبیح‌الله صفا، حمید عنایت و مرتضی مطهری)، علل شکست ایرانیان، این که ایرانیان چه‌گونه اسلام آوردند، و علل نهادینه شدن اسلام در ذهینت ایرانی را- در بخش‌های جداگانه‌ی به‌هم‌پیوسته، آناتومی کرده است:

❖ دکتر کاظم علمداری، ***چرا اعراب بر ایران دست یافتند***، در کتاب «چرا ایران عقب ماند و غرب پیش رفت؟» تهران: نشر گام نو، ۱۳۷۹، صص ۲۹۵ تا ۳۳۷.

[۱۱۹] این سخن شاید در فرهنگ ایران من، به «خودستایی» یا «فضل‌فروشی» تعبیر شود، اما به پشتوانه‌ی نظری که در این جا ابراز کردم، باید بگویم که من برای تدوین کتابِ هرگز منتشرنشده‌ی «***خود در خط برکه، در خط جام***»، که تحلیلی تطبیقی از دو آینه‌ی نمادین غربی و ایرانی است، تا به فرهنگ و تمدن زادگاه اسطوره‌ی «نارسیسوس» نشت کنم، و تا فرهنگ و تمدن یونان و رم باستان در ذهن من تصویر شود، ده‌ها کتاب و ده‌ها مقاله در زمینه‌ی تاریخ و فرهنگ و ادبیات یونان و رم باستان، و پیدایش و زوال این فرهنگ‌ها خواندم، که میان آن‌ها، ۲۸ مأخذ درباره‌ی سقوط امپراتوری‌ی رم غربی بود. متن بسیار فشرده‌ای از کتاب یادشده، با همین عنوان، در شماره‌ی ۱ نشریه‌ی «سنجش»، بهار ۱۳۷۶/ ۱۹۹۷، آلمان، به ویراستاری/ مدیریتِ محمود فلکی و علی صیامی، منتشر شد.

که به قول تورج دریائی/ امیرمصدق کاتوزیان: «تاریخ سیاست‌زده» را تحویل می‌دهد؛ به ویژه در مورد تمدن ایران باستان، با این همه گم‌گوشه‌های خاموش. اما پیش از این داوری‌های متقن که «ایرانی‌ها به زور شمشیر اسلام آوردند» یا «ایرانیان از قوم مهاجم استقبال کردند، و با میل به اسلام گرویدند»، شاید پرسش نخستین این باشد که ما از کدام «ایرانی‌ها» سخن می‌گوئیم. چرا که دست کم به شهادت همان طبقه‌بندی‌ی اجتماعی، می‌توان گفت که «ایرانی‌ها» در آستانه‌ی هجوم تازیان، متشکل از گروه‌های ناهمگونی بوده‌اند. افزون بر اجرای پانصد ساله‌ی قوانین پر از تبعیض در ایرانِ ساسانی- به گزارش کتاب‌های تاریخ، و حتا به گزارش شاهنامه‌ی فردوسی- خرافه‌پنداری و نابخردی‌های پادشاهان واپسین ساسانی، ناراضیان فراوانی در میان درباریان، نخبگان، خدمتگزاران، و مردم زیر سلطه پدید آورده بود؛[۱۲۰] همان گروه‌هائی که حالا ما می‌توانیم مجموعه‌ی آن‌ها را به زبان مناسبات سیاسی/ اجتماعی‌ی عصر ساسانی، با عنوان‌های «بِخرد/ دانا» و «فرومایه»، و اکثراً ناراضی، شناسایی کنیم.[۱۲۱]

منتها، اگر حضور زنده‌ی کهن‌الگوهای «وحدت دین و دولت»، «بینش اسطوره‌ای»، «خوی تبعیت»، «فقر تفاهم» (در غیاب گفت‌وگو و مشارکت)، «فقر مفاهمه» (در غیاب حق آموزشِ همگانی)، «قدرت‌طلبی» و «استبداد فکری» را در نهانگاه آگاهی و ناخودآگاهی‌ی فرهنگ ایرانی بپذیریم، باز به گواهی‌ی عظمت امپراتوری‌های پیش از اسلام، باید حضور کهن‌الگوهای «دانش‌طلبی»، «عظمت خواهی»، «غرور ملی»، «اتکاء به نفس فرهنگی»، و «استقلال‌طلبی»ی سیاسی را نیز در روان جمعی‌ی ایرانی (از «بخرد» و «فرومایه»)، بپذیریم. کما این که پس از شکست هخامنشیان از اسکندر، در کارکرد مجموعه‌ی همین کهن‌الگوها، کوشش مداوم و همه‌جانبه‌ی سلوکیان در یونانی‌کردنِ زبان و فرهنگ ایران به جایی نرسید،[۱۲۲] و ایرانِ اشکانی- البته در غیاب وحدت دین/ دولت- با توشه‌ای گرانبها از تمدن‌های یونانی و پیرامونی، بر سوخته‌های هخامنشی روئید، و امپراتوری‌ی ایران، باز به بزرگترین رقیب امپراتوری‌ی رم تبدیل شد؛ قدرتی که بعدها هم، با دولت متمرکز ساسانی، سده‌ها ادامه یافت، اما نهایتاً با پیامدهای خودکامگی‌های همان وحدت دین/ دولت (به عنوان ابزاری سیاسی)، و در غیاب خرد سیاسی‌ی پادشاهان پیشین، از پا درآمد.[۱۲۳]

اگر نبوغ خیره‌کننده‌ی سیاسی، نظامی، تشکیلاتی، و خردِ روادارِ پادشاهان باستانی در غیاب صدای توده‌های اجتماعی و در حضور حس عظمت‌خواهی در روان جمعی، توانست «امپراتوری‌ی ایران» را بسازد؛ ایرانی را از زیر بار اشغالگران

---

[۱۲۰] جلال متینی در یکی از پژوهش‌های ارجمند خود، نابخردی‌های هرمزد، خسرو پرویز، و یزدگرد سوم را علت نابه‌سامانی‌های دولت ساسانی، و مهمترین علت سقوط ایران در برابر تازیان می‌داند. او پس از اشاره به رفتار هرمزد با بهرام چوبینه، و ایجاد نارضایتی در خدمتگزاران صادق، شواهدی از خرافه‌پنداری‌ی خسرو پرویز و به اقدامات نابخردانه‌ی او به رأی پیشگویان، بدست می‌دهد. به مأخذ زیر نگاه کنید: جلال متینی، ***یکی داستان است پر آب چشم: حمله‌ی عرب به ایران***، در مجله‌ی ایران‌شناسی، سال هفتم، شماره‌ی ۱، بهار ۱۳۷۴، صص ۱۰۹ تا ۱۵۱.

[۱۲۱] از میان انبوه آثاری که در زمینه‌ی تاریخ و فرهنگ ساسانیان و مناسبات اجتماعی در دوران این سلسله‌ی پادشاهی نوشته شده، خواننده‌ام را به سه کتاب نسبتاً تازه‌ی زیر رجوع می‌دهم:

- تورج دریائی، ***سقوط ساسانیان: فاتحین خارجی، مقاومت داخلی، و تصویر پایان جهان***، ترجمه از انگلیسی به فارسی از منصور اتحادیه (نظام مافی) و فرحناز امیرخانی، تهران: نشر تاریخ ایران، ۱۳۸۱. (فصل چهارم این کتاب به مقاومت ایرانیان در برابر مهاجمان اختصاص دارد.)
- تورج دریائی، ***تاریخ و فرهنگ ساسانیان***، ترجمه از انگلیسی به فارسی از مهرداد قدرت دیزجی، تهران: نشر ققنوس، ۱۳۸۲.
- اردشیر خدادایان، ***ساسانیان***، تهران: انتشارات به دید، ۱۳۸۱.

[۱۲۲] در زمینه‌ی تفاوت‌های دو فرهنگ ایرانی و یونانی، و علت‌های عدم پذیرش ایرانیان از فرهنگ یونانی در زمان سلوکیه، پژوهش‌های بسیاری از سوی پژوهشگران ایرانی انجام شده است، که مأخذ زیر یکی از آن‌هاست:

- غفور میرزائی، ***فردا در اسارت دیروز (تاریخ ایران: بررسی‌ی عوامل سازنده‌ی ساختار فرهنگی و حکومتی)***، کالیفرنیا: انتشارات مزدا، ۱۳۷۶، مقاله‌های «بخش اول»، صص ۱۳ تا ۳۰۷.

[۱۲۳] برای آگاهی‌ی بیشتر پیرامون جدائی‌ی دین از حکومت در زمان اشکانیان و وحدت دین با حکومت در زمان ساسانیان، به مأخذ زیر نگاه کنید. با این توضیح که احمد تفضلی دین را **در کنار** حکومت/ دولتِ اشکانیان توضیح داده است:

- احمد تفضلی، ***کرتیر و سیاست اتحاد دین و دولت در دوره‌ی ساسانی***، در «یکی قطره باران- جشن‌نامه‌ی استاد زریاب خوئی»، به کوشش دکتر احمد تفضلی، تهران: نشر نو، ۱۳۷۰، صص ۷۲۱- ۷۳۷.

یونانی برهاند؛ و حدود دوازده سده، امپراتوری‌ی ایران را به عنوان رقیب سرسخت قدرت‌های سیاسی و نظامی‌ی غربِ زمانه‌ی خودش بر پا نگه دارد، و اگر اتکاء به نفس فرهنگی و میل به حفظ هویت دینی/ فرهنگی در ناخودآگاه مردم ایران، توانست در برابر زبان و فرهنگ یونانی مقاومت کند، تداوم تک‌صدایی، سکوت مدنی‌ی اکثریتِ توده‌ها، و ذهنیتی آمیخته با «شایست/ نشایست»‌های ساسانی، در زمان هجوم تازیان بر ایران و پس از آن، پیامدهای اسفبار خود را به نمایش تاریخ گذاشت. به ویژه که از سویی، در فرایند شکست، الگوی هزار ساله‌ی سَروری‌ی ملی در ذهن ایرانی ترک برداشت، و از سوی دیگر، دین قوم اشغالگر (برخلاف دین و فرهنگ یونانی)، هم با کهن‌الگوی «تک‌خدائی» در ذهن او سازگار می‌آمد، و هم ندای برابری‌ی انسان‌ها در آن، فروریختن سدّ هزاران ساله‌ی «طبقات» را وعده می‌داد. گرچه در عمل چنین نشد. چرا که افزون بر تاراج سرمایه‌های ملی توسط تازیان، و افزون بر یوغ بردگی‌ی بیگانه بر گردن ایرانی، بسیاری از همان ثروتمندان و مالکان ایرانی نیز پس از باور به قطعیت شکست، در تثبیت امتیازات طبقاتی‌ی خود با قوم اشغالگر سازشی ناخجسته داشتند. اما در آغاز کار، ذهنیتِ آکنده از تقدس‌های مذهبی و بی‌عملی‌ی فرهنگی‌ی ناشی از آن نیز، به پیامدهای زیان‌بار اشغال ایران، نیرویی مضاعف بخشیده بود.

گروه نجبگانِ طبقه‌های فرادست، یعنی همان «بخردان»، که نسل اندر نسل از نعمت‌های معنوی‌ی برآمده از عظمت امپراتوری بهره داشت، و از رهگذر بهره‌وری از آموزش، به دانش و درک تاریخی مجهز بود، نسبت به اهمیتِ استقلال دینی، فرهنگی، و سیاسی به حد فراشناخت رسیده بود؛ در نتیجه، در ابتدای یورش تازیان- و تا پیش از آن که برخی از آنان برای حفظ منافع خود با قوم اشغالگر سازش کنند- تا پای جان برای راندن اشغالگران ایستاد؛ پس از «تسلیم» نیز، ظرف دو سده زبانش را بازسازی کرد؛ برای زبان عربی دستور نوشت؛ و با پذیرش خط و نحو این زبان، با شعر و نثری به زبان خود، به تبیین خود و جهان پرداخت؛ نه تنها ورق‌های هویت خود را که در «گنجینه‌ها» سوخته یا پوسیده بود، دوباره نوشت، بلکه اسلام اشغالگران را هم بر سیاق جهان‌بینی‌ی سیاووشی‌ی خود دوباره نوشت،[۱۲۴] تا به تدریج نسبت به «جهان اسلام» (نه نسبت به قوم اشغالگر) احساس تعلق کرد؛ جهانی که، با همه‌ی کشتارهای خونینی که به خود دید، به یاری و همکاری‌ی همین نخبگان و نخبگان تمدن‌های دیگری که به اسلام آمدند، برای چند سده، جهانِ گفت‌و گو و مبادله‌ی دانش و اندیشه شد. و در عین حال، و شوربختانه- همین جا باید اشاره کرد- که همین «نخبگان» ایرانی بودند که با گزینش زبان و خط عربی برای نوشته‌های «تاریخی/ علمی/ فلسفی»‌ی خود، بزرگ‌ترین گسل فرهنگی را در تاریخ ایران پدید آوردند. محمد بن جریر طبری (۲۲۴- ۳۱۰ هجری قمری)، تاریخ‌نگار و پژوهشگری که در شهر آمل طبرستان (مقاوم‌ترین منطقه‌ی ایران در برابر پذیرش اسلام) به دنیا می‌آید؛ سر از بغداد درمی‌آورد؛ نخستین مفسر قرآن می‌شود؛ تاریخ عظیم خود را به زبان عربی می‌نویسد؛ و در تاریخ خود، نه تنها پیامبر اسلام را یک خط درمیان، «پیامبر ما» می‌نامد، بلکه از ایرانیان، با ضمیر «آن‌ها» یاد می‌کند؛ به گونه‌ای که انگار خودش ایرانی نیست. از طبری گذشته، کافی است به «الفهرستِ» ابن ندیم مراجعه کنیم و ببینیم که در «دوره‌ی طلائی‌ی اسلام»، به جز معدودی اثر فارسی‌زبان، آثار مهم علمی و فلسفی‌ی همه‌ی اندیشه‌ورزان ایرانی به زبان عربی نوشته شده است. از این روست که کلیه‌ی این اندیشه‌ورزان- با افزودنِ یک «اَل» به نام خود - به عنوان «دانشمندان عرب» یا «دانشمندان اسلامی» به جهان معرفی شده‌اند. اما صرف نظر از تقابل «ایرانی/ عرب»- که سزاوار است به «نژادپرستی» متهم شود- غبن بزرگ تاریخ اندیشه و فرهنگ ایران در آن جاست که به سبب همین عربی‌نویسی، غیرنخبگان و مردم معمولی‌ی ایران به طور کامل از تأثیر آراء و اندیشه‌های این نخبگان- که برخی‌شان هم به ساختار الاهی اسلام دست برده بودند- بی‌بهره ماندند؛ یعنی همان مردمی که از یوغ ممنوعیتِ آموزش و آگاهی رها شده بودند، و چونان یعقوب لیث صفاری در آرزوی ادبیات و دانشی به زبان خود بودند. با این آگاهی که در زمان ساسانیان، دانشگاه گندی شاپور مرکز علمی‌ی ایران و همه‌ی منطقه بود، و با

---

[۱۲۴] اسماعیل نوری علا، ***پیدایش و نقش دینکاران امامی در ایران***، لس‌انجلس: انتشارات شرکت کتاب، ۲۰۰۶.

این خبر که نیشابور در سده‌های نخستین اسلام، مرکز علمی/ ادبی‌ی ایران بود، پرسش این است که چرا و با چه انگیزه‌ای نظامیه‌ی بغداد برای دانشمندان ما جایگزین گندی شاپور و مدرسه‌های متعدد نیشابور و ری شد؟ اصلاً چرا نخبگان ایرانی، مرکزی از آنِ خودِ اسلامی‌شان در ایران تأسیس نکردند و در نظامیه‌ی بغداد تحصیل کردند؟ چرا آثار خود را به زبان فارسی ننوشتند؟ چرا- مثلاً- ابن سینا، در بخارای زمان سامانیان که زبان فارسی رسمیت یاداشت، یا در قلب خوارزم و گرگان و ری و اصفهان و همدان، که سلسله‌های ایرانی نیز در آن‌ها حکومت داشتند، مهم‌ترین آثار خود را به زبان عربی آفرید؟ آیا این خردورزان هم- بنا بر الگوی ایرانِ ساسانی- مردم را درخور آگاهی و گسترش دانش نمی‌دانستند؟ یا مردم ایران را در فهم و درک گزاره‌های فلسفی‌ی خود ناتوان می‌دیدند؟ تردید نیست که همه‌ی مردم یونانِ سده‌های پیش از میلاد، جزئیات علمی/ سیاسی/ فلسفی‌ی فیلسوفانی چون افلاتون و ارسطو و دموکریت و ... را نمی‌فهمیدند. اما نمی‌توان انکار کرد که نگارش همین فیلسوفان به زبان مردم یونان، در ارتقاء مدنیت و فرهنگ یونان باستان سهم انکارناپذیر داشت. حال پرسش دیگر این است که مخاطبان آثار عربی‌زبان فیلسوفان ما چه کسانی بودند، اگر قدرت‌های دینی/ علمی/ سیاسی‌ی زمانه نبودند؟ به باور من، کهن‌الگوهای دینخوئی و اراده‌ی معطوف به قدرت، که منشاء اصلی‌ی آن «ترس» است، در نهانگاه روان جمعی‌ی ایرانی، در این کار بی‌کار نبوده است. از این دربار به آن دربار و از این «استاد» به آستانه‌ی آن «استاد» مشرّف شدنِ دانشمندان عربی‌نویس ما، این داوری را تأیید می‌کند. شعرهای فارسی‌زبانی که به ابن سینا نسبت داده‌اند- چه سروده‌ی خود او باشد و چه سروده‌ی شاعر دیگری- نمائی از دینخوئی و اراده‌ی معطوف به قدرت را به نیکی تصویر کرده است:

زورکی چند در جهان بودم/ بر سر خاک باد پیمودم
ساعتی لطف و لحظه‌ای در قهر/ جان پاکیزه را بیالودم
باخرد را به طبع کردم هجو/ بی‌خرد را به طمع بستودم

اما شهروندان محروم از نعمت‌های امپراتوری و محروم از دانش، و گرانبار از ستم، یعنی همان «کهتران» و «فرومایگانِ» عهد ساسانی، همان‌هایی بودند که تاریخ به خیانت یا به تسلیمِ بی‌چون و چرای آن‌ها در برابر تازیان گواهی داده است؛ و گواهی داده است که در پیکار نهاوند (که در درازنای آن، ارتش ایران بیش‌ترین تلفات را تحمل کرد)، سپهسالاران ارتش ایران، «برای جلوگیری از عقب‌نشینی و فرار سربازان از برابر تازیان، پای آن‌ها را با زنجیر به هم بسته بودند.»[۱۲۵] و گواهی داده است که در جنگ‌های «سلاسل» و «فتح‌الفتوح» عملاً مقاومتی از سوی سپاه ایران صورت نپذیرفت؛ و پس از سقوط کامل امپراتوری و پس از معکوس شدنِ «اخوت و مساوات»ی که دین تازیان وعده داده بود، باز هم تاریخ گواهی داده است که آیندگانِ همان مردم عادی- که در عین حال آکنده از هویت قومی/ فرهنگی/ دینی، و آکنده از سرافرازی‌ی استقلال و عظمت امپراتوری هم بودند- قیام‌های پس از اشغال را از این سده تا آن سده‌ی تاریخ و از این شهر تا آن شهر ایران‌زمین تداوم بخشیدند؛ منتها، و باز شوربختانه، برای پیشبرد مبارزه با اشغالگران، ابزاری جز «دین» و توجیه «دینی» نمی‌شناختند.

تاریخ سده‌های نخستین ایرانِ اسلامی آکنده است از نام دلاورانی که ضمن کوشش برای رساندن نَسَبِ خود به خاندان‌های ایرانی‌ی پیش از اسلام، به نام «پیامبر»، برای استقلال ایران و نجات هویت ایرانی جنگیدند. زید بن علی، به‌آفرید، سنباذ، استاذ سیس، مقنّع (رهبر سپیدجامگان)، خِداش، سیاه‌جامگان و خرم‌دینان یا سرخ‌جامگان، با آمیزش عناصر آئین «مِهری» (میترائیسم)، تزهای «زندگی‌ی جاویدان» در زرتشیت، «تناسخ» در آیین‌های بودا، و «نور و ظلمت» در آیین مانی و

---

[۱۲۵] برتولد اشپولر، ***تاریخ ایران در قرون نخستین اسلامی***، جلد اول، ترجمه‌ی جواد فلاطوری، تهران: شرکت انتشارات علمی و فرهنگی،چاپ چهارم، ۱۳۷۳، ص ۱۸.

مزدک، و عناصری از دین اسلام، در درازنای سه/ چهار سده، در یکدیگر «حلول» کردند، و با نام دینِ تازه، با اشغالگران مبارزه کردند. «ابومسلم»، دلاور ایرانی نیز، که خود ادعای پیامبری یا «دین تازه» را هم نداشت، گرچه با تعیین جانشین ایرانی‌تبار برای خلیفه‌ی وقت، به تبارشناسی‌ی خلافتِ عربی دست برد، و گرچه از رهگذر آن، در تغییر ساختارهای ذهنی و سامانه‌های عینی‌ی اسلامِ عربی مؤثر بود، اما تا لحظه‌ای که به دست خلیفه بر خاک بیافتد، به نظم «خلافت»، یعنی به مفهوم «شهریارِ الاهی» وفادار ماند، و بعد از مرگش هم، از سوی مبارزان ایرانی به مقام پیامبری «مبعوث» شد، تا ادامه‌ی حرکت او میسر باشد. به عنوان مثال، بابک خرمدین، یکی از برجسته‌ترین مبارزان تاریخ ایران- که «نزدیک بود خلافت عباسی را از پیش بردارد و مسلمانی را تغییر دهد»[۱۲۶]- با باور به اصل تناسخ و «بازگشت روان از پیکری به پیکر دیگر پس از مرگ» در درازنای ۲۳ سال ایستادگی و مبارزه‌ی خونین با اشغالگران، در انتظار ظهور مجدد ابومسلم بود.[۱۲۷] غلامحسین صدیقی در پژوهش گسترده‌ی خود، جنبش‌های ایرانی در سده‌های دوم و سوم هجری را «جنبش‌های دینی» شناسائی می‌کند. و علی میرفطروس، این تشخیص را «بحث‌انگیز» می‌داند و می‌نویسد: «ما بر آنیم که جنبش‌هائی مانند جنبش بابک خرمدین را نخست باید جنبش‌های اجتماعی نامید. زیرا که رهبران این جنبش‌ها بیش‌تر مبارزان اجتماعی بوده‌اند تا «مجاهدین دینی».[۱۲۸] منتها، پذیرش این واقعیت که رهبران جنبش‌ها بیش‌تر «مبارزان اجتماعی» بودند، تا «مجاهدین دینی» نیز، چیزی از بار «دینی/ مذهبی»ی این جنبش‌ها نمی‌کاهد.

تقدس «شاه/ مغ» و شاکله‌ی اطاعت بی‌چون و چرا از آموزه‌های نهادینه شده‌ی آن، در روان جمعی‌ی ایرانی (اعم از فرادست و فرودست، آگاه و ناآگاه)، چنان دیرینه و دیرپا بود که اکثر این مبارزان برای «خلیفه» تقدسی آسمانی قائل بودند. به عنوان مثال، یکی از سازه‌های شکست یعقوب لیث ایرانی از ارتش خلیفه‌ی وقت این بود که یعقوب، به دلیل اعتقاد سپاهیانش و برادرش، «عمرو»، به تقدس و الوهیت خلیفه، از همان ابتدای حرکت به سوی بغداد، قصد جنگیدن با خلیفه را با برادرش و با سپاهیانش مطرح نکرد، و چنان که تاریخ سیستان می‌گوید، اعلام کرد که برای دیدار خلیفه به بغداد می‌رود.[۱۲۹] البته خود یعقوب هم در تقدس‌اندیشی نسبت به «دین خلیفه»، دست کمی از برادرش نداشت. او بارها علیه غیرمسلمانان («کفار») جنگید، و در گسترش و تثبیت اسلام در ایران شرقی (سمرقند، بخارا، مرو و ...) نقش مهمی داشت. در واقع، با وجود هجوم‌های ناموفقی که ارتش تازی به کابل داشت، این یعقوبِ ایرانی بود که با قلع و قمع بودائیان کابل، اسلام را در آن منطقه رویاند. و طرفه این که، برخی از تاریخنویسان زمانه، به پاس این رشادت‌ها (که البته استقلال‌طلبانه بود، اما در جهت گسترش دین تازه هم پیش می‌رفت)، اصل و نسب او را به «خسرو پرویز ساسانی» رسانده‌اند.[۱۳۰] مشابه گرایش‌های ذهنی‌ی یعقوب لیث را در پادشاهان خردگرای سامانی نیز می‌بینیم. به عنوان مثال، خواندن نماز به زبان فارسی، ابتدا از تصویب شاه سامانی می‌گذرد، اما زمانی که با مخالفت فقهای اسلام روبه‌رو می‌شود، شاه مقاومت نمی‌کند، و حرف خود را پس می‌گیرد. سید جواد طباطبایی به نقل از تاریخ بخارا، درباره‌ی اسماعیل سامانی می‌نویسد:

---

[۱۲۶] مروج‌الذهب، جلد دوم، ص ۴۷۱. برگرفته از: علی میرفطروس، ***هفت گفتار***، مکان نشر ؟ نشر فرهنگ، ۲۰۰۱ (۱۳۸۰)، ص ۶۳.

[۱۲۷] حمید حمید، ***نهضت خرمدینی در ایران***، از جمله کتاب‌های نشر الکترونیکی‌ی تارنمای «مرز پرگهر»، به نشانی‌ی زیر: https://derafsh-kaviyani.com/books/khoramdin.pdf . همچنین، نگاه کنید به: ناصر انقطاع، ***منم، بابک: مردی به استواری‌ی کوه سبلان***، لس‌انجلس: شرکت چاپ محدود، ۱۹۹۹، ص ۲۱.

[۱۲۸] علی میرفطروس، ***هفت گفتار***، مکان نشر ؟، نشر فرهنگ، ۲۰۰۱ (۱۳۸۰)، ص ۹۰.

[۱۲۹] پروین ترکمنی آذر و دکتر صالح پرگاری، ***تاریخ تحولات سیاسی، اجتماعی، اقتصادی، و فرهنگی‌ی ایران در دوره‌ی صفاریان و علویان***، تهران: سازمان مطالعه و تدوین کتب علوم انسانی‌ی دانشگاه‌ها، ۱۳۷۸، ص ۴۰.

[۱۳۰] عباس اقبال آشتیانی، ***تاریخ مفصل ایران: از صدر اسلام تا انقراض قاجاریه***، به کوشش دکتر محمد دبیرسیاقی، تهران: انتشارات خیام، چاپ نهم، ۱۳۸۰، ص ۱۸۹. در مورد تاریخ صفاریان، مراجعه کنید به: * پروین ترکمنی آذر و دکتر صالح پرگاری، ***تاریخ تحولات سیاسی، اجتماعی، اقتصادی و فرهنگی‌ی ایران در دوره‌ی صفاریان و علویان***، تهران: انتشارات سازمان مطالعه و تدوین کتب علوم انسانی‌ی دانشگاه‌ها (سمت)، تابستان ۱۳۷۸.

پیوسته خلیفه را اطاعت نمودی و در عصر خویش، یک ساعت بر خلیفه عاصی نشدی و فرمان او به غایت استوار داشتی. [۱۳۱]

کارکرد کهن الگوی تک‌صدایی و وابسته‌های آن در روان جمعی سبب شد که شاهان، حکمرانان، و استقلال‌طبان ایرانی، که با هدف آزادی‌ی ایران از سلطه‌ی بیگانه، یا با هدف کاستن از قدرت بغداد و افزودن به قدرت ایرانی، یا با هدف رهایی از تعصب شریعت‌مداران، یا علیه ستم حکمرانان غیرایرانی، در میدان‌های نظامی و فرهنگی جنگیدند، نه به وسیله‌ی دستگاه خلافت بغداد، بلکه اکثراً به دست یکدیگر، یکی پس از دیگری حذف شدند؛ طاهریان به وسیله‌ی صفاریان، صفاریان به وسیله‌ی سامانیان، آل زیار به وسیله‌ی آل بویه و آل بویه به وسیله‌ی سامانیان و... بابک، رهبر سرسخت‌ترین گروه نهضت مقاومت (خرم‌دینان) به وسیله‌ی افشینِ ایرانی، حسنک وزیر به وسیله‌ی بوسهل زوزنی؛ عبدالرزاقِ سربدار، توسط برادرش وجیه‌الدین مسعود سربدار (قرن هشتم هجری)؛ و ... این رشته سر دراز دارد تا برسد به رویاروئی‌ی مرگبارِ «محمدرضا شاه پهلوی» با «دکتر محمد مصدق»، «حزب توده/ فدائیان خلق- اکثریت» با «فدائیان خلق- اقلیت»، و ...

کهن الگوی وحدت دین و دولت و عناصر ذهنی‌ی وابسته به آن، پس از اشغال ایران، از راه دیگری نیز رؤیای رسیدن به استقلال، و بازگشت ایرانی به یک‌پارچگی‌ی فرهنگی و عظمت باستانی را به خاکستر نشاند. چرا که دین‌یارانِ زمان ساسانی، در غیبت نیمه‌ی دیگر خود، یعنی شهریاران، برای حفظ هویت دینی و فرهنگی، از دست زدن به هرگونه عمل تشکیلاتی ناتوان مانده بودند. در نتیجه، یا به ناگزیر از ایران گریختند، و یا پس از حدود چهار سده مقاومت‌های پراکنده در برابر دین تازه، تحلیل رفتند، و نیایشگاه‌های آنان یکی پس از دیگری به مسجد جا سپردند، تا در عصر مغولان و تیموریان به زاویه و تکیه و خانقاه تبدیل شوند؛ کتاب‌ها و کتابخانه‌ها دود شوند؛ فرهیختگان و دگراندیشان از دم تیغ صحرانشینان بگذرند یا از ایران بگریزند.

***

از همان ابتدای تسلط تازیان بر ایران، حضور پررنگ مفهوم «شهریار الاهی» در حافظه‌ی جمعی‌ی ایرانی، فقط به دین‌یاران و به جنگجویان استقلال‌طلب منحصر نبود. تاریخ فلسفه‌ی چهار/ پنج سده‌ی نخست ایران اسلامی، ضمن این که به جهش درخشان تفکر و رشد خرد ذهن ایرانی‌ی بعد از اسلام گواهی می‌دهد، به این نکته نیز گواهی می‌دهد که تحول بینش فلسفی و رشد اندیشه‌ی عقلی، در بالاترین نقطه‌های اوج خود، به ضرب رسوب جهان‌شناسی‌ی دینی و شناخت‌شناسی‌ی شهریار الاهی دهن‌بند خورده است.

جنبش فکری‌ی «شعوبیه»، واکنش روشنفکران ایرانی (و دیگر ملت‌های تحت سلطه‌ی تازیان) بود در برابر نژادپرستی‌ی قوم پیروز، که به خاطر انتساب پیامبر اسلام و قرآن به خود و زبان عربی، خود را برترین نژاد و برترین قوم می‌دانست، و ایرانیان را به خاطر نداشتن «کتاب آسمانی» و انتساب آنان به کفر و شرک، تحقیر می‌کرد. جنبش شعوبیه، تزهای «**مساوات بشری صرف‌نظر از نَسَب و نژاد**»، و «**تمایز بین دین و جامعه**» را سرلوحه‌ی مطالبات خود قرار می‌دهد. منتها، با

---

[۱۳۱] سید جواد طباطبایی، ***زوال اندیشه‌ی سیاسی در ایران***، تهران: انتشارات کویر، ۱۳۷۳، ص ۹۵.

استنادی تأویلی به بخش کوتاهی از آیه‌ی ۱۳ در سوره‌ی «حجرات» به مصاف مشکل می‌رود.[۱۳۲] در این رهگذر، نه تنها به تفسیر اخلاقی‌ی اسلام می‌رسد، بلکه با نگرش باطنی/ تأویلی، در پیاده کردن تز «تمایز بین دین و ملت»، به تز «تمایز بین جامعه و حقیقت» می‌رسد، و از درونه‌ی این تفکیک، از فردگرایی‌ی بریده از جامعه، سر بر می‌کند. این جنبش، ضمن این که در زمان خیزش و گسترش، به تحول حیات علمی و جوشش فرهنگی‌ی ایران به صورت چشمگیری یاری می‌دهد، و ضمن این که بر حرکت علیه نژادپرستی‌ی عرب و اصولاً سلطه‌ی تازیان در تاریخ ایران اثر می‌گذارد، به عقیده‌ی بسیاری از پژوهشگران، از نظر گسترش اندیشه‌های باطنی، خاستگاه جنبش‌های صوفیه و اسماعیلیه و اخوان‌الصفا نیز می‌شود.

این جنبش‌ها، ضمن توجه به برهان فلسفی و اندیشه‌ی عقلی، از تمام فلسفه‌ی یونان، اصول باطنی و عرفانی‌ی فیثاغورسی، رواقی (در رُم)، و نوافلاطونیان را ملاک قرار می‌دهند؛ برداشت‌های فلسفی‌ی خود را با گرایش‌های تند شیعی می‌آمیزند؛ و به شناخت‌شناسی‌ی «عالم کبیر و عالم صغیر» می‌رسند، که با جهان‌بینی‌ی ایرانی بسیار سازگار می‌آید. و شگفتا که در طول راه، تز والای مبارزه با «عصبیت نژادی» در اسماعیله و تز «وحدت بشری و عشق و شفقت عام» در اخوان‌الصفا، به تدریج به فتوای «قتل مخالفان» می‌انجامد. شگفت‌انگیزتر این که، تز «تمایز بین دین و جامعه»، حدود یک هزاره بعد از شعوبیه، گوهر جنبش «روشنگری» در اروپا می‌شود، تا بعد، تز «مساوات بشری، صرف‌نظر از نَسَب و نژاد»، مهم‌ترین سازه‌ی «منشور حقوق بشر» را تشکیل دهد. اما در ایرانِ زمان خود، با همه‌ی خروشی که در جامعه می‌آفریند، زیر سلطه‌ی کهن‌الگوهای قدسی از یک سو، و تکفیر دین‌یاران و فقیهان از سوی دیگر، بیش و پیش از هر چیز به انسجام فکرت‌های صوفیانه/عارفانه دامن می‌زند.

در قلمرو فلسفه، ابونصر فارابی (۲۶۰- ۳۳۹ قمری)، با این که نخستین کس نیست، اما برجسته‌ترین شخصیتی است که مبانی‌ی فلسفه‌ی افلاتون و ارسطو،[۱۳۳] و البته، نوافلاتونیان را در هم می‌آمیزد و با ادراکی که از آن آمیزه دارد، «فلسفه» را با دین اسلام می‌آمیزد. ذبیح‌الله صفا، با ارجاع به منابع متعدد، درباره‌ی فارابی می‌نویسد:

> در حقیقت فارابی فلسفه را در چشم مسلمین بیاراست و از ابهام و اشکال آن بسی کاست و با تقلیدی که در تطبیق عقاید افلاتون و ارسطو از افلاتونیان جدید کرد، و نیز با تطبیق بسیاری از اصول عقاید قدما بر مبانی‌ی اسلامی و تفسیر و توضیح و تدوین همه‌ی منطقیات ارسطو و اجزاء مختلف علوم، خدمت بزرگی به تحکیم روش منطقی در فلسفه‌ی اسلامی و ایجاد مقدمات دوره‌ی اسکولاستیک در علوم انجام داد.[۱۳۴]

فارابی، با بار گرانی از همه‌ی علوم عقلی‌ی زمانه‌ی خود، در صدد ساختن بنیادهای نظری‌ی «مدینه‌ی فاضله» برمی‌آید، و با همه‌ی درخششی که در ادراک فلسفه‌ی سیاسی و در استدلال به نمایش می‌گذارد، و با این که در برابر تصوف زندگی‌ستیز می‌ایستد، «مدینه»‌ی او - در میان همهمه‌ی دوردست اما زنده‌ی «شهریار/ مغ» - دارای «رئیس اول» می‌شود؛ رئیسی که، با مفهوم «نبوت» و مسئله‌ی جانشینی پیامبر در اندیشه‌ی اسلامی پیوندی ناگسستنی دارد. یعنی درست خلاف جهتی که افلاطون در تدوین فلسفه‌ی سیاسی پیموده بود. افلاطون سیاست عقلی را جانشین سیاست اسطوره‌ای

---

[۱۳۲] دکتر سید محمد قانعی راد، ***جامعه‌شناسی‌ی رشد و افول علم در ایران***، تهران: انتشارات مدینه، ۱۳۷۹، ص ۲۷۳. یادآوری می‌کنم که در نوشتن کل پاراگراف مربوط به «شعوبیه»، از این کتاب ارجمند و همچنین از کتاب «تاریخ ایران بعد از اسلام» نوشته‌ی عبدالحسین زرین‌کوب، استفاده کرده‌ام.

[۱۳۳] در منابع آمده است که او یکی از کتاب‌های افلاتون را نیز به جای کتابی از ارسطو گرفته بود.

[۱۳۴] دکتر ذبیح‌الله صفا، ***تاریخ علوم عقلی در تمدن اسلامی تا اواسط قرن پنجم***، تهران: انتشارات امیرکبیر، چاپ چهارم، ۲۵۳۶، ص ۱۹۴.

کرد، و ارسطو، اخلاق را مقدمه و زمینه‌ای برای سیاست برآورد کرد. اما فارابی، نتوانست از بینش و سیاست اسطوره‌ای فراتر رود. این است که، در سازواره‌ی «مدینه»‌ی او، «اخلاق» بر «سیاست» پیشی می‌گیرد. به ضرب بینش اسطوره‌ای است که فارابی، با همه‌ی بهایی که برای آزادی و اختیار آدمی قائل است، «اجرام سماوی» را در تعیین سرنوشت انسان دخیل می‌بیند. و به ضرب اخلاق الاهی است، که ریاست مدینه‌ی فاضله‌اش را، به امامت و ولایت می‌سپارد. سیدجواد طباطبایی- پژوهشگر این دوره از تاریخ فرهنگ ایران- درباره‌ی فارابی می‌نویسد:

> هدف فارابی، بررسی‌ی بحرانی بود که لرزه بر ارکان دستگاه خلافت انداخته بود؛ خلافتی که، تلاشی‌ی آن، مانند همه‌ی نظام‌های مبتنی بر باورهای دینی، بیش‌تر از آن که سیاسی و در قلمرو عمل باشد، در نظر و در قلمرو باورهای دینی و آئینی بود. فارابی، با تکیه بر اندیشه‌ی فلسفی‌ی یونانی، تفسیری از نبوت ارائه کرد که بیش‌تر با نظریه‌ی امامت شیعی سازگار بود.[۱۳۵]

افزون بر این که اندیشه‌ورزان مسلمان و یهودی و مسیحی‌ی سده‌های نخستینِ تمدن اسلامی، در سراسر تصرفات پهناور اسلام، مداوماً در احاطه‌ی متکلمان و فقیهان زمانه بودند، محمد زکریا رازی و ابونصر فارابی، با یکی از مهم‌ترین متکمان شیعی، یعنی با «شیخ کلینی رازی» (۲۵۸- ۳۲۹) نیز هم‌دوره بودند. کلینی رازی، که در عصر حسن عسکری (یازدهمین امام شیعیان) به دنیا آمد،[۱۳۶] بین ۱۵ تا ۱۶ هزار حدیث از پیامبر و امامان شیعه در کتاب هنگفتِ «الکافی» گردآورد،[۱۳۷] که حتا اگر قرآن هم در کار نبود، همین «الکافی» برای کنترل اندیشه و گفتار و کردار مسلمانان «کافی» بود. علامه محمدتقی مجلسی درباره‌ی کلینی گفته است: «کلینی در نظم و ترتیب کتابش «الکافی»، بی‌نظیر بوده، و این مزایا دلیل است که وی از جانب خداوند متعال تأییدات خاصی داشته است.»[۱۳۸] جالب است بدانیم که فارابی نیز مجموعه‌ای از کلام پیامبر اسلام گردآورد که در آن‌ها به علم منطق اشاره شده بود. ذبیح‌الله صفا، پس از درج این گزاره (به نقل از کتاب «طبقات‌الاطباء»)، انگار از سر دردی تاریخی، می‌پرسد:

> آیا نمی‌توان باور داشت که این کلمات و احادیث از زمره‌ی احادیث مجعولی بود که علمای منطق و فلسفه برای حفظ خود در قبال متعصبین جعل کرده و به حضرت رسول نسبت داده باشند؟[۱۳۹]

در این تردید نیست که جانِ اندیشه‌ورزانِ علوم عقلی همواره از سوی «متعصبین» در خطر بوده است. اما این واقعیت

---

[۱۳۵] سید جواد طباطبایی، ***زوال اندیشه‌ی سیاسی در ایران***، پیشین، ص ۱۴۰. **توضیح:** افزون بر این بازگفت، در بدست آوردن تصویری از فلسفه‌ی فارابی، از کل این کتاب ارجمند بیش از منابع مشابه سود برده‌ام. در زمینه‌ی فلسفه‌ی فارابی، هم چنین نگاه کنید به: رضا داوری، ***فارابی مؤسس فلسفه‌ی اسلامی***، تهران: انتشارات انجمن فلسفه‌ی ایران، ۱۳۵۳.

[۱۳۶] حجت‌الاسلام علی دوانی می‌نویسد: «ثقة‌الاسلام کلینی در عصر امام حسن عسکری علیه السلام متولد شد، و با چهار سفیر و نماینده‌ی خاص امام زمان علیه السلام ــ که در طول غیبت کوتاه آن حضرت، رابط بین شیعیان و امام زمان علیه السلام بودند ــ هم‌عصر بود. با این که آن چهار تن، از فقها و محدثان بزرگ شیعه بودند و شیعیان آن‌ها را به جلالت قدر می‌شناختند، ولی کلینی مشهورترین شخصیت عالی‌مقامی بود که در آن زمان، میان شیعه و سنی با احترام می‌زیست و به صورت آشکار به ترویج مذهب حق و نشر معارف و فضایل اهل‌بیت علیهم‌السلام همت می‌گماشت.» به مأخذ زیر نگاه کنید:

- حجت‌الاسلام علی دوانی، **ثقة‌السلام کلینی رحمة‌الله**، تارنمای «کلینی»، ۱ شهریور ۱۳۸٦:

http://www.kulayni.com/persian/index.php?option=com_content&task=view&id=14&Itemid=37

[۱۳۷] در دانشنامه‌ی ویکی‌پدیا، زیر عنوان «الکافی» می‌خوانیم: «گفته شده که اختلاف در اعداد حدیث‌های روایت شده در کافی، ناشی از شیوه‌ی شمردن احادیث است. به این معنی که برخی، روایاتی را که با دو سند ذکر شده است، دو روایت، و بعضی، آن را یک روایت به حساب آورده‌اند.»

[۱۳۸] برگرفته از: حجت‌الاسلام علی دوانی، **ثقة‌السلام کلینی رحمة‌الله**، تارنمای «کلینی»، ۱ شهریور ۱۳۸٦:
http://www.kulayni.com/persian/index.php?option=com_content&task=view&id=14&Itemid=37

[۱۳۹] دکتر ذبیح‌الله صفا، ***تاریخ علوم عقلی در اسلام تا اواسط قرن پنجم***، پیشین، ص ۱٤٦.

عینی، این واقعیت را نمی‌زداید که ذهنیتِ خودِ این افراد نیز آکنده از کهن‌الگوهای فرهنگی بود. کما این که جا پای رسوب جهان‌شناسی‌ی ایرانشهری، در فلسفه‌ی عمومی و فلسفه‌ی سیاسی‌ی خردگراترین فیلسوفان ما، مثل فارابی، مسکویه‌ی رازی، ابن سینا، ابوریحان بیرونی، مطهربن طاهر مقدسی، خواجه نصیرالدین طوسی، تا ملاصدرا، به روشنی قابل ردیابی است؛ و در سه دهه‌ی گذشته، پژوهشگران بسیاری برای یافتن و نشان دادن نمودهای آن همت گذاشته‌اند. محمد رضا فشاهی، بعد از شرح کوتاه اما گویائی که از نظر ابوریحان بیرونی (۳۵۲- ۴۲۷ قمری) پیرامون فکرتِ «خورشیدمرکزی» به دست می‌دهد، باز انگار از سر دردی تاریخی، می‌پرسد:

> اما چرا بیرونی در اواخر زندگی، نظر خویش مبنی بر «مرکزیتِ خورشید» را پس گرفت، و همچون گالیله با ایماء و اشاره اظهار نداشت که «با این همه، می‌چرخد»؟ آیا قرن دهم و یازدهم بیرونی بیدادگرانه‌تر از قرن هفدهم گالیله بود؟ یا این که تفاوت «روح شرقی» و «روح غربی» در همین جاست؟ یعنی تفاوت برونو و گالیله با بیرونی، همان تفاوت «تسلیم» و «طغیان» است؟ یا این که نه، شاید عوامل دیگری در کار بوده است؟[۱۴۰]

البته، در روایت دیگری می‌خوانیم که ابوسعید سَجزی (ریاضی‌دان و ستاره‌شناس ایرانی- از مردم سیستان- ۳۳۰ تا ۴۱۵ قمری) نخستین کسی بود که بر اساس عقیده به حرکت وضعی‌ی زمین، اسطرلاب تازه‌ای ساخته بود، و ابوریحان بیرونی، به گفته‌ی خودش، آن را «ستوده» بود؛ منتها، این نظریه را «شُبهه»‌ای می‌دانست که «تحلیل‌اش دشوار، و رفع و ابطالش مشکل است.»[۱۴۱] با این وصف، همین اظهار «شبهه» و «ستودن»، مورد انتقاد دانشمند دیگری به نام «ابوعلی حسن بن علی مراکشی» (از دانشمندان سده‌ی هفتم قمری) قرار می‌گیرد:

> [...] از بیرونی عجیب است که چه‌گونه رد کردن شبهه‌ای را که نادرستی‌اش بی‌اندازه آشکار است، دشوار می‌شمارد. حال آن که نادرستی‌ی این سخن را ابن سینا در کتاب شفا و رازی در کتاب ملخص و بسیاری دیگر از آثارش روشن کرده‌اند.[۱۴۲]

وقتی این انتقاد/ سرزنش، حدود سه سده پس از مرگ بیرونی به متن می‌نشیند، می‌توان تصور کرد که اگر بیرونی در زمان خود بر این نظریه پافشاری می‌کرد، چه بلائی به سرش می‌آمد. منتها، اگر گالیله با یک دستگاه- دستگاه تفتیش عقاید کلیسا- روبه‌رو بود، بیرونی، افزون بر فشار تکفیر فقها، از درون (خود) و بیرون (جامعه‌ی دانشمندان زمانه) درگیر خوی تبعیت از سنت بود. اول این که: با پذیرش حرکت وضعی‌ی زمین، متن‌های مقدس نفی می‌شدند، و دوم این که افلاتون و ارسطو و بطلمیوس و که و که‌ها چنان گفته‌اند، نه چنین؛ و تا جهان باقی است، «درِ» دانش و آگاهی باید بر «پاشنه»‌ی یافته‌های آن‌ها بگردد. یعنی این که، یافته‌ها و گفته‌های بزرگان پیشین (آن چنان که تفسیر و فهم شده) نیز در ذهنیت جامعه‌ی اندیشه‌ورزان به مرحله‌ی قدوسیت رسیده است. در این صورت است که هر اندیشه‌ی نو- از هر دو سوی فیلسوف‌ها و فقیهان- یا به دیده‌ی «شبهه» نگریسته می‌شود و یا چیزی جز «کفر» برآورد نمی‌شود. من، رابطه‌ی «تسلیم» با «روح شرقی» (در سخن محمدرضا فشاهی) را نمی‌دانم، اما- بنا بر تحلیل بالا- بر این باورم که ترس نهادینه شده از قدرت‌های قدسی (آسمانی و زمینی) در روان جمعی‌ی ایرانی، در «تسلیم» خردورزان ما دستی توانا داشته است. نظامی

---

[۱۴۰] محمد رضا فشاهی، ***ارسطوی بغداد: از عقل یونانی به وحی قرآنی (کوششی در آسیب‌شناسی‌ی فلسفه‌ی ایرانی-اسلامی)***، سوند: نشر باران، ۱۹۹۸، ص۲۴.

[۱۴۱] مهندس یونس کرامتی، ***کارنامه‌ی ایرانیان: در زمینه‌ی نوآوری‌های ریاضیات، نجوم و گاه‌شماری***، زیر نظر اکبر ایرانی و علیرضا مختارپور، تهران: مؤسسه‌ی فرهنگی‌ی اهل قلم، ۱۳۸۰، ص ۱۰۱.

[۱۴۲] مهندس یونس کرامتی، ***کارنامه‌ی ایرانیان: در زمینه‌ی نوآوری‌های ریاضیات، نجوم و گاه‌شماری***، پیشین، ص ۱۰۲.

عروضی سمرقندی در کتاب چهارمقاله، داستانی را از ابوریحان بیرونی در برابر سلطان محمود غزنوی شرح می‌دهد، که با همه‌ی افسانه‌پردازی‌های احتمالی، جنس اِعمال قدرت، و تسلیم خردورزان را به کمال نمادینه می‌کند.[۱۴۳] شاه خودکامه‌ی غزنوی، که هم خود را عقل کل می‌داند و هم در برابر دانش ابوریحان بیرونی احساس حقارت می‌کند، اینک در «کوشکی» با «چهار در» نشسته است و به ابوریحان می‌گوید: «من ازین چهار در، از کدام در بیرون خواهم رفت؟ حکم کن و اختیار آن بر پاره‌ی کاغذ نویس و در زیر نهالی می‌نِه.» ابوریحان بر تکه کاغذی می‌نویسد: «از این چهار در هیچ بیرون نشود، بر دیوار مشرق دری کنند، و از آن در بیرون شود»، و «کاغذ پاره» را در زیر نهالی دفن می‌کند. محمود غزنوی که از پاسخ بیرونی بی‌خبر است، به قصد تحقیر این دانشمند، فرمان می‌دهد تا در سمت شرقی قصر در پنجمی بسازند، و از آن راه از قصر خارج می‌شود، و سپس می‌گوید تا «آن کاغذ پاره بیاورند.» شاه غزنوی با دیدن «حکمِ» درستِ ابوریحان، چنان خشمگین می‌شود که دستور می‌دهد که ابوریحان را «به میان سرای فرو اندازند.» ابوریحان در «دام»ی که برای ایمنی کاخ ساخته بودند می‌افتد؛ «دام» را پاره می‌کند و بدون هیچ آسیبی به زمین فرود می‌آید:

> محمود گفت: «او را برآرید». برآوردند. گفت: «یا بوریحان! ازین حال باری ندانسته بودی.» ابوریحان گفت: «ای خداوند دانسته بودم.» گفت: «دلیل کو؟» غلام را آواز داد و تقویم از غلام بستد و تحویل خویش از میان تقویم بیرون کرد، در احکام آن روز نوشته بود که «مرا از جای بلند بیاندازند، و لیکن به سلامت به زمین آیم و تندرست برخیزم.»[۱۴۴]

خشم شاه خودکامه، که این بار هم در برابر ابوریحان احساس حقارت کرده، مضاعف می‌شود، و دستور اسارت ابوریحان را صادر می‌کند. ابوریحان شش ماه در زندان باقی می‌ماند، و «در این شش ماه، کس حدیث بوریحان پیش محمود نیارست کرد.» تا این که:

> خواجه‌ی بزرگ احمدِ حسن میمندی در شکارگاه سلطان را خوش طبع یافت و سخن را گردان گردان همی آورد تا به علم نجوم، آن گاه گفت: «بیچاره بوریحان که چنان دو حکم بدان نیکوئی بکرد، و بدل خلعت و تشریف، بند و زندان یافت.» محمود گفت: «خواجه بداند که من این دانسته‌ام، و می‌گویند که این مرد را در عالم نظیر نیست مگر بوعلی سینا؛ لکن هر دو حکمش برخلاف رأی من بود و پادشاهان چون کودکِ خرد باشند، سخن بر وفق رأی‌ی ایشان باید گفت، تا از ایشان بهره‌مند باشند. آن روز که آن دو حکم بکرد، اگر از آن دو حکم او یکی خطا شدی، بِه [بهتر] افتادی او را. فردا بفرمای تا او را بیرون آرند و اسب و ساخت زر و جُبّه‌ی مَلِکی و دستار قصب [پارچه‌ای که از نوع حریر] دهند و هزار دینار و غلامی و کنیزکی.» پس همان روز بوریحان را بیرون آوردند و این تشریف بدین نسخت به وی رسید، و سلطان عذر خواست و گفت: «یا بوریحان! اگر خواهی از من برخوردار باشی سخن بر مراد من گوی، نه بر سلطنتِ علم خویش.» بوریحان از آن پس سیرت بگردانید. (پیشین، صص ۹۳ تا ۹۴.)

در چنین جوّی بود که ابوریحان بیرونی «سلطنت علم خویش» به فراموشی سپرد، و « از آن پس سیرت بگردانید.» اگر تغییر رفتار ابوریحان شگفت‌انگیز است، هشدار نظامی عروضی (در ۵۵۰ هجری قمری) به مخاطبان نوشته‌اش شگفت‌انگیزتر است. او در دنباله‌ی این داستان می‌نویسد:

---

۱۴۳ من نمی‌دانم که ابوریحان بیرونی، فیلسوف، ریاضی‌دان، و اخترشناسی که حتا در زمانه‌ی خود از بزرگان و صاحب‌نظران این دانش‌ها برشمرده می‌شد، ادعای پیش‌گوئی هم داشت، یا نه. اما این داستان، شاید نشانه‌ای باشد از شرایط چیره بر «روح تاریخ اندیشه» در ایران.

۱۴۴ احمد بن عمربن علی نظامی عروضی سمرقندی، ***چهار مقاله***، به اهتمام دکتر محمد معین، چاپ دهم، تهران: انتشارات امیرکبیر، ۱۳۶۹، ص ۹۲.

> و این یکی از شرایط خدمت پادشاه است، در حق و باطل با او باید بودن، و بر وفق کار، او را تقریر باید کرد. (پیشین، ص ۹۴)

الگوی تغییر رفتار ابوریحان بیرونی در «پس گرفتن» نظرش (یا در دنبال نکردن ایده‌ی ابوسعید سجزی)، در بسیاری از خردورزان ایرانی‌ی سده‌های نخست ایران اسلامی دیده می‌شود. به عنوان مثال، ابن سینا (۳۵۹- ۴۱۶ قمری)، در اوج گرایش به فلسفه‌ی ارسطو، نقد خردورزانه‌ی زکریای رازی و ابوریحان بیرونی بر ارسطو را برنمی‌تابد.[۱۴۵] و این در حالی است که خود او هم به سبب گرایش به فلسفه‌ی یونان (با این که همان فلسفه‌ی ارسطوئی‌ی او آکنده است از التقاط با اندیشه‌ی قدسی/ اسلامی) مدام در معرض تکفیر است، و پس از تحمل گریزها و دربه‌دری‌های بسیار، بالأخره «تسلیم» می‌شود، و از فلسفه‌ی مشایی، یکسره به فلسفه‌ی «رواقی»‌ی رُمی‌شده/ اسلامی‌شده و نمادِ عمیقاً عرفانی‌ی «حیّ بن یقضان» (زنده‌ی بیدار) سر برمی‌کند. و تازه، این زمانی است که «امام محمد غزالی»، هنوز به جهان نیامده، و فکرت‌های «تکفیرگرانِ» جهان اسلام را در کتاب‌هایش جمع‌بندی نکرده است. اگر شیخ کلینی، یک سره به دنبال فقه و کلام شیعی و انتظار ظهور امام زمان رفته بود، محمد غزالی طوسی (۴۵۰- ۵۰۵)، با تسلط بر علوم عقلی‌ی زمانه‌ی خود، به ویژه دانش منطق، و با بهره‌گیری از اصول «منطق»، منطق و فلسفه و ریاضیات و نجوم و علوم طبیعی و حتا «مناظره» را به عنوان «آفت» شناسائی کرد. غزالی طوسی، افزون بر این که در کتاب «تهافت‌الفلاسفه»، با حمله به روش استقرائی در استدلال، بسیاری از اصول فلسفه‌ی مشائی را نفی کرده بود، و فیلسوفان ارسطوئی را زندیق و ملحد و کافر نامیده بود، در کتاب های دیگرش نیز تا دم مرگ همین گزاره ها را به بیان های مختلف به خورد فرهنگ ایران داد. به عنوان مثال، به گفته‌ی ذبیح‌الله صفا، غزالی در «باب شروط مناظره و مضار آن» در کتاب «فاتحة‌العلوم» می‌نویسد:

> اگر کسی گوید که فوائد این فن [مناظره] تشحیذ ذهن است، باید گفت که اگر چیزی سودی تنها و زیان‌هائی بسیار دارد، جایز نیست برای این منفعت خود را به زیان‌های بزرگ دچار کرد. چنان که شراب لاشک در تعدیل مزاج و تقویت طبع و دماغ، و قمار در تشحیذ خاطر، مؤثر است. و با این حال، هر دو حرام‌اند. و حتا مداومت در بازی‌ی شطرنج، با آن که ذهن را نیرومند می‌سازد، ممنوع و محظور است، و همچنین است نظر در علم اقلیدس و المجسطی و دقائق حساب و هندسه و ریاضیات که خاطر را تشحیذ و نفس را نیرومند می‌کند، و با این حال، ما آن را به سبب یک آفت که در پی دارد منع می‌کنیم. زیرا از مقدمات علم اوائل است، که مذاهب فاسدی در پی دارد. و اگرچه در خودِ علم هندسه و حساب مذهب فاسدی که متعلق به دین باشد وجود ندارد، لیکن می‌ترسم که بدان منتهی گردند.[۱۴۶]

به فشرده‌ترین کلام می‌توان گفت که مجموعه‌ای از بن‌مایه های الهی (مانند وحی) و «مذهب انتظار» در ذهنیت خود اندیشه‌ورزان ما، در کنار نفوذ «دین‌کاران» در ذهنیت جامعه، در کنار همنشینی‌ی اندیشه‌ورزان با دین‌کاران و قدرت‌مداران سیاسی، فلسفه‌ی را دست‌مایه قرار داد، و ریشه‌های تدوین و انسجام مذهب شیعه را در منظومه‌ی ذهنی‌ی ایرانی فراهم آورد. محمدرضا نیکفر، پژوهشگر قلمرو فلسفه، انگیزه و فرآورده‌ی تلاش‌های دانشمندان این دوره را به شرح زیر فشرده کرده است:

---

[۱۴۵] محمد زکریا رازی، پیش از ابوریحان بیرونی و ابن سینا (که هم‌دوره بوده‌اند) می‌زیست. اما زمانی که ابوریحان بیرونی در ادامه‌ی نقدهای زکریای رازی از فلسفه‌ی ارسطو، پانزده سئوال را برای اظهار نظر و مشورت نزد ابن سینا می‌فرستد، ابن سینا نه تنها نظرات او را رد می‌کند، و پرسنده را «فضول» می‌خواند. و این در حالی است که خود ابن‌سینا در زمان زندگی، هم مورد تمسخر عارفان بود، و هم شیخ عمر سهروردی (متکلم اسلامی) به او لقب «کافر» عطا کرده بود؛ لقبی که تا سده‌های متمادی بعد از مرگ نیز، از سوی متکلمان و فقیهان اسلامی تکرار شد.

[۱۴۶] دکتر ذبیح‌الله صفا، ***تاریخ علوم عقلی در اسلام تا اواسط قرن پنجم***، پیشین، ص ۱۴۹.

دگرنمائی‌ی دین، از همان ورود علم‌های غیرعربی به حیطه‌ی جهان‌بینی‌ی عرب آغاز شده است. دانشمندان، بزرگ‌ترین تحریف‌کنندگان دین بوده‌اند؛ چون خواسته‌اند پویش و شور و خودانگیختگی‌ی ایمانی را در قالب تأمل و درنگِ علمی بریزند. [...] استدلال ناب دینی فقط به این گونه است: اگر نپذیری، گرفتار عقوبت خواهی شد! این نکته‌ی کانونی‌ی منطق ایمانی، در زیر قشری از مفهوم‌ها و گزاره‌ها منطق یونانی پنهان است. کافی است اندکی مقاومت کنیم تا پوشش تزئینی کنار زده شود، و ایمان، برهان قاطع خود را بنماید.[۱۴۷]

البته موضوع سخن محمدرضا نیکفر در این نوشته، گزارش و تحلیل تفکر این دوره از تاریخ نیست. با این همه، نکته‌ی جالب از نظر من این است که او به «تحریفِ» آگاهانه یا ناآگاهانه‌ی این دانشمندان از «فلسفه‌ی یونان» نمی‌پردازد؛ و در عوض، بر تحریف آنان از «دین» تکیه می‌کند. به عنوان نمونه از پژوهش‌های گسترده‌ای که پیرامون پیامدهای عینی‌ی ذهنیتِ ایمانی- از دیدگاه‌های مختلف- در تبعید نوشته شده است، می‌توان به کار فرشاد صدری اشاره می‌کرد. فرشاد صدری در پژوهش خود، فلسفه‌ی ارسطو را بازخوانی می‌کند، برداشت فیلسوفان دنیای مسیحیت از فلسفه‌ی ارسطو را با ترجمان فیلسوفان ایرانی/ اسلامی از این فلسفه به مقایسه می‌گذارد، و خوانش متفکران اولیه‌ی اسلامی از ارسطو را، هم برآمده از ذهنیت دینی/ فرهنگی‌ی این اندیشه‌ورزان برآورد می‌کند و هم این خوانش را سبب‌ساز ذهنیتی شناسائی می‌کند که تداوم هزارساله‌ی آن، در حکومت جمهوری‌ی اسلامی به عینیت نشسته است.[۱۴۸] نمونه‌ی دیگر، متن «فلسفه چیست؟» نوشته‌ی محمدحسین صدیق یزدچی است. این پژوهشگر از دیدگاه هستی‌شناختی به چیستی‌ی «فلسفه»، و کارکرد آن در فرهنگ و تمدن اسلامی می‌پردازد، و در این رهگذر نشان می‌دهد که چه‌گونه بدخوانی‌ها و بدفهمی‌های اندیشه‌ورزان سده‌های نخست اسلام از مفاهیم کلیدی در متافیزیک افلاتون و ارسطو، فکرت‌های ربوبی و قدسی را با فلسفه درآمیخت؛ و نتیجه این شد که: «مدافعان آتشین دیانت [...] این حق را به خود داده‌اند که با بی‌ریشه کردن فلسفه، یعنی تفکر ناب عقلانی، باورهای دینی را به جای فلسفه بنشانند و آن آموزه‌ها را قرن‌ها به انسان‌های این فرهنگ (مسلمانان) بیاموزانند.»[۱۴۹]

و این چنین است که زکریای رازی در قلمرو فلسفه‌ی طبیعی، ابوالقاسم فردوسی در قلمرو فلسفه‌ی تاریخ، و فخرالدین گرگانی در قلمرو ادبیاتی با بینش گیتیانه و زندگی‌ی تنانه، و هر سه از نظر استقلال فکری، در تاریخ ایران بعد از اسلام، چهره‌هایی شاخص باقی می‌مانند. این سه، هر یک به گونه‌ای، بر عنصر «تسلیم در روح ایرانی» طغیان می‌کنند.

حکیم ابوبکر محمد بن زکریای رازی (۲۵۱- ۳۱۳ قمری)، پزشک، شیمیست، و فیلسوف، از راه علم و تجربه‌های علمی به فلسفه می‌رسد. با توجه به فهرستی که از آثار رازی در دست داریم، تردید نیست که کیهان‌شناسی‌ی این فیلسوف نیز، از اندیشه‌های دینی متأثر است. منتها، رازی، نه پیرو ارسطوئیان زمانه بود و نه پیرو متکلمان اسلامی زمانه‌ی خود. محمدرضا فشاهی- که محمد زکریا رازی را «تنها متفکر اصیل، به معنای واقعی‌ی کلمه به معنی‌ی مستقل» برآورد کرده- در این زمینه می‌نویسد:

---

[۱۴۷] محمدرضا نیکفر، ذات یک پندار: انتقاد از ذات‌پنداری‌ی اصلاح‌طلبان دینی در نمونه‌ی سروش، ص ۹ از فایل زیر:
http://www.drsoroush.com/PDF/P-CMO-13830000-Zaat_Yek_Pendaar-Nikfar.pdf

[148] Farshad Sadri, ***How Early Muslim Scholars Assimilated Aristotle and Made Iran the intellectual Center of the Islamic World: A Study of Falsafah***, Edwin Mellen Press, 2010

[۱۴۹] محمدحسین صدیق یزدچی، ***فلسفه چیست؟*** فصل‌نامه‌ی «باران»، سوئد: شماره‌ی ۳۰-۳۱، پائیز- زمستان ۱۳۹۰، صص ۱۴۶- ۱۶۵.

> رازی، بنای فلسفه‌ی خویش را نه بر مبنای دو فرهنگ مسلط ، یعنی فرهنگ یونانی و فرهنگ اسلامی، بلکه بر مبنای فلسفه‌های ایرانی و بابلی و هندی بنیان‌گذاری نموده بود.[۱۵۰]

در فهرست آثار رازی از دو کتاب «فی‌النبوات» (در باب پیامبری‌ها) و «فی حیل‌المتنبئین» (در باب نیرنگ‌های پیامبرنماها) نام برده شده، که مخالفان او، اولی را «نقض‌الادیان» (دین‌ستیزی) و دومی را «مخاریق‌الانبیاء» (نیرنگ‌های پیامبران) نامیده‌اند. از این دو کتاب، جز بخش‌هائی که به منظور تمسخر یا ردّیه در کتاب‌های مخالفان او نقل قول شده، اثری به جا نمانده است. اما از همین نقل‌قول‌ها پیداست که رازی، مهم‌ترین گفتمان غالب بر زمانه‌ی خود، یعنی مفهوم «حدوث» جهان را نفی کرده است. اصول پنج‌گانه‌ی متافیزیک رازی که به «قُدمای خمسه» معروف‌اند، عبارت‌اند از: خالق، نفس کلی، ماده‌ی اولیه، مکان مطلق (خلاء)، و زمان مطلق (دهر، یا زمان بی‌کرانه). اصل «ماده‌ی اولیه» («اجزاء ذره‌ای»)، به اتمیست‌های یونان باستان برمی‌گردد، و اصل مطلقیت زمان (در برابر زمان محدود)، به زروان در اوستا. فشرده‌ترین شرحی که از جهان‌شناسی‌ی رازی- استوار بر نظریه‌ی «قدمای خمسه»- در دست دارم، باز از محمدرضا فشاهی است:

> به اعتقاد رازی در میان آن پنج اصل، «خالق» و «نفس کلی»، حی و فاعل هستند. «هیولی اولی»[ماده‌ی نخستین] فاقد حیات و منفعل است و تمام اجسام از آن پدید آمده‌اند. «خلاء» و «دهر» نیز نه حی هستند و نه فاعل. خلاصه این که در جهان چیزی پدید نمی‌آید مگر از چیز دیگر، و محال است که جهان از عدم بوجود آمده باشد. و چون چنین است، لازم است که ماده نیز «قدیم» بوده باشد تا اجسام از آن پدید آمده آیند، و چون ماده به «مکان» احتیاج دارد، پس «مکان» نیز قدیم است. (ارسطوی بغداد، پیشین، ص ۲۶)[۱۵۱]

بدین ترتیب، رازی، بر خلاف نص صریح متون مقدس (تورات و تلمود و قرآن) و بر خلاف روند غالب بر تفکرِ زمانه‌ی خود، جهان هستی را نه «حادث»، بلکه «قدیم» شناسایی می‌کند. و با بها دادن به خرد و شعور انسانی، امور قدسی، مانند وحی و پیامبری، را یکسره نفی می‌کند. از این گذشته، رازی، برای نخستین بار (و نُه سده پیش از آن که در غرب اتفاق افتد)، با نگاهی مستقل، فلسفه‌ی ارسطو را با روش فلسفی به چالش می‌گیرد. با این باورهاست که رازی از دید متکلمان و روحانیان «ملحد» است، و از دید برخی از فیلسوفان متألّه، بی‌سواد و نادان و «فضول». این داستان تکراری، که «رازی در سن ۴۰ سالگی به تحصیل پرداخت» هم احتمالاً از همین فتوای نوع دوم برآمده است. در حالی که اگر سال ۲۵۱ را (از قول ابوریحان بیرونی) به عنوان سال تولد رازی بپذیریم، باید بپذیریم که رازی در حدود ۳۰ سالگی یا کم‌تر، رئیس بیمارستان ری بوده است.[۱۵۲] البته در دوره‌های بعد از رازی، برخی از نویسندگان کوشیدند تا متون فلسفی‌ی طبیعی‌ی

---

[۱۵۰] محمدرضا فشاهی، ***ارسطوی بغداد: از عقل یونانی به وحی‌ی قرآنی (کوششی در آسیب‌شناسی‌ی فلسفه‌ی ایرانی- اسلامی)***، پیشین، ص ۲۵.

[۱۵۱] بخش مربوط به رازی در کتابِ «ارسطوی بغداد» بسیار کوتاه و فشرده است. خواننده‌ی علاقه‌مند به مطالعه‌ی بیش‌تر پیرامون این شخصیت استثنائی را به کتاب‌های زیر رجوع می‌دهم:
* دکتر مهدی محقق، ***شرح حال و آثار رازی***، مقدمه‌ی ترجمه‌ی کتاب «السیرة الفلسفیة رازی»، تهران: انتشارات آموزش انقلاب اسلامی، ۱۳۷۱.
* مهدی محقق، ***فیلسوف ری: محمد بن زکریای رازی***، تهران: انتشارات دانشگاه تهران، ۱۳۴۹.
* پرویز سپیتمان (اذکائی)، ***حکیم رازی: حکمت طبیعی و نظام فلسفی***، تهران: انتشارات طرح نو، ۱۳۸۴.

[۱۵۲] عبدالحسین حائری، استاد فلسفه و پژوهشگر تاریخ فلسفه، پیرامون رساله‌ی رازی در مجموعه‌ی تازه‌یافته‌شده‌ی «داء خفی» می‌نویسد: رازی در این رساله در ضمن سخن درباره‌ی امکان تبدیل جنس زن و مرد و این که بعضی از زنان و مردان تکامل نیافته‌اند، و زنان یا مردان تکامل نیافته نشان‌هایی از جنس مخالف با خود دارند، می گوید: « من خود زنی ریشدار دیدم که از کردستان برای تماشای معتضد آورده بودند.» این گفته‌ی رازی ثابت می کند که او در عهد خلافت معتضد، در بغداد بوده و ما می‌دانیم که معتضد در ۲۷۹ خلیفه شد و در ۲۸۹ هـ. ق درگذشت. نتیجه آن است که رازی در بین سال های ۲۷۹- ۲۸۹ در بغداد بوده و این خود بسیاری از سخنان را درباره‌ی زندگی رازی قابل تردید می‌سازد، به‌خصوص گفته‌ی ابوریحان را که تاریخ تولد او را در ۲۵۱ می داند، و نیز داستان معروف، که آغاز تحصیل او پس از ۴۰ سالگی بوده است .

رازی را کار «دشمنان» او معرفی کنند.[۱۵۳] همچنین، برخی از مفسران اسلامیِ معاصر- مانند مرتضی مطهری- کوشیده‌اند با هزار توجیه، شیعه بودنِ رازی و اعتقاد او به معاد و نبوت و امامت را اثبات کنند و نفیِ رازی نسبت به وحی و پیامبری را نفی کنند،[۱۵٤] یا برخی دیگر- مانند سیدحسین نصر- در پژوهش‌های خود، رازی را «مشمول توطئه‌ی سکوت سازند.»[۱۵۵] پرویز اذکائی، رازی‌شناس و کارشناس «رازی‌شناسی»، در این زمینه می‌نویسد:

> دکتر سیدحسین نصر، استاد علوم و معارف اسلامي و پژوهشگر اندیشمند جهانیِ ایرانِ امروز، که در شناساییِ دین و دانش و حکمت و عرفان مسلمانان به مغرب زمین، مصدر برجسته‌ترین خدمات ممکنه بوده که اکنون نیز چنین باشد. دکتر نصر یك سالی استاد من در رشته‌ی علوم و معارف اسلامی بود، در خصوص ابوریحان بیرونی نوشته‌های او برایم بس گرامی است؛ اما درباره‌ی حکیم رازی بهترین و روشنگرترین نوشته‌ی وی همانا گفتار معروف «از کیمیای جابری تا شیمیِ رازی» است (معارف اسلامی در جهان معاصر، تهران، ۱۳۵۳، ص ۹۵ ــــ ۱۰۱) که در آن، نتایج تحقیقات استادش هانری کُربن را هم بازتاب می‌کند؛ و نیز شرح حال موجز رازی افزون بر گزارش «سنّت کیمیایی»ِی وی که هم چه‌گونه آن را به «شیمیِ نوین» فرارویاند (علم و تمدّن در اسلام، ترجمه احمد آرام، تهران، ۱۳۵۰، ص ۲۹ ــــ ۳۰ و ۲۹۱ ــــ ۳۰٦)، از نمونه‌های والای پژوهش علمی در این موضوع است. لیکن دکتر نصر در کتاب گرانمایه‌ی دیگر خود نظر متفکران اسلامی درباره‌ی طبیعت (تهران، خوارزمی، ۱۳۵۹) که لابد انتظار می‌رفت یا می‌رود از «حکمت طبیعی»ِی رازی هم در جزو متفکّران اخوان الصفا، ابوریحان بیرونی و ابن‌سینا سخن بگوید، به دلایلی دم فرو بسته و [می] توان گفت که رازی را مشمول «توطئه‌ی سکوت» ساخته است. شاید علّت این باشد که استادم دکتر نصر نسبت به حکمت دهری و مادی، به طور اعمّ، و نسبت به دین‌گریزی و پیامبرستیزیِ حکیم رازی به طور اخصّ حساسیّت دارد، و گوئی از این بابت بُغضی در گلوی اوست که این از سیره‌ی حکیمان به دور باشد؛ و گرنه چه سبب دارد که به قول انجیل

ولی به عقیده‌ی این بنده، تنها، بودن رازی در بغداد، در سال های ۲۷۹- ۲۸۹ که مقتضای نوشته‌ی خود اوست در این رساله، نمی‌تواند در مقابل عقاید گوناگونی که درباره‌ی زندگی‌ی وی ابراز شده، راهنمای روشنی برای ما باشد؛ مگر این که بدانیم وی هنگامی که به بغداد رفت در آغاز تحصیل طب نبود بلکه بدان پایه از شهرت در طب نایل آمده بود که به ریاست بیمارستان معتضدی برگزیده شود، و یا اصولاً برای این سمت و یا برای بنای بیمارستان (اگر به گفته‌ی آقای محیط طباطبائی، «عضدی» در نقل ابن ابی اصیبعه را محرّف «معتضدی» بدانیم) دعوت شود . برای اثبات این مطلب نیز سندی معتبر در دست است. ابن ابی اصیبعه و قفطی نقل کرده‌اند که رازی پیش از سفر به بغداد ریاست مارستان [= بیمارستان] ری را داشت. (عیون الانباء ، ج ۱، صص ۳۱۰ ، چاپ اول و تاریخ الحکماء) بنابراین یا باید تولد رازی را از ۲٤۰ نیز زودتر بدانیم و یا معتقد شویم که رازی در کودکی به درس طب پرداخته و حتا در کودکی نبوغ یافته و در آغاز جوانی و شاید در حدود ۳۰ سالگی و یا ۲۵ سالگی به ریاست مارستانِ ری برگزیده شده، و تصور می کنم اشکال احتمال دوم بیش‌تر باشد. زیرا علاوه بر این که نبوغ وی در جوانی نقل نشده، مسلّم است که وی قبل از پرداختن به تحصیل، به برزگری و کیمیاگری و شاید به رشته‌های دیگر پرداخته بوده.» به مأخذ زیر نگاه کنید:

- ❖ استاد عبدالحسین حائری، ***معرفیِ یکی از آثار بازیافته‌ی محمد زکریا رازی و نکته‌ای درباره‌ی زندگیِ او***، تارنمای «دانش و زندگی»، ۱/ ۵/ ۱۳۸٤.

http://www.tebyan.net/index.aspx?pid=12186

[۱۵۳] **از کتاب مرتضی مطهری نقل قول می‌کنم که:** «ابن ابی اصیبعه [نویسنده‌ی سده‌ی هفتم هجری] ضمن این که نسبت چنین کتابی را به رازی انکار می‌کند احتمال می‌دهد که برخی «اشرار» این کتاب را ساخته و از روی دشمنی به رازی نسبت داده باشند و تصریح می‌کند که نام «مخاریق الانبیاء» را دشمنان رازی، نظیر علی بن رضوان مصری به این کتاب داده‌اند نه خود رازی.» و سپس خود مرتضی مطهری می‌افزاید: «از سخن ابن ابی اصیبعه پیدا است که کتاب نبوات و کتاب حیل المتنبئین غیر این کتابی است که این نام به او داده شده است، و **آن دو کتاب وضع روشنی دارد.**» در این جا معلوم نیست منظور مرتضی مطهری از «آن دو کتاب وضع روشنی دارد» چیست؟ کدام دو کتاب وضع روشنی دارند؟ «وضع روشن» کدام است، چیست؟ به مأخذ زیر نگاه کنید:

- ❖ مرتضی مطهری، ***خدمات متقابل اسلام و ایران***، تهران: انتشارات صدرا، چاپ دوازدهم، ۱۳۶۲، صص ۵۳۵.

[۱۵٤] مرتضی مطهری می‌نویسد: «در فهرست کتب رازی ، کتابی «فی النبوات» آمده، که دیگران به طعن و استهزاء نام او را «نقض الادیان» نهاده‌اند و کتاب دیگری به نام «فی حیل المتنبئین" و دیگران به طعن نام او را «مخاریق الانبیاء» گذاشته‌اند. این کتاب‌ها در دست نیست ، ولی متکلمین اسماعیلی از قبیل ابوحاتم رازی و ناصر خسرو (و شاید منقول از ابوحاتم) در کتب خود به نقل قول از رازی مطالبی آورده مبنی بر این که او منکر نبوات بوده است. هر چند ابوحاتم نام رازی را نبرده است و از او با کلمه‌ی «ملحد» یاد کرده است، ولی مسلم است که منظور او محمدبن زکریای رازی است. نظر به این که آن کتب در دست نیست، نمی‌توان اظهار نظر قطعی کرد ، ولی از مجموع قرائن می‌توان بدست آورد که رازی منکر نبوات نبوده و با «متنبئین» (مدعیان دروغی‌ی نبوت) در ستیزه بوده است.» نگاه کنید به:

- ❖ مرتضی مطهری، ***خدمات متقابل اسلام و ایران***، پیشین.

[۱۵۵] دکتر سیدحسین نصر، ***نظر متفکران اسلامی درباره‌ی طبیعت***، تهران: انتشارات خوارزمی، ۱۳۵۹.

«چون است که خس را در چشم برادر خود می‌بینی، اما چوبی که در چشم خود داری نمی‌بینی» (متّی، ۲/۱۰ ـــ ٤) و از کجا که ابوریحان بیرونی در علم طبیعی سرآمدتر از حکیم ری بوده است؟ ولی در نگاه دکتر نصر چون گویا بیرونی طبیعت را «صُنع» اِلاهی می‌دانسته، در حالی که رازی آشکارا اعتقادی به اِبداع و خلق و صنع نداشته، توفان خشم و کینه‌ی استادِ اِلاهی و مینوگرای ما را برانگیخته، بدین‌سان او را در جزو متفکّران طبیعیِ ایران لایق تحقیق ندیده است.[۱۵٦]

اما همین که آثار فلسفی/ کیهان‌شناختی‌ی رازی نابود شده، همین که رازی، در متن دین‌باوران مسلمان (متکلمان، و فیلسوفان متألّه) و حتا روحانیان یهودی (مانند ابن میمون- فیلسوف متألّه‌ی یهودی- قرطبه‌ی اسپانیا- سده‌ی دوازدهم میلادی) تکفیر، یا- دست کم- سرزنش شده، همین که مکان آرامگاه او معلوم نیست، همین که در زمان ما، سیدحسین نصر پیرامون فلسفه‌ی «طبیعی»ی رازی «سکوت» می‌کند، ناموجه بودنِ توجیه‌ها، و بیهودگی‌ی تلاش‌ها در تحریف آراء رازی را نشان می‌دهند. در حالی که کتاب‌های پزشکی و شیمی‌ی رازی از دیرباز مشمول عنایت دانشمندان بوده است. مثلاً، «فرج بن سلیم» (Farragut) سیسیلی، پزشک یهودی، در سال ۱۲۷۹ میلادی، کتاب الحاوی (فی‌الطبّ) رازی را با عنوان Continents به زبان لاتین ترجمه کرد؛ و «آبراهام بن سولومون» (اویگدور A. Avigdor)، خاخام‌زاده‌ی یهودی و پزشک/ مترجم معروف زمانه‌ی خود در فرانسه نیز، بخش‌هایی از آثار پزشکی‌ی رازی و ابن سینا را به زبان لاتین ترجمه کرد.[۱۵۷] اما شگفتا، نخستین کسی که با پژوهش و نشر آثار فلسفی‌ی بازمانده از رازی، او را به عنوان یک «فیلسوف» به جهان معاصر شناساند، «پاول کراوس» (P. Kraus)، نابغه‌ی اتریشی، دانشمند شرق‌شناس یهودی (۱۹۰۲- ۱۹٤٤)، متخصّص در فلسفه و علوم اسلامی بود، که خود به عنوان «بزرگ‌ترین رازی‌شناس» شناسائی شده است.[۱۵۸]

ابوالقاسم فردوسی، در کوران هجوم‌های فراموشی‌ی ملی، برگ‌هائی از تاریخ گذشته‌ی ایران باستان را از این جا و آن جا می‌یابد و ورق می‌زند؛ و در این رهگذر- ضمن این که با نمایش تضادهای سرشت آدمی، از مرزهای فرهنگی‌ی زمان و مکان خود فراتر می‌رود، و ضمن این که به مآخذ خود وفادار می‌ماند- ذات نابخردی را شخصاً به چالش می‌گیرد. در اندیشه‌ی انتقادی‌ی ابوالقاسم فردوسی، یکه‌تازی‌های قدرت (چه دینی و چه سیاسی)، به عنوان دشمن مصلحت همگانی، تبیینی تحلیلی می‌گیرد و با درشت‌ترین نشانه‌های زبانی مردود شناخته می‌شود. سوای ناپرسائی‌ی فردوسی از چه‌گونگی‌ی حذفِ دوره‌ی ۵۰۰ ساله‌ی اشکانیان در منابع ساسانی (که شاید اصولاً از چنین تحریفی خبر نداشته است، و در منابع او به آن اشاره نشده بوده است)، شاهنامه، آکنده است از صدای نقادانه‌ی سراینده‌اش نسبت به شرایط سیاسی و عملکردهای نابخردانه‌ی شخصیت‌های اسطوره‌ای و تاریخی؛ که در گزینش واژگان فردوسی تعیّن یافته است. به عنوان مثال، کافی است به بخش «داستان مزدک و قباد» در شاهنامه نگاه کنیم و همدلی‌ی فردوسی با تز اجتماعی‌ی مزدک را دریابیم. درست در زمانی که تاریخ‌نگارانِ بعد از اسلام، مزدک و افکار او را به سخت‌ترین کیفرها محکوم می‌کردند، فردوسی، مزدک را «بادانش و رأی» و «گران‌مایه» می‌خواند، و با کاربرد صفتِ «نگون‌بخت» در زمان اعدام مزدک، با

---

[۱۵٦] پرویز اذکائی، ***رازی‌شناسی در عصر حاضر***، پایگاه تخصصی‌ی نور، مجله‌ی آیینه‌ی میراث، دوره‌ی جدید، شماره‌ی ۲۲، پائیز ۱۳۸۲، ص ۵۰. برگرفته از تارنمای «بانک اطلاعات اسلامی»:
http://www.islamicdatabank.net/engine/View_article.asp?ID=A65803

[۱۵۷] پرویز اذکائی، ***رازی‌شناسی در عصر حاضر***، پیشین، ص ۳۹:

[۱۵۸] پرویز اذکائی، ***رازی‌شناسی در عصر حاضر***، پیشین، ص ٤۰:
توضیح: همین جا باید- به نقل از پرویز اذکائی در مقاله‌ی یادشده، ص ٤۰- یادآوری کنم که: ت. ج. دی بور (T.J. De Boer) هلندی، استاد فلسفه‌ی دانشگاه آمستردام (۱۸٦٦- ۱۹٤۲)، نخستین دانشمند اروپائی است که اهمیت جوانب فلسفی‌ی رازی را دریافت و در مقاله‌هائی که پیرامون «طب روحانی‌ی رازی» نوشت، بخش‌هائی از کتاب سیرت فلسفی‌ی رازی را بازگو کرد (مجله‌ی فرهنگستان علوم هند، ۱۹۲۰، ص ۱۷۱). این دانشمند، همچنین، در کتاب «تاریخ فلسفه در اسلام» (اشتوتگارت، ۱۹۰۱)- که به انگلیسی (۱۹۰۳) و به عربی (۱۹۳۸) نیز ترجمه شد- در فصل یکم (فلسفه‌ی طبیعی) از باب سوم (فلسفه‌ی فیثاغوری) شرحی جامع از حکمت دهری/ طبیعی/ و اخلاقی‌ی زکریا رازی را فرانمود.

او همدلی می‌کند. فردوسی که در عبرت‌آموزی‌های خود همواره «خردمندی» را شرط می‌داند و مدام از واژه‌ی «خرد» سود می‌جوید، در ندائی که درباره‌ی پایان کار مزدک به خواننده‌اش می‌دهد، نه از واژه‌ی «خرد»، بلکه از واژه‌ی «باهوش» استفاده می‌کند: «**تو گر باهُشی، راه مزدک مگیر**». همدلی‌ی فردوسی با مزدک، نه به خاطر طرفداری از «تاراج»ی است که از سوی تاریخ گزارش شده، و نه از آن روست که الزاماً با نظم جامعه‌ی جمشیدی مخالف است، بلکه به سبب درک روشنی است که از مصلحت همگانی دارد. او در مبحث مزدک، ابتدا به «خشک‌سالی» و فقر مردم اشاره می‌کند، و از زبان مزدک، فقر را برای سلامت جامعه به «زهر» تشبیه می‌کند، و احتکار ثروت را با عبارتِ «در نهفت» (در مصراع «**که جایی که گندم بود در نهفت**») نشان می‌دهد. در مرحله‌ی اجرای تز مزدک، به «گرسنه» بودن تاراج‌گران و انبارهای پر و پیمان محتکران اشاره می‌کند (**دویدند هر کس که بُد گرسنه/ به تاراج گندم شدند از بُنه**)، و سپس، دلیل هراس قدرت از برقراری‌ی عدالت اجتماعی را از زبان خود خسرو انوشیروان چنین باز می‌گوید که اگر همه‌ی مردم با هم برابر باشند، پس چه کسی برای ما «مهتران»، «مزدوری» کند؟

چو مردم سراسر بود در جهان/ نباشند پیدا کهان و مهان/
که باشد که جوید در کهتری/ چه‌گونه توان یافتن مهتری/ [...]/
همه کدخدایند و مزدور کیست/ همه گنج دارند و گنجور کیست[۱۵۹]

در این بافت و ساخت است که اطلاق صفت‌های «با دانش و گرانمایه» به مزدک، و کاربرد واژه‌ی «نگون بخت» در مورد پایان کار او، و مصراع «تو گر باهُشی راه مزدک مگیر» در شاهنامه، رنگ همدلی می‌گیرد. این همدلی، آن هم در رواج مزدکی کشی، نه تنها طغیان علیه نُرم‌های زمانه است، بلکه از خرد سیاسی‌ی فردوسی خبر می‌دهد. بینش سیاسی‌ی فردوسی و اعتقاد او به مصلحت عمومی، و البته در قالب همان نظم جمشیدی، بیش از همه در ارزیابی‌های او از خودکامگی‌های جمشید رخ می‌کند، و مبارزه‌ی او با تصوفِ زندگی‌ستیز، در شرح کناره‌گیری‌ی عارفانه‌ی کیخسرو از سلطنت خود را نشان می‌دهد.

فردوسی، کناره‌گیری‌ی کیخسرو را به زیان مصلحت همگانی برآورد می‌کند، و از زبان مردم و با بیان سپهسالاران دربار، این محبوب‌ترین شاه شاهنامه‌ی خود را به خاطر «ترک دنیا» به باد انتقاد می‌گیرد. فردوسی در زمانه‌ای که بینش عرفانی و باطنی‌گری، در قطب دیگرِ بینش «کلامی»، فضای زمانه را انباشته است، به مأخذ خود وفادار می‌ماند و از زبان «زال»، عرفان و ترک دنیای عارفانه را «راه دیو» می‌خواند، و آشکارا «کیخسرو» را از سلطنت عزل می‌کند:

گر این باشد ای شاه سامان تو/ نگردد کسی گرد فرمان تو
پشیمانی آید ترا زین سخن/ براندیش و فرمان دیوان مکن
و گر نیز جویی چنین راه دیو/ ببُرد ز تو فر کیهان خدیو
بمانی پر از درد و تن پرگناه/ نخوانند از این پس ترا نیز شاه

(به عنوان معترضه، و تا تفاوت فرهنگ و سیاست در دوره‌های «کیانیان» و «ساسانیان» را نشان دهم، همین جا خواننده‌ام را به مقایسه‌ی این صدای مقاوم با صدای مقاوم «دبیر»ی که در بارگاه انوشیروان ساسانی با کوفتن «دوات» بر سرش برای همیشه خاموش شد، فرامی‌خوانم.) طرفه این که فردوسی، درست برخلاف آن چه که در فلسفه‌ی دوران او دیده

---

[۱۵۹] *شاهنامه‌ی فردوسی*، بر اساس چاپ مسکو، به کوشش و زیر نظر دکتر سعید حمیدیان، تهران: نشر قطره، چاپ سوم، ۱۳۷۵، جلد هشتم، ص ۴۸.

می‌شود، بینش اسطوره‌ای را - که هم خاص ژانر حماسه است و هم در متن‌های پیشین و مآخذ او وجود داشته- با اندیشه‌ی عقلی در هم می‌آمیزد. در نتیجه، تقدیرگرایی‌ی اجتناب‌ناپذیر در ژانر «حماسه»، به منظوری که فردوسی از مصلحت همگانی در سیاست مدنی دارد، خدشه‌ای وارد نکرده است.

ادبیات فارسی در زمینه‌ی بینش گیتیانه (و در همان حوالی‌ی زمانی‌ی فردوسی) نام تکستاره‌ی دیگری را هم ثبت کرده است: **«فخرالدین اسعد گرگانی»**، پدید آورنده‌ی «ویس و رامین». البته، به تشخیص پژوهشگران، اصل این اثر متعلق به دوره‌ی اشکانی است. اما، در زمانه‌ای که از سه سو در محاصره‌ی حماسه‌سرایی، عرفان، و شریعت است، گرگانی با انتخاب این اثر برای بازسازی، سوی چهارم را می‌گیرد: سویه‌ای که نقطه‌ی عزیمتِ آن، هم با حماسه‌سرایی‌ی فردگریز در تقابل قرار می‌گیرد، هم با عرفان و تصوفِ تن‌ستیز و هم با شریعت زن‌ستیز. فخرالدین اسعد گرگانی، در عبور از این گذرگاه تنگ، اولاً «ویس»ی می‌آفریند که بر خلاف «گردآفرید» فردوسی، یک «زن» تمام عیار است؛ زنی که هم به جنسیت خود آگاه است، هم به آن وفادار است، و هم بی‌پروای اخلاق حاکم، بر نُرم‌های زن‌ستیز شریعت می‌شورد. ثانیاً، خارج از استانداردهای فردیت‌زدای حماسه و تصوف، «رامین»ی می‌آفریند که با تمام پارادایم‌های «روان‌شناسی»ی هزار سال بعد، قابلیت و ظرفیت ملاقات دارد.

با توجه به تعامل بی‌وقفه میان وجوه تاریخی/ فرهنگی‌ی یک جامعه، این فرزانگان، محصول همان جنبش‌های هستند که درخشش اندیشه‌ی عقلی‌شان ایران سده‌های سوم تا تا پنجم را نورباران کرده است؛ گرچه، پرتو آن درخشش‌ها، در پیوند با بینش دینی/ اسطوره‌ای، یا به ضرب تکفیر، مدام، ساحتِ تاریخ تفکر ما را روشن وُ خاموش می‌کند. داستان تکفیر رازی و فردوسی از سوی قدرت‌های سیاسی و دینی‌ی زمانه، داستان مکرری است، که دامان بیرونی و ابن‌سینا و دیگر متفکران حوزه‌ی فلسفه، و حتا دامان برخی از متکلمان اسلامی (مانند «ابن حزم»)، از متکلمان فرقه‌ی ظاهریه، که نگاهی مساعد به فلسفه و منطق داشت) را نیز می‌گیرد. اما در این میان آن چه شگفت‌انگیز است، تکفیرها و ردیّه‌هایی است که از سوی متفکران حوزه‌ی فلسفه بر اندیشه‌ورزان نوجوی حوزه‌ی فلسفه روا می‌شد. محمدرضا فشاهی شگفتی‌ی خود را به شرح زیر ابراز کرده است:

> آن چه که از دیدگاه تاریخ فلسفه حائز اهمیت است، یعنی غیرقابل درک است، حملات شدید ارسطوئیان و اسماعیلیان، یعنی خردگراترین متفکران جهان اسلام، به متفکرانی نظیر بیرونی و رازی است. [...] پاسخ‌های ابن سینا به ابوریحان بیرونی، یعنی به انتقادات درست بیرونی به ارسطو، چنان خودپسندانه و لجوجانه و بی‌ادبانه است، که خواننده‌ی امروزی دچار حیرت می‌شود. ردّیه‌نویسی بر آثار زکریای رازی، یکی از کارهای روزمره‌ی متفکران جهان اسلام بود. ابن سینا، در پاسخ دوم بیرونی، رازی را «فضول» نامیده است. «ابن میمون»، فیلسوف یهودی، رازی را «بیمار مبتلا به هذیان» نامید. ناصر خسرو، متفکر و متکلم و شاعر نامدار اسماعیلی، او را «هوس‌باز و نادان و غافل و جسور» خواند. و سرانجام، متفکر دیگر اسماعیلی به نام «ابوحاتم رازی»، به زکریای رازی لقب «ملحد» را اعطا نمود. هنگامی که فیلسوفان خردگرا و ارسطوگرا این چنین دست به تکفیر فیلسوفان دیگر بزنند، دیگر چه انتظاری از «محکمه‌ی تفتیش عقاید» می‌توان داشت؟[۱۶۰]

و از همین جمله است برخورد ابومعشر بلخی، منجم بزرگ، نسبت به یعقوب ابن اسحاق الکندی، مترجم و مفسر ارسطو؛ و از همین جمله است برخورد «مطهربن طاهر مقدسی» با اندیشه‌ی علمی‌ی «زکریا رازی»؛ و شگفتا که زیر نام «خِرد».

---

[۱۶۰] محمد رضا فشاهی، ***ارسطوی بغداد: از عقل یونانی به وحی قرآنی (کوششی در آسیب‌شناسی‌ی فلسفه‌ی ایرانی- اسلامی)***، سوئد: نشر باران، ۱۹۹۸، ص ۲۷.

هنگامی که زکریا رازی «خوارق عادتِ» منسوب به «انبیاء» و «مشایخ» را به دلیل مغایرت با عقل رد می‌کند، مقدسی مدعیِ خردگرایی چنین برمی‌آشوبد:

> و بدان که محمدبن زکریا را کتابی است که آن را «مخاریق‌الانبیاء» خوانده و نقل کردن از مطالب آن روا نیست. و هیچ دین‌باوری و صاحب مروتی گوش فرادادن بدان را رخصت نمی‌دهد، چرا که مایه‌ی تباهی‌ی دل و از میان برنده‌ی دین و نابودکننده‌ی مروت است و انگیزنده‌ی خشم بر پیامبران [...] و پیروان ایشان است. و ما آن چه را که در حدود گنجایش خِردمان باشد، بر خِرد خویش تحمیل نمی‌کنیم.[۱۶۱]

می‌بینیم، الگوی تکفیر (یا دست کم، ترور شخصیت) نه تنها از سوی فقیهان و شریعت‌مداران برای اهل فلسفه و عارفان و حتا متکلمان اسلامی به کار می‌رفت، بلکه از سوی خردورزان برای خردورزان دیگر، و از سوی عارفان، برای عارفان فرقه‌ی دیگر کاربرد داشت. کما این که هجویری در «کشف‌المحجوب...» کاربرد این الگو را میان «طبقاتِ» صوفیان/ عارفان، به ویژه بین دو «طبقه»ی معتقد به «سُکر» و «صحو»، نشان داده است.[۱۶۲]

***

تصوف/ عرفان ایرانِ اسلامی: گرچه تعریف، تبارشناسی، و دسته‌بندی‌ی شاخه‌های تصوف ایران اسلامی در این جا موضوع سخن من نیستند، اما با هدف بدست دادن زمینه‌ای از وجوهِ گسترده‌ی عرفان ایرانی/ اسلامی به چند نکته اشاره می‌کنم: «آن ماری شمیل»، اسلام‌شناس آلمانی، در کتاب «ابعاد عرفانی‌ی اسلام»، پیش از آن که خود «تعریف»ی بدست دهد، می‌نویسد:

> پدیده‌ای که معمولاً به نام تصوف خوانده می‌شود، آن چنان گسترده، و ظهور آن به حدی متنوع و رنگارنگ است، که هیچ کس جرأتِ توصیف کامل آن را به خود نمی‌دهد.[۱۶۳]

نظر پژوهشگران و دانشمندان علوم و معارفِ ایرانِ اسلامی – از هجویری گرفته تا علامه قزوینی، صفا، زرین کوب، اقبال آشتیانی، غنی، مرتضوی، آژند، نصر، طباطبائی، خیاوی، تا پطروشفسکی، نیکلسُن، دوزی، آربری، ماسینیون، شمیل، کُربن، براون- پیرامون «تبارشناسی»ی این پدیده نیز- تا جائی که من خوانده‌ام- با هم تفاوت دارد. برخی، سرچشمه‌ی آن را به عروج پیامبر اسلام و خود قرآن رسانده‌اند؛ برخی دیگر، علی، امام اول شیعیان، را حلقه‌ی ارتباط بین تشیع و تصوف و باطنی‌گری دانسته‌اند؛ برخی دیگر آن را «واکنش آریائی علیه عربیت و اسلام و دین اعرابِ سامی» می‌دانند؛ برخی دیگر، ریشه‌های تصوف ایرانی را در عرفان یهود (کابالا) و مسیحیت و فلسفه‌ی نوافلاتونیان یافته‌اند؛ برخی دیگر، ریشه‌های آن را در حکمت خسروانی و زرتشیت و مانی و مزدک شناسائی کرده‌اند؛ برخی دیگر، آمیزه‌ای

---

[۱۶۱] مطهربن طاهر مقدسی، ***آفرینش و تاریخ***، ترجمه‌ی محمدرضا شفیعی کدکنی، جلد اول تا سوم، تهران: انتشارات آگاه، ۱۳۷۴، ص ۴۷۷.

[۱۶۲] علی بن عثمان هجویری (نیمه‌ی دوم سده‌ی پنجم قمری) در کتاب «کشف‌المحجوب»، صوفیان اسلامی را تا پایان سده‌ی چهارم هجری به دوازده «طبقه» تقسیم کرده است. «طیفوریه» (یکی از آن دوازده طبقه) که پیرو راه بایزید بسطامی بوده‌اند، خود را اهل «غلبه» یا «سکر» شناسائی می‌کردند؛ و دیگری، «جنیدیه»، که از پیروان راه جنید بودند، خود را اهل «صحو» یا «هشیاری» می‌دانستند. به گفته‌ی هجویری، جنیدیان می‌گفتند: «سکر بازی‌گاه کودکان است، و صحو فناگاه مردان». نگاه کنید به:

❖ علی بن عثمان بن المهجوری، ***کشف المحجوب***، از روی متن تصحیح شده‌ی والنتین ژوکوفسکی، ویراستار علی‌اصغر عبداللهی، تهران: دنیای کتاب، ۱۳۸۱، ص ۱۷۸.

[۱۶۳] آن ماری شمیل، ***ابعاد عرفانی‌ی اسلام***، ترجمه‌ی دکتر عبدالرحیم گواهی، تهران: دفتر نشر فرهنگ اسلامی، جلد اول، ۱۳۷۴، ص ۳۵. برگرفته از:

❖ روشن خیاوی، ***حروفیه: تاریخ، عقاید و آراء***، تهران: نشر آتیه، ۱۳۷۸، فصل‌های دوم و سوم، ص ۷۸.

از همه یا بخشی از هر یک از این‌ها را در عرفان ایرانی دیده‌اند. با این وصف، با تکیه بر متن‌های صوفیان و عارفان نامدار تاریخ ایران، همه‌ی این شارحان معتبر، در جستارهای خود پذیرفته‌اند که تصوف/عرفان ایرانِ اسلامی، پیوند عمیقی با دین اسلام و قرآن دارد.[۱۶۴] از نظر «گروه‌بندی»، هجویری در کشف‌المحجوب، شاخه‌های عرفان اسلامی تا پایان سده‌ی چهارم قمری را به دوازده «طبقه» تقسیم کرده است، که در میان آن‌ها، طبقه‌های «سُکر» (آن که «در جلال متحیر بود») و «صحو» (آن که در «افعال متفکر بود») بیش‌ترین تقابل را با هم داشته‌اند. «آن ماری شمیل»، اسلام‌شناس آلمانی، (شاید با در نظر گرفتن دو «طبقه»ی «صحو» و «سکر»)، کل عرفان/ تصوف اسلامی را در دو درجه‌ی «اراده‌گرایانه» و «عارفانه» (گنوستیک) دیده است؛ و رینولد نیکلسُن، خاورشناس انگلیسی، «تصوفِ زهد و ورع» را از «تصوف فلسفه و فکر» جدا کرده است. روشن خیاوی، از «آن ماری شمیل» چنین نقل قول می‌کند:

> صوفی‌ی نوع «اراده‌گرایانه» در پیِ آن است که، آن گونه که در حدیث نبوی آمده، «خود را به اوصاف الاهی متصف کند»، و اراده‌ی خویش را کاملاً با خواست و اراده‌ی خداوندی یکی نماید، تا بدین ترتیب با کمال، به معضلات فرضی‌ی حاصل از دوگانگی‌ی فی مابینِ جبر و اختیار فائق آید. این گونه از عرفان و تصوف را می‌توان به مثابه یک فرایند عملی‌ی حیات مورد توجه قرار داد. اما صوفی‌ی معرفت «گنوستیک»، در تلاش دستیابی به معرفتی عمیق‌تر [باطنی] از خداوند است: وی سعی می‌کند تا ساختار عالم مخلوقِ الاهی را شناخته و یا درجه و میزان الهامات و اشراقات را تفسیر کند. [...] در تصوف اسلامی، این هر دو وجه به قوت دیده می‌شوند و در دوران بعد نیز با یکدیگر امتزاج پیدا می‌کنند.[۱۶۵]

روشن خیاوی، از جمله مورخان و شارحان جنبش «حروفیه»، در دنباله‌ی این بازگفت می‌نویسد:

> همین گرایش اراده‌گرایانه است که در برهه‌های مختلفی از زمان، حلاج و مولوی و عین‌القضاة و شهاب‌الدین سهروردی و نعیمی و نسیمی را پرورش داد. (مأخذ پیشین، ص ۷۹)

اما صرف نظر از تعریف، سرچشمه، و دسته‌بندی‌ی دیدگاه‌ها،عرفان ایران، از همان سده‌های نخستینِ بروز (برای زنده کردنِ حکمت خسروانی) تا عرفان اسلامی، در ساحت عمل، سرشتی زایا و جوشنده داشت و در ساحت نظر، سرشتی شورشی. شورش در قلمرو نظر، تلاشی - آگاهانه یا ناخودآگاهانه- بود علیه فکرتِ «تک خدائی»؛ به ویژه که «توحیدِ» اسلامی، با مفاهیم «الله اکبر» و «لااله اله الله»، نه تنها خدای مسلمان را برتر اعلام می‌کرد، بلکه او را تنها خدای برحق می‌شناخت. نشانه‌های این شورش، در عرفان ایران اسلامی، به ویژه شاخه‌ی وحدت وجودی‌ی آن، در نوشته‌های عارفانی مانند منصور حلاج و ابوسعید ابوالخیر و شهاب‌الدین سهروردی و ، و ... به چشم می‌آید؛ که در سده‌های بعد، در سخنان «دیوانه»های عطار نیشابوری، در نوشته‌های «شمس تبریزی»، «**غزل**»های مولانا، فضل‌الله نعیمی، و شعرهای عمادالدین نسیمی متبلور می‌شود. سرشت شورش علیه قطعیت‌های «اصول» و «فروع» دین نیز، حتا در نوشته‌های مذهبی‌ترین متصوفان و عارفان دوره‌ی اسلامی قابل ردیابی است. به عنوان مثال، بارقه‌های طغیان بر آموزه‌های شرعی را در روایت‌های مربوط به بایزید بسطامی، و شگفتا که مرید «امام جعفر صادق»، می‌توان دید:

> چون [بایزید] به شهر آمد، قرصی نان از دکانی بستد و می‌خورد. ماه رمضان بود. خلق چون چنان دیدند، به یکبار

---

[۱۶۴] برای آگاهی از آراء دانشمندان یادشده پیرامون تصوف/ عرفان ایرانی، به مأخذ زیر نگاه کنید:
- روشن خیاوی، ***حروفیه: تاریخ، عقاید و آراء***، پیشین، فصل‌های دوم و سوم، صص ۶۷ تا ۱۱۶.

[۱۶۵] روشن خیاوی، ***حروفیه: تاریخ، عقاید و آراء***، تهران: نشر آتیه، ۱۳۷۹، ص ۷۸.

برمیدند. شیخ با اصحاب گفت: دیدید که مسئله‌ای شرعی را به کار نبستم، همه‌ی خلق مرا رد کردند.[۱۶۶]

این نظریه‌ی شورشی در سده‌های نخستینِ بروز، در قلمرو عمل نیز در تأسیس مدرسه و کتابخانه و ترویج بحث و گفت‌وگو در خانقاه‌ها متبلور شد، که به نوبه‌ی خود، سبب‌ساز نوعی جوشش فرهنگی علیه شریعت‌مداران بود. منتها، عرفان وحدت وجودی‌ی ایرانی/ اسلامی، در رهگذر تلاش برای شکستن قطعیت‌های شرعی، و کلاً برای بریدن بند ناف خود از «احد/ واحدِ» آسمانی، و از «شاه/ مغ/ شهریار/ خلیفه»‌ی زمینی‌ی آن تک‌قدرت - که در هر حال، این دومی، در زمان خود موجودیتی عینی و کارکردهای اجتماعی داشت- زیر تیغه‌ی دولبه‌ی کهن‌الگوهای فرهنگی از یک سو، و تکفیر شریعت‌مداران، از سوی دیگر، به آن «شهریار»‌ی رأی داده بود، که یکسره مجرد، انتزاعی، و ناکجایی بود. و با این بینش بود که **در رهگذر زمان،** نه تنها امکان فهم مشترک را در «راز» خود منحل کرد و «فردگرایی»‌ی بریده از جامعه را پدید آورد، بلکه با تز «فناء فی‌الله»، به نفی‌ی همان«فردِ» بریده هم رسید. بسیاری از پژوهشگران ما (از جمله علی میرفطروس، در کتاب «حلاج»، چاپ چهاردهم ۱۹۹۸؛ و روشن خیاوی، در کتاب «حروفیه»، ۱۳۷۸)[۱۶۷]، از زاویه‌ی انسان‌مداری‌ی رنسانس و مطالبات عصر روشنگری‌ی اروپا (مثل حق و حقوق فردی)، در «اَناالحقِ» حلاج، «انسان‌خدایی» را دیده‌اند. اما از چشم‌انداز عرفان ایرانی- که از یک سو «عالم صغیر» و «عالم کبیر»، یا «کثرت» و «وحدت» را به عنوان دو پدیده‌ی مجزا تلقی می‌کند، و از سوی دیگر «وصل» و انحلال در «عالم کبیر» را هدف نهایی‌ی «عالم صغیر» قرار می‌دهد- «اناالحق»، چیزی جز انحلال «من» در «حق» را متبادر نمی‌کند، و این «حق»، هیچ ربطی با مکانیسم اندیشگی‌ی «انسان‌خدایی» و یا «حق و حقوق فردی» در مدرنیته‌ی غربی نمی‌یابد. چرا که، نوزایی‌ی فرهنگ غربی، دقیقاً بر عرفان مسیحیت شورید، که در «قرون وسطا» هستی‌ی انسان را از زمین بریده بود. اما عرفان اسلامی- حتا در والاترین شاخه‌های شورشی‌ی خود- انسان را نه تنها از اندیشه‌ی عقلی، بلکه از «خودِ» انسان هم برید.

طرفه این که، عرفان در اوج دفاع از اندیشه‌ی شهودی و ستیز با اندیشه‌ی عقلی و استدلالی، خودش از عقل، به عنوان ابزار، سود می‌جوید تا بتواند اندیشه‌ی عقلی را باطل کند و حقانیت اندیشه‌ی شهودی را مستدل دارد. مثال بارز این معرفت شناسی، «مثنوی‌ی معنوی»‌ی مولانا جلال‌الدین محمد بلخی است. از قول علی میرفطروس می‌گویم:

> مولوی با همه‌ی علاقه و احترامش به «اندیشه» (ای برادر! تو همه اندیشه‌ای...)، سرانجام، دنیا را «مردار» و علم و عقل را «آخور»‌ی می‌دانست زیبنده‌ی «اُشتران»: خُرده کاری‌های علم هندسه/ یا نجوم و علم طب و فلسفه/ این‌همه، علمِ بنای آخورست/ که عمادِ بودِ گاو و اُشترست».[۱۶۸]

این دستگاه نظری، با تکیه بر «خودشناسی»، اختیار و مسئولیت فرد را به رسمیت می‌شناسد، و از سوی دیگر، به ضرب و زور همان «راز»، و با **اثبات** خصوصی بودنِ تجربه‌های فردی، راه فهم مشترک را می‌بندد. اما در تحلیل نهایی، این راوی یا گوینده‌ی تمثیل است که به ضرب استدلال‌های سلبی و ایجابی، جهان‌بینی‌ی خود را به مخاطب دیکته می‌کند، و با این انتقال، بر تز خودشناسی از راه تجربه‌های مستقیم (فردیت) خط بطلان می‌کشد. حتا داستان‌هایی مانند «فیل در تاریکی» (که به نظر برخی از تحلیل‌گران، نشان نسبی‌نگری و باور مولانا به تز تکثرگرائی تلقی شده)، از یک سو اهمیت

---

[۱۶۶] عطار نیشابوری، ***تذکرة‌الاولیاء***، تصحیح دکتر محمد استعلامی، تهران: انتشارات زوار، ۱۳۶۰. ص ۱۶۳.

[۱۶۷] روشن خیاوی در کتاب «حروفیه» می‌نویسد: «ما اکنون، یک سال و اندی مانده به پایان قرن بیستم میلادی، دریافته‌ایم که یک مفهوم بیش‌تر برای حق وجود ندارد، و آن «انسان» است. و حتا ترازوی حق و ناحق برای خدا نیز، شأن و شرف انسان است.» به مأخذ زیر نگاه کنید:
❖ روشن خیاوی، ***حروفیه: تاریخ، عقاید و آراء***، پیشین، ص ۸۳.

[۱۶۸] علی میرفطروس، ***وظیفه‌ی روشنفکر فرهنگ سازی است نه سیاست بازی***، گفت‌وگو با نشریه‌ی «نیمروز»، شماره‌ی ۷۸۵، ۱ خرداد ۱۳۸۳/ ۲۱ مه ۲۰۰۴.

ادراک حسی‌ی انسان را به زیر سئوال می‌برد، و از سوی دیگر، جهل «رهرو» را در برابر دانایی‌ی «مرشد» قرار می‌دهد. در واقع، استدلال برای فهم فلسفی‌ی جهان است که در عرفان مردود برشمرده می‌شود، نه استدلال برای پندآموزی‌ی مراد به مرید. با این که مولوی مفهوم «از مقلد تا محقق فرق‌هاست» را بارها و به بیان‌های مختلف تکرار کرده است، اما در دستگاه نظری‌ی «مثنوی‌ی معنوی»، این «مراد» است که جهان را به تمامی و با قطعیت فهمیده است و به حکم «راز»داری، باید که این فهم را از قلمرو شعور عوام (همان «کهتران» و «فرومایگانِ» ایرانِ ساسانی) پنهان دارد؛ مگر این که «عوام»، گوش به آموزه‌هائی که مراد «تحقیق» کرده است، «هفت» مرتبه‌ی کندن از زندگی‌ی زمینی را بپیمایند، و در مرتبه‌ی نهایی، در لحظه‌های تأمل و مراقبه، به طور کامل در خدا مستحیل شود، یعنی «خدا» شود. و این یعنی، نفی‌ی کامل جلوه‌های «انسانی».

به لحاظ نظری، واپسگرایی‌ی عرفان ایرانِ اسلامی در همین خط مشی بروز می‌کند. چرا که از سویی به سبب هستی‌شناسی‌ی ربوبی، از اصل «سیمرغی»‌ی حکمت خسروانی جا می‌ماند، از سوی دیگر، به سبب تجرد محض در بنای «هفت‌مرتبه»‌ی خود، از هفت مرتبه‌ی زمینی‌ی «آیین مهر» واپس می‌ماند، و باز از سوی دیگر، به سبب بریدن کامل از اندیشه‌ی عقلی، حتا، هم از «قانون» زرتشتیِ ساسانی عقب می‌افتد، و هم از «فقه و کلام» اسلامی، که حالا به سوی استیلا بر ذهنیت فرد مسلمان چهارنعل می‌تازد.

البته در سوفیسم یونانی نیز، از سویی، اصل اختیار و مسئولیتِ فرد در «خود»شناسی، با اصل «تغییر مداوم پدیده‌های هستی»، در تقابل قرار می‌گیرد، و از سوی دیگر، در اصل «خصوصی بودن تجربه‌های فردی»، امکان دریافت و ادراک مشترک نفی می‌شود. اما از آن جا که سوفیسم فراتر از انسان و زندگی‌ی زمینی‌ی او نیروی دیگری را به رسمیت نمی‌شناسد، «شناخت» در سوفیسم، منبای ادارک حسی دارد و نه شهودی. این است که با وجود رگه‌های مشترک در جهان‌بینی‌ی سوفیسم و عرفان ایرانی، بین این دو، خط مرزی به فاصله‌ی زمین و آسمان ترسیم می‌شود. تفاوت آشکار در این دو شناخت‌شناسی، بین روش‌شناسی‌ی آن‌ها هم دره‌ای عمیق‌تر ایجاد می‌کند: سوفیسم «می‌پرسد»، و عرفان، در عین حال که جغرافیای راه را «می‌داند» و آن را دیکته می‌کند، نه قادر است بپرسد و نه حتا در مرتبه‌ی هفتم این جغرافیا، قادر است تجربه را به مرتبه‌های پایین منتقل کند. چرا که دانش تجربی‌ی عارفِ رسیده به «اصل» در لحظه‌های مراقبه، اصولاً قابل انتقال به «مفهوم» نیست:

> [دانش حاصل از مراقبه] نه دانشی مجرد و متافیزیکی است، که خدا را علت نخستین هستی می‌گیرد، و نه دانشی برآمده از یزدان‌شناسی، که بر الوهیتی استوار بر داده‌های وحی و مکاشفه گمانه‌زنی می‌کند. دانش حاصل از مراقبه، دانشی شهودی است که ریشه در عشق دارد و به سختی به مقولات ساختگی فرو کاستنی است. عارف، عنصر فوق طبیعی را تجربه می‌کند، ولی قادر به مفهوم سازی از این تجربه نیست. زیرا تجربه‌ای است کاملاً یگانه، که شبیه هیچ یک از تجارب پیشین نیست. و لذا، به دیگری نیز انتقال‌پذیر نیست.[۱۶۹]

جای شگفتی نیست که شناخت‌شناسی‌ی عقلی و متکی بر داده‌های حسی در سوفیسم، عملاً به اصل آزادی و برابری‌ی حقوق سیاسی‌ی انسان برسد، و روش‌شناسی‌ی پُرسای آن، هر فرد را به مثابه «مراد» خودِ آن فرد تلقی کند. و باز جای شگفتی نیست که شناخت‌شناسی‌ی شهودی و نفی کننده‌ی ادراک حسی در عرفان اسلامی، «حقوق سیاسی» که هیچ، حق زندگی‌ی زمینی را از فرد بستاند، و روش‌شناسی‌ی مطبّق آن، از اصل «مراد و مریدی» سر برکند، و به انسجام هر چه

---

[۱۶۹] آنتونیو مونرِو، ***یونگ، خدایان و انسان مدرن***، ترجمه‌ی داریوش مهرجویی، تهران: نشر مرکز، چاپ دوم، ۱۳۸۰، ص ۱۷۲.

بیش‌تر خوی تبعیت در ذهنیت ایرانی بیانجامد. و باز جای شگفتی نیست که «سوفیسم» در یونان، یعنی در سرزمین دیالوگ و خواندن و نوشتن و فلسفه و قانون اساسی و دموکراسی بروید، و عرفان اسلامی، در تمدن تک‌صدای ایرانشهری ببالد، و با ریشه‌ای چنین عمیق از ذهنیت مراد و مریدی، خود را در طول تاریخ بازتولید کند. این گونه است که به قول اکبر سعیدی سیرجانی «در محیطهائی چنین، زمین هرگز خالی از بت نیست: معاویه برود، یزید می‌آید»؛ فقط کافی است که شیوه‌ی فریفتنِ «پیرو» و راه مشروعیت‌یابی را آموخته باشد. با این بازتولید تاریخی، اصلاً جای شگفتی نیست که حدود هزار و دویست سال پس از منصور حلاج، در درون نظام اسلامی‌ی ایران، «جمعیت آل یاسین»، در قالب «مذهب/علم»، به پیامبری و رهبری‌ی معنوی/ سیاسی‌ی جوانی متولد سال ۱۳۵۲، به نام «پیمان فتاحی»، ملقب به لقب‌های «ایلیا میم»، «رام‌الله»، و «آواتار»، از سال ۱۳۷۵ تا سال ۱۳۹۰ خورشیدی، با ده‌ها دفتر و تشکیلاتی عریض و طویل و با داشتن سخنگوی رسمی، ۱۶۰هزار پیرو دست و پا کرده، که «عشق الاهی» و «مغناطیس الاهی» را در رهبرشان می‌بینند؛ «رهبر/ پیامبر»ی که، می‌گوید: «اسرار را به وسیله‌ی فکر و تشخیص نمی‌توان شناخت. اسرار را باید به وسیله‌ی عشق و آگاهی دریافت. اسرار، مربوط به عالم غیب است. عالم غیب که عالم مرئی نیست. فکر و استدلال، وسیله‌ی شناسائی‌ی عالم مرئی (ماده و انرژی) است؛ و حال و شهود، وسیله‌ی کشف ناشناخته‌هاست.»[۱۷۰]

***

با خاموشی‌ی تدریجی‌ی جنبش‌های استقلال‌طلبانه در دوره‌های غزنویان و سلجوقیان، و با گسترش شریعت‌نامه‌نویسی و انسجام فقه و کلام اسلامی، و با اشاعه‌ی فرقه‌های تصوف و عرفان در میان لایه‌های مختلف اجتماعی، ریشه‌های اندیشیدن فلسفی و بینش علمی بی‌آب می‌ماند، و با به خاک افتادن «شهاب‌الدین سهروردی» (که هنوز بارقه‌های فلسفه در عرفان او می‌درخشید)، و با مرگ «خیام نیشابوری»ی شاعر، متفکر و ریاضیدان، به خشکی می‌گراید. «عمر خیام نیشابوری»، ریاضی‌دان، ستاره‌شناس، و شاعر، در دهه‌های آخر سده‌ی پنجم هجری، جامعه‌ی خود را این گونه ترسیم می‌کند:

> ما گرفتار روزگاری هستیم که از اهل علم، فقط عده‌ی کمی، مبتلا به هزاران رنج و محنت، باقی مانده، که پیوسته در اندیشه‌ی آنند که غفلت‌های زمان را فرصت جسته، به تحقیق در علم و استوار کردن آن بپردازند. و بیش‌تر عالم‌نمایان زمان ما حق را جامه‌ی باطل می‌پوشانند و [...] اگر ببینند که کسی جستن حقیقت و برگزیدن راستی را وجهه‌ی همت خود ساخته و در ترک دروغ و خودنمایی و مکر و حیله جهد و سعی دارد، او را خوار می‌شمرند و تمسخر می‌کنند.[۱۷۱]

بازتابِ عملی‌ی این نگرش خردستیز، بر حیات علمی - نه تنها در ایران بلکه در سراسر جهان اسلام- این است که از میانه‌ی سده‌ی دوم هجری تا پایان سده‌ی پنجم، تعداد ۱۰۰ تن دانشمند (که بیش‌تر آن‌ها نیز ایرانی هستند) در قلمروهای ستاره‌شناسی، تاریخ طبیعی، جغرافیا، زیست‌شناسی، شیمی، فیزیک، و ریاضیات در این «جهان» فعالیت داشته‌اند، اما از سده‌ی ششم تا سیزدهم، تعداد ۵۵ نفر.[۱۷۲] بازتاب متقابل اندیشه‌ی علمی، بر سیاست، اجتماع، و فرهنگ، در تصویر کلی‌ی تاریخ، خود را بهتر نشان می‌دهد: تاریخ شش دهه‌ی نخست اسلامی، آکنده است از رویش و جوشش فکر در فرقه‌های گوناگون مذهبی/عرفانی، رویش و جوشش دانش، از ایران تا اندلسِ اسپانیا. و شگفتا که در اوج این رویش و

---

[۱۷۰] برگرفته از جستار:

- رضا پرچی‌زاده، ***جمعیت آل یاسین: فرقه‌ای مذهبی- عرفانی در خرقه‌ی علم***، فصل‌نامه‌ی «باران»، شماره‌ی ۳۰- ۳۱، پائیز- تابستان ۱۳۹۰، صص ۵٦- ٦٦. برای آگاهی‌ی بیش‌تر پیرامون این «جمعیت»، به جستار زیر نیز نگاه کنید:
- رامین احمدی، ***چه کسی از «آل یاسین» می‌ترسد***، تارنمای «گویا نیوز»، ۵ خرداد ۱۳۸۷:

http://www.news.gooya.com/politics/archives/2008/06/072838print.php

[۱۷۱] دکتر سید محمد امین قانعی راد، ***جامعه‌شناسی‌ی رشد و افول علم در ایران*** تهران: انتشارات مدینه، ۱۳۷۹، ص ۵۱۰.

[۱۷۲] دکتر سید محمد امین قانعی راد، ***جامعه‌شناسی‌ی رشد و افول علم در ایران***، پیشین، ص ۵۱٦.

جوششِ «جهان اسلام» بود که «غرب»، این میراث‌خوار فلسفه‌ی یونان، در ژرفای تاریکی و سکوت «قرون وسطایی» به خواب رفته بود- و تنها صدایی که سکوت آن را می‌شکست، صداهای هیولاییِ دادگاه‌ها و شکنجه‌گاه‌های «تفتیش عقاید» بود. و شگفت‌انگیزتر این که در حوالی‌ی بیداری‌ی غرب، با جا افتادن نظام فقاهتی و افزایش «خبر» و «حدیث» برای محکم‌تر کردن پشتوانه‌ی «تکفیر» از یک سو، و با اوجگیری‌ی تفکر «عرفان»‌ی تهی‌شده از جوشش و شورش، از سوی دیگر، صدای هر نوع اندیشه‌ی عقلی در «جهان اسلام» به طور اعم، و در ایران به طور اخص، رو به خاموشی می‌رفت.

در حمله و استیلای مغول، ایرانی، یک بار دیگر خود و تمدن و کتاب‌هایش را در معرض آتش‌سوزی می‌یابد؛ در این مرحله، گرچه موفق می‌شود که مغول را دست کم در محدوده‌ی سرزمین خود، «ایرانی» کند، و، گرچه با بهره‌وری از تمدن‌های زیر سلطه‌ی مغولان و سپس تیموریان، به غنای علم و هنر و صنعت و تجارت خود می‌افزاید، اما یأس ناشی از این شکست، و ناتوانی در برابر موقعیتِ خونبار تاریخی، با بینش اسطوره‌ای/شهودی و کهن‌الگوی تقدیرگرایی در ذهنیت او دست همکاری می‌دهد، تا به خانقاه وُ دِیر وُ زاویه‌ی ده‌های شاخه‌ی عرفان، سلامی پانصد ساله دهد؛ سلامی که، در زمان صفویان شیعی، به ضرب شمشیر به سجده تبدیل می‌شود.

اما صداهایی که در امتداد این سلام وُ سجده، هر یک به گونه‌ای، سلام و سجده را به سود حیات تپنده‌ی اجتماعی موج انداختند، عمدتاً، در قلمرو دینی/شیعی، جنبش «سربداران» بود؛ در قلمرو شیعی/عرفانی، صدای «حروفیه»؛ در قلمرو ادبیات، صدای سعدی، مولوی، و حافظ؛ در قلمرو اندیشه، صدای ملاصدرا از مکتب اصفهان؛ و در قلمرو سیاست، صدای شاه عباس صفوی؛ که این آخری، درست در یکی از خطرناک‌ترین بزنگاه‌های تاریخی برخاست، و ضمن سرکوب هر نوع اندیشه‌ی عقلی، چنان طنینی داشت که استقلال ایران را از دهان گشوده‌ی استعمار اروپایی (پرتقال، هلند، فرانسه، و انگلستان) رهانید. البته این طنین نیز، هم زمزمه‌ای از خردورزی‌ی سیاسی‌ی کوروش و داریوش را به همراه داشت، و هم زمزمه‌ای از قدرت مطلقه‌ی آن‌ها را؛ بدون آن که از مداراگری‌ی مذهبی‌ی شاهان هخامنشی بوئی برده باشد. کما این که افزون بر کشتار هزاران تن از یهودیان و سُنی‌مذهبان ایران، و کوچاندن هزاران هموطن کُرد و ارمنی، جنگ مدام و فرساینده او با دولت عثمانی، در درجه‌ی نخست، جنگ تشیع با سنت بود.[۱۷۳]

جنبش سربداران، با وجود باور ژرف به اسلام شیعی، از آن رو که هم با اشغالگران مغول درافتاد، و هم خاستگاه مردمی داشت، با بدست آوردن گوشه‌ای از قدرت سیاسی‌ی زمان خود، به سرعت میان مردم فرودست جا باز کرد. این جنبش به سبب اختلاف میان سردارانش به زودی محکوم به نابودی شد؛ و در زمان تیموریان جای خود را به «مرعشیان» سپرد، که البته آن‌ها نیز مسلمان شیعه بودند، و آن‌ها نیز به دست تیموریان تار و مار شدند. منتها در همان مدت اندک، با استفاده از آموزه‌های شیعی، علیه ستم اشغالگران تیموری جنگیدند. اگر این جنبش‌ها جنبه‌ی صرفاً مذهبی داشتند و به مکان معینی (مازندران) محدود بودند، جنبش «حروفیه»، هم به مذهب شیعه دست برد، هم اشغالگران را هراساند، و هم تا دوردست‌های شرق و غرب زادگاه خود (باز، مازندران) گسترید.

جنبش «حروفیه»، در میانه‌های سده‌ی هشتم هجری و در زمانه‌ی ستم و رعب و وحشتِ حکومت تیمور گورکانی، و از میان همان تصوف اسلامی، خیز برداشت. فضل‌الله استرآبادی، متخلص به «نعیمی»، رهبر این جنبش، خود از خانواده‌ای شیعی‌ی دوازده امامی بود. اما با شناخت‌شناسی‌ی تقدس رازگونه‌ی صدا و حروف و کلمات و اعداد- وام گرفته از عارفان

---

[۱۷۳] برای دیدن این ویژگی‌ها مراجعه کنید به: راجر سیوری، ***ایران عصر صفوی***، ترجمه‌ی کامبیز عزیزی، تهران: نشر مرکز، چاپ دوازدهم، ۱۳۸۳.

مسلمان و یهودی و مسیحی-[۱۷۴] به قِدَم عالم و قرآن معتقد بود؛ انسان را مظهر مجسم خدا برشمرد؛ و ادعا کرد که معانی‌ی باطنی و حقیقی‌ی حروف و واژگان قرآن را دریافته است، و با ادعای آگاهی بر «غیب‌الغیوب»- از جمله «علم جفر» و «علم سیمیا»- و با تکیه بر اصل تناسخ، خود را ادامه‌ی تسلسل «الوهیت» نامید.

در دانشنامه‌ی اسلامی، پیرامون اعتقادات حروفیان چنین می‌خوانیم:

> درباره‌ی حروفیان و بنیان‌گذار مکتب آنان گزارش‌های ضد و نقیضی به چشم می‌خورد که تمیز درست را از نادرست دشوار می‌کند. مثلاً در پاره‌ای منابع، از تقید سخت آنان به اعتقادات و مبانی اسلام سخن رفته و در پاره‌ای دیگر به انکار اعتقادات دینی و عدم تقید آنان اشاره شده است. [...] آنان متهم‌اند که محرّمات را مباح دانسته و واجبات را ترک گفته‌اند. [... پاره‌ای از منابع] حروفیه را متهم به انکار خدا، یا اعتقاد به خدائی‌ی فضل‌الله حروفی [کرده‌اند][۱۷۵]

در گروهی از منابع، «تقید سخت حروفیه» به مبانی شریعت شیعه، به عنوان «تقیه» شناسائی شده است، و در برخی دیگر، «ترک واجبات» به رهبرانِ پس از نعیمی منتسب شده است.[۱۷۶] اما فرقی نمی‌کند که «مباح دانستن محرمات، و ترک واجبات» از سوی چه شخصیتی در این فرقه عنوان شده باشد. همین که فضل‌الله نعیمی کتاب‌های خود را به زبان گرگانی نوشت (جاودان‌نامه، محبت‌نامه و عرش‌نامه)، همین که قاسم انوار (شاعر طرفدار حروفی) به زبان گیلکی شعر سرود، همین که گفته شده «حروفیان هنگام وضو، اشعاری به زبان فارسی می‌خواندند» (دانشنامه‌ی اسلامی)، همین که تفکر حروفی در مدتی حدود نیم سده، از استراباد (مازندران) به شمال خراسان بزرگ و اصفهان و آذربایجان تا سوریه و آناتولی و حتا منطقه‌ی بالکان در اروپا میان مردمِ- اکثراً فرودست- نفوذ کرد، و همین که «علما»ی اسلام در ایران و مصر و عثمانی با فتوای کشتار و سوزاندن حروفیان، به برکندن بنیاد این اندیشه عزم جزم کرده بودند، نشان می‌دهد که جنبش حروفیه، یک جنبش اجتماعی بود، که یک‌جا، با نظام غارتگر دین/دولت (در ایران: نظام اشغالگر تیموری/ شریعتمداران زمانه) درافتاده بود. احسان طبری در پژوهشی پیرامون جنبش حروفیه می‌نویسد:

> در «مزارات تبریز» در باره‌ی فرقه‌ی حروفیه آمده است :«این طبقه، مشهور به اباحت و تزندق‌اند و در آن زمان با پادشاه خیلی اختلاط داشته‌اند. مردم به این قوم بسیار گرویده بودند. آخر علماء هجوم کرده، فتواها نوشتند که شرعاً خون این قوم را باید ریخت و **اگر پادشاه احتمال کند دفع پادشاه نیز فرض است.**[۱۷۷] مولانا نجم الدین اسکوئی که از گزیده‌ی علماست در نوشتن فتوا به قتل این جماعت، ملاحظه نموده، [فتوا] ندا. پادشاه معتقد به فتوای وی بود. گویند در آن زمان مجذوبی بود در کوه سرخاب که هرگز به شهر عبور نمی‌کرد. در خلال این حال روزی مجذوب در کمال حدّت به شهر آمد و به خانه‌ی مولانا نجم الدین رفت و از روی عتاب تمام گفت که حضرت رسالت پناهی (صلعم) امشب به واقعه‌ی [خوابِ] من آمد و

---

[۱۷۴] احسان طبری با استفاده از منابع متعدد، اندیشه‌ی حروفی و «علوم» سری و رازآمیز در تاریخ را از فلسفه‌ی فیثاغورس، متن‌های زبان پهلوی، کابالای توراتی، اسماعیلیان، «علم جفر» در اسلام، تا صوفیان وحدت وجودی، ریشه‌یابی کرده است:

❖ احسان طبری، ***درباره‌ی جنبش حروفیه (افکار و حوادث)***، تارنمای «احسان طبری»، بازدید ۲۰ سپتامبر ۲۰۱۱:
http://tabari-ehsan.blogfa.com/post-43.aspx

[۱۷۵] «دانشنامه‌ی اسلامی»، بازدید: ۱۷ دسامبر ۲۰۱۱:
http://www.encyclopaediaislamica.com/madkhal2.php?sid=6046

[۱۷۶] در دانشنامه‌ی اسلامی می‌خوانیم: «پس از قتل فضل‌الله به فرمان تیمور، بنا به وصیت فضل‌الله هوادارانش به اطراف و اکناف پراکنده شدند و پنهانی به نشر افکار حروفی‌گری پرداختند»:
http://www.encyclopaediaislamica.com/madkhal2.php?sid=6046

[۱۷۷] روشن خیاوی در کتاب «حروفیه» (۱۳۷۹- ص ۱۸۷)، به نقل از «مجله‌ی دانشکده‌ی ادبیات تهران، سال ۲، شماره‌ی ۲» واژه‌ی «احتمال» در متن طبری را به صورت «اهمال» ثبت کرده است.

فرمود که برو به نجم الدین بگو که حکم به قتل این جماعت کن که این‌ها مخرب دین‌اند. چون مولانا این سخن بشنید گریه بسیار کرد و حکم قتل فرمود. گویند قریب به پانصد کس کشتند و سوختند. و اهل حقیقت بر این‌اند که در فضل‌الله نعیمی فتوری نبود و در کمال تزهّد بود و نان کسی نمی‌خورد و به طاقیه‌دوزی اوقات می‌گذرانید.»[۱۷۸]

احسان طبری در ادامه‌ی بازگفتِ بالا می‌نویسد:

از این شرح جالب در «مزارت تبریز» چند چیز فهمیده می‌شود :۱- حروفیه (مانند زمان کوات ساسانی که به مزدکیان رابطه‌ی نزدیك داشت) با میرانشاه [گورکانی] روابط نزدیك داشتند. شاید میرانشاه می‌خواسته است از آن‌ها برای تضعیف روحانیت، چنان که شیوه‌ی متداول در ایران بوده است، استفاده کند. ۲- مانند همان دوران که مؤبدان اعمال فشار کردند، این بار نیز علماء جنجال برداشتند و پیروان مردی را که از راه طاقیه (کلاه)دوزی ارتزاق می‌کرد و به زهد و ورع معروف و تمام عمر در شروان زیسته، در شهر هرات به «اباحه» و «زندقه» و «اعتقاد به تناسخ» منسوب و یا متهم کردند؛ یعنی تقریباً همان اتهامات دوران مزدک را تکرار کردند. (پرانتزها از متن طبری است و قلاب از من.)

روشن خیاوی، که مفهوم «أناالحق» را از دیدگاه جامعه‌شناسی‌ی «حقوق» و «انسان‌مداری»ی عصر مدرنیته بررسی کرده، جنبش حروفیه را ادامه‌ی راهِ حسین بن منصور حلاج و «تعهدِ» انسانی/ اجتماعی‌ی او برآورد می‌کند و می‌نویسد:

آغاز جنبش حروفیه، آغاز توجه تاریخ ایران به این مسئولیت بوده؛ مسئولیتی که می‌توان آن را با شعاع جهانی مورد نظر و توجه قرار داد. سخن «اناالحق» از زبان اندیشمند سوخته‌دلِ جان‌نثار، حلاج، بیرون آمد، و او با این سخنش صلا در داد که ای انسان‌ها! حق منم، حق تو هستی، حق اوست، حق همه‌ی ما هستیم؛ حق انسان‌هاست! و انسان‌ها حق هستند. و این فریاد جهان‌شمول حلاج را چهار صد سال بعد، گوش نعیمی و نسیمی به جان شنید. یعنی چهار صد سال طول کشید تا گوش جامعه به آن حساسیتی برسد تا ندا و پیام حلاج را بشنود.[۱۷۹]

علی میرفطروس، ضمن جدا کردن گروه‌های مختلف در درون فرقه‌ی حروفیه، بر وجه اومانیستی‌ی فلسفه‌ی فضل‌الله نعیمی، و بر وجوه سیاسی‌ی جنبش حروفیه تکیه می‌کند؛ آن را «آئینی نو» می‌نامد؛ و معتقد است که حروفیه، «ختم دین محمدی را اعلام کرد.»[۱۸۰] میرفطروس در متن دیگری، حتا «آته‌ایسم» را در زوایای آموزه‌های حروفیه دیده است. من این متن اخیر را ندیده‌ام. اما روشن خیاوی در این زمینه نوشته است:

حروفیه، انسان را جامع کمالات و در واقع وجودی کامل و جامع می‌دانند، و ضرورتاً سمبل یا نمونه‌ای نیز برای انسان کامل ارائه می‌دهند، که همانا «فضل‌الله نعیمی» است. خود نعیمی، در اشعار زیادی از خود به عنوان «خدا» یا «خدای مجسم» یاد می‌کند. اما می‌توان تصور کرد که منظور او همانا «انسان کامل» یا «انسان‌خدائی‌ی حلاج» است. [...] تعالیم حروفی در رابطه با انسان به آن جا کشیده که بعضی از محققین [مانند علی میرفطروس]، باورهای «آته‌ایستی» را در

---

[۱۷۸] احسان طبری، ***درباره‌ی جنبش حروفیه (افکار و حوادث)***، پیشین.

[۱۷۹] روشن خیاوی، ***حروفیه: تاریخ، عقاید و آراء***، پیشین، ص ۸۱.

[۱۸۰] علی میرفطروس، ***جنبش حروفیّه: بررسی‌ی منابع و مآخذ و تحقیقات جدید (۱)***، فصل‌نامه‌ی «ایران‌شناسی»، سال ششم، شماره‌ی ۳، پائیز ۱۳۷۳، ص ۵۸٤.

لابه‌لای این تعالیم سـراغ گرفته‌اند. با این توضیح که «هر چند به خاطر شرایط خاص مذهبی/سیاسی، به مضامین و اصطلاحات عرفانی آمیخته است»، اما مطالعه‌ی دقیق این آثار، عقاید «آته‌ایستی»ی حروفیه را نشان می‌دهد.[۱۸۱]

ذبیح‌الله صفا، در شرح عقاید صوفیان می‌نویسد: «هر کس بخواهد مبانی‌ی اعتقادهای صوفیان ایران اسلامی را از دایره‌ی شرع بیرون بَرد و درباره‌ی بعضی از کارهای آنان دست به تأویل‌ها و توجیه‌های ادعائی بزند، دچار اشتباه شده است.»[۱۸۲] با این وصف، با خواندن متن‌های مربوط به «حروفیه»ی منسوب به نعیمی، ناگزیریم بپذیریم که این جنبش از «دایره‌ی شرع بیرون» رفت، به مبانی‌ی شریعت فقها دستبرد زد، و برای مدتی خواب دین/ دولتِ زمان و مکان خود را برآشفت. کما این که درافتادنِ حروفیان با فقهای زمانه، از این تک بیتِ قاسم انوار (شاعر هوادار حروفیه) پیداست:

هر چه که گویم، فقیه گوید:«هی هی!»/
هر چه که گوید فقیه، گویم:«هیهات!»[۱۸۳]

حتا اگر تحلیل طبقاتی‌ی احسان طبری را نپذیریم، یا اگر تحلیل‌های حقوقی/انسان‌مدارانه‌ی میرفطروس و خیاوی را نپذیریم، با خواندن متونِ نظری‌ی «فرقه‌ی حروفیه» (مثلاً با تکیه بر برابری‌ی انسان‌ها)، و با خواندن متون مربوط به خیزش و خاموشی‌ی آن، و با توجه به سرگذشت دردناک نعیمی و نسیمی و هواداران آن‌ها، نمی‌توانیم بر سرشت شورشی/جنبشی‌ی آن (نسبت به «دین/ دولتِ» زمانه‌اش) دیده‌پوشی کنیم. اما در عین حال، با توجه به افکار و آرائی که پژوهشگران و تحلیل‌گران (نه دشمنان شریعت‌مدار) به نعیمی و کلاً به «حروفیه» نسبت داده‌اند، دو واقعیت را نیز نمی‌توان نادیده گرفت:

یک) جنبش حروفی- ضمن دست بردن به کیفیتِ ظهور «امام زمان» در شیعه‌ی دوازده امامی- با قرائت باطنی از متن‌های مقدس اسلام، جای اندیشه‌ی عقلی را در ژرفای ذهنیت جامعه به «سحر» و «جادو» و «اوراد مقدس» و خرافات سپرد. به بیانی دیگر، کیهان‌شناسی و فکرت‌های فلسفی‌ی فضل‌الله نعیمی و پیروان نخبه‌ی او هر چه که بود، به هواداران عام او (یعنی مردم عادی، که از فهم و درک راز و رمز نهفته در «حرف» و «کلمه» ناتوان بودند)، چندان مربوط نمی‌شود. چرا که، بنا بر قرائن، پیروان عامِ این جهان‌بینی، اکثراً از پیشه‌وران خرده‌پای شهرها بودند، و طبیعتاً- مانند بسیاری از پیروان عام فرقه‌های دیگر صوفی- از این آموزه‌های فلسفی چیزی نمی‌فهمیدند؛ در نتیجه، به سحر و جادو و طلسم رسیدند، و از خرافات، و اندیشه‌های غیرعقلانی نیز سر برکردند. ذبیح‌الله صفا بدون این که از «حروفیه» سخنی به میان آورد، به نقل از کتاب «نفایس‌الفنون فی عرائیس‌العیون» نوشته‌ی شمس‌الدین محمد آملی (دانشمند قرن هشتم هجری و همزمان با جنبش حروفیه) می‌نویسد:

> صوفیان برای هر حرف از حروف هجا معنائی و خواصی قائل‌اند. مثلاً [...] هر کس به وقت طلوع آفتاب و در وقت گرما هر اسمی را از اسمای حق که اول او «ح» باشد- همچو یا حی یا حکیم یا حنان یا حلیم- بخواند، گرما بر او اثر نکند. و آن چه ارباب احوال بر سر آتش نشینند و روند و بدان بازی کنند، در ایشان اثر نکند، هم به واسطه‌ی این معنی است.[۱۸۴]

---

[۱۸۱] روشن خیاوی، ***حروفیه: تاریخ، عقاید و آراء***، پیشین، صص ۱۹۶ تا ۱۹۷. **توضیح:** روشن خیاوی بازگفت مربوط به علی میرفطروس را از مأخذ زیر برگرفته است:

- علی میرفطروس، ***جنبش حروفیه و نهضت پسیخانیان (نقطویه)***، ناشر: بامداد، بی‌تاریخ.

[۱۸۲] ذبیح‌الله صفا، ***تاریخ ادبیات در ایران***، پیشین، زیرنویس ص ۱۷۹.

[۱۸۳] برگرفته از: احسان طبری، ***درباره‌ی جنبش حروفیه (افکار و حوادث)***، پیشین.

[۱۸۴] ذبیح‌الله صفا، ***تاریخ ادبیات در ایران***، جلد سوم، بخش اول، تهران: چاپ ششم، انتشارات فردوس، ۱۳۶۸، صص ۱۸۲ تا ۱۸۳.

دو) حروفیه از یک سو، با تأکید بر مفهوم «انسان کامل» و گنجاندن «فضل‌الله نعیمی» در این مفهوم، به جاذبه‌ی کهن‌الگوی «مراد» و «مرشد» و «پیر» در ذهنیت ایرانی نیرو بخشید، و از سوی دیگر، با تکیه‌ی مدام بر آیات قرآن، مفهوم «مهدویت»، و «علم جفر»،[۱۸۵] به عنوان مؤثری برای ادامه‌ی فکرت دینی/شیعی عمل کرد. روشن خیاوی، در دنباله‌ی توضیح پیرامون مفهوم «اراده‌گرایانه» در عرفان ایران، و پس از گنجاندن نعیمی و نسیمی در کنار حلاج و سهروردی (به عنوان عمل‌گرایانی که «برای پیاده کردن دیدگاهاشان به فکر بدست گرفتن قدرت سیاسی‌ی جامعه بودند»)، می‌نویسد:

> به جرأت می‌توانم بگویم که حتا نهضت حروفیه در شکلی خاص، تقریباً بعد از سده‌ای، به شکل حکومت صفویان در جریان تاریخ ظهور کرد. بررسی‌ی اشعار شاه اسماعیل صفوی (با تخلص خطائی)، که در بین فدائیان خود، یعنی قزل‌باش‌ها، لقب «مرشد کامل» یا «مرشد اعظم» را داشت، نشان می‌دهد که شاه اسماعیل خطائی، کاملاً با اندیشه‌های نعیمی و نسیمی، یعنی رهبران نهضت حروفیه آشنائی داشته است. (روشن خیاوی، پیشین، ص ۷۹.)

البته، همین جا باید یادآور شد که آشنائی با فکرت حروفی و باطنی‌گری منحصر به «شاه اسماعیل» نبود. بنیادگذار «طریقت صفوی»، و جانشینان او، مدت‌ها پیش از جنبش نعیمی، یعنی به مدت دویست سال پیش از به دست آوردن قدرت سیاسی، خود را مرشد کامل و صاحب کرامات معرفی می‌کردند؛ صاحب ملک و آبادی و خدم و حشم فراوان بودند؛ در دوره‌ی مغولان و تیموریان از پرداخت مالیات معاف بودند؛ و در بارگاه‌های عظیمی که توسط مریدان برای آن‌ها ساخته می‌شد، به ضرب فکرت «الوهیت»- و به عکس زندگی‌ی ساده‌ی نعیمی و نسیمی- از دسترنج زحمتکشان در ناز و نعمت روزگار می‌گذراندند. «راجر سِیوُری Roger Savory»، ایران‌شناس انگلیسی و کارشناس تاریخ صفویه، پیش از نقل سه خط از شعرهای شاه اسماعیل- مبنی بر ادعای خدائی‌ی او- در این زمینه می‌نویسد:

> هیچ شکی نیست که طی‌ی نیمه‌ی آخر قرن نهم (پانزدهم میلادی)، قبل از برقراری‌ی دولت صفویه، رهبر صفویه- در تبلیغات این طریقت- صرفاً نماینده‌ی امام غایب نبود. بلکه خود امام غایب بود؛ حتا رهبر صفویه را تا آن جا می‌رساندند که ادعا می‌کردند خداوند در او حلول کرده است. ادعا شده است که مریدان جنید آشکارا از وی به عنوان «خدا» و از پسرش به عنوان «پسر خدا» یاد می‌کردند. [...] مضمون اشعار خود اسماعیل گواه مسلمی است که او تمایل داشته پیروانش او را وجودی الاهی بدانند.[۱۸۶]

در قلمرو شعر، حضور صدای زمینی، سیاستمدرانه، و حتا ماکیاولیستی‌ی سعدی، در سده‌ی هفتم هجری، چندان شگفت‌انگیز نیست؛ چرا که از یک سو هنوز با جوش و خروش اندیشه‌های فلسفی و علوم عقلی در سده‌های پیشین پیوند دارد، و از سوی دیگر، صدای مستبد قرون و اعصاری را به نفع قدرت و حفظ قدرت منتشر می‌کند. سعدی به «قدرت»، درس عدالت می‌دهد که: «برو پاس درویش محتاج دار/ که شاه از رعیت بود تاجدار»، اما «درویش محتاجِ» سعدی، تسلیم و فرمانبردار بی‌چون و چرای «تاجدار» است: «مهتری در قبول فرمان است/ ترک فرمان دلیل حرمان است/ هر که سیمای راستان دارد/ سر خدمت بر آستان دارد»؛ یا: «خدا را ندانست و طاعت نکرد/ که بر بخت و روزی

---

[۱۸۵] به روایت احسان طبری: «علمِ» طلسم آمیز جفر را- بنا به روایت حاملان و مصنفان این علم- پیمبر بر پوست بزغاله‌ای نگاشت و به علی سپرد؛ و هم از این جهت جفر نام گرفت؛ زیرا در عربی به بزغاله «جفر» می‌گویند:
❖ احسان طبری، ***درباره‌ی جنبش حروفیه (افکار و حوادث)***، پیشین.

[۱۸۶] راجر سیوری، ***ایران عصر صفوی***، ترجمه‌ی کامبیز عزیزی، تهران: نشر مرکز، چاپ دوازدهم، ۱۳۸۳، صص ۲۱ تا ۲۲.

قناعت نکرد»؛ یا: «چو نتوان بر افلاک دست آختن/ ضروری‌ست با گردشش ساختن». پادافره‌ی سعدی به فرد شورشی و نافرمان، همیشه و همواره تا امروز دستورالعمل قدرت‌مداران بوده است:

اولین باب تربیت پند است/ دومین، نوبه‌خانه و بند است
سومین، توبه وُ پشیمانی/ چارمین، شرط وُ عهد وُ سوگند است
پنجمین، گردنش بزن که خبیث/ به قضای بد آرزومند است[۱۸۷]

اما شاید از شگفتی‌های بی‌پاسخ تاریخ باشد که صدای مولوی عارف در «غزل»هایش بتواند از «مثنوی معنوی»ی او تجاوز کند، بر «یاحق و یاهو»ی آن بر بخش زندگی‌گریز عرفان خط بیاندازد، و موجی از شور هستی را در لم‌یزرع زمانه برویاند. مولوی در غزل‌هایش، آشکارا، صدای تعلیمی در «مثنوی معنوی» را وامی‌گذارد، به عنصر دیالکتیکی عرفان میدان می‌دهد، و با به‌هم زدن «بَرّ وُ بحر» ذهنی و زمین وُ آسمان عینی، و دوختن شرق وُ غرب وُ سفید وُ سیاه عالم به یکدیگر، جوششی را به عرفان بازمی‌گرداند که با جنبه‌ی شورشی‌ی نخستینِ عرفان ایرانی همخانواده است، و بر هر گونه خشک‌اندیشی‌ی خواب‌آلود (حتا بر «مثنوی معنوی»ی خود مولانا) خط می‌اندازد. منتها این بینش هم نهایتاً سرشتی سلسله مراتبی و تعلیمی دارد و دامنه‌ی هِرَم را از جست‌وجو و پرسش بازمی‌دارد.

حافظ، باوجود بارقه‌های تند عرفانی در شعرش، با قرار دادن مخاطب بر باریکه‌ی میان«هست» یا «نیست»، به ساختارهای ذهنی‌ی جزم‌گرایانه دست می‌برد. البته، همان‌طور که قبلاً هم اشاره کردم، شکستن جزم‌های شریعت، از همان آغاز، در سرشت عرفان ایران اسلامی حضوری انکارناپذیر داشت. منتها، همان «شک» هم، همواره از سوی مراد به مرید دیکته می‌شد. مثلاً زمانی که ابوالحسن خرقانی می‌گوید: «اسرار ازل را نه تو دانی و نه من»، در درجه‌ی نخست، به اصل «حدوث عالم» در اسلام، و «قِدَم عالم» در شاخه‌های فلسفه‌ی اسلامی، شک کرده است. منتها، این شک را به عنوان یک گزاره‌ی ایقانی و در دایره‌ای بسته به مخاطب خود القاء می‌کند. اما حافظ، از نشانه‌های زبانی، سیستم معنایی خود را می‌آفریند، و در این رهگذر، دو سوی زنجیره‌ی گفتمان تحلیلی را باز می‌گذارد؛ به یاری‌ی شگردهای وارونه‌گویی، شک شخصی را جایی بین نفی و اثبات در درون شعر معلق نگه می‌دارد، و به یاری نظام نشانه‌شناختی‌ی خود، شکی مضاعف را به بیرون شعر منتقل می‌کند. این است که مخاطب حافظ، نه تنها مداوماً با این پرسش روبه‌روست که «منظور حافظ این است یا آن»، بلکه با این پرسش‌ها هم در کلنجار است که: گیرم منظور حافظ در فلان بیت، «این» یا «آن» باشد، اما آیا خودش به «این» باور دارد یا به «آن»؟ چرا که در فلان بیت دیگر، «آن» وُ «این» حافظ جایگاه‌های متفاوتی دارند. این تعلیق از آن رو پیش آمده که سیستم نشانه‌های شخصی‌ی حافظ با سیستم نشانه‌های زبان متعارف، در ذهن مخاطب مدام به هم می‌پیوندند و مدام از هم می‌گریزند. اشاره‌های صریح حافظ به مفاهیم قرآن، در کنار کاربرد مفاهیم عرفانی، چنان در سیستم نشانه‌شناسی‌ی این شاعرِ همه‌ی اعصار دویده، که نمی‌گذارد بدانیم که این معشوقی که او، مثلاً در بیتِ «**معشوق چون نقاب ز رخ برنمی‌کشد/ هر کس حکایتی به تصور چرا کنند؟**» به ما نشان می‌دهد، آیا «خدا»ی یزدان‌شناختی است، یا همان «اصل» است که در شناخت شهودی باید به آن «وصل» شد، یا همانا «حقیقت» مورد جست‌وجوی خود حافظ است، که هر آن در منظر او چهره‌ای دیگر می‌نمایاند. با این معرفت‌شناسی‌ی روشمندانه است که شعر حافظ، ضمن بخشیدن لذتِ پایان‌ناپذیرِ زیبایی‌شناختی، طعم سهمگین/شیرینِ شک‌گرایی‌ی هرگز نداشته را به ایرانی می‌چشاند.

در قلمرو فلسفه، مکتب فلسفی‌ی اصفهان، صدای اندیشه‌ی عقلی را یک بار دیگر در فضای ذهنی‌ی ایران پژواک می‌دهد.

---

[۱۸۷] برگرفته از شیرین بیانی، استاد و پژوهشگر تاریخ: «شمس‌الدین از سعدی در مورد مجازات مجدالملک یزدی سئوال کرد و سعدی با این سه بیت پاسخ گفت.» نگاه کنید به: شیرین بیانی، ***دین و دولت در ایران در عهد مغول***، تهران: مرکز نشر دانشگاهی، ۱۳۶۷.

ستاره‌ی این مکتب، یعنی ملاصدرا، با این که عناصر فلسفه‌ی یونان را با عناصر کلامی و اشراقی و قرآنی می‌آمیزد، و با این که تز «حرکت جوهری»ی خود را در رابطه‌ی مستقیم با قرآن می‌نویسد و در خدمت الاهیات شیعی قرار می‌دهد، هنوز پرتوی از اندیشه‌ی عقلی را بازتاب می‌دهد. این صدا، با همه‌ی باری که از مذهب شیعه دارد، از سوی «شاه/مغ» زمانه (همان شاه عباس سیاستمدار) تبعید می‌شود. اما این صدا، در فضای فرهنگی‌ی ایران می‌ماند، تا در جنبش‌های بعدی (عمدتاً، جنبش‌های شیخیه و باب، و در هر یک به گونه‌ای) پژواک یابد. البته فکر و سخن در جنبش‌های یادشده، ضمن این که از سوی الاهیات به سوی الاهیات در حرکت است، اما مونولوگ ملاصدرا را به دیالوگ نزدیک می‌کند، و در کنار آشنایی‌ی ایرانی با حرکت‌های فکری و اجتماعی‌ی غرب، زمینه را برای «نقد» ایرانی فراهم می‌آورد، که بازتاب عملی‌ی آن در اجتماع و سیاست، همانا جنبش مشروطیت است.

در این حوالی‌ی زمانی بود که آمیزه‌ای از کهن‌الگوهای بینش اسطوره‌ای و جهان‌بینی‌ی «شهریار الهی» ، و حس عظمت‌خواهی و میل درونی به حفظ هویت ملی، یک بار دیگر، از زیر خاکستر قرون به درآمد. یعنی: آمیزه‌ای از ناتوانی در اندیشه‌ی عقلی، دین‌خویی، تعبدخواهی از فرودست و تعبدگرایی نسبت به فرادست، تک‌روی، تک‌صدایی، و نامداراگری، از یک سو، و میل به سازندگی و لزوم عبور از این بینش سنتی از سوی دیگر، در ذهنیت ایرانی سربرداشت، تا در جنبش‌های فکری‌ی دوره‌ی مشروطیت، در مکانیسم جنبش مشروطیت، در فهم وُ درک وُ پذیرش وُ کاربست ما از عناصر «مدرنیته»، در نهضت‌های چپ‌گرای ما، در جنبش‌های فکری‌ی حوالی‌ی انقلاب ۱۳۵۷، در انقلاب سال ۱۳۵۷، در مبارزه‌ی اپوزیسیون کنونی‌ی ما علیه رژیم اسلامی، در «جنبش اصلاحات» سال ۱۳۷۶ و در «جنبش سبز» سال ۱۳۸۸ در درون‌مرزهای ایران، و بالأخره، در فهم و درک و پذیرش و کاربست ما از عناصر «پست مدرن»، اعلام حضور کند.

خواننده‌ی متن حاضر، با مرور این تصویر ذهنی حق دارد بپرسد: آیا این تصویر، بن‌بستی ابدی را القا می‌کند؟ به دیگر سخن، آیا فرهنگ ایران در چرخه‌ای بدون روزنِ فرار از کهن‌الگوها گرفتار است؟

از آن جا که این پرسش با هدف نوشته‌ی حاضر پیوند دارد، همین جا می‌گویم که در قانون طبیعی‌ی تکامل، «بن‌بست ابدی»، حتا برای موجود تک‌یاخته‌ای مردود است. حتا شناخت‌شناسی‌های توراتی و قرآنی و عرفانی (نه هستی‌شناختی‌ی آن‌ها) هم بر بن‌بست ابدی و ایستایی‌ی هیچ باشنده‌ای صحه نمی‌گذارند، چه رسد به باشنده‌ی تپنده‌ای که در طول تاریخ، برای «تصلب شرائین» خود، مداوماً، مداوایی پیدا کرده است. همه‌ی پژوهشگران ما، که در دو سده‌ی گذشته بن بست‌ها را دیده‌اند، حتا مأیوس‌ترین آن‌ها (که به نظر می‌رسد «آرامش دوستدار» باشد)، با اجرای عمل «پژوهش»، آگاهانه یا ناخودآگاهانه به «ابدی» بودن «بن‌بست» پاسخ منفی داده‌اند. البته، سرشت «روزن» برای حرکت و تحول را تنها می‌توان در مقایسه‌ی نوشته‌های همین پژوهشگران پرشمار جست و جو کرد، و نه شاید در تک‌تک آن‌ها. به عنوان مثال، در مقایسه‌ی نوشته‌های انتقادی‌ی «فتحعلی آخوندزاده» با نوشته‌های انتقادی‌ی «آرامش دوستدار» است که این «روزنِ» خجسته خود را نشان می‌دهد. من بر این باورم که اگر پژوهشگران ما این روزن را نمی‌دیدند، از خواندن و جست‌وجو کردن و نوشتن درباره‌ی فرهنگ و ادبیات فارسی، آن هم در این حجم عظیم، ناتوان می‌ماندند.

شاید با دیدن این روزنه‌ی امید بوده که به ویژه در طول سه دهه‌ی گذشته، پژوهشگران بسیاری، چه در ایران و چه در برون‌مرزهای ایران، از چشم‌اندازهای متفاوت، در پیداکردن و نشان دادن تأثیرهای مثبت و منفی‌ی فرهنگ تواراثی در انقلاب مشروطیت، در برخورد ما با «مدرنیته»، و در شکل‌گیری‌ی انقلاب مشروطیت، در خوانش ما از مفاهیم «آزادی» و «عدالت اجتماعی»، در شکست جنبش‌های سوسیالیستی، در انقلاب ۱۳۵۷، در جنبش‌های مناسبتی و مقطعی، و قیام

خرداد ۱۳۸۸ قلم زده‌اند. و تاریخ این جنبش‌ها و قیام‌های مردم ایران و مطالبات آن‌ها شــهادت می‌دهند که این تلاش‌ها در رشــد تدریجی‌ی مردم ایران و ارتقاء آگاهی‌ی آن‌ها دســتی توانا داشــته اســت. به گونه‌ای که، اگر داشــتن «عدالتخانه» سرلوحه‌ی مطالبات انقلاب مشروطیت بود، داشتن «استقلال و آزادی»ی ملی، سرلوحه‌ی مطالبات انقلاب ۵۷ شد، که در طول ســه دهه، در قیام خرداد ۱۳۸۸، به مطالبه‌ی آزادی‌های فردی و برابری‌ی حقوقی جا ســپرد. اگر شــعار ایرانیان در حمایت از نهضـت ملی‌ی دکتر مصـدق (۳۰ خرداد ۱۳۳۱)، «یا مرگ یا مصـدق» بود، حالا، یعنی حدود نیم سده بعد، در یکی از پیام‌های مبارزاتی‌ی درون‌مرزی (پس از انتخابات ۸۸) به «مرگ یا آزادی» تغییر کرده اســت. در متنی با عنوان «نام‌گذاری‌ی سی‌ی تیر به روز ندای آزادی»- که در کوران مبارزات مردم ایران در تیر ماه ۱۳۸۸ منتشر شد- می‌خوانیم:

> [...] بیش از نیم قرن پیش، هنگامی که شـاه و نخسـت وزیر انتصـابی‌اش [قوام‌السـلطنه در ۳۰ تیر ۱۳۳۱] کوشـیدند دکتر مصــدق نخســت وزیر محبوب مردم را عزل کنند، مردم آزادی‌خواه ایران با نادیده گرفتن حکومت نظامی، به خیابان‌ها ریختند و شاه را وادار به عقب نشینی کردند. آن روز یکی از جوانانی که تیر خورده بود با خون خود بر دیوار این شعار را نوشت :
>
> *از جان خود گذشتم، با خون خود نوشتم، یا مرگ یا مصدق*
>
> امروز ما به بزرگداشت آن روز، با شعار زیر همه‌ی شهر را اشغال خواهیم کرد:
>
> **از جان خود گذشتم، با خون خود نوشتم، یا مرگ یا آزادی**[۱۸۸]

گوهری که در بازگفت بالا می‌درخشـد، و در عمل نیز با برگذشـتن مردم ایران از «جنبش سـبز» با رهبری‌ی سـیدحسـین موسوی و شیخ کروبی، و رسیدن به حق‌طلبی‌ی بدون «رهبری» تأیید می‌شـود، همان اندک روزنی است که از برگذشتـنِ نسبی‌ی ایرانی از کـیش شـخصیت خبـر می‌دهد. در این تحول- در کنار عوامل دیگر رشد ذهنی- نمی‌توان تلاش سی ساله و هدفمند متفکران و نویسندگان آزادی‌خواه درون و برون‌مرزهای ایران را نادیده گرفت. فرآورده‌ی این تلاش‌ها، که اینک به صــورت مجموعه‌ای گرانبها، ما را در بازشــناســی‌ی خود و فرهنگ‌مان یاری می‌دهد، شــاید که حرف ناگفته‌ای باقی نگذاشته باشد. اما من هم به سهم خود، تلاش می‌کنم که در این جلد از مجموعه، فشرده‌ای از حضور یا غیاب این الگوها و کهن‌الگوهای فرهنگی را در دوره‌های مختلف تاریخ معاصر ایران بازشناسی کنم، و نقش آن‌ها را در سمت وُ سو دادن به فهم وُ درک وُ پذیرش وُ گیرش وُ گوارشِ پیشـاهنگان و نخبگان فرهنگی و سـیاسـی‌مان بفهمم و نشـان دهم. و البته با این هدف که توشـه‌ی مطالعه‌ی من در این رهگذر، آن ریشـه‌ها و زمینه‌های فرهنگی‌ای را بازتاب دهد، که ذهنیت‌های نهفته در سی و پنج سال «متن فارسی در تبعید» را رقم زده اند.

---

[۱۸۸] *نام‌گذاری‌ی سی‌ی تیر به روز ندای آزادی*، تارنمای «هسته‌های مقاومت ملی»، ۱۵ ژوئیه ۲۰۰۹، به نشانی‌ی زیر:
http://moghavematmelli.wordpress.com/

انقلاب‌های ناتمام ایران

تاریخ ایرانِ قرن سیزدهم [هجری] بسیار پیچیده‌تر از مبارزه‌ی ساده بین چند گروه عمده بود.
این تاریخ، شاهد کشمکش‌های چندگانه بین مجامع کوچکِ بی‌شمار، طایفه بر ضد طایفه، ایل بر ضد ایل، ایل بر ضد روستا، ایل بر ضد شهر، شهر بر ضد روستا، روستا بر ضد روستا،
روستا بر ضد محله‌ی شهر، و محله‌ی شهر بر ضد محله‌ی شهر بوده است.
[...] اعتمادالسلطنه، وقایع‌نگار درباری، همه‌ی نواحی‌ِ جنوب شرقی را که بر اثر
نفاق شوم محلی خالی از سکنه شده بود، نام می‌بَرَد.
[...] ملکم در طول سفرهای فراوانش دریافت که تقسیم شهرهای بزرگ به محله‌هائی
با نام حیدری و نعمتی، که نویسنده‌ای به شاه عباس نسبت داده بود، هنوز وجود دارد
و مثل گذشته خصومت‌انگیز است. همیشه بین این گروه‌ها تعصبی وجود دارد و در روز آخر ماه محرم با خشونت به یکدیگر حمله می‌کنند. اگر یک گروه مسجدی را می‌آراید،
گروه دیگر اگر بتواند مانع‌اش می‌شود، و علم و کتل‌شان را خراب می‌کند. اگر رقبایشان را
از خانه‌هایشان بیرون کنند، به نشانه‌ی پیروزی با تبر علامتی روی هر در می‌گذارند. این دعواها اغلب بسیار جدی است و قربانیان زیادی می‌گیرد. مأمور مالیات اصفهان شرح می‌دهد که چه‌طور هر سال در روز عید قربان هزاران نفر حیدری و نعمتی که در میدان اصلی نزاع می‌کنند، اغلب تلفات زیادی می‌دهند. حسن فسائی، وقایع‌نگار شیرازی می‌گوید که طرفین این دعواها در شهر زادگاه وی تلفات را «صدقه» برای خداوند می‌دانند.

(یرواند آبراهامیان)[۱۸۹]

افزون بر کارجویان ایرانی که به طور قانونی به روسیه مهاجرت می‌کردند،
و در سال ۱۸۹۶/ ۱۲۷۵ تعدادشان به ۵۶۳۷۱ نفر می‌رسید، فرماندار ایالت الیزاپتول در روسیه‌ی تزاری، در سال ۱۸۸۷/ ۱۲۶۶ گزارش داد: «هر سال در طول فصل بهار و بر روی کوه‌های مرزی، می‌توان هزاران نفر از ایرانیان را- با پاهای برهنه و لباس‌های پاره پوره- در گروه‌های چهل تا پنجاه نفری مشاهده کرد، که برای یافتن کار به طور غیرقانونی
از مرزهای امپراتوری‌ِ روسیه می‌گذرند. [...] هرگونه اقدام برای بستن این گذرگاه کارجویان، نتایج بسیار وخیمی برای اقتصاد رو به رشد امپراتوری‌ِ روسیه خواهد داشت.»[۱۹۰]

به حکم فلسفه‌ی تاریخ و دانش جامعه‌شناسی، که یک رویداد را پیامد شبکه‌ای از فرایندهای درازدامن گذشته برآورد می‌کنند، هر گزارشی از مقطع معینی از تاریخ معاصر ایران، گزارشگر را به ناگزیر لایه به لایه تا زمینه‌ها و مقدمه‌های

---

[۱۸۹] یرواند آبراهامیان، ***ایران بین دو انقلاب: از مشروطه تا انقلاب اسلامی***، ترجمه‌ی کاظم فیروزمند، حسن شمس‌آبادی، و محسن مدیر شانه‌چی، تهران: نشر مرکز، چاپ هشتم، ۱۳۸۳، صص ۲۵ تا ۲۸.

[۱۹۰] بهزاد کاظمی، ***سوسیالیسم و استالینیسم در ایران، بخش نخست***، فصل‌نامه‌ی «سامان نو، نشریه‌ی پژوهش‌های سوسیالیستی، شماره‌ی ۱۳/ ۱۴، پائیز/ تابستان ۱۳۸۹، ص ۱۱۱.

انقلاب مشروطیت، یعنی- دست کم- به حدود صد و پنجاه سال پیش به عقب می‌برد. یعنی به زمانی می‌برد که ایرانی از خوابی گران پرید، و دید که نه تنها در زنجیر قدرت‌مداران بومی برده‌ی مفلوکی بیش نیست، نه تنها فرهنگ و تمدنش از کاروان جهان جا مانده است، بلکه «پیش‌رفتگان» هم، به یاری‌ی قدرت‌های بومی، ماده و معنای او را به تجاوز و تحقیر گرفته‌اند. از این زمان بود که اندیشه‌ورز و پیشاهنگ ایرانی کوشید تا هر چه زودتر جهان تازه را بازشناسد، خود را در متن این جهان بازتعریف کند، و بر پایه‌ی یافته هایش راه را بیابد و خود را به کاروان برساند. در این رهگذر بود که آسیب‌شناسی‌ی آن خوابِ گران- در هیئت «نقد»- نیز در دستور کار قرار گرفت. به بیانی دیگر، در نخستین مرحله‌ی بیداری، بایستگی‌ی «شناخت» از چند سو ایرانی را در محاصره داشت: شناخت خود؛ شناخت نشانه‌ها و انگیزه‌های خواب ماندن، از راه نقد گذشته؛ شناخت مفهوم‌هائی که جهان «پیش رفته» را ساخته بود؛ و شناخت راه و ابزار رسیدن؛ که همه‌ی این‌ها- طبیعتاً- باید با ملات شناخت‌شناسی‌ی دیرینه و بر شاکله‌های ذهنی‌ی از پیش بسته‌شده‌ی او می‌روئید. در یک نگاه سراسری می‌توان دید آن چه که ایرانی از همان دوران تا دقیقه‌ی اکنون بر پیشانی‌ی این تلاش درازدامن و توان‌فرسای خود نوشته و خوانده و سروده، آرزوی رسیدن به حاکمیت «قانون»، «عدالت»، «آزادی»، «استقلال ملی»، و «ایران متمدن، آباد و سربلند» بوده است. به شهادت تاریخ، از میان هزاران پیکارگر سیاسی/ فرهنگی/ اجتماعی‌ی مُعمّم و مُکلّای صد و پنجاه سال گذشته، تنها شخصیتی که با ایران و ایرانیت و تمدن ایرانی در نظر و عمل، آشکارا و مکرراً دشمنی نشان داد، آیت‌الله روح‌الله خمینی بود؛[۱۹۱] که جانشینان او نیز بنا بر «مصلحت نظام»، ضمن استفاده‌ی ابزاری از مفهوم «ایرانیت»، این دشمنی را دنبال کرده‌اند.[۱۹۲] اما صرف نظر از این استثناء هنگفت، می‌توان گفت که ایرانی، تحقق عملیِ

---

[۳] تاریخ صد و پنجاه سال گذشته‌ی ایران، از شخصیت‌های روحانی و غیرروحانی‌ای نشانی می‌دهد که یا از آغاز با جنبش‌های آزادی‌خواهانه‌ی مردم مخالف بودند، و یا در نیمه راه مبارزه، به دلایل مختلف، به آن پشت کردند، یا در تبانی با قدرت سیاسی، و گاه با بیگانگان، به سرکوبگران جنبش یاری دادند. اما تا جائی که من خوانده‌ام، هیچ یک از آن‌ها مانند آیت‌الله خمینی ایران و ایرانیت را نفی نکردند و در برابر «تمدن ایرانی» نایستادند (شاید هم فرصت این کار را نیافتند). ایران‌ستیزی‌ی آیت‌الله خمینی، در ادبیات سیاسی‌ی جمهوری‌ی اسلامی نمونه‌های فراوان دارد. از جمله، روز ۱۵ مرداد ۱۳۵۹ با لحنی فریادگونه گفت: «کسانی که می‌خواهند ملیت را احیا کنند در مقابل اسلام ایستاده‌اند. اسلام آمده که این حرف‌های نامربوط را از بین ببرد» (صحیفه‌ی نور، جلد ۱۲، ص ۲۷۴.) و روز ٦ خرداد ۱۳٦۰ در دیدار با نمایندگان مجلس شورای اسلامی گفت: «ما دانشگاهی را که شعارش این باشد که می‌خواهیم ایران متمدن و آباد داشته باشیم و رو به تمدن بزرگ برویم، نمی‌خواهیم.» افزون بر مجموعه‌ی «صحیفه‌ی نور»، که این سخنان آیت‌الله در آن منعکس است، اینک انبوهی از متن نیز در دست است که نویسندگان هر یک از آن‌ها، مجموعه‌هائی از سخنان ایران‌ستیز و دروغ‌های آشکار این آیت‌الله را (البته با استفاده از همان «صحیفه» و یا نشریات سال‌های ۵۷ تا زمان مرگ او) گردآوری کرده‌اند. به عنوان نمونه‌ای از این گونه مجموعه‌ها، به مأخذ زیر- که شامل هلهله و هورای رسانه‌ها و شخصیت‌های غربی پیرامون این آیت‌الله نیز هست- نگاه کنید:

- ❖ ***پیامبر دروغین نوفل لوشاتو***، گرد آوری و تنظیم از سعید ترکمان، تارنمای «خبرنامه‌ی گویا»، ۲۳ تیر ۱۳۸۹:
HTTP://NEWSMANAGER.GOOYA.COM/POLITICS/ARCHIVES/2010/07/107599.PHP

[٤] تز ایران‌زدائی‌ی آیت‌الله، با مرگ او فراموش نشد، و توسط بازماندگان معمم و مکلای او ادامه یافت: مثلاً، افزون بر تحریف تاریخ ایران باستان در کتاب‌های درسی و غیردرسی‌ی منتشرشده در جمهوری‌ی اسلامی، یکی از نشانه‌های عملی‌ی ضدیت با مظاهر ایران پیش از اسلام، تلاش حکومت اسلامی برای از بین بردن بناها و یادبودهای ایران باستان و مراسم نوروز و چهارشنبه سوری است که از همان سال نخست این رژیم شروع شد و در درازنای سی و چهار سال گذشته ادامه یافته است. نمونه‌ی بارز آن، تخریب بناهای تاریخی و ساختن سد سیوند در کنار آرامگاه کورش هخامنشی است. و نمونه‌ی ادامه‌ی سیاست‌های ایرانی‌زدای آیت‌الله خمینی، نظر آیت‌الله خامنه‌ای و چند تن دیگر از مراجع تقلید است که در آستانه‌ی نوروز ۱۳۸۹ به شرح زیر منتشر شد: «خامنه‌ای، به سئوالات مردم درباره‌ی مراسم چهارشنبه‌ی آخر سال پاسخ داد. به گزارش روز یکشنبه ایرنا، این استفتاء که در پایگاه اطلاع رسانی‌ی دفتر وی منتشر شده، به شرح ذیل است: سئوال: نظر جنابعالی درباره‌ی چهارشنبه سوری چیست؟ جواب: علاوه بر آن که هیچ مبنای شرعی ندارد، مستلزم ضرر و فساد زیادی است که مناسب است از آن‌ها اجتناب شود.علاوه بر استفتاء ، از دفتر برخی مراجع عظام تقیلد نیز در این زمینه سئوال شد که پاسخ دادند: مراسم چهارشنبه‌ی آخر سال، علاوه بر این که مبنای شرعی ندارد، نوعی آتش پرستی است و خواندن اشعاری مانند «زردی‌ی من از تو و سرخی‌ی تو از من» مصداق حاجت خواستن از آتش است.» نگاه کنید به:

- ❖ ***خامنه‌ای: چهارشنبه سوری مبنای شرعی ندارد و مستلزم ضرر و فساد زیادی است***، تارنمای «آسمان دیلی نیوز»، ٢٤ اسفند ۱۳۸۸:
http://asemandailynews.com/?p=34874

به دنبال این فتواها، زین‌العابدین قربانی، نماینده‌ی ولی‌ی فقیه در استان گیلان و امام جمعه‌ی رشت، در خطبه‌های نماز جمعه‌ی رشت گفت: «مراسم چهار شنبه سوری و پریدن از روی آتش خرافه پرستی بوده و این مراسم از گذشتگان برای ما مانده و هرچیزی که از گذشته مانده مقدس نیست و هر چیز عتیقه‌ای محبوب نیست ...این که از روی آتش می‌پرند و می‌گویند زردی‌ی من از تو سرخی‌ی تو از من، این بت پرستی است. زرتشتی‌ها فکر می‌کردند آتش نشانه‌ی خدا و مقدس است. توی مسلمان هم اگر این گونه فکر احمقی.» این سخنان در روزنامه‌ی دولتی‌ی «ایران»، روز ۲۲ اسفندماه ۱۳۸۸، یعنی پس از تولد «جنبش سبز» مردم ایران، منتشر شد. اما از آن جا که بخشی از بدنه‌ی این جنبش، در همان سال ۱۳۸۸ شعار داده بود: «نه شرقی، نه غربی، جمهوری‌ی ایرانی»، و از آن جا که بسیاری از جوانان ایران نوروز ۸۹ را در کنار آرامگاه کورش و در تخت جمشید برگزار کردند و از آن جا که تصویر این برگزاری‌ها در سراسر جهان منتشر شد، (به اضافه‌ی علت‌های پنهان سیاسی)، سکانداران را، که

عملی‌ی این مفهوم‌های نظری را شرط رسیدن به جامعه‌ی جهانی و بازیافتِ کرامتِ تحقیرشده‌ی خود تشخیص داده است. در رهگذر تلاش برای تحقق این آرمان‌های توأمان بود که پیکار خونین با قدرت سیاسی از یک سو، و کشمکش‌های خونینِ همرزمان بر سر راهکارهای پیکار، از دیگر سو، تاریخ صد و پنجاه سال گذشته‌ی ایران را آکنده است. از این چشم‌انداز، بدیهی است که گزینش «راهکارهای پیکار»، در درجه‌ی نخست، بستگی‌ی مستقیم داشته است به این که پیکارگران سیاسی/ اجتماعی/ فرهنگی‌ی ما، در رهگذر جستوجوهای خود، از «هویت»، و از مفهوم‌های «عدالت»، «قانون»، «آزادی»، و «برابری» به چه تعریف‌هائی رسیده بودند و رسیده‌اند. آن چه که از دورترین سواد این برش از تاریخ به دید می‌آید، خط فاصل خونینی است که- **عمدتاً**- شش نوع جهان‌بینی- در گزینش راهکارهای این پیکار- رسم کرده‌اند: ۱) بینش بنیادگرای ملی (باستان‌گرا)، که خود و هویت ایرانی را با سنجه‌های دوران عظمت «ایران باستان» می‌سنجد و راهکارش بریدن از کلیه‌ی مظاهر ذهنی و عینی‌ی ایران اسلامی است؛ ۲) بینش ملی/ مذهبی، که در شناخت هویت، دوران شوکت «ایران اسلامی» (سده‌های چهارم تا ششم هجری) را نقطه‌ی عزیمت قرار داده است، و بر اساس آن، عناصر مدرن/غربی را در قالب فرهنگ «ایران اسلامی» می‌ریزد و می‌پذیرد؛ ۳) بینش بنیادگرای اسلام سیاسی، بی‌توجه به ملیت، «اسلام» را به عنوان یک «دین جهانی»، سنجه‌ی شناسائی‌ی هویت می‌داند و بر اساس آن، با نمودهای ذهنی‌ی عناصر مدرنیته- که مهم‌ترین شاخصه‌ی آن جدائی‌ی دین از دولت بود و هست- سر ستیز دارد؛ ۴) بینش سوسیالیستی/ کمونیستی، با هدف رسیدن به عدالت اجتماعی، که اصولاً هویت را در «طبقه»، و موقعیت هر طبقه را در ساختار اقتصادی‌ی جامعه برانداز می‌کند، و تکیه بر هویت‌های فردی و ملی و دینی را در راه رسیدن به فرودگاه خود زیانبار می‌داند. ۵) بینش قوم‌گرا، که «زبان» و فرهنگ قومی را معیار «هویت»شناسی قرار می‌دهد، و بر اساس این شناخت، خواستار «حق تعیین سرنوشت» برای «ملیت‌ها» است، بدون آن که الزاماً سودای جدائی از ایران را داشته باشد. ۶) بینش انسان‌گرا، که می‌توان آن را در فرهنگ سیاسی‌ی ایران پدیده‌ای نسبتاً تازه تلقی کرد، و با قید احتیاط گفت که اگر هم از پیش وجود داشت، اما پس از شکست پیکارگران سکولار در انقلاب ۵۷، نمودهای گسترده یافت. این بینش- که ضمن تفاوت‌های عمده با «اومانیسم» دوره‌ی رنسانس ایتالیا، شباهت‌هائی هم با آن دارد- هر فرد را، در درجه‌ی نخست و در ورای دین و ملیت و جنسیت،با هویت «انسان»ی تعریف می‌کند، و طبیعتاً، رسیدن به جامعه‌ی آرمانی را به ارتقاء آگاهی‌های سیاسی، حقوقی، اقتصادی و فرهنگی‌ی یکان جامعه، در به دست آوردن حق انسانی و شهروندی‌ی خود، منوط می‌داند.

در مجموعه‌ی حاضر، و به فراخور هر مبحث، نمودهای عینی‌ی هر یک از این بینش‌ها، و بستر ذهنی‌ی هر یک را بررسی کرده‌ام، و در رهگذر آسیب‌شناسی‌ی شکست‌های مکرر پیشاهنگان مبارزه در پیکارهای پیگیرشان، ضمن دیدن افق‌های باز، بن‌بست‌های چرخشی و دایره‌وار را هم دیده‌ام؛ بن‌بست‌هائی که، به سبب حضور زنده‌ی انگیزه‌های ذهنی‌شان، به نظر ابدی می‌آیند. اما بنا به قانون تکوین- که هم تاریخ سراسری‌ی ایران به آن شهادت می‌دهد، هم «افق‌های باز» صد و پنجاه سال گذشته‌ی ما، و هم تاریخ تمدن‌های دیگر- بر این باورم که هیچ بن‌بستی در جوامع انسانی محتوم و ابدی نیست. چنان که، جنبش آغازین رنسانس، در قلب فرهنگی جوانه زد که هیولای هزارساله‌ی «قرون وسطا» از آن جا سر برکرده بود؛ و تا حدود دو سده، همان دوپارگی‌ها و آشفتگی‌های ذهنی‌ای را در جامعه‌ی ایتالیا پدید آورده بود که ما صد و پنجاه سال است در آن غوطه‌ور هستیم. یاکوب بورکهارت، پژوهشگر و نویسنده‌ی «فرهنگ رنسانس در ایتالیا» در این زمینه گفته‌ای دارد که سال‌هاست آویزه‌ی امیدهای من است:

همواره با تمهیدِ فن بدل، خود را بر پا نگه‌داشته‌اند، سیاستی دگر آمد. به این ترتیب که محمود احمدی نژاد، رئیس جمهور وقت، ناگهان از ایران و ایرانیت و کوروش بزرگ و نوروز به دفاع برخاست، و با اعلام این که به «مکتب ایرانی» اعتقاد دارد، و از نژاد رستم و سهراب و آرش است، و با سر و صدای بسیار، در هفته‌ی نخست فروردین ۱۳۹۰ به برگزاری‌ی «جشن‌های نوروزی» در تهران و در تخت جمشید اقدام کرد.

کدام چشم می‌تواند به اعماقی که سیرت و سرنوشت اقوام در آن جا معین می‌شوند، نفوذ کند: به آن جا که ویژگی‌ی فطری و تجربی به هم می‌آمیزد و به صورت یک کل واحد درمی‌آید و طبیعت دوم یا سوم می‌شود؛ به آن جا که حتا استعدادهای روحی، که در نظر اول همچون خصوصیتی فطری می‌نماید، در واقع به تدریج در زمانی نسبتاً مؤخرتر پدید آمده است. [...] چه‌گونه می‌توانیم در باره‌ی آن رگ ها و مجرا های ظریفی داوری کنیم که از طریق آن ها سیرت فطری و عقل و معرفتِ مکتسب به طور لاینقطع به هم می‌آمیزند. [...] بهتر است از تعمیم‌های ناروا بپرهیزیم؛ زیرا اقوامی که در نظر ما بیمار می‌نمایند، ممکن است به زودی تندرستی‌ی خود را بازیابند، و در درون ملتی به ظاهر تندرست، ممکن است بذر مرگ نهفته باشد، که با نزدیک شدن نخستین خطر سر برآورد.[۱۹۳]

---

[۱۹۳] یاکوب بورکهارت، ***فرهنگ رنسانس در ایتالیا***، ترجمه‌ی محمد حسن لطفی، تهران: انتشارات طرح نو، ۱۳۷٦، ص ۳۹٤.

انقلاب مشروطه

اجنبی حرف بزن!

بگو من چه باید بکنم که ایرانیان را هشیار نمایم؟

(عباس میرزا قاجار به ژوبر، نمایندهی دولت فرانسه در ایران)[۱۹۴]

در مملکتی که جنگ اصنافی نیست/ آزادیِ آن منبسط و کافی نیست/

در جشن به کارگر چرا ره ندهند/ این مجلس اگر مجلس اشرافی نیست.

(فرخی یزدی)

از پشت بام باغ اتابک / تا کوچه باغ‌های امیرخیز/ یک جاده خون / یک کاروان شهید را /

همپای شب‌گریزیِ این فوج‌های بی‌سردار/ همراه می‌برد/ تا آستانه‌ی «ستار»/ «ستار»/ بر کوهه‌ی دریده‌ی زین / [...]/ با آن گلوی خونین چه تلخ می‌خواند/

آواز این قبیله چه زیباست./ [...]/

باد از هراس شب/ در زیر چتر خونیِ باران / پر می‌کشد به کوه / تا خفیه‌گاه ایمن خورشید/

و از ستیغ سربیِ البرز/ این صبح سربلند/ که می‌روید/ آواز تازه‌ی عاشق‌هاست /

آواز این قبیله چه زیباست.

(ایرج جنتی عطایی)

[...] با این وضع مجالس [دوره‌های مجلس شورای ملی] سئوالی که پیش می‌آید این است که آیا تاریخ صد ساله‌ی اخیر را می‌توان به عنوان تاریخ مشروطیت نوشت؟ یا آن که مشروطیت تنها همان دوره‌ی کوتاهی بود که جنبه‌ی آرمانیِ آن غالب بود؟ [...] من تعجب می‌کنم که تاریخ صد ساله‌ی اخیر را به عنوان مشروطیت می‌نویسند. مجلس البته کم و بیش باقی ماند، اما اصول آزادی، اصول دمکراسی و اصول مشروطیت باقی نمانده بود.[...]

ما برای همان مشروطه‌ای هم که مشروطه نبود، کتاب اساسی نداریم.

(ایرج افشار، ۷ دی ۱۳۸٤)[۱۹۵]

---

۱۹٤ عبدالهادی حائری، ***نخستین رویارویی‌ی ایران با دورویه‌ی تمدن بورژوازی‌ی غرب***، تهران: انتشارات امیرکبیر، ۱۳٦۷، ص ۳۰۸.

۱۹۵ سینا سعدی، ***سخنان ایرج افشار در باب انقلاب مشروطه***، تارنمای «بی بی سی/ فارسی»، ۲۹ دسامبر ۲۰۰۵، بازدید، ۲ ژانویه ۲۰۰٦:
http://www.bbc.co.uk/persian/arts/story/2005/12/051229_pm-cy-iraj-afshar.shtm

در سپیده دمان بیداری، آلیاژی با ترکیبی نابرابر از پنج بینش نخستِ فهرستی که در مقدمه‌ی این مبحث آوردم، انقلاب مشروطه را رقم زد، و ایرانی، پس از تلاش‌های خونین پیشاهنگان مبارزه، برای نخستین بار در درازنای دراز تاریخ خود حق «رأی دادن» را به دست آورد (۱۴ مرداد ۱۲۸۵)، و اندکی بعد نیز آن را عملاً آزمود (۲۵ شهریور ۱۲۸۵).[۱۹۶] نشانه‌های نظری‌ی این بینش‌ها (باستان‌گرا، ملی/ مذهبی، بنیادگرای اسلامی، سوسیالیستی/ کمونیستی، قوم‌گرا) در متن‌های تفسیری/ تحلیلی‌ی مربوط به دوران مشروطیت، و نشانه‌های عملی‌ی آن‌ها، در تاریخ سیاسی‌ی مشروطه‌ی ایران قابل ردیابی هستند. انبوهی از پژوهشگران ایرانی، هر یک کم یا بیش، و از زاویه‌های متفاوت، در درازنای زمان این ردیابی‌ی گرامی را انجام داده‌اند،[۱۹۷] و من در این مختصر در صدد تکرار یافته‌های آن‌ها نیستم؛ و درنگ من بر برخی از شرایط و رویدادهای تاریخی، تنها از آن روست که نقشه‌ی شناخت‌شناسی‌ی آن رویدادها را چنان که در ذهن دارم برای خواننده‌ام ترسیم کنم.

ایرج افشار، پژوهشگر، ایران‌شناس، و کتاب‌شناس، می‌گوید: «ما برای همان مشروطه‌ای هم که مشروطه نبود، کتاب اساسی نداریم.» البته که این داوری، در قیاس با تاریخ‌نگاری‌ی غرب، جای چون و چرا ندارد. اما با توجه به کل شرایط فرهنگی/ اجتماعی/ سیاسی‌ی ایران در حوالی‌ی مشروطیت، باید گفت همین که داریم هم از برکت ذهنیت فرهیختگانی است که هر یک به میزانی از بار آن فرهنگ توارثی/ حیدری/ نعمتی‌ی زمان صفویه رها شده بودند. افزون بر تشخیص کارشناسانه‌ی ایرج افشار، که به درستی، به کاستی‌ی «وقایع‌نگاری» و بی‌دقتی، یا پرده‌پوشی‌ی تاریخ‌نگاران دوران مشروطیت نظر دارد، باید به این نکته هم توجه داشت که برخی از نویسندگان متن‌های «تفسیری و تحلیلی»ی مربوط به این دوران، از چشم‌اندازی به انقلاب مشروطه نگاه کرده‌اند که انگیزه‌ی آرمانی‌ی ایرانیان در این جنبش عظیم را در سایه نگه می‌دارد. به عنوان نمونه، کتاب سه جلدی‌ی «فراموشخانه و فراماسونری در ایران» نوشته‌ی اسماعیل رایین، در بخش‌هائی که به انقلاب مشروطه‌ی ایران مربوط هستند، نیروی محرکه‌ی کلیت این انقلاب (از جنبش تنباکو گرفته تا پایان انقلاب مشروطه)، یکسره از سوی لژهای فراماسونری‌ی انگلستان و فرانسه تأمین شده است. و به این ترتیب، شبکه‌های مرتبط با اصل تکوین تاریخی‌ی ملت ایران و پیشاهنگان مبارزه، به کلی از قلم «تاریخ» افتاده است. متن‌های فراوانی نیز در دست داریم که برخی از سلحشوران و رزمندگان حوالی‌ی مشروطیت (مانند خیابانی، میرزا کوچک‌خان، و پسیان) را یکسره عامل همسایه‌ی شمالی قلمداد کرده‌اند. (به ویژه از زمانی که همسایه‌ی شمالی‌ی ایران پرچم «عدالت اجتماعی» یا «سوسیالیسم» را در جهان برافراشت.) از سوی دیگر، متن‌هائی در دست داریم که اخلال‌های انکارناپذیر همسایه‌ی شمالی (زمانی که با نام «اتحاد جماهیر شوروی» شناخته می‌شد) را – در پیدایش بحران‌های پس از مشروطه نادیده می‌گیرند. در بیش‌تر متن‌هائی از این دست، انحلال قرارداد شوم ۱۹۰۷، به دستور و امضاء لنین، برجسته شده، اما پیرامون این نکته‌ی مهم که «اتحاد جماهیر شوروی» جنبش‌های جمهوری‌خواه آذربایجان و کردستان و گیلان و خراسان را از نظر ایدئولوژی مصادره به مطلوب کرد، و در عین حال، برای حفظ منافع خود آنان را در بزنگاه پیکار تنها گذاشت، و حتا در سرکوب آنان با حکومت ایران و رقبای بین‌المللی‌خود همکاری کرد، یا سکوت شده است، یا تاریخ به کلی تحریف شده است. و پیامد این مجموعه، به قول فریدون آدمیت، چیزی نبوده به جز «آشفتگی در فکر تاریخی»ی ما.

با این همه، به استنادِ متن‌های حوالی‌ی مشروطیت (از گزارش‌های کسروی و ناظم‌الاسلام و دولت‌آبادی گرفته تا گزارش‌های سفیران کشورهای بیگانه، از شعارها و اعلامیه‌ها و شبنامه‌ها گرفته تا کاریکاتور، از شعر گرفته تا

---

[۱۹۶] البته، ناظم‌الاسالم کرمانی وجود «دست تقلب و تدلیس» را در نخستین انتخابات مجلس شورای ملی هم گزارش داده است.

[۱۹۷] ناظم‌الاسلام کرمانی، احمد کسروی، یحیی دولت آبادی، مهدی ملک زاده، فریدون آدمیت، هما ناطق، رحیم رضازاده ملک، اسماعیل رایین، ژانت آفاری، آرامش دوستدار، سید جواد طباطبائی، محمدرضا نیکفر، باقر مؤمنی، ماشاالله آجودانی، احمد اشرف، احمد توکلی، محمد توکلی طرقی، یرواند آبراهامیان، حمید حمید، علی میرفطروس، تورج اتابکی، رحیم نامور، عبدالحسین میرزا صالح، به اضافه‌ی ده‌ها تن از مورخان و پژوهشگرانی که به مناسبت صدمین سالگرد مشروطه‌ی ایران سخن گفتند، و نوشتند، نمونه‌های بارز اندیشه‌ورزانی هستند که با رویکردهای متفاوت، نمودهای عملی‌ی این بینش‌ها را یا فقط گزارش کرده‌اند، یا گزارش‌ها را بررسیده‌اند.

داستان‌واره‌ها و مقاله‌ها و جستارهای اجتماعی)- و البته به برکت آموخته‌های تطبیقی/ استنتاجی‌ی خودم از دسترنج همان پژوهشگران و مفسران یادشده و یادنشده- نقشه‌ی زیر را می‌بینم:
«مدرنیته»، و فضائی که «مدرنیسمِ» نیمه‌کاره بر انسان غربی گشود،[۱۹۸] همان جهان تازه‌ای است که انسان ایرانی در سپیده دم بیداری، خود را از آن جامانده می‌بیند. اما پیش‌زمینه‌های علمی، و انگیزه‌هائی که این جهان تازه برای شدن در زادگاه خود داشت، و بسیاری از راهکارهائی که برای تحقق آرمان‌های خود برگزیده بود، با ذهنیت روشنفکران دوره‌ی مشروطیت بیگانگی می‌کند. به بیانی دیگر، در این برش از تاریخ، روان جمعی‌ی ایرانی و حتا پیشگامان مبارزه، نه تنها زیرساخت علمی‌ی مظاهر «مدرنیته» (تا جائی که به او رسیده، مانند صنعت چاپ یا عکاسی یا اسلحه‌ی گرم، و سپس‌تر، سینما یا راه آهن) را نمی‌شناسد، نه تنها به روش علمی، و به «فلسفه»- که زمینه‌ی نظری‌ی «مدرنیسم» بودند- مجهز نیست، نه تنها با مفهوم‌های درونی‌ی مهم‌ترین فرزند «مدرنیته/ مدرنیسم»، یعنی مارکسیسم (که فرآورده‌ی رشد «کارخانه» و «کار» و «کارگر» بود) آشنا نیست، بلکه بار هنگفت فرهنگِ مذهبی، قبیله‌ای، و «شبان/ رَمگی» بر ذهنیت او سنگینی می‌کند. اما در عین حال، هم دستیابی به مظاهر «مدرنتیه» را لازمه‌ی «پیشرفت» برآورد می‌کند، و هم لزوم آزادی از خودکامگی‌ی «دولت‌مداران» و «دین‌کاران» را- که جان و مال و «وطن» آن‌ها را به حراج گذاشته‌اند- با گوشت و پوست خود تجربه کرده، و هم به برکت نسیم «مدرنیته/ مدرنیسم» و یکی از فرزندانش، «مارکسیسم»، دریافته است. در نتیجه‌ی خلاء تفکر پیرامون زیرساخت‌ها، تفکر انتقادی در این دوره، عمدتاً، به کارکردها معطوف است، و نه به عناصر درونی‌ی کلان‌پدیده‌های سیاسی/ اجتماعی، مانند «دین/ مذهب»، «حکومت»، و بنیادهای عینی و ذهنی‌ی ازدواج باستانی‌ی آن‌ها، و پیامدهای آن در تاریخ ایران.

البته، بنا بر یافته‌های هما ناطق- پژوهشگر دوران قاجار و تاریخ مشروطیت- حدود دوازده سال از تاریخ قاجار، دوران شکوفائی‌ی اندیشه پیرامون پدیده‌ی «دین» بود، و تأثیری که این شکوفائی بر «حکومت» گذاشت، در عین حال، لزوم راهجوئی برای ابطال آن تأثیر را نیز به دنبال داشت. هما ناطق، به فرمان محمدشاه قاجار (در سال ۱۸۴۰/ ۱۲۱۹) مبنی بر «برابری‌ی همه‌ی ادیان» اشاره می‌کند و می‌افزاید: جنبش بابیان- که برخلاف تصور رایج بیش‌تر جنبه‌ی سیاسی/ اجتماعی داشت تا جنبه‌ی مذهبی- حاصل این فرمان و آزادی‌های آن دوازده سال بود.[۱۹۹] (نقل به معنی از یک مصاحبه در فیلم) منتها می‌دانیم که روحانیت، با شناخت و استفاده از ذهنیت عمیقاً مذهبی/ شیعی‌ی مردم (از شاه تا «امیرکبیر» تا «رعیت»)، با کشتار بابیان، و دگراندیشان فرهنگی و سیاسی، به آن آزادی‌ی نسبی پاسخی خونین داد.

در حالی که غرب، به برکتِ فرهنگ گفت‌وگو، کشف‌های علمی، و گفتمان‌های فلسفی‌ی برآمده از آن کشف‌ها، دست کم حدود پنج سده وقت داشت تا به آگاهی‌ی خردبنیادِ تاریخی **بیاندیشد**؛ با برانداز کردنِ این «آگاهی»، از تاریکی‌ی «قرون وسطا» به درآید، و به تدریج، هم به لحاظ نظری از «مذهب» و «حکومت» تقدس‌زدائی کند، و هم به لحاظ عملی، قلمرو آن‌ها را از یکدیگر جدا کند. (همین جا به عنوان معترضه بیافزایم که «اندیشیدن» به مفهوم ذهنی‌ی «آگاهی‌ی خردبنیاد»، ضمن این که در آن «تقدس‌زدائی»ها کارساز بود، الزاماً به معنای «دست یافتنِ» کامل به آن نبود. چرا که انسان غربی‌ی دوره‌ی «مدرنیته»، در مسیر حرکت برای این «دست‌یابی»، به پدیده‌های عینی و ذهنی‌ای برخورد، که از گرانیگاه اندیشه‌ی روشنگری- تا حد ملموسی- فاصله داشتند. در جلد دوم مجموعه‌ی حاضر بر این فرایند درنگ کرده‌ام.)

---

[۱۹۸] پیرامون اصطلاحات «مدرنیته» و «مدرنیسم»، تفاوت‌های این دو واژه/ مفهوم، و همچنین پیرامون چرائی‌ی کاربرد «مدرنیسم نیمه‌کاره»، در جای دیگری از مجموعه‌ی حاضر سخن گفته‌ام. اما همین جا نیز یادآور می‌شوم که عبارت «مدرنیسم نیمه‌کاره در غرب» را در سراسر این مجموعه با این استدلال بکار برده‌ام که مناسبات سیاسی/ اقتصادی/ اجتماعی‌ای که در دوران موسوم به «مدرنیته» در غرب به ظهور رسید، مفهوم «مدرنیسم» (با تعریفی که پروژه‌ی «روشنگری» برای آن ارائه داده بود) را در زیر گرفت و ایده‌ی بنیادی‌ی آن، یعنی، «جرأت اندیشیدن داشته باش» را نابود کرد. بنا بر این برداشت، «مدرنیسمِ» ایرانی، برداشتی «ایرانی» بود از «مدرنیسم»ی که حتا در زادگاه خود «نیمه‌کاره» به ظهور رسید.

[۱۹۹] هما ناطق، در فیلم مستند ***شب بعد از انقلاب***، ساخته‌ی رضا علامه‌زاده، یوتیوب:
http://www.youtube.com/watch?v=_7t3mgf3Pco

با خوانش انطباقی/ استنتاجی از تاریخچه‌ی «حزب اجتماعیون عامیون» (که بعداً به «حزب سوسیال دمکرات» تغییر نام داد)، و عملکرد پایه‌گذاران و هواداران آن، نمونه‌ی مشخص عمل‌گرائی‌ی بی‌پشتوانه‌ی نظریه، به چشم می‌آید. «حزب سوسیال دمکرات»- که با ملاحظه‌ی ذهنیت مذهبی‌ی جامعه و با پروا از نفوذ مجتهدان در مردم، خود را «حزب دمکرات» معرفی می‌کرد- اصل «انفکاک کامل قوای سیاسی از روحانیون» را بر پیشانی‌ی اساسنامه‌ی مبارزاتی‌ی خود ثبت کرده بود. این حزب، با وجود کارشکنی‌های روحانیان و اعضای حزب «اجتماعیون اعتدالیون»، در مجلس دوم، فراکسیونی متشکل از ۲۸ نماینده داشت، و دو تن از پایه‌گذاران آن (سید حسن تقی زاده و علی اکبر دهخدا) نیز به سبب پافشاری بر اصل تفکیک دین از دولت- یا «شرع» از «عرف»- توسط مجتهدان مجلس ، ابتدا حکم تکفیر گرفتند و سپس از ایران تبعید شدند. با این وصف، از این جا و آن جای مجموعه‌ی نوشته‌های پایه‌گذاران این حزب، و گزارش‌هائی که پیرامون عملکرد آن‌ها در دست داریم، نشانه‌های رسوب آموزه‌های مذهبی/ سنتی- مانند «تقیه‌های سیاسی و پنهان‌کاری‌های ریز و درشت» و صادر کردن حکم قتل مخالفان- قابل ردیابی است، و ماشاءالله آجودانی در کتاب گرامی‌ی «مشروطه‌ی ایرانی» (۱۹۹۷) نمونه‌های بسیاری از آن را ثبت کرده است.[۲۰۰] با این که در وجود درخشش‌های ذهنی‌ی هیچ یک از این پیشاهنگان جای تردید نیست، اما من در خوانش‌های تطبیقی/ استنتاجی‌ی خود از این مجموعه، تنها علی اکبر دهخدا را، به میزان قابل توجهی، از این رسوب مبرا دیده‌ام. مهم‌ترین تفاوت او با دیگر اعضای حزب «اعتدالیون عامیون»، و بعد، «فرقه» یا «حزب دموکرات»، باور او به مبارزه‌ی فرهنگی برای گسترش آگاهی از راه هنر و قلم و نوشتار است؛ باوری که، در کارنامه‌ی او نیز جلوه‌های آشکاری دارد.

چنین بود که راهکارهای پیشنهادی‌ی «مدرنیست»های ما، از کانال همان ذهنیتی عرضه شد که آکنده بود از تقدس «دین/ مذهب/ دولت»؛ یعنی تقدس‌های غیرقابل انتقاد، غیرقابل پرسش، و رها از هر چون و چرا. در نتیجه، صرف نظر از چند استثناء، همه‌ی کاستی‌ها، ناشی از **اجرای** نادرستِ مجریان این دو نهادِ پیوسته برآورد می‌شد، و نه در ذات این دو نهاد. با این ذهنیت بود که بسیاری از پیشگامان دوره‌ی مشروطیت، مفاهیم «مدرنِ» سیاسی/ اجتماعی را در قالب «شریعت» معنی کردند، و نمادها و نمودهای مدرنیسم را در آیه‌های قرآن دیدند؛ یا برای اثبات نظرهای تازه‌ی خود، از آیه‌های قرآن یا از خبرها و حدیث‌های مربوط به منش و کنش پیامبر اسلام و امامان شیعه سود جستند؛ یا برای عملی‌کردن ایده‌های نو، هر یک به نوعی، نیازمند موافقت روحانیت بودند. در جای جای متون مربوط به این دوره- چه در متن‌های همان زمان، و چه در متن‌های تفسیری‌ی بعدی- انگیزه‌ی این «نیاز» را در نظرگرفتنِ «ذهنیت مذهبی‌ی عامه‌ی مردم» برآورد کرده‌اند. به عنوان یک مثال از صدها، عباس میرزای قاجار، در تأیید اصلاحات پیشنهادی‌ی خود، از روحانیت فتوا می‌گیرد. یرواند آبراهامیان ، ترس از «قیام مذهبی» را سبب درخواستِ این فتوا می‌داند و می‌نویسد:

> [عباس میرزا] برای جلوگیری از تکرار قیام مذهبی که سلطان سلیم سوم [عثمانی] را ساقط کرده بود، فتوای روحانیت را در موافقت با نظام جدید بدست آورد. دوستش، شیخ‌الاسلام تبریز اعلام داشت که بازسازی‌ی قشون کاملاً با اسلام مطابقت دارد، مگر نه این که قرآن می‌فرماید خداوند کسانی را که در صفوفی استوار در راه او می‌جنگند، دوست دارد؟ وقایع‌نگار دربار عباس میرزا نیز می‌نویسد که وی با «ذهن وقاد» خود از طریق اروپائیان تدابیر جنگی را که پیامبر اختراع کرده بود، مجدداً کشف کرد. [...] به این ترتیب، قشون جدید، وارث غیرمستقیم اما مشروع پیامبر اسلام بود. (ایران بین دو انقلاب، ۱۳۸۳، ص ۴۸)

تردید نیست که «قیام مذهبی»، گویای ذهنیت مذهبی‌ی عامه‌ی مردم است، که البته با فتوای روحانیت به عینیت درمی‌آید، و تاریخ ایران و تاریخ جهان اسلام نیز بارها به این نوع فتواها و قیام‌ها شهادت داده است. اما پرسش این جاست که ذهنیت پیشروان نوسازی‌ی ایران، تا چه میزان از روان جمعی/ مذهبی‌ی ایرانی پیشروتر بوده است؟ یکی از «اروپائیان»ی که

---

۲۰۰ نشانه‌های عملی‌ی این رسوب در ذهنیت افراد یادشده، در جای جای کتاب زیر بررسی شده است:

❖ ماشاءالله آجودانی، ***مشروطه‌ی ایرانی و پیش‌زمینه‌های نظریه‌ی «ولایت فقیه»***، لندن: انتشارات فصل کتاب، ۱۳۷۶/ ۱۹۹۷.

عباس میرزا دربارهٔ «تدابیر جنگی» با او مشورت می‌کرد، ژوبر فرانسوی بود. عباس میرزا در نشستی از ژوبر می‌پرسد:

> نمی‌دانم این قدرتی که شما اروپائی‌ها را بر ما مسلط کرده چیست، و موجب ضعف ما و ترقیِ شما چه؟ شما در قشون جنگیدن و فتح‌کردن، و بکاربردنِ تمام قوای عقلیه متبحرید؛ حال آن که ما در جهل و شغب غوطه‌ور؛ و به ندرت آتیه را در نظر می‌گیریم. مگر جمعیت و حاصل‌خیزی و ثروت مشرق زمین از اروپا کم‌تر است؟ یا آفتاب، که قبل از رسیدن به شما به ما می‌تابد، تأثیرات مفیدش در سر ما کم‌تر از سر شماست؟ یا خدائی که مراحمش بر جمیع ذرات عالم یکسان است خواسته شما را بر ما برتری دهد؟ گمان نمی‌کنم. اجنبی حرف بزن! بگو من چه باید بکنم که ایرانیان را هشیار نمایم؟
> (عبدالهادی حائری، ۱۳۶۷، ص ۳۰۸)

به برکت این بازگفت، می‌دانیم که عباس میرزای تاریخ ایران «گمان نمی‌کند» که «موجب ضعف ما» و «برتری»ی آن‌ها، کار «خدا» باشد. اما نمی‌دانیم که این پیشاهنگ، برای نوسازیِ ایران، تنها از هراس «قیام مذهبی» به فتوای مجتهدان نیاز داشته، یا ذهنیت خود او نیز به این «استفتاء» نیازمند بوده است. کما این که مجموعهٔ «اعلامیه» ها و «شب‌نامه»‌های پیشروان مبارزه در دوران مشروطه آکنده است از نقد عملکرد «شاهِ **لامذهب**» و «علما»ئی که «از دین و **مسلمانی** بوئی نبرده‌اند».[۲۰۱] به بیانی دیگر، رفتار بر اساس اصل «مسلمانی»ی متکی به احکام قرآن، مورد هیچ انتقاد و عتابی نیست؛ هر چه هست، «شاه» و «علمائی» هستند که به نظر نویسندگان این متن‌ها، رفتارشان با آموزه‌های اسلامی مغایرت داشته است. گذشته از شب‌نامه‌ها و اعلامیه‌ها- که طبیعتاً توده‌ها را مخاطب قرار می‌دهند- پل‌زدنِ ناخودآگاهانه از اندیشه‌های نو به قرآن و مبانیِ مذهب شیعه، در متن‌های نظریِ نواندیشان آن زمان، اگر آسان‌یاب نباشد، دست کم در بطن اکثریتِ آن‌ها قابل ردیابی است.

با این همه، انقلاب مشروطهٔ ایران، در فضا/ زمان خود، از نظر چیرگی بر سلطانیسم هزاران ساله، چیرگی بر مناسبات فئودالیستیِ کهن (از نوع ایرانیِ آن)، و ورودِ ناقصِ جامعه/ تاریخ ایران به دوران سرمایه‌داری[۲۰۲]، انقلابی پیشرو بود. منتها- با این که ظاهراً بر دین‌کارانِ «مشروعه‌خواه» نیز پیروز شد- سهم دین‌کاران را در «قانون اساسیِ مشروطهٔ ایران» به رسمیت شناخت. از مهم‌ترین اسباب پیروزیِ دین‌کاران در بدست آوردن این سهم، استیلای همان تقدس‌های موروثی بر ذهنیت مردم و پیشاهنگان مبارزه بود، که به ترفندها و دو دوزه بازی‌های برخی از شخصیت‌های لایهٔ روحانی مجال بروز می‌داد؛ همان شخصیت‌هائی که یک دست در دست بازار و دست دیگر در دست دربار، و دست سوم در دست نمایندگان استعمار، راه را برای استحمار و استثمار فرودستان باز می‌خواستند. و طرفه این که آن گروهی از شخصیت‌های روحانی، که هم در فرایند شورش‌های پیش از انقلاب مشروطه، هم در جریان انقلاب مشروطه، و هم در جریان استبداد صغیر، با هدف‌های روشنفکران و پیشاهنگان مبارزه و مردم معمولی همسوئی و همیاری نشان دادند، اکثراً از سوی حامیان همیشگیِ خود، یعنی بازاریان و بازرگانان، برانگیخته و حمایت می‌شدند. چرا که حالا، روند تکامل تاریخی، لزوم سرمایه‌گذاری‌های مستقل و شخصی را پیش آورده بود، که نه نظام فئودالی/ سلطانی- بنا بر ماهیت- می‌توانست با رشد و توسعه آن موافق و همگام باشد، و نه استعمار خارجی با شکل مستقلِ این توسعه. به بیانی دیگر، و از دیدگاه جامعه‌شناسیِ اقتصادی، بازاریان و بازرگانان کلانی که در کنار مردم و روحانیت در این مبارزه شرکت داشتند،

---

۲۰۱ همین جا باید بی‌درنگ این معترضه را بیافزایم که «شعر» دورهٔ مشروطیت، به نسبت متن‌های دیگر این دوره، بسیار پیشروتر بود. چرا که اندک‌شماری از شعرهای این دوره، از نقد «دین‌کاران» به نقد «دین»، و از نقد «سلطانیسم» به نقد «شهریار الاهی» هم رسیده بودند. مثلاً برخی از شعرهای ملک‌الشعرای بهار، و دهخدا (با نام «دخو»).

۲۰۲ احمد اشرف، ***موانع تاریخیِ رشد سرمایه‌داری در ایران، دورهٔ قاجاریه***، تهران: انتشارات زمینه، ۱۳۵۹.

با دگرگون شدن شیوه‌ی تولید ایلی/ عشایری، رسالت تاریخی‌ی خود را در پیدایش دوره‌ی نخست سرمایه‌داری (بورژوازی‌ی ملی) و نزدیک کردن ایران به «کاروان پیش‌رفته» به انجام رساندند. گرچه بسیاری از تحلیل‌گران سیاسی/ اقتصادی‌ی ما، آن «بورژازی‌ی ملی» را موجودی ناقص‌الخلقه تلقی می‌کنند. مثلاً احمد اشرف در پژوهش گرامی‌ی خود می‌نویسد: «استبداد داخلی [مانع دموکراسی‌ی بورژوازی]، همراه با ویژگی‌های شیوه‌ی تولید در اجتماعات ایلی، شهری، و روستائی از یک سو، و استعمار خارجی از دیگر سوی، مانع رشد سرمایه‌داری‌ی جدیدِ صنعتی و تحقق رسالت تاریخی‌ی سرمایه‌داری‌ی ملی در کشور ما گردیدند.»[۲۰۳] البته، تا جائی که به جامعه‌ی روحانیت مربوط است، از این نکته هم نباید غافل ماند که در میان روحانیان (از مجتهدان گرفته تا لایه‌های فروتر)، شخصیت‌های فراوانی هم بودند که ضرورت زمانه را دریافتند و بدون وابستگی به قدرت‌های داخلی یا خارجی، با خواست مردم و نیاز تاریخ همراهی کردند و جان خود را در این راه از دست دادند.[۲۰۴] همچنین، از این نکته‌ی مهم نمی‌توان غافل شد که همین انقلاب ناتمام، همین موجود «ناقص‌الخلقه»، به برکت شور و شعور آن ایرانیانی به مرحله‌ی اجرائی رسید که کم یا بیش، با پیامدهای عینی‌ی «مدرنیته»ی غربی آشنا بودند، و برای تأسیس نهادهای «دولت مشروطه» و «حکومت قانون»، و در رویاروئی با روحانیتِ جاگرفته در «مشروطیت»، از تمام توان خود سود جستند. به عنوان نمونه، و فقط یک نمونه از این تلاش‌ها، بندی از خطابه‌ی محمدعلی فروغی را که در سال ۱۳۱۵ در دانشکده‌ی حقوق ایراد کرده بود، در این جا بازگو می‌کنم. با این توضیح که این سخنرانی، یک سال پس از تأسیس دانشکده‌ی حقوق ایراد شده است. به بیانی دیگر، از تاریخ امضاء فرمان مشروطیت تا سال ۱۳۱۴ ایران از چنین نهادی محروم بود. محمدعلی فروغی، چرائی‌های این فرایند را در جای جای خطابه‌ی خود- البته، اشاره‌وار- بازگو می‌کند. مثلاً، در فرازی از این خطابه، که به مجلس دوم (پس از عزل محمدعلی شاه) مربوط است، ابتدا به شرایط حاکم بر مجلس قانون‌گذاری می‌پردازد، و سپس، گوشه‌ای از کوشش «متجددین» برای رهائی از بن‌بست‌ها را ترسیم می‌کند. من بخش بزرگی از این فراز را در این جا باز می‌گویم و یادآور می‌شوم که اهمیت این بازگفتِ بلند در این است که حدود هفتاد سال پس از تاریخی که فروغی از آن سخن گفته، یعنی در انقلاب سال ۱۳۵۷، اکثریتِ خاص و عامِ مردم ایران، به «قانون»ی رأی دادند که پیکارگران سیاسی و خبرگان آزادی‌خواهِ دوران مشروطیت، آن را با هزار «لطائف‌الحیل» باطل کرده بودند:

> [...] حکومت واقعی را علمای دین حق خود می‌دانستند و نمی‌خواستند از دست بدهند. در صورتی که، هر روز در حکومت خودشان، احکام ناسخ و منسوخ صادر می‌کردند. و اگر عدلیه‌ی صحیح درست می‌شد، یا حکومت از دست آن‌ها بیرون می‌رفت، مجبور می‌شدند با قید به نظامات و اصولی حکومت کنند، [که] آن هم منافی با صرفه و مصالح آن‌ها بود. مخالفت آقایان با حکومت قانون چنان اساس و استحکامی داشت که تا مدت مدیدی، محاکم عدلیه، احکامی را که صادر می‌کردند، «حکم» نمی‌نامیدند و جرأت نمی‌کردند عنوان صدور حکم به خود بدهند؛ و رأی‌ی خود را در دعاوی، «راپرت به مقام وزارت» عنوان می‌کردند. [...] بهانه این بود که با وجود قانون شرع، قانونِ دیگر احتیاج و جایز نیست، و حتا چیز دیگر را «قانون» نمی‌توان نامید. این بود که در مجلس شورای ملی، وضع قوانین برای عدلیه، مشکل، بلکه محال بود؛ یعنی، عدلیه نمی‌توانست اساس پیدا کند. از آن طرف، اقتضای روزگار و عقیده‌ی متجددین، قانون را لازم می‌دانست، و

---

۲۰۳ احمد اشرف، ***موانع تاریخی‌ی رشد سرمایه‌داری در ایران: دوره‌ی قاجاریه***، تهران: انتشارات زمینه، ۱۳۵۹، بخش «طرح مسئله».

۲۰۴ افزون بر گواهانی که در «تاریخ مشروطه‌ی ایران» نوشته‌ی احمد کسروی و در «تاریخ بیداری‌ی ایرانیان» نوشته‌ی ناظم‌الاسلام کرمانی، و «حیات یحیی» نوشته‌ی یحیی دولت آبادی در زمینه‌ی همراهی‌ی روحانیان در تحقق مشروطیت آمده است، حمید حمید نیز در جستار «علماء در اعلامیه‌ها» می‌نویسد: «از اعتراف به این واقعیت‌ها نمی‌توان گذشت که در میان خیل علمائی که به هر مقصود به انقلاب پیوسته بودند، کسانی را نیز می‌توان یافت که تنگاتنگ در کنار مردم قرار داشتند، و از آغاز تا پایان، به بهای جان خویش از آرمانی که مردم به پای آن سرنهاده بودند پیروی کردند؛ در نبرد شرکت جستند، و مصائب فراوانی را نیز تحمل کردند. از میان این گروه معدود می‌توان از شیخ علی اصغر لیلاوالی، ضیاءالعلماء، شیخ سلیم و ثقةالاسلام تبریزی، آن شیخی‌ی شهید، نام برد.» نگاه کنید به :حمید حمید، ***علماء در اعلامیه‌ها***، تارنمای «نشر کارگری‌ی سوسیالیستی»، تاریخ مقاله: ۲۴ آوریل ۱۹۹۴، تاریخ بازدید: ۱۰ مه ۲۰۱۰:
www.iwsn.org/aashr/2/hmid/olma/0.pdf

> وزیر عدلیه‌ی بیچاره، میان دو سنگ آسیا گرفتار بود. بالأخره، مرحوم مشیرالدوله‌ی اخیر، که وزیر عدلیه شد، تدبیری اندیشید و در مجلس عنوان کرد که عدلیه محتاج به قوانینی است، و آن قوانین مفصل است، و اگر بخواهیم آن‌ها را ماده به ماده از مجلس بگذرانیم، سال‌ها بلکه قرن‌ها طول می‌کشد. از این گذشته، ما که در این طریق جدید تازه‌کار هستیم، در وضع قوانین ممکن است اشتباه بکنیم و قوانین بد بگذرانیم. بهتر آن است که مجلس به کمیسیون عدلیه‌ی خود مأموریت بدهد که قوانینی را که دولت برای عدلیه پیشنهاد می‌کند، مطالعه و تصویب کنند و پس از تصویبِ کمیسیون، آن قوانین موقتاً در عدلیه مجری باشد و به آزمایش گذاشته شود، و پس از تنقیح و تهذیب به مجلس پیشنهاد شود و به تصویب رسیده، صورت قانونیت پیدا کند. این طریقه به زحمت زیاد در مجلس تصویب شد. اما مشکلات کمیسیون هم کم‌تر از خود مجلس نبود. [...] تصور نکنید که این کارها به آسانی انجام گرفت. کشمکش‌ها کردیم، لطائف‌الحیل بکار بردیم، با مشکلات و دسیسه‌ها تصادف کردیم. [...] مِن‌جمله این که مقدسین، یعنی مزدورهای آنان، چماق شریعت را نسبت به قوانین بلند کردند و در ابطال و مخالفت آن‌ها با شرع شریف، حرف‌ها زدند و رساله‌ها نوشتند، که از جمله به خاطر دارم که یکی از آن رساله‌ها، اول‌اعتراض و دلیلش بر کفری بودن آن قوانین، این بود که در موقع چاپ کردنِ آن‌ها، فراموش شده بود که ابتدا به بسمِ‌الله الرحمن الرحیم بشود. [...][۲۰۵]

***

ابزار بیداری‌ی ایرانیان در حوالی‌ی انقلاب مشروطیت، که از درونه‌ی رویدادهای نیک و بد تاریخی سر برکرد، عمدتاً عبارت بودند از: **یک)** مجموعه‌ی جنبش‌های شیخیه و باب و منشعبات آن‌ها، در نیمه‌ی نخست سده‌ی دوازدهم خورشیدی. این جنبش‌ها، با این که مانند بسیاری از جنبش‌های رهائی‌بخش مردم ایران از مذهب به مذهب روئید، اما با دست بردن به برخی از اصول فقه و کلام شیعی، چهار ستون روحانیت شیعه را لرزاند. صرف نظر از آموزه‌های صرفاً مذهبی‌ی این دو مکتب (که در مقوله‌ی «کلام اسلامی» می‌گنجیدند؛ اکثراً به زبان عربی نوشته شده بودند؛ و طبیعتاً مردم عادی از فهم آن‌ها عاجز بودند)، بیش‌ترین تکیه‌ی پیروان این دو مکتب و مکتب‌های منشعب از آن‌ها، تبلیغِ مفهوم برابری‌ی حقوقی و مدنی و جنسیتی از یک سو، و توسعه‌ی اقتصادی، از سوی دیگر، بود.[۲۰۶] **دو)** اعزام دانشجو به اروپا، که از سال ۱۱۹۱ خورشیدی و با دو دانشجو آغاز شد و در سال‌های بعد ادامه یافت. **سه)** ورود صنعت چاپ به ایران (۱۱۹۵). **چهار)**

---

[۲۰۵] متن کامل خطابه‌ی فروغی، از سوی داریوش کارگر، روز ۲۵ ژانویه ۲۰۱۲ به من رسید. داریوش کارگر در ابتدای متن نوشته است: « در میان مجله‌های قدیمی و مطالب آرشیو به خطابه‌ی محمدعلی فروغی در دانشکده‌ی حقوقِ دانشگاه تهران برخوردم، که وی در سال ۱۳۱۵ ایراد کرد. متن این سخنرانی ابتدا در مجله‌ی «یغما»، و سپس به نقل از یغما، در جاهای دیگر تجدید چاپ شد.»

[۲۰۶] شیخ احمد احسائی (۱۱۲۹ تا ۱۲۰۵ خورشیدی) پایه‌گذار مکتب شیخی بود. او در دیداری با فتحعلی‌شاه قاجار نظرات تازه‌ی خود را ابراز کرد و مورد مرحمت او هم قرار گرفت. اما پس از چندی که از تبلیغ و خطابه‌های او در شهرهای ایران گذشت، و نظراتش مورد توجه مردم قرار گرفت، از سوی مجتهدان زمان تکفیر شد. شاگرد و جانشینی او، سید کاظم رشتی (۱۲۱۲ تا ۱۲۵۹ خورشیدی) و سپس کریم خان کرمانی، نظرات او را در کتاب‌های متعدد بسط دادند. این مکتب، معاد جسمانی، عروج جسمانی‌ی پیامبر، و الهی‌بودن قرآن را رد کرده است. پس از مرگ سید کاظم رشتی، سید علی محمد شیرازی، با استفاده از زمینه‌های فلسفی و اجتماعی‌ی مکتب شیخیه، در سال ۱۲۲۳ خورشیدی، مکتب باب را معرفی کرد. از آن رو که اینک جامعه‌ی ایران، بیش از زمان شیخ احمد احسائی، آماده‌ی تحول و تغییر بود، اندیشه‌های سیاسی/ اجتماعی‌ی باب و پیروان او به سرعت در لایه‌های متوسط جامعه جا باز کرد. شیخ احمد روحی (۱۲۷۲ تا ۱۳۱٤ قمری)، نیز، در ترویج فرقه/ مذهب «ازلی»، که از بابیت منشعب می‌شد، و باز البته در قالب تز «اتحاد اسلام»، نقش مهمی در گسترش آگاهی‌های مدنی، حقوقی و جنسی در میان ایرانیان بازی کرد؛ به طوری که برخی از پیکارگران مشروطیت در «کمیته‌ی انقلابی» از هواداران فرقه‌ی او بودند. در این جا اشاره به این نکته را بایسته می‌دانم که فریدون آدمیت، تاریخ‌پژوهش مشروطیت، در جای جای آثار متفاوت خود، در سخن گفتن پیرامون باب، و به ویژه پیرامون بهائیان (شاخه‌ای از مکتب باب)، بدون توجه به تأثیر مثبت آموزه‌های اجتماعی‌ی این جنبش‌ها در بیداری‌ی ایرانیان، این جنبش‌ها را یکسره برساخته‌ی «استعمار» برآورد کرده است، و از سوی برخی از پژوهشگران تاریخ نیز پاسخ رد یا قبول گرفته است. من وارد این مقوله نمی‌شوم، اما برای آگاهی‌ی بیش‌تر در زمینه‌ی این دو جنبش، و پیامدهای آن‌ها، خواننده‌ام را به مآخذ زیر، که با دیدگاه‌های متفاوت نوشته شده‌اند، رجوع می‌دهم:

* دکتر محمد علی اکبری، ***شیخیه: از اعتراض تا تأسیس فرقه‌ی مذهبی***، تهران: پژوهش‌نامه‌ی علوم انسانی، دانشگاه شهید بهشتی، شماره‌ی ۳٤، ۱۳۸۳؛ دکتر علی محمد اکبری، ***نقش اندیشه‌های شیخیه در ظهور جنبش بابیه***، تهران: پژوهش‌نامه‌ی علوم انسانی، دانشگاه شهید بهشتی، شماره‌ی ۳۸، ۱۳۸٤.

* محمد رضا فشاهی، ***واپسین جنبش قرون وسطائی در دوران فئودال (اخباری و اصولی، شیخی و بابی)***، تهران: انتشارات جاویدان، ۱۳۵٦.

* احسان طبری، جنبش بابیان، آخرین و بزرگترین جنبش قرون وسطائی، بخش ۳۸ از کتاب ***برخی بررسی‌ها درباره‌ی جهان‌بینی‌ها و جنبش‌های اجتماعی در ایران***، انتشارات حزب توده‌ی ایران، ۱۳۸۹

* دلارام مشهوری، ***رگ تاک: گفتاری درباره‌ی نقش دین در تاریخ اجتماعی‌ی ایران***، پاریس: انتشارات خاوران، ۱۳۸۲، جلد اول.

حضور کارشناسان خارجی در نهادهای دولتی، و معلمان و مدرسان خارجی در مدرسه‌ی دارالفنون. **پنج)** سفرهای مکرر بازرگانان ایرانی به خارج از کشور، که پیامد اوج‌گیری‌ی اقتصاد تجاری در ایران بود.[۲۰۷] **شش)** قراردادهای «گلستان» (۱۸۱۳/ ۱۱۹۲)، «ترکمانچای» (۱۸۲۸/ ۱۲۰۷)، و «آخال» (۱۸۸۱/ ۱۲۶۰)، که مجموعاً ۲۷ شهر/ ایالت ثروتمند (از نظر معادن و ژئوپلیتیک) و بخش عمده‌ی دریای خزر را از نقشه‌ی ایران زدود، و به خاک روسیه‌ی تزاری افزود؛ همچنین، قرارداد «پاریس»، (۱۸۵۶/ ۱۲۳۵) که هرات و کلاً افغانستان را از ایران جدا کرد، و بعداً بخش‌هائی از بلوچستان و مکران را به انگلستان واگذاشت (۱۸۸۷/ ۱۲۶۶). و بالأخره، قرارداد روسیه‌ی تزاری با بریتانیا بر سر تقسیم ایران به دو منطقه‌ی نفوذ این دو کشور (۱۹۰۷/ ۱۲۸۶)، یعنی، عملاً تجزیه‌ی ایران؛ و درست در بحبوحه‌ی پیکار مشروطه‌خواهان با محمدعلی شاه قاجار. **هفت)** مسابقه و تعارض دولت‌های انگلستان، فرانسه، و روسیه‌ی تزاری، برای تسلط بر منابع و امکانات ارضی و اقتصادی‌ی ایران.[۲۰۸] چرا که از یک سو، طرفین این مسابقه‌ی مرگبار، مدام در حال افشاء و انحلال توطئه‌ها و خنثا کردن امتیازهای یکدیگر بودند، و از سوی دیگر، تراکم امتیازهای انحصاری به بیگانگان به میزانی رسیده بود که حتا ناآگاه‌ترین قشرهای ملت ایران را با شتاب هر چه بیش‌تر به حقوق از دست رفته‌ی خود آگاه می‌کرد. **هشت)** برخی از اهرم‌های اجرائی‌ی این استعمارِ چند ملیتی- مانند ورود مُبلّغانِ دینی و تأسیس مدرسه‌های دینی در ایران- حامل پدیده‌های پارادوکسیکالی بودند که ضمن پدید آوردن زمینه‌های مناسب برای تحققِ هدفِ استعمارگران، خیزش پرهیبی از آگاهی را نیز در مردم ایران سبب شدند. افزون بر باب گفت‌وگوئی که مبلغان مذهبی‌ی اروپائی با کتاب‌های خود و در مناظره‌های خود با «علماء» و روحانیان مسلمان باز کردند، و افزون بر این که ردیه‌نویسی‌های روحانیان مسلمان، بارآور بحث‌های تازه‌ای در قلمرو نظری‌ی اسلام شد،[۲۰۹] تأسیس مدرسه‌های میسیونری از سوی این

---

۲۰۷ پیرامون تأثیر متقابل اقتصاد تجاری و بروز افکار دموکراتیک در ملت ایران، به مأخذ زیر نگاه کنید:
خسرو شاکری، ***پیشینه‌ی اقتصادی- اجتماعی‌ی جنبش مشروطیت و انکشاف سوسیال دموکراسی در آن عهد***، تهران: نشر اختران، ۱۳۸۵.

۲۰۸ پیرامون حرکت‌های استعماری‌ی بریتانیا و روسیه‌ی تزاری در کتاب‌های مربوط به این دوره از تاریخ ایران سخن بسیار گفته شده است، اما پیرامون سوءاستفاده‌ی فرانسویان از منابع ملی‌ی ما کم‌تر سخن رفته است. به عنوان نمونه، در سال ۱۲۶۳ خورشیدی (۱۸۸٤ میلادی)، فرانسویان، امتیاز انحصاری‌ی عملیات باستان‌شناسی در شهر شوش را از ناصرالدین‌شاه و بعد از مظفرالدین شاه گرفتند و ظرف ٤۳ سال، پانصد تُن از آثار تاریخی‌ی سه هزار ساله‌ی این شهر باستانی را به موزه‌ی لوور پاریس منتقل کردند. این قرارداد شوم در زمان رضا شاه پهلوی (۱۳۰٦ خورشیدی) توسط مجلس شورای ملی لغو شد. برای آگاهی‌ی بیش‌تر از این رویداد درازمدت به مأخذ زیر، با عنوان «***شوش در لوور***»، نگاه کنید:

http://www.jadidonline.com/images/stories/flash_multimedia/Susa_shush_test/susa_high.html

۲۰۹ فرستادن مأموران دینی برای اشاعه‌ی مسیحیت در کشورهای خاور، به فرمان پاپ، رهبر کاتولیک‌ها، در پایانه‌های سده‌ی ۱۵ میلادی (در عصر صفویه) آغاز شد. اندکی بعد (۱۰۳٦ه. ق/ ۱٦۲٦ م) پادشاه فرانسه، لویی سیزدهم، برای تبلیغ مذهب کاتولیک و کسب امتیازهای تجاری و ایجاد نفوذ سیاسی برای فرانسه، «لویی دهی Lovies des Hags» را به ایران اعزام کرد. کمپانی‌ی فرانسوی‌ی هند شرقی نیز توسط کشیشی فرانسوی به نام «رافائل دومان»- که در سال‌های ۱۰۵۵ تا ۱۱۰۸ هجری (۱٦٤۵ تا ۱٦۹٦ میلادی) در ایران بود- تأسیس شد. پس از آن بود که تعداد مسیونرهای شاخه‌های مختلف مسیحیت، عمدتاً از کشورهای فرانسه، بریتانیا، و سپس‌تر، ایالات متحده‌ی امریکا، روانه‌ی ایران شدند و در شهرهای مختلف ایران به فعالیت پرداختند. «هنری مارتین» نیز از معروف‌ترین کشیش‌های انگلیسی در عصر قاجاریه بود که با پشتیبانی‌ی سفیران انگلیس در ایران (سِر جان ملکم، و بعد، سِر گُر اُزلی)، در اجرای هدف‌های استعماری‌ی بریتانیا نقش مؤثری ایفاء کرد. در ورای اجرای هدف‌های استعماری، و افزون بر تأسیس مدرسه‌های دینی، یکی از فعالیت‌های فرهنگی‌ی این مبلغان، (از همان عصر صفویه) نوشتن کتاب‌های دینی، و ترتیب دادن جلسه‌های بحث و مناظره با روحانیان مسلمان بود، که همواره هم با «ردیه‌نویسی»ی روحانیان ایران روبه‌رو می‌شد. تا جائی که تاریخ این دوره نشان می‌دهد، تأثیر تبلیغات مسیونرها اروپائی در مسیحی کردن ایرانیان بسیار کم‌تر از تأثیر «ردیه»های مجتهدان مسلمان در مسلمان کردن یهودیان و مسیحیان ایرانی بود. عبدالهادی حائری در پژوهش خود می‌نویسد: «درست در هنگامی که ایران برای نخستین بار گام در گرداب سیاست جهانی گذاشته بود و با فقدان آزمودگی و آگاهی‌های بسنده پیرامون دیپلماسی‌ی اروپا با دولت‌های استعمارگر و فزون‌خواهی مانند انگلیس و روس و فرانسه دست به گریبان بود، [...] تبلیغ کیش مسیح، سست ساختن بنیاد باورهای مذهبی‌ی ایرانیان، متوجّه ساختن اندیشه‌های همگانی، به ویژه دستگاه‌های رهبری‌ی سیاسی و مذهبی‌ی ایران، به مسائل فکری و عقیدتی و معنوی که در کشور انگلیس ریشه داشت و از آن جا سرچشمه می‌گرفت، و به یک سخن بازداشتن جامعه‌ی ایران از گزینش راهی درست [بود] برای آشنائی‌ی ژرف و بنیادی بر ژرفای دو رویه‌ی تمدن بورژوازی‌ی غرب و رویاروئی‌ی همه سویه با آن. اسناد و مدارک تاریخی نیک گزارشگر آن است که هنری مارتین در درازای درنگ ۱٦ ماهه اش (از مه ۱۸۱۱ تا سپتامبر ۱۸۱۲) در ایران این وظائف استعماری را در چارچوب توانائی خویش به بهترین شیوه انجام داده است.» (حائری، ص ۵۱٦) عبدالهادی حائری البته وارد این مقوله نمی‌شود که در صورت عدم حضور این میسونرها، «گزینش راهی درست برای آشنائی با تمدن غرب» در آن سکون و سکوت حاکم بر «جامعه‌ی ایران»، چه‌گونه و از چه راه‌هائی می‌توانست پدید آید. در حالی که با رویکردی متفاوت با رویکرد عبدالهادی حائری، می‌توان گفت که مبادله‌ی نظر بین روحانیان دین اسلام (از جمله شاخه‌ی «اخباریون») و این کشیش‌ها، به تدریج نخستین روزنه‌ها را، برای اندیشیدن به جوانب «دین» و گفت‌وگو و چون و چرا درباره‌ی آن، رو به ایرانیان گشود. این «روزنه»، در کنار رواج آموزش نوین (که به ویژه در اواخر عصر قاجار در مدرسه‌های مسیونری اجرا می‌شد) و دیگر ابزار بیداری، راه را برای دیدن و شناسائی‌ی

کشورهای استعماری نیز، به حکم جریان دیالکتیکیِ تاریخ، افق تازه‌ای را رو به ایرانیان گشود. چرا که، برنامه و روش نوین آموزش و پرورش در این مدرسه‌ها، روش «تعلیم مکتبی» در ایران را پس زد، و به زودی از سوی برخی از روشنفکران فرهنگی- مانند میرزا حسن تبریزی مشهور به رشدیه و محمدعلی تربیت و علی اکبر دهخدا- در شهرهای مختلف ایران گرته‌برداری شد.[۲۱۰] **نُه)** نوشته‌های آن گروه از نویسندگان ایرانی که پس از قراردادهای «گلستان» و «ترکمانچای» شهروند روسیه برشمرده شدند. این نویسندگان آزادی‌خواه، در کنار نویسندگان تبعیدی/ مهاجر، از یک سو از داغ و درفش «شاه/ مجتهد» در ایران در امان بودند، و از سوی دیگر، تلاش پیگیر توده‌های فرودست روسیه را- برای دست‌یابی به آزادی و حقوق اقتصادی و سیاسیِ خود- می‌دیدند، و از سوی سوم، با رفت و آمد به کشورهای غربی و خواندن متن‌های آن‌ها، جهان‌بینی‌ها و فضاهای تازه‌ی زندگی در کشورهای اروپائی را نفس می‌کشیدند. کتاب‌های این نویسندگان- افزون بر ترجمه‌ی آثار نویسندگان غیرایرانی- هم شرایط اسفبار زندگیِ مردم ایران را به رخ می‌کشیدند، و هم با تکیه بر ساختار سیاسیِ کشورهای اروپائی، «قانون» و «قانون اساسی» را شرط نخستِ برقراریِ عدالت و مدنیت و ترقی و سربلندیِ ایران معرفی می‌کردند. (که پژوهشگران بسیاری در دوران کنونی بر نمودهای ذهنیت مذهبی در اکثر این آثار انگشت گذاشته‌اند.) در این زمینه، می‌توان از روشنگرانی مانند میرزا یوسف‌خان مستشارالدوله تبریزی، عبدالرحیم طالبوف، زین‌العابدین مراغه‌ای، میرزا ملکم خان ناظم‌الدوله، سیدجمال‌الدین اسدآبادی (در دوره‌ی نخست فعالیتش)، میرزا آقاخان کرمانی (در دوره‌ی متأخر زندگی)، و فتحعلی آخوندزاده نام برد. در کنار آثار این نویسندگان، باید از «سیاحت‌نامه»های ایرانیانی یاد کرد که به امپراتوری‌های تزاری و عثمانی و به کشورهای غربی سفر کرده بودند. (که البته به دلیل مشکلات مربوط به چاپ و توزیع و حضور سانسور دولتی، این کتاب‌ها در سطح محدودی به دست پیشاهنگان درون‌مرزی می‌رسید.) افزون بر این‌ها، نشریه‌های پرشماری که از سوی آزادی‌خواهان ایرانی با همین درون‌مایه‌ها در دسترس مردم باسواد ایران قرار می‌گرفت، و به گفته‌ی سعید نفیسی، «باسوادها برای بی‌سوادها می‌خواندند و مردم حلقه می‌زدند و روی خاک می‌نشستند و گوش می‌دادند.»[۲۱۱] ادوارد براون، پژوهشگر تاریخ ادبیات ایران، از ۳۷۱ نشریه‌ی فارسی و ترکی‌زبان نام برده است که در فاصله‌ی ۱۲۶۸ تا ۱۳۲۹ هجریِ قمری (۱۸۵۰ تا ۱۹۱۱میلادی) توسط ایرانیان درون‌مرزی یا برون‌مرزی منتشر می‌شد.[۲۱۲] با مطالعه‌ی شرح کوتاهی که ادوارد براون برای معرفیِ هر نشریه نوشته است، در می‌یابیم که به جز انگشت‌شماری روزنامه‌های دولتی، بقیه‌ی این نشریه‌ها در جهت آگاهی‌رسانی و روشنگری‌های سیاسی/ اجتماعی/ فرهنگی پیش می‌رفته‌اند.

به یاریِ این مجموعه از ابزار بود که نسیمی از پیامدهای مدنی و حقوقیِ انقلاب فرانسه، انقلاب‌های صنعتیِ اروپا، انقلاب استقلال امریکا، ایده‌ی عدالت اقتصادی در سوسیالیسم و کمونیسم، مبارزات فمینیستی در امریکا و اروپا، خیزش‌های دهقانی و سپس، انقلاب ۱۹۰۵ در روسیه، به پیشاهنگان سیاسی و فرهنگیِ ایران وزید؛ به آگاهی‌های حقوقی و جنسی و طبقاتیِ آن‌ها افزود؛ و آن‌ها نیز خبر را، دهان به دهان به گوش مردم بی‌سواد اعماق جامعه رساندند.

هدف پنهان مسیونرها، یعنی وجوه استعماریِ مأموریت آن‌ها، باز کرد. برای آگاهیِ بیش‌تر پیرامون مسیونرهای اروپائی و تأثیر پارادوکسیکال فعالیت آن‌ها مآخذ زیر را بخوانید و خود استنتاج کنید:

* عبدالهادی حائری، ***نخستین رؤیائی‌های اندیشه‌گران ایران با دورویه‌ی تمدّن بورژوازیِ غرب***، تهران: انتشارات امیرکبیر، ۱۳۶۲.
* مریم میراحمدی، ***دین و مذهب در عصر صفویه***، تهران: انتشارات امیر کبیر، ۱۳۶۳.
* هما ناطق، ***ایران در راهیابیِ فرهنگی، ۱۸۳۴ - ۱۸۴۸***، پاریس: انتشارات خاوران، ۱۹۹۰.

۲۱۰ برای آگاهی در این زمینه، به مأخذ زیر نگاه کنید:

❖ هما ناطق، ***ایران در راه‌یابیِ فرهنگی، ۱۸۳۴ تا ۱۸۴۸***، پاریس: انتشارات خاوران، ۱۹۹۰.

۲۱۱ سعید نفیسی، اشرف‌الدین، مجله‌ی «سپید و سیاه»، شهریور ۱۳۳۴. برگرفته از:

❖ پرفسور ادوارد برون، ***تاریخ مطبوعات و ادبیات ایران در دوره‌ی مشروطیت***، ترجمه و تحشیه و تعلیقات تاریخی و ادبی، به قلم محمد عباسی، تهران: انتشارات کانون معرفت، ۱۳۳۵، ص ۱۲۲. **توضیح:** متن سعید نفیسی از جمله افزوده‌های مترجم، محمد عباسی، به کتاب ادوارد براون است.

212 Edward G. Browne, ***The Press and Poetry of Modern Persia***, Cambridge: at the University Press, 1914.

مطالبه‌ی حکومت «جمهوری»، کنش‌های پیگیر مردم در شورش بر «امتیازنامه‌ی رژی»، در مبارزه با حکومت سلطانی، در مبارزه با پیشنهاد «حکومت مشروعه»، و تشکیل فزاینده‌ی گروه‌های سیاسی (که خود را با نام‌هائی مانند «حزب» یا «کمیته» یا «جمعیت» شناسائی می‌کردند و به صورت‌های «سِرّی» یا «غیبی» یا «نیمه مخفی» یا علنی در مبارزه شرکت داشتند)، به این آگاهی‌ی نسبی گواهی می‌دهند. به عنوان نمونه، همان نیروهای «سوسیال دمکرات»، شاخه‌ی تبریز، به آن حد از آگاهی و رشد سیاسی رسیده بودند که در دوره‌ی کوتاه «استبداد صغیر» (پس از به توپ بستن مجلس اول به فرمان محمدعلی شاه قاجار (۱۲۸۷ خورشیدی) این پرسش را مطرح کنند که:

> آیا تشکیل یک سازمان مستقل و خالص، که افکار و سیاست سوسیال دموکراسی را در ایران نمایندگی کند، ضرورت دارد، یا باید به صفوف سایر نیروهای دموکرات و ملی بپیوندند؟[۲۱۳]

گرچه این پرسش هنوز میان گروه‌های چپ ایران مطرح است، و هنوز بر سر پاسخ آن بحث و حتا مجادله وجود دارد، اما ذات **طرح** چنین پرسش معتبری در اوان کودکی‌ی جنبش چپ ایران، از شـــعور سیاسی‌ی پیکارگران یک سده پیش تاریخ ایران خبر می‌دهد.

پس از استقرار همان مشروطه‌ی نیم‌بند- یا به تعبیر ماشاءالله آجودانی، مشروطه‌ی «اسلامی شده»- تا پیش از آن که رضا شاه پهلوی بر تخت طاووس ایران بنشیند، و شور و شوقِ دست یافتن به افق‌های تازه را از «قلم» ایرانیان برگیرد- انبوه پیکارگران و پیشگامان مبارزه، به آن میزان از آگاهی‌های سـیاسـی رسـیده بودند که در شب‌نامه‌ها، اعلامیه‌ها، شعرها و نشریه‌های خود، در کنار افشاگری پیرامون «ظلم حکام»، «دستِ دراز اجانب»، «شیطان‌صفتی‌ی مُلا» و «وطن‌فروشان»، از حق و حقوق «کارگر»، از «آزادی‌ی قلم و اجتماعات»، و از اجرای درسـت قانون اسـاسـی دفاع می‌کردند. به عنوان مثال، در تاریخ ۱۳۰۱/۲/۸ «اتحادیه‌ی مرکزی‌ی کارگران ایران» به رهبری‌ی «محمد دهگان» برای نخسـتین بار، اول ماه مه را به عنوان «روز کارگر» مطرح کرد و کارگران را به شـرکت در تظاهرات اول ماه مه فراخواند.[۲۱۴] روزنامه‌ی «حقیقت» در این روز نوشت:

> اول ماه مه باید تعطیل شـود. این تعطیلی هرج مرج نیسـت. این تعطیل، انقلاب هم نیسـت، این تعطیل اسـت که باید ملت از حکومت با زور حقوق خود را مسترد دارد. این عید نیست بلکه دادخواهی است. این روزی است که دولت باید موجودیت ملت را بفهمد، باید به حکومت فهماند که تو نوکر ملت هستی، باید موافق خواهش ملت رفتار کنی، تو نمی‌توانی از آزادی‌ی قلم، آزادی مطبوعات و آزادی اجتماعات جلوگیری کنی؛ زیرا آن حق مشـروع ملت اسـت. تو نباید بدون رضـا و خواهش ملت بر خلاف مصـالح ملت با اجانب معاهده عقد کنی؛ زیرا آن حق را ملت به تو نداده اسـت. تو نباید و نمی‌توانی حکومت را برای شـخص خود آلت استفاده قرار داده، اولاد اتباع خود را وکیل کنی و قوم و خویش خود را در ادارات دولتی جابه‌جا نمایی.[۲۱۵]

---

۲۱۳ حسن ماسالی، ***سیر تحول جنبش چپ ایران و عوامل بحران مداوم آن***، ص ۵۱. این کتاب شناسنامه ندارد. تاریخ پیش‌گفتار این کتاب، اردی‌بهشت ۱۳۸۰/ مه ۲۰۰۱ است.

۲۱۴ برگرفته از بیانیه‌ی کارگران «فلزکار مکانیک»: ***فراخوان برگزاری‌ی مراسم روز کارگر***، تارنمای «گزارشگر»، ٦ اسفند ۱۳۸۸: http://www.gozareshgar.com/10.html?&tx_ttnews%5Btt_news%5D=8683&tx_ttnews%5BbackPid%5D=23&cHash=8851b4702a

۲۱۵ برگرفته از بیانیه‌ی کارگران «فلزکار مکانیک»، پیشین.

چند روز بعد (۱۱/ ۲/ ۱۳۰۱) همین روزنامه، همان خواسته‌هائی را مطرح کرد که پس از ۹ دهــه هنوز که هنوز اسـت از دل و زبان و قلم پیشگامان سیاسی و کارگری‌ی ایران برمی‌تراود:

به عقیده‌ی ما: ۱- فردا باید بدون تأخیر در تمام نقاط ایران حکومت‌های نظامی لغو شود، زیرا مخالف قانون اساسی است. ۲- محبوسین سیاسی که به جرم آزادی‌خواهی یا هر نوع مسلک سیاسی در ایران توقیف شده‌اند، آزاد گردند. ۳- جرایدی که تا به حال بدون محاکمات هیئت منصفه در مرکز ولایت توقیف شده‌اند، منتشرگردند. ۴- اصول امتیاز [دادن به] روزنامه که بر خلاف قانون اساسی است ملغا گردد.۵- نظارت و جلوگیری از هر قبیل آزادی‌خواه [کذا] لغو بشود. ۶- کنفرانس، میتینگ، اجتماعات در همه جا آزاد باشد.۷- مأمورین دولتی که به آن‌ها اتهام دزدی و خیانت زده شده و اعم از وزیر و وکیل یا مستشار تحت محاکم بیرون آیند.۸- قانون برای تعیین حدود کارگر و کارفرما وضع شود، به طور کامل از مظالم و غارتگری‌ی حکام و مأمورین دولت عموماً جلوگیری و در صورت تجدید فجایع آن‌ها، مجازات به آن‌ها داده شود. (مأخذ پیشین)

اما در کنار تأکید بر روشنگری‌های قلمی و بیانی‌ی پیکارگران مشروطیت، و تأثیر آن در گسترش آگاهی و ایجاد مقاومت در مردم معمولی، باید از سلحشوران و رزمندگانی مانند ستارخان و باقرخان یاد کرد، که با نبرد مسلحانه در دوره‌ی «استبداد صغیر»، در سرنوشت نهائی‌ی این انقلاب نقشی تعیین‌کننده داشتند. این جنبش ملی و بی‌پشتوانه‌ی هر نوع حمایت بیگانه، زمانی خیز برداشت، که کشتار و قلع و قمع مشروطه‌خواهان توسط محمدعلی شاه قاجار و حامیان خودی و بیگانه‌ی او از یک سو، و فرصت طلبی‌ی گروه مؤثری از «مشروعه»خواهان و مالکان بزرگ از سوی دیگر، مردم را به سوی ناامیدی و سستی در مبارزه سوق داده بود. پس از آن که محمدعلی شاه قاجار مجلس را به توپ بست و انحلال مشروطه را اعلام کرد، ستارخان، مردی بی‌بهره از سواد خواندن و نوشتن، فرزند روستائی دورافتاده از مرکز استان آذربایجان، فرماندهی‌ی «مجاهدان تبریز و قفقاز و ارمنی‌ها» را در محله‌ی «امیرخیز» تبریز به عهده گرفت، و در کنار همتای خود باقرخان (که در محله‌ی «خیابان» تبریز با نیروهای دولتی می‌جنگید)، حدود یازده ماه در برابر نیروهای عظیم محمدعلی شاه، که این دو محله را محاصره کرده بودند، جنگید. تصویر طاق نصرت‌ها و پذیرائی‌های ستایش‌آمیز مردم شهرها بر سر راه ستارخان و ۳۰۰ تن از مجاهدان همراهش به تهران، و تصویب لقب «سردار ملی» برای ستارخان و «سالار ملی» برای باقرخان در مجلس شورای ملی، اهمیت و تأثیر نبرد سرسختانه‌ی این دو، به ویژه ستارخان، را به تاریخ مشروطیت گزارش داده‌اند. فشرده‌ترین شرحی که پیرامون وضعیت این دو پیکارگر در متن‌های مربوط یافته‌ام، مقاله‌ای از میرهدایت حصاری است که بخشی آن را در این جا بازمی‌گویم:

[...] آغاز یورش نیروهای دولتی به پایگاه‌های آزادی‌خواهان تبریز در همان روز به توپ بستن مجلس در تهران، نشانگر این بود که طرح این حمله از پیش تنظیم شده بود. آن‌ها فکر می‌کردند همان طور که مجلس شورای ملی را در تهران در عرض چند ساعت مضمحل و حتا مشروطه را در همان روز در سرتاسر ایران برانداختند، کار تبریز را نیز با یك حمله یکسره خواهند کرد. ولی به زودی به اشتباه خود پی بردند. دیدیم که تا پایان کار نیز با این که از همه‌ی شهرها نیرو بر سر تبریز ریخته بودند، کوچك‌ترین موفقیتی به دست نیاوردند و حتا سرانجام شکست نیز خوردند. با رسیدن خبر به توپ بستن مجلس در تهران و برافتادن مشروطه در آن جا و حمله‌ی نیروهای دولتی به تبریز، نمایندگان انجمن ایالتی‌ی تبریز نیز دست و پای خود را گم کرده و عده‌ای مخفی و تنی چند در سفارت‌خانه‌ها بست نشستند، ولی مجاهدان بی‌باکانه در مقابل نیروهای استبداد ایستادند و قدمی عقب ننهاده و به هر سختی که بود ماندند تا شاهد پیروزی را در آغوش کشیدند. [...] دراین میان، پاخیتانوف کنسول روس در تبریز ظاهراً به عنوان میانجی‌گری و دلسوزی به فعالیت پرداخته و مجاهدان را تشویق می‌کرد که دست از جنگ برداشته و از پادشاه ایران طلب بخشش نموده و امنیت خود را بدست آورند. همین

موضوع موجب اختلاف بین آزادی‌خواهان شد و عده‌ای اسلحه‌ی خود را تسلیم کردند، و دایره‌ی آزادی‌خواهان محدودتر شد، و تنها محلات «امیرخیز» و «خیابان» و «دو گرد آزادی»، ستارخان و باقرخان باقی ماندند. مجاهدان نوبر و مارالان نیز مرعوب شده، تصمیم به تسلیم اسلحه‌ی خود گرفتند، و راه «خیابان» را به روی نیروهای دولتی به سرکردگی رحیم خان چلبیانی قره‌داغی باز کردند، و او با دبدبه و کبکبه وارد شهر شده در باغ شمال اقامت گزید (۲۲ تیر ماه ۱۲۸۷) و به جمع‌آوری‌ی سلاح پرداخت. [...] رحیم خان خبر فتح تبریز را به محمدعلی شاه تلگراف زد. بدین ترتیب محله‌ی امیرخیز تنها نقطه‌ای بود که هرگز حاضر به تسلیم نشد. ستارخان که از سال‌ها پیش در تبریز به دلیری معروف شده بود، در این جنگ‌ها مردانگی و قهرمانی‌ی زیادی از خود نشان داد. هیچ کس گمان نمی‌کرد که ستارخان با آن عده‌ی کم در مقابل آن همه نیروی دولتی تاب مقاومت داشته باشد؛ و همه فکر می‌کردند که یکی دو روزه او نیز یا تسلیم خواهد شد و یا فرار کرده جان خود را به در خواهد برد؛ ولی چنین نشد. [...] دولتیان که گمان می‌کردند گرفتن یك محله‌ی کوچك و پیروزی بر چند مجاهد محصور و با کم‌ترین امکانات کار سختی نخواهد بود، با تمام نیرو به امیرخیز حمله‌ور شدند، ولی پس از یك روز جنگ شدید، کاری نکرده و عقب نشستند. فردای آن روز پاخیتانوف که از این همه سماجت متعجب شده بود، به محله‌ی امیرخیز آمده و به نصیحت ستار پرداخت و گفت بیرق از کنسول‌خانه فرستاده‌ام، به بالای در خانه‌ی خود بزن و در زینهار دولت روس باش؛ و حتا قره‌سوارانی‌ی تمام آذربایجان را وعده داد که از شاه به نام او بگیرد. در این جا بود که ستارخان آن جمله‌ی معروف خود را خطاب به کنسول روس گفت: «آقای جنرال کنسول! من می‌خواهم هفت دولت به زیر بیرق ایران بیایند، من زیر بیرق بیگانه نروم.»[۲۱۶]

***

از زنان آزادی‌خواه و مبارز این دوره مانند «زرین تاج- قرة‌العین»[۲۱۷] و «بی بی خانم استرآبادی»[۲۱۸] و «رستمه»[۲۱۹] و «بی بی مریم بختیاری»[۲۲۰] که بگذریم، بارقه‌هائی از رشد را در حرکتِ همگانی و پیگیر زنان ایران- در شورش بر «امتیازنامه‌ی رژی»[۲۲۱]، در فرایند انقلاب مشروطه، در زُدایش ماده‌های زن‌ستیزانه‌ی قانون اساسی و مصوبه‌های مجلس

---

۲۱۶ میرهدایت حصاری، ***پاسخ سردار ملی به سفیر روس***، تارنمای «ستارخان»، بازدید ۲ تیر ۱۳۸۸:
http://sattarkhan2.blogfa.com/post-6.aspx

۲۱۷ پیرامون شخصیت زرین‌تاج، ملقب به «قرة‌العین»، در پاره‌ای دیگر از همین کتاب سخن گفته‌ام. در این جا فقط اشاره می‌کنم که او زنی دانشمند، شاعر و سخنوری توانا، آزادی‌خواهی مبارز، رهبری فداکار برای جنبش باب، و آزادی‌خواهی مبارز علیه حکومت ستم‌پیشه‌ی قاجار بود. او نخستین زن ایرانی است که در حضور مردان نقاب از رو برگرفت. گرچه در اوج جوانی به فجیع‌ترین وجه ممکن کشته شد، اما برایند آموزه‌های او در رشد آگاهی‌ی زنان- از زنان فرودست گرفته تا زنان درباری- در شرکت مؤثر زنان در جنبش‌های اجتماعی‌ی بعدی عینیت یافت.

۲۱۸ مبارزه‌ی بی بی خانم استرآبادی، نویسنده‌ی کتاب «معایب‌الرجال» (۱۳۰۹ قمری / ۱۲۷٤ خورشیدی؟) مبارزه‌ای فرهنگی برشمرده می‌شود. او، که بزرگ‌شده‌ی دربار قاجار بود، در این کتاب اشاره‌ای به امور سیاسی ندارد. اما پیکان تیز زبان را عمدتاً به سوی نابرابری‌ی جنسی نشانه رفته است. او مدرسه‌ی دخترانه‌ای در تهران تأسیس کرد، و اندیشه‌های برابری را بیش‌تر از راه همین مدرسه اشاعه داد. اما کتاب معایب‌الرجال، در زمان زندگی‌ی او تنها در نسخه‌هائی معدود در دسترس گروه نخبگان درباری قرار گرفت، که آن هم در بیداری‌ی همان نخبگان بی‌تأثیر نبود.

۲۱۹ رستمه، زنی که «در تیراندازی و شمشیرزنی اشتهار داشت.» و در قیام زنجان علیه استبداد صغیر، از سران قیام برشمرده می‌شد. در این مورد به کتاب زیر نگاه کنید:

- عبدالحسین ناهید، ***زنان ایران در جنبش مشروطه***، آلمان غربی، انتشارات نوید، ۱۳٦۸/ ۱۹۸۹، ص ۱۲.

۲۲۰ سردار بی بی مریم بختیاری، در جریان انقلاب مشروطه، در قیام مردم علیه استبداد صغیر، و سپس، علیه قرارداد ۱۹۱۹ همدوش مردان جنگید. به مأخذ زیر نگاه کنید:

- نورالله دانشور علوی، ***جنبش وطن‌پرستان اصفهان و بختیاری***، تهران، نشر آنزان، ۱۳۷۷، ص ۱۷۹.

۲۲۱ قرار دادِ «امتیازنامه‌ی رژی»، در تاریخ ۲۷ رجب ۱۳۰۷ قمری، برابر با ۲۰ مارس ۱۸۹۰ میلادی (۱۲٦۹ خورشیدی) در تهران به امضاء ناصرالدین شاه قاجار رسید. بر اساس این قرارداد استعماری، خرید و فروش توتون و تنباکوی ایران به صورت انحصاری به کمپانی رژی واگذار شد. این کمپانی پس از امضاء قرار داد، نمایندگان خود را به شهرهای مختلف ایران فرستاد، و کار خود را شروع کرد. اما به رغم حمایت صد در صد شاه و دولتمردانش و نیز به رغم حمایت بسیاری از مجتهدان طراز اول شهرهای ایران از این کمپانی، یک سال مبارزه‌ی پیگیر مردم در شهرهای بزرگ شاه را وادشت که با قبول پرداخت خسارت به کمپانی، قرارداد را منحل کند. برای اطلاع بیش‌تر از پیش‌زمینه‌های سیاسی‌ی این قرارداد و شرح مبارزه‌ی مردم ایران با آن، به مآخذ زیر مراجعه کنید:

قانون‌گذاری- می‌بینیم. از میان ده‌ها نمونه‌ای که در کتاب‌های مربوط به این دوران به ثبت رسیده، به یک نمونه از شرکت زنان در شورش بر «امتیازنامه‌ی رژی» بسنده می‌کنم. با این که شرکت زنان تهران در این جنبش بسیار گسترده‌تر از شهرهای دیگر بود، من در این جا، با استفاده از پژوهش گرامی‌ی فریدون آدمیت، از موردی که در شهر صد در صد مذهبی‌ی مشهد روی داد، یاد می‌کنم: «کمپانی‌ی رژی»، پس از این که امتیاز خرید و فروش توتون و تنباکو را از ناصرالدین شاه قاجار دریافت می‌کند، نماینده‌های خود را به شهرهای ایران روانه می‌دارد. نماینده‌ی این کمپانی در خراسان، می‌تواند «حمایت حکمران خراسان و مجتهد بزرگ مشهد و علمای آن جا را به دست آورد و برخلاف انتظار، با ایشان مناسبات دوستانه‌ی خصوصی برقرار کند». در نتیجه، کوشش مردم و «یک واعظ و یک پیشنماز و یک مدرس دینی و دسته‌ای از طلاب» برای جلب همکاری‌ی «مجتهد بزرگ» به جائی نمی‌رسد. «ژنرال مَکلین انگلیسی، که خود شاهد صحنه‌ی حوادث بوده» در «گزارش خصوصی»ی خود می‌نویسد:

> [...] به عقیده‌ی صاحب‌دیوان، حادثه‌ی روز چهارشنبه خیلی جدی بود. زیرا قضیه‌ی تنباکو کنار رفته بود و ذهن مردم سرشار از عناد سیاسی و دینی بود. **جنبه‌ی غریب این ماجرا حضور زنان بود**. اما آن‌ها از گروه زنان هرزه‌ای بودند، چوب در دست آمدند که مردان را بزنند، مگر به حرکت آیند. [...][۲۲۲] (تأکید از من است.)

البته که از دید قدرت‌های مسلط، چه خارجی باشند و چه داخلی، مبارزه‌ی مردم علیه آن‌ها، علاوه بر سرکوب‌های دیگر، با برچسب «هرزگی» نیز روبه‌رو می‌شود؛ حال این مبارزان چه زن باشند و چه مرد. کما این که در شورش بر امتیازنامه‌ی رژی، پیکارگران مرد نیز، هم از سوی استعمارگران، هم از سوی حکومتیان و هم از سوی مجتهدانی که به خاطر شرکت در سرکوب جنبش، از « عنایت ملوکانه» بهره بردند، با عنوان‌هائی مانند «یاغیان»، «آشوبگران»، «لات‌ها» و «اوباش» شناسائی شدند. با این همه، پیکار مردم در مبارزه با «امتیازنامه‌ی رژی» به ثمر نشست و چپاولگران بیگانه را دست کم در یک زمینه از ایران راند، و پیش‌زمینه‌های انقلاب مشروطه را فراهم آورد. اما نکته‌ی درخور اهمیت در بحث حاضر، حضور زنان در این جنبش است؛ آن هم در تاریخ دوم ربیع‌الاول سال ۱۳۰۹ هجری‌ی قمری، (مهر ۱۲۷۰ خورشیدی، ۶ اکتبر ۱۸۹۱ میلادی)، یعنی تقریباً همزمان با حضور زنان اروپا و امریکا در صحنه‌ی مبارزه‌های حقوقی، سیاسی، اقتصادی؛ آن هم زمانی که، ناصرالدین شاه در تلگراف خود به صاحب دیوان مشهد نوشته بود: «همه‌ی یاغیان را بدون استثناء دستگیر نمائید، صد نفر آن‌ها را جلو توپ بگذارید و پدرشان را بسوزانید». (عبارت‌های درون گیومه‌ها را از صفحات ۶۰ تا ۶۵ کتاب «شورش بر امتیازنامه‌ی رژی»، نوشته‌ی فریدون آدمیت، ۱۳۶۰، برگرفته‌ام.)

زنان پیشاهنگ، حتا پیش از انقلاب مشروطه، با تأسیس کلاس‌ها و مدرسه‌های دخترانه به انتشار آگاهی‌های جنسی، علمی، بهداشتی، و خانوادگی همت گذاشتند،[۲۲۳] و گروهی از آن‌ها (حتا زنان درباری)، گردهم‌آئی‌های خصوصی را به تفهیم آراء و اندیشه‌های تازه اختصاص دادند. در جریان جنبش مشروطیت نیز با رهبری‌ی مردان درافتادند، و در برابر عناصر

- ❖ فریدون آدمیت، ***شورش بر امتیازنامه‌ی رژی***، تهران: انتشارات پیام، ۱۳۶۰.
- ❖ فریدون آدمیت و هما ناطق، ***افکار اجتماعی و سیاسی و اقتصادی در آثار منتشرنشده‌ی دوران قاجار***. (**توضیح:** من این کتاب را ندیده‌ام، اما بازگفت‌هائی از آن را در کتاب‌ها خوانده‌ام.)
- ❖ ابراهیم تیموری، ***تحریم تنباکو: اولین مقاومت منفی در ایران***. (**توضیح:** من این کتاب را ندیده‌ام.)
- ❖ عبدالحسین ناهید، ***زنان ایران در جنبش مشروطه***، پیشین، صص ۳۰ تا ۴۰.
- ❖ ناظم‌الاسلام کرمانی، ***تاریخ بیداری‌ی ایرانیان***، به اهتمام علی اکبر سعیدی سیرجانی، تهران: نشر پیکان، چاپ پنجم، ۱۳۷۶، در بیان واقعه‌ی رژی، صص ۱۹ تا ۶۰.

[۲۲۲] فریدون آدمیت، پیشین، ص ۶۴.

[۲۲۳] هما ناطق، ایران در راهیابی‌ی فرهنگی از ۱۸۳۴ تا ۱۸۴۸ میلادی، لندن: ۱۹۸۸ (۱۳۶۷)؛ هما ناطق و فریدون آدمیت، ***افکار اجتماعی و سیاسی و اقتصادی در آثار منتشرنشده‌ی دوران قاجار***، تهران: نشر آگاه، ۱۳۵۶.

محافظه‌کار ایستادند. پس از تشکیل مجلس نیز، با قانون انتخابات ۱۳۲۴ قمری (۱۲۸۵ خورشیدی- ۱۹۰۶ میلادی)، که «با صراحت کامل، زنان را از تلاش‌های سیاسی باز می‌داشت»،[۲۲۴] مقابله کردند؛ «انجمن‌های نیمه سِرّی» تشکیل دادند؛ «در مورد وام از روس و انگلیس به مخالفت برخاستند»؛ با اهداء پول و طلا و جواهرات خود، در تأسیس بانک ملی‌ی ایران مشارکت کردند؛ تصویب حق طلاق برای زنان و تجدید نظر در «تعدد زوجات» را از مجلس خواستار شدند؛ مدرسه‌های دخترانه، با برنامه‌های مدرن درسی، تأسیس کردند. مسعود آقائی، در کتاب گرامی‌ی «انجمن‌های نیمه‌سِرّی‌ی زنان در نهضت مشروطیت» فهرستی از نام ۶۳ مدرسه‌ی دخترانه در تهران را ثبت کرده است که در سال ۱۲۹۲ خورشیدی (۱۹۱۳ میلادی) فعال بوده‌اند.[۲۲۵] چند تن از زنان پیشرو، پس از مشروطیت، به انتشار روزنامه‌ی مخصوص زنان روی آوردند، و افزون بر مقاله‌های آموزشی و پندآموز، در برابر مسائل سیاسی، مثلاً، قرارداد ۱۹۱۹، بازتاب مخالف نشان دادند.[۲۲۶] و طرفه این که، همه‌ی این کوشش‌ها، زیر حمله و تیغ محافظه‌کاران معمم و مکلائی پیش می‌رفت که چه در مجلس و چه در سطح جامعه، بر این نظر پافشاری داشتند که: «آزادی‌ی زنان به تضعیف نظم سنتی‌ی حاکم بر روابط مرد و زن می‌انجامد و بر فرهنگ اسلامی و مخصوصاً تشیّع، ضربه‌ی مهلک می‌زند.»[۲۲۷] و البته، قانون اساسی‌ی مشروطه‌ی ایران به سرکوبگران حق این اعمال نفوذ را داده بود. از این رو، می‌توان گفت که زنان آگاه‌شده‌ی ایران با طرح این مطالبات، نه تنها اصل‌ها و ماده‌های قانون اساسی، بلکه- دانسته یا نادانسته- اصول فقهی را به چالش گرفته بودند.

***

با این همه، در نگاهی شناخت‌شناسانه به متن‌های دوران مشروطیت، می‌بینیم حضور ملموس این آگاهی‌های نسبی، به معنای رهائی‌ی روان جمعی‌ی مردم ایران از **رسوبات** فرهنگ توارثی- یعنی فرهنگ استوار بر شریعت و پیوند «دین/ دولت»- نبود. بسیاری از تحلیل‌گران تاریخ فکر، نشانه‌های این رسوب را در نوشته‌های روشنگرانی مانند آخوندزاده و میرزا ملکم‌خان، طالبوف، و ... ردیابی و تحلیل کرده‌اند. اما تا جائی که من می‌دانم، این کار، در زمینه‌ی نامه‌ها و شب‌نامه‌ها و اعلامیه‌ها و شعرهای آن دوره، به صورت گسترده انجام نشده است.[۲۲۸] من هم در این مختصر بر آن نیستم. اما بایسته است که در همین جا به چند نمونه اشاره کنم. در مطالعه‌ی ادبیات دوران مشروطیت به نامه‌هائی برمی‌خوریم که از سوی لایه‌های فرودست جامعه برای دادخواهی به مسئولان امر نوشته شده بود؛ به اعلامیه‌ها و شب‌نامه‌هائی بر می‌خوریم که از سوی گروه‌ها و جمعیت‌ها و کانون‌های مشروطه‌خواه منتشر شده بود؛ همچنین، مقاله‌های مندرج در نشریه‌ها، و شعرها را هم داریم، که به عنوان مهم‌ترین متن‌های این دوران، ما را در شناخت ذهنیت پیشروان مبارزه، و

---

۲۲۴ در نخستین نظام‌نامه‌ی انتخابات، که در سال ۱۳۲۷ قمری (۱۲۸۸ خورشیدی/ ۱۹۰۹ میلادی) به امضاء محمدعلی شاه قاجار رسید، افراد محروم از شرکت در انتخابات به قرار زیر معرفی شده بود: «نسوان، اشخاص خارج از رشد و آن‌هائی که در تحت قیمومیت شرعی هستند، ورشکستگان به تقصیر، مرتکبین قتل و سرقت، مقصرینی که مستوجب مجازات قانون اسلامی شده‌اند...» نگاه کنید به: صدیقه ببران، ***سیر تاریخی‌ی نشریات زنان در ایران معاصر***، تهران: انتشارات روشنگران و مطالعات زنان، ۱۳۸۱، ص ۲۲.

۲۲۵ ژانت آفاری، ***انجمن‌های سری‌ی زنان در نهضت مشروطه***، ترجمه به فارسی از: دکتر جواد یوسفیان، تهران: نشر بانو، ۱۳۷۷، صص ۱۷ تا ۲۰.

۲۲۶ در سال ۱۹۱۹ (۱۲۹۸ خورشیدی) قراردادی بین وثوق‌الدوله (نخست وزیر احمد شاه قاجار) و لرد کرزن (وزیر خارجه‌ی انگلستان) امضاء شد که طی‌ی آن نهادهای نظامی و مالی‌ی کشور، امتیاز راه آهن و راه‌های شوسه‌ی ایران در اختیار انگلستان قرار می‌گرفت. وثوق‌الدوله در برابر این وطن‌فروشی مبلغ دویست هزار تومان از انگلستان رشوه دریافت کرد. برای اطلاع بیش‌تر از زمینه‌های سیاسی/ اجتماعی‌ی این قرارداد و پیامدهای آن، از جمله، به کتاب زیر مراجعه کنید:

- حسین مکی، ***تاریخ بیست ساله‌ی ایران***، جلدهای اول تا سوم، تهران: انتشارات علمی، ۱۳۷۴.

۲۲۷ در این پاراگراف، عبارت‌های درون گیومه‌ها را از کتاب «انجمن‌های سری‌ی زنان در نهضت مشروطه» نوشته‌ی ژانت آفاری برگرفته‌ام.

۲۲۸ یادآوری می‌کنم که پیرامون شعرهای دوران مشروطیت، کتاب‌های فراوانی نوشته شده، که موارد ستیز شاعران را نیز تحلیل کرده‌اند. اما تا جائی که من خوانده‌ام، در هیچ یک از این آثار، حضور رسوبات فرهنگی در این شعرها، یعنی آن چه که شاعران آن دوره، خود با مظاهر آن در ستیز بودند، بررسی نشده است.

بافتار اجتماعی/ سیاسی/ فرهنگی‌ی دوره‌ی مشروطیت یاری می‌دهند. تا جائی که بافت اجتماعی/ فرهنگی مربوط می‌شود، با دقت در این متن‌ها، دو واقعیت به دید می‌آید: ۱) مردم ایران، لایه‌ی روحانی را پناهگاه نهائی‌ی خود می‌دانستند. مثلاً در شکایت‌نامه‌ای که گروهی از کشاورزان جهرم به حکمران فارس نوشتند می‌خوانیم: «اگر به عرض ما نرسیدید، عریضه به **شاه نجف** می‌نمائیم و اگر قبول نشد، عریضه به اولیای دولت خواهیم کرد.»[۲۲۹] ۲) در اثر فشار مردم ایران و پیشگامان آن‌ها بود که برخی از شخصیت‌های روحانی، به صف مبارزان پیوستند. چرا که در درازنای سلطنت دودمان قاجار (به استثنای دوره‌ی محمد شاه قاجار)،[۲۳۰] بیش از هر زمانی در تاریخ ایران، این لایه‌ی اجتماعی، هم در میان مردم فرودست جامعه و هم در شاهان خاندان قاجار و دربارهای آن‌ها نفوذ داشتند، و رأی برگزیدگان آن‌ها در سیاست‌گذاری‌های داخلی و خارجی‌ی ایران نقش تعیین‌کننده داشت. ناصرالدین شاه قاجار پیرامون جنگ با کشور روسیه‌ی تزاری که با قراردادهای «گلستان» و «ترکمانچای»، به قیمت از دست رفتن بخش عظیمی از سرزمین ایران تمام شد، می‌گوید: «آن فقره‌ی جهادیه‌ی علمای کربلا و نجف که آمدند طهران و فتحعلی شاه بیچاره را واداشته با دولت روسیه به جنگ و جدال انداخته، از نظرها فراموش نشده است.»[۲۳۱] خرده‌پاهای این لایه نیز به برکت همین نفوذ و به برکت ناآگاهی‌ی مردم، در سراسر شهرها و روستاهای ایران از مال و مکنت و اعتبار برخوردار بودند؛ در نتیجه، جای شگفتی نیست که در حفظ وضع موجود می‌کوشیدند. بی‌سبب نیست که با مطالعه‌ی تاریخ‌ها و تفسیرهای این دوران درمی‌یابیم که جز انگشت‌شماری از شخصیت‌های این لایه‌ی اجتماعی که با مردم و خواسته‌های آن‌ها هم‌گام شدند، اکثر شخصیت‌های بانفوذ روحانی، یا در برابر یاری‌خواهی‌ی مردم سکوت می‌کردند، یا عملکردشان مصداق «شریک دزد و رفیق قافله» بود، و یا آشکارا به سود حکومت در سرکوب جنبش‌های مردمی گام می‌زدند. البته زمانی هم رسید که بسیاری از پیشگامان مردم، این «علماء» را شناختند و افشا کردند؛ اما در همین حالت هم پناهگاهی به جز «اسلام» و «مسلمانی» نمی‌شناختند. افزون بر متن‌هائی که از سوی گروه‌های صرفاً مذهبی (مانند «هیئت ملّیه‌ی اسلامی») در افشاء «علما»ی وابسته منتشر می‌شد، شب‌نامه‌ها و اعلامیه‌ها و «بیان‌نامه»ها و شعرهای این دوران آکنده است از نمونه‌های نقد روحانیت و مبارزه با این لایه‌ی اجتماعی از یک سو، و پناهندگی به اسلام و مسلمانی و قرآن، و حتا هراس از سلب اعتقاد مردم نسبت به «علماء»، از سوی دیگر. چند نمونه‌ی کوتاه را در این جا درج می‌کنم: گروهی با نام «هواخواهان ملت»، که قبلاً در اعلامیه‌ای از عدم واکنش «حجج اسلام نجف» نسبت به مبارزه‌ی مردم و سرکوب آن توسط حکومت، انتقاد کرده بودند، در شب‌نامه‌ی بعدی خود می‌نویسند:

> [...] این است حال و روز وزرای پایتخت سلطنت، ظلم حکام در بلاد؛ چاره منحصر است به اقدامات مجدانه‌ی علمای اعلام، که برحسب غیرت مسلمانی جلو افتاده، تا مردم متابعت نمایند، عقب آن‌ها باشند. افسوس! که آن‌ها همه به اغراض شخصی رفتار می‌نمایند. چیزی که در میان نیست رضای خداوند و خدمت بشر یا حفظ وطن، یا ملاحظه‌ی توهم، یا غیرت یا فتوت است و غافلند از این که نزدیک است عقاید مردم به کلی از آن‌ها قطع شود.[۲۳۲]

گروه «ندای فرشته‌ی بشری»، در یکی از اعلامیه‌های خود «وارونه‌گوئی»ی چهار تن از «وعاظِ رؤسای روحانی» را

---

[۲۲۹] فریدون آدمیت، ***شورش بر امتیازنامه‌ی رژی***، پیشین، ص ۲۶.

[۲۳۰] ماشاءالله آجودانی، ***مشروطه‌ی ایرانی و پیش‌زمینه‌های نظریه‌ی «ولایت فقیه»***، پیشین، ص ۱۴۹.

[۲۳۱] فریدون آدمیت، ***شورش بر امتیازنامه‌ی رژی***، پیشین، ص ۳۰.

[۲۳۲] حمید حمید، ***علماء در اعلامیه‌ها***، تارنمای «نشر کارگری‌ی سوسیالیستی»، صص ۸ تا ۹، تاریخ مقاله: ۲۴ آوریل ۱۹۹۴، تاریخ بازدید: ۱ آوریل ۲۰۱۰:
www.iwsn.org/aashr/2/hmid/olma/0.pdf
مأخذ حمید حمید عبارت است از: محمد مهدی شریف کاشانی، واقعیات اتفاقیه در روزگار، به کوشش منصوره‌ی اتحادیه (نظام مافی) و سیروس سعدوندیان، مکان نشر (؟)، نشر تاریخ ایران، ص ۲۷.

افشا می‌کند و در جمع‌بندی‌ی سخن می‌نویسد:

> خلاصـه، منادی‌ی فرشـته‌ی بشـری هر گاه بخواهد اقدامات کفرآمیز و شـرک‌انگیز هر یک از چهار نفر را از بدو تولد الی کنون، جزء و کلاً، بر خلق عالم محسوس و روشن بدارد، با براهین قوی‌ی بدون معارض، می‌تواند. ولی اندک ستاریت را از شرایط مذهب خود شمرده، نقداً در افشاء اعمال آن چهار نفر خاموش خواهد بود.[۲۳۳]

همین گروه به دنبال اعلامیه‌ی پیشین، اعلامیه‌ی دیگری منتشر می‌کند که در بخشی از آن چنین می‌خوانیم:

> عجب بدبختی شـامل حال ما مردم شده است که دچار و گرفتار دو نمره از مردم بی‌فتوتِ بی‌حمیت شـده‌ایم. یکی رجال ظالم خـون‌خـوار قدار متعدی‌ی بی‌شـرم و بی‌حیای دولت، و یکی بعضی از علمای طماع، بی‌دیانت، بی‌غیرتِ ملت که هیچ کدام اصلاً معتقد به خدا و رسول و مردمی و صواب و عقاب و مؤاخذه‌ی الهی نیستند. [...] این علماء ... به ملاحظه‌ی دخل‌های خیالی که دارند اقدام مجدانه نخواهند کرد. پس باید ما مردم در خیال اصلاح کار خود باشیم و کاوه‌ی آهنگری پیدا نمائیم.[۲۳۴]

از اعلامیه‌ها و شـب‌نامه‌های گروه‌های آزادی‌خواه گذشـته، این دوگانگی‌ی ذهنی را در آثار فرهیختگانی که با برایندهای فکری‌ی عصر روشنگری، و با بنیادهای ساختار سیاسی در کشورهای غربی ابراز آشنائی می‌کردند نیز می‌بینیم. میرزا ملکم خان ناظم‌الدوله- یکی از نظریه‌پردازان مهم و مؤثر در شـروع و ادامه‌ی جنبش مشـروطیت- نمونه‌ی بارز این میان‌ماندگی است. ملکم خان در درازنای پنـجاه سال فعالیت سیاسی و نشر نظرات سیاسی/ اجتماعی‌ی خود- که «اندیشه‌ی ترقی و پیشرفت ایران» را بر پیشانی داشت- آموزه‌های تازه‌اش را با آموزه‌های توارثی چنان در هم و برهم عرضه کرده اسـت که مخاطب نوشـته‌های او (حتا تحلیل‌گران زبده‌ی تاریخ فکر) در جمع‌بندی‌ی دسـتگاه نظری‌ی او وامی‌مانند.[۲۳۵] یرواند آبراهـامیان با پشتـوانه‌ی نوشته‌ی ملکم خان در نشریه‌ی «قانون»، شماره‌ی ۱، بهمن ۱۲۶۸ می‌نویسد: «قصد اصلی‌ی وی بیان فلسفه‌ی غرب به کلام مقدس قرآن، حدیث و امامان شیعه بود.»[۲۳۶] و سپس، به متن سخنرانی‌ی ملکم- در لندن- اشاره می‌کند و بخشی از آن را به شرح زیر بازمی‌نویسد:

> ما دریافته‌ایم که آن دسـته از افکار که هنگام ورود از طریق عوامل شـما در اروپا، به هیچ وجه پذیرفتنی نبود، زمانی که **ثابت شد در ذات اسلام وجود دارد**، به یکباره با کمال میل پذیرفته می‌شد. می‌توانم به شما اطمینان دهم که اندک پیشرفتی که در ایران و عثمانی خصوصاً در ایران می‌بینید، به واسطه‌ی این حقیقت است که **مردم**، اصول اروپائی‌ی شما را گرفته، و

---

[۲۳۳] حمید حمید، ***علماء در اعلامیه‌ها***، پیشین، صص ۱۰ تا ۱۱.

[۲۳۴] حمید حمید، ***علماء در اعلامیه‌ها***، پیشین، صص ۱۲ تا ۱۳.

[۲۳۵] به عنوان مثال، هما ناطق، کارشـناس تاریخ و متون مشـروطیت، در سـال ۱۳۵٤ متنی در تأویل نوشـته‌های ملکم خان- در روزنامه‌ی «قانون»- منتشر کرد که مؤید درک درست ملکم خان از اومانیسم عصر روشنگری بود. من این متن را در زمان انتشار آن خوانده‌ام، اما آن را در حال حاضر در اختیار ندارم. هما ناطق اما چند سال پس از انقلاب ۵۷، در تبعید، متن دیگری در زمینه‌ی روزنامه‌ی «قانون» و نظرهای ملکم خان نوشـت، و در آن، پس از پوزش‌خواهی‌ی ضـمنی از برداشـت‌های نادرسـت خود در مقاله‌ی نخسـت، نظرهای ملکم را به عنوان یکی از انگیزه‌های برایش حکومت ولایت فقیه شـناسـائی کرد. همچنین، فریدون آدمیت در کتاب «فکر آزادی و مقدمه‌ی نهضـت مشـروطیت»، دسـتگاه نظری‌ی ملکم خان را چنین می‌خواند که او مجلس شورای ملی و اراده‌ی ملت را منشاء قانون می‌دانسته است. در حالی که تورج امینی، با بازخوانی‌ی آثار ملکم خان، این نظر فریدون آدمیت را- با استناد به نوشته‌های خود ملکم خان- رد می‌کند. نشانی‌ی متن‌های هما ناطق و تورج امینی به قرار زیر است:

- ❖ هما ناطق، ***روزنامه‌ی قانون پیش‌درآمد حکومت اسـلامی:*** نشـریه‌ی «دبیره»: جُنگ انجمن بهروز، چاپ افق، کلن/ آلمان غربی، شماره‌ی ٤، پاییز ۱۳٦۷، صص ۷۲ تا ۱۰۲.
- ❖ تورج امینی، ***ارزیابی‌ی ملکم خان و روزنامه‌ی قانون***، تارنمای «گفتمان ایران»، ۲۳ فروردین ۱۳۸۵: http://www.goftman-iran1.info/-othermenu-13/371

[۲۳٦] یرواند آبراهامیان، ***ایران بین دو انقلاب: از مشـروطه تا انقلاب اسـلامی***، ترجمه‌ی کاظم فیروزمند، حسـن شـمس‌آوری، دکتر محسـن شانه‌چی، تهران: چاپ هشتم، نشر مرکز، ۱۳۸۳، ص ٦۲.

به جای این که بگویند این اصـــول از انگلیس، فرانســـه یا آلمان آمده، گفته‌اند «ما هیچ کاری با اروپائیان نداریم اما این‌ها اصول حقیقی‌ی دین ماست (و در واقع این امر درست است) که اروپائیان آن‌ها را اخذ کرده‌اند!» این امر اثر حیرت‌انگیزی داشته است.[۲۳۷] (پرانتز در بازگفت آبراهامیان هست. تأکیدها از من است.)

از این بازگفت می‌توان نتیجه گرفت که ملکم خان پیرامون ذهنیت «مردم» سـخن گفته اسـت. اما، افزون بر متعرضـه‌ی او (تأیید او در داخل پرانتز در گفتاورد بالا)، از نوشـته‌های دیگر او چنین برمی‌آید که برای خود او نیز «ثابت شـده» بود که «افکار» اروپائیان، «در ذات اسـلام وجود دارد.» او از سـوئی، از لزوم «مجلس شـورای ملی» و «اراده‌ی ملت» سـخن می‌راند، و از سوی دیگر، در حفظ بنیادهای سنتی در ساختارهای سیاسی‌ی موجود قلم می‌زند. مثلاً:

ترتیب قوانین در ایران باید کار مخصوص مجلس شورای دولت باشد. مجلس شورای دولت یعنی این مجلس دربار اعظم که از بناهای عمده سلطنت قاجاریه است.[۲۳۸]

ملکم خان در «دفتر تنظیمات»، حکومت جمهوری را معرفی می‌کند. اما از آن جا که این شیوه‌ی حکومت اصـولاً در ذهنیت او نمی‌گنجد، از این الگو می‌گذرد، و سپس تعریفِ دو گونه از حکومت سلطنتی را به دست می‌دهد:

سـلطنت دو ترکیب دارد: در هر حکومتی که، هم اختیار وضـع قانون و هم اختیار اجرای قانون در دسـت پادشـاه است، ترکیب آن حکومت را سلطنت مطلق گویند. مثل سلطنت روس و عثمانی. و در حکومتی که اجرای قانون با پادشاه و وضع قانون با ملت است، ترکیب آن حکومت را سلطنت معتدل می‌نامند. مثل انگلیس و اتریش و فرانسه. [...] اوضـاع سـلطنت‌های معتدل به حالت ایران اصـلاً مناسـبتی ندارد، چیزی که برای ما لازم اسـت، تحقیق اوضاع سلطنت‌های مطلق است[۲۳۹]

ملکم خان، اما، در عین دفاع از «سـلطنت مطلقه» برای ایران، بارها از لزوم «قانون»، «حقوق ملت»، «حقوق برابر»، «آزادی‌ی فردی»، «آزادی‌ی قلم»، «آزادی‌ی بیـان»، «آزادی‌ی اجتمـاعـات»، ««آزادی‌ی عقیـده و فکر» و «اجتهـاد شخصـی» دفاع می‌کند. مثلاً در شماره‌ی ۱۳ نشریه‌ی «قانون» می‌نویسد:

ما می‌گوییم خداوند عالم همه‌ی ما را یعنی همه‌ی افراد بشر را انسان آفریده است و به هر یك از ما این مأموریت مبارك را کرامت فرمود که خود را به اجتهاد شخصی‌ی خود از پایه‌ی انسانیت به مقام آدمیت برسانیم.[۲۴۰]

همچنین، در گزارشی که فتحعلی آخوندزاده از سخنان ملکم ارائه می‌دهد، می‌خوانیم:

---

۲۳۷ یرواند آبراهامیان، ***ایران بین دو انقلاب: از مشروطه تا انقلاب اسلامی***، پیشین.

۲۳۸ نشریه‌ی «قانون»، شماره‌ی ۲. برگرفته از جستار زیر:
- تورج امینی، ***ارزیابی‌ی ملکم خان و روزنامه‌ی قانون***، پیشین.

۲۳۹ حسن قاضـی‌مرادی، ***ملکم‌خان و لیبرالیسم پیش از مشروطه***، ۲٤ مارس ۲۰۰۹/ ٤ فروردین ۲۵٦۸ شاهنشـاهی، (٤ فروردین ۱۳۸۸ خورشیدی)، تارنمای «سکولاریسم نو»:
http://www.irancpi.net/digran/matn_3109_0.html
حسن قاضی‌مرادی این بازگفت را از مأخذ زیر برگرفته است:
- ***رساله‌های میرزا ملکم خان ناظم‌الدوله***، به کوشش حجت‌الله اصیل، تهران: نشر نی، ۱۳۸۱، ص ۱۲٤.

۲٤۰ نشریه‌ی «قانون»، شماره‌ی ۱۳. برگرفته از جستار زیر:
- حسن قاضی‌مرادی، ***ملکم‌خان و لیبرالیسم پیش از مشروطه***، پیشین.

سعادت و فیروزی نوع بشر وقتی رو خواهد کرد که عقل انسانی کلیتاً، خواه در آسیا خواه در اروپا، از حبس ابدی خلاص شود و در امورات و خیالات تنها **عقل بشری** سند و حجت گردد و حاکم مطلق شود **نه نقل**.[۲۴۱] (تأکیدها از من است.)

اما، با تکیه‌ی بی‌چون و چرا بر لزوم مطابقت قوانین ایران با «قوانین عدل الهی» و لزوم دادنِ «قدرت کامل به مجتهدین»، «اجتهاد شخصی» را- که قرار است کارکرد آن «سند سعادت نوع بشر» باشد- باطل می‌کند؛ و با این پیشنهاد، «عقل بشری» را به جایگاه تاریخی‌ی «نقل» وامی‌گذارد:

* آن **مجتهدین** و آن عقلا و آن شاهزادگان و آن بزرگان که دارای فضل و امین آدمیت هستند موافق قواعد مخصوص جزء مجلس خواهند بود.[۲۴۲] (تأکید از من است.)
* باید اقلاً ۱۰۰ نفر از **مجتهدین بزرگ** و فضلای نامی و عقلای معروف ایران را در پایتخت دولت در یک مجلس شورای ملی جمع کرد، و به آن‌ها مأموریت و قدرت کامل داد که اولاً آن قوانین، آن اصولی که از برای تنظیم ایران لازم است، تعیین و تدوین و رسماً اعلام نمایند.[۲۴۳] (تأکید از من است.)
* این مجلس دربار اعظم، مقدمه‌ی شورای کبرای ملی است. شما جزو وزرای دولت نیستید، شما مشیران نظام ایران هستید. عدد شما کم است. باید اقلاً هفتاد نفر باشید. **مجتهدین بزرگ** و فضلای ملت باید لامحاله داخل این مجلس باشند. احیای ایران موقوف به **اجرای قوانین عدل الهی** است. ترتیب قوانین بر عهده‌ی مجلس شماست.[۲۴۴] (تأکیدها از من است.)

گروهی از تحلیل‌گران، از دیدگاه روان‌شناسی، این دوگانگی‌های ملکم خان را به حساب فرصت‌طلبی و خصلت‌های فردی‌ی او می‌گذارند، و برخی دیگر، از دیدگاه جامعه‌شناسی، ریشه‌ی این دوپارگی را به سرشت طبقاتی‌ی او، و به خصلت‌های «لیبرالیسم» و «طبقه‌ی بورژوا» مربوط می‌کنند؛ و برخی دیگر، آن را به عنوان «تاکتیک» برآورد می‌کنند. اما مخاطب نوشته‌های ملکم خان، از دیدگاه معرفت‌شناسی، در برابر این پرسش‌های ساده قرار دارد که آیا این فرهیخته‌ی عاشق «ترقی»، مفهوم و کارکرد «اجتهاد شخصی» را نمی‌شناخته؟ یا، قرآن و «نقل» را به عنوان پشتوانه‌ی «مجتهدان بزرگ» در «اجرای قوانین عدل الهی» شناسائی نمی‌کرده است؟ آیا این متفکر و نظریه‌پرداز «مدرن» و شیفته‌ی فلسفه‌ی سیاسی/ اجتماعی‌ی «جان استوارت میل» و مکتب انسانگرای اگوست کنت، از کارکرد حکم «تکفیر» در دستگاه نظری‌ی معنی‌کنندگان «قوانین عدل الهی» در طول تاریخ ایران، و حتا در دوره‌ی معاصر خود بی‌خبر بوده است؟ یعنی نمی‌دانسته است، که «مجتهدان بزرگ و فضلای نامی»ی زمانه‌ی خودش، در کشتار دگراندیشان منتقدِ حاکمیت، و شیخی‌ها و بابیان، دستی توانا داشتند؟ نمی‌دانسته است که این دگراندیشان به خاطر «اجتهاد شخصی» و ابراز «عقیده و فکر» با تکفیر «مجتهدان بزرگ و فضلای نامی» به خاک و خون غلتیده‌اند؟

اما طبیعتا، ملکم خان در میدان این پریشانی تنها نبود؛ سیدجمال‌الدین اسدآبادی/ افغانی در دوره‌ی متأخر زندگی، و میرزا آقاخان کرمانی در دوره‌ی متقدم زندگی‌ی خود، در اثبات سازگاری بین اصول قرآنی با دانش‌های نوین اروپائی کوشیدند.

---

[۲۴۱] حسن قاضی‌مرادی، ***ملکم‌خان و لیبرالیسم پیش از مشروطه***، پیشین. مأخذ حسن قاضی‌مرادی برای این بازگفت، به قرار زیر است:
❖ آخوندزاده، میرزا فتحعلی، ***الفبای جدید و مکتوبات***، تصحیح مجید محمدزاده، فرهنگستان علوم شوروی، آذربایجان، ۱۹۶۳، ص ۲۹۰

[۲۴۲] نشریه‌ی «قانون»، شماره‌ی ۳۵. برگرفته از جستار زیر:
❖ تورج امینی، ***ارزیابی‌ی ملکم خان و روزنامه‌ی قانون***، پیشین.

[۲۴۳] نشریه‌ی «قانون»، شماره‌ی ٦. برگرفته از جستار زیر:
❖ تورج امینی، ***ارزیابی‌ی ملکم خان و روزنامه‌ی قانون***، پیشین

[۲۴۴] نشریه‌ی «قانون»، شماره‌ی ۱۸. برگرفته از جستار زیر:
❖ تورج امینی، ***ارزیابی‌ی ملکم خان و روزنامه‌ی قانون***، پیشین.

اگر مردم محروم روستائی در جهرم، «به پادشاه نجف» پناه می‌بردند، اگر آزادی‌خواهان کم‌تجربه در شهرها و روستاهای ایران، در راه مبارزه علیه ستم و خودکامگی به دامان «دین اسلام» و«مجتهدان بزرگ» و «مسلمانی» می‌آویختند، سیدجمال‌الدین دنیادیده و آگاه از چند و چون غارت بیگانگان، تنها راه نجات را در اتحاد «جهان اسلام»، و در عین حال، نزدیک شدن به دانش‌ها و یافته‌های همان بیگانگان (یا «دشمنان اسلام» یا «کفار») می‌بیند. یا میرزا ملکم خان «مترقی» و طرفدار «عقل» و «آدمیت»، بین «جان استوارت میل» و «اگوست کنت» و مجریان «قوانین عدل الهی» در ایران چنان سرگردان است که نمی‌بیند گرانیگاه اندیشه‌های جان استوارت میل را ابطال احکام و ارباب کلیسا، و دفاع از آزادی‌های فردی تشکیل می‌داد، و اندیشه‌های اگوست کنت نیز در جهت آزادی‌ی انتخاب فردی حرکت می‌کرد، اما اندیشه و عمل به «قوانین عدل الهی»، در درازنای تاریخ ایران ریشه‌های «اجتهاد شخصی» را خشکاند. و شگفتا که سرلوحه‌ی تلاش‌های همه‌ی این اندیشه‌ورزان- چنان که بارها و با بیان‌های مختلف در نوشته‌های خود تکرار کرده‌اند- تحقق ایران آباد و آزاد و مستقل و سربلند بوده است.

البته تاریخ ایران، پیرامون وابستگی یا عدم وابستگی‌ی سیدجمال‌الدین اسدآبادی و میرزا ملکم خان به بیگانگان، چون و چراها و تردیدهائی دارد که داوری درباره‌ی هدف‌ها و آرزوهای واقعی‌ی این دو تن را با مشکل روبه‌رو می‌کند. اما این دوپارگی‌ی ذهنی، در آثار و رفتار صمیمی‌ترین، و در عین حال پیشرفته‌ترین پیشاهنگان سیاسی/ فرهنگی‌ی آن زمان، مانند فتحعلی آخوندزاده، یا، میرزا آقاخان کرمانی (پس از تحول شگفت‌انگیز او)، یا روشنفکران طراز اولی که «جامع آدمیت» یا «کمیته‌ی انقلاب ملی» را بنیان گذاشته بودند، یا حتا رزمندگان مسلحی که با «مشروعه‌خواهان» جنگیدند و به عنوان «نجات‌دهندگان» انقلاب مشروطه معروف شدند، نیز قابل ردیابی است:

* میرزا فتحعلی آخوندزاده، در معرفی‌ی واژه‌ی «پنزور» (به گفته‌ی بهرام چوبینه، منظور آخوندزاده واژه‌ی فرانسوی‌ی «پانسور» یعنی متفکر بوده است.) می‌نویسد:

> پنزور عبارت از فیلوسوف و یا حکیم فیلوسوف مانند و کثیرالفکر و صاحب خیال که به اقتضای عقل سلیم به جهت نمودن خیر و شر مردم تصنیفات بنویسد، خواه در امور پولیتیک و خواه در باب عقاید. در عقیده‌ی فیلوسوفان متأخرین فرنگستان، پنزور حقیقی و مستحق تنظیم عبارت از وجودیست که در ارائت خیر و شر ابنای جنس خود از هیچ گونه ملامت و عداوت تقاعد نورزد و در افشای خیالات حکمیانه‌ی خود از هیچ گونه واهمه احتراز نکند. یعنی بر طبق مضمون آیه‌ی شریفه‌ی یُجاهِدونَ فی سبیل‌الله و لایَخافونَ لومَةَ لائِم ذلِکَ فضلُاللهِ یُؤتیه مَن یَشاءُ وَاللهُ واسِعٌ عَلیم، وجودی باشد ذوفضل.[۲۴۵]

از تعریف/ ترجمه/ برداشتِ ابتدائی‌ی آخوندزاده از واژه/ مفهوم «متفکر» که بگذریم، ارجاع او به «آیه‌ی شریفه»، در تأیید سخن، آن هم در ابتدای متنی که به خاطر ازدواج پیامبر اسلام با زن پسرخوانده‌اش، خدای واعظان را با لقب «جاکشِ محمد نام، یک نفر عرب» می‌نوازد، و به خاطر «حرام» بودن «نغمه‌پردازی و ساز و تأتر و رقص و نقاشی و مجسمه‌سازی و شطرنج»، به فقه اسلامی می‌تازد، نشان دهنده‌ی ذهنیتی است که میان «آیه‌ی شریفه»ی قران و

---

[۲۴۵] میرزا فتحعلی آخوندزاده، ***مکتوبات: نامه‌های شاهزاده کمال‌الدوله به شاهزاده جلال‌الدوله***، به کوشش و با مقدمه‌ی بهرام چوبینه، فرانکفورت: انتشارات البرز، مه ۲۰۰۶/ ۱۳۸۵، ص ۲۸۷. **توضیح اول:** آخوندزاده در زیرنویس این متن، پس از ترجمه‌ی این آیه به فارسی، آن را آیه‌ی ۵۷ از سوره‌ی مائده معرفی می‌کند؛ که بهرام چوبینه هم آن را عیناً نقل کرده است. اما شماره‌ی این آیه با نسخه‌ای که من از ترجمه‌ی قرآن (به ترجمه‌ی قمشه‌ای) دارم، مطابقت نمی‌کند. **توضیح دوم:** در مقدمه‌ی بهرام چوبینه (ص ۱۷۱) می‌خوانیم که کتاب «مکتوبات»، نخستین بار توسط باقر مؤمنی به طور پنهانی در ایران منتشر شد. اما گرفتار سانسور رژیم گذشته شد. متن کنونی نیز با همکاری‌ی زنده یاد محمد جعفر محجوب تهیه شده بود، و در خرداد ۱۳۶۴/ ۱۹۸۵ توسط انتشارات «مرد امروز» در آلمان به چاپ رسید. بهرام چوبینه، مؤسس انتشارات «مرد امروز»، متن حاضر را با حروف‌چینی‌ی تازه با مقدمه‌ای در ۲۷۲ صفحه به تاریخ ایران عرضه کرده است.

«سیویلیزاسیون فرنگستان» معلق مانده است. (به صفحه‌های ۳۶۸ و ۳۳۳ مکتوبات نگاه کنید.)

* میرزا آقا خان کرمانی، شاگرد آخوندزاده، از یک سو، «مساوات در مالکیت» را می‌ستاید و مزدک بامدادان را به عنوان طراح آن می‌ستاید، و «فرنگستان امروزی را در استعداد قبول مساوات و مواسات»، در «مقام ایران باستان» می‌نشاند، و از سوی دیگر، به پشتوانه‌ی سخنش در مقوله‌ی ستم و ستم‌پذیری، به نامه‌ی «امیرالمؤمنین»، نماینده‌ی بی‌چون و چرای مالکیت خصوصی، استناد می‌کند.[۲۴۶]

* در گزارش دکتر مهدی ملک زاده (پسر ملک‌المتکلمین مشروطه‌خواه) می‌خوانیم که نخستین نشست «کمیته‌ی انقلاب ملی» (جمعیتی نیمه مخفی، در آستانه‌ی انقلاب مشروطه)، ۵۴ تن از آزادی‌خواهان تحصیل‌کرده و «روشنفکران رادیکال»، با اهدافی غیرمذهبی، و با هدف اشاعه‌ی مفاهیم آزادی و دمکراسی و مشروطه در میان توده‌ها، گرد هم آمدند، و تک به تک، در یک دست قرآن و در دست دیگر پرچم ایران (که روی آن نوشته شده بود «قانون- عدالت»)، نسبت به اهداف «کمیته» و حفظ اسرار آن سوگند وفاداری یاد کردند. و از این فراتر، «اولین اقدام کمیته، فرستادن نمایندگان به حوزه‌ی علمیه‌ی عتبات، و به ویژه نجف بود که نظر آنان را نسبت به فعالیت‌های خود جلب کنند.»[۲۴۷]

دوپارگی‌ی ذهنی، همچنین، در رفتار سوسیالیست/ کمونیست‌های مستقل آن دوران جلوه‌های انکارناپذیر دارد. جست‌وجوگر این دوره از تاریخ ایران، از یک سو، به آگاهی‌ی سیاسی و رشد نسبی‌ی نخستین نیروی چپ ایران برمی‌خورد،[۲۴۸] و از سوی دیگر، به وابستگی‌ی بنیادگذاران آن نیرو، به «محافظین اسلام». از هر دو وجه این ادعا نمونه‌ای بدست می‌دهم:

* در زمان «استبداد صغیر» و اوج مبارزه‌ی مشروطه‌خواهان برای استقرار دوباره‌ی مشروطیت، در گروه «اجتماعیون عامیون»،[۲۴۹] مدافعان «سوسیال دمکراسی- کمونیستی»، شاخه‌ی تبریز، پیرامون تحلیل سرشت انقلاب ایران و شرکت این حزب در پیکار مشروطه‌خواهان، «دو نقطه نظر» متضاد پدید می‌آید. پیامد این اختلاف نظر، سردرگمی‌ی نخبگان این

---

۲۴۶ عابرت‌های داخل گیومه در این پاراگراف را از مأخذ زیر برگرفته‌ام:
- فریدون آدمیت، ***اندیشه‌های میرزا آقا خان کرمانی***، آلمان: انتشارات نوید، بازچاپ، ۱۹۹۲، صص ۲۵۵ و ۲۶۳.

۲۴۷ من مجموعه‌ی کتاب‌های ملک زاده را به امانت از کتابخانه خوانده‌ام. اما متأسفانه آن را در اختیار ندارم، و این بازگفت را نیز میان یادداشت‌هایم (از آن مجموعه) ندیدم. اما آن را از بازنویسی‌ی محمد حسیبی- کوشنده‌ی سیاسی در تبعید- از متن «***تاریخ انقلاب مشروطیت ایران نوشته‌ی مهدی ملک زاده***» برگرفته‌ام. این متن در ۱۴ مرداد ۱۳۸۶ در تارنمای «رشد» منتشر شد:
http://www.zinati.de/Images/Images/Azadi%20Khahan.pdf

۲۴۸ متن کامل نامه‌ی سوسیال دمکرات‌های تبریز به کارل کائوتسکی که در تاریخ ۱۶ ژوئیه‌ی ۱۹۰۸ نوشته شده، با ترجمه از فرانسوی به فارسی در کتاب زیر آمده است:
- حسن ماسالی، ***سیر تحول جنبش چپ ایران و عوامل بحران مداوم آن***. این کتاب شناسنامه ندارد. تاریخ پیش‌گفتار آن اردیبهشت ۱۳۸۰ برابر با مه ۲۰۰۱ است. متن یادشده، همراه پاسخ کائوتسکی به تاریخ ۱ اوت ۱۹۰۸، در صفحات ۵۲ تا ۵۹ این کتاب آمده است.

۲۴۹ احمد کسروی پیرامون این سوسیال دموکرات‌ها می‌نویسد: «یک سال پیش از جنبش مشروطه‌خواهی، ایرانیان قفقاز در باکو، از روی مرامنامه‌ی سوسیال دموکرات روس، دسته‌ای به نام «اجتماعیون عامیون» پدید آوردند که نریمان نریمانوف پیشوای آنان بود. سپس چون در ایران جنبش مشروطه برخاست، در تبریز، شادروان علی مسیو و حاجی علی دوافروش و حاجی رسول صدقیانی و دیگران، همان مرامنامه را به فارسی ترجمه و دسته‌ی «مجاهدان» را پدید آوردند و خود یک انجمن نهانی به نام «مرکز غیبی» برپا کردند، که رشته‌ی کارهای دسته را در دست داشت و آن را راه می‌برد. در همان هنگام کسانی از همان ایرانیان قفقاز به تبریز و دیگر شهرها آمدند. بدین سان مجاهدان در تبریز دو تیره می‌بودند: یکی آنان که از قفقاز آمده و دیگری آنان که از خود تبریز برخاسته بودند. آن تیره هم جز از تبریزیان نمی‌بودند، ولی چون از قفقاز رسیده رخت قفقازی به تن می‌کردند، «قفقازی» نامیده می‌شدند، و خودآزمودەتر و چابکتر می‌بودند و به ملایان و کیش پروا نمی‌داشتند و از این رو مردم از آنان رمیده می‌بودند.» کسروی سپس به اختلاف این گروه با سران «مرکز غیبی» اشاره می‌کند و در پایان این بند می‌نویسد: «ولی چون سردستگان از هر دو سو کسان بافهم و آزموده‌ای می‌بودند، از خونریزی جلو گرفتند و بدون آن که در بیرون دانسته شود با یکدیگر آشتی نمودند» نگاه کنید به:
- احمد کسروی، ***تاریخ مشروطه‌ی ایران***، با پیش‌گفتاری از رحیم رضازاده ملک، تهران: انتشارات صدای معاصر، ۱۳۷۸، صص ۴۰۰ تا ۴۰۱.

حزب است در مورد پیوستن به پیکارگران مشروطه‌خواه، یا، تشکیل سازمان مستقل و «خالص» برای حزب خود. آن‌ها، در تاریخ ۱۶ ژوئیه‌ی ۱۹۰۸ (۱۲۸۷ خورشیدی) به کارل کائوتسکی- نظریه‌پرداز آلمانی‌ی مارکسیسم- نامه می‌نویسند، و پس از شـــرح «دو نقطه نظر» خود، نظر او را در دو مورد جویا می‌شـــوند: اول این که آیا خصـــلت انقلاب ایران «قهقرائی» است یا «پیشرو و مترقی»؟ و دوم این که «شرکت سوسیال دمکرات‌ها در یک جنبش پیشرو و مترقی، یا در یک جنبش قهقرائی از چه نوع می‌تواند باشد؟» بر خلاف نظر حسن ماسالی (که متن کامل این نامه را در کتاب گرامی‌ی خود آورده، و محتوای آن را «ابتدائی» و کودکانه برآورده کرده است)، تحلیل شرایط، و راه حل نویسندگان نامه- با توجه به تاریخ آن- از آگاهی‌ی سیاسی‌ی نخستین پیکارگران چپ ایران خبر می‌دهد. به ویژه آن جا که می‌نویسند:

> [...] اگر چه با توجه به آن که در ایران هنـــوز صنایع ســـرمایه‌داری به وجود نیامده‌اند، پرولتاریای صنعتی (به معنای اروپائی‌ی کلمه)، که گروه ما بتواند بر آن تکیه کند، وجود ندارد، لکن برخی از رفقا به درستی بر آن عقیده‌اند که گروه می‌تواند از چارچوب فعالیت منفعل (پروپاگاند) خارج شده، و نه تنها می‌تواند، بلکه باید در ضمن کوشش به نفع دمکراسی و پیشرفت اقتصادی و اجتماعی‌ی کشور، بدون چشم‌پوشی از اصول اساسی‌ی خود، فعالانه در جنبش‌ها شرکت جوید. این طبیعی است که یک نفر سوسیال دمکرات، از آن جا که نه تنها فردی‌ست سوسیالیست، بلکه به علاوه دمکرات، پیگیرترین دمکرات‌ها نیز هست، نمی‌تواند در یک جنبش دمکراتیک بیکار بنشیند. از این روست که گروه، اصل شرکت در جنبش‌ها را مورد قبول قرار داد. اگر چه برخی از رفقا از دفاع از این نظریه خودداری کنند، امتناع آنان به هیچ وجه مطلق نبوده، نسبی و مشروط است. [...][۲۵۰] (پرانتزها در متن اصلی وجود دارند.)

ممکن اســـت زبان این نامه اکنون فرســـوده به نظر آید؛ اما دلیل من در ادعای بلوغ نســـبی‌ی نویســـندگان این نامه، همانا، تشـخیص درسـت آن‌ها نسبت به شـرایط طبقه‌ی کارگر در ایران آن روزگار، و تردید آن‌ها پیرامون ضـرورت وجود یک حزب ســـوســـیالیســـتی اســـت. در روزآمد بودن نویســـندگان این نامه همین بس که نگرانی‌ها و تردیدهای آن‌ها، دقیقاً همان دغدغه‌ای را بازتاب می‌دهند که در همان ســـال‌ها، بین نظریه‌های لنین (به ویژه در کتاب «چه باید کرد») و نظریه‌های‌ی رزا لوکزامبورگ (به ویژه در کتاب «مسائل تشـکیلاتی‌ی سـوسـیال دموکراسـی‌ی روسـیه») وجود داشـت، و سـوسـیالیسـم جهانی را با بحرانی روش‌شناختی روبه‌رو کرده بود.

با این وصـــف، پس از پیروزی‌ی پیکارگران بر محمدعلی‌شـــاه قاجار و بازگشـــت مشـــروطیت، در «اعلامیه»‌ای از همین گروه می‌خوانیم:

> شـما محرومین متحد شـوید. ما، سـوسـیال دموکرات‌ها، **محافظین اسـلام** و ایران، در این روزهای جشـن و سـرور اعلام مشـــروطیت، به همه‌ی دوســـتانِ آزادی، در هر کجا که باشـــند، درود می‌فرســـتیم. ما قبل از هر چیز به **علما و تجار**، این همکاران خستگی‌ناپذیر در مبارزه برای ملت، **این محافظین اسلام در تهران**، که زندگی و هستی‌ی خود را تقدیم این هدف مقدس کرده‌اند، درود می‌فرستیم.[۲۵۱] (تأکیدها از من است.)

خواننده‌ی این متن، اگر از پاسخ کائوتسکی به نامه‌ی «سوسیال دمکرات‌های کمونیستِ» ما با خبر باشد، چنین می‌اندیشد که نویسـندگان آن نامه، پیشـنهاد کائوتسـکی را مبنی بر لزوم شـرکت نیروهای چپ در کلیه‌ی جنبش‌های مردمی به عنوان

---

۲۵۰ حسن ماسالی، ***سیر تحول جنبش چپ ایران و عوامل بحران مداوم آن***، پیشین، ص ۵۷.

۲۵۱ حسن ماسالی، ***سیر تحول جنبش چپ ایران و عوامل بحران مداوم آن***، پیشین، ص ۵۱.

یک «تاکتیک» پذیرفته بودند، و تأکید آن‌ها بر «محافظین اسلام»، دنباله‌ی همان «تاکتیک» است . چرا که کائوتسکی در پاسخ خود، و به پشتوانه‌ی نظر خود، از تاکتیکِ موفق «مارکس در ۱۸۴۸ در آلمان» یاد کرده بود. اما شگفتی زمانی رخ می‌کند که بدانیم نویسندگان آن نامه، نظر کائوتسکی را نپذیرفته بودند و مخالفت خود را نیز طی نامه‌ای به پلخانف اعلام داشته بودند،[۲۵۲] و به دنبال آن نیز، حزب سوسیالیستی‌ی «خالص» خود را تشکیل داده بودند. به بیانی دیگر، ابراز تعلق آن‌ها به «محافظین اسلام»، نمی‌تواند به عنوان یک تاکتیک برآورد شود. بلکه این ابراز تعلق، در قلمرو معرفت‌شناسی به عنوان نمودی برخاسته از بنیادهای ذهنیت و بینش مذهبی‌ی آن‌ها برآورد می‌شود؛ نمودی که، نمایانگر میان‌ماندگی‌ی ذهنی‌ی این گروه «پیشرو» بود، بین تازه‌ترین و کهنه‌ترین آموزه‌های سیاسی/ اجتماعی/ فرهنگی. البته ریشه‌های سخت جان این ذهنیت، با بنیادی‌ترین عنصر اندیشگی‌ی بزرگ‌آموزگارشان، لنین، هم‌خانواده است؛ چرا که لنین،- فردی که مأموریت «تغییر جهان» را پذیرفته بود- در کتاب «انقلاب پرولتری و کائوتسکی‌ی مرتد»، به کائوتسکی همان لقبی را داده است که «امام فخرالدین رازی» به زکریا رازی داده بود. گیرم که مأخذ فتوای آن یکی، قرآن و حدیث بود، و مأخذ فتوای این یکی، آموزه‌های مارکس.

* ستارخان، گرچه از نعمت سواد بی‌بهره بود، اما شعور مبارزه با استبداد، و نبوغ نظامی از گزارش‌های مربوط به شیوه‌ی مبارزه‌ی او پیداست، و آرمان‌های آزادی، استقلال، و سربلندی ایران از گزارش کردار سیاسی و گفته‌هائی که از او نقل شده است، می‌بارد. ستارخان، که آوازه‌ی مبارزه و شجاعت و سخت‌کوشی‌ی او از مرزهای ایران بیرون رفته و در روزنامه‌های خارجی با «گاریبالدی» (قهرمان ملی‌ی ایتالیا) مقایسه شده، در پایان محاصره‌ی تبریز، به دعوت مشروطه‌خواهان تهران با نیروهای زیر فرمانش از تبریز راهی‌ی تهران می‌شود. در تهران از او تجلیل می‌شود، و او و نیروهایش را در «باغ اتابک» اسکان می‌دهند. اما چندی بعد، در حالی که محمدعلی شاه قاجار از سلطنت «خلع» شده و مشروطه و مجلس شورا به قدرت بازگشته، صحبت از «خلع سلاح» پیش می‌آید، که بعد معلوم می‌شود حکم آن توسط «آیات عظام نجف» صادر شده بود. ستارخان تسلیم نمی‌شود، در حمله‌ی نیروهای دولتی زخم برمی‌دارد، و دستگیر می‌شود. «وزارت داخله»، طی‌ی اطلاعیه‌ای «سردار ملی» را «متمرد» می‌خواند، و اعلام می‌کند:

> **در اجرای احکام آیات عظام نجف**، مبنی بر خلع سلاح مجاهدین، قوای دولتی عده‌ای متمرد را در باغ اتابک محاصره و ظرف سه ساعت متمردین کلاً مغلوب و سی‌صد و پنجاه نفر گرفتار و در نظمیه محبوس شدند.[۲۵۳]

البته ستارخان- از جنس «شیرآهنکوه»های احمد شاملو- که در این ماجرا از ناحیه‌ی پا زخم برداشته، آزاد می‌شود؛ پس از چند سال درمان‌های بی‌نتیجه، در ۴۸ سالگی از همان زخم می‌میرد. شگفتا که درمی‌یابیم این آزادی‌خواه، «مطابق احکام صادره‌ی علماء اعلام عظام مرجع **تقلید** شیعه» برای کسب **آزادی** جنگیده بود. در متنی که (به گفته‌ی همنشین بهار) ستارخان «به یکی از یاران خود انشاء کرده بود»، و بخشی از آن بر سنگ گور او نیز نوشته شده است، می‌خوانیم:

> عموم اهالی داخله خاصه و عامه، سیماً اولیای امور و رؤسای عظام کرام فخام و اهالی ممالک خارجه کاملا مسبوق و مستحضرند که این بنده‌ی عاصی، ستار، برای اجرای حکم شریعت غراء احمدی و حفظ بیضه اسلام **مطابق احکام**

---

[۲۵۲] حسن ماسالی، ***سیر تحول جنبش چپ ایران و عوامل بحران مداوم آن***، پیشین، ص ۵۹.
توضیح: نامه‌ی دموکرات‌ها و پاسخ کائوتسکی، در تارنمای «مارکسیست‌ها» نیز در دسترس است:
www.marxists.org/farsi/history/sosyal-demokrasiye-iran/chilingarian-nameh.pdf
www.marxists.org/farsi/archive/kautsky/works/1908/pasokh-sd-tabriz.pdf

[۲۵۳] برگرفته از: همنشین بهار، ***رد پای علمای اعلام بر سنگ قبر ستارخان***، تارنمای «دیدگاه»، بازدید ۲ اوت ۲۰۱۱:
http://www.didgah.net/maghalehMatnKamel.php?id=26206

> **صادره‌ی علماء اعلام عظام مرجع تقلید شیعه**، از جان و مال و اولاد و هستی خود صرف نظر کرده فوق الطاقه کوشیده تا دولت جابره تبدیل بر دولت عادله، به عبارت آخری دولت شورویه دایر شود، تا مگر آب رفته به جو بازگردد و قوانین حضرت سیدالمرسلین که سرمشق اهل کره از کفار و غیره گردیده، رویّه و مسلک اهل اسلام و کافه‌ی مسلمین و مسلمات بشود؛ و برای معرفی‌ی خود به اهل عالم پس از تبدیل دولت جابره اطاعت اوامر مطاعه‌ی دولت عادله را کرده، به مرکز که پایتخت ایران شناخته شود، حاضر شده و برای تأکید بر معرفی‌ی خود به عالمیان در گوشه‌ی انزوا و عزلت هر قسم تعدیات وارده را محتمل، در این موقع برای پیشرفت قانون ، مظلومیت اختیار نمود. [...][۲۵۴]

* با این که به لحاظ شناخت‌شناسی، می‌توان «شعر» را از پیشروترین متن‌های دوران مشروطیت برآورد کرد، در مشاهده‌ای از نزدیک، شعر مشروطیت را نیز از این گونه بینش‌های میان‌مانده آکنده می‌بینیم. چند نمونه از آن‌ها را در این جا درج می‌کنم:

«اشرف‌الدین گیلانی» یکی از معروف‌ترین و اثرگذارترین شاعران مبارز دوره‌ی مشروطیت بود. او در زمان «استبداد صغیر» در شماره‌ی ۹ نشریه‌ی خود- «نسیم شمال»- به تاریخ ۱۱ دی ماه ۱۲۸۶ خورشیدی (۲ ژانویه ۱۹۰۸) مستزادی منتشر کرد که درد و دریغ از «گمنام شدن و پایمال شدن اسلام»، با درد و دریغ از «خون جوانان کشته شده» در مبارزه، در هم آمیخته‌اند:

گردید وطن غرقه‌ی اندوه و محن وای/ ای وای وطن وای
خیزید و روید از پی‌ی تابوت و کفن وای/ ای وای وطن وای
از خون جوانان که شده کشته درین راه/ رنگین طبق ماه
خونین شده صحرا و تل و دشت و دمن وای/ ای وای وطن وای
کو همت و کو غیرت و کو جوش فتوت/ کو جنبش ملت
دردا که رسید از دو طرف سیل فتن وای/ ای وای وطن وای
افسوس که اسلام شده از همه جانب/ پامال اجانب
مشروطه‌ی ایران شده تاریخ زَمَن وای/ ای وای وطن وای
تنها نه همین گشت وطن ضایع و بدنام/ **گمنام شد اسلام**
پژمرده شد این باغ و گل و سرو و سمن وای/ ای وای وطن وای [...][۲۵۵]

همین شاعر، چند روز پس از پیروزی‌ی مشروطه‌خواهان و عزل محمدعلی شاه قاجار، جانشین او- احمد شاه قاجار- را در شعری مخاطب قرار می‌دهد و به او سفارش می‌کند:

ای شهنشاه جوان شیران جنگ‌آور نگر/ در نگر/ عالمی دیگر نگر
ملتی را راحت از مشروطه سرتاسر نگر/ در نگر/ عالمی دیگر نگر
پادشاهی کن که دوران جهان بر کام تست/ رام تست/ شاه احمد نام تست

---

[۲۵۴] ***رنج‌نامه‌ی ستارخان سردار ملی***، روزنامه‌ی «ایران»، شماره‌ی ۶۲۵، ۱۷ فروردین ۱۳۷۵. برگرفته از تارنمای «سردار ملی»، بازدید ۱۰ خرداد ۱۳۸۸:

/http://sardaremelli.persianblog.ir

[255] Edward G. Browne, ***The Press and Poetry of Modern Persia***, Cambridge: at the University Press, 1914, p. 183.

در محامد **خویش را همنام پیغمبر نگر**/ در نگر/ عالمی دیگر نگر [...][۲۵۶] (تأکید از من است.)

در شعری منسوب به میرزا تقی خان دانش، شاعر آزادی‌خواه دیگر، که در شماره‌ی ۹۳ نشریه‌ی «ایران نو» (آذر ۱۲۸۸ خورشیدی / دسامبر ۱۹۰۹ میلادی) منتشر شد، شاعر، قانون اساسی‌ی مشروطه را «قانون الهی» می‌خواند که به راهنمائی‌ی «قرآن محمد» متحقق شده است:

صد شکر حقوق وطن امروز ادا شد/ بَه بَه چه به‌جا شد
هنگام وفا وقت صفا دفع جفا شد/ به به چه به‌جا شد
الحمد که قانون الهی جریان یافت/ ملت هیجان یافت/ شد کشته و جان یافت
قرآن محمد همه را راهنما شد/ مشروطه به پا شد/ به به چه به‌جا شد [...][۲۵۷]

البته نقطه‌ی اشتراک شعر مشروطیت (همان طور که نقطه‌ی اشتراک اکثر نثرهای این دوره)، عمدتاً واژگان «وطن»، «استقلال»، «آزادی»، «قانون» و «تجدد» بود؛ در همان قلمرو هم گام برداشت؛ و در میدان معنائی که برای مطالبات یادشده داشت، ظاهراً پیروز هم شد. اما از آن جا که واژگان یادشده، در زبان و فرهنگ ایران به «مفهوم» و «گفتمان» تبدیل نشده بود، میدان معنائی‌ی آن‌ها تا دامان «دین»، «اسلام» و «مسلمانی» کش می‌آمد. کما این که در شعر شاعران آزادی‌خواه این دوره- مانند محمدتقی بهار، عارف قزوینی، میرزاده عشقی، و ...، حتا ایرج میرزا- نیز، گرایش‌های ژرف مذهبی حضوری انکارناپذیر دارد.

به عنوان مثال، در دیوان محمدتقی بهار (ملک‌الشعرای آستان قدس)، بیش از دیوان شاعران دیگر، به واژگان «تجدد» و «تمدن» و «متمدن» برمی‌خوریم. او در قصیده‌ی «جهنم»، نگاه مذهبی به زندگی‌ی متجدد و مدنی را به سخره می‌گیرد:

جز شیعه هر که هست به عالم خداپرست/ در دوزخ است روز قیامت مکان او
وز شیعه نیز هر که فکل بست و شیک شد/ سوزد به نار هیکل پرنیان او
آن کس که شد وکیل و ز مشروطه حرف زد/ دوزخ شود به روز جزا پارلمان او
و آن کس که روزنامه‌نویس است و چیزفهم/ آتش فتد به دفتر و کلک و بنان او

اما خود او نیز از این ذهنیت گریزی ندارد. بهار در مبارزه با نفوذ دولت‌های روس تزاری و بریتانیا در شمال و جنوب ایران، قصیده‌ی «ایران ما شماست» را می‌سازد، که آمیزه‌ای است از مفاهیم ایران پیش از اسلام، «تمدن»، و «دین محمد»:

هان ای ایرانیان، ایران اندر بلاست/ مملکت **داریوش** دستخوش نیکلاست
مرکز **ملک کیان** در دهن اژدهاست/ **غیرت اسلام** کو، جنبش ملی کجاست؟ [...]
به کین **اسلام** باز خاسته بر پا صلیب/ خصم شمال و جنوب داده ندای مهیب
روح تمدن به لب آیه‌ی اَمَن یجیب/ **دین محمد** یتیم، کشور ایران غریب

---

256 Ibid, p.217.

257 Ibid, p. 222.

نمونه‌های این ذهنیت در سراسر دیوان بهار به آسانی قابل دیدار است. مثلاً، در ترجیع‌بندی که در سوگ شیخ محمد خیابانی نوشت، می‌خوانیم:

پامال نمودند و زدودند وستردند/ آزادی‌ی ایران و **مسلمانی‌ی ایران**

نمونه‌ی دیگر، شعر «زرتشت» از عارف قزوینی است. با این که در دیوان این شاعر آزادی‌خواه کم‌تر به نمادهای اسلامی برمی‌خوریم، اما این شعر، نمود برجسته‌ای از «دین‌خواهی» و «دین‌خوئی»ی شاعر آن را به تماشا گذاشته است:

به نام آن که در شأنَش کتاب است/ چراغ راه دینش آفتاب است
مهین دستور دربار خدائی/ شرف‌بخش نژاد آریائی
دوتا گردیده چرخ پیر را پشت/ پی‌ی پوزش به پیش نام زرتشت

گرچه عارف قزوینی در شعر زرتشت، به ورطه‌ی نژادپرستی هم غلتیده است، اما از مفاهیم سراسر این شعر چنین برمی‌آید که مشکل «این کشور» را در فراموش کردن دینِ «به‌دینان» و گرویدن به دینِ «بیگانه» برآورد کرده است:

به ایمانی ره بیگانه جوئی/ رها کن، تا به کی بی‌آبروئی
به قرن بیست گر در بند آئی/ همان به، دین به‌دینان گرائی
به چشم عقل آن دین را فروغ است/ که خود بنیان گن دیو دروغ است[...]
در آتشکده دل بر تو باز است/ درآ، کاین خانه‌ی سوز و گداز است [...]
در این کشور چوشد این شعله خاموش/ فتادی دیگ ملیت هم از جوش [...]
کنونت نیست چون گوش شنفتن/ مرا هم گفته‌ها باید نهفتن
بسی اسرار در دل مانده مستور/ که بی‌تردید بایستی برم گور

بدین ترتیب، تصادفی نیست که محمدتقی بهار، با وجود «حبس» و تبعیدهای کوتاه مدت، تا پایان زندگی (و خوشبختانه) با قدر و منزلتی در شأن یک ادیب و کوشنده‌ی سیاسی زیست؛ اما عارف قزوینی، «بسی اسرار»ش را در فقر و تهی‌دستی و انزوا با خود به «گور» برد.

***

بنا بر مجموعه‌ی شرایط تاریخی، در این تردید نیست که پیشگامان مبارزه در آن دوره، جهت همراه کردن مردم عادی و کشاندن آن‌ها به میدان مبارزه، نشان دادن همدلی با باورهای آن‌ها را بایسته می‌دانستند؛ و در این راه، همچنین، به همگامی‌ی پیشوایان دینی نیاز داشتند. بنابراین، فراخواندن، و گاه، واداشتن «علما» به شرکت در مبارزه امری اجتناب‌ناپذیر و حتا هوشمندانه بود. در این هم تردید نیست که برخی از شخصیت‌های مترقی‌ی این لایه‌ی اجتماعی- مانند ملک‌المتکلمین واعظ، یا سیدجمال‌الدین واعظ اصفهانی، و بعداً، شیخ محمد خیابانی[۲۵۸]- در پراکندن آگاهی و در پیروزی‌ی

[۲۵۸] میرزا نصرالله بهشتی، ملقب به «ملک‌المتکلمین»، واعظ، بنیان‌گذار چندین مدرسه با برنامه‌ی جدید آموزشی، و عضو گروه نیمه مخفی‌ی «کمیته‌ی انقلاب ملی» بود. او در آغاز «استبداد صغیر»، در تیر ماه ۱۲۸۷ خورشیدی به فرمان محمدعلی شاه قاجار، به طرز فجیعی اعدام شد. شیخ محمد خیابانی نیز، پس از استقرار مشروطه، در زمان احمدشاه قاجار و نخست‌وزیری‌ی «مخبرالسلطنه هدایت»، به هواداری از حکومت جمهوری، علیه «حالت اسف‌آمیز مملکت و اختلاسات بی‌حد و حصر مالیه، و...» ، از جمله قرارداد ۱۹۱۹، در فروردین ۱۲۹۹ در تبریز قیام کرد. او همچنین، به عنوان احیاکننده‌ی حزب دموکرات آذربایجان شناسائی شده است. او در اشاعه‌ی آگاهی‌های سیاسی و حقوق مدنی، افزون بر سخنرانی‌ها و نوشته‌های خود، از موسیقی و تئاتر یاری می‌جست. شاید بتوان او را به عنوان نخستین روشنفکری تلقی کرد که ضمن پذیرش تمامیت ارضی‌ی ایران، به خودمختاری‌ی قومی باور داشت. برای آگاهی بیش‌تر پیرامون این شخصیت، به مآخذ زیر نگاه کنید:

جنبش‌های این دوره سهمی غیرقابل انکار داشتند. به این نکته هم باید اشاره کرد که «علمای نجف» در پاسخ به تلگراف محمدعلی‌شاه (پیش از به توپ بستن مجلس شورا) نوشتند: «همراهی با مخالفین مشروطه و اطاعت حکمشان در تعرض به مجلس‌خواهان، به منزله‌ی اطاعت یزید بن معاویه است.»[۲۵۹] اما در این جا بحث من پیرامون ذهنیت همگانی‌ی جامعه، از جمله «روشنفکران» و پیشاهنگان مبارزه است، که در سپهر آن، انگار همه‌ی جهان بر مدار «مذهب/ دولت» می‌گردد. این ذهنیت (که صدها نمونه‌ی آن را می‌توان- دست کم- در کتاب‌های «تاریخ مشروطه‌ی ایران» نوشته‌ی احمد کسروی و «تاریخ بیداری‌ی ایرانیان» نوشته‌ی ناظم‌الاسلام کرمانی و «حیات یحیی» نوشته‌ی یحیی دولت آبادی یافت) دو «شاه» دارد که باید در کنار هم و با هم بر «رعایا» حکمرانی کنند. در دوران مشروطیت، یکی از این «شاهان» در دربار نجف، و دیگری در دربار تهران بر تخت قدرت نشسته‌اند؛ که انگار، «شاه نجف» دست بالا را دارد. البته ادبیات دوران مشروطیت به این طرفگی شهادت می‌دهد که مبارزان و نواندیشان این دوره به آن میزان از آگاهی و جرأت رسیده بودند که ستمکاری، رشوه‌خواری، وطن‌فروشی و کمکاری‌ی (به قول خودشان: «بی‌غیرتی‌ی») هر دو «شاه» و کارگزارانشان را افشاء کنند، و در صورت رام نشدن، آن‌ها را از تخت قدرت به زیر آورند. سرنگونی‌ی محمدعلی شاه قاجار و سرنگونی‌ی شیخ فضل‌الله نوری- مجتهد صاحب‌نفوذی که «قانون مشروعه» را به جای «قانون مشروطه» تجویز می‌کرد- نمود عینی‌ی این آگاهی و توانائی است. منتها، چنان که قبلاً اشاره کردم، متر و معیار ذهنی‌ی اکثریت این مبارزان، «دین اسلام»، «حفظ قرآن» «پیغمبر اسلام» و «مسلمانی» بود. بی‌سبب نیست که در این ادبیات، مثلاً، به این فریاد زنان تهرانی علیه ناصرالدین‌شاه برمی‌خوریم که: «ای شاه‌باجی سبیلو، ای لچک به سر، **ای لامذهب**، ما ترا نمی‌خواهیم!»[۲۶۰] همان گونه که عنوان‌های تحقیرآمیز «شاباجی» و «لچک به سر»، از زبان زنانی که خود سراپا غرق در لچک و چادر و چاقچور و روبنده به میدان نبرد آمده‌اند، از ناآگاهی‌ی جنسی خبر می‌دهد، عبارت «لامذهب»، به عنوان یک ناسزا، نمودار ذهنیتی است که تقدسِ «مذهب» در نُه توی آن خانه کرده است. کما این که در ادبیات شورش علیه قرارداد رژی، یا واقعه‌ی مربوط به «نوز»، یا در واگذاری‌ی امتیاز راه آهن و بانک به بیگانگان، به جای شکایت از «فروش مملکت» به بیگانان، بارها از «فروش مملکت به **کافرها**» شکایت شده است؛ حتا برخی از پاره‌های این ادبیات به حکم اسلامی‌ی تکفیر آلوده است؛ و حتا یکی از نشریاتی که در طول «استبداد صغیر» با خشن‌ترین کلمات علیه استبداد و خودکامگی‌ی محمدعلی شاه قاجار افشاگری می‌کرد، با نام اسلامی‌ی «**جهاد اکبر**» منتشر می‌شد.[۲۶۱]

به فرمان همین ذهنیت بود که الگوی «کنستی‌توسیونِ» کشورهای اروپائی (که در عین جدائی دین از دولت نوشته شده بود) در ایران به قانون اساسی‌ی دین/ دولت جا سپرد. به بیانی دیگر، این ذهنیت، با تمام تلاش درازدامانی که برای تحقق «قانون مشروطه» به خرج داد، و با تمام خونی که برای رسیدن به این آرزو صرف کرد، در قله‌ی پیروزی‌ی خود به «قانون اساسی»ای رسید، که اصل‌های اول و دوم متمم آن، جایگاه «شاه نجف» و «شاه تهران» را بر تخت حکمرانی استوار کرد؛ و «شاه نجف» را تا «ظهور حضرت حجة عصر عجل الله فرجه» بر فراز سر «عامه‌ی ملت» و «مجلس مقدس شورای ملی» نشاند؛ و آشکارا بر حقوق هزاران شهروند غیرمسلمان ایران- و حتا مسلمانان اهل سُنت- خط کشید.

---

* فرامرز خیابانی اصل، ***چهره‌ای ناشناخته از شیخ محمد خیابانی***، تارنمای «خبرنامه‌ی گویا»، ۵ مرداد ۱۳۸۵:
http://news.gooya.com/politics/archives/051288.php

*علی آذری، ***قیام محمد خیابانی در تبریز***، تهران: نشر مرکز، چاپ چهارم، ۱۳۵۴.

۲۵۹ احمد کسروی، ***تاریخ مشروطه‌ی ایران***، پیشین، ص ۶۸۶.

۲۶۰ عبدالحسین ناهید، ***زنان ایران در جنبش مشروطه***، پیشین، ص ۳۲.

261 Edward G. Browne, ***The Press and Poetry of Modern Persia***, Cambridge: at the University Press, 1914, p. 71.

اصل اول و دوم متمم قانون اساسی‌ی مشروطه‌ی ایران

اصل اول: مذهب رسمی‌ی ایران اسلام و طریقه‌ی حقه‌ی جعفریه‌ی اثنی عشریه است. باید پادشاه ایران دارا و مروج این مذهب باشد.

اصل دوم: مجلس مقدس شورای ملی که به توجه و تأیید حضرت امام عصر عجل‌الله فرجه و بذل مرحمت اعلیحضرت شاهنشاه اسلام خلدالله سلطانه و مراقبت حجج اسلامیه کثرالله امثالهم و عامه‌ی ملت ایران تأسیس شده است، باید در هیچ عصری از اعصار، مواد قانونیه‌ی آن مخالفتی با قواعد مقدسه‌ی اسلام و قوانین موضوعه‌ی حضرت خیرالانام صلی الله علیه و آله و سَلم نداشته باشد و معین است که تشخیص مخالفت قوانین موضوعه با قواعد اسلامیه بر عهده‌ی علمای اعلام ادام الله برکات وجود هم بوده و هست. لهذا رسماً مقرر است در هر عصری از اعصار، هیأتی که کمتر از پنج نفر نباشد از مجتهدین و فقهای متدینین، که مطلع از مقتضیات زمان هم باشند، به این طریق که علمای اعلام و حجج اسلام مرجع تقلید شیعه اسامی‌ی بیست نفر از علماء که دارای صفات مذکوره باشند معرفی به مجلس شورای ملی بنمایند. پنج نفر از آن‌ها را، یا بیش‌تر به مقتضای عصر، اعضای مجلس شورای ملی بالاتفاق یا به حکم قرعه تعیین نموده به سمت عضویت بشناسند، تا موادی که در مجلس عنوان می‌شود به دقت مذاکره و غوررسی نموده، هر یک از آن مواد معنونه که مخالفت با قواعد مقدسه‌ی اسلام داشته باشد طرح و رد نمایند که عنوان قانونیت پیدا نکند و رأی این هیأت علماء در این باب مطاع و بتبع خواهد بود و این ماده تا زمان ظهور حضرت حجة عصر عجل الله فرجه تغییرپذیر نخواهد بود.

جای شگفتی نیست که علی اکبر ولایتی (دولتمرد همیشه در صحنه‌ی جمهوری‌ی اسلامی) صد سال بعد، اصل دوم متمم قانون اساسی‌ی مشروطه را «سلفِ» نهادِ «شورای نگهبان» در جمهوری‌ی اسلامی برآورد می‌کند.[۲۶۲] و با توجه به این مجموعه از شرایط ذهنی و عینی، جای شگفتی نیست که شمار نمایندگانِ «علما و طلاب» در مجلس اول، از ۵ لایه‌ی اجتماعی‌ی دیگر، حتا از لایه‌ی «اعیان» یا «عمال دیوانی»، بیش‌تر بود.[۲۶۳] و جای شگفتی نیست که این مجلس، «قانون انتخابات»ی را تصویب کند که در آن، «زن» در ردیف «محجوران»، از حق انتخاب کردن و انتخاب شدن محروم شود. (۱۵ مهر ۱۲۸۵ خورشیدی)

اما ناگفته نباید گذاشت که انگشت‌شماری هم از اندیشه‌ورزان آن روزگار بودند که چه به عنوان نماینده‌ی مجلس اول، و چه در مقام ژورنالیست، با بندهای غیردمکراتیک در قانون اساسی درافتادند. نمونه‌های برجسته‌ی نمایندگان مجلس اول، تقی زاده و دهخدا بودند، و نمونه‌های برجسته‌ی روزنامه‌نگاران، میرزا جهانگیرخان صوراسرافیل، و نویسندگان روزنامه‌ی تبعیدی‌ی «حبل‌المتین» در کلکته بودند، که هم شاه و هم روحانیان را سبب‌ساز جهل و عقب‌ماندگی‌ی مردم ایران شناسائی کردند، و حضور پررنگ روحانیان در مجلس را به باد انتقاد گرفتند. صاحبان و همه‌ی نویسندگان «حبل‌المتین» که در ایران نبودند، اما میرزا جهانگیرخان، صاحب نشریه‌ی صوراسرافیل، در دوره‌ی استبداد صغیر، بهای آزادی‌خواهی و شهامت خود را با خون خود پرداخت.

در این جا، با این هدف که نمائی از ذهنیت مذهبی‌ی زنان آزادی‌خواه- یعنی عنصر مهمی از چرائی‌های جامعه‌شناختی‌ی تدوین این قانون اساسی- ترسیم شود، بایسته است که به داوری‌ی آن‌ها و بینش‌هائی که در کنش‌های صرفاً زنانه‌شان تجلی

---

۲۶۲ علی اکبر ولایتی، ***اصل دوم متمم قانون اساسی‌ی مشروطه سلف شورای نگهبان به حساب می‌آید***، خبرگزاری‌ی دانشجویان ایرانی- تهران، برگرفته از تارنمای «خبرنامه‌ی گویا»، ۱۹ آذر ۱۳۸۵:
http://news.gooya.com/politics/archives/050424.php

۲۶۳ احمد اشرف، ***موانع تاریخی‌ی رشد سرمایه‌داری در ایران، دوره‌ی قاجاریه***، تهران: انتشارات زمینه، ۱۳۵۹، ص ۱۱۹.

می‌کرد نیز اشاره کنم:

نشریه‌ی «شکوفه»، دومین نشریه‌ی مخصوص زنان، از سوئی، از «نمایش زنانه در لندن» سخن می‌گوید، و از سوی دیگر، در شماره‌ی ۲۲ سال دوم در تاریخ ۱۳۳۲ قمری (۱۲۹۳ خورشیدی) در مقاله‌ای با عنوان «فلسفه‌ی حجاب» می‌نویسد:

> همه کس می‌داند که رفع حجاب، باعث اختلاط زن و مرد با یکدیگر می‌شود و مفاسد مترتبه بر این اختلاط را هیچ عاقلی نمی‌تواند انکار نماید. چه می‌بینیم در اروپا که حجاب مرفوع و اختلاط زن و مرد موجود است، هیچ عائله و خانواده نیست که دچار مشکلات فوق‌العاده و مخدورات مالایطاق این مسئله نشده باشد... وقتی که در فلسفه‌ی همین یک حکم محکم حجاب که در حق ما طایفه‌ی نسوان صادر شده است، تفکر نمائیم، می‌فهمیم که پیغمبر اکرم به واسطه‌ی این حکم، تا چه اندازه جلوگیری از فساد اخلاقی و اعمال ماها فرموده و تا چه پایه، اسباب رستگاری و فلاح ما را تهیه نموده است.[۲۶۴] (نقطه چین در مأخذ من وجود دارد.)

از این نمونه گذشته، مجموعه‌ی نشریه‌های انگشت‌شمار زنانه در دهه‌ی اول مشروطه، آکنده است از آرزوی «ترقی» و «تعالی» و «پیشرفت» و رسیدن به جهان کنونی، از سوئی، و اندرزهای اخلاقی/ مذهبی و مردسالارانه از سوی دیگر. «خانم کحال»، سردبیر نخستین نشریه‌ی زنان- به نام «دانش»- به زنان توصیه می‌کند:

> انقلاب هایدر ترتیبات راحتی‌ی شوهر مواظب باشید. مثلاً غذای او را به وقت حاضر نمائید و در زمستان، کرسی یا بخاری‌ی او را گرم و حاضر بدارید، اطاق را پاک و تمیز نگاه دارید. کلیةً طوری باشید که وقتی مرد وارد خانه می‌شود، از هر جهة راحت باشد.[۲۶۵] (در این بازگفت، کتابت متن را عیناً منتقل کرده‌ام.)

پند و اندرزهای آکنده از آموزه‌های اخلاق مذهبی ، مانند راه و رسم «مواظبت از شوهر»، «اطاعت از شوهر»، «تمکین از شوهر»، در شماره‌های نشریه‌ی «زبان زنان»- سومین نشریه‌ی زنان در ایران- به سردبیری‌ی صدیقه دولت آبادی، بارها تکرار شده است.[۲۶۶] چرا که مبنای آموزه‌های اجتماعی‌ی او، قوانین اسلامی و خطاب‌های «پیغمبر ما» است. مثلاً:

---

[۲۶۴] حمیرا رنجبر عمرانی، ***نشریات زنان در دوران قاجار و رضا خان***، تارنمای «مؤسسه‌ی مطالعات تاریخ معاصر ایران»، بازدید ۱۰ شهریور ۱۳۸۸:

http://www.iichs.org/index.asp?id=1059&doc_cat=

[۲۶۵] صدیقه ببران، ***سیر تاریخی‌ی نشریات زنان در ایران معاصر***، تهران: انتشارات روشنگران و مطالعات زنان، ۱۳۸۱، ص ۳۷. (**توضیح**: با این که در صفحه‌ی عنوان این کتاب می‌خوانیم: «پژوهش و نگارش: صدیقه ببران»، این کتاب، جز یک زیرنویس ناقص در بخش «پیش‌گفتار مؤلف»، نه زیرنویس دارد، نه بخش «منابع» یا «کتاب‌شناسی». فقط پیش از هر گفتاورد، نام نویسنده‌ی گفتاورد و نام کتاب او، و گاهی هم ناقص، آمده است؛ مثل: «در کتاب تاریخ مشروطیت تألیف احمد کسروی می‌خوانیم»، یا «چنان‌چه مورگان شوستر امریکائی در کتاب اختناق ایران در مورد زنان ایران می‌نویسد». از آن جا که این نوشته، «پایان‌نامه‌ی فوق لیسانس نویسنده بوده»، و از آن جا که تصور یک «پایان‌نامه»ی دانشگاهی بدون ذکر کامل منابع، حتا در جمهوری‌ی اسلامی، بسیار دور از ذهن می‌نماید، این احتمال گشوده می‌ماند که ممکن است ناشر به دلایلی، بخش یادداشت‌ها و منابع را از قلم چاپ انداخته باشد. در هر حال، من در مطالعه‌ی کتاب‌های مربوط به نشریات زنان ایران به این نکته برخوردم که بسیاری از نقل قول‌های صدیقه ببران، برگرفته از آثار زیر است. متنها، از آن رو که من در هنگام نگارش این مبحث، هیچ یک از آن پژوهش‌ها را در اختیار نداشتم، از نقل قول نویسنده‌ی این کتاب سود جستم:

- ❖ پری شیخ‌الاسلامی، ***زنان روزنامه‌نگار و اندیشمندان ایران***، تهران: مؤلف، ۱۳۵۱؛ محمد صدر هاشمی، ***تاریخ جراید و مجلات در ایران***، اصفهان، انتشارات کمال، ۱۳۶۳.

[۲۶۶] مجموعه‌ی سه جلدی‌ی زیر در ۷۳۶ صفحه، شامل زندگی‌نامه، کارنامه‌ی اجتماعی، مقاله‌های «زبان زنان»، سخنرانی‌ها، نامه‌ها، یادواره‌ها و عکس‌هائی از صدیقه دولت آبادی است:

- ❖ ***صدیقه دولت آبادی: نامه‌ها، نوشته‌ها، و یادها***، ویراستاران: مهدخت صنعتی، افسانه نجم آبادی، محمد توکلی طرقی، امریکا: انتشارات «نگرش و نگارش زن»، تابستان ۱۳۷۷.

اگر عمیق شویم اولین کسی که بر ضد تعدد زوجات قیام نمود، پیغمبر ما محمد بن عبدالله بود. چنان که عرض شد، قبل از پیغمبر، یک نفر مرد می‌توانست چندین زن، بدون این که حد معینی داشته باشد، اختیار نماید.[...] تا این که پیغمبر اسلام با شیوع آن در تمام ممالک بزرگ دنیا و در مقابل آن همه تعصب جاهلانه‌ی عرب‌ها، ارکان آن را شکست داد. در بادی امر به اقتضای زمان، محدود، و بعد با قید شرط مهمی آن را ممنوع فرمود. بدین معنا، در اول امر قدغن نمود هیچ کس نمی‌تواند بیش‌تر از چهار زن انتخاب نماید؛ ولی بعد، لزوم رعایت عدالت را در رفتار با زن‌ها شرط حتمی و اساسی قرار داده، ازدواج بیش از یک زن را بدان طریق ممنوع داشت. [...][۲۶۷]

و این در حالی است که با مطالعه‌ی زندگی‌نامه و نوشته‌های سیاسی/ اجتماعی‌ی این شخصیت درمی‌یابیم که او یکی از پیشروترین زنان روزگار خود بوده است؛ به طوری که رئیس شهربانی‌ی تهران در زمان دستگیری‌ی او به او می‌گوید: «خانم، شما صد سال زود به دنیا آمده‌اید.» و او پاسخ می‌دهد: «آقا، من صد سال دیر به دنیا آمده‌ام.» بازتاب صدیقه دولت آبادی- البته سال‌ها پس از استقرار مشروطیت و پس از تبعید رضا شاه- نسبت به یکی از سخنرانی‌های مریم فیروز (که متن آن در روزنامه‌ی «ستاره»، ۱۴ تیر ماه ۱۳۲۴ منتشر شده بود)، بیش از آن که به آگاهی‌ی جنسی‌ی او و بیش از آن که به رهائی‌ی ذهنیت او از سنت‌های پدرسالارانه گواهی دهد، نشانگر آگاهی و آینده‌نگری‌ی ژرف او در قلمروهای آموزش، و روش‌های ارتقاء فرهنگ عمومی است. مریم فیروز در آن جا گفته بود:

قبل از زمامداری‌ی رضا شاه، زنان و مردان روشنفکر آزادی‌خواه برای رفع حجاب و آزادی‌ی بانوان اقداماتی نموده و با بیداری‌ی نسوان مشغول کار آزادی‌ی زنان بودند. افسوس که در دوران حکومت دیکتاتوری، کانون بانوان، استخرهای شنا، و پیشاهنگی مانع ترقی‌ی زنان شد [...][۲۶۸]

صدیقه دولت آبادی، پایه‌گذار «کانون بانوان»، طی‌ی مقاله‌ای طولانی، از کانون بانوان، و از «استخر شنا و پیشاهنگی»، و تأثیر بالقوه‌ی آن‌ها در ارتقاء رشد زنان ایران، دفاع می‌کند و سوءاستفاده از این امکانات را ناشی از «بد تفسیر کردن آزادی» برمی‌شمارد، و سپس، بدون آن که از مریم فیروز نام بَرد، او و زنان همفکرش را مخاطب قرار می‌دهد و می‌نویسد:

[...] دنبال خیال باطل می‌روید که پرچمدار یک اساسی می‌شوید که در حقیقت گرویدن به بیگانگان است. بیگانگان شمال و جنوب و مشرق و مغرب، علمدار آزادی‌ی ما نمی‌شوند و راه حلی برای بیچارگی‌ی کنونی‌ی کشور به دست شما نمی‌دهند. همان آزادی‌ی ایام دیکتاتوری که امروز شما از آن تنقید می‌کنید، یک نعمت غیرمترقبه‌ای بود که به حکم اجبار نصیب زنان ایران شد و اگر آن را به هوسرانی تفسیر و تعبیر نکرده بودند، امروز بعد از ده سال به نتایج مطلوب رسیده و ثمر شیرین دربرداشت. و باز هم می‌گویم: [...] آزادی[ای] که امروز دیگران برای ما تأمین کنند، مطمئن باشید که تا صد سال دیگر هم برای ما به جای شکر حنظل بار می‌آورد. [...][۲۶۹]

---

۲۶۷ ***صدیقه دولت آبادی: نامه‌ها، نوشته‌ها، و یادها***، پیشین، جلد دوم، ص ۳۹۸.

۲۶۸ برگرفته از: صدیقه دولت آبادی، ***خانم مریم فیروز با دقت بخوانند***، در کتاب: صدیقه دولت آبادی: نامه‌ها، نوشته‌ها و یادها، ویراستاران: مهدخت صنعتی و افسانه نجم آبادی، شیکاگو: انتشارات نگرش و نگارش زن، جلد دوم، ۱۳۷۷، ص ٤٤١.

۲۶۹ مأخذ پیشین، ص ٤٤٣.

رضا شاه پهلوی

(۲۴ اسفند ۱۲۵۶ آلاشت/ مازندران- ۴ مرداد ۱۳۲۳ ژوهانسبورگ/ افریقای جنوبی)

واگذاری‌ی امتیازهای انحصاری به انگلیسی‌ها و روس‌ها از جمله نشانه‌های وضعیت
نیمه مستعره‌ی کشور بود. اجازه دهید چند نمونه دهم:
امتیازهائی که در دوره‌ی قاجار به انگلیسی‌ها داده شد:
خطوط تلگرافی از تهران تا خانقین، بوشهر، بلوچستان، تبریز- جلفا
و نیز خط بندرهای گوادر - جاسک - بندرعباس، به شرکت انگلیسی‌ی تلگراف
اروپا - هندوستان (۱۸۶۲- ۱۸۶۸)؛ بانک شاهنشاهی و نشر اسکناس (۱۸۸۹)؛
امتیاز صنایع تنباکوی کشور به شرکت تنباکوی پادشاهی انگلستان به بهای پانزده هزار پوند (۱۸۹۰)؛ احداث راه و راه آهن تهران - اهواز، تهران - قم - اصفهان، بروجرد - اصفهان و دیگر؛ امتیاز انحصاری‌ی اکتشاف و بهره‌برداری از منابع نفت و گاز به ویلیام ناکس دارسی برای
مدت ۶۰ سال (توسط مظفرالدین شاه در سال ۱۹۰۱)؛ فانوس‌های دریائی در خلیج فارس (۱۹۱۳)؛
واگذاری‌ی کنترل کامل ارتش، خزانه، شبکه‌ی ترابری و مخابرات کشور
(در زمان احمدشاه، سال ۱۹۱۹) و دیگر.
امتیازهای که در دوره‌ی قاجار به روس‌ها داده شد:
هفت امتیاز برای استفاده‌ی خطوط تلگراف شمال و شمال شرقی کشور (۱۸۸۱- ۱۹۰۲)؛ بهره برداری از شیلات دریای مازندران (۱۸۸۶- ۱۹۰۶)؛ تأسیس بانک استقراضی (۱۸۹۰)؛
بیمه‌ی ترابری‌ی انزلی - قزوین - همدان و تهران (۱۸۹۱ تا ۱۸۹۵)؛
استخراج معادن قراجه داغ در آذربایجان (۱۸۹۸)؛ احداث و بهره‌برداری‌ی
راه شوسه و راه آهن در منطقه‌ی آذربایجان (۱۹۰۲- ۱۹۱۳)؛
احداث خط لوله‌ی انتقال نفت از انزلی به رشت (۱۹۱۱)؛ و دیگر.

(جمشید اسدی)[۲۷۰]

هیچ چیز شگفت‌انگیزتر از این نبود [....] که وقتی وارد عربستان (خوزستان)
یا یکی از بنادر ایرانی‌ی خلیج فارس شدم، مشاهده کردم که هیچ قدرت خارجی به جز بریتانیای کبیر (به هر دلیلی که باشد) وجود ندارد. [...]
اگر بتوانند به زبان خارجی صحبت کنند،
آن زبان انگلیسی است؛ اگر خرید و فروش بکنند، بیش‌تر از روپیه

---

[۲۷۰] ***استقلال و منفعت ملی در روزگار جهانی شدن، گفت‌وگوی سوم جمشید اسدی با علیرضا موسوی***، تارنمای «خبرنامه‌ی گویا»، ۲ فروردین ۱۳۹۱:

http://news.gooya.com/columnists/archives/137819.php

[پول رایج در هند، مرکز حکومت بریتانیا در شرق] استفاده می‌کنند تا تومان؛
سایر قدرت‌ها را فقط به اسم می‌شناسند؛ [...] هند به آن‌ها نزدیک‌تر از تهران است؛
و به مأمورین ادارات کنسولی‌ی بریتانیا به چشم دوست می‌نگرند در حالی که مردم شمال ایران به آن‌ها به چشم سوءظن نگاه می‌کنند.
(ویکتور مالِت، سفیر بریتانیا در تهران ۱۹۱۱ تا ۱۹۱٤/ ۱۲۹۰ تا ۱۲۹٤)[۲۷۱]

[...] اگر یک مرکز قوی و ایران‌شناس و ایران‌پرستی وجود داشت،
البته این وسایل را درهم می‌شکست. ولی چه سود که دولت ایران از آوازه و شهرت این وسایل
سه گانه چنان مرعوب شده که اساساً جرأت نمی‌کرد تحقیقی کند و عملاً امتحان نماید.
عشایر کوچک در مراکز ایالات و اوباش و الواط در داخله‌ی شهرها از دولت
باج سبیل می‌گرفتند و مزد غارتگری و قتل و بی‌ناموسی‌ی خود را
به نام قراسورانی و غیره می‌ستاندند
(رضا خان سردار سپه، ۱۳۰۳ خورشیدی)[۲۷۲]

سالیان دراز و سنوات متمادی است که
روی نعش این مملکت تاخت و تاز کرده‌اند. تمام سلول‌های حیاتی‌ی آن را
غبار کرده و به هوا پراکنده‌اند، و حالا من گرفتار آن ذراتی هستم که اگر بتوانم،
باید آن‌ها را از هوا گرفته و به ترکیب مجددِ آن‌ها بذل توجه نمایم. [...] من مسئولیت یک اصلاح مهمی را بر روی یک تل خرابه و ویرانه بر عهده گرفته‌ام.
این کار شوخی نیست. و سر من در حین تنهائی،
گاهی در اثر فشار فکر در حال ترکیدن است.
(رضا شاه پهلوی، به خامه‌ی فرج‌الله بهرامی)

من میل به تظاهر ندارم و نمی خواهم از اقداماتی که
شده است اظهار خوشوقتی کنم و نمی‌خواهم فرقی بین امروز
با روزهای دیگر بگذارم. ولی شما خانم‌ها باید این روز را یک روز
بزرگ بدانید و از فرصت‌هایی که دارید برای ترقی‌ی کشور استفاده کنید. [...]
سعادت آتیه در دست شماست.
(رضا شاه پهلوی- ۱۷ دی ۱۳۱٤، فرمان کشف حجاب)

چه بی‌عدالتی از این بیش‌تر که اعلیحضرت شاه فقید <u>۵٦۰۰</u> رقبه املاک مردمی
از هر طبقه را به زور و بدون این که یک اعلان ثبت در روزنامه‌های وقت منتشر شود،

---

[۲۷۱] سر پرسی لورین، ***شیخ خزعل و پادشاهی‌ی رضا خان***، ترجمه‌ی محمد رفیع مهرآبادی، تهران: نشر فلسفه، ۱۳٦۳، ص ۵۷.
توضیح: پرسی لورین، نماینده‌ی بریتانیا در تهران، این سخنان را از قول ویکتور مالت، نماینده‌ی پیشین بریتانیا در تهران- نقل کرده است. کتاب «شیخ خزعل و پادشاهی‌ی رضا خان»، ترجمه‌ی بخشی از کتاب زیر است:

❖ Gordon Waterfield, ***Professional Diplomat: Sir Persy Loraine of Kirkharle, Bt., 1880- 1961***, London: John Murray Publishers Ltd, 1973.

[۲۷۲] ***سفرنامه‌ی خوزستان، سخنان رضا شاه پهلوی، به خامه‌ی فرج‌الله بهرامی***؛ تجدید چاپ شده توسط مرکز پژوهش و نشر فرهنگ سیاسی‌ی دوران پهلوی، ۱۳۵٤؛ تجدید انتشار در «نشر تلاش آنلاین»، ۱۳۸۳.

مالک شده باشند و اعلیحضرت محمدرضا شاه پهلوی به عنوان ارث پدر این املاک را به زارعین بفروشند و وجهی بدین طریق بر ثروت خود اضافه کنند.

(دکتر محمد مصدق، در پاسخ به محمدرضا شاه پهلوی، تأکید از من است.)[۲۷۳]

پس از کناره‌گیری‌ی رضا شاه از سلطنت، مسئله‌ی املاک او، که قریب دو هزار رقبه بود، مطرح شد. این املاک را رضا شاه در دوران سلطنت خود به عناوین مختلف از مالکیت صاحبان آن‌ها بیرون آورده و تصاحب کرده بود.

(سرهنگ غلامرضا نجاتی، تأکید از من است.)[۲۷۴]

حالا سال ۱۹۱۷ میلادی، برابر با ۱۲۹۶ خورشیدی، است. انقلاب «سوسیالیستی» در روسیه پیروز شده است. رهبران دولت نوپای شوروی، در ۱۴ دسامبر ۱۹۱۷ (آذر ۱۲۹۶)، کلیه قراردادهای دولت تزاری با کشورهای دیگر را لغو می‌کنند؛ و این خبر را در ۲۸ ژانویه ۱۹۱۸ توسط کنسول روسیه‌ی تزاری در خوی (که به انقلاب پیوسته بود) به تهران می‌رسانند. در نتیجه، از سوئی، قراردادِ روسیه و انگلستان، مبنی بر تقسیم ایران به دو منطقه‌ی نفوذِ روسیه‌ی تزاری و بریتانیا- که در سال ۱۹۰۷ بین این دو دولت بسته شده بود- از اعتبار می‌افتد، و از سوی دیگر، حق قضاوت کنسولی‌ی اتباع روسیه در ایران (کاپیتولاسیون)، که از جمله مفاد قرارداد «ترکمانچای» بود، رسماً لغو می‌شود؛[۲۷۵] گرچه مدتی طول می‌کشد تا دولت شوروی سفیری با استوارنامه‌ی محکم به تهران بفرستد، اما دولتمردان میهن‌دوست و هوشیار ایران در مجلس و دولتِ صمصام‌السلطنه، نبض زمان و موقعیت را می‌گیرند، و طی‌ی «مصوبه‌ی برج اسد» (مرداد ۱۲۹۷)، قرارداد ۱۹۰۷، و کلّ قرارداد «ترکمانچای» را باطل اعلام می‌کنند، و حکم تخلیه‌ی ایران را برای سفارت انگلستان در تهران نیز می‌فرستند.[۲۷۶] منتها، انگلستان که حالا در غیاب رقیب، قدرت بلامنازع در ایران است، نه تنها این «مصوبه» را به هیچ می‌گیرد، بلکه در برابر پرداخت حقوق ماهیانه‌ی پانزده هزار تومان به احمد شاه، برکناری‌ی صمصام‌السلطنه و انتصاب حسن وثوق‌الدوله را به احمد شاه قاجار دیکته می‌کند؛[۲۷۷] و در این میان، صدای دادخواهی‌ی ایران نسبت به قرارداد «ترکمانچای» نیز بی‌پژواک می‌ماند. وثوق‌الدوله آمده است تا با یاری‌ی اشراف و ثروتمندانی مانند خود، ظرف دو سال آینده، با امضاء یک قرارداد، بریتانیا را از «منطقه‌ی نفوذ»اش فراتر بَرَد و کل ایران را برای نخستین بار به مستعمره‌ی رسمی‌ی این کشور تبدیل کند: حالا سال ۱۲۹۸ خورشیدی، برابر با ۱۹۱۹ میلادی است. جنگ اول جهانی پایان یافته، و در حالی که کشور نوپای شوروی با جنگ داخلی دست به گریبان است، انگلستان، با بیگاری گرفتن از مردم

---

۲۷۳ دکتر محمد مصدق، ***خاطرات و تألمات مصدق***، چاپ دوم، لندن: انتشارات جبهه: نشریه‌ی ملیون ایران، ۱۹۸۶، ص ۳۵۴

۲۷۴ سرهنگ غلامرضا نجاتی، ***تاریخ بیست و پنج ساله‌ی ایران: از کودتا تا انقلاب***، تهران: خدمات فرهنگی رسا، ۱۳۷۱، زیرنویس ص ۱۸۳.

۲۷۵ در اوت ۱۹۰۷ / مرداد ۱۲۸۶، در حالی که مجلس نوپای ایران با هزار مسئله دست به گریبان بود، عهدنامه‌ی تقسیم ایران بین روسیه‌ی تزاری و بریتانیا امضاء شد. بنا بر این قرارداد، جنوب ایران منطقه‌ی نفوذ انگستان شد؛ شمال ایران منطقه‌ی نفوذ روسیه؛ و منطقه‌ی میانی نیز «بی‌طرف» اعلام شد. و پس از آن بود که هر یک از این دولت‌ها در ایران ارتش خود را در منطقه‌ی نفوذ خود پیاده کردند. اعلامیه‌ی لنین، نه تنها این «عهدنامه» را ملغا کرد، بلکه الغای کلیه‌ی امتیازاتی را که دولت تزاری از دولت ایران گرفته بود- البته غیر از سرزمین‌هائی که ایران با معاهده‌های گلستان و ترکمنچای از دست داده بود- باطل کرد.

۲۷۶ عبدالرضا هوشنگ مهدوی، ***تاریخ روابط خارجی‌ی ایران از ابتدای دوره‌ی صفویه تا پایان جنگ دوم جهانی (۱۵۰۰ تا ۱۹۴۵)***، تهران: انتشارات امیرکبیر، ۱۳۸۴.

۲۷۷ شاپور رواسانی، ***دولت و حکومت در ایران***، تهران: انتشارات شمع، بی‌تاریخ، ص ۱۱.

شـــهرهای سـر راه، نیروهای خود را تا شـمال ایران پیش رانده و به مخالفان انقلاب سـوسـیالیسـتی یاری می‌دهد.[۲۷۸] وثوق‌الدوله با دریافت دویست هزار تومان رشوه‌ای که می‌گیرد، همراه با دو تن از وزرای کابینه‌اش (علی‌اکبر صارم‌الدوله و نصـرت‌الله فیروز، که آن‌ها هم هریک از رشـوه‌ی صـدهزار تومانی بهره‌مند شـدند)، مخفیانه قراردادی را با نماینده‌ی انگلستان امضاء می‌کند که بر اساس آن، در برابر یک وام دو میلیون پوندی به ایران، حق نظارت بر همه‌ی نهادهای مالی و نظامی‌ی ایران، و امتیاز راه آهن و راه‌های شوسه‌ی ایران به انگلستان واگذار شده است. انگلستان منتظر تصویب مجلس و امضاء شاه ایران نمی‌ماند، و هیئت‌های مالی و نظامی‌ی خود را برای اجرای قرارداد به ایران روانه می‌کند. خبر منتشر می‌شود و افکار عمومی را علیه این قرارداد برمی‌انگیزد. قرارداد، توسط مجلس و شاه تأیید نمی‌شود. وثوق‌الدوله استعفا می‌دهد؛ و احمد شاه مشیرالدوله را به نخست وزیری برمی‌گزیند. در حالی که قرارداد (با امضـاء نخسـت وزیر «ممالک محروسه‌ی ایران»)، از نظر انگلیسی‌ها هنوز معتبر است، نخست وزیر تازه الغاء آن را **اعلام** می‌کند. مستشاران مالی و نظـامی‌ی انگلیس، (مجریـان قرارداد) ایران را ترک می‌کنند. امـا این کـار، التهاب آزادی‌خواهـان سـراسـر ایران را فرونمی‌نشاند. چرا که نه از گستره‌ی نیروهای نظامی‌ی بریتانیا در ایران کاسته شده و نه از نفوذ این کشور در تار و پود اقتصـاد و سـیاسـت ایران. در این بلبشـو، برخی از دولتمردان بانفوذ با شـتاب هر چه بیش‌تر به فروش امتیازهای ملی به بیگانگان سرگرم‌اند، و از سوی دیگر، امتیازها، به ضرب مقاومت آزادی‌خواهان در مجلس (که بسیاری‌شان از فرهیختگان خاندان قاجار بودند) و بیرون از مجلس، یکی پس از دیگری لغو می‌شود. جنگ و جدالِ سران ایلات و عشایر با یکدیگر، و گاه با دولت مرکزی، ویژگی‌ی دولت در دولت را بیش از پیش تعیّن بخشیده است. قتل و غارت و تجاوز و ناامنی، تورم، و قحطی و بیماری‌های واگیر در شـهرها و روسـتاهای ایران بی‌داد می‌کند. فسـاد و ضـعف دولت مرکزی در تسـلط بر نابه‌سـامانی‌های سیاسـی/ اقتصـادی/اجتماعی، همه‌ی پیکارگران مستقل و حزب‌ها و گروه‌های سیاسـی را برای «نجات ایران» از یک سـو، و دولت اسـتعماری‌ی انگلسـتان را برای حفظ و گسـترش منافع خود از سـوی دیگر، سـخت به تکاپو واداشته است. «رضاخان میرپنج»، خارج از حلقه‌ی «سلطنه»ها و «دوله»ها و «فرنگ دیده‌ها»ی قاجار، فرمانده‌ی بریگاد قزاق در قزوین، مردی سنتی، خودساخته، بلندپرواز، مقتدر، میهن‌دوست، آگاه از شرایط کنونی‌ی ایران، مسلط به گویش چند زبان ایرانی، اما بی‌بهره از سوادِ خواندن و نوشتن، مردِ این لحظه‌ی آشفته از تاریخ ایران است؛ لحظه‌ی آشفته‌ای که، در اثر نابخردی‌های پادشاهان قاجار و وابستگان‌شان، ایران، استقلال سیاسی و اقتصادی‌ی خود را تا بن دندان به استعمار بریتانیا باخته است.

سـرهنگ «رضا خان میرپنج»، به تازگی از سوی ژنرال ادموند آیرونساید، فرمانده‌ی نیروهای انگلیسی در بریگاد قزاق، به درجه‌ی سرهنگی و به مقام فرماندهی رسیده است.[۲۷۹] او با تشویق و تدارک ژنرال آیرونسـاید، در شامگاه سوم اسفند ۱۲۹۹ خورشیدی با نیروی سه هزار نفره‌ی زیر فرمان خود، به همراهی و راهنمائی‌ی سیدضیاءالدین طباطبائی، روزنامه نگار سیاسـی (سـردبیر نشـریه‌های «شـرق»، «برق»، و «رعد»)، مردی با ادعای ایران‌دوسـتی، اما مدافع سیاسـت‌های انگلستان)، ظرف چند ساعت، نهادهای اداری و نظامی در تهران را اشغال می‌کند؛ دولت وقت را برمی‌اندازد؛ و چنان که

---

[۲۷۸] ژنرال دنسـترویل، ***امپریالیسـم انگلیس در ایران و قفقاز***، ترجمه‌ی حسـین انصـاری، با مقدمه‌ی حسین ابوترابیان، تهران: انتشـارات کتابخانه‌ی منوچهری، ۱۳۵۸، ص ۱۴۰.

[۲۷۹] «بریگاد قزاق»، که مهم‌ترین و منسجم‌ترین نهاد نظامی‌ی ایرانِ عصر قاجار برشمرده می‌شود به درخواست ناصرالدین شاه در سال ۱۲۵۸ توسط روسیه‌ی تزاری در ایران دایر شد. در زمان محمدعلی شاه، سرهنگ لیاخوف، فرمانده‌ی بریگاد قزاق بود، و به دستور شاه، مجلس شورای ملی را به توپ بست. پس از پیروزی‌ی انقلاب اکتبر در روسیه، و ابطال قراردادهای استعماری‌ی روسیه‌ی تزاری با ایران (توسط لنین و تروتسـکی)، انگلیسـی‌ها به این نهاد نیز تسلط یافتند. ژنرال آیرونسـاید، فرمانده‌ی انگلیسـی‌ی این نهاد، در سال ۱۲۹۹ پست فرماندهی را به رضـا خان میرپنج واگذاشت. در واقع، رضا خان میرپنج نخستین فرمانده‌ی ایرانی‌ی این نهاد بود. چرا که تا آن زمان، فرماندهی‌ی تمام شعبه‌های بریگاد قزاق در ایران، در اختیار افسران روسی و بعد هم انگلیسی قرار داشت. به مأخذ زیر نگاه کنید:

- دکتر باقر عاقلی، ***رضا شاه و قشون متحدالشکل***، تهران: نشر نامک، ۱۳۸۶.

به ژنرال آیرونساید قول داده است،[۲۸۰] به احمد شاه قاجار اطمینان می‌دهد که «کودتا برای نجات سلطنت است.» احمد شاه که از ضعف خود و دولت مرکزی آگاه است، به کودتا روی موافق نشان می‌دهد؛ سیدضیاءالدین طباطبائی را به نخست وزیری منصـوب می‌کند، و «رضـا خان» را در مقام وزیر جنگ، لقب «سـردار سـپه» می‌بخشـد. یرواند آبراهامیان می‌نویسد:

سیدضیـاء و رضـاخان در اعلان تشکیل حکومت خود اظهار داشتند که با پایان دادن به تجزیه‌ی داخلی، انجام دگرگونی‌های اجتماعی و نجات کشور از اشغال بیگانگان، عصر احیای ملی را آغاز می‌کنند. (ایران بین دو انقلاب، ۱۳۸۳، ص ۱۰٦)

نکته‌ای که در زمینه‌ی شـرایط سـیاسـی‌ی این لحظه از تاریخ ایران نباید فراموش کرد، نقش دولت نوپای شـوروی در برخورد با دولت ایران است. شوروی، که در ابتدای پیروزی‌ی انقلابِ اکتبر ۱۹۱۷ کوشیده بود که با کاستن از بار گران تعهدات ایران، نظرِ موافق بلندپایگان و مردم ایران را نسبت به خود جلب کند، حدود یک هفته پس از کودتای سـوم اسـفند (یعنی ۸ اسـفند ۱۲۹۹/ ۲۷ فوریه ۱۹۲۱) قراردادی با دولت ایران به امضـاء رسـاند، که زنگ خطرِ «تقسیم ایران به دو منطقه‌ی نفوذ» را در گوش ایرانیان تجدید می‌کرد. در فصل ششم از این پیمان‌نامه آمده است:

طرفین معظمتین متعاهدین موافقت حاصل کردند که هرگاه ممالک ثالثی بخواهند به وسیله‌ی دخالت مُسلّحه سیاست غاصبانه را در خاک ایران مجری دارند، یا خاک ایران را مرکز حملات نظامی بر ضد شوروی قرار دهند [...] اگر حکومت ایران پس از اخطار دولت شوروی خودش نتواند این خطر را رفع نماید، دولت شوروی حق خواهد داشت قشون خود را به خاک ایران وارد نماید تا این که برای دفاع از خود اقدامات لازمه‌ی نظامی را به عمل آورد.[۲۸۱]

قول‌های مساعد شوروی در عدم تعرض به ایران، و سپس، امضاء این قرارداد، درست در دوره‌ای انجام شد، که از سوئی، نیروهای سیاسی و نظامی‌ی بریتانیا هنوز در ایران بودند و ورودِ نیروهای شـوروی به خاک ایران خطری بالقوه بود، و از سـوی دیگر، پیشـاهنگان سـیاسـی‌ی آذربایجان و خراسـان و گیلان، با هدف دسـت‌یابی‌ی ایران به اسـتقلال و آزادی و حکومت جمهوری قیام کرده بودند، و به امید کمک‌های دولت «خلقی‌ی شوروی»، علیه نفوذ انگستان، فساد دولتمردان، و فقر و بی‌عدالتی در ایران، با نیروهای دولتی می‌جنگیدند. اما زد و بندها و بده بسـتان‌های پنهانی‌ی دولت شـوروی با دولت ایران، از حد این «قرارداد» فراتر رفت: جنبش آذربایجان، به رهبری‌ی شـیخ محمد خیابانی، پیش از رسـمیت یافتن این قرارداد، در شهریور ۱۲۹۹ سرکوب شد؛ و چند ماه پس از امضاء این قرارداد بود که جنبش‌های خراسان و گیلان نیز از کمک‌های شوروی بی‌بهره ماندند، و شگفتا که به اتهام تجزیه‌ی ایران و پیوستن به «شوروی‌ی سوسیالیستی»، منهدم شدند. کلنل محمدتقی پسیان، رهبر جنبش خراسان، در مهر ۱۳۰۰ جان خود را از دست داد؛ و میرزا کوچک خان، رهبر جنبش جنگل در گیلان، در آذر ۱۳۰۰. چرا که این پیکارگران، نه تنها از سـوی «کمیته‌ی صـدور سـوسـیالیسـم» (در حزب کمونیسـت شـوروی) مأموریت نداشـتند، بلکه- بنا بر اسـناد- این قیام‌ها با هدف اسـتقلال ایران و برقراری‌ی یک حکومت مردمی در ایران شـکل گرفته بود.[۲۸۲] (و شـگفتا که خطای معرفت‌شـناختی‌ی این پیکارگران نسـبت به حکومتِ «خلقی‌ی

---

[۲۸۰] ***خاطرات سری‌ی آیرونساید، به انضمام ترجمه‌ی شاهراه فرماندهی***، تهران: مؤسسـه‌ی پژوهش و مطالعات فرهنگی، و مؤسسـه‌ی خدمات فرهنگی‌ی رسا، ۱۳۷۳، ص ۲۱۹.

[۲۸۱] وحید مازندرانی، ***راهنمای عهود و عهدنامه‌ی تاریخی‌ی ایران***، تهران: انتشارات ابن سینا، ۱۳٤۱، ص ۳۸.

[۲۸۲] با مطالعه‌ی زندگی‌ی سیاسـی‌ی قیام‌کنندگان در خراسـان (محمدتقی پسیان)، آذربایجان (شیخ محمد خیابانی)، و گیلان (میرزا کوچک خان)- با وجود ابهام‌ها و پرسش‌های بی‌پاسخ- در عدم وابستگی‌ی این شخصیت‌ها تردیدی به جا نمی‌ماند. چرا که هر سه تن این پیکارگران، علیه ظلم و فساد حکومت، و در راستای حفظ استقلال و تمامیت ارضی‌ی ایران، حرکت می‌کردند. میرزا کوچک خان می‌گوید: «من و رفقایم محال است آلت دست آن‌ها [روس‌ها] بشویم. [...] من استقلال ایران را خواهانم و بقای اعتبارات کشور را طالبم. آسایش ایرانی و همه‌ی ابنای بشر را

شورویِ سوسیالیستی»، تا فروریزیِ شورویِ سوسیالیستی، گریبان‌گیر معرفت‌شناسیِ انبوهی از پیکارگران سیاسیِ ما باقی ماند؛ و جوی خونِ پسیان‌ها و میرزاها و خیابانی‌ها را زنده و جاری نگه داشت.)

***

سید ضیاءالدین طباطبائی، که حالا عبا و عمامه را کنار گذاشته، هم برای بهبود وضع کارگران و کشاورزان و فرودستان جامعه پیشنهادهای اصلاحی ارائه می‌کند، و هم مدافع سرسخت قرارداد ۱۹۱۹ است. او، به رغم حمایت نمایندگان انگلستان، حدود سه ماه بعد (٤ خرداد ۱۳۰۰) به سبب دفاع از منافع بریتانیا، به سوئیس تبعید می‌شود.[۲۸۳] احمد قوام‌السطنه، از زندان آزاد می‌شود و به نخست وزیری می‌رسد. اما «رضاخان سردار سپه»، که در طول دو سال گذشته، توانائیِ انجام تعهداتِ اعلام‌شده را نشان داده است، در سوم آبان ۱۳۰۲ به فرمان احمد شاه به نخست وزیری منصوب می‌شود و در آبان ۱۳۰۳ عنوان فرماندهیِ کل قوای مسلح را از مجلس شورای ملی می‌گیرد. واپسین سفر احمد شاه قاجار به اروپا، همزمان است با اوج قحطیِ نان و شورش سراسریِ مردم ایران علیه محتکران بازار از یک سو، تاخت و تاز سران عشایر و ادامه‌ی ناامنی از سوی دیگر، و رشد گرایش‌های سوسیالیستی- با وجود سرکوب جنبش‌های گیلان و آذربایجان و خراسان- در میان پیکارگران سیاسی، از سوی سوم. این شرایط، اشراف، زمین‌داران، دولتمردان، نمایندگان مجلس شورای ملی، و حزب‌ها و گروه‌های ملی‌گرا، و البته نمایندگان استعمار در ایران را- با هدف‌های متفاوت و متضاد- به چاره‌اندیشی وامی‌دارد. و چاره، عزل شتابزده‌ی احمد شاه است. بنا بر قانون اساسیِ مشروطه‌ی ایران، عزل و نصب پادشاه به عهده‌ی «مجلس مؤسسان» است. با پشتوانه‌ی این اصل، مجلس مؤسسان اول، احمد شاه، هفتمین و واپسین پادشاه دودمان قاجار را از سلطنت خلع می‌کند (۱۳۰۴)، و به گفته‌ی یرواند آبراهامیان، با «پشتیبانیِ چشمگیر مردم کشور» و «همدستیِ علنیِ گروه‌های مختلف در درون و بیرون مجالس چهارم و پنجم»، «رضا خان سردار سپه»، نخست وزیر او را، که توانائیِ سازمان‌دهیِ خود را در پنج سال گذشته به نمایش گذاشته- با عنوان «رضا شاه پهلوی»- به سلطنت برمی‌گزیند.[۲۸٤]

بدون تفاوت دین و مذهب شایقم.» یا شیخ محمد خیابانی می‌گوید: «آذربایجان جزء لاینفک ایران است و ایران جزء لاینفک آذربایجان.» در عین حال، با مطالعه‌ی اسناد مربوط به ادامه‌ی حرکت آن‌ها، در این هم تردیدی به جا نمی‌ماند که همسایه‌ی شمالی، چه در زمان تزاری و چه در زمان «شوروی»، به کمک مزدوران خود برای حفظ و گسترش نفوذ خود در ایران از کلیه‌ی این حرکت‌ها سوءاستفاده کرد، و باز برای حفظ منافع خود، در تبانی با بریتانیا، و در تبانی با دولتمردان ایران، این شخصیت‌ها و دنبال‌کنندگان راه آن‌ها را تنها گذاشت. به مآخذ زیر نگاه کنید:

- ❖ دکتر شاپور رواسانی، ***نهضت میرزا کوچک خان جنگلی و اولین جمهوریِ شورائی در ایران***، تهران: نشر چاپخش؛ شهریور ۱۳۶۳.
- ❖ بابک امیرخسروی و محسن حیدریان، ***مهاجرت سوسیالیستی و سرنوشت ایرانیان***، چاپ دوم، تهران: نشر پیام امروز، ۱۳۸۲.
- ❖ خانبابا بیانی، ***غائله‌ی آذربایجان***، تهران: انتشارات زریاب، ۱۳۷۵.
- ❖ حمید شوکت، ***در تیررس حادثه: زندگیِ سیاسیِ قوام‌السلطنه***، تهران: نشر اختران، ۱۳۸۵، بخش سوم، صص ۷۵ تا ۱۰۹.

۲۸۳ شخصیت سیاسیِ سیدضیاءالدین طباطبائی و چرائیِ خلع و تبعید او، از دیدگاه‌ها و زاویه‌های متناقض در تاریخ ایران ثبت شده است. مسعود بهنود، نویسنده‌ی کتاب «از سیدضیاء تابختیار» ، در مقاله‌ای می‌نویسد: «سید ضیا می‌گوید که رضا خان وزیر جنگ را فراخوانده و نارضایتیِ خود را از سید ضیا به او می‌گوید. پاسخ، یک سلام نظامیِ محکم بود: "امر بفرمائید همین الان اعدامش می‌کنم."شاه با دستپاچگی فریاد زد "اعدام نه نه... برود فرنگ برود به هر جا." و خود سید ضیا در مصاحبه‌ای می‌گوید: "وقتی نماینده‌ی سردار سپه بدون وقت قبلی وارد کاخ بادگیر شد فهمیدم خبری شده است. وقتی گفت به فرمان اعلیحضرت اتومبیل آماده است، زیر لب فحشی دادم. خدایار خان دستش به اسلحه‌اش رفت، خیال کرد سردار سپه را می‌گویم؛ در حالی که مقصودم کسی بود که نفهمید چه بر سر خود آورده، خودش تاج را دو دستی تحویل کسی داد که هرگز جلو من ننشست. از من می‌ترسید." در مورد وابستگیِ این شخصیت به انگلستان نیز از قول خود او چنین می‌خوانیم: «می‌گویند من انگلوفیل هستم، درست است، تکذیب هم ندارد؛ اما من انگلوالاغ نیستم، از کسی اطاعت ندارم، انگلیسی‌ها را از همسایه‌ی شمالی برای ایران بهتر می‌دانم. اما فیل هستم.» شاید کوتاه‌ترین توصیفی که می‌توان پیرامون شخصیت میان‌مانده‌ی سیدضیاء به دست داد، بازنوشته‌ی مسعود بهنود باشد: «با فرار محمد علی شاه از کشور روزنامه‌ی شرق را منتشر کرد. بالای آن نوشت "این روزنامه طرفدار استقلال ایران و آیینه‌ی حقیقت نمای ایرانیان است." همان جا برای اولین بار از سوسیالیسم و کمونیسم نوشت. روزنامه نگاری بی‌پروا و انقلابی بود. چنان کرد که با سومین شماره، دولت تصمیم به توقیف شرق گرفت. سید ضیا زود دست به کار انتشار روزنامه‌ی برق شد.» نگاه کنید به:

- ❖ مسعود بهنود، ***سید ضیا و صد روز صدارتی که تاریخ ایران را دگرگون کرد***، برگرفته از تارنمای «تاریخ ایرانی»، بازدید: ۱۰ اسفند ۱۳۸۹: http://tarikhirani.ir/fa/news/4/bodyView/428

توضیح: یادآوری می‌کنم که مسعود بهنود در مقاله‌ی یادشده هیچ سندی را به عنوان مأخذ گفته‌های خود ارائه نداده است.

۲۸٤ البته، سرهنگ غلامرضا نجاتی، به استناد تاریخ بیست ساله‌ی ایران، نوشته‌ی حسین مکی، جلد سوم، انقراض قاجاریه و تشکیل سلسله‌ی پهلوی، صص ۴۱۸-۴۱۹، و به استناد نطق مخالف دکتر محمد مصدق، در زمینه‌ی رأی مجلس به خلع احمد شاه و گزینش رضا شاه به

بدین ترتیب، ایده‌ی «جمهوری»، که از دوره‌ی انقلاب مشروطه زمزمه‌اش برخاسته بود، و میرزا کوچک خان، شیخ محمد خیابانی و محمد تقی پسیان را همراه با انبوهی از همراهان آن‌ها قربانی گرفته بود، و حتا علی اکبر دهخدا را به عنوان نخستین «رئیس جمهور ایران» نامزد کرده بود، عملاً به فراموشی سپرده می‌شود. شگفتی در این جاست که خود «رضا خان سردار سپه» (در دوره‌ی نخست وزیری) نیز در زمره‌ی جمهوری‌خواهان بود. از متن‌های مربوط به این دوره چنین برمی‌آید که برایندی از چند نیرو ، رژیم پادشاهی را ابقاء کرد: یک) پیکارگران فرهنگی و دولتمردان باتجربه‌ی دودمان قاجار- که بسیاری از آن‌ها با مشروطه‌خواهان همراه بودند، و در میان مردم نفوذ و اعتبار داشتند، و در عین حال، «رضا خانِ» بی‌نام و نشان را چندان جدی تلقی نمی‌کردند، هنوز بازگشتِ سلطنت به خاندان خود را امکان‌پذیر می‌دیدند. دو) اعمال نظر سران ایلات و عشایر و روحانیان و بازار، به عنوان محافظان سرسخت سنتِ پادشاهی. سه) اعمال نظر نمایندگان بریتانیا در ایران، که از تمرکزِ قدرت در سنت پادشاهی در راستای حفظ منافع خود تجربه‌های گرانبهائی داشتند. با این همه، رضا خان سردار سپه، برای تحقق حکومت جمهوری چندی هم با مخالفان آن مبارزه می‌کند. اما افزون بر سه نیروی یادشده، انگار دو نیروی دیگر نیز در عقب‌نشینی‌ی او از این ایده مؤثر بوده‌اند: جذابیت تاج و تخت شاهنشاهی‌ی ایران برای خودِ «رضا خان سردار سپه»؛ و لزوم شتابزدگی و سرعت عملِ لازم برای تدارک تغییر در غیاب احمد شاه قاجار- که در اروپا به سر می‌بَرد و در آستانه‌ی بازگشت به ایران است. با این همه، ایده‌ی جمهوری‌خواهی یکسره به فراموشی سپرده نمی‌شود؛ و افزون بر مبارزه‌ی خونینِ برخی شخصیت‌های آزادی‌خواهِ آن زمان برای تحقق حکومت جمهوری، صدای تمنایش تا سال ۱۳۵۷ در سپهر سیاسی‌ی ایران تاب می‌خورد.

و چنین است که نظام پادشاهی با رضا شاه پهلوی ادامه می‌یابد؛ و مرحله‌ی نوسازی‌ی ساختارهای سیاسی/ اجتماعی/ فرهنگی‌ی ایران بر بنیادهای «مدرنتیه»، از یک سو، و پیکار درازدامن مردم ایران با استبدادِ دو پادشاه خاندان پهلوی از سوی دیگر آغاز می‌شود.

***

بینش، منش و کنش‌های سیاسی‌ی رضا شاه پهلوی در درازنای بیست سال قدرتمداری‌ی او را شاید بتوان در دو گروه متضاد زیر شناسائی کرد:

سلطنت، می‌نویسد: «برای طرح و تصویب ماده‌ی واحده‌ی تغییر سلطنت، زمینه‌ی کافی از پیش فراهم شده بود. تروریست‌های دولتی، اطراف بهارستان را محاصره کرده بودند. مأمورین انتظامی نیز مجلس را زیر نظر داشتند. با ترور واعظ قزوینی، در پایان جلسه‌ی روز هفتم آبان [۱۳۰۴] در جلوی مجلس به جای ملک‌الشعرای بهار، که در جلسه‌ی آن روز مجلس قسمتی از توطئه‌های پشت پرده را برای به سلطنت رسیدن رضا شاه فاش ساخته بود، نمایندگان مجلس سخت مرعوب شده بودند. عده‌ای از نمایندگان طرفدار سردار سپه، حضور و غیاب نمایندگان را در جلسه‌ی رسمی نظارت می‌کردند.» به مأخذ زیر نگاه کنید:

- ❖ سرهنگ غلامرضا نجاتی، ***جنبش ملی شدن صنعت نفت ایران و کودتای ۲۸ مرداد ۱۳۳۲*** ، تهران: چاپ هشتم، شرکت سهامی‌ی انتشار، ۱۳۷۸، ص ۱۴۹.

برای اطلاع بیش‌تر از زندگی و شخصیت رضا شاه پهلوی و آثار نیک و بدی که در دوران صدارت و سطنت خود بر ایران و ایرانیان گذاشت، خواننده‌ام را به منابع زیر که از دیدگاه‌های مختلف نوشته شده‌اند، رجوع می‌دهم:

- ❖ نجفقلی پسیان و خسرو معتضد، ***از سوادکوه تا ژوهانسبورگ: زندگی‌ی رضا شاه پهلوی***، تهران: نشر ثالث، چاپ سوم، ۱۳۸۲.
- ❖ حسین مکی، ***تاریخ بیست ساله‌ی ایران***، تهران: انتشارات علمی، ۱۳۸۰
- ❖ ملک‌الشعرا- بهار (محمدتقی بهار) ***تاریخ مختصر احزاب سیاسی‌ی ایران: انقراض قاجاریه***، تهران: امیرکبیر، ۱۳۶۳. چاپ نخست این اثر (۱۳۲۳) در اینترنت نیز منتشر شده است.
- ❖ یحیی دولت آبادی، ***حیات یحیی***، تهران: انتشارات عطار و فردوسی، ۱۳۶۲، جلد ٤.
- ❖ یرواند آبراهامیان، ***ایران بین دو انقلاب: از مشروطه تا انقلاب اسلامی***، ترجمه از انگلیسی به فارسی از : کاظم فیروزمند، حسن شمس‌آوری، محسن مدیر شانه‌چی، تهران: نشر مرکز، چاپ هشتم، ۱۳۸۳.
- ❖ استفانی کرونین، ***رضا شاه و شکل‌گیری‌ی ایران نوین***، ترجمه‌ی مرتضی ثاقب فر، تهران: نشر جامی، ۱۳۸۲.
- ❖ سیروس غنی، ***ایران: برآمدن رضاخان، برافتادن قاجار و نقش انگلیسی‌ها***، ترجمه‌ی حسن کامشاد، تهران: انتشارات نیلوفر، ۱۳۸۵.
- ❖ تورج اتابکی، ***تجدد آمرانه: جامعه و دولت در عصر رضا شاه***، ترجمه‌ی مهدی حقیقت‌خواه، تهران: نشر ققنوس، ۱۳۸۷.
- ❖ احسان طبری، ***جامعه‌ی ایران در دوران رضا شاه***، تارنمای «راه توده»:

http://www.rahetudeh.com/rahetude/Tabari/iran-rezashah/html/jameehiran-16.html

گروه ۱) رضا شاه پهلوی، با تصرف زمین‌های حاصلخیز و املاکِ زمین‌داران و خرده مالکان و کشاورزان خُرد و کلانِ سراسر ایران، به یک فئودال تمام عیار و به ثروتمندترین مردِ ایرانِ فقیر و ویران تبدیل شد؛[۲۸۵] شاعران و نویسندگان و روزنامه‌نگاران آزادی‌خواه و روشنگر را به زندان انداخت؛ برای مرعوب کردن نویسندگان آزادی‌خواه، میرزاده‌ی عشقی و فرخی‌ی یزدی (هر دو شاعر) را کشت؛ ابوالقاسم لاهوتی، پیکارگر دوره‌ی مشروطیت، شاعر، و سردبیر روزنامه‌ی «بیستون» را غیاباً به اعدام محکوم کرد؛ نشریه‌های مستقل، و مهم‌ترین نهاد کوشندگان زن (انجمن نسوان وطن‌خواه) را تعطیل کرد؛ نخستین اعتصاب ۲۰ هزار نفره‌ی کارگران نفت جنوب و کسبه‌ی محلی را که خواهان بالابردن دستمزدها و حق داشتن اتحادیه بودند، به شدیدترین وجه ممکن سرکوب کرد (۴ اردی‌بهشت ۱۳۰۸)؛[۲۸۶] با ممنوع کردن فعالیت‌های «مرام اشتراکی» (کمونیستی)، بسیاری از کوشندگان میهن‌دوست و آزادی‌خواه ایران را به مهاجرتی ناخواسته به شوروی ناگزیر کرد و به دست تصفیه‌های استالین سپرد (۱۳۱۰)؛ ۵۳ تن از کوشندگان سیاسی را (که با افکار سوسیالیستی/ کمونیستی و به صورت مخفی فعالیت داشتند، و از راه نوشتار به انتشار آگاهی مشغول بودند) به زندان انداخت، و تقی ارانی، یکی از شریف‌ترین اعضای آن را در زندان کشت (۱۳۱۶)؛[۲۸۷] به گفته‌ی آبراهامیان: «مالیات کشاورزی را از دوش مالکان برداشت و بر کشاورزان روستائی بار کرد»؛ با نادیده گرفتن بند مربوط به «انجمن‌های ایالتی و ولایتی» در قانون اساسی، و با تمرکزگرائی‌ی فارس‌محور، حق تعیین سرنوشت سیاسی/ اجتماعی/ فرهنگی را از «اقلیت‌های قومی» (ملیت‌های ایرانی) گرفت و آن‌ها را از پوشش محلی و کاربرد زبان مادری محروم کرد؛ آزادی‌ی انتخابات و نمایندگی‌ی مجلس را به رأی و تشخیص خود محدود کرد؛ مصونیت پارلمانی را از نمایندگان مجلس گرفت؛ بسیاری از خبرگان سیاسی و سیاست‌آموختگان وفادار به مشروطیت را (که برخی‌شان از دودمان قاجار بودند) به بهانه‌های مختلف از صحنه‌ی سیاست ایران راند؛ و با این ابزار، راه هرگونه اندیشه‌ی مستقل و توسعه‌ی سیاسی و مدنی را سد کرد. افزون بر

---

[۲۸۵] دکتر محمد مصدق، در دوران اسارت در احمدآباد، به برخی از گفته‌های محمدرضا شاه در کتاب «مأموریت برای وطنم» پاسخ‌هائی نوشته که در پایان بند ۹ آن چنین می‌خوانیم: «و باز چه بی‌عدالتی از این بیش‌تر که اعلیحضرت شاه فقید ۵۶۰۰ رقبه املاک مردمی از هر طبقه را به زور و بدون این که یک اعلان ثبت در روزنامه‌های وقت منتشر شود، مالک شده باشند و اعلیحضرت محمدرضا شاه پهلوی به عنوان ارث پدر این املاک را به زارعین بفروشند و وجهی بدین طریق بر ثروت خود اضافه کنند.» در حالی که غلامرضا نجاتی، رقم املاک رضا شاه را «قریب دو هزار» ثبت کرده است. نشانی‌ی هر دو مأخذ را در ابتدای همین مبحث به دست داده‌ام..

[۲۸۶] یونس پارسا بناب، ***تاریخ صد ساله‌ی جنبش‌های سوسیالیستی، کارگری، و کمونیستی در ایران (از انقلاب مشروطیت ۱۲۸٤ تا انقلاب ۱۳۵۷)***، ویراستار: ساسان دانش، فصل‌نامه‌ی «سامان نو»، شماره‌ی ۱۳/ ۱٤، آوریل ۲۰۱۱، ص ۱٤۷: www.saamaan-no.org/pdf

[۲۸۷] گروه موسوم به «پنجاه و سه نفر» داستان پیچیده‌ای دارد؛ و من به هیچ وجه جرأت نمی‌کنم آن را در چند جمله جمع‌بندی کنم. چرا که پیرامون تاریخچه‌ی آن، و گرایش‌های سیاسی‌ی اعضای آن، به ویژه پیرامون گرایش سیاسی‌ی دکتر تقی ارانی، در کتاب‌های مختلف اظهار نظرهای کاملاً ضد و نقیضی ابراز شده است. من در جای دیگری از مجموعه‌ی حاضر به این موضوع اشاره کرده‌ام، و در این جا به این توضیح ناقص بسنده می‌کنم: این ۵۳ تن، در دوره‌ی دانشجوئی در کشورهای اروپائی (عمدتاً آلمان) به عنوان اپوزیسیون برون مرزی، به مارکسیسم گرایش یافته بودند. اما دیدگاه و روش همه‌ی آن‌ها در مبارزه یک سان نبود. بلکه اکثر آن‌ها با گرایش به کمونیسم بین‌المللی، عضو «حزب کمونیست ایران» شدند، (که به لحاظ ایدئولوژیک، به حزب کمونیست شوروی وابسته بود)، و تعداد اندکی، که تقی ارانی یکی از آن‌ها بود، «فرقه‌ی جمهوری‌ی انقلابی‌ی ایران» را بنیاد گذاشتند. منتها پس از بازگشت به ایران با یکدیگر همکاری داشتند (و پیچیدگی، در تفسیرِ همین همکاری رخ می‌کند)، و به دنبال انتشار نشریه‌ی «دنیا»، به سردبیری‌ی تقی ارانی، و تماس با گروه‌های دانشجوئی و کارگری، و ایجاد موجی از اعتراض‌های دانشجوئی در دانشگاه تهران، در سال ۱۳۱۶ زندانی شدند. به جز تقی ارانی که در سال ۱۳۱۸ در سن ۳۶ سالگی ظاهراً به سبب ابتلا به بیماری‌ی تیفوس و عدم مراقبت‌های پزشکی در زندان جان سپرد، پس از شهریور ۲۰ و با فرمان «عفو عمومی»، همه‌ی نفرات این گروه آزاد شدند. همین جا بایسته است بیافزایم که اکثریت اعضای این گروه، به عنوان پدیدآورندگان حزب توده‌ی ایران شناسائی می‌شوند؛ حزبی که هنوز معتقد است که ارانی عضو «حزب کمونیست ایران» شده بود. در حالی که پژوهش حمید احمدی خلاف این نظر را گزارش می‌دهد. نکته‌ی دیگر این که: بلافاصله پس از تبعید رضا شاه، مردم ایران از طریق نشریات، محاکمه و مجازات بازجویان و شکنجه‌گران و عاملان کشتار دوره‌ی او را خواستار شدند. از جمله محاکمه شوندگان، «سرپاس مختاری»، بازجو و شکنجه‌گر، و «پزشک احمدی»، پزشک بدنام در زندان دوره‌ی رضا شاه بودند. تا جائی که گزارش‌های مختصر احمد کسروی خبر می‌دهند، در این دادگاه‌ها، از طریق دفاع از مطالب نشریه‌ی «دنیا»، از نویسندگان آن، و از تقی ارانی نیز دفاع شده است. در زمینه‌ی گروه «پنجاه و سه نفر» و تقی ارانی به منابع زیر، که با دو دیدگاه متضاد نوشته شده‌اند، نگاه کنید:

- حمید احمدی، ***تاریخچه‌ی فرقه‌ی جمهوری‌ی انقلابی‌ی ایران و گروه ارانی (۱۳۰٤ تا ۱۳۱٦)***، تهران: نشر آتیه، ۱۳۷۹.
- ***ویژه‌ی صدمین سالگرد تولد دکتر تقی ارانی***، نشریه‌ی دنیا، شماره‌ی ٦، برلین: انتشارات حزب توده‌ی ایران، تابستان ۱۳۸۲.

در زمینه‌ی دادگاه‌های پس از رضا شاه، و دفاع از نشریه‌ی «دنیا»، به اثر زیر نگاه کنید:

- ***دفاعیات احمد کسروی از سرپاس مختاری و پزشک احمدی، برگرفته از [نشریه‌ی] پرچم روزانه و هفتگی (۱۳۲۱ و ۱۳۲۲)***، به کوشش باهماد آزادگان، پاریس: انتشارات خاوران، ۱۳۸۳/ ۲۰۰٤، ص ۱۱۸.

اِعمال این سیاست‌های آهنین در مواجه با مسائل داخلی‌ی ایران، رضا شاه، به رغم میل به حفظ منافع ایران، در فرایند «الغاء/ تمدید قرارداد دارسی» چنان ناتوان و نابخردانه عمل کرد، که راه، برای انتساب او به «خیانت» برای همیشه‌ی تاریخ گشوده ماند.[۲۸۸] و این در حالی است که هیچ متنی حاکی از خودفروشی و رشوه‌خواری در پرونده‌ی او ثبت نشده

---

[۲۸۸] امتیاز حفاری، کشف، و بهره‌برداری از نفت ایران، در سال ۱۲۸۰ خورشیدی (۱۹۰۱ میلادی) از سوی دولتمردان و دلالان دربار مظفرالدین شاه قاجار و به امضاء او، در برابر حق‌الامتیاز ۱٦ درصد از سود خالص فروش نفت برای ایران، به مدت ٦۰ سال به یکی از شهروندان استرالیائی (انگلیسی تبار) به نام ویلیام دارسی واگذار شد. حدود هفت سال بعد، درست در زمانی که دارسی از رسیدن به نفت در ایران مأیوس شده بود، چاهی در مسجد سلیمان فوران کرد. در سال ۱۲۸۸ خورشیدی (۱۹۰۹) این کمپانی با نام شرکت «انگلو- پرشیا» استخراج و فروش نفت ایران را آغاز کرد. چندی بعد، دولت انگلستان با خرید ۵۱ درصد از سهام این شرکت، آن را عملاً در اختیار گرفت، و نام کمپانی را به «شرکت نفت ایران و انگلیس» تغییر داد (۱۳۱٤/ ۱۹۳۵). این همان شرکتی است که پس از شکست بریتانیا از دکتر محمد مصدق و استقلال‌طلبان همراه او، پس از ملی شدن نفت ایران، و از آغاز فعالیت «کنسرسیوم» به بعد، با نام «بریتیش پترولیوم» شناسائی شد (۱۳۳۳/ ۱۹۵٤). «قرارداد تمدید امتیازنامه‌ی دارسی»، که در ۸ اردی‌بهشت ۱۳۱۲ به فرمان رضا شاه، به وسیله‌ی حسن تقی زاده (وزیر دارائی‌ی وقت) و سِر جان کدمن (رئیس هیئت مدیره‌ی شرکت) امضاء شد، داستان دراز و پیچیده‌ای دارد که تاکنون از چشم‌اندازهای متفاوت و متناقض بررسی شده است. فشرده‌ی این داستان را در این جا بازمی‌گویم، و برای آگاهی‌ی بیش‌تر خواننده‌ام را به منابعی که در پی می‌آورم رجوع می‌دهم: از سال ۱۳۰۷، سخن بر سر افزودن به سهم ایران از درآمدهای نفت، و لزوم تغییراتی در «امتیازنامه‌ی دارسی» در مجلس شورای ملی درگیر شد. رضا شاه مذاکره را به عهده‌ی تیمورتاش (وزیر دربار) گذاشت. این مذاکرات ٥ سال به درازا کشید و به جائی نرسید، اما پرونده‌ی قطوری از شرایط بین دولت ایران و کمپانی پدید آورد. شرکت، به جای هر نوع افزایش، به بهانه‌ی نداشتن سود، در سال ۱۳۱۱، حق‌السهم ایران را کاهش داد. صدای مجلس و مردم به اعتراض برخاست. رضا شاه روز ٦ آذر ۱۳۱۱ در حضور اعضاء کابینه، پرونده‌ی نفت را خواست و از روی «عصبانیت» و اعتراض به کمپانی، کل پرونده را «در آتش بخاری انداخت»، و الغاء قرارداد را خواستار شد. نمایندگان دولت بریتانیا و شخصیت‌های مربوط به کمپانی، برای مذاکره‌ی رسمی با نمایندگان ایران معرفی شدند. نمایندگان دولت ایران، محمدعلی فروغی (وزیر خارجه)، علی‌اکبر داور (وزیر دادگستری)، حسن تقی‌زاده (وزیر دارائی) و حسین علاء (رئیس بانک ملی) بودند، که مبنای حق‌الامتیاز ایران را میزان استخراج نفت قرار دادند. آن‌ها پیشنهادهای ایران را به شرح زیر به نمایندگان شرکت نفت انگلیس و ایران ارائه دادند: ۱- حق‌الامتیاز ایران، نه بر مبنای «سود خالص»، بلکه بر مبنای میزان استخراج نفت پرداخت شود (٦ شلینگ در هر تُن نفت برای دولت ایران). ۲ــ پرداخت مالیات بر درآمد از سوی شرکت به دولت ایران. ۳- تضمین حداقل درآمد سالانه برای دولت ایران به مبلغ یک میلیون و ۲۰۰هزار لیره. ٤ــــ تربیت کارشناسان ایرانی، و افزایش کارکنان ایرانی‌ی شرکت، به‌طوری که تدریجاً جای کارکنان خارجی را بگیرند. ٥ــــ توسعه‌ی فروش فرآورده‌های نفتی در سراسر ایران به قیمت ارزان. ٦- محدودکردن حوزه‌ی جغرافیائی‌ی قرارداد، و لغو حق انحصار به خلیج‌فارس. ۷- پرداخت مبلغ عادلانه‌ای بابت حساب‌های گذشته. نمایندگان شرکت نفت انگلیس و ایران این پیشنهادها را نپذیرفتند و از لندن دستور گرفتند که مذاکرات را متوقف کنند و به انگلستان بازگردند، تا موضوع را به «جامعه‌ی ملل» احاله دهند. به گزارش «سر جان کدمن» رئیس هیئت مدیره‌ی شرکت، و بنا به نوشته‌های مصطفی فاتح (نماینده‌ی ایران در شرکت) و حسن تقی‌زاده ، رضا شاه، که تا آن زمان مصممانه بر سر پیشنهادهای هیئت ایران استوار ایستاده بود، پس از طرح احاله‌ی دعوا به «جامعه‌ی ملل»، و پس از یک ملاقات خصوصی با کدمن، کوتاه آمد، و با توافق بر سر برخی از ماده‌های پیشنهادی‌ی هیئت ایران، تمدید قرارداد- تا سی سال پس از انقضاء قرارداد اولیه‌ی دارسی- را پذیرفت، و حق‌الامتیاز ایران را به ۲ شلینگ کم‌تر از پیشنهاد هیئت ایران (یعنی ٤ شلینگ در هر تُن) کاهش داد. سعید رهنما در این زمینه می‌نویسد: «انگلیسی‌ها بر روی کاغذ چند تغییر جزئی را پذیرفتند، ولی در عمل هیچ تغییر جدی‌ای [به نفع ایران] روی نداد.» اما به نفع انگلستان سی سال دیگر به مدت قرارداد افزوده شد؛ یعنی، قراردادی که قرار بود در سال ۱۳٤۲ به پایان رسد، تا سال ۱۳۷۲/ ۱۹۹۳ تمدید شد. پیرامون این قرارداد که به «متمم قرارداد دارسی» یا «قرارداد ۱۳۱۲/ ۱۹۳۳» معروف شد، از دیدگاه‌های متفاوت، مقاله‌ها و کتاب‌های فراوان نوشته شده است. مخالفان رضا شاه، به آتش سپردن پرونده‌ی نفت و پیشنهاد «الغاء قرارداد» از سوی رضا شاه را توطئه‌ای برای تمدید قرارداد برآورد می‌کنند. مثلاً حسین مکی، آن را «خیمه‌شب‌بازی»‌ی رضا شاه می‌نامد، که در جهت منافع انگلستان طراحی شده بود. جالب توجه است که پشتوانه‌ی بسیاری از این نوع تحلیل‌ها، گزارش‌ها و خاطرات شخصیت‌های انگلیسی‌ای است که در مذاکرات مربوط به این پرونده حضور داشته‌اند. برخی دیگر از تحلیل‌گران مخالف، با تکیه بر فرض دست‌نشانده بودن رضا شاه، این امکان را مطرح می‌کنند که انگیزه‌ی کوتاه آمدن او، ترسِ از دست دادن قدرت و خلع از پادشاهی بود. برخی دیگر، که با انصاف و با دید تاریخی به این قضیه نگاه کرده‌اند، بنا بر اسناد و مدارکی که از آرشیو اسناد بریتانیا منتشر شده است، فراز تکراری‌ی «دست‌نشانده بودن رضا شاه» را رد می‌کنند، برخی از مواد قرارداد ۱۹۳۳ را به نفع ایران می‌دانند، و کوتاه آمدن رضا شاه در برابر ارجاع پرونده به دادگاه بین‌المللی را به فقدان اسناد و مدارکی منوط می‌دانند که در آتش سوخته بود. با توجه به برخورد قاطعانه‌ی رضا شاه در مورد شیخ خزعل در خوزستان و خان‌های بختیاری (که از دیرباز با سیاست‌های استعماری‌ی بریتانیا همسو بودند و با شرکت نفت رابطه‌ای دوستانه داشتند)، و با توجه به این که رضا شاه در جنگ دوم جهانی به دشمن بریتانیا پیوست، نظر اخیر پذیرفتنی‌تر است. اما، حتا اگر این نظر را بپذیریم که فقدان مدارک برای ارائه در دادگاه بین‌المللی شاه را به پذیرش این قرارداد واداشت، یعنی اگر مسئله‌ی «توطئه» و «خیانت آگاهانه» را منتفی بدانیم، ناآگاهی‌ی سیاسی و نابخردی‌ی رضا شاه در سوزاندن یک پرونده مهم سیاسی/ اقتصادی را نمی‌توان نادیده گرفت.

در این زمینه به مآخذ زیر نگاه کنید:

- سعید رهنما، ***بریتیش پترولیوم: صد سال واماندگی‌ی اخلاقی***، (مقاله)، تارنمای «عصر نو»، ۳ تیر ۱۳۸۹/ ۲٤ ژوئن ۲۰۱۰:
- http://asre-nou.net/php/view.php?objnr=10444
- محمد حسن‌نیا، ***بررسی‌ی عملکرد شرکت نفت ایران و انگلیس در اسناد ۱۹۰۱- ۱۹۱۴***، (مقاله)، تارنمای «کتابخانه، موزه و مرکز اسناد مجلس شورای ملی»، بازدید: ۱۷ خرداد ۱۳۹۰:
- www.ical.ir/index.php?option=com_k2&view=item&id=2235:%D8%A8%D8%B1%D8%B1%D8%B3%D9% &Itemid=9
- مصطفی فاتح، ***پنجاه سال نفت ایران***، تهران شرکت سهامی‌ی چاپ، ۱۳۳٥. (من نشر الکترونیکی‌ی این کتاب را دیده‌ام.)
- شاهرخ وزیری، ***نفت و قدرت در ایران***، ترجمه‌ی مرتضی ثاقب‌فر، تهران: انتشارات عطائی، ۱۳۸۰.
- ***نفت از آغاز تا به امروز***، تهران: انتشارات شرکت نفت، بهمن ۱۳٦۱.

است، و هر چه که هست، از میهن‌دوستی و آرزوی او برای «سعادتِ آینده»ی ایران حکایت می‌کند.

گروه ۲) رضا شاه پهلوی، ساختار یک ارتش مدرن را- مشتمل بر نیروهای سه گانه- پایه‌گذاری کرد؛ متمم دوم قانون اساسی، و نفوذ «پنج مجتهد» بر قوانین مجلس شورای ملی را عملاً خنثا گذاشت، و بدین ترتیب راه هر گونه نفوذ به سیاستگذاری‌های کشور را بر لایه‌ی روحانیت بست؛ راه زد و بندهای سودجویانه‌ی دولتمردان با بیگانگان و با بازار را بست؛ راه هرگونه سوءاستفاده و فساد مالی و سیاسی را بر دولتمران وقت- حتا شخصیت‌هائی که در برکشیدن او به مقام پادشاهی مؤثر بودند- بست؛ قرار داد «کاپیتولاسیون»، قرارداد ۱۹۱۹، و قرارداد انحصار باستان‌شناسی در شهر باستانی‌ی شوش را لغو کرد؛ امتیاز چاپ اسکناس را از انگلستان گرفت؛ برای بازستاندن جزایر بحرین، با بریتانیا کشمکشی- البته ناموفق- داشت؛[۲۸۹] مناسبات «خان خانی» و دولت در دولت را برچید و به این وسیله بزرگ‌ترین مانع رشد «بورژوازی‌ی ملی» را از سر راه برداشت. به ضرب «فرمان» یا با تشویق، به تأسیس کارخانه‌های متعدد و به صنعت و تولید داخلی یاری داد، و با این کار- خواسته یا ناخواسته- رشد کمّی و کیفی‌ی «طبقه‌ی کارگر»، با مفهوم مدرن آن را سبب شد.[۲۹۰] حجاب را از سر و روی زن ایرانی برگرفت، و ورود او را به قلمروهای آموزشی و کارهای اجتماعی ممکن کرد؛ در تأسیس نخستین بانک ملی، نخستین دانشگاه، نخستین فرهنگستان زبان، نخستین فرستنده‌ی رادیوئی، و راه آهن سراسری و هزاران کیلومتر راه‌های شوسه بین شهرهای ایران همت گذاشت؛ آموزش دوره‌ی ابتدائی را اجباری کرد و مدارس متوسطه‌ی دولتی را در همه‌ی شهرهای ایران بر پا داشت؛ ساختار آموزش و پرورش و دیگر دستگاه‌های اداری‌ی کشور را مدرنیزه کرد،[۲۹۱] و در این رهگذر کوشید تا حد امکان، دست دین‌کاران را از دستگاه‌های آموزش و دادگستری‌ی کشور کوتاه کند. (گرچه به سبب تنیده‌بودنِ قوانین مذهبی در بافت حقوقی‌ی ایران- به ویژه در قلمرو «ثبت اسناد و احوال»، ناگزیر بود در دادگستری از روحانیان هم استفاده کند)؛ حتا اگر نیک بنگریم، با شرط تربیت کادرهای تخصصی از میان کارکنان ایرانی‌ی شرکت نفت توسط انگلیسی‌ها، که در قرارداد ۱۳۱۲ گنجانیده بود، زمینه‌های نهضت ملی کردن نفت را فراهم آورد؛ به طوری که در زمان اخراج انگلیسی‌ها از ایران (۱۳۳۱/ ۱۳۳۲)، کارشناسان ایرانی- که در دانشگاه انگلیسی‌ی «صنعت نفت آبادان» تحصیل کرده بودند، کارهائی مانند استخراج نفت، حفظ پالایشگاه، تنظیم قراردادهای فروش نفت، و تنظیم امور اداری و مالی‌ی شرکت را مستقلاً از عهده برآمدند. این هم که نوآوری‌های رضا

❖ ***ماجرای لغو قرارداد نفتی‌ی دارسی در زمان رضا خان چه بود***، تارنمای «آفتاب»، ٦ آذر ١٣٨٦/ ٢٧ نوامبر ٢٠٠٧:

❖ http://www.aftab.ir/articles/politics/plitical_history/c1c1196181316_oil_iran_p1.php

❖ مظفر شاهدی، ***نفت ایران از امتیاز دارسی تا قرارداد گس- گلشائیان***، تارنمای «باشگاه اندیشه»، ١ اردیبهشت ١٣٨٧:

http://www.bashgah.net/pages-17541.html

توضیح: منبع تارنمای «باشگاه اندیشه»، «مؤسسه‌ی مطالعات تاریخ معاصر ایران» بوده است. و جالب این است که در دانشنامه‌ی ویکی پدیا نیز زیر عنوان «پیشینه‌ی صنعت نفت ایران» از همین متن استفاده شده است:

http://fa.wikipedia.org/wiki/%D8%B5%D9%86%D8%B9%D8%AA_%D9%86%D9%81%D8%AA_%D8%A7%DB%8C%D8%B1%D8%A7%D9%86

[289] Christin Marschall, ***Iran's Persian Gulf Policy: From Khomeini to Khatami***, chapter 1: Foundations of Iran's Persian Gulf Policy, London & New York: RoutledgeCurzon, 2003, p. 6.

[۲۹۰] از جمله منابعی که به رشد کمی و کیفی‌ی کارخانه‌ها و کارگاه‌ها و به اعتصابات مطالبه‌محور کارگران در زمان رضا شاه اشاره کرده‌اند، خواننده‌ام را به متن‌های زیر رجوع می‌دهم:

❖ رامین رحیمی، ***حزب توده‌ی ایران، رفرمیسم بورژوازی‌ی «چپ» علل غیبت طبقاتی‌ی کارگران در مبارزات ضد دیکتاتوری – بخش پنجم***، تارنمای «اتحاد کارگری»، بازدید: ٢٥ مه ٢٠١١:

http://etahad.wordpress.com/2011/05/22/%d8

❖ یونس پارسا بناب، ***تاریخ صد ساله‌ی جنبش‌های سوسیالیستی، کارگری، و کمونیستی در ایران (از انقلاب مشروطیت ١٢٨٤ تا انقلاب ١٣٥٧)***، پیشین.

[۲۹۱] به گزارش یرواند آبراهامیان، در سال ١٣٠٤، تعداد ٥٥ هزار و ٩٦٠ دانش‌آموز دبستانی و ١٤٤٨٨ دانش‌آموز دبیرستانی در ایران تحصیل می‌کردند، و شمار طلاب دینی ٥٩٨٤ تن بود. در حالی که در سال ١٣٢٠، بیش از ٢٨٧ هزار و ٢٤٥ دانش‌آموز در ٢٣٣٦ دبستان، و ٢٨١٩٤ دانش‌آموز در ١١٠ دبیرستان به تحصیل مشغول بودند، و شمار طلاب دینی به ٨٧٥ تن کاهش یافته بود. نگاه کنید به: یرواند آبراهامیان، ***ایران بین دو انقلاب: از مشروطه تا انقلاب اسلامی***، پیشین، ص ١٣٢.

شاه پهلوی را به قول تورج اتابکی «تجدد آمرانه»[۲۹۲] برآورد کنیم یا برآورد نکنیم، در ذات تغییرات مثبتی که رضا شاه در ایران پیاده کرد، تفاوتی ایجاد نمی‌کند. (من- به حکم یافته‌های جامعه‌شناسی، و با توجه به شرایط ذهنیِ انبوه روشنفکران و مردم شــهریِ آن زمان ایران- برچســبِ «تجدد آمرانه» را فراگیر نمی‌دانم. چرا که زمینه‌های اجتماعیِ بسـیاری از نوآوری‌های رضا شاه- مانند تغییر در سیستم آموزشی- از حوالیِ مشروطیت و حتا پیش از آن هموار شده بود؛ که تأسیس دارالفنون یکی از نشانه‌های آن است.)

در هر حال، نتیجه‌ی اِعمال مجموعه‌ی این سیاست‌ها بود که رضا شاه پهلوی- به رغم این که در طول سلطنت خود ایران را از شـکل مجموعه‌ای از روستاهای عقب‌مانده و ایل‌نشین‌های مخــروبه و ویران‌شهرها، به هئیت یک «کشورِ» نیمه صنعتی تبدیل کرد- در میان تمامیِ لایه‌های اجتماعیِ ایران، مخالف و معتــرض داشــت؛ و به این ترتیب بــود که تا آخرین روزهای ســـلطنتـــش، لایه‌های محروم و تهی‌دست، لایه‌های متوسط سنتی، لایه‌های ایلی/ عشـــایری/ قومی، زمین‌دارانِ ســابق، کشــاورزان و خرده مالکان، دولتمردان و لایه‌های بالای اداری، بازاریان و بازرگانان، و از همــــه مشـخص‌تر، دو لایه‌ی روحانیت، و پیکارگران آزادی‌خواه و عدالت‌جو (با تمام تفاوت‌های معرفت‌شناختی و روش‌شناختی) با او ضدیتی آشتی‌ناپذیر داشتند؛ و آن چنان «آشتی‌ناپذیر»، که به محض استعفا/ عزل او، پروژه‌های همه‌جانبه در زدایش سیاست‌های او آغاز به کار کرد؛ آن چنان «آشتی‌ناپذیر»، که اکثریت اعضاء همه‌ی این لایه‌های اجتماعی، هنوز که هنوز است، یعنی هفتاد سال پس از استعفا/عزل «رضا شاه پهلوی» از «سلطنت» ایران، او را «رضا خان» می‌نامند، و بدون توجه به مجموعه‌ی اسناد موجود، و با استفاده از اسناد گزینشیِ خود، او را «دست‌نشانده‌ی انگلیس‌ها» می‌خوانند. حتا دانشمندی مانند دکتر سیروس بینا، ضمن تکرارِ گزاره‌ی «دست‌نشاندگی»ی رضا شاه، بدون توجه به مجموعه‌ی شرایط سیاسی/ اجتماعیِ ایرانِ آن زمان، کودتای سوم اسفند را «سرآغاز سیاه‌روزیِ مردم ایران» برآورد می‌کند.[۲۹۳]

البته، با مراجعه به کتاب‌های تاریخ و پژوهش‌های تاریخیِ مربوط به این دوره، تردیدی باقی نمی‌ماند که دولت‌های روسیه و بریتانیا مسائل ایران را لحظه به لحظه زیر نظر داشتند، و برای حفظ منافع خود، و با داشتن ارتشی از آن خود در ایران، هر جا که لازم می‌دیدند از دخالت پنهان و آشکار در سیاست‌های ایران ابائی نداشتند. همچنین، نویسندگان کتاب «شاه سازان Kingmakers»، برکشیدنِ «شاهان» و «امیران» و «سلطان»های منطقه‌ی خاورمیانه- از جمله ایران و رضا شاه پهلوی- توسط کشورهای غربی را به تفصیل برملا کرده‌اند.[۲۹۴] از این گذشته، تمامیِ متن‌های تاریخیِ این دوره، دخالت و تأثیر شـخصـیت‌های سـفارت بریتانیا در ایران را در کودتای اسـفند ۱۲۹۹ تأیید می‌کنند. مثلاً به گفته‌ی محمدتقی بهار (ملک‌الشعراء)، چندی پیش از کودتای سوم اسفند ۱۲۹۹، «مستر اسمارت» مستشار سفارت انگلیس، در دو ملاقات جداگانه، پیرامون «ایجاد حکومتی مقتدر»، «ثابت» و «نیمه دیکتاتوری» با خودِ بهار مذاکره کرده بود؛ محمدتقی بهار هم این پیشنهاد را پذیرفته بود. بهار در این جا می‌نویسد: «ولی در انتخاب افراد و اعضاء آن دولت، سلیقه‌ی ما راست نیامد.» ملک‌الشعراء بهار البته ننوشته است که این «افراد و اعضـاء» پیشنهادی چه کسـانی بودند.[۲۹۵] منتها، ملاقات و مذاکره‌ی ژنرال ادموند آیرونساید با «رضـا خان میر پنج»، و حمایت او از کودتای ۱۲۹۹ در همه‌ی سندها ذکر شده است. کما این

---

[۲۹۲] تورج اتابکی، ***تجدد آمرانه: جامعه و دولت در عصر رضا شاه***، (گردآوری و تألیف)، ترجمه‌ی مهدی حقیقت‌خواه، تهران: انتشارات ققنوس، ۱۳۸۵.

[۲۹۳] ***مصاحبه‌ی محمد حسیبی با دکتر سیروس بینا***، بخش دوم برنامه‌ی تلویزیونیِ «چه باید کرد؟»، ۲۳ فوریه ۲۰۱۴/ ٤ اسفند ۱۳۹۲، فایل صوتی:

http://www.chebayadkard.com/chebayadkardfilm.php

[294] Karl E. Meyer & Shareen Blair Brysac, ***Kingmakers: The Invention of the Modern Middle East***, New York: W. W. Norton & Company, 2008. pp. 297, 310-12, 320-21.

[۲۹۵] محمدتقی بهار (ملک‌الشعراء)، ***تاریخ مختصر احزاب سیاسیِ ایران***، جلد اول، تهران: امیرکبیر، ۱۳۲۳، ص ۶۳.

که به گفته‌ی یحیی دولت آبادی، پس از این کودتا، نشان درجه‌ی اول شیر و خورشید با حمایل سبز، به پاس یاری به کودتا، از سوی دولت ایران به ژنرال آیرونساید اهدا شده بود.[۲۹۶] با این وصف، تا جائی که من می‌دانم، ریزِ مذاکرات آیرونساید با «رضا خان میرپنج» هرگز منتشر و مشخص نشده است. مدارک آرشیو بریتانیا نیز نشان می‌دهند که مقامات بریتانیا و وزیر خارجه‌ی این کشور به شخص «رضا خان» اعتماد نداشته‌اند. همایون کاتوزیان (استاد تاریخ در دانشگاه آکسفورد) با تکیه بر همین اسناد، کودتای سوم اسفند ۱۲۹۹ را خارج از کنترل و اراده‌ی دولت و وزارت خارجه‌ی بریتانیا برآورد می‌کند، و در یک مصاحبه می‌گوید «بریتانیا نه نقشی در برآمدن رضا شاه داشت و نه دخالتی در فروافتادن احمد شاه»؛ و می‌افزاید:

> سِر پرسی لورن [سفیر وقت بریتانیا در ایران] در یکی از نامه‌هایش به لرد کرزن [وزیر خارجه‌ی بریتانیا] از رضا خان به عنوان مردی درستکار و باعرضه یاد می‌کند که دزد نیست و با بریتانیا هم دشمنی ندارد. اما لرد کرزن در جوابش به او توصیه می‌کند که گول نخورد، رضا خان «بلد است شیرین حرف بزند و ترش رفتار کند (talking sweet and acting sour)».[۲۹۷]

منصور بیات‌زاده (کوشنده‌ی سیاسی برون‌مرزی، و از مدافعان و پیروان راه دکتر مصدق)، در واکنش نسبت به این سخنِ همایون کاتوزیان پرسش معتبری را پیش می‌کشد، که تا جائی که من می‌دانم تاکنون به آن پاسخی داده نشده است. بیات‌زاده می‌پرسد:

> آیا اسنادی که در اختیار این استاد قرار گرفته‌اند بیانگر این موضوع هستند که، در زمانی که برنامه‌ی کودتای سوم اسفند ۱۲۹۹ در ایران در دستور کابینه‌ی دولت بریتانیا قرار می‌گیرد، در آن جلسات، هیئت دولت با امر کودتا در ایران مخالفت کرده است؟ و یا این که بنا بر سِرّی بودن کارِ سازمان‌های جاسوسی، این موضوع اصلاً در کابینه‌ی دولت مطرح نشده است و در نتیجه مدرکی که دلالت بر دخالت «هیئت دولت وقت بریتانیا » در آن ماجرا باشد، وجود ندارد؟[۲۹۸] (فشرده‌ی سخن بیات‌زاده)

از سوی دیگر، می‌بینیم سرپیچی‌های «رضا خان سردار سپه» از راهنمائی‌ها و اجرای خواسته‌های نمایندگان انگلستان در ایران نیز در متن‌ها به ثبت رسیده است. مثلاً، بنا بر کتاب سیروس غنی (مورخ مقیم امریکا)- که نویسنده، آن را بر اساس اسناد آرشیو بریتانیا نوشته است- زمانی که مجلس ایران سیدضیاء طباطبائی (نخست وزیر وقت) را عزل و تبعید می‌کند، و «سردار سپه» وزیر جنگ است، هرمن نورمن، وزیر مختار انگلستان در ایران، به دولت متبوع خود گزارش می‌دهد که:

> همه‌ی مساعی‌ی من برای منصرف کردن توطئه‌گران از این دسیسه‌ی فاجعه‌آمیز شکست خورد؛ شکست من ناشی از این واقعیت است که از هنگام فراخوانی‌ی نیروی ما، **وزیر جنگ، دیگر از ما واهمه‌ای ندارد.**[۲۹۹] (تأکید از من است.)

---

۲۹۶ یحیی دولت آبادی، ***حیات یحیی***، تهران: جلد چهارم، چاپ چهارم، تهران: انتشارات عطار و فردوسی، ۱۳۶۲، ص ۲۲۷.

۲۹۷ همایون کاتوزیان (استاد تاریخ در دانشگاه آکسفورد)، ***بریتانیا نه نقشی در برآمدن رضا شاه داشت و نه دخالتی در فروافتادن احمد شاه***، تارنمای «بی بی سی»، ۳۱ اکتبر ۲۰۰۵:
http://www.bbc.co.uk/persian/iran/story/2005/10/051031_mf_katouzian.shtml

۲۹۸ دکتر منصور بیات‌زاده، ***خدا رحمت کند خلیل ملکی را!*** تارنمای «اخبار روز»، ۱۱ تیر ۱۳۸۶/ ۲ ژوئیه‌ی ۲۰۰۷:
http://www.akhbar-rooz.com/article.jsp?essayId=10191

۲۹۹ سیروس غنی، ***ایران: برآمدن رضا خان، برافتادن قاجار و نقش انگلیسی‌ها***، ترجمه از انگلیسی به فارسی از حسن کامشاد، تهران: انتشارات نیلوفر، ۱۳۷۶، ص ۲۳۴.

همایون کاتوزیان نیز در پژوهش‌های خود به این نتیجه رسیده که برآیش رضا شاه پهلوی، مطلقاً از خواست دولت بریتانیا تبعیت نمی‌کرده است. هم‌چنین، جلال متینی در کتاب «نگاهی به کارنامه‌ی سیاسی‌ی دکتر محمد مصدق» با تکیه بر مبارزه‌ی رضا شاه با اهرم‌های بریتانیا در ایران (مانند شیخ خزعل و برخی از خان‌های بختیاری) قاطعانه، قضاوتِ دست‌نشاندگی‌ی رضا شاه را باطل می‌داند.[۳۰۰]

بد نیست همین جا ثبت کنم که- برخلاف تمامی‌ی «مورخان» رسمی‌ی جمهوری‌ی اسلامی، که سی و چهار سال است برای پادشاهان پهلوی پرونده‌های سراسر «نوکری» می‌سازند- دکتر صادق زیباکلام (استاد تاریخ در دانشگاه‌های ایران) نخستین، و شاید تنها کارشناس حاضر در جمهوری‌ی اسلامی است که به عدم دخالت «دولت انگستان» در کودتای ۱۲۹۹ و به قدرت رساندن رضا شاه شهادت داده است. او از اسفند ۱۳۸۸ به بعد، در گفت‌وگو با تلویزیون صدا و سیما و برخی از نشریه‌های درون‌مرزی، ضمن تکیه‌ی بی‌چون و چرا نسبت به «دیکتاتوری»ی رضا شاه، و ضمن برشمردنِ آثار نیک او در ساختن ایران مدرن، بر این گزاره پافشاری کرده است که «روح انگلستان هم در جریان به قدرت رسیدنِ رضا شاه نبود»؛ و به قول معروف: «پای لرزَش هم نشسته است.»[۳۰۱]

اما اگر کودتای سوم اسفند ۱۲۹۹ و برآیشِ رضا شاه پهلوی را در متن شرایط و تجربه‌های تاریخی برانداز کنیم، هیچ یک از داوری‌های قاطعانه با فعلِ «بود» یا «نبود»، قانع‌کننده به نظر نمی‌رسند. شرایط سوق‌الجیشی و ژئوپلیتک ایران؛ نظر منفی‌ی رقبای سیاسی‌ی بریتانیا (یعنی دولت‌های امریکا، فرانسه، و روسیه‌ی شوروی، که این آخری، حالا نه «رقیب»، بلکه «دشمن» تلقی می‌شد) نسبت به قرارداد ۱۹۱۹؛ فرسایش نیروهای نظامی‌ی بریتانیا در جنگ اول جهانی؛ پیدایش دولت سوسیالیستی در شمال ایران؛ لغو امتیازات روسیه‌ی تزاری توسط این نظام؛ معاهده‌ی روسیه‌ی شوروی با ایران پیرامون لشگرکشی به ایران در صورت ضعف دولت مرکزی در راندن مهاجمان از خاک خود؛ هراسی که ثروتمندان ایران از نفوذِ ایده‌های انقلابی/ سوسیالیستی در ایران داشتند؛ هراسی که گروهی از فرهیختگانِ میهن‌دوست از تجزیه‌ی خاک ایران داشتند؛ تصویب «قانون برج اسد» در مجلس شورای ملی و حکم اخراج نیروهای انگلیسی از ایران؛ عدم اجرای این حکم از سوی نیروهای انگلیسی و لشگرکشی‌ی آن‌ها به سوی مرزهای شوروی (که به ارتش شوروی اجازه‌ی ورود به ایران را می‌داد)؛ در کنار ضعف دولت مرکزی در چیرگی به ده‌ها عامل آشوب و فساد و بی‌سامانی در اقصا نقاط کشور ایران؛ مجموعه‌ی شرایطی را به نمایش می‌گذارند که حضور «رضا شاه پهلوی» را در تاریخ ایران سبب شد.

در واقع، قرائن موجود در خاطرات آیرونساید، گزارش‌های یحیی دولت آبادی و محمدتقی بهار، و پژوهش‌های سیروس غنی، نیکی کدی، جان فوران، عبدالرضا هوشنگ مهدوی، و دیگران،[۳۰۲] سه گزاره‌ی زیر را تأیید می‌کنند: ۱) عوامل بریتانیا در ایران در برکشیدن «رضا میرپنج»- دست کم تا کودتای سوم اسفند ۱۲۹۹- تأثیری غیرقابل انکار داشته‌اند. این

---

[۳۰۰] جلال متینی، ***نگاهی به کارنامه‌ی سیاسی‌ی دکتر محمد مصدق***، لس‌انجلس: انتشارات شرکت کتاب، ۱۳۸۵، پیوست سوم.

[۳۰۱] ***روح انگلستان هم در جریان به قدرت رسیدن رضا شاه نبود***، مصاحبه با صادق زیبا کلام، نشریه‌ی «نسیم بیداری»، شماره‌ی ۲۳، دی ماه ۱۳۹۰.

[۳۰۲] به مآخذ زیر نگاه کنید:

- ❖ ادموند آیرونساید، ***خاطرات سری‌ی آیرونساید***، تهران: مؤسسه‌ی پژوهش و مطالعات فرهنگی، با همکاری‌ی مؤسسه‌ی خدمات فرهنگی‌ی رسا، ۱۳۷۳.
- ❖ نیکی کدی، ***ریشه‌های انقلاب ایران***، ترجمه‌ی عبدالرحیم گواهی، تهران: انتشارات قلم، چاپ دوم، ۱۳۷۷.
- ❖ نیکی کدی، ***ایران دوران قاجار و بر آمدن رضاخان***، ترجمه‌ی، مهدی حقیقت‌خواه، تهران: انتشارات ققنوس، چاپ اول، ۱۳۸۱.
- ❖ جان فوران، ***مقاومت شکننده: تاریخ تحولات اجتماعی‌ی ایران از سال ۱۵۰۰ میلادی مطابق با ۸۷۹ شمسی تا انقلاب***، ترجمه‌ی احمد تدین، تهران: مؤسسه‌ی خدمات فرهنگی‌ی رسا، چاپ پنجم، ۱۳۸۹.
- ❖ عبدالرضا هوشنگ مهدوی، ***سیاست خارجی‌ی ایران در دوران پهلوی (۱۳۰۰-۱۳۵۷)***، تهران: انتشارات البرز، ۱۳۷٤.

که فرایند یادشـــده با اطلاع یا بدون اطلاعِ «دولت و مجلس بریتانیا» بوده، تفاوتی در ذاتِ این قضـــیه ایجاد نمی‌کند. ۲) توانائی‌های خودِ «رضـا میرپنج» در سـازمان‌دهی، و منش نظامی و میهن‌دوسـتانه‌ی او، در این گزینش دسـتی توانا داشـته اسـت. ۳) مذاکرات مقامات بریتانیائی- از جمله آیرونسـاید- با خود «رضـا میرپنج» به گونه‌ای نبوده اسـت که او خود را رسماً دست‌نشانده‌ی دولت انگلستان بداند. کما این که گزارش‌هائی مانند «واهمه نداشتنِ وزیر جنگ» از عوامل انگلستان در ایران، همچنین مبارزه‌ی «رضا خان سردار سپه» با سیدضیاءالدین طباطبائی و ایل‌های انگلوفیل، و نیز، گرایش آشکار رضـا شـاه پهلوی به آلمان (به عنوان «نیروی سـوم»)، به اسـتقلال فکر و عمل رضـا شـاه- شـهادت می‌دهند. منتها- باز بر اساس مجموعه‌ی گزارش‌ها و پژوهش‌ها و تفسیرهائی که در دست داریم- در این هم تردید نیست که رضا شاه پهلوی، خود بهتر از هر کسی، عوامل بریتانیائی را در برکشیدنِ خود مؤثر می‌دانسته است. با این تحلیل است که من- برخلافِ برخی از مفسـران، که این نقل قول دکتر مصـدق از رضـا شـاه را باور ندارند-[۳۰۳] بعید نمی‌دانم که رضـا شـاه گفته باشـد: «مرا انگلیسی‌ها آوردند، ولی ندانستند که را آوردند.»[۳۰۴]

سیاست خارجی‌ی رضـا شاه پهلوی نیز به تشخیص مستقل او شهادت می‌دهد. او- که مانند همه‌ی مردم ایران- از استعمار بریتانیا و روسیه و آثار مخرب آن در ایران تجربه‌های تلخی داشت، به آلمان به عنوان «نیروی سوم» می‌نگریست و مانند بسیاری از فرهیختگان ایران، به یاری‌های این کشور چشم امید بسته بود؛[۳۰۵] به ویژه که آلمان، نه تنها پیشینه‌ی استعماری در ایران نداشـت، بلکه در زمان جنگ اول جهانی نیز ماده‌ای در قراردادِ «برسـت لیتوفسـک» (۱۹۱۸) گنجانیده بود که اسـتقلال و حاکمیت ملی‌ی ایران را تضـمین می‌کرد.[۳۰۶] با این انگیزه‌ها بود که رضـا شـاه به جمهوری‌ی وایمار آلمان جلب شـد و کوشـید تا پروژه‌های نوسـازی‌ی ایران را با علم و صـنعت و تکنولوژی‌ی این کشـور به پیش بَرد. در جریان اوج‌گیری‌ی «رایش سـوم» و تز برتری‌ی نژاد آریائی در آلمان، که به تاخت و تاز آدولف هیتلر و به جنگ دوم جهانی انجامید، رضـا شـاه پهلوی، بنا بر بینش باسـتان‌گرای خود و با توهّم برتری‌ی قوم آریائی، و شـاید هم برای رهائی از فشـار انگلسـتان، از هیتلر جانبداری کرد، و بر اسـاس همین توهم نیز کلمه‌ی « پرشـیا» را- که در زبان‌های اروپائی معرّف کشـور ایران بود- به «ایران» تغییر داد. و این در حالی بود که بی‌طرفی‌ی ایران در این جنگ، از سـوی مجلس شـورای ملی تصویب و اعلام شده بود. رضا شاه، از سوئی به آلمانی‌ها و نیروی ارتش هیتلر، روی خوش نشان داد، و از سوی دیگر با پشتوانه‌ی مصوبه‌ی مجلس در «بی‌طرفی‌ی ایران»، با ورود نیروهای «متفقین» (امریکا و انگلیس و شوروی) به خاک ایران مخالفت کرد. «متفقین» نیز در یک حمله‌ی ضربتی، ظرف چند ساعت، پنج لشگر ارتش نوپای ایران را منهدم کردند؛ تهران و شـهرهای بزرگ و کوچک ایران را اشـغال کردند؛ رضـا شـاه را به اسـتعفاء واداشـتند؛ و با پادرمیانی‌ی محمدعلی فروغی، با بی‌میلی و شاید از سرِ ناچاری، با ادامه‌ی سلطنت در خاندان پهلوی موافقت کردند. رضا شاه پهلوی، در مجلس ایران سـلطنت را به ولیعهد خود واگذاشـت، و بدون هیچ مقاومتی از سـوی مجلس و مردم، روز ۲۵ شـهریور

---

[۳۰۳] به عنوان نمونه، به مصاحبه‌ی دکتر صادق زیباکلام نگاه کنید:
❖ ***روح انگلستان هم در جریان به قدرت رسیدن رضا شاه نبود***، مصاحبه با صادق زیبا کلام، نشریه‌ی «نسیم بیداری»، شماره‌ی ۲۳، دی ماه ۱۳۹۰.

[۳۰۴] ***تقریرات مصدق در زندان درباره‌ی حوادث زندگی‌ی خویش، یادداشت‌شده به اهتمام سرهنگ جلیل بزرگمهر***، به کوشش ایرج افشار، تهران: انتشار زمینه، ۱۳۵۹، ص ۱۰۲. **توضیح:** این جمله را حسین مکی به شکل زیر ثبت کرده است: «مرا انگلیسی‌ها آورده‌اند، ولی ندانستند با چه کسی سر و کار دارند.» نگاه کنید به: حسین مکی، ***تاریخ بیست ساله‌ی ایران***، تهران: انتشارات علمی، ۱۳۸۰، جلد اول، زیرنویس ص ۱٦٤.

[۳۰۵] به مأخذ زیر نگاه کنید:
❖ ژرژ لنچافسکی، ***سی سال رقابت غرب و شوروی در ایران***، ترجمه‌ی حورا یاوری، تهران: انتشارات سحر، ۱۳۵۱، صص ۱۸۵ تا ۱۸۸.

[۳۰٦] قرارداد صلحِ «برست لیتوفسک Brest-Litovsk» در تاریخ ۳ مارس ۱۹۱۸ بین روسیه‌ی شوروی، و امپراتوری‌های آلمان و اتریش- مجارستان و عثمانی (با عنوان «قدرت‌های مرکزی») امضـاء شـد، که ماده‌ی دهم آن، استقلال و حق حاکمیت «پرشیای بی‌طرف» را به رسمیت می‌شناخت. به مأخذ زیر نگاه کنید:
❖ John W. Wheeler-Bennett, ***Brest-Litovsk: The Forgotten Peace, March 1918***, New York: W. W. Norton & Co.,1971, pp. 379- 384, 403-408.

۱۳۲۰ با «یک مشت از خاک ایران» برای همیشه به تبعید رفت.[۳۰۷] بدین ترتیب، محمدرضا شاه پهلوی، در سن ۲۲ سالگی میراث‌دار کشوری شد که از یک سو در اشغال ارتش‌های بیگانه بود، و از سوی دیگر در محاصره‌ی انبوه رانده‌شدگان یا سرکوب‌شدگانِ پدرش، که همه، برای بازیابی‌ی منافع مادی یا معنوی‌ی از دست رفته‌ی خود خیز برداشته بودند.

---

[۳۰۷] رضا شاه پهلوی در تاریخ ۲۵ شهریور ۱۳۲۰ با کشتی به بندر موریس فرستاده شد، و دو سال آخر زندگی‌ی تبعیدی‌ی خود را نیز در ژوهانسبورگ گذراند. هر دو مکان، از مستعمرات امپراتوری‌ی بریتانیا بود. رضا شاه پهلوی در سال ۱۳۲۳ درگذشت، و پیکر او را به امانت در مصر دفن کردند. در اردی‌بهشت ۱۳۲۹، پیکر او به ایران منتقل شد، و در آرامگاه نه چندان مجللی که برای او ساخته بودند، دوباره دفن شد. محمد رضا شاه پهلوی در سفر بی‌بازگشت خود، پیکر پدرش را دوباره به مصر برد. تاریخ هم نشان داد که نگرانی‌ی او چندان بی‌دلیل نبوده است؛ چرا که، آرامگاه رضا شاه پهلوی در سال نخست جمهوری‌ی اسلامی، با فتوا و دخالت صادق خلخالی و لشگر حزب‌الله ویران شد.

محمد رضا شاه پهلوی

(۴ آبان ۱۲۹۸ تهران- ۵ مرداد ۱۳۵۹ مصر)

روزی در این کشور

مرد نیرومندی برخاسته رشته‌ی کارها را بدست می‌گیرد.

در آن روز، همگی ستایش‌گر می‌شوند، همگی چاپلوسی می‌کنند، کارهای بد او را مدح می‌کنند. [...] روزی هم آن مرد نیرومند، افتاده از کشور بیرون می‌رود. در این هنگام، همگی نکوهش‌گر

می‌گردند، همگی بدگوئی می‌آغازند، کارهای نیک آن دوره را نیز نمی‌پسندند. بلکه می‌کوشند

همه‌ی کارهای آن دوره را بازگردانند. زن‌ها دوباره با چادر و چاقچور بیرون می‌آیند. مردها کلاه پوستی به سر می‌گذارند. سید بچه‌ها و آخوند بچه‌ها، که چغاله‌های گدائی و مفتخوری هستند، به خیابان می‌ریزند، روضه‌خوانی‌ها فراوان می‌گردد. قمه‌زنان و زنجیرزنان دوباره پیدا می‌شوند.

عشایر به استقلال خود بازمی‌گردند. هرج و مرج در هر سو نمایان می‌شود.

این کارها رخ می‌دهد تنها برای آن که آثار آن مرد نیرومند از میان رود.

این است نمونه‌ی رآکسیون در کارهای این کشور.

(احمد کسروی، ۱۳۲۱)[۳۰۸]

[...] وظیفه‌ی خود می‌دانم به نام رئیس قوای سه‌گانه‌ی مملکتی،

استقرار این اصلاحات را از طریق مراجعه به آراء عمومی- پیش از انتخابات مجلسین- از ملت ایران که حاکم بر مجلسین و منشاء اقتدارات ملی‌ست، تقاضا کنم.

(محمدرضا شاه پهلوی، اعلام انقلاب سفید، بهمن ۱۳۴۱)

[...] تو و یارانت با بُـرّه‌های حنجره‌ی مسلسل‌ها/

فریاد برداشتید/ چنان عظیم، چنان عظیم/ که خلق خسته تکان خورد/

و قصرهای خون و ستم به لرزه درآمد/ تو در دل‌های خلق می‌گشتی/

و همچنان می‌خواندی/ آوازهای سرخ و بلندت را/ پر شور/

و در مرکز ستم، به قلب دشمن شلیک می‌کردی/

با گلوی کینه فریاد برمی‌داشتی/ و خاک میهنت در هیجان و امید می‌سوخت/

سه هزار رنجر/ سه هزار چترباز/ لیک آن‌ها تنها جنازه‌ات را یافتند/

---

[۳۰۸] ***دفاعیات احمد کسروی از سرپاس مختاری و پزشک احمدی، برگرفته از [نشریه‌ی] پرچم روزانه و هفتگی (۱۳۲۱ و ۱۳۲۲)***، به کوشش باهماد آزادگان، پاریس: انتشارات خاوران، ۱۳۸۳/ ۲۰۰۴، ص ۱۱۳.

چرا که تو با آخرین گلوله‌ی خود/ به شهادت رسیده بودی/

با این همه پیش از آن که جرأت کنند/ به تو نزدیک شوند/

جنازه‌ات را به گلوله بستند/

چقدر می‌ترسیدند/ [...]

(سیعد سلطان‌پور)[۳۰۹]

کسی که وارد این تشکیلات سیاسی [حزب رستاخیز] نشود

و معتقد و مؤمن به این سه اصلی که من گفتم نباشد دو راه برایش وجود دارد:

یا یک فردی است متعلق به یک تشکیلات غیر قانونی، یعني به اصطلاح خودمان توده‌ای؛

یعنی- باز به اصطلاح خودمان و با قدرت اثبات- بی‌وطن. او جایش یا در زندان ایران است، یا اگر بخواهد، فردا با کمال میل بدون اخذ حق عوارض، گذرنامه را در دستش می‌گذاریم

و به هر جائی که دلش می‌خواهد برود. چون ایرانی که نیست، وطن که ندارد،

و عملیاتش هم که قانونی نیست، غیر قانونی است،

و قانون هم مجازاتش را معین کرده است. [...]

(محمدرضا شاه پهلوی، اعلام تأسیس حزب رستاخیز، اسفند ۱۳۵۳)

[...] خونم را به توده‌های گرسنه و پابرهنه‌ی ایران تقدیم می‌کنم.

و شما آقایان فاشیست‌ها [...] ایمان داشته باشید که خلق محروم ایران

انتقام خون خود را خواهد گرفت. [...] ایمان داشته باشید که حکومت غیرقانونی‌ی ایران

توسط امریکا تحمیل شده و در حال احتضار است، و دیر یا زود با انقلاب قهرآمیز

توده‌های ستم‌کشیده‌ی ایران واژگون خواهد شد.

(از وصیت‌نامه‌ی خسرو گلسرخی- ۲۸ بهمن ۱۳۵۲)[۳۱۰]

[...] انقلاب ملت ایران نمی‌تواند مورد تأیید من، به عنوان پادشاه ایران،

به عنوان یک فرد ایرانی نباشد. من نیز پیام انقلاب شما ملت ایران را شنیدم.

تضمین می‌کنم که حکومت ایران در آینده بر اساس قانون اساسی، عدالت اجتماعی،

و اراده‌ی ملی، و به دور از استبداد، ظلم، و فساد باشد.

بار دیگر در برابر ملت ایران سوگند خود را تکرار می‌کنم و متعهد می‌شوم که

خطاهای گذشته و بی‌قانونی و ظلم و فساد دیگر تکرار نشده

بلکه خطاها از هر جهت جبران نیز گردد. [...]

(واپسین خطابه‌ی محمدرضا شاه پهلوی، ۱۶ آبان ۱۳۵۷)

[...] می‌خواستم هدف ملت ایران پیش برود و کشور ایران همان

---

۳۰۹ سعید سلطان‌پور، ***در یادبود امیر پرویز پویان***، برگرفته از نشریه‌ی «آلترناتیو»، شماره‌ی ۳، ۲۱ خرداد ۱۳۹۰:
http://alternative-magazine.blogspot.com

۳۱۰ آخرین دفاع و مجموعه‌ی شعر، نقد، ترجمه، و مصاحبه‌ی گلسرخی، گردآورنده و تنظیم از بزرگ خضرائی، تهران: انتشارات آرمان، ۱۳۵۷. برگرفته از: علی‌اکبر قاضی‌زاده، ***جان‌باختگان روزنامه‌نگار***، تهران: انتشارات جامعه‌ی ایرانیان، ۱۳۷۹، ص ۶۲۸.

مقامی را که داشته، مجدداً بدست آورد؛ می‌خواستم شاه بر مملکتی سلطنت کند
که در اعداد ملل مستقل و آزاد دنیا باشد؛ و اگر روزی به شاه گفتند برو، بگوید نمی‌روم. [...]
(دکتر محمد مصدق در دادگاه تجدید نظر، ۲۰ اردی‌بهشت ۱۳۳۳،
برگرفته از تألیف جلیل بزرگمهر، وکیل مصدق)

آرزوی من این بود که آینده‌ی ملت ایران افتخارآمیز، سعادتمند و پررونق باشد؛
آینده‌ای فراخور تاریخ چند هزار ساله‌ی کشورم، که همواره یکی از سازندگان اصلی‌ی تمدن جهانی بوده است. آرزو داشتم که در آستانه‌ی هزاره‌ی سوم، ایران کاملاً نوسازی شده، اقتصادش پر رونق، جامعه‌اش متحول و پیشرو باشد؛ مردمش از یک سطح آموزش مترقی برخوردار باشند، و نظام سیاسی‌اش حکومت بر قوام مردم، یعنی بر یک دموکراسی‌ی واقعی استوار باشد.
(محمد رضا شاه پهلوی، ۱۳۵۹، در تبعید بی‌بازگشت)[۳۱۱]

در یک ویدیو کلیپ بسیار کوتاه،
آیت‌الله کاشانی را در مجلس ضیافت دربار دیدم.
دکتر محمد مصدق ایستاده، و او نشسته بود، و به رقص میهمانان ،
و دست به دست شدنِ گیلاس‌های مشروب نگاه می‌کرد؛
دهانش نیمه باز، نگاهش مبهوت، و چشمانش آن چنان گرد، که به دایره پهلو می‌زد.
در میان‌ماندگی‌ی ما بین سنت و تجدد، نمائی از این گویاتر ندیده‌ام.
(ملیحه تیره گل)

در مورد سنت، این تصور را باید کاملاً کنار گذاشت که گویا
چیزی است در پشت سر ما؛ یا چیزی است که
همان گونه که بوده از گذشته به اکنون می‌رسد.
سنت فعال می‌شود، ساخته می‌شود، تحریف می‌شود، بر این جا یا آن جایش
تأکیدهائی غیر سنتی می‌یابد، ارزشی سمبلیک می‌یابد، و در بازار مدرن،
خود به صورت یک کالای مدرن از زمره‌ی «صنایع دستی» درمی‌آید.
سنت اغواگر است، و برای اغواگری ابائی ندارد که
از شیوه‌های مدرن آوازه‌گری استفاده کند.
(محمدرضا نیکفر)[۳۱۲]

بیش‌تر کارشناسان تاریخ‌های سیاسی، اجتماعی، و فرهنگی‌ی ایران بر این واقعیت پافشاری دارند که ۱۲ سال نخستِ پادشاهی‌ی محمدرضا شاه پهلوی (از ۲۵ شهریور ۱۳۲۰ تا کودتای ۲۸ مرداد ۱۳۳۲)، به نسبت زمان رضا شاه، دست کوشندگان سیاسی و فرهنگی‌ی ایران بازتر بود؛ آزادی‌های مدنی رو به رشد می‌رفت، و به رشد آگاهی‌ی اجتماعی در ایران سرعت می‌بخشید. صرف نظر از گروهی از مفسران، که آزادی‌های موجود در این سال‌ها را به «هرج و مرج» معنی می‌کنند، گروهی از مفسران سیاسی- از چشم‌انداز طبقاتی- بر این تشخیص پافشاری دارند که آزادی‌های نسبی در

---

[۳۱۱] محمد رضا شاه پهلوی، ***پاسخ به تاریخ***، ترجمه‌ی حسین ابوترابیان، تهران: ناشر (؟)، ۱۳۷۱.

[۳۱۲] محمدرضا نیکفر، ***انقلاب بهمن: دو روح در یک کالبد***، تارنمای «رادیو زمانه»، ۱۷ بهمن ۱۳۹۲/ ۷ فوریه ۲۰۱۴:
http://www.radiozamaneh.com/124026#.UvZBRmyx4y4

دهه‌ی نخست سلطنت محمدرضا شاه، نه به سبب آزادی‌خواهی‌ی او، بلکه برآیند جوانی و بی‌تجربگی‌ی او، حضور نیروهای بیگانه، و کوشش‌های فرهنگی‌ی حزب‌های کوچک و بزرگ چپ‌گرا در ایران بود؛ کما این که به محض تسلط بر ارکان کشور، به عنوان نماینده و کارگزار «سرمایه‌داری»، کاربستِ روشِ خفقان و سرکوب از سوی او، امری اجتناب‌ناپذیر بود. گروه دیگر، آزادی‌های آن دهه را برخاسته از آزادی‌خواهی‌ی محمدرضا شاه می‌دانند، و رشد ایده‌های کمونیستی، ایجاد و گسترش «حزب توده‌ی ایران»، وابستگی‌ی این حزب به اتحاد جماهیر شوروی، خیزش ایده‌ی جدائی‌خواهی و خطر تجزیه‌ی ایران را به عنوان سبب‌سازهای محدودیتِ آزادی شناسائی می‌کنند. این گروه بر این باورند که اگر روشنفکران و نخبگان جامعه، همه‌ی کوشش‌های خود را بر روشنگری‌های مدنی و حقوقی و گسترش آگاهی‌های فرهنگی متمرکز می‌کردند، و بعدها نیز با «انقلاب سفیدِ» پیشنهادی‌ی شاه مدارا می‌کردند و در پیاده کردن ماده‌های آن- به سود گسترش شعور سیاسی/ فرهنگی‌ی جامعه و رشد جامعه‌ی مدنی- سهیم می‌شدند، نه دیکتاتوری ضرورت تاریخی می‌یافت، و نه رویدادِ «انقلاب اسلامی» پیش می‌آمد. به باور من، برای شناخت چه‌گونگی‌ها و چرائی‌های آن آزادی‌ی نسبی، و تبدیل آن به دیکتاتوری‌ی مطلق، و سپس، رویداد انقلاب ۱۳۵۷ ایران، هیچ یک از این رویکردها به تنهائی گویا نیست، و در عین حال هیچ یک از آن‌ها را نیز نمی‌توان از دایره‌ی شناختِ تاریخی و داوری خارج گذاشت. چرا که هر یک از آن‌ها- حتا رویکردِ یک‌سویه‌ی مفسرانی که با نگاهی غیرتاریخی به موضوع شناخت نگاه کرده‌اند- پاره‌هائی از واقعیت را در خود دارند، که تنها با نگاهی تطبیقی/انتقادی/استنتاجی به مجموعه‌ی آن‌ها، به دید می‌آیند. اما در قلمرو شناخت‌شناسی، بزرگ‌ترین پاره‌ی واقعیت، که از ورای تمام رویدادهای این دوره‌ی دوازده ساله به چشم می‌آید، باز همانا هنوز، سرگشتگی‌ی ذهن ایرانی است در تفسیر مفاهیمی چون «آزادی»، «دموکراسی»، «استقلال»، «پیشرفت» و «سربلندی»؛ از شاه کشور گرفته تا پیکارگران سیاسی در «چپ» و «راست»؛ از دولتمردان سنتی گرفته تا دولتمردان «متجدد»؛ از نخبگان فرهنگی در درون رژیم شاه گرفته تا نخبگان فرهنگی در اپوزیسیون آن رژیم.[۳۱۳]

***

محمد رضا شاه جوان، پرورش یافته در خانواده‌ای مذهبی/ نظامی/ مستبد، و در عین حال، دانش‌آموخته در کشور سوئیس، و مدرسه‌ی نظام در تهران، از سنّ شش سالگی ولیعهدِ پادشاهی‌ی ایران بود. او، با این که از سال ۱۳۱۸ عملاً با برخی از امور کشورداری آشنا شده بود، اما در آغاز سلطنت- که به ناگهان به او رسیده بود- در احاطه‌ی دولتمردان و سیاست‌کارانِ کارکشته‌ای مانند محمدعلی فروغی، عبدالحسین هژیر و محمد ساعد مراغه‌ای، و بقایای «سلطنه»ها و «دوله»های قاجاریه، قدرتی دست پائین داشت. افزون بر این، حضور نیروهای بیگانه در ایران و پیامدهای زیانبار این اشغال، حضور سران متفقین در تهران بدون دیدار رسمی با او،[۳۱۴] خیزش مخالفان و زخم‌خوردگان پدرش، اوج‌گیری‌ی

---

[۳۱۳] از میان آثاری که از دیدگاه‌های مختلف و با رویکردهای مختلف، از نزدیک به این بحران نگاه کرده‌اند، خواننده‌ام را به مآخذ زیر رجوع می‌دهم:

- ❖ اصغر شیرازی، ***مدرنیته، شُبهه و دموکراسی: بر مبنای یک بررسی‌ی موردی درباره‌ی حزب توده‌ی ایران از آغاز تا سال ۱۳۷۸***، تهران: نشر اختران، ۱۳۸۶.
- ❖ فخرالدین عظیمی، ***بحران دموکراسی در ایران (۱۳۲۰ تا ۱۳۳۳)***، ترجمه‌ی عبدالرضا هوشنگ مهدوی و بیژن نوذری، تهران: نشر آسیم، ۱۳۸۷.

[۳۱۴] روزهای ٤ تا ۹ آذر ۱۳۲۲، فرانکلین رزولت (رئیس جمهور امریکا)، ژوزف استالین (رئیس اتحاد جماهیر شوروی) و وینستون چرچیل (نخست وزیر انگستان) برای شرکت در یک کنفرانس سری علیه آلمان نازی در تهران بودند. این کنفرانس که به نام «کنفرانس تهران» رقم خورد، در روزهای ششم تا نهم آذر در محل سفارت شوروی در ایران برگزار شد؛ شاه ایران ناگزیر شد که برای شرکت در این کنفرانس به سفارت شوروی در تهران برود. اما جز استالین، هیچ یک از دو مقام دیگر، خارج از «کنفرانس تهران» با او ملاقات نداشتند. چنان که ارتشبد حسین فردوست می‌نویسد، استالین هم با شرط حضور گارد خود به جای گارد شاه، در کاخ **مرمر** با او ملاقات کرد. «ملکه‌ی مادر»، مادر محمدرضا شاه پهلوی، در خاطرات خود می‌گوید: «در آن موقع محمدرضا جوان بود و انگلیسی‌ها و امریکائی‌ها هم چون ایران را اشغال کرده بودند خود را حاکم ایران می‌دیدند و حاضر نشدند به دیدن محمدرضا بیایند، بلکه محمدرضا را وادارکردند تا به دیدن رئیس جمهوری‌ی آمریکا و نخست وزیر انگلستان برود. اما مرحوم"یوسف استالین" شخصاً به کاخ **سعد آباد** آمد و با شاه جوان ایران و من که مادرش بودم و دختران و سایر فرزندان رضا ملاقات کرد وعصرانه خورد.» گرچه تفاوت در مکان این دیدار در دو نقل قول یادشده، قابل تأمل است، و گرچه هیچ یک از دو مأخذ زیر به صورت صد در صد قابل اطمینان نیستند، اما در خبر دیدار استالین از محمد رضا شاه، که در هر دو مأخذ آمده، و فرح پهلوی نیز سی و سه سال پس از انقلاب در مصاحبه با «بی بی سی» آن را تأیید کرد، جای تردید نیست. به مآخذ زیر نگاه کنید:

گرایش‌های چپ و شکل‌گیری‌ی «حزب توده‌ی ایران»، مقاومت اتحاد جماهیر شوروی در پس کشیدن نیروهای خود از ایران (بعد از پایان جنگ)،[۳۱۵] مجموعاً فضائی پدید آورده بودند، که از یک سو، هیچ نوع رفتار مستبدانه را امکان بروز نمی‌دادند، و شگفتا که از سوی دیگر، امکان رشد نهادهای مدنی، و گسترش روشنگری‌های سیاسی/ اجتماعی/ فرهنگی را میسر می‌کردند. باقر مؤمنی (که در شهریور ۱۳۲۰، ۱۵ ساله بود و به عنوان شاهدی زنده تا همین دقیقه‌ی اکنون – یعنی ۲۰ مهر ماه ۱۳۹۱- وجود پربار از دانشِ تاریخی‌ی او برای ادبیات فارسی در تبعید گوهر گرانبهائی برشمرده می‌شود) در این زمینه می‌نویسد:

> سقوط نظام استبدادی که با خلع و تبعید رضاشاه به وسیله‌ی متفقین صورت گرفت، فضائی باز به وجود آورد که در آن تمام نیروهای فکری اجتماعی ــــ سیاسی، از مذهبی‌ها و فاشیست‌ها گرفته تا لیبرال‌ها و دموکرات‌ها و سوسیال دموکرات‌ها و کمونیست‌ها همگی امکان فعالیت یافتند و با ایجاد سازمان‌های سیاسی - اجتماعی به ترویج اندیشه‌های خود پرداختند.[۳۱۶]

و اسماعیل پوروالی، روزنامه‌نگار، که در سال ۱۳۲۵ در هیئت نویسندگان روزنامه‌ی «ایران ما»- به مدیریت خسرو اقبال- قلم می‌زده، در تبعید می‌نویسد: بنا به دعوت محمدرضا شاه پهلوی، همراه اعضاء دیگر هیئت تحریریه‌ی «ایران ما» «روز ۲ مرداد ۱۳۲۵» در کاخ سعدآباد با شاه ملاقات کرده بود. او در این ملاقاتِ «فراموش‌نشدنی»، شاه ایران را «جوان ساده و دمکرات»ی دیده بود که چند ساعت با روزنامه‌نگاران گفتوُ شنود داشته، با آن‌ها در باغ گشتوُگذار کرده بود، عکس گرفته بود، گفته بود و خندیده بود.[۳۱۷]

منتها، در کنار «امکان فعالیت برای کمونیست‌ها» و «ترویج اندیشه‌های خود» توسط «سازمان‌های سیاسی- اجتماعی»، ادعای امتیاز نفت شمال، که استالین در همان کنفرانس تهران (آذر ۱۳۲۲) آن را مطرح کرده بود، و از سوی نمایندگان حزب توده در مجلس شورای ملی هم تکرار می‌شد؛ خیزش فرقه‌ی دموکرات در آذربایجان و تشکیل «حکومت ملی‌ی آذربایجان»، و «جمهوری‌ی مهاباد کردستان»، و این که حزب توده‌ی ایران با فرقه‌ی دموکرات آذربایجان همکاری داشت؛ شورش عشایر جنوب (بختیاری و قشقائی) به تأسی از فرقه‌ی دموکرات آذربایجان،[۳۱۸] و بالأخره، ترور نافرجام شاه (۱۵

❖ ارتشبد (سابق) حسین فردوست، ***ظهور و سقوط سلطنت پهلوی***، تهران: مؤسسه‌ی مطالعات و پژوهش‌های سیاسی، ۱۳۷۰، فصل دوم.
❖ ***مصاحبه و خاطرات تاج‌الملوک داناترین سیاستمدار دربار دو پهلوی***، مصاحبه‌کنندگان: ملیحه خسروداد، تورج انصاری، محمودعلی باتمانقلیج، تارنمای «پیک نت»، تاریخ بازدید نوامبر ۲۰۰۹:
http://www.peiknet.com/1384/hafteh/06mehr/hafteh_page/83tajolmoluk.htm

توضیح: کتاب خاطرات ملکه مادر، به نشانی‌ی زیر، مدتی پس از نگارش این یادداشت به دستم رسید:
❖ ***خاطرات ملکه پهلوی، تاج‌الملوک آیرملو***، تهران: نشر به آفرین، ۱۳۸۰.

۳۱۵ رویداد مهمی، که با درایتِ محمدعلی فروغی و نمایندگان مجلس شورای ملی، در پنج روز اقامت سران متفقین در تهران رخ داد، امضاء سند تخلیه‌ی ایران بود به وسیله‌ی سران سه کشور. بنا بر این سند، استقلال و تمامیت ارضی‌ی ایران از سوی امریکا، شوروی، و بریتانیا به رسمیت شناخته شد و نیروهای متفقین موظف شدند که به محض پایان جنگ، ایران را تخلیه کنند. پس از پایان جنگ، امریکا و بریتانیا به این تعهد وفادار ماندند، اما شوروی مدت‌ها از انجام این تعهد سرپیچی کرد، و عاقبت نیز با اولتیماتوم امریکا و با امید کسب امتیاز نفت شمال، از ایران خارج شد.

۳۱۶ باقر مؤمنی، ***نقش حزب توده در گسترش فرهنگ و هنر***، تارنمای «بی بی سی»، ۱ فوریه ۲۰۱۲/ ۱۲ بهمن ۱۳۹۰:
http://www.bbc.co.uk/persian/iran/2012/02/120131_l44_tudeh_party_culture_art.shtml

۳۱۷ فشرده‌ی سخن اسماعیل پوروالی. به مأخذ زیر نگاه کنید:
❖ اسماعیل پوروالی، ***مرگ داوود نوروزی***، روزگار نو، دفتر نهم، سال دوازدهم، شماره‌ی ۱۴۱، آبان ۱۳۷۲، ص ۲۸.

۳۱۸ ناصر خان قشقائی پیرامون شورش جنوب همزمان با اوج فعالیت فرقه‌ی دموکرات آذربایجان در شمال ایران، می‌گوید: «ابوالحسن خان بختیاری و بنده و جهانشاه خان بختیاری در چشمه‌ی شهباز، نزدیک شهرضا، قسم خوردیم که متحداً اگر شمال را کمونیست‌ها بردند، لااقل از اصفهان به پائین را ما نگه داریم. [...] قرار شد که اصفهان را بختیاری‌ها بگیرند و شیراز را ما.». محمد ناصر قشقائی، اما، در مصاحبه با حبیب لاجوردی (تاریخ شفاهی دانشگاه هاروارد، ۳۱ ژانویه ۱۹۸۳) گفته است «هدف شورش، نه مقابله با دولت مرکزی، بلکه فراهم ساختن شرایطی بوده است که قوام بتواند به مسئله‌ی فرقه‌ی دموکرات [آذربایجان] پایان بخشد.» به مأخذ زیر نگاه کنید:

بهمن ۱۳۲۷)[۳۱۹] واقعیت‌هائی هستند که هم در تصمیم شاه در غیرقانونی اعلام کردن حزب توده و «شورای متحده‌ی مرکزی‌ی اتحادیه‌های کارگران ایرانی»[۳۲۰] (۱۳۲۷)، و هم در دستکاری‌ی او در قانون اساسی و افزودن به اختیارات خود (تا حق انحلال مجلس شورای ملی و مجلس سنا در سال ۱۳۲۸) بی‌تأثیر نبودند. از سوی دیگر، می‌دانیم که «حزب توده‌ی ایران» در آغاز تأسیس، نه تنها «وابسته» نبود، بلکه به قانون اساسی‌ی مشروطه و ارزش‌های مشروطیت باور داشت و تلاش پایه‌گذاران آن (اکثراً از بازماندگان گروه «۵۳ نفر») در سال‌های نخستِ تشکیل این حزب، بیش‌تر به اصلاحات سیاسی و مدنی و انتشار آگاهی معطوف بود. احسان طبری‌ی جوان، مسئول مطبوعاتی‌ی حزب توده در همان سال‌ها نوشت:

> حزب ما [...] خود را نه تنها موجد یک رستاخیز اجتماعی و سیاسی و اقتصادی بلکه در عین حال پرچمدار یک رستاخیز عظیم معنوی و روحی می‌داند. [...]. این رستاخیز معنوی و فکری، به عینه مانند رستاخیز اجتماعی، تنها در نتیجه‌ی مبارزه‌ی سخت و جدی در جبهه‌های ایدئولوژیک، فلسفه، هنر، علم و غیره عملی می‌شود.[۳۲۱]

اما چشم‌اندازِ ایدئولوژیک این حزب و جنبش‌هائی که در سپهر کارگری‌ی ایران پدید آورد، از یک سو، ترس آشکار شاه و کلاً جناح راست را نسبت به این حزب برانگیخت و محدودیت و سپس سرکوب آن را سبب شد؛ و از سوی دیگر، همین

❖ حمید شوکت، ***در تیررس حادثه: زندگی‌ی سیاسی‌ی قوام‌السلطنه***، تهران: نشر اختران، ۱۳۸۵، صص ۲۵۵ تا ۲۵۶. **توضیح:** حمید شوکت برای بازگفت از «ناصرخان قشقائی» مرجعی ارائه نداده است. اما در این نقطه از کتاب حاضر، و از منظر من، برای نشان دادن شرایط دهه‌ی آغازین پادشاهی محمدرضا شاه پهلوی، نه الزاماً چه‌گونگی و انگیزه‌های شروع شورش‌های جنوب، بلکه در درجه‌ی نخست، وجود این شورش‌ها اهمیت دارد.

[۳۱۹] ترور نافرجام شاه در ۱۵ بهمن ۱۳۲۷، توسط ناصر فخرآرائی (خبرنگار نشریه‌ی «پرچم اسلام» وابسته به آیت‌الله کاشانی) انجام شد. فخرآرائی، پس از شلیک ۵ تیر به شاه، در حالی که دست‌هایش را به علامت تسلیم بالا برده بود، توسط نیروهای محافظ شاه کشته شد. اما همان کارت خبرنگاری و نشانی‌ی خانه‌ی یکی از اعضاء حزب توده به نام عبدالله ارگانی، که در جیب او بافتند، سر نخی شد برای دستگیری و تبعید آیت‌الله کاشانی، و دستگیری‌ی سران حزب توده، و «منحله» اعلام کردن این حزب. البته بابک امیرخسروی، از اعضاء پیشین حزب توده، بنا به دلایلی که در فصل نهم از کتاب «نظر از درون به نقش حزب توده‌ی ایران» ارائه می‌دهد، بر این باور است که تلاش شاه برای غیرقانونی اعلام کردن حزب توده، مدتی پیش از ترور نافرجام او آغاز شده بود. در هر حال، مجموعه‌ی گزارش‌هائی که بعداً در زمینه‌ی ترور شاه منتشر شد نشان می‌دهد که کمیته‌ی مرکزی‌ی حزب توده از این توطئه بی‌خبر بوده است. منتها، نورالدین کیانوری، از کمیته‌ی اجرائی حزب، بدون خبر کمیته‌ی مرکزی‌ی حزب در این توطئه دست داشته است. فریدون کشاورز، از بلندپایگان حزب توده، در کتاب «من متهم می‌کنم کمیته‌ی مرکزی‌ی حزب توده‌ی ایران را» گزارش داده است که کیانوری در جلسه‌ی کمیته‌ی مرکزی‌ی حزب توده که پس از تبعید در مسکو تشکیل می‌شد، گفته بود: «من عقیده دارم که اگر رفقای شوروی یکی از ماها را صدا کنند و به او بگویند فلان کار را بکن ولی به رفقای کمیته‌ی مرکزی‌ی خودت نگو، ما باید حرف‌شنوی داشته باشیم و آن کار را انجام بدهیم.» عبدالله ارگانی نیز حدود ۵۰ سال پس از واقعه، با محمود تربتی سنجابی گفت‌وگوئی دارد که دخالت نورالدین کیانوری در این ترور را مستدل می‌کند. پیرامون گزاره‌های بالا به مآخذ زیر نگاه کنید:

❖ بابک امیرخسروی، ***نظر از درون به حزب توده‌ی ایران: نقد خاطرات نورالدین کیانوری***، تهران: انتشارات اطلاعات، ۱۳۷۵، صص ۱۹۴ تا ۲۰۸.

❖ فریدون کشاورز، ***من متهم می‌کنم کمیته‌ی مرکزی‌ی حزب توده ی ایران را***، تهران: انتشارات رواق، زمستان ۱۳۵۷، ص ۴۷.

❖ ***پنج گلوله برای شاه، گفت‌وشنود عبدالله ارگانی و محمود تربتی سنجابی***، تهران: نشر خجسته، ۱۳۸۱.

[۳۲۰] «شورای متحده‌ی مرکزی‌ی اتحادیه‌های کارگران ایرانی»، متشکل از سازمان‌دهندگان اتحادیه‌های کارگری و نمایندگان کارگران در کارخانه‌های مختلف، که هر یک از آن‌ها قبلاً هم فعال بودند، در ۱۱ اردی‌بهشت ۱۳۲۳ توسط حزب توده تشکیل شد. این شورا از سوی فدراسیون جهانی‌ی اتحادیه‌های کارگری (W.F.T.U.) به عضویت پذیرفته شد. مهم‌ترین نشریه‌ی ارگان این شورا، «ظفر» نام داشت و مقتدرترین فرد آن نیز رضا روستا بود. در گزارشی که این شورا به دومین کنگره‌ی جهانی‌ی اتحادیه‌های کارگری (به سرپرستی‌ی فدراسیون اتحادیه‌های کارگری‌ی چپ) ارائه داد، فعالیت‌های انجام شده‌ی زیر منعکس بود: اعتصاب کارگران ساختمانی در تهران در سال‌های ۱۳۲۱ و ۱۳۲۲؛ اعتصاب کارگران شهرداری‌ی تهران در سال ۱۳۲۳؛ اعتصاب کارگران کارخانه‌های پارچه‌بافی در تهران، مازندران، و آذربایجان در سال‌های ۱۳۲۲ و ۱۳۲۳؛ اعتصاب ۲۰ هزار نفره‌ی کارگران پارچه‌باف اصفهان در پائیز ۱۳۲۳؛ اعتصاب‌های پی در پی در صنعت نفت کرمانشاه، آبادان، و آغاجاری در سال‌های ۱۳۲۴ و ۱۳۲۵. به مآخذ زیر نگاه کنید:

❖ علی منوچهری و مهدی احمدی، ***اعتصابات کارگری در دوره‌ی نخست وزیری‌ی دکتر مصدق***، فصل‌نامه‌ی «پیام بهارستان»، شماره‌ی ۵، پائیز ۱۳۸۸، صص ۳۷۰ تا ۳۷۱. **توضیح:** من این متن را از تارنمای «انسانی» برگرفته‌ام:
http://www.ensany.ir/storage/Files/20101205113600-Pages%20from%20payam5-19.pdf

[۳۲۱] **برگرفته از:** باقر مؤمنی، ***نقش حزب توده در گسترش فرهنگ و هنر***، تارنمای «بی بی سی»، ۱ فوریه ۲۰۱۲/ ۱۲ بهمن ۱۳۹۰:
http://www.bbc.co.uk/persian/iran/2012/02/120131_l44_tudeh_party_culture_art.shtml

سرکوب‌ها (یا محدودیت‌ها)، بینش و کنش این حزب را با شتابی فزاینده به سوی کشور «مادر سوسیالیسم» کشاند، که به نامِ «دفاع از خلق‌های محروم جهان»، در واقع، در ساز وُ کارِ «جهان»گشائی بود و به خاک و منابع و آب‌های ایران نیز چشم داشت.

***

پیش از سلطنت رضا شاه پهلوی، بر اساس اختیاراتی که در بندهای ۹۱ و ۹۲ در قانون اساسی‌ی مشروطه برای «انجمن‌های ایالتی و ولایتی»، پیش‌بینی شده بود، قوم‌های غیرفارس ایران، در برخی از موارد، مانند پوشش، کاربرد زبان محلی، انتخاب پرسنل نهادهای دولتی، و صَرفِ بودجه، مستقل از مرکز عمل می‌کردند. از زمانی که رضا شاه بر این بخش از قانون اساسی در عمل خط بطلان کشید، ناخشنودی‌ی قوم‌های غیرفارس- به ویژه در آذربایجان، کردستان، و خوزستان- آتشی بود که در زیر سرکوب‌های مداوم دولت مرکزی پنهان بود. با رفتن رضا شاه از ایران، این آتش، در کنش‌های پیکارگران ما شعله کشید و بلافاصله هم مورد سوءاستفاده‌ی دولت‌های بریتانیا و اتحاد جماهیر شوروی قرار گرفت، و به ویژه در آذربایجان، با کوشش و هدایت گروهی از پیکارگران چپ، در پدیده‌ای با نام «فرقه‌ی دموکرات آذربایجان» تجلی یافت. این «فرقه»، با بیانیه‌ی ۱۲ شهریور ۱۳۲۴ در تبریز اعلام حضور کرد؛ و از «حزب توده‌ی ایران» نیز- که در آن زمان قانونی بود و در مجلس هم نماینده داشت- خواست (یا به آن دستور داد) تا کمیته‌ی ایالتی‌ی خود در آذربایجان را منحل کند و به فرقه بپیوندد. البته به رغم تلاش‌های پیدا و پنهانِ عوامل شوروی در ایران برای زیر نفوذ گرفتنِ حزب توده، کم‌تر از دو سال پیش از این تاریخ (یعنی ۱۷ اسفند ۱۳۲۲)، رهبران این حزب در سرمقاله‌ی روزنامه‌ی «رهبر»، ارگان کمیته‌ی مرکزی، نوشته بودند:

> [...] ما دوستی‌ی خود را چه با بریتانیا وچه با شوروی، مشروط به یک شرط می‌کنیم. و آن این که این دولت‌ها منافع خود را درحدود منافع ملی ما، در حدود ارتقاء و سعادت عمومی‌ی ما حفظ کنند. که این دو دولت، حامی‌ی هیچ گونه سیاست ارتجاعی یا افراطی در ایران نباشند.... ما هر روز که احساس کنیم همسایه‌ی شمالی‌ی ما برخلاف تصور ما می‌خواهد در ایران منافع استعماری برای خود فرض نماید، یا قصد آن را داشته باشد که رژیم خود را به زور بر ملت ایران تحمیل کند، یا بخواهد ایران را منضم به خاک خود سازد، ما با این روش‌ها سخت مبارزه خواهیم کرد.[۳۲۲]

به دنبال این سیاست بود که کمیته‌ی مرکزی‌ی حزب توده ابتدا با پیشنهادِ پیوستن به فرقه مخالفت کرد. فریدون کشاورز، عضو کمیته‌ی مرکزی‌ی وقت در حزب توده، و نماینده‌ی دوره‌ی چهاردهم در مجلس شورای ملی، در زمینه‌ی این ادغام می‌نویسد:

> روز قبل از اعلام تشکیل فرقه‌ی دموکرات آذربایجان، کمیته‌ی مرکزی‌ی حزب در منزل من جلسه داشت، زیرا من مصونیت پارلمانی داشتم و کلوپ حزب در اشغال سربازان بود. [...] شوفر من مرا صدا کرد و گفت آقائی به نام پادگان از تبریز آمده و با شما کار فوری دارد. [صادق] پادگان، دبیر تشکیلات ایالتی‌ی حزب در آذربایجان بود. [...] پادگان به من گفت: من همین امروز از تبریز رسیده‌ام و پیغام خیلی فوری برای کمیته‌ی مرکزی دارم و نمی‌دانم کجا می‌توانم رفقا را پیدا کنم. [...] او را وارد اتاق جلسه کردم. او چنین گفت: «من از تبریز حالا رسیده‌ام و فوری باید برگردم. من آمده‌ام به شما اطلاع بدهم که فردا تمام سازمان حزب ما در آذربایجان، از حزب توده‌ی ایران جدا شده و با موافقت رفقای شوروی به فرقه‌ی دموکرات آذربایجان، که تشکیل آن فردا اعلام خواهد شد می پیوندد.» شما می‌توانید نزد خود مجسم کنید چه ضربه‌ای به همه‌ی ما وارد شد. [...] بالأخره تصمیم گرفتیم که نامه‌ای به حزب کمونیست اتحاد شوروی بنویسیم. [...] ایرج

---

[۳۲۲] برگرفته از: بابک امیرخسروی، ***پادزهری به نوشته‌ی آقای خسرو شاکری***، تارنمای «گویا نیوز»، ۱۸ بهمن ۱۳۹۰:
http://news.gooya.com/politics/archives/2012/02/135673.php

اسکندری مأمور نوشتن این نامه شد و پس از قرائت و تصویب آن در کمیته‌ی مرکزی، ارسال شد. ولی هیچ وقت جواب این نامه نرسید.[۳۲۳]

اما حزب توده که، دست کم در مورد شاخه‌ی آذربایجان، در برابر کار انجام‌شده قرار گرفته بود، به رغم این مخالفت، سرانجام تسلیم شد، و به فرقه‌ی دموکرات آذربایجان پیوست. این فرقه، با گُردان‌های مسلحی به نام «فدائیان»، پایگاه‌های نظامی‌ی مهم آذربایجان، و سپس تمامی‌ی نهادهای این استان را تسخیر کرد؛ «حکومت ملی‌ی آذربایجان» را به نخست وزیری‌ی سیدجعفر پیشه‌وری تشکیل داد؛ به قاضی محمد، رهبر کردهای ناراضی‌ی ایران، برای تشکیل حکومتی جداگانه در کردستان یاری رساند؛ و در حالی که اصلاحات فرهنگی، سیاسی، اجتماعی و ارضی‌ی قابل مشاهده‌ای در آذربایجان انجام داده بود، روز ۲۳ آذر ۱۳۲۵ با ورود ارتش شاهنشاهی‌ی ایران به آذربایجان منهدم شد. با انهدام فرقه‌ی دموکرات آذربایجان، هزاران تن از طرفداران بی‌نام و نشان، یا پیکارگران نامدار این فرقه و حزب توده‌ی ایران- که اکثراً با آرمان تحقق آزادی و عدالت اجتماعی به این نهادها پیوسته بودند- یا کشته شدند و یا به کشور «حامی‌ی خلق‌های تحت ستم» پناه بردند، و در آن جا اکثراً یا به تیغ تصفیه‌های استالین گرفتار آمدند، و یا در اردوگاه‌های مهاجران ایرانی در شرایط پلیسی و با خفت و خواری زندگی را به پایان بردند. اگر این گروه عظیم از پیکارگران صادق و صمیمی‌ی ایران از چه‌گونگی و هدف نهائی‌ی «تأسیساندنِ» این فرقه بی‌خبر بودند، اگر شخصیت‌های مطلع در «فرقه» و «حزب توده»، پیرامون واقعیت‌های این رویداد خونین سکوت کردند، یا با تحریف واقعیت‌ها، مردم ایران را از چه‌گونگی‌ی آن بی‌خبر نگه داشتند، محمدرضا شاه پهلوی- که با رقبای بین‌المللی‌ی شوروی نیز در تماس دائم بود- بی‌تردید از واقعیت‌های پشت پرده‌ی این رویداد بی‌خبر نبود. چرا که اسنادِ قرار و مدارهای تقسیم جهان- که پیش از جنگ دوم جهانی بین آلمان و شوروی و ژاپن و ایتالیا امضاء شده بود- در سال ۱۹۴۸ (۱۳۲۷) منتشر شد.[۳۲٤] سند مربوط به ایران در این مجموعه، به نیکی و به کمال نشان می‌دهد که هدف شوروی‌ی استالین، نه تنها دستیابی به منابع زیرزمینی‌ی شمال ایران، بلکه دست یافتن به سراسر خاک ایران تا خلیج فارس و دریای عمان بود. این کتاب، بعدها تجدید چاپ شد، و بابک امیرخسروی، عضو برجسته‌ی آن زمانی‌ی حزب توده، بند ۴ از پروتکل سِرّی‌ی مربوط به سهم شوروی از این غنایم ارضی را، که در ۱۳ نوامبر ۱۹۴۰ نوشته شده بود، از صفحه‌ی ۲۵۹ آن، به شرح زیر ترجمه کرد:

اتحاد شوروی اعلام می‌کند که خواست‌های ارضی‌ی او به سوی بخش جنوبی‌ی سرزمین ملی‌ی اتحاد شوروی در جهت اقیانوس هند متمرکز است. چهار قدرت اعلام می‌کنند، با حفظ حق حل و فصل موارد خاص، متقابلاً این خواست‌های ارضی را محترم شمرده و مانع دستیابی به آن‌ها نخواهند شد.[۳۲٥]

ماده‌ی ۳ از این بندِ پروتکل نیز که روز ۲۶ نوامبر ۱۹۴۰ «مورد پذیرش» و امضاء چهار دولت قرار گرفت، مرز «خواست ارضی» را از سوی شوروی تعیین کرده است:

---

[۳۲۳] فریدون کشاورز، ***من متهم می‌کنم کمیته‌ی مرکزی‌ی حزب توده ی ایران را*** (مصاحبه)، تهران: انتشارات رواق، چاپ دوم، زمستان ۱۳۵۷، صص ٦۱ تا ٦۳.

افزون بر این گونه نشانه‌ها که در گوشه و کنار خاطرات سیاسی دیده می‌شود، در اسناد آرشیوهای شوروی نیز به مخالفت و مقاومت برخی از سران حزب توده نسبت به این ادغام و نسبت به سیاست‌های فرقه و دخالت‌های حزب کمونیست شوروی، اشاره شده است. به مأخذ زیر نگاه کنید:

❖ جمیل حسنلی، ***فراز و فرود فرقه دموکرات آذربایجان: به روایت اسناد محرمانه‌ی آرشیوهای اتحاد جماهیر شوروی***، ترجمه‌ی منصور همامی، تهران: نشر نی، ۱۳۸۳، صص ۴۷، ۵۵، ۶۰، ۱۱۱.

[324] ***Nazi- Soviet Relations 1939-1941***, Documents from the Archives of the German Foreign Office, Edited by Raymond James Sontag and James Stuart Beddie, New York: Department of State Publication 3023, 1948, Chapter 6.

[۳۲٥] بابک امیرخسروی، ***نظر از درون به نقش حزب توده‌ی ایران: نقدی بر خاطرات نورالدین کیانوری***، تهران: انتشارات اطلاعات، ۱۳۷۵، ص ۱۱٤.

مشروط بر این که منطقه‌ی جنوب باطوم و باکو، در جهت کلی‌ی خلیج فارس به مثابه مرکز تقاضاهای اتحاد شوروی مورد پذیرش قرار بگیرد. (پیشین)

بابک امیرخسروی، به دنبال این بازگفت می‌نویسد:

> من تا دستیابی به این سند، بر این گمان بودم که دولت شوروی عمدتاً می‌خواهد از مسئله‌ی آذربایجان به صورت ابزار فشار برای کسب امتیاز نفت شمال استفاده کند و چندان پای‌بند الحاق آذربایجان و کردستان به شوروی نیست. بر این باور بودم که موضوع آذربایجان واحد و الحاق آذربایجان ایران به اتحاد شوروی صرفاً وسوسه‌های ذهنی و بلندپروازی‌های میرجعفر باقراوف [دبیر کمیته‌ی مرکزی‌ی حزب کمونیست آذربایجان شوروی] است. بارها این سئوال را مطرح ساخته بودم که در این صورت چرا شوروی‌ها پای کردها را نیز به این ماجرا کشاندند؟ این سند پاسخ آن است و می‌رساند که نه تنها آذربایجان، بلکه کردستان و سرتاسر ایران تا خلیج فارس و اقیانوس هند مد نظر «رفیق استالین» و دولت «حامی‌ی ملت‌های تحت ستم» بود! (پیشین، صص ۱۱۴ تا ۱۱۵- گیومه‌ها از بابک امیرخسروی است.)

منتها، ماده‌ی خامی که نمی‌توان از این فرایند حذف کرد (اما از مجموعه‌ی برآوردهای شاه ایران حذف شده بود)، زمینه‌ی مساعدی بود که نارضایتی و طغیان فروخورده‌ی مردم آذربایجان و کردستان (علیه ستم ملی) در اختیار «رفیق استالین» گذاشته بود.[۳۲۶] پس از رفتن رضا شاه پهلوی از ایران و پس از پایان جنگ دوم جهانی، دولت شوراها، که از سال‌ها پیش برای یافتن منابع نفت در شمال ایران جست‌وجو کرده بود، از این زمینه‌ی آماده برای بذرپاشی سود جست. اینک اسناد «کاملاً سِرّی»ی حکومت شوراها به تاریخ ایران می‌گویند که دولت شوروی، پیش از بیرون کشیدن ارتش خود از ایران، با استفاده از این زمینه‌ی مساعد، و با استفاده از ایمان بی‌چون و چرای پیکارگران چپ ایران به آرمان‌های سوسیالیسم و به حقانیت دولت شوروی (که به ویژه از زمان لنین و با الغای قرارداد ۱۹۰۷ و کاپیتولاسیون و چشم‌پوشی از بدهی‌های ایران به دولت تزاری، در دل‌ها کاشته شده بود)[۳۲۷] «فرقه‌ی دموکرات آذربایجان» را پدید آورد، و رهبران ایرانی‌ی این

---

[۳۲۶] جمیل حسنلی در مصاحبه‌ای که پس از انتشار کتاب «فراز و فرود فرقه‌ی دموکرات آذربایجان به روایت اسناد محرمانه‌ی آرشیوهای اتحاد جماهیر شوروی» با او انجام شد، ضمن تکیه بر نقش شوروی در ایجاد فرقه‌ی دموکرات آذربایجان، پیرامون نقش «اراده‌ی ملی» در تشکیل این فرقه، می‌گوید: «در سال ۱۹۴۵ آذربایجان جنوبی شاهد حرکتی ملی بود که این حرکت تداوم بلاواسطه‌ی حرکت دموکراتیک نهضت مشروطه، جنبش ستارخان و شیخ محمد خیابانی بود. [...] علاوه بر این، نه تنها بازماندگان جنبش خیابانی بلکه بیش‌تر اشخاص که در جنبش ستارخان شرکت داشتند هنوز در قید حیات بودند. آن‌ها می‌دانستند که چه ظلم‌هائي بدان‌ها شده و استبداد بر سر اینان چه آورده است. از دیگر طرف رسمیت یافتن زبان فارسی و انکار و قدغن شدن زبان، تاریخ و مدنیت آذربایجان از سوی رژیم پهلوی نیز موجب تحقیر غرور ملی‌ی مردم شده بود. از دیدگاه اقتصادی نیز تبریز که روزگاری دومین شهر ایران به حساب می‌آمد بر اثر بی‌توجهی‌ی رژیم به یکی از ده‌ها شهر عادی‌ی ایران تبدیل شده بود؛ و همه‌ی این‌ها از دید مردم نمی‌توانست پنهان بماند. به طورکلی زبان ترکی در ایران زبان زندان به حساب می‌آمد چون اکثر زندانیان سیاسی ترک‌ها بودند و همه‌ی این‌ها نارضایتی‌هایی را فراهم می‌آورد که به محض وجود فرصت بروز می‌نمود. [...] فرقه‌ی دموکرات آذربایجان يك حزب با ماهیت کمونیستی نبود؛ این يك حرکت ملی و يك حزب ملی بود. حتا کنسول انگلیس جناب *Uoll* در مکاتبات خویش با لندن به طور صریح این نکته‌ی مهم را مورد تأکید قرار مي دهد که: "مبارزه با حزب توده به دلیل داشتن ماهیت کمونیستی آسان است اما مبارزه با فرقه‌ی دموکرات به دلیل ماهیت ملی و مردمی‌ی آن چندان هم آسان نمی‌باشد و در این حزب طبقات مختلف مردم اشتراك دارند و این مسئله، مبارزه با گسترش ایده‌های فرقه را غیرممکن می‌سازد." [...] فرقه‌چی‌ها متشکل از تجار، زمیندار، صاحبکار، روشنفکر، معلم، روستائی، شهری، کارگر، کشاورز و ... و توده‌های دیگر مردم بود.» به مأخذ زیر نگاه کنید:

- ❖ ***فرقه‌ی دموکرات آذربایجان اهمیت ملی داشت***، مصاحبه با دکتر جمیل حسنلی، و ترجمه: ص.رضایی، م.عباسی:

http://www.achiq.org/m.hukumet/hesenli.htm

[۳۲۷] نصرت‌الله جهانشاهلو، معاون پیشه‌وری (از حزب توده)، در خاطراتش می‌نویسد: «ما همه میهن‌پرور بودیم و آزادی و آبادی‌ی "ایران" میهن‌مان را می‌خواستیم، چرا این گونه قدم در راهی گذاشتیم که بیراهه بود؟ سبب این بود که ما نادرست، شیفته نگرشی شده بودیم که به گمان ما، تنها راه رهایی‌ی میهن‌مان از چنگ این یا آن بیگانه یا دست نشاندگان آن ها بود. غافل از آن که در عمل، واقعیت‌ها با بسیاری از نظریه‌ها، فرسنگ‌ها فاصله دارد و تلاش ما چیزی به جز از چاله به چاه ویل بردگی و بندگی افتادن نبود. بسیاری از مردم میهن‌پرور ایران، گمان می‌کردند که حزب توده و فرقه‌ی دموکرات آذربایجان، ساخته و پرداخته خود ایرانیان‌اند. از این روی بدان‌ها روی آوردند و از آن‌ها چشم امید داشتند. آری مردم ما نمی‌دانستند که برپادارنده و گرداننده‌ی حزب توده، بیگانگانند و آگاه نبودند که فرقه‌ی دموکرات آذربایجان را میرجعفر باقراوف (رئیس جمهور شوروی آذربایجان)، به اغوای عبدالصمد کامبخش (از رهبران حزب خائن توده) در باکو طرح ریزی کرد.» به مأخذ زیر نگاه کنید:

فرقه- غافل از این که استالین آمده بود که لنین را محو کند- جز مهره‌هائی برای اجرای همان طرح توسعه‌طلبانه‌ی (ارضی و اقتصادی) شوروی نبودند: جمیل حَسَنلو، استاد دانشگاه در باکو، با استناد به اسناد «آرشیوهای کمیساریای وزارت خارجه‌ی اتحاد شوروی، کمیته‌ی دفاع دولتی، کمیته‌ی مرکزی‌ی حزب کمونیست اتحاد شوروی، شورای کمیساریای خلق شوروی، و نیز ارگان‌های مختلف آذربایجان شوروی»، در کتاب «فراز و فرود فرقه‌ی دموکرات آذربایجان»[۳۲۸] نشان می‌دهد که برنامه‌ی سیاسی‌ی این فرقه، اساس‌نامه‌ی داخلی، چارچوب تشکیلاتی، ترکیب رهبری‌ی فرقه، دستور انحلال کمیته‌ی محلی‌ی حزب توده در آذربایجان و پیوستن آن به فرقه، گروه‌های اجتماعی‌ای که فرقه بایستی جذب می‌کرد،[۳۲۹] نشریه‌هائی که بایستی منتشر می‌کرد، و حتا عبارت‌های تبلیغی در این نشریه‌ها، شعارهائی که بایستی می‌داد یا نمی‌داد، مو به مو در مسکو یا در آذربایجان شوروی تنظیم شده بود. (صص ۶۵ تا ۶۷) پیرامون نخستین گام این حرکت در این کتاب می‌خوانیم که میرجعفر باقراوف، دبیر کمیته‌ی مرکزی‌ی حزب کمونیست آذربایجان شوروی، به مسکو فراخوانده می‌شود تا دستورالعمل محرمانه‌ای مبنی بر «تدابیر لازم در مورد سازماندهی‌ی جنبش جدائی‌خواهانه در آذربایجان جنوبی و سایر شهرهای ایران» را از دفتر سیاسی‌ی کمیته‌ی مرکزی‌ی حزب کمونیست شوروی دریافت کند؛ و گام نخست اجراء این «تدابیر» نیز، «تشکیل فرقه‌ی دموکرات آذربایجان بود.» (ص ۵۲) و با پشتوانه‌ی همان فرمان مسکو است که میرجعفر باقراوف، دبیر کمیته‌ی مرکزی‌ی حزب کمونیست آذربایجان شوروی، در یک سخنرانی می‌گوید:

> شما می‌دانید که ارتش سرخ در مدتی کوتاه بسیاری از مناطق شمالی‌ی ایران را اشغال کرده است. تمام این سرزمین‌ها آذربایجان ماست. بر اساس داده‌ی تاریخی بخش‌های بسیاری از مناطق شمالی‌ی ایران خاک آذربایجان ماست. شهرهای بزرگ ایران چون قزوین، ارومیه، میانه، مراغه، تبریز، اردبیل، سلماس، خوی، انزلی و غیره زادگاه آبا و اجداد ماست. اگر حقیقت را بخواهید تهران از شهرهای قدیمی‌ی آذربایجان است. (حسنلی، ۱۳۸۳، ص ۲۱)

البته قرار بر این بوده که به سبب «حساسیتی که ایرانیان به وحدت ملی» دارند، از شعارهای جدائی‌طلبانه در آذربایجان ایران احتراز شود، اما بر پایه‌ی همین هدف بود که دستورالعمل‌های مسکو، زیر نظر ۷۰۰ تن از کارشناسان شوروی (افزون بر ارتش این کشور که پس از پایان جنگ دوم جهانی هنوز شمال ایران را ترک نکرده بود) توسط اهرم‌های ایرانی‌ی فرقه‌ی دموکرات و با پشتیبانی‌ی کامل حزب توده‌ی ایران، در آذربایجان و کردستان اجرا شد. (حسنلی، ص ۱۲۸) پیشه‌وری برای قرار و مدار «خودمختاری‌ی وابسته به دولت مرکزی»، با هواپیمای شوروی به تهران رفت و با احمد قوام (نخست وزیر وقت) دیدار کرد. قوام بر اساس ماده‌ی «انجمن‌های ایالتی و ولایتی» در قانون اساسی‌ی مشروطه، تمامی اختیارات یک استان خودمختار را برای آذربایجان پذیرفت، اما پذیرش پیشنهاد پیشه‌وری در مورد استقلال ارتش و «تقسیم اراضی» را که مغایر با قانون اساسی بود، به «تصویب مجلس» موکول کرد. از سوی دیگر، قوام، که حل مسئله‌ی آذربایجان را در دستور دولت خود گذاشته بود، به فراصت دریافته بود که اگر امتیاز نفت شمال ایران به شوروی واگذار شود، به احتمال زیاد، شوروی حمایت خود را از فرقه برخواهد گرفت. این بود که با سادچیکُف (سفیر شوروی در تهران) وارد مذاکره شد؛ به مسکو رفت و با سران شوروی دیدار کرد؛ و نهایتاً، روز ۱۵ فروردین ۱۳۲۵ قراردادی برای «ایجاد یک شرکت نفت مشترک بین ایران و شوروی» را- البته به شرط تصویب در مجلس پانزدهم که هنوز هفت ماه به تشکیل آن باقی مانده بود- در مسکو امضاء کرد؛ و در برابر آن، خروج ارتش شوروی از ایران و عدم مداخله‌ی این کشور در

ما و بیگانگان، سرگذشت دکتر نصرت‌الله جهانشاهلو افشار، نشر ورجاوند، ۱۳۸۰، ص ۱۰۵.

[۳۲۸] جمیل حسنلی، ***فراز و فرود فرقه دموکرات آذربایجان: به روایت اسناد محرمانه‌ی آرشیوهای اتحاد جماهیر شوروی***، ترجمه‌ی منصور همامی، تهران: نشر نی، ۱۳۸۳.

[۳۲۹] مثلاً این که: «در درجه‌ی نخست به دین و خدمتگزاران دین توجه بشود.» نگاه کنید به:

- جمیل حسنلی، ***فراز و فرود فرقه‌ی دموکرات آذربایجان***، پیشین، ص ۳۹.

مسائل داخلی‌ی ایران را خواستار شد.[۳۳۰] این قرارداد، همان گونه که قوام پیش‌بینی کرده بود- در مجلس پانزدهم ابتدا شامل مرور زمان شد و نهایتاً هم «کم لن یکن» اعلام شد. اما تا به آن جا برسد، ذات این قرارداد در زمان خود، در کنار فشارهای بین‌المللی (عمدتاً امریکا)،[۳۳۱] سبب شد که شوروی نه تنها ارتش خود را از خاک ایران خارج کند، بلکه با بهانه‌هائی مانند «مصالح صلح جهانی» و «مصالح پرولتاریا»، و «مصالح جبهه‌ی صلح و سوسیالیسم»، ناگهان به «فرقه‌ی دموکرات آذربایجان» دستور تسلیم دهد، و آذربایجان را (لابد تا فرصتی دیگر) به دولت ایران بسپارد. جعفر پیشه‌وری و چهار تن از اعضاء کابینه‌اش (پادگان، شبستری، جاوید، دانشیان)- که رهنمودها و یاری‌های شوروی را به حساب یاری‌های «انسان‌دوستانه» و «برادرانه» به جنبش حق‌طلبانه‌ی مردم آذربایجان واریز کرده بودند- روز ۱۷ آذر ۲۵ از طریق سرکنسول اتحاد شوروی در تبریز، به رهبران شوروی نامه می‌نویسند و ملتمسانه تقاضای کمک می‌کنند. جمله‌های زیر از این نامه‌ی طولانی، حضور گسترده‌ی مردم معمولی‌ی آذربایجان در این جنبش را- فارغ از نقشه‌های شوم شوروی- به تاریخ گزارش می‌دهند:

> [...] ما هشت ماه تمام است که بر خلاف احساسات مردم ما، بر خلاف آرزوها و تمایلات اعضا و فعالان فرقه‌مان؛ به خاطر پیشرفت امور و حل مسالمت‌آمیز اختلافات؛ با در نظرداشتِ سیاست جهانی‌ی دوست بزرگمان اتحاد شوروی و با توجه به میانجیگری دولت شوروی، کوشیده‌ایم سیمای قوام را دموکراتیک و مترقی جلوه دهیم و حتا در مواقعی، بر خلاف فکر و اعتقاد خویش از او تعریف و تمجید نیز نموده‌ایم. هدف این بوده است که کار از جانب ما مختل نشود. حتا زمانی که فدائیان ما امکان تسخیر قزوین، رشت و تهران را نیز داشتند، ما از نفوذ و احترام خویش استفاده کرده و جلوی آن‌ها را گرفته‌ایم تا بهانه به دست او نیافتد. این گذشت‌های ما را جهانیان می‌دانند و شما بهتر از همه می‌دانید. ما در اجرای این موافقتنامه، حکومت ملی خود را ملغی کردیم، مجلس ملی مان را به انجمن ایالتی تبدیل نمودیم، دسته‌جات فدائی را به سازمان نگهبان مبدل ساختیم؛ آماده‌ی سپردن اختیار و فرماندهی‌ی قشون ملی‌مان به آنان شدیم و شروع به تحویل همه‌ی عایدات خود به خزانه‌ی آن‌ها، یعنی بانک ملی کردیم. این همه به این خاطر بود که دستاویزی به دست آن‌ها داده نشود. قوام با مشاهده این کوتاه آمدن‌های ما هر روز بر خواست‌های خود افزود و سرانجام کار را به آن‌جا رسانیده است که می‌خواهد با یک حمله، به یکباره به آزادی خاتمه دهد. او مسئله نفت را با این قصد پیش کشیده است که خروج ارتش سرخ را از ایران تأمین کند و نهضت ملی‌ی آذربایجان را در هم بکوبد. [...] حمله‌ی خائنانه‌ی نیروی اعزامی‌ی قوام به ما، هیجان شدیدی در میان مردم ما به وجود آورده است. مردم گروه گروه به فرقه مراجعه می‌کنند و برای دفاع از آزادی سلاح می‌خواهند. این نیز بیانگر جدی‌ی روحیه‌ی مردم ماست. روحیه‌ی چند فئودال و یا چند عنصر ارتجاعی دیگر مانند امیرنصرت اسکندری، جمال امامی، سرلشکر مقدم و ذوالفقاری‌ها ، نمی‌تواند بیانگر روحیه خلق باشد. روحیه‌ی آن‌ها ــ که آقایی و زمین‌هایشان را از دست داده اند ـ روشن است که چه‌گونه می‌تواند باشد. ولی توده‌های شهری و روستائی که آزادی و زمین به دست آورده‌اند، آماده‌ی هر گونه فداکاری در راه دست‌آوردهایشان هستند. اگر ما امروز امکان دهیم که آزادی‌ی آنان از بین برود، دیگر به پا خیزاندن آنان ممکن نخواهد گشت. آن‌ها دیگر به کسی اعتماد نخواهند کرد. توده نه فقط از ما،

---

[۳۳۰] برای آگاهی‌ی بیش‌تر در زمینه‌ی مذاکره‌های قوام با پیشه‌وری و با شوروی‌ها به مآخذ زیر نگاه کنید:
- مصطفی فاتح، ***۵۰ سال نفت ایران***، تهران: نشر علم، ۱۳۸۴.
- حمید شوکت، ***در تیررس حادثه: زندگی‌ی سیاسی‌ی قوام‌السلطنه***، تهران: نشر اختران، ۱۳۸۵، صص ۱۹۳ تا ۲۶٤.
- خانبابا بیانی، ***غائله‌ی آذربایجان***، ویرایش سعید قائمی، تهران: انتشارات زریاب، ۱۳۷۵، ص ۵۲۱ تا ۵٤۲. **توضیح:** کتاب «غائله‌ی آذربایجان» شامل کلیشه یا رونوشت ده‌ها سند معتبر است.»

[۳۳۱] ارتشبد حسین فردوست در خاطرات خود نوشته است که نماینده‌ی آمریکا در سازمان ملل به شوروی اولتیماتوم داد که اگر تا تاریخ معینی نیروهایش را از ایران خارج نکند جنگ سوم جهانی رخ خواهد داد. اما جیمز بیل، پژوهشگر امریکائی، وجود چنین التیماتومی را نفی می‌کند و می‌نویسد هشدارهای امریکا به شوروی تنها شامل «ابراز نگرانی» بوده است. به مأخذ زیر نگاه کنید:
- حسین فردوست، ***ظهور و سقوط سلطنت پهلوی***، تهران: انتشارات اطلاعات، ۱۳۷۰، جلد ۲، ص۱٤۹.
- جیمز بیل، ***شیر و عقاب***، ترجمه‌ی مهوش غلامی، تهران: انتشارات کوبه، ۱۳۷۱، ص ٦٤.

بلکه از همه‌ی نیروهائی که با شـــعار آزادی به میدان می‌آیند ناامید و مأیوس خواهد گشـــت. نیرو و قدرت ما نیز در گرو اعتماد و ایمان مردم به ماسـت. [...] شـما خوب می‌دانید که توده را همیشـه نمی‌توان به پا خیزاند، و [نهضـت] را همیشـه نمی‌توان به وجود آورد؛ زمینه برای نهضت عظیم توده‌ای همه وقت فراهم نمی‌گردد. [...] امکان امروزی را نباید از دست داد. [...] بگذارید از تهران کـاملاً قطع رابطـه کنیم و حکومت ملیِ‌ی خویش را بـه وجود آوریم. [...] اگر کمـک اتحاد شوروی مخفیانه انجام گیرد، آن گاه در صورت مراجعه‌ی دولت ایران به شورای امنیت، سندی در دست نخواهد داشت.[۳۳۲]

(قلابِ شامل کلمه‌ی «نهضت» از سیروس مددی، مترجم متن است.)

کنسول شوروی در تبریز نیز تلگراف کوتاهی از سوی شخص استالین را برای سران فرقه می‌برد: «انقلاب فراز و نشیب دارد. اکنون باید بدین نشـیب تن در دهید و خود را برای فراز آینده آماده کنید.»[۳۳۳] نصـرت‌الله جهانشـاهلو افشـار (معاون جعفر پیشه‌وری)، در زمینه‌ی مقاومت پیشه‌وری، در برابر این دستور، می‌نویسد:

آقای قلی‌اوف [کنسـول شـوروی در تبریز] در اتاق کوچکی ما را پذیرفت. آقای پیشـه‌وری که از روش ناجوانمردانه‌ی روس‌ها سـخت برآشـفته بود، به سـرهنگ قلی‌اوف پرخاش کرد و گفت شـما ما را آوردید میان میدان و اکنون که سـودتان اقتضـا نمی‌کند، ناجوانمردانه ما را رها کردید؛ از ما که گذشـته اسـت، اما مردمی را که به گفته‌های ما سـازمان یافتند و فداکاری کردند، همه را زیر تیغ داده‌اید. به من بگوئید پاسخگوی این همه نابه‌سامانی‌ها کیست؟ آقای سرهنگ قلی‌اوف که از جسارت آقای پیشه‌وری سخت برآشفته بود، زبانش تپق زد و یک جمله بیش نگفت: «سنی گتـبرن، سنه دییر گت (کسی که تو را آورد، به تو می‌گوید برو.)»[۳۳٤]

و چنین است که پیشـه‌وری و یارانش نیز مانند صدها تن از پیکارگران صـمیمی یا مزدبگیرِ این «فرقه»، به دامان «نجات دهنده‌ی خلق‌های تحت ستم» می‌گریزند، و هزاران تن از مردم آزادی‌خواه آذربایجان و پیکارگرانی که امکان فرار نداشتند یا از دم تیغ ارتش شاهنشاهی ایران می‌گذرند، یا زندان‌های ایران را پر می‌کنند. جعفر پیشه‌وری در باکو نیز آرام نمی‌ماند و علیه سیاست شوروی در مورد «فرقه»، افشاگری می‌کند. استالین، در تاریخ هشتم ماه مه ۱۹۴۷ (۱۳۲۶)- یعنی حدود پنج ماه پس از سـقوط حکومت فرقه در آذربایجان- شـخصـاً نامه‌ای به او می‌نویسـد، و ضـمن شـرح علت بیرون کشـیدن نیروهای شـوروی از ایران، علل عدم حمایت از فرقه را برای او شـرح می‌دهد. بنا بر یادداشت عباس جوادی (مترجم متن از انگلیسـی به فارسـی) این نامه جزء اسـناد «فوق‌العاده محرمانه»ی حزب کمونیسـت بود، که پس از فروریزیِ‌ی اتحاد

---

[۳۳۲] ***درخواست کمک‌های مخفیانه‌ی تسلیحاتی از استالین توسط جعفر پیشه‌وری برای جدا کردن آذربایجان از ایران***، ترجمه از زبان ترکی توسـط سـیروس مددی، گُلن (آلمان): دی ماه ۱۳۸۵، تهیه‌ی نسـخه‌ی P.D.F. نشـر الکترونیکی توسـط وبگاه «تاریخ ایران». برگرفته از: http://aleborzma.wordpress.com/ آخرین بازدید، ۲۴ سپیتامبر ۲۱۰۱۴.

[۳۳۳] بابک امیرخسروی، ***نظر از درون به نقش حزب توده‌ی ایران: نقدی بر خاطرات نورالدین کیانوری***، تهران: انتشارات اطلاعات، ۱۳۷۵، ص ۹۹.

توضیح: بابک امیرخسروی، از متنی استفاده کرده که قبلاً نوشته شده بوده است. اما در حال حاضر، دسترسی به نامه‌ها و تلگراف‌های «شخص استالین» برای مورخان و پژوهشگران غیرممکن است. خسرو شاکری، پژوهشگر تاریخ معاصر ایران، که پس از فروپاشیِ‌ی «اتحاد جماهیر شوروی» به بایگانی‌های شوروی‌ها- بخش مربوط به ایران- دست یافت، در متنی که پیرامون چه‌گونگیِ‌ی تشکیل حزب توده و ارتباط آن با ارتش سرخ، نوشت، تأکید کرده است که «به من گفته شد که تمام مکاتبات استالین در بایگانیِ‌ی ریاست جمهوری است و تاریخ‌شناسان را امکان دست‌یابی به این بایگانی نیست.» به مأخذ زیر نگاه کنید:

❖ خسرو شاکری، ***اندر پایه‌گذاریِ‌ی حزب توده به دست اداره‌ی اطلاعاتِ ارتش شوروی***، بخش دوم، زیرنویس شماره‌ی ٤٦، تارنمای «گویا نیوز»، ۱۱ بهمن ۱۳۹۰:

http://news.gooya.com/politics/archives/2012/01/135345.php

[۳۳٤] **ما و بیگانگان، سرگذشت دکتر نصرت‌الله جهانشاهلو افشار**، پیشین، ص ۲۵۷

شوروی در دسترس عموم قرار گرفت.[۳۳۵] استالین در این نامه، خطاب به «رفیق پیشه‌وری»، به او گوشزد می‌کند که از الگوی لنین مبنی بر تبدیل «خواست‌های انقلابی به خواست‌های عملی» پیروی نکند؛ چرا که شرایط روسیه در سال‌های ۱۹۰۵ و ۱۹۱۷ با «وضع کنونی‌ی ایران کاملاً فرق می‌کند». در بخش‌های دیگری از این نامه می‌خوانیم:

به رفیق پیشه‌وری

به نظر می‌رسد شما در بررسی‌ی وضع داخلی‌ی ایران و همچنین بُعد بین‌المللی‌ی مسئله دچار اشتباه شده‌اید. [...] در ایران هیچ وضع عمیقاً انقلابی موجود نیست. در ایران تعداد کارگران کم است و آن‌ها سازماندهی‌ی خوبی ندارند. دهقانان ایران هنوز فعالیت جدی از خود نشان نمی‌دهند. ایران در حال جنگی بر علیه دشمن خارجی نیست که باعث تضعیف دایره‌های انقلابی (حکومتی؟ - مترجم) از طریق یك شکست نظامی شود. نتیجتاً در ایران شرایطی که کارآمد بودنِ تاکتیك‌های سال های ۱۹۰۵ و ۱۹۱۷ را تأیید کند موجود نیست. ثانیاً: مطمئناً اگر قوای شوروی در ایران باقی می‌ماندند شما می‌توانستید روی موفقیت در امر خواست‌های انقلابی‌ی خلق آذربایجان حساب کنید. اما ما دیگر نمی‌توانستیم نیروهای شوروی را در ایران نگهداریم و آن هم در وهله نخست بدین سبب که ادامه‌ی حضور آن‌ها در ایران بنیاد سیاست‌های آزادسازانه‌ی ما در اروپا و آسیا را مختل می‌کرد. بریتانیائی‌ها و امریکائی‌ها به ما گفتند اگر نیروهای شوروی می‌توانند در ایران بمانند در آن صورت چرا نیروهای بریتانیا در مصر، سوریه، اندونزی، یونان و به همین ترتیب نیروهای امریکا در چین، ایسلند و دانمارك نتوانند بمانند. از این جهت ما تصمیم گرفتیم نیروها را از ایران و چین بیرون ببریم تا این که این بهانه را از دست بریتانیائی‌ها و امریکائی‌ها بگیریم، جنبش آزادی‌بخش در مستعمرات را دامن بزنیم و بدین ترتیب سیاست آزادسازی‌ی خود را حق به جانب‌تر و مؤثرتر نمائیم. [...] ما در این جا شاهد نزاعی بین حکومت قوام و دوایر طرفدار انگلیس در ایران هستیم که نماینده ارتجاعی‌ترین عناصر ایران هستند. قوام در گذشته هر قدر هم که ارتجاعی بوده باشد، باید امروزه برای حفظ خود و حکومتش بعضی اصلاحات دمکراتیك را انجام داده و حمایت نیروهای دمکراتیك ایران را جلب کند. تاکتیك ما در چنین شرایطی چه باید باشد؟ به نظر من ما باید از این نزاع استفاده کنیم تا این که از قوام امتیاز بگیریم، از او حمایت کنیم تا نیروهای طرفدار انگلیس را منزوی نمائیم و زمینه‌ای برای ادامه‌ی دمکراتیزه کردن ایران را مهیا کنیم. تمام توصیه‌های ما به شما مبتنی بر این تشخیص است. البته در پیش گرفتن تاکتیك دیگری هم ممکن بود: تف کردن به همه چیز، قطع رابطه با قوام و با این ترتیب تضمین پیروزی مرتجعین طرفدار انگلیس. اما این دیگر نه یك تاکتیك بلکه حماقت می‌بود. این در واقع خیانت به امر خلق آذربایجان و دمکراسی ایرانی می‌بود. رابعا: طوری که شنیده‌ام شما می‌گوئید که ما شما را ابتدا به عرش اعلا بردیم و سپس به قعر ادنی پرت کرده به شما بی‌احترامی نمودیم. اگر این شنیده‌هایم درست باشد، برای ما جای تعجب است. واقعاً چه اتفاقی افتاده است؟ در این جا ما تکنیکی را به کار برده‌ایم که هر انقلابی با آن آشناست. در هر شرایطی که شبیه شرایط امروز ایران باشد، اگر کسی بخواهد حداقل معینی از طلب‌هائی را از حکومت به دست آورد، در آن صورت جنبش باید به راه خود ادامه دهد، از خواست‌های حد اقل فراتر رود و خطری (فشاری- مترجم) برای حکومت ایجاد کند، تا این که دادن امتیاز از سوی حکومت تأمین گردد. اگر شما خیلی پیش نمي‌رفتید در شرایط کنونی ایران نمي‌توانستید به اهدافی (امتیازاتی- مترجم) نائل شوید که حکومت قوام امروزه ناچار به تأمین آن است. قانون جنبش انقلابی همین است. بی‌حرمتی به شما اصلاً و ابداً مطرح نیست. بسیار عجیب است که شما تصور مي‌کنید ما شما را آلوده به لکه‌ی ننگ و بی‌احترامی کرده‌ایم. بر عکس، اگر شما عاقلانه رفتار کنید و با حمایت معنوی ما خواهان قانونی شدن وضع واقعی

---

[۳۳۵] عباس جوادی، ***نامه‌ی تاریخی‌ی استالین به پیشه‌وری***، مشخصات اصل روسی‌ی سند در آرشیو وزارت خارجه‌ی روسیه: AVP RF, f. 06, op. 7, p. 34, d. 544, ll. 8-9، تارنمای «چشم‌انداز»، ۱۰ دسامبر ۲۰۱۳:
http://cheshmandaz.org/2013/12/10/%d9%86%d8%a7%d9%85%d9%87-%d8%aa%d8%a7%d8%b1%db%8c%d8%ae%db%8c-%d8%a7%d8%b3%d8%aa%d8%a7%d9%84%db%8c%d9%86-

و فعلی در آذربایجان شوید در آن صورت هم آذری‌ها و هم ایران به شما به عنوان پیشاهنگ جنبش مترقی و دمکراتیك در خاورمیانه احترام خواهد گذاشت.
ی. استالین

این نامه، نه تنها استفاده‌ی ابزاری‌ی استالین از «فرقه‌ی دموکرات آذربایجان» و «حزب توده‌ی ایران» را در پیشبرد تاکتیک‌های دست‌یابی به نفت ایران گزارش می‌دهد، بلکه استفاده‌ی ابزاری‌ی اتحاد شوروی از «جنبش‌های آزادی‌بخش در مستعمرات» را- که بعداً به وقوع پیوستند- به تاریخ معرفی می‌کند.

عباس جوادی، مترجم این متن، در انتهای تحلیل خود از نامه‌ی استالین به پیشه‌وری می‌نویسد:

> لازم به توضیح است که سیدجعفر پیشه‌وری تنها حدود یک ماه بعد از این نامه‌ی استالین (یازدهم ژوئن ۱۹٤۷) در یک تصادف ماشین‌سواری در آذربایجان شوروی به قتل رسید. اگرچه هیچ دلیل کافی و مشخصی درباره‌ی سوءقصد بودنِ این حادثه در دست نیست، اما بعضی‌ها بر آنند که دستگاه اطلاعاتی‌ی شوروی از تصادف‌های رانندگی به خصوص در این راه برای قتل مخالفین خود استفاده می‌کرده است.

از همه‌ی این فاجعه‌ها فراتر، سایه‌ی شوم «وابستگی»‌ی فرقه دموکرات آذربایجان و حزب توده است، که تا پایان سلطنت محمدرضا شاه پهلوی بر فراز سر همه‌ی پیکارگران راه آزادی و برابری در ایران، باقی می‌ماند. اگر بابک امیرخسروی، که همواره مخالف جناح وابسته‌ی حزب توده بود، پس از نزدیک به پنجاه سال، به چاپ دوم کتاب «روابط نازی- شوروی» دست می‌یابد، دلیلی در دست نیست که محمدرضا شاه پهلوی، به عنوان پادشاه یک کشور، که با رقبای جهانی‌ی شوروی نیز در ارتباط بود، از چاپ نخست این کتاب و واقعیت‌های مورد اشاره‌اش بی‌خبر مانده باشد، و فرقه‌ی دموکرات آذربایجان را به عنوان فرآورده‌ی هدف‌های شوروی برآورد نکرده باشد. تصادفی نیست که محمدرضا شاه تا پایان سلطنت خود، با چشم بستن بر ستمی که از سوی حکومت مرکزی بر مردم آذربایجان و کردستان می‌رفت، و بی‌توجه به خواسته‌های برحق مردم این استان‌ها، نه تنها مطمئن بود که فرقه و حزب توده وابسته به شوروی بوده‌اند، بلکه دچار این فوبیا بود که همه‌ی کمونیست‌های ایران وابسته به شوروی هستند، و حتا همه‌ی منتقدان او «توده‌ای» و به قول خودش «بی‌وطن» هستند.

اما، در دوازده سال نخست سلطنت محمد رضا شاه پهلوی، فرایندهای دیگری نیز در جریان بود که ظاهراً به «متفقین اشغال‌گر» یا «فرقه‌ی دموکرات آذربایجان» یا «خطر بلشویک‌ها» ربطی نداشت؛ منتها، بر آن چه «آزادی‌های نسبی» نام گرفت تأثیری تعیین‌کننده گذاشت. ناصر پاکدامن، «رضا خان زدائی» را از زمره‌ی مهم‌ترین این فرایندها برآورد کرده است. من، واژه‌ی «شاه» را به جای واژه‌ی «خان» می‌گذارم و با بهره‌گیری از جستار گرامی‌ی او،[۳۳٦] «رضا شاه زُدائی» را به عنوان یکی از مهم‌ترین عواملی که دهه‌ی نخست سلطنت محمدرضا شاه را به دوره‌ی «نسبتاً آزاد» مشهور کرد، شناسائی می‌کنم؛ دوره‌ای با پیامدهای متضاد؛ دوره‌ای که، از نظر عینی، زمینه‌ی ملی کردن نفت ایران را فراهم کرد، و از نظر ذهنی و در درازمدت، زمینه‌ی عقب‌گرد بخش عظیمی از پیکارگران فرهنگی/ اجتماعی/ سیاسی‌ی ما را پدید آورد.

---

[۳۳٦] ناصر پاکدامن، ***قتل کسروی***، چاپ دوم با تصحیحات و اضافات، آلمان: انتشارات فروغ، ۱۳۸۰/ ۲۰۰۱.

به محض خروج رضا شاه پهلوی از ایران، پروژه‌های «رضا شاه زدائی»، نه تنها از سوی همه‌ی ناراضیانِ به حق و ناب‌حق در همه لایه‌های اجتماعی، بلکه از سوی پسرش محمد رضا شاه، شکل اجرائی یافت. گوئی ایران بدون رضا شاه پهلوی، به مثابه‌ی فنر رهاشده‌ای بود که تا منتها درجه‌ی ممکن فشرده شده باشد؛ انگار انرژی‌ی نهفته در این فنر فشرده، مخلوطی (نه آمیزه‌ای) بود از دو ماده‌ی ترکیب ناشدنی. این انرژی، از یک سو، از توقف و انباشت جوششی سرچشمه می‌گرفت که برای رسیدن به «کاروان جهان» جامعه‌ی دوره‌ی مشروطیت را فرا گرفته بود، و از سوی دیگر، از غبنی ناخودآگاه سرچشمه می‌گرفت که در زمان رضا شاه، حافظه‌ی دینی/ مذهبی‌ی ایرانی را آزرده بود. پس از رفتن رضا شاه، از دولتمردان کشور گرفته تا بازار؛ از روحانیت گرفته تا «فرنگ‌رفته‌ها»، از فرهنگیان مستقل گرفته تا سازمان‌های سیاسی؛ از چپ گرفته تا راست؛ از عشایر گرفته تا لایه‌های شهری، بر بند بند و حلقه حلقه‌ی این فنرِ رها شده، در فضاهای اقتصادی، فرهنگی و سیاسی‌ی ایران تاب می‌خوردند و کرده‌های نیک و بد رضا شاه را می‌زودند. حالا، دولتمردان و بازاریان و ثروتمندان کلان، همان‌هائی که رضا شاه راه فساد مالی و زد و بندهای سیاسی/ اقتصادی‌ی آشکار و نهان را بر آن‌ها بسته بود (همان‌هائی که احمد کسروی آن‌ها را «کمپانی‌ی خیانت» نامیده)، در کنار لایه‌ی روحانی، (همان لایه‌ای که رضا شاه بساط نفوذ فرهنگی‌شان را برچیده بود و بساط «اوقاف» و «سهم امام»شان را به خطر انداخته بود)، در کنار روشنفکران سیاسی و نویسندگان معترض (همان‌هائی که در درون و بیرون از زندان قدرت نفس کشیدن از آن‌ها سلب شده بود)، سرکردگان عشایر و خان‌ها (همان‌هائی که تسلط مطلق‌شان بر جان و مال مردم زیر سلطه‌ی خود شکسته بود)، بزرگ مالکان و خرده مالکان و کشاورزان (همان‌هائی که زمین‌شان به تاراج رفته بود)، برای کسب مطالبات معوقه‌ی خود، یک‌جا به پا خاسته بودند. برای آشنائی با همه‌ی جانب‌های این قیام متکثر، خواننده‌ام را به کتاب «قتل کسروی» نوشته‌ی ناصر پاکدامن، به کتاب‌های احمد کسروی، به کتاب «ایران بین دو انقلاب» نوشته‌ی یرواند آبراهامیان، و به کتاب‌های خاطرات سیاسی‌ی مربوط به این دوران رجوع می‌دهم. اما همین جا، به مقتضای هدف کتاب حاضر، بایسته است به چند مورد مؤثر، که به محض خروج رضا شاه از ایران اجرا شد، و زمینه‌ی انقلاب دوم ایران را ساخت، اشاره کنم.

* محمدعلی فروغی، نخستین نخست وزیر محمد رضا شاه پهلوی؛ همان شخصیتی که نخستین نخست وزیر رضا شاه پهلوی هم بود و سپس به بهانه‌ی جانبداری از فساد مالی‌ی بستگانش از درگاه او رانده شد؛ همان که با تنفیذ محمدرضا شاه - به عنوان شاه ایران- در آن دوره‌ی آشوب‌زده از خطر تجزیه‌ی ایران جلوگیری کرد؛ همان که در «کنفرانس تهران» تعهد تخلیه‌ی ایران را به امضاء سران متفقین رسانید؛ همان که دانشکده‌ی حقوق را تأسیس کرد؛ همان که ترجمه‌ها و تألیف‌های او در رشد آگاهی‌ی چند نسل پس از خودش تأثیری انکارناپذیر گذاشت؛ در اعلام سیاست‌گذاری‌های دولت خود می‌گوید: «باید به مسئله‌ی دین هم اهمیت داد. در بیست سال گذشته، یکی هم دین از میان رفت» (پاکدامن، قتل کسروی، ۱۳۸۰، ص ۷۶، به نقل از کتاب «دادگاه» نوشته‌ی کسروی)

* در همان روزها، مجلس دوازدهم که «لایحه‌ی قانونی‌ی جدید اوقاف را در دست بحث و تصویب داشت، آن را از دستور کار بیرون گذاشت.» (پاکدامن، ص ۷۶)،

* «آنان که رخت، دیگر گردانیده بودند، دوباره با عبا و عمامه بازگشتند. آنان که گوشه‌ای خزیده بودند، بیرون آمدند. بار دیگر با قانون‌ها و دانش‌ها و همه‌ی نیک‌ها نبرد آغاز کردند.» (پاکدامن، ص ۷۹، به نقل از «دادگاه» نوشته‌ی کسروی)

* نشریه‌های مذهبی دایر می‌شود.

* «مدارس قدیمه، با معدودی از طلاب که ... به سختی و گرسنگی می‌گذراندند»، احیا می‌شوند. (پاکدامن، ص ۹۳، به نقل از بیانیه‌ی آیت‌الله ابوالقاسم کاشانی)

* حوزه‌های علمیه رونق می‌گیرند.

* آیت‌الله حاج آقا حسین قمی، که در سال ۱۳۱۴ در اعتراض به سیاست‌های فرهنگی‌ی رضا شاه پهلوی، از جمله «کشف

حجاب»، از او اجازه‌ی ملاقات خواسته بود، و «شاه فقید روی نشان نداده بود»، حالا (تیر ماه ۱۳۲۲)، ظاهراً به قصد «زیارت مشهد» از «عتبات عالیات» (بخوانید: «نجف») روانه‌ی ایران می‌شود.[۳۳۷] رهگذر او، شهر به شهر، چراغانی و آذین‌بندی است؛ به طوری که «در تاریخ اسلام کم سابقه است [...و] اگر قربانی‌ی فرزند را اسلام تجویز کرده بود، هزاران فرزند قربانی‌ی مقدمش می‌کردند.» (پاکدامن، ص ۹۲، نقل قول از کتاب «آثارالحجة»). رادیوی رسمی‌ی کشور، در «تجلیل و تکریم» او سنگ تمام می‌گذارد. دولتمردان، بازاریان، و روحانیان، مردم را «به دیدار او فرامی‌خوانند»، تاجران بازار «هزینه‌ی پذیرائی‌ی او را پذیرا می‌شوند»، و حاج آقا حسین قمی، با این جلال و جبروت در این شهر و آن شهر ایران می‌گردد و این جا و آن جا ضمن اعتراض به تمام دستاوردهای مدرن رضا شاه پهلوی، پنج خواسته را مطرح می‌کند و تصویب آن‌ها را از دولت وقت می‌خواهد:

۱- دولت، زنان ایران را در انتخاب حجاب آزاد بگذارد و مجبور به جابه‌جائی نکند.

۲- مدارس مختلط را که به دستور رضا خان در تمام ایران دایر بود، ببندد و نماز در مدارس برگزار کند.

۳- دروس دینی جزو برنامه‌ی دبستان‌ها و دبیرستان‌ها شود.

۴- مردم را از فشار اقتصادی و کمبود غذائی و خواربار نجات دهد که در زحمت نباشند.

۵- حوزه‌های علمیه را آزاد بگذارند و مزاحم طلاب دینی نگردند. (پاکدامن، ص ۹۳، به نقل از «نهضت روحانیون ایران، نوشته‌ی دوانی»)

* چهار خواسته از فهرست خواسته‌های آیت‌الله، به اضافه‌ی موضوع اوقاف- که او در خواسته‌های خود نگنجانیده بود- از تصویب مجلس شورای ملی می‌گذرد و توسط نخست‌وزیر وقت (علی سهیلی) به آگاهی‌ی همگان می‌رسد. (البته، فقره‌ی ۴ از این مطالبات، یعنی، رفع «فشار اقتصادی و کمبود غذائی»ی مردم، که کلیدش به دست تجار و محتکران بازاری است، کماکان مسکوت می‌ماند، و این یا آن آیت‌الله هم با این قضیه درگیر نمی‌شوند.)

* برآورده شدن این خواسته‌ها، روحانیت را به قدرت خود می‌آگاهاند، و به زودی، به ضرب تومارهای طویل از مردم شهرهای مختلف ایران، لزوم چادر و روبنده برای زنان را در جامعه مطرح می‌کنند.

* «دولت در اداره‌ی رادیو، دستگاهی به نام "تبلیغات دینی" بر پا می‌گرداند.» (پاکدامن، ص ۶۰، به نقل از «دادگاه»، کسروی)

* البته روزنامه‌نگاران و پیکارگران در ادامه‌ی کنش‌های آزادی‌خواهانه‌ی دوره‌ی مشروطیت، با روشنگری پیرامون شرایط زندگی‌ی مردم و عملکرد دولتمردان و دین‌کاران، خشم هر دو، به ویژه دین‌کاران را برمی‌انگیزند.

* محمدرضا شاه پهلوی، روز ۲۱ بهمن ۱۳۲۳ برای «عیادت و احوال‌پرسی از آیت‌الله بروجردی» به بیمارستان فیروزآبادی در شهر ری می‌رود. آیت‌الله در فرصت این دیدار، شاه را به رفع «غفلت‌های گذشته» و قلع و قمع روزنامه‌های آزادی‌خواه، که «با کمال شدت و گستاخی همه چیز را مورد تاخت و تاز خود قرار داده و حریم مقدس روحانیت و دین هم از تجاوز آنان مصون و محفوظ نمانده» فرامی‌خواند. «شاه جوانبخت»، به او قول همکاری می‌دهد و برای توفیق در این راه، «از قدرت‌های معنوی‌ی آیت‌الله استمداد می‌نماید.» (پاکدامن، ص ۷۸، نقل قول از «خاطرات زندگی‌ی آیت‌الله العضما آقای بروجردی»)

* محمد رضا شاه، پس از شکست فرقه‌ی دموکرات آذربایجان به تبریز سفر می‌کند، و روز ۶ خرداد ۱۳۲۶ به مدرسه‌ی «طالبیه» (مدرسه‌ی دینی‌ی تبریز) می‌رود تا از تلاش‌های روحانیت در تحریم استفاده از زمین‌های تقسیم شده میان روستائیان و صدور حکم «قتله» (حکم جهاد علیه آزادی‌خواهان تبریز)، از آن‌ها قدردانی کند. جامعه‌ی روحانیان نیز به نوبه‌ی خود، در مجله‌ی «جهان اسلام» با سرمقاله‌ای با عنوان «سلطان تشیع به کانون تشیع می‌رود»، از «شاهنشاه

---

[۳۳۷] عباس میلانی در پژوهش‌های خود یافته است که این آیت‌الله به دعوت مستقیم محمدرضا شاه به ایران آمد. من این سخن را در یکی از برنامه‌های تلویزیونی‌ی عباس میلانی شنیدم، که متأسفانه، نشانی‌ی آن را یادداشت نکردم.

جوانبخت اسلام‌پناه» قدردانی می‌کند.[۳۳۸]
* و بدین ترتیب است که «شاه نجف» و «شاه تهران» یک بار دیگر با هم آشتی می‌کنند، و نشانه‌های آشتی‌ی «مذهب» و «دولت»، تا نوروز ۱۳۴۲ خورشیدی این فهرست را همچنان ادامه می‌دهد. بی‌سبب نیست که در دانشنامه‌ی حوزه‌ی علمیه‌ی قم می‌خوانیم: «نفع آن [قضیه‌ی شهریور ۲۰ و رفتن رضا شاه] برای اسلام و به‌خصوص حوزه‌ی علمیه‌ی قم کم‌تر از نفع آفتاب بر ذرات نبود.» (پاکدامن، ص ۷۹)

این «آفتابِ» هنوز غروب نکرده‌ی دوباره دمیده، این «شاهان نجف»دیده، حالا در «شاه تهران»، و همچنین، در میان دولتمردان وقت، و همچنین، میان مردم مذهبی (در لایه های متفاوت اجتماعی)، آن قدر نفوذ دارند که نه تنها بر ژرفای ذهن ایرانی حکومت می‌کنند، نه تنها بر پوشش زن، نه تنها بر آموزش و پرورش، نه تنها در قلمرو «نشر» نقش تعیین کننده دارند، بلکه کشتار و آزار نواندیشان و دگراندیشان و یهودیان و مسیحیان، و به ویژه بهائیان ایران را نیز در دستور کار دارند، و آن قدر قدرت و فرصت دارند که نشسته در بارگاه‌های حوزوی‌ی خود، هر زمان که اراده کنند، به کمک لشگریان پیاده و سواره (مردم مذهب‌زده‌ی کوچه و خیابان و ماشین تروری به نام فدائیان اسلام، و دولتِ دین‌مدار) هر یک از این برنامه‌ها را با یک فتوا به اجرا بگذارند. مثال بارز این نوع فتواها را در کتاب «کشف‌الاسرار- ۱۳۲۳» نوشته‌ی روح‌الله خمینی (که هنوز به درجه‌ی «آیت‌الله»ی هم نرسیده بود) می‌بینیم. او در این کتاب، فرمان «رضا شاه زدائی» را با جمله‌هائی مانند «**باید حتا قانون‌هائی که در زمان او** [رضا شاه] **از مجلس گذشته، اوراقش را سوزاند و محو کرد**»،[۳۳۹] صادر می‌کند، و نخستین گام او به سوی «محو» دیکتاتوری، نه به سود آزادی‌ی بیان و اندیشه، بلکه به سود دیکتاتوری از نوع مذهبی است:

> یکی از چیزهایی که نیازمند به اصلاح است، همین روزنامه و مجلات و هفتگی‌هاست که امروز به این صورت اسف‌آور است و در حقیقت بعضی از آن‌ها را باید کانون پخش فساد اخلاق و فحشا گفت، برای نشر بی‌عفتی‌ها و افسارگسیختگی‌ها هیچ چیز امروز بیش‌تر از این اوراق ننگین کمک کاری نمی‌کند. (پیشین، ص ۲۸۳)

روح‌الله خمینی بلافاصله پس از انتشار این کتاب، در نخستین بیانه‌ی زندگی‌ی خود، با عنوان «بخوانید و بکار بندید» (اردی‌بهشت ۱۳۲۳)- که آن هم بعداً به صورت یک جزوه منتشر شد- فرمان تدارک برای تشکیل «لشگر حزب‌الله» را صادر می‌کند:

> امروز روزی است که نسیم روحانی‌ی الاهی وزیدن گرفته و برای قیام اصلاحی بهترین روز است. اگر مجال را از دست بدهید و قیام برای خدا نکنید و مراسم دینی را عودت ندهید، فرداست که مشتی هرزه گرد شهوتران بر شما چیره شوند و تمام آیین و شرف شما را دستخوش اغراض باطله‌ی خود کنند.[۳۴۰]

---

[۳۳۸] سیروس مددی، ***دیدار شاه با روحانیون آذربایجان پس از سرکوب نهضت ۲۱ آذر- خرداد ۱۳۲۶*** ، برگرفته از تارنمای «آذربایجان آنلاین» توسط تارنمای «سبز یعنی وطن»، ۷ خرداد ۱۳۸۹.

[۳۳۹] روح‌الله خمینی، جزوه‌ی کشف‌الاسرار را در پاسخ به رساله‌ی «اسرار هزار ساله» (۱۳۲۲)، نوشته‌ی علی‌اکبر حکمی‌زاده، نوشت. حکمی‌زاده ، که خود «طلبه»ای بود در فیضیه‌ی قم، در این رساله، اصول شیعه و مکتب کلامی و فقهی‌ی آن را به باد انتقاد گرفته بود. نگاه کنید به :

❖ روح‌الله خمینی، ***کشف‌الاسرار***، بی‌جا، نشر ظفر، ۱۳۲۳، ص ۲۱٤. **توضیح:** من متن چاپی‌ی این کتاب را ندیده‌ام. نشانی‌ی مأخذ الکترونیکی‌ی آن به قرار زیر است:

http://www.4shared.com/document/yq_WIvtx/__online.html

[۳۴۰] **صحیفه‌ی نور**، جلد ۱، ص ۲۳.

کم‌تر از یک سال پس از این بیانیه است که طلایه‌ی لشگر حزب‌الله با تشکیل «جمعیت فدائیان اسلام»، با شعار «کشتن و کشته‌شدن در راه اسلام»، اعلام حضور می‌کند (۱۳۲۴)، و با قتل احمد کسروی، نخستین مأموریت خود را به انجام می‌رساند (اسفند ۱۳۲۴). قاتل احمد کسروی (سیدحسین امامی) به دستور «آقایان علماء» و با وساطت نخست‌وزیر وقت (قوام‌السلطنه) و وزیر دربارِ «مدرن» و نوگرای وقت (عبدالحسین هژیر) آزاد می‌شود؛[۳۴۱] آزاد می‌شود، تا چندی بعد خودِ عبدالحسین هژیر را در مراسم سوگواری‌ی عاشورا در مسجد سپهسالار تهران به ضرب یک گلوله به قتل رسانَد. (۱۳ آبان ۱۳۲۸) و چنین است که در انتخابات مجلس شانزدهم، از ۵۰ عضو در «سازمان نظارت بر انتخابات»، ۲۵ نفر آنان از جمعیت فدائیان اسلام هستند.

***

سهم قدرتی که به نفع مذهب و روحانیت در قانون اساسی‌ی مشروطه گنجانده شد، در کنار پتانسیلی که لایه‌ی روحانیت برای حفظ و گسترش نفوذ خود در میان مردم محروم از سواد و آگاهی داشت، در کنار رسوب جان‌سخت آموزه‌های مذهبی در ذهنیت بسیاری از پیکارگران نوسازی‌ی ایران (از جمله، نواب صفوی، بنیادگذار جمعیت فدائیان اسلام و عامل اصلی‌ی قتل احمد کسروی، و از جمله، عبدالحسین هژیر، دولتمرد نوگرائی که عامل اصلی‌ی آزادی‌ی قاتل احمد کسروی شد)، در کنار زد و بندهای آشکار و نهان دولتمردان، زمینداران، و بازاریان کلان کشور، مرتباً در همان آزادی‌های نسبی‌ی دهه‌ی نخست پادشاهی‌ی محمدرضا شاه پهلوی اخلال می‌کرد. قتل احمد کسروی، پژوهشگر، مورخ، و منتقد سیاسی/ اجتماعی، با حکم تکفیر مجتهدان، در روز روشن و در کاخ دادگستری‌ی پایتخت ایران، توسط گروه «فدائیان اسلام»، و این که قاتل او از زندان آزاد شد، و این که هیچ گورستانی دفن پیکر کسروی را نپذیرفت، و این که فقط چند نشریه به قتل کسروی و آزادی‌ی قاتلان او اعتراض کردند، تنها یکی از نشانه‌های ذهنیت مذهبی‌ی دولتمردان (از جمله خود محمدرضا شاه پهلوی) ایران و روزنامه‌نگاران مستقل یا سازمانی، و قدرت‌نمائی‌های روحانیت در آن دوازده سال بود.[۳۴۲] البته دشمنی‌ی روحانیت با احمد کسروی، و سکوت دولت و رسانه‌های وقت در قبال قتل او، تنها به خاطر نظرات

---

[۳۴۱] ایرج اسکندری، یکی از رهبران حزب توده و وزیر پیشه و هنر در کابینه‌ی قوام‌السطنه، در خاطراتش نوشته است: «قتل کسروی قبل از این که ما وارد کابینه شویم انجام گرفته بود. در کابینه‌ی ائتلافی‌ی قوام‌السلطنه که ما شرکت داشتیم قبلاً قاتل کسروی را گرفته بودند. امامی [قاتل کسروی] توقیف بود و شبی در جلسه‌ی هیئت وزیران، قوام‌السلطنه به عادت مألوف کاغذی درآورد و نشان داد که آقایان علماء نوشته و حاکی از آن بود که تقاضا کرده‌اند امامی را که در توقیف می‌باشد مرخص نمایند. لذا عقیده‌ی آقایان وزراء را می‌پرسید. [عبدالحسین] هژیر بلافاصله گفت به عقیده‌ی من صحیح است و باید موافقت نمود که این فرد از زندان آزاد شود. من اجازه‌ی صحبت خواستم و گفتم در روز روشن و در دادگاه و با حضور قاضی و دیگران، يك آدمی را زده و با کارد شکمش را پاره کرده و کشته‌اند. حالا حکم توقیف این فرد را دادستان و قاضی داده‌اند و من نمی‌فهمم ما در هیئت وزیران چه‌گونه می‌توانیم در این مسئله دخالت کنیم. [...] گفتم بنابراین معلوم نیست چرا يك چنین مطلبی در هیئت وزیران باید مطرح بشود؟ هژیر اظهار داشت که نخیر آقا، بنده عقیده دارم که این آدم مهدورالدم بوده و اگر هم او را کشته‌اند کار صحیحی بوده (يك همچو عبارتی). من اوقاتم تلخ شد. گفتم یعنی چه آقا؟ مهدورالدم یعنی چه؟ و تازه تشخیص آن با چه کسی است؟ هژیر جواب داد با خود شخص! گفتم اگر این جوره بنده هم تشخیص می‌دهم که شما مهدورالدم هستید و همین الان اگر اجازه بدهید شکم شما را سفره بکنم چون به قول شما تشخیص آن با خود من است. قوام‌السلطنه محکم زد زیر خنده. گفتم این که قانون نشد، مذهب نشد. شما يك فرد تحصیل‌کرده‌ای هستید و از شما بعید است که در قرن بیستم يك همچو حرف‌هائی می‌زنید. مهدورالدم یعنی چه؟ ما قانون جزاء، قانون مجازات داریم و تمام اصول محاکماتی را معین کرده‌اند برای این که ما دیگر از این حرف‌ها نزنیم...قوام‌السلطنه گفت بسیار خوب. و قضیه را مسکوت گذاشتند. و بعد از این که ما از کابینه بیرون آمدیم و موسوی‌زاده را وزیر دادگستری کردند، فوری این‌ها را مرخص نمودند.» به مأخذ زیر نگاه کنید:

- ❖ ***خاطرات ایرج اسکندری، دبیر اول حزب توده (۱۳۴۹ - ۱۳۵۷)***، تهران: ویراستار و ناشر: مؤسسه‌ی مطالعات و پژوهش‌های سیاسی، چاپ سوم، ۱۳۸٤، صص ٦٠ تا ٦١. **توضیح**: این کتاب حاصل خاطرات شفاهی‌ی ایرج اسکندری است که توسط خسرو امیرخسروی و فریدون آذرنو از روی نوار پیاده شده است.

[۳۴۲] ناصر پاکدامن، پژوهشگر زندگی و مرگ احمد کسروی، می‌نویسد: «در ۸ اردی‌بهشت ۱۳۲٤، به زندگی‌ی احمد کسروی سوءقصد شد. سوءقصدکنندگان نواب صفوی و احمد خورشیدي بودند. نواب صفوی از پشت سر به کسروی دو بار تیراندازی کرد و سپس با کارد به او حمله آورد و وی را به سختی زخمی کرد. در ۲۰ اسفند همان سال زمانی که بازپرس شعبه‌ی هفت دادسرای تهران، بلیغ، که رسیدگی به شکایت علیه کسروی را برعهده داشت، وی را به بازپرسی به کاخ دادگستری خواسته بود، گروهی از جمله دو برادر، سیدحسین و سیدعلی امامی، به دفتر بلیغ ریختند و کسروی و منشی وی حدادپور را کشتند.» ناصر پاکدامن، همچنین، حکم دادگاه مبنی بر آزادی‌ی قاتلان کسروی را در این چند جمله خلاصه کرده است: «فرشته‌ی عدالتِ آن دوران، نواب صفوی و خورشیدیان را به هنگام ضرب و جرح کسروی دنبال نکرد، و پس از قتل کسروی نیز برادران امامی و یاران را آزاد کرد، و چنین حکم داد که کسروی و همراهش با گلوله‌های خطارفته‌ی سلاح‌های خویش کشته شده‌اند.» باز به گفته‌ی ناصر پاکدامن، تنها نشریاتی که به قتل کسروی و حکم دادگاه برای آزادی‌ی قاتل او اعتراض کردند، نشریه‌ی «رهبر» (ارگان حزب توده‌ی

کسروی پیرامون اسلام و شیعه‌گری نبود. کسروی- که با همه‌ی دین‌ها و مذهب‌های سازمان‌یافته درافتاده بود- در راستای دفاع از وحدت و یگانگی، و برای از بین بردن نفاق و نفرت بین گروه‌های مختلفِ ملت ایران، از حقوق مدنی‌ی پیروان همه‌ی دین‌ها و مذهب‌ها- از جمله بهائیان- و از حقوق اقلیت‌های قومی در کاربرد زبان‌شان دفاع می‌کرد. در شانزده اصلی که کسروی به عنوان هدف‌های حزب خود- یعنی «آزادگان» (یا: «باهماد آزادگان»)- اعلام کرده بود، افزون بر لزوم حکومتی استوار بر «نمایندگی» و «قانون»مندی با موازین قانون اساسی «برای جلوگیری از استبداد»؛ افزون بر لزوم آموزش به مردم پیرامون حقوق شخصی و اجتماعی و ثروت‌های ملی؛ افزون بر لزوم توسعه‌ی صنعت و تجارت و اقتصاد و بهداشت عمومی؛ هم بر لزوم مبارزه با تفرقه‌های عقیدتی پا فشرده بود، و هم بر «سهم» هر شهروند «از اقتصاد» – «بر اساس امتیاز او و کار او»- تأکید کرده بود.[۳۴۳] همچنین، در نوشته‌های احمد کسروی هم به مبارزه‌ی او علیه «تقلید از ساختارهای مدنی/ فرهنگی‌ی اروپا» برمی‌خوریم و هم به مبارزه‌ی او علیه «فلسفه‌ی مادی» و دیگر «تندرو»انی که «زندگی را به عنوان میدان جنگ تصور می‌کنند».[۳۴۴] بنا بر این آراء بود که نه تنها روحانیت، بلکه هم اروپامحوران ایران، و هم چپ ایران (که در آن زمان عمدتاً با حزب توده نمایندگی می‌شد) با احمد کسروی مرزبندی داشتند.

با این همه، پیامد منطقی‌ی همان آزادی‌های نسبی در همان دهه، در جریان «نهضت ملی کردن نفت ایران» خود را به مشاهده‌ی تاریخ گذاشت. با اوج‌گیری‌ی همین جریان بود که زندگی و نام محمدرضا شاه پهلوی با زندگی و نام محمد مصدق، تا پایان عمرِ هر دو ، به هم گره خورد؛ و به گونه‌ای گره خورد، که بررسی‌ی زندگی‌ی سیاسی‌ی هیچ یک از آن‌ها، بدون بررسی‌ی زندگی‌ی سیاسی‌ی آن دیگری امکان‌پذیر نیست.

***

جنبش ملی‌کردن نفت ایران: گرچه ایده‌ی ملی کردن نفت ایران به نام دکتر محمد مصدق و جبهه‌ی ملی به ثبت تاریخ رسید، اما خواست و لزوم آن، سال‌ها پیش از اجراء، فضای سیاسی‌ی ایران را آکنده بود، و با هر تلنگری زنده‌تر و کاراتر می‌شد. قرارداد «گس- گلشائیان»، به عنوان ضمیمه‌ی قرارداد اصلی‌ی سال ۱۳۱۲، یکی از همان تلنگرها بود. این قرارداد، که در برابر افزایشی جزئی به سهم ایران، تمدید قرارداد را مطالبه می‌کرد، در ۲۶ تیر ۱۳۲۸، زمان نخست وزیری‌ی ساعد مراغه‌ای، بین عباسقلی گلشائیان (وزیر دارائی) و سِر نویل گس (نماینده‌ی بریتانیا) امضاء شد و در هفته‌های پایانی‌ی مجلس پانزدهم برای تصویب به مجلس رفت.[۳۴۵] بحث بر سر این قرارداد، بین اقلیت مخالف و اکثریت

ایران)، «ایران ما» (روزنامه‌ای با یاری‌ی روشنفکران و نویسندگانی با مواضع چپ و همکارانی از اعضاء حزب توده)، و نشریه‌ی «سخن»، بود. پاکدامن می‌نویسد: «نخستین کنگره‌ی نویسندگان ایران هم که از ۳ تا ۵ تیرماه ۱۳۲۵ در خانه‌ی فرهنگ شوروی برگزار شد، از [کنار] این قتل به سکوت گذشت.» به مأخذ زیر نگاه کنید:

- ناصر پاکدامن، ***قتل کسروی، چند سند***، فصل‌نامه‌ی «چشم‌انداز»، چاپ پاریس، شماره‌ی ۱۶، بهار ۱۳۷۵، صص ۱۱۳ تا ۱۳۰.

[۳۴۳] احمد کسروی، به عنوان بنیادگذار حزب «آزادگان»، این شانزده اصل را طی‌ی یک سخنرانی اعلام کرد، و متن آن نیز در روزنامه‌ی «پرچم»، ارگان حزب «آزادگان»، منتشر شد. به مأخذ زیر نگاه کنید:

- Mohammad Ali Jazayery, ***Kasravi, Iconoclastic Thinker of Twentieth-Century Iran***, in Ahmad Kasravi, On Islam and Shi'ism, Translated from Persian by M. R. Ghanoonparvar, California: Mazda Publishers, 1990, pp. 11-12.

[344] Ibid, P.16.

[۳۴۵] روز ۲۶ تیر ۱۳۲۸، بین وزیر دارایی‌ی دولت وقت ایران (عباسقلی گلشائیان) و نماینده‌ی کمپانی‌ی نفت انگلیس («گس») قراردادی به امضاء رسید که به معاهده «گس ـــ گلشائیان» معروف شد، و قراردادی الحاقی بود به پیمان‌نامه‌ی سال ۱۳۱۲، که در زمان رضا شاه پهلوی بین ایران و انگلستان بسته شده بود. به موجب این معاهده، ایران در مقابل فروش هر تُن نفت، به جای ٤ شلینگ قبلی ٦ شلینگ دریافت می‌کرد. فروش نفت در داخل ایران نیز ۲۵ درصد ارزان‌تر از فروش آن در خارج از کشور تعیین شد. ضمناً شرکت نفت ایران و انگلیس موظف بود مبلغ ۵ میلیون لیره استرلینگ یک‌جا به ایران بپردازد. در مقابل این تعهداتِ انگلستان، دولت ایران نیز موظف شد تعهدات امتیاز سال ۱۳۱۲ را دوباره تأیید کند. این پیمان ، زیر فشار نمایندگان اقلیت (از جمله دکتر محمد مصدق و آیت‌الله کاشانی)، نه تنها در مجلس‌های پانزدهم و شانزدهم به تصویب نرسید، بلکه به تدریجی شتابنده، فکر ملی کردن صنعت نفت ایران را، که از مدت‌ها پیش در فضای سیاسی‌ی ایران برانگیخته شده بود، نیرو بخشید. به گفته‌ی دکتر مصدق، نخستین کسی که پیشنهاد ملی کردن نفت ایران را مطرح کرد، دکتر حسین فاطمی بود. (البته نام خسرو اقبال

موافق، مجلس پانزدهم را متشنج کرد، و آن قدر ادامه یافت تا مجلس پانزدهم پایان یافت. شاه در مدت کوتاهی دو نخست وزیر عوض کرد؛ و سپهبد حاج‌علی رزم آرا، دومین آن‌ها بود (۵ تیر ۱۳۲۹). او نیز با مخالفت ملی‌گرایان در مجلس شانزدهم، که اینک به «ملی کردن نفت» می‌اندیشیدند، نتوانست به مسئله‌ی این قرارداد سر و سامان دهد. نظر رزم آرا پیرامون ملی کردن نفت را شاید بتوان در این جمله‌ی او خلاصه کرد که: «ایران نمی‌تواند یک لولهنگ بسازد، چه طور می‌خواهد صنعت نفت را اداره کند!» (نقل از حافظه‌ی دوردستِ کودکی.) رزم آرا روز ۱۶ اسفند ۱۳۲۹ توسط عضوی از فدائیان اسلام (خلیل طهماسبی) ترور شد، و در دم جان سپرد. کم‌تر از دو هفته بعد، دکتر محمد مصدق، نماینده‌ی تهران و رئیس کمیسیون نفت در مجلس شانزدهم، به پیشنهاد دکتر حسین فاطمی و حمایت گروهی از ملی‌گرایان، لایحه‌ی «ملی کردن صنعت نفت ایران» را به مجلس داد. این لایحه، که فقط به نفت جنوب مربوط نبود و «تمام مناطق کشور بدون استثناء» را شامل می‌شد، در روزهای ۲۴ و ۲۹ اسفند ۱۳۲۹ به تصویب مجلس‌های شورای ملی و سنا رسید. بنا بر این قانون، ایران با پذیرش پرداخت غرامتِ دارائی‌های شرکت نفت، «شرکت نفت ایران و انگلیس» را منحل اعلام کرد، و با تصویب قانون «خلع ید»، کارکنان انگلیسی‌ی آن باید از ایران اخراج می‌شدند (۱۰ اردیبهشت ۱۳۳۰)؛ و شدند. دکتر محمد مصدق در سال ۱۳۳۰ به نخست وزیری رسید و اجرای این قانون را (به اضافه‌ی اصلاح قانون انتخابات) در دستور کار دولت خود قرار داد. با ادامه‌ی دسیسه‌ی نمایندگان بریتانیا در ایران، دکتر مصدق روابط دیپلماتیک ایران با بریتانیا را قطع کرد (۳۰ مهر ۱۳۳۱). تحریم خرید نفت از ایران، که توسط دولت‌های غربی- در رأس آن‌ها انگلستان و امریکا- انجام گرفت، و توسط «اتحاد جماهیر شوروی» هم عملاً تأیید شد، اقتصاد کشور را به مخاطره انداخت. دکتر مصدق، با وجود کارشکنی‌های نمایندگان طرفدار بریتانیا در مجلس، کوشید تا در غیاب درآمد نفت، با اصلاحات اقتصادی و با مشارکت مردم، ایران را برپا نگه‌دارد. بدین ترتیب دکتر مصدق، افزون بر پیکار در جبهه‌ی خارجی، مدام در تلاش برای تأمین بودجه از یک سو، خنثا کردن کارشکنی‌های نمایندگان طرفدار بریتانیا، از سوی دیگر، و محدود کردن اختیارات شاه، از سوی سوم بود، که او را به مطالبه‌ی درآمدهای دربار و شخص شاه (مثل درآمدی که از «آستان قدس رضوی» یا از فروش املاکش به کشاورزان داشت) هم کشید. دخالت ارتش در امور انتخاباتی‌ی کشور سبب شد که دکتر مصدق، هم الحاق وزارت جنگ به دولت را از شاه مطالبه کند، و هم اختیار طرح و تصویب و اجرای لوایحی که خود و دولتش صلاح می‌دانند برای مدت شش ماه از مجلس مطالب کرد. شاه درخواست واگذاری‌ی وزارت جنگ به او را نپذیرفت؛ و مصدق، به جای باز کردن دیالوگی همدلانه با شاه، به ویژه در کوران مبارزه با استعمار، با پشتوانه‌ی حمایت مردم و آیت‌الله کاشانی، در ۲۵ تیر ماه ۱۳۳۱ از مقام نخست وزیری استعفا داد. شاه نیز، به جای باز کردن دیالوگی همدلانه با مجلس و با دولت مصدق و با مردم ایران، استعفای او را پذیرفت، و به توصیه و با فشار انگلستان، احمد قوام‌السطنه را به نخست وزیری برگزید. با اعلامیه‌ی جبهه‌ی ملی، و همیاری‌ی حزب توده، انبوه طرفداران مصدق در شهرهای بزرگ ایران به خیابان‌ها ریختند، و فریاد «یا مرگ یا مصدق» فضای ایران را آکند. دولت قوام، به دنبال چهار روز دستگیری و ضرب و شتم تظاهرکنندگان، روز ۳۰ تیر ماه ۱۳۳۱، به روی انبوه مردم، که حالا با حکم «جهادِ» آیت‌الله ابوالقاسم کاشانی انبوه‌تر شده بودند، آتش گشود.[۳۴۶] شاه، پس از چند روز به ناگزیر، با شرط دکتر مصدق موافقت

و عباس اسکندری، به عنوان مطرح کننده‌ی این پیشنهاد، بسی پیش‌تر ار نام دکتر فاطمی در مآخذ آمده است.) در هر حال، دکتر حسین فاطمی، صاحب امتیاز و سردبیر نشریه‌ی «باختر امروز»، عضو برجسته‌ی جبهه‌ی ملی، نماینده‌ی تهران در مجلس شورای ملی، و وزیر امور خارجه‌ی دولت مصدق بود. او پس از کودتای ۲۸ مرداد اعدام شد.

[۳۴۶] در این زمینه به دو مأخذ زیر مراجعه کنید:

- حمید شوکت، ***در تیررس حادثه: زندگی‌ی سیاسی‌ی قوام‌السطنه***، تهران: نشر اختران، ۱۳۸۵، صص ۲۷۵ تا ۳۰۳.
- خسرو شاکری زند، ***استالین و ترومن: غروب شوکت قوام‌السطنه، حضرت اشرف: نقدی بر تاریخ‌نگاری‌ی ایدئولوژیک***، تارنمای «میلیونیوم»، بازدید ۱۰ خرداد ۱۳۹۰:

http://www.melliun.org/ketab/k10/ketabeghawam.htm

توضیح: پیرامون دوره‌های پنج‌گانه‌ی نخست‌وزیری‌ی احمد قوام، متن‌های فراوانی نوشته شده است، که از میان آن‌ها، شاید تنها متنی که به طرفداری، یا بهتر است گفته شود، به اعاده‌ی حیثت این شخصیت چندرویه‌ی تاریخ معاصر ایران پرداخته است، کتاب «در تیررس حادثه»، نوشته‌ی حمید شوکت باشد. برخی از تاریخ‌پژوهان دیدگاه این کتاب را ستودند و بسیاری نیز به آن تاختند. اکثر مخالفان این کتاب، البته به کمبود

کند و او را به نخست وزیری بازگرداند. مجلس شورای ملی نیز اختیارات شش ماهه به مصدق را – به رغم مغایرت با قانون اساسی- تصویب کرد؛ و در جلسه‌ی ۱۶ دی ماه ۱۳۳۱ یک بار دیگر به او رأی اعتماد داد. اما هنوز یک ماه به پایان اختیارات شش ماهه باقی مانده بود، که دکتر مصدق تمدید یک ساله‌ی اختیارات را از مجلس خواست (۱۸ دی ماه ۱۳۳۱). در کنار مجموعه‌ای از فعالیت‌های عوامل خارجی، این درخواست، افزون بر نمایندگان طرفدار شاه و نمایندگانی که به سود امریکا و انگلستان با مصدق مخالفتی دائمی داشتند، بین حزب‌ها و گروه‌های جبهه‌ی ملی و طرفداران مصدق نیز شکاف انداخت.

از سوی دیگر، پس از تصویب قانون ملی کردن نفت ایران، بریتانیا حاضر نشد حق ایران در حاکمیت بر نفت و نظارت بر درآمدهای آن را بپذیرد، و افزون بر غرامت دارائی‌های خود در شرکت نفت، درآمد سال‌های آینده تا پایان قرارداد را مطالبه کرد. از این رو، دکتر مصدق به همه‌ی پیشنهاداتِ سودجویانه‌ای که از سوی بریتانیا و با وساطت امریکا برای حل مسئله‌ی نفت مطرح شد، پاسخ منفی داد. مذاکرات حضوری‌ی او با رئیس جمهور امریکا (ترومن- ۲۳ تا ۲۶ مهر ۱۳۳۰ در واشنگتن) و بعد، با سفیر و نمایندگان رئیس جمهور بعدی (آیزنهاور) برای کسب حمایت و دریافت وام از امریکا نیز به جائی نرسید. دکتر مصدق در همین حال بود که از سوی نمایندگان طرفدار شاه و بریتانیا و گروهی از طرفدارانِ بریده‌ی خودش در مجلس هفدهم نیز در محاصره بود. روز ۹ اسفند ۱۳۳۱، خانه‌ی دکتر مصدق مورد حمله‌ی گروهی از اوباش قرار می‌گیرد که با چاقو و چماق به قصد کشتن مصدق رفته بودند. مصدق از مهلکه می‌گریزد، و در مجلس شورا اقامت می‌گزیند و به شاه ۴۸ ساعت وقت می‌دهد که نخست وزیر دیگری برگزیند، و گرنه موضوع حمله به خانه‌اش را با ملت در میان خواهد گذاشت. روز بعد آیت‌الله بروجردی، طی بیانیه‌ای اظهار امیدواری می‌کند که «بین اعلیحضرت و نخست وزیر وحدت نظر برقرار شود.» این پیام، در کنار ناآرامی‌های سراسر کشور، مجلس را به چاره‌جوئی وامی‌دارد، و فراکسیون‌های مخالف با یکدیگر را به هم نزدیک می‌کند. از هر فراکسیون، نمایندگانی برای دیدار و مذاکره با مصدق و شاه انتخاب می‌شوند. این «هیئت هشت نفره» گزارشی را به امضاء شاه و مصدق می‌رسانند و آن را برای تصویب به «ساحت مقدس مجلس شورای ملی» می‌برند. دکتر عباس توفیق (حقوقدان و خبرنگار پارلمانی‌ی نشریه‌ی توفیق در مجلس‌های شانزدهم و هفدهم) پس از درج گزارش این رویداد در مقاله‌اش، می‌نویسد:

> با این گزارش، در حقیقت نمایندگان تمام گروه‌های مختلف، اعم از طرفداران مصدق، یا طرفداران شاه، یا طرفداران آیت‌الله کاشانی تأیید کردند که «شاه سلطنت می‌کند نه حکومت.» تصویب این گزارش، که موجب تسجیل و تثبیت چند اصل مهم متمم قانون اساسی‌ی ایران بود، یکی از پیروزی‌های بزرگ دموکراسی و «حکومت مردم» به شمار می‌رفت و ایران

منابع دست اول، و ارجاع نویسنده به متن‌های نامعتبر با این کتاب برخورد کرده‌اند. از جمله، منوچهر بختیاری، داده‌های این کتاب پیرامون حضور قوام در دوره‌ی انقلاب مشروطه را زیر ذره بین برده و برداشت‌های حمید شوکت را نادرست دیده است. اما گسترده‌ترین نقدی که بر این کتاب نوشته شد، از سوی خسرو شاکری زند بود که بخش‌هائی از آن در رسانه‌های الکترونیکی منتشر شد. خسرو شاکری زند، این نوع تاریخ‌نگاری را «ایدئولوژیک» نامیده، «مبانی‌ی ارجاع مؤلف» را به زیر سئوال برده، و در فصل‌های مختلف کتابِ ««استالین و ترومن: غروب شوکت قوام‌السطنه، حضرت اشرف»»، عملکرد سیاسی‌ی قوام را از شهریور ۲۰ تا دوره‌ی مورد بحث (۳۰ تیر ۱۳۳۱) بررسیده، و سیمائی از قوام را نشان داده است که با سیمای ترسیمی‌ی حمید شوکت مغایرت دارد. منتها، صرف نظر از گرایش آشکار حمید شوکت در ستایش یا تطهیر قوام و نفی‌ی شخصیت‌هائی مانند حسن تقی‌زاده، و گذاشتن تلویحی‌ی بار مسئولیت خونریزی در روز ۳۰ تیر ۱۳۳۱ بر دوش دکتر مصدق، در کتاب او مدارکی هست که خواننده می‌تواند از ورای مجموعه‌ی آن‌ها، هم با ویژگی‌های قوام آشنا شود و هم نمائی از زمینه‌های سیاسی/ اجتماعی و پیامدهای آخرین دور نخست وزیری‌ی او بدست آورد. به باور من، مشکل کتاب «در تیررس حادثه» در همان جانبداری‌ی حمید شوکت نهفته است که به ضرب و زور اسناد گزینشی و عبارت‌هائی مانند «چنین به نظر می‌رسد»، باورهای نویسنده را به خواننده تحمیل کرده است. اما اهمیت کتاب در این است که یک شخصیت سیاسی را به گونه‌ای کالبدشکافی کرده است، که در رهگذر آن، شرایط فرهنگی/ مذهبی‌ی حاکم بر سپهر سیاسی‌ی ایران، به ویژه در دوره‌ی «نهضت ملی کردن نفت» نیز ترسیم شده است؛ شرایطی که، نقشه‌های عینی و ذهنی‌ی بروز «حکومت اسلامی» را پیش روی خواننده باز می‌کنند. به بیانی دیگر، صرف نظر از موضوع «قوام‌السطنه»، با خواندن کتاب «در تیررس حادثه»، به ویژه فصل هشتم آن، خواننده درمی‌یابد که «انقلاب اسلامی» پدیده‌ای ناگهانی نبوده و آبشخور داخلی‌ی آن نیز چیزی جز ذهنیت مذهبی‌ی اکثر نخبگان سیاسی‌ی ما نبوده است.

را در عداد یکی دیگر از کشورهای مترقی‌ی مشروطه‌ی سلطنتی‌ی جهان قرار می‌داد. سیاست‌هائی که موفقیت خود را در اختلاف شاه و مصدق می‌دانستند [...] برای جلوگیری از مطرح شدن و تصویب آن در مجلس شورای ملی به هر عمل خلاف شنیع و حتا هر جنایتی دست زدند و با تمام امکانات مالی و غیرمالی‌ی خود به توطئه پرداختند. [...] هر بار در جلسه‌ی علنی، با جنجال، توهین، فحاشی، سیلی زدن، عینک شکستن، مشت و لگد زدن، شکستن سر و خونین کردن صورت، و حتا حمله به رئیس مجلس برای پائین کشیدن او از پشت میز ریاست مجلس، جلسات مجلس را به هم می‌زدند. دشمنان دولت دکتر مصدق، برای متزلزل کردن دولت او و تقویت روحیه‌ی مخالفانش، حتا اقدام به ربودن و قتل رئیس شهربانی‌ی مملکت [سرتیپ محمود افشارطوس] کردند.[۳۴۷]

همزمان با این کشمکش‌ها در مجلس شورای ملی، حمله‌های بی‌امان نشریات خریداری شده، به مصدق و دولت او به اوج رسید؛ اکثر این متن‌ها به وسیله‌ی تبلیغات سیا نوشته می‌شد. ریچارد کاتم، یکی از این تبلیغگران، می‌نویسد:

چهار از پنج روزنامه‌ای که در تهران منتشر می‌شد، زیر نفوذ سیا بود. [...] هر مقاله‌ای که می‌نوشتم، تقریباً فوراً، روز بعد در مطبوعات ایران ظاهر می‌شد. این مقاله‌ها طراحی شده بودند که مصدق را کمونیست و فناتیک نشان دهند.»[۳۴۸]

از سوی دیگر، بلواها و ناامنی‌هائی بود که عوامل بریتانیا و امریکا در ایران، «به نام حزب توده» در تهران و برخی از شهرهای ایران ایجاد می‌کردند، که پس از شکست کودتای اول به اوج رسید. مازیار بهروز، تاریخ‌پژوه و استاد دانشگاه سانفرانسیسکو، در ضمن شرح جست‌وجوهای بی‌نتیجه‌ی خود پیرامون این پدیده- یا «تظاهرات سیاه»- در یک مصاحبه می‌گوید:

نکته‌ی خیلی تاریکی در مورد کودتا هست و آن چیزی است که به نام «تظاهرات سیاه» معروف است. تظاهرات سیاه، یعنی این که سیا پول بدهد به یک عده که خودشان را در نقش جبهه‌ی ملی یا حزب توده دربیاورند و به نمادهای سلطنت حمله کنند. بعد این عده، مردم و توده‌های واقعی را به صحنه بکشانند و نشان بدهند جنبش بعد از شکست مرحله‌ی اول کودتا، چنان تند و رادیکال شده که کنترل دارد از دست مصدق خارج می‌شود. در گزارش‌هائی که الان آمده و در خیلی از مصاحبه‌ها با افراد درگیر کودتا، گفته شده که سیا حدود ۵ هزار دلار برای این تظاهرات هزینه کرد. بنابراین، این تظاهرات سیاه به عنوان یک موفقیت بزرگ برای امریکا تعبیر می‌شود. [...] من در این قسمت از جریان کودتا علامت سئوال می‌گذارم. تاریخ سرانجام پاسخ خواهد داد.[۳۴۹]

نشریه‌ی «انقلاب اسلامی در هجرت»، پس از نقل کامل این بخش از سخنان دکتر مازیار بهروز، می‌نویسد:

---

[۳۴۷] دکتر عباس توفیق، ***درباره‌ی قانونی بودن یا نبودن فرمان عزل دکتر مصدق***، نشریه‌ی ره آورد، شماره‌ی ۷۹، تابستان ۱۳۸٦/ ۲۰۰۷، صص ۱۱۷ تا ۱۱۹. **توضیح**: سرتیپ محمود افشارطوس، از «افسران ملی» و از طرفداران سرسخت دکتر مصدق بود. او روز ۳۱ فروردین ۱۳۳۲ طی یک توطئه ربوده شد و روز ٦ اردی‌بهشت ۱۳۳۲ پیکر شکنجه‌شده‌ی او را در غار «تلو» در حوالی‌ی لشگرک تهران یافتند. در رابطه با این قتل تعدادی از افسران بازنشسته‌ی ارتش بازداشت و زندانی شدند، و در بازجوئی‌ها، سرنخی از حضور مظفر بقائی، حتا شاه، در این ماجرا بدست آمد. اما کودتای ۲۸ مرداد همان سال دررسید، زندانیان این ماجرا آزاد شدند، و قضیه‌ی این قتل هم تا سال‌ها سر به مهر باقی ماند.

[348] Stephen Ki nzer, ***All the Shah's Men: An American Coup and the Roots of Middle East Terror***, New Jersey: John Wiley & Sons, Inc., 2nd. ed. 2008, p. 6.

[۳۴۹] دکتر مازیار بهروز این مصاحبه را در تاریخ ۲۸ مرداد ۱۳۸۳ با «گروه فرهنگ» انجام داده است. به مأخذ زیر نگاه کنید:

- نشریه‌ی الکترونیکی‌ی «انقلاب اسلامی در هجرت»، شماره‌ی ٦۰۱، بازدید ۱۰ مهر ۱۳۸۹:

http://goto.glocalnet.net/banisadr_arkiv/matn1-601.htm

[...] غیر از تظاهراتی که به نام حزب توده در تهران ، به قصد زمینه‌سازی‌ی کودتا به راه انداختند و بسیار مهم‌تر از آن، نوشتن نامه‌ها به روحانیان شهرهای ایران بود. این کار را روضه‌خوان‌های تحت امر [آیت‌الله] بهبهانی انجام می‌دادند؛ به قصد ایجاد وحشت در روحانیان و بر انگیختن‌شان بر ضد مصدق؛ نامه‌ای تهدید آمیز («با استقرار جمهوری‌ی توده‌ای، دست‌های شما را که عوام نادان می‌بوسند قطع خواهیم کرد»، «عمامه‌های شما را طناب دار شماها می‌کنیم» و...) . بعد از کودتا بود که برخی - و نه همه‌ی آن‌ها - از واقعیت آگاه شدند. بر این کار افزوده می‌شود شایعه‌پراکنی و «مدرک»سازی درباره‌ی قصد حزب توده به کودتا بر ضد حکومت مصدق، و برقراری‌ی «جمهوری‌ی توده‌ای» بر اساس شعاری که حزب توده می‌داد؛ عوامل دربار تمبرهای جمهوری‌ی توده‌ای را چاپ نیز کردند. می‌دانیم که ملاتاریا همین روش را از دوران انقلاب تا امروز بکار می‌برند (از آتش زدن سینما رکس آبادان و به پای ساواک نوشتن تا انفجار حزب جمهوری اسلامی و ترورها که به پای «اختلافات درون گروهی» نوشته شده و می‌شوند و... تا تظاهرات ۲۱ تیر ۱۳۷۸ را به حساب دانشجویان گذاشتن و ...)[۳۵۰] (پرانتزها در متن اصلی وجود دارند.)

«مارک گزیوروسکی Mark Gasiorowski » استاد علوم سیاسی و پژوهشگر تاریخ سیاسی، در بازتاب نسبت به مقاله‌ای که نشریه‌ی نیویورک تایمز در ۱۶ آوریل ۲۰۰۰ پیرامون اسناد آرشیو شورای امنیت ملی‌ی امریکا منتشر کرد، مقاله‌ای نوشت و در آن، به «حزب توده‌ی قلابی» (fake Toudeh Party)، که توسط سازمان سیا ساخته شده بود، اشاره کرد. او در این مقاله نوشت:

مقاله‌ی نیویورک تایمز و اسنادی که منتشر کرده، پیرامون دو نکته‌ی مورد مناقشه چیزی نمی‌گوید. از جمله این که آیت‌الله کاشانی در سازمان‌دهی‌ی جمعیت‌های خیابانی [۲۸ مرداد ۳۲] دست داشته است، و دیگر این که تیم سیا، حزب توده‌ی «قلابی» را برای گردآوری‌ی جمعیت‌های خیابانی سازمان داده بود.[۳۵۱]

در چنین فضائی بود که کارشکنی‌های روزافزون نمایندگان مخالف یا مخالف‌شده در مجلس بالا گرفت و بعداً به استیضاح مصدق هم رسید؛[۳۵۲] و فکر «انحلال» مجلس را در دکتر مصدق نیرو بخشید. او، روز ۹ اسفند ۱۳۳۱ در جلسه‌ی غیرعلنی‌ی مجلس موضوع انحلال مجلس را مطرح کرد. این پیشنهاد مورد مخالفت اکثریت نمایندگان قرار گرفت. با این وصف، دکتر مصدق که تنها راه چاره را در انحلال مجلس می‌دید، یک بار روز ۴ تیر ماه ۱۳۳۲ و یک بار ۲۳ تیر ۱۳۳۲ در جلسه‌ای در خانه‌ی خود، موضوع رفراندم برای انحلال مجلس هفدهم را با نمایندگان فراکسیون نهضت ملی در میان گذاشت، و با این که نظر او هر دو بار از سوی همه، حتا یاران و مشاوران خودش، رد شد، رفراندم را روز ۱۲ مرداد ۱۳۳۲ انجام داد؛ و انحلال مجلس، از سوی مردم نیز تصویب شد. و این در حالی بود که تدارک کودتا از سوی فرستاده‌ی سیا و کارگزاران ایرانی‌اش، و چندی از امیران ارتش انجام شده بود و روز ۲۵ مرداد ۱۳۳۲ به اجرا گذاشته شد؛ که البته خبر آن پیشاپیش به مصدق و دولتمردانش رسیده بود، و با هشیاری‌ی آن‌ها عملیات کودتا ناکام ماند، و برخی از عوامل آن دستگیر شدند. اما این پایان ماجرا نبود. سازمان‌های اطلاعاتی‌ی بریتانیا و امریکا، به یاری‌ی مأموران خود و مأمورانی که در میان ایرانیان داشتند، و با تبانی‌ی برخی از امیران ارتش که طرفدار شاه بودند، یا با «دلار» طرفدار شاه شده بودند، و با دستیاری‌ی گروه‌های مذهبی (عمدتاً، طیف آیت‌الله کاشانی که حالا به بهانه‌ی «خطر کمونیسم برای

---

۳۵۰ نشریه‌ی الکترونیکی‌ی «انقلاب اسلامی در هجرت»، شماره‌ی ۶۰۱، بازدید ۱۰ مهر ۱۳۸۹:
http://goto.glocalnet.net/banisadr_arkiv/matn1-601.htm

351 Professor Mark Gasiorowski, ***What's New on the Iran 1953 Coup in New York Time Article (April 16, 2000 front page) and the Documents Posted on the Web***, April 19, 2000:
http://www.gwu.edu/~nsarchiv/NSAEBB/NSAEBB28/

۳۵۲ دولت دکتر مصدق در ۱۵ تیر ماه ۱۳۳۲ از سوی علی زهری، نماینده‌ی مجلس، استیضاح شد.

اسلام»، علیه مصدق برخاسته بود و از سوی کودتاچیان نیز- برای اجیر کردن اوباش- پول گرفته بود)،[۳۵۳] روز ۲۸ مرداد ۱۳۳۲- در کمال ناباوریِ مردم ایران- دولت دکتر مصدق را سرنگون کردند.[۳۵۴] خسرو شاکری (زند) در متنی پیرامون «کودتای ۲۸ مرداد»،[۳۵۵] در زمینه‌ی موفقیت این کودتا، به نقش حزب توده و نفوذ «جاسوسان بریتانیا در کمیته‌ی مرکزیِ این حزب، اشاره می‌کند و می‌نویسد:

یکی از دلایل موفقیت کودتای ۲۸ مرداد این است که بلافاصله پس از شکست کودتا در ۲۵ مرداد، به دنبال یک اعلامیه‌ی مفصل کمیته‌ی مرکزیِ حزب توده درباره‌ی کودتا، ارگان علنیِ آن حزب، یعنی «به سوی آینده»، مشخصاً توجه را از تکرار کودتا در پایتخت منحرف کرد.

خسرو شاکری در ادامه‌ی سخن، از سرمقاله‌ی همان هفته‌ی نشریه‌ی «شجاعت» (که به جای «به سوی آینده» منتشر می‌شد) به شرح زیر نقل قول می‌کند:

بعد از این که توطئه‌ی کودتا در مرکز مواجه با شکست شد، صحنه‌ی فعالیت عمال آن‌ها که هنوز دستگیر نشده‌اند به شهرستان‌ها منتقل گردید. به قرار اطلاعی که به دست آوردیم، یکی از صحنه‌های مهم این فعالیت خوزستان است. فرمانده‌ی لشکر خوزستان سرتیپ مغروری که با کودتاچیان در تهران ارتباط دارد، به دستور آن‌ها در صدد است که آشوبی در این استان حساس و مهم کشور ایجاد کند و با اعلام استقلال خوزستان برای ساقط کردن دولت وارد عمل شود. اخبار دیگری نیز حکایت می‌کند که سرلشکر زاهدی، به اصطلاح نخست وزیر شاه خائن، هم بعد از این که در تهران دچار ورشکستگی گردید عازم خوزستان گردیده است، تا در آن جا به اتفاق سرتیپ مغروری و با کمک‌هایی که می‌تواند از مناطق [زیر] تسلط انگلیسی‌ها، یعنی بصره، کویت، و بحرین به دست آورند به توطئه‌ی خائنانه‌ی خود ادامه دهند.... قرار است شاه فراری هم از خارج به اهواز وارد شود تا حکومتی را که استعمارگران با سرکوبیِ استقلال و حاکمیت ملیِ ما برای او تهیه می‌بینند، تحویل بگیرد.[۳۵۶] (نقطه‌چین از خسرو شاکری است.)

خسرو شاکری با توجه به شرایط حاکم بر «سازمان افسریِ حزب توده»، این «اطلاعات» را «نادرست» می‌داند و می‌نویسد:

[...] اعلامیه‌ی کمیته‌ی مرکزیِ حزب توده و متعاقب آن سرمقاله‌ی ارگان علنیِ آن حزب به راستی یک تاکتیک انحرافی بود که جاسوس(های) بریتانیا در سطحِ کمیته‌ی مرکزی به اجرا گذاشتند. [...] مطمئناً، نمی‌توان

---

[353] Stephen Ki nzer, ***All the Shah's Men: An American Coup and the Roots of Middle East Terror***, New Jersey: John Wiley & Sons, Inc., 2nd. ed. 2008, p. 178.

[۳۵۴] نشریه‌ی «نیویورک تایمز» در سال ۲۰۰۰ میلادی بخشی از اسناد سازمان سیا را منتشر کرد که شرکت سازمان‌های اطلاعاتیِ امریکا و انگلیس در کودتای ۲۸ مرداد ۱۳۳۲ و سرنگونیِ دولت دکتر مصدق را تأیید می‌کرد. در این زمینه، افزون بر مآخذی که بعداً به دست خواهم داد، به دو مأخذ زیر نگاه کنید:

* دکتر غلامرضا وطن دوست، ***اسناد سازمان سیا*** (دو زبانه)، تهران: انتشارات رسا، ۱۳۷۹.

* یرواند آبراهامیان، ***ملی شدن نفت- کودتا و دیوار بی‌اعتمادی***، ترجمه‌ی جعفر خیرخواهان، در کتاب: محمد جعفر محمدی، «راز پیروزیِ کودتای ۲۸ مرداد،» کلن: انتشارات فروغ، تاریخ (؟)، تاریخ پیش‌گفتار ۱۳۸۲، صص ۱۶۹ تا ۲۱۲.

[۳۵۵] خسرو شاکری (زند) ***یادداشتی پیرامون کودتای ۲۸ مرداد و پلنوم چهارم حزب توده به سال ۱۳۳۶ - ۱۹۵۷***، تارنمای «گویا نیوز»، ۲۸ مرداد ۱۳۹۲:

http://news.gooya.com/politics/archives/2013/08/165450.php

[۳۵۶] شجاعت، به جای به سوی آینده، شماره‌ی ۱۹- ۲۸ مرداد ۱۳۳۲، [گروه پژوهش] جامی، گذشته چراغ راه آینده، ص ۶۸۶.

> ادعا کرد که این دو اطلاع غلط از سوی سازمان افسری‌ی حزب رسیده بوده باشند؛ پس، چه کسی مسئول این تاکتیک انحرافی در کمیته‌ی مرکزی بود؟ هنوز قطعاً نمی‌دانیم؛ اما این مسئول(ان) نمی‌توان(ند) جز جاسوس(ان) بریتانیا در کمیته‌ی مرکزی بوده باش(ن)د.

همین جاست که موضوع مرموز «حزب توده‌ی قلابی» به یاد می‌آید و این گمانه را نیرو می‌بخشد که کلِ کمیته‌ی مرکزی‌ی حزب توده در آن برش تاریخی، همانا همان «حزب توده‌ی قلابی» بوده است.

***

شاه که پس از شکست کودتای اول و پیش از به ثمر رسیدن کودتای دوم ایران را ترک کرده بود و امیدی به بازگشت خود نداشت، در هتل محل اقامتش در رُم خبر موفقیت کودتای دوم را شنید و- بنا بر یک روایت- گفت:

> Everyone who is not a communist is favorable to my stand. (هر کس که کمونیست نیست، طرفدار من است.)[۳۵۷]

و- بنا بر روایت دیگر- گفت:

> I knew it! I knew it! They love me! (می‌دانستم! می‌دانستم! آن‌ها مرا دوست دارند.)[۳۵۸]

هر دوی این روایت‌ها در واقع یک سخن می‌گویند؛ سخنی که بعدها نیز با عبارت‌های «رستاخیز ملی» و «قیام ملی» توسط شاه و اطرافیانش تکرار شد. این سخن، بدان معناست که مصدق کمونیست بود و تنها کمونیست‌ها بودند که با او سر مخالفت داشتند. انگار نه انگار که مسئله‌ی نفت و ملی کردن آن، به عنوان یک آرزو برای ملت ایران مطرح بوده است. این سخن، حتا اگر به فرمان «سیاست» ابراز شده باشد، باز از توهم و خودفریبی‌ی محمدرضا شاه پهلوی (که از چه‌گونگی‌ی روند کودتا خبر داشت)، و در شناخت پایگاه خودش در میان ملت خودش نشانی می‌دهد. البته، بخش بزرگی از بازار و طبقه‌ی متوسط سنتی، عمدتاً به خاطر مخالفت شخصیت‌های روحانی، و شعارها و تبلیغات گسترده‌ی حزب توده (یا به نام حزب توده)، و تبلیغات منفی علیه مصدق که به طور روزمره و سیل‌آسا از سوی سازمان‌های اطلاعاتی‌ی امریکا و بریتانیا به نشریه‌های رسمی‌ی ایران دیکته می‌شد، از دولت مصدق دلسرد شده بودند؛ اما بدون تردید، جمعیتی که روز ۲۸ مرداد ۳۲، اکثراً با چوب و چماق و قمه، سوار بر تانک‌های شِرمن (از پادگان سلطنت‌آباد) و کامیون‌های ارتش، خیابان‌های تهران را اشغال کردند و خانه‌ی مسکونی‌ی دکتر مصدق را ویران کردند و اموال شخصی‌ی او را به تاراج بردند، همه‌ی «آن‌ها»، یعنی همه‌ی ملت ایران نبودند. در هر حال، شاه، با امضاء قرارداد «کنسرسیوم» و با به رسمیت شناختن سهم «شرکت نفت ایران و انگلیس» و چند کمپانی‌ی امریکائی و اروپائی، بر کوشش‌های مصدق و یارانش و بر آرزوی میلیون‌ها ایرانی‌ی آزادی‌خواه خط بطلان کشید؛ استقلال سیاسی و اقتصادی‌ی ایران را آشکارا گرو گذاشت؛ پویش

---

[۳۵۷] بنا به گزارش عباس میلانی (بر مبنای اسناد سفارت انگلستان در تهران)، «زمانی که تلگراف موفقیت کودتا، توسط گزارشگر اسوشیتد پرس به شاه داده شد. رنگ شاه پرید، دست‌هایش به گونه‌ای می‌لرزید که نمی‌توانست متن تلگراف را بخواند. ناباورانه پرسید: " می‌تواند حقیقت داشته باشد؟" و تکرار کرد: "این شورش نیست، این حکومت من است که به قدرت برمی‌گردد. هر کس که کمونیست نیست طرفدار من است." دیری نگذشت که تلگرافِ ژنرال زاهدی، نخست وزیر جدید را دریافت کرد که او را در اسرع وقت به بازگشت به ایران فرامی‌خواند.» به مأخذ زیر نگاه کنید:

❖ Abbas Milani, ***The Shah***, New York: Palgrave Macmillan, 2011, p. 189.

[۳۵۸] Stephen Kinzer, ***All the Shah's Men***, New Jersy: John Wiley & Sons, Inc., 2008, p. 184.

طبیعیِ رشد و تکوین تاریخیِ ملت ایران را منحرف کرد؛ و خواسته یا ناخواسته، داغی همیشگی بر روان ملت و تاریخ ایران کاشت.[۳۵۹]

روز ۲۸ مرداد ۳۲، نیروهای کودتا نهادهای دولتی و ارتش را یکی پس از دیگری تسخیر کردند، و آن گاه بود که فرمان عزل مصدق و نصب سپهبد زاهدی (به عنوان نخست وزیر) چند بار از رادیوی رسمی کشور پخش شد. در شامگاه این روز، در پیِ حملهی گروه خریداریشدهی اوباش به سرکردگیِ شعبان جعفری («شعبان بیمخ»)، که پس از کودتا با عنوان «تاجبخش» شناسائی شد)[۳۶۰] به خانهی مسکونیِ دکتر مصدق، نخست وزیر مورد تأییدِ ۹۳/ ۹۹ درصد مردم تهران در رفراندم ۱۲ مرداد ۳۲،[۳۶۱] همراه با چند تن از یارانش که تا پایان با او مانده بودند، دیوار به دیوار و بام به بام گریخت، به خانهای پناهنده شد، و پیش از موعدِ اعلام شده، خود را به دولت کودتا معرفی کرد. اما پادشاه ایران، دکتر محمد مصدق، این فسادناپذیرترین و غیرقابل خریدترین شخصیت سیاسیِ ایران معاصر را- که با همهی ضعفها و اشتباهات احتمالی در تاکتیکِ مبارزه- برای حفظ منافع ایران یک تنه در برابر قدرت استعماری/ امپریالیستیِ بریتانیا قد علم کرده بود، در دادگاه لاهه این غول را شکست داده بود، در مورد امتیاز نفت شمال در برابر شوروی ایستاده بود، علیه او به ائتلاف با حزب توده تن نداده بود، و به نظام مشروطهی ایران وفادار بود و از شاه میخواست که فقط «سلطنت» کند و «حکومت» را به مردم واگذارد، مانند یک خیانتکار یا یک جنایتکار جنگی، در دادگاه نظامی محاکمه کرد، و او را پس از سه سال زندان انفرادی، تا پایان زندگی در روستای احمدآباد به اسارت گرفت، و با ممنوع کردن نام و یاد و تصویر او در رسانهها، کوشید که موجودیت او را از حافظهی جمعی بزداید.[۳۶۲] غافل از این که از همین تاریخ، خودِ او، مشروعیت

---

[۳۵۹] روز 22 فروردین ۱۳۳۳ تشکیل کنسرسیوم بینالمللی، برای فروش نفت ایران، اعلام شد، و ۲۲ نفر از نمایندگان ۸ کمپانیِ نفتیِ امریکایی، انگلیسی، هلندی و فرانسوی وارد تهران شدند. در تیر ۱۳۳۳ مذاکرات دولت با کنسرسیوم پایان گرفت. در ۲۸ شهریور همان سال، قرارداد بین دکتر علی امینی و «هوارد پیج» رئیس گروهی که نمایندگیِ کمپانیهای نفتی را برعهده داشتند در تهران امضاء شد، و فردای آن روز شرکتهای آمریکائی در نیویورك آن را امضاء کردند. در ۲۹ مهر مجلس هجدهم که انتخابات آن را حکومت زاهدی برگزار کرده بود، قرارداد را (که در لندن و به زبان انگلیسی تهیه شده بود و بعد به زبان فارسی ترجمه شده بود) تصویب کرد. قرارداد سپس در ٦ آبان، به تصویب سنا رسید و در بهمن همان سال؛ بهرهبرداریِ وسیع از نفت ایران توسط کنسرسیوم غربی آغاز شد. طبق پیمان کنسرسیوم، ٤٠ درصد سهام نفت ایران متعلق به ٥ کمپانیِ آمریکائی، ٤٠ درصد متعلق به شرکت نفت ایران و انگلیس، ١٤ درصد متعلق به یك کمپانیِ هلندی و ٦ درصد باقیمانده متعلق به یك کمپانیِ فرانسوی بود. از نظر درآمدهای نفتی، ایران ٥٠ درصد عایدات نفت را دریافت میکرد. اما فقط نفت نبود. به موجب قرارداد کنسرسیوم کمپانیهای یادشده اجازه یافتند در هر نقطهی ایران عملیات اکتشاف و استخراج را با هزینه دولت ایران انجام دهند. این کمپانیها همچنین اختیارات وسیعی در بندرها، راه آهن، سرویس تلفن و تلگراف و بیسیم و هواپیمائیِ ایران بدست آوردند. طبق این قرارداد، حوزهی امتیاز و شعاع عملیات کنسرسیوم شامل قسمتی از خاك بلوچستان، قسمت جنوبیِ استان کرمان، تمام استان فارس، قسمت جنوبیِ استان اصفهان، سراسر استانهای خوزستان و لرستان، بروجرد، ملایر، صفحات جنوبیِ استان کرمانشاه، جزایر خارك، کیش، قشم، هرمز، شعیب، هنگام ،و چند جزیرهی کوچكتر در جنوب کشور بود. البته، در قرارداد «کنسرسیوم دوم» که در سال ۱۳۵۲ (۱۹۷۳) ، بین ایران و ١٤ کمپانیِ غربی، و به مدت دو سال، بسته شد، گسترهی عملیات حفاری یا ساختمانیِ این کمپانیها به میزان قابل توجهی کاهش یافت.
برای نگارش «قرارداد کنسرسیوم»، پس از تطبیق اطلاعات با کتاب عبدالرضا هوشنگ مهدوی، از نوشتهی مؤسسهی مطالعات و پژوهشهای سیاسی سود بردهام:
قرارداد کنسرسیوم، تارنمای «مؤسسهی مطالعات و پژوهشهای سیاسی»، بازدید ۱۱ بهمن ۱۳۸۹:
http://www.ir-psri.com/Show.php?Page=ViewArticle&ArticleID=139

- ❖ عبدالرضا هوشنگ مهدوی، ***سیاست خارجی ایران در دوران پهلوی***، تهران: نشر البرز، ۱۳۷۳.
- ❖ نفت از آغاز تا امروز، تهران: انتشارات وزارت نفت، بهمن ۱۳۶۱.

[۳۶۰] هما سرشار، **شعبان جعفری**، چاپ دوم، لسانجلس: نشر ناب، ۱۳۸۱.

[۳۶۱] در رفراندومی که روز ۱۲ مرداد ۱۳۳۲ به پیشنهاد دکتر مصدق برای انحلال مجلس، در تهران انجام شد، ۹۳/ ۹۹ درصد رأیدهندگان به انحلال مجلس رأی دادند. گزارش مربوط به نتیجهی این رفراندوم، در سند شمارهی ٤ از مجموعهی آرشیو شورای امنیت ملیِ امریکا، در تارنمای «انقلاب اسلامی در هجرت»، شمارهی ٦٠١ منتشر شده است:
http://goto.glocalnet.net/banisadr_arkiv/matn1-601.htm

[۳۶۲] برای آگاهی از این نقطهی شوریده از تاریخمان، خوانندهام را به منابع زیر- که با دیدگاههای مختلف (له و علیه مصدق) پیرامون «نهضت ملی کردن نفت» و کودتای ۲۸ مرداد، و محاکمات دکتر مصدق نوشته شدهاند- رجوع میدهم:

- ❖ همایون کاتوزیان، ***مصدق و مبارزه برای قدرت در ایران***، ترجمهی فرزانه طاهری، چاپ سوم، تهران: نشر مرکز، ۱۳۷۸. **توضیح:** کتابی با عنوان «مصدق و نبرد قدرت»، به ترجمهی احمد تدین، توسط نشر خدمات فرهنگیِ رسا، در سال ۱۳۷۰ نیز منتشر شده است. من این کتاب را ندیدهام و تفاوت آن را با ترجمهی فرزانه طاهری نمیدانم.

سلطنت را در دل و جان مردم ایران- به گونه‌ای بازگشت‌ناپذیر- از دست داده است.

نظر برخی از تحلیل‌گران تاریخ این دوره بر این است که شاه با ایده‌ی کودتا مخالف بود، و پیش از خروج از ایران، طی دو یادداشت جداگانه دکتر مصدق را از مقام نخست وزیری عزل کرده بود، و سپهبد زاهدی را به جای او برگزیده بود؛ در نتیجه دولت دکتر مصدق روز ۲۸ مرداد ۳۲ دولتی غیرقانونی بود. بنا بر خاطرات کرمیت روزولت (مأمور سیا برای انجام کودتا)، و بنا بر اسناد منتشر شده‌ی «آرشیو شورای امنیت ملی‌ی امریکا»،[۳۶۳] این درست است که شاه با کودتا موافق نبود؛[۳۶۴] این هم درست است که برگه‌هائی با عنوان «فرمان»‌های عزل مصدق و نصب زاهدی با امضاء شاه در دست مجریان کودتا وجود داشت. اما این نیمه‌واقعیت‌های تاریخی، نظر تحلیل‌گرانی را که در نفی‌ی «کودتا» بودنِ رویداد ۲۸ مرداد ۱۳۳۲ و در اثبات غیرقانونی بودن دولت مصدق، بر آن انگشت گذاشته‌اند، مستدل نمی‌کنند.[۳۶۵] در کتاب کرمیت روزولت می‌خوانیم زمانی که تمام کوشش‌های سیا برای جلب رضایت شاه به کودتا و امضاء فرمان‌ها بی‌نتیجه می‌مانَد،[۳۶۶] روزولت در دیداری پنهانی، شاه را از تبدیل ایران به «یک کشور کمونیستی، یا مانند کشور کُره»، می‌ترسانَد

- غلامرضا نجاتی، ***مصدق: سال‌های مبارزه و مقاومت***، دو جلد، تهران: انتشارات رسا، ۱۳۷۶؛ ***جنبش ملی شدن صنعت نفت ایران و کودتای ۲۸ مرداد ۱۳۳۲*** ، تهران: شرکت سهامی‌ی انتشار، چاپ هشتم، ۱۳۷۸.
- یرواند آبراهامیان، ***ملی شدن نفت- کودتا و دیوار بی‌اعتمادی***، ترجمه‌ی جعفر خیرخواهان، در کتاب: محمد جعفر محمدی، «راز پیروزی‌ی کودتای ۲۸ مرداد،» کلن: انتشارات فروغ، تاریخ (؟)، تاریخ پیش‌گفتار ۱۳۸۲، صص ۱۶۹ تا ۲۱۲.

توضیح: اصل این مقاله به زبان انگلیسی منتشر شد، و بازتاب یرواند آبراهامیان است نسبت به اسناد منتشرشده‌ی سیا توسط نیویورک تایمز در زمینه‌ی کودتای ۲۸ مرداد، در آوریل و ژوئن ۲۰۰۰. ترجمه‌ی این مقاله ابتدا در نشریه‌ی «آفتاب» شماره‌ی ۱۳، اسفند ۱۳۸۰ منتشر شد، و محمد جعفر محمدی نیز آن را با عنوان «پیوست شماره‌ی ۱» به کتاب خود افزوده است. اصل این مقاله را در مأخذ زیر بخوانید:
Ervand Abrahamian, ***The 1953 Coup in Iran***, science & Society, Vol. 65, No. 2, Summer 2001, pp. 182-215: http://www.webcitation.org/5kg6nFIXE

- بهزاد کاظمی، ***ملی‌گرایان و افسانه‌ی دموکراسی: کارنامه‌ی مصدق در پرتو جنبش کارگری و دموکراسی‌ی سوسیالیستی***، لندن: نشر نظم کارگر، ۱۹۹۹.
- جلال متینی، ***نگاهی به کارنامه‌ی سیاسی‌ی دکتر محمد مصدق: تحقیق***، لس‌انجلس: انتشارات شرکت کتاب، ۱۳۸٤.
- علی میرفطروس، ***آسیب‌شناسی‌ی یک شکست (از انقلاب مشروطه به انقلاب اسلامی)***، مونترآل: انتشارات فرهنگ، ۲۰۰۸.
- دکتر محمد مصدق، ***خاطرات و تألمات دکتر محمد مصدق***، به کوشش ایرج افشار، چاپ دوم، لندن: انتشارات جبهه: نشریه‌ی ملیون ایران، تاریخ انتشار (؟).
- جلیل بزرگمهر، ***دکتر مصدق در دادگاه نظامی***، تهران: شرکت سهامی‌ی انتشار، ۱۳۶۵؛ ***دکتر مصدق در دادگاه تجدید نظر***، تهران: شرکت سهامی‌ی انتشار، ۱۳۶۵.
- ماشاءالله ورقا، ***ناگفته‌هائی پیرامون فروریزی‌ی حکومت مصدق و نقش حزب توده‌ی ایران***، تهران: انتشارات بازتاب نگار، ۱۳۸٤.
- محمدعلی موحد، ***خواب آشفته‌ی نفت: دکتر مصدق و نهضت ملی‌ی ایران***، دو جلد، تهران: نشر کارنامه، چاپ دوم، ۱۳۸٤.
- Mark J. Gasiorowski, ***U.S. Policy and the Shah: Building a Client State in Iran***, New York: Cornell University Press, 1991.
- ***Mohammad Mosaddeq and the 1953 Coup in Iran***, Edited by Mark J. Gasiorowski and Malcolm Byrne, Syracuse University Press, 2004.
- Abbas Milani ,***The Shah***, New York: Palgrave Macmillan, 2011, Chapters 9 & 10, PP. 141- 202.

[363] Dr. Donald Wilber, ***CIA Clandestine Service History, "Overthrow of Primier Mossadeq of Iran, November 1952- August 1953"***, March 1954, Electronic Briefing Book No. 28: http://www.gwu.edu/~nsarchiv/NSAEBB/NSAEBB28/#documents

[364] Jamse Risen, ***Secrets of History: The C.I.A. in Iran***, in New York Times on the web, April 16 2000: http://www.nytimes.com/library/world/mideast/041600iran-cia-index.html

[۳۶۵] به عنوان نمونه از این گونه آثار، به کتاب‌های زیر مراجعه کنید:
- سپهر ذبیح، ***ایران در دوره‌ی دکتر مصدق: ریشه‌های انقلاب ایران***، ترجمه‌ی محمد رفیعی مهرآبادی، تهران: نشر آشیانه‌ی کتاب، ۱۳۸۱.
- علی میرفطروس، ***آسیب‌شناسی‌ی یک شکست (از انقلاب مشروطه به انقلاب اسلامی)***، مونترآل: انتشارات فرهنگ، تاریخ انتشار (؟).
- جلال متینی، ***نگاهی به کارنامه‌ی سیاسی‌ی دکتر محمد مصدق***، لس‌انجلس: انتشارات شرکت کتاب، ۱۳۸٤.

[۳۶۶] بنا بر کتاب «ضدکودتا: تلاش برای کنترل ایران» نوشته‌ی کرمیت روزولت (صص ۱٤٦-۱٤۷) سیا برای راضی کردن شاه به امضاء فرمان‌های عزل مصدق و نصب زاهدی، اشرف پهلوی را برای راضی کردن برادرش از پاریس به تهران می‌فرستد. اما ترغیب اشرف پهلوی نیز در شاه مؤثر نمی‌افتد. واشنگتن/ سیا، ژنرال نورمن شوارتسکف را به ایران می‌فرستد. مذاکرات شوارتسکف با شاه هم بی‌نتیجه می‌ماند. به گفته‌ی استفان کینزر در کتاب «همه‌ی مردان شاه»: «شاه مطمئن نبود که [در جریان کودتا] ارتش از او حمایت کند.» (ص ۸) بنا بر گفته‌ی روزولت: «شاه از جنگ ویرانگر داخلی» اظهار نگرانی می‌کرد. (ص ۱٤۷) بنا به گفته‌ی کینزر، روزولت اسدالله رشیدیان را با این پیام نزد

و می‌گوید اگر شاه به کودتا رضایت ندهد، سیا «با طرح دیگری» وارد عمل خواهد شد.[۳۶۷] شاه حتا پس از موافقت نیز- پیش از رسیدن «فرمان»ها، که قرار بود روزولت برای امضاء نزد او بفرستد- تهران را به قصد ویلای خود در کلاردشت ترک می‌کند. اما کرمیت روزولت کوتاه نمی‌آید و سرهنگ نعمت‌الله نصیریان، رئیس گارد شاهنشاهی را با هواپیما به محل اقامت شاه می‌فرستد. نصیریان امضاءها را از شاه می‌گیرد و فرمان‌ها را به روزولت می‌رساند. شگفت‌آور این که در سراسر کتاب روزولت، سخن بر سر «گرفتن امضاء» است، و نه «گرفتن فرمان‌ها»؛ انگار فرمان‌ها قبلاً نوشته شده بوده و در دست کودتاچیان در انتظار امضاء شاه بوده است. مثلاً، زمانی که رفتن شاه به شمال را (پیش از امضاء فرمان‌ها) شرح می‌دهد، می‌نویسد: «فرمان‌ها هنوز در کاخ بود» (ص ۱۷۰). «فرمان» عزل دکتر مصدق، که در جریان هجوم به خانه‌اش در روز ۲۸ مرداد از دورن «گاو صندوق» او ربوده شد، و هرگز به رؤیت تاریخ نرسید. اما شکل نوشتاری‌ی «فرمانِ» نصب زاهدی بر سربرگ دربار- که عیناً در کتاب‌های روزولت و اردشیر زاهدی گراور شده- با این که با امضاء شاه است، بسیار تردید برانگیز به نظر می‌آید. چرا که هم فاصله‌ی کلمات در خطهای این متن ناهمسان است، هم تاریخ، در دل امضاء شاه دویده، هم تاریخ روز در آن دستکاری شده و هم واژه‌ی «مرداد»، به صورت «مراداد» نوشته شده است. درست مثل این که به قول مصدق در دادگاه، سربرگ‌های بدون متن، قبلاً به صورت «سفید مُهر» در اختیار کودتاچیان بوده، و (به قول دکتر عباس توفیق) انگار که نویسنده در نگارش متن- که باید در بالای امضاء قرار می‌گرفت- در سطرهای سوم و چهارم دچار کمبود جا بوده است؛ و «تا متن از امضاء تجاوز نکند، یا متن فرمان در روی امضاء نوشته نشود، در این دو خط، تا حد ممکن کلمات را ریز و به هم نزدیک نوشته است.»[۳۶۸] البته، با وجود همه‌ی حدس و گمان‌ها، چند و چون واقعی‌ی این «فرمان»ها هنوز به عرض تاریخ ایران نرسیده است. چرا که در درجه‌ی نخست، این گزاره که شاه برگه‌ی «سفید مهر» در اختیار کسی گذاشته باشد، سخت محل تردید است. از این گذشته، درست است که شاه در آن زمان در کلاردشت به سر می‌برد، اما آیا باورکردنی است که او سربرگ دیگری در اختیار نداشت تا متن نامرتب را پاره کند و آن را به صورت مرتب و با فاصله‌های لازم روی برگه‌ی تازه بنویسد و بعد امضاء کند؟ فراتر از این، اگر امضاءها قبلاً در دست کودتاچیان بوده، و متن بعد از امضاء نوشته شده، چرا روزولت در جای جای کتابش از «گرفتن امضاء» از شاه تأکید کرده است. در هر حال، ماهیت مشکوک این فرمان‌ها، و لحن قاطعانه و حتا تهدیدآمیز فرستادگان سیا (البته در قالب زبان دوستانه و محترمانه و «شاهنشاه»گو در صحبت‌هائی که با شاه داشتند)، بی‌اختیار ما را به تنگنائی می‌کشاند که شاه ایران در آن گرفتار بود؛ تنگنائی از همان جنس که در سال ۱۳۱۲ رضا شاه پهلوی را به تمدید قرارداد نفت ناگزیر کرده بود؛ تنگنائی که، میراث‌خوار سیاست‌های نابخرانه و آزمندانه‌ی شاهان قاجار، حدود دویست سال نفوذ و دخالت استعمار در ایران، و بر فراز همه، نابخردی‌های برخاسته از خوی استبدادی در خود شاه بود که تا آن لحظه‌ی تاریخی پشتوانه‌ی ملت خود را از دست داده بود. در نتیجه، اگر هم می‌خواست، نمی‌توانست به کودتاچیانِ نفتی/ استعماری بگوید: «نه».

شاه می‌فرستد که : «بریتانیا و امریکا کودتا را طراحی کرده‌اند و هیچ جور هم قابل جلوگیری نیست.» (ص ۸) در هر حال، عدم رضایت شاه به امضاء فرمان‌ها، سبب می‌شود که خود روزولت، به صورت پنهانی (که فیلم‌های جیمز باند را به ذهن متبادر می‌کند) با شاه دیدار کند، و شاه- با این شرط که بتواند در طول مدت کودتا از تهران خارج باشد و در محلی امن سکنا کند- به امضاء فرمان‌ها رضایت می‌دهد. اما صبح روز بعد، زمانی که رابط، فرمان‌ها را برای امضاء به کاخ سعدآباد می‌برد، متوجه می‌شود که شاه و ملکه ثریا (همسر دوم شاه) قبلاً به ویلای خود در کلاردشت پرواز کرده‌اند. (روزولت، ص ۱۶۹- ۱۷۰) شاید تفاوت‌هائی که در گزارش‌های کینزر و روزولت دیده می‌شود، از آن رو پیش آمده که کنیزر به مآخذ متعددی، از جمله گزارش شوراتسکف و اسناد آرشیو امنیت ملی‌ی امریکا نیز، مراجعه کرده است. به مآخذ زیر نگاه کنید:

* Kermit Roosevelt, ***Countercoup: The Struggle for Control of Iran***, New York: McGraw-Hill, 1979.

❖ Stephen Kinzer, ***All The Shah's Men***: ***An American Coup and the Roots of Middle East Terror***, New Jersey: John Wiley & Son, Inc., 2008.

[367] Stephen Kinzer, Ibid, p. 10.

[۳۶۸] دکتر عباس توفیق، ***درباره‌ی قانونی بودن یا نبودنِ فرمان عزل دکتر مصدق***، ره‌آورد، شماره‌ی ۷۹، تابستان ۱۳۸۶/ ۲۰۰۷، صص ۱۱۹ تا ۱۲۴.

پیرامون این سـخن که «رویداد ۲۸ مرداد کودتا نبود» نیز، جالب اسـت بدانیم که عنوان اول کتاب خاطرات کرمیت روزولت، «ضد کودتا» است. یعنی که مصدق علیه شاه کودتا کرده بود، و عملیات آژاکس برای خنثا کردن این کودتا انجام گرفت؟ در حالی که زیرعنوانِ همین کتاب، «تلاش برای کنترل ایران» است، و سراسر این کتاب آکنده است از اعتراف آشکار نویسنده به توطئه‌ی سیا و وزارت امور خارجه‌ی امریکا برای «کنترل» موج عظیم ضداستعماری و استقلال‌طلبی مصممانه در ایران، که در سـازش‌ناپذیری‌ی دکتر مصـدق متبلور بود. افزون بر گفته‌های کرمیت روزولت در کتابش، و افزون بر اسنادی که نیویورک تایمز از کتاب «دونالد ویلبر» (سرپرست عملیات آژاکس در سیا) منتشر کرد، کتاب‌های برخی از مفسران سیاسـی در امریکا، هر یک به گونه‌ای، خواسته یا ناخواسته، بر هدف سیا در کنترل موج عظیم تلاش مردم ایران برای دسـت‌یابی به حاکمیت ملی صحه گذاشـته‌اند،[۳۶۹] و اسـناد منتشر شـده‌ی شورای امنیت ملی‌ی امریکا نیز نشـان می‌دهند که ادعای «خطر کمونیسم»، آخرین تیر ترکش این سـازمان و سـازمان اطلاعاتی‌ی بریتانیا بوده است برای موجه جلوه دادن سـرنگونی‌ی دولت مصـدق در افکار عمومی‌ی ایرانِ مذهبی، غرب، و کلاً در کشـورهای غیرکمونیستی در کشـاکش «جنگ سـرد».[۳۷۰] در متن‌های مربوط به کودتا آمده اسـت که رئیس جمهور امریکا، ترومن، با کودتا مخالف بود و گفته بود که مسئله‌ی نفت باید با دولت مصـدق حل و فصـل شـود. اما با خواندن متن‌های منتقدان سیاسـت خارجی‌ی امریکا، درمی‌یابیم که نقشـه‌ی تسلط بر ذخایر انرژی در جهان، و بر آب‌هائی که حمل این ذخایر به سـوی غرب را ممکن می‌کنند، خاص هیتلر و اسـتالین نبود، و از همان پایان جنگ دوم جهانی (در زمان ریاسـت جمهوری‌ی فرانکلین روزولت) سـرلوحه‌ی سـیاسـت‌های امریکا را نیز رقم زده بود. مشـاور فرانکلین روزولت، «بِرل A. A. Berle»، گفته بود: «کنترل ذخایر بی‌مانند خاورمیانه، به کنترل اسـاسـی‌ی جهان می‌انجامد.»[۳۷۱] بر این اسـاس، دلیل امتناع رئیس جمهور امریکا در سـرنگونی‌ی مصـدق در آغاز کار این بود که سـیا، زمان بیش‌تری لازم داشـت تا ابتکار عملیات را از چنگ بریتانیا به در آورد و هژمونی‌ی امپراتوری‌ی امریکا را بر بریتانیا و کلاً، کشـورهای غربی نیز تثبیت کند. کما این که در زمان ریاسـت جمهوری‌ی آیزنهاور ابتکار عملیات کودتا در ایران عملاً به سیا منتقل شده بود. درسـت در همین دوران است که مشاوران

---

[۳۶۹] به عنوان مثال از این نوع متن‌ها به مأخذ زیر، که توسط یکی از کارمندان سیا نوشته شده، نگاه کنید:
Richard W. Cottam, ***Nationalism in Iran***, Pittsburgh: University of Pittsburgh Press, 1979.

[۳۷۰] در مدارک متعدد این واقعیت تکرار شده است که ترومن، رئیس جمهور وقت امریکا، می‌خواست مسئله‌ی نفت با حکومت مصدق حل شود. در اغاز کار، رئیس سـازمان سیا در ایران، و سفیر وقت امریکا در ایران نیز با سرنگونی‌ی دولت مصدق مخالف بودند. آیزنهاور، رئیس جمهور بعدی نیز در ابتدای دوره‌ی ریاسـت جمهوری، با سـرنگونـی‌ی مصـدق موافق نبود. برادران دالس، آلن ولش دالس و جان فاستر دالس، از سرمایه‌گذاران چندین بانک و شرکت‌های نفتی، .که در دوره‌ی آیزنهاور به قدرت رسیدند، مأموران پیشین امریکا در ایران را برکنار کردند و به رغم گزارش‌های محرمانه‌ای که پیرامون عدم کفایت حزب توده در رسـیدن به قدرت در دسـت داشـتند، به عنوان یک تاکتیک در جلب رضـایت آیزنهاور (که افزون بر دنبال کردن سیاست «تسلط بر جهان»، سخت درگیر جنگ سرد و «ترس سرخ» هم بود)، مسئله‌ی خطر کمونیسم را عمده کردند. الن دالس، رئیس سازمان سیا بود و جان فاستر دالس، وزیر خارجه‌ی دولت آیزنهاور. افزون بر این گزارش‌ها، پنج دهه پس از کودتای ۲۸ مرداد، مجموعه‌ای سند (و البته نه همه‌ی اسناد) از بایگانی‌ی شورای امنیت ملی‌ی امریکا (مربوط به سال‌های ۱۹۵۱ تا ۱۹۵۴) منتشر شد، که در سند شماره‌ی ٤ آن، به تاریخ ۱۰ اوت ۱۹۵۳ (۵ روز پیش از نخستین کودتا)، ضـمن بررسـی‌ی اوضـاع سیاسـی و اقتصـادی‌ی ایران، امکان به قدرت رسیدن حزب توده (خطر کمونیسم) منتفی برشمرده است. در جائی از این سند آمده است: «حزب توده نه به اندازه‌ی کافی قوی است و نه سـازمان‌دهی‌ی درخوری دارد.» ترجمه‌ی سند شـماره‌ی ٤ از این مجموعه، که به موضـوع «خطر کمونیسـم» مربوط اسـت، در تارنمای «انقلاب اسلامی در هجرت» شماره‌ی ٦۰۱ منتشر شده است:
http://goto.glocalnet.net/banisadr_arkiv/matn1-601.htm
بخشی از اسناد یادشده در کتاب زیر نیز گردآوری و تنظیم شده است:
Mohammad Mosaddeq and the 1953 Coup in Iran, edited by Mark J. Gasiorowski and Malcolm Byrne:
http://www.huffingtonpost.com/joan-e-dowlin/americas-role-in-irans-un_b_216831.html
برای آشنائی‌ی بیش‌تر با الن دالس و سیاست‌های او در سازمان سیا به دو مأخذ زیر نگاه کنید:

- Allen Dulles, ***The Craft of Intelligence***, New York: Harper and Row, 1963.
- Peter Grose, ***Gentleman Spy: The Life of Allen Dulles***, Boston: Houghton Mifflin, 1994.

[371] Noam Chomsky, ***Is the World Too Big to Fail?*** Noam Chomsky explains how the global order of power has been created and describes the mechanisms behind its continuity, originally published in ***TomDispatch.com***, taken from: Aljazeera site, Sep. 29, 2011:
http://english.aljazeera.net/indepth/opinion/2011/09/201192514364490977.html

آیزنهاور به مسئله‌ی «نفرتِ مردم خاورمیانه» از امریکا اشاره می‌کنند، و آیزنهاور می‌گوید: «تا زمانی که دیکتاتورهای این کشورها دموکراسی و رشد را سرکوب می‌کنند، ما نگران نفرت مردم این کشورها از امریکا نیستیم.»[۳۷۲] با توجه به این که اطلاعات یادشده تازه نیستند، و نویسندگان و مورخان امریکائی از دهه‌ها پیش بر آن‌ها انگشت گذاشته‌اند،[۳۷۳] خواننده‌ی متن‌هائی که با استناد به «عزل مصدق از نخست وزیری»، و با تکیه بر خاطرات اردشیر زاهدی، ابلاغ می‌کنند که رویداد ۲۸ مرداد ۳۲ «کودتا نبود» بلکه «رستاخیز» مردم ایران بود، اگر این نظر را حمل بر جانب‌داری نکند، دست کم به گستردگی‌ی دامنه‌ی «تحقیق» تردید می‌کند. صرف نظر از خاطرات اردشیر زاهدی که خود و پدرش در کودتا درگیر بودند، شگفت‌انگیز است که این گونه تاریخ‌نگاری، از دو قطب متضاد می‌آید: در یک قطب، مورخان رسمی‌ی جمهوری‌ی اسلامی، و در قطب دیگر، زخم‌خوردگان جمهوری‌ی اسلامی؛ شگفتا که این دو قطب، پیرامون شخصیت و کارنامه‌ی سیاسی‌ی «دکتر مصدق» به یک نظر واحد رسیده‌اند. نمونه‌ی قطب اول، محمدعلی موحد، تاریخ‌نگار درون‌مرزی، است که در کتاب «خواب آشفته‌ی نفت»، با تکیه بر سندهای گزینشی، کل نهضت ملی کردن نفت، آرزوی ایرانیان در رسیدن به استقلال، و عمل دکتر مصدق در تحقق آن را به «خوابی آشفته» تشبیه کرده است.[۳۷٤] کتاب «کارنامه‌ی سیاسی‌ی دکتر محمد مصدق» نوشته‌ی دکتر جلال متینی، استاد و رئیس سابق دانشگاه فردوسی در سال‌های پیش از انقلاب، نمونه‌ای از قطب دوم است. جلال متینی در این کتاب، محمد مصدق را با صفت‌های «قُد»، «یک دنده» و به عنوان نمونه‌ی «عصبیت تاریخی‌ی ما» نواخته است؛ چرا که مصدق «با تمام طرح‌ها و پیشنهادات در مجلس مخالفت می‌کرد»؛ با احداث «راه آهن سراسری‌ی جنوب به شمال» مخالف بود؛ تفاوت «لوله‌کشی برای آب» و «لوله‌کشی برای فاضلاب» را نمی‌دانست؛ «با هیچ پیشنهادی در مورد مسئله‌ی نفت موافقت نکرد تا بتواند خود را وجیه‌المله نشان دهد»؛ و به این نتیجه می‌رسد که در اثر اشتباهات مصدق، مردم حمایت خود را از او بریده بودند و شعار «یا مرگ یا مصدق» را در روز ۲۸ مرداد به فراموشی سپردند. البته، بسیاری از بازگفت‌های جلال متینی در این کتاب، مانند سخن مصدق خطاب به سپهد رزم‌آرا و تهدید او به مرگ- که متینی در صفحه‌ی ۲۱۳ کتاب خود آورده است- درست است، و با «متن مذاکرات مجلس شانزدهم، ۸ تیر ماه ۱۳۲۹» پشتیبانی شده است. اما شگفتا از دکتر جلال متینی، که همیشه و همواره، واژه/ مفهومِ «پژوهش» بر نوشته‌های او برازنده بوده است، در این جا، به رغم ادعای «بی‌طرفی»، از فراز هزار مأخذ و مدرک و سند معتبر می‌جهد و به دامان بازگفت از مراجع نامعتبر می‌آویزد؛ تا عقب‌ماندگی و عوام‌فریبی‌ی دکتر مصدق و حمایت او از استعمار انگلستان را «مستند» کند.[۳۷۵] البته بر این کتاب نیز در تبعید نقدهای متعدد و مفصلی نوشته شد که نقد محترم ناصر شاهین‌پر یکی از آن‌ها است.[۳۷٦]

علی میرفطروس، نویسنده‌ی تبعیدی و پژوهشگر تاریخ، نمونه‌ی دیگری از قطب دوم (یعنی از زخم‌خوردگان جمهوری‌ی اسلامی) است. او در کتاب «دکتر محمد مصدق: آسیب‌شناسی‌ی یک شکست»- که به گفته‌ی خودش آن را با «انگیزه و

---

372 Ibid.

۳۷۳ خواست و برنامه‌ی «رهبری‌ی جهان»، همواره مورد اشاره‌ی رئیس جمهورهای امریکا بوده است. به عنوان مثال از صدها متنی که ماهیت این مطالبه را بررسی کرده‌اند، به مآخذ زیر نگاه کنید.

- William Appleman Williams, ***America and the Middle East: Open Door Impeialism or Enlighened Leadership***, New York: Rinehart, 1958.
- *Sheldon L. Richman, ***"Ancient History": U.S. Conduct in the Middle East since World War II and the Folly of Intervention***, Policy Analysis no.159. Cato Institute site, August 16, 1991:

http://www.cato.org/pub_display.php?pub_id=1019

۳۷٤ محمدعلی موحد، ***خواب آشفته‌ی نفت: دکتر مصدق و نهضت ملی‌ی ایران***، ۲ جلد، تهران: نشر کارنامه، چاپ دوم، ۱۳۸۴.

۳۷۵ جلال متینی، ***کارنامه‌ی سیاسی‌ی دکتر محمد مصدق***، لس‌انجلس: انتشارات شرکت کتاب، ۱۳۸۴.

۳۷٦ ناصر شاهین پر، ***نگاهی به کارنامه سیاسی‌ی دکتر محمد مصدق***، تارنمای « ایران امروز»، ٦ شهریور ۱۳۸۵:
http://www.iran-emrooz.net/index.php?/politic/more/9938http://www.iran-emrooz.net/index.php?/politic/more/9938

الهام دوست و استاد بزرگوار خود، دکتر جلال متینی» نوشته است- پیرامون انگیزه‌ی دکتر مصدق، در مبارزه با محمدرضا شاه پهلوی، می‌نویسد:

مصدق که احمد شاه را به عنوان «پادشاه جوان‌بخت» و «شاه وطن‌پرست» بارها مورد ستایش و تمجید قرار داده بود، **چه بسا** که در سودای بازگشت و استقرار مجدد سلطنت قاجارها بود.[۳۷۷] (گیومه از میرفطروس است. تأکید از من است.)

میرفطروس برای اثبات این «چه بسا»، از «صفحه‌ی ۱۹۱ جلد اول کتاب حسین مکی» چنین شاهد می‌آورد (بدون آن که نام و عنوان کتاب مکی را یادآور شود):

«دکتر مصدق، می‌خواست شاه را برکنار کند و مطمئناً چنین بود. از اوایل مرداد ماه ۱۳۳۱، اکبر میرزای صارم‌الدوله را فرستادند به اروپا تا با بچه‌های محمدحسن میرزا- ولیعهد احمد شاه- ملاقات کند. دکتر صحت، که طبیب مخصوص محمدحسن میرزا بود، گفت: بچه‌های محمدحس میرزا قبول نکردند.»

برای میرفطروس اهمیت ندارد که از خود بپرسد و به مخاطبش بگوید که «اکبر میرزای صارم‌الدوله» را چه کسانی به اروپا «فرستادند»؟ «بچه‌های محمدحسن میرزا» چه نام دارند؟ «دکتر صحت» در کجا، و به چه کسی «گفت»؟ در عوض، بلافاصله پس از این نقل قولِ پر از پرسش، می‌نویسد:

با توجه به مخالفت‌های پایدار مصدق با رضا شاه (به خاطر نقش وی در برکناری‌ی احمد شاه و انقراض سلسله‌ی قاجار) و با توجه به مجموعه‌ی عملکردهای مصدق در طول سلطنت محمدرضا شاه، آیا مصدق با حمایت حزب توده و قشقائی‌های فارس، در **سودای سیاسی‌ی دیگری** بود؟ این گونه سوءظن‌ها و بدگمانی‌ها، فضای سیاسی‌ی جامعه را عمیقاً آشفته کرده بود. لذا مصدق به مشاوران معتدل و فرهیخته‌ای مانند غلامحسین صدیقی یا اللهیار صالح نیاز داشت؛ اما او بر افراد رادیکالی مانند حسین فاطمی، علی شایگان، زیرکزاده، حسیبی و رضوی تکیه کرد، که **در جمهوری‌خواهی‌ی آنان تردیدی نبود**. این امر، اگر چه موجب خشنودی‌ی و حمایت حزب توده بود، اما ناخشنودی‌ی بسیاری از یاران مصدق، و خصوصاً نگرانی‌های دولت امریکا را همراه داشت. آیا انتخاب این افراد و اتکای مصدق به آنان، ناآگاهانه بود؟ چنان که خواهیم دید، **حوادث بعدی** (خصوصاً در ۲۵ مرداد ۳۲) **تمایلات پنهان مصدق** یا انگیزه‌های درونی‌ی یاران نزدیک او (خصوصاً حسین فاطمی) را آشکار ساخت. (پیشین، صص۱۲۵ تا ۱۲۶) (پرانتزها از میرفطروس؛ تأکید از من است.)

نکته‌ی دیگری که می‌تواند به «تحریف» تعبیر شود، نظر میرفطروس است پیرامون تعطیل مدرسه‌های مختلطِ دخترانه و پسرانه به دستور دکتر مهدی‌ی آذر (وزیر فرهنگ دولت مصدق). گذشته از این که دکتر آذر یکی از سکولارترین دولتمردان دولت مصدق بود، می‌دانیم که تعطیل کردنِ مدرسه‌های یادشده هشت سال پیش از دوره‌ی مصدق، و در زمان نخست‌وزیری‌ی سهیلی در مجلس عنوان شده بود و جواز تصویب گرفته بود. البته، محمد امینی، پژوهشگر تاریخ ایران، در کتاب «سوداگری با تاریخ»، با «سند» وُ مدرک «ثابت» کرده است که بسیاری از «سند»های کتابِ میرفطروس «جعلی» است.[۳۷۸] با این وصف، فرض من بر این است که تمام سندهای میرفطروس در این کتاب «واقعی» هستند. منتها، بر این باورم که «واقعی» بودن، امر «گزینشی» عمل کردن در اسناد یک پژوهش را لاپوشانی نمی‌کند. همچنین، بر این

---

[۳۷۷] علی میرفطروس، ***دکتر محمد مصدق: آسیب‌شناسی‌ی یک شکست (از انقلاب مشروطه به انقلاب اسلامی)***، مونترآل- کانادا، نشر فرهنگ، ژانویه ۲۰۰۸/ ۱۳۸۶، ص ۱۲۵.

[۳۷۸] محمد امینی، ***سوداگری با تاریخ: پاسخی به «آسیب‌شناسی‌ی یک شکست»***، لس‌انجلس: انتشارات شرکت کتاب، ۱۳۹۱/ ۲۰۱۲.

باورم که تمایل یا عدم تمایل دکتر مصدق به بازگشتِ خاندان قاجار، سوژه‌ای معتبر است؛ و رسیدگی به چه‌گونگی‌های این احتمال، از وظایف پژوهشگرانِ بی‌طرف تاریخ است. اما علی میرفطروس، نه تنها در بازگفت بالا، بلکه در شرح و توصیف «حوادث بعدی» نیز مطلقاً از عهده‌ی اثبات آن برنیامده است، و کتابش را به گمانه‌های نامستدل آلوده است. اگر بپذیریم که دکتر مصدق «سودای» بازگشت قاجار را داشت، چه‌گونه بپذیریم که برای تحقق این «تمایلات پنهان»، به شخصیت‌هائی «اتکاء» کرد که «در جمهوری‌خواهی‌ی آنان تردیدی نبود»؟ نمی‌دانم که میرفطروس این تضاد آشکار را چه‌گونه توضیح می‌دهد. و طرفه این که بسیاری از سندها و پشتوانه‌های میرفطروسِ در تبعید، برگرفته از جلد اول کتاب «خواب آشفته‌ی نفت»، نوشته‌ی محمدعلی موحد است؛ یعنی کتابی که وزارت ممیزی در جمهوری‌ی اسلامی، نه تنها با انتشار آن مشکل ندارد، بلکه با انتشار «نقد»های تأییدکننده پیرامون آن هم مشکل ندارد.[۳۷۹]

اما حافظه‌ی تاریخ ایران نه تنها هنوز نتوانسته آن «تمایلات پنهان مصدق» را آشکار کند، بلکه «تمایل»‌ی به جز تمایل به استقلال اقتصادی‌ی ایران را هنوز در کارنامه‌ی دکتر محمد مصدق ثبت نکرده است. به عنوان نمونه، در غیبت چند روزه‌ی شاه (۲۵ مرداد ۳۲ تا پیروزی‌ی کودتاگران)، به دستور دکتر مصدق و به سرپرستی‌ی دکتر حسین فاطمی (وزیر خارجه‌ی دولت مصدق)، تمامی‌ی کاخ‌های خانواده‌ی سلطنتی به وسیله‌ی نیروهای انتظامی مهر و موم شد. از این گذشته، مفهوم «شاه باید سلطنت کند نه حکومت»، از همان نطقی که دکتر مصدق در مخالفت با به سلطنت رسیدنِ «سردار سپه رئیس‌الوزراء» در روز ۹ آبان ۱۳۰۴ در مجلس ایراد کرده بود تا واپسین لحظه‌های زندگی، با بیان‌های مختلف از او شنیده شده بود. تکرار این مفهوم از سوی مصدق، و گام‌هائی که برای جلوگیری از فساد مالی در دربار برمی‌داشت- گرچه شاید از نظر زمانی نابه‌هنگام بود- نشان می‌داد که رویاروئی‌ی او با شاه، نه به خاطر «سلطنت» او، بلکه به خاطر محدود کردن اختیارات شاه و جلوگیری از دخالت‌های منفی‌ای بود که او در انتخابات، و در روند ملی کردن نفت (به روش مصدق) اعمال می‌کرد.

یکی دیگر از پژوهشگرانِ «کارنامه‌ی مصدق»، بهزاد کاظمی است؛ که حدود سی سال در تبعید، با تمام توان خود علیه جمهوری‌ی اسلامی کوشید، پژوهید، و منتشر کرد. بهزاد کاظمی نیز با تکیه بر اسناد گزینشی‌ی خود، و با تکیه بر پایگاه طبقاتی‌ی دکتر مصدق، به این برداشت رسیده است که «دکتر مصدق برای جلوگیری از فروپاشی‌ی نظام پادشاهی، **فعالانه** به پیروزی‌ی کودتاگران یاری رساند.» بهزاد کاظمی، ضمن این که روی واژه‌ی «فعالانه» تأکید کرده است، به عنوان یکی از دلایل این «یاری رساندن فعالانه»، به شرکت دکتر مصدق در کابینه‌ی پس از کودتای ۱۲۹۹ اشاره می‌کند، و می‌نویسد:

> وی در کنار یکی از کودتاگران (رضا خان سردار سپه)، که پست وزارت جنگ را داشت، به کار سرگرم شد. او حتا برای سرکوب «جنبش چپ» در آذربایجان، با حمایت انگلیسی‌ها و رضا خان، به آن دیار رفت.[۳۸۰] (نشانه‌های سجاوندی از بهزاد کاظمی است.)

بهزاد کاظمی با پشتوانه‌ی اسناد گزینشی‌ی خود تا آن جا پیش می‌رود که پایداری‌ی دکتر مصدق در برابر بریتانیا را به عنوان کوشش آگاهانه‌ی او برای جابه‌جائی‌ی هژمونی‌ی امریکا بر بریتانیا در ایران معرفی می‌کند.

---

۳۷۹ محمدعلی موحد، ***خواب آشفته‌ی نفت: دکتر مصدق و نهضت ملی‌ی ایران***، تهران: نشر کارنامه، ۱۳۷۸.

۳۸۰ بهزاد کاظمی، ***ملی‌گرایان و افسانه‌ی دموکراسی: کارنامه‌ی مصدق در پرتو جنبش کارگری و دموکراسی‌ی سوسیالیستی***، لندن: نشر نظم کارگر، ۱۳۷۸، صص۳۵۲ تا ۳۵۳ .

و این در حالی است که دکتر سید محمود کاشانی، از قطب اول- یعنی یکی از «پژوهشگران»ی که برای «روحانیان مبارز» و برای جمهوری‌ی اسلامی «تاریخ» می‌نویسند، دکتر مصدق را عامل انگلستان قلمداد می‌کند، و آیت‌الله کاشانی را مرجع و مدافع اصلی‌ی «نهضت ملی»؛ و سپس به این «نتیجه» می‌رسد که:

> در خلال ۵۰ سال گذشته وابستگان سیاست‌های بیگانه برای توجیه سقوط پیش‌بینی نشده[ی دولت مصدق]، تبلیغات گمراه کننده‌ای به راه انداخته؛ رهبران نهضت، مجلس و مردم را متهم ساخته و مدعی شده‌اند مُشتی اراذل و اوباش و روسپیان به خیابان‌ها ریختند و دولت ملی را سرنگون‌کردند! این فریب‌کاری‌ها برای آن است که همکاری‌ی مصدق با دولت انگلستان برای براندازی‌ی نهضت ملی‌ی ایران آشکار نشود. [...] در انتخابات مجدد دوره‌ی شانزدهم در تهران آیت‌الله کاشانی‌که در تبعید لبنان به سر می‌برد به نمایندگی‌ی مجلس انتخاب شد وبا استقبال تاریخی‌ی بی‌مانندی به ایران بازگشت و خانه‌ی او کانون اصلی‌ی مبارزات ملت ایران گردید. دراین انتخابات مصدق نیز با کمک هواداران نهضت ملی‌ی ایران به مجلس شانزدهم راه یافت و با خواندن پیام‌های آیت‌الله کاشانی در این مجلس هرچه بیش‌تر خود را به کانون قدرت نزدیک کرد و اعتماد سران نهضت ملی‌ی ایران را به دست آورد. دولت انگلستان که خود را در برابر امواج خروشان نهضت مردمی در ایران ناتوان یافت، استراتژی‌ی تازه‌ای در پیش گرفت. نخست شخص مصدق که خود را پیش از این بازنشسته سیاسی معرفی می‌کرد به صحنه آورده و او را بر موج نهضت سوار کردند. (۸) انگلیس‌ها از این پس گروه قابل توجهی از مهره‌های وابسته‌ی خود را در دولت و مجلس و دیگر پست‌های کلیدی بسیج کرده و به تدریج برای نخست وزیری‌ی مصدق زمینه‌چینی کردند و او هم توانست نقش خود را به سان یک بازیگر ماهر به مورد اجرا گذارد.[۳۸۱]

خواننده‌ی این متن- متنی که ۴۴ فقره زیرنویس ارائه دارد- برای دیدن سندِ این ادعا به زیرنویس‌ها مراجعه می‌کند، و در فقره‌ی ۸ آن به جای سند، باز با ادعای بی‌پشتوانه‌ی دیگری مواجه می‌شود؛ و نهایتاً، نخواهد دانست که رابطه‌ی «استاندار» بودنِ مصدق با مسئله‌ی «نهضت ملی کردن نفت» چیست، و حتا نخواهد دانست که نامه‌ی حمایتِ «مستر نورمان» از مصدق در کجا منتشر شده است. چرا که در زیرنویس شماره‌ی ۸ این متن «تحقیقی» خوانده است :

> مصدق از گذشته‌های دور روابط پنهانی و نزدیک با انگلیس‌ها داشت و بر همین پایه او را در دوران جوانی به استانداری‌ی فارس رساندند که زیر کنترل سیاسی و نظامی‌ی انگلستان بود. حتا «مستر نورمان» وزیر مختار این کشور در ایران در نامه‌ای به نخست وزیر وقت ایران در آبان ۱۲۹۹ خورشیدی خواستار ادامه‌ی استانداری او در فارس گردید.[۳۸۲]

شگفت‌انگیز است که این «محقق»، چشم در چشم تاریخ می‌دوزد و تا رهبری‌ی «نهضت ملی کردن نفت» را به سود «روحانیت» و «آیت‌الله کاشانی» بگرداند، و بی‌هیچ واهمه‌ای از قضاوت تاریخ، آن را تحریف می‌کند. من نمی‌دانم در آن «کنفرانس» شنونده‌ای از او پرسید یا نپرسید که اگر مصدق «بازیگر انگلستان» بود، پس چرا در برابر منافع این کشور سرسختانه ایستاد؟ آیا این پایداری، با همه‌ی ناکامی‌هایش، به سلطه‌ی بی‌منازغ بریتانیا بر نفت و نفتگرانِ زحمت‌کش ایران پایان نداد؟ این «محقق»، در حالی سهم آیت‌الله کاشانی در نهضت ملی‌کردن نفت را ارتقاء می‌دهد که حتا میزان پولی را که کودتاچیان به خانه‌ی او فرستاده بودند، در مآخذ مختلف آمده است. یرواند آبراهامیان، پژوهشگر تاریخ و مورخ این

---

۳۸۱ دکتر سیدمحمود کاشانی، ***مداخله‌ی انگلستان و امریکا برای براندازی‌ی نهضت ملی‌ی ایران***، (متن سخنرانی در کنفرانس ۸ تا ۱۰ ژوئن ۲۰۰۲، در مرکز مطالعات خاورمیانه، کالج سنت آنتون در دانشگاه آکسفورد)، تارنمای «مرکز اسناد انقلاب اسلامی»، واپسین بازدید: ۱۹ سپتامبر ۲۰۱۳/ ۲۸ شهریور ۱۳۹۲:

http://www.irdc.ir/fa/content/4750/default.aspx

۳۸۲ دکتر سیدمحمود کاشانی، ***مداخله‌ی انگلستان و امریکا برای براندازی‌ی نهضت ملی‌ی ایران***، پیشین.

دوره از تاریخ ایران، نیز در کتاب «کودتا» در بخش معرفی‌ی شخصیت‌های کلیدی در ماجرای نهضت ملی نفت و کودتای مرداد ۱۳۳۲، پیرامون آیت‌الله ابوالقاسم کاشانی می‌نویسد: «انگلیسی‌ها او را دشمن تلخ نامیده بودند؛ منتها دشمنی که قابل خریداری است.»[۳۸۳]

متنی از عرفان قانعی‌فرد- نویسنده‌ای در میانِ درون مرز و برون‌مرز- نیز نمونه‌ی دیگری است از این نوع «پژوهش»های طرف‌گیرانه. این «پژوهشگر»، در متنی که ظاهراً به تاریخچه‌ی تأسیس «ساواک» مربوط است، هدف دکتر مصدق و نهضت ملی کردن نفت را به شکل زیر به خواننده‌اش عرضه می‌کند:

> [...] در امریکا، سازمان مرکزی‌ی اطلاعات امریکا (سیا - CIA) به مثابه بازوی اطلاعاتی‌ی دولت امریکا در سال ۱۳۲۶ تأسیس شد و برخی از مورخان بر این عقیده‌اند که برکناری‌ی محمد مصدق در ۲۸ مرداد ۱۳۳۲ – **که می‌خواست شاه را از قدرت خلع کند**- به خاطر همکاری‌ی این سازمان بوده است، و برخی دیگر از دولتمردان ایرانی – مانند اردشیر زاهدی - این امر را در آن دوران، امری تبلیغاتی و اغراق‌آمیز و برای قدرت‌نمائی‌ی این سازمان نوپای اطلاعاتی می‌دانند . اما جدای از این اختلاف نظر تاریخی و سلیقه در بیان روایت،[...] حوادث داخلی ایران پس از شهریور ۱۳۲۰ و خصوصاً **غائله‌ی مصدق** و آغاز رابطه‌ی نوین با امریکا و احساس خطر از قدرت شوروی، حمایت از شاه و دربار و حفظ امنیت رژیم ، ضرورت وجود تشکیلاتی منسجم را دوچندان می کرد. [...][۳۸۴] (تأکیدها از من است.)

برخی دیگر از پژوهشگران، از چشم‌انداز «ناسیونالیسم» («ناسیونالیسم»ی که بعد از اوج‌گیری‌ی نهضت‌های ملی در ایران و کشورهای خاورمیانه و امریکای لاتین و افریقا، همتراز با «فاشیسم» معنا شد) به «نهضت ملی کردن نفت ایران» و به «دکتر مصدق» نگاه کرده‌اند. دکتر سیروس ابراهیم‌زاده، پژوهشگر مقیم کالیفرنیا، یکی از آن‌هاست. این نویسنده در کتابی با عنوان «مصدق در دیوان دادگستری‌ی بین‌المللی‌ی لاهه»، ملی‌گرائی‌ی مصدق و یارانش را با «فاشیسم» همتا می‌کند؛ و به این جا می‌رسد که دکتر مصدق در مقام وکیل مجلس، با سکوت در برابر فرقه‌ی دموکرات آذربایجان، از تصمیم شوروی‌ها در جداکردنِ آذربایجان از ایران پشتیبانی کرد. این پژوهشگر، از سوئی، تکرار گزاره‌ی «ملی‌کردنِ نفت ایران» از سوی پژوهشگران دیگر را نشانه‌ی «خودفریبی»، «ساده‌اندیشی»، و «سطحی‌نگری»ی آن‌ها می‌داند، و از سوی دیگر، خود همین گزاره را تکرار می‌کند تا بگوید:

> از ملی کردن نفت ایران، در درجه‌ی اول، روسیه‌ی شوروی بالاترین بهره‌برداری‌ها را کرد. پس از دو قرن رقابت روسیه و بریتانیا در ایران، برای بدست آوردن امتیازات مالی و معنوی، سرانجام دولت اتحاد جماهیر شوروی موفق شده بود که به دست عناصر به اصطلاح ملی‌گرا شرکت بزرگ نفت انگلیس را از ایران بیرون راند و نزدیک چهار هزار و پانصد کارشناس، مدیر و تکنیسین انگلیسی را از کشور بیرون کند. [...] مصدق و دار و دسته‌اش این خواست شوروی را جامه‌ی عمل پوشاندند و «به نام سعادت ملت ایران»، شرکت نفت انگلیس را ملی اعلام کردند. همسایه‌ی شمالی موفق شده بود که پس از ۳۳ سال از انقلاب بلشویکی به هدف خود برسد.[۳۸۵]

---

383 Ervand Abrahamian, ***The Coup: 1953 the CIA, and the Roots of Modern U.S.-Iranian Relations***, New York: The New Press, 2013. P.xviii.

۳۸۴ فرد، ***تولد ساواک (سازمان اطلاعات و امنیت کشور)***، تارنمای «گویا نیوز»، ۳ مهر ۱۳۹۰:
http://news.gooya.com/politics/archives/2011/09/128635.php

۳۸۵ دکتر سیروس ابراهیم‌زاده، ***مصدق در دیوان دادگستری‌ی بین‌المللی‌ی لاهه***، لس‌انجلس: ناشر: ندارد، ۱۳۸۵/ ۲۰۰۶، ص ۲۶.

البته کارِ تخریبِ شخصیت و کارنامه‌ی دکتر مصدق به این متن‌های ظاهراً «مستدل» و «مستند» ختم نمی‌شود، بلکه به ناسزاگوئی و تمسخر هم می‌کشد. به عنوان نمونه، «پرفسور پیروز مجتهدزاده» (از قطب اول)، دکتر مصدق را به عنوان شخصیتی برساخته‌ی «بی بی سی» معرفی می‌کند و می‌نویسد: «تف بر مصدق شارلاتان».[۳۸۶] و نادره افشاری، (نویسنده‌ی تبعیدی و از قطب دوم)، بارِ همکاری شخصیت‌های «دولت موقت» با آیت‌الله خمینی، و کلاً، برایش حکومت جمهوری‌ی اسلامی را به دوش شخص مصدق می‌گذارد؛[۳۸۷] و در متن دیگری با عنوان «مصدق در گیومه»، با عبارت‌هائی مانند «نخست وزیر پیژاما/ شلواری»، مصدق را به باد تمسخر می‌گیرد.[۳۸۸]

از سوی دیگر، بسیاری از پژوهشگرانِ طرفدار جبهه‌ی ملی و دکتر مصدق، بدون توقف بر ضعف‌ها و اشتباهات تاکتیکی‌ی دکتر مصدق و «جبهه‌ی ملی»، با تکیه بر اسناد گزینشی‌ی خود، بار شکست نهضت مصدق و کودتا را یکسره به دوش شاه و امریکا و بریتانیا و «مزدوران» آن‌ها گذاشته‌اند؛ به گونه‌ای که، در این جا نیز خواننده‌ای که اسناد این دوره را خوانده باشد، بدون آن که حضور «مزدوران» را نفی کند، و بدون آن که نقش شاه و امریکا و بریتانیا را نادیده بگیرد، به بی‌نظری، یا به اصالت پژوهش آن‌ها تردید می‌کند. چرا که این گروه از پژوهشگران ما- از جمله دکتر فخرالدین عظیمی- نیز از نگاه کردن به ذهنیت مذهبی‌ی خود دکتر مصدق، و به اشتباهات استراتژیک و تاکتیکی‌ی او- به عنوان سبب‌سازهای شکست- غافل مانده‌اند. (در ادامه‌ی بحث به نظر فخرالدین عظیمی اشاره خواهم کرد.)

در میان این دو قطب، دکتر عباس میلانی را هم داریم که کوشیده‌است از داوری‌ی قطعی پیرامون رویداد ۲۸ مرداد ۳۲ خودداری کند. عباس میلانی در بخش دهم از کتاب انگلیسی‌زبانِ «شاه»[۳۸۹] و ترجمه‌ی فارسی‌ی آن با عنوان «نگاهی به شاه»،[۳۹۰] ابتدا نمائی فشرده از روندهای زمینه‌چینی‌ی سازمان‌های اطلاعاتی‌ی امریکا و بریتانیا برای نفوذ در دربار ایران و سپس برای سرنگونی‌ی دولت مصدق ترسیم می‌کند؛ سپس به گزارش نماینده‌ی سیا در ایران که در شب ۲۸ مرداد به رئیس جمهور امریکا- آیزنهاور- فرستاده شده بود استناد می‌کند که گفته بود:

> موجی غیرمنتظره از واکنش نسبت به دولت مصدق در میان مردم و ارتش سبب شد که بنا بر آخرین گزارش‌ها از تهران، شهر به تصرف نیروهائی دربیاید که خود را وفادار به شاه می‌دانند.

عباس میلانی آن گاه، خاطرات اردشیر زاهدی در این زمینه را به شرح زیر نقل به معنی می‌کند:

> انگیزه‌ی پدرش نه اجرای طرح غربی‌ها، [بل]که حفظ وطن از خطر سوء مدیریت مصدق و برآمدن توده‌ای‌ها بود. می‌گوید بدون همراهی و همدلی میهن‌پرستانی چون آیت‌الله کاشانی و مظفر بقائی، مصدق هرگز سرنگون نمی‌شد. و این وحدت نظر و عمل بود که کار مصدق را یکسره کرد نه تلاش‌های طرح آژاکس.

---

۳۸۶ پرفسور پیروز مجتهدزاده، ***تف بر مصدق شارلاتان***، هفته‌نامه‌ی «نگاه پنجشنبه»، شماره‌ی ۳۷، ۲۳ آذر ۱۳۹۱.

۳۸۷ نادره افشاری، ***دوستان مصدق/ یاران خمینی***، تارنمای «نادره افشاری»، ۱۷ اوت ۲۰۱۰/ ۲۷ مرداد ۱۳۸۹:
http://nadereh-afshari.org/index.htm

۳۸۸ نادره افشاری، ***مصدق در گیومه***، تارنمای «نادره افشاری»، پیشین.

389 Abbas Milani, ***The Shah***, New York: Palgrave Macmillan, 2011, pp 171- 202.

۳۹۰ من ترجمه‌ی فارسی‌ی این کتاب را، که با عنوان «نگاهی به شاه» در امریکا منتشر شد، ندیده‌ام. و آن چه که در این مبحث از آن کتاب نقل کرده‌ام، پس از تطبیق با روایت انگلیسی‌ی آن، از نشریه‌ی «باران» برگرفته‌ام. با این توضیح که در این متن، زیرنویس‌های میلانی ثبت نشده است. نگاه کنید به:

❖ ***تیپای آژاکس: بریده‌ای از فصل دهم کتاب تازه‌منتشرشده‌ی «نگاهی به شاه»***، فصل‌نامه‌ی «باران»، شماره‌ی ۳۶ و ۳۷، بهار و تابستان ۱۳۹۲، صص ۹۰- ۹۴.

عباس میلانی از این داده‌ها چنین نتیجه می‌گیرد که:

> بی‌اغراق می‌توان گفت که در تمام سال‌های پس از ۲۸ مرداد، زندگی‌ی شاه تا حد زیادی تحت‌الشعاع رخدادهای آن روز، و مهم‌تر، تحت‌الشعاع تصور حامیان و دشمنانش از آن چه به گمانشان در آن چند روز رخ داد، بوده است. کودتا بود، یا ضد کودتا؟ رستاخیز و قیام ملی، یا کودتای ننگین استعماری؟ شاید باید پذیرفت که هر دو قطب این روایتِ مطلق‌اندیش گره بر باد می‌زنند؛ هزارتوی تاریخ را به احکامی ساده و گاه حتا ساده‌انگارانه تقلیل می‌دهند. شاید سودای این قضاوت‌های مطلق، ریشه در فرهنگ مانوی دارد که جهان را عرصه‌ی نبرد نیک و بد، خیر و شر، تاریکی و روشنائی می‌داند و عرصه‌ی خاکستری‌ی هستی را برنمی‌تابد. [...] به گمانم تردید نمی‌توان داشت که انگلیس و امریکا، هر دو در مقطعی، عزم حزم کردند که مصدق را از کار برکنار کنند. آن چه به دقت نمی‌توان تعیین کرد، وزن و نقش هر یک از این تلاش ها در برافتادن مصدق بود. به دیگر سخن، در مجموعه عواملی که در تعیین فرجام ۲۸ مرداد نقشی داشتند- از دخالت بیگانه و بی‌عملی‌ی مصدق و حزب توده در آن روز، تا نقش نیروهای مذهبی چون کاشانی و نگرانی‌های بازاری‌ها از تندروی‌های حزب توده، و کسانی چون حسین فاطمی در فاصله‌ی ۲۵ تا ۲۸ مرداد- وزن مخصوص هر کدام در آن روز تاریخی چه بود. [...] برای بحث تازه و جدی در باب ۲۸ مرداد به گمانم دو پیش شرط لازم‌اند. اول این که باید این رخداد را «تاریخی» کرد. به دیگر سخن، عواطف گاه برخاسته از تجربیات شخصی را وا باید گذاشت و به چیزی جز داده‌ها عنایت نکرد. [...] شرط دوم این است که اسناد و مدارک متعددی که تاکنون مخفی مانده‌اند باید در دسترس محققان و همه‌ی علاقمندان قرار گیرد. [...] (برگرفته از فصل‌نامه‌ی «باران»، پیشین، صص ۹۲- ۹۳)

در این تردید نیست که ریشه‌ی اندیشگی در بخش پرشماری از نوشته‌ها پیرامون این رویداد تاریخی، از منطق دوئالیستی آب می‌خورد. و در این هم تردید نیست که به قول عباس میلانی:

> تا زمانی که اسناد و گزارش‌های دفتر شاه، دفتر آیت‌الله کاشانی و بروجردی و بهبهانی، اسناد پلیس و رکن دو و ارتش ایران، همه‌ی اسناد حزب توده، حزب سومکا، نیروی سوم، اسناد سفارت امریکا و شوروی و مهم‌تر از همه، اسناد سیا، کا گ ب و سرویس اطلاعاتی‌ی انگلستان- که هیچ کدام از قضا تاکنون شامل قوانین مربوط به علنی‌کردن گزارش‌های دولتی نبوده‌اند- و نیز خاطرات و یادداشت‌های اطرافیان شاه، مصدق، و زاهدی قابل دسترس نباشند، صدور حکم و حرف تازه و قطعی در مورد رخدادهای ۲۸ مرداد به گمانم نامیسر است. (فصل‌نامه‌ی «باران»، پیشین، ص ۹۳)

اما تا همین دقیقه‌ی اکنون، و تا همین حد که رخداد ۲۸ مرداد سال ۱۳۳۲ به وسیله‌ی عباس میلانی، و شاهدان عینی، و پژوهشگران بی‌طرف دیگر، و با سندِ عذرخواهی‌ی وزیر خارجه‌ی امریکا از ملت ایران بابت همین رویداد، «تاریخی» شده است، مسئله‌ی «کودتا بودنِ» رخداد ۲۸ مرداد، بیش‌تر به عنوان یک واقعیت نمایان می‌شود تا یک پرسش؛ و این که چه نیروئی یا مجموعه‌ی چه نیروهائی در آن دخیل بوده‌اند، و هر یک تا چه میزان دخیل بوده‌اند، در ذات این واقعیتِ تاکنونی تغییری ایجاد نمی‌کند. عباس میلانی حدود یک دهه پیش از کتاب «شاه» نیز ذات کودتا بودن این رویداد را به زیر پرسش برده بود و پاسخ را به آینده‌ای نامعلوم محول کرده بود. من در جلد پنجم از مجموعه‌ی حاضر، پیرامون آراء این پژوهشگر در همین زمینه، بیش‌تر توضیح داده‌ام، اما همین جا نیز بایسته است اشاره کنم که از سخنان عباس میلانی چنین برمی‌آید که او دو مقوله‌ی **روندهای جاری** در شدنِ کودتا را با **شدنِ کودتا** یکی گرفته است. البته که رسیدگی به «روندهای جاری در شدنِ کودتا»، ابعاد «کودتا» را بیش‌تر باز خواهد کرد؛ و البته که رسیدگی به اسناد و مدارک تازه، گم‌گوشه‌های تاریک این ماجرا را بر تاریخ آشکارتر خواهد کرد. به نظر من، عملکرد، و ذهنیت پشت تصمیم‌های خود دکتر محمد

مصدق در درازنای دوران جنبش ملی، و سپس در روز واقعه، **یکی** از عناصری است که در زمینه‌ی بررسی «روندهای جاری» باید بازخوانی شود.

***

دکتر محمد مصدق- برآمده از خاندان اشرافی/ مذهبی/ سنتی‌ی قاجار، و در عین حال، دانش‌آموخته‌ی حقوق در اروپا- مانند همه‌ی آرزومندانِ «استقلال و تعالی و ترقی»ی ایران، فرزند «مدرنیته»ی دوپاره‌ی ایران بود. ذهنیت مذهبی‌ی دکتر مصدق، رجوعِ مکرر او به قرآن، و استفاده‌ی او از واژگان/ مفاهیم فقهی (مانند اجرای حکم «محاربه با خدا» که در مورد وثوق‌الدوله از مجلس تقاضا کرد)، از همان ابتدای شکل‌گیری‌ی جبهه‌ی ملی، در ترکیب این جبهه و فرآورده‌های بینش و کنش آن نقشی تعیین کننده داشت. تا ادعای مذهبی بودنِ دکتر مصدق و سران جبهه‌ی ملی را مستند کرده باشم، از خاطرات یدالله سحابی، یکی از یاران مصدق (و بعداً، از پایه‌گذارانِ «نهضت آزادی»)، و سپس، از «ملی/ مذهبی»های سرشناس در جمهوری‌ی اسلامی)، نقل قول می‌کنم:

> در آن دوران، یعنی ترور رزم‌آرا، فدائیان اسلام در ارتباط نزدیک با جبهه‌ی ملی بودند. ترور رزم‌آرا هم در جلسه‌ای که با حضور مرحوم نواب صفوی، مرحوم دکتر فاطمی، دکتر بقایی، مکی، دکتر شایگان و سایر رهبران جبهه‌ی ملی- البته بدون حضور دکتر مصدق و آیت‌الله کاشانی- برگزار شده بود، مطرح شد. در آن جلسه بنا به دلایلی دکتر مصدق شرکت نداشت و دکتر فاطمی را به نمایندگی خود فرستاده بود. آیت‌الله کاشانی هم در آن جلسه حضور نداشت که این هم به دلیل اختلافات میان کاشانی و نواب بود. به هر صورت در آن جلسه سران جبهه‌ی ملی، تحلیلی از وضعیت سیاسی‌ی کشور را ارائه می‌کنند که نتیجه‌ی کلی‌ی آن‌ها این بود که خطر اصلی‌ی روز، شخص رزم‌آرا است و رزم‌آرا است که قصد آن دارد که ایران را به انگلستان بفروشد. آنان معتقد بودند که شاه فعلاً خطرناک نیست و همه‌ی کارها زیر سر رزم‌آرا است. در پاسخ به تحلیل‌های سران جبهه، نواب اظهار می‌دارد که فرض کنیم رزم‌آرا امروز ساقط شد و در این حال فنجان خود را برمی‌گرداند توی نعلبکی و می‌گوید حالا رزم‌آرا ساقط شد، بعدش چی، آیا شما قول می‌دهید که پس از سقوط وی، احکام اسلامی را اجراء کنید، که آن‌ها جواب مثبت می‌دهند.[۳۹۱]

بی‌درنگ اشاره کنم که فخرالدین عظیمی (استاد دانشگاه کنیتیکت در امریکا، و نویسنده‌ی کتاب «بحران دمکراسی در ایران»)، این سخنان سحابی را آمیخته به «اوهام و خیالات» می‌داند، و در مصاحبه‌ای می‌گوید:

> [...سحابی] در مجموع طوری حرف زده است که گویی واقعه‌ای را که تمام و کمال رخ داده و خود هم ناظر آن بوده بیان می‌کند. ادعاهای او این تصور را القا می‌کند که آن چه می‌گوید سندیت دارد. اما اصلاً این طور نیست. درباره‌ی چنین ملاقاتی و شرکت‌کنندگان و موضوعات مطرح شده، هیچ سندی یافت یا ارائه نشده است. [...] این حرف‌ها اغلب مبتنی بر ادعاهای کسانی مانند خلیل طهماسبی و نواب صفوی و شنیده‌ها و مطالب گرد آمده در بازجویی‌های سال ۱۳۳۴ درباره‌ی قتل رزم‌آرا است. هدف اصلی و مشخص آن بازجویی‌ها هم پرونده‌سازی برای درگیر جلوه دادن مصدق و نزدیکان او در قتل رزم‌آرا بود. [...] بی‌گمان، بعد از کودتای ۲۸ مرداد دولتیان از هیچ تلاشی برای درگیر قلمداد کردن مصدق و اطرافیان او در آدم‌کشی و تباهکاری خودداری نکردند. نکته‌ای که برای من روشن نیست این است که چرا باید کسی مانند سحابی روایت فدائیان از نقش آن‌ها را بی‌هیچ تأملی بپذیرد و ادعاهای موجود را بدون آزمودن و سنجیدن در خور ذکر بداند. بی‌گمان همدلی‌ی او با فدائیان، به رغم انتقادهایی که به آن‌ها دارد، آشکار است ولی کار خاطره‌نگار این است که در برابر

---

۳۹۱ عزت‌الله سحابی، ***نیم قرن خاطره و تجربه: خاطرات مهندس عزت‌الله سحابی***، جلد اول، تهران: نشر فرهنگ صبا، ۱۳۸۶، ص ۹۳.

آیندگان احساس مسئولیت کند و هر شنیده‌ای را که در اثر گذشت زمان با تصورات و اوهام و خیالات زیادی آمیخته شده است، به عنوان واقعیت یا به شکلی که دیگران آن را واقعیت تصور کنند، منعکس نکند. [...][۳۹۲]

اما چه یدالله سحابی این گزاره‌ها را با «اوهام» خود آمیخته باشد و چه نه، می‌دانیم که حدود دو ماه بعد از جلسه‌ای که یدالله سحابی گزارش آن را داده است، رزم آرا، نخست وزیر ایران به دست عضوی از فدائیان اسلام (خلیل طهماسبی) به قتل می‌رسد؛ قاتل در کمال سربلندی به عمل خود اعتراف می‌کند؛ هشت ماه بعد، در تاریخ ۲۴ آبان ۱۳۳۰، زمان نخست‌وزیری‌ی دکتر محمد مصدق، مجلس شورای ملی سپهبد رزم آرا را «مهدورالدم» می‌شناسد، و حکم آزادی‌ی قاتل او را تصویب می‌کند. حکم «مهدورالدم»، به خاطر رویداد خونین ۳۰ تیر ۱۳۳۱، برای احمد قوام نیز از سوی شخصیت‌های جبهه‌ی ملی در مجلس شورای ملی تکرار می‌شود. گرچه همراهی‌ی آیت‌الله کاشانی و فدائیان اسلام با دکتر مصدق و جبهه‌ی ملی را- در روند انتخابات مجلسی که قانون ملی شدن نفت را تصویب کرد- نمی‌توان نادیده گرفت؛ همچنین، نمی‌توان از کنار همکاری و همراهی‌ی دکتر مصدق با آیت‌الله کاشانی در روزهای پایانی‌ی تیر ماه ۳۱ با سکوت گذشت، اما این «همراهی»، بر چنان ذهنیتی استوار بود که حتا پس از بروز اختلاف بین آیت‌الله کاشانی و فدائیان اسلام، و پس از بریدن هر دو از مصدق و جبهه‌ی ملی، نهادی به نام «نهضت آزادی» را پدید آورد که «دین را از سیاست جدا نمی‌دانست»، و نهایتاً، سرآغازِ ذوب‌شدنِ شخصیت‌های کلیدی‌ی آن شد در بینش آیت‌الله خمینی؛ بینشی که، نه تنها مشروطیتِ مورد دفاع دکتر مصدق و سران جبهه‌ی ملی را از بین برد، بلکه مفهوم «ملی» را نیز «خیانت به اسلام» تلقی کرد. اما ذهنیت دکتر مصدق هم یکسره مذهبی/ سنتی نبود. او مرد زمانه‌ی خود نیز بود. سیاست آزادی‌ی بیان و اندیشه، که دکتر مصدق در زمان صدارت خود پیرامون نشریه‌ها و حزب‌ها و سازمان‌ها به اجرا گذاشت، و این که اعلام کرد: «در جراید ایران آن چه راجع به شخص این‌جانب نگاشته می‌شود، هر چه نوشته باشند و هر که نوشته باشد، به هیچ‌وجه نباید مورد اعتراض و تعرض قرار گیرد»؛[۳۹۳] و این که به یاران و هوادارانش گفت «از من بت نسازید»، در تاریخ معاصر ایران بی‌همتا است، و از بخش «مدرنِ» ذهنیت مصدق خبر می‌دهد. (گرچه هواداران او به این سفارش اهمیت ندادند و از همان زمان تاکنون در رسانه‌های خود از دکتر محمد مصدق «بت» ساخته‌اند.) این ذهنیت دوپاره و میان‌مانده، از یک سو، مصدق را به آیت‌الله کاشانی و فدائیان اسلام و رهنمودهای آن‌ها وصل کرد، و از سوی دیگر، چون پاره‌ی «مدرن» ذهنیت او نمی‌توانست و نمی‌خواست «**احکام اسلامی را اجراء**» کند، در بزنگاه مبارزه از سوی آنان رانده شد، و حتا از سوی فدائیان اسلام به مرگ تهدید شد.[۳۹۴] دکتر مصدق در دور دوم نخست وزیری (پس از ۳۰ تیر ۱۳۳۱)، روندهائی را در اصلاحات اجتماعی پی گرفت که نه تنها با «احکام اسلامی»ی فدائیان اسلام مغایر بود، بلکه از حضور ذهنیت و دولتی سکولار خبر می‌داد؛ که مهم‌ترین آن‌ها، آزادی‌ی بیان بود. او در این دوره، وزارت کشور، وزارت کشاورزی، و وزارت راه را به رهبران حزبِ غیرمذهبی‌ی «ایران» سپرد؛ وزارت دادگستری را به عبدالعلی لطفی سپرد، که قاضی‌ای ضد روحانی بود و در دوره‌ی رضا شاه پهلوی نظام قضائی‌ی ایران را بازسازی کرده بود؛ وزارت فرهنگ را به دکتر مهدی آذر، استاد دانشگاه و هوادار حزب توده واگذار کرد؛ وزرای کابینه‌ی او نیز یکی پس از دیگری، اصلاحاتی را در برنامه‌ی کار گنجاندند که هر یک به نوعی با منافع روحانیان در تضاد قرار می‌گرفت (مانند ملی کردن شرکت‌های تلفن کشور، یا، دایر کردن نانوائی‌های جدید برای کاهش «قیمت ارزاق»، یا، رفع ممنوعیت از فروش

---

[۳۹۲] فخرالدین عظیمی: ***جبهه‌ی ملی نقشی در ترور رزم‌آرا نداشت***، دو ماهنامه‌ی «اندیشه‌ی پویا») تارنمای «تاریخ ایرانی»، ۲۵ مرداد ۱۳۹۰، http://tarikhirani.ir/fa/news/4/bodyView/3461/.html

[۳۹۳] ***پیام دکتر مصدق به ملت ایران***، روزنامه‌ی کیهان، ٤/ ۱۱/ ۱۳۳۱. برگرفته از: سرهنگ غلامرضا نجاتی، جنبش ملی شدن صنعت نفت ایران و کودتای ۲۸ مرداد ۱۳۳۲، پیشین، ص ۱۵۵.

[۳۹۴] پژوهشگرانی که به «بست نشستنِ» دکتر مصدق در مجلس (اتاق بودجه)، یا به این که خانه‌ی خود را با تانک و محافظان پرشمار به شکل یک «دژ» درآورده بود، خرده گرفته‌اند، به این مهم توجه ندارند که دکتر مصدق، از ماهیت «فدائیان اسلام» و روش مقابله‌ی آن‌ها به نیکی خبر داشت.

مشروبات الکلی با هدف افزایش به مالیات کشور). مشاوران دکتر مصدق نیز پیشنهاد کردند که با توجه به روح قانون مشروطه، که همه‌ی آحاد ملت را برابر می‌داند، به زنان حق رأی داده شود.[۳۹۵]

با این همه، مسائل پرسش‌برانگیز در سیاست‌های دکتر مصدق کم نبودند. مثلاً، رویاروئی‌ی مصرانه‌ی او با شاه، بر سر املاکی که از پدرش به ارث برده بود، و ثروت او و خانواده‌اش، آن هم در اوج مبارزه با نیروهای خارجی، باز به باور من، نابه‌هنگام بود، و در بسیاری موارد (مثل درآمد شاه از فروش املاک غصب شده توسط پدرش)، به ملی کردن نفت و تأمین کسر بودجه ربطی فوری نداشت؛ به ویژه که می‌دانیم «ضبط اموال پادشاه سابق به نفع مردم ایران»، یکی از مفادی بود که توسط کمیته‌ی موقت حزب توده در مهر ماه ۱۳۲۰ در مرامنامه‌ی این حزب نوشته شده بود. مطالبه‌ی وزارات جنگ از سوی مصدق نیز، ضمن این که به عنوان یک چاره‌جوئی برای جلوگیری از مداخله‌ی شاه و دربار در انتخابات مطرح شد، اما مسئله و دغدغه‌ی همیشگی‌ی دکتر مصدق بود. او، در ۲۸ بهمن ۱۳۰۰ که از سوی مشیرالدوله به استانداری‌ی آذربایجان منصوب شده بود، «به شرطی» آن شغل را پذیرفته بود که «ارتش آن ناحیه تحت امر او باشد»؛ و زمانی از این شغل استعفا داد که «سردار سپه» این اختیار را از او گرفت (اواسط سال ۱۳۰۱).[۳۹۶] در هر حال، پافشاری‌ی دکتر مصدق در خلع ید شاه از ارتش، در این بزنگاه تاریخی، یا: به نظر مخالفانش- مبنی بر انحصارطلبی‌ی او- صحه می‌گذارد، و یا بی‌خبری او را از موقعیتی که مسئله‌ی «ملی‌کردن نفت ایران» در میان ارتشیان ایران داشت گزارش می‌کند؛ چرا که بنا به گزارش محمدجعفر محمدی، عضو آن‌زمانی‌ی سازمان نظامی‌ی حزب توده، بسیاری از افسران و امیران ارتش نیز پیشاپیش با شاه و سیاست‌های او مخالف شده بودند. محمدجعفر محمدی، که پس از پنجاه سال، و در تبعید، «رازهای پیروزی‌ی کودتای ۲۸ مرداد» را- صرفاً از دیدگاه نظامی- بررسی کرده است، در کتاب خود، ابتدا از ۵ تیپ رزمی در تهران و حومه، و از فرماندهان آن‌ها (در زمان کودتا) نام می‌برد و سپس می‌نویسد:

> آری در تهران و حومه ۵ تیپ رزمی وجود داشت و کودتاچیان نتوانستند حتا یکی از این تیپ‌ها را با خود همراه سازند. زیرا: جنبش آزادی‌خواهی در ایران پس از توطئه‌های درباری‌ی سی‌ام تیر، نهم اسفند، و ربودن و کشتن رئیس شهربانی‌ی کل کشور، سرتیپ محمود افشارطوس در اردیبهشت ماه سال ۱۳۳۲، به شدت در بین افسران و درجه‌داران اوج گرفت و عده‌ی زیادی از افسران، نه تنها به شاه و دربار تمایلی نداشتند، که به شدت از دکتر مصدق و جنبش ملی‌شدن صنعت نفت پشتیبانی می‌کردند. در حقیقت می‌توان گفت که در کل ارتش ایران، نه تنها در آن پنج واحد رزمی‌ی مستقر در تهران و حومه، در صدِ پائینی از شاه و دربار طرفداری می‌کردند، بلکه در کلِ ارتش، این در صد، بسیار ضعیف بود.[۳۹۷]

مسئله‌ی بحث‌برانگیز دیگر در سیاست‌های دکتر مصدق، درخواست اختیارات یک ساله‌ای بود که در واقع، فلسفه‌ی وجودی‌ی مجلس را منتفی می‌کرد. از آن مهمتر، مسئله‌ی انحلال مجلس هفدهم است، که بسیاری از نمایندگان فراکسیون نهضت ملی و مشاوران و نزدیک‌ترین یاران دکتر مصدق- مانند دکتر عبدالله معظمی، دکتر علی شایگان، دکتر غلامحسین صدیقی، دکتر کریم سنجابی، خلیل ملکی، احمد رضوی و محمود نریمان- با توجه به مفاد قانون اساسی- با آن مخالف بودند. دکتر غلامحسین صدیقی، وزیر کشور دولت مصدق و یکی از شریف‌ترین شخصیت‌های نهضت ملی، چندی پیش

---

۳۹۵ اطلاعات مربوط به اصلاحات دور دوم نخست وزیری‌ی دکتر مصدق را از مأخذ زیر برگرفته‌ام:

❖ یرواند آبراهامیان، ***ایران بین دو انقلاب: از مشروطه تا انقلاب اسلامی***، ترجمه‌ی کاظم فیروزمند، حسن شمس‌آوری، محسن مدیرشانه‌چی، تهران: چاپ هشتم، نشر مرکز، ۱۳۸۳، ص ۲۴۸.

۳۹۶ سرهنگ غلامرضا نجاتی، ***جنبش ملی شدن صنعت نفت ایران ...*** ، پیشین، ص ۱۴۸.

۳۹۷ محمدجعفر محمدی، ***پس از نیم قرن: راز پیروزی‌ی کودتای ۲۸ مرداد***، آلمان- کلن: انتشارات فروغ، ۱۳۸۲/ ۲۰۰۳، صص ۲۶ تا ۲۷.

از درگذشت، در گفت‌وگوئی که با حمید سیف‌زاده داشت، یادآور شد که دکتر مصدق را از انحلال مجلس برحذر داشته بود:

دکتر مصدق با التماس از من خواست که تا فردا پس فردا که پنج‌شنبه و جمعه بود، مخالفتی نکنم تا باز با هم صحبت کنیم و اگر نتیجه‌ی مطلوب به دست نیامد، برای اتخاذ هر رویه و عملی مختار باشم. من هم قبول کردم. در فاصله‌ی این دو روز، ایشان دستور دادند وکلا استعفا بدهند و حدود سی چهل نفر پیشقدم شدند که به تدریج شمار آن‌ها به ۵۸ نفر رسید. روز شنبه که برای ادامه‌ی مذاکره با دکتر مصدق به دیدار او رفتم، گفت: «آقا ما نمی‌خواهیم مجلس را منحل کنیم. این وکلا هستند که خودشان استعفا داده‌اند و چون مملکت نمی‌تواند بلاتکلیف بماند، ما ناچاریم از مردم سئوال کنیم که چه باید کرد؟» و بدین ترتیب قرار رفراندم گذاشته شد.[۳۹۸]

در هر حال، رفراندم انحلال مجلس- با همه‌ی تنگنائی که این مجلس برای دولت مصدق پدید آورده بود- با این که از سوی اکثریت مردم نیز پاسخ مثبت گرفت، از نُرم‌های دمکراتیکِ دولت مصدق تجاوز کرد، و او را در عمل، به سوی نوعی از استبداد سوق داد. به ویژه اگر این رفراندم انجام نشده بود، و مجلس عملاً در مرحله‌ی «انحلال» قرار نداشت، «فرمان»های شاه در عزل مصدق و نصب سپهبد زاهدی، بهانه‌ای به دست کودتاچیان نمی‌داد که دولت مصدق را غیرقانونی اعلام کنند؛ زیرا بر مبنای قانون اساسی‌ی مشروطه، «فرمان»های شاه با تصوب مجلس مشروعیت می‌یافت؛ در حالی که با انجام رفراندم انحلال مجلس، در آن زمان عملاً مجلسی در کار نبود که این «فرمان»ها را تصویب کند یا نکند. افزون بر این، در غیاب مجلس، و در جوّ نظامی/ امنیتی‌ی پس از کودتا، دولت زاهدی توانست انتخابات مجلس بعدی را آن طور که می‌خواست و لازم بود که قرارداد کنسرسیوم را تصویب کند، انجام دهد.

مسئله‌ی پرسش‌برانگیز دیگر، درخواست کمک مالی از امریکا بود؛ یعنی از دولتی که هم در تحریم خرید نفت ایران دست داشت، و هم از آن پیروی کرده بود. اگر سخن مخالفان دکتر مصدق- حاکی بر عمده کردن «خطر کمونیسم در ایران» از سوی خود دکتر مصدق- را نپذیریم، و نپذیریم که او این «خطر» را به عنوان گروکشی در برابر ترس امریکا از چیرگی‌ی شوروی در ایران عمده کرده بود، دست کم به عنوان یک واقعیت انکارناپذیر تاریخی می‌دانیم که او برای تأمین کسر بودجه، از امریکا درخواست وام کرده بود، و برای آن «موعد» هم تعیین کرده بود. این درخواست، آن هم در اوج «جنگ سرد»، به همان سیاستی دامن زد که سازمان‌های اطلاعاتی‌ی بریتانیا و امریکا، با خلق پدیده‌ای به نام «حزب توده‌ی قلابی» در ایران، و با گزارش‌های خود، برای جلب رضایت رئیس جمهور امریکا- برای سرنگونی‌ی دولت مصدق- دنبال می‌کردند. خسرو شاکری زند، مورخ این دوره از تاریخ ایران، این فرایند را در مقاله‌ای طولانی و با زیرنویس‌های متعدد بررسی کرده است. در فرازهائی از این مقاله و زیرنویس‌های آن آمده است:

در پاسخ به این پرسش که آیا، چنان که بریتانیا و ایالات متحده علناً و مصرانه تبلیغ می‌کردند، ایران در عهد مصدق در خطر کمونیسم قرار داشت و حزب توده تخته‌ی پرش فتح ایران توسط اتحاد شوروی بود یا نه؟ باید یادآور شد که تبلیغات مستمر بریتانیا و امریکا و روزنامه‌های عمده‌ی غربی این نکته را ترجیع‌بند مقالات خود پیرامون مسئله‌ی نفت می‌کردند و حتا بریتانیا در مذاکرات خود با امریکا، با توجه به ضعف فکری‌ی امریکا در زمینه‌ی جنگ سرد و رواج مکارتیسم، بر این مسئله تأکید می‌ورزید تا هر چه زودتر امریکا را متقاعد سازد که ادامه‌ی دولت مصدق به کمونیسم در ایران منتج خواهد شد و هیچ راهی جز کودتا برای جلوگیری از افتادن ایران در چنگ شوروی نخواهد بود. [...] در تلگرافی به تاریخ بیست و یکم ژوئیه/ سی‌ام تیر ۱۳۳۲ از سفارت امریکا- که ضمیمه به گزارش‌های دفتر تحقیقاتی‌ی سیا، اول اکتبر ۱۳۳۲/ بیست و سوم مهر ۱۳۳۲- است، درباره‌ی تظاهرات یادبود سی‌ام تیر (در سال ۱۳۳۲)، که هواداران دولت مصدق در

---

۳۹۸ بامشاد، ***قصه‌ی پرغصه‌ی من و ایران من***، ماهنامه‌ی «روزگار نو»، دفتر دوازدهم، سال یازدهم، شماره‌ی ۱۳۲، بهمن ۱۳۷۱، ص ۹۶.

> نوزدهم ژوئیه برگزار کردند، آورده شده است که تعداد شرکت کنندگان هوادار مصدق «تنها تقریباً سه هزار تن» بود، اما هوادارن حزب توده در تظاهراتی جداگانه به همان مناسبت «دوازده هزار تن» بودند، که با دیسیپلین خود و حمل پرچم‌های متعدد ضدِ امریکائی در آن شرکت داشتند. هواداران برجسته‌ی مصدق تحت تأثیر نمایش توده‌ای‌ها و از بابت نمایش هواداران خود سرخورده شدند. اما در اظهار نظر سیا درباره‌ی آن تلگراف آمده است که گزارش سفارت در تضاد با خبر رادیو تهران و روزنامه های تهران بود، که تعداد هوادارن دولت مصدق را صد هزار گفته و به زد وُ خورد در بین هواداران مصدق و توده‌ای‌ها اشاره کرده بودند. در این اظهار نظر همچنین گفته می‌شود که نمایش صفوف منظم حزب توده «تأثیر گذار»تر و «نامیمون»تر از «خشونت عوام» بود.[۳۹۹]

گرچه خسرو شاکری زند نیز بنا بر پرسشی که مطرح کرده، به سهم دکتر مصدق در «برجسته» کردن این «خطر» نپرداخته است. اما بنا بر این گونه اسناد- که اکثراً تا امروز منتشر شده و در اختیار مورخان قرار دارند- در این تردید نیست که «خطر کمونیسم» توسط سازمان‌های اطلاعاتی‌ی امریکا و بریتانیا عمده می‌شد. منتها، باز بنا بر اسناد، در این واقعیت هم تردید نیست که خود دکتر مصدق نیز در فرایند درخواست مصرانه‌ی وام از امریکا و در مذاکراتِ مربوط به آن، به این فکر دامن زد. البته، شیفتگان دکتر مصدق برای همه‌ی این‌ها توضیحاتی دارند که در همه‌ی موارد قانع‌کننده نیستند. مثلاً گروهی بر این باورند که عمده کردن «خطر کمونیسم» یکسره از سوی سازمان‌های اطلاعاتی‌ی غرب و یا حزب توده القاء می‌شد، و خود دکتر مصدق از آن مبرا بود. اما برای حذف دکتر مصدق از شرکت در این «القاء»، باید سخن همه‌ی دیپلمات‌های امریکائی را که در این ماجرا درگیر بوده‌اند، و هر یک، شنیده‌های خود از دکتر مصدق را جداگانه به دولت خود و به سازمان اطلاعاتی‌ی آن گزارش داده‌اند، یکسره دروغ بپنداریم؛ که البته نه تاریخ چنین اجازه‌ای به پژوهشگر خود پیش‌کش کرده است، و نه دیپلمات‌های همه‌ی کشورها- مانند برخی از دولتمردان ما- به دولت خودشان گزارش دروغ می‌دهند.

***

به طور کلی، پیرامون زندگی و شخصیت و عملکرد سیاسی‌ی دکتر مصدق، و رویداد ۲۸ مرداد ۳۲ و سقوط دولت مصدق، و محاکمه‌ی او در دادگاه نظامی، در شصت سال گذشته صدها متن، مخالف یا موافق، از دیدگاه‌های علمی/ تاریخی، یا تحقیقی/ ایدئولوژیک، یا صرفاً تبلیغی، نوشته شده است، و به مناسبتِ سالگردهای تصویب «ملی شدن نفت» یا «درگذشت دکتر مصدق» یا «۲۸ مرداد ۳۲»، صدها گفتار با دیدگاه‌های مختلف ایراد شده است. در کنار این مجموعه، اسناد مجلس شورای ملی در آن سال‌ها، گزارش‌های سفیران و نمایندگان بریتانیا و ایالات متحده‌ی امریکا، اسناد منتشرشده از سوی شورای امنیت ملی‌ی امریکا، اسناد مربوط به «دادگاه لاهه»، دفاعیه‌های مصدق در دادگاه نظامی، متن‌های مفسران و خبرنگاران خارجی، خاطرات اعضاء خانواده‌ی دکتر مصدق،[۴۰۰] خاطرات شخصیت‌های سیاسی‌ی آن دوران، خاطرات و یادداشت‌های خود دکتر مصدق هم در دسترس هستند، که مجموعاً ادبیات هنگفتی را تشکیل می‌دهند. تا جائی که من در گوشه و کنار این مجموعه‌ی شلوغ پرسه زده‌ام، «دکتر مصدق»های متعددی به دید می‌آید: در یک قطب، دولتمردی را می‌بینیم که به رغم سفارش خود او، که «از من بت نسازید»، در چشم پرستندگانش در هیئت یک قدیس، یک

---

[۳۹۹] خسرو شاکری (زند)، ***نقدی بر پاره‌ای از نظرات پیرامون نقش حزب توده در روزهای ۲۵ تا ۲۸ مرداد***، بخش اول و دوم، برگرفته از تارنمای «البرز نیوز»، واپسین بازدید: ۲۲ اکتبر ۲۰۱۲:
http://www.alborznews.eu/index.php/2012-09-19-09-03-19/8912-safehate-vizhe11.html
توضیح: به مأخذ مورد اشاره‌ی خسرو شاکری زند، توجه کنید:
Communists demonstrate impressively in Iran, 21 June [sic July] 1953, Current Inteligence Bulletin (C.I.B.), 3 March 1953.

[۴۰۰] افزون بر خاطرات دکتر غلامحسین مصدق (پسر دکتر محمد مصدق)، کتاب «در خلوت مصدق»، نوشته‌ی شیرین سمیعی (همسر محمود مصدق، نوه‌ی دکتر محمد مصدق) را در دست داریم که به باور من، یکی از مآخذی است که می‌توان وجهی از شخصیت محمد مصدق را در آن دید:
- شیرین سمیعی، ***در خلوت مصدق***، لس‌انجلس: انتشارات شرکت کتاب، ۱۳۸۴/ ۲۰۰۶.

اَبَر مرد، عاری از هر ضعف و خطا، با سرشتی فراانسانی، رو در روی پدیده‌های شَرّی به نام‌های «محمد رضا شاه پهلوی» و «امپریالیسم انگلیس» و «امپریالیسم امریکا» ایستاده است. در قطب روبه‌رو، دکتر مصدق را در هیئت دولتمردی می‌بینیم، نیمه معلول، عقب‌مانده، باستانی، دو- دوزه باز، عوام‌فریب، توطئه‌گر، فراماسونر، دیکتاتورمآب، کینه‌توز، انتقام‌جو، امامزاده‌ی روشنفکران سطحی، عاشق هورای مردم، که هدفی نداشت جز نابودی‌ی پدیده‌ی خِیری به نام «خاندان پهلوی» در قالب شخصیتی «وجیه‌الملّه». در میانه‌ی این دو قطب، و به برکت مجموعه‌ی پژوهش‌های بی‌طرفانه و با رویکرد علمی- و حتا به برکت استنتاج از «تحقیق»های جهت‌دار و طرف‌گیرانه‌ی مخالفان مصدق- دولتمردی را می‌بینم با همه‌ی قوت‌ها و ضعف‌های انسانی، که برای بازپس‌گرفتن حقوق حقه‌ی مردم ایران، در برابر استبداد رو به رشدِ داخلی و استعمار خارجی تمام قد ایستاد، و در این رهگذر، صدای مردم غارت‌شده‌ی ایران را به گوش جهانیان نیز رساند؛ و در عین حال، با همه‌ی نابخردی‌های حتمی و احتمالی در تاکتیک مبارزه، با هیچ ترفندی قابل تطمیع و قابل خریداری نبود؛ و به هیچ قیمتی حاضر نشد منافع ملت ایران را با منافع شخصی‌ی خود تاخت بزند. این «دکتر مصدق» می‌توانست- دست کم در دور دوم مذاکره، که انگلستان حاضر شد بدون حق بررسی‌ی اسناد فروش نفت، حق مالکیت نفت ایران را به رسمیت بشناسد- با استعمار سازش کند، و بعد، مانند سپهبد زاهدی در زمان طرح لایحه‌ی کنسرسیوم در مجلس، بگوید: ما با این قرارداد «در واقع سر انگلیس و امریکا کلاه گذاشته‌ایم»، و با این نوع مردم‌فریبی‌ها، «وجیه‌الملّه» هم باقی بماند. اما نه تنها چنین نکرد، بلکه برای جلوگیری از خونریزی و یا جنگ داخلی، مردم را بیانیه داد که روز ۲۸ مرداد از خانه‌هاشان بیرون نیایند. این «دکتر محمد مصدق»، در روزهای پایانی‌ی دولتش دیده بود که در تنهائی‌ی محض، و در محاصره‌ی کامل مخالفان داخلی و خارجی، در رسیدن به نهایتِ هدفش شکست خورده است. با این وصف، ادامه‌ی مبارزه را در دفاعیات خود در دادگاه نظامی، به عرض مردم ایران رساند.

در هر حال، از جمعیت‌های هزاران نفره‌ای که در هر فرصت ممکن و غیرممکن و زیر چوب و چماق جمهوری‌ی اسلامی، در سالگرد ملی کردن نفت، یا تولد یا درگذشت مصدق، احمد آباد را از امواج انسانی پر می‌کنند، چنین به نظر می‌آید که روان جمعی‌ی ملت ایران، تصویر سوم از «دکتر مصدق» را، به عنوان مرد فسادناپذیر تاریخ معاصر، و به عنوان نماد بلندقامتِ مقاومت ملی، به حافظه‌ی تاریخی‌ی خود سپرده است. و این حکم تاریخ است، که از فراسوی ضعف‌ها و قوت‌های دکتر مصدق، و از فراسوی تحریف‌های آگاهانه یا ناآگاهانه‌ی مخالفان، تمام قد عرض اندام می‌کند. به حکمِ همین حکمِ تاریخی است که حدود ۶۰ سال بعد از سقوط مصدق، سینماگر جوانی از نسل دوم مهاجران، به نام روزبه دادوند، که «در امریکا بزرگ شده و تا سال ۲۰۰۳ هرگز اسم مصدق را هم نشنیده بود»، ابتدا با خواندن کتاب «همه‌ی مردان شاه»، و سپس با مطالعه‌ی تاریخ قرن بیستم و متن‌های مخالف و موافق با مصدق، چنان تحت تأثیر شخصیت این مرد تاریخی قرار می‌گیرد، که از قلب امریکا به احمدآباد سفر می‌کند؛ تبعیدگاه و محل مرگ مصدق را از نزدیک می‌بیند؛ و از سال‌های واپسین زندگی‌ی او فیلم می‌سازد. من، همه‌ی این فیلمِ ۲٤ دقیقه‌ای را که از جشنواره‌های متعدد جایزه گرفت، ندیده‌ام. اما در متنی که فیروزه خطیبی (روزنامه نگار مقیم لس‌انجلس) در معرفی‌ی این فیلم و تهیه‌کننده‌ی آن نوشت، از قول روزبه دادوند خواندم:

> من از مجموع خوانده‌هایم درباره‌ی مصدق، چه مثبت و چه منفی، نهایتاً به این نتیجه رسیدم که او حقیقتاً تنها امید رسیدن به دمکراسی در ایران و یکی از معدود رهبران سیاسی ۱۰۰ سال گذشته‌ی ایران بود که ذره‌ای فساد و انحراف در وجودش دیده نمی‌شد. [...] احساس می‌کنم افکار و ایده‌آل‌های مصدق در وجود هر ایرانی زندگی می‌کند. بارها به این مسئله فکر کرده‌ام که اگر مصدق بر مسند قدرت باقی می‌ماند تاریخ و سرنوشت مردم ایران امروز چه شکلی پیدا می‌کرد؟[۴۰۱]

---

[۴۰۱] فیروزه خطیبی، ***فیلم کوتاه مصدق، نگاهی خیالی به روزهای آخر زندگی‌ی او***، تارنمای «بی بی سی»، ۲۷ آوریل ۲۰۱۳/ ۷ اردیبهشت ۱۳۹۲:
http://www.bbc.co.uk/persian/arts/2013/04/130427_l41_cinema_mosaddegh_interview.shtml

همین جا به عنوان معترضـه بیافزایم که مقایسـه‌ی آرامگاه آیت‌الله خمینی، با آرامگاه دکتر محمد مصـدق (در فیلم روز به دادوند) این پرسـش را نیز در بیننده می‌انگیزد که چرا آرامگاه چنین شـخصـیتی، پس از این همه سـال و پس از سـقوط حکومت کودتا، هنوز این گونه سـاده و متروک و دورافتاده وانهاده شـده اسـت. من به نوبه‌ی خود، همین جا به عرض می‌رسانم که برای یافتن پاسخ به این پرسش، باید به راه و روش و اندیشه‌ای نگاه کرد که زیر شعار «مرگ بر امریکا»، سی و چهار سال است که از علت‌العلل سقوط مصدق درس آموخته است، تا «بر مسند قدرت» باقی بماند. (پایان معترضه)

با این همه، باز، این حکم تاریخ است که ۶۰ سال پس از سقوط دولت مصدق، یعنی شش دهه پس از کودتای ۲۸ مرداد ۱۳۳۲، یعنی آن چه که محمدرضا شاه پهلوی آن را «رستاخیز ملی» خواند، شاهزاده رضا پهلوی- نوه‌ی رضا شاه پهلوی، پسر و ولیعهد محمدرضا شاه پهلوی- را در تبعیدگاه خود واداشت که نسبت به دکتر محمد مصدق و تلاش او و یارانش در راه ملی کردن نفت ایران، تمام قد ادای احترام کند.[۴۰۲]

***

محمدرضـا شـاه پهلوی پس از کودتا، «حزب توده» و «جبهه‌ی ملی» را غیرقانونی اعلام کرد؛ گروهی از پیکارگران را اعدام یا زندانی کرد؛ و آن‌هائی را که از اعدام و زندان جان به در برده بودند از ایران تاراند؛ و سـپس، تا راه هر امکانی را بر رشـد آگاهی و اندیشـه‌های مدنی سـد کند، بیش از پیش، راه هر امکانی را به رشـد احسـاسـات و اندیشـه‌های مذهبی گشود. (خواهم گفت که چه‌گونه گشود.)

البته این دوره، یکی از پیچیده‌ترین دوره‌های زندگی‌ی «حزب توده» بود، که ریز چه‌گونگی‌ی آن موضوع سخن من نیست. منتها بایسته است که چند نکته را اشاره‌وار یادآوری کنم: بنا بر گوشه و کنارهای اسناد منتشرشده‌ی شورای امنیت ملی‌ی امریکا، در کوران مبارزه‌ی بریتانیا و امریکا با دکتر مصـدق- و کلاً، با جنبش ملی‌کردن نفت- سـازمان‌های اطلاعاتی‌ی این کشورها، پدیده‌ای به نام «حزب توده‌ی قلابی» با «تظاهرات سیاه» در ایران بوجود آورده بودند، که نقش آن، در قالب دفاع از دکتر مصدق، ایجاد نفرت و انزجار و ترس و بی‌اعتمادی در لایه‌های مختلف مردم نسبت به دکتر مصدق و حزب توده بوده اسـت. البته، به گفته‌ی دکتر مازیار بهروز، خرد و کلان حزب توده از وجود چنین پدیده‌ای اظهار بی‌خبری می‌کنند.[۴۰۳] اما ذات این اظهار بی‌خبری نیز، سخت به زیان حزب توده است. چرا که خواسته یا ناخواسته می‌پذیرد که این خودِ «حزب توده» بوده که با آشـوب‌ها و بلواهای پیاپی (مانند حمله با چوب و چماق به مغازه‌ها و گروه‌های سـیاسـی و مکان‌های عمومی ظاهراً به نفع جنبش ملی و دکتر مصـدق)، خود عامل ایجاد آن بی‌اعتمادی و دلسـردی در مردم ایران نسبت به سیاست‌های دکتر مصدق بوده است. از این گزاره‌ی مشکوک که بگذریم، پیرامون خودِ «حزب توده» و عملکرد آن در این دوره از تاریخ ایران، متن‌های پژوهشـی‌ی فراوانی در دسـت داریم که ما را از چند و چون برخورد منفی‌ی این حزب با دکتر مصـدق و مسـئله‌ی نفت آشـنا می‌کنند. برخی از پژوهشـگران، در چرائی‌ی عدم حمایت حزب توده از دولت

---

۴۰۲ در بیانیه‌ی رضا پهلوی (۲۹ اسفند ۱۳۹۰) چنین می‌خوانیم:
«بیست و نهم اسفند ماه، سالروز ملی شدن صنعت نفت ایران، بر کارکنان، متخصصـان و فعالان این عرصـه و بر ملت ایران فرخنده باد. در دوران شـکوفایی و پیشرفت اقتصـادی‌ی کشورمان، به کوشش و همت بزرگ‌مردانی، همچون دکتر محمد مصدق، رهبر جنبش ملی کردن نفت ایران و اعضـای کمیسیون مخصـوص نفت، در ۲۹ اسفند ۱۳۲۹ قانون ملی شدن صـنعت نفت، [با قطع‌نامه‌ی زیر] به تصـویب مجلس شـورای ملی ایران رسـید: "**به نام سـعادت ملت ایران و به منظور کمک به تأمین صـلح جهانی، ما امضـاکنندگان ذیل پیشـنهاد می‌نمائیم که صـنعت نفت ایران در تمام مناطق کشور بدون استثنا ملی اعلام شود؛ یعنی تمام عملیات اکتشـاف، استخراج و بهره‌برداری در دست دولت قرارگیرد.**" ضمن تجلیل از خدمات دکتر محمد مصدق و همه‌ی کسانی که در این کار عظیم و تاریخی ایفای نقش نمودند و همچنین، با قدردانی از فعالیت‌ها و فداکاری‌های برجسته و ارزشمند کارکنان سخت‌کوش، شرافتمند و دلسوز صنعت نفت و گاز کشورمان، این روز تاریخی و ملی را به تمام هممیهنانم شادباش می‌گویم.» به مأخذ زیر نگاه کنید:
❖ رضا پهلوی، ***بیست و نهم اسفند ماه، سالروز ملی شدن صنعت نفت ایران***، تارنمای «رضا پهلوی»، ۱۹ مارس ۲۰۱۲:
http://www.rezapahlavi.org/details_article.php?persian&article=583

۴۰۳ نشریه‌ی الکترونیکی‌ی «انقلاب اسلامی در هجرت»، شماره‌ی ۶۰۱، بازدید ۱۰ مهر ۱۳۸۹:
http://goto.glocalnet.net/banisadr_arkiv/matn1-601.htm

مصدق، به وابستگی‌ی این حزب به اتحاد جماهیر شوروی اشاره می‌کنند و این عدم حمایت را به مسئله‌ی نفت شمال و منافع دولت شوروی، که با ملی شدن صنعت نفت برای همیشه منتفی می‌شد، مربوط می‌دانند؛[۴۰۴] بنا بر پژوهش گسترده‌ی اصغر شیرازی، تا زمانی که مصدق (در پست نماینده‌ی مجلس) با دادن امتیاز نفت شمال به شوروی‌ها مخالفت نکرده بود، ارگان‌های نوشتاری‌ی حزب توده، او را «مظهر اراده‌ی ملت» و مظهر «مبارزه بر علیه ارتجاع و دسایس ارتجاعی» معرفی می‌کردند. اما زمانی که دکتر مصدق، در تاریخ ۱۱ آذر ۱۳۲۳ قانون ممنوعیت مذاکره و واگذاری‌ی هر نوع امتیاز به «دول مجاور و غیر مجاور» را در مجلس مطرح کرد و آن را به تصویب رساند، و سپس‌تر، به دنبال سیاست «موازنه‌ی منفی»، امتیاز شوروی در شیلات ایران را لغو کرد، نظر و رفتار این حزب نسبت به دکتر مصدق دگرگون شد؛ به طوری که درست در کوران مبارزه با استعمار، مصدق و جبهه‌ی ملی را «عامل استعمار» نامید و ارگان نوشتاری‌ی آن (به سوی آینده، ۷ آذر ۱۳۲۹) مصدق را «پیرمرد مکاری» خواند که «نیم قرن است به اغفال و فریب خلق مشغول است.» این حزب، همچنین، تمام اصلاحات اقتصادی‌ی دولت مصدق را، که توانسته بود ایران را بدون درآمد نفت به مدت دو سال سر پا نگهدارد، (حتا قانونی را که از سهم مالکانه کاست و به سهم کشاورز افزود)، با زبانی منفی در قالب الگوهای سوسیالیستی سنجید و آن‌ها را «رفرمیستی» در سطح «فئودالیسم» تلقی کرد.[۴۰۵] همایون کاتوزیان، پژوهشگر این دوره از تاریخ ایران، نیز می‌نویسد:

> از نخست وزیری‌ی مصدق در اردیبهشت ۱۳۳۰ تا قیام تیر ۱۳۳۱، حزب توده از هیچ‌گونه تهمت شفاهی و کتبی نسبت به مصدق و طرفدارانش خودداری نکرد. فقط در یک کاریکاتورِ یک صفحه‌ای، مصدق را به شکل رقاصه‌ی نیمه‌لختی کشیدند که دارد برای امریکا و انگلیس می‌رقصد.[۴۰۶]

بدین ترتیب، جای شگفتی نیست که حزب توده، روز ۲۸ مرداد ۳۲ از صحنه‌ی نبرد غایب بود. البته توجیه این غیبت، بیانیه‌ی دکترمصدق بود مبنی بر «در خانه ماندنِ مردم». اما، بدون آن که بخواهیم استقلال‌طلبی و صداقتِ انبوه مبارزان در این حزب را نادیده بگیریم، تاریخ نشان می‌دهد که دست کم از زمان اوج‌گیری‌ی فرقه‌ی دموکرات آذربایجان، کمیته‌ی مرکزی‌ی این حزب، برای هر اقدام یا آکسیونی که لازم می‌دانست، منتظر دستور هیچ مرجعی- به جز «حزب کمونیست شوروی»- نمی‌ماند. جالب است بدانیم که فرخ نگهدار (از بخش «اکثریتِ» سازمان چریک‌های فدائی‌ی خلق ایران، و ذوب‌شده در حزب توده‌ی ایران) نزدیک به شش دهه پس از ۲۸ مرداد ۳۲، در گفتاری با عنوان «حمایت توده‌ای‌ها از مصدق موجب کودتا شد، نه عدم حمایت آن‌ها»، در حمایت حزب توده از مصدق (به ویژه پس از ۳۰ تیر ۱۳۳۱) تردید ندارد؛ و همین حمایت را سبب سقوط دولت مصدق برآورد می‌کند.[۴۰۷] البته اگر- با پشتوانه‌ی اسناد موجود- عبارت «حمایت حزب توده از مصدق» را از گفته‌ی فرخ نگهدار برداریم، تشخیص او بخشی از واقعیت را برملا می‌کند. چرا که حزب توده، در فضای دموکراتیک صدارت دکتر مصدق، با این که هنوز رسماً حزبی «غیرقانونی» بود، از کمای سیاسی به درآمد، و دوباره قدرتمند شد، و در درازنای دو سال، ده‌ها آکسیون کارگری و خیابانی را در شهرهای مختلف ایران

---

۴۰۴ در پاراگراف پایانی‌ی پیشنهاد جبهه‌ی ملی برای ملی کردن نفت ایران که با امضای حائری‌زاده، اللهیار صالح، دکتر شایگان، دکتر محمد مصدق، و حسین مکی در تاریخ ۴ آذر ۱۳۲۹ توسط محمد مصدق (وکیل مجلس) در کمیسیون نفت مجلس خوانده شد، عبارت «صنعت نفت در مناطق کشور **بدون استثناء** ملی اعلام شود» آمده بود. به مأخذ زیر نگاه کنید:

- سرهنگ غلامرضا نجاتی، ***جنبش ملی شدن صنعت نفت ایران و کودتای ۲۸ مرداد ۱۳۳۲***، چاپ هشتم، تهران: شرکت سهامی انتشار، ۱۳۷۸، ص ۱۱۰.

۴۰۵ اصغر شیرازی، ***مدرنیته، شُبهه و دموکراسی: بر مبنای یک بررسی‌ی موردی درباره‌ی حزب توده‌ی ایران***، تهران: نشر اختران، ۱۳۸۶، فصل چهارم، صص ۲۴۱ تا ۲۶۸.

۴۰۶ همایون کاتوزیان، ***حزب توده در آئینه‌ی تاریخ***، تارنمای «رادیو فردا»، ۱۲ مهر ۱۳۹۰:
http://www.radiofarda.com/content/f3_todehparty_in_history/24348954.html

۴۰۷ فرخ نگهدار، ***حمایت توده‌ای‌ها از مصدق موجب کودتا شد نه عدم حمایت آن‌ها***، تارنمای «رادیو فردا»، ۱۹ اوت ۲۰۱۰، بازدید ۱۰ سپتامبر ۲۰۱۰:
http://www.radiofarda.com/content/f4_Farokh_Negahdar_Tudeh_Party_Mossadegh/2131900.html

تدارک دید و به اجراء گذاشت؛ در ارگان‌های نوشتاریِ خود علیه شاه و رژیم سلطنتی و «امپریالیسم امریکا» و به نفع گرایش‌های «سوسیالیستی» تبلیغ کرد. و به این وسیله، بارآور تهدیدی بود که «خطر کمونیسم» نام گرفت، و یکی از عوامل مهمی شد که از یک سو، طیف مذهبی را از مصدق دور کرد، و از سوی دیگر، در بحبوحه‌ی «جنگ سرد» امکان کودتا علیه دولت او را نیرو بخشید. شگفتا که این حزب، حتا در روزهای ۲۵ تا ۲۷ مرداد ۱۳۳۲ پس از شکست کودتای اول، با انبوه هواداران خود، در تهران و در شهرهای بزرگ ایران علیه شاه و نظام سلطنت تظاهرات هنگفتی را هدایت کرد؛ شعارهای «ما شاه نمی‌خواهیم» و «مرگ بر شاه» را همگانی کرد؛ و بدون «دستور» دکتر مصدق، در پائین کشیدن مجسمه‌های شاه و پدرش نقش اساسی داشت، اما روز ۲۸ مرداد، یعنی روز کودتا، خیابان‌های ایران از تظاهرات این حزب خالی بود. بیست و پنج سال بعد، نورالدین کیانوری، دبیر کل حزب توده، ضمن این که اشتباه دکتر مصدق در عدم شناخت از «امپریالیسم امریکا» را برآمده از پایگاه طبقاتیِ او برشمرد (و البته بدون اشاره به وابستگیِ سران حزب توده به سیاست‌ها و رهنمودهای «امپریالیسم شوروی»)، به اشتباه حزب توده اعتراف کرد. در بخشی از این متن آمده است:

> حزب توده‌ی ایران طرح شعار ملی شدن نفت در «سراسر ایران» را یک توطئه‌ای ارزیابی کرد که هدفش پیدا کردن راه جدیدی برای واگذاریِ منابع نفتیِ **سراسر ایران** به انحصارهای نفت‌خوار امریکائی بود. این اشتباه هم جزئی از اشتباه اساسیِ رهبریِ حزب درباره‌ی یکی دانستن جناح ملیِ جبهه‌ی ملی، یعنی دکتر مصدق و یارانش، با جناح امریکائیِ جبهه‌ی ملی، یعنی بقائی، مکی، و عمیدی نوری و همه‌ی دار و دسته‌ای [بود] که بعداً به صفوف کودتاچیان ۲۸ مرداد پیوستند.[۴۰۸] (گیومه در متن اصلی وجود دارد. تأکید از من است.)

توجه خواننده، بی‌اختیار، به عبارت «ملی شدن نفت در سراسر ایران» در نوشته‌ی کیانوری جلب می‌شود؛ که «نفت شمال» و منافع شوروی را نیز شامل می‌شد. کیانوری در این متن، اشاره می‌کند که خبر کودتای اول (۲۵ مرداد) را روز پیش او به مصدق داده بود، و به یاریِ حزب توده بود که کودتا خنثا شد؛ و خبر کودتای دوم را نیز او به اطلاع مصدق رسانده بود و حتا به او پیشنهاد ائتلاف داده بود؛ به این ترتیب که، اگر مصدق حزب توده را مسلح کند، حزب با کودتاچیان مقابله خواهد کرد. البته، بابک امیرخسروی، یکی از دبیران کمیته‌ی مرکزیِ آن زمانیِ حزب توده، هم در کتاب نقد خاطرات کیانوری و هم در گفت‌وگوهایش، با ارائه‌ی چند دلیل، این ادعای کیانوری را «ساخته‌ی ذهن» او برآورد می‌کند، و می‌گوید:

> روز ۲۴ مرداد حزب توده به مریم فیروز [همسر کیانوری و دختر عمه‌ی دکتر مصدق، که معمولاً رابط حزب با مصدق بود] دسترسی نداشته است. [...] به احتمال فراوان، خود سرهنگ مبشری به صورت ناشناس و از تلفن عمومی با منزل مصدق تماس گرفته و این اطلاع را به ایشان داده است.[۴۰۹]

حزب توده در تبعید می‌گوید که خود مریم فیروز خبر را به مصدق رسانده بود و از او خواسته بود که با اعلامیه‌ای مردم را به خیابان فراخواند.[۴۱۰] در هر حال، استیفن کینزر در کتاب «همه‌ی مردان شاه» می‌نویسد: مصدق به کیانوری گفته

---

[۴۰۸] نورالدین کیانوری، ***حزب توده و دکتر محمد مصدق***، تهران: ۱۳۵۷، برگرفته از تارنمای «رحمان هاتفی»، بازدید ۱۰ بهمن ۱۳۸۹:
www.rahman-hatefi.net/mossadegh-kia-230-86022.pdf

[۴۰۹] بابک امیرخسروی، ***گفت‌وگو با «شهروند امروز»، درباره‌ی مریم فیروز***، متن کامل، تارنمای «گویا»، ۳۰ فروردین ۱۳۸۷:
http://news.gooya.com/politics/archives/2008/04/070526.php

[۴۱۰] ***فیلم آخرین دیدار و گفت‌وگو با*** مریم فیروز ***در خانه‌ی میدان «سنائی»***، تارنمای «راه توده»، ۱۷ مارس ۲۰۰۸:
http://www.rahetudeh.com/rahetude/Sarmaghaleh-vasat/HTML/2008/mars/maryam.html

بود: «خدا دست راستم را قطع کند اگر یک حزب سیاسی را مسلح کنم.» (۲۰۰۸، ص ۱۷۹) شاید این گفت‌وگو در زمان دیگری بین کیانوری و مصدق انجام شده باشد. شاید هم انگیزه‌ی دکتر مصدق در اعلامیه‌ی مبنی بر «خانه ماندن مردم»، هراسی بود که از هژمونی یافتنِ حزب توده داشت. زیرا که می‌دانست این حزب، هم وابسته است، و هم، خود «شاخه‌ی نظامی» دارد و پیشاپیش «مسلح» است.

در هر حال، این یک واقعیتِ عینی است که همان گونه که شوروی‌ی «ضد امپریالیست» و مدافع «خلق‌های محروم»، در بحبوحه‌ی تحریم خرید نفت از ایران، از خرید نفت ایران سر باز زد، و مصدق و مردم ایران را در برابر «امپریالیسم به سرکردگی‌ی امریکا» تنها گذاشت، رهبری‌ی حزب توده نیز پس از ۳۰ تیر ۱۳۳۱ دولت مصدق و مردم ایران را در میدان نبرد با استعمار/ امپریالیسم تنها گذاشت، و با این کار، انبوهی از پیکارگران جوان، صادق، و آرمان‌خواه ایران را (به ویژه در شاخه‌ی نظامی‌ی حزب) در زندان‌ها و جوخه‌های اعدام تنها و بی‌پناه رها کرد. آن‌هائی نیز که زندان و اعدام جان به در بردند، باز به دامان کشور شوروی پناهنده شدند، و به جز اندک‌شماری از رهبران فراری‌ی این حزب که در شوروی «قدر دیدند» و در کنار «رفیق استالین» به صدر نشستند، بقیه، اگر شانس پذیرشِ اقامت در شوروی را داشتند، با قید کلمه‌ی «بدون تابعیت» در برگه‌ی اقامت، در کشور بیگانه ویلان و سرگردان و بی‌هویت باقی ماندند.[۴۱۱]

خسرو شاکری، پژوهشگر تاریخ معاصر ایران- با استفاده از مدارک موجود در بایگانی‌های شوروی‌ی سابق- ضمن اشاره به «خواست اصیل» پایه‌گذاران این حزب در ایجاد «یک حزب سیاسی‌ی مترقی»، وابستگی‌ی این حزب به ارتش سرخ را مستند می‌کند، و پیرامون برخورد آن با نهضت ملی کردن نفت ایران می‌نویسد:

> رودررو‌ئی‌ی تندخویانه‌ی حزب توده با مصدق و زدن برچسبِ «عروسك امریکا» به وی- بدون تـردید خط مشی‌ای که آموزگارِ حزب [یعنی] شوروی، توصیه می کرد- به قیمت گزافی برای آن حزب تمام شد، و آن را به نحوی روزافزون پشتیبان منافع اتحاد شوروی می‌شناساند. از آن زمان تاکنون اکثریت مردم ایران، از جمله بسیاری از روشنفکران حزب توده، آن سازمان را ازین بابت مقصر می‌دانند که سهم مهمی در موفقیت کودتای ۲۸ مرداد ۱۳۳۲ داشت. برخلاف آن چه معمولاً ادعا شده است، شکست حزب توده، و از جمله سازمان نظامی‌ی آن، حاصل کار حکومت نظامی‌ی مولود کودتای سیا نبود، بلکه نتیجه‌ی بحران آئینی و خط مشی‌ای بود که گریبان کادرها و اعضای حزب را در زمان مخالفت آن حزب با مصدق گرفته بود و آنان را از اعتماد به رهبرانی محروم داشت که بعضاً لاقیدانه در مسکو می‌زیستند و بعضاً به زندگی مخفیانه در وطن ادامه می‌دادند. فرمانداری نظامی و سپس ساواك فقط تکه‌های شکسته‌ی يك سازمانِ از درون ازهم‌پاشیده را رُفتند، که از داخل، در مقابله با فرآیند هم‌آوردی‌ی میهن‌دوستانه و دمکراتیكِ مصدق پیشاپیش مضمحل شده بود.[۴۱۲]

ناصر انقطاع، پژوهشگر تبعیدی، که در زمان کودتا عضو حزب «پان‌ایرانیست‌ها» و هوادار دکتر مصدق بوده، می‌نویسد:

> در شامگاه روز ۲۹ امرداد، مرا بازداشت کردند، و مدت پنجاه و هشت روز در بازداشت بودم. در این جا باید اقرار کنم که در درازای مدتی که در بازداشت به سر می‌بردم، هیچ گونه رفتار خشن و یا شکنجه‌ای نسبت به من و گروهی چشمگیر از هواداران مصدق (از جمله روان‌شاد حیدر رقابی، «هاله»، که با من در یک جا بازداشت بود، و خیلی زودتر از من آزاد شد) انجام نشد؛ و جز سه- چهار بازجوئی‌ی سطحی (و البته بی‌ادبانه) کار دیگری با من نداشتند. ولی آن گونه که شنیدم،

---

[۴۱۱] بابک امیرخسروی و محسن حیدریان، ***مهاجرت سوسیالیستی و سرنوشت ایرانیان، مهاجران حزب کمونیست ایران، فرقه‌ی دموکرات آذربایجان، حزب توده‌ی ایران، سازمان فدائیان اکثریت***، چاپ دوم، تهران: انتشارات پیام امروز، ۱۳۸۲، ص ۲۲.

[۴۱۲] خسرو شاکری، ***اندر پایه‌گذاری‌ی حزب توده به دست اداره‌ی اطلاعاتِ ارتش شوروی***، دو بخش، تارنما ی«گویا نیوز»، ۱۱ بهمن ۱۳۹۰: http://news.gooya.com/politics/archives/2012/01/135345.php

توده‌ای‌ها را به سختی می‌زدند و شکنجه می‌کردند.[۴۱۳]

و یرواند آبراهامیان نیز در زمینه‌ی برخورد حکومت کودتا با حزب توده می‌نویسد:

> به جز [دکتر حسین] فاطمی که اعدام شد، و [عبدالعلی] لطفی وزیر دادگستری که [در هجوم تیم شعبان جعفری- شعبان بی‌مخ- به خانه‌اش] به قتل رسید، با دیگر رهبران جبهه‌ی ملی مدارا شد- اغلب به حبس‌هائی تا پنج سال محکوم شدند. اما با حزب توده سخت‌تر رفتار شد. چون اعضای مخفی‌ی حزب توده در چهار سال بعد کم کم آفتابی شدند، نیروهای امنیتی چهل مقام حزبی را اعدام کردند، چهار تن دیگر را زیر شکنجه کشتند، حدود دویست نفر را به زندان ابد محکوم کردند، و بیش از سه هزار نفر از اعضای حزب را دستگیر کردند. رژیم توانست مطمئن باشد که هم سازمان حزب توده و هم جبهه‌ی ملی را، اگر نه جاذبه‌ی آن‌ها را، از بین برده است. محمدرضا شاه چون پدرش رضا شاه، اکنون می‌توانست بدون مخالفانی سازمان‌یافته حکومت کند. تاریخ دور کامل زده بود.[۴۱۴] (قلاب‌ها از من است.)

اما تاریخ نشان داد که نه حزب توده برای همیشه خاموش شد و نه جبهه‌ی ملی. البته، بازسازی‌ی مؤثر حزب توده در تبعیدِ سران آن، به درازا کشید، که بعداً در پوششِ «سازمان نوید» فعالیت خود را از سر گرفت. اما جبهه‌ی ملی و مخالفان ملی‌گرای باقی مانده از هجوم، بلافاصله در صدد تدارک دفاع برآمدند و «نهضت مقاومت ملی» را تشکیل دادند و کم‌تر از یک ماه پس از کودتا، روز ۷ شهریور ۱۳۳۲، نخستین اعلامیه‌ی خود را با عنوان «نهضت ادامه دارد» توزیع کردند. منتها، فعالیت این گروه نیز به سبب تشتت آراء اعضای آن، در آن جوّ پلیسی، به قول آبراهامیان، «سازمان‌یافته» نبود، اما چنان که غلامرضا نجاتی شرح می‌دهد، در تداوم مقاومت مردمی بی‌تأثیر هم نبود. در هر حال، اگر شاه ایران برای این اعدام‌ها و غیرقانونی اعلام کردن «حزب توده‌ی ایران»، حربه‌ی «وابستگی به بیگانگان» را در دست داشت، در مورد «جبهه‌ی ملی‌ی ایران»- که از چندین نهاد و حزب و جمعیت و سازمان ملی‌گرای مستقل تشکیل شده بود، و با وفاداری به رژیم مشروطه، اجرای قانون اساسی، انتخابات آزاد، و استقلال ایران را مطالبه می‌کرد[۴۱۵] - به جز نابخردی‌ی ناشی از خودکامگی و وابستگی‌ی خودش به بیگانگانی که جنبش‌های استقلال‌طلبانه‌ی منطقه را یکی پس از دیگری سرکوب می‌کردند، چه انگیزه‌ای داشت؟ کما این که از این پس بود که شاه ایران، بی‌پروای مفاد قانون اساسی، به هر کاری که لازم

---

[۴۱۳] ناصر انقطاع، ***پنجاه سال تاریخ با پان‌ایرانیست‌ها: آرمان‌خواهان و آرمان‌فروشان***، لس‌انجلس: انتشارات شرکت کتاب، ژانویه ۲۰۰۱/ دی ۱۳۷۹، ص ۸۲.

[۴۱۴] یرواند آبراهامیان، ***ایران بین دو انقلاب: از مشروطه تا انقلاب اسلامی***، ترجمه‌ی کاظم فیروزمند، حسن شمس‌آوری، محسن مدیر شانه‌چی، تهران: نشر مرکز، چاپ هشتم، ۱۳۸۳، ص ۲۵۲.
در مورد دستگیری‌های پس از ۲۸ مرداد ۱۳۳۲ به اسناد موجود در کتاب زیر نیز نگاه کنید:
بهروز طیرانی، ***محاکمات سیاسی در ایران از سال ۱۳۳۳ تا ۱۳۵۷***، تهران: نشر علم، ۱۳۸۱.

[۴۱۵] عبدالحسین آذرنگ در جستار گرامی‌ی خود حزب‌ها و جمعیت‌های درونی‌ی جبهه‌ی ملی را به قرار زیر ثبت کرده است:

> جبهه‌ی ملی اول: در بدو تشکیل (اول آبان ۱۳۲۸)، اساسنامه‌ی جبهه‌ی ملی و آئین‌نامه‌ی آن انتشار یافت. [...] در مدت کوتاهی چند حزب و تشکل سیاسی به جبهه پیوستند و ترکیب نخستین آن را به وجود آوردند، از جمله حزب ایران ، به رهبری‌ی اللهیار صالح و کریم سنجابی و دیگران؛ حزب ملت ایران بر بنیاد پان‌ایرانیسم ، به رهبری‌ی داریوش فروهر؛ حزب پان ایرانیست، به رهبری‌ی محسن پزشکپور (همکاری با جبهه تا ۳۰ تیر ۱۳۳۰)؛ سازمان نظارت بر آزادی‌ی انتخابات ، به رهبری مظفر بقایی ، که بعداً با گروه انشعابی از حزب توده‌ی ایران به رهبری‌ی خلیل ملکی ادغام شد و حزب زحمتکشان ملت ایران به رهبری‌ی آن دو پدید آمد؛ جمعیت آزادی‌ی مردم ایران ، به رهبری‌ی محمد نخشب ، که بعداً به نهضت خداپرستان سوسیالیست معروف شد؛ جمعیت فدائیان اسلام به رهبری‌ی سیدمجتبی نواب صفوی؛ مجمع مسلمانان مجاهد به رهبری‌ی شمس قنات‌آبادی، وابسته به آیت الله سیدابوالقاسم کاشانی (همکاری با جبهه تا تیر ۱۳۳۱)؛ سازمان هیئت علمیه‌ی تهران، متشکل از عده‌ای روحانی و مجتهد؛ جامعه‌ی بازرگانان و اصناف تهران ؛ و نیز چند تشکل دیگر از دانشگاهیان، فرهنگیان ، کارگران و دهقانان [...]از این میان ، حزب ایران ، که از همه سازمان یافته‌تر بود، هسته‌ی اصلی‌ی جبهه‌ی ملی را تشکیل می‌داد. [...] به مأخذ زیر نگاه کنید:

- عبدالحسین آذرنگ، ***جبهه‌ی ملی‌ی ایران، بزرگ‌ترین ائتلاف نیروهای سیاسی در تاریخ معاصر ایران تا پیش از انقلاب اسلامی ۱۳۵۷ ش.*** تارنمای «دایرةالمعارف اسلامی»، بازدید اردی‌بهشت ۱۳۸۹:

http://www.encyclopaediaislamica.com/madkhal2.php?sid=4503

می‌دید، دست می‌زد؛ به سفارش و یا اجازه‌ی رئیس جمهور وقت امریکا، نخست وزیر عوض می‌کرد؛ انتخابات مجلس را- مثلاً به این دلیل که اللهیار صالح (عضو برجسته‌ی حزب ایران و جبهه‌ی ملی) از کاشان بر رقیب خود پیروز شده- نیمه کاره متوقف می‌کرد؛ و یا انتخابات انجام شده را کلاً منحل می‌کرد؛ تا برسد به موارد دیگر خودکامگی.

***

دین‌کارانِ همراه با کودتاچیان، که حالا به اعتبار یاری به سقوط دولت مصدق، در میهمانی‌های شاه دعوت می‌شدند، و در طلب دستمزد بودند، برای اجرای خواسته‌های خود از این فرصت طلائی سود بردند. به عنوان نمونه، از شاه، وقتِ ملاقات گرفتند و موافقت او را- در حمله به بهائیان و زدودن آن‌ها- به دست آوردند. در این رهگذر، مسجد «سلطانی» و رادیوی کشور برای تهییج مردم در اختیار محمد تقی فلسفی (واعظ و نماینده‌ی آیت‌الله بروجردی در تهران) قرار گرفت. و پس از آن که با خطابه‌های آتشینِ این واعظ، پیمانه‌ی مردم از نفرت نسبت به بهائیان پر شد، اداره‌ی سیاسی‌ی وزارت کشور، با استناد به اصل اول متمم قانون اساسی و اصل ۲۱ از قانون اساسی،[۴۱۶] طی‌ی بخشنامه‌ای به تاریخ ۲۶ اردی‌بهشت ۱۳۳۴ به استانداری‌ها و فرمانداری‌های کشور فرمان حمله را صادر کرد.[۴۱۷] اما مردم مذهبی و تهییج شده- که در شهرهای ایران به شکارچی‌ی بهائیان تبدیل شده بودند- در این حمله‌ی شوم تنها نماندند، بلکه سپهبد نادر باتمانلقیچ، رئیس ستاد ارتش شاهنشاهی هم کلنگ به دست گرفت و همراه با لشگر زیر فرمانش در تخریب عبادتگاه بهائیان تهران (حظیرةالقدس) با آن‌ها همداستان شد. البته این کشتار و تخریب، پایان حمله به بهائیان ایران نبود. مدرسه‌ی «حجتیه» نیز به توصیه‌ی شخصیت‌های عالی‌مقام روحانی و البته با اجازه‌ی شاه تأسیس شد تا خطابه‌های آتشین فلسفی را تداوم بخشد، و تنور نفرت نسبت به دگراندیشان را داغ نگهدارد. در تغافل یا تجاهل محمدرضا شاه پهلوی- در تکیه به روحانیت- همین بس که نمی‌دید در صورت نافرمانی، همین منبرها و مدرسه‌های مذهبی، به ضرب «مکر» و ترفندهای هزار ساله، نقشه‌ی سرنگونی‌ی او را به تصویب ملت ناراضی‌ی ایران خواهند رساند.

پس از شوک کودتا، به مناسبت تصویب «کنسرسیوم نفت» در مجلس و نیز سفر ریچارد نیکسون (معاون رئیس جمهور وقت امریکا) به ایران، صدای اعتراضِ «آن‌ها»ی محمد رضا شاه، یعنی مردم ایران به ساحت علنی و رویاروئی‌ی مستقیم کشیده شد؛ چنان علنی، که محمدرضا شاه پهلوی، «اداره‌ی سیاسی‌ی وزارت کشور» را برای کنترل و سرکوب دگراندیشان و آزادی‌خواهان و مخالفان خود کافی ندید، و قانون تأسیس سازمان اطلاعات و امنیت کشور (ساواک) را در ۲۳ اسفند ۱۳۳۵ از مجلس نوزدهم گذراند و آن را بر تمام نهادهای دولتی و مدنی‌ی ایران حاکم کرد؛ صدها مأمور و بازجو و شکنجه‌گر (دانش‌آموخته تا لمپن‌های میدانی) را تربیت کرد تا هزاران جوان معترض ایران را در سیاهچال‌های این نهاد مخوف زیر شکنجه آش و لاش کنند، بسوزانند، و بکشند. این نهاد که ظاهراً به نهاد نخست‌وزیری وابسته بود، گرچه از نظر گزارش به صورت سلسله مراتبی عمل می‌کرد، اما مقصد نهائی‌ی گزارش‌هایش خود شاه بود، و تنها از او فرمان می‌گرفت. حالا، شاه ایران، یک «سلطان»، و یک دیکتاتور تمام عیار بود، و با نادیده گرفتن اصل‌های مدافع حقوق مردم در قانون اساسی، شخصاً، بر تمامی‌ی ارگان‌ها و نهادهای وابسته به ارتش و قوای سه گانه‌ی کشور تسلطی تعیین‌کننده داشت. از خاطرات دولتمردان شاه و اسنادی که پس از سقوط پادشاهی منتشر شد پیداست که مسائل کلان اقتصادی، مانند نفت یا خرید تجهیزات نظامی یا سرمایه‌گذاری‌های خارجی، نه از کانال مجلس و وزارت نفت، یا وزارت

---

[۴۱۶] اصل بیست و یکم قانون اساسی‌ی مشروطه را باقر مؤمنی به قرار زیر فشرده کرده است:
«تشکیل انجمن‌ها یا احزاب و اجتماعات نیز به موجب قانون "در تمام مملکت آزاد" اعلام شده است به شرط آن که "مولدّ فتنه‌ی دینی و دنیوی و مخلّ به نظم نباشند"؛ اجتماع کنندگان با خود اسلحه نداشته باشند و "ترتیباتی را که قانون در این خصوص مقرر می‌کند متابعت نمایند"؛ به علاوه "اجتماعات در شوارع و میدان‌های عمومی هم باید تابع قوانین نظمیه باشند."» به جستار زیر نگاه کنید:
❖ باقر مؤمنی، ***قانون اساسی‌ی مشروطه‌ی ایران: روند تدوین و تحول***، تارنمای «سامان نو»، ۴ خرداد ۱۳۸۵:
http://www.saamaan-no.org/HTML/shomareh01/08.htm

[۴۱۷] تورج امینی، ***جوابی طولانی به یک نوشته‌ی کوتاه***، تارنمای «گفتمان ایران»، ۱۰ خرداد ۱۳۸۶، بازدید: ۲ تیرماه ۱۳۸۹:
http://www.goftman-iran1.info/-othermenu-13/661

جنگ و با مشورت فرماندهان ارشد ارتش، یا وزارت خارجه، بلکه مستقیماً از سوی شخص شاه تصمیم‌گیری می‌شد.[۴۱۸] او که خود (پس از کودتای ۲۸ مرداد) برکشیده‌ی یک «توطئه» بود، برای جلوگیری از توطئه‌ی کودتا علیه خود، نه تنها دولت را از ارتش کاملاً جدا و بی‌خبر نگه می‌داشت، بلکه دولتمران یا امیران نیروهای سه گانه‌ی ارتش را جداگانه به حضور می‌پذیرفت و فرمان‌های خود را تک به تک به آن‌ها ابلاغ می‌کرد. بدین ترتیب، رابطه‌ی سلسله مراتبی در سطوح بالای اداری و ارتش عملاً منحل بود، و رابطه‌ی ارگانیکی میان مجلس و دولت و ارتش برقرار نبود. شاه از طریق دولت‌های دست‌نشانده‌ی خود، در انتخابات مجلس شورای ملی، و حتا در تصمیم‌گیری‌های همان مجلس فرمایشی نیز، اعمال نفوذی بی‌چون و چرا داشت. به بیانی دیگر، پدیده‌ای به نام «دولت پارلمانی»، که ایجاد آن هدف اصلی انقلاب مشروطه بود، در عمل جای خود را به همان حکومت پادشاهی/ سلطانی‌ی پیش از مشروطیت سپرد. اما ساواک و چاره‌اندیشی‌های دیگر شاه، نه تنها نتوانست حرکت آزادی‌خواهانه‌ی مردم ایران را برای همیشه از نفس بیاندازد، بلکه به تدریج خیزگاه حرکت‌هائی شد که تنها هدفشان حذف خود شاه و نظام پادشاهی بود؛ و آن چه روند این حرکت‌ها را سرعت بخشید و نهایتاً ابزار سقوط رژیم او را در اختیار مخالفان داخلی و خارجی گذاشت، همانا حکومت تک‌قدرتی‌ی خودش بود که به ارتش و مجلس و دولت، بدون داشتن رابطه‌ای ارگانیک با یکدیگر، و به مثابه تکه‌های جداگانه از ملک شخصی‌ی خود می‌نگریست. فراورده‌ی همین بینش بود که پس از واپسین خروج شاه از ایران در دی ماه ۱۳۵۷، نه تنها رئیس ستاد ارتش و امیران ارشد نیروهای سه گانه‌ی ارتش، نخست وزیر انتخابی‌ی او (شاپور بختیار) و مورد تأیید مجلس را به هیچ گرفتند، بلکه آن قدر در میدان رقابت با یکدیگر تاب خوردند، تا ژنرال رابرت هویزر امریکائی به دادشان رسید و امضاء «بی‌طرفی‌ی ارتش» در برابر انقلابِ اسلامی‌شده را از آن‌ها گرفت.

***

هنوز داغ کودتا بر دل مردم ایران تازه است، و هنوز دستگیری‌های پس از کودتا به ادامه دارد، که روز ۲۴ آبان ۱۳۳۲ دولت ارتشبد فضل‌الله زاهدی از سفر قریب‌الوقوع ریچارد نیکسون، معاون وقت رئیس جمهور ایالات متحده، به ایران خبر می‌دهد. روز ۱۴ آذر خود ارتشبد زاهدی رسماً اعلام می‌کند که دولت ایران روابط سیاسی‌ی خود را با بریتانیا تجدید می‌کند، و «دنیس رایت» به عنوان کاردار سفارت انگلستان، به زودی وارد ایران خواهد شد. این پیام‌ها، به مردم شکست‌خورده‌ی ایران و انبوه هواداران جنبش ملی گران می‌آید، و به تظاهراتی در جای جای تهران انجامد، که توسط نیروهای انتظامی سرکوب می‌شود، و چندی از کوشندگان سیاسی را روانه‌ی زندان می‌کند. دانشجویان دانشکده‌های فنی، پزشکی، حقوق و علوم سیاسی در دانشگاه تهران، روز ۱۵ آذر در خیابان‌های اطراف دانشگاه به تظاهرات می‌پردازند، و گروهی از آن‌ها نیز توسط مأموران دولت دستگیر یا مجروح می‌شوند. رژیم که به دنبال ایجاد فضای امنی برای ورود ریچارد نیکسون به ایران است، به هشدار اعتراض‌آمیز رئیس دانشگاه تهران (دکتر علی‌اکبر سیاسی) وقعی نمی‌گذارد، و سربازان ارتش و نیروهای انتظامی را در پیرامون دانشگاه تهران مستقر می‌کند. بامداد روز ۱۶ آذر دانشجویان در درون دانشگاه با نیروهای امنیتی روبه‌رو می‌شوند؛ گروهی از نیروهای امنیتی، به این بهانه که توسط سه دانشجوی دانشکده‌ی فنی مورد تمسخر قرار گرفته‌اند، به این دانشکده وارد می‌شوند، و قصد دارند تا آن سه دانشجو را با خود ببرند، که با اعتراض یکی از استادان ناموفق می‌مانند. رئیس دانشکده، برای حفظ آرامش و جان دانشجویان، زنگ تعطیل را زودتر از موعد مقرر به صدا درمی‌آورد؛ دانشجویان از کلاس‌ها خارج می‌شوند و به شعار دادن می‌پردازند. یورش مسلحانه‌ی نظامیان (با گلوله و سرنیزه) به دانشجویان، به زخمی شدنِ انبوهی از دانشجویان و مرگ سه تن از آنان می‌انجامد: مصطفی بزرگ‌نیا، دانشجوی دانشکده‌ی فنی، ۱۹ ساله، از فعالان «سازمان جوانان و دانشجویان حزب توده ایران»، مهدی شریعت رضوی، ۲۱ ساله، از «نهضت ملی به رهبری‌ی دکتر مصدق»، و احمد قندچی ۲۰ ساله، کوشنده‌ی

---

[۴۱۸] به عنوان مثال پیرامون خرید جنگ‌افزار، و این که بیش‌تر اقلام برای خرید، از سوی امریکا پیشنهاد می‌شد و فقط به تصویب شاه می‌رسید، خواننده‌ام را به کتاب زیر، که توسط وزیرمشاور و رئیس سازمان برنامه و بودجه‌ی کشور (از سال ۵۱ تا ۵۶) نوشته شده، رجوع می‌دهم:

❖ عبدالمجید مجیدی، ***خاطرات عبدالمجید مجیدی***، تهران: انتشارات گام نو، ۱۳۸۱، صص ۱۴۶ تا ۱۷۰.

«جبهه‌ی ملی‌ی ایران». مرگ این سه جوان دانشجو نه تنها شب «سوم» و «هفتم» و «چهلم» این قربانیان به تظاهرات گسترده‌ی ایرانیان می‌انجامد، بلکه حمایت دانشجویان برخی از دانشگاه‌های جهان را نسبت به دانشجویان ایران برمی‌انگیزد. رژیم، از بیم افکار عمومی در ایران و جهان، تیراندازی به دانشجویان را به «چند تیر هوائی» و «حرکت سر خودِ» چند تن ارتشی نسبت می‌دهد. و چنین است که روز ورود ریچارد نیکسون، (۱۷ آذر ۱۳۳۲)، دانشگاه تهران (که در مسیر عبور او قرار داشت)، در محاصره‌ی ارتش و نیروهای انتظامی، «امن وُ امان» به نظر می‌رسد؛ و دو روز بعد، ریچارد نیکسون از همان دانشگاه دکترای افتخاری دریافت می‌کند.

دکتر علی‌اکبر سیاسی، رئیس وقت دانشگاه تهران، به دنبال شرح اقدامات خود در گذار این رویداد، در خاطرات خود می‌نویسد:

> [...] از شاه وقت خواستم و در نظر داشتم نسبت به عمل جنایتکارانه‌ی قوای انتظامی اعتراض کنم. شاه مجال نداد و به محض رسیدن من، دست پیش گرفت و گفت: «این چه دسته گلی است که همکاران دانشکده‌ی فنی‌ی شما به آب داده‌اند، چند صد دانشجو را به جان سه چهار نظامی انداخته‌اید که این نتیجه نامطلوب را به بار آورد؟» گفتم معلوم می‌شود که جریان را آن طور که خواسته‌اند، ساخته و پرداخته، به عرض رسانده‌اند. شاه گفت: »به دروغ نگفته‌اند، عقل هم حکم می‌کند که جریان همین بوده است.» [...][۴۱۹]

اما نخستین حرکت بزرگ و «مطالبه‌محور»ی که پس از کودتای ۲۸ مرداد در ایران روی داد، خیزش معلمان سراسر کشور بود که به رهبری و با درایت دکتر محمد درخشش به پیروزی رسید. دستگاه شاه، ابتدا با فرمان گلوله به مصاف این خیزش آمد. اما با پیگیری‌ی معلمان- که جبهه‌ی ملی و اعضاء بازمانده از حزب توده و مخالفان لایه‌های دیگر اجتماعی نیز به آن‌ها پیوسته بودند- و با کشته شدن دکتر ابوالحسن خانعلی (دبیر فلسفه‌ی دبیرستان جامی در تهران در تظاهرات روز ۱۲ اردی‌بهشت ۱۳۴۰ در میدان بهارستان تهران)، عقب نشست؛ نخست‌وزیر وقت (جعفر شریف امامی) استیضاح شد؛ استعفا داد؛ و دولت تازه (به نخست وزیری‌ی علی امینی) به افزایش حقوق ماهانه‌ی معلمان تن داد؛ اما طبق معمول، تشکل و حرکت صنفی‌ی آنان را- که در «باشگاه مهرگان» متمرکز بود- متوقف کرد. دو هفته بعد از رویداد میدان بهارستان، یعنی روز ۲۸ اردی‌بهشت ۱۳۴۰ و به دعوت «جبهه‌ی ملی‌ی دوم»، و همکاری‌ی حزب توده، اجتماع صد هزار نفره‌ی مردم در میدان «جلالیه»ی تهران (پارک لاله‌ی بعدی) صدای اعتراض همگانی را یک بار دیگر به گوش شاه رساند. سیر نابخردی‌ی شاه- با سرکوب حرکت‌های پراکنده اما پیوسته‌ی دانشجویان، و زندانی کردن چندی از هواداران و اعضاء شورای عالی‌ی جبهه‌ی ملی- همچنان ادامه یافت. زمانی هم که شاه به فکر سازش با جبهه‌ی ملی افتاد، و اسدالله علم را برای مذاکره با اللهیار صالح مأمور کرد، شرط‌های سه‌گانه‌ی این «جبهه» را نپذیرفت و پس کشید. شرط‌های جبهه‌ی ملی عبارت بودند از: « ۱) اجرای کامل قانون اساسی؛ ۲) آزادی‌ی انتخابات در سراسر کشور؛ ۳) دخالت نکردن شاه در اموری که مطابق قانون در حیطه‌ی مسئولیت او نیست.» عدم پذیرش این سه شرط نشان داد که شاه در اندیشه‌ی دخالت دادن جبهه‌ی ملی در امور کشور نبود، و انگیزه‌ی پیشنهاد او نیز چیزی جز خریدن و ساکت کردن صدای جبهه‌ی ملی و هواداران انبوه آن نبود؛ چرا که پیشاپیش می‌دانست این سه شرط، گرانیگاه اساسنامه‌ی جبهه‌ی ملی

---

۴۱۹ در نگارش این بند از سخن، از زبان و بیان مأخذ زیر سود جسته‌ام:
❖ شصتمین سالگرد ۱۶ آذر، ***۱۶ آذر؛ یک روز تاریک با سه نام روشن***، ۱۶ آذر ۱۳۹۲/ ۶ دسامبر ۲۰۱۳، تارنمای «دویچه وله»:
http://www.dw.de/%DB%B1%DB%B6-%D8%A2%D8%B0%D8%B1-%DB%8C%DA%A9-%D8%B1%D9%88%D8%B2-%D8%AA%D8%A7%D8%B1%DB%8C%DA%A9-%D8%A8%D8%A7-%D8%B3%D9%87-%D9%86%D8%A7%D9%85-%D8%B1%D9%88%D8%B4%D9%86/a-17274529

را تشکیل می‌دهد.[۴۲۰]

انقلاب سفید، یا «انقلاب شاه و مردم»: شاه ایران، به عنوان یک ایرانی، در آرزوی ایرانی آباد و مترقی و متمدن و همپا با جهان نیز بود؛ و چنان که می‌گفت: «سلطنت بر ملتی پابرهنه» برای او «افتخار» نداشت. از سوی دیگر، خواسته‌های معیشتیِ لایه‌های محروم اجتماعی را با اسلحه و زندان و تبعید پاسخ می‌گفت. این پاسخ نیز خیزش‌های کارگران و زحمتکشان ایران را مکرر می‌کرد. تکرار اعتصاب‌های مطالبه‌محور در شهرهای بزرگ صنعتیِ ایران به جائی رسیده بود که به روایت رضا روستا: روزنامه‌ی انگلیسیِ «ایونینگ استاندارد» در شماره‌ی ۱۵ مه ۱۹۶۱ (اردی‌بهشت ۱۳۴۰) خود این خیزش‌ها را توصیف کرد و نوشت: «همه‌ی این‌ها روزهای واپسین روسیه‌ی تزاری را به خاطر می‌آورد.»[۴۲۱]
در چنین شرایطی بود که شاه ایران با همفکریِ مشاوران خود (یا به قول مخالفانش: «به دستور ارباب خود، امریکا»،[۴۲۲] یا شاید از آن رو که به قول لنین: «حکومتی که خود را در سراشیب سقوط می‌بیند به اصلاحات روی می‌آورد»؛ یا شاید به قول الکساندر دوم، تزار روسیه: «تا ویرانیِ بساط ارباب و رعیتی از پائین صورت نگرفته، بهتر است خودمان آن را از بالا شروع کنیم»)،[۴۲۳] دست به اصلاحاتی زد که خود آن را «انقلاب سفید» یا «انقلاب شاه و مردم» نامید. شاه روز ششم بهمن ۱۳۴۱، در یک سخنرانیِ تاریخی تصویب این طرح را از مردم ایران «تقاضا» کرد. او در این سخنرانی، از این که وضع دهقان‌های ایران به نسبت زمان «طفولیت و دوران مدرسه»‌ی او بهبود یافته ابراز خوشحالی کرد؛ به «شخصیت فرد فرد دهقان‌های گردن‌فراز» ایران بالید، و اصلاحات پیشنهادیِ خود را ضامن «الغای رژیم ارباب و رعیتی» و «آزادیِ کشاورزان» و «تأمین‌کننده‌ی آینده‌ای بهتر و عادلانه‌تر و مترقی‌تر برای طبقه‌ی شریف کارگر، و بهبود وضع کارمندان صدیق و زحمتکش دولت، و رونق زندگیِ پیشه‌وران، با حفظ سنت‌های ملی» معرفی کرد. و گفت:

> برای من این ساعت شاید گرامی‌ترین و شریف‌ترین ساعات زندگیِ من باشد. چون هم، یکی از آرزوهای دیرینه‌ی خود را برآورده می‌بینم و هم این که، لااقل ۷۵ در صد جمعیت این مملکت را آزاد و خوشبخت و امیدوار به آینده می‌بینم. [...] وظیفه‌ی خود می‌دانم به نام رئیس قوای سه‌گانه‌ی مملکتی، استقرار این اصلاحات را از طریق مراجعه به آراء عمومی- پیش از انتخابات مجلسین- از ملت ایران که حاکم بر مجلسین و منشاء اقتدارات ملی‌ست، تقاضا کنم.

مجموعه‌ی اصول این «اصلاحات»، که در دو نوبت اعلام شد، به قرار زیر بود:

---

۴۲۰ برای اطلاع بیش‌تر پیرامون گزاره‌های مختصر من در زمینه‌ی فعالیت‌های جبهه‌ی ملی و برخوردهای محمدرضا شاه پهلوی با این جبهه، پس از کودتا، به مآخذ زیر رجوع کنید:

- غلامرضا نجاتی، ***تاریخ سیاسیِ بیست و پنج ساله‌ی ایران: از کودتا تا انقلاب***، تهران: مؤسسه‌ی خدمات فرهنگیِ رسا، چاپ هفتم، ۱۳۸٤، فصل‌های سوم و پنجم.
- مهدی آذر، ***به یاد اللهیار صالح: مذاکرات صالح و علم***، تهران: انتشارات آینده، ۱۳٦۸.

۴۲۱ رضا روستا، ***تاریخچه‌یِ پیدایش سندیکاهای ایران و وظایف اجتماعیِ اتحادیه‌های کارگری***، بخش ٦، تارنمای «راه توده»، 18 فوریه ۲۰۰۸، بازدید ۲ خرداد ۱۳۹۱:
http://www.rahetudeh.com/rahetude/mataleb/rusta/html/aghaz-sendika.html

۴۲۲ در مبارزات انتخابی سال ۱۹٦۰ «جان اف. کندی» از حزب دمکرات در امریکا به ریاست جمهوری رسید، و در ژانویه‌ی ۱۹٦۱ (دی ماه ۱۳۳۹) به کاخ سفید رفت. یکی از راه‌های پیشنهادیِ او در سیاست‌های خارجیِ امریکا، اصلاحات سیاسی و اقتصادی در کشورهای «جهان سوم» بود.

۴۲۳ الکساندر دوم، تزار روسیه، در سال ۱۸۵٦ پیشنهاد اصلاحات ارضی و پایان دادن به رژیم ارباب و رعیتی را مطرح کرد. او در این زمینه گفته بود: «بهتر است تا این رژیم از پائین ویران نشده، آن را از بالا ویران کنیم.» این طرح البته تا مدت‌ها اجرا نشد، و زمانی هم که به اجرا گذاشته شد، فراگیر نبود، و با همه‌ی کوشش‌های دولت تزاری در انجام آن، تا انقلاب ۱۳۱۷ روسیه، زمینداران کلان به آن تن ندادند. جمله‌ی لنین بازتابی است به این رُفرم ناقص و درازمدت.

اصـــلاحات ارضـــی و الغای رژیم ارباب و رعیتی ؛ ملی کردنِ جنگل‌ها و مراتع ؛ تبدیل کردن کارخانه‌های دولتی به شرکت‌های سهامی، و فروش سهام آن جهت تضمین اصلاحات؛ سهیم کردنِ کارگران در سودِ کارخانه‌ها؛ ،ایجادِ سپاهِ دانش به منظورِ مبارزه با بی‌سوادی؛ تأسیس انجمن‌های ایالتی و ولایتی، که شامل تجدید نظر اساسی در قانون انتخابات بود؛ که شامل حق رأی به زنان و حقوق برابر سیاسی‌ی آن‌ها با مردان نیز بود. (در آیین‌نامه‌ی مربوط به انتخابات، سه نکته‌ی واقعاً انقلابی پیش‌بینی شـده بود: ۱) کلمه‌ی «باسـواد» به جای کلمه‌ی «ذکور» به عنوان شـرط انتخاب کردن و انتخاب شـدن نماینده؛ ۲) حذف قید «اسـلام» از شـرایط انتخاب کنندگان و انتخاب شـوندگان؛ ۳) تغییر مرجع سـوگندِ نمایندگان از «قرآن»، به «کتاب آسمانی». تا پیش از آن، نمایندگان زردشتی، کلیمی، و مسیحی، در مراسم تحلیف خود به قرآن سوگند می‌خوردند.)

افزوده‌های سال ۴۲:

ایجادِ سـپاهِ بهداشـت؛ ایجادِ سـپاهِ ترویج و آبادانی؛ ملی کردنِ آب‌های کشـور؛ ایجاد خانه‌های اصـناف و شـوراهای داوری؛ فروش سهامِ کارخانه‌ها به کارگران؛ نوسازی‌ی شهرها و روستاها با کمک سپاه ترویج و آبادانی؛ انقلابِ اداری و آموزشی؛ ایجاد شرکت‌های تعاونی برای مبارزه با گران فروشی و دفاع از منافع مصرف کنندگان؛ آموزشِ رایگان و اجباری در هشت سال اول تحصیل؛ مبارزه با فساد و رشوه‌خواری؛ تغذیه‌ی رایگان برای کودکان خردسال در مدرسه‌ها و تغذیه‌ی رایگان شیرخوارگان تا دو سـالگی با مادران؛ بیمه‌های اجتماعی برای همه‌ی ایرانیان؛ پیش‌گیری از افزایش بهای مسکن.

البته شاه، همان ۷۵ در صدِ خیالی‌ی خود را «مردم» و «ملت» به حساب می‌آورد. آینده نیز- مانند گذشته- نشان داد که از دیدگاه او نه تنها «ملت ایران»، بلکه «مجلسین» هم «منشاء اقتدارات ملی» به حساب نمی‌آیند، و در بزنگاه تصمیم‌گیری، تنها خودش «منشاء اقتدارات ملی» است. با این وصف، حتا اگر اصلاحات پیشنهادی‌ی شاه به «دستور امریکا» صورت گرفته بود، و یا حتا اگر انگیزه‌ی او «کمونیسم ستیزی»، یا جلوگیری از خطر سقوط خودش بود، باز، (در خوانش من) محتوای مردمی‌ی اصـول «انقلاب سـفید» از یک سو، و متن و لحن سـخنرانی‌ی او در هنگام اعلام این طرح از سـوی دیگر، بر «آرزوی‌ی قلبی‌ی» او در داشتن «ایرانی آباد و پیشرفته و سربلند» گواهی می‌دهند.

اما در سایه‌ی چرکین کودتای ۲۸ مرداد ۳۲، کشتار و سرکوب مداوم کوشندگان فرهنگی و سیاسی، و کارگری‌ی ایران، در کنار وابستگی‌ی آشکار شاه به امریکا- که دامنه‌ی فعالیت‌های امپریالیستی‌ی آن در کشورهای موسوم به «جهان سوم» گسترشی فزاینده داشت- این «آرزو»ی شاه، از دید اکثریت مردم و سازمان‌های سیاسی‌ی ایران معنائی جز «عوام‌فریبی» و «دروغ» نیافت. از سوی دیگر، اجرای بسیاری از اصول «انقلاب سفید»- که نفوذ و اقتدار روحانیت را کاهش می‌داد- مخالفت و کارشکنی‌های «مراجع تقلید» و انبوه «مقلدان» آن‌ها را برانگیخت. چرا که در فرایند اجرای اصلاحات ارضی، هم به منافع زمینداران لایه‌ی روحانی نیز آسیب می‌رسید، و هم دست روحانیان از املاک «موقوفه»- که محل درآمدی هنگفت بود- در سطح کشور کوتاه می‌شد. همچنین، با تأسیس خانه‌های انصاف و سپاه دانش در روستاهای کشور، نقش دیرینه‌ی روحانیت در نفوذ به، و تسلط بر، زندگی‌ی لایه‌های دورافتاده و ناآگاه ملت ایران به خطر می‌افتاد. حجت‌الاسلام روح‌الله خمینی- بدون داشتن درجه‌ی «مرجعیت»، اما آگاه از نفوذ روحانیت در ذهنیت محمدرضا شاه- ابتدا از موضعی مطمئن به او هشدار داد. او در تلگرافی به شاه نوشت:

> حضور مبارک اعلیحضرت همایونی، پس از اهداء تحیت و دعا، به طوری که در روزنامه‌ها منتشر شده است، دولت در انجمن‌های ایالتی و ولایتی، اسـلام را در رأی‌دهندگان و منتخبین شـرط نکرده و به زنان حق رأی داده اسـت. و این امر موجب نگرانی‌ی علمای اسلام و سایر طبقات مسلمین است. مستدعی است امر فرمایند مطالبی را که مخالف دیانت مقدسه

و مذهب رسمی‌ی کشور است را از برنامه‌های دولتی و حزبی حذف نمایند تا موجبات دعاگوئی‌ی ملت مسلمان شود.[۴۲۴]

اما شاه، این بار در برابر روحانیت و همگام همیشگی‌ی آن، یعنی بازار، کوتاه نیامد، و مواد «انقلاب سفید» را، پس از رفراندم و تصویب «مجلسین»، به اجرا گذاشت. حجت‌الاسلام خمینی، که از «اعلیحضرت همایونی» انتظار این بی‌اعتنائی را نداشت، و از سوی دیگر، از پشتیبانی‌ی حوزه‌ی علمیه‌ی قم و بازار («هیئت‌های مؤتلفه‌ی اسلامی»)[۴۲۵] اطمینان داشت، نوروز ۱۳۴۲ را «عزای ملی» اعلام کرد و طی‌ی بیانیه‌ای به امضاء ۹ تن از روحانیان طراز اول، بدون کوچک‌ترین اشاره‌ای به «اصلاحات ارضی» (که در آن زمان کشاورزان فرودست را تا حدی راضی کرده بود)، «برابری‌ی زنان و مردان» را «موجب ارتداد» دانست، حذف شرط «رجولیت» و «ذکوریت» برای «قضاوت» را «کفر» نامید و گفت «**دستگاه جبار بداند اگر بخواهد به اسلام تجاوز کند و احکام کفر را در بلاد اسلامی جاری سازد، من در کمین آن ایستاده‌ام.**»[۴۲۶] پس از این بیانیه و نامه‌های تحریک‌آمیز حجت‌الاسلام خمینی به «علمای» شهرهای مختلف، و ایراد سخنرانی‌های معترضانه‌ی آن‌ها، ستادهای مقاومت در اندک زمانی در حوزه‌های علمیه و مدرسه‌های مذهبی و نشریه‌های آن‌ها فعال شدند، و حرکت آن‌ها از سوی همه‌ی طیف‌های مبارزه و پیکارگران سیاسی‌ی «چپ» و «راست» نیز تأیید شد. اگر مخالفت لایه‌های روحانی و زمینداران و بازاریان کلان به خاطر به خطر افتادن منافعشان توجیهی تاریخی دارد، اگر مخالفت همه‌ی طیف‌های چپِ درگیر در مبارزه، با «اصلاحاتِ» پیشنهادی‌ی شاه، به خاطر ستیز آن‌ها با بنیادهای نظم «سرمایه‌داری» توجیهی تاریخی دارد، جانبداری‌ی سوسیالیست/ کمونیست‌های ایران از روحانیتی که مدافع سرسخت مالکیت خصوصی و نظام سرمایه‌داری است، تاکنون با هیچ توجیه موجهی به عرض تاریخ ایران نرسیده است. علی

---

[۴۲۴] بهزاد کاظمی، ***انقلاب و ضدانقلاب در ایران***، نشریه‌ی الکترونیکی‌ی «خیابان»، شماره‌ی ۶۲، ۲۲ اسفند ۱۳۸۸:
www.xyaban62.pdf

[۴۲۵] «هیئت مؤتلفه‌ی اسلامی» در فرایندی شبکه‌وار و در مدتی کوتاه، از ائتلاف چندین «هیئت اسلامی» در بازار و مناطق دیگر تهران تشکیل شد. هسته‌های اولیه‌ی آن، «هئیت مسجد امین‌الدوله»، «هیئت مسجد شیخ علی» و «هیئت اصفهانی‌ها» در بازار تهران بودند که از سال ۱۳۳۹ در بازار فعالیت داشتند. بنا بر «تاریخ شفاهی‌ی هیئت‌های مؤتلفه»: «هیئت مسجد امین الدوله، از کسبه و تجار بازار تهران و شاگردان آن‌ها تشکیل می‌شد که به دلایل متفاوت، تحصیل علوم جدید را در مراحل ابتدائی رها کرده و در بازار تهران به کار پرداخته و شب‌ها پس از پایان کار، به تحصیل علوم دینی نزد شیخ حسین زاهد و مرحوم آیت‌الله شیخ عبدالکریم حق‌شناس در مسجد امین‌الدوله می‌پرداختند. در میان شاگردان این دو، عده‌ای مانند حبیب‌الله عسگراولادی، ابوالفضل توکلی بینا و حبیب‌الله شفیق با یکدیگر آشنا شدند و بعدها مهدی عراقی نیز به آن‌ها پیوست. مهدی عراقی، در جمعیت فدائیان اسلام سابقه‌ی فعالیت داشت و تحت تعقیب قرار گرفته و به زندان نیز رفته بود.» اما پس از تصویب لایحه‌ی «انجمن‌های ایالتی و ولایتی» در سال ۱۳۴۱، آیت‌الله خمینی نمایندگان همین سه هیئت اسلامی‌ی بازار تهران را به قم فراخواند و آن‌ها را برای مبارزه با آن لایحه، به اتحاد عمل تشویق کرد. این فرمان اجرا شد؛ در ابتدای کار، دوازده هیئت اسلامی از اقصا نقاط تهران، زیر عنوان «جبهه‌ی مسلمانان آزاده» با هم ائتلاف کردند، و با تکثیر و انتشار اعلامیه‌های آیت‌الله خمینی به مبارزه علیه شاه پرداختند؛ تعداد این هیئت‌ها به زودی، به «بیست و هفت و بیست و هشت و بیست و نه» هم رسید که همگی هنوز زیر نام «جبهه‌ی مسلمانان آزاده»، فعالیت داشتند و همگی نیز «مورد تأیید امام هم بودند.» اساسنامه‌ی این «جبهه» نیز توسط مرتضی مطهری، محمدجواد باهنر و آیت‌الله بهشتی تدوین شد، و فعالیت‌های آن با حوزه‌ی علمیه‌ی قم و امام‌های جمعه و واعظان خرده‌پای منبرها هم‌آهنگ شد، و در انگیزش شورش ۱۵ خرداد ۱۳۴۲ نقش اساسی داشت. یکی از عملیاتی که این «جبهه» در کارنامه‌ی خود به آن افتخار می‌کند، ترور حسنعلی منصور، نخست وزیر، است. پس از دستگیری‌ی اعضای برجسته‌ی این «جبهه»، محمد جواد باهنر و محمد علی رجائی آن را با نام «جمعیت مؤتلفه‌ی اسلامی‌ی دوم» احیاء کردند. در دوران انقلاب، آیت‌الله بهشتی اساسنامه‌ی آن را تنظیم کرد. این هیئت، در واقع، هسته‌ی مرکزی‌ی ستاد آیت‌الله خمینی در دوران انقلاب ۵۷ بود، و زیر پوشش عملیات فرهنگی، شاخه‌ی نظامی‌ی خود را تقویت کرد و به کار گماشت، و در نهایت نیز «ستاد انقلاب» و «ستاد استقبال از امام خمینی» را در تهران تشکیل داد. این «جمعیت» پس از انقلاب نیز به حزب «جمهوری‌ی اسلامی» جذب شد، و حتا پس از انفجار در این حزب (۷ تیر ۱۳۶۰)، با قدرت بیش‌تری موجودیت خود را حفظ کرد. این «جمعیت»، که بعدها با نام‌های «هیئت‌های مؤتلفه‌ی اسلامی» و «جمعیت هیئت‌های مؤتلفه‌ی اسلامی»، و در حال حاضر (۱۳۸۹)، با نام «حزب مؤتلفه‌ی اسلامی» نیز خوانده شده، با تأسیس نهادهای موازی در شهرهای مختلف ایران، و با در دست داشتن نبض اقتصاد ایران، یکی از نیروهای مؤثر در استقرار و تداوم جمهوری‌ی اسلامی برشمرده می‌شود. به مأخذ زیر نگاه کنید:

- ❖ حکیمه امیری، ***تشکیل هیئت‌های مؤتلفه‌ی اسلامی تحت نظر امام خمینی (ره)***، تاریخ شفاهی‌ی هیئت‌های مؤتلفه‌ی اسلامی، مرکز اسناد انقلاب اسلامی، تابستان ۱۳۸۶. برگرفته از تارنمای «آفتاب»، ۲۹ خرداد ۱۳۸۷:

http://www.aftabir.com/articles/view/politics/plitical_history/c1c1213767421_iran_p1.php/%d8%aa%d8%b4%da%

[۴۲۶] به مأخذ زیر نگاه کنید. با این توضیح که منبع نقل قول اکبر گنجی، دو جلد کتاب نهضت امام خمینی، نوشته‌ی سیدحمید روحانی است:

- ❖ اکبر گنجی، ***«آیت‌الله خمینی؛ بی‌گناه یا ...»***، تارنمای «گویا نیوز»، ۲۲ خرداد ۱۳۸۹:

http://newsmanager.gooya.com/politics/archives/2010/06/106381.php

کشتگر، پیکارگر «چپ» ایران در تبعید، از روز دوم خرداد ۴۲ چنین یاد می‌کند:

> [...] با نام او [خمینی]، نخستین بار، در دوم خرداد ۴۲ آشنا شدم. چه روز خونین و ترسناکی بود، دوم خرداد ۴۲. برای نخستین بار آدم‌هائی دیدم که در خون خود بر آسفالت خیابان‌ها سینه خیز می‌رفتند. جلوی بازار تهران از هرسو که فرار می‌کردی مسلسل‌ها آواز مرگ به گوشت می‌خواندند. فشنگ‌ها به سان پرنده‌های نامرئی به سرعت در اطراف سرم پرواز می‌کردند. بال‌هایشان به سر و صورتم می‌خورد اما نمی‌دیدمشان. وحشت مرگ، تا اعماق وجودم را می‌شکافت. دهانم خشک خشک بود، از بس دویده بودم قلبم با بی‌تابی می‌خواست از قفس سینه‌ام فرار کند، خودم را به درون کوچه‌ای انداختم و محکم به دیوار چسبیدم. مسلسلی که بر زره پوش سوار بود و از وسط خیابان همه جا را گلوله باران می کرد کوچه را به رگبار بست و رفت؛ و من از شادی‌ی زنده‌ماندن، آدم‌هائی که روی فرش خیابان‌ها جان می‌کندند فراموش کرده بودم. این نخستین تجربه‌ی «مبارزاتی»‌ی زندگی‌ی من بود. عجیب است آن روز نیز، هم آن‌هائی که به خون غلتیدند و هم آن‌هائی که جان سالم به دربردند یا حسین می‌گفتند...[۴۲۷]

البته باید بی‌درنگ افزود که تنها بخش راست «جبهه‌ی ملی‌ی ایران» بود که گفت: «اصلاحات ارضی آری، دیکتاتوری‌ی شاه نه!» اما در این زمان، بخش بزرگی از این «جبهه» یا به «چپ» پیوسته بود و با تحلیل‌های آن همسوئی داشت، و یا با نام‌های مختلف به اسلامیست‌ها وصل بود. در این شرایط بود که رویاروئی‌ی مخالفان با شاه، در ۱۵ خرداد ۱۳۴۲ به اوج رسید و با به جا گذاشتن انبوهی کشته و زخمی و زندانی، به دستگیری و حصر حجت‌الاسلام خمینی انجامید، و احتمال محاکمه و اعدام او بر سر زبان‌ها افتاد. برای پیش‌گیری از این احتمال، مراجع سه گانه‌ی قم (آیت‌الله شریعتمداری، آیت‌الله مرعشی، و آیت‌الله گلپایگانی) و به کوشش آیت‌الله حسینعلی منتظری، «به عنوان یک مصلحت»، او را به درجه‌ی «آیت‌الله» ارتقاء دادند و «مرجعیت» او را به رسمیت شناختند. و این چنین بود که «آیت‌الله خمینی»، به عنوان «مرجع تقلید شیعیان»، از تیررس محاکمه و اعدام خارج شد.[۴۲۸] آیت‌الله روز ۱۷ فروردین ۱۳۴۳ با پادرمیانی‌ی سرلشگر پاکراون (رئیس وقت ساواک)، آزاد شد، و به قم رفت. آیت‌الله خمینی، که تاکنون مخالفتش با «انقلاب سفیدِ» شاه، در بند مربوط به «رجولیت» و «ذکوریت» و «سوگند نمایندگان مجلس به کتاب آسمانی» خلاصه شده بود، چند ماه بعد از آزادی (۴ آبان ۱۳۴۳)، و پس از تصویب وام دویست میلیون دلاری از یک بانک امریکائی (با تضمین دولت امریکا) در مجلس

---

۴۲۷ علی کشتگر، ***خدعه، خمینی و انقلاب***، تارنمای «گویا نیوز»، ۱۷ بهمن ۱۳۹۱:
http://news.gooya.com/politics/archives/2013/02/154917

۴۲۸ سحاب سپهری، پژوهشگر انقلاب ۵۷ ، در این زمینه می‌نویسد: «بعد از فوت آیت‌الله بروجردی در سال ۱۳۴۰، موضوع وحدت مرجعیت تقلید در ایران از بین رفت و همزمان تعدادی مرجع تقلیدِ هم‌تراز در ایران و عراق ظهور کردند که از جمله می‌توان به سه مرجع در قم (معروف به مراجع ثلاثه) اشاره کرد: آیت‌الله شریعتمداری، آیت‌الله مرعشی و آیت‌الله گلپایگانی. در ضمن علاوه بر این سه مرجع در قم، مرجع‌های دیگری مثل آیت‌الله خویی در نجف و آیت‌الله قمی و آیت‌الله میلانی هم در مشهد ظهور کردند. نقش عامل‌هایی که به تکثر مرجع‌های تقلید در دوران بعد از فوت مرجع واحد (آیت‌الله بروجردی) منجر شد هنوز به خوبی بررسی نشده است. شخصیت سیاسی‌ی مستقل آیت‌الله خمینی بعد از فوت آیت‌الله بروجردی در سال ۱۳۴۰ ظهور کرد. در آن زمان آیت‌الله خمینی ۶۰ ساله و شخصیتی کم‌تر شناخته شده بود. به این ترتیب او جزو گروه برگزیده‌ی مراجع تقلید نبود. [...] بعد از آن که شورش ۱۵ خرداد سرکوب شد و موضوع محاکمه‌ی نظامی و احتمال اعدام آیت‌الله خمینی پیش آمد، مراجع ثلاثه مقیم قم به خوبی توجه کردند که نباید به یک حکومت کلاهی اجازه بدهند که یک عمامه‌ای ارشد را محاکمه کند. قراین نشان می‌دهد که آنها به عنوان یک مصلحت به مرجعیت آیت‌الله خمینی رضایت دادند. آیت‌الله حسینعلی منتظری (به نقل خاطراتش) در کشاکش‌های داخلی با روحانیت بالا برای به رسمیت شناخته شدن آیت‌الله خمینی به عنوان یک مرجع تقلید، نقشی کلیدی بازی کرد. به رسمیت شناختن مرجعیت تقلید برای آیت‌الله خمینی زمینه.ی کار را فراهم آورد. با این تمهید و با وساطت سرلشکر پاکروان (رئیس وقت ساواک) و به فرمان محمدرضا شاه، آیت‌الله خمینی در سال ۱۳۴۳ ابتدا به ترکیه و بعد از آن به شهر تجف (در عراق) تبعید شد. ولی آیت‌الله خمینی بعد از استقرار در نجف به مخالفت خود با محمدرضا شاه ادامه داد. آیت‌الله خمینی در ایران شبکه‌ای قوی از پیروان و مقلدان داشت که منابع مالی برای ساختار حوزه‌ی او در نجف را تامین می‌کردند و رهنمودهای او را هم به مقلدانش منتقل می‌کردند. در این مورد هم آیت‌الله منتظری نقشی ویژه داشت.» به مأخذ زیر نگاه کنید:

- ❖ سحاب سپهری، ***سه روز تاریخ‌ساز، بیست تا بیست و دو بهمن ۵۷، بخش اول: بررسی‌ی زمینه‌ها***، تارنمای «رادیو زمانه» ۵ بهمن ۱۳۸۹:

http://radiozamaneh.com/specials/revolution/2011/01/25/1178

ایران، و به بهانه‌ی تصویب لایحه‌ی مصونیت قضائی‌ی مستشاران امریکائی (کاپیتولاسیون)، و باز، بدون این که کم‌ترین اشاره‌ای به اصلاحات ارضی داشته باشد، تیزترین و آشکارترین حمله‌های کلامی به «انقلاب سفید»، به رژیم، و شخص شاه را آغاز کرد. او در یک سخنرانی‌ی بلند، برای انگیزش مردم ایران علیه شاه، از تمامی‌ی امکانات بلاغی‌ی خود سود جست، و به صورت بندگردان، گفت:

> [...] «اگر نفوذ روحانیون باشد، نمی‌گذارند این‌ها خودسرانه چنین قرضه‌ی سنگینی را بر ملت ایران تحمیل کنند»؛ «اگر نفوذ روحانیون باشد، نمی‌گذارند در بیت‌المال چنین هرج و مرجی واقع شود»؛ «اگر نفوذ روحانیون باشد نمی‌گذارند هر دولتی هر کاری که خواست انجام دهد»؛ «اگر نفوذ روحانیون باشد نمی‌گذارند مجلس به این صورت مبتذل درآید»؛ «اگر نفوذ روحانیون باشد نمی‌گذارند دختر و پسر در آغوش هم کشتی بگیرند»؛ «اگر نفوذ روحانیون باشد نمی‌گذارند عده‌ای به اسم وکیل بر ملت تحمیل شده بر سرنوشت مملکتی حکومت کنند»؛ «اگر نفوذ روحانیون باشد نمی‌گذارند یک دست‌نشانده‌ی امریکائی این غلط‌ها را بکند، از ایران بیرونش می‌کنند».[۴۲۹]

با خواندن متن این سخنرانی‌ی بلند و تهییجی، اذعان می‌کنیم که آیت‌الله خمینی، آخرین هشدارهایش را به شاه ایران رسانده بود. او در جائی از این سخنرانی می‌گوید: «ای ملل اسلام، ای سران ملل اسلام، ای رؤسای جمهوری‌ی ملل اسلامی، ای سلاطین ملل اسلامی، به داد ما برسید، ای شاه ایران، به داد خودت برس!»[۴۳۰] متن این سخنرانی بلافاصله به صورت مخفیانه چاپ شد و به سراسر ایران رسید.

این سخنرانی، بین آیت‌الله خمینی و محمدرضا شاه پهلوی مرزی آشتی‌ناپذیر کشید. نُه روز پس از آن سخنرانی، (یعنی روز ۱۳ آبان ۱۳۴۳)، کماندوهای ارتش شاهنشاهی، آیت‌الله خمینی را در خانه‌اش دستگیر کردند و بلافاصله او را به ترکیه فرستادند، تا از آن جا به عراق منتقل شود. اگر ملت ایران «کودتای ۲۸ مرداد ۳۲» را بر شاه نبخشیده بود، اینک، در چشم لایه‌های اعماق جامعه، و لایه‌ی فرودست جامعه با باورهای عمیقاً مذهبی، و در چشم گروه‌های سیاسی‌ی صرفاً مذهبی، و گروه‌های ملی/ مذهبی، و در چشم همه‌ی طیف‌های مارکسیستی، و در چشم انبوه دانشجویان و دانش‌آموختگان ناراضی‌ی ایران، آن زخم مکرر شده بود. (بدون آن که بین عناصر درونی‌ی جنبش «ملی کردن نفت» و جنبش «۱۵ خرداد» و انگیزه‌های آن‌ها کوچک‌ترین شباهتی وجود داشته باشد.) با این که لایحه‌ی کاپیتولاسیون مستشاران امریکائی از سوی اسدالله علم، نخست وزیر وقت، به مجلس داده شده بود، و به رغم مخالفت برخی از نمایندگان مجلس شورای ملی، با تنفیذ او و دولت او به تصویب رسیده بود، اما روز اول بهمن ۱۳۴۳ برابر با ۱۷ ماه رمضان (سالگرد جنگ بدر) حسنعلی منصور (نخست وزیر بعدی)، به بهانه‌ی تصویب کاپیتولاسیون، توسط عضوی از شاخه‌ی نظامی‌ی «هیئت مؤتلفه‌ی اسلامی» و با فتوای آیت‌الله حسینی میلانی، ترور شد.[۴۳۱] شاه نیز، روز ۲۱ فروردین ۱۳۴۴ در کاخ اختصاصی‌ی خود (کاخ مرمر)، از سوی یک گروه مائوییستی مورد سوءقصدی نافرجام قرار گرفت.[۴۳۲] این رویدادهای پی در پی نیز به

---

۴۲۹ برگرفته از: سرهنگ غلامرضا نجاتی، ***تاریخ سیاسی‌ی بیست و پنج ساله‌ی ایران: از کودتا تا انقلاب***، تهران: انتشارات خدمات فرهنگی‌ی رسا، چاپ هفتم، ۱۳۸٤، جلد اول، زیرنویس صفحه‌های ۳۰۵ تا ۳۱۰.

۴۳۰ برگرفته از: سرهنگ غلامرضا نجاتی، ***تاریخ سیاسی‌ی بیست و پنج ساله‌ی ایران: از کودتا تا انقلاب***، پیشین.

۴۳۱ شرح لایحه‌ی کاپیتولاسیون و نقش شاه و علم و حسنعلی منصور در تنفیذ تصویب آن در مجلس، و همچنین شرح ترور حسنعلی منصور را در مآخذ زیر بخوانید:
- عباس میلانی، **معمای هویدا**، تهران: نشر اختران، چاپ هفدهم، ۱۳۸۰، صص ۱۹۳ تا ۲۱۷.
- ***خاطرات عسگراولادی از اجرای فتوای انقلابی‌ی اعدام حسنعلی منصور*** (بخش ۱)، تارنمای «خبرگزاری‌ی فارس»، ۱۵ بهمن ۱۳۸۹:

http://www.farsnews.com/newstext.php?nn=8911130480

۴۳۲ عامل این ترور، رضا شمس‌آبادی، سرباز وظیفه در گارد شاهنشاهی بود. بعداً ساواک کشف کرد که طراحی‌ی این ترور توسط یک گروه مائوییستی به سرکردگی‌ی پرویز نیکخواه انجام شده است. پرویز نیکخواه، عضو «کنفدراسیون جهانی‌ی دانشجویان و محصلین ایرانی» بود و در پایه‌گذاری‌ی این نهاد جهانی نقش مؤثری داشت. او پس از مدتی تحمل زندان، خط مشی‌ی مبارزه‌ی خود را تغییر داد، و تا پیش از اعدام در نظام جمهوری‌ی اسلامی، با نهادهای رژیم شاه همکاری کرد؛ اما از سوی پیکارگران سیاسی، به مثابه یک لکه‌ی ننگ، مورد شماتت و نفرت و

خشونت رژیم نسبت به مخالفان و منتقدان افزود، و خشونت رژیم هم به نوبه‌ی خود، بین شاه و پیشاهنگان مبارزه مرز آشتی‌ناپذیری رسم کرد. و شگفتا که در ۲۴ شهریور همین سال بود که دو مجلس شورا و سنا، لقب «آریا مهر» را برای «شاهنشاه» تصویب کردند؛ غافل از این واقعیت که، فکرتِ براندازی‌ی او و نظام پادشاهی، دارد در اندیشه‌ی نسل جوان ایران از حالت جنینی خارج می‌شود.

***

حماسه‌ی خونین «سیاهکل»، که با وجود شکست، فصل نوینی در مبارزات مارکسیستی‌ی ایران گشود، در ۱۹ بهمن ۱۳۴۹، به وسیله‌ی ۲۲ تن از جوانان مارکسیست اجراء تاریخی یافت. این حرکت که پیش از رسیدن به هدف، توسط همان مردم فرودست و «زحمتکش»ی که چریک‌ها برای احقاق حقوق آن‌ها و به نام آن‌ها با دستگاه می‌جنگیدند، لو رفت، و از سوی ارتش و ژاندارمری به شدت سرکوب شد.[۴۳۳] حمله‌های بعدی‌ی ساواک به بازماندگان گروه سیاهکل- که حالا «سازمان چریک‌های فدائی‌ی خلق ایران» را تشکیل داده بودند- و به پایه‌گذاران و اعضاء «سازمان مجاهدین خلق ایران»، انبوهی از جوانان را به زندان و شکنجه و اعدام سپرد. تظاهرات دانشجویان- با شعارِ «مبارزین جنگل، ما همه با شمائیم»- در اسفند ۱۳۴۹ و نیز در اردی‌بهشت ۱۳۵۰، با حمله‌ی پلیس ضدشورش به خون کشیده شد؛ و در مهر ماه همان سال بود که گارد ضد شورش در دانشگاه تهران مستقر شد. نقشه‌ی «ربودن شهبانو و ولیعهد»، به عنوان گروگان در برابر آزادی‌ی زندانیان سیاسی- که توسط دوازده تن از جوان‌های پرشورِ انقلابی، اما مستقل و غیر سازمانی، طراحی شده بود-[۴۳۴] پیش از اجرا به وسیله‌ی عامل نفوذی‌ی ساواک (امیرحسین فطانت) کشف و گزارش شد، و روز ۱۴ مهر ماه ۱۳۵۲

دشنام قرار گرفت. مثال بارز این شماتت و نفرت را در شعر «پیشواز» سروده‌ی نعمت میرزازاده (مرداد ۱۳۴۹)- که عبارت «برای پ. ن» را بر پیشانی دارد- می‌توان ملاحظه کرد. چهل و پنج سال پس از انتشار این شعر، و حدود سی و پنج سال پس از اعدام نیکخواه، جمشید انور، (از پایه‌گذاران کنفدراسیون) نوشت:

> «پرویز نیکخواه بعدها پس از کشیدن نیمی از محکومیت ده سال زندانش، تغییر عقیده داد و از زندان بیرون آمد و با رژیم [شاه] به همکاری پرداخت. علت این حرکت وی هنوز برای دوستانش کاملاً روشن نیست . مرحوم پرویز اوصیا می‌گفت که دو شب تا صبح با نیکخواه صحبت کرده بود . می‌گفت که پرویز هنوز موضع سیاسی‌اش همان است؛ ولی معتقد است ، با تماسی که در زندان با مذهبیون داشته، که این‌ها بارها خطرناکتر از شاه هستند و مملکت را به قرون وسطا بر خواهند گرداند . بنا بر این می‌بایست به طور تاکتیکی از شاه پشتیبانی کرد تا خطر قشریون اسلامی منتفی شود. در ظاهر نیکخواه با نبوغش به نتیجه‌ای رسیده بود که ما سال‌ها بعد وقتی رفتار خمینی و دار و دسته‌اش را دیدیم متوجه آن شدیم! من متأسفانه با وجود نامه‌ی سرگشاده‌ی وی که از زندان برای من و فرانسواز نوشته بود، از ملاقات با وی امتناع کردم و توسط فیروز فولادی پیغام بدی برایش فرستادم . با وجود این چند بار که فامیل و آشنایان مشترک را دیده بود سلام فرستاده بود. بعد از مرگ دردناک او متوجه اشتباه خود شدم. دیر شده بود و چاره‌ای جز بردن وجدان گناهکارم به گور ندارم.» به مآخذ زیر نگاه کنید:
>
> - نعمت میرزازاده (م. آزرم)، ***سحوری***، تهران: چاپ دوم، انتشارات رواق، تابستان ۱۳۵۷، صص ۱۶۸ تا ۱۷۱.
> - ***نامه‌ی جمشید انور به برگزارکنندگان جشن پنجاهمین سالگرد کنفدراسیون***، تارنمای «جامعه‌ی رنگین کمان»، ۱۲ ژانویه ۲۰۱۳:
>
> http://www.rangin-kaman.org/v1/index.php?option=com_content&view=article&id=10121:2013-01-19-22-15-59&catid=34:politique

[۴۳۳] رویداد سیاهکل را از زبان زیبای یرواند آبراهامیان و مترجمانش در این جا بازمی‌گویم: «در شامگاه سرد زمستانی‌ی ۱۹ بهمن ۱۳۴۹، سیزده مرد جوان مسلح به تفنگ و اسلحه‌ی کمری به یک پاسگاه ژاندارمی در روستای سیاهکل در کناره‌ی جنگل‌های گیلان حمله کردند.». شاه با لشگری مرکب از هلیکوپترها و کماندوهای ارتش «شاهنشاهی»، به فرماندهی‌ی برادرش، درست مانند این که به جنگ با سپاه دشمن می‌رود، با این افراد و معدود یاران دیگر آن‌ها در منطقه برخورد کرد. در این حمله، ۳۰ تن از چریک‌ها کشته شدند، ۱۱ تن اسیر شدند، که از میان آن‌ها، ده نفر به زندان نرسیده به ضرب گلوله از پای درآمدند، و یک تن نیز که به زندان رسید، در زیر شکنجه جان داد. روز ۱۹ بهمن ۴۹ و رویداد «سیکاهکل»، در واقع، نه تنها روز تولد «سازمان چریک‌های فدائی‌ی خلق ایران»، بلکه روز تولد بسیاری از سازمان‌ها و گروه‌های چریکی در زمان محمدرضا شاه برشمرده می‌شود.

[۴۳۴] به روایت عباس سماکار و رضا علامه‌زاده، طرح گروگان‌گیری‌ی شهبانو و ولیعهد در برابر آزادی‌ی زندانیان سیاسی، ابتدا به صورت یک فکر زودگذر و (شاید آرمانی) در ذهن این دو جرقه زده بود، که به گونه‌ای نیاندیشیده توسعه یافته بود. عباس سماکار و رضا علامه‌زاده و طیفور بطحائی، سه طراح اصلی و نخستین افراد این گروه بودند. این افراد پس از مشورت‌های طولانی با یکدیگر موفق شدند نظر هشت تن دیگر از ناراضیان را به همکاری جلب کنند، که بیش‌تر آن‌ها کارمند تلویزیون یا روزنامه‌نگار بودند. آن‌ها به خاطر بدست آوردن اسلحه، با کرامت دانشیان، از سازمان چریک‌های فدائی‌ی خلق ایران- که پیشینه‌ی زندان هم داشت- رابطه می‌گیرند. شخصی به نام امیرحسین فطانت- که بعداً معلوم شد عامل نفوذی‌ی ساواک بوده- انتقال اسلحه را به عهده می‌گیرد. یکی دیگر از اعضای این گروه، به نام منوچهر مقدم سلیمی، پیش‌تر در جریان ترور شاه در کاخ مرمر بازداشت شده بود و سه سال زندان را گذرانده بود. اما هنوز اسلحه به گروه نرسیده، هر دوازده نفر توسط ساواک دستگیر می‌شوند. از این ۱۲ نفر، به جز کرامت الله دانشیان و خسرو گلسرخی که اعدام شدند، طیفور بطحایی، رضا علامه زاده، و عباس سماکار به حبس ابد محکوم شدند، و بقیه‌ی افراد گروه، با درخواست عفو از شاه و شهبانو به یک تا چند سال زندان محکوم شدند. لازم است بدانیم که خسرو گلسرخی (متولد ۱۳۲۲) از جوانی شعرهای سیاسی می‌سرود و آن‌ها را با نام‌های مستعار منتشر می‌کرد. او سر دبیر بخش هنری‌ی روزنامه‌ی کیهان بود؛ در سال ۱۳۴۷ با عاطفه گرگین، شاعر، نویسنده، و پژوهشگر ازدواج کرد. مقاله‌های سراسر انتقادی‌ی او- از جمله «گرفتاری‌ی شعر

خبر آن به اطلاع مردم ایران رسید. دو تن از این جوانان که زیر شکنجه به توبه تن ندادند- به نام‌های کرامت‌الله دانشیان و خسرو گلسرخی- بعد از محاکمه، که به صورت علنی و با حضور خبرنگاران ایرانی و خارجی صورت گرفت، و بخش‌هائی از آن نیز از تلویزیون ایران پخش شد- روز ۲۹ بهمن ۱۳۵۲ اعدام شدند. دفاعیه‌های این دو مبارز جوان در دادگاه، و سپس خبر اعدام آن‌ها، بر نفرت مردم و پیکارگران سیاسی نسبت به شاه افزود. حدود دو سال بعد، روز ۳۰ فروردین ۵۴- در اوج مبارزه‌ی مسلحانه‌ی سازمان‌های «چریک‌های فدائی‌ی خلق ایران» و «مجاهدین خلق ایران»، مأموران ساواک، بیژن جزنی و شش تن از یارانش، به همراه دو تن از پیکارگران مجاهد را در حالی که پس از شکنجه و بازجوئی محاکمه شده بودند و دوران زندان خود را می‌گذراندند، بر تپه‌های اوین به گلوله بست.[۴۳۵] چرا که- به قول ناصر مهاجر (پژوهشگر زندان و ادبیات زندان):

> از چشم ساواک پنهان نبود که این‌ها در زندان سخت مشغول فعالیت‌اند؛ که به رغم سخت‌گیری‌ها و مراقبت‌ها، به بیرون زندان نقب زده‌اند؛ که ارتباط با رهبری‌ی بیرون از زندان چریک‌ها را بدست دارند؛ و به شکلی سازمان‌یافته، نیازمندی‌های هم‌رزمانشان را فراهم می‌کنند؛ کادرسازی و تربیت چریك، تدوین مبانی‌ی نظری و مواضع سیاسی‌ی جنبش مسلّحانه، تنظیم جزوه‌های آموزشی، خبررسانی، و خبرگیری، ارائه‌ی رهنمودهای عملی و... این اَعمال برای حکومتی که عزم جزم کرده بود که جنبش چریکی را نابود کند، نابخشودنی بود.[۴۳۶] (نقطه‌چین از ناصر مهاجر است.)

روزنامه‌ی کیهان روز ۳۰ فروردین ۵۴ نوشت: «امروز مقامات انتظامی اعلام کردند ۹ نفر از زندانیانی که قصد فرار داشتند، کشته شدند. [...]»[۴۳۷] اما این ادعا، بنا بر تجربه، برای مخالفان رژیم و پیکارگران سیاسی مطلقاً پذیرفتنی نبود. کما این که چهار سال بعد، چند تن از شکنجه‌گران ساواک (تهرانی، شاهین، آرش کمالی) چه‌گونگی‌ی این جنایت را به مردم ایران گزارش دادند. مثلاً، بهمن نادری‌پور، معروف به «تهرانی»، شکنجه‌گر و سربازجوی ساواک و سرپرست زندان سیاسی‌ی اوین، در شب اول خرداد ۱۳۵۸ در دادگاه انقلاب اسلامی به این جنایت ساواک اعتراف کرد:

> بعد از ترور رضا زندی‌پور، رئیس کمیته‌ی شهربانی و راننده‌اش در اواخر سال ۵۳ [به دست چریک‌ها] و پایان یافتن مراسم عزاداری، یک روز در هفتم فروردین ۵۴، محمدحسین ناصری، معروف به «عضدی» مرا به اتاق خود خواست و

در شِبه جزیره‌ی روشنفکران» و «سیاست هنر، سیاست شعر»- نیز در نشریه‌ی نگین منتشر شده بود. او در هنگام دستگیری، دارای پسری خردسال بود. عباس سماکار و رضا علامه‌زاده، هر یک جداگانه، روایت خود از شکل‌گیری‌ی گروه، اجرای این پروژه‌ی خام، و پیامدهای آن را در کتاب‌های زیر به تاریخ سپرده‌اند. به مآخذ زیر نگاه کنید:

- ❖ عباس سماکار، ***من یک شورشی هستم: خاطرات زندان، یادمان خسرو گلسرخی و کرامت دانشیان و گروه دوازده نفره***، لس‌انجلس: انتشارات شرکت کتاب، بهار ۱۳۸۰ (۲۰۰۱).
- ❖ رضا علامه‌زاده، ***دستی در هنر، چشمی بر سیاست***، لس‌انجلس: انتشارات شرکت کتاب، زمستان ۱۳۹۰ (۲۰۱۲).

[۴۳۵] نام این مبارزان به قرار زیر است: بیژن جزنی (یکی از بنیادگذاران نظری‌ی سازمان چریک‌های فدائی‌ی خلق ایران)، سعید کلانتری (مشعوف)، عزیز سرمدی، عباس سورکی، محمد چوپان‌زاده، حسن ضیاء ظریفی، و جلیل افشار (از سازمان چریک‌های فدائی‌ی خلق ایران)، کاظم نورالانوار و مصطفی جوان خوشدل (از سازمان مجاهدین خلق ایران). ناصر مهاجر در این زمینه، می‌نویسد: « در روز پانزدهم اسفند ۱۳۵۳، درست یک روز پس از این که عباس شهریاری، «مرد هزار چهره» و عنصر نفوذی‌ی ساواک در گروه‌های چپ، به دست چریک‌های فدائی‌ی خلق از پا درآمد، و سه روز پس از این که شاه نظام تک‌حزبی بوجود آورد، و حزب رستاخیر را بر پا کرد، از بلندگوهای بند چهارم و پنجم و ششم زندان شماره‌ی یک قصر شنیده شد: افراد زیر [سی و چهار نفر] وسائل خود را جمع کنند و به زیر هشت بروند.» مهاجر در ادامه، به نقل از پرویز نویدی می‌نویسد: «[در زیر هشت] صدای سرهنگ زمانی، رئیس زندان قصر بلند شد که: آقایان! شما از این زندان به زندان دیگری منتقل می‌شوید. ممکن است برخی‌تان باز به این جا برگردید و برخی‌هاتان هم هرگز برنگردید. به هر حال خیال بعضی‌ها، مثل آقای جزنی دیگر از دست ما راحت می‌شود و خیال ما از دست بعضی‌ها. دیگر به ما گزارش نخواهند داد که آقای جزنی با کی نشسته، با کی حرف می‌زده، با کی راه می‌رفته...» بدین ترتیب، این افراد را به زندان اوین منتقل می‌کنند و ۹ تن آن‌ها را شبانه بر تپه‌های اوین به گلوله می‌بندند. به مآخذ زیر نگاه کنید:

- ❖ ناصر مهاجر، ***گزارش یک جنایت***، نشریه‌ی «نقطه»، شماره‌ی ۱، بهار ۱۳۷٤، ص ۷۱.

[۴۳۶] ناصر مهاجر، ***گزارش یک جنایت***، پیشین، ص ۷۳.

[۴۳۷] برگرفته از: ناصر مهاجر، ***گزارش یک جنایت***، پیشین، ص ۷۰.

گفت: قرار است عملیاتی انجام شود که آقای [پرویز] ثابتی گفته شما هم باید در عملیات باشید... در روز پنج‌شنبه ۲۹ فروردین بود که رضا عطارپور با همان حسین‌زاده تلفنی به من اطلاع داد که [...] بعد از پایان وقت اداری در رستوران هتل امریکا، واقع در خیابان تخت جمشید، روبه‌روی سفارت امریکا برای صرف نهار حاضر باشم. [...] وقتی ساعت دو و نیم به رستوران رسیدم، رضا عطاپور، محمدحسن ناصری، بهمن فرنژاد، معروف به «دکتر جوان»، سعدی جلیل اصفهانی، معروف به «بابک»، ناصر نوذری، معروف به «رسولی» و محمدعلی شعبانی، معروف به «حسینی» هم تقریباً همزمان با من آمده بودند... در ضمن صرف ناهار، عطارپور گفت آن عملیاتی را که قرار بود، الان موقع آن است و جزئیات کار را ثابتی بررسی کرده و تصویب شده و سرهنگ وزیری [رئیس زندان اوین] در جریان قرار گرفته و باید همان‌طور که آن‌ها در دادگاه‌های انقلابی‌ی خود، وقت و بی‌وقت، تصمیم به ترور می‌گیرند، ما هم چند نفر از اعضای این سازمان‌ها را بکشیم. عطاپور ادامه داد که شعبانی (حسینی) و رسولی... زندانیان را از زندان اوین تحویل می‌گیرند و ما هم به قهوه‌خانه‌ی اکبر آوینی، در نزدیکی‌ی بازداشتگاه [اوین] منتظر می‌شویم و با سرهنگ وزیری به محل می‌رویم. رسولی و حسینی زودتر حرکت کردند و [ما] بعد از نیم ساعت به سوی قهوه‌خانه راه افتادیم و به قهوه‌خانه رسیدیم. رسولی و حسینی زندانیان را تحویل گرفته و سرهنگ وزیری در حالی که لباس نظامی به تن داشت، خود را آماده‌ی کارزار با عدّه‌ای کرده بود که هم دستشان بسته بود و هم چشمشان. با راهنمایی‌ی او و به دنبال مینی‌بوسِ حامل زندانیان، به بالای ارتفاعات بازداشتگاه اوین رفتیم... زندانیان را پیاده کرده، به ردیف روی زمین نشاندند؛ درحالی که دست‌ها و چشمانشان بسته بود. سپس، رضا عطاپور، فاتحانه، پا پیش گذاشته و گفت همان‌طور که شما و رفقای شما در دادگاه‌های انقلابی‌ی خود رهبران و همکاران ما را محکوم کرده و حکم را اجرا می‌کنید، ما هم شما را محکوم کرده و می‌خواهیم حکم را اجرا کنیم. بیژن جزنی و چند نفر دیگر به این عمل شدیداً اعتراض کردند. اولین کسی که رگبار مسلسل یوزی را به سوی آن‌ها بست، سرهنگ وزیری بود و از آن جائی که گفتند همه باید شلیك كنند، همه شلیك کردند... بعد، سعدی جلیل اصفهانی بالای سر همه رفت و تیر خلاص را شلیك کرد... من و رسولی چشم‌بند شهدا را سوزاندیم و اجساد را داخل مینی‌بوس گذاشتیم و حسینی و رسولی جنازه‌ی شهدا را به بیمارستان شماره‌ی ۵۰۱ ارتش بردند و پزشکی‌ی قانونی، آقای دکتر قربانی، از اجساد بازدید کرد و اجازه‌ی دفن صادر شد. (روزنامه‌ی اطلاعات، اول خرداد ۱۳۵۸- پرانتز و نقطه‌چین‌های بدون قلاب از عبدالعلی معصومی، نویسنده‌ی مأخذ من است.)[۴۳۸]

افزون بر این اعتراف‌های مشابه، «دکتر سید رحمت‌الله میرحقانی» معاون سرپرست پیشین پزشکی‌ی قانونی، چند روز پیش از «پیروزی‌ی انقلاب ۵۷»، پیرامون دروغِ «فرار» (در کیهان ۱۸ بهمن ۵۷) افشاگری کرده بود.[۴۳۹] همچنین، در سال ۱۳۵۴ (پس از فاجعه‌ی تیرباران ۹ نفر زندانی)، شاه و ساواکش از سوی سازمان عفو بین‌الملل به نقض حقوق بشر متهم شده بودند. با این همه، پرویز ثابتی مدیر کل امنیت داخلی‌ی ساواک- که بیست سال از سیاه‌ترین سال‌های دیکتاتوری‌ی محمدرضا شاه پهلوی در کلیه‌ی امور امنیتی و اطلاعاتی‌ی داخلی حرف نخست را می‌زد- سی و سه سال پس از انقلاب، از مخفیگاه خود خروج کرد، و در گفت‌وگو با عرفان قانعی فرد (پژوهشگر تاریخ معاصر ایران)، که به صورت کتاب

---

[۴۳۸] عبدالعلی معصومی، ***سازمان چریک‌های فدایی‌ی خلق ایران***، تارنمای «ایران نبرد»، بازدید ۱۵ دسامبر ۲۰۱۱:
http://www.iran-nabard.com/40%20sal/ali_masoumi.htm
توضیح: ناصر مهاجر در متن ***گزارش یک جنایت***، پیشین، مشابه همین متن را از روزنامه‌ی کیهان، دوشنبه ۲۸ خرداد ۱۳۵۸، بازگو کرده است.

[۴۳۹] میرحقانی روز ۱۸ بهمن ۵۷ گفته بود: «شما می‌دانید گروه مبارز ۹ نفری‌ی جزنی- ظریفی، که در زیر شکنجه‌های سبعانه‌ی ساواک چون کوهی استوار مقاومت کرده بودند و حاضر نشدند شرف و حرمت انقلابی‌ی خود را از دست بدهند، به عنوان این که در حین فرار کشته شده‌اند، تیرباران شدند. و پزشک قانونی به دستور رئیس و معاون سازمانی‌اش اجازه نداشت به صراحت بنویسد چرا گلوله از پشت وارد بدن نشده است (اگر در حال فرار باشد). در حالی که این‌ها از جلو گلوله خورده بودند. و شما می‌دانید این صورت جلسه‌ها را آقای رئیس چند روز قبل از رفتنشان به ساواک تحویل می‌دهند تا از خلال اظهار نظر پزشک قانونی نتوان موضوع فرار یا تیرباران را مشخص کرد.» برگرفته از: ناصر مهاجر، ***گزارش یک جنایت***، پیشین، ص ۷۵.

منتشر شد،[۴۴۰] در برابر چشم صدها تن از زندانیان نجات‌یافته‌ی آن دوران و از همبندان بیژن جزنی، دست داشتن ساواک در کشتار گروه جزنی را نفی کرد، و آن را به «سازمان زندان‌ها» نسبت داد. صدای بی‌چهره‌ی او نیز در روز ۱۸ بهمن ۱۳۹۰/ ۷ فوریه ۲۰۱۲، در برابر پرسش مصاحبه‌گر «صدای امریکا» (سیامک دهقانپور) پیرامون «کشتار و شکنجه در ساواک»، مرگ شایعه‌برانگیز تختی و شریعتی و بهرنگی و مصطفی خمینی (پسر آیت‌الله خمینی) را پیش کشید، تا کشتارهای ثابت‌شده‌ی ساواک را در لفاف «شایعه» بپوشاند؛ و درباره‌ی شکنجه در ساواک نیز بگوید:

> بنده همیشه به سهم خودم با شکنجه که یک چیز غیرقانونی بود مخالفت کرده‌ام و چون حقوق خوانده بودم به سهم خودم همیشه با هر چیزی که منجر به شکنجه شود مخالفت کرده‌ام و هیچ وقت هم خودم نه شکنجه دیده‌ام و نه بازجوئی کرده‌ام. من اهل بازجوئی نبودم من فقط هفت هشت ده نفر آدم را دیده‌ام که کسانی بودند که می‌خواستند مصاحبه‌ی تلویزیونی بکنند، آن هم تازه محدود بود. مثلاً آقای [پرویز] نیکخواه بود، آقای [کوروش] لاشایی، آقای [سیاوش] پارسانژاد بود، بهرام مولایی و سه چهار نفر دیگر که یک موقعیتی داشتند و بهشان تضمین داده بودند که اگر همکاری بکنید تعقیب نمی‌شوید. [...][۴۴۱]

به قول سهراب مبشری در مقاله‌ی «تلنگری ضروری به وجدان عمومی‌ی جامعه‌ی سیاسی‌ی ایران»: «مگر ادولف آیشمن صرفاً با اثبات نقش او به عنوان جنایتکارِ پشتِ میزنشین محکوم نشد؟»[۴۴۲]

در هر حال، گرچه در دوران اسارت بیژن جزنی و یارانش، سازمان چریک‌های فدائی‌ی خلق توسط حمید اشرف و دیگر پیکارگرانِ مبارزه‌ی مسلحانه بازسازی شده بود، اما مرگ این گروه و اسارت انبوهی از هموندان چریک، ضربه‌ی سنگینی بر پیکر این سازمان و اصولاً بر پیکر مبارزه‌ی مسلحانه وارد کرد. منتها، این جنایت بزرگ و دروغ بزرگِ «فرار»، آتش خشم و نفرت پیکارگران و قشرهای آگاهِ مردم ایران را نسبت به رژیم تیزتر کرد.

***

پس از ۲۸ مرداد ۳۲، به ویژه پس از ۱۵ خرداد ۴۲، با صدارت امیرعباس هویدا (که شخصیتی بود دوستدار هنر و ادبیات و آشنا با فرهنگ غربی) و با اجرای ماده‌های «انقلاب سفید»، انبوهی از نویسندگان، هنرمندان، ژورنالیست‌ها، و شخصیت‌های دانشگاهی‌ی ایران، با این که اکثراً با دیکتاتوری‌ی شاه مخالف بودند، بدون گرایش‌های سازمانی، و با هدف گسترش آگاهی و دانائی در جامعه، در نهادهای دولتی مانند رادیو، تلویزیون، کارگاه‌های سینما و تئاتر و موسیقی، و رسانه‌های نوشتاری‌ی مورد تأیید رژیم، و در پست‌های فرهنگی/ دانشگاهی/ پژوهشی- که به برکت «انقلاب سفید» و البته به برکت درآمد نفت، رو به افزایش داشت- به کار مشغول شدند. معرفی و تفسیر نوین از تاریخ و ادبیات کلاسیک، و تفسیر آثار شاعران و نویسندگان نوپرداز، و کلاً، هنر و ادبیات معاصر ایران (که عمدتاً سرشتی معترض داشت، و بنا به سیاست روز همواره در سایه باقی مانده بود)، و حتا ورود این متن‌ها به درس‌ها و بحث‌های دانشگاهی، نمونه‌ای از کوشش‌های این گروه برشمرده می‌شود.[۴۴۳] افزون بر قلمروهای ژورنالیستی و آکادمیک، انبوهی از هنرمندان و

---

[۴۴۰] ***در دامگه حادثه: گفت‌وگوئی با پرویز ثابتی مدیر امنیت داخلی‌ی ساواک*** (بررسی‌ی علل و عوامل فروپاشی‌ی حکومت شاهنشاهی)، گفت‌وگوکننده: عرفان قانعی فرد، با پیش‌گفتاری از دکتر نادر انتصار، لس‌انجلس: انتشارات شرکت کتاب، ۲۰۱۲.

[۴۴۱] سیامک دهقانپور، ***اولین گفت‌وگو با پرویز ثابتی در برنامه‌ی افق***، صدای امریکا، ۱۸ بهمن ۱۳۹۰/ ۷ فوریه ۲۰۱۲:
http://www.youtube.com/watch?v=bTA0hsWTy9M

[۴۴۲] سهراب مبشری، ***تلنگری ضروری به وجدان عمومی‌ی جامعه‌ی سیاسی‌ی ایرانی: پیرامون مصاحبه‌ی صدای آمریکا با پرویز ثابتی***، تارنمای «اخبار روز»، ۲۳ بهمن ۱۳۹۰/ ۱۲ فوریه ۲۰۱۲:
http://www.akhbar-rooz.com/news.jsp?essayId=43628

[۴۴۳] در زمینه‌ی معرفی‌ی ادبیات نوین ایران و جهان، از جمله می‌توان از رضا براهنی (شاعر، نویسنده و منتقد ادبی) در قلمرو دانشگاه؛ نادر نادرپور (شاعر) و فرهنگ فرهی (ادیب، هنرشناس و سخنور) در قلمرو رادیو و تلویزیون، نام برد؛ و در زمینه‌ی معرفی‌ی ادبیات کلاسیک،

نویسندگان، و کارشناسان رشته‌های بهداشتی و پزشکی در ۳۵ نهادی که توسط شهبانو فرح پایه‌گذاری شد و زیر نظر او اداره می‌شد، به کار مشغول بودند. از جمله این نهادها، که فهرست ۳۵ گانه‌ی آن به کتاب «کهن دیارا، خاطرات فرح پهلوی» پیوست شده است، می‌توان از نهادهای «جشن هنر شیراز»، «جشنواره‌ی توس»، نام برد که گروه انبوهی از هنرمندان و نویسندگان را به خود جذب کرده بود. نمونه‌ی دیگر از این انبوه، حضور گروهی از نامدارانِ شعر و قصه‌نویسی و نقاشی و موسیقی و فیلمسازی و تئاتر در «کانون پرورش فکری‌ی کودکان و نوجوانان» است. این کانون نیز که به پیشنهاد شهبانو فرح پهلوی ساخته شد و زیر نظر او اداره می‌شد، افزون بر انتشار کتاب‌ها و فیلم‌ها و برپائی‌ی جشنواره‌های متعدد،این نهاد در آستانه‌ی انقلاب ۵۷، بیش از بیست و نه کتابخانه‌ی ثابت و ده کتابخانه‌ی سیار، با ده هزار عضو و بیش از سه میلیون نفر مُراجع، فقط در تهران داشت. شعبه‌های این کانون و کتابخانه‌های آن، به تدریج در شهرهای دیگر ایران هم دایر شد که به وسیله‌ی شخصیت‌های ادبی و هنری‌ی محلی اداره می‌شد. جالب است یادآور شوم که انتشار کتاب «ماهی سیاه کوچولو» نوشته‌ی صمد بهرنگی، که به نوعی، راهنمای ادبی‌ی چریک‌ها برشمرده می‌شد- گرچه با مشکلات فراوان، اما- توسط انتشارات این کانون انجام شد. افزون بر این کانون، شمار قابل توجهی از نویسندگان و هنرمندان، در نهادهای وابسته به تلویزیون یا وزارت فرهنگ و هنر، مانند «کارگاه نمایش»، «اداره تئاتر»، «تالار ۲۵ شهریور»،[٤٤٤] «تالار رودکی»،[٤٤٥] موزه‌هائی مانند «موزه‌ی فرش» یا «موزه‌ی رضا عباسی»،[٤٤٦] در قلمروهای آفرینش آثار هنری یا پژوهش‌های تاریخی، به پرورش و گسترش آگاهی‌ی همگانی یاری می‌دادند. اما، کار کردن در نهادهای دولتی یا وابسته به دربار نیز به معنای امنیت نبود. شخصیت‌های این گروهِ هنگفت، مداوماً بر لبه‌ی تیغی حرکت می‌کردند، که در یک سوی آن حفره‌ی سیاه ساواک دهان گشوده بود، و در سوی دیگر آن، سرزنش و طرد اپوزیسیونِ آشتی‌ناپذیر. این شخصیت‌ها از سوی نخست، مداوماً در معرض بازداشت و در خطر برکناری از کار قرار داشتند، و از سوی دوم، در معرض اتهام «وابستگی به رژیم» و «خیانت به مردم». نمونه‌های برجسته از عابران این «لبه‌ی تیغ»، که پس از انقلاب ۵۷ نیز در ایران ماندند، فریدون آدمیت و پرویز ناتل خانلری هستند. فریدون آدمیت، هم به سبب پست‌های

از جمله می‌توان از پرویز ناتل خانلری، زهرا کیا (خانلری)، محمدجعفر محجوب، و جلال متینی نام برد؛ و در زمینه‌ی پژوهش‌های تاریخی، از جمله می‌توان به فریدون آدمیت اشاره کرد.

[٤٤٤] ساخت بنای تالار ۲۵ شهریور (در محله‌ی سنگلج تهران، کنار پارک شهر) توسط آرشاویر بابائیان انجام گرفت و پس از تکمیل به وزارت فرهنگ و هنر واگذار شد. این مجموعه از ۱۸ مهر ۱۳۴۴، همزمان با آغاز نخستین جشنواره‌ی نمایش‌های ایرانی، گشایش یافت. با تشکیل «اداره‌ی برنامه‌ریزی و تولید تئاتر حرفه‌ای» (بعداً «اداره‌ی تئاتر») در سال ۱۳۴۳ و گشایش تالار ۲۵ شهریور، یک سال بعد از آن، بسیاری از دست‌اندرکاران فعال تئاتر به استخدام دولتی‌ی این اداره درآمدند و در تالار ۲۵ شهریور مشغول به کار شدند. ۱۱۴ کارگردان و بازیگر و ۲۰ کارمند اعم از مدیر، مدیر صحنه، گریمور، طراح دکور و نور و سازندهٔ دکور در این تالار فعالیت داشتند. از جمله هنرمندانی که در این مجموعه فعال بودند می‌توان به خلیل موحد دیلمقانی، داود رشیدی، بهرام بیضائی، جلال ستاری، اسماعیل شنگله، عظمت ژانتی، عباس جوانمرد، جعفر والی، علی نصیریان، عزت‌الله انتظامی، داود رشیدی، حسین کسبیان، هرمز هدایت، اکبر یادگاری، پرویز فنی‌زاده، ثریا قاسمی، اسماعیل داورفر، فرزانه تأییدی، پرویز تأییدی، محمدعلی جعفری، سعید امیرسلیمانی، سعید راد، اکبر زنجان‌پور، سهراب سلیمی، جمیله شیخی، مهین شهابی، حمید طاعتی و فرهاد مجدآبادی اشاره کرد. نویسندگان سرشناسی نیز چون غلامحسین ساعدی، اکبر رادی، بهرام بیضایی، بیژن مفید، محسن یلفانی، منوچهر رادین، بهمن فرسی، محمود دولت‌آبادی، عنایت‌الله احسانی، کوروس سلحشور، حسین مکی، بهزاد فراهانی، محمد رهبر، حمید نعمت و آرمان امید در تالار ۲۵ شهریور، و در راستای توسعه‌ی نمایشنامه‌های ایرانی کار کردند. با اوجگیری‌ی سانسور فرهنگی و خفقان سیاسی، و با اوجگیری جوهر اعتراض در آثار هنری در دهه‌ی ۱۳۵۰، این تئاتر نتوانست آثار هنرمندان «ایرانی» را به نمایش بگذارد؛ و برای اولین بار نمایشی خارجی با عنوان «بازرس» اثر نیکلای گوگول و به کارگردانی عزت‌الله انتظامی در آن به روی صحنه رفت. در نگارش این توضیح، از متن زیر سود جسته‌ام:

❖ محمد امین خرمی، ***تماشاخانه‌ی سنگلج***، تارنمای «جدید آنلاین»، ۱۶ تیر ۱۳۹۰:
http://www.jadidonline.com/story/07072011/frnk/sangelaj_theatre

[٤٤٥] مجموعه‌ی عظیم، فنی، و مجلل تالار رودکی، بر اساس نمونه‌ی «اُپرا هال وین»، با گنجایش نزدیک به ۹۰۰ تماشاگر، ساخته شد و در سال ۱۳٤٦ توسط محمدرضا شاه پهلوی و شهبانو فرح پهلوی گشایش یافت. این تالار مکانی بود برای اجرای برنامه‌های باله‌ی ملی‌ی ایران، باله‌ی کلاسیک غربی، اپرا، کنسرت، که توسط هنرمندان ایرانی، و بیش‌تر توسط هنرمندان و گروه‌های غیرایرانی انجام می‌شد، از جمله هنرمندان ایرانی که در این تالار برنامه اجرا کردند، حشمت سنجری (رهبر ارکستر سمفونیک تهران)، بنان، مرضیه، محمد رضا شجریان، پری زنگنه (خواننده‌ی سوپرانو)، منیر وکیلی، و حسین سرشار بودند.

[٤٤٦] از میان موزه‌های معتبری که در این دوره ساخته شد، موزه‌ی رضا عباسی بود، که ساختن بنای مدرن آن و تجهیز آن با بودجه‌ای هنگفت سال‌ها به درازا کشید. این موزه، که آثار هنری‌ی ایران را از پیش از تاریخ تا سده‌ی سیزدهم هجری در تالارهای مختلف دربرمی‌گرفت، در سال ۱۳٥٦ رسماً گشایش یافت.

بالای اداری و دیپلماتیک، مورد تردید و سوءظن اپوزیسیون شاه بود، هم به خاطر نامه‌ی اعتراض به اعلام استقلال بحرین و پذیرش آن از سوی دولت ایران، به اجبار ساواک بازنشسته شد، و هم در حکومت اسلامی به گوشه‌گیری و انزوا محکوم بود. فریدون آدمیت (۱۲۹۹ تا ۱۳۸۷)، فرزند یکی ار بنیادگذاران «جامع آدمیت» در عصر مشروطه بود. او افزون بر داشتن دانشنامه از دانشکده‌ی حقوق دانشگاه تهران، مدرک دکتری در رشته‌ی تاریخ و فلسفه‌ی سیاسی را از دانشگاه لندن دریافت کرد. فریدون آدمیت، تا زمان بازنشستگی‌ی اجباری، در پست‌های سفیر ایران در سازمان ملل متحد، سفیر ایران در هند، و مشاور وزیر امور خارجه خدمت کرد. آثار پژوهشی‌ی او- در ژانر تاریخ فکر در دوران مشروطیت- مجموعه‌ی گرانبهائی را تشکیل می‌دهند، که صرف نظر از کاستی‌های احتمالی (که هر کتابی ممکن است داشته باشد)، کیستی و چیستی‌ی ما را در سپیده دمان بیداری نقش زده است، و هیچ پژوهشگری از رجوع به آن بی‌نیاز نیست. با این وصف، هم از سوی کوشندگان سیاسی‌ی سکولار و هم از سوی کوشندگان مذهبی مورد حمله قرار داشت. برای آگاهی از برخورد تلخ اعضای کانون نویسندگان ایران (دوره‌های دوم و سوم) با فریدون آدمیت، به جلد دوم مجموعه‌ی «بخشی از تاریخ روشنفکری‌ی ایران» نوشته‌ی مسعود نقره کار (۲۰۰۱) مراجعه کنید. پرویز ناتل خانلری (۱۲۹۲ تا ۱۳۶۹)، ادیب، زبان‌شناس، پژوهشگر تاریخ زبان و ادبیات فارسی، و سردبیر ۲۷ دوره از نشریه‌ی اثرگذار «سخن» نیز به سبب پذیرش پست‌های وزارت و سناتوری، از سوی اپوزیسیون شاه همواره مورد تردید و گاه تهمت و ناسزا قرار داشت. در حالی که او پیشنهاددهنده‌ی طرح «سپاه دانش»، بنیادگذار «بنیاد فرهنگ ایران»، نویسنده‌ی کتاب‌های گرانبهای «تاریخ زبان فارسی» و «فرهنگ تاریخی‌ی زبان فارسی» بود، و بسیاری از همان منتقدان او، کار خود را از نشریه‌ی «سخن» آغاز کرده بودند. باقر مؤمنی، از اعضاء و هواداران همیشگی‌ی حزب توده، سی و سه سال پس از انقلاب ایران و حدود بیست سال پس از درگذشت پرویز ناتل خانلری، در حالی که شعر «عقابِ» خانلری را بازتاب فضای مبارزاتی‌ی حزب توده تلقی می‌کند، خودِ خانلری را با واژگانی مانند «فرصت‌طلب»، و پناهنده به «خورشگاه زاغ» می‌نوازد:

> در زمان فعالیت آشکار و وسیع حزب [توده] نه تنها انسان‌های صدیق و پاکبازی چون هدایت به میدان جدال مثبت با بی‌عدالتی‌ها و خفقان سیاسی ــــ اجتماعی و مبارزه در راه اعتلای انسان ایرانی قدم نهادند، بلکه این حزب فضایی بوجود آورده بود که فرصت‌طلبانی همچون پرویز خانلری نیز وارد عرصه‌ی مبارزه‌جویی شده و به سرودن اشعاری همچون «عقاب» می‌پرداختند. او که در دوران اوج آزادی‌ی فعالیت‌های سیاسی ــــ اجتماعی و سلطه‌ی فرهنگی‌ی حزب توده‌ی ایران، در این شعر، که آنرا به صادق هدایت تقدیم می‌کند، چهره‌ی «زاغ زشت بد اندام و پلشت» را به بهترین شکل به تصویر می‌کشد و «گند و مُردارخواری» را ارزانی او می‌دارد و می‌خواهد همچون عقاب بر باد سبک سیر سوار شود و در اوج سپهر، جایگاه پیروزی و زیبایی مهر، پرواز کند. پس از سلطه‌ی سیاهی‌ی استبداد و پس از سرکوبی‌ی جنبش‌های توده‌ای و ملی، به خورشگاه زاغ پناه می‌برد و در خدمت دستگاه استبداد به وزارت فرهنگ و سناتوری می‌رسد و به عنوان خدمت به فرهنگ آن دستگاه، فعالانه «بنیاد فرهنگ» پهلوی و «فرهنگستان ادب و هنر» حکومت استبدادی را پایه‌گذاری می‌کند.[۴۴۷]

اما آدمیت و خانلری تنها رهروانِ «لبه‌ی تیغ» نبودند. نادر نادرپور، حسن شهباز، فرهنگ فرهی، و بسیاری دیگر نیز بودند، که ایرج گرگین (۱۳۱۳- ۱۳۹۰) در گفت‌وگو با ماندانا زندیان از آن‌ها نام برده است. ایرج گرگین، که به سبب کار در رادیوهای ایرانِ دوره‌ی پادشاهی، خود یکی از همین رهروان بود- در آن گفت‌وگو، به گونه‌ای ضمنی به وظیفه‌ی

---

۴۴۷ باقر مؤمنی، ***نقش حزب توده در گسترش فرهنگ و هنر***، تارنمای «بی بی سی»، ۱ فوریه ۲۰۱۲/ ۱۲ بهمن ۱۳۹۰:
http://www.bbc.co.uk/persian/iran/2012/02/120131_l44_tudeh_party_culture_art.shtml

«وزارت اطلاعات»، یعنی به مسئله‌ی نظارت دولت بر رسانه‌ها، اشاره می‌کند، و سپس، از گروهی از این رهروان لبه‌ی تیغ نام می‌برد:

> [...] در اواسط دهه ۱۳۳۰ تحولی در این زمینه پدید آمد، وزارت اطلاعات تأسیس شد و رادیو به عنوان یک اداره‌ی کل، زیر نظر این وزارت قرار گرفت. باید توضیح داد که وظیفه‌ی این وزارت - به عکس اکنون- دخالت در امور اطلاعاتی و امنیتی‌ی کشور نبود و حوزه‌ی کار آن منحصر به رادیو و نشریات می‌شد.[...] رادیو علاوه بر نقش رسمی‌ی خود به عنوان سخنگوی دولت و ارگان حکومت، وظایف دیگری در جهت ارائه‌ی برنامه‌های سرگرم کننده و تفریحی و خدماتی و فرهنگی به عهده گرفت و جمعی بزرگ از بهترین هنرمندان تئاتر و موسیقی و نیز دانشمندان و استادان دانشگاه در این برنامه‌ها شرکت می‌جستند. در اوائل دهه ۱۳۴۰ تأسیس «برنامه‌ی دوم - رادیو تهران» که سرپرستی و مسئولیتش به عهده من واگذار شد، به رادیو در ایران معنای تازه‌ای بخشید. برای نخستین بار فرستنده‌ای به طور کامل به طرح مباحث فرهنگی و هنری و علمی و اقتصادی اختصاص یافت و این رادیو که نگاهی نو به مسائل و رویدادها داشت، به پایگاهی برای معرفی هنر و ادبیات جدید ایران، تئاتر و موسیقی جهان و برخی مباحث تاریخی و اجتماعی تبدیل شد که پیش از آن پرداختن به آن‌ها مرسوم نبود. از همان آغاز تأسیس برنامه‌ی دوم رادیو، گروهی از نخبه‌ترین، برجسته‌ترین و بهترین ادیبان، نویسندگان، هنرمندان و دانشگاهیان، به دعوت من با آن به همکاری‌ی پیوسته پرداختند. شاید مناسب باشد نام برخی از آنان را در این جا ذکر کنم: فرخ غفاری، فریدون رهنما، دکتر محمدجعفر محجوب، علی‌اصغرحاج سید جوادی، دکتر علی‌محمد کاردان، علی‌اصغر سروش، مهدی اخوان ثالث، دکتر هوشنگ نهاوندی، حسن هنرمندی، دکتر شاپور راسخ، دکتر جمشید بهنام، عبدالله توکل ... و گروهی دیگر از شاعران و نویسندگان و هنرمندان که «برنامه‌ی دوم» از وجود گرانقدر آن‌ها در برنامه‌هایش بهره می‌جست. فروغ فرخزاد، احمد شاملو، نادر نادرپور و سیمین بهبهانی از آن جمله بودند. [...] این احساس پس از گذشت سال‌ها همچنان در من باقی ست. هیچ کس از خطا مصون نیست، من هم نبوده‌ام. ولی وقتی به پشت سر نگاه می‌کنم و به قضاوت خویش می‌نشینم می‌بینم از زندگی حرفه‌ای خود راضی بوده‌ام، گرچه حاصل کار، هرگز آرزوهای مرا برآورده نکرده است.[۴۴۸]

آری. «هیچ کس از خطا مصون نیست»، و گرچه- به دلایلی که ایرج گرگین از آن‌ها نام نبرده- ممکن است حاصل کارشان آرزوی آن‌ها را برآورده نکرده باشد، اما در تأثیری که این گروه از نخبگان- درست به همان اندازه که منتقدان آن‌ها در قلمرو چپ- بر گسترش شعور اجتماعی‌ی مخاطبانشان برجا گذاشتند، جای تردید نیست. (ملاحظه‌ی تاریخ‌های خروج بسیاری از این شخصیت‌ها از ایران، نشان می‌دهد که آن‌ها، در حین انقلاب و حتا پس از «پیروزی»‌ی آن، بلافاصله از ایران خارج نشدند؛ بلکه یکی/ دو سال اول حکومت اسلامی را تجربه کردند، و با رسیدن به بن‌بست برای هر نوع فعالیت فرهنگی، به خودتبعیدی دست زدند. به بیانی دیگر، بسیاری از شخصیت‌های این گروه، به انقلاب و بهبود شرایط سیاسی/ فرهنگی در حکومت تازه چشم امید داشتند.)

اما آن ۳۵ نهادی که به پیشنهاد شهبانوی ایران تأسیس شدند و زیر نظر او اداره می‌شدند- مانند بسیاری از نهادهای مشابهی که افراد خانواده‌ی دربار با ظاهری خدماتی پایه‌گزاری کرده بودند- سویه‌ی دیگری هم داشت، که با سویه‌ی مثبت آن (یادشده در بند بالا) در تقابل قرار می‌گرفت. سیاوش اوستا (حسن عباسی)، نویسنده و ژورنالیستِ مقیم فرانسه، که با

---

[۴۴۸] ***درباره‌ی رادیو و تلویزیون در ایران: گفت‌وگوی ماندانا زندیان با ایرج گرگین***، تارنمای «ایران امروز»، ۲۳ اکتبر ۲۰۰۷:
http://farhang.iran-emrooz.net/index.php?/farhang/more/14474/
با این توضیح که این گفت‌وگوی بلند به پیشنهاد فصل‌نامه‌ی «ره آورد»، چاپ کالیفرنیای جنوبی، به سردبیری‌ی شعله شهباز (همسر حسن شهباز) انجام شد، و در سه شماره‌ی پیاپی‌ی این نشریه به چاپ رسید. من متأسفانه به این شماره‌های «ره آورد» دسترسی نیافتم. فایل پی دی اف آن را نیز نتوانستم باز کنم. اما بخش نخست آن را در تارنماهای «ایران امروز» و «صدای امریکا» خواندم.

بسیاری از شخصیت‌های ایرانی (در ایران و برون‌مرزهای ایران) مصاحبه‌ی نوشتاری یا تلویزیونی داشته- و در نوشته‌های خود، گاه به گاه، فرح پهلوی را «شهبانوی نازنین» نیز خطاب می‌کند- در این زمینه می‌نویسد:

> [...] در هنگامی که دولت شاهنشاهی ایران بیش از بیست وزارتخانه و وزیر داشت، شهبانو فرح دقیقاً ۳۵ تشکیلات بزرگی چون وزارتخانه را به نام خود کرده و سرپرست آن‌ها بود؛ که هر یك هم بودجه‌های بسیار بالائی در اختیار داشتند، و هم میدان فعالیتشان بسیار گسترده‌تر از یك وزارتخانه بود. فرح پهلوی که تجربه‌ی تاریخی‌ی ثریا اسفندیاری زن دوم پادشاه را می‌شناخت و چون اکثر ایرانیان و جهانیان می‌دانست که ثریا در دربار و حکومت تنها و بی‌یاور بود [...] به محض ورود به کاخ محمدرضا شاه، امپراتوری‌ی مستقل خود را در برابر دولت شاهنشاهی پایه نهاد؛ به گونه ای که یکی از وزرای امیرعباس هویدا به من می‌گفت که در یکی از میهمانی‌های دربار، هویدا به پادشاه می‌گوید که قربان اجازه بفرمائید من و کل کابینه استعفای خود را تقدیم کنیم. پادشاه با عصبانیت دلیل می‌خواهد و هویدا با خنده می‌گوید قربان شهبانو در برابر هر یك از وزارتخانه‌های ما یك یا دو سازمان تشکیل داده‌اند و هم بهتر از ما کار می‌کنند و هم دردسرشان برای کسب بودجه و امکانات بسیار کم‌تر از ماست.[۴۴۹]

اما شهبانو فرح پهلوی در ساختن «امپراتوری»‌ی اقتصادی تنها نبود، و افراد دیگری از خانواده‌ی دربار- و در رأس همه، خود پادشاه- بسی پیش‌تر و بیش‌تر از او، در بنیادگذاری‌ی این گونه نهادهای ظاهراً خدماتی/ خیریه دستی توانا داشتند. افزون بر کثرت فزاینده‌ی سرمایه‌گذاری‌های خارجی در قلمروهای ساختمانی، بانکداری، تجاری، کشاورزی، صنعتی، و مؤسسات فرهنگی در سطح کشور، مجموعه‌ی این نهادهای درباری نیز آسیب بزرگی به اقتصاد کل کشور وارد کرد؛ به گونه‌ای که در طول زمان، سرمایه‌گذاری‌های کوچک ملی را به خطر انداخت، و دست بازار سنتی را عملاً از اقتصاد کشور کوتاه کرد. برخی از این نهادها، ضمن این که ابزاری بودند برای کنترل حرکت‌های مدنی (مثل سازمان زنان)، به نام «خیریه» نیز سودهای کلانی به صاحبانان خود می‌رساندند. (مانند «سازمان شاهنشاهی» و بلیط «بخت‌آزمای»‌اش، که متعلق به شاهزاده اشرف پهلوی بود.) اما مهم‌ترین و مؤثرین این نهادها، «بنیاد پهلوی»، متعلق به خاندان پهلوی بود، که به نام «سازمان غیرانتفاعی/ خیریه» ثبت شده بود. این نهاد، در دهه‌ی پایانی‌ی رژیم پادشاهی، افزون بر سرمایه‌گذاری در کشورهای خارجی، در ۲۰۷ شرکت بزرگ و پردرآمد ایران- در زمینه‌های تجارت، معدن، بیمه، بانک، کشاورزی، شهرسازی، هتل سازی، تفریحات، سرگرمی و توریسم، سهم داشت؛[۴۵۰] و آن قدر کلان شده بود که ویلیام راجرز، وزیر خارجه‌ی اسبق امریکا، وکیل دعاوی آن بود.[۴۵۱] و این در حالی بود که این نهاد، نه تنها از پرداخت مالیات معاف بود، نه تنها سالیانه مبلغ ۴۰ میلیون دلار «اعانه» دریافت می‌کرد، نه تنها از مبلغ هنگفتی از درآمد نفت را به صورت اعتبار بانکی در اختیار داشت، بلکه سرمایه‌ی اولیه‌ی آن نیز متعلق به مردمی بود که اموال و املاک و مستغلات و کارخانه‌هاشان توسط رضا شاه پهلوی توقیف و ضبط شده بود. محمدرضا شاه پهلوی در آغاز سلطنت، در اثر اعتراض و مطالبه‌ی مردم، (که در مجلس و مطبوعات منعکس می‌شد)، بخش بزرگی از اموال و املاکی را که از پدرش ارث برده بود، به دولت واگذاشت، تا درآمد آن «صرف عمران و آبادی‌ی کشور و امور خیریه» شود؛ اما به محض استقرار در قدرت سیاسی، آن را به نام «موقوفه‌ی خاندان پهلوی» از دولت پس گرفت (۳۰ تیر ۱۳۲۸)، تا بعداً از محل فروش همان املاک به کشاورزان، و دیگر درآمدهای آن «موقوفه»، مثلاً، جزیره‌ی کیش برای استراحت و سرگرمی و تفریحات «خواص»

---

۴۴۹ سیاوش اوستا (حسن عباسی)، ***مروری بر خاطرات شهبانو فرح: بی‌وفائی‌ی جهان با شاه ایران: امپراتوری‌ی بانو فرح پهلوی در برابر دولت شاهنشاهی***، تارنمای «سیاوش اوستا»، بازدید ۱۰ سپتامبر ۲۰۱۱:
http://www.aria7000.com/farah-ziba.htm

450 Ervand Abrahamian, ***Radical Islam: The Iranian Mojahedin***, London: I.B. Tauris & Co Ltd., 1989, p.14.

۴۵۱ غلامرضا نجاتی، ***تاریخ سیاسی‌ی بیست و پنج ساله‌ی ایران: از کودتا تا انقلاب***، تهران: نشر مؤسسه‌ی خدمات فرهنگی رسا، چاپ هفتم، ۱۳۸٤، جلد اول، ص ۳٦۸.

ساخته شود؛ سرتاسر سواحل دریای خزر در استان‌های گیلان و مازندران «شهرسازی» شود و ویلاهای «بساز و بفروش» به «عوام» ایران فروخته شود، یا برخی از مناطق آن، به نام نامیِ «والاحضرت»ها و به ضرب سیم خاردار و نگهبان مسلح، برای مردم ایران به کلی «ممنوع‌الورود» شود.[۴۵۲]

در درازنای همین دوران بود که واژه/ واژه‌ی کتاب‌های شعر و داستان و نمایش‌نامه و روزنامه، از سوی ساواک به زیر ذره‌بین می‌رفت و حتا واژگانی مانند «گل سرخ» یا «شقایق»، حساسیت این نهاد را برمی‌انگیخت. به عنوان یک نمونه، و فقط یک نمونه، به خاطره‌ای از ابراهیم گلستان اشاره می‌کنم. پیشاپیش بگویم که عنصر صرفاً سیاسی، نه از داستان‌های گلستان بیرون می‌زند و نه از فیلم‌هایش. گلستان شهادت می‌دهد:

> سال ۱۹۷۴ (۱۳۵۳) مرا گرفتند بردند. [...] بعد از این که آزاد شدم، از یکی از رفقایم پرسیدم که اصلاً چرا مرا گرفتند؟ او گفت تنها کاری که می‌توانم بکنم، این است که به آقای ثابتی، مقام امنیتی، تلفن کنم و وقت بگیرم که تو پیش او بروی، با او حرف بزنی و ببینی چرا تو را گرفته‌اند. همین کار را کرد و من هم رفتم آقای ثابتی را در محلی در سلطنت‌آباد که نزدیک خانه‌مان هم بود، دیدم. ثابتی گفت: «آقای گلستان، آیا می‌دانید که از وقتی ما به اسم شما برخورد کرده‌ایم تا وقتی شما را گرفتیم، فقط ۱۱ دقیقه طول کشید؟» گفتم: «شما اسم این را چی می‌گذارید؟ از وقتی شما روی ماشه‌ی هفت تیرتان فشار بیاورید و مغز من پر از خون، روی دیوار پشت سر شما بپرد، ۱۱ ثانیه هم طول نمی‌کشد. اما اصلاً چرا مرا گرفتید؟» گفت: «وقتی [غلامحسین] ساعدی را گرفتیم، در نامه‌هایش به جمله‌ای از شما برخوردیم که جمله‌ی بسیار مرموزی است و فوری شما را گرفتیم.» البته من با ساعدی رابطه نداشتم، فقط دوبار او را دیده بودم. [...] آن جمله این است: «بگو رفتم تماشای آتش‌بازی؛ باران آمد، باروت‌ها نم برداشت.» به ثابتی گفتم: آقای ثابتی، این جمله را من ۲۶ سال پیش نوشته‌ام. خطاب به آقای ساعدی هم ننوشته‌ام، آن را آخر یک قصه نوشته‌ام و این قصه تا کنون چهار یا پنج بار چاپ شده است. آقای ساعدی این قصه را خوانده است، اما شما که مقام امنیتی و اطلاعاتی هستید، نخوانده‌اید. من نوشته بودم که شما بخوانید، اما نخوانده‌اید و اطلاع نداشتید. من چه‌کار کنم[۴۵۳].

***

در چنین فضای خودآفریده‌ای بود که شاه، از کودتای ۲۸ مرداد ۱۳۳۲ تا واپسین لحظه‌ی خروجش از ایران، پیوسته و به طور فزاینده در محاصره‌ی پنج نیروی پیکارگر قرار داشت: ملّی‌گرایان سکولار (که هم استقلال ایران را در خطر می‌دیدند، و هم شاهد نقض آشکار قانون اساسیِ مشروطیت بودند)؛ نیروهای سوسیالیستی/ کمونیستی (که با وابستگیِ شاه به امپریالیسم امریکا و با شکاف فزاینده‌ی طبقاتی در نبرد بودند)؛ انبوه شاعران و داستان‌نویسان و هنرمندان موسیقی

---

[۴۵۲] در ۳۰ تیر ۱۳۲۸، دولت لایحه‌ای به مجلس برد که بازگشت این اموال به خاندان پهلوی را مطالبه می‌کرد. این لایحه تصویب شد و این بخش از ثروت مردم ایران به «موقوفه‌ی خاندان پهلوی» تعلق گرفت، تا در سال ۱۳۳۷، با نام «بنیاد پهلوی» در قلمروهای فرهنگی و اقتصادیِ ایران اعلام حضور کند. از جمله منابعی که از وجوه مختلف به ضبط املاک توسط رضا شاه پهلوی و به نهاد «بنیاد پهلوی» پرداخته‌اند، به مآخذ زیر نگاه کنید:

- محمد ترکمان، ***تاریخ معاصر ایران*** (مجموعه‌ی مقالات)، کتاب هفتم، تهران: انتشارات مؤسسه‌ی پژوهش و مطالعات فرهنگی، ۱۳۷٤، فصل «نگاهی به اموال منقول و غیرمنقول رضا شاه».
- منیژه ربیعی، ***بنیاد پهلوی***، تارنمای «دانشنامه‌ی اسلام»، بازدید ۲۲ مه ۲۰۱۰: http://www.encyclopaediaislamica.com/madkhal2.php?sid=1951
- غلامرضا نجاتی، ***تاریخ سیاسیِ بیست و پنج ساله‌ی ایران: از کودتا تا انقلاب***، تهران: مؤسسه‌ی خدمات فرهنگی رسا، چاپ هفتم، ۱۳۸۴، جلد اول، صص ۱۳۸ تا ۱۳۹، ۴۹۱ و ۴۹۳؛ جلد دوم، ص ۸۱.
- ***انتقال بنیاد پهلوی به دولت***، گفت‌وگو با دکتر شاپور بختیار در تبعید، تارنمای «نهضت مقاومت ملی»، بازدید: ۲۹ ژوئن ۲۰۱۲: http://www.namir.info/home/pdf/akbar_rooz5/b_bonyad.htm

[۴۵۳] ***گفته‌های ناگفته‌ی گلستان، باروتی که نم کشید!*** بخش پنجم از مجموعه‌ی گفت‌وگوهای الهه خوشنام با ابراهیم گلستان، با عنوان «در قلمرو ادبیات»، تارنمای «دویچه وله»، http://www.dw.com/fa-ir/باروتی-که-نم-کشیدbrگفتههای-ناگفتهی-گلستان/a-6310542?maca=per-rss-per-all-1491-rdf

و سینما و تئاتر و آزادی‌خواهان مستقل (که به گونه‌ای آشتی‌ناپذیر با خفقان سیاسی در نبرد بودند)؛ شخصیت‌ها و سازمان‌های وابسته به لایه‌ی روحانی و بازار (به دلایلی که برخی از آن‌ها را برشمردم)؛ نیروی «کنفدراسیون جهانی‌ی دانشجویان ایرانی» (متشکل از همه‌ی نیروهای چپِ مستقل یا سازمانی، و انجمن‌های اسلامی). نارضایتی‌ی همگانی به میزانی رسیده بود که بسیاری از دانشجویان، حتا آن‌ها که از وزارت علوم و نهادها و بنیادهای وابسته به دربار (مانند «بنیاد فرهنگ ایران» و «بنیاد پهلوی») بورس تحصیلی دریافت می‌کردند، به محض خروج از ایران، به «کنفدراسیون جهانی‌ی دانشجویان ایرانی» می‌پیوستند. دانشجویان بورسیه و بسیاری از دانشجویانی که با هزینه‌ی شخصی در خارج از ایران تحصیل می‌کردند، به سبب فعالیت علیه رژیم، پس از پایان تحصیل نیز قادر به بازگشت به ایران نبودند، و پس از پایان تحصیل در کنفدراسیون باقی می‌ماندند. این دانشجویان و دانش‌آموختگان، وظیفه‌ای دوجانبه برای خود قائل بودند: افشاگری‌ی نمودهای دیکتاتوری‌ی شاه در برون مرزهای ایران، از یک سو، و ارسال گزارش‌هائی از «انقلاب‌های فرهنگی» در کشورهای غربی، انقلاب کوبا، جنبش‌های آزادی‌خواهانه در مکزیک، شیلی، آرژانتین، فلسطین، کنگو و الجزایر، به ایران، از سوی دوم. در نتیجه می‌توان گفت که تلاش بی‌وقفه‌ی کنفدراسیون در افشاء دیکتاتوری‌ی شاه و جلب حمایت روشنفکران جهان و نهادهای حقوق بشر، حلقه‌ی پنجم محاصره‌ای بود که شاه، به ویژه در دهه‌ی پنجاه خورشیدی، موجودیت خود را در آن گرفتار می‌دید؛ پنج حلقه‌ای که به لحاظ نظری، به سه حلقه قابل فروکاستن بود: پیکارگران مذهبی، پیکارگران کمونیست، و پیکارگران ملی/ مذهبی (چه سازمانی، و چه مستقل)؛ که با وجود تفاوت‌های عظیم در هدف مبارزه، از نظر ذهنیت، در نقطه‌ی «مذهب» به هم می‌رسیدند. به بیانی دیگر، هیچ یک از این گروه‌های هنگفت و از درون ناهمگون، با «مذهب» مشکلی نداشت، و اگر در راه پیکار خود لازم می‌دید، بی‌درنگ به آن می‌آویخت. منتها، تابوی پادشاه ایران، تا پیش از سال ۱۳۵۷، نبردِ «کمونیست‌ها» بود، که آشکارا سرنگونی‌ی او، نظام شاهنشاهی، و نظام سرمایه‌داری را طلب می‌کرد.

* در درازنای همین دوران بود که کتاب «شرح زندگی‌ی من» با نام ابوالقاسم لاهوتی، پیرامون اردوگاه‌های کار اجباری و تصفیه‌های استالین، در تهران به بازار آمد (پائیز ۱۳۳۲) که به زودی جعلی بودن آن نیز بر مردم و پیکارگران سیاسی آشکار شد. این گونه ترفندهای دستگاه حکومتی/ امنیتی، که کم هم نبودند، به نوبه‌ی خود سبب شدند که مفاد کتاب‌های راستینی چون «استالین و تصفیه‌ی ارتش سرخ» (۱۳۴۵) یا «سفری در گردباد» (۱۳۴۸ پیرامون اردوگاه‌های کار اجباری در شوروی) از دید پیکارگران چپ مورد تردید قرار گیرند و از زمره‌ی دروغ‌پراکنی‌های سیا- و بعداً- ساواک تلقی شوند.[۴۵۴]

* در ادامه‌ی همین ناباوری‌های دوسویه بود که پچپچه‌ی بیماری‌ی سرطان شاه، در میان لایه‌هائی از مردم معمولی‌ی ایران درگرفت، و اکثریت آن‌ها، که از سوئی با تبلیغات ضد شاه آشنا بودند، و از سوی دیگر، نشانه‌ای از بیماری در سیما و قامت و صدای شاه نمی‌دیدند، این گزاره را برساخته‌ی مخالفان رژیم برآورد کردند. (معترضه: من، ملیحه تیره گل، و حلقه‌ی دوستان و خانواده‌ام، از جمله‌ی آن «مردم معمولی» بودیم. بدین ترتیب، شگفت‌انگیز می‌نماید که سال‌ها بعد «گری سیک Gary Sick»، کارمند شورای امنیت ملی در دوره‌های ریاست جمهوری‌ی جرالد فورد و جیمی کارتر، در کتابش چنین وانمود کرد که تا زمان اوج‌گیری‌ی بیماری‌ی شاه در تبعید، محافل اطلاعاتی‌ی امریکا و حتا فرانسه، از بیماری‌ی او خبر نداشتند؛ «با این که هر دو پزشکِ شاه، فرانسوی بودند.»[۴۵۵] «هنری پرشت Henry Precht»، مستشار نظامی/

---

[۴۵۴] کتاب «استالین و تصفیه‌ی ارتش سرخ» نوشته‌ی ویکتور الکساندروف، و کتاب «سفری در گردباد»، خاطرات ی. گینزبورگ. در این زمینه به مأخذ زیر نگاه کنید:
بابک امیر خسروی و محسن حیدریان، ***مهاجرت سوسیالیستی و سرنوشت ایرانیان***، چاپ دوم، تهران: انتشارات پیام امروز، ۱۳۸۲، ص ۱۰۴.

[455] Gary Sick, ***All Fall Down: America's Tragic Encounter with Iran***, New York: Random House, 1985, pp. 181-186.

سیاسیِ امریکائی نیز که از سوی وزارت دفاع کشورش سال‌ها در ایران اقامت داشت، و در حوالیِ انقلاب ایران به ریاست میز ایران در وزارت خارجه‌ی امریکا برگزیده شد، همین بی‌خبری را ابراز کرده است.[456])

* در درازنای همین دوران بود که نویسندگان آزادی‌خواه و مستقل، زیر بار «کنگره‌ی جهانیِ شعرا و نویسندگان»- کنگره‌ی فرمایشیِ دربار- نرفتند؛ بیانیه‌ی آن را تحریم کردند؛ با کوششی پیگیر، نخستین «کانون نویسندگان ایران» را بنا نهادند؛ و مطالبه‌ی «آزادیِ اندیشه و بیان، بی‌حصر و استثناء» را بر پیشانیِ منشور آن به ثبت رساندند.[457] البته حکومت سانسور به این کانون مجوز رسمی نداد. اما «کانون نویسندگان ایران» در همان جوّ امنیتی، مجمع عمومیِ خود را تشکیل داد و هیئت دبیران خود را برگزید. منتها، به سبب خفقان فزاینده، این کانون، به رغم خواست و نیت بسیاری از اعضاء آن، از مطالبات صنفی بسی فراتر رفت، و به تدریج (در قلمرو آزادیِ بیان) به نهادی سیاسی تبدیل شد؛ اعضای مقاوم آن یکی پس از دیگری به زندان و بازجوئی و ممنوع‌القلم شدن یا تبعید محکوم شدند؛ و همین‌ها بودند که در شروع انقلاب ۵۷ سهم به سزائی پرداختند. (در جلد سوم مجموعه‌ی حاضر، به تفصیل پیرامون فرایندهای جاری در «کانون نویسندگان ایران» سخن گفته‌ام.)

* در درازنای همین دوران بود که به رغم مطالبه‌ی «آزادیِ اندیشه و بیان بی‌حصر و استثناء»، از سوی شعرِ «متعهد»

---

[456] ***Change Will Come From Within***, Interview with former American diplomat in Tehran, by Fariba Amini, June 17, 2003:
http://www.iranian.com/FaribaAmini/2003/June/Precht/

[457] از گزارش‌های پرشماری که پیرامون تشکیل «کانون نویسندگان ایران» منتشر شده است، چنین برمی‌آید که دو رویداد توأمان و تقریباً همزمان، نویسندگان مستقل و آزادی‌خواه ایران را به تشکیل این کانون واداشت. به روایت رضا براهنی، اولی در سال ۱۳۴۵ بود که دولت وقت (دولت امیرعباس هویدا) به ناشران دستور داد که کتاب را پس از چاپ و پیش از انتشار به اداره‌ی سانسور وزارت فرهنگ و هنر نشان دهند. و دومی در سال ۱۳۴۶ روی داد، که به پیشنهاد و کوشش شهبانو فرح پهلوی، برای برگزاریِ «کنگره‌ی جهانیِ شعرا و نویسندگان» تدارک لازم دیده شد. افزون بر گروهی از نویسندگان ایرانی، قرار بود چند نویسنده‌ی سرشناس از «انجمن جهانیِ قلم» در این کنگره شرکت کنند. در میان نویسندگان ایرانیِ پیش‌بینی شده برای شرکت در این کنگره، شخصیت‌های فهرست زیر در آن زمان از همه نامدارتر بودند: فریدون آدمیت، داریوش آشوری، جلال آل احمد، هوشنگ ابتهاج، مهدی اخوان ثالث، محمود اعتمادزاده (به آذین)، رضا براهنی، بهرام بیضائی، باقر پرهام، فریدون تنکابنی، اسماعیل خوئی، سیمین دانشور، یدالله رؤیائی، غلامحسین ساعدی، محمدعلی سپانلو، احمد شاملو، سیاوش کسرائی، نادر نادرپور، و اسماعیل نوری علا. اما اکثریت همین نویسندگان، که کنگره‌ی یادشده را «درباری» و «فرمایشی»، و به منظور ساکت کردن نویسندگان ایرانی در اعتراض به خفقان رژیم برآورد کرده بودند، پیش از انجام این کنگره، به تشکیل کانونی از آن خود اقدام کردند. این نویسندگان، با همکاریِ گروه‌ها و جمع‌های کوچکتری مانند گروه ادبیِ «طرفه»، جمع ادبیِ «کافه فیروز»، جمع ادبیِ «کافه نادری»، و گروه «تالار قندریز»، با گرایش‌های هنری و سیاسیِ مختلف، اما با هدف مشترکِ مبارزه با سانسور و نهادی کردن آزادیِ بیان و اندیشه، گردآمدند، و جمع ۴۰ نفره‌ی آنان در نخستین بیانیه‌ی خود در اواخر سال ۱۳۴۶، ضمن محکوم کردن «کنگره جهانی»ی دربار، زیر نام «کانون نویسندگان ایران»، اعلام موجودیت کردند. البته این کانون، که در درجه‌ی نخست به استقلال و عدم وابستگی به دستگاه می‌اندیشید، با تمام کوشش‌ها و دوندگی‌های شخصیت‌های محوریِ آن نتوانست از دولت وقت (امیرعباس هویدا) مجوز رسمی بگیرد. با این همه، پس از تدوین منشور کانون و پس از نشاندن عبارت «آزادیِ اندیشه و بیان، بی‌حصر و استثناء» بر پیشانیِ آن منشور، که به امضاء ۵۲ نویسنده رسیده بود، در سال ۱۳۴۷ مجمع عمومی خود را تشکیل داد و هیئت دبیران خود را برگزید. از سال ۱۳۴۹ به بعد، که جوّ پلیسی دوباره بالا گرفت و اعضاء این کانون مرتباً در معرض دستگیری و بازجوئی و زندان و ممنوع‌القلم شدن قرار داشتند، کانونیان، عملاً، به گردهم‌آئی‌های کوچک و پراکنده ناگزیر شدند؛ تا که سال ۱۳۵۶ فرابرسد و در «فضای باز سیاسی»، در رویداد «ده شب شعر گوته» دوباره با هم گرد آیند، و با یک صدا، در برابر رژیم خفقان اعلام حضور کنند؛ و در ۲۳ آبان ۱۳۵۶ بیش از ده هزار نفر از دانشجویان و جوانان معترض را به مدت ۲۴ ساعت برای تحصن در دانشگاه «آریا مهر» («شریف» بعدی) گرد هم آورند. برای آگاهیِ گسترده در زمینه‌ی کانون نویسندگان ایران، به جلد اول مجموعه‌ی « **بخشی از تاریخ روشنفکریِ ایران**» تحقیق و تدوین مسعود نقره کار (نشر باران ۲۰۰۲) مراجعه کنید. من در نگارش فشرده‌ی بالا، هم از نوشته‌ی کوتاهی از مسعود نقره کار و هم از نوشته‌ای در وبگاه شخصیِ محمد محمدعلی (نویسنده‌ی درون‌مرزی) سود جسته‌ام. متن اول را مسعود نقره کار به مناسبت چهلمین سالگرد تأسیس کانون منتشر کرد، و نوشته‌ی دوم، متن سخنرانیِ محمد محمدعلی است، که او آن را روز ۹ مهر ۱۳۸۸ در نشست کانون نویسندگان ایران در تبعید، در شهر ونکوور- کانادا ایراد کرده بود:

- ❖ مسعود نقره کار، ***چراغی که خاموش شدنی نیست***، تارنمای «کانون نویسندگان ایران- در تبعید»، بازدید ۱۸ خرداد ۱۳۸۸: http://www.iwae.org/index.htm
- ❖ http://www.mohammadmohammadali.com/articles/01102009.htm

صدا برخاست که: «هنگام عزل و بوسه‌ی عاشقانه نیست».[۴۵۸] چرا که، «امه سزر» (شاعر و نمایشنامه‌نویسِ انقلابی-لاتینی‌تبارِ فرانسوی‌زبان) هم گفته بود: «باید تکلیف خود را روشن کرد./ افعال عاشقانه، با زمان‌های استعماری صرف نمی‌شوند.»[۴۵۹] با چنین دستورالعمل‌هائی بود که صدای شاعران «موج نو» که «هنر» را از «سیاست» جدا می‌دیدند و به هستی‌ی «شعر» و به هستی‌ی انسان عام در هنر توجه داشتند، به لحاظ «اجتماعی»، نه تنها بی‌پژواک ماند، بلکه شاعران این «موج» از سوی گروه‌های «متعهد»، به «عدم تعهد» نیز متهم شدند. به ضرب و زور چنین دستورالعمل‌هائی بود که «تعهدِ» رئالیسم سوسیالیستی، عمدتاً از نوع «روسی/ استالینیستی»ی آن نیز، فضای ذهنی و عینی‌ی ادبیات و هنر ما را آکند. بر فراز تک مقاله‌های منتقدان چپ‌گرا، که دست کم از سال‌های دهه‌ی ۱۳۳۰ به بعد، با زبان و بیان ژورنالیستی در نشریه‌ها، با کوبیدن و نفی‌ی «بوف کور» صادق هدایت و «اسیر» فروغ فرخزاد و آثار بهرام صادقی و ... ، تز رئالیسم سوسیالیستی را به ادبیات فارسی تزریق می‌کردند، باید از کتاب «رئالیسم و ضد رئالیسم در ادبیات» نوشته‌ی سیروس پرهام (دکتر میترا) یاد کرد. نخستین چاپ این کتاب در سال ۱۳۳۴ منتشر شد، و تا پیش از انقلاب به چاپ پنجم، و تا سال ۱۳۶۲، به چاپ هفتم رسید. تحلیل دانشورانه‌ی سیروس پرهام از آثار ادبی‌ی ایران و جهان در این کتاب، به گونه‌ای ظریف و پوشیده، آغشته است به نگاه ایدئولوژیک و تجویز تز «رئالیسم سوسیالیستی»، بدون این که از آن نامی به میان آورده شود. برای دیدن این ویژگی‌ها باید سراسر کتاب را خواند. اما من تنها دو فراز از متن این کتاب را در این جا ثبت می‌کنم:

> [...] پس نویسنده‌ی رئالیست نخست می‌کوشد تا بفهمد که چرا مرد ثروتمند پاکیزه و «خوش سلیقه» و مرد بینوا ادبار و ناخوش‌آیند است. همین که این حقیقت دریافته و نمایانده شود، همه چیز دگرگون خواهد شد. «کثافتِ» فقرا دیگر «مهوّع و نفرت‌انگیز» نخواهد بود؛ بلکه حس همدردی‌ی ما را برخواهد انگیخت؛ همچنان که «پاکیزگی»ی اغنیا، به عوضِ «دل‌انگیزی»، دلگیر و خشم‌آورخواهد گشت. (ص ٤۱) [...] هنرمندی که برای درک ماهیت اشیاء به «جادوی کلمات» متوسل می‌شود، گریزی نخواهد داشت [... که] مانند رمبو و مالارمه و ورلن با لولیدن در زیر حباب شفاف ماوراءالطبیعه‌ای‌ی خود به زندگی‌ی بی‌ثمر و پرشکنجه‌ی خویش ادامه دهد. [مثلا] رمبو که در هفده سالگی اشعار فناناپذیری می‌سرود، در نوزده سالگی یکسره دست از شعر و شاعری شست، کشور به کشور آواره گردید و در گرسنگی و شکنجه جان سپرد. (ص ۱٤۲)[۴۶۰] (گیومه‌ها از متن اصلی است.)

معنای مخالفِ مثال مربوط به «رمبو» این است که به جای «اشعار فناناپذیر»، اشعار تاریخ مصرف‌دار بسازید؛ وگرنه، «کشور به کشور آواره» می‌شوید و در «گرسنگی و شکنجه جان خواهید سپرد.» اگر این دستورالعمل مرعوب‌کننده برخاسته از دیدگاه اختیاری‌ی شخص نویسنده بود، شاید با ده‌ها ردّیه و مقاله‌ی انتقادی روبه‌رو می‌شد. اما از آن جا که این نگاه برخاسته از دستورالعمل «حزب مترقی و طراز نوینِ توده» بود، و از آن جا که بدنه‌ی اصلی‌ی جامعه‌ی ادبی‌ی آن

---

۴۵۸ خطی از شعر «دیریست گالیا» سروده‌ی هوشنگ ابتهاج (ه. ا. سایه). چنان که از متن‌های مربوط به تفسیر این شعر برمی‌آید «گالیا» نام دختری بوده که شاعر در جوانی به او عشق می‌ورزیده. در نتیجه، می‌توان این شعر را به عنوان گواهی بر یک تحول شخصی برشمرد. منتها، جوّ انتقادی‌ی زمانه، آن را به مثابه یک مانیفست ادبی/ هنری/ اجتماعی تعبیر کرد. بخش‌هائی از این شعر را در این جا ثبت می‌کنم: دیریست گالیا!/ در گوش من فسانه‌ی دلدادگی مخوان!/ دیگر ز من ترانه‌ی شوریدگی مخواه!/ دیریست گالیا! به ره افتاد کاروان/ عشق من و تو؟ این هم حکایتی‌ست/ اما در این زمانه که درمانده هر کسی/ از بهر نان شب/ دیگر برای عشق و حکایت مجال نیست/ شاد و شکفته در شب جشن تولدت/ تو بیست شمع خواهی افروخت تابناک/ امشب هزار دختر همسال تو ولی/ خوابیده‌اند گرسنه و لخت روی خاک/ زیباست رقص و ناز سرانگشت‌های تو/ بر پرده‌های ساز/ اما هزار دختر بافنده این زمان/ با چرک و خون زخم سرانگشت‌هایشان/ جان می‌کنند در قفس تنگ کارگاه/ از بهر دستمزد حقیری که بیش از آن/ پرتاب می‌کنی تو به دامان یک گدا [...] دیریست گالیا! هنگام غزل و بوسه‌ی عاشقانه نیست/ هر چیز رنگ آتش و خون دارد این زمان/ هنگامه‌ی رهائی‌ی لب‌ها و دست‌هاست/ عصیان زندگی‌ست/ در روی من مخند/ شیرینی‌ی نگاه تو بر من حرام باد!/ بر من حرام باد از این پس شراب و عشق!/ بر من حرام باد تپش‌های قلب شاد!/ یاران من به بند/ در دخمه‌ی تیره و غمناک باغشاه/ در عزلت تب‌آور تبعیدگاه خارک/ در هر کنار و گوشه‌ی این دوزخ سیاه/ زودست گالیا!/ در من فسانه‌ی دلدادگی مخوان!/ [...]

۴۵۹ امه سزر، ***مجموعه‌ی گفتار***، در کتاب زمان، کتاب اول، ویژه‌ی امه سزر، فروردین ۱۳٤۸.

۴۶۰ سیروس پرهام (دکتر میترا)، ***رئالیسم و ضد رئالیسم در ادبیات***، تهران: چاپ هفتم، انتشارات آگاه، ۱۳۶۲.

روزگار ایران، به این نوع «ترقی» می‌بالید، نه تنها در برابر این استدلال هولناک سکوت کرد، بلکه سر بر آستان آن سائید. چرا که به گفته‌ی احسان طبری (ایدئولوگ حزب توده، که پس از حدود پنجاه سال پراکندن آموزه‌های استالینیستی، در زندان جمهوری‌ی اسلامی به «دین اسلام» مشرف شد):

> او [استالین] به این نتیجه رسیده بود که جریانات «مدرنیستی» در هنر، نمودار انحطاط هنر بورژوائی است. [...] و گفته شد که مدرنیسم نقش ذهنیت هنرمند را بر انعکاس عینیت زندگی و طبیعت مرجّح می‌کند و لذا نوعی ایده‌آلیسم هنری است و با جهان‌بینی‌ی انقلابی در تضاد بنیادی است.[٤٦١]

* در درازنای همین دوران بود که غلامرضا تختی، قهرمان جهانی‌ی کُشتی و عضو شورای عالی جبهه‌ی ملی، خودکشی کرد (۱۷ دی ۱۳۴۶)؛ تا از خاص و عامی که از احضارهای او به ساواک خبر داشتند، صدا برخیزد که «جهان پهلوان را کشتند.»[٤٦٢] و در مراسم چهلم درگذشت او، از انجمن‌های دانشجوئی صدا برخیزد که: «تختی نکشت خود را/ او را شهید کردند».[٤٦٣] در درازنای همین دوران بود که صمد بهرنگی، (از جمله مارکسیست‌های حلقه‌ی تبریز، که بعداً در تشکیل «سازمان چریک‌های فدائی‌ی خلق ایران» نقش به سزائی داشتند)، در رودخانه‌ی ارس غرق شد، (۹ شهریور ۱۳۴۷)، و این بار، هم در جامعه‌ی «روشنفکری» و هم میان محرومان و فرودستان جامعه (یعنی، مخاطبان اصلی‌ی آثار صمد بهرنگی، که ضمناً از درگیری‌های او با ساواک هم بی‌خبر نبودند) زمزمه در گرفت که کار، کار ساواک است؛ زمزمه‌ای که هنوز پس از نزدیک به پنج دهه، از سویه‌های مختلف و با گرایش‌های مختلف بر گرداگرد مرگ مشکوک صمد بهرنگی پیچ و تاب می‌خورد.[٤٦٤] در درازنای همین دوران بود که مرگ جلال آل احمد (۱۸ شهریور ۱۳۴۸)، و علی

---

[٤٦١] احسان طبری، ***از دیدار خویشتن*** (۱۳٦۰ پیش از زندان)، به کوشش ف. شیوا، سوئد: نشر باران، چاپ دوم، ۱۳۷۹/ ۲۰۰۱، ص ۱۳۲.

[٤٦٢] غلامرضا تختی، برنده‌ی چندین مدال طلا و نقره در مسابقات جهانی‌ی کُشتی، یکی از محبوب‌ترین چهره‌های مردمی‌ی زمانه‌ی خود بود. او، که از طرفداران راه مصدق بود و پس از رویداد ۱۵ خرداد ۱۳٤۲ نیز به عضویت شورای مرکزی‌ی جبهه‌ی ملی برگزیده شده بود، بارها توسط ساواک احضار می‌شد. در بسیاری از متن‌های مربوط به این شخصیت چنین آمده است که دستگاه ساواک، برای جلوگیری از افزایش محبوبیت او، او را از حقوق و مزایا و امکانات تمرین و آماده‌سازی محروم داشت؛ و این محرومیت‌ها، در مسابقات بعدی به شکست تختی انجامید. غلامرضا تختی یک روز پیش از خودکشی (۱٦ دی ۱۳٤٦) وصیت‌نامه‌ی خود را به ثبت رساند و روز ۱۷ دی، در حالی که دارای فرزندی سه ماهه بود، در هتل آتلانتیک تهران خود را کشت. مفسران رژیم گفتند و نوشتند که ناتوانی در کسب امتیاز قهرمانی، او را به خودکشی واداشت، عطاءالله بهمنش، مفسر ورزشی، بعداً گفت که ساواک حتا از پخش خبر خودکشی‌ی تختی در رادیو جلوگیری کرد. در هر حال، طرفداران بی‌شمار او نوشتند و هنوز می‌نویسند که در هر حالت، رژیم شاه غلامرضا تختی را کشت؛ فرقی هم نمی‌کند که مستقیماً، یا با ایجاد محرومیت برای او. بابک تختی، تنها فرزند غلامرضا تختی، که پدرش را به یاد نمی‌آورد، می‌گوید: «مرگ تختی برای خود من هم روشن نیست. ولی فکر می‌کنم کشتن یک آدم فقط تیرخالی کردن توی مغزش نیست. این جا خودکشی عین کشتن است، و حکومت پهلوی بدون تردید در مرگ تختی مقصر بود. فکرش را بکنید آدمی با موقعیت تختی کارش را از دست بدهد، توی استادیوم راهش ندهند، نگذارند حقوق بگیرد و نگذارند کشتی بگیرد. [...]» یادآوری کنم که بابک تختی، صاحب امتیاز، مدیر مسئول و مدیر فروشگاه نشر «قصه» در تهران، به همراه همسرش، منیرو روانی‌پور (داستان نویس)، و پسرشان، غلامرضا تختی، پس از سال‌ها دست و پنجه نرم کردن با عوامل فرهنگی‌ی رژیم اسلامی، بالأخره به خیل مهاجران پیوست.

[٤٦٣] مهدی سامع، ***سه رویداد: تختی، حمید اشرف، و سالگرد سیاهکل***، تارنمای «بی بی سی»، ۱٤ بهمن ۱۳۸۹/ ۳ فوریه ۲۰۱۱:
http://www.bbc.co.uk/persian/iran/2011/02/110203_l42_siahkal_part_eight.shtml

[٤٦٤] صمد بهرنگی، افزون بر شرکت در هسته‌ی مارکسیست‌های تبریز، معلم روستا و نویسنده‌ی ادبیات کودکان نیز بود. اما قصه‌های انتقادی و روشنگرانه‌ی او شهر و روستا نمی‌شناخت، و در میان همه‌ی لایه‌های اجتماعی‌ی ایران طرفدار داشت. او بارها به ساواک فراخوانده شده بود؛ و بنا بر گفته‌های برادرش، اسد بهرنگی- در کتاب «برادرم صمد، روایت زندگی و مرگ او»- مورد شکنجه هم واقع شده بود. صمد بهرنگی بنا بر اظهار حمزه فراهتی، که دوست و هموند او در همان هسته‌ی مارکسیستی بود، در شهریور ۱۳٤۷ در برابر دیدگان او (به عنوان تنها شاهد) در رودخانه‌ی ارس غرق شد. در مراسم تشییع پیکر او به گورستان، جمعیت عظیمی از مردم شرکت داشتند، که به احتمال قوی، اکثر آن‌ها از فعالیت سیاسی‌ی او بی‌خبر بودند. چرا که محبوبیت او در میان مردم غیرسیاسی، تنها به خاطر این بود که صدای اعتراض خود را از کتاب‌های او شنیده بودند. و به سبب کشتار و خفقانی که وجود داشت، او را به عنوان «شهید»ی شناسائی کردند، که به خاطر روشنگری‌هایش مورد خشم ساواک بوده است. در همان زمان، جلال آل احمد در مقاله‌ی «صمد و افسانه‌ی عوام»، با اشاره به فضای ذهنی‌ی جامعه، این شک را «مستمسکی» برای «گیردادن» به رژیم و «شهیدنمائی»ی عوام تعبیر می‌کند. او در این مقاله، از داستان برادرش که در مدینه مرده بود، و بعداً شهید قلمداد شده بود، آغاز می‌کند و می‌نویسد: «**گیر آمد. مستمسک گیر آمد. فلانی که از کربلا آمده بود، از فلان دیگری که از مدینه برگشته بود، نقل کرده بود که فلانی را سُنّی‌ها چیزخور کرده‌اند. و چه زود قضیه پیچید، از این دهن به آن گوش، و شد یک اعتقاد. [... در مورد شایعه‌ی قتل عمدی‌ی صمد] ، من هنوز باورم نمی‌شود. یعنی رمانتیک بازی‌ی ذهنی؟ یا فرار از واقعیت؟ یا افسانه‌ی عوامانه؟ نمی‌دانم. فقط می‌دانم که آهای مناف!**

شریعتی (۲۹ خرداد ۱۳۵۶) از سوی مردم، یکی پس از دیگری به ساواک نسبت داده شد. شگفتا که دست کم در مورد شریعتی هیچ کس گمانش به «علمای اسلام» نرفت؛ چرا که علی شریعتی، به خاطر تز «دین منهای روحانیت»، از سوی روحانیان بلندپایه مورد حمله بود و یکی از آن‌ها او را «اَعدی عدوّ اسلام» خوانده بود.[۴۶۵] کما این که بعدها و در کوران انقلاب ۵۷، یکی از شرایط گزینش اعضاء «شورای انقلاب» به دستور مخفیانه‌ی آیت‌الله خمینی این بود که عضو شورای انقلاب نباید «از طیف شریعتی» باشد؛[۴۶۶] و پس از فرونشستن تب انقلاب نیز، آیت‌الله خمینی با نام و کتاب‌های شریعتی میانه‌ی خوبی نشان نداد. منتها، بنا به «مصلحت»، با نام و کتاب‌های شریعتی رفتاری کژ دار و مریزی پیشه کرد؛ چرا که می‌دانست بسیاری از جوان‌های حزب‌اللهی که در حال ساختن نهادهای «جمهوری‌ی اسلامی» بودند، به آموزه‌های شریعتی گرایش داشتند، و از پیروان اندیشه‌های او برشمرده می‌شدند. در حالی که با مقایسه‌ی کتاب‌ها و متن سخنرانی‌های این دو شخصیت پی می‌بریم که آیت‌الله خمینی به بسیاری از اندیشه‌ها، تعبیرها، و حتا واژگان کاربردی‌ی شریعتی دستبرد زده بود. (ساده‌ترین نمونه‌ی آن، واژه‌ی «مستضعف» است، که نخستین بار- دست کم در دوران معاصر- در بیان شریعتی به کار رفته بود.) و بالأخره، در پایانه‌ی همین دوران بود که سیدمصطفی خمینی، پسر آیت‌الله خمینی در نجف درگذشت (۱ آبان ۱۳۵۶)، و در تمام محافل مذهبی‌ی ایران و خارج از ایران، این مرگ به ساواک نسبت داده شد. با این که در پیام کوتاه آیت‌الله خمینی کوچک‌ترین نشانه‌ای از «شهادتِ» فرزندش نبود، اما پس از دریافت پیام‌های تسلیتی که این مرگ را نیز به دستگاه امنیتی‌ی ایران نسبت داده بودند، در پاسخ به پیام تسلیت یاسر عرفات که آرزو کرده بود «محنت‌های او پایان گیرد»، نوشت: «درد و محنت من روزی پایان می‌گیرد که ملت من از شرِ این آدمِ فاسد فارغ شود.»[۴۶۷] و با این جمله، نسبتِ این مرگ به دستگاه را تلویحاً تأیید کرد. و طرفه این که ساواک، حتا اگر در این قتل‌ها دست نداشت، در آن زمان هیچ یک از این شایعه‌ها را تکذیب نکرد، تا وحشت و رعب را در مخالفان و پیکارگران سیاسی زنده نگه دارد؛ تا سی و سه سال پس از انقلاب، صدای پرویز ثابتی، مدیرکل امنیت داخلی‌ی ساواک، ناگهان از مخفی‌گاه خود خروج کند، و به محضی که سخن از «کشتارهای ساواک» می‌شود، شایعه‌های مربوط به این مرگ‌های مشکوک را دست‌مایه کند، و بگوید که «همه شایعه بود.»[۴۶۸]

برای تو می‌گویم، من فقط این را می‌دانم که صمد نباید مرده باشد. صمد نمی‌تواند مرده باشد.». در هر حال، حمزه فراهتی، ۲۳ سال پس از مرگ صمد بهرنگی، در سال ۱۳۷۰، «شایعه»‌ی مرگ صمد بهرنگی توسط ساواک را ناشی از شایعه‌پراکنی‌ی آل احمد علیه ساواک برآورد کرد، و نشریه‌ی آدینه، به سردبیری‌ی فرج سرکوهی نیز -احتمالاً بدون مراجعه به متن آل‌احمد- این خبر را منتشر کرد. حمزه فراهتی، مبسوط این رویداد را در کتاب خاطرات خود نیز آورد. من در جلد هفتم مجموعه‌ی حاضر، مفصلاً به این مسئله پرداخته‌ام. اما همین جا خوانندهام را به چاپ دوم کتاب ***«راز» مرگ صمد...!؟ (چه‌گونه ارتجاع، مرگ مشکوک صمد را دستاویز حمله به یاران او قرار داده است)***، نوشته‌ی اشرف دهقانی، از انتشارات چریک‌های فدائی خلق، و نیز به مقاله‌ی زیر رجوع می‌دهم:

❖ آیدین، ***حمزه فراهتی، مقاله‌ی آل احمد، فرج سرکوهی و «راز» مرگ صمد***، تارنمای «سیاهکل»، شهریور ۱۳۸۳:
http://www.siahkal.com/publication/Samad/Idyn.pdf

[۴۶۵] مهدی بازرگان در مقدمه‌ای که بر کتاب «شخصیت و اندیشه‌ی دکتر علی شریعتی» نوشته، می‌گوید: « دکتر شریعتی وقتی حرف از اسلام منهای روحانیت می‌زند مرتکب ذنب لایغفری می‌شود که همه‌ی روحانیت را علیه خود بر می‌انگیزاند. و چون به اعتقاد و بنا به مصالح آقایان، «اسلام مساوی است با روحانیت»، یکی از افاضل معروف و از معاودین عراق حکم «اَعدی عدوّ اسلام» را درباره‌ی او صادر می‌نماید. سِرّ مخالفت شدید و دشمنی با دکتر شریعتی در این جا است. حملات و تهمت‌ها به راه افتاد. نزد بزرگان حوزه و صاحب نظران می‌رفتند تا فتوای ارتداد بگیرند و ساواک آن‌ها را پخش می‌کرد.» البته مهندس بازرگان از «یکی از افاضل معروف» نام نمی‌برد. اما ما اکنون می‌دانیم که آیت‌الله ناصر مکارم شیرازی و آیت‌الله شهاب‌الدین نجفی مرعشی، شریعتی را نافی‌ی امام زمان می‌دانستند، و آیت‌الله مرتضی انصاری قمی نیز به اعدام او فتوا داده بود. برای دیدن بازگفت از مهدی بازرگان به مأخذ زیر نگاه کنید:

❖ مقدمه‌ی کتاب: جعفر سعیدی، ***شخصیت و اندیشه‌ی دکتر علی شریعتی***، تهران: انتشارات چاپخش، ۱۳۷۲.

[۴۶۶] محمد جعفری، ***گروگان‌گیری و جانشینان انقلاب، تحول انقلاب از آزادی به استبداد- ۲***، لندن: انتشارات برزاوند، تیر ماه ۱۳۸۶، نشر الکترونیکی، ص ۴۹.

[۴۶۷] احسان نراقی، ***انقلاب اسلامی به روایت اسناد صوتی***، برنامه‌ای از مهرداد حقیقی، لس‌انجلس. برگفته از: مهدی اصلانی، احمد رشیدی مطلق کیست؟ علی شعبانی؟ فرهاد نیکخواه؟ محمود احمدی‌نژاد؟ تارنمای «راه کارگر»، بازدید ۱۴ ژوئیه ۲۰۱۲:
http://www.rahekaregar.com/maghalat/201001/motlagh.html

[۴۶۸] سیامک دهقانپور، ***اولین گفت‌وگو با پرویز ثابتی در برنامه‌ی افق***، صدای امریکا، ۱۸ بهمن ۱۳۹۰/ ۷ فوریه ۲۰۱۲:
http://www.youtube.com/watch?v=bTA0hsWTy9M

* در درازنای همین دوران بود که از یک سو، پوشیدنِ لباس‌های مدل غربی، از جمله شلوار «جین»، نشان «امروزی بودن» تلقی شد؛ موسیقی‌ی پاپ با سازهای غیرایرانی در میان مردم جا باز کرد؛ رفتن به دانسینگ و کاباره، باب روز شد؛ و کاراکترهائی در نقش فاحشه‌ی کافه و کاباره، با بدن‌های نیمه برهنه در «فیلمفارسی»ها برای «کلاه مخملی‌ها» و «کنگر/ ماست»خورها و «آبگوشت»خورهای «کافه‌های لاله‌زاری» به رقص مشغول بودند؛ و از سوی دیگر، تقدیس نمادهای مذهبی، مانند «گنبدهای طلا»، «مسجد»، «نماز»، «لامپ سبز الله»، «اذان پاک سحرگه»، «عبای وحدت»، و وعده‌ی «طنینِ ناب اذان با صدای خوب بلال» در ترانه‌ها و شعرها پدیدار شد.[٤٦٩] در درازنای همین دوران بود که صدای اعتراض هنرمندان قلمرو موسیقی و ترانه‌سرائی، در کوی و برزن‌های ایران پیچید که- مثلاً- «داره از ابر سیا خون میچکه/ جمعه‌ها خون جای بارون می‌چکه»؛ تا پچپچه در کوچه درافتد که: این «جمعه»، همان جمعه‌ی خونین سیاهکل است.[٤٧٠] یا: «از صدا افتاده تار و کمونچه/ مرده می‌بَرَن کوچه به کوچه»؛ تا خفقان سیاسی و اعدام‌ها را واگویه کند،[٤٧١] و به پچپچه‌های مربوط به ترانه‌ی «مرا ببوس/ برای آخرین بار» بپیوندند که توسط مردم به وصیت‌نامه و آخرین وداع یک زندانی‌ی سیاسی‌ی رو به اعدام معنی شده بود.[٤٧٢]

* در درازنای همین دوران بود که فیلم «خانه سیاه است» (پیرامون جذام و جذامخانه)، ساخته‌ی فروغ فرخزاد، نه الزاماً به لحاظ ارزش‌های هنری، بلکه به خاطر همدردی با این بیماران و به خاطر واتعهدای سیاسی/اجتماعی، میان منتقدان رژیم جا باز کرد، اما هیچ یک از این منتقدان، به درمانگاه‌ها و تیم‌های پزشکی‌ی وابسته به «بنیاد مبارزه با جذام» و «شهرک جذامیان درمان‌شده» که زیر نظر شهبانو فرح پهلوی ساخته و اداره می‌شد، توجهی نشان نداد؛ و خبر این فعالیت‌ها در رسانه‌ها نیز، از سوی پیکارگران و مردم ناراضی به عنوان «تبلیغات رژیم» تلقی می‌شد.

* در درازنای همین دوران بود که زن ایرانی به پست‌های نمایندگی‌ی مجلس، وزارت، سفارت، و به عرصه‌های مختلف علمی و تخصصی (از کارشناسی‌ی برنامه‌ریزهای آموزشی و حقوقی گرفته تا خلبانی‌ی جت‌های نظامی) راه یافت؛ تا به نوبه‌ی خود راهی گشاید برای حضور محترم و فعال زنان در خانواده و جامعه. به عنوان نمونه، «قانون حمایت از خانواده» (۱۳۴۶) و «قانون حمایت از کودکان بدون سرپرست» (۱۳۵۳) توسط گروهی از همین زنان نوشته شد. در همین دوران بود که «سازمان زنان ایران»، به صورت رسمی در ایران تشکیل شد، و با وجود وابستگی‌ی آشکار به دربار، دست کم در ارتقاء آگاهی‌های جنسی در زنانِ شهرهای دورافتاده‌ی کشور مؤثر بود. و طرفه این که از دید مردم ناراضی، و به ویژه پیکارگران طیف چپ، همه‌ی این تحولات، حتا تصویب «قانون حمایت از خانواده»- که برای نخستین بار پس از ۱۴۰۰ سال، برخی از قوانین زن‌ستیز، مانند «تعدد زوجات» را به نفع زن تعدیل کرده بود- «فرمایشی»، «فریبکاری» و پیامد «فساد دربار» تلقی شد.

---

[٤٦٩] نمونه‌هائی از این نوع شعرها را در کتاب زیر به دست داده‌ام، و در این جا آن‌ها را تکرار نمی‌کنم:

❖ ملیحه تیره گل، ***اندیشه در شعر اسماعیل خوئی و خاستگاه اجتماعی‌ی آن***، تکزاس: چاپ دوم، انتشارات «یوتاچ»، ۱۳۷۵/ ۱۹۹٦، ص ۲٤٥.

[٤٧٠] ترانه‌ی «جمعه» (۱۳۵۰)، سروده‌ی شهیار قنبری، آهنگساز: اسفندیار منفردزاده، با صدای فرهاد مهراد.

[٤٧١] ترانه‌ی «شبانه» یا «کوچه‌ها» (۱۳۵۳)، سروده‌ی احمد شاملو، آهنگساز: اسفندیار منفردزاده، با صدای فرهاد مهرداد.

[٤٧٢] شعر «مرا ببوس» در سال ۱۳۲۹ در مجموعه اشعار حیدر رقابی- با نام مستعار «هاله» منتشر شده بود. اما پس از کودتای ۱۳۳۲ بود که مجید وفادار بر روی آن آهنگ گذاشت، و با صدای حسن گلنراقی اجرا شد؛ و به عنوان نمادی از مقاومت مبارزان، سخت مورد توجه مردم ایران قرار گرفت. به مأخذ زیر نگاه کنید:

❖ دکتر منصور بیات‌زاده، ***کنفدراسیون، جنبش دانشجوئی، بخش دوم: ساواک شاه و روزنامه‌ی کیهان***، تارنمای «جنبش سوسیالیستی»، ۱٦ بهمن ۱۳۸۵/ ۵ فوریه ۲۰۰۷:

http://www.tvpn.de/sa/sa-ois-iran-1045.htm

* در این دوران بود که «سازمان شاهنشاهی و خدمات اجتماعی» زیر نظر شاهزاده اشرف پهلوی تأسیس شد، و پیش و بیش از آن که «خدمات»ی به «اجتماع» ارائه دهد، عبارت‌های «لاتاری»، «بلیت بخت‌آزمائی»، و «برنده‌ی خوشبخت» را وارد زبان روزمره کرد؛ تا بعد، روز «چهارشنبه»، یعنی روز قرعه‌کشی‌ی این لاتاری، به تمسخر از شعر و ترانه‌ی متعرض سر برکند که: «عصر چارشنبه‌ی من/ عصر خوشبختی‌ی ما/ فصل گندیدن من/ فصل جون‌سختی‌ی ما»[۴۷۳]

* در درازنای همین دوران بود که فیلم نیرومند و تأثیرگذارِ «قیصر»، حضور چاقوکشی و قداره‌بندی و تجاوزکاری‌ی باج‌بگیران را از یک سو، و دادخواهی‌ی شخصی- در قالب انتقام‌جوئی (قصاص)- را از سوی دیگر، در محله‌ها و لایه‌های عقب‌مانده‌ی جامعه به رخ کشید؛ و شخصیتِ «مردانه»، «غیرتمند» و «ناموس‌پرست»ی چونان «قیصر» را- با کفش‌های پاشنه خوابیده و زبان عامیانه‌ی زیر بازارچه‌ای- به عنوان قهرمان مردم اعماق شناسائی کرد.[۴۷۴] در درازنای همین دوران بود که فیلم‌های «آرامش در حضور دیگران»، «گاو»، «حسن کچل»، «طوقی»، «آقای هالو»، «صمد آقا»، «رگبار»، «مغول‌ها»، «اسرار گنج دره جنی»، «تنگنا»، «شازده احتجاب»، «دایره‌ی مینا»، «آب توبه»، «گوزن‌ها»، و نمایشنامه‌هائی مانند «چوب به دست‌های ورزیل»، «روزنه‌ی آبی»، «چهار صندوق»، و «آموزگاران»- که به وسیله‌ی زبده‌ترین نخبگان هنرهای نمایشی نوشته شدند، و در سالن‌ها و تالارهای تازه‌سازِ مجلل و حرفه‌ای به اجرا درآمدند- هر یک به گونه‌ای- حتا تلویحی و با نماد و استعاره- استبداد سیاسی، فقر فرهنگی و اقتصادی، جهل و خرافه‌پنداری، نوچه‌پروری و بردگی‌ی اختیاری، تضاد وحشتناک فرهنگی در بافتار اجتماعی، نوآوری‌های بی‌ریشه، ضایعات هجوم روستائیان به شهرها، بهره‌کشی از توده‌های فرودست، و بی‌پناهی‌ی قربانیان آن را نشان می‌دادند؛ و فیلم «شازده احتجاب»، ضمن انتقال این فریاد قرون و اعصاری، زوال اشرافیت و اقتدار پادشاهی را هم پیش‌بینی می‌کرد.[۴۷۵] در پایانه‌های همین دوران بود که هر شب برنامه‌ی طنزی چند دقیقه‌ای، به نام «آقای مربوطه» از تلویزیون پخش می‌شد و ضمن نقد فرهنگی، گاهی گوشه‌ای هم به مسائل سیاسی می‌زد، که با سانسور و خفقان حاکم سخت در تضاد قرار می‌گرفت؛[۴۷۶] یا برنامه‌ی انتقادی‌ی دیگری با عنوان «پنج و سه دقیقه»- که بعداً به «همه روز، همین ساعت، همین جا» تغییر نام داد- از رادیو تهران پخش می‌شد که نارسائی‌های حکومت را با طنزی آشکار نشانه می‌گرفت؛[۴۷۷] تا باز، میان مردم ناباور به انتهای کار رژیم پچپچه درافتد که این‌ها «سوپاپ اطمینان»اند. در پایانه‌های همین دوران بود که سریال‌های

---

[۴۷۳] از ترانه‌ی «هفته‌ی خاکستری»، با صدای فرهاد مهرداد، ترانه از: شهیار قنبری.

[۴۷۴] نویسنده و کارگردان فیلم «قیصر» مسعود کیمیائی است. بهروز وثوقی، ناصر ملک مطیعی و پوری بنائی از جمله هنرپیشه‌های این فیلم هستند.

[۴۷۵] فیلم «قیصر» به نویسندگی و کارگردانی‌ی مسعود کیمیائی، ۱۳۴۸؛ فیلم «آرامش در حضور دیگران»، به کارگردانی‌ی ناصر تقوائی و بر اساس داستانی از غلامحسین ساعدی، ۱۳۴۷؛ فیلم «گاو» با برداشتی از رمان «عزاداران بیل» نوشته‌ی غلامحسین ساعدی، با کارگردانی‌ی داریوش مهرجوئی، ۱۳۴۸؛ فیلم «حسن کچل» با نویسندگی و کارگردانی‌ی علی حاتمی، ۱۳۴۸؛ فیلم «طوقی» با کارگردانی‌ی علی حاتمی، ۱۳۴۹؛ فیلم «آقای هالو» با نویسندگی و کارگردانی‌ی داریوش مهرجوئی، ۱۳۴۹؛ فیلم «صمدآقا» با نویسندگی و کارگردانی‌ی پرویز صیاد، ۱۳۵۰؛ فیلم «رگبار» با نویسندگی و کارگردانی‌ی بهرام بیضائی، ۱۳۵۱؛ فیلم «مغول‌ها» به نویسندگی و کارگردانی‌ی پرویز کیمیاوی، ۱۳۵۲؛ فیلم «تنگنا» با کارگردانی‌ی امیر نادری، ۱۳۵۲؛ فیلم « اسرار گنج دره جنی» با نویسندگی و کارگردانی‌ی ابراهیم گلستان، ۱۳۵۳؛ فیلم «دایره‌ی مینا» با کارگردانی‌ی داریوش مهرجوئی، ۱۳۵۳؛ فیلم «شازده احتجاب» نوشته‌ی هوشنگ گلشیری و با کارگردانی‌ی بهمن فرمان آرا، ۱۳۵۳؛ فیلم «آب توبه» با کارگردانی‌ی محمدرضا فاضلی، ۱۳۵۳؛ فیلم «گوزن‌ها» با نویسندگی و کارگردانی‌ی مسعود کیمیائی، ۱۳۵۳. نمایش «چوب به دست‌های ورزیل» نوشته‌ی غلامحسین ساعدی، با کارگردانی‌ی جعفر والی، ۱۳۴۴ (در برخی مآخذ: ۱۳۴۵)؛ نمایش «روزنه‌ی آبی» نوشته‌ی اکبر رادی، با کارگردانی‌ی شاهین سرکیسیان و آربی آوانسیان، ۱۳۴۵؛ نمایش «چهار صندوق» با نویسندگی و کارگردانی‌ی بهرام بیضائی، ۱۳۴۶؛ نمایش «آموزگاران» نوشته‌ی محسن یلفانی با کارگردانی‌ی سعید سلطان‌پور، ۱۳۴۹.
توضیح: از میان این فیلم‌ها، فیلم «آرامش در حضور دیگران»، تا سال ۱۳۷۲ در سانسور ساواک باقی ماند.

[۴۷۶] برنامه‌ی «آقای مربوطه» به نویسندگی و کارگردانی و باریگری‌ی بهزاد اشتیاقی، که گاه همسر او (فرشته مهبان) و گاه مادر همسر او (فرخ لقا هوشمند) هم در آن شرکت داشتند، از سال ۱۳۵۳ تا ۱۳۵۷ هر شب از تلویزیون ملی‌ی ایران پخش می‌شد. به مأخذ زیر نگاه کنید:
❖ ***مصاحبه‌ی خواندنی با بهزاد اشتیاقی، بازیگر نقش آقای مربوطه***، تارنمای «خبرنگار»، بازدید شهریور ۱۳۸۹:
http://ali1345.blogfa.com/post-190.aspx

[۴۷۷] تهیه‌کننده‌ی این برنامه دکتر محمود عنایت بود.

«سلطان صاحبقران»[۴۷۸] و «دائی‌جان ناپلئون» قدرت متوهم دربار و اشرافیت را در تلویزیون ایران به سُخره گرفتند.[۴۷۹] البته دستگاه سانسور پخش سریال «دائی جان ناپلئون» را متوقف کرد. اما دنباله‌ی این مجموعه پس از چندی دوباره اجازه‌ی پخش یافت؛ و مردم ایران، از همین توقیف/ پخش، وجود دو دستگی در ساواک را گمانه زدند؛ و پچپچه درگیر شد که دستی بالای دست شاه در ساواک در کار است. و بالأخره در پایانه‌ی همین دوران بود که در فیلم «سفر سنگ»، مردی با شالی سبز بر گردن، با ظاهری شبیه شمایل امام اول شیعیان، با نام «غریبه»- که معلوم نشد از کجا- به دهکده‌ای می‌آید؛ «عمومِ» مردم ستمدیده را علیه اربابِ ده می‌شوراند؛ به یاری‌ی خشم و خروش مردم، کاخ اربابی را ویران می‌کند؛ و بعد، مانند «هفت تیر کِش» فیلم‌های وسترن امریکائی، راهش را می‌گیرد و می‌رود. تا میان انبوه ناراضیان رژیم پچپچه درافتد که: انگار نزدیک است! و این، سال ۱۳۵۶ است؛ یعنی همان سالی که شهرداری‌ی تهران برای «زیباسازی»ی شهر، آلونک‌های حاشیه‌نشین‌های بی‌سرپناه را با بولدوزور ویران کرد، و اعتراض حاشیه‌نشین‌ها، نخستین جنبش عینی علیه «ارباب» شد؛ یعنی یک سال پیش از آن که عمامه به جای تاج بنشیند؛ و «اربابِ» پسین، جای «اربابِ» پیشین را پر کند؛ و بر خلاف «غریبه» در «سفر سنگ»، بماند و کاخ آرزوی پیکارگران راه آزادی را همراه با پیکر خود آن‌ها به خاک بسپارد.

همین جا باید بیافزایم که همه‌ی «پچپچه»هائی که از آن یاد کردم- به اضافه‌ی پچپچه‌های روزافزون در مورد زندگی‌ی خصوصی/ جنسی‌ی شاه و مادر و خواهر او- عمدتاً در میان ناراضیان لایه‌های متوسط و تحصیل‌کرده‌ی شهری درمی‌گرفت؛ و در مواردی (مانند مرگ شریعتی یا سیدمصطفی خمینی) نیز توسط سازمان‌های اسلامی (عمدتاً نهضت آزادی) و انجمن‌های اسلامی در درون کنفدراسیون جهانی‌ی دانشجویان ایرانی شایع می‌شد. به بیانی دیگر، در همان حال که جذابیت مبارزه‌ی مسلحانه برای «ویرانی‌ی کاخ اربابی» در میان جوانان شهری رو به افزایش بود، پیش از بروز نشانه‌های انقلاب ۵۷، به دلایل زیر، آرزوی «ویرانی»ی رژیم، جنبه‌ی همگانی نداشت: ۱) شکوفائی‌ی اقتصاد نفتی، برای بسیاری از لایه‌های اجتماعی، از جمله توده‌های کارگری، به نسبت گذشته، رفاهی نسبی فراهم کرده بود؛ ۲) ابعاد ناآگاهی نسبت به حقوق شهروندی و طبقاتی در میان مردم اعماق و لایه‌های فرودست گسترده‌تر و عمیق‌تر از آن بود، که حتا پیام رزمندگان کمونیست و پیشاهنگان و هنرمندان سکولار را دریافت کنند. کما این که، بنا به اعتراف کنونی‌ی برخی از پیکارگران آن زمانی، بسیاری از کارگران و مردم کوچه و بازار، پیکارگران مسلح را، به زبان خودِ شاه، «خرابکار» می‌خواندند، و در برخی از موارد، آن‌ها را در حین عملیات مسلحانه، متوقف می‌کردند.[۴۸۰] ۳) بسیاری از مردم- حتا در

---

[۴۷۸] سریال «سلطان صاحبقران»، به نویسندگی و کارگردانی‌ی علی حاتمی، در تلویزیون (در زمان ریاست رضا قطبی) ساخته شد و در سال ۱۳۵۴ در شبکه‌ی دوم تلویزیون به نمایش درآمد. این فیلم که در ۱۳ بند ساخته شده بود، استبداد، طمطراق توخالی و عقب‌ماندگی‌ی ناصرالدین شاه قاجار و دربارش را به سخره گرفت. در این مجموعه، بند «امیر کبیر»، توطئه‌ها و نخبه‌کُشی‌های دربار قاجار، و بند «میرزا رضا کرمانی» (قاتل ناصرالدین شاه) تلاش مخالفان برای نابودی‌ی شاه را مستدل می‌کردند. این مجموعه در سال ۵۶ یک بار دیگر در تلویزیون ایران به نمایش گذاشته شد.

[۴۷۹] مجموعه‌ی «دائی جان ناپلئون» نوشته‌ی ایرج پزشک زاد، و با کارگردانی‌ی ناصر تقوائی، ۱۳۵۵. شخصیت اول این داستان، ستوان بازنشسته‌ی قزاق، بزرگ خانواده‌ای نیمه اشرافی، که ادعا می‌کرد در جوانی در جنگ قراق‌ها با انگلیسی‌ها شرکت داشته و در قلع و قمع انگلیسی‌ها رشادت‌ها کرده، حالا مدام در این توهم بسر می‌برد که انگلیسی‌ها برای انتقام از او در حال توطئه هستند. پس از نمایش این مجموعه بود که توهم توطئه، حتا در برخی از جدی‌ترین نقدهای ایرانی، با اصطلاح «فکرهای دائی جان ناپلئونی» شناسائی شد، و هنوز می‌شود. در حالی بود که اکنون می‌دانیم همزمان با انتشار این مجموعه در جهان واقعی، «توطئه»ای واقعی علیه رشد مردم و پیشرفت ایران در حال «چیده» شدن بود.

[۴۸۰] افزون بر مورد دستگیری‌ی چریک‌های سیاهکل توسط روستائیان، افزون بر مورد حمایت مردم از شهرام شفیق، که حمله‌ی مجاهدین به او را ناکام گذاشت، نمونه‌های دیگری نیز از این کیفیت در دست داریم. به عنوان مثال، «مصطفی شعاعیان، در مقاله‌ی "دو یادداشت"، از حادثه‌ای سخن به میان می‌آورد که در جریان آن، مجاهدی برای خلع سلاح به پاسبانی هجوم می‌برد، ولی در اثر حمله‌ی مردم، ناکام می‌شود. مجاهد، در حالی که از تهدید مردم با نارنجک ناامید می‌شود، به حیات خود با بلعیدن قرص سیانور خاتمه می‌دهد.» نگاه کنید به :

❖ انوش صالحی، ***مصطفی شعاعیان و رمانتیسم انقلابی***، سوئد: نشر باران، ۱۳۸۹، ص ۳۸۲.

توضیح: بازگفت بالا را از متن زیر، که کتاب انوش صالحی را معرفی و نقد کرده است، برگرفته‌ام:

میان همان ناراضیان لایه‌های متوسط شهری و حتا در میان کوشندگان ملی‌گرا (سیاسی یا فرهنگی)، پیش از آن که «اربابِ ارباب» به انبار باروت کبریت بکشد، و پیش از رسیدن جامعه به فاز قیام جمعی- نه در پیِ «ویرانی» و براندازیِ دستگاه شاه، بلکه به دنبال اصلاح وضع موجود بودند. کما این که در نامه‌ی سرگشاده‌ای که شاپور بختیار، داریوش فروهر و کریم سنجابی در خرداد ۵۶ به شاه نوشتند، و جمعیت صدهزاران نفره‌ای که با حضور در تظاهرات، آن را تأیید کرد، اجرای قانون اساسیِ مشروطه مطالبه شده بود.

* در درازنای این دوران بود که حزب توده‌ی ایران، از یک سو به جنبش‌های کارگری نیرو داد و کارگران را در احقاق حقوق صنفیِ خود یاری رساند، و از سوی دیگر، از سال ۴۲ به بعد، در نشریه‌ی «دنیا» (ارگان تئوریک حزب)، افزون بر شرح یک یک جنبش‌های مردم در طول تاریخ ایران، و افزون بر مقابله با سازمان‌های چپ مستقل، «مقاله‌هائی پیرامون اسلام و نقش جنبش‌های اسلامی "در نهضت رهائی‌بخش میهن ما" [...]، تفکیک روحانیت، به مترقی و ارتجاعی، و تعلق طبقاتیِ هر یک از آن‌ها، توضیح لزوم وحدت بین نیروهای مترقیِ اسلامی و مارکسیست‌ها، تعیین وجوه توافق بین اسلام و سوسیالیسم» را ندا درداد.[481]

*در درازنای همین دوران بود که مدرسه‌های دینی، مانند «حجتیه»- به عنوان پوششی برای فعالیت‌های سیاسیِ لایه‌ی روحانیت- تجدید سازمان و ساختار کردند؛ نشریه‌های «مکتب اسلام» و «مکتب تشیع» تأسیس شد؛ مدرسه‌ی «حقانی» به عنوان ضمیمه‌ای بر حوزه‌ی علمیه‌ی قم، و با پول یکی از بازاریان تهران پایه‌گذاری شد، و به تربیت کادرهائی پرداخت که پس از انقلاب ۵۷، یا از بلندپایگان حکومت جمهوریِ اسلامی شدند، یا از «سربازان گمنام امام زمان»، و یا از تربیت‌شدگان «سربازان گمنام امام زمان»، که به عنوان بازجو، شکنجه‌گر، و اعدام‌کننده (جلاد)، در زندان‌های جمهوریِ اسلامی به نسل‌کشیِ مبارزان خدمت کنند.[482] در درازنای همین دوران بود که «هیئت مؤتلفه‌ی اسلامی»، از دل بازار روئید و با استفاده از ماشین تروری که «فدائیان اسلام» در اختیار روحانیت قرار داده بود، در میان مردم مذهبی نفوذ و گسترش یافت، تا بعداً با تقدیم پول‌های کلان به کمپ آیت‌الله، به تحقق «جنبش اسلامی» یاری دهد، و تا پس از انقلاب، با

❖ محمد حسین خسروپناه، ***اینک مصطفی شعاعیان***، نشریه‌ی باران، چاپ سوئد، شماره‌ی ۲۸/ ۲۹، زمستان ۱۳۸۹/ بهار ۱۳۹۰، ص ۲٤٦.

[481] اصغر شیرازی، ***مدرنیته، شبهه، و دموکراسی: بر مبنای یک بررسیِ موردی درباره‌ی حزب توده‌ی ایران از آغاز تا ۱۳۷۸***، تهران: نشر اختران، ۱۳۸٦، صص ۹۵ تا ۹٦.

[482] محمد تقی شهرام، یکی از پایه‌گذاران سازمان «پیکار در راه رهائیِ طبقه‌ی کارگر» (بخش مارکسیست‌شده‌ی سازمان مجاهدین خلق ایران)، که در تیر ۱۳۵۸ دستگیر شد و در ۳ مرداد ۱۳۵۹ به جوخه‌ی اعدام سپرده شد، در یکی از یادداشت‌های زندان خود، که آن را در زندان سپاه نوشته است، ابتدا به «سازمان امل» (سازمانی شیعی) در لبنان، و پایه‌گذار آن، مصطفی چمران، و رابطه‌ی این سازمان با «تعلیم» بخشی از سپاه پاسداران انقلاب اسلامی در «نقاطی مانند علی‌آباد قم» اشاره می‌کند، و ضمن تشریح عملکرد و موقعیت سپاه پاسداران و کمیته‌های انقلاب، می‌نویسد: «نکته‌ی جالب توجه این است که شما در تمام این مراحل یا چشم‌تان بسته است و یا با افرادی که سرو صورت‌شان پوشیده شده روبه‌رو هستید. افرادی که همه همدیگر را با اسم کوچك خطاب می‌کنند و ظاهراً بسیاری از آن‌ها با آن که در مواضع و مسئولیت‌های بسیار مختلف و دور از هم قرار دارند یکدیگر را می‌شناسند. مثلاً کافی است پیش بازجویتان بگویید که مرا با فردی به نام عبدالله از انفرادیِ قصر به اوین منتقل کردند تا او بلافاصله عبدالله را بشناسد؛ و یا همین طور به یکی از این کارکنان قضائیِ سپاه، مانند افراد این خانه، نام کوچك و احیاناً هیئت ظاهریِ فلان مسئول زندان اوین را بگویید تا او را به خاطر آورد و بشناسد. در تلفن‌هایی که از مراکز مختلف و به افراد و مقامات گوناگون زده می‌شود عموماً از افراد یا اسامیِ کوچك آن‌ها نام برده می‌شود، درست **به مثابه یك خانواده یا فامیل بزرگ** که همه یکدیگر را با اسامی کوچك صدا می‌کنند و هیچ‌گاه هم اشتباهی پیش نمی‌آید. این جا نیز رابطه‌ها آن قدر نزدیك است که مشاغل و پست‌ها هر چند دور از هم و غیرمرتبط باشند، افراد شاغل آن برای مسئولین دیگر به خوبی شناخته شده هستند. دستگیری خود من نمونه بسیار خوبی است از عملکرد این گروه ویژه‌ی چپ در کمیته‌ی مرکزی... » (تأکیدها از من است.) **توضیح:** یادداشت‌های زندان تقی شهرام، که به بیرون از زندان منتقل شده بود، سی سال پس از اعدام او، به کوشش تراب حق شناس و یارانش در گروه «اندیشه و پیکار»، در بهمن ۱۳۸۹ در هفت دفتر منتشر شد. برگرفته‌ی بالا در دفتر شماره‌ی ٤ این مجموعه دیده می‌شود. به مأخذ زیر نگاه کنید:

❖ محمدتقی شهرام، ***دفترهای زندان: یادداشت‌ها و تأملات در زندان‌های جمهوریِ اسلامی***، بخش ۴، تارنمای «اندیشه و پیکار»، ۲۲ اسفند ۱۳۸۹/ ۱۳ مارس ۲۰۱۱:

http://www.peykarandeesh.org/free/573-taghi4.html

در دســت گرفتن نبض بازار و اقتصــاد ایران، وام مادی و معنوی‌ی خود را از مردم ایران پس بگیرد. در درازنای همین دوران بود که «نهضــت آزادی‌ی ایران»، از دل «جبهه‌ی ملی» پدیدار شــد، [۴۸۳]و در مسیر حرکت خود موج عظیمی از گرایش‌های مذهبی‌ی ضــداســتبدادی را در جامعه پدید آورد. در درازنای همین دوران بود که دبیرســتان‌های «علوی» و «کمال» و «رفاه» تأسیس شدند، و پایگاه‌هائی فراهم آوردند برای کاردسازی‌ی نیروهای مذهبی/ سیاسی، و انتشار ده‌ها کتاب و مقاله پیرامون قرآن و تطبیق آن با علم و سیاست «مدرن».[۴۸۴] این دو مدرسه، به اضافه‌ی مدرسه‌های «رفاه» و «حجتیه»، و «مؤسســه‌ی خیریه‌ی اخلاق»، از کمک‌های مالی‌ی بازاریانِ کلان بهره‌های کلان می‌بردند. در مسیر فعالیت فرهنگی‌ی «نهضــت آزادی» و مدرســه‌های مذهبی بود که مرکزی به نام «حســینیه‌ی ارشــاد» به وســیله‌ی ســه تن از شــخصــیت‌های مذهبی و با هزینه‌ی «بازرگانانِ» کشــور ســاخته شــد (۱۳۴۳)،[۴۸۵] تا اســلام‌گرایان معمم و مکلائی چون مطهری و بهشتی و باهنر و هاشمی رفسنجانی و علی شریعتی، آراء اسلام راستین/ جهانی/ انقلابی را تبلیغ کنند.

«نواندیشــان دینی و روشــنفکران بومی‌گرا»: در درازنای همین دوران بود که آراء ســیدجمال‌الدین اســدآبادی، در میان گروهی از باهوش‌ترین و مستعدترین متفکران ما بیدار شد. سیدجمال‌الدین اسدآبادی در دوران مشروطیت، در مبارزه با اســتعمارِ «انگلیز» و «فرنســا»، و عقب‌ماندگی‌ی ایران و «جهان اســلام» از کاروان جهان، و در راه اشــاعه‌ی «اتحاد اسلام»، به «فقهای دیانت اسلام» تاخته بود که:

چه بسیار تعجب است که مسلمانان آن علومی که به ارسطو منسوب است، آن را به غایتِ رغبت می‌خوانند؛ گویا که ارسطو

---

[۴۸۳] پس از کودتای ۲۸ مرداد ۳۲، مجموعه‌ای از نیروهای ملی، «نهضــت مقاومت ملی‌ی ایران» را تشــکیل دادند. این نیروها در ســال ۱۳۳۹ «جبهه‌ی ملی‌ی دوم» را تأسیس کردند. اما به سبب اختلاف در مشی‌ی مبارزه بود که در اردیبهشت ۱۳۴۰ گروهی از «ملی/ مذهبی»های شــورای عالی‌ی جبهه‌ی ملی‌ی دوم، به زعامت مهندس مهدی بازرگان، دکتر یدالله ســحابی، ســیدمحمد طالقانی (ســپس آیت‌الله طالقانی)، مهندس منصــور عطائی، حسن نزیه، رحیم عطائی، و عباس سمیعی، سازمان «نهضت آزادی‌ی ایران» را با عنوان «تشکل دموکراتیک مسلمان» بنا نهادند. شعاری که مهندس بازرگان برای این سازمان برگزید، عبارت بود از: «ما ایرانی هستیم، ما مسلمانیم، ما مصدقی هستیم». یک سال بعد (۱۳۴۱) با بالاگرفتن اختلاف پیرامون جنبه‌های تشکیلاتی، «جبهه‌ی ملی‌ی دوم» منحل شد. و پس از آن بود که «جبهه‌ی ملی‌ی سوم»، با شرکت ٤ سازمان ملی اعلام حضــور کرد. این ســازمان‌ها عبارت بودند از: «نهضــت آزادی‌ی ایران» (بازرگان و یارانش)؛ «جامعه‌ی ســوســیالیســت‌ها» (خلیل ملکی و یارانش)؛ «حزب ملت ایران» (داریوش فروهر و یارانش)؛ «حزب مردم ایران» (حبیب‌الله پیمان و کاظم ســامی و یارانشــان). با این که «جبهه‌ی ملی‌ی سوم» زیر فشار اختناق سیاسی، عملاً نتوانست فعالیت سیاسی‌ی علنی داشته باشد، و بیش‌تر اعضاء شورای عالی‌ی آن، از جمله مهدی بازرگان، در دادگاه نظامی محاکمه و زندانی شدند، اما دفترهای نهضت آزادی و جبهه‌ی ملی در خارج از ایران فعال بودند. دفترهای برون‌مرزی‌ی نهضت آزادی، به رهبری‌ی علی شریعتی، ابراهیم یزدی، و مصطفی چمران اداره می‌شدند. با اوجگیری‌ی اعتراضــات مردم در ســال ۱۳۵۷ بود که هم «جبهه‌ی ملی‌ی چهارم» تشــکیل شــد، و هم «نهضــت آزادی‌ی ایران» تجدید حیات کرد. مهندس مهدی بازرگان در کتاب «خاطرات» خود تک تک این موارد را شرح داده است، و همایون کاتوزیان نیز این تاریخچه را در مقاله‌ی فشرده‌ی زیر ثبت کرده است. به مآخذ زیر نگاه کنید:

- ***شصت سال خدمت و مقاومت، خاطرات مهدی بازرگان در گفت‌وگو با سرهنگ غلامرضا نجاتی***، تهران: ۱۳۷۷.
- همایون کاتوزیان، ***«نهضــت آزادی» تشــکل «دموکرات مسلمان» ایران و پنج دهه کوشــش ســیاســی***، تارنمای «رادیو فردا»، ۲۶ اردیبهشت ۱۳۹۰:

http://www.radiofarda.com/content/f3_katouzian_on_nehzat_azadi/24176060.html

[۴۸۴] مدرسه‌ی علوی، به وسیله‌ی سه تن، با نام‌های علی اصغر کرباسچیان، رضا روزبه و علی گلزاده غفوری، در سال ۱۳۳۵ تأسیس شد. عبدالکریم ســروش، یکی از دانش‌آموختگان این مدرســه بود، که پس از پایان این مدرســه، مدتی هم به عضــویت حلقه‌ی درس شــیخ محمود حلبی، رئیس انجمن حجتیه درآمد. و مدرســه‌ی «کمال» در سال ۱۳۳۶ توسط مهدی بازرگان و یدالله سحابی تأسیس شد. تدریس در این دبیرستان نیز به عهده‌ی خود بازرگان و سحابی و دبیران مذهبی بود. نوشته‌های همین افراد در کنار مواد آموزشــی‌ی دیگر نیز در این دبیرستان‌ها تدریس می‌شد. در تارنمای ویکی‌پیدیا، در کارنامه‌ی مهدی بازرگان ۱۰۵ اثر ثبت شــده، که آثار مربوط به پیش از ســال ۵۷، در این دبیرســتان توزیع و تدریس می‌شده است. به مأخذ زیرنگاه کنید:

- ***خاطرات منتشرنشده‌ی عزت‌الله سحابی از مدرسه‌ی کمال، خاندان عسگراولادی و جناح بازار***، تارنمای «آفتاب»، بازدید ۱ مرداد ۹۰: http://www.aftabnews.ir/vdci3uazut1apv2.cbct.html

[۴۸۵] حسینیه‌ی ارشاد، توسط محمد همایون، ناصر میناچی و عبدالحسین علی‌آبادی تأسیس شد. آیت‌الله مرتضــی مطهری نیز با این حسینیه همکاری داشت و عهده‌دار انتشارات این حسینیه بود. تدوین مجموعه‌ای پیرامون «محمد خاتم پیغمبران»، نخستین گام انتشارات حسینیه‌ی ارشاد بود که مطهری تحقیق و نگارش بخش هجرت تا وفات پیامبر را به علی شــریعتی ســپرد. پس از انقلاب، آیت‌الله مرتضــی مطهری، رئیس شــورای انقلاب شد، و ناصر میناچی، نخستین وزیر «فرهنگ و ارشاد ملی» در دولت موقتِ جمهوری اسلامی.

یکی از اراکین مسلمانان بوده است. و اما اگر سخنی به کلیلو [گالیله؟] و نیوتون و کپلر نسبت داده شود، آن را کفر می‌انگارند. [...این‌ها] به زعم خود، صیانت دیانت اسلامیه را می‌نمایند. آن‌ها فی‌الحقیقة دشمن دیانت اسلامیه هستند. نزدیک‌ترین دین‌ها به علوم و معارف دیانت اسلامیه است. [...] خاک بر سر این گونه حکیم و خاک بر سر این گونه حکمت. حکیم آن است که جمیع حوادث و اجزای عالم ذهن او را حرکت بدهد، نه آن که مانند کورها در یک راهی راه برود که هیچ نداند که پایان آن کجاست. علم فقه مسلمانان حاوی است مر جمیع حقوق منزلیه و حقوق بلدیه و حقوق دولیه را؛ پس می‌باید شخصی که متوغل در علم فقه شود، لایق آن باشد که صدراعظم ملکی شود یا سفیر کبیر دولتی گردد. و حال آن که ما فقهای خود را می‌بینیم بعد از تعلیم این علم از اداره‌ی خانه‌ی خود عاجز هستند بلکه بلاهت را فخر می‌شمارند.[۴۸۶]

جوهر این آموزه‌ها که حدود یک سده پیش از زمان مورد بحث، توسط سیدجمال‌ابدین اسدآبادی (افغانی) ترویج می‌شد، در گفتارهای اسلامی/ عرفانی/ غرب‌ستیزانه‌ی متفکران این دوره، مانند احمد فردید و جلال آل احمد و داریوش شایگان و احسان نراقی و علی شریعتی و مرتضی مطهری و سیدحسین نصر و فخرالدین شادمان و رضا داوری و حمید عنایت- که همه‌شان ظاهراً «دینی/ مذهبی» هم نبودند- از «خواب غفلت» بیدار شد. اگر مخاطب جمال‌الدین اسدآبادی تنها «خواص» بودند، آموزه‌های بسیاری از این متفکران، که تمامی‌ی هویت ایرانی را در هویت بومی/ اسلامی خلاصه می‌کردند، از طریق نشست‌ها و سخنرانی‌ها و کتاب‌هاشان، بین جوان‌ها و لایه‌های مختلف مردم ما برق‌آسا جا باز کرد، و تبلیغ مفاهیمی مانند «اسلام راستین»، «خویشتن خویشِ اسلامی»، «معنویتِ شرقی»، «میراث معنوی»، «اسلام انقلابی»ی بر ساخته‌ی این متفکران، سینه‌ی دونیمه‌ی تجدد ایرانی را بیش از پیش شکافت. و شگفتا که اکثر شخصیت‌های کُلاهی‌ی این گروه، دانش‌آموخته‌ی دانشگاه‌های کشورهای «استعماری» بودند؛ و شگفت‌انگیزتر این که با دستاوردهای علمی‌ی غرب و با تقلید از روش و نگرش منتقدان فلسفی و اجتماعی‌ی غرب، به جنگ غرب می‌رفتند. شاید مؤثرترین فرد از مجموعه‌ی یادشده، علی شریعتی باشد، که تأثیر تز «اسلام انقلابی» و شهادت‌طلب او در جوان‌های پیش از انقلاب را باید از زبان مهدی بازرگان شنید:

[...] در هر حال اشتیاق و استقبال از شهادت که در گفتارها و نوشتارهای دکتر [شریعتی] به جالب‌ترین گونه، روح و رنگ یافته و هدیه به جوانان شده بود، اگر وجود نداشت، حماسه‌های سرنوشت‌ساز و تاریخی‌ی میدان ژاله [در جمعه‌ی سیاه]، خیابان سرچشمه‌ی تهران و نظائر آن در قزوین، سنندج، مشهد، تبریز و جاهای دیگر ایران به وجود نیامده کمر استبداد شکسته نمی‌شد، و سپس جنگ عراق با چنین تعداد داوطلبان عاشق و کفن‌پوش آغاز و دوام نمی‌یافت، اگر دکتر شریعتی در کتاب امام و امت تکیه و تأکید روی نیاز امت به امام و به رهبر مرشد و مطاع همگان نمی‌کرد رهبری و ولایت در انقلاب و نظام حاکم چنین قداست و قدرت نمی‌یافت. همچنین اگر ستیزه‌گری‌ی او با سازشکاری، با سرمایه‌داری و با مظاهر استثمار و استعمار جاری و ساری در دل و دیده‌های امت ایران نشده بود تداوم انقلاب پا نمی‌گرفت، یا به سوی دیگری متمایل می‌شد.[۴۸۷]

اگر آل احمد، شریعتی، مطهری، شادمان، شایگان، نراقی، نصر و عنایت با انتشار کتاب‌های خود، دست کم فرصت نقد را پدید آوردند، احمد فردید- که جلال آل احمد عنوان «غرب‌زدگی» را از او گرفت- چنین نکرد. فردید که چندین دهه مدرس فلسفه در دانشگاه بود، آراء خود را به صورت سخنرانی در مجامع آکادمیک یا در کلاس‌های درس، گاهی هم در

---

[۴۸۶] سیدجمال‌الدین اسدآبادی، ***مقالات جمالیه***، به کوشش ابوالحسن جمالی، تهران: چاپ دوم، انتشارات اسلامی، ۱۳۵۸، صص ۹۴ و ۹۵.

[۴۸۷] مهدی بازرگان، مقدمه‌ی کتاب: جعفر سعیدی، ***شخصیت و اندیشه‌ی دکتر علی شریعتی***، تهران: انتشارات چاپخش، ۱۳۷۲

مناظره‌های تلویزیونی ابلاغ می‌کرد، بدون آن که آن‌ها را به چاپ بسپارد. چند سال پس از مرگ فردید، یکی از شاگردان و پیروان او، متن سخنرانی‌ها و درس‌گفته‌های او را از روی نوار پیاده کرد و آن را با مؤخره‌ای طولانی، در کتابی با عنوان «دیدار فرهی و فتوحات آخرالزمان» به چاپ سپرد. داریوش آشوری، با وجود این کتاب امکان یافت که رساله‌ی روشنگری، با عنوان «اسطوره‌ی فلسفه در میان ما ...»، پیرامون این شخصیت و در رَدّ اندیشه‌های او بنویسد.[۴۸۸] عبدالکریم سروش (نواندیش دینی‌ی پس از انقلاب ۵۷) نیز، البته با رویکردی متفاوت با رویکرد آشوری، بارها در سخنرانی‌ها و مصاحبه‌های خود، آراء این شخصیت فرهنگی را معرفی و رَدّ کرده است.[۴۸۹] نصرالله پورجوادی (اندیشه‌ورز فرهنگی/ ادبی‌ی درون‌مرزی)، نیز که در دوره‌ی فوق لیسانس، دانشجوی احمد فردید بوده، حدود نُه سال بعد از مقاله‌ی آشوری («اسطوره‌ی فلسفه میان ما...»)، با تأیید نظر داریوش آشوری در مقاله‌ی یادشده، سخنان احمد فردید و چرخش‌های او را در دوران جمهوری‌ی اسلامی«شارلاتانیسم» خوانده است.[۴۹۰]

در این جا مجال بازبینی‌ی این متن‌ها، و پاسخ طرفداران فردید به آن‌ها، نیست.[۴۹۱] اما شاید بازگفت کوتاه زیر- برگرفته از یکی از واپسین سخنرانی‌های احمد فردید (بهمن ۱۳۶۹)- جهان‌بینی‌ی او را در دوران جهوری‌ی اسلامی نمایندگی کند:

> امام خمینی‌ی فقید از نوادر تاریخ بود که با انقلاب اسلامی نخستین تزلزل را در بنیان غرب‌گرائی ایجاد کرد. اما این بحران همچنان ادامه دارد. از این رو مبارزه‌ی بی‌سابقه با غرب‌زدگی باید تا ظهور مهدی‌ی موعود، که پایان بحران غرب‌زدگی است، ادامه یابد.[۴۹۲]

بیهوده نیست که نصرالله پورجوادی، در مقاله‌اش به این نتیجه می‌رسد که احمد فردید «بیش از هر کس به تاریخ معنویت ما ظلم کرده است.» پورجوادی در این متن، احمد فردید را به «پیش از انقلاب» و «بعد از انقلاب» تقسیم می‌کند و ضمن

---

۴۸۸ داریوش آشوری، ***اسطوره‌ی فلسفه در میان ما: بازدیدی از احمد فردید و نظریه‌ی غرب‌زدگی***، ۲۰۰٤/ ۱۳۸۳ در تارنمای شخصی‌ی آشوری با نام «ملکوت»:

www.ashouri.malakut.org/archives/fardid.pdf

۴۸۹ به عنوان مثال، به مأخذ زیر نگاه کنید:

- ***متن مصاحبه‌ی داریوش سجادی با دکتر سروش***، ۱۸ اسفند ۱۳۸٤، تارنمای «سروش»:

http://www.drsoroush.com/Persian/Interviews/P-INT-13841218-HomaTV.html

۴۹۰ نصرالله پورجوادی، ***تفاوت‌های فردید قبل و بعد از انقلاب اسلامی*** (مقاله‌ی انتقادی‌ی نصرالله پورجوادی درباره‌ی احمد فردید)، تارنمای «خبر آنلاین»، ۲۸ مرداد ۱۳۹۲:

http://www.khabaronline.ir/detail/309013/culture/religion

۴۹۱ به عنوان نمونه از متن‌های مدافع احمد فردید، به مآخذ زیر نگاه کنید:

- محمد مددپور، ***مؤخره*** در کتاب «دیدار فرهی و فتوحات آخرالزمان»، تهران: مؤسسه‌ی فرهنگی پژوهشی‌ی چاپ و نشر نظر، چاپ دوم، ۱۳۸۷.
- طاها مبین، ***فردید و مخالفانش***، تارنمای «طاها نیوز»، بازدید ۵ خرداد ۱۳۹۰:

http://www.taha-mobin.parsfa.com/post-295689.html

- مسعود آقائی، ***تفکرات و اندیشه‌های دکتر فردید و نقش آن در انقلاب اسلامی***، تارنمای «جاد نیوز» ارگان انجمن اسلامی‌ی دانشجویان، بازدید ۲ اردی‌بهشت ۱۳۹۰:

http://www.jadnews.org/index.php?option=com_content&view=article&id=189:1389-05-09-07-22-49&catid=42:maghalat

۴۹۲ این متن، دومین پارگراف از متن کوتاهی است که با عنوان «احمد فردید دار فانی را وداع گفت»، در تارنمای یکی از پیروان اندیشه‌ی فردید، از یک نشریه یا از یک خبرنامه، عیناً کلیشه شده است:

- طاها مبین، ***فردید و مخالفانش***، تارنمای «طاها نیوز»، بازدید ۵ خرداد ۱۳۹۰:

http://www.taha-mobin.parsfa.com/post-295689.html

توضیح: احمد فردید در رژیم پیشین ایران، شاه را دارای «فره‌ی ایزدی» شناسائی می‌کرد. در این زمینه به سخنان احسان نراقی در کتاب زیر توجه کنید. من این کتاب را ندیده‌ام، اما بخش‌هائی از آن را در مقاله‌های مختلف خوانده‌ام:

- سیدابراهیم نبوی، ***در خشت خام: مصاحبه با احسان نراقی***، تهران: جامعه‌ی ایرانیان، چاپ سوم، ۱۳۷۹، صص ۱۱۸ و ۱۲۴.

اشاره به نمونه‌هائی از «پریشان‌گوئی»ها و «مهملاتِ» او در سال‌های پیش از انقلاب، معتقد است که فردید در آن سال‌ها «گاهی ناگهان دریچه‌ای را به روی شاگردان و مستمعان خود می‌گشود که خستگی‌ی ناشی از تحمل یک ساعت پریشان‌گوئی را از اذهان ایشان به در می‌کرد.» و خلاصه این که: «فردید دستش به کلی خالی نبود. گاهی حرفی برای گفتن داشت. ولی بعد از انقلاب، آن چه داشت در برابر سیاست روز و در پیش پای قدرتمندان قربانی کرد.» پورجوادی پیرامون فردیدِ پس از انقلاب می‌نویسد:

> [...] بعد از انقلاب، ظاهراً کلاس‌های او پررونق شده بود. دلیل آن هم این بود که فردید آراء خود را سیاسی کرده بود و از افکاری که داشت، برای توجیه انقلاب اسلامی استفاده می‌کرد. اگر یک کلمه به تمام معنی در حق او صادق باشد، آن کلمه‌ی «شارلاتانیسم» است. کلمه‌ای که بر پیشانی او حک شده بود، و او تا می‌توانست از آن برای جلب مستمع استفاده می‌کرد، غرب‌زدگی بود. داریوش آشوری در نقد شدیداللحنی که چند سال پیش از او کرده بود، او را با پیرمرد خنزرپنزری‌ی «بوف کورِ» صادق هدایت مقایسه کرده است. پیرمرد، بعد از انقلاب بساطی پهن کرده بود از یک مشت فحش و ناسزا که نثار روشنفکران مسلمان و نامسلمان می‌کرد. نیست‌انگاری و خودبنیادی و طاغوت‌زدگی از دهانش نمی‌افتاد. از عبدالکریم سروش که می‌خواست بدگوئی کند، به کارل پوپر فحش می‌داد. مرحوم حسن حبیبی را که می‌خواست تحقیر کند، گورویچ را به یهودی‌بودن متهم می‌کرد. به جبهه‌ی ملی و دکتر مصدق بد می‌گفت تا خود را مدافع امام‌خمینی جلوه دهد. کار تمدن غرب را تمام‌شده می‌انگاشت. نفرت خود را از امریکا هیچ وقت پنهان نمی‌کرد. شاید یکی از دلایلی که چپ‌ها به‌سراغش می‌آمدند، همین امریکاستیزی‌ی او بود. هر که را می‌خواست بکوبد، او را یهودی و صهیونست و فراماسون می‌خواند. از تفکر کسی انتقاد نمی‌کرد. اگر از کسی خوشش نمی‌آمد، او را زبون‌اندیش می‌خواند. زمانی که نمی‌بایست از اومانیسم بد بگوید، زشت‌ترین حرف‌ها را به اسم خدا و پیغمبر درباره‌ی اومانیسم می‌گفت. پشت این بدگویی از اومانیسم، جهل و حماقت نبود، بلکه خبث طینت و شرارت نهفته بود. برای عده‌ای دم از تزکیه‌ی انقلابی می‌زد. اگر قدرت به دست او می‌افتاد، از پل پت در کامبوج نه، ولی از موسولینی عقب نمی‌افتاد. پیرمرد خنزرپنزری آبرو برای اهل فلسفه در مملکت نگذاشته بود. [...] در اوایل انقلاب، روحانیون را مسخره می‌کرد و می‌گفت: «کلرژی نمی‌تواند مملکت را اداره کند.» لفظ فرنگی‌ی «کلرژی» را به جای آخوند و روحانی به کار می‌برد. بعداً که جمهوری‌ی اسلامی مستقر شد، از طرفداران روحانیت شد. [...] فردید با طرح نظریه‌ی غرب‌زدگی‌ی خود و اطلاق آن به تاریخ معنویت ایران، بیش از هر کس به تاریخ ما ظلم کرده است. [...] (نصرالله پورجوادی، مرداد ۱۳۹۲، مأخذ پیشین)

داریوش آشوری در بازتاب به تقسیم‌بندی‌ی نصرالله پورجوادی در این مقاله، متنی منتشر کرد با عنوان «یادکری دیگر از فردید»، و در آن، با اشاره به چند نمونه از ترجمه‌ی نادرست فردید در همان زمانِ «پیش از انقلاب»، «داعیه‌هایِ زبان‌دانی» و کلاً، فلسفه‌دانی‌ی او (به ویژه شناخت او از هایدگر) را به زیر سئوال برد. منتها، در پایان متن خود به نکته‌ای اساسی پیرامون ذهنیت فردید اشاره کرد، که به باور من، به لحاظ تاریخ فکر ما بسیار قابل تأمل است. آشوری در پایان این مقاله نوشت:

> با این همه، در میانِ همه‌ی استادانِ فلسفه‌ی دانشگاهی در میانِ ما، یک امتیازِ شایان می‌باید به فردید داد. و آن این که او در درس‌گفتارهایِ پریشانِ خود، در کلافِ سر-در- گمِ معلومات‌فروشی‌های بی‌پایان، یک مسئله‌ی اساسی نیز طرح می‌کرد که برای ذهن‌های جوینده و پوینده‌ی جوان کشش داشت و آنان را به کلاس‌های او و پای سخنرانی‌های او می‌کشید. و آن این بود که در ورایِ فرمول‌بندی‌های مهندسانه و کارشناسانه در بابِ توسعه‌نیافتگی‌ی ما در برابرِ جهانِ توسعه‌یافته، یا فرمول‌بندی‌های مارکسیست- لنینیستی در بابِ رابطه‌ی امپریالیسم و کولونی- که بنیانِ آن هم همان پی‌جوئی‌ی ایدئولوژیکِ

> مانع‌های توسعه‌یافتگی بود- با فرمول‌بندیِ فردید از آسیب‌شناسیِ تاریخیِ ذهنیِ ما به عنوانِ انسانِ «غرب‌زده»، مسئله‌ی «ما» یک بُعدِ فلسفیِ اگزیستانسیل پیدا کرد. اما فردید با آن زبانِ گُنگ و شخصیّتِ نقش‌بازِ نااستوارِ کین‌توز هرگز نتوانست از این مسئله شرحی درست و روشن بدهد. [...] مسئله‌ای که او به شیوه‌ی خود طرح می‌کرد، یعنی پرسشِ «ما کیستیم؟ و در جهانِ کنونی کجا جای داریم؟» همان است که ذهن کسانی، از جمله مرا، در درازنای این سالیان به خود مشغول داشته است. امّا در دورانِ انقلاب با نقش‌بازی‌های سیاسی و مذهبی‌اش خیلِ مریدانی از جنسِ دیگر یافت. در حقیقت به چیزی مانندِ شیخِ فرقه‌ی حَقّه‌ی (یا حُقّه‌ی؟) فردیدیه بدل شد که هایدگرِ صوفی هم گویا از سلسله‌ی مشایخِ آن است![۴۹۳]

نقطه‌ی اشتراک در نوشته‌های بسیاری از مفسرانِ آراء احمد فردید، اشاره به پریشان‌گوئی، و در عین حال، جذابیتِ بیان این شخصیت، و توان بالای او در نفوذ به مخاطب از طریق بمباران ذهن او با ترم‌ها و مفاهیم فلسفی است.[۴۹۴] سیدجواد طباطبائی، استاد کنونی‌ی دانشگاه و پژوهشگر تاریخ، و از جمله شاگردان فردید، پیرامون او می‌گوید:

> [...] در مورد فردید باید بگویم که درباره‌ی او، هم به افراط و هم به تفریط، بسیار سخن گفته‌اند. اما من از محضر فردید بسیار استفاده کردم، با این که این استفاده بسیار پراکنده بود. اولین باری که در کلاس فردید شرکت کردم، عنوان درس او پدیدارشناسی هگل بود. من با اشتیاق در آن درس حضور پیدا کردم، اما متوجه شدم که در تمام مدت در مورد هایدگر سخن می‌گوید. سال دیگر، عنوان درس پدیدارشناسی هوسرل بود. این بار نیز همان مطلب را تکرار کرد. البته همین تکرار هم برای من مفید بود. [...] فردید آدمی بود که ذهن پریشانی داشت، شاید بهتر باشد بگویم ذهن سامانی داشت که برای خود او مفهوم بود، اما ظرایف فلسفی‌ی بسیاری را دریافته بود. کلاس او نیز از طراوت خاصی برخوردار بود. [...] قبل از این که کلاس شروع شود همگی دور هم جمع می‌شدیم و در مورد حرف‌های فردید در جلسه‌ی گذشته صحبت می‌کردیم. یک بار صحبت از تقدیر تاریخی بود، یکی از دانشجویان گفت: من متوجه نمی‌شوم که منظور استاد از تخدیر تاریخی چیست؟ بیان نه چندان فصیح و پریشان‌گویی‌های او به این گونه بدفهمی‌ها دامن می‌زد، اما این که گفته‌اند هیچ نمی‌دانست و... سخن درستی نیست. هر کسی می‌بایست بتواند ارتباطی با او برقرار کند که البته کار آسانی نبود. [...] زبان اصلی‌ی او فرانسه بود که بسیار هم بد تلفظ می‌کرد. اگر بخواهم از تجربه شخصی‌ی خودم این مسئله را برای شما بازگو کنم، باید بگویم تلفظ فردید از بعضی کلمات فلسفی‌ی فرانسه در ذهن مانده بود. اما وقتی برای تحصیل به پاریس رفتم همان اولین روزها دریافتم که همه‌ی آن‌ها را غلط یاد گرفته‌ام.[۴۹۵]

در هر حال، نفوذ کلام فردید به گونه‌ای بود که داریوش آشوری- که در جوانی چندی در نشست‌های او شرکت می‌کرد و گویا در جرگه‌ی مریدان او بود- در شرح انگیزه‌های خود در نگارش رساله‌ی «اسطوره‌ی فلسفه در میان ما ...» می‌نویسد:

---

[۴۹۳] داریوش آشوری، ***یادکردی دیگر از فردید***، (در حاشیه‌ی مقاله‌ی نصرالله پورجوادی در مجله‌ی اندیشه‌ی پویا)، تارنمای «گویا نیوز»، ۱۲ بهمن ۱۳۹۲:
http://news.gooya.com/politics/archives/2014/02/174632.php

[۴۹۴] گویاترین متنی که پیرامون این ویژگی‌های فردید خوانده‌ام، بخشی از مقاله‌ی زیر است، که نویسنده، آن را به رضا براهنی نسبت داده است:
محمدرضا ضاد، ***فردید از دید براهنی***، تارنمای «فردید نامه»، ۲۴ شهریور ۱۳۸۸:
http://fardidnameh.blogfa.com/post-34.aspx

[۴۹۵] ***گفت‌وگوی مهرنامه با سیدجواد طباطبایی: تسویه حساب با چریک‌ها***، تارنمای «مرکز دایرةالمعارف اسلامی»، ۱۵ تیر ۱۳۹۲:
http://www.cgie.org.ir/fa/news/3521

این کار را همچنین می‌بایست به عنوان نوعی روان‌پالائی می‌کردم، برای پاک کردن حساب خودم با دورانی از زندگی‌ام، چه بسا با آلایش‌هائی که هنوز از آن دوران در من مانده است. (آشوری، اسطوره‌ی فلسفه ...، ۱۳۸۳، پیشین)

با این نفوذ کلام و موقعیتِ پیامبرگونه‌ای که احمد فردید در آن دوران در میان مریدانش داشت، جای شگفتی نیست اگر بگوئیم که اندیشه‌های او در جهت‌گیری‌ی انقلاب، عاملی مؤثر بوده است. به چرخش او به سوی حکومت «کلژی»ها، و تزهای بعد از انقلاب او در این جا کاری ندارم که اندیشه‌ی امام‌زمانی‌اش میان لشگر حزب‌الله چنان گرفت که برای امام زمان بشقابی خالی بر سفره‌ی خود می‌گذارند، تا بیاید، اول شام بخورد، و بعد با شمشیر آخته‌اش «امپریالیست‌ها و صهیونیست‌ها»، و کل «غرب» را «از صفحه‌ی زمین محو کند» و حاکمیت «اسلام» را بر سراسر زمین محقق سازد.[۴۹۶]

* در درازنای همین دوران بود که تز قرضی‌ی «از خود بیگانگی» و «شیئ‌شدگی»‌ی علی شریعتی از مارکسیسم، از پیکر «سرمایه و کار و کارگر و مناسبات تولیدی» جدا شد، به بدنه‌ی «اسلام علوی» چسبید، و دامان زنان دانش‌آموخته را نیز گرفت؛ و بحث «آزادی‌ی زن»، به بحث «کالاشدگی‌ی زن» در فرهنگ‌های غربی، فروکاهید. و بحث «آزادی‌های جنسی»، از «فریب‌های بی‌شمار استحمار» برشمرده شد. و شگفتا! بسیاری از زن‌هائی (مانند برخی از گویندگان تلویزیون در سال ۱۳۵۷) که از این تزها دفاع می‌کردند، خود سراپا به مظاهر فرهنگ غربی آراسته بودند. و در درازنای همین دوران بود که تز «دموکراسی‌ی هدایت شده» در کتاب «امت و امامت» نوشته‌ی علی شریعتی، «دموکراسی» را از معنا و مفهوم فراگیر و هم‌زمانی و هم‌مکانی‌ی خود خالی کرد،[۴۹۷] و خواسته یا ناخواسته، زمینه‌ی تز «دیکتاتوری‌ی صُلحا»[۴۹۸] را برای بنیادگذاران جمهوری‌ی اسلامی (از جمله آیت‌الله خمینی و آیت‌الله بهشتی) فراهم آورد. و باز، در درازنای همین دوران بود که در پناه مبارزه با «استعمار»، این جمله‌ی مارکس که «دموکراسی از ترّهات سرمایه‌داری (یا بورژوازی) است»، از کل دستگاه نظری‌ی این متفکر بیرون کشیده شد، و در پناه آن، مفاهیم «آزادی و حقوق بشر» و ارزش‌های دموکراتیک، به ارزش‌های «بورژوائی»، «لیبرالی» و «امپریالیستی» تعبیر شدند، و حتا با عنوان‌هائی مانند «شوخی‌های بزرگ»،[۴۹۹] یا «خر رنگ کن» به سخره گرفته شدند؛ که البته جنبش چریکی‌ی ایران نیز بر این گزاره‌ها صحه می‌گذاشت.

رسیدگی‌ی دقیق به اندیشه‌های متفکران این دوره و یافتن وجه اشتراک یا تفارق در آن‌ها، البته، مجال دیگری می‌طلبد. اما همین جا باید اشاره کنم که صرف نظر از تفاوت‌های چشم‌گیری که در آراء و راه حل‌های این اندیشه‌ورزان دیده می‌شود، نقطه‌ی عزیمت اندیشه‌های این مجموعه را ضدیت با مظاهر «مدرنیته»‌ی غرب- به عنوان ابزار «استعمار»- رقم می‌زند، که رگه‌ی مشترک در بیش‌تر جنبش‌های کشورهای «جهان سوم» آن زمان را نیز رقم می‌زد؛ و به روایت «شموئل آیزنشتات» (جامعه‌شناس روسی/ لهستانی‌تبار)، خود جنس و جنمی «مشخصاً مدرن داشت».[۵۰۰] بنابراین، می‌توان گفت که

---

[۴۹۶] این سخن من مطلقاً از سر طنز یا تمسخر یا کنایه نیست. محمود احمدی نژاد، رئیس جمهور دوره‌های نهم و دهم در جمهوری‌ی اسلامی، این ادعا را مطرح کرده و «بشقاب خالی» بر میز شام خود را نمادی برای انتظار بر ظهور مهدی موعود معرفی کرده است. در این زمینه در جلد سوم مجموعه‌ی حاضر با استدلال و سند کافی سخن گفته‌ام.

[۴۹۷] علی شریعتی، ***امت و امامت***، انتشارات قلم، تهران: ۱۳۵۸، صص ۱۶۶ تا ۱۶۷.

[۴۹۸] این اصطلاح در بیان آیت‌الله بهشتی تکرار شده است. در این زمینه به مأخذ زیر نگاه کنید:

دکتر غلام علی صفاریان و مهندس معتمد دزفولی، ***سقوط دولت بازرگان***، تهران: قصیده سرا، ۱۳۸۲ ص ۱۴۳.

[۴۹۹] علی شریعتی، ***فاطمه، فاطمه است***، نشر الکترونیکی توسط تارنمای «دکتر علی شریعتی»، ص ۴۹.

[500] Shmuel N. Eisenstadt, ***Multiple Modernities***, Daedalus, vol. 129, No. 1, Winter 2000, pp. 1-29. (p. 2) http://www.jstor.org/discover/10.2307/20027613?uid=3739920&uid=2&uid=4&uid=3739256&sid=21103971595743

«شناسائیِ مشکل» در این دستگاه نظری، معتبر، قابل بررسی و تأمل بود. اما این اندیشه‌ورزانِ ما تنها به شناسائیِ مشکل بسنده نکردند، و «راه حلِ» مشکل را نیز در بازگشتی قاطعانه نشان دادند. گرانیگاه «راه حل»های پیشنهادیِ آن‌ها (به جز فخرالدین شادمان، و تا حدی نیز داریوش شایگان، که بیش‌تر به حفظ فرهنگ و سنت‌های ایرانی در استفاده از آموزه‌های مدرنیسم توجه داشتند) همانا رویکرد به اسلام و مذهب تشیع- به عنوان بازگشت به هویت خویش- نه تنها به مثابه سَدّی در برابر استعمار، بلکه در عین حال، به عنوان راهی برای اعتلای از دست‌رفته‌ی اسلام بود. در رهگذر آن فهم نظری و اجرای این راهکار است، که آن نقطه‌ی عزیمتِ گرامی (مبارزه با استعمار)، به سود پروژه‌های «استعمار نو» پیش می‌رود: در سده‌های هجدهم و نوزدهم میلادی، کشورهای استعمارگر با هدف گسترش نفوذ اقتصادی و سیاسی و فرهنگیِ خود در ایران و در همه‌ی کشورهای غنی از نظر منابع، و برای پیشی گرفتن بر رقبای خود، به ناگزیر از پروژه‌های پارادوکسیکالی سود بردند که چون برآیند پیامدهای علمی و نظریِ رنسانس، عصر روشنگری، و پیشنهادهای «مدرنیسم» بودند، برخلاف هدف و خواست استعمارگران، به رشد آگاهیِ مردم این کشورها یاری دادند. و از سوی دیگر، گسترش و تعمیق آگاهی‌های اجتماعی و سیاسی در این ملت‌ها- حتا در قالب همان «مدرنیته»یِ ناموزون بومی- بزرگ‌ترین مانع در برابر هدف‌های استعمارگران را پدید آورد. چرا «استعمار»- که حالا به مرحله‌ی «امپریالیسم» رسیده بود، و برای حفظ منافع خود راه‌هائی بهتر از اشغال فیزیکیِ سرزمین‌های غنی یافته بود- برای جلوگیری از گسترش درک مردم این سرزمین‌ها در تغییر آگاهانه‌ی شرایط (رسیدن به «خرد خودبنیاد»)، از ایده‌های ضد «مدرن» استقبال نکند؟[۵۰۱] اما «نواندیش» ما که این «خط» را نخوانده است، تمامیِ دستاوردهای فرهنگی و علمی و فلسفیِ غرب را- که با همه‌ی مطلقیت‌هایش، دست کم جدائیِ دین و حکومت را در زادگاه خود به کرسیِ عمل نشانده بود- یکسره به زیر ضرب می‌گیرد؛ و با هر ضربه، از یک سو، «مدرنیسم» هنوز نهادینه نشده در گستره‌ی ادراک ایرانی را ویران می‌کند و به دَرّه‌ی دهان‌گشوده بین سنت و تجددِ ایرانی ژرفا می‌بخشد؛ و از سوی دیگر، پایه‌ای از هزارپایه‌ی «اسلام سیاسی» (ایدئولوژیک، سرکوبگر، ضد زن، ضد آزادی‌های فردی و اجتماعی و سیاسی) را بنا می‌نهد. و شگفتا که «دَرّه‌ی دهان‌گشوده» در ذهنیت خودِ شخصیت‌های این گروه، به ویژه شخصیت‌های کُلاهیِ آن، در نوشته‌های تک تک آن‌ها قابل ردیابی است. این دانش‌آموختگان در «غرب»، یک پا بر پله‌ی شناخت خود از «هایدگر» یا «سارتر» یا «مارکس» و یک پا بر پله‌ی «وحی» و «قرآن» و «مولا علی» و «تشیع علوی» و «اسلام وحدانی» و «عرفان اسلامی»یِ «هانری کربن»یِ، از ستیز با «استعمار» و نماینده‌ی آن در ایران، به ستیز با «مدرنیسم نوپای ایرانی» سر برکردند، و میراث خود را برای نسلِ جوانِ درگیر در انقلاب ۵۷ نیز باقی گذاشتند. البته جلال آل احمد (فرزند یک شخصیت روحانی) که دانش‌آموخته‌ی «غرب» نبود، زمانی که پس از ۲۸ مرداد ۳۲ به قول خودش «به جِد در خویشتن نگریست»، انگار به تدریج متوجه شد که «خویشتن» او نه تنها در آموزه‌های پدری، بلکه در «نعش به دار آویخته»یِ شیخ فضل‌الله نوریِ مشروعه‌خواه نهفته است. از این رو بود که از «خویشتن خود» به «کلیت تشیّع اسلامی»، پل زد:

---

[۵۰۱] در پاره‌هائی از ادبیات سیاسیِ کشورهای امریکای لاتین- که در رابطه با استعمار، مشابهت‌های چشمگیری با شرایط سیاسیِ ایران دارند- آن چه که من به عنوان «پروژه‌های پارادوکسیکال استعمارگران» شناسائی کرده‌ام، به عنوان پروژه‌هائی شناسائی شده است که از آغاز، با هدف بارور کردن «هویت خدعه‌آمیز، شکسته، و متزلزل» در مردم کشورهای مستعمره، آگاهانه از سوی استعمارگران به اجرا گذاشته شده بود. مثلاً «بولیوار اِچه‌وِریا»، یکی از متفکران رادیکال امریکای لاتین، در مقاله‌ای که به مناسبت جشن‌های دویستمین سالگرد استقلال کشورهای امریکای لاتین نوشت، بر این باور است که پس از شکست امپراتوریِ اسپانیا و پس ار جنگ‌های استقلال در کشورهای امریکای لاتین، «خالقان جمهوری‌های پسا استعماری» برای پیشبرد هدف‌های خود، هویتی برای ملت‌های امریکای لاتین رقم زدند که «ظاهراً می‌تواند تضادهای همیشگی و پایدار میان ستمگر و ستمدیده را سازش‌پذیر جلوه دهد. [...] هویتی که هر غروری در آن، باید از نوع شکسته و متزلزل خود باشد؛ چون ما با هویتی سر و کار داریم که از بیماری‌هائی رنج می‌برد که آن را به منبع شرم بدل کرده است؛ به هویتی که آرزوی پرهیز از آن را در فرد تحریک می‌کند.» شگفت‌انگیز است که این متفکر مارکسیست، در این مقاله (که چند هفته پیش از مرگش – بهار ۲۰۱۰- به زبان اسپانیائی منتشر شد)، در نقش «نواندیشان مذهبی»یِ ما ظاهر شده، و مسئله‌ی بازگشت به هویت بومی را (به عنوان یک چاره) نه البته «پیشنهاد»، بلکه فقط مطرح کرده است. به مأخذ زیر نگاه کنید:
Bolivar Echeverria, ***Potemkin Republics: Reflextion on Latin America's Bicentenary***, New Left Review, No. 70, July / August 2011, p p. 53- 61.

> من با دکتر «تندر کیا» موافقم که نوشت شهید نوری نه به عنوان مخالف مشروطه، که خود در اوایل امر مدافعش بود، بلکه به عنوان مدافع مشروعه باید بالای دار برود؛ و من می‌افزایم! و به عنوان کلیّت تشیع اسلامی. [...] من نعش آن بزرگوار را بر سر دار همچون پرچمی می‌دانم که به علامت استیلای غرب‌زدگی پس از دویست سال کشمکش بر بام سرای این مملکت افراشته شد.[502]

جلال آل احمد در رهگذر پل‌سازی، تاریخ را هم تحریف می‌کند و از قول تندر کیا (از نواده‌های شیخ فضل‌الله نوری) می‌نویسد: «شیخ نوری نه به عنوان مخالف مشروطه...». در حالی که شیخ فضل‌الله نوری، بارها «مخالفت» خود با مشروطیت را گفته بود و نوشته بود و حتا در سخنرانی‌ی هنگام اعدام خود ابراز کرده بود. شیخ فضل‌الله نوری، البته در آغاز جنبش با مشروطیت مخالف نبود. اما- به قول مهدی قلی هدایت در کتاب «خاطرات و خطرات»- زمانی که «از قالیچه بیرون ماند»، با مشروطیت به مخالفت برخاست. کما این که علامه محمد قزوینی در حاشیه‌نویسی بر کتاب «انقلاب ایران»، اثر ادوارد براون، نوشته است که «شیخ به محاکمه‌کنندگان گفته بود: "نه من مرتجع بودم و نه سیدعبدالله بهبهانی و سیدمحمد طباطبائی مشروطه‌خواه. فقط محض این بود که مرا خوار و ذلیل بکنند و کنار بزنند. موضوع ارتجاع و اصول مشروطه در میان نبود.» پس از بیرون ماندن از دایره‌ی قدرت بود که او با «دلایل عقلی و نقلی»‌ی خود، کلاً با مفاهیم «قانون» و «قانون‌گذاری» در مشروطه مخالفت کرد، و دو اصل «حرّیت» و «مساوات» در قانون اساسی‌ی مشروطه را «شوم» نامید، و گفت: «بنای قرآن بر آزاد نبودن قلم و لسان است.» یا: «یک کلمه در نظام‌نامه‌ی قانون اساسی در آزادی‌ی قلم ذکر شد، این همه مفاسد روزنامه‌ها [پیش آمد]، وای اگر آزادی در عقاید بود.» یا: «خلط مبحث اشاعه می‌دهند که اسلام‌طلبان مستبد هستند. حال آن که البته باید مستبد باشند. اساس اسلام، بلکه هر دینی، بر استبداد است.» یا: «میان اسلام و مشروطه، در ذات، تعارض وجود دارد. زیرا: ولایت، خاص نواب امام و فقهاست.» و «پس از ختم رسالت، جعل قانون، به هر دلیل و از سوی هر کس، با اسلام منافات دارد.» فضل‌الله نوری، حتا با واژه‌ی «روزنامه» (مهم‌ترین وسیله‌ی گردش اطلاعات) آشکارا سر دشمنی نشان داد؛ به طوری که، نشریه‌ی خود را به جای «روزنامه»، «لایحه» نام‌گذاری کرد.[503] او در «این لوایح، سران مشروطه را بابی، بهائی، خارجی، مادی، بی‌دین، لامذهب، شیفته‌ی فرنگ و ... می‌خواند.» از جمله اتهام‌هائی که در زمان محاکمه‌ی شیخ فضل‌الله نوری مطرح شد، «تکفیر مشروطه‌خواهان، بابی‌خواندن وکلا، تشویق اوباش بر ضد مجلس، و نوشتن رساله در تحریم مشروطیت» بود. پیرم خان در همین دادگاه از او می‌پرسد: «تو بودی که مشروطه را حرام کردی؟ شیخ پاسخ داد: بله! من بودم و تا ابد هم حرام خواهد بود. مؤسسان این مشروطه همه لامذهب هستند و مردم را فریب داده‌اند.» شیخ فضل‌الله نوری، حتا در پای چوبه‌ی دار همین سخن را تکرار کرد: «در این دم آخر هم باز به این مردم می‌گویم که مؤسسان این اساس، لامذهبانی هستند که مردم را فریب داده‌اند.»[504] با این همه شواهد آشکار، بر من پوشیده است که جلال آل احمد با چه منطقی توانسته «نعش آن بزرگوار» را به مثابه «پرچم»ی برای «غربزدگی»ی ما و دلیل تسلط استعمار برانداز کند. غافل از این که «آن بزرگوار»، گورستان موقوفه‌ی

---

[502] جلال آل احمد، ***غربزدگی***، نشر الکترونیکی توسط تارنمای «تاریخ ما»، ص ۴۱:
http://tarikhema.ir/books/adab/jalal_aleahmad/gharbzadegi%20.pdf

[503] علی‌اکبر قاضی‌زاده در کتاب ***جان‌باختگان روزنامه‌نگار***، تهران: انتشارات جامعه‌ی ایرانیان، ۱۳۷۹، ص ۲۲۱ با استفاده از منابعی که از آن‌ها یاد می‌کند، می‌نویسد: «مشروعه‌خواهان با چاپ و انتشار روزنامه مخالف بودند. بنا بر این نشریه‌ی خود را "لایحه" نام گذاشته بودند.» قاضی‌زاده در زیرنویس مربوط به این جمله نوشته است: حاج شیخ محمدحسین تبریزی از مخالفان مشروطه، در رساله‌ی تذکرةالغافل و ارشادالجاهل نوشته است :"آزادی‌ی جراید، مایه‌ی توهین دولت و خفت ملت و قوت دشمنان دین است."» اما ادوارد براون از «لایحه» نام نمی‌برد، بلکه در کتاب ***تاریخ مطبوعات و ادبیات ایران در دوره‌ی مشروطیت***، ترجمه و تحشیه و تعلیقات به قلم محمد عباسی، تهران: انتشارات کانون معرفت، ۱۳۳۷، جلد دوم، ص ۱۵۸ می‌نویسد: «[...] و اعلامیه‌های شیخ فضل‌الله نوری و پیروان وی را که به سال هزار و سی‌صد و بیست و هشتم هجری‌ی قمری (۱۹۰۷) در زاویه‌ی مقدسه‌ی حضرت عبدالعظیم تحصن داشتند، و بر ضد مجلس شورای ملی آن‌ها را منتشر می‌ساختند، در صورتی که این‌ها را روزنامه بدانیم، از مهم‌ترین ارگان‌های ارتجاع بود و اهمیت خاصی در تاریخ انقلاب ایران داشت.»

[504] علی‌اکبر قاضی‌زاده، ***جان‌باختگان روزنامه‌نگار***، پیشین، صص ۲۱۳ تا ۲۲۹.

«مسلمانان» را (در محله‌ی پامنار تهران)، «به مبلغ هفت صد و پنجاه تومان» برای ساختمان بانک استقراضی «به روس‌ها فروخت.» و این درحالی بود که مجتهدانی مانند طباطبائی و «ملاهای دیگر»، از این کار امتناع کرده بودند. (فقط قاضی و فقیه یا متولی‌ی ملک موقوفه می‌توانست به نام «تبدیل به احسن» در ملک وقفی تصرف کنند.)[۵۰۵] و غافل‌تر از این واقعیت که، اندیشه‌ی سرزنشِ اهل دین نسبت به حرکت‌های آزادی‌خواهانه، به خودی خود، اندیشه‌ای وارداتی از «غرب» است: چرا که در آغاز سده‌ی نوزدهم میلادی، ملاهای غربی- مانند بونالدو دومستر- که با جدائی دین از حکومت، اتوریته‌شان به خطر افتاده بود، «سعی می‌کردند گسستی را محکوم کنند که عصر روشنگری و انقلاب فرانسه در تاریخ غرب به وجود آورده بود.»[۵۰۶]

با مطالعه‌ی مجموعه‌ای از گفتارها و نوشتارهای این اندیشه‌ورزان نخبه، می‌بینیم که آبشخور فهم نظری‌ی آن‌ها از جهان، و از جمله «استعمار»، در فرهنگ مذهبی و آموزه‌های اسلامی سرچشمه‌های ژرفی دارد. و شگفتا که نفوذ اندیشه‌ها، و نوع صورت‌بندی‌ی مفهومی‌ی آن‌ها در رویاروئی با «غرب»، از مردم معمولی (مذهبی، و یا نیمه مذهبی) بسی فراتر رفت، و گستره‌ای وسیع از روشنفکران چپ و راست آن روزگار را پیمود: از قلمرو آفرینش‌های ادبی و هنری و پژوهش‌های آکادمیک گرفته تا قلمرو مبارزه‌ی پیشاهنگان سیاسی. در قلمرو آفرینش‌های ادبی، این تأثیر و نفوذ را- مثلاً- می‌توان در داستان‌های سیمین دانشور، احمد محمود، نمایشنامه‌های غلامحسین ساعدی و در بسیاری از شعرهای آن روزگار دید؛ و در قلمرو نوشتارهای آکادمیک، مثلاً- می‌توان از «تاریخ مذکر» (۱۳۴۹)، نوشته‌ی رضا براهنی یاد کرد؛[۵۰۷] و در قلمرو پیشاهنگان مبارزه‌ی سیاسی، می‌توان به این واقعیت نگاه کرد که اکثریت پیکارگران سیاسی‌ی آن روزگار، در لبنان و سوریه و فلسطینِ «مسلمان» آموزش نظامی دیدند و برای آزادسازی‌ی سرزمین فلسطین، دوش به دوش جنگ‌آوران فلسطینی، با اسرائیلِ «یهودی» جنگیدند؛ اما آن‌ها را با ویتنام و ویتکنگِ «غیرمسلمان»، و مبارزه‌ی بی‌امانش با «استعمار» و « امپریالیسم» چندان کاری نبود. شخصیت بیش‌تر این «نواندیشان» تا آن جا جامعه‌ی روشنفکری‌ی ایران را مجذوب و- انگار- مرعوب کرده بود، که هیچ یک از اندیشه‌ورزان یارای برخورد انتقادی با پیشنهادهای آن‌ها را در خود نمی‌دید. البته، چند «نقد» بر کتاب «غرب‌زدگی»ی آل احمد نوشته شد؛ که مهم‌ترین آن‌ها را داریوش آشوری نوشت. اما او نیز به بنیادهای ذهنی‌ی اثر نپرداخت، و نگاه او بیش‌تر بر ناروشنی‌ی منظور آل احمد از مفاهیم موجود در کتاب غرب‌زدگی تمرکز داشت. شاید متن «خشمگین از امپریالیسم، ترسان از انقلاب» نوشته‌ی امیرپرویز پویان، یکی از موارد نادری باشد که به گونه‌ای بنیادی با نظرات آل احمد برخورد کرده است؛ که آن هم پس از درگذشت آل احمد منتشر شد.[۵۰۸] برای نشان دادن زمینه‌ی «چشم و گوش بسته‌ای» که کلام جلال آل احمد در آن تخم پاشید، از یادداشت‌های دوران دانشجوئی‌ی علی‌اشرف درویشیان (داستان‌نویس درون‌مرزی) نقل قول می‌کنم که مدت کوتاهی در روزهای «سه شنبه»ی هر هفته در دانشسرای عالی شاگرد آل احمد بوده است:

---

۵۰۵ مهدی بامداد، شرح حال رجال ایران. برگرفته از: علی‌اکبر قاضی‌زاده، پیشین، ص ۲۱۷.

۵۰۶ سمیر امین، ***اسلام سیاسی در خدمت امپریالیسم***، تارنمای «نشر بیدار»، ۱۰ فوریه ۲۰۰۸:
http://nashrebidar.com/gunagun/ketabha/eslam%20siyasi/eslamsiyasi%20der%20khatmate.htm

۵۰۷ رضا براهنی در صفحه‌ی ۱۱۰ کتاب «تاریخ مذکر» چاپ تهران (۱۳۴۹) می‌نویسد:
«چه باید کرد؟ می‌توانم سخت بدبین باشم و بگویم که کاری نمی‌توان کرد؛ و می‌توانم خوشبین باشم و بگویم باید این کارها را کرد. و شاید باید فقط یک کار کرد. درون مردم، هنوز چیزی به صورت ایمان می‌جوشد، این ایمان در خاورمیانه دینی است؛ این ایمان به کمک روشنفکر واقعی‌ی منطقه و روحانیتی دست برداشته از خرافات و مویه و زاری، و تجددطلبان واقعی‌ی فرهنگی و اجتماعی، باید مردم را علیه استعمار تمدن غربی به سلاح جهاد مجهز کند، در مردم غرور جهاد با فساد تمدن غربی و مؤسسان آن و سردمداران آن ایجاد کند؛ این عقده‌ی مفعولیت فرهنگی و اجتماعی را از بین ببرد؛ و فرهنگی با ایمان، سازنده و خلاق را براساس یک زیربنای صحیح اقتصادی و اجتماعی بنیان گذارد.»

۵۰۸ امیرپرویز پویان، ***خشمگین از امپریالیسم، ترسان از انقلاب***، تارنمای «آرشیو اسناد اپوزیسیون ایران»:
http://www.iran-archive.com/start/2

> امروز برنامه دادند. در میان جدول، درسی داریم با نام آئین نگارش. در زیرش اسم آشنائی به نظرم می‌رسد. بدون عنوان دکترا. کتاب‌هایش را تا آن جا که به شهرستان می‌رسیده، خوانده‌ام: مدیر مدرسه، سه تار، هفت مقاله، غرب زدگی. خوشحال می‌شوم که خودش را هم خواهم دید. با سایر دوستان در میان می‌گذارم و معرفی‌اش می‌کنم. کم‌تر کسی او را می‌شناسد. ما ترکیبی هستیم از همه‌ی شهرستان‌ها، در حدود ده سال معلم دهات و شهرک‌ها بوده‌ایم و حالا آمده‌ایم دانشسرای عالی برای ادامه‌ی تحصیل و دیدن دوره‌ی یک ساله ی مدیریت. همه چشم و گوش بسته هستیم. چیزی نخوانده‌ایم. کسی را نمی‌شناسیم. راحتت کنم، هالو هستیم. [...] ساعت دوم با او درس داریم. چهار کلاس هستیم و صد و هشتاد نفر. همه‌ی ما را به آمفی تئاتر می‌برند. هجوم می‌بریم، نه برای درس، بلکه برای این که جلوتر بنشینیم. [...] روزهای سه‌شنبه کلاسمان صورت دیگری به خود می‌گیرد. مثل این که از خواب یک هفته بیدار می‌شویم. اصلاً از خواب همیشگی بیدار می‌شویم. پر از هیجان هستیم. احساس شهامت می‌کنیم. حتا کسانی که یک خط چیز ننوشته‌اند، دو صفحه مطلب می‌نویسند. [...] یکی از بچه‌ها بلند می‌شود و می‌گوید: «استاد من نمی‌توانم چیزی بنویسم. استعداد ندارم، چکار کنم؟» آل احمد می‌گوید: «اولاً استاد خودتی، ما معلمیم رئیس. ثانیاً استعداد یعنی کشک، این را هم غربی‌ها توی دست و پای ما انداخته‌اند. ثالثاً چرا نمی توانی بنویسی؟» [...] خواسته‌هائی داریم که رئیس دانشسرا با آن مخالف است. زمزمه‌ی اعتصاب بلند شده است. با آل احمد در میان می‌گذاریم. می‌گوید: «از حق خودتان دفاع کنید. بلند شوید اعتصاب کنید. من هم به دنبالتان.» این جمله‌ی :«من هم به دنبالتان»، هنوز در گوشم زنگ می‌زند. قرار می‌گذاریم در سر کلاس‌ها سکوت کنیم. سکوت می‌کنیم. [...حالا] همه‌ی ما را بیرون کرده‌اند. خیلی زود. در عرض یک روز ۱۸۰ ورقه‌ی پایان مأموریت تحصیلی به ما داده‌اند. چه زود!! در حالی که وقتی می‌خواستم ورقه‌ی معرفی به یکی از بیمارستان ها را بگیرم یک ماه طول می‌کشید. پشت میله‌ها ایستاده‌ایم و به همدیگر آدرس می‌دهیم برای مکاتبه. آل احمد را هم از دانشسرا بیرون کرده‌اند. [جز یکی از دانشجویان] دیگران مثل روز اول نیستند. فهرستی از کتاب‌های خوب تهیه دیده‌اند که به یکدیگر می‌دهند. چشم و گوششان باز شده. با سینه‌ای پر از امید و پر از کینه به شهرستان برمی‌گردیم. شوق مبارزه در لباس معلمی در چهره‌ی یکایک رفقا پیداست. وقتی که قدم برمی‌دارند حس می‌کنی که زمین زیر پایشان می‌لرزد و پایه‌های پوسیده‌ی خیلی چیزهای دیگر هم می‌لرزد.[۵۰۹]

در تأثیر پایداری که آموزه‌های این گروه از اندیشه‌ورزان بر بسیاری از روشنفکران و پیکارگران سیاسی‌ی ما گذاشت، همین بس که نسیم خاکسار در سال‌های نخستینِ تبعید می‌نویسد:

> در طی‌ی این چند سال اخیر، نامه‌های زیادی از برخی دوستان چپم که در سازمان‌های مختلف فعالیت می‌کرده یا هنوز هم فعالیت می‌کنند، داشته‌ام که از خودشان با بیان‌های مختلف انتقاد می‌کردند. آن‌ها به طور فردی، برخی‌شان به نظرات «آل احمد» رسیده‌اند، برخی به نظرات «خلیل ملکی» و دیگران.[۵۱۰] (یادآوری کنم که خلیل ملکی در زمره‌ی «نواندیشان دینی» برشمرده نمی‌شود؛ و بحث نسیم خاکسار در آن متن نیز به مقوله‌ی «نواندیشان دینی» مربوط نبوده است.)

تأثیر آموزه‌های متفکران مذهبی‌ی این دوره، چنان پایدار است که صرف نظر از کارکرد آن‌ها در بروز انقلاب ۵۷ و در شکل‌گیری‌ی نظام جمهوری‌ی اسلامی، بنیاد اندیشه‌های اکثریت قریب به اتفاق «اصلاح‌طلبان» جمهوری‌ی اسلامی، حتا در جایگاه «اپوزیسیونِ» سرکوب‌شده را نیز رقم زده‌اند؛ سیدمحمد خاتمی و مصطفی تاجزاده، به آیت‌الله مرتضی مطهری اقتداء می‌کنند؛ عبدالکریم سروش، راه علی شریعتی را می‌پیماید و پیشنهادهای نظری‌ی او را بسط می‌دهد؛ محمد قوچانی،

---

۵۰۹ علی‌اشرف درویشیان، ***چون و چرا: دست‌نوشته‌های سال*** ۱۳۴۵، تهران: نشر اشاره، ۱۳۸۱. **توضیح:** من این کتاب را ندیده‌ام. البته فشرده‌ای از آن به صورت یک مقاله، نخستین بار در نشریه‌ی «کلک»، شماره‌ی ۶ شهریور ۱۳۶۹ به چاپ رسیده بود. در عین حال، این متن در سال ۱۳۹۲ از سوی پست الکترونیکی‌ی «سهیلا ناجی» هم به من رسید.

۵۱۰ مجموعه‌ی **نظر آزمائی**، به پیشنهاد ناصر پاکدامن، نشریه‌ی «چشم‌انداز»، پاریس، بهار ۱۳۷۱/ ۱۹۹۲.

احمد فردید و رضا داوری را به عنوان «پست مدرن‌های معنوی» می‌ستاید؛ و این فهرست همچنان تا امروز ادامه دارد؛ به طوری که هنوز که هنوز است (۱۳۹۲)، هر نوع تفسیر دیگر از تاریخ، حتا از سوی پژوهشگر بی‌طرفی مانند جواد طباطبائی، به مثابه «آب به آسیای دشمن» ریختن است. جواد طباطبائی در پاسخ به این گونه معترضان می‌گوید:

> با شایعه‌سازی و افسانه‌بافی که نمی‌توان تاریخ نوشت یا با تحقیق تاریخی درافتاد. دو نمونه‌ی بارز این جعل تاریخ و افسانه‌بافی در دهه‌های اخیر، آل احمد و شریعتی بوده‌اند و از نوشته‌های آنان تاکنون هیچ نکته‌ای از تاریخ ایران روشن نشده است. اگر کسی آبی به آسیاب کسی ریخته، آل احمد بود با جعل اعتبار برای شیخ شهید.[۵۱۱]

در مقایسه‌ی کلیت اندیشه‌ورزان یادشده با اندیشه‌ورزان‌مان در سده‌های چهارم و پنجم هجری، از چشم‌انداز من، عقب‌گردی هولناک به دید می‌آید: ابن سینا و رازی و فارابی و بیرونی و ... کوشیدند تا با پل زدن بین آموزه‌های اسلام و آموزه‌های فلسفی‌ی یونان (مادر غرب)، و سهروردی، با پل زدن بین آموزه‌های اسلامی و حکمت خسروانی‌ی پیش از اسلام، فضائی برای تنفس از جبرِ «باید»های مذهبی‌ی اشغالگران ایران، و مجالی برای اندیشیدن فردی بیابند؛ اما اندیشه‌ورزان این دوره، با پل زدن بین آموزه‌های اسلامی و غربی، فضای تنفسی را که (گرچه هنوز تَنگ) به بهای یک سده تلاش ایرانی برای به دست آوردن آزادی‌ی گزینش پدید آمده بود، ناخواسته بستند. اگر اسیر تئوری‌ی توطئه نباشیم (که من امیدوارم نباشم) و اگر این اندیشه‌ورزان را «عامل امپریالیسم روس و انگلیس و امریکا» ندانیم، و اگر- مثلاً- از دعوا بر سر احتمال یا حتمیتِ «همکاری‌ی علی شریعتی با ساواک»[۵۱۲] فراتر رویم، تردید نیست که آن‌ها هم در آرزوی ایران آباد و آزاد و مستقل بوده‌اند. منتها، در گرد و غبارِ طوفانی که بین زیرساخت‌های معرفت‌شناسی و آموزه‌های نوینِ غربی در ذهنشان بر پا بود، «استقلال و هویت مستقل» را در گرو خوانش ویژه‌ی خود از آموزه‌های اسلام شیعی می‌دیدند. مثلاً، علی شریعتی، بالیده در یک خانواده‌ی روحانی- که افزون بر «استعمار»، با «استحمار» نیز در نبرد بود- تفسیرهائی از «اسلام راستین» عرضه می‌کند و راهکارهائی می‌نمایاند که سازه‌های هر یک در تناقضی آشکار با یکدیگر قرار دارند. به عنوان نمونه، در جلد اولِ «اسلام شناسی»، تشکیل شورای پس از درگذشت پیامبر اسلام و انتخاب خلیفه را «تحقق دمکراسی» ارزیابی می‌کند و در «بازشناسی‌ی هویت ایرانی- اسلامی»، به امر «خلافت» می‌تازد و آن را «اسلام ظالم» می‌نامد؛ او از سوئی، در یک سخنرانی می‌گوید: «آراء مردم هنوز نمی‌تونه رهبری‌ی شایسته را انتخاب کنه؛ گروه‌ها و مردم، رهبری‌ی شایسته را نمی‌تونه تشخیص بده»؛ از سوی دیگر، رهبری‌ی روحانیت را نیز سبب‌ساز استبداد سیاسی و نابودکننده‌ی دگراندیشان برآورد می‌کند؛ و از سوی سوم، «تشیع علوی» و تز «اجتهاد» در آن را در برابر «تشیع صفوی»

---

۵۱۱ ***گفت‌وگوی مهرنامه با سیدجواد طباطبایی: تسویه حساب با چریک‌ها*** ، تارنمای «مرکز دایرةالمعارف اسلامی»، ۱۵ تیر ۱۳۹۲: http://www.cgie.org.ir/fa/news/3521

۵۱۲ حجت‌الاسلام سید حمید روحانی (انارکی)، نویسنده‌ی کتاب دو جلدی‌ی «بررسی و تحلیلی از: نهضت امام خمینی»، در مقاله‌ای که در آذر ماه ۱۳۷۲ نوشت، یادآوری کرد که: در سال ۱۳۶۱ «بنا بر امر امام» اسناد ساواک را تحویل گرفته بود و «به بخش‌های از زندگی و اسناد پشت پرده‌ی شریعتی دست» یافته بود. و سپس افزود: «نگاهی عمیق‌تر به آثار شریعتی و زندگی‌ی پرفراز و نشیب علمی و سیاسی‌ی او نشان می‌دهد که او چه کار پرعظمت و بی‌نظیری کرد هاست. حالا ممکن است ارتباطی با رژیم و ساواک داشته، ولی نباید از نظر دور داشت که از روی تقیه بوده، و می‌خواسته آن‌ها را فریب دهد تا کار خودش را بکند.» دکتر جلال متینی- رئیس آن‌زمانی‌ی دانشکده‌ی ادبیات دانشگاه فردوسی در مشهد، که در همان دانشکده از نزدیک شریعتی را می‌شناخته- نیز در زمستان ۱۳۷۲ در پیرامون شریعتی متنی در ٦٥ صفحه نوشت، و همین سخنانِ حجت‌الاسلام حمید روحانی را بازگفت. اما تازه‌ترین تکرار این گزاره را در نوشته‌ی اکبر گنجی (از جمله معتقدان سابق به آراء شریعتی، و از جمله منتقدان این زمانی‌ی «فرهنگ ایرانی») می‌خوانیم، که افزون بر مسئله‌ی «همکاری با ساواک»، به «دروغ»های شریعتی پیرامون تخصیلات و ... نیز پرداخته است. به مآخذ زیر نگاه کنید:

- حجت‌الإسلام حمید روحانی، ***شریعتی از نگاهی دیگر***، کیهان هوائی، شماره‌ی ۱۰٦۰، ۱۷ آذر ۱۳۷۲، ص ۱۸.
- جلال متینی، ***خاطرات: دکتر علی شریعتی در دانشگاه مشهد (فردوسی)***، فصل‌نامه‌ی «ایران‌شناسی»، چاپ امریکا، سال پنجم، شماره‌ی ۴، زمستان ۱۳۷۲، صص ۸۳۴- ۸۹۹.
- اکبر گنجی، ***چه‌گونه شریعتی، شریعتی نمی‌شد؟*** تارنمای «روز آنلاین»، ۶ مهر ۱۳۹۰: http://www.roozonline.com/persian/opinion/opinion-article/archive/2011/september/28/article/-b2bc997d84.html

می‌ستاید؛ به طوری که معلوم نیست آن «اجتهاد» در کجای تز «اسلام بدون روحانیت» جا می‌گیرد. علی شریعتی، از سوئی، آزادی در پوشش و آرایش را به الگوبرداری از «عروسک فرنگی» متهم می‌کند؛ زن‌های مخاطب خود را به درستی و به زیبائی، به زیان‌های تقلید می‌آگاهاند؛ آن‌ها را به آزادیِ گزینش ترغیب می‌کند؛ اما خود، الگوی «فاطمه» را به آن‌ها تجویز می‌کند؛ آن هم نه «فاطمه»ی تاریخی و آن گونه که در متن‌های موجود آمده، بلکه «فاطمه»‌ای را که خود، در ذهن دوپاره‌ی «اسلامی/ اروپائی»ی دهه‌ی ۱۹۶۰ خود، برساخته بود.[۵۱۳] در این گونه بزنگاه‌هاست که سخن کارل مارکس درباره‌ی این «نواندیشان» ما به تمامی صدق می‌کند؛ با این تفاوت که پرش نواندیشان ما حتا به اندازه‌ی پرش «لوتر» بُرد نداشت:

> آدمیان هستند که تاریخ خود را می‌سازند ولی نه آن گونه که دلشان می‌خواهد، یا در شرایطی که خود انتخاب کرده باشند؛ بلکه در شرایط داده شده‌ای که میراث گذشته است و خود آنان به طور مستقیم با آن درگیرند. بار سنتِ همه‌ی نسل‌های گذشته با تمامی‌ی وزن خود بر مغز زندگان سنگینی می‌کند. و حتا هنگامی که این زندگان گوئی بر آن می‌شوند تا وجود خود و چیزها را به نحوی انقلابی دگرگون کنند، و چیزی یکسره نو بیافرینند؛ درست در همین دوره‌های بحران انقلابی است که با ترس و لرز از ارواح گذشته مدد می‌طلبند؛ نام‌هایشان را به عاریت می‌گیرند، و شعارها و لباس‌هایشان را؛ تا در این ظاهر آراسته و در خور احترام، و با این زبان عاریتی، بر صحنه‌ی جدید تاریخ ظاهر شوند. به همین ترتیب بود که لوتر نقاب پولس حواری را به چهره زد.[۵۱۴]

در مقایسه‌ی آراء اندیشه‌ورزان دوره‌ی مشروطیت با آراء اندیشه‌ورزان این دوره نیز به «وزنِ گذشته» برمی‌خوریم. منتها، اندیشه‌ورزان دوره‌ی مشروطه (همان‌ها که جلال آل احمد آن‌ها را «منتسکیوهای وطنی» نامید)، از مفاهیم اسلامی یاری گرفتند تا «مدرنیته»ی ایرانی را در جامعه‌ای سراسر «سنت»، موجه جلوه دهند و به رواج مفاهیمِ «آزادی»، «قانون» و «مدنیت» یاری رسانند. اما اندیشه‌ورزان این دوره، به یاریِ مفاهیم اسلامی/ شیعی به جنگ «مدرنیسمِ» نیم‌بندِ ایرانی رفتند، و در این رهگذر خطرناک، دانسته یا نادانسته، خواسته یا ناخواسته، از نفیِ مفهوم «آزادی» سر برکردند. در یک جمع‌بندیِ کلی می‌توان گفت: یکی از علت هائی که آموزه‌های علی شریعتی، جلال آل احمد، احمد فردید، مهدی بازرگان، و کلاً شخصیت‌های این گروه از اندیشه‌ورزان، به سرعت در میان مردم، به ویژه جوان‌های آن روزگار، جا باز کرد، همین دوپارگیِ ذهنی در کل جامعه‌ی ایران بود؛ چرا که این اندیشه‌ورزان، با استفاده‌ی از مصالح ناهمگونِ سنتی و مدرن برای «پُل»سازی‌های بی‌پایه، و با زبانی آکنده از واژگان و عبارت‌هائی مانند «سوسیولوژیسم»، «بیولوژیسم»، «ماشینیسم»، «اکونومیسم»، و «از خود بیگانگی»، «جانا سخن از» ذهنیت دوپاره‌ی مردم می‌گفتند؛ ذهنیتی که از یک سو قرن‌ها به ژرفای باورهای مذهبی/ مسجدی فروکشیده شده بود، و از سوی دیگر، به سوی ایده‌آل‌های «مدرنیسم»- مانند آزادی و عدالت اجتماعی و پیشرفت و استقلال- پر می‌کشید. در مجموعه‌ی این آرمان‌ها، دست کم، مفهوم «آزادی»، به معنای فردی و مدنیِ آن، از مفاهیم کلیدیِ «مدرنیسم» غربی بود، که با قانونمندی‌های «اسلام شیعی» - از «صفوی» تا «علوی»اش- سخت بیگانگی می‌کند. شاید به سبب درک همین بیگانگی بود که بسیاری از شخصیت‌های این گروه از اندیشه‌ورزان، برای پل زدن بین این دو، از مصالح «عرفان اسلامی»- مانند «وجود قدسیِ آدمی»- سود می‌جستند. غافل از این واقعیت آشکار که مفهوم «آزادی» در «عرفان اسلامی» (ضمن این که «مقید» به «راز»ی است که فقط «مرادِ به نور رسیده» آن را می‌شناسد)، با مفاهیم مربوط به «آزادی‌های مدنی»، فرسنگ‌ها فاصله

---

۵۱۳ برای دیدن مجموعه‌ی این گزاره‌ها، باید سراسر کتاب‌های «فاطمه، فاطمه است»، و «زن» را خواند.

۵۱۴ کارل مارکس، ***هژدهم برومر لوئی بناپارت***، «بازنویسی با پاره‌ای تغییرات، از روی ترجمه‌های باقر پرهام و محمد پورهرمزان و با استفاده از متن انگلیسی» توسط تارنمای «مارکس/ انگلس»:
http://marxengels.public-archive.net/fa/ME0682fa.html

دارد. کما این که بعداً دیدیم «مرادِ به نور رسیده»ای چونان روح‌الله خمینی، البته حق داشت هم از «خال لب معشوق» سخن براند، و هم به عنوان «ولی‌ی مطلقه» به کشتار هزاران تن از آدمیان دگراندیش فتوا دهد؛ تا ته ذهن و اتاق خواب مردم ایران را به دست «مریدان» بی‌شمار خود کنترل کند؛ با «استعمار» و «امپریالیسم» زد و بند کند؛ و در همان حال، «خال لب معشوقِ» دیگران را از کنار لب‌ها و حتا از صفحه‌ی کتاب‌ها خط بزند. اگر آزادی‌خواهان و استقلال‌طلبانی مانند علی شریعتی یا جلال آل احمد یا حمید عنایت آن قدر زنده می‌ماندند تا «مجلسِ» این «مراد به نور رسیده» را بیازمایند، تردید دارم که مانند احمد فردید به مرگ طبیعی می‌مردند. کما این که داریوش شایگان پس از ظهورِ «مراد»- که عوضی درآمده بود- به دامان همان «غرب»ی گریخت که از آن می‌گریخت و مردم را از آن می‌گریزاند؛ و طرفداران فعال اندیشه‌های شریعتی (مثلاً در گروه‌های «پیشتازان» و «موحدین») نیز در همان دهه‌ی ۱۳۶۰ از سوی لشگر حزب‌الله به زندان و شکنجه و اعدام محکوم شدند. در هر حال، تا که همجنسی‌ی ذهنیت این گروه از اندیشه‌ورزان را با ذهنیت جوان‌های آن دوره (یعنی مخاطبان آن‌ها) و نیز تأثیر آموزه‌های «اسلام حقیقی»ی این متفکران بر جوان‌های آن دوره را نشان دهم، بخش‌هائی از آخرین دفاع خسرو گلسرخی در دادگاه را، که خود نیز از طریق تلویزیون شاهدش بوده‌ام، از زبان علی‌اکبر قاضی‌زاده در این جا باز می‌گویم. پیش از آن اشاره کنم که بنا بر قرائن، این پیکارگر دلیر عضوِ رسمی‌ی هیچ یک از گروه‌ها و سازمان‌های مذهبی یا مارکسیستی نبود. اما در ابری از گرایش به هر دو سو، در دفاعیه‌ی خود، شرق و غرب تاریخ جنبش‌های مردم ایران را به هم می‌دوزد، و «اسلام حقیقی» را به آن چهل تکه، وصله می‌کند:

> در آخرین دفاع، گلسرخی، سخن خود را با حدیثی از امام حسین (ع): «ان‌الحیوة عقیدة والجهاد» آغاز کرد و افزود: «من ... نخستین بار، عدالت اجتماعی را در مکتب اسلام جستم و آن گاه به سوسیالیسم رسیدم. من ... برای جانم چانه نمی‌زنم و حتا برای عمرم. من قطره‌ای ناچیز از عظمت و حرمان خلق های مبارز ایران هستم؛ خلقی که مزدک‌ها، مازیارها، بابک‌ها، یعقوب لیث‌ها، ستارها، حیدرعمواوغلی‌ها، پسیان‌ها، میرزا کوچک‌ها، ارانی‌ها، روزبه‌ها، و وارطان‌ها داشته است. ... اسلام حقیقی در ایران همواره دِین خود را به جنبش‌های رهائی‌بخش ایران پرداخته است: سیدعبدالله بهبهانی و شیخ محمد خیابانی نمودار صادق این جنبش‌ها هستند و امروز نیز اسلام حقیقی، دِین خود را به جنبش‌های آزادی‌بخش ایران ادا می‌کند.» گلسرخی پس از اشاره به یک حدیث علوی در مورد فقر و غنا، نتیجه گرفت: «می‌توان در این تاریخ، از مولا علی (ع) به عنوان نخستین سوسیالیست جهان نام برد؛ نیز از سلمان پارسی و ابوذر غفاری. زندگی‌ی مولا حسین (ع) نمودار زندگی‌ی کنونی‌ی ماست که جان بر کف برای خلق‌های محروم میهن خود در این دادگاه محکوم می‌شویم. او در اقلیت بود و یزید، بارگاه و قشون و حکومت و قدرت داشت. او ایستاد و شهید شد. هر چند یزید گوشه‌ای از تاریخ را اشغال کرد، اما آن چه در تداوم تکرار شد، راه مولا حسین (ع) و پایداری‌ی او بود، نه حکومت یزید.»[۵۱۵] (نقطه‌چین‌ها از قاضی‌زاده است.)

در حالی که در درازنای سی و پنج سال گذشته پژوهشگران دینی در ایران و در تبعید، تناقض‌ها یا اشتباهات یا ناکارائی‌ی برخی از آراء دکتر شریعتی را در کتاب‌ها و مقاله‌های خود مستند کرده‌اند، آموزه‌های او در روشنفکران ما چنان تأثیر پایداری گذاشت که برخی از آن‌ها سال‌های متمادی پس از انقلاب و در حالی که در تبعید به سر می‌برند، و در حالی که با جمهوری‌ی اسلامی مبارزه می‌کنند، هنوز (خرداد ۱۳۹۱) از او به عنوان «آموزگار» یاد می‌کنند. به عنوان مثال، همنشین بهار، تاریخ‌پژوه (پژوهشگری که من از اطلاعات وسیع او در نوشته‌هایش، بسیار سود برده‌ام)، به محضی که انتقادی علیه علی شریعتی می‌شنود، چنان برآشفته می‌شود، که به جای برخورد با سخنِ مورد انتقاد، به سراغ پیشینه و حالِ شخص منتقد می‌رود؛ به جای نگاهی پژوهشگرانه به نظریه‌های علی شریعتی، از «محبوبیتِ» او در میان مردم، و از این که «در

---

۵۱۵ علی‌اکبر قاضی‌زاده، ***جانباختگان روزنامه‌نگار***، تهران: انتشارات جامعه‌ی ایرانیان، ۱۳۷۹، ص ۶۲۵.

خاطره‌ها باقی مانده» سخن می‌گوید؛ و از او به عنوان «آموزگاری مهربان» یاد می‌کند. این برآشفتگی زمانی روی داد که دکتر عباس میلانی در مصاحبه‌ای با سیامک دهقانپور در صدای امریکا، به تناقض‌های شریعتی (به ویژه در نظریه‌ی «امت و امامت» او) تاخت و از او به عنوان «جاده صاف کنِ تز ولایت فقیه» یاد کرد.[۵۱۶] همین جا بگویم که عباس میلانی در این مصاحبه، خود به گونه‌ای قاطعانه، شریعتی را «فرزند زمانه‌ی خود، زمانه‌ی پرگوئی، زمانه‌ی پرمدعائی‌هائی‌های بی‌پایه، زمانه‌ی قاطع‌گوئی، زمانه‌ی شهادت‌طلبی» خواند. البته، سخن قاطعانه در نکوهشِ سخن قاطعانه، به جای خود جای چون و چرا دارد. من در مبحث «گفتمان روشنفکر و روشنفکری» به شیوه‌ی برخوردهای قاطعانه‌ی عباس میلانی با «روشنفکران» پرداخته‌ام، و در این جا وارد آن مبحث نمی‌شوم. اما تا جائی که به بحث حاضر مربوط می‌شود، اشاره می‌کنم که در آن مصاحبه، سروش دباغ، پژوهشگر دینی و مدرس فلسفه در دانشگاه تورنتو، و حسن یوسفی اشکوری، پژوهشگر دینی (نویسنده‌ی کتاب «شریعتی، ایدئولوژی، استراتژی»، و بنیادگذار «دفتر پژوهش‌های فرهنگی دکتر علی شریعتی»)- هم حضور داشتند. یوسفی اشکوری، ضمن انتقاد به «کیفرخواستِ دکتر عباس میلانی» در این مصاحبه، به تناقض‌های شریعتی و به این که «برخی از آموزه‌های شریعتی تاریخ مصرفش گذشته و بعضی نیز قابل انتقاد هستند»، تکیه کرد. اما همنشین بهار، مقاله (یا دفاعیه‌اش) را با بحث «دیالتیک» گشود، تا درک درستِ شریعتی را از این گفتمان نشان دهد؛ و نشان دهد که چون سنتز (شدن)، از ویرانی‌ی کاملِ «تز» در برابر «آنتی تز» پدید نمی‌آید، پس شریعتی نیز آموزه‌های دینی را که بخش عمده‌ی هویت ایرانی بر آن استوار است، به همان سبب نگه داشته و آن را پایه‌ی آموزه‌های خود قرار داده است. تا این جا- چه با استدلال همنشین بهار موافق باشیم و چه نباشیم- با مقاله‌ای نظری روبه‌رو هستیم. اما همنشین بهار، که از عبارت/ برچسبِ «جاده صاف کن» و اشاره‌ی عباس میلانی به تناقض‌ها و «بندبازی‌ها» و «قاطعیت»های شریعتی، برآشفته است، ناگهان وارد مقوله‌هائی می‌شود که حیرت خواننده را برمی‌انگیزد. او پیشینه‌ی میلانی را «که به جای معارضه با رژیم آخوندپرور شاه، مدآحی‌ی رژیم سلطنتی را کرد تا از زندان آزاد شود»، ملاک قرار می‌دهد تا اندیشه‌های علی شریعتی را « که عمری با دستگاه ستم و روحانیون مرتجع درافتاد»، حقانیت بخشد؛ و به جای آن که در رد نظرات میلانی سند و مدرک و استدلال (که در آن دانش و دستی توانا دارد) ارائه دهد، مقاله‌اش را با ناسزاگوئی نسبت به منتقدانِ شریعتی به پایان می‌برد:

> بر خلاف کیفرخواست آقای میلانی که «شریعتی قبل از زندان هم آدم افسرده‌ای بود»، شور و ایستادگی‌ی آن آموزگار مهربان و هوشیار هنوز هم در خاطره‌ها باقی است و نوکران ارتجاع و استعمار اگر چه بیش از ۳۰ سال است پشت سرش صفحه می‌گذارند و هر کدام به نوعی مزّه می‌ریزند، نتوانستند و نمی‌توانند از محبوبیت وی بکاهند. وقتی برخی آگاهانه سوراخ دعا را گم می‌کنند، و عملکرد استبدادِ زیر پرده‌ی دین را به حساب امثال او [شریعتی] می‌گذارند، من بی اختیار به یاد انقلاب کبیر فرانسه می‌افتم: پس از بگیر و ببندهای «روسپیر» و اعدام امثال «دانتون»، و به ویژه بعد از آن که نظایر ناپلئون بناپارت، رنج و شکنج انقلابیون را به جنگ‌افروزی آلودند، برخی به جّد و طنز می‌گفتند: «**خوردم زمین تقصیر ولتر بود. افتادم توی جوب تقصیر روسو بود.**»[۵۱۷] (تأکید از همنشین بهار است.)

چنان که پیش از این اشاره کردم، تمامی‌ی اندیشه‌ورزان بومی‌گرای این دوره، ظاهراً «دینی/ مذهبی» نبودند؛ و همه‌ی آن‌ها، صرفاً بر اساس آموزه‌های شناخته‌شده‌ی مذهبی و در جهت تبلیغ آن‌ها حرکت نمی‌کردند. اما به علت رسوب معرفت‌شناسی‌ی دینی در ذهنیت خودشان (در میان همه‌ی علت‌های احتمالی)، از «اسلام» و «اسلامیت» و کارکردِ استبدادِ زیرِ پرده‌ی دین سر برکردند. مثلاً، شریعتی‌ی ضد «روحانیت» از «فاطمه»ی اسلام الگو می‌سازد و آن را به زنان ایران

---

۵۱۶ علی شریعتی: ***اسلام سیاسی و اسلام بدون روحانیت***، مصاحبه‌ی سیامک دهقانپور با عباس میلانی، حسن یوسفی اشکوری، و سروش دباغ، صدای امریکا، برنامه ی افق، ۲۹ خرداد ۱۳۹۱/ ۱۸ ژوئن ۲۰۱۲:
http://www.youtube.com/watch?v=SXQJ4PQ8Ick&feature=player_embedded

۵۱۷ همنشین بهار، ***علی شریعتی و «آوف هه بونگ Aufhebung»***، تارنمای «دیدگاه‌ها»، بازدید ۱۱ آذر ۱۳۹۱/ ۱ دسامبر ۲۰۱۲:
http://www.didgah.net/maghalehMatnKamel.php?id=27112

تجویز می‌کند؛ یعنی، خودش عملاً در جایگاه «روحانیت»ی می‌نشیند که برای مهار کردن آزادی های جنس «زن»، الگوهای فراوانی را تجویز می‌کند؛ و آل احمدِ کمونیستِ عضو حزب توده، «بر نعش آن عزیز»ی «نماز» می‌گزارد، که لفظ «آزادی» را با «اسلام» مغایر می‌دید، و «اسلام، و هر دینی» را آشکارا با «استبداد» این‌همان می‌دانست.

اما، گذشته از نواندیشانی که صرفاً در قلمرو دین گام می‌زدند، نقد روشنفکری‌ی بومی‌گرایانه‌ی این دوره یک سویه خواهد بود اگر در عین حال به انگیزه‌های بروز و پیامدهای مثبت این موج نگاه نکنیم. عبدی کلانتری، نویسنده و جامعه‌شناس تبعیدی، نقشه‌ی روان- جامعه‌شناختی‌ی بروز گروهی از روشنفکرانِ این دوره را- در متنی که به بهانه‌ی هفتاد و پنجمین سالگرد تولد داریوش آشوری نوشت- به زیبائی ترسیم کرده است؛ و اثرات مثبت این موج را نیز از دیدگاه خود برشمرده است. در بخشی از متن یادشده می‌خوانیم:

> [...] شجره‌ی سیاسی‌ی این تیره از روشنفکری‌ی معاصر ایرانی به گروهی باز می‌گردد که بعد از گذشت چند سال از تأسیس حزب توده‌ی ایران (حزب کمونیست)، از رهبری‌ی این حزب کنده شدند و با پیشوائی‌ی خلیل ملکی و جلال آل احمد، نیروی «سوّمی» را شکل دادند تا مُروّج نوعی از سوسیالیسم یا سوسیال دموکراسی‌ی ایرانی باشند. اعضای این گروه به مرور مثل مهره‌های رهاشده از یک نخ، در محیط روشنفکری‌ی سال‌های چهل و پنجاه شمسی پخش و پراکنده شدند و به دنبال علایق شخصی‌ی خویش رفتند. اگر این گروه پا به عرصه‌ی وجود نمی‌گذاشت، فعالیت فکری‌ی روشنفکران چپ در محدوده‌ی آثار لنین، استالین، مائو، و نظریه‌پردازان احزاب رسمی‌ی مسکو و پکن باقی می‌ماند. اما به یاری‌ی نیروی سومی‌ها (یا به تعبیر رسمی «رویزیونیست‌ها»)، نسلی از جوانان روشنفکر ایرانی این اقبال را یافتند تا با نام و نوشته‌های بزرگانی آشنا شوند همچون آنتونیو گرامشی، روزا لوکزامبورگ، نیکلای بوخارین، لئون تروتسکی، گئورک لوکاچ، آرنولد هاوزر، ژان پل سارتر، برتولت برشت، هربرت مارکوزه، کریستوفر هیل، اریک هابسبام، شارل بتلهایم، پل سوئیزی، و پل باران؛ و دریابند که جهانِ فکری‌ی متأثر از مارکسیسم بسیار وسیع‌تر و متنوع تر از جزوه‌های حزبی و درس‌نامه‌های مبتنی بر «ماتریالیسم دیالکتیکِ» آکادمیسین‌های روسی است. در دهه‌های چهل و پنجاه شمسی در ایران، در نشریات روشنفکرانه‌ای چون «اندیشه و هنر» و«جهان نو» با همکاری‌ی گروهی از نویسندگان و مترجمانِ خوش‌فکر و مستقل، نظیر خلیل ملکی، حسین ملک، ناصر وثوقی، منوچهر هزارخانی، مصطفی رحیمی، ابوالحسن نجفی، جلال آل احمد، امین عالیمرد، احمد اشرف، ناصر پاکدامن، هما ناطق، فریبرز سعادت، محمود کیانوش، باقر پرهام، رضا براهنی، مصطفی شعاعیان، داریوش آشوری، و چند تنی دیگر توجه به تحقیقات اجتماعی‌ی مردم‌شناسانه، نشر رساله‌های جامعه‌شناختی، و توجه به تئوری‌های مدرنیزاسیون از جدیتی برخوردار شد که پیش از آن از مباحث روشنفکری و عمدتاً «ادبی» غایب بود. سرانجام از درون بحث‌های روشنفکری و غیرآکادمیکِ همین گروه بود که مسئله‌ی مهم «نسبت فرهنگِ ما با مُدرنیته»، یا همان «گفتمان غربزدگی» (و نقد این گفتمان) متولد شد؛ گفتمانی که در صدد بود نخست دلایل وابستگی و واپسماندگی‌ی اقتصادی، علمی، و فرهنگی‌ی ایران را بفهمد (آسیب‌شناسی کند)، و آن گاه برای آن‌ها درمان یا راه حلّی اصیل و بومی پیدا کند: راه سومی برای رشد و توسعه‌ی اقتصادی و فرهنگی، متمایز از کمونیسم روسی و وابستگی‌ی نواستعماری به غرب. توجه به نویسندگان ضداستعماری نظیر فرانس فانون، امه سزر، آلبر مِمّی، مهاتما گاندی، و جواهر لعل نهرو، ترجمه‌ی «ادبیات ملتزم»، و معرفی‌ی مبارزات آزادی‌بخش ملی در جهان سوّم، برای برخی از این روشنفکران که «بومی‌گرا»تر بودند از فوریتی خاص برخوردار شد. [...][۵۱۸] (تمامی‌ی علامت‌های سجاوندی از عبدی کلانتری است.)

عبدی کلانتری، پس از این مقدمه، به سراغ نوشته‌های کسی می‌رود که نخستین نقد منفی را بر «غربزدگی»ی آل احمد نوشته بود؛ یعنی به سراغ برخی از نوشته‌های کلیدی‌ی دیروز و امروز داریوش آشوری می‌رود، و با تحلیلی علمی،

---

[۵۱۸] عبدی کلانتری، ***داریوش آشوری، سرگشته میان جهان‌های شرقی و غربی***، تارنمای«بی بی سی»، ۱۱ نوامبر ۲۰۱۳/ ۲۰ آبان ۱۳۹۲:

http://www.bbc.co.uk/persian/arts/2013/11/131111_l44_ashouri_anniversary_kalantari.shtml

«جایگاه استیصال‌آمیز» آشوری را در «سرگشتگی»ی هنوز بین «جهان‌های شرقی و غربی» نشان می‌دهد. در خوانش من، عبدی کلانتری در این متن، ضمن نشان دادن پایداری‌ی درازمدت تأثیر «نقد گفتمان غربزدگی»ی آل احمد در فاهمه‌ی آشوری (به عنوان نمونه‌ای از اندیشه‌ورزانِ تز «بازگشت به خود و به میراث گذشته و به فرهنگ دینی»)، ذات ناکارای «راه حل» این اندیشه‌ورزان را نیز به نقد کشیده است.

***

هما ناطق، در پیش‌گفتار کتاب «کارنامه‌ی فرهنگی‌ی فرنگی در ایران»، ص ۹، می‌نویسد:

> [در این کتاب] بی‌آن که پاسخی داشته باشم، این پرسش را پیش کشیده‌ام که آنان که بی‌چون و چرا به ستایش و الگوبرداری از فرنگ برآمدند، چه طرفی از دانش و پیشرفت فرنگی بستند که به کار نبستند؛ و یا آنان که دانش و پیشرفت فرنگ را به هیچ گرفتند و نکوهیدند، برای رهایی از واماندگی، چه کالای بهتری در بساط داشتند که رو ننمودند؟

اگر نتوانیم برای بخش اول این پرسش پاسخی قانع‌کننده و سرراست پیدا کنیم، پاسخ بخش دوم را همین روشنفکران مذهبی/ دینی/ بومی‌گرا و ضدغربی، به تاریخ عرضه کرده‌اند؛ یعنی، «کالای بهتر» را با نام «معنویت شرقی»، «اسلام راستین»، «اسلام حقیقی»، «اسلام رحمانی» شناسائی کرده‌اند. پرسش من اما این است که آیا این متفکران تنها در مخالفت با تجددگرائی‌ی شاه به این رویکرد رسیده بودند، یا کلاً تابوی تجدد و دورشدن از ریشه‌های دینی/ مذهبی، ذهنیت آنان را برآشوبیده بود؟ تا به پاسخ احتمالی‌ی این پرسش نزدیک شوم، به یکی از واپسین گفت‌وگوهای احسان نراقی مراجعه می‌کنم. پیشاپیش بگویم که احسان نراقی (۱۳۰۵- ۱۳۹۱) یکی از شخصیت‌های برجسته‌ی آکادمیک ایران بود. این دانش‌آموخته‌ی رشته‌ی حقوق در دانشگاه‌های تهران و ژنو و سوربن، در دوران پادشاهی‌ی محمدرضا شاه پهلوی در پست‌هائی مانند ، مدیریت «مؤسسه‌ی مطالعات و تحقیقات اجتماعی»، مسئول «اداره‌ی جوانان» در یونسکو (سازمان آموزش علمی و فرهنگی‌ی سازمان ملل متحد)، و ریاست «مؤسسه‌ی تحقیقات و برنامه‌ریزی‌ی علمی و آموزشی‌ی کشور» خدمت کرد؛ با شاه و دربار حشر و نشر داشت؛ و از دو رئیس جمهور فرانسه هم نشان لژیون دو نور گرفته بود. احسان نراقی، اما در عین حال، از خانواده‌ای پشت اندر پشت روحانی می‌آمد و با آیت‌الله ابوالقاسم کاشانی بستگی‌ی خانوادگی داشت؛ ابوالحسن بنی‌صدر، حسن حبیبی، و صادق قطب‌زاده، از ملی/ مذهبی‌های آن دوره (و از سردمداران انقلاب ۵۷)، از جمله تربیت‌یافته‌های مکتب او بودند. نراقی، به شهادت کتاب‌هایش، اگر نه در گروه نواندیشانِ صرفاً «مذهبی»، دست کم، در گروه «سنت‌پرستان/ غرب‌ستیزان/ شرق‌ستایانِ» این دوره جایگاهی بی‌چون و چرا داشت.[۵۱۹] در گفت‌وگوئی که در سال پایانی‌ی زندگی با یکی از نشریه‌های ایران داشت، مصاحبه‌گر از احسان نراقی می‌پرسد:

> - فکر نمی‌کنید که همین نگاه شیفته‌وار به سنت و جوامع شرقی باعث شد که نتوانید به پدیده‌ی ایدئولوژیک‌شدنِ سنت و انقلاب اسلامی پی ببرید؟
>
> **احسان نراقی**: من مطابق با شرایط آن زمان سخن می‌گفتم. من که به صورت ذاتی از تفاوت‌های جوامع شرقی و غربی سخن نگفتم [...] آن زمان یکی از مسائلی که گریبانگیر جامعه بود، موج غرب‌گرائی‌ی افراطی و ریتم غربی‌شدنِ سریعی بود که در همه‌ی ابعاد در جامعه نفوذ و رسوخ می‌کرد و تمام تلاش‌ها و دیدگاه‌های من بر این زمینه استوار بود که

---

[۵۱۹] برای آشنائی با آراء احسان نراقی ، از جمله، به کتاب‌های موجود در فهرست زیر نگاه کنید:
- احسان نراقی، ***علوم اجتماعی و سیر تکوینی‌ی آن***، تهران: انتشارات دانشگاه تهران، ۱۳۴۴.
- احسان نراقی، ***غربت غرب***، تهران: امیرکبیر، ۱۳۵۳.
- احسان نراقی، ***آن چه خود داشت***، تهران: انتشارات امیرکبیر، ۱۳۵۵.
- احسان نراقی/ اسماعیل خوئی، ***آزادی، حق عدالت*** (مناظره‌ی اسماعیل خوئی با احسان نراقی) تهران: انتشارات جاویدان، ۱۳۵۶.

توضیح: من کتاب اخیر را ندیده‌ام.

چشم‌بسته و کورکورانه از هر چه که غربی است پیروی نکنیم و یک تعادلی در عملکردهایمان داشته باشیم. تمام حرف من این بود که سعی کنیم درباره‌ی امور غربی و شرقی دست به گزینش بزنیم.[۵۲۰]

اما از سخنان بعدی‌ی او در همین گفت‌وگو چنین برمی‌آید، که نه تنها برای خود او «گزینشِ» آگاهانه‌ای در کار نبوده، بلکه او نیز «چشم‌بسته» از ذهنیت مذهبی‌ی رایج در خانواده‌ی معمم خود «پیروی» کرده است:

در میان شخصیت‌های مذهبی‌ی مؤثر بر نهضت مشروطه، من شخصاً به سیدجمال‌الدین اسدآبادی هم به دیده‌ی احترام می‌نگرم که همو بود که ابراز کرد: وحدت اسلام به همراه اخذ علوم تجربی؛ و این که تجدد با اسلام منافاتی ندارد. اصولاً خانواده‌ی من اعم از پدربزرگ، پدر و عمویم (ملاعلی نراقی) همگی تحت تأثیر سیدجمال بودند. او در عین حال دچار اشتباه خیلی از مشروطه‌طلبان ما چون آخوندزاده و... نشد که خواهان ترویج مفاهیمی چون آزادی در خارج از چارچوب سنت بودند و حتا در مواردی ضد مذهب عمل می‌کردند. [...] (مأخذ پیشین.)

و با این ذهنیت، جای شگفتی نیست که احسان نراقی زمانی بر گفته‌ی اسدآبادی صحه بگذارد، که «منافاتِ» «اسلام» و «تجدد» را شخصاً در جمهوری‌ی اسلامی تجربه کرده است. اما آن چه را که متفکرانی مانند احسان نراقی، از آموزه‌های پدرخوانده‌ی خود (سیدجمال‌الدین اسدآبادی- افغانی) نخوانده بودند- و گویا که نوآمدگانِ این فکرت هنوز هم آن را نخوانده‌اند- این پیام نهانی است که اسدآبادی در نامه‌ای محرمانه نوشته بود:

ما سرِ مذهب را نمی‌بُریم، مگر به وسیله‌ی خود مذهب. بنابراین اگر اکنون به ما بنگرید، ما را پارسایانی تارک دنیا، و پرستندگانی نمازخوان که هرگز از فرمان خدا سر نمی‌پیچند، می‌بینید.[۵۲۱]

با پیدایش و عملکرد اسلام سیاسی در ایران، برخلاف آرمان مهدی بازرگان و شریعتی و آل احمد و نراقی و دیگر «نواندیشان دینی»، چنین به نظر می‌آید که هدف نهائی‌ی این معلم و قائد اعظم سی و سه سال است که در حال شدن است. به عنوان نمونه، نه هنوز از «بریدنِ سرِ مذهب»، بلکه از بریدن مردم از تقدس این نوع «پرستندگانِ نمازخوان» و البته ایده‌های قرون وسطائی‌شان، خواننده‌ام را به خبر زیر رجوع می‌دهم:

[...] آیت‌الله مهدوی کنی، رئیس مجلس خبرگان، در بخش دیگری از سخنان خود که در مراسم عمامه‌گذاری‌ی جمعی از دانشجویان دانشگاه امام صادق [۲٤ آبان ۹۰] بود گفت که وی هنگامی که پانزده ساله بوده روحانی شده است. وی سپس با ذکر خاطره‌ای گفت که در قدیم مردم به روحانیت فحش نمی‌دادند: «آیت‌الله برهان لباس خود را به من عاریه داد و من فقط یک عمامه خریدم. پس از این که مراسم عمامه‌گذاری به پایان رسید و با اتوبوس به منزل باز می‌گشتم، همه به من می‌گفتند آخوند کوچولو. در قدیم مردم روحانیت را مسخره نمی‌کردند بلکه خوشحال شده بودند که کسی در این سن کم روحانی و معمم شده است.» رئیس مجلس خبرگان در پایان نیز گفت که در حال حاضر «عده‌ای ممکن است بر ما صلوات بفرستند و عده‌ای هم فحش دهند.»[۵۲۲]

---

۵۲۰ علی عظیمی نژادان، ***بی‌منطق غرب‌ستیز نیستم: گفت‌وگوئی منتشرنشده با احسان نراقی***، روزنامه‌ی «اعتماد»، ۲۹ بهمن ۱۳۹۱.

521 Elie Kedouri, ***Afghani and 'Abduh: An Esaay on Religious Unbelief and Political Activism in Modern Islam***, New York: The Humanities Press, 1966, P. 15.

توضیح: مترجم این جمله‌ها، فروزنده فرزاد است. به مأخذ زیر نگاه کنید:
http://www.rahetudeh.com/rahetude/baziye-sheytani/html/baziye-sheytani-2.html

۵۲۲ سروش جعفری، ***رییس مجلس خبرگان: همه بیایید جمهوری‌ی اسلامی را حفظ کنیم***، تارنمای «خودنویس»، ۲٤ آبان ۱۳۹۰:

* در درازنای همین دوران بود که جوانان انقلابیِ سرخورده از سازمان‌های کوچک و بزرگی مانند «نهضت علی»،[۵۲۳] «نهضت آزادی»، «جبهه‌ی ملی» و «حزب توده»، به مارکسیسم انقلابی روی آوردند، و از پیوستنِ هسته‌های کوچکی از آن‌ها- در شهرهای مشهد و تبریز و ساری و تهران- سازمان عظیم «چریک‌های فدائیِ خلق ایران» فراروئید، و جوان‌های معترض و به ویژه کنشگران جنبش دانشجوئی را گروه گروه به خود فراخواند.[۵۲۴] در درازنای همین دوران بود که مجموعه‌ی نهادهای مذهبی، عمدتاً، «نهضت آزادی» و مدرسه‌ها و نوشتارهایش، زمینه‌ی پیدایش و رشد سازمان عظیم «مجاهدین خلق ایران» با ایده‌ی «اسلام رهائی‌بخش» را فراهم آورد. این سازمان- به ویژه پس از کشته شدن احمد رضائی (از چریک‌های مجاهد) در حمله‌های ساواک (۱۱ بهمن ۱۳۵۰)، به سرعت در میان مردم مذهبیِ ایران جا باز کرد. در درازنای همین دوران بود که ساواک، با هدف شناسائیِ دانشجویان چپ و راه یافتن به سازمان‌های چپ، چند نهاد، از جمله «سازمان انقلابیِ حزب توده» را آفرید،[۵۲۵] که البته، در شناسائیِ برخی از دانشجویان و پیکارگران طیف چپ (به ویژه در کنفدراسیون جهانیِ دانشجویان ایرانی) موفق بود؛ اما با این کار، و با هجوم به نهادهای مذهبی و زندانی کردن کوشندگان سیاسیِ چپ و راست، زندان‌هایش را با توشه‌ی اندیشه‌های جوان با گرایش‌های چپ، از یک سو، و با گرایش‌های سنتی/ مذهبی از سوی دیگر، مجهز کرد؛ به گونه‌ای که، انسجام بسیاری از سازمان‌ها و گروه‌ها، و دگرگونی در آرایش نیروهای مخالف، عمدتاً در زندان صورت پذیرفت. به عنوان نمونه، محمد حنیف‌نژاد و سعید محسن (پایه‌گذاران سازمان مجاهدین خلق ایران)، که به جرم شرکت در تظاهرات جبهه‌ی ملیِ دوم و پخش تراکت دستگیر شده بودند، در گفت‌وگوی حضوری با سران جبهه‌ی ملی و نهضت آزادی در زندان، بن‌بست را دیدند، از موضع مسالمت‌آمیزِ جبهه‌ی ملی و نهضت آزادی برگذشتند، و به موضع آشتی‌ناپذیرِ مبارزه‌ی مسلحانه رسیدند.[۵۲۶] ردّ پای این تغییر را می‌توان در شخصیت‌های سازمان چریک‌های فدائیِ خلق ایران، مانند بیژن جزنی- که ابتدا در محدوده‌ی سازمان جوانان حزب توده و نیز در چارچوب سیاست‌های جبهه‌ی ملی فعالیت داشت، و پس از اسارت‌های مکرر به مارکسیسم گرایش یافت- دنبال کرد. جزنی، حتا «تاریخ سی ساله‌ی ایران» را در زندان و بر روی کاغذ سیگار نوشت، و تکه تکه از زندان به بیرون فرستاد.[۵۲۷] همچنین، گرویدن فرخ نگهدار- عضو ارشد کمیته‌ی مرکزیِ سازمان چریک‌ها- به حزب توده و

---

http://www.khodnevis.org/persian/%D8%B1%D8%B3%D8%A7%D9%86%D9%87%E2%80%D9%5.html

[۵۲۳] امیرپرویز پویان، از جمله پایه‌گذاران «سازمان چریک‌های فدائیِ خلق ایران»، پیش از تشکیل هسته‌ی این سازمان در مشهد، در گروه مذهبیِ «نهضت علی» عضویت داشت؛ و مسعود احمدزاده، همفکر او در مشیِ مبارزه، دارای گرایش شدید ملی- مذهبی بود. به مأخذ زیر نگاه کنید:

❖ ***روایت محمدتقی سیداحمدی از «سازمان چریک‌های فدائیِ خلق ایران» در گفت‌وگو با سهلا بهاردوست***، (بخش دوم)، تارنمای «اخبار روز»، ۱۶ اردیبهشت ۱۳۹۰:

http://www.akhbar-rooz.com/article.jsp?essayId=37721

[۵۲۴] به عنوان نمونه از متن‌هائی که به چه‌گونگیِ گرایش دانشجویان ایران به مبارزه‌ی مخفی پرداخته‌اند، به متن زیر نگاه کنید:

❖ مهدی فتاپور، ***جنبش دانشجویی در سال های ۴۷ تا ۵۲***، تارنمای «عصر نو»، ۱۰ ژوئیه ۲۰۱۰:

http://asre-nou.net/php/view_print_version.php?objnr=10607

برگرفته از نشریه‌ی آرش، چاپ پاریس.

[۵۲۵] عباس میلانی، که مدت کوتاهی عضو این سازمان بوده، در کتاب «داستان دو شهر» به ساختگی‌بودن این سازمان اشاره کرده است. همچنین، در بسیاری از متن‌هائی که در دهه‌ی ۱۳۸۰ خورشیدی منتشر شد، این موضوع تأیید شده است. اما یرواند آبراهامیان در کتاب معتبر «ایران بین دو انقلاب: از مشروطه تا انقلاب اسلامی» بدون اشاره به قلابی بودن آن، از این سازمان سخن گفته است. من در جلد چهارم مجموعه‌ی حاضر پیرامون این سازمان به تفصیل سخن گفته‌ام.

[۵۲۶] محمد حنیف‌نژاد روز اول بهمن ۱۳۴۱ در رابطه با عضویت در نهضت آزادی دستگیر شد، و تا زمان آزادی-۱۱ شهریور ۱۳۴۲- همبندِ مهندس مهدی بازرگان، یدالله سحابی و آیت‌الله بهشتی بود. سعید محسن نیز یک بار در ۱۴ آذر ۱۳۴۰ به جرم پخش تراکت و شرکت در متینگ جبهه‌ی ملی بازداشت شد، و بار دوم، نیز در اول بهمن ۱۳۴۰، به جرم عضویت در «کمیته‌ی دانشجویان نهضت آزادی» به زندان افتاد.

[۵۲۷] در چند مأخذ به این واقعیت اشاره شده است. به عنوان مثال به مأخذ زیر نگاه کنید:

❖ محمود باباعلی و ناصر مهاجر، ***تاریخ را چگونه نباید نوشت (مروری بر حاشیه‌نویسی‌های آقای سرکوهی درباره‌ی بیژن جزنی و سازمان فدائی)***، تارنمای نشریه‌ی «آرش»، بازدید ۱۴ شهریور ۱۳۸۸:

http://www.arashmag.com/content/view/421/47/1/12/

گروانیدنِ «اکثریت» اعضاء سازمان چریک‌ها به این حزب، در زندان فرصت عمل یافت. تغییر جهان‌بینیِ خسرو گلسرخی و تقی شهرام نیز نمونه‌های دیگری از تأثیر گردهم‌آئی‌ها و مذاکرات این جوانان در کمون‌های زندان هستند. به عنوان نمونه، لطف‌الله میثمی (از مجاهدین اولیه) پیرامون تغییر جهان‌بینیِ خسرو گلسرخی می‌نویسد:

> گلسرخی در زندان شماره‌ی ۳ قصر با کاظم ذوالانوار [از مجاهدین خلق] هم‌بند بود. کاظم خیلی با او کار کرده بود، حتا خطبه‌های نهج‌البلاغه را برایش خوانده بود. [...] یك روز مهندس عبدالعلی بازرگان [پسر مهدی بازرگان] تعریف می‌کرد که وقتی [در زندان] با گلسرخی قدم می‌زدم، می‌گفت: این روشنفکران ما خیلی ذهنی هستند. اگر من آزاد بشوم، اولین کاری که می‌کنم، می‌گویم روشنفکران باید نسبت به اسلام تجدید نظر کنند.[۵۲۸]

البته، خسرو گلسرخی- متأسفانه- «آزاد» نشد، اما متن آخرین دفاعیه‌ی او، شاهد گویائی بر این «تجدید نظر» در زندان است.

***

پس از اعلام مواد «انقلاب سفید» و پس از رویداد خونین ۱۵ خرداد ۴۲، ایده، تئوری، و پرَکتیس مبارزه با دستگاه شاه تغییری اساسی یافت. محمدرضا شاه پهلوی که مطالبه‌های جبهه‌ی ملی و نهضت آزادی- در چارچوب قانون اساسیِ مشروطه- را برنمی‌تابید، و فعالیت‌های صرفاً فرهنگیِ نویسندگان و دانش‌آموختگان مستقل، و خبرگان هوادار- یا سابقاً هوادارِ- حزب توده را سرکوب می‌کرد، با شتابی فزاینده با پدیده‌ای روبه‌رو شد که هم مطالباتش از چارچوب «اجراء قانون اساسیِ مشروطه» برگذشته بود، و هم ابزار رویاروئی را از «تظاهرات» و «راهپیمائی» و «اعلامیه»، به اسلحه تبدیل کرده بود. البته، جمعیت «فدائیان اسلام»، حدود دو دهه پیش از این تاریخ، «پاسخ» را در«لوله‌ی تفنگ» یافته بود، و بذر مشیِ مسلحانه را در زمین سرسخت مبارزه با رژیم شاه کاشته بود. در درازنای دهه‌ی ۱۳۴۰ خورشیدی، اما، این «پاسخ»- در کنار پاسخ‌های مشابهی که از سوی جنبش‌های رهائی‌بخش مردم کشورهای دیگر جهان به حکومت‌های خودکامه و به استعمار داده شده بود و داده می‌شد، از سوی انبوهی از جوانان ناراضی و مبارز ایران- و البته با ایدئولوژی‌های متفاوت- استقبال شد. در این دوره، افزون بر گروه‌های مذهبی/ سنتی- مانند «جمعیت مؤتلفه‌ی اسلامی» (که ترکیبی بود از ائتلاف شش هیئتِ بازاری/ مذهبی- از جمله فدائیان اسلام- و طرفدار آیت‌الله خمینی)، هسته‌های کوچکی از مبارزان سیاسی- و شگفتا که بدون خبر از وجود یکدیگر، در این جا و آن جای ایران تشکیل شد، که مشیِ مبارزه‌ی مسلحانه را تنها راه برخورد با این رژیم برآورد می‌کردند. گرچه نخستین مرحله‌ی هدف همه‌ی این گروه‌ها براندازیِ رژیم شاه بود، و خط مشیِ همه‌ی آن‌ها مبارزه‌ی مسلحانه بود، اما بنا بر ایدئولوژی‌ای که هر یک دنبال می‌کرد، می‌توان مجموعه‌ی آن‌ها را عمدتاً – و با اندکی مسامحه- در سه دسته‌ی «مذهبی/ سنتی»، «مارکسیست»، و «مذهبی/ نواندیش» به ملاحظه گذاشت. هدف یا چشم‌انداز نهائیِ گروه‌های سنتی/ مذهبی، رسیدن به حکومت اسلامی، به زعامت مرجع تقلید شیعیان (آیت‌الله خمینی) بود؛ هدف یا چشم‌انداز نهائیِ همه‌ی شاخه‌های مارکسیست، رسیدن به حکومت سوسیالیستی بود؛ و هدف یا چشم‌انداز نهائیِ مذهبی‌های نواندیش، رسیدن به حکومتی بود بر اساس الگوئی که از حکومتِ «علی» (امام اول شیعیان) می‌شناختند. برخی از گروه‌های این دسته‌ی اخیر، آموزه‌های مارکسیستی را در آموزه‌های علی و دیگر امامان مذهب شیعه (یا برعکس) یافته بودند. از این چشم‌انداز کلی بود که ایدئولوژیِ هیچ یک از این پیکارگران، به ویژه از نیمه‌ی دوم دهه‌ی ۱۳۴۰ خورشیدی، برای «سلطنت مشروطه» و تبعاً، برای محمدرضا شاه پهلوی و خاندانش، جائی باقی نگذاشته بود. به بیانی دیگر، رویاروئیِ پیکارگران، حالا کلِ «نظام» سیاسی/ اقتصادی/ فرهنگیِ شاه را نشانه گرفته بود؛ و برخورد شاه و رزمندگان مخالف او نسبت به یکدیگر- آشکارا به عنوان دو

[۵۲۸] خاطرات لطف‌الله میثمی، *آن‌ها که رفتند*، انتشارات صمدیه، ۱۳۸۲، ص ۳٤٤.

«دشـمن»- به فاز مرگ یا زندگی رسـیده بود. و این نکته‌ای اسـت که در مطالعه و داوری پیرامون این برش از تاریخ، نمی‌تواند از دایره‌ی دید پژوهشگر/ داور غایب بماند.

***

جنبش چریکی: گرچه رسـیدگی به روند تشـکیل سـازمان‌های سـیاسـی، تئوری/ پرَکتیس هر یک، و چه‌گونگی‌ی ادغام/ ائتلاف/ انشعاب‌های این سازمان‌ها در دستور کار نوشته‌ی حاضر نیست، اما بنا به «هدفِ» مجموعه‌ی حاضر، مروری بر ساخت و بافت و عملکرد آن‌ها را در این جا بایسته می‌دانم. از آن رو که در بندهای پیشین و نیز در بندهای پسین کتاب حاضـر، پیرامون مهم‌ترین گروه از دسـته‌ی «مذهبی/ سـنتی»، یعنی «هیئت مؤتلفه‌ی اسـلامی»، و نقش آن در مبارزه با رژیم شاه اشاره‌وار سخن گفته‌ام، در این جا به مروری گذرا بر دو سازمان مهم و اثرگذارِ دیگرِ آن دوران، یعنی «سازمان چریک‌های فدائی‌ی خلق ایران» و «سازمان مجاهدین خلق ایران» بسنده می‌کنم.
در درازنای سـه دهه‌ی گذشـته، بی‌اغراق، ده‌ها «تاریخچه»، صـدها متن در ژانرهای «جسـتارِ گزارشـی/ تفسـیری»، «یادواره»، «خاطرات»، و «گفت‌وگو»، از سـوی پژوهشـگرانِ تاریخ، یا از سـوی پیکارگرانِ بازمانده از آن دوران، با دیدگاه‌های مختلف پیرامون این دو سازمان سیاسی (به ویژه «سازمان چریک‌های فدائی‌ی خلق ایران»)، در تبعید، منتشر شـده اسـت. با پرسـه زدن در گوشـه و کنار این گروه از متن‌ها، پیرامون برخی از گزاره‌های معین، به تفاوت‌ها و گاه به تناقض‌هائی برمی‌خوریم که- در کنار خلاء اطلاعاتی پیرامون این دو سازمان زیرزمینی- از ترسیم یک نقشه‌ی مشخص از هر یک از آن‌ها جلوگیری می‌کنند. از سـوی دیگر، «پژوهشـگرانِ» نظام بعدی، یعنی جمهوری‌ی اسـلامی، نیز با اسـتفاده‌ی گزینشـی از منابع سـاواک (از جمله، متن بازجوئی‌ی زندانیانِ زیر شـکنجه‌ی سـاواک)، یا از متن بازجوئی‌های زندانیانِ زیر شـکنجه در زندان‌های همین نظام، پیرامون هر یک از این دو سـازمان و شـخصـیت‌های کلیدی‌ی هر یک از این دو سـازمان، کتاب‌های قطوری منتشـر کرده‌اند، که در تصـویر نهائی‌ی مجموعه‌ی آن‌ها، زُدایشِ اندیشـه‌ی چپ و مقاومتِ رادیکال، از یک سو، و تاریخ‌سازی برای جمهوری‌ی اسلامی از دیگر سو، آشکارا به دید می‌آیند. در نتیجه، تنها راهی که برای شـناختن نسـبی‌ی این دو سـازمان باقی می‌ماند، خواندن متن‌های موجود، با خوانشـی تطبیقی و اسـتنتاجی، توسط کسی است که بی‌نظرانه در این راه گام می‌گذارد. من بدون ادعای «رهروی» در این راهِ خونین، در فشرده‌ی زیر می‌کوشم که تا جای ممکن، بر متن‌هائی تکیه کنم که خودِ این سازمان‌ها در کوران مبارزه، به شـکل‌های جزوه یا کتاب یا بیانیه و اطلاعیه منتشر کرده‌اند؛ یا، در صورت عدم دسترسی به متن‌های اصیل، گزاره‌هائی را منعکس کنم که در اکثر متن‌های مخالف و موافق مشترک هستند. هم‌چنین، با آگاهی از کنشِ «چپ‌زُدائی» و هدفِ «تاریخ‌سازی» در دسـتگاه‌های تبلیغاتی‌ی جمهوری‌ی اسـلامی، خود را از اسـتفاده از برخی گزاره‌های اطلاعاتی (به عنوان مواد خام) در کتاب‌هائی که این دستگاه‌ها پیرامون مبارزه‌ی این دو سازمان با رژیم محمدرضا شاه پهلوی نوشته‌اند، بی‌نیاز نمی‌بینم.
پیرامون این گزاره که سازمان چریک‌های فدائی‌ی خلق ایران- و بعداً، «بخش مارکسیست‌شده‌ی سازمان مجاهدین خلق» (سازمان «پیکار»)- پیرو کدام یک از شاخه‌های «مارکسیسمِ» موجود بودند، من در این جا سکوت می‌کنم. چرا که یافتن پاسخ احتمالی، نیازمند کند وُ کاو در معیارهای هر شاخه از مارکسیسم، و مقابله‌ی آن‌ها با عناصر درونی‌ی تئوری‌های هر یک از این سازمان‌ها است؛ که البته موضوع سخن من در این مجموعه نیست. منتها همین جا اشاره می‌کنم که «سازمان چریک‌های فدائی‌ی خلق»، خود را «مارکسیست/ لنینیست» می‌خواند؛ اما برخی از تحلیل‌گران، این سـازمان را (پیش از انقلاب ۵۷) متأثر از «مارکسیـسم/ مائوئیسـم» هم برآورد کرده‌اند. در خوانش من از متن‌های تئوریک این سـازمان نیز، (عمدتاً در مقوله‌ی مبارزه در «روستا» یا «شـهر»)، رگه‌هائی از هر دو طیف به دید می‌آید. نکته‌ی گمراه‌کننده‌ی دیگر در برخی از تاریخچه‌ها این است که هر یک از گروه‌های منشعب از این سازمان عظیم (که پس از انقلاب ۵۷ به چندین شاخه تقسـیم شـد)، تاریخچه‌ی متفاوت و متناقضـی برای این سـازمان قائل هسـتند و آن دیگری را به «تحریف تاریخ» و به «مصـادره‌ی نام سـازمان» متهم می‌کنند؛ نام‌هائی را از تاریخچه‌ی سـازمان حذف می‌کنند، یا کم بهاء می‌دهند؛ خطاها را به

حساب گروه مقابل می‌ریزند و اعتبارها را به حساب خود. من در جلد چهارم مجموعه‌ی حاضر نمونه‌هائی از این روش برخورد را شکافته‌ام و این ویژگی را نشان داده‌ام. اما هدف من در این بخش از سخن، نه نگارش «تاریخچه»، نه تکیه بر این یا آن شخصیت در «پایه‌گذاری» یا «رهبری»ی سازمان‌ها، بلکه- عمدتاً- ترسیم گوشه‌هائی از ذهنیت جاری در سپهر اندیشگی‌ی انبوهی از جوان‌های ایران است که در مقام اپوزیسیونِ آشتی‌ناپذیرِ محمدرضا شاه پهلوی تمام قد ایستاد؛ تمام قد به خاک افتاد؛ و- با این که به هدف نهائی/ آرمانی‌ی خود نرسید- در پیدایش انقلاب ایران و نابودی‌ی رژیم پادشاهی سهمی انکارناپذیر داشت. البته در این رهگذر نیز- به ناگزیر- بزنگاه‌های تاریخی‌ای را ثبت خواهم کرد، که ممکن است مرا هم در عنوان «تحریف‌گر تاریخ»- یا دست بالا، در عنوان‌های «ناآگاه» یا «گمراه»- بگنجاند. از این رو، می‌کوشم تا نظرهای متناقض پیرامون گزاره‌های مورد اختلاف را در متن یا در زیرنویس بیاورم.

سازمان چریک‌های فدائی‌ی خلق ایران: به فشرده‌ترین کلام می‌شود گفت که: شالوده‌ی بزرگ‌ترین سازمان‌های مارکسیستی‌ی ایران، یعنی «سازمان چریک‌های فدائی‌ی خلق ایران»، از سوی شخصیت‌های جوان و دانش‌آموخته‌ای پی‌ریزی شد که در دوران تحصیل در دبیرستان و دانشگاه، عضو حزب توده یا جناح چپ جبهه‌ی ملی‌ی دوم، یا هر دو، بودند؛ در محدوده‌ی سیاستِ این نهادها در انجمن‌های دانش‌آموزی و دانشجوئی با دیکتاتوری‌ی شاه مبارزه کرده بودند؛ برخی‌شان در نوجوانی، زندان و بازجوئی را تجربه کرده بودند؛ این نوع مبارزه را بی‌ثمر یافته بودند؛ در ضمن مطالعه‌ی فردی و گروهی، با مفاهیم مارکسیست/ لنینیستی و مارکسیست/ مائویستی، و با کارکرد مبارزه‌ی موفق آن‌ها در کشورهای دیگر، آشنا شده بودند؛ از شرایط عینی و ذهنی‌ی جامعه‌ی ایران- به زعم خود- تحلیل مشخصی داشتند؛ این شرایط را در چارچوب اصول دریافتی‌ی خود- از مارکسیسم- سنجیده بودند؛ و بر اساس همه‌ی این یافته‌ها، مشی‌ی مسلحانه را تنها راه مبارزه با رژیم «وابسته»ی شاه - به عنوان نماینده‌ی امپریالیسم در ایران- تشخیص داده بودند. صرف نظر از این اطلاعات کلی، و تا جائی که به «تاریخچه»ی این سازمان مربوط می‌شود، ما هم‌اکنون- عمدتاً- دو روایت در دست داریم که پیرامون مسئله‌ی پایه‌گذاران این سازمان و بینش و کنش مبارزاتی‌ی آن‌ها، با هم در تضاد و تقابل قرار دارند. مبنای یکی از روایت‌ها (که من به گونه‌ای قراردادی، در این جا، آن را «تاریخچه‌ی نخست» می‌نامم)، مجموعه‌ی متن‌های دست اولی است که توسط پیشاهنگان این سازمان نوشته شده بود، در کنار انبوهی متن که از شهریور ۱۳۵۳ تا زمان انقلاب در نشریه‌های «نبرد خلق» و «۱۹ بهمن تئوریک» پیرامون گزاره‌هائی منتشر می‌شدند که به عنوان منبع تدوین یک تاریخچه به کار می‌آیند. این سازمان منتشر می‌شد. پاراگراف زیر- برگرفته از شماره‌ی ۴ «۱۹ بهمن تئوریک»، تیر ماه ۱۳۵۴- شاید فشرده‌ترین متنی باشد که چه‌گونگی‌ی روند تشکیل این سازمان را در «تاریخچه‌ی نخست» متعین می‌کند:

> سازمان چریک‌های فدائی‌ی خلق از رشد و پیوند دو جریان و یا دو گروه، که قبل از وحدت در فروردین ماه ۵۰ مستقل از هم عمل می‌کردند، بوجود آمد. این دو گروه عبارت بودند از گروه پیشتاز جزنی- ظریفی و گروه پیشاهنگ احمدزاده- پویان- مفتاحی، که قبل از ادغام، هر کدام مراحل تکاملی‌ی پُر فراز و نشیبی را پشت سر گذاشته، و از اواسط سال ۴۹ تا فروردین ۵۰، طی‌ی یکسری همکاری‌های عملی در مبارزه و تبادل نظرهای تئوریک، سازمان چریک‌های فدائی‌ی خلق را بوجود آوردند.

اکنون ما می‌دانیم که به لحاظ بینش تئوریک و استراتژی‌ی مبارزه، در مرکزیت این سازمان هرگز اتفاق نظر کاملی روی نداد؛ اما پس از ادغام این دو گروه، کلیتی با نام «سازمان چریک‌های فدائی‌ی خلق ایران»، دارای تاریخچه‌ای بود که تا پیش از انشعاب بزرگ، و تقسیم سازمان به «اقلیت» و «اکثریت» (۱۳۵۹)، «روایتِ دوم»ی از آن وجود نداشت. در نتیجه، هر تفاوتی که بین روایت‌های «اکثریت» و «اقلیت» پیرامون تاریخچه‌ی این سازمان بروز کرد، عمدتاً به مقطع آن انشعاب مربوط می‌شود؛ که رسیدگی به چه‌گونگی‌ی آن به بحث حاضر مربوط نیست. منتها، مبنای «روایت دوم»ی که من

در این جا به گوشه‌هائی از آن می‌پردازم، عمدتاً، گواهی‌ها و یادمانده‌های اشرف دهقانی است، از آن چه که در همان دوران «ادغام» بر این سازمان گذشته بود؛ و البته در رابطه با گزاره‌های «روایت نخست». اشرف دهقانی، از نوجوانی در حلقه‌ی مارکسیست‌های تبریز و در پیوند با گروه احمدزاده/ پویان در این سازمان فعالیت داشت؛ به زندان ساواک گرفتار آمد؛ از زندان گریخت؛ در سال‌های پایانی‌ی رژیم سلطنتی، از سوی مرکزیت سازمان- با هموند دیگری به نام «محمد حرمتی‌پور»- به عنوان «نماینده‌ی سازمان در خارج از کشور» فعالیت داشت؛ بنا به روایت‌ها، پس از قیام ۲۲ بهمن و در اسفند ۱۳۵۷ به ایران بازگشت؛ با خط مشی‌ی تازه‌اعلام‌شده‌ی سازمان، و برخورد آن با نظام جمهوری‌ی اسلامی مخالفت کرد؛ و در جزوه‌ای که با عنوان «مصاحبه با رفیق اشرف دهقانی» (خرداد ۱۳۵۸) منتشرشد، با پافشاری بر مواضع تئوریک احمدزاده/ پویان، خط مشی‌ی تازه‌ی سازمان (مبارزه‌ی سیاسی/ ایدئولوژیک به جای مبارزه‌ی مسلحانه/ نظامی) را رد کرد. او، که پس از انتشار آن «مصاحبه» تاکنون، رهبری‌ی سازمانی با عنوان «چریک‌های فدائی‌ی خلق ایران» (چفخا) را به عهده دارد، در تمام سال‌های تبعید نیز بر سر آن مواضع (یعنی مبارزه‌ی مسلحانه، هم استراتژی و هم تاکتیک) باقی مانده است. در این جا البته، سخن از چرائی‌ها و چه‌گونگی‌های این گزینش مطرح نیست. اما انگیزه‌ی حضور او در مبحث حاضر، «تاریخچه»‌ای است که او در سخنرانی‌ها و نوشتار خود- به ویژه در دهه‌ی اخیر- برای «جنبش جنگل» و آغاز سازمان چریک‌های فدائی‌ی خلق نوشته است. اشرف دهقانی با بیان‌های متفاوت بر این گزاره‌ها پافشاری دارد که:

«تئوریسین‌های اصلی‌ی چریک‌های فدائی‌ی خلق، امیرپرویز پویان و مسعود احمدزاده بودند»؛ یا: «مؤسس اصلی‌ی گروه جنگل [سیاهکل] رفیق کبیر و تا حدی گمنام، رفیق غفور حسن‌پور بود»؛ یا: «بدعت گذاران این روش کار [تحلیل مناسبات حاکم بر جامعه] در دهه‌ی ۴۰ در ایران هم، رفقای گرانقدر ما بهروز دهقانی و صمد بهرنگی بودند»؛ یا: «رفیق جزنی و رفقای انقلابی‌ی همراهش به وظیفه‌ای که تاریخ در نیمه‌ی اول دهه‌ی چهل به عهده‌شان گذاشته بود به خصوص با مقاومتشان در زندان، به خوبی پاسخ دادند. و به همین خاطر نامشان به عنوان رفقای انقلابی همواره در یادها زنده خواهد ماند. اما آن رفقا و گروهشان، هر چه که بود و بودند، ربطی به چریک‌های فدائی‌ی خلق نداشته و ندارند.»

با این که تاریخچه‌ی اشرف دهقانی (و البته، همفکران او) مورد انتقادهای فراوانی قرار دارد،[۵۲۹] اما من- تا حقی از آیندگان باطل نشود- در این فشرده، «تاریخچه‌ی نخست» را (که بیش‌ترِ اندیشه‌ورزان سیاسی در مفاد آن اتفاق نظر دارند) مبنای گزارش خود قرار می‌دهم، و در حین گزارش‌هایم، به استدلال‌های اشرف دهقانی (به عنوان «تاریخچه‌ی دوم») می‌پردازم. همین جا یادآوری می‌کنم که متن‌هائی که من به عنوان مبنای «تاریخچه‌ی دوم» از آن‌ها سود می‌جویم، عمدتاً عبارت‌اند از: یک) مقاله‌ی «از پاسخ به ضرورت زمان تا گسست از تئوری»، که اشرف دهقانی آن را به مناسبت چهلمین سالگرد سیاهکل منتشر کرد؛[۵۳۰] دو) متن مقاله‌ی او، با عنوان «فرخ نگهدار و تحریف تاریخ چریک‌های فدائی‌ی خلق».[۵۳۱]

---

[۵۲۹] به عنوان نمونه‌ای از انتقادها- که از زبانی سالم و مستدل نیز برخوردار است- به مأخذ زیر نگاه کنید:
❖ شباهنگ راد، ***بازنویسی تاریخ چریک‌های فدائی‌ی خلق توسط «اشرف دهقانی»***، تارنمای «آزادی‌ی بیان»، آرشیو دوم، ۲ ژوئیه ۲۰۱۱/ ۱۱ تیر ۱۳۸۹:
http://azadi2011b.wordpress.com/2011/07/02/%D8%A8%D8%A7%D8%B2%D9%86%

[۵۳۰] اشرف دهقانی، ***از پاسخ به ضرورت زمان تا گسست از تئوری: تجربه‌ای تاریخی از چریک‌ها***، تارنمای «بی بی سی»، ۱۷ ژوئن ۲۰۱۱/ ۲۷ خرداد ۱۳۹۰:
www.bbc.co.uk/persian/iran/2011/110617_siahkal_ashrar_dehghani.shtml
این متن در تارنمای «سیاهکل» نیز- البته با عنوان کامل- منتشر شد:
❖ اشرف دهقانی، ***از پاسخ به ضرورت زمان تا گسست از تئوری (تجربه‌ای تاریخی از چریک‌های فدائی‌ی خلق در دهه‌ی ۵۰)***، تارنمای «سیاهکل»، خرداد ۱۳۹۰:
http://www.siahkal.com/index/mid-col/az-pasokh-be-zarorat-ta.pdf

[۵۳۱] اشرف دهقانی، ***فرخ نگهدار و تحریف تاریخ چریک‌های فدائی‌ی خلق***، نشریه‌ی «پیام فدائی» از انتشارات «چریک‌های فدائی‌ی خلق ایران»، شماره‌ی ۱۴۴، بهمن ۱۳۹۱، صص ۵ تا ۱۱.

***

بیژن جزنی (۱۳۱۶- ۱۳۵۴)، با توشه‌ای از دانش فلسفی و مارکسیستی و تجربه‌هائی که از نوجوانی در حزب توده، در جبهه‌ی ملی، و در دوران مکرر اسارت در زندان بدست آورده بود،[۵۳۲] پس از رسیدن به این دریافت که حزب توده‌ی پس از کودتای ۲۸ مرداد ۳۲ عملاً خنثا شده، و رژیم شاه با هر نوع انتقاد و مقاومتِ مسالمت‌آمیزِ جبهه‌ی ملی نیز سر ستیز دارد، با همفکری‌ی چند تن از یارانش، به لزوم مبارزه‌ی قهرآمیز رسید. این بود که از سال ۱۳۴۵ به بعد، با همفکری‌ی حسن ضیا ظریفی، عباس سورکی، علی‌اکبر صفائی فراهانی، محمد صفاری آشتیانی، زرار(ضرار) زاهدیان و حمید اشرف،[۵۳۳] با این تحلیل که رژیم محمدرضا شاه- افزون بر دیکتاتوری و استبداد سیاسی- «سرمایه‌داری‌ی وابسته» است و در راستای منافع امپریالیسم حرکت می‌کند، خط مشی‌ی مبارزه‌ی چریکی را به عنوان تنها راه درهم شکستن اتوریته‌ی رژیم، کشاندن توده‌ها به مبارزه، و گشودن راهی برای تحقق جامعه‌ای رها از استثمار و استعمار تشخیص داد، و نظر خود را در تابستان ۱۳۴۹ در متنی که در زندان نوشت، با عنوان «آن چه یك انقلابی باید بداند»، فرموله کرد.[۵۳۴] من این کتاب (یا جزوه) را ندیده‌ام. اما یک گزاره‌ی مهم از آن را به اعتبارِ بازگفتِ اشرف دهقانی، در این جا منعکس می‌کنم: «هر گونه خیال‌بافی در اوضاع فعلی پیرامون زمینه‌های بالفعل انقلاب دهقانی و جنگ‌های دهقانی با ناکامی روبه‌رو خواهد شد.»[۵۳۵] اما نوشته‌های تئوریک بعدی‌ی بیژن جزنی نشان می‌دهند که این تشخیص، الزاماً به منزله‌ی نفی‌ی بیژن جزنی نسبت به مبارزه‌ی مسلحانه‌ی پیشاهنگان در روستا و شهر نبوده است. کما این که او در سلسله مقاله‌هائی که- باز در زندان- نوشت و به نام خودش منتشر شد، گفته است:

---

[۵۳۲] عبدالعلی معصومی- با استفاده از مقاله‌های «جنگی درباره‌ی زندگی و آثار بیژن جزنی» و به ویژه مقاله‌ی ناصر مهاجر- در تاریخچه‌ی مختصر خود می‌نویسد: پدر، دایی‌ها و عموهای بیژن عضو حزب توده بودند. مادر بیژن نیز از فعالان حزب توده بود. پس از شکست حزب دموکرات در آذربایجان در آذر ۱۳۲۶، پدرش به‌علّت همکاری با حزب دموکرات آذربایجان به شوروی پناهنده شد. [آغاز نقل قول از ناصر مهاجر]: بیژن «در ده سالگی به صفوف سازمان جوانان حزب توده پیوسته (سال۱۳۲۶) و تا آخرین روزهای زندگی‌ی این سازمان، جزء اعضای ازخودگذشته‌ی آن بوده. با کودتای ۲۸ مرداد ۱۳۳۲، در هسته‌های مقاومتِ "حزب" نام نوشته و تا روزی که مسئله‌ی مقاومت مسلّحانه در برابر کودتا منتفی نشده، در خانه‌ی حزبی و در حالت آماده‌باش زیسته. در یکی دو سال اول کودتا هم چند بار بازداشت شده و بار اول چند روز و بار دوم چند هفته و بار سوم شش ماه حبس کشیده؛ با این که هژده سالش تمام نشده بود. در سال‌های ۳۸- ۱۳۳۴ به همراه شماری از جوانان همسن و سالش ــ که همدیگر را در زندان شناخته بودند و همدست و همداستان شده بودندــ به بازبینی و جمع‌بندی‌ی مشی و عملکرد حزب توده پرداخته؛ از موضعی انقلابی از این جریان بریده و همراه با رفقایش در جنبش‌های مردمی‌ی این دوره و مهمتر از همه، اعتصاب کارگران کوره‌پزخانه‌های تهران و رانندگان اتوبوس شرکت داشته. در تنفّس کوتاه سال‌های ۴۲- ۱۳۳۸ و تحرّك سیاسی‌ی این دوره، یکی از رهبران مورد احترام جنبش دانشجوئی شده و از سرآمدان جناح چپ غیرتوده‌ای و گردانندگان "جبهه‌ی ملّی‌ی دانشگاه"؛ و هم از این رو زیر ذرّه‌بین پلیس سیاسی و در معرض آزار و بازداشت‌هایی قرارگرفته، که گاه چندین ماه به‌درازا می‌کشید. با این که از برجسته‌ترین سازمان‌دهندگان جنبش‌های اجتماعی و بسیج‌کننده‌ی اعتراض‌های توده‌ای به شمار رفته. نمونه‌ی آخرش برگزاری‌ی آئین هفتم و چهلم جهان پهلوان تختی بود که بیژن جزنی و گروهش نقش به سزائی در آن داشتند... (جُنگی درباره‌ی زندگی و آثار بیژن جزنی، پاریس: انتشارات خاوران، ۱۳۷۸، مقاله‌ی ناصر مهاجر، ص۳۹۶)». به مأخذ زیر نگاه کنید:

- عبدالعلی معصومی، ***سازمان چریك‌های فدائی‌ی خلق ایران***، تارنمای «ایران نبرد»، بازدید: ۱۰ ژوئیه ۲۰۱۲:

http://www.iran-nabard.com/40%20sal/ali_masoumi.htm

توضیح: من کتاب «جنگی درباره‌ی زندگی و آثار بیژن جزنی» را دیده‌ام و در اختیار دارم. اما در این جا ترجیح دادم که از عبدالعلی معصومی نقل کنم، تا فشرده‌ای از اطلاعات خانوادگی‌ی جزنی نیز در این جا منعکس شود.

[۵۳۳] در مصاحبه‌ای که شهلا بهاردوست با فرخ نگهدار انجام داد، فرخ نگهدار می‌گوید که او حمید اشرف را به بیژن جزنی معرفی کرده بود و بعداً هم خودش او را عضوگیری کرده بود. اما تا جائی که من دیده‌ام، در هیچ «تاریخچه»‌ای، نام فرخ نگهدار در فهرست «پایه‌گذارانِ»این سازمان قید نشده است. به مأخذ زیر نگاه کنید:

- شهلا بهاردوست، ***به یاد و گرامی‌داشت حمید اشرف: مصاحبه با فرخ نگهدار یار نزدیک حمید اشرف***، تارنمای «عصر نو»، ۲۰ آذر ۱۳۸۹:

http://www.asre-nou.net/php/view.php?objnr=12615

[۵۳٤] کتاب ***آن چه یک انقلابی باید بداند***، تا سال‌ها به «علی اکبر صفائی فراهانی» نسبت داده می‌شد. میهن جزنی (همسر بیژن جزنی)، در صفحه‌ی ٦٧ کتاب «جنگی درباره‌ی زندگی و آثار بیژن جزنی» نوشت، که نویسنده‌ی این کتاب، بیژن جزنی بود، اما چون خود او در زندان بود، آن را به نام «ابوعباس» (نام مستعار علی اکبر صفائی فراهانی) منتشر کرد.

[۵۳۵] اشرف دهقانی، ***فرخ نگهدار و تحریف تاریخ چریک‌های فدائی‌ی خلق***، نشریه‌ی «پیام فدائی»، شماره‌ی ١٦٤، بهمن ۱۳۹۱، زیرنویس، ص ۱۱.

> چون هدف از اولین اقدامات مسلحانه تغییر فضای سیاسیِ جامعه و به طور کلی تبلیغ مسلحانه است، عملیات مسلحانه در روستا و شهر می‌توانند یکدیگر را کامل کنند. و گذشته از آن، وجود سلول‌های مسلح در کوه و شهر، به مثابه یك عامل حمایت‌کننده‌ی تاکتیکی، می‌تواند مورد استفاده قرارگیرد. [...] جنبش روستایی می‌تواند کادرهایی را که در شهر امکان ادامه‌ی مبارزه ندارند، به خود جلب کنند و با اجرای عملیات مسلحانه، قوای دشمن را در مناطق وسیعی به خود مشغول دارد و این مناطق را به طور وسیعی «سیاسی» کند. همچنین، جنبش چریکیِ شهری با برهم‌زدن نظم شهرها، می‌تواند قسمتی از قوای دشمن را تجزیه کرده و سیستم عصبیِ دشمن را نیز مورد آسیب قراردهد.[۵۳۶]

در هر حال، این گروه- که در ابتدای کار، میان اعضاء با نام رمزیِ «شرکت» شناسائی می‌شد.[۵۳۷] - پیش از دست زدن به عمل مسلحانه، از سوی نیروهای امنیتی ضربه‌ی سنگینی خورد. بدین ترتیب که، روز ۱۷ بهمن ۱۳٤٦- حدود سه هفته پس از برگزاریِ مراسم شبِ هفتِ «جهان‌پهلوان تختی» (۲۳ دی ۱۳٤۸)- بیژن جزنی و عباس سورکی- که از برگزارکنندگان این مراسم بودند، دستگیر شدند. ساواك از طریق «ناصر آقایان»- همشهریِ عباس سورکی و از هموندان او در «سازمان جوانان حزب توده»- که با ساواک همکاری می‌کرد، به فعالیت‌های این «شرکت» پی برده بود. روز ۱۸ بهمن ٤٦، ساواک تعداد دیگری از اعضاء بازمانده‌ی گروه، به نام‌های سعید (مشعوف) کلانتری (دائیِ بیژن جزنی)، محمد چوپانزاده، حسن ضیاء ظریفی، عزیز سرمدی، احمد جلیل افشار، زرار (ضرار) زاهدیان، دکتر سیروس شهرزاد، را (که در صدد خروج از کشور بودند) دستگیر کرد. این اعضاء نیز «در نتیجه‌ی تماس با "تشکیلات تهرانِ" حزب توده، که ساواک در آن نفوذ کرده بود، در دام شبکه‌ی عباس شهریاری افتادند و دستگیر شدند.»[۵۳۸] تمام این زندانیان، در دادگاه نظامی محاکمه شدند و بیژن جزنی به ۱۵ سال زندان محکوم شد. بیژن جزنی، تا زمانی که بر تپه‌ی اوین تیرباران شود، در زندان بسر برد؛ متن‌های تئوریک را در زندان نوشت؛ و بنا بر «تاریخچه‌ی نخست»، پروژه‌های عملیاتیِ گروه را از درون زندان هدایت کرد.

حمید اشرف، علی‌اکبر صفائی فراهانی، و محمود صفاری آشتیانی، بازمانده‌های گروه جزنی بودند، که اولی به جذب نفرات تازه پرداخت، و دو تن دیگر برای آموزش‌های نظامی و کمک به نهضت آزادی‌بخش فلسطین از ایران خارج شدند. گروهی که حمید اشرف گردآورد، با سلاح‌هائی که آن دو تن از فلسطین وارد ایران کردند، در سال ۱۳٤۹ آماده‌ی نبرد مسلحانه علیه رژیم شده بود. این گروه، که بعدها به «گروه جنگل» معروف شد، رویداد موسوم به «سیاهکل» را پدید آورد. یکی از اختلاف نظرها، در این بزنگاه تاریخی ریشه دارد که پروژه‌ی «سیاهکل» زمانی به عمل گرائید که بیژن جزنی در زندان بود. اشرف دهقانی بر این گزاره تأکید دارد که حمید اشرف و یارانش، پس از زندانی شدنِ بیژن جزنی، اصولاً «گروه جدیدی را متکی بر تجارب گروه پیشین با خط مشیِ تازه» سازمان داده بودند، و رویداد سیاهکل فرآورده‌ی خط مشیِ این گروه تازه- به نام «گروه جنگل»- بود.[۵۳۹] اشرف دهقانی، علت جدانگریِ خود را این گونه

---

[۵۳٦] بیژن جزنی، ***جمع‌بندیِ مبارزات سی ساله‌ی اخیر ایران***، تهران: انتشارات سازمان چریک‌های فدائیِ خلق ایران، ۱۳۵۷، ص ۱۰.
توضیح: بخش‌هائی از متن «جمع‌بندی...»، در نشریه‌ی زیرزمینیِ «۱۹ بهمن» یا در رادیوهای برون‌مرزی در همان دوران منتشر شده بود. تنها در سال ۱۳۵۷ بود که مجموعه‌ی آن بخش‌ها به صورت کتاب در ایران چاپ شد و توزیع همگانی یافت.

[۵۳۷] محمدرضا شالگونی می‌نویسد: «آن طور که من از عزیز سرمدی و عباس سورکی در زندان برازجان در سال ۱۳۵۰ شنیدم، اسم رمز آن [گروه جزنی] در میان خود اعضاء گروه "شرکت" بود.» به مأخذ زیر نگاه کنید:
- ❖ محمدرضا شالگونی، ***متن‌هائی که ما را به فضای دهه‌ی چهل می‌برند***، نشریه‌ی «آرش»، چاپ پاریس، شماره‌ی ۱۰۸، تیر ۱۳۹۱/ ژوئیه ۲۰۱۲، ص ۱۰۸.

[۵۳۸] محمدرضا شالگونی، ***متن‌هائی که ما را به فضای دهه‌ی چهل می‌برند***، پیشین.

[۵۳۹] به عنوان نمونه، به منابع زیر نگاه کنید:
- ❖ اشرف دهقانی، ***از پاسخ به ضرورت زمان تا گسست از تئوری (تجربه‌ای تاریخی از چریک‌های فدائیِ خلق در دهه‌ی ۵۰)***، پیشین.
- ❖ رفیق پولاد، ***نکاتی درباره‌ی تاریخ سازمان چریک‌های فدائیِ خلق ایران***، نشریه‌ی «پیام فدائی»، ارگان چریک‌های فدائیِ خلق ایران، شماره‌ی۵۹، فروردین ۱۳۸۳ :

http://www.siahkal.com/history/ipfg-history-speech.htm

تبیین می‌کند که: «نه خود رفیق جزنی و نه رفقای هم‌گروهش در زندان، حتا کم‌ترین اطلاعی هم از چه‌گونگی‌ی شکل‌گیری‌ی گروه جنگل نداشتند.»[۵۴۰] دانسته نیست که اشرف دهقانی از کجا و به حکم کدام سند می‌داند که جزنی و یارانش «کم‌ترین اطلاعی از چه‌گونگی‌ی شکل‌گیری‌ی گروه جنگل نداشتند». همان گونه که ریزنوشته‌های بیژن جزنی از زندان بیرون می‌آمد، آیا نمی‌توانست خبر بازسازی‌ی گروه، به صورت رمز به او رسیده باشد؟ آیا اشرف دهقانی- که خود از رموز مخفی‌کاری در کار مبارزه آگاه است- انتظار دارد که مثلاً حمید اشرف (بازمانده‌ی آزادِ گروه جزنی و مسئول تدارکات سیاهکل) در جائی می‌نوشت که خبرها را به بیژن جزنی رسانده است؟ یا مثلاً می‌نوشت که ما به بیژن جزنی خبر دادیم که گروهی برای حمله‌ی مسلحانه به سیاهکل تشکیل داده‌ایم؟ از این گذشته، افزون بر شهادت یاران جزنی، که خلاف ادعای اشرف دهقانی را ثابت می‌کند، اگر این ادعا را بپذیریم، در برابر این پرسش قرار می‌گیریم که اگر رهنمودهای تئوریک بیژن جزنی در عملیات سیاهکل و سپس در عملیات شهری، نقش مؤثری نداشت، چرا پس از رویداد سیاهکل، مدت محکومیت او از ۱۵ سال به «حبس ابد» تبدیل شد؟ یا در ادامه‌ی عملیات چریک‌ها در شهر، چرا جزنی‌ی زندانی بر تپه‌های اوین اعدام شد؟ این درست است که حمید اشرف، تا جُرمِ بیژن جزنی در زندان افزایش نیابد، در جزوه‌ی «تحلیل یک سال مبارزه‌ی چریکی در شهر و کوه» (۱۳۵۰)، از او نام نبرده است. اما او را به عنوان یکی از «رهبران اصلی» شناسائی کرده است:

> گروه جنگل بر مبنای فعالیت سه تن از کادرهای سابق تشکیل گردید. این سه تن، بازماندگان گروهی بودند که در سال ۴۵ با هدف ایجاد جنبش قهرآمیز در ایران تشکیل شد و در زمستان ۴۶ این گروه ضربه شدیدی خورد و رهبران اصلی‌اش دستگیر شدند.[۵۴۱]

منتها، در همین دوران، جوان‌های مارکسیست دیگری در هسته‌های کوچک، و در گوشه و کنار ایران نیز با همان تحلیل سیاسی، به راه حل مسلحانه رسیده بودند. مجموعه‌ی مسعود احمدزاده (۱۳۲۶- ۱۳۵۰)، عباس مفتاحی (۱۳۲۴- ۱۳۵۰) و امیرپرویز پویان (۱۳۲۵- ۱۳۵۰) یکی از آن هسته‌ها بود. این سه تن، در اندک زمانی، هسته‌های مارکسیستی‌ی هم‌اندیش خود را در شهرهای مشهد، ساری، تبریز، و تهران،[۵۴۲] در یک گروه گردآوردند، و تئوری و پرکتیس این مبارزه را در جزوه‌ی «ضرورت مبارزه‌ی مسلحانه و رد تئوری‌ی بقا» (نوشته‌ی امیرپرویز پویان، بهار ۱۳۴۹)[۵۴۳] و

---

[۵۴۰] اشرف دهقانی، ***فرخ نگهدار و تحریف تاریخ چریک‌های فدائی‌ی خلق***، نشریه‌ی «پیام فدائی»، شماره‌ی ۱۶۴، بهمن ۱۳۹۱، صص ۵-۱۱، برگرفته از تارنمای «سیاهکل»:

http://www.siahkal.com/index/mid-col/Farrokh-Negahdaar-va-tahrife-taarikhe-IPFG.htm

[۵۴۱] حمید اشرف، ***تحلیل یک سال مبارزه‌ی چریکی در شهر و کوه***، آثار و انتشارات چریک‌های فدائی‌ی خلق ایران، تارنمای «سیاهکل»، بازدید: ژانویه ۲۰۰۵:

http://www.siahkal.com/publication/list2-Farsi.htm

[۵۴۲] مهم‌ترین و اثرگذارترین هسته‌هائی که به گروه احمدزاده پیوستند، هسته‌های تبریز و مشهد بودند. افراد هسته‌ی تبریز، پیش و پس از جذب به گروه احمدزاده، از طریق فعالیت‌های فرهنگی، بیش‌ترین توجه را به آگاهاندن و جذب توده‌های محروم روستاهای آذربایجان نشان دادند. افراد این هسته عبارت بودند از: بهروز دهقانی، علیرضا نابدل، کاظم سعادتی، مناف فلکی، صمد بهرنگی، اشرف دهقانی، روح‌انگیز دهقانی (همسر کاظم سعادتی)، و بعداً، اسدالله مفتاحی و تقی افشانی. افراد اولیه‌ی هسته‌ی مشهد نیز عبارت بودند از: حمید توکلی، بهمن آژنگ، غلامرضا گلوی، مهدی سوالونی و سعید آریان. البته پس از تشکیل سازمان چریک‌ها، هر یک از این هسته‌ها نیز تعداد قابل ملاحظه‌ای از روشنفکران انقلابی، به ویژه در دانشگاه‌های تبریز و مشهد را به خود جذب کردند.

[۵۴۳] امیرپرویز پویان، ***ضرورت مبارزه‌ی مسلحانه و رد تئوری‌ی بقاء***، آثار و انتشارات چریک‌های فدائی‌ی خلق ایران، تارنمای «سیاهکل»، ژانویه ۲۰۰۵، آخرین بازدید: ۳ فوریه ۲۰۱۲:

http://www.siahkal.com/publication/list2-Farsi.htm .

توضیح: از جمله تارنماهائی که این متن را منتشر کرده است، «دوزخی»، نام دارد. جالب توجه است که در پروفایل نویسنده‌ی «جهنمی/ دوزخی» می‌خوانیم که متولد ۱۳۵۹ است. به تارنمای او نگاه کنید:

http://dozakhi.blogfa.com/post-8.aspx

کتاب «مبارزه‌ی مسلحانه هم استراتژی هم تاکتیک» (نوشته‌ی احمدزاده، تابستان ۱۳۴۹) تدوین کردند.[۵۴۴] چنان که از این دو متن برمی‌آید، این گروه، با تکیه بر تئوری‌ی «دو مطلق» (سکون سیاسی‌ی مطلق در اثر استبداد سیاسی‌ی مطلق)، و با این استدلال که «موتور کوچکِ» پیشاهنگ می‌تواند «موتور بزرگ»، یعنی جامعه را به حرکت درآوَرد، مبارزه‌ی مسلحانه‌ی پیشاهنگان را سرلوحه‌ی فعالیت‌های خود قرار داد. مسعود احمدزاده در کتاب «مبارزه‌ی مسلحانه هم استراتژی هم تاکتیک» می‌نویسد:

> گروه، قبل از اتخاذ مشی‌ی مسلحانه، شیوه‌ی دیگری را تجربه کرده بود. گروه، از روی مدل چینی [یعنی] ابتدا حزب و سپس دست زدن به عمل نظامی، به کار سیاسی میان دهقانان و کارگران پرداخت. رفقا به روستاها و میان کارگران رفته و به ایجاد ارتباط با آنان می‌کوشیدند. برخورد عینی‌ی ما با تجاربِ این شیوه از عمل، نشان‌دهنده‌ی بی‌ثمری‌ی مطلقِ این شیوه بود.[...] در شرایط کنونی هر مبارزه‌ی سیاسی، به ناچار باید بر اساس مبارزه‌ی مسلحانه سازمان یابد؛ و تنها موتور کوچک مسلح است که می‌تواند موتور بزرگ توده‌ها را به حرکت درآورد. شرایط ذهنی‌ی انقلاب، در طی عمل مسلحانه به کمال شکل خواهد گرفت.

امیرپرویز پویان نیز در کتاب «مبارزه‌ی مسلحانه و رد تئوری‌ی بقاء»، ضمن شرح شرایط سیاسی/ اجتماعی‌ی آن دوره، یعنی استبداد مطلق سیاسی، از یک سو، و سکوت و سکون مطلق مردم از سوی دیگر، و در رد نظر مخالفان مشی‌ی مسلحانه، از سوی سوم، وظیفه‌ی پیکارگرانِ پیشاهنگ در آن شرایط را چنین فرموله می‌کند:

> پنهان‌کاری بی‌آن که با اِعمال قدرت انقلابی همراه باشد، دفاعی غیرفعّال و نامطمئن است؛ و اگر می‌باید پنهان‌کاری و قدرت انقلابی، توأماً، شرط بقاء ما باشند، ناگزیر باید اصل بنیانی‌ی "تئوری‌ی بقاء"، یعنی، اصل عدم تعرّض را نفی کنیم. به این ترتیب، نظریه‌ی «تعرّض نکنیم تا باقی بمانیم»، لزوماً، جای خود را به مشی‌ی «برای این که باقی بمانیم مجبوریم تعرّض کنیم»، می‌دهد. [...] برای ما پیروزی در نقطه‌ای بسیار دور، در فراسوی راهی دشوار، قرار دارد. ما با آگاهی به این دشواری‌ها قدم به این راه نهاده‌ایم. ما به خوبی آگاهیم که برای گسترش مبارزه‌ی مسلحانه در میان توده‌ها و شرکت مستقیم آنان در این پیکار رهائی‌بخش، هنوز راه درازی در پیش داریم. ما در این گذرگاه سرخ و پرشکوه، شهدای بسیاری خواهیم داد، که همواره جای آنان را رزمندگان راستین دیگری خواهند گرفت. جنبش، از فراز و نشیب‌های بسیار خواهد گذشت و باز چون سیلی خروشان پیش خواهد رفت؛ و در این رهگذر است که توده به مبارزه روی می‌آورد و با شرکت فعالانه‌ی خود در پیکار مسلحانه، شرایط ایجاد حزب سراسری طبقه‌ی کارگر را فراهم می‌سازد و بدین گونه است که حزب طبقه‌ی کارگر نه در «حرف» بلکه در «عمل» تشکیل خواهد شد. [...]

بنابراین، در اوایل سال ۱۳۴۹، مجموعه‌ی مارکسیست‌هائی که سال‌ها روی متون مارکسیستی و بررسی‌ی شرایط سیاسی/ اجتماعی‌ی ایران کار کرده بودند، و به لحاظ نظری به لزوم مشی‌ی چریکی رسیده بودند، دارای دو گروه عمده بود، که بعداً با نام‌های «گروه جزنی» و «گروه احمدزاده» شناسائی شدند؛ و پس از ادغام نیز «سازمان چریک‌های فدائی‌ی خلق ایران» را پدید آوردند. اما این «لزوم»، در دستگاه نظری‌ی هر یک از تئوریسین‌های این دو گروه- صرف نظر از مشابهت‌ها- از چشم‌اندازها و با کیفیت‌های اجرائی‌ی متفاوتی عرضه شد، که به رغم تلاش‌های بسیار برای ایجاد هم‌آهنگی، همیشه و همواره به قوت خود باقی ماندند. به عنوان مهم‌ترین تفاوت (و البته در خوانش من از متن‌های جزنی و تحلیل‌های

---

[۵۴۴] مسعود احمدزاده، ***مبارزه‌ی مسلحانه هم استراتژی، هم تاکتیک***، تابستان ۱۳۴۹، بازچاپِ الکترونیکی توسط «چریک‌های فدائی‌ی خلق ایران»، تارنمای سیاهکل:
http://www.siahkal.com/publication/notes.htm
توضیح: این متن با فرمتِ «Word» منتشر شده، نه با فرمتِ pdf . در نتیجه، من در بازگفت از این کتاب، از ثبت شماره‌ی صفحه معذورم.

بعدی از آثار او)، بیژن جزنی، با تکیه بر تغییراتی که پس از اصلاحات ارضی در سرشت رژیم و در جامعه‌ی ایران روی داده بود، شاه را، ضمن وابستگی به «امپریالیسم»، به عنوان «دیکتاتور»ی برانداز می‌کرد که از استقلال نسبی برخوردار است. از این رو، تضاد اساسی را نه «تضاد خلق با امپریالیسم»، بلکه «تضاد خلق با دیکتاتوری‌ی شاه» برآورد می‌کرد؛ شرایط عینی‌ی انقلاب را فراهم نمی‌دید؛ و با تأکید بر لزوم مبارزه‌ی مسلحانه، به فعالیت‌های صنفی/ سیاسی و تلاش برای ایجاد تشکل‌های کارگری نیز اهمیت می‌داد. او در رساله‌ی «نبرد با دیکتاتوری‌ی شاه» می‌نویسد:

> در شرایط حاضر، تضاد اساسی‌ی جامعه‌ی ما، یعنی تضاد خلق با بورژوازی‌ی کمپرادور و امپریالیسم، به تمامی، تضاد عمده محسوب نمی‌شود، و دیکتاتوری‌ی رژیم که وجهی از این تضاد است، نقش عمده را ایفاء می‌کند. در پروسه‌ی مبارزه با این عامل عمده است که تضاد اساسی [تضاد خلق با امپریالیسم] به تمامی عمده می‌شود. در چنان شرایطی، ما در آستانه‌ی انقلاب قرار خواهیم داشت و یا به عبارت دیگر، شرایط ضروری برای انقلاب فراهم خواهد بود.[٥٤٥]

جزنی در جای دیگر همین متن می‌نویسد:

> اعمال قهر انقلابی از یک سو، نیازمند رشد پیشاهنگ و نیرومند شدن اوست، و از سوی دیگر مستلزم آمادگی‌ی توده‌ها در پذیرفتن این حمایت است. [...] مبارزات گروهی و قهرمانی‌های فردی، بدون پیوند فشرده و تنگاتنگ با مردم و خواست توده‌ها سرانجامی نخواهد داشت.

با پشتوانه‌ی چنین عبارت‌هائی در نوشته‌های جزنی است که می‌توان گفت مشی‌ی مسلحانه در دستگاه نظری‌ی او جنبه‌ی تاکتیکی داشت. (گرچه باید بی‌درنگ اشاره کرد که در جای جای نوشته‌های جزنی، مبارزه‌ی مسلحانه (به عنوان «محور تاکتیک‌ها»)، به جنبه‌های استراتژیک هم نزدیک می‌شود. مثلاً در صفحه‌ی ۱۱۰ از «نبرد با دیکتاتوری‌ی شاه ...» می‌نویسد:

> حتا اگر در شرایطی تاکتیک‌های سیاسی امکان گسترش فوق‌العاده پیدا کند، باز تاکتیک‌های نظامی و جریان‌های مسلح جنبش اهمیت محوری و نقش استراتژیک خود را حفظ خواهند کرد.

اما مسعود احمدزاده و امیرپرویز پویان (دو نظریه‌پرداز «گروه احمدزاده»)، شاه را به مثابه دست‌نشانده‌ی امپریالیسم برانداز می‌کردند. از این رو، خیزش‌های مقطعی و مطالبه‌محوری، مانند خیزش دانشجویان و معلمان و کارگران شرکت واحد اتوبوسرانی‌ی تهران، را به حسابِ «رشد تضادها» (به تبیین مارکسیستی: «تضاد کار و سرمایه») و آمادگی‌ی «شرایط ذهنی‌ی در حال تکوین» می‌گذاشتند؛ شرایط عینی‌ی انقلاب را مهیا می‌دیدند؛ و معتقد بودند که در بن‌بستِ سیاسی‌ی موجود، ایجاد تشکل‌های کارگری و نهایتاً تشکیل «حزب پرولتاریا»، تنها می‌تواند از درون مشی‌ی مبارزه مسلحانه زاده شود. مسعود احمدزاده در «مبارزه‌ی مسلحانه، هم استراتژی هم تاکتیک» می‌نویسد:

> در شرایط کنونی‌ی ایران نمی‌توان عدم وجود جنبش‌های خودبه‌خودی‌ی وسیع را به معنی‌ی عدم وجود شرایط عینی‌ی انقلاب دانست. ما در بررسی‌ی شرایط عینی‌ی میهن خود نشان دادیم که هر گونه توسل به آماده نبودن شرایط عینی‌ی انقلاب مبین اپورتونیسم و سازش‌کاری و رفرمیسم، نشانه‌ی فقدان شهامت سیاسی و توجیه بی‌عملی است. من فکر می‌کنم که علت عدم وجود چنین جنبش‌هایی را اساساً باید از یک طرف در سرکوب قهرآمیز و اختناق مداوم و ناشی از

---

[٥٤٥] بیژن جزنی، ***نبرد با دیکتاتوری‌ی شاه به مثابه نیروی عمده‌ی امپریالیسم و ژندارم منطقه***، تهران: انتشارات چمن، ۱۳۵۷، ص ۱۰۱.

> دیکتاتوری‌ی امپریالیستی به مثابه عامل اساسی‌ی ابقاء سلطه‌ی امپریالیستی همراه با تبلیغات وسیع سیاسی و ایدئولوژیک ارتجاعی دانسته، و از طرف دیگر ضعف‌های عمده‌ای را که عامل انقلابی، سازمان‌ها و رهبری‌های مبارزه دچار آن بودند، باید در نظر داشت. [...] اما دلائل ما برای این که شرایط عینی‌ی انقلاب وجود دارد چیست؟ آیا ما با تحلیل شرایط عینی این امر را نشان ندادیم؟ و نشان ندادیم که توده‌ها به علت شرایط مادی زندگی‌شان، بالقوه حاضرند که بار انقلاب ضدامپریالیستی را حمل کنند؟ آیا این شور و شوق انقلابیون، این جستجوهای خستگی‌ناپذیر نیروهای روشنفکری‌ی طبقات انقلابی و مترقی در پیدا کردن راه انقلاب، این یورش‌های پی‌درپی پلیس، این زندان‌ها، این شکنجه‌ها، این قتل‌ها، انعکاس ذهنی‌ی آماده بودن شرایط انقلابی نیستند؟ آیا طرح مسئله‌ی انقلاب در این مقیاس وسیع، آیا این همه محافل و گروه‌های مبارز متعلق به همه‌ی طبقات ستمدیده می‌توانستند وجود داشته باشند بدون آن که شرایط عینی‌ی حل مسئله‌ی انقلاب را در دستور قرار داده باشد؟ و بالاخره آیا این جنبش‌های جرقه‌دار و پراکنده‌ی توده‌ها دال بر وجود شرایط عینی انقلاب نیست؟

تفاوت دیگر در چشم‌اندازهای دو گروه این بود که بیژن جزنی، ضمن این که عملیات مسلحانه در شهر و روستا را مکمل هم می‌دانست، عملیات چریکی در کوه را برتری می‌داد و آن را برای تبلیغ و توده‌ای کردنِ این مشی مؤثرتر برآورد می‌کرد. اما مسعود احمدزاده، ضمن این که عملیات مسلحانه‌ی خودِ چریک‌ها را- به عنوان «موتور کوچک»- در آغاز کار کافی می‌دید، بر گزینه‌ی انجام آن در شهر، پافشاری داشت.

همین تفاوت‌ها و اختلاف نظرها، در آستانه‌ی عملیات سیاهکل- که توسط بازمانده‌های گروه جزنی پیشاپیش طراحی شده بود- موضوع مذاکره‌های چند ماهه‌ای شد بین مرکزیت گروه جزنی و مرکزیت گروه احمدزاده، برای رسیدن به یک تاکتیکِ واحد. این مذاکره، در فاصله‌ی شهریور تا دی ماه ۱۳۴۹ بین دو گروه صورت گرفت. اما پیش از رسیدن به توافق تئوریک، یک تن، به نام احمد فرهودی، از گروهِ احمدزاده برای شرکت در عملیات سیاهکل فرستاده شد.[۵۴۶] منتها، هنوز «ادغامِ» دو گروه صورتِ رسمی نیافته، و پدیده‌ای به نام «سازمان چریک‌های فدائی‌ی خلق ایران»، برای زاده شدن از بطن تاریخ، منتظر عملیات چریک‌ها در «جنگل سیاهکل» است. پیش از ورود به «جنگل سیاهکل»، اما، مایلم با نقل قول از یکی از چریک‌های فدائی‌ی خلق در تبعید، «تسلیحاتِ» نخستینِ این پیکارگران جوان ایران را در این جا بازنمائی کنم:

> با پذیرش مبارزه‌ی مسلحانه به عنوان شیوه‌ی عمده‌ی مبارزه، گروه احمدزاده تدارک آغاز نبرد را شروع نمود. گروه با سه کُلت - که به واقع برخی از آن‌ها کاملاً کهنه و فرسوده بود - کار را شروع کرد. مصادره‌ی بانک ونک، حمله به کلانتری‌ی [۵] تبریز و در آخر حمله به کلانتری‌ی قلهک، از جمله عملیات‌های گروه بود، که از نظر مالی و تسلیحاتی تشکیلات را تقویت نمود. اجازه بدهید که در همین جا کمی حاشیه بروم و حادثه‌ای را برایتان تعریف کنم. همان طور که گفتم، سلاح‌های گروه فرسوده بود. به همین دلیل هم در جریان مصادره‌ی بانک ونک، وقتی که رفیق کاظم سلاحی (در این عملیات رفقا کاظم سلاحی، احمد فرهودی، حمید توکلی و احمد زیبرم شرکت داشتند.) پس از پایان عملیات می‌خواست چخماق اسلحه‌اش را بخواباند تا سلاحش از حالت مسلح خارج شود، تیری از سلاحش درمی‌رود که پوست سر رفیق احمد زیبرم را خراش می‌دهد. خوشبختانه در این حادثه صدمه‌ای جدی به رفیق زیبرم وارد نشد، اما شیشه‌ی ماشین شکست و رفقا مجبور شدند ماشین را کنار خیابان رها کرده و منطقه را ترک نمایند. با این که ماشین از طریق شناسنامه‌ی جعلی خریده شده بود، اما ساواک دنبال خط شناسنامه را گرفت و متوجه شد که شناسنامه از اداره‌ی پدر رفیق احمد فرهودی برداشته شده است. و به همین دلیل نام احمد فرهودی لو رفت و او مجبور شد مخفی شود.[۵۴۷]

---

[۵۴۶] در برخی از منابع گفته شده که ٤ تن از گروه احمدزاده برای شرکت در عملیات جنگل فرستاده شدند. در برخی از منابع آمده است که «قرار شد بعداً ده نفر دیگر به گروه عملیاتی بپیوندند.»، به مآخذ زیر نگاه کنید:
- غلامرضا نجاتی، ***تاریخ سیاسی‌ی بیست و پنج ساله‌ی ایران: از کودتا تا انقلاب***، پیشین، ص ۳۸۶؛

[۵۴۷] رفیق پولاد، ***نکاتی درباره‌ی تاریخ سازمان چریک‌های فدائی‌ی خلق ایران***، نشریه‌ی « پیام فدائی»، ارگان چریک‌های فدائی‌ی خلق ایران، شماره‌ی۵۹، فروردین ۱۳۸۳ :
http://www.siahkal.com/history/ipfg-history-speech.htm

تازه، محموله‌ای که صفاری آشتیانی و صفائی فراهانی، زیر چشم ساواک و با هزار مرارت از مرز خرمشهر به ایران وارد کردند، عبارت بود از «پنج اسلحه‌ی کمری، دو قبضه مسلسل دستی، دوازده عدد نارنجک دستی، مقداری فشنگ و دینامیت»؛[۵۴۸] و البته، کوله‌باری از تجربه‌ی نظامی/ پارتیزانی. هزینه‌ی تدارکات پروژه‌ی سیاهکل، با حمله به بانک ملی- شعبه‌ی خیابان وزرا- و مصادره‌ی ۶۰ هزار تومان تأمین شد، و تاکتیک عملیاتِ نیز به صورت حمله به پاسگاه ژاندارمری و جنگلبانی‌ی سیاهکل و خلع سلاح آن‌ها طراحی شده بود، که بایستی با پشتوانه‌ی تیم شهر، توسط تیم کوه اجراء می‌شد؛ نه آن گونه که اشرف دهقانی می‌اندیشد: برای آغاز یک «انقلاب دهقانی»؛ که مثلاً بیژن جزنی در آن شرایط آن را عملی می‌دانست یا نمی‌دانست. (مقاله‌ی «فرخ نگهدار و ...»)

چند روز پیش از اجراء عملیات، اما، ساواک با دستگیری و شکنجه‌ی تا حد مرگِ غفور حسن‌پور- یکی از کادرهای تیم شهری‌ی گروه- پیشاپیش اطلاعاتی پیرامون گروه بدست آورده بود، و حتا سه تن از کادرها را در گیلان و هفت تن را در تهران دستگیر کرده بود؛ و خبر این دستگیری‌ها نیز به تیم کوه رسیده بود. در همین حال بود که روز ۱۹ بهمن ۱۳۴۹ تیم کوه، «با توجه به این موضوع که ممکن است در هر لحظه از عمل نابود شود»، به فرماندهی‌ی علی‌اکبر صفائی فراهانی، با حمله به پاسگاه ژاندارمری‌ی سیاهکل پروژه را به اجراء گذاشت. در این عملیات، چریک‌ها موفق شدند موجودی‌ی سلاح پاسگاه (۹ قبضه تفنگ و ۱ قبضه مسلسل) را مصادره کنند و بگریزند. که البته، در ضمن این عملیات دو تن ژاندارم (و به قولی دیگر، سه تن ژاندارم) کشته شدند. اما حالا، کل منطقه در محاصره‌ی هوائی و زمینی‌ی نیروهای انتظامی، ژاندارمری، و امنیتی بود. درگیری‌ی نظامی بین این نیروها و چریک‌ها، تا ۸ اسفند ۴۹ به درازا کشید، و طی‌ی این مدت، افزون بر یک تن از چریک‌ها که به قول حمید اشرف، «در جنگل گم شد»، دو تن از آن‌ها (رحیم سماعی و مهدی اسحاقی) تا آخرین گلوله جنگیدند و «با انفجار نارنجک، خودشان را با چند تن از عوامل دشمن را نابود ساختند»، و هفت تن دیگر دستگیر شدند. «در مجموع، از افراد گروه ۲۲ نفری‌ی جنگل در کوه و شهر، جمعاً ۱۷ نفر دستگیر شدند.» ۱۳ تن از دستگیرشدگان، نیز پس از محاکمه در دادگاه نظامی، روز ۲۷ اسفند ۱۳۴۹، به جوخه‌ی اعدام سپرده شدند. (در بسیاری از منابع، نام غفور حسن‌پور، به شرح زیر، در فهرست اعدام شدگان آمده است: علی اکبر صفائی فراهانی، احمد فرهودی، غفور حسن‌پور، محمدهادی فاضلی، هادی بنده‌خدا، هوشنگ نیری، اسکندر رحیمی، جلیل انفرادی، عباس دانش، اسماعیل معینی، شعاع‌الدین مشیدی، ناصر سیف‌دلیل صفایی و محمدعلی محدث قندچی. و این در حالی است که می‌دانیم غفور حسن‌پور در زیر شکنجه جان باخته بود. حمید اشرف نیز در «تحلیل یک سال...» تأکید کرده است که این پیکارگر در زیر شکنجه «به شهادت» رسید.)[۵۴۹] (در این پاراگراف، عبارت‌های داخل همه‌ی گیومه‌ها را از متن «تحلیل یک سال ...» نوشته‌ی حمید اشرف برگرفته‌ام.)

پس از این اعدام‌ها، تیم شهری‌ی گروهِ احمدزاده، روز ۱۴ فروردین ۱۳۵۰، به کلانتری‌ی قلهک حمله کرد، و مسلسل یک سرپاسبان را به غنیمت گرفت. چهار روز بعد، یعنی روز ۱۸ فروردین ۱۳۵۰، پنج نفر (اسکندر صادقی‌نژاد، حمید اشرف، محمد صفاری آشتیانی، منوچهر بهائی‌پور، رحمت پیرونذیری) از هشت تن بازمانده‌ی گروه جنگل، طرح اعدام انقلابی‌ی سرتیپ ضیاء فرسیو (رئیس اداره‌ی دادرسی‌ی ارتش و دادستان دادگاه اعدامیان) را اجراء کردند. پس از این دو حمله‌ی موفقیت‌آمیز بود که بازماندگان سیاهکل و گروه احمدزاده رسماً در هم ادغام شدند؛ و نهادی به نام «چریک‌های

---

[۵۴۸] محمود نادری، ***چریک‌های فدائی‌ی خلق: از نخستین کنش تا بهمن ۱۳۵۷***، تهران: مؤسسه‌ی مطالعات و پژوهش‌های سیاسی، ۱۳۸۷، صص ۱۴۹ تا ۱۵۲.

[۵۴۹] افزون بر یادآوری‌ی حمید اشرف، گزاره‌ی کشته شدنِ غفور حسن‌پور در زیر شکنجه، در منابع دیگر هم آمده است. مثلاً، به مأخذ زیر نگاه کنید:

❖ ***مروری بر تاریخچه‌ی سازمان از سیاهکل تا کنفرانس دهم سازمان (۱۳۸۵)***، تارنمای «پیشگام» هواداران سازمان فدائیان اقلیت، ۳ فوریه ۲۰۱۱:

http://pishgaam13.wordpress.com/2011/02/03/siyahkal/

فدائی‌ی خلق ایران» را پدید آوردند (۲۲ فروردین ۱۳۵۰)؛[۵۵۰] و طی‌ی بیانیه‌ای تاریخی، ضمن اعلام رسمی‌ی جنگ مسلحانه با رژیم، مسئولیت هر دو این عملیات را به عهده گرفتند:

> [...] هر جا ظلم هست، مقاومت و مبارزه هم هست. [...] ما فرزندان انبوه زحمت‌کشانی هستیم که در طول صدها سال با افشاندن خون‌شان به‌ما یاد داده‌اند که چه‌گونه می‌توان به آزادی و زندگی‌ی شرافتمندانه دست یافت. [...] مبارزه‌ی چریکی شروع شده است. [...] یورش قهرمانانه‌ی چریک‌های از جان گذشته به پاسگاه سیاهکل در گیلان بار دیگر، به روشنی‌ی تمام، نشان می‌دهد که مبارزه‌ی مسلحانه تنها راه آزادی‌ی مردم ایران است. ما چریک‌های فدائی‌ی خلق با حمله به پاسگاه کلانتری‌ی قُلهک و اعدام فرسیو جنایتکار نشان دادیم که راه قهرمانانه‌ی سیاهکل را ادامه خواهیم داد. [...][۵۵۱]

روز ۲۶ فروردین ۵۰، در جریان پخش این بیانیه و چند بیانیه‌ی دیگر در تهران، یک تن از چریک‌ها (جواد سلاحی) در درگیری با مأموران در خیابان مجبور به خودکشی شد، و یک تن دیگر (علیرضا نابدل) دستگیر شد. روز ۳ خرداد، امیرپرویز پویان و رحمت‌الله پیرونذیری، در خانه‌ی تیمی‌ی خود در محاصره‌ی نیروهای انتظامی/ امنیتی قرار گرفتند و پس از ساعت‌ها نبرد، خودکشی کردند. ۴ اردی‌بهشت ۵۰، چریک‌ها با حمله به بانک آیزنهاور تهران موجودی‌ی آن را مصادر کردند. از تابستان تا پائیز ۵۰، مسعود احمدزاده، اسدالله مفتاحی، عباس مفتاحی، مجید احمدزاده، حمید توکلی و غلامرضا گلوی نیز دستگیر شدند، و روز ۱۱ اسفند ۱۳۵۰ به جوخه‌ی اعدام سپرده شدند. از آن پس، حمید اشرف- بازمانده‌ی گروه جزنی و گروه جنگل- با همکاری‌ی کادرهای باقی‌مانده، به بازسازی‌ی سازمان پرداخت، و سازمان، به جذب کادرهای تازه، تجدید نظر در ساختار تشکیلاتی، و تدارک عملیات مسلحانه در سطح شهری ادامه داد. به عنوان مثال، روز ۱۲ اسفند ۱۳۵۳ (سالروز تیرباران احمدزاده‌ها و اسدالله مفتاحی و ...)، چریک‌های فدائی‌ی خلق، سروان یدالله نوروزی، فرمانده‌ی گارد مستقر در دانشگاه صنعتی، را اعدام انقلابی کردند، و پس از به جا گذاشتن اعلامیه‌های توضیحی- برای آگاهی‌ی مردم از علت این اعدام- به سلامت از صحنه دور شدند.[۵۵۲]

با توجه به شکست عملیات سیاهکل، و انعکاس گسترده‌ای که عملیات چریکی‌ی شهری روی جامعه- به ویژه در محافل دانشجوئی- می‌گذاشت، از سال ۱۳۵۰ تا سال ۱۳۵۳، تز احمدزاده/ پویان در سازمان چریک‌های فدائی‌ی خلق هژمونی یافته بود. اما از سال ۱۳۵۳، زمزمه‌های تجدید نظر در تز مبارزه‌ی مسلحانه و گذاشتن تکیه بر مبارزه‌ی ایدئولوژیک (که به تزهای بیژن جزنی نزدیک‌تر بود)، از سرمقاله‌های نشریه‌ی «نبرد خلق» (ارگان سازمان) برخاست، و از وجود بحران در این سازمان خبر داد. یرواند آبراهامیان در این زمینه می‌نویسد:

> فدائیان در بحث از نحوه‌ی خروج از این بن‌بست، دو شاخه شدند. اکثریت، به رهبری‌ی حمید اشرف تا زمان مرگش در نیمه‌ی سال ۱۳۵۵، بر ادامه‌ی مبارزه‌ی مسلحانه، تا برانگیختن خیزش توده‌ای تأکید داشت. اما اقلیت طرفدار اجتناب از

---

[۵۵۰] به گفته‌ی اشرف دهقانی در «حماسه مقاومت» ۱۳۸۳، ص ۲۲، نام این نهاد نخستین بار بدون واژه‌ی «سازمان» به کار رفت. بر من پوشیده است که این واژه در چه زمانی و به پیشنهاد چه کسانی به آن افزوده شد، و مخففِ «سچفخا» را پدید آورد. اشرف دهقانی همچنین در ص ۱۳ همان کتاب نوشته است که آرم اولیه‌ی سازمان داس و چکش نداشت. داس و چکش در اوایل سال ۵۴ به آرم سازمان اضافه شد.

[۵۵۱] من به اصل این بیانیه دسترسی نیافتم و این بازگفت را از تارنمای دانشنامه‌ی ویکی پدیا، زیر عنوانِ «سازمان چریک‌های فدائی‌ی خلق» برگرفته‌ام.

[۵۵۲] اعدام سروان یدالله نوروزی در سالروز اعدام مجید احمدزاده و دیگر رهبران سازمان انجام شد. چرا که مجید احمدزاده، دانشجوی دانشگاه صنعتی بود، و چنان که در اعلامیه‌ی توضیحی‌ی چریک‌ها آمده است، یدالله نوروزی، «یکی از خوش‌خدمت‌ترین و منفورترین مهره‌های گارد در دانشگاه بود.» به مأخذ زیر نگاه کنید:

❖ ***رفیق مجید احمدزاده: اولین دانشجوی شهید دانشگاه صنعتی***، تارنمای سازمان اتحاد فدائیان خلق ایران، اسفند ۱۳۸۳:
http://www.etehadefedaian.org/archive/bargiaztarikh/Majidahmadzadeh.htm

درگیری‌ی مسلحانه، افزودن بر کار سیاسی به ویژه در میان کارگران کارخانه‌ها، و برقراری‌ی ارتباط نزدیک‌تر با حزب توده بود. (ایران بین دو انقلاب، پیشین، ص ۴۵۱)

اما تا این زمزمه‌ها به مرحله‌ی تصمیم برسد، زمان لازم بود. با تیرباران بیژن جزنی و یارانش (۱۳۵۴) و سپس با ضربه‌های مهلک سال ۵۵ به کادرهای فعال سازمان، و با مرگ حمید اشرف و ده تن از یارانش در مرکزیت (در روز ۸ تیر ۵۵)،[۵۵۳] سازمان چریک‌های فدائی‌ی خلق ایران، به بن‌بست کامل رسید؛ بسیاری از همونددانی که فعالیت علنی داشتند و برای ساواک شناخته‌شده نبودند، به زندگی‌ی عادی برگشتند؛ اکثریت اعضای وفادار به مبارزه‌ی مسلحانه، در زندان بودند؛ بسیاری از پیکارگرانِ مخفی یا نیمه‌علنی‌ی این سازمان، به امید فعالیت مؤثر در خارج از کشور، از ایران خارج شده بودند؛ و تماس بازماندگانِ سازمان با نمایندگان برون‌مرزی‌ی خود عملاً قطع شده بود؛[۵۵۴] یا به قول اشرف دهقانی، یکی از نمایندگان برون‌مرزی‌ی سازمان: کادرهای مرکزیت سازمان «گویا نیازی هم به ایجاد رابطه با نمایندگان سازمان در خارج از کشور (نویسنده‌ی این سطور و رفیق حرمتی‌پور) به خرج نمی‌دادند».

در چنین شرایطی است که این بزنگاه از تاریخ سازمان چریک‌ها، در هاشوری از تأیید و تکذیب رقم خورده است. من از میان متن‌های موجود در این زمینه، دو راویت را برگزیده‌ام: روایت حزب توده، و روایت اشرف دهقانی. فشرده‌ی روایت نخست می‌گوید: با مرگ حمید اشرف و کادر رهبری، و اوج‌گیری‌ی ناامیدی از کارائی‌ی مبارزه‌ی مسلحانه در اکثر کادرهای بازمانده‌ی سازمان چریک‌ها، در مهر ماه ۱۳۵۵ گروه مخالف با مشی‌ی مسلحانه، با نام «گروه منشعب از سازمان چریک‌های فدائی‌ی خلق وابسته به حزب توده‌ی ایران» از سازمان جدا شد. رهبری‌ی این انشعاب را تورج حیدری بیگوند (۱۳۳۲-۱۳۵۵) به عهده داشت،[۵۵۵] که از مدتی پیش، مشی‌ی مسلحانه را در جزوه‌ای رد کرده بود. این جزوه، در مهر ماه ۱۳۵۵، (پس از مرگ حیدری بیگوند در نبردی خیابانی)- با مقدمه‌ای به قلم هم‌فکران او، و «تحلیلی از اوضاع ایران» به قلم رحمان هاتفی (رهبر سازمان «نوید»)- منتشر شد. در بخش «مقدمه»‌ی این جزوه، از جنبش مسلحانه به عنوان «انقلاب روشنفکرانه» و «آتش بازی‌ی هیجان‌انگیز» یاد شده، که «در حقیقت جز توفانی در لیوان آب نبود.»[۵۵۶]
پیوستنِ تورج حیدری بیگوند و یارانش به «سازمان نوید» (بخش درون‌مرزی‌ی حزب توده، به رهبری‌ی رحمان هاتفی)، داستانی دارد که هم جدال خاموشِ طیف‌های مختلف چپ با یکدیگر را آشکار می‌کند، و هم تلاش توان‌فرسای مبارزانِ آن دوره را- برای یافتن راهی بهتر و درست‌تر در مبارزه- و هم ذهنیت جاری در سپهر اندیشگی‌ی گروه‌هائی از پیکارگرانِ آن‌زمانی/ این‌زمانی را. گزارش این انشعاب- از دیدگاه حزب توده- حدود سه دهه پس از انقلاب سال ۵۷، از زبان علی خدائی، یکی از اعضاء قدیمی‌ی سازمان نوید و حزب توده، در یک «گفت‌وگو» در تبعید، به متن نشست؛ و من با هدفِ نشان دادنِ تصویری نسبتاً دقیق از ذهنیت‌های جاری در این روایت، بخش بزرگی از سخنان او را در این جا ثبت کنم. یکی از پرسش و پاسخ‌های این «گفت‌وگو» به قرار زیر است:

---

۵۵۳ حمید اشرف در ۸ تیر ۱۳۵۵ در جریان یورش ساواک به محل کمیته‌ی مرکزی‌ی سازمان چریک‌های فدائی‌ی خلق ایران در خانه‌ای تیمی در مهرآباد جنوبی‌ی تهران همراهِ ده تن از یارانش (طاهره خرّم، محمّدرضا یثربی، غلامعلی خرّاط پور، علی‌اکبر وزیری، محمّدمهدی فوقانی، یوسف قانع خشکه بیجاری، فاطمه حسینی، عسگر حسینی ابرده، محمّد حسین حق‌نواز، و غلامرضا لایق مهربانی) تا آخرین نفس جنگید و کشته شد.

۵۵۴ ***پیش به سوی مبارزه‌ی ایدئولوژیک: پاسخ به «مصاحبه با رفیق اشرف دهقانی»***، سازمان چریک‌های فدائی‌ی خلق ایران، مرداد ۱۳۵۸، ص ۷؛ برگرفته از تارنمای «آرشیو اپوزیسیون ایران»، بازدید: ۲۰ بهمن ۱۳۹۱:
http://www.iran-archive.com/sites/default/files/sanad/cherikha-ta-enghelab-pasokh_be_ashraf.pdf

۵۵۵ اعضای دیگر گروه منشعب، فریبرز صالحی، حسین قلمبر (سیامک)، فرزاد دادگر، سیما بهمنش و فاطمه ایزدی بودند.

۵۵۶ ***میراث انقلابی‌ی تورج حیدری بیگوند، نسل جوان چپ بخواند تا بداند چرا نباید گذشته را بار دیگر تکرار کرد***، تارنمای «راه توده»، ۲۸ ژوئیه ۲۰۰۸:
http://www.rahetudeh.com/rahetude/mataleb/beigwand/html/elamiyeh_11.html

- چه‌گونه سازمان نوید که یک سازمان به شدت بسته، و زنجیره‌ای از حلقه‌های مستقل بود، به خانه‌های تیمیِ سازمان چریک‌های فدائی وصل شد؟

- ماجرا خیلی ساده شروع شد، اما شَمّ بسیار تیز و ابتکار عمل و قدرت تصمیم‌گیریِ فوریِ [رحمان] هاتفی، که فاصله‌ی زیادی با مهدی پرتوی داشت، از همین اتفاق و یا اطلاع ساده توانست راه به خانه‌های تیمیِ چریک‌ها باز کند. ماجرا این گونه شروع شد که یکی از نویسندگان و خبرنگاران روزنامه‌ی اطلاعات که اهل شعر و ادبیات نیز بود، و با هاتفی نیز دوستی داشت، اولین اطلاعات مربوط به بحث جدی در خانه‌های تیمیِ چریک‌ها را به هاتفی خبر داد. این شخص «عسگر آهنین‌جگر» بود که خوشبختانه جان سالم بدر برده و اکنون در مهاجرت زندگیِ ادبیِ خود را دنبال می‌کند. او، تا آن جا که اطلاع دارم با «امیر معزز»، از رفقای چریک، تماس برقرار کرده بود. یعنی از قبل با هم دوست بودند و مدت‌ها هم از هم بی‌خبر بودند، اما یک بار که همدیگر را می‌بینند، معزز گله و شکوه از وضع سیاسیِ خود می‌کند و می‌گوید که دیگر مشیِ مسلحانه را قبول ندارد و موقعیت نامناسبی نیز در خانه‌ی تیمیِ خود دارد. [...] هاتفی از همین طریق، یعنی از طریق عسگر آهنین‌جگر موفق شد اطلاعات دیگری در باره‌ی بحث‌های درونیِ رفقای چریکِ برخی خانه‌های تیمی به دست آورد. در جریان همین پیگیری، معزز توانست جزوه‌ی حیدری بیگوند را از طریق آهنین‌جگر به هاتفی برساند. البته با این اطلاعات که بیگوند به دلیل نظراتی که پیدا کرده در سازمان چریک‌ها منزوی شده و حتا او را در یک خانه‌ی تیمی نیمه‌زندانی کرده‌اند و معزز مسئول ارتباط های او با خارج از خانه و خرید و دیگر امور است. این جزوه یک تکان بزرگ به ما بود. در حقیقت بیگوند همان چیزهائی را نوشته بود و به همان راهی گام گذاشته بود که زنده یاد [هوشنگ] تیزآبی سال‌های قبل به آن رسیده و با جسارتی کم نظیر آن‌ها را در نشریه‌ی «به سوی حزب» طرح کرده بود.[۵۵۷] این جزوه بلافاصله کپی شده و توسط یک مسافر به خارج از کشور منتقل شد تا به دست رهبریِ حزب برسد. چون بیگوند اطلاع داده بود که صلاح نمی‌داند در آن خانه‌ی تیمی بماند و حتا اشاره کرده بود که نسبت به جان خود هم بیمناک است، تصمیم گرفته شد، مکانی برای او در نظر گرفته و به صورت ضربه‌ای او را از خانه‌ی تیمی‌اش خارج کرده و به این مکان منتقل کنیم و در واقع بیاید در پناه نوید. معزز برای رساندن این پیام و انتقال بیگوند اعلام آمادگی کرده بود و این در شرایطی بود که معزز در حقیقت نگهبان بیگوند در آن خانه‌ی تیمی بود. بیگوند در این فاصله اصرار کرده بود که یک قراری را اجراء کند و سپس منتقل شود به نزد نوید. با کمال تأسف و تأثر بسیار، او سر این قراری که حداقل من از آن دقیقاً اطلاع ندارم، کشته شد. ظاهراً قراری بوده که به دلیل دستگیریِ دیگران توسط ساواک لو رفته بوده و وقتی بیگوند سر قرار حاضر می‌شود احساس می‌کند در تله افتاده و پیش از آن که موفق به فرار شود، مأموران ساواک او را به گلوله می‌بندند و کشته می‌شود. [۱۲ مهر ۱۳۵۵]. این خبر واقعاً برای ما یک ضربه‌ی روحیِ بزرگ بود. پس از این حادثه، ما موفق شده بودیم امیر معزز را از خانه خارج کرده و به شبکه‌ی نوید وصل کنیم. من و هاتفی او را در یک بعد از ظهر در انتهای خیابان نواب سوار اتومبیل کردیم و به یکی از محلات نارمک، که محل چاپ نوید بود و فلاصله‌ی کمی از خانه‌ی پرتوی داشت، منتقل کردیم. [...] معزز با نام مستعار «علی»، در زیرزمین خانه که محل چاپ نوید بود، مستقر شد. تا روزهای انقلاب که از این خانه دیگر بیرون آمد، در همین زیرزمین ماند. زیرا نباید منطقه و محل را می‌شناخت و نباید هم به صورت اتفاقی در شهر توسط رفقای سابقش شناسائی می‌شد. با بردباریِ زیادی این شرایط را تحمل کرد. [...] معزز قبل از خروج از آن خانه [ی تیمیِ چریک‌ها] و پیوستن به نوید، موفق شد قرار و رابطه‌ای میان ما و یکی دیگر از

---

۵۵۷ هوشنگ تیزابی، متولد ۱۳۲۲، از اعضاء حزب توده بود. او، در مقاله‌های نشریه‌ی زیرزمینی «بسوی حزب»، هم کار سیاسی و تشکیل حزب کارگر را شرط موفقیت در مبارزه‌ی «مارکسیست/ لنینیستی» برآورد می‌کرد، و هم آگاهیِ طبقاتی را میان کارگران و توده‌های زحمتکش گسترش می‌داد. او پس از چند بار دستگیری و زندان‌های کوتاه مدت، بالأخره به دام سازمان امنیت گرفتار آمد، و پس از تحمل شکنجه‌های سخت، روز ۷ تیر ماه ۱۳۵۳ اعدام شد.

رفقای همان خانه‌های تیمی، که اتفاقاً آن‌ها نیز بسیار به مشی‌ی حزب و نوید نزدیک شده بودند، برقرار کند. از این مرحله به بعد بود که عسگرآهنین‌جگر به خواست هاتفی از ایران خارج شد و فکر می‌کنم به همراه یک نسخه‌ی دیگر از کتاب بیگوند- که ما قبلاً هم آن را به اروپا فرستاده بودیم تا به حزب برسانند- و رفت به آلمان دمکراتیک و زیر پوشش حزب در برلین شرقی قرار گرفت. [...] ارتباط ما با رفقای منشعب در تهران منظم شد. آن‌ها سئوالاتی داشتند که تا گرفتن پاسخ آن‌ها و قانع‌شدن حاضر نبودند مشی‌ی مسلحانه را به کلی کنار بگذارند و به حزب بپیوندند. از سوی این گروه، زنده یاد فرزاد دادگر به همراه سیامک (حسین قلمبر) با نوید در ارتباط قرار گرفتند. زنده یاد قلمبر، که واقعاً هیبت یک چریک شهری را داشت، سوار بر موتوری پرقدرت، فرزاد دادگر را به سر قرار آورده و من او را تحویل گرفته و با ماشین خودم به محلی می‌بردم که هاتفی منتظر او [و سئوال‌هایش] بود. [...] سرانجام این گروه پذیرفتند که مشی‌ی مسلحانه را کنار بگذارند و زندگی‌ی عادی و توده‌ای را شروع کنند. روز آخر یادم هست که هاتفی اصرار زیادی کرد که فرزاد دیگر اسلحه حمل نکند و به این وضع خطرناک خاتمه بدهد و دیگر همفکرانش در خانه‌ی تیمی و گروهی که با آن‌ها در ارتباط بود را هم تشویق کند اسلحه و سیانور را کنار بگذارند، چون کارهای مهمتری هنوز در پیش است و حزب به نیرو و کادر جوان نیاز دارد. [...] هسته یا گروه دیگری از چریک‌ها با گروهی که فرزاد در میان آن‌ها بود در ارتباط بود، که سرسخت‌تر از فرزاد پاسخ‌های هاتفی را می‌پذیرفت. رابط این گروه را هم چند بار به همان شیوه‌ای که گفتم به همین خانه برای مذاکره با هاتفی بردم. اهل بندر انزلی بود. واقعاً دیگر سئوالی نداشتند که پاسخ داده نشده باشد، اما باز هم تعلل می‌کرد در کنار گذاشتن سلاح و سیانور و بازگشت به زندگی عادی و توده‌ای. [...][۵۵۸] (قلاب‌های شامل نوشته از من هستند.)

روایت اشرف دهقانی: پیشاپیش بگویم که اشرف دهقانی (اگر نگوئیم از جمله «پایه‌گذارانِ» سازمان چریک‌های فدائی‌ی خلق ایران، دست کم، از قدیم‌ترین همواندن این سازمان)، در دوره‌ی مورد بحث، به عنوان یکی از نمایندگان سازمان چریک‌ها، در خارج از ایران به سر می‌برده است، و پشتوانه‌ی روایت او از این بزنگاه تاریخی (به ویژه موضوع «گروه منشعب» و حیدری بیگوند)، عمدتاً عبارتند از: ۱- شناخت از مناسبات درونی‌ی سازمان خود؛ ۲- شناخت تجربی از حزب توده و سازش سران آن با جمهوری‌ی اسلامی؛ و ۳- قرائن تاریخی. این نکته نیز درخور یادآوری است که اشرف دهقانی روایت خود را ضمنِ انتقاد به «توضیحِ» تراب حق‌شناس در مقدمه‌ی انتشار نوارهای صوتی در تارنمای «اندیشه و پیکار» گزارش داده است.[۵۵۹] از این رو، بخش هائی از متن بلند دهقانی را در این جا ثبت می‌کنم که تنها به «گروه

---

[۵۵۸] بخش دوم از یادمانده‌های علی خدائی در دیدار و گفت‌وگو با «ن. کیانی» و «ع. خیرخواه»، ***پیوستن گروه منشعب به نوید، روزگاری که آسان سپری نشد***، تارنمای «راه توده»، شماره‌ی ۱۷۴، ۲۸ آوریل ۲۰۰۸:

http://www.rahetudeh.com/rahetude/mataleb/nagofteha/html/nagofteha-2.html

توضیح: رحمان هاتفی، با نام مستعار «حیدر مهرگان» در حزب توده‌ی ایران فعالیت داشت. او، افزون بر فعالیت‌های حزبی، در دوران انقلاب ۵۷ سردبیر روزنامه‌ی کیهان بود. رحمان هاتفی، در جریان دستگیری‌های گسترده‌ی اعضاء و مرکزیت حزب توده توسط رژیم جمهوری‌ی اسلامی، در اردیبهشت سال ۱۳۶۲ دستگیر و زندانی شد، و زیر شکنجه در زندان‌های رژیمی جان سپرد، که برای تحقق آن بسیار کوشیده بود.

[۵۵۹] «گفت‌وگوهای درونی بین دو سازمان چریک‌های فدائی‌ی خلق ایران و مجاهدین خلق ایران»، از سال ۱۳۵۴ آغاز شده بود، و نوار آن‌ها نیز روی ۱۲ کاست ضبط شده بود. تراب حق‌شناس، از سوی «گروه تنظیم و انتشار آرشیو سازمان پیکار در راه آزادی‌ی طبقه‌ی کارگر»، لینک‌های این ۱۲ کاست را (هر یک در چند پرونده‌ی فرعی) در سپتامبر ۲۰۱۰ در تارنمای اندیشه و پیکار منتشر کرد:

http://www.peykarandeesh.org/PeykarArchive/Mojahedin-ML/mojahed_fadaii.html

سری‌ی بعدی این آرشیو با عنوان «گفت‌وگو بین سازمان مجاهدین خلق ایران و گروه منشعب از سازمان چریک‌های فدائی‌ی خلق ایران (معروف به گروه تورج بیگوند)»- که به اواخر شهریور ۱۳۵۵ مربوط هستند- در ۸ نوار و ۱۵ قسمت در مرداد ۱۳۹۰/ اوت ۲۰۱۱ در تارنمای «اندیشه و پیکار» در اختیار تاریخ قرار گرفت:

http://peykarandeesh.org/PeykarArchive/Mojahedin-ML/mojahed_fadaii-dore2.html

بخش سوم این آرشیو نیز، با عنوان «دور دوم گفت‌وگو بین سازمان چریک‌های فدائی‌ی خلق و سازمان مجاهدین خلق ایران- سال ۱۳۵۶» در ۱۵ فایل و ۴۵ قسمت در مرداد ۱۳۹۰/ اوت ۲۰۱۱ بر تارنمای انتشارات «اندیشه و پیکار» نشست:

http://peykarandeesh.org/PeykarArchive/Mojahedin-ML/mojahed_fadaii-dore2.html

تراب حق‌شناس از سوی گروه تنظیم و انتشار آرشیو سازمان پیکار، پیرامون هر یک از این پرونده‌ها، «توضیح»‌ی نیز نوشت. محور مقاله‌ی اشرف دهقانی عمدتاً «توضیح»‌هائی است، که تراب حق‌شناس در بخش دوم این گفت‌وگوها آورده است:

- اشرف دهقانی، ***ملاحظاتی درباره‌ی یک سند تاریخی!*** تارنمای «اشرف دهقانی»، شهریور ۱۳۹۰/ اوت ۲۰۱۱:

http://www.ashrafdehghani.com/pdf/PF148-molahezate-yek-sanad-tarikhi.pdf

منشعب» و «تورج حیدری بیگوند» مربوط هستند:

> [...] بیگوند کسی است که حزب توده مدعی شد که می‌خواسته است از سازمان چریک‌های فدائی‌ی خلق انشعاب کند ولی قبل از آن در مهر ماه ۱۳۵۵ در درگیری با ساواک کشته شد. نام بیگوند را در واقع حزب توده با انتشار کتابی به نام او بر سر زبان ها انداخت. [...] واقعیت این است که آن چه به نام «گروه منشعب از سازمان چریک‌های فدائی‌ی خلق ایران» معروف شد، توسط حزب توده از میان افرادی که با [عنوان هموندانِ] سازمان چریک‌های فدائی‌ی خلق شناخته می‌شدند، ساخته و پرداخته شده بود. [...] کتابی که «توده‌ای»ها پس از شهادت تورج بیگوند به نام وی منتشر کردند را نمی‌توان حقیقتاً نوشته‌ی خود وی به حساب آورد. آن‌ها مدعی‌اند که رفیق وی به نام امیر معزز نوشته‌ی بیگوند را به حزب توده داده است. ولی موقعی که حزب توده به نام بیگوند کتاب منتشر کرد، وی شهید شده بود و ریش و قیچی در دست «توده‌ای»ها بود که می‌خواستند از شهادت او به نفع اشاعه‌ی اندیشه‌های خود استفاده کنند. هدف حزب توده در واقع، مقابله با نظرات انقلابی‌ی چریک‌های فدائی‌ی خلق، با سوءاستفاده از محبوبیت نام خود آن‌ها بود.[...] بیگوند در درون سازمان، گروهی نداشت که یک ماه پس از شهادت وی «انشعاب» را اعلام کند! «توده‌ای»ها [...] تعداد دوستان بیگوند را سه نفر ذکر کرده‌اند که البته آن‌ها هم یک گروه نبودند. اما با داده‌های موجود- که البته نمی‌توان آن‌ها را کامل به حساب آورد- می‌توان گفت که پس از شهادت رفیق حمید اشرف و رفقای دیگر، در شرایط پراکندگی و قطع ارتباط ها و به طور کلی با به هم ریختن اوضاع سازمان، تعدادی که درستی‌ی مشی‌ی مسلحانه را مورد سئوال قرار داده و تردیدهایشان پس از ضربه‌های سنگین سال ۱۳۵۵ هم تقویت شده بود، در آبان ماه آن سال حساب خود را از بقیه‌ی رفقای سازمان جدا کردند. این عده که هنوز به صورت گروهی منسجم در نیامده بودند، جدائی خود را نیز با اطلاعیه‌ای اعلام نکردند. در طی‌ی مدتی بین آن‌ها و عناصری از حزب توده ارتباطی بر قرار می‌شود. این موضوع را «توده‌ای»ها به این شکل مطرح می‌کنند که آن‌ها از طریق امیر معزز- کسی که قبلاً با تورج بیگوند هم خانه بود- توانسته‌اند با افراد دیگری از سازمان چریک‌های فدائی‌ی خلق تماس بر قرار بکنند. بی‌تردید، ادعاهای حزب توده را بدون بررسی و تحقیق کامل نمی‌توان و نباید پذیرفت؛ ولی به طور کلی، به گونه‌ای که واقعیت های بعدی بیانگرند، ارتباط حزب توده با جداشدگان از سازمان، یک واقعیت و امر محرزی است. [...] آن چه مسلم است این است که آن چه به نام گروه منشعب از سازمان چریک‌های فدائی‌ی خلق معروف شده نه در آبان ماه همان سالی که سازمان چریک‌های فدائی خلق مورد حملات شدید ساواک قرار گرفت، یعنی در سال ۱۳۵۵، بلکه آن گروه پس از آن تاریخ و بعد از یک سال ارتباط مداوم با حزب توده شکل گرفت. در واقعیت امر نیز اعلام موجودیت گروهی به نام «گروه منشعب از سازمان چریک‌های فدائی‌ی خلق» نه در سال ۱۳۵۵، بلکه در آبان ماه سال ۱۳۵۶ بود. تازه همین به اصطلاح «گروه منشعب» در سال ۱۳۵۶ نیز [...] پیوستن به سازمان نوید حزب توده را اعلام نکرد. به هیچ‌وجه! اگر با تعمق لازم به هدفی که حزب توده از اعلام انشعاب یک گروه از سازمان چریک‌های فدائی‌ی خلق تعقیب می‌نمود، توجه کنیم، خواهیم دید که اتفاقاً حزب توده تا جائی که برایش مقدور بود می‌خواست از به اصطلاح «برگی» که به دست آورده بود، حداکثر استفاده را بکند و به راحتی حاضر نبود نام «چریک‌های فدائی‌ی خلق» در دنباله‌ی گروه دست‌ساز خود را از دست بدهد. این به اصطلاح حزب، با همه‌ی کینه اش نسبت به چریکهای فدائی خلق، به خوبی از محبوبیت عنصر فدائی در میان مردم مطلع بود (و هست) [...] این مردم آگاه و مبارز ایران بودند که پس از علنی شدن سازمان‌های مخفی در سال ۵۷ ، گروه منشعب را وادار کردند که نام چریک‌های فدائی خلق را از دنباله‌ی اسم خود برداشته و بعد رسماً به حزب توده بپیوندد. [...] بر اساس اطلاعات تا کنون موجود، آن چه به نام «گروه منشعب از سازمان چریک‌های فدائی‌ی خلق ایران» شهرت یافته، گروهی بود که حزب توده طی تماس و کار روی افراد جدا شده از سازمان چریک‌های فدائی‌ی خلق بعد از ضربه‌های سنگین ۸ تیر ۵۵، برای اشاعه نظرات خود به وجود آورد، و بلافاصله پس از علنی شدن سازمان‌های سیاسی‌ی مخفی پس از سقوط رژیم شاه، بر اثر فشار توده‌های مبارز و آگاه ایران مجبور شد آن گروه دست‌ساز خویش را در درون خود جای دهد.

این یادآوری را مکرر می‌کنم که محور سخنان اشرف دهقانی در این مقاله، انتقاد به تراب حق‌شناس و گروه تنظیم‌کننده‌ی آرشیو اندیشه و پیکار است به خاطر تکرار برخی از داده‌های حزب توده در «توضیح»ی که در «مقدمه»ی لینک‌های مربوط به آن «گفت‌وگو»ی تاریخی نوشته بودند. از این رو، سخن او پیرامون «حزب منشعب» و «تورج حیدری بیگوند»، در جای جای مقاله و حتا در زیرنویس آن، پراکنده است. منتها، در همین پراکندگی، و در خلال افشاگری‌های دهقانی نسبت به حزب توده، می‌توان به این گزاره‌ی متقن ره یافت که پس از ضربه‌های کمرشکنی که سازمان چریک‌های فدائی‌ی خلق ایران در سال ۵۵ تحمل کرد، اندیشه‌ی تجدید نظر در مشی‌ی چریکی، دوران جنینی‌ی خود را- دست کم در بخشی از این سازمان- پشت سر نهاده بود.

یادآوری‌ی این نکته نیز بایسته است که در آن دوران، حزب «نوید» (بخوانید: حزب توده) یا «گروه منشعب»، تنها حزب‌ها یا سازمان‌های مارکسیستی‌ی مخالف با مشی‌ی چریکی نبودند؛ بلکه گروه‌های دیگری نیز- به ویژه در «کنفدراسیون جهانی‌ی محصلین و دانشجویان ایرانی»- بودند، که با وجود گرایش به «مارکسیسم/ لنینیسم/ مائوئیسم»، با مشی‌ی چریکی‌ی سازمان چریک‌های فدائی‌ی خلق (و البته نه مانند حزب نوید، و با ذات مبارزه‌ی مسلحانه) مرزبندی داشتند. به عنوان نمونه، «سازمان انقلابیون کمونیست»، در اوایل سال ۱۳۵۰ متنی در مخالفت با این مشی منتشر کرد، با عنوانِ «مارکسیست- لنینیست‌ها و مشی‌ی مسلحانه» نوشته‌ی سیامک زعیم.[۵۶۰] همچنین، گروه «پویا»، در فرایند ادغام با «سازمان انقلابیون کمونیست» و در آستانه‌ی تشکیل «اتحادیه‌ی کمونیست‌های ایران»، متنی به قلم حسین ریاحی[۵۶۱] منتشر کرد با عنوان «سخنی با پویندگان راه انقلاب» (۱۳۵۵)، که شیوه‌ی چریکی‌ی سازمان فدائیان خلق را زیر سئوال برده بود.[۵۶۲]

در کشاکش چنین فضا و شرایطی بود که روز ۱۶ آذر ۱۳۵۶ سازمان چریک‌های فدائی‌ی خلق ایران در نشریه‌ی «پیام دانشجو»، شماره‌ی ۳ اعلام کرد که «تئوری‌های رفیق جزنی به عنوان رکن اساسی و رهنمون فعالیت‌های سازمان شناخته شده است.»[۵۶۳] اشرف دهقانی، در حالی که این «اعلامیه» را «فتوا» می‌نامد، این گزاره را تصدیق می‌کند:

---

۵۶۰ سیامک زعیم (یا: زعیمی)، در ابتدا از شاخه‌ی چپ جبهه‌ی ملی بود؛ در زمان دانشجوئی در امریکا، در جنبش ضد جنگ ویتنام فعالیت داشت؛ بعد به «سازمان انقلابیون کمونیست» پیوست و از رهبران این سازمان شد؛ سپس مسئولیت ایدئولوژیکی- سیاسی در نهاد «اتحادیه‌ی کمونیست‌های ایران» را پذیرفت. او در سال ۱۳۵۷ به ایران بازگشت و به عنوان طراح اصلی، «قیام سربداران در آمل» را رهبری کرد. سیامک زعیم، یک روز پس از سرکوب قیام سربداران توسط رژیم اسلامی (۷ بهمن ۱۳۶۰) دستگیر شد و در سال ۱۳۶۳ اعدام شد.

۵۶۱ حسین تاجمیر ریاحی، از ۱۳۳۹ تا ۱۳۴۲ از کوشندگان جنبش دانشجوئی در ایران ؛ از جمله برگزارکنندگان مراسم چهلم تختی، و سپس از جمله مؤسسان گروه «فلسطین» بود، که از ضربه‌ی ساواک به این نهاد جان سالم به در برد؛ برای آموزش نظامی به اردوگاه‌های فلسطینی رفت؛ مسئولیت «رادیو میهن‌پرستان» در عراق را به عهده داشت؛ در اواخر سال ۱۳۵۷ به ایران بازگشت؛ از جمله رهبران «قیام سربداران در آمل» بود؛ در تیر ماه ۱۳۶۰ دستگیر شد، و در ۵ بهمن ماه ۱۳۶۰ تیرباران شد.

۵۶۲ مریم جزایری، ***قیام آمل و اتحادیه‌ی کمونیست‌ها: دو تاریخ‌نگاری، دو جهان‌بینی***، نشریه‌ی «آرش»، چاپ پاریس، شماره‌ی ۱۰۸، تیر ۱۳۹۱/ ژوئیه ۲۰۱۲، ص ۱۱۳.
توضیح: من دو متن یادشده در مقاله‌ی مریم جزایری را نخوانده‌ام. اما برخی از متن‌های منتشرشده توسط «اتحادیه‌ی کمونیست‌ها» را که در دوران انقلاب و در حوالی‌ی قیام‌های کردستان و به ویژه «قیام آمل- از ۲۲ آبان ۱۳۶۰ تا ۵ بهمن ۱۳۶۰» در ایران منتشر می‌شد، دیده‌ام. همچنین، کتاب «***پرنده‌ی نوپرواز: گفت‌وگو با یکی از رفقای شرکت‌کننده در مبارزه‌ی مسلحانه‌ی سربداران و قیام آمل***»- که در سال ۱۳۸۳ در تبعید منتشر شد- را نیز خوانده‌ام. و از همین راه می‌دانم (امیدوارم درست بدانم) که با الهام از پیشنهادهای تاکتیکی‌ی مائوتسه دون، مشکل «اتحادیه‌ی کمونیست‌های ایران» با «چریک‌های فدائی‌ی خلق ایران»، نه بر سر ذات مبارزه‌ی مسلحانه، بلکه بر سر تاکتیک‌های اجرائی‌ی مشی‌ی چریکی بوده است. یادآوری کنم که بازماندگان «اتحادیه‌ی کمونیست‌های ایران»، در تبعید، «حزب کمونیست ایران» را تشکیل دادند، که خود را تشکیلاتی «مارکسیست- لنینیست- مائوئیست» شناسائی می‌کند.

۵۶۳ به دو مأخذ زیر نگاه کنید:

- ***پیش به سوی مبارزه‌ی ایدئولوژیک: پاسخ به «مصاحبه با رفیق اشرف دهقانی»***، سازمان چریک‌های فدائی‌ی خلق ایران، مرداد ۱۳۵۸، ص ۷؛ برگرفته از تارنمای «آرشیو اسناد اپوزیسیون ایران»، بازدید: ۲۰ بهمن ۱۳۹۱:
http://www.iran-archive.com/sites/default/files/sanad/cherikha-ta-enghelab-pasokh_be_ashraf.pdf

پس از ضربه‌های سنگینی که در سال ۱۳۵۵ به سازمان ما وارد شد، پس از گذشت دوره‌هائی، در شرایطی که من و رفیق حرمتی‌پور به مثابه اعضای قدیمی‌ی سازمان در خارج از کشور به سر می‌بردیم، سه تن، به اسامی‌ی منصور غبرائی، قربانعلی عبدالرحیم‌پور، و رفیق احمد غلامیان لنگرودی، در رأس باقی‌مانده‌ی سازمان قرار گرفته و در ۱۶ آذر ۱۳۵۶ اعلام کردند که نظرات رفیق بیژن جزنی را جایگزین نظرات شناخته‌شده‌ی پیشین سازمان چریک‌های فدائی‌ی خلق کرده‌اند. (مقاله‌ی «فرخ نگهدار و ...» ص ۸)

پیرامون بازتاب آن‌زمانی‌ی اشرف دهقانی و حرمتی‌پور نسبت به این تصمیم سازمان، در متن بلند «پیش به سوی مبارزه‌ی ایدئولوژیک» (که سازمان چریک‌های فدائی‌ی خلق در «پاسخ به مصاحبه با رفیق اشرف دهقانی» در مرداد ۱۳۵۸ منتشر کرد)، چنین می‌خوانیم:

وقتی که رفقای خارج مطلع می‌شوند [که] سازمان نظرات رفیق جزنی را پذیرفته و رسماً اعلام کرده است، دلایل این تغییر مواضع را از سازمان سئوال می‌کنند. سازمان در تماس‌های بعدی از آن‌ها می‌خواهد که به ایران بیایند و مواضعشان را به بحث بگذارند. آن‌ها چندین ماه به دلایل مختلف از بازگشت خودداری کرده، و بالأخره به سازمان اطلاع می‌دهند که تنها پس از انتشار نظراتشان، که رکن اساسی‌ی آن همان نظرات رفیق مسعود احمدزاده است، به ایران خواهند آمد. و در مورد نحوه‌ی انتشار جزوه‌ی حاوی نظراتشان («درباره‌ی شرایط عینی‌ی انقلاب») از سازمان سئوال می‌کنند که آن را با آرم یا بدون آرم سازمان انتشار دهند؟ به دنبال این امر، سازمان تصمیم می‌گیرد چنان‌چه رفقا این حرکت غیرتشکیلاتی را به اجرا گذارند، آن‌ها را از سازمان اخراج نماید. و جهت اعلام این تصمیم، یکی از رفقا را در اواخر پائیز ۵۷ به خارج می‌فرستد. چون رفقا قبل از دریافت پاسخ از سوی سازمان، جزوه‌ی «درباره‌ی شرایط عینی‌ی انقلاب» را بدون اطلاع از نظر سازمان با آرم و نام سازمان انتشار داده بودند، رفیق تصمیم سازمان را به اطلاع آنان می‌رساند. رفقا، ضمن پذیرش، از حرکت غیرتشکیلاتی‌ی خود انتقاد می‌کنند. همچنین آن‌ها به تصمیم اخراج اعتراض می‌کنند و سازمان ضمن تعلیق نظر خود مبنی بر اخراج، یک بار دیگر از آن‌ها می‌خواهد جهت حل قضیه به ایران بیایند. آن‌ها حدوداً اوایل اسفند ۵۷ به ایران آمدند. [...] اما رفقا پذیرش مسئولیت و ادامه‌ی عضویت را موکول به این می‌کردند که سازمان بپذیرد که همواره دو نظر را به عنوان مواضع خویش در سطح جنبش اعلام کنند. [۵۶۴]

اما خوانش کادرهای رهبری‌ی سازمان در سال ۱۳۵۶ از تز بیژن جزنی هر چه که بود، هژمونی‌ی این تز، به اضافه‌ی نفوذ اندیشه و مشی‌ی حزب توده در این سازمان، در دو/ سه سال آینده نقش مهمی در انشعاب بزرگ و تجزیه‌ی نهائی‌ی سازمان چریک‌های فدائی‌ی خلق ایران بازی کرد.[۵۶۵] «توکل»، از شخصیت‌های دیرینه‌ی «سازمان چریک‌های فدائی

❖ عبدالعلی معصومی، ***سازمان چریک‌های فدائی‌ی خلق ایران***، تارنمای «ایران نبرد»، بازدید: ۱۰ ژوئیه ۲۰۱۲:
http://www.iran-nabard.com/40%20sal/ali_masoumi.htm

۵۶۴ ***پیش به سوی مبارزه‌ی ایدئولوژیک: پاسخ به «مصاحبه با رفیق اشرف دهقانی»***، سازمان چریک‌های فدائی‌ی خلق ایران، مرداد ۱۳۵۸، پیشین، صص ۷ تا ۸.

۵۶۵ من در این جا وارد جزئیات این مبحث نمی‌شوم. برای آگاهی از کم و کیف اندیشه‌های جزنی و احمدزاده، و تفاوت‌هائی که انتخاب تز جزنی در سازمان ایجاد کرد، باید آثار نوشتاری‌ی هر یک از این تئوریسین‌ها را خواند، و پیرامون پیامدهای هژمونی‌ی هر یک از دو تز در سازمان، باید یادمانده‌های کادرهای سابق و کارشناسان تاریخ سیاسی را خواند. از جمله به آثار زیر نگاه کنید:

❖ مسعود احمدزاده، ***مبارزه‌ی مسلحانه هم استراتژی هم تاکتیک***، تهران: انتشارات هواداران چریک‌های فدائی‌ی خلق، چاپ هفتم، ۱۳۵۶، ص ۶۵.
❖ امیرپرویز پویان، ***ضرورت مبارزه‌ی مسلحانه و رد تئوری‌ی بقاء***.
❖ بیژن جزنی، ***تاریخ سی ساله‌ی ایران***، تهران: انتشارات هواداران چریک‌های فدائی‌ی خلق، ۱۳۵۷.
❖ اشرف دهقانی، ***از پاسخ به ضرورت زمان تا گسست از تئوری: تجربه ای تاریخی از چریک‌ها***، تارنمای «بی بی سی»، ۱۷ ژوئن ۲۰۱۱ (۲۷ خرداد ۱۳۹۰):
http://www.bbc.co.uk/persian/iran/2011/06/110617_siahkal_ashraf_dehghani.shtml
❖ ***جُنگی درباره‌ی زندگی و آثار بیژن جزنی***، به همت کانون گردآوری و نشر آثار بیژن جزنی، پاریس: انتشارات خاوران، ۱۳۷۸.
❖ نقی حمیدیان، ***سفر با بال‌های آرزو: شکل‌گیری‌ی جنبش چریکی‌ی فدائیان خلق***، سوئد: چاپ آرش، ۱۳۸۳.
❖ محمود باباعلی و ناصر مهاجر، ***تاریخ را چگونه نباید نوشت (مروری بر حاشیه‌نویسی‌های آقای سرکوهی درباره‌ی بیژن جزنی و سازمان فدائی)***، تارنمای نشریه‌ی «آرش»، بازدید ۱۴ شهریور ۱۳۸۸:

خلق ایران» (سچفخا)،[٥٦٦] آشفتگی‌ی نظری در این سازمان در این دوره را، به شرح زیر ترسیم کرده است:

[...سچفخا] از یک طرف، در نتیجه‌ی ضربات سال ۵۵ به شدت تضعیف شده است، و از طرف دیگر اوضاع سیاسی‌ی جدید، وظایف، تحلیل‌ها و تاکتیک‌های نوینی را می‌طلبد؛ چرا که مشی و تاکتیک‌های گذشته‌ی سازمان با شرایط جدید دیگر هیچ همخوانی نداشت. سچفخا اما نتوانست از پس این وظیفه برآید و نقشی را که شایسته‌ی آن برای رهبری و تأثیرگذاری بر جنبش بود، در جریان اعتلای مبارزات قبل از قیام انجام دهد. با وجود این، در نتیجه‌ی همان مبارزات دوران پیش از قیام بود که در روزها و ماه‌های پس از قیام و سرنگونی‌ی رژیم شاه توانست به بزرگ‌ترین سازمان کمونیست، نه فقط در ایران، بلکه در کل خاورمیانه تبدیل شود. اما [...] نداشتن برنامه و تاکتیک‌های منسجم، منطبق بر شرایط نوین، سچفخا را فلج کرد؛ به بروز اختلافات جدی در سازمان انجامید؛ و سرانجام بر سر مهمترین این اختلافات، انشعابی بزرگ در سازمان چریک‌های فدایی خلق ایران، در وهله نخست بر سر ماهیت طبقاتی‌ی رژیم جمهوری‌ی اسلامی و موضع‌گیری در قبال آن، و البته همچنین در ارزیابی‌ی مبارزات گذشته‌ی سازمان رخ داد. جناح موسوم به فدائیان اکثریت، به حمایت از جمهوری‌ی اسلامی برخاست و جناح فدائیان اقلیت به مبارزه علیه آن. این انشعاب در خرداد ماه سال ۵۹ رسمیت یافت.[٥٦٧]

انشعاب بزرگ این سازمان، روز ۲۱ خرداد ۱۳۵۹ در شماره‌ی ۶۲ نشریه‌ی «کار، ارگان سراسری‌ی سازمان چریک‌های فدائی‌ی خلق ایران»، رسماً اعلام شد. در بندی از «بیانیه و اطلاعیه»‌ی مربوط به این انشعاب می‌خوانیم:

[...] انشعابی که در سازمان به وقوع پیوست، بر اساس تضاد ایدئولوژیک میان دو جریان شکل گرفت؛ که یکی بر پایه‌ی بینش گذشته‌ی سازمان، دفاع از اپورتونیسم چپ را به عهده گرفت و در عرصه‌ی مبارزه‌ی طبقاتی‌ی جاری، خط مشی‌ی ماجراجویانه را پیشنهاد کرد (و هم‌اکنون نیز در پیش گرفته است)؛ و دیگری، با تجهیز به مارکسیسم لنینیسم، بینش و نظریات گذشته‌ی سازمان را انحراف از اصول تشخیص داد و کوشش خود را بر این قرار داد که در عرصه‌ی مبارزه‌ی طبقاتی‌ی جاری، خط مشی‌ی پرولتاریائی و متکی بر قوانین عینی‌ی ناظر بر روند مبارزه‌ی طبقاتی را در پیش گیرد. [...] (ص ۲)[٥٦٨]

که البته منظور از واژه‌ی «ماجراجویانه» در این متن، «مبارزه‌ی مسلحانه» علیه رژیم اسلامی است؛ و منظور از «خط مشی‌ی پرولتاریائی» نیز عملاً، دفاع از سیاست‌های آیت‌الله خمینی و جمهوری‌ی اسلامی از کار درآمد، که در رهگذر انجام آن، بسیاری از هموندان پیشین این سازمان به مرگ و تبعید رهسپار شدند.

اما تا به این «انشعاب»- که انشعاب‌های متعدد را به دنبال آورد- برسیم، باید همین جا به نقش کارآمد این سازمان مسلح

---

http://www.arashmag.com/content/view/421/47/1/12/

❖ ***روایت محمدتقی سیداحمدی از «سازمان چریک‌های فدائی‌ی خلق ایران» در گفت‌وگو با شهلا بهاردوست***، تارنمای «اخبار روز»، در چند بخش، از ٤ اردیبهشت ۱۳۹۰ به بعد:

http://www.akhbar-rooz.com/article.jsp?essayId=37472

[٥٦٦] توکل، از دوران دانشجوئی به مبارزه‌ی مسلحانه گرایش یافت؛ به تبعید و زندان محکوم شد؛ در جریان انقلاب، با دیگر زندانیان سیاسی از زندان ساواک آزاد شد؛ بعد از انقلاب، مشاور کمیته‌ی مرکزی‌ی سچفخا بود و در تحریریه‌ی نشریه‌ی کار، قلم می‌زد؛ بعد از انشعاب خرداد ۵۹ عضو کمیته‌ی مرکزی‌ی «اقلیت» بود. او در تبعید نیز عضو «سازمان فدائیان- اقلیت» است. برگرفته از تارنمای «بی بی سی»، ۸ فوریه ۲۰۱۱/ ۱۹ بهمن ۱۳۸۹:

http://www.bbc.co.uk/persian/iran/2011/02/110203_l42_siahkal_tavakol.shtml

[٥٦٧] توکل، ***سازمان چریک‌های فدائی‌ی خلق ایران از سیاهکل تا قیام ۵۷***، تارنمای «بی بی سی»، ۸ فوریه ۲۰۱۱/ ۱۹ بهمن ۱۳۸۹:
http://www.bbc.co.uk/persian/iran/2011/02/110203_l42_siahkal_tavakol.shtml

[٥٦٨] آرشیو اسناد «چریک‌های فدائی‌ی خلق ایران»، ***اسناد خیانت اکثریت***- تارنمای «سیاهکل»:
http://www.siahkal.com/index/left-col/Asnade-Khianate-Aksariat.pdf

در «پیروزیِ انقلاب» اشاره کنم: گرچه پایه‌گذاران و تئوریسین‌ها و بسیاری از کادرهای عملیاتیِ «سازمان چریک‌های فدائیِ خلق ایران» در مقاطع مختلف توسط رژیم شاه اعدام شدند، یا در زیر شکنجه جان باختند، یا در درگیری با مأموران امنیتی با کپسول سیانور خودکشی کردند، و با وجود انشعاب گروه حیدری بیگوند، و با وجود اختلاف‌های نظری‌ای که از بدو ادغام، بین دو گروه احمدزاده و جزنی در درون رهبری و کادرهای این سازمان جریان داشت، و با وجود این که سازمان چریک‌های فدائیِ خلق ایران در سال ۵۷ «مرکزیتِ» منسجم و پلاتفرم مشخصی نداشت،[۵۶۹] اما با محبوبیتی که میان انبوه هواداران و سمپات‌های خود داشت، نه تنها در گیرشِ انقلاب ۵۷ کارآمد و مؤثر بود، بلکه با ذخیره‌ی هنگفتی که از تجربه‌های نظامی داشت در رهبریِ قیامِ مردم و سازمان‌های سیاسیِ دیگر در روزهای ۱۹ تا ۲۲ بهمن ۵۷ و در سقوط نهائیِ رژیم پادشاهی، نقشی غیرقابل انکار ایفاء کرد. مسعود احمدزاده هفت سال پیش از این روزهای سرنوشت‌ساز، در کتاب «مبارزه‌ی مسلحانه، هم استراتژی هم تاکتیک» نوشته بود:

> شکست یک گروه مبارز مسلح، تأثیری تعیین‌کننده بر سرنوشت مبارزه ندارد. اگر قبول داریم که مبارزه طولانی است، اگر قبول داریم که مبارزه با تشکل گروهی آغاز می‌شود، چه اهمیتی دارد که گروهی در این میان از بین بروند. مهم این است که اسلحه‌ای که از دست رزمنده‌اش می‌افتد، رزمنده‌ای دیگر باشد که آن را بردارد، اگر گروهی شکست می‌خورد، گروهی دیگر باشد که راه او را دنبال کند. این مهم نیست که گروه یا گروه‌هائی پیشاهنگ‌تر به زندگی خود ادامه دهند تا بتوانند نتایج عمل خود را ببینند، از اثرات آن بهره‌برداری کنند، و حمایت معنوی را که ایجاد کرده‌اند با سازماندهی خود مبدل به حمایت مادی کنند. این را می‌توانند **گروه‌های دیگر** انجام دهند؛ گروه‌هائی که می‌خواهند به وظایف انقلابیِ خویش عمل کنند. (تأکید از من است.)

منتها، همه‌ی این «گروه‌های دیگر»، حالا از جنسی نیستند که مسعود رزمنده‌ی ما در انتظارشان بود. حالا، در آستانه‌ی انقلاب ایران، اعلامیه‌ی خطِ گروی آیت‌الله خمینی از همان شهر نجف، جنس بخش اکثریت این «گروه‌های دیگر» را دستکاری کرده است:

> من صریحاً اعلام می‌کنم که از این دستجات خائن چه کمونیست و چه مارکسیست و چه منحرفین از مذهب تشیع و از مکتب مقدس اهل بیت عصمت علیهم الصلوه و السلام به هر اسم و رسمی باشند متنفر و بیزارم و آن‌ها را خائن به مملکت و اسلام و مذهب می‌دانم.[۵۷۰]

گرچه تنها هشدار و خط گروی آیت‌الله و کارکردِ آن ابراز «بیزاری» نبود که جنس بخشی عظیمی از «گروه‌های دیگر» (یعنی بخش عظیمی از «چریک‌های فدائیِ خلقِ» بعد از احمدزاده) را در زمان انقلاب «دیگر» کرده بود، بلکه- در خوانش من- رسوب بینش مذهبی/ سنتیِ نهادینه شده در ذهنیت خودشان و در ذهنیت فرهنگ توده‌های مذهبی/ سنتی- که از درون هزاران مسجد و انجمن اسلامی، آیت‌الله را بر روی دست و سر خود به کرسی نشاندند- نیز در آن دگرگونی عیار بالائی داشت. اما انگار خبرِ «نفرت و بیزاری» از یک سو، و حضور ذهنیت مذهبیِ خود و توده‌های مردم به باورِ

---

[۵۶۹] از جمله تاریخچه‌هائی که عدم انسجام کمیته‌ی مرکزی و نداشتن یک پلاتفرم مشخص در سازمان چریک‌های فدائیِ خلق در سال‌های ۵۶ و ۵۷ را بازنمائی کرده‌اند، به دو مأخذ زیر نگاه کنید:

- گفت‌وگو با مهدی فتاپور پیرامون ***روند شکل‌گیری رهبریِ سازمان چریک‌های فدائیِ خلق ایران پس از انقلاب و شکل‌گیریِ اولین کمیته‌ی مرکزیِ آن***، تارنمای «مهدی فتاپور»، ۲۴ اکتبر ۲۰۱۰:

http://fatapour.blogspot.com/2010/11/blog-post.html

- ***تداوم (گفت‌وگوئی با مهدی سامع)***، تنظیم و تدوین علی ناظر، جلد اول، انتشارات نبرد خلق، ۱۳۷۶، ص ۸.

[۵۷۰] ***مبارزات امام خمینی به روایت اسناد (در دوران تبعید در نجف)***، تدوین غلامعلی پاشازاده، تهران: مرکز اسناد انقلاب اسلامی، ۱۳۷۸، سند شماره ی۱۰۱، ص ۳۱۵.

اکثریت پیکارگران این سازمان و سازمان‌های چپ دیگر ننشسته بود، که آنان را در نقطه‌ای از راهِ انقلابِ ۵۷ در حمایت از آیت‌الله خمینی (پیش از «پیروزیِ انقلاب») به تأمل وادارد. این است که عبارت‌هائی مانند «مصادره‌ی انقلاب» در لابه‌لای متن‌های تحلیلیِ همه‌ی طیف‌های چپ ایران جا خوش کرده است. اشرف دهقانی، از جمله «گروه‌های دیگر»، که بر راه احمدزاده و پویان رفت و «دیگر» نشد، سی و چهار سال پس از انقلاب، در متن «پاسخ به ضرورت زمان ...» می‌گوید:

> در سال ۱۳۵۷ که مردم مبارز ایران برای کسب استقلال، آزادی، رفاه و برابری دست به انقلاب زدند، **هر چند که کمونیست‌ها در شرایطی نبودند که بتوانند رهبریِ آن انقلاب را به دست بگیرند**، اما در آن زمان کمونیسم از چنان **پشتوانه‌ی توده‌ای** و از چنان اعتباری در جامعه برخوردار بود که **حتا خمینی** که با دخالت مستقیم قدرت‌های بزرگ به حکومت رسید نیز، **در آغاز جرأت نکرد علیه کمونیست‌ها سخنی بر زبان راند**. واقعیت این بود که از سال ٤۹ به بعد نام کمونیسم در ایران با نام چریک‌های فدائیِ خلق عجین شده بود؛ با نام کمونیست‌هائی که در میان وسیع‌ترین توده‌های مردم ایران (و نه فقط ایران) محبوبیت بی‌نظیری کسب کرده بودند. [۵۷۱] (پرانتز از اشرف دهقانی است. تأکیدها از من است.)

اگر آن ابراز «نفرت و بیزاری»ی آیت‌الله را در برابر جمله‌ی «حتا خمینی در آغاز جرأت نکرد علیه کمونیست‌ها سخنی بر زبان راند» قرار دهیم، به غیبت ذهنی و فیزیکیِ اشرف دهقانی در روندهای انقلاب ۵۷ ایران می‌رسیم. از این گذشته، پرسیدنی است که اگر «کمونیسم پشتوانه‌ی توده‌ای و اعتبار داشت»، چرا «کمونیست‌ها در شرایطی نبودند که رهبریِ انقلاب را به دست بگیرند»؟ برای درکِ جوانبِ این پرسش که چرا «کمونیست‌ها در شرایطی نبودند که بتوانند رهبریِ انقلاب را به دست گیرند»، به دو جا سرک می‌کشم. اولی آماری است که یرواند آبراهامیان از ترکیب قربانیان جنبش چریکی (از سازمان‌های فدائی و مجاهد و پیکار) به دست داده است:

> بین واقعه‌ی سیاهکل و مهر ۱۳۵٦، که انقلاب اسلامی به خیابان‌های تهران راه گشود، ۳۴۱ چریک و عضو گروه‌های مسلح سیاسی جان باختند. [...] درباره‌ی ۳۰٦ نفر از ۳۴۱ نفر چریک مقتول، خویشان آنان و سازمان‌های چریکی اطلاعاتی داده‌اند. از ۳۰٦ نفر، ۲۸۰ نفر (۹۱%) را می‌توان جزو روشنفکران دانست. ۲٦ نفر (۹%) بقیه، شامل ۲۲ کارگر کارخانه، ۳ مغازه‌دار، و یک روحانی است. (ایران بین دو انقلاب، پیشین، ص ۴۴۳)

البته تعداد اندکِ «کارگرانِ» جان‌باخته، دلیل متقنی برای کمرنگ بودن حضور آنان در مبارزه نیست. اما با توجه به این واقعیت که آغاز بحث نظری پیرامون مشیِ مسلحانه به سال‌های آغازین دهه‌ی چهل می‌رسد، نسبت ۹۱% «روشنفکر» به ۹% «کارگر» و پیشه‌ور، در طول این زمان دراز نیز می‌تواند گویای ناتوانیِ سازمان‌های چریکیِ ما در جذب لایه‌های کارگریِ جامعه باشد. برای دیدن این ناتوانیِ چریک‌ها در جذب لایه‌های روستائی/ کشاورزی و پراکندن آگاهی میان قشرهای محروم جامعه، به «جنگل سیاهکل» نقب می‌زنم. جزئیات عملیات سیاهکل و پیامدهای دردناک آن - که من در این فشرده از فراز آن پریدم- را باید در کتاب‌های تاریخ و تاریخچه‌ها، همچنین، در گفت‌وگوها و یادمانده‌های کادرهای باقی مانده از سازمان چریک‌ها خواند. اما همین جا باید به گزاره‌ای اشاره کنم که به باور من، دردناک‌تر از مرگ ققنوس‌های جوانی است، که پادشاه ایران در اوج توهم و در کمال نابخردی، آن‌ها را «جوجه‌های پرریخته»‌ای خوانده بود که «قدرت پرواز ندارند»:

---

[۵۷۱] اشرف دهقانی، ***از پاسخ به ضرورت زمان تا گسست از تئوری (تجربه‌ای تاریخی از چریک‌های فدائیِ خلق در دهه‌ی ۵۰)***، تارنمای «سیاهکل»، خرداد ۱۳۹۰:
http://www.siahkal.com/index/mid-col/az-pasokh-be-zarorat-ta.pdf

در کشاکش جنگ و گریز و اختفای چریک‌ها، در حالی که جنگل سیاهکل در محاصره‌ی مأموران ساواک و ژاندارمری است؛ در حالی که اعلامیه‌ها و بیانیه‌های دولتی، چریک‌ها را «اشرار مسلح» معرفی کرده‌اند؛ در حالی که فرمانده‌ی ژاندارمری‌ی کل کشور و امیران ژاندارمری‌ی تهران و گیلان برای هر چه زودتر به دام انداختن چریک‌ها، کارگزاران خود را تهدید و تطمیع می‌کنند؛ علی‌اکبر صفائی فراهانی، هوشنگ نیری، جلیل انفرادی، برای تهیه‌ی خوراک، از جنگل بیرون می‌آیند و به خانه‌ی یک روستائی پناه می‌برند. سرهنگ غلامرضا نجاتی، با استفاده از منابع خودِ چریک‌های فدائی، این صحنه‌ی دردناک را به شرح زیر ترسیم کرده است:

> روستائیان با اطلاع از حضور چریک‌ها در آن جا، خانه را محاصره می‌کنند. صفائی فراهانی برای مردم حرف می‌زند و هدف و آرمان‌های چریک‌ها را از اقدام به نبرد مسلحانه شرح می‌دهد. چند تن از روستائیان خواستار آزادی‌ی آن‌ها می‌شوند. ولی کدخدا و سپاهی‌ی دانشِ روستا، مردم را از کمک به آن‌ها برحذر می‌دارند و آن‌ها را از مجازاتی که در انتظارشان است می‌ترسانند. سرانجام، چریک‌های مسلح، بی‌آن که برای آزادی‌ی خود به اسلحه متوسل شوند، تسلیم می‌شوند. مدتی بعد، ژاندارم‌ها و مأموران ساواک سرمی‌رسند و آن‌ها را دستگیر می‌کنند و به تهران می‌فرستند.[۵۷۲]

صفائی فراهانی در برگ بازجوئی‌ی ساواک اشاره کرده است که به هنگام صرف غذا متوجه می‌شود که روستائیان زیادی به اتاق آمد و رفت می‌کنند. وقتی سبب را جویا می‌شود، صاحب‌خانه می‌گوید: «چیزی نیست، شب‌نشینی داریم!»[۵۷۳] مهرعلی نوروزی، میزبان آن شبِ چریک‌ها، در بازجوئی‌ی خود صحنه‌ی «شب‌نشینی» را چنین بازنمائی کرده است:

> [...] شام که خوردند، چائی هم خوردند، ساعت نزدیک به ۱۲ شب گفتند می‌خواهیم برویم. گفتیم آقایان چکاره هستید که می‌خواهید شب بروید؟ گفت شما چکار دارید که ما چکاره هستیم. گفتیم هر کاره که باشید نمی‌گذاریم امشب بروید. باید صبح بروید. چون قصد داشتیم آن‌ها را نگه داریم تا مأمورین بیایند. آن‌ها قصد رفتن کردند و می‌خواستند کفش خودشان را بپوشند، که یک دفعه چند نفر ریختیم سر آن‌ها و دست‌هایشان را گرفتیم. یکی از آن‌ها دستش را درآورد و اسلحه‌ی خود را کشید و تیراندازی کرد. به پای من زد که مجروح شدم. ولی بقیه آن‌ها را گرفتند و دست و پای آن‌ها را بستند تا مأمورین آمدند.[۵۷۴]

البته گزارش حمید اشرف شهادت این فرد را درباره‌ی کاربرد اسلحه نفی می‌کند. او، در «تحلیل یک سال مبارزه‌ی چریکی در شهر و کوه»، ضمن انتقاد از «ملایمت و ملاطفتِ» نا به‌جای این چریک‌ها، می‌نویسد:

> [...] چهار نفرشان توسط روستائیان ناآگاه دستگیر شدند و این رفقا به خاطر طرز تفکر ذهنی‌ی خود و به خاطر این که مبادا یک روستائی آسیب ببیند، با آن‌ها رفتار خشن نظامی نکردند، آن‌ها فکر می‌کردند که به هیچ وجه به هیچ روستائی در هیچ شرایطی نباید آسیبی برسد. لذا وقتی دهقانان در صدد دستگیری‌ی آنان برآمدند مسلحانه اقدام نکردند.[۵۷۵]

---

۵۷۲ سرهنگ غلامرضا نجاتی، ***تاریخ سیاسی‌ی بیست و پنج ساله‌ی ایران: از کودتا تا انقلاب***، پیشین، ص ۳۸۹. منابع غلامرضا نجاتی برای این گزاره عبارت‌اند از: ***تاریخ مبارزات مردم ایران: حقایقی درباره‌ی جنبش جنگل و حماسه‌ی سیاهکل***، انتشارات سازمان چریکی‌ی فدائیان خلق ایران، صص ۱۶ تا ۲۴ (من این مأخذ را ندیده‌ام)؛ حمید اشرف، ***جمع‌بندی‌ی سه ساله***، انتشارات نگاه، ۱۳۵۷، صص ۹۵ تا ۱۰۱.

۵۷۳ محمود نادری، ***چریک‌های فدائی‌ی خلق: از نخستین کنش تا بهمن ۱۳۵۷***، تهران: مؤسسه‌ی مطالعات و پژوهش‌های سیاسی، ۱۳۸۷، ص ۲۰۲.

۵۷۴ محمود نادری، ***چریک‌های فدائی‌ی خلق: از نخستین کنش تا بهمن ۱۳۵۷***، پیشین، ص ۲۰۳.

۵۷۵ حمید اشرف، ***تحلیل یک سال مبارزه‌ی چریکی در شهر و کوه***، ۱۳۵۰، تارنمای «سیاهکل»، بازدید ۱۰ فوریه ۲۰۱۲: http://www.siahkal.com/publication/Hameed%20Ashraf.htm

در حالی که به گفته‌ی خود چریک‌ها، یکی از دلایل گزینش جنگل‌های گیلان و مازندران برای عملیات، این بود که مردم این منطقه، در برخوردِ رادیکال با حکومت، دارای سابقه‌ی تاریخی بودند. البته، بنا بر منابع چریک‌های فدائی، آن‌ها در همان زمان، بر این امر آگاه بودند که اثرگذاری بر روستائیان منطقه، یک شَبه، و با اجراء یک حمله‌ی مسلحانه ممکن نیست، و جلب اعتماد و کمک و همکاری‌ِ آن‌ها، مستلزم جنگ و گریزهای مکرر در منطقه، و تماس‌های مکرر و طولانی‌مدت با شبانان و کشاورزان و مردم محلی است. در این صورت، پرسیدنی است که آن‌ها با چه اطمینانی به خانه‌ی آن روستائی پناهنده شدند؟ چرا موضوع «شب‌نشینی داریم» را باور کردند؟ آیا انتظار داشتند که با یک «سخنرانی» و شرح «آرمان‌ها»، روستائیان و کشاورزان را با خود همراه کنند؟ در این جا به ناگزیر، گریزی می‌زنم به موقعیت مشابه ارنستو چه گوارا و تیم ۱۷ نفره‌ی او در واپسین روزهای زندگی در جنگل‌ها و کوهپایه‌های بولیوی که توسط ۱۷هزار سرباز محاصره شده بودند: «چه گوارا مداوماً این نکته را در نظر داشت که مهم‌ترین خطر برای او و تیمش، روستائیانی هستند که به علت هراس از جنگ چریکی، از آن‌ها می‌گریزند.» از این رو بود که او و تیم او- در حالی که «از فرط تشنگی ادرارشان را می‌نوشیدند و از فرط گرسنگی گوشت پوسیده‌ی کرم‌آلود را می‌بلعیدند»، و یکی پس از دیگری از پا درمی‌آمدند، به جای رفتن به خانه‌ی روستائیان، در کوهستان‌ها اطراق می‌کردند. و شگفتا که سرانجام نیز «توسط یک روستائی، که آن‌ها را در حوالی‌ِ مزرعه‌ی سیب‌زمینی‌ِ خود دیده بود» لو رفتند.[۵۷۶]

از سوی دیگر، برخورد ناموافق مردم آن روستا با چریک‌های ما را نمی‌توان یکسره به حسابِ دیکتاتوری‌ِ شاه و تبلیغات دولت گذاشت- که در طول این مدت، چریک‌ها را «خرابکار» و «اشرار» و «تروریست‌های خدانشناس» معرفی کرده بود، و روستائیان گیلان و مازندران را با اعلامیه‌های تهدیدآمیز (در صورت همکاری با چریک‌ها) بمباران کرده بود- این برخورد دردناک، شاید نمودی هم بود از عدم خواست مردم اعماق به تغییر وضع موجود؛ که البته از دید چریک‌ها فقط به «ناآگاهی» تعبیر می‌شد. بنا بر این تحلیل، این تنها دیکتاتوری نبود که مانع جنبش‌های خودجوش یا عدم همدلی‌ِ مردم با چریک‌ها می‌شد، بلکه (در تبیینِ مارکسیستی)، این «ناآگاهی»، مبیّنِ «عدم رشد تضادها»ی «کار و سرمایه»، یا به بیانی دیگر، عدم وجود و نارسیدگی‌ِ شرایط عینی‌ِ انقلاب در جامعه بود. البته، چنان که قبلاً اشاره کردم، بیژن جزنی معتقد بود که شرایط عینی‌ِ انقلاب در جامعه‌ی ایران هنوز فراهم نیست. با این همه، او نیز، بر محوریت مبارزه‌ی مسلحانه «علیه دیکتاتوری»ی شاه- به عنوان نماینده‌ی «سرمایه‌داری» در ایران- پافشاری داشت. و اگر من درست فهمیده باشم، به فشرده‌ترین کلام می‌توان گفت که او نیز چنین می‌پنداشت که در فرایند مبارزه با دیکتاتوری‌ِ شاه، تضادها رشد خواهد کرد؛ شرایط عینی‌ِ انقلاب سوسیالیستی فراهم خواهد شد؛ و نهایتاً، به مبارزه با نظم سرمایه‌داری و امپریالیسم خواهد انجامید.

از این گذشته، مشکل در این جا بود که چریک‌های کمونیست ما، می‌دانستند که نه تنها روستائیان، بلکه انبوهی از مردم شهرنشین و تحصیل‌کرده اما غیرسازمانی‌ِ ایران از جزئیات برنامه برای پیاده کردن حکومت آرمانی‌ِ آن‌ها بی‌خبر هستند. چرا که در سراسر متن‌های تئوریک و بیانیه‌های مهمِ این سازمان، نه تنها نشانه‌های ملموسی از چه‌گونگی‌ِ برپائی‌ِ این حکومت آرمانی ترسیم نشده، بلکه پیرامون شیوه‌های سازمان‌یابی‌ِ توده‌ها در هنگام مبارزه نیز کوچک‌ترین اشاره‌ای دیده نمی‌شود. شرکت مردم شهر و روستا در باطل کردن بسیاری از پروژه‌های چریک‌ها در حین اجراء- یا دست کم، عدم همکاری با آن‌ها- در جای جای تاریخ این سازمان، نشان می‌دهد که انگیزه‌ی نخستینِ بسیاری از مردمی که

---

[۵۷۶] اولیویه برانسُن و میشل لووی، ***میراث انقلابی‌ِ چه گوارا***، ترجمه‌ی نیکو پور ورزان، نشر الکترونیکی‌ِ «آلترناتیو»، مرداد ۱۳۹۱، صص ۱۷ تا ۲۷.

حرکت چریک‌ها را در دل می‌ستودند و حتا بسیاری از «هواداران» این سازمان- چه در زمان شاه و چه در آغاز جمهوری‌ی اسلامی- مخالفت با دستگاه حاکم و ضربه زدن به آن بوده است، و نه صرفاً رسیدن به «آرمانِ» چریک‌ها، که در غیاب حزب و سندیکا و اتحادیه‌های کارگری و تشکل‌های دهقانی، شاید شیوه‌های عملی‌ی تحقق آن برای خود چریک‌ها هم چندان روشن نبود.

با این همه، واقعیتِ انکارناپذیر این است که مجموعه‌ی عملیات مسلحانه- در کنار بیانیه‌های روشنگرانه نسبت به ماهیت رژیم و «اعلامیه‌های توضیحی»‌ی چریک‌ها (پس از اجرای هر پروژه‌ی عملیاتی) در کنار خبرِ مکررِ تیرباران‌ها و زمزمه‌های شکنجه‌ی پیکارگران اسیر در زندان‌ها، در کنار خیزش‌های دانشجوئی، در کنارِ فرهنگی که با شعر و ادبیات و هنر پدید آورد- هم جوّ سیاسی‌ی ضد رژیم را در لایه‌های متوسط شهری به شدت دامن زد، و هم نیروی «سیاهکل» را به صورت یک جنبش سراسری به گوشه و کنار محافل دانشجوئی‌ی ایران منتقل کرد. به طوری که، به رغم کوشش‌های ساواک و تبلیغات مسموم رژیم علیه چریک‌ها[۵۷۷]، از سیاهکل تا انقلاب ۵۷، پدیده‌هائی به نام «فعالیت مخفی» و «مبارزه‌ی مسلحانه»، و «مشی‌ی چریکی» در فرهنگ سیاسی‌ی ایران به مفهومی آشنا و در عین حال حماسی تبدیل شد. فداکاری و از جان‌گذشتگی‌ی دلیرانِ سیاهکل (و البته، چریک‌های سازمان مجاهدین خلق)، در پژواک حماسه‌های «پاتریس لومومبا» رهبر انقلابی‌ی کنگو، «چه گوارا»‌ی امریکای لاتین، «هوشی مینه» ویتنام، و «جمیله بوپاشا»‌ی الجزیره، تا آن جا میان جوانان ایران جذابیت پیدا کرده بود که حتا دانش‌آموزان دبیرستانی را (که نمی‌توان پذیرفت به اندازه‌ی خود چریک‌ها بر دانش‌های مارکسیستی، یا بر ویژگی‌های «نظم توحیدی»‌ی مجاهدین، مسلط بوده باشند) به زندگی‌ی چریکی می‌کشید. مثلاً در اوایل این دهه، تعداد اندکی از دانش‌آموزان دبیرستانی در شهر نهاوند، «گروه ابوذر» را تشکیل دادند، که به زودی توسط ساواک کشف شد و تمام اعضاء آن دستگیر و کشته شدند.[۵۷۸] یا، سازمان چریک‌های فدائی‌ی خلق ایران، در بهمن ماه ۱۳۵۲، یعنی در کوران مبارزه‌ی مسلحانه، از گروهی به نام «گروه عیار» در نهاوند، یاد کرد و در اثبات همگانی شدنِ گرایش به مشی‌ی چریکی، در شماره‌ی ۱ نشریه‌ی داخلی‌ی سازمان نوشت:

---

[۵۷۷] افزون بر تکرار واژه‌ی «خرابکاران» و «اشرار» و «دزدان مسلح» در یادکردن از چریک‌ها، و افزون بر توطئه‌های گوناگون برای بَدنمائی‌ی چریک‌ها در انظار مردم، ساواک، که به هیچ روی نتوانسته بود تهمت جاسوسی و وابستگی‌ی چریک‌ها را در افکار عمومی جا بیاندازد، از ۲۹ اردی‌بهشت تا اول خرداد ۵۵ در روزنامه‌های کیهان و اطلاعات و رستاخیز دو نامه منتشر کرد، و مدعی شد که آن‌ها را در حمله‌ی روزهای ۲۶ و ۲۸ اردی‌بهشت ۵۵ به پایگاه چریک‌ها بدست آورده است. فریبرز سنجری، چریک فدائی‌ی خلق، در متن مستدلی که در چهلمین سالگرد سیاهکل نوشت، با رجوع به ترمنولوژی‌ی این دو نامه و تفاوت آن با زبان و ادبیات کمونیست‌های فدائی، و با تکیه بر رواج رمزنویسی در سازمان چریک‌های فدائی‌ی خلق، جعلی بودن این نامه‌ها را ثابت کرد. در فرازهائی از متن فریبرز سنجری می‌خوانیم: «ساواک در این نامه‌ها نوشته بود که "صد هزار آفیش امپریالیستی رسید و به موقع هم رسید" که البته منظورشان "صد هزار دلار" بود. و یا، جهت نسبت دادن جاسوسی به چریک ها نوشته بودند که "راجع به اطلاعاتی که دوستان بزرگتر درباره‌ی ارتش ضد خلقی‌ی ایران خواسته بودند باید بگویم فعلاً چند نفر از افسران وظیفه را در اختیار داریم." [...] البته گذشت زمان لازم بود تا این شاهکارِ ساواکساخته "تعمیق" یافته و حال [در جمهوری‌ی اسلامی] ادعا شود که این نامه‌ها در جریان دستگیری‌ی رفیق اشرف دهقانی در آلمان به دست پلیس آلمان افتاده و نهادهای امنیتی‌ی آلمان در چارچوب روابط خود با رژیم شاه، اسناد و میکروفیلم‌های به دست آمده را در اختیار ساواک قرار داده اند .[...] این ادعا در کتابی به نام "نهضت امام خمینی" نیز مطرح شده است. سید حمید روحانی نویسنده‌ی کتاب مزبور در صفحه ۴۹۷ کتاب مدعی شده که با دستگیری‌ی اشرف دهقانی در ۲۳ دی ماه ۵۴ در آلمان "تعدادی میکروفیلم حاوی‌ی نامه‌ها از ایران" که گویا رفیق اشرف با خود حمل می کرده "به دست پلیس آلمان افتاده است." روشن است که این ادعای دشمنان ماست. ولی اجازه بدهید بر خلاف همه‌ی این دروغ ها، تاکید کنم رفیق اشرف دهقانی موقعی که در سال ۵۴ از منطقه به آلمان آمد و به وسیله پلیس آلمان دستگیر شد، هیچ میکروفیلم و نامه‌ای که از ایران فرستاده شده باشد با خودش حمل نمی‌کرد و مدتی پس از دستگیری هم آزاد می -شود. حالا شما به تاریخ دستگیری‌ی این رفیق در آلمان و تاریخی که در زیر نامه‌ها گذاشته شده توجه کنید که خود این امر دروغ بودن چنین ادعایی را در این زمینه ثابت می کند. چه‌طور ممکن است کسی که خودشان نوشته‌اند در تاریخ ۲۳ دی ۵۴ دستگیر شده می‌توانسته نامه‌ی مورخه‌ی ۱۷ فروردین ۵۵ را با خودش حمل کند؟» به مأخذ زیر نگاه کنید:

❖ فریبرز سنجری، ***رزم سیاهکل و نامه‌های ساواک‌ساخته***، تارنمای «بی بی سی»، ۹ فوریه ۲۰۱۱/ ۲۰ بهمن ۱۳۸۹:
http://www.bbc.co.uk/persian/iran/2011/02/110204_l13_siahkal_fariborz_sanjari.shtml

[۵۷۸] حسین زرینی، ***گروه ابوذر***، تهران: انتشارات انقلاب اسلامی، ۱۳۸۱. (همراه با اسناد بازجوئی‌ی شهربانی و ساواک از افراد این گروه.) برای آگاهی بیش‌تر پیرامون گروه‌های چریکی، از سیاهکل تا یک سال به انقلاب، خوانندهام را به صفحات ۴۴۲ تا ۴۵۷ از کتاب «ایران بین دو انقلاب» نوشته‌ی یرواند آبراهامیان، چاپ هشتم، ۱۳۸۳ رجوع می‌دهم

> [...] ما شاهد مبارزه‌ی جوانانی هستیم که از طریق عملیات انقلابی‌ی مبارزین فدائی، اعدام‌ها و درگیری‌های شجاعانه‌ی آن‌ها، با مفهوم مبارزه آشنا شده‌اند. آن‌ها با همه‌ی صداقت و پاکباختگی‌شان، که ملهم از پاکباختگی‌ی چریک‌هاست، به مبارزه روی می‌آورند. گروه «عیار» در نهاوند، نمونه‌ی بارز از فعالیت‌های این گونه مبارزین جوان است. این گروه که از عده‌ای جوانان ۱۸ تا ۲۰ ساله تشکیل شده بود، چند عمل موفقیت‌آمیز مسلحانه انجام داد. خلع سلاح یک پاسبان در قم، اعدام انقلابی‌ی یکی از ثروتمندان منفور در نهاوند، و انفجار سازمان زنان ارتجاعی‌ی نهاوند، از عملیات این گروه بود. گروه‌های دیگری نیز در یزد، دزفول، مراغه، و بروجرد و ... فعالیت می‌کنند که اکثراً از مبارزین جوان تشکیل شده‌اند. پیوستن مبارزین جوان و محصلین به مبارزه، آثار پروسه‌ی توده‌ای شدن مبارزه‌ی مسلحانه است. زیرا محصلین در مقیاسی وسیع‌تر از مثلاً دانشجویان، در سطح [سراسر؟ این کلمه در فرمت پی دی اف به درستی قابل خواندن نیست] کشور پراکنده‌اند.[۵۷۹]

جای شگفتی است که این سازمان «مارکسیست لنینیست»، که بنا بر تعریف، در «پروسه‌ی توده‌ای شدن مبارزه» می‌بایست بر «طبقه‌ی کارگر و زحمتکشان جامعه» تکیه کند، لایه‌ی دانش‌آموز و دانشجو را تکیه‌گاه قرار داده بود، و روی خیزش‌های آن‌ها حساب باز کرده بود. و بدین ترتیب اما، جای شگفتی نیست که در دوران انقلاب و پس از پیروزی‌ی آن، اکثریت کارگران و زحمتکشان و لایه‌های فرودست جامعه، از اردوگاه «حزب‌الله» سر در آوردند، و روبه‌روی چریک‌ها و هواداران دانش‌آموز و دانشجوشان ایستادند. و باز، با آن بینش چیره بر سپهر مبارزه، جای شگفتی نیست که در نیمه‌ی اول دهه‌ی پنجاه، هر پیکارگری که- بر اساس تز تقدم «آگاهی‌ی طبقاتی» و «اولویتِ تشکل‌های کارگری»- راه مبارزه‌ی صنفی/ سیاسی را پیشنهاد می‌کرد، و یا مشی‌ی جاری در سازمان را به چالش می‌کشید، و یا مانند مصطفی‌شعاعیان، به تقدیس لنین و الگوکردنِ آموزه‌های او در سازمان خرده می‌گرفت و «نظراتِ ضدِ لنینی» ابراز می‌کرد، صدایش بی‌پژواک می‌ماند؛ و در صورت پافشاری، با عنوان‌هائی مانند «مارکسیست امریکائی»، یا «عضو مسئله‌دار»، یا «فرصت‌طلب»، از درگاه این «چپ» رانده می‌شد.[۵۸۰] البته یادآوری‌ی مجدد این نکته را بایسته می‌دانم که «چریک‌های فدائی‌ی خلق ایران» (موسوم به جریان اشرف دهقانی) و «فدائیان خلق ایران- اقلیت» (به رهبری‌ی «توکل»)، یا «سازمان چریک‌های فدائی‌ی خلق ایران» (به رهبری‌ی مهدی سامع)- که به خاطر سازش «اکثریتِ» چریک‌ها با نظام جمهوری‌ی اسلامی، از پیکر ستبر «سازمان چریک‌های فدائی‌ی خلق ایران» جدا شدند- هنوز پس از سی و چهار سال (و البته با همه‌ی اختلاف نظرهائی که اکنون با هم دارند) به حقانیت مشی‌ی مسلحانه باور دارند، و سبب‌ساز باختِ انقلاب به روحانیت را کوتاه آمدن بخش «اکثریتِ» چریک‌ها در اجرای مشی‌ی مسلحانه و تحویل اسلحه به حاکمیت و حمایت از حکومت جدید برآورد می‌کنند. در هر حال، چند ماه پس از «پیروزی‌ی انقلاب»، در حالی که هنوز انشعاب بزرگ رسماً اعلام نشده بود،

---

۵۷۹ فهرست مطالب دوره‌ی اول نبرد خلق (بهمن ۱۳۵۲ تا خرداد ۱۳۵۵)، گردآوری و تنظیم از مهدی سامع، شماره‌ی ۱ نبرد خلق، صص ۱ و ۲، برگرفته از تارنمای «آرشیو اسناد اپوزیسیون»، بازدید ۱۷ اسفند ۱۳۸۹:
http://www.iran-archive.com/fadaiiane_khalgh/cherikha_ta_1357/nabarde_khalgh/nabarde_khalgh.html

۵۸۰ برچسب «مارکسیست امریکائی» نخستین بار از سوی بیژن جزنی به مصطفی شعاعیان زده شد. مصطفی شعاعیان، که به ضرورت تشکیل یک «جبهه» در مبارزه علیه شاه می‌اندیشید، در کتابی با عنوان «شورش»، با تکیه بر لزوم مبارزه‌ی مسلحانه، اهمیت کار سیاسی و روشنگری‌ی مبارزان بین طیف‌های مختلف طبقه‌ی کارگر را یادآور شد، و در این رهگذر ، تزها و عملکرد لنین (به ویژه نفی‌ی انترناسیونالیسم کمونیستی)، همچنین، اجرای مو به موی آموزه‌های لنین و لنینیسم در سازمان چریک‌های فدائی‌ی خلق را به باد انتقاد گرفت. حمید مؤمنی، چریک فدائی‌ی خلق در سال ۱۳۵۳ در کتابی با عنوان «شورش نه، قدم‌های سنجیده در راه انقلاب»، در دفاع از تزهای سازمان و از لنینیسم، و در دفاع از این نظر که مصطفی شعاعیان اصولاً لنین و لنینیسم را نخوانده یا نفهمیده، به او پاسخ داد. من کتاب «شورش» نوشته‌ی مصطفی شعاعیان را ندیده‌ام. اما- افزون بر مآخذ زیر- بازگفت‌هائی از آن را در کتاب حمید مؤمنی (شورش نه؛ قدم‌های سنجیده در راه انقلاب) خوانده‌ام:

- حمید مؤمنی، ***شورش نه، قدم‌های سنجیده در راه انقلاب***، بهار ۱۳۵۳؛ انتشار مجدد به صورت کتاب و نشر الکترونیکی از سوی چریک‌های فدائی‌ی خلق، با مقدمه‌ای از اشرف دهقانی، تارنمای «سیاهکل»، آذر ۱۳۹۱:
http://www.siahkal.com/publication/shooresh-na-Part1.pdf
- انوش صالحی، ***مصطفی شعاعیان و رمانتیسم انقلابی***، سوئد: نشر باران، ۲۰۱۰.
- خسرو شاکری (ویراستار)، ***مصطفی شعاعیان، هشت نامه به چریک‌های فدائی‌ی خلق، نقد یک منش فکری***، تهران: نشر نی، ۱۳۸۶.
- پیمان وهاب‌زاده، ***مصطفی شعاعیان: سیاست جبهه‌ای، استالینیسم و نقش روشنفکران ایران***، ترجمه به فارسی از محسن صفاری، فصل‌نامه‌ی «باران»، سوئد: شماره‌ی ۳۴- ۳۵، پائیز و زمستان ۱۳۹۱، صص۱۳۵- ۱۶۰.

سازمان چریک‌های فدائی‌ی خلق- که حالا با بینش و منش و روشِ چریک‌های اولیه (تا پایان حمید اشرف) فاصله گرفته بود- سبب‌های شکست این سازمان را در «فقدان ارتباط و پیوند با توده‌ها» برآورد کرد:

> در آستانه‌ی قیام، به علت فقدان صف‌بندی‌ی طبقاتی‌ی مشخص، فقدان هژمونی‌ی پرولتاریائی بر جنبش، فقدان تشکل و آگاهی‌ی توده‌ها، فقدان سازمان‌های سیاسی‌ی انقلابی که با توده‌های خود در ارتباط همه جانبه و نزدیک باشند، خصوصیات طبقاتی و قشری‌ی رهبری‌ی جنبش، و بالأخره، احساس خطر بورژوازی در برابر توده‌ها و مبارزه‌ی اوجگیرنده‌ی آن‌ها، زمینه‌های عینی‌ی سازش بین بورژوازی و رهبری‌ی خرده بورژوازی‌ی جنبش را فراهم ساخت.[۵۸۱]

و فاجعه آن جا دهان باز می‌کند که بدانیم این تشخیص نابه‌هنگام، از نخستین زمزمه‌هائی بود که درست در زمان شکل‌گیری‌ی حکومت اسلامی، به پاره شدن «سازمان چریک‌های فدائی‌ی خلق ایران»، و گرویدن بخشی از «اکثریتِ» آن به «حزب توده»‌ای انجامید، که هم به سبب تبعید درازمدت، پایگاه گسترده‌ای میان مردم ایران نداشت، و هم قرار بود که حکومت ولایت فقیه را با تمام نیروی خود حمایت کند. تا سیاست حزب توده در انقلاب سال ۱۳۵۷ در این جا مستدل شود، معترضه‌ی زیر را بایسته می‌دانم: در آستانه‌ی انقلاب، ایرج اسکندری، دبیر اول کمیته‌ی مرکزی‌ی حزب توده، با دستورالعملِ همراهی و همکاری‌ی این حزب با آیت‌الله خمینی مخالفت کرد، و نورالدین کیانوری، نواده‌ی شیخ فضل‌الله نوری، در همان تبعیدگاه ربع قرنی‌اش- آلمان شرقی- به جای او به رهبری‌ی حزب توده برگزیده شد. احسان طبری، ایدئولوگ حزب توده، پیش از اسارت در زندان جمهوری‌ی اسلامی، در این زمینه می‌نویسد:

> در آستانه‌ی انقلاب ایران، کاملاً روشن شد که رفیق اسکندری (که جانشین دکتر رادمنش شده بود) در انقلاب ایران خواستار پیروی از شعارهای جناح لیبرالی‌ی جبهه‌ی ملی است. در برابر او، رفیق کیانوری با مشی درستی که پلنوم ۱۵ و ۱۶ و ۱۷ حزب [توده] و **حوادث واقعی‌ی صحنه‌ی انقلاب** ایران صحت آن را تأیید کرد، قرار داشت. شکست مشی‌ی لیبرالی و **پیروزی‌ی مشی‌ی انقلابی**، ابتکار را به طور نهائی از دست گروه مقابل خارج ساخت و به اختلاف درازنفس و رنج‌آور حزب نقطه‌ی ختامی گذاشت. [...] رفیق اسکندری در آستانه‌ی انقلاب ایران در اثر لجاج در دفاع از مشی‌ی لیبرالی (دادن شعار «دموکراسی» و «قانون اساسی» به جای سرنگونی‌ی سلطنت) حتا با رأی‌ی خودش مسند را تهی ساخت.[۵۸۲] (گیومه‌ها و پرانتزها از احسان طبری است. تأکیدها از من است.)

برای روشن شدن عبارتِ «به رأی‌ی خودش»، باید به خاطرات ایرج اسکندری مراجعه کرد؛ تا هم معنی‌ی تفکر «دموکراتیک» را فهمید، و هم دردِ اجبار را در «تهی کردن مسند» چشید.[۵۸۳] البته، همین جا باید یادآوری کنم که ایرج اسکندری، در مقام رئیس کمیته‌ی مرکزی‌ی حزب توده، پیش‌تر از این تاریخ، در راه مبارزه با رژیم شاه به دامان آیت‌الله

---

[۵۸۱] نشریه‌ی «کار»، سال دوم، شماره‌ی ٦١، ١٤ خرداد ١٣٥٩، ص ٥ ضمیمه. برگرفته از تارنمای «مرکز اسناد اپوزیسیون ایران»، بازدید خرداد ۱۳۸۹:

www.iran-archive.com/fadaiie-khalgh/fadaiian-aksariiat/kar/dowre-1-61-150/061pdf

[۵۸۲] احسان طبری، ***از دیدار خویشتن***، (١٣٦٠- پیش از زندان)، به کوشش ف. شیوا، چاپ دوم، سوئد: نشر باران، ١٣٧٩/ ٢٠٠١، ص ٨٢.

[۵۸۳] کتاب «خاطرات ایرج اسکندری» حاصل گفت‌وگوی او با بابک امیر خسروی و فریدون آذرنور (دو تن از کادرهای پیشین حزب توده) است. متن نوارها را محسن عاشورپور (عضو پیشین کمیته‌ی مرکزی حزب توده) و شیوا فرهمند راد (عضو پیشین حزب توده) تنظیم کرده‌اند، و مجلدات آن بین سال‌های ۱۳٦۷ و ۱۳٦۸ توسط انتشارات «حزب دموکراتیک مردم ایران» در آلمان منتشر شد. مفاد این مجلدات با «ویرایش» جمهوری‌ی اسلامی نیز در سال ۱۳۸٤ منتشر شد. من مجلدات پیشین این خاطرات را ندیده‌ام. اما کتاب زیر را دیده‌ام:

- ❖ خاطرات ایرج اسکندری، دبیر اول حزب توده‌ی ایران (١٣٤٩- ١٣٥٧)، تهران: مؤسسه‌ی مطالعات و پژوهش‌های سیاسی، ١٣٨٤.

خمینی در نجف، نیز آویخته بود؛[۵۸۴] منتها، به خاطر مقاومت در برابر «سرنگونی‌ی سلطنت» و تأسیس حکومت اسلامی به رهبری‌ی آیت‌الله خمینی است که حالا وادار می‌شود «مسند را تهی» کند. مسئله در این جا البته «مسندِ» این یا آن نیست؛ بلکه درد بی‌درمانی که حزب توده، و به ویژه با همکاری‌ی بخش «اکثریت» سازمان چریک‌های فدائی‌ی خلقِ آن زمانی، بر دل تاریخ ایران گذاشت، در این است که «مشی‌ی انقلابی»ی حزب توده، با پایان «انقلاب» پایان یافت، و با تکیه بر «ضدامپریالیست» بودنِ آیت‌الله خمینی، به مشی‌ی سازش با نظام ولایت فقیه جا سپرد. با توجه به چنین شرایطی است که نظریه‌ی «دزدیده‌شدنِ انقلاب توسط لایه‌ی روحانی»، استناد و اعتبار خود را از دست می‌دهد. تا نمونه‌ای از ابراز این «نظریه» را (که در درازنای سی و پنج سال گذشته صدها بار در متن‌های همه‌ی طیف‌های مختلف چپ در تبعید تکرار شده است و هنوز تکرار می‌شود) این جا ثبت کرده باشم، به سراغ ناهید سروستانی، فیلمساز مقیم سوئد، می‌روم. ناهید سروستانی، عضو خانواده‌ی چپ در روزهای قیام بهمن ۵۷، و سازنده‌ی فیلم‌های مستندِ «فحشا زیر چادر» و «من و ملکه» در دوران تبعید، سومین فیلم خود را «انقلاب دزدیده شده‌ی من» نامیده است. محمد عبدی در مصاحبه‌ای با سروستانی، از او می‌پرسد: «از نام فیلم شروع کنیم؛ "انقلاب دزدیده شده من"...» و سروستانی در پاسخ می‌گوید:

> خب دزدیدند از ما. کسانی که انقلاب کردند بیش‌تر بچه‌های مبارز چپ بودند. حتا اگر اسلامی‌ها هم بودند، باز چپ بودند. من یادم هست آن روزی که انقلاب شد، همه خیلی خوشحال بودند، اما چند دقیقه بعد گفتند **آن‌ها** بودند که انقلاب کردند و اصلاً **ما** گیج بودیم که چه‌طور شد که این اتفاق افتاد و به یک شکل‌هایی از ما دزدیدن‌اش.[۵۸۵]

از پرسش و پاسخ در این مصاحبه چنین برمی‌آید که بن‌مایه‌ی این فیلم به سوژه‌های «زندان» و «اعدام» مربوط می‌شود، و نه الزاماً به روندهای انقلاب ۵۷. اما، جمله‌های ناهید سروستانی در بازگفت بالا، از سرگشتگی‌ی ذهنِ گوینده بین دو مفهومِ «اسلامی» و «چپ»، بین «آن‌ها» و «ما»، خبر می‌دهد؛ سرگشتگی‌ای که نه تنها در زمان انقلاب، بلکه سی و چهار سال بعد از انقلاب نیز ذهن گوینده را اشغال کرده است. البته، ناهید سروستانی- چنان که در فیلم مستند «من و ملکه» خود را معرفی کرده است- از هواداران فعال در سازمان چریک‌های فدائی‌ی خلق بوده است و نه از اعضاء کمیته‌ی مرکزی و تصمیم‌گیر در این سازمان. اما وجود این «گیجی» و تحیر از باختن به «آن‌ها»، به نوبه‌ی خود، خواننده را گیج و متحیر می‌کند که این «چپ» چه‌گونه ندید که با تأیید یک «مجتهد شیعی» در مقام «رهبری»ی انقلاب- دست کم از روزهای عید فطر و تاسوعا/عاشورای ۵۷ به بعد- «انقلاب»اش را دو دستی به «آن‌ها»ئی که «اسلامی»اش را می‌خواستند، تقدیم کرده بود. و تازه، این گیجی و حیرت و حسرت شامل برخی از افراد آن طیفِ چپ هم هست که با نام‌های «اکثریت» و «حزب توده»، آیت‌الله را در مقام رهبری‌ی انقلاب تأیید کردند؛ و حتا زمانی که خود مورد تاخت و تازِ نظام تازه واقع شدند، و حتا در سالیان دراز تبعید، هنوز هم از وجود و حضور جمهوری‌ی اسلامی دفاع می‌کنند، و امیدوار هستند که این نظام، از «راه رشد غیرسرمایه‌داری»، مردم ایران را به «انقلاب دموکراتیکِ» موعود برساند.

---

۵۸۴ حجت‌الاسلام سیدمحمود دعایی که در نجف از نزدیکان آیت‌الله خمینی بود، پیرامون همکاری‌ی حزب توده (به دبیر کلی‌ی ایرج اسکندری) با رژیم صدام، در مبارزه با رژیم شاه، می‌نویسد: «بعد از آن که رژیم بعث عراق تصمیم گرفت با ایران وارد درگیری بشود، کانون‌هائی بوجود آورد که از مبارزین ایرانی نیز دعوت به فعالیت کردند. نمایندگان عراق سراغ خیلی‌ها رفتند. صدام، تیمور بختیار را دعوت کرد. [...] در کنار او عراقی‌ها در اروپا سراغ کنفدراسیون و دانشجویان ناراضی‌ی ایران رفتند. سراغ جبهه ملی‌ی دوم در اروپا و نیز حزب توده رفتند. علی‌نقی منزوی، نماینده حزب توده در آلمان شرقی [...] از طرف ایرج اسکندری به عراق آمده بود و این‌ها اصرار داشتند که از امام هم دعوت کنند، که امام نپذیرفت.» به مأخذ زیر نگاه کنید:

- ❖ ***فصل‌نامه‌ی مطالعات تاریخی***، تهران: مؤسسه‌ی مطالعات و پژوهش‌های سیاسی، سال سوم، شماره‌ی پانزدهم، زمستان ۱۳۸۴، صص ۱۸ - ۱۹ و ۲۹.

۵۸۵ محمد عبدی، ***انقلابی که دزدیده شد***، تارنمای «بی بی سی»، ۱۰ بهمن ۱۳۹۱/ ۲۹ ژانویه ۲۰۱۳: http://www.bbc.co.uk/persian/arts/2013/01/130129_l44_nahid_sarvestani_move.shtml

سازمان مجاهدین خلق ایران[۵۸۶] از درون کانون‌ها و هیئت‌های مذهبی، مدرسه‌های دینی، انجمن‌های اسلامی‌ی دانشگاه‌ها، کمیته‌های دانشجوئی‌ی جناح مذهبی‌ی «جبهه‌ی ملی‌ی دوم»، «نهضت آزادی» و «حوزه‌ی علمیه‌ی قم» بیرون آمد. هسته‌های آغازین این سازمان را جوانانی، اکثراً از خانواده‌های بازاری یا روحانی، و عمیقاً مذهبی/ سنتی تشکیل می‌دادند، که در عین باورِ بی‌چون و چرا به تعالیم اسلام شیعی، دانش‌آموخته، اهل مطالعه، آشنا با جنبش‌های رهائی‌بخش کشورهای جهان، و بر فراز همه، معترض به شرایط حاکم بر ایران بودند. اعتراض آن‌ها، به خفقان سیاسی، نابرابری‌های اقتصادی/ اجتماعی، و «وابستگی‌ی رژیم شاه به امپریالیسم» بود؛ و اعتراض فرهنگی‌ی آن‌ها نیز، به تسلط «اسلام سنتی» بر جامعه‌ی روحانیت، و عدم توجه این جامعه به وجه سیاسی‌ی اسلام برای مقابله با آن شرایط بود. حضور مقتدر آیت‌الله بروجردی، به عنوان تنها مرجع تقلید شیعیان، و تز او مبنی بر عدم مداخله‌ی روحانیت در سیاست، از یک سو، و ناتوانی‌ی جبهه‌ی ملی و نهضت آزادی در مقابله با خودکامگی‌های شاه، از سوی دیگر، سبب شد که این جوانان آزادی‌خواه و عدالت‌جو، علیه اسلامِ سنتی‌ی پدران خود برخیزند؛ مفهوم «اسلام راستین» را که از نوشته‌های نواندیشان دینی (کلاهی و روحانی[۵۸۷]) گرفته بودند، به مفهوم «اسلام انقلابی» (که به ویژه پس از ۱۵ خرداد ۴۲ در نام آیت‌الله خمینی متبلور شده بود) گره بزنند؛ و این «اسلام راستین/ انقلابی» را- در وجه ستم‌ستیزی- با مارکسیسم، همخانواده ارزیابی کنند.

از این چشم‌انداز کلی بود که محمد حنیف‌نژاد (۱۳۱۸- ۱۳۵۱)، سعید محسن (۱۳۱۸- ۱۳۵۱)، اصغر بدیع‌زادگان (۱۳۱۹- ۱۳۵۱)، علیرضا نیک‌بین رودسری (متولد ۱۳۲۱)- دانش‌آموخته‌های رشته‌های مختلف مهندسی و ریاضی، پس از چند سال مطالعه، در سال ۱۳۴۴ هسته‌ی نخستین این سازمان را شکل دادند.[۵۸۸] (از حسن افتخاری جهرمی- که پس از

---

۵۸۶ **توضیح:** نگارش فشرده‌ای که از تاریخچه‌ی «سازمان مجاهدین خلق ایران» در این جا آوردم، در سال ۲۰۱۲/ ۱۳۹۱ به پایان رسید. در مه ۲۰۱۳/ خرداد ۱۳۹۲، تاریخچه‌ی فشرده‌ای از این سازمان از سوی «سازمان پیکار» در اینترنت منتشر شد. از آن رو که در تطبیق متن خودم با متن‌های «سازمان پیکار» متوجه تفاوت معنی‌داری نشدم، در ویرایش نهائی به متن حاضر دست نزدم. به سه مأخذ زیر نگاه کنید.

- https://www.youtube.com/watch?v=65WO5QHIusM
- https://www.youtube.com/watch?NR=1&v=CKDFP7YaPyw&feature=endscreen
- https://www.youtube.com/watch?v=maW2lOf6fR8

۵۸۷ افزون بر آیت‌الله طالقانی و آیت‌الله مطهری، که قبلاً به فعالیت‌های دینی/ فرهنگی‌ی آن‌ها اشاره کردم، به روایت تراب حق‌شناس، که خود در سال‌های ۱۳۳۸- ۱۳۳۹ در حوزه‌ی علمیه‌ی قم تحصیل می‌کرده، در این حوزه، روحانیان جوانی بودند که «تلاش می‌کردند چهار چوب کهنه و قدیمی و سنتی را بشکنند و به اصطلاح " اصلاح‌طلبان مذهبی"ی آن دوره بودند. یکی محمد حسین بهشتی بود. [...] و نیز رفسنجانی، مکارم شیرازی، جعفر سبحانی تبریزی و .. .[...] می‌خواهم بگویم که به هر حال حرکتی که بعدها به رهبری‌ی خمینی شروع شد و به صورت یک جنبش سیاسی در آمد، ابتداء به صورت یک جنبش فرهنگی در بین روحانیون جوان شکل گرفت. مانند بیرون آوردن مجله‌ای با جلد رنگی به نام مکتب اسلام یا بر پا کردن کلاس درس انگلیسی برای طلبه ها؛ و این کارهائی بود که مکارم و بهشتی و امثال آن‌ها می‌کردند. یا مثلاً مطرح کردن بحث درباره‌ی داروینیسم و مارکسیسم، در کلاس درس ایدئولوژی‌ی مکارم شیرازی.» به مأخذ زیر نگاه کنید:

- ***گفت‌وگوی پرویز قلیچ‌خانی با تراب حق‌شناس، از اعضای اولیه‌ی مجاهدین خلق***، نشریه‌ی «آرش» چاپ پاریس، شماره‌ی ۷۹، آبان ۱۳۸۰/ نوامبر ۲۰۰۱، ص۲۱.

توضیح: یادآوری کنم که تراب حق‌شناس، در سلسله‌گفتارهائی که چند سال بعد پیرامون تغییر مواضع ایدئولوژیک این سازمان و جدائی‌ی گروه مارکسیست‌شده از بدنه‌ی آن، ایراد کرد، ضمن تأکید بر «مذهبی بودن» پایه‌گذاران سازمان مجاهدین، مکرراً تأکید می‌کند که «نباید پایه‌گذاران این سازمان را با «مبارزان روحانی یکی گرفت»؛ این سازمان «با جریان‌های دیگر مذهبی تفاوت داشت»؛ «ما روی مبارز بودن خودمان تأکید داشتیم»؛ «مجاهدین را نمی‌توان در رده‌ی "نواندیشان دینی" قرار داد»، «با این که ما تحت تأثیر آن‌ها بودیم، اما با گرایش مبارزه‌ی انترناسیونالیستی وارد میدان شدیم.» به مأخذ زیر نگاه کنید:

- ***گفتارهائی از خاطرات تراب حق‌شناس پیرامون سازمان مجاهدین (م.ل): اهمیت و فراز و فرود آن***، ضبط شده در شهریور ۱۳۹۲، انتشار در تارنمای «پیکار»: ۲۲ شهریور ۱۳۹۲/ ۱۳ سپامبر ۲۰۱۳:

http://peykar.org/files/voice/article/MojahedinML.mp3

۵۸۸ از آن رو که عبدالرضا نیک‌بین، پیش از شروع عملیات مسلحانه‌ی مجاهدین، از گروه کناره گرفته بود، در متون رسمی‌ی سازمان مجاهدین خلق، نام علی‌اصغر بدیع‌زادگان به عنوان یکی از سه تن پایه‌گذاران این سازمان ثبت شده است. اما در بیش‌تر تاریخچه‌های سازمان مجاهدین خلق، نام «عبدالرضا نیک بین رودسری»، در شمار سه تن پایه‌گذاران این سازمان آمده است، و گفته شده که او تا پیش از کنارگیری از سازمان، نگارش متن‌های تئوریک و تهیه‌ی جزوه‌های درسی برای حوزه‌های آموزشی را به عهده داشته است. حسین احمدی روحانی، از قدیمی‌ترین اعضاء این سازمان نیز، در صفحه‌ی ۲۳ کتاب ***سازمان مجاهدین خلق***، (تهران: انتشارات مرکز اسناد انقلاب اسلامی، ۱۳۸۴)، از «عبدالرضا نیک‌بین (معروف به عبدی)» به عنوان یکی از سه تن بنیادگذاران اولیه‌ی این سازمان نام برده است. نکته‌ی دیگر پیرامون پایه‌گذاران این سازمان به حضور حسن افتخاری جهرمی مربوط است که او نیز پس از چندی از سازمان کناره گرفت. تراب حق‌شناس، پیرامون تاریخ تشکیل این سازمان نیز به نکته‌ی مهمی اشاره کرده است: «به نظر من، [تشکیل سازمان امری] تدریجی است. درست است که سازمان مجاهدین از زمان رضا رضایی اعلام کرده که تأسیس سازمان از سال ۱۳۴۴ است، ولی این جنبه‌ی تبلیغی دارد و هیچ تاریخ دقیقی را نمی‌توانیم در این مورد ثبت کنیم. اما شروع تدارک برای عمل مسلحانه، باید گفت سال‌های ۴۸-۴۹ است. بدین معنا که از سال ۴۴ تا سال ۴۸ سازمان، فعالیت آموزشی سیاسی و

چندی از سازمان کناره گرفت- نیز در مجموعه‌ی پایه‌گذاران نام برده شده است.)[۵۸۹] تپش مخالفت با رژیم محمدرضا شاه پهلوی و تعداد مخالفان مذهبی‌ِ او به گونه‌ای بالا بود که در اندک زمان، انبوهی از دانشجویان و دانش‌آموختگانِ جوان- لایه به لایه- به این هسته‌ی نخستین پیوستند، و مجموعاً، در شکل‌بندی‌ِ ساختاری، تدوین ایدئولوژی، تدوین خط مشی‌ِ مبارزه، تهیه و تنظیم متن‌های آموزشی، ساختن بمب دستی و مواد انفجاری، ساختن تکنولوژی‌ِ شنود برای گردآوری‌ِ اطلاعات، رمزنگاری، گردآوری‌ِ منابع مالی، آموزش نظامی، اجراء عملیات چریکی، و همچنین، در فراز و نشیب‌های ایدئولوژیک سازمان مجاهدین خلق ایران نقش داشتند.

هدف نهائی‌ِ این گروه، رسیدن به جامعه‌ی بی‌طبقه، در چارچوب «نظم توحیدی» در ایران بود؛[۵۹۰] و راه تحقق آن را نیز براندازی‌ِ رژیم موجود در ایران، با مشی‌ِ مسلحانه (به عنوان «یک ضرورت تاریخی») و با جلب حمایتِ «روحانیت مبارز»، برای تبلیغ پیرامون مفاهیم اسلام سیاسی تشخیص داده بودند.

گرچه پیکارگران سازمان چریک‌های فدائی‌ِ خلق، برای تشخیص و توضیح شرایط عینی و ذهنی‌ِ جامعه‌ی ایران و برای تدوین اصول استراتژیک و تاکتیک مبارزه، نیازمند خلاقیت‌های فردی بودند، اما ایدئولوژی‌ای به نام «مارکسیسم/ لنینیسم»، و منابعی مانند نوشته‌های ارنستو چه گوارا[۵۹۱] و «رژی دبره»[۵۹۲] را در اختیار داشتند. در حالی که پیشتازان سازمان مجاهدین خلق، باید هم ایدئولوژی و هم متدولوژی‌ِ مبارزه را از همین «اسلام راستین» استنتاج و استخراج می‌کردند؛ که به نوبه‌ی خود، مفهومی تازه، نامشخص و تعریف‌نشده بود. تراب حق‌شناس، یکی از شخصیت‌های اولیه‌ی این سازمان، در این زمینه می‌گوید:

مطالعاتی دارد، و خوب کسانی که در زمینه‌های اقتصاد، سیاست، فلسفه، دین و سایر مسائل واردتر بودند، دیگران را آموزش می‌دادند.» به مأخذ زیر نگاه کنید:

- ❖ ***گفت‌وگوی پرویز قلیچ‌خانی با تراب حق‌شناس، از اعضاء اولیه‌ی مجاهدین خلق***، پیشین، ص ۲۳.

[۵۸۹] یرواند آبراهامیان (در کتاب ***ایران بین دو انقلاب: از مشروطه تا انقلاب اسلامی***، پیشین، ص ۴۵۱) پایه‌گذاران سازمان مجاهدین را «شش تن» ذکر کرده، و به ترتیب زیر از آن‌ها نام برده است: محمد حنیف‌نژاد، سعید محسن، محمد [محمود] عسگری‌زاده، رسول [عبدالرسول] مشکین‌فام، علی‌اصغر بدیع‌زادگان، و احمد رضائی. من این ترکیب را در هیچ یک از مآخذ مربوط به این سازمان نیافتم. یرواند آبراهامیان، اما در کتاب «مجاهدین» (به زبان انگلیسی) غیر از سه تن پایه‌گذاران اولیه (حنیف‌نژاد، محسن و بدیع‌زادگان)، از ۹ تن دیگر، به عنوان اعضاء نخستین کمیته‌ی مرکزی‌ِ این سازمان- که کتاب‌های ایدئولوژیک سازمان را تدوین کردند- یاد کرده است. این ۹ نفر عبارت‌اند از: محمود عسگری‌زاده، عبدالرسول مشکین‌فام، علی میهن‌دوست، احمد رضائی، ناصر صادق، علی باکری، محمد بازرگانی، بهمن بازرگانی، و مسعود رجوی، که اندکی بعد، رضا رضائی، حسین روحانی، و تراب حق‌شناس به آن‌ها افزوده شدند. به مأخذ زیر نگاه کنید:

- ❖ Ervand Abrahamian, ***Radical Islam: The Iranian Mojahedin***, London: I.B. Touris Publishers, 1989, P. 89.

[۵۹۰] پیرامون «حکومت اسلامی»، به عنوان حکومت آرمانی‌ِ این سازمان (تا پیش از تغییر ایدئولوژی)، از جمله، در بازجوئی‌های به جا مانده از محمد حنیف‌نژاد و سعید محسن در زندان ساواک، یادداشت‌های آیت‌الله بهشتی، یادداشت‌های حسین احمدی روحانی، سخن رفته است. به دو مأخذ زیر نگاه کنید:

- ❖ حسین احمدی روحانی، ***سازمان مجاهدین خلق***، تهران: مرکز اسناد انقلاب اسلامی، انتشارات مرکز اسناد انقلاب اسلامی، ۱۳۸٤، ص ٤۹.
- ❖ گروه پژوهشگران، ***سازمان مجاهدین: از پیدائی تا فرجام، گفتار سوم از ۱۳٤٤ تا ۱۳۵۰***، تهران: سازمان مطالعات و پژوهش‌های سیاسی، ۱۳۸٤، صص ۲۷۶- ۲۸٤.

[۵۹۱] کتاب «جنگ چریکی» نوشته‌ی ارنستو چه گوارا (Ernesto "Che" Guevara)، پزشک، کوشنده‌ی سیاسی، و نویسنده‌ی آرژانتینی، متولد ۱۹۲۸، همرزم فیدل کاسترو در انقلاب کوبا، است. چه گوارا در این کتاب- که کتاب بالینی‌ِ چریک‌های امریکای لاتین شده بود- مبارزه‌ی قهرآمیز را تنها راه رویاروئی با امپریالیسم برآورد کرده و تاکتیک‌های آن را برشمرده بود. به مأخذ زیر نگاه کنید:

- ❖ ***Che Guevara: Radical Writings on Guerrilla Warfare, Politics and Revolution***, Filiquarian Publishing, 2006,

[۵۹۲] رژی دبره (Regis Debray)، فرانسوی، متولد ۱۹۴۰، روشنفکر، نویسنده، شاگرد لوئی آلتوسر، آکادمسین رشته‌ی فلسفه، فعال سیاسی و همرزم ارنستو چه گوارا، در کتاب «انقلاب در انقلاب؟ مبارزه‌ی مسلحانه و مبارزه‌ی سیاسی در امریکای لاتین»، مشی‌ِ مسلحانه‌ی پیشاهنگان مبارزه را به عنوان «موتور کوچک»ی برآورد کرد که «موتور بزرگ»، یعنی جامعه، را نهاتیاً به حرکت وامی‌دارد. افزون بر این بن‌مایه، که بن‌مایه‌ی کتاب «مبارزه‌ی مسلحانه هم استراتژی و هم تاکتیک» نوشته‌ی مسعود احمدزاده را تشکیل داد، رد پای درون‌مایه‌های آن کتاب- مانند برخورد با تروتسکیسم- نیز در کتاب احمدزاده قابل شناسائی است. به مأخذ زیر نگاه کنید:

- ❖ Regis Debray, ***Revolution in the Revolution? Armed Struggle and Political Struggle in Latin America***, translated into English by: Bobbye Ortiz, New York: Monthly Review Press and Grove, 1967.

> [...] بخشی از بند ناف ایدئولوژیک ما به برداشتی که بازرگان از اسلام داشت بسته بود. ما به تدریج به این نتیجه رسیده بودیم که حالا باید مطالعه کنیم و ببینیم راه مبارزه چه‌گونه است؟ ما نمی‌دانستیم که چه‌گونه باید مبارزه کرد؛ و این نقطه‌ی آغاز اساسی در آن دوره‌ی اول بود. در یکی از نخستین جزوه‌های آموزشی آمده بود که «ما راه و استراتژی مبارزه بلد نیستیم ولی این بدان معنا نیست که صلاحیت یادگیری آن را نداریم.» برای ما در این که باید مبارزه کرد حرفی نبود؛ بلکه در چه‌گونه مبارزه کردن حرف داشتیم. [...] ضمناً هیچ مدرسه‌ای هم نبود که بتوان در آن درس انقلابی آموخت، مگر خود زندگی. برای ما، مثلاً مرجعی مانند تجارب و آموزش حزب توده و جنبش جهانی‌ی کمونیستی وجود نداشت. ایدئولوژی‌ی دینی‌ی موجود هم مورد پذیرش ما نبود. در واقع ، نه تنها استراتژی‌ی مبارزه‌ی سیاسی ، بلکه جهان‌بینی‌مان را خودمان باید تدوین می‌کردیم.[۵۹۳]

در تکاپوی تدوین «جهان‌بینی» و «استراتژی‌ی مبارزه» است که این جوانان، به مهم‌ترین مرجع خود در «اسلام راستین»، یعنی مهندس مهدی بازرگان، پناه می‌برند. مهدی بازرگان- که در پل‌زدن بین عقل و علم و قرآن و فقه شیعی، عمری صرف کرده است (حتا مسئله‌ی «طهارت» در فقه را با «میکروب‌شناسی»ی عصر مدرن توجیه «علمی» کرده است)، و نوشته‌ها و سخنان او مهم‌ترین انگیزه‌ی خیزش این جوانان است- انگار که از خواب پریده باشد، به آن‌ها گوشزد می‌کند که «تدوین اسلام و بکاربستن آن در عمل کار **ساده‌ای نیست**.» لطف‌الله میثمی، یکی از اعضاء اولیه‌ی این سازمان، در خاطرات خود می‌نویسد:

> مهندس گفت: [...] این حرفی که شما می‌زنید، یعنی روش تحلیل اسلامی، و این قبیل مسائل، خیلی وقت می‌خواهد و خرج دارد. خود من در ماه ۴۰۰۰ تومان هزینه‌ی زندگی دارم، و باید در شرکت کار کنم تا آن را تأمین کنم. [...] تدوین اسلام و به کار بستن آن در عمل، کار ساده‌ای نیست. ما مثل کسی هستیم که قصد دارد کفش بدوزد، ولی نه چرم و نخ دارد، نه شماره و اندازه‌ی کفش را. این کار بسیار ظریف و دقیق است و باید متناسب با ویژگی‌های جامعه‌ی ما صورت گیرد. چنین کاری تاکنون انجام نشده است.[۵۹۴]

به عنوان معترضه همین جا بگویم که برخی از منابع موجود، پذیرش این خاطره‌ی میثمی را به مخاطره می‌اندازند. یکی از این منابع، کتاب مهم و اثرگذارِ «بعثت و ایدئولوژی»، نوشته‌ی مهندس بازرگان است. من جز پاره‌هائی از این اثر را نخوانده‌ام. اما، در همان پاره‌ها دیده‌ام که مهدی بازرگان برای دوختنِ «کفش»، هم «چرم» را دارد و هم «نخ» را، و هم «دوختن» را امری «سَهل» برآورد کرده است. خود مهدی بازرگان پیرامون این کتاب گفته است:

> یکی از برنامه‌های جشن بعثت که در زندان شاه در سال‌های ۴۰ تا ۴۲ ایراد شد و به صورت کتاب درآمد، عنوانش را بعثت و ایدئولوژی گذارده بودم که مورد استقبال و موجب تحرک‌هایی شد. هدف از تألیف آن کتاب، نشان دادن این مطلب بود که از اصول و احکام اسلام می‌توان به **سهولت** ایدئولوژی استخراج کرد و آئینی یا مکتبی برای مبارزان خودمان علیه استبداد و استیلای خارجی ارائه کرد.[۵۹۵]

در هر حال، واقعیت این است که پایه‌گذاران سازمان مجاهدین، و نخبگانی که بعداً به آن‌ها پیوستند، خود کمر همت بربستند، و برای یافتن ابزار نظری، مطالعه‌ی گسترده و همه‌جانبه‌ای را آغاز کردند.[۵۹۶] آن‌ها، با مطالعه‌ی تفسیرهای قرآن، نهج‌البلاغه، حدیث‌های قدسی، کتاب‌های «نواندیشان دینی»، تاریخ اسلام، تاریخ معاصر ایران، تاریخ جنبش‌های

---

۵۹۳ ***گفت‌وگوی پرویز قلیچ‌خانی با تراب حق‌شناس ...***، پیشین، ص ۲۳.

۵۹۴ خاطرات لطف‌الله میثمی، ***از نهضت آزادی تا مجاهدین***، جلد اول، محل نشر؟ نشر صمدیه، ۱۳۷۸، صص ۹۶- ۹۷.

۵۹۵ برگرفته از: سروش دباغ، ***بازرگان متأخر در برابر بازرگان متقدم***، نشریه‌ی «مهرنامه»، چاپ تهران، شماره‌ی ۴.

۵۹۶ محسن نجات‌حسینی در کتاب ***برفراز خلیج فارس***، پیشین، صص ۴۱۸ تا ۴۲۱، نام و نشان بسیاری از این آثار را ثبت کرده است. همچنین، یرواند آبراهامیان در کتاب «مجاهدین» (به زبان انگلیسی)، پیرامون برخی از این آثار توضیح داده است:

- Ervand Abrahamian, ***Radical Islam: The Iranian Mojahedin***, London: I.B. Touris Publishers, 1989, PP. 88-89.

جاری در جهان، گزیده‌ای از آثار مارکس، لنین، استالین، مائو، ایدئولوژی و متدولوژی‌ی سازمان را عمدتاً در سه کتاب زیر تدوین کردند: «شناخت»، نوشته‌ی حسین احمدی روحانی؛ «تکامل ما»، نوشته‌ی علی میهن‌دوست؛ و «راه انبیاء راه بشر»، نوشته‌ی محمد حنیف‌نژاد. مقاله‌ها و جزوه‌ها و کتاب‌هائی مانند «مقدمه‌ی مطالعات مارکسیستی»، نوشته‌ی سعید محسن، «اقتصاد به زبان ساده» ترجمه‌ی آزاد از کتاب «کارمزدی و سرمایه» نوشته‌ی مارکس، به قلم عسگری‌زاده، و «سیمای یک مسلمان» یا «نهضت حسینی»، نوشته‌ی مسعود رجوی و احمد رضائی نیز مکملی بر آن سه کتاب بودند. شیوه‌ی ساخت و پرداخت این ایدئولوژی/ متدولوژی، خوانش ویژه‌ای بود از آیات گزینشی‌ی قرآن و خطبه‌هائی از نهج‌البلاغه، که با مفاهیم پایه‌ای‌ی مارکسیسم همخوانی داشت؛ یا برعکس: سنجشِ تطبیقی‌ی مفاهیم مارکسیستی با برخی از متن‌های مقدس اسلامی.

از آن رو که آشنائی با منابع الهام‌بخش نوشته‌های یادشده از اهمیت معرف‌شناختی برخوردار است، در این جا به برخی از آن‌ها اشاره می‌کنم: «اصول مقدماتی‌ی فلسفه»، نوشته‌ی ژرژ پُلیتسر (فیلسوف مارکسیست، که ضمن شرح فلسفه‌ی «مادی» به زبان ساده، «ایده‌آلیسم فلسفی» را به سود «ماتریالیسم» رد کرده، اما «ایده‌آلیسم اخلاقی» را به معنای «فداکاری در راه عقیده و آرمان» لازم دانسته و ستوده است)؛ «ماتریالیسم دیالکتیک»، نوشته‌ی استالین؛ «دیالکتیک طبیعت و تاریخ: دینامیسم جهش- تضاد»، نوشته‌ی انور خامه‌ای؛ «درباره‌ی تضاد»، نوشته‌ی مائوتسه دون؛ کتاب‌های «خلقت انسان» و «قرآن و تکامل موجودات زنده»، نوشته‌ی یدالله سحابی؛ «حکومت از نظر اسلام» و «اسلام و مالکیت»، نوشته‌ی آیت‌الله طالقانی (که در دومی، بر سازگاری‌ی سوسیالیسم با مذهب تأکید شده است.)[۵۹۷]؛ «ذره‌ی بی‌انتها»، «اصل انسان»، و «راه طی‌شده»، نوشته‌ی مهدی بازرگان. در کتاب «تکامل ما»، روند تکامل انواع در داروینیسم، توجیهی قرآنی یافته است. از کتاب «راه طی شده»، نوشته‌ی مهدی بازرگان (در کنار آثاری چون «کتابچه‌ی سرخ مائو») نیز، به عنوان عمده‌ترین مأخذ برای سلسله جزوه‌هائی نام برده شده است، که بعداً به صورت کتابِ «راه انبیاء راه بشر» منتشر شد. گوهر مذهبی‌ی ایدئولوژی‌ی مجاهدین، از جمله، در پارگراف زیر تعیّن یافته است:

> ما پس از سال‌ها مطالعه‌ی وسیع در تاریخ اسلام و ایدئولوژی‌ی تشیع، به این نتیجه رسیده‌ایم که اسلام، به ویژه اسلام تشیع، در برانگیختن توده‌ها به انقلاب نقش عمده‌ای ایفا خواهد کرد. زیرا تشیع، به ویژه شهادت و مقاومت تاریخی‌ی حسین، هم دارای پیامی انقلابی است و هم جایگاه خاص در فرهنگ رایج ما دارد.[۵۹۸]

برگرفته‌ی زیر نیز، خویشاوندی‌ای را که مجاهدین خلق بین «اسلام تشیع» و «مارکسیسم» می‌دیدند، تا حدی بازنمائی می‌کند:

> [...] اسلام و مارکسیسم هر دو یک درس واحد می‌دهند؛ زیرا با بی‌دادگری مبارزه می‌کنند. اسلام و مارکسیسم هر دو یک پیام دارند؛ زیرا الهام‌بخش شهادت، مبارزه و ایثارند. کدام یک به اسلام نزدیک‌ترند: آن ویتنامی که با امپریالیسم می‌جنگد یا شاه که به صهیونیسم کمک می‌کند؟ از آن جا که اسلام دشمن ستمگری است، با مارکسیسم که او نیز دشمن ستمگری است، همکاری خواهد کرد. این هر دو یک دشمن دارند و آن امپریالیسم مرتجع است.[۵۹۹]

---

۵۹۷ یرواند آبراهامیان، ***ایران بین دو انقلاب: از مشروطه تا انقلاب اسلامی***، پیشین، ص ۴۲۱.
توضیح: من کتاب «اسلام و مالکیت» نوشته‌ی آیت‌الله طالقانی را ندیده‌ام. اما بنا به قول یرواند آبراهامیان (در کتاب ***مجاهدین ایرانی***، انگلیسی، ۱۹۸۹، ص ۸۲)، آیت‌الله طالقانی در این کتاب بر این باور است که اسلام مالکیت خصوصی را پذیرفته است، اما با فئودالیسم، سرمایه‌داری و زیاده‌خواهی‌ی آزمندانه مخالف است. این را هم باید بیافزایم که مجاهدین در طراحی‌ی ایدئولوژی‌ی خود این نظر آیت‌الله را نپذیرفتند، و راجع به «مالکیت خصوصی» و الغاء آن به نظر تازه‌ای رسیدند، که در متن حاضر به آن پرداخته‌ام.

۵۹۸ سازمان مجاهدین، «شرح تأسیس و تاریخچه و وقایع سازمان مجاهدین»، تهران: ۱۳۵۸، ص ۴۴، برگرفته از: یرواند آبراهامیان، ***ایران بین دو انقلاب***، پیشین، ص ۴۵۳

۵۹۹ سازمان مجاهدین، ***پاسخ به اتهامات اخیر رژیم***، ۱۳۵٤، ص ۱۰ تا ۱۳، برگرفته از یرواند آبراهامیان، ***ایران بین دو انقلاب***، پیشین، ص ٤۵۵.

با چنین درکی بود که مجاهدینِ اولیه، کل مارکسیسم را «علم مبارزه» شناسائی کردند: علمی که، «بدون آگاهی از» آن، «اعجاز قرآن [...] را به درستی نمی‌توان درک کرد.» یا: «بدون آشنائی با فرهنگ انقلابیِ عصر حاضر، درک عظمت آیات قرآن هیچ ممکن نیست.»[۶۰۰] و منظور از «فرهنگ انقلابیِ عصر حاضر»، البته، همانا همان فرهنگ مارکسیستی بود که با امیدِ امروز/ فردائی در نابود کردن «امپریالیسم» و مادرش: «سرمایه‌داری»، جای جای جهان آن روز را با آرزوی عدالت اجتماعی موج انداخته بود.

مهم‌ترین عنصر قابل تأمل در دستگاه نظری‌ی مجاهدین خلق، موضوع «مالکیت» است، که در قرآن، به وضوح از «خصوصی» بودنِ آن دفاع شده است. از آن رو که در حال حاضر، متأسفانه، بسیاری از متن‌های تئوریک این سازمان از دسترس من خارج است، پیرامون ربطی که مجاهدین بین پارادایم‌های «فرهنگ انقلابیِ عصر حاضر» و «اسلام/ قرآن» برقرار کرده بودند- به ویژه بین «مالکیت خصوصی» در اسلام و «الغاء مالکیت خصوصی» در مارکسیسم- در این جا از جمع‌بندی‌ی یرواند آبراهامیان سود می‌جویم. فراز فشرده‌ی زیر ترجمه‌ی خامی است از صفحه‌ی ۹۳ کتابِ « The Iranian Mojahedin» ۱۹۸۹، نوشته‌ی یرواند آبراهامیان:

> مجاهدین اولیه در کتاب‌های خود چنین استدلال می‌کردند که خداوند، نه تنها- همان گونه که ادیان یکتاپرست باور دارند- جهان را آفرید، بلکه قانون تکامل تاریخی را در جهان جاری کرد؛ تاریخ در روند تکامل، مالکیت خصوصی و نابرابری‌ی طبقاتی را آفرید، و جوامع نابرابر، جای جوامع مساوات‌طلب اولیه را گرفت؛ تقسیم طبقات سبب شد که حکومت‌های سرکوب‌گر، ایدئولوژی‌های کاذب، تضادهای بنیادین بین مالکان و کارگران و بین شیوه و روابط تولید پدید آیند؛ این تضادهای بنیادین، سرچشمه‌ی دینامیسم تاریخی، پیش‌برنده‌ی تغییرات کمّی به سوی تغییرات کیفی، ویرانی‌ی همه‌ی سیستم‌های عقب‌مانده- مانند برده‌داری، فئودالیسم و سرمایه‌داری- است، و حضور عدالت و مساواتی را تضمین می‌کند که قرآن وعده‌اش را داده است؛ یعنی، «مستضعفان وارثان زمین هستند.» مجاهدین، این فرایندِ تکاملی را به عنوان «جبر تاریخ» شناسائی می‌کردند. با این تحلیل بود که حنیف‌نژاد در آخرین بیانیه‌ی زندگی‌ی خود اعلام کرد که «جدا کردن مبارزه‌ی طبقاتی از اسلام، خیانت به اسلام است.»

می‌بینیم که انتقاد مجاهدین به روحانیتِ سنتی، و به خوانش سنتی‌ی آن‌ها از متن‌های مقدس، و خوانش زمینی و عرفی‌ی خودشان از این متن‌ها، مطلقاً بدان معنا نیست که ایمان مذهبی/ شیعی بر ذهنیت پایه‌گذاران، ایدئولوگ‌ها، و اعضاء این سازمان حکمفرما نبود. ترجمه و تفسیر آن‌ها از بینش و کنش امامان شیعه- به ویژه علی و حسین و امام دوازدهم- به گونه‌ای بود که حتا «سُنی‌ها را نیز خائن به نظام توحیدی‌ی محمد می‌دانستند.» تراب حق‌شناس، در زمینه‌ی تلفیق/ تطبیق اسلام و مارکسیسم در این سازمان، می‌نویسد:

> [...] مثلا اگر بچه‌ها با درک رادیکال، این تئوری‌ی قدیمی[ی مارکسیستی] را می‌پذیرفتند که «کار منشاء ارزش است»، بله‌اش را از قرآن می‌گرفتند. برخی کتاب‌های مارکسیستی، از لنین تا مائو، همچنین کتاب‌هایی که با دید مادی به بحث درباره‌ی پیدایش جهان و تئوری‌های تکامل انواع پرداخته‌اند، از جمله کتاب‌های آموزشی‌ی سازمان بود؛ ولی مواظبت می‌شد که این مباحث، اعتقادات دینی‌ی افراد را سست نکند؛ و لذا به توجیهات و تفسیرهائی از دین و قرآن می‌پرداختیم که مخصوص خودمان بود. [...] ما عملاً سازمان انقلابیون حرفه‌ای‌ی مدل لنینی را با تفسیر اسلامی مطابق می‌کردیم و پای آن هم محکم ایستاده بودیم.[۶۰۱]

بر اساس این ایدئولوژی/ متدولوژی بود که هسته‌های نخستینِ این سازمان، ساختار تشکیلاتی و متون توضیحی و آموزشی‌ی آن را نوشتند؛ «امپریالیسم» را به عنوان «سدّ بزرگ» در «راه تکامل بشریت» شناسائی کردند، و «رهائی‌ی ملت‌ها از چنگال امپریالیسم» را سرلوحه‌ی «مبارزه در عصر کنونی» قرار دادند.

---

۶۰۰ از کتاب «شناخت»، برگرفته از: ***سازمان مجاهدین: از پیدائی تا فرجام***، پیشین، فصل دوم، صص ۳۲۶- ۳۲۷.

۶۰۱ ***گفت‌وگوی پرویز قلیچ‌خانی با تراب حق‌شناس ...***، پیشین، ص ۲۳.

اعتقاد راسخ به اسلام، اعتقاد راسخ به مبارزه، عدم وابستگی به خانواده و مظاهر زندگی‌ی عادی، اطاعت، انضباط پذیری، پنهان‌کاری، و اطمینان از نظر امنیتی، از جمله معیارهائی بودند که توسط هسته‌های نخستین این سازمان برای عضوگیری تعیین شده بود.[۶۰۲] عبدالله محسن، از مجاهدین اولیه، پیرامون مرحله‌ی نخستِ گزینشِ عضو می‌گوید:

> انگیزه‌های مذهبی مبنا بود. ما در افرادی که می‌خواستیم انتخاب کنیم، این را معیار قرار می‌دادیم... در دانشگاه هم با این که برنامه‌ها مذهبی نبود، ولی اگر می‌دیدند که کسی روزه می‌گیرد یا نماز می‌خواند یا کتاب‌های مهندس بازرگان و دکتر سحابی (مثل خلقت انسان) یا آقای طالقانی (مثل جهاد و شهادت) را در دست کسی می‌دیدیم، به دنبال او می‌رفتیم.[۶۰۳]
> (نقطه‌چین و پرانتزها در مأخذ من وجود دارند.)

با این شرایط بود که هسته‌های نخستین این سازمان، با تشکیل شاخه‌های «ایدئولوژی»، «سیاسی»، «نظامی»، «کارگری»، «روحانیت»، و «بازار»، و با حمایت برخی از روحانیان نواندیش و بازاریان مخالف با رژیم، طی شش سال موفق شدند بسیاری از دانشجویان مذهبی و ناراضی را از درون انجمن‌های اسلامی‌ی دانشگاه‌ها و نهضت آزادی (و حتا از میان سربازها و افسرانِ «نظام وظیفه») در شهرهای بزرگ ایران (و همچنین، در کنفدراسیون جهانی‌ی دانشجویان ایران)، به این سازمان جذب کنند؛ در مانورهای آزمایشی، شجاعت و میزان استقامت آن‌ها را بیازمایند؛ پس از اطمینان، آن‌ها را به عنوان عضو در خانه‌های تیمی مستقر کنند؛ و در کمال پنهان‌کاری، و با مقررات و نظمی آهنین، آن‌ها را به لحاظ ایدئولوژیک و پذیرش مسئولیت‌های چریکی آموزش دهند. محسن نجات‌حسینی، که به زودی یکی از شخصیت‌های مؤثر این سازمان شد، پیرامون دوره‌ی آزمایشی/ آموزشی‌ی خود در این سازمان می‌نویسد:

> در آن زمان می‌دانستم که به شاخه‌ای از یک گروه سیاسی وصل هستم. آرزوی دیرینِ ریشه‌کن کردنِ فقر و بدبختی، به حرکت و مبارزه‌ی ما نیرو می‌داد، و از سوی دیگر، تفکر مذهبی به آن جلا می‌بخشید، و به ما وعده می‌داد که نه تنها از گسترش عدالت و دیدن رستگاری‌ی مردم لذت خواهیم برد، بلکه خود نیز از پاداش خداوندی بهره‌مند خواهیم شد. ناشناخته بودن تشکیلات همواره سئوال‌برانگیز بود. ولی در آن جوّ وحشتناک پلیسی، که ساواک با شبکه‌ی گسترده‌ی خود، در به در به دنبال هر گروه و تشکل سیاسی‌ی ضد رژیم می‌گشت تا آن را در نطفه خفه کند، این حس طبیعی‌ی کنجکاوی در هاله‌ی مسئله‌ی امنیتی محو می‌شد. من و ما و امثال ما همراه گروهی ناشناخته و بی‌نام و نشان، به دنبال گمشده‌ای که آزادی و برابری بود، به راه افتاده بودیم. این که اسم گروه چیست، رهبر آن کیست، در کجا و در چه زمانی آغاز به کار کرده است، و چند نفر عضو دارد، همه پرسش‌های بی‌پاسخ بود و ما به خاطر حفظ امنیت تشکیلات، به خود اجازه‌ی طرح آن را نمی‌دادیم. [...] من به عنوان پای ثابت خانه‌ی جمعی در شهرآرا، میزبان ناشناس افرادی بودم که با نام‌های مستعار به آن جا رفت و آمد می‌کردند. هیچ کس نباید بیش از سه نفر از یاران تشکیلاتی را می‌شناخت. رفت و آمد در بین اتاق‌ها با دادن علامت و کوبیدن مرس به دیوار انجام می‌شد، تا از برخورد و رویاروئی‌ی افراد جلوگیری شود. [...] بعدها با ابداع یک سیستم الکترونیکی، رفت و آمدها را به این خانه، و در درون خانه، از اتاقی به اتاق دیگر یا به دستشوئی و آشپزخانه، کنترل می‌کردیم.[۶۰۴]

شاخه‌ی نظامی‌ی این سازمان نیز- در ایران و لبنان و فلسطین- اعضاء آزمایش‌شده‌ی خود را برای عملیات پارتیزانی و نبرد مسلحانه آموزش داد. نخستین گام برای آموزش نظامی در ایران، آموختن ورزش‌های رزمی، و انجام خدمت سربازی (با هدف آشنائی با نظم نظامی و کاربرد اسلحه) بود. نخستین تماس بخش برون‌مرزی‌ی این سازمان با سازمان آزادی‌بخش فلسطین نیز، در زمستان ۱۳۴۸ روی داد، و آموزش مبارزه‌ی مسلحانه به اعضاء قابل اعتماد این سازمان- که اکثراً با شناسنامه و پاسپورت جعلی، یا از راه‌های پنهانی، از ایران خارج می‌شدند- در دوره‌های سه ماهه تا شش ماهه آغاز شد.

---

۶۰۲ خاطرات محسن نجات‌حسینی (۱۳۴۵ تا ۱۳۵۵)، ***بر فراز خلیج فارس***، تهران: نشر نی، ۱۳۷۹، صص ۳۷ تا ۶۳؛ گروه پژوهشگران، ***سازمان مجاهدین: از پیدائی تا فرجام، گفتار سوم از ۱۳۴٤ تا ۱۳۵۰***، پیشین، صص ۲۹۴ تا ۲۹۶.

۶۰۳ عبدالله محسن، «گفت‌وگوها»، برگرفته از: ***سازمان مجاهدین: از پیدائی تا فرجام، گفتار سوم از ۱۳۴٤ تا ۱۳۵۰***، پیشین، ص ۲۹۴.

۶۰٤ خاطرات محسن نجات‌حسینی (۱۳۴۵ تا ۱۳۵۵)، ***بر فراز خلیج فارس***، پیشین، صص ۵۲ تا ۵۸.

از مهم‌ترین عملیات گروه برون‌مرزی‌ی این سازمان، ربایش یک هواپیمای دوموتوره‌ی ایرانی بود که شش تن از اعضاء برون‌مرزی‌ی این سازمان را – زنجیرشده به یکدیگر و همراه با یک پلیس ناظر- برای تحویل به دولت ایران، از زندان دُبی به بندرعباس می‌بُرد. (۱۸ آبان ۱۳۴۹) اتهام این افراد، که مدت‌ها در زندان دبی بسر برده بودند، جعل سند، از جمله گذرنامه و شناسنامه بود. چرائی‌ها، چه‌گونگی‌ها، و پیامدهای این ماجرا را- که گرچه به دشواری، اما با موفقیت انجام شد و زندانیان را به سلامت به اردوگاه‌های فلسطینی در بیروت رساند- باید در خاطرات محسن نجات‌حسینی (یکی از زندانیان سوار بر همان هواپیما) خواند.[۶۰۵] اما همین جا باید اشاره کنم که امکانات این هواپیماربائی را حسین احمدی روحانی (با هزینه‌ی شخصی) و تراب حق‌شناس، از رهبران برون‌مرزی‌ی سازمان، فراهم آورند، و عمل آن نیز به وسیله‌ی حسین احمدی روحانی، رسول مشکین‌فام، و محمد سادات دربندی انجام شد، که هر سه، با نام و نشان مستعار و سندهای جعلی، و با حمل اسلحه‌ی گرم و سرد و مواد آتش‌زا، جزء مسافران همان هواپیما بودند.

اما در کشاکش مطالعه‌های تئوریک، آموزه‌های چریکی‌ی مجاهدین تا مرداد ۱۳۵۰ در ایران فرصت عمل نمی‌یابد. پس از رویداد سیاهکل است که مرکزیت این «سازمانِ» هنوز بی‌نام، عملیات چریکی را در ایران آغاز می‌کند. بمب‌گذاری در کارخانه‌ی صنایع الکترونیکی‌ی تهران، در مقابله به مراسم جشن‌های ۲۵۰۰ سال شاهنشاهی، نخستین طرحی است که در روزهای پایانی‌ی مرداد ۱۳۵۰ اجراء می‌شود. اما این طرح، و طرح ربودن یک هواپیمای ایران اِیر، پیش از اجراء، توسط یک عضو نفوذی لو می‌رود (۱ شهریور ۱۳۵۰)، و عده‌ای از مجاهدین دستگیر می‌شوند. بازمانده‌های سازمان، عملیات انفجاری را در این جا و آن جای تهران ادامه می‌دهند، تا هر ۱۱ نفر عضو مرکزیت، به همراه انبوهی از اعضاء سازمان، به صورت زنجیره‌ای دستگیر می‌شوند. (بنا بر نخستین بیانیه‌ی این سازمان، از ۱ شهریور تا ۲۰ بهمن ۱۳۵۰ تعداد ۷۵ تن از کادرهای آن دستگیر شده بودند. حسین احمدی روحانی، تعداد دستگیرشدگان سال ۵۰ را «حدود ۱۲۰ نفر» ثبت کرده است.[۶۰۶] آبراهامیان، «۶۶ نفر»،[۶۰۷] و حسن راهی، که از جمله دستگیرشدگان بود، تعداد دستگیرشدگان را «حدود ۷۰ نفر» ثبت کرده است.) به روایت حسن راهی، همین هموندانِ زندانی، که آن‌ها را پس از بازجوئی و شکنجه در دو اتاق از بند ۲ زندان اوین مجتمع کرده بودند، با بدن‌های شکنجه‌شده، به ارزیابی‌ی موقعیت پرداختند، و تصمیم‌های تازه- از جمله گزینشِ نام «سازمان مجاهدین خلق ایران» برای این سازمانِ هنوز بی‌نام- را، با رأی‌گیری، به بازمانده‌های بیرون از زندان منتقل کردند.[۶۰۸]

روز اول مهر ماه ۱۳۵۰ طرح ربودن شهرام شفیق («شهرام پهلوی‌نیا»)، پسر شاهزاده اشرف پهلوی)- با هدف آزاد کردن یاران زندانی- از سوی اعضاء بازمانده اجراء می‌شود. این طرح نیز با مقاومت شهرام شفیق، دخالت مسئول پارکینگِ او، جمع شدن مردم، سررسیدن پلیس، و گریز چریک‌ها از مهلکه، به شکست می‌انجامد.[۶۰۹]

رضا رضایی (۱۳۲۶ - ۱۳۵۲)، که روز ۴ شهریور ۵۰ دستگیر شده بود، روز ۲۷ آذر ۵۰، با کوله‌باری از تجربه‌های بدست آمده از تماس با سایر رهبران سازمان در زندان، و آشنائی با تاکتیک‌های ساواک در بازجوئی‌ها، از زندان فرار می‌کند؛[۶۱۰] به احمد آرام (۱۳۲۸-۱۳۵۵)، رهبر شاخه‌ی نظامی‌ی سازمان، و کاظم ذوالانوار و احمد رضائی (برادر

---

۶۰۵ خاطرات محسن نجات‌حسینی، ***برفراز خلیج فارس***، پیشین، صص ۹۳ تا ۱۷۱.
توضیح: فهرست نام شش نفر زندانی به قرار زیر است: سیدجلیل سیداحمدیان، موسی خیابانی، کاظم شفیعی‌ها، حسین خوشرو، محمود شامخی، و محسن نجات‌حسینی.

۶۰۶ حسین احمدی روحانی، ***سازمان مجاهدین خلق***، تهران: انتشارات مرکز اسناد انقلاب اسلامی، ۱۳۸٤، ص ۱۱۷.

۶۰۷ یرواند آبراهامیان، ***ایران بین دو انقلاب***، پیشین، ص ٤۵۳.

۶۰۸ حسن راهی، ***با استقرار حکومت اسلامی مجدداً به زیرزمین خزیدیم***، نشریه‌ی «آرش»، چاپ پاریس، شماره‌ی ۱۰۸، تیر ۱۳۹۱/ ژوئیه ۲۰۱۲، ص ۱۷۱.
توضیح: حسن راهی در همان جا یادآوری می‌کند: «دو نفر از بچه‌ها را هیچ‌گاه به عمومی نیاوردند و تا زمان اعدامشان در انفرادی نگه‌داری می‌شدند. این دو، یکی رسول مشکین‌فام و دیگری محمد حنیف‌نژاد بود.»

۶۰۹ خاطرات محسن نجات حسینی، ***بر فراز خلیج فارس***، پیشین، صص ۲۹۹ تا ۳۰۲.

۶۱۰ خاطرات محسن نجات‌حسینی، ***بر فرار خلیج فارس***، پیشین، صص ۳۰۵ تا ۳۰۷.

بزرگ خود) می‌پیوندد؛ و از مرکزیت شاخه‌ی برون‌مرزی‌ی سازمان (تراب حق‌شناس، محمود شامخ، و حسین احمدی روحانی) نیز یاری می‌خواهد. با پیوستن محمود شامخ به این جمع، بازاندیشی به عملکردِ تاکنونی‌ی سازمان و بازسازی‌ی تشکیلات آن آغاز می‌شود. اما پیش از هر اقدام مؤثری، روز ۱۱ بهمن ۱۳۵۰ احمد رضائی (متولد ۱۳۲۴) در درگیری با مأموران ساواک طی‌ی عملیات انتحاری کشته می‌شود. پیامد بازاندیشی و نخستین مرگ در سازمان این است که این گروهِ تاکنون بی‌نام، در نیمه‌ی دوم اسفند ۱۳۵۰، با انتشار نخستین بیانیه‌ی سیاسی، با نامِ «سازمان مجاهدین خلق ایران» در ساحت اپوزیسیون مسلح محمدرضا شاه پهلوی رسماً اعلام حضور می‌کند.[۶۱۱]

نخستین «بیانیه‌ی سیاسی‌ی سازمان مجاهدین خلق ایران»، با عبارت‌های «به نام خدا و به نام خلق قهرمان ایران» و ترجمه‌ی آیه‌ای از قرآن آغاز می‌شود. در این بیانیه، ابتدا به سوژه‌های زیر اشاره شده است: «استعمار قدیم و جدید»، «برنامه‌های اصلاحی‌ی رژیم شاه، که چیزی جز خواست‌های اربابان امپریالیست‌اش در استثمار بیش‌تر مردم ایران نبوده»، «پیمان‌های سیاسی/ نظامی»ی رژیم با «امپریالیست‌ها»، شرکت ارتش ایران در «توطئه» برای سرکوبِ «خلق‌های منطقه، به ویژه خلق‌های قهرمان فلسطین و ظفار»، «سیستم پلیسی و نیروی ارتش که رژیم پیوسته سعی نموده از آن به عنوان عامل سرکوب توده‌ها استفاده نماید». بیانیه، سپس، با یادآوری از «رزمندگان قهرمان سیاهکل، که پیش از ما جان خویش را در این راه فدا کرده‌اند»، «فداکاری» را به عنوان شرط نخستِ رسیدن به «آزادی» شناسائی می‌کند. و شگفتا! در حالی که انبوهی از کادرهای اسیر، برای حفظ اطلاعات و اسرار سازمان، شکنجه را به جان می‌خرند، در این بیانیه، به «برقراری‌ی ارتباطات عمیق انقلابی با جنبش پیشرو منطقه، یعنی انقلاب فلسطین» اعتراف شده است. در بخشی از این بیانیه می‌خوانیم:

> [...] هسته‌ی اولیه‌ی سازمان ما که هم اکنون برای اولین بار نام آن را فاش می‌کنیم، در ۶ سال قبل، و با شرکت برخی از کادرهای سابق نهضت آزادی‌ی ایران، که پس از زندانی شدن سران مؤمن و فداکارش، دیگر فعالیتی نداشت- پس از انتقادی اساسی نسبت به شیوه‌ی مبارزات گذشته- به شکل مخفی بنیاد یافت. از همان بدو تشکیل، با استفاده از تجربیات ارزنده‌ی تاریخ مبارزات خلق‌های انقلابی‌ی جهان عموماً، و خلق خودمان خصوصاً، و همچنین با بررسی و تحلیل علمی از شرایط جامعه‌ی ایران به این حقیقت پی برد که: اولاً، در شرایط کنونی تضاد اصلی و آشتی‌ناپذیر جامعه‌ی ما را تضاد بین توده‌های خلق از یک طرف، و امپریالیسم جهانی به سرکردگی‌ی امریکا و رژیم دست‌نشانده‌ی شاه از طرف دیگر تشکیل می‌دهد. ثانیاً، به خاطر پیروزی در مبارزه‌ی ضدامپریالیستی، بسیج همه‌ی رنجبران و ستمدیدگان خلق، امری ضروری و اجتناب‌ناپذیر است. سازمان ما در روشنائی‌ی این دو اصل اساسی، شیوه‌ی مبارزه‌ی مسلحانه‌ی توده‌ای را به عنوان تنها راه کسب آزادی و نابودی‌ی استثمار انسان از انسان، انتخاب و دنبال نمود؛ و از آن روز تاکنون، تحت شکل سازماندهی‌ی مخفی و در پرتو فداکاری‌ی خلق و فرزندان پیشتاز آن، و با سعی در بکار گرفتنِ حداکثر امکانات موجود، و با برقراری‌ی ارتباطات عمیق انقلابی با جنبش پیشرو منطقه، یعنی انقلاب فلسطین، موفق گردید علارغم شرایط پلیسی‌ی ایران، در زمینه‌های نظامی و انقلابی تجارب ارزنده‌ای کسب نماید.[...] (مأخذ پیشین)

افزون بر این اعترافِ سازمانی، دستگیرشدگان نیز در دادگاه نظامی به شرکت خود در مبارزه‌ی مسلحانه مهر تأیید می‌زنند، و با شهامتی خیره‌کننده، از حقانیت آن دفاع می‌کنند. به عنوان نمونه، علی میهن‌دوست، خطاب به برگزارکنندگان دادگاه نظامی می‌گوید: «اگر مسلسلی در دست داشتم الان همه‌ی شما را نابود می‌کردم.»[۶۱۲]

این است که افزون بر کشته شدن برخی از کادرها در جنگ با مأموران در بیرون از زندان، و افزون بر ده‌ها عضو زندانی در زیر شکنجه، بهار و تابستان ۱۳۵۱ برگریزانِ این گروه از فرزندان جوان ایران نیز می‌شود: روز ۳۱ فروردین ۵۱ تعدادی از اعضاء مرکزیت سازمان (ناصر صادق، علی باکری، محمد بازرگانی، و علی میهن‌دوست) اعدام

---

۶۱۱ این بیانیه در تاریخ ۲۰ بهمن ماه ۱۳۵۰ نوشته شده، و در نشریه‌ی «باختر امروز»، دوره‌ی دوم، شماره‌ی ۲۴ ، اسفند ۱۳۵۰ منتشر شده است.

۶۱۲ خاطرات محسن نجات‌حسینی، ***بر فراز خلیج فارس***، پیشین، ص ۳۱۰.

شـدند؛ روز ۴ خرداد ۵۱ نیز پایه‌گذاران آن (حنیف‌نژاد، محسـن، بدیع‌زادگان، عسـکری‌زاده، و مشـکین‌فام) با بدن‌های شکنجه‌شده و سوخته، به جوخه‌ی اعدام سپرده شدند.

البته این اسارت‌ها و مرگ‌ها، ضربه‌ی کمرشکنی بود، اما به معنای پایان کار «سازمان مجاهدین خلق ایران» نبود. رضا رضـائی، کاظم ذوالانوار، و بهرام آرام- باز با یاری شـاخه‌ی برون مرزی- به بازسـازی‌ی تشـکیلات و تجدید نظر در تاکتیک‌های سازمان پرداختند. عضوگیری‌ی رسمی‌ی زنان نیز در این دوره آغاز شد. بر اساس این تاکتیک‌ها و رهنمودها، سازمان یک سری عملیات ساده تا پیچیده‌ی نظامی را در دستور کار قرار داد. حمله به پاسگاه‌های پلیس راهنمائی، گذاشتن مواد انفجاری‌ی دست‌ساز در وسائل نقلیه‌ی نظامی و پلیسی و تأسیسات حساس تهران، انفجار سفارتخانه‌ی اردن در تهران، انفجار در مسیر حرکت سلطان قابوس در تهران، ترور ژنرال هارولد پرایس (مستشار عالی‌ی نظامی‌ی امریکا در ایران)، و ترور سرهنگ سعید طاهری (از عوامل کشتار ۱۵ خرداد ۴۲)، از مهم‌ترین‌های این عملیات بودند. سازمان مجاهدین، طی‌ی «بیانیه»‌ای مسـئولیت هر یک از این عملیات را به عهده می‌گرفت و چرائی های آن را به عرض مردم ایران می‌رسـاند. به عنوان نمونه، پس از حمله‌های پیاپی‌ی چریک‌های فدائی و مجاهدین به پاسـگاه‌های پلیس راهنمائی، سـازمان مجاهدین خلق ایران روز ۴ خرداد ۱۳۵۱ بیانیه‌ای به شرح زیر منتشر کرد:

> [...] هدف عمده‌ی این حملات پاسخ دادن به زورگوئی‌ی دستگاه پلیس راهنمائی به رانندگان زحمت‌کش و نیز به همکاری‌ی پلیس راهنمائی در امر سـرکوب انقلابیون با سـایر نیروهای ضـدانقلاب بود. [...] ما اخطار می‌کنیم [...] در صـورتی که پلیس راهنمائی به زورگوئی و چپاولگری‌ی خودش علیه برادران زحمت‌کش راننده ادامه دهد، و در صـورتی که پلیس راهنمائی باز هم به طور مسلح قصد تعرض و کشتار فرزندان انقلابی‌ی خلق را داشته باشد، از حملات انتقامی‌ی ما مصون نخواهد بود. [...]
>
> درود به رانندگان زحمت‌کش تهران
>
> پیروز باد مبارزه‌ی عادلانه‌ی خلق علیه زورگوئی و چپاولگری
>
> مرگ بر شاه دزد و زورگو و دار وُ دسته‌ی چپاولگرش[۶۱۳]

دستگاه سـاواک نیز، البته، بی‌کار نماند؛ مهدی رضـائی‌ی ۲۰ سـاله را در دادگاه‌های بدوی و تجدید نظر، به سه بار اعدام محکوم کرد، و خبر تیرباران او را روز ۱۶ شهریور ۵۱ به گوش و چشم مردم ایران رساند. و رضا رضائی نیز- که در نیمه‌شـب ۲۵ خرداد ۱۳۵۲ در محل اسـتقرار خود در خانه‌ی تیمی مورد حمله‌ی مأموران سـاواک قرار گرفت- تا آخرین نفس جنگید و کشته شد. عصر همان روز، مردم ایران این خبر را نیز در صفحات اول روزنامه‌ها خواندند. (من، به عنوان فردی معمولی و غیرسازمانی، همان روزها خدا خدا می‌کردم که «برادرانِ رضائی» برادر دیگری نداشته باشند؛ غافل از این که حالا خواهرِ رضائی‌ها- صدیقه رضائی- نیز وارد سازمان مجاهدین شده و در صف زندان و شکنجه است؛ غافل از این که به زودی «انقلابِ» آرمانی‌ی پیکارگران سیاسـی واقعیت عملی خواهد یافت و ۶ فرزندِ «مادر بهکیش» را در کنار هزاران جوان دیگر، خواهد بلعید.)

پس از مرگ رضـا رضـائی، و دسـتگیری‌ی کاظم ذوالانوار (مهر ۵۱) اسـت که تقی شـهرام، بهرام آرام، و مجید شـریف واقفی رهبری‌ی سـازمان را به عهده می‌گیرند، و به یاری شـاخه‌ی برون‌مرزی‌ی سـازمان، ضـمن تدارک‌های همه‌جانبه برای حمله‌های مسلحانه، با تأسیس نشریه‌ی «پیام مجاهد»، تجدید چاپ متن‌های پیشین، استفاده از برنامه‌های رادیوئی، و

---

۶۱۳ برگرفته از: اشرف دهقانی، ***بذرهای ماندگار***، لندن: انتشارات چریک‌های فدائی‌ی خلق ایران، ۲۰۰۵، ص ۱۷۸.

تبلیغات گسترده در کنفدراسیون و انجمن‌های اسلامی‌ی دانشجویان در اروپا، به نشر آگاهی‌های سیاسی و تبلیغ برنامه‌ها و هدف‌های سازمان می‌پردازند؛ منتها، در روند بازاندیشی به ایدئولوژی‌ی سازمان- به قول تقی شهرام- به این دریافت می‌رسند که: «پیراهن اسلام را از هر کجا وصله‌ی علمی زدیم، از جای دیگر پاره شد.» در نتیجه، اکنون زمزمه‌هائی در سازمان پیچیده است که از تغییر مواضع ایدئولوژیک سازمان، از حذف تمام ایده‌های اسلامی‌ی آن، و از گرایش بخشی از رهبری و کادرهای سازمان به مارکسیسم خبر می‌دهند؛ متن‌های «جزوه‌ی سبز» و «پرچم مبارزه‌ی ایدئولوژیک را افراشته‌ایم»، این زمزمه‌ها را عینیت کلامی می‌بخشند؛ و سازمان مجاهدین را از درون و برون متلاطم می‌کنند: در درون، دو دستگی در میان شخصیت‌های رهبری، و به تبع، بین اعضاء سازمان؛ و در بیرون، از دست دادن حمایت بازار، نهضت آزادی، و برخی از روحانیان مدافع سازمان (مانند آیت‌الله طالقانی و حجت‌الاسلام هاشمی رفسنجانی).[۶۱۴] حالا، بهرام آرام و تقی شهرام و بسیاری از شخصیت‌های مهم درون‌مرزی‌ی سازمان، با گرایش به مارکسیسم، در برابر مجید شریف واقفی و همفکران او- با گرایش به همان ایدئولوژی‌ی «اسلامی»- قد علم کرده‌اند. مجید شریف واقفی (متولد ۱۳۲۷)، رهبر شاخه‌ی کارگری و مذهبی‌ی سازمان، که به تغییر ایدئولوژی و تحویل نام و منابع سازمان به ایدئولوژی‌ی مارکسیسم تن نمی‌دهد، از سوی رهبری به کار در کارخانه گمارده می‌شود؛ اما مخفیانه، امکانات تسلیحاتی و مالی‌ی سازمان را به محلی امن منتقل می‌کند و به گردآوری‌ی کادرهای مردد می‌پردازد. این عملیات، به آگاهی‌ی رهبری‌ی سازمان می‌رسد؛ و رهبری‌ی وقت سازمان، او را به عنوان «خائن» شناسائی می‌کند؛ روز ۱۶ اردی‌بهشت ۱۳۵۴ توسط همسرِ سازمانی‌اش (لیلا زمردیان) به یک قرارِ سازمانی فراخوانده می‌شود، و همان جا همراه با هموند همفکرش، محمدصمد لباف، توسط دو تن از هموندان رده‌های پائین‌ترِ سازمان به طرز فجیعی به قتل می‌رسد. پس از این تصفیه است که «بیانیه‌ی اعلام مواضع ایدئولوژیک»، نوشته‌ی محمدتقی شهرام در مهر ماه ۱۳۵۴، «مواضع ایدئولوژیک مارکسیستی» را- به عنوان «نتیجه‌ی منطقی‌ی ایدئولوژی‌ی گذشته»ی سازمان- اعلام می‌کند. تراب حق‌شناس پیرامون دلایل این چرخش می‌گوید:

> [...] ما از قرآن می‌خواستیم چیزهایی را در بیاوریم که مبارزه‌ی اجتماعی‌ی ما را تأیید کند. تجربه به ما آموخت و هر کدام از مجاهدین که کلاه خود را قاضی می‌کردند، این را می‌توانستند بفهمند که ما چندین سال بالای اعلامیه‌ها آیه‌ی قرآن می‌نوشتیم و معتقد بودیم که از قرآن الهام می‌گیریم ، ولی آن جا که یک سال می‌گذرد و تو برای هیچ یک از کارهائی که به مبارزه روزمره‌ات مربوط می‌شود، لازم نمی‌بینی که لای قرآن را باز کنی! یعنی در واقع غیرقابل استفاده است. (همین حرف را مجید شریف واقفی در خانه‌ی تیمی‌ی مشترک در تابستان ۱۳۵۲ به پوران بازرگان زده است). چرا به خودمان دروغ بگوئیم؟ به نظر من در آن جریان تغییر ایدئولوژی یک اصل وجود داشت که نادیده گرفته شده است. آن این است که نباید به دیگران و خودمان دروغ بگوئیم. درست است که ما در این کار اشتباهاتی کردیم و خطاهایی مرتکب شدیم و خودمان هم در سال ۵۷ گفتیم و نقد کردیم؛ ولی اصل کار در تغییر ایدئولوژی این بود که نباید به مردم دروغ گفت. وقتی ما می‌رسیم به این اصل که راهنمای ما دیگر اندیشه‌ی مذهبی نیست و کارآیی ندارد تا در امر مبارزه ما را یاری دهد، باید این را صریح به همه بگوئیم، حتا اگر بسیاری از امکانات را هم از دست بدهیم، و حتا اگر بسیاری از هواداران ما از ما زده شوند. این مسئله در مقدمه‌ی کتاب «بیانیه‌ی اعلام مواضع...» با صراحت کامل گفته شده است.[۶۱۵] (پرانتز و گیومه از تراب حق‌شناس است.)

---

[۶۱۴] حجت‌الاسلام علی‌اکبر هاشمی رفسنجانی در کتاب «دوران مبارزه، ۱۳۶۷، صص ۱۰۲ تا ۱۰۳» می‌نویسد: «به وسیله‌ی همین آقای غیوران، که اواخر رابط من بود، در منزل ایشان ملاقاتی با بهرام آرام، یکی از سران کافرشده آن‌ها، کردم [...] نشسته بود جلو من، پاهایش را دراز کرده بود و اسلحه‌اش را گذاشته بود و با من صحبت می‌کرد. [...] دیدیم نقطه‌ی اتفاق نداریم. [...] اعلام کردم که از این تاریخ به بعد هیچ گونه کمکی و حمایتی از طرف ما و دوستان ما به شما نخواهد رسید.

[۶۱۵] ***گفت‌وگوی پرویز قلیچ‌خانی با تراب حق‌شناس، از اعضای اولیه‌ی مجاهدین خلق***، پیشین، ص ۲۴.

البته، با نگاهی به نخستین بیانیه‌ی سیاسی‌ی سازمان، این لاپوشانی‌ی نادانسته به روشنی به دید می‌آید؛ به گونه‌ای که، اگر ترجمه‌ی آیه‌ی قرآن در مطلع آن نبود- به لحاظ کاربردِ واژگان و اصطلاحات و نشانه‌های نمادینِ زبان- کوچک‌ترین تفاوتی با اعلامیه‌های «سازمان چریک‌های فدائی‌ی خلق ایران» نداشت؛ و صرف نظر از آن آیه، کم‌ترین نشانی از ملاحظات مذهبی (مانند اعتراض به وجود کازینو و بار و کاباره در ایران و یا پوشش زنان؛ یعنی آن چه که بعداً احمد خمینی آن را «مفاسد قبیح اجتماعی در خیابان‌ها» نامید) در آن دیده نمی‌شد. بی‌سبب نبود که مسعود احمدزاده در زندان، هوشمندانه به مهدی ابریشمچی (از مجاهدین خلق) گفته بود:

> شما یك پوسته‌ی ایده‌آلیستی دارید؛ و مثل جوجه که رشد می‌کند و پوسته را می‌شکند، این پوسته در حال شکستن است و به زودی هسته‌ی ماتریالیستی‌ی آن بیرون می‌زند و نمایان می‌شود.[۶۱۶]

این گروه تازه، خود را به عنوان «وارث هویت گذشته»ی سازمان نیز برانداز می‌کند. و از این روست که تمامی‌ی اعلامیه‌ها و جزوه‌های سازمانی‌ی پس از «اعلامیه تغییر مواضع...»، به نام «سازمان مجاهدین خلق ایران»، البته، با حذف آیه‌ی طلیعه‌ی آرم مجاهدین، منتشر می‌شود. از این گذشته، اعضاء سازمان در گزینش یکی از این دو ایدئولوژی آزاد نیستند؛ بدین ترتیب که، با هدف زدودنِ «خصلت بورژوائی‌ی مذهب از افراد»، نمایندگانی از سوی رهبری‌ی تازه (تقی شهرام و بهرام آرام)، اعضاء درون‌مرزی و برون‌مرزی‌ی سازمان را- که به گرایش تازه تن نمی‌دهند- در کلاس‌ها و نشست‌هائی طولانی به ایدئولوژی‌ی تازه متقاعد می‌کنند؛ و در صورت عدم موفقیت، آن‌ها را به شکل‌های مختلف از حوزه‌ی عمل و تصمیم‌گیری پس می‌رانند. (معترضه: گرویدن پسر آیت‌الله طالقانی به مارکسیسم، و مذاکره‌ی تقی شهرام با حمید اشرف- با هدف تشکیل یک «جبهه»ی مارکسیستی- در همین دوره رخ داد.) خط مشی‌ی این جریان، «مبارزه‌ی مسلحانه‌ی پیشتاز» بود و «در رابطه با تحلیل شرایط جامعه، مشی مسلحانه پیشتاز را تا سال ۱۳۵۳ (با این اعتقاد که تا آن زمان شرایط عینی انقلاب وجود داشته است) درست و از آن به بعد نادرست ارزیابی می‌کرد.» اما این جریان هم در سازمان مجاهدین بخش مارکسیست در حال پوست انداختن بود. بهرام آرام در پائیز ۱۳۵۵ در یک تعقیب و گریز با مأموران ساواک تا آخرین گلوله جنگید و نهایتاً خود را با نارنجک منفجر کرد. پس از مرگ بهرام آرام، گروه معترضی که در درون بخش مارکسیستی رشد کرده بودند، در اسفند ۱۳۵۶ طی‌ی بیانیه‌ای حضور خود را به عنوان یک جریان تازه اعلام کردند:

> پس از طی یک دوره مبارزه ایدئولوژیک درون سازمانی و با اتکاء به آموزش‌های مارکسیسم – لنینیسم ، مشی‌ی سازمان از مشی‌ی چریکی (مبارزه‌ی مسلحانه پیشتاز) به مشی توده ای- انقلابی تغییر یافته است.[۶۱۷]

این جریان- با مسئولیتِ « جمعی مرکب از مسئولین شاخه‌های سازمان که مجموعاً نظراتشان مورد تأیید توده‌های سازمانی بود»- در مهر ۱۳۵۷ نیز پیرامون تغییر خط مشی و چرائی‌های آن، بیانیه‌ی تازه‌ای منتشر کرد، و طی‌ی آن «انحرافات و عملکردهای غیرپرولتری‌ی ۵ سال گذشته‌ی سازمان» را- در رابطه با «رهبری»ی آن- برشمرد؛ مشی‌ی چریکی‌ی «پیشتاز» و جدا از توده را کلاً «سکتاریستی»، «انحرافی» و «غیرپرولتری» خواند؛ و استراتژی‌ی «کار سوسیال

---

۶۱۶ لطف الله میثمی، *آن‌ها که رفتند کاری حسینی کردند*، انتشارات صمدیه، ۱۳۸۲، ص ۷۹.

۶۱۷ من این بیانیه را ندیده‌ام. آن را از مأخذ زیر برگرفته‌ام:
اطلاعیه‌ی بخش مارکسیستی- لنینیستی سازمان مجاهدین خلق ایران، مهر ماه ۱۳۵۷، آرشیو سازمان پیکار در راه آزادی‌ی طبقه‌ی کارگر، تارنمای «اندیشه و پیکار»:

http://peykar.info/PeykarArchive/Mojahedin-ML/etelaiyeh-1357.html

دموکراتیک و فعالیت تربیتی و آگاه‌گرانه در بین طبقه و توده‌ها» و «مشـی مبارزه‌ی مسـلحانه‌ی توده‌ای» را برگزید. در بخش‌هائی از این بیانیه می‌خوانیم:

> [...] این جریان توده‌ای و انقلابی که از بهار سـال ۵۶ به تدریج نضـج گرفته و تکامل می‌یافت، علیرغم مقاومت‌هائی از جانب مرکزیت سازمان (به خصوص و در درجه اول از سوی عنصر مسلط مرکزیت که توانسته بود طی سالهای ۵۲ تا ۵۷، هژمونی‌ی ایدئولوژیک، سیاسی و تشکیلاتی‌ی خود را بر مرکزیت سازمان اعمال نماید) و علیرغم تلاش و کوشش این مرکزیت در ادامه‌ی حاکمیت اندیشه و عمل غیرکمونیستی، سکتاریستی و تفرقه‌افکنانه‌ی گذشته، توانست با اتکاء به نیروی اکثریت قاطع مسئولین و توده‌های سازمانی، مقاومت آن را در هم شکسته و سرانجام آن را وادار به استعفا نماید.[...][٦١٨]

در همین بیانیه بود که این جریان، «سوسیال امپریالیسم شوروی» را «در کنار امپریالیسم امریکا» نشاند؛ هر دو را «دشمنان اصلی‌ی خلق‌های جهان، و کانون‌های اصلی‌ی جنگ و آتش‌افروزی» برآورد کرد، که «برای غارت و استثمار خلق‌های جهان با یکدیگر رقابت و مبارزه می‌کنند.» با این بینش بود که «دار و دسـته‌ی کمیته‌ی مرکزی‌ی حزب توده‌ی ایران» را «اپورتونیست»، «خائن به جنبش کمونیستی»، و «ستون پنجم بورژوازی لیبرال در درون جنبش کمونیستی» ارزیابی کرد و «هر گونه همکاری با آن را مردود» شـمرد. و در همین بیانیه بود که این «جریان»، تکلیف خود را پیرامون «وحدت» با «سـازمان چریک‌های فدائی‌ی خلق ایران»- که مذاکرات آن از سـال ٥٤ با حضـور نمایندگان دو سازمان (از جمله حمید اشرف با تقی شهرام) آغاز شده بود- نیز روشن کرد:

> [...] ما قبل از این که این مبارزه‌ی ایدئولوژیک را ، مبارزه با مشی‌ی سکتاریستی و غیرپرولتری‌ی سازمان چریک‌های فدائی خلق بدانیم، در مجموع یک مبارزه‌ی رقابت‌آمیز، چپ‌روانه، و سلطه‌طلبانه ارزیابی می‌کنیم، که برای تحقق اهداف غیرپرولتری‌ی خویش (ولی در پوشش «وحدت»)، به شیوه‌های نادرستی نظیر شانتاژ، جدل و گاه تهمت متوسل می‌شد. این مبارزه‌ی ایدئولوژیک، از آن جا که اساساً و در بهترین حالت، در چارچوب مشی‌ی چریکی و در متن تمام انحرافات آن، نظیر سکتاریسم و ولونتاریسم (اراده گرائی) صورت می‌گرفت ، طبیعتا نمی‌توانست بر موازین لنینی‌ی مبارزه‌ی ایدئولوژیک استوار بوده و ناظر بر وحدت اصولی‌ی نیروهای انقلابی‌ی جنبش باشد. [...] چنین برخوردی از جانب ما ، به اختلافات بین دو سازمان دامن زده و مناسبات بین آن‌ها را به بن بست می‌کشانید. ما مسئولیت تیرگی، به بن بست رسیدن، و بحرانی شدن روابط دو سازمان را، به خصوص بعد از ضربات وارد بر رفقای فدائی در سال ۵۵ ، به طور عمده به عهده می‌گیریم. [...]

همین «جریان» در همین بیانیه بود که اطلاق نام «سازمان مجاهدین خلق ایران» را به خود «نادرست» دانست، و نوشت: «تا روشن شدن نام سازمان، فعالیت‌های ما با هویت «بخش مارکسیستی – لنینیستی‌ی سازمان مجاهدین خلق ایران»- که به نظر ما با واقعیت امر انطباق دارد- صورت خواهد گرفت.» این بیانیه، همچنین اعدام‌های درون‌سازمانی را که در زمان رهبری‌ی پیشین اجرا شده بود، محکوم کرد:

> [...] در ارتباط با نگرش غیرطبقاتی و غیرمارکسیستی‌ی ما به نیروهای مذهبی و هم چنین گرایشات سلطه‌طلبانه و چپ‌روانه‌ی سازمان، عده‌ای از رفقای سازمانی که در جریان تحول ایدئولوژیک، حاضر به پذیرش مارکسیسم نشده و در

---

٦١٨ ***اطلاعیه‌ی بخش مارکسیستی- لنینیستی سازمان مجاهدین خلق ایران***، مهر ماه ۱۳۵۷. پیشین.

> صدد تشکل گروهی‌ی خویش بودند، از سوی رهبری، به عنوان خائن و توطئه گر، اعدام شدند. ما ضمن این که «اعدام» را به مثابه یک سیاست و شیوه‌ی عمومی، در برخورد با تضادهای درون سازمانی و اختلافات ایدئولوژیک، محکوم می‌کنیم، اعدام این رفقا را توسط رهبری‌ی سازمان، اقدامی ضدانقلابی ارزیابی کرده و آن را توطئه‌گرانه و تروریستی می‌دانیم. بدین ترتیب، اطلاق «خائن» و «توطئه گر» و «اپورتونیست» را به رفقای شهید «مجید شریف واقفی»، «مرتضی صمدیه لباف» و «محمد یقینی» نادرست دانسته و آن‌ها را جزو شهدای انقلابی محسوب می‌داریم. [...]

اما تحولات بینشی و کنشی‌ی ناشی از بزنگاه‌های بحرانی در این سازمان، و تشکیل سازمانی با عنوان «بخش مارکسیستی – لنینیستی‌ی سازمان مجاهدین خلق ایران»، به مثابه پایانِ بخشِ اسلامی‌ی مجاهدین خلق نبود. این بخش نیز با استفاده از تجربیات هنگفتی که داشت، و با استفاده از حمایت بازار و روحانیت و انقلابیون فلسطینی و یمن جنوبی و عراق و لیبی، به بازسازی‌ی خود پرداخت. به طوری که، در کشاکش انقلاب ۵۷- به ویژه پس از آزادی‌ی مسعود رجوی و موسی خیابانی از زندان-[۶۱۹] شانه به شانه‌ی بخش مارکسیست/ لنینیستی‌ی این سازمان، در میدان عمل برای سرنگونی‌ی رژیم شاه حضوری فعال داشت؛ و پس از «پیروزی‌ی انقلاب» نیز، به لحاظ تعدادِ اعضاء و هوادار، و به لحاظ حمایتی که از سوی برندگان انقلاب دریافت کرد، بر بخش «منشعب» (که حالا خود را با عنوان «سازمان پیکار برای آزادی‌ی طبقه‌ی کارگر» شناسائی می‌کرد) بسی برتری یافته بود. در واقع، در روزهای ۱۹ تا ۲۲ بهمن ۵۷، که سیل خروشان خاص و عام مردم خیابان‌های ایران را می‌پیمود، هر دو بخش سازمان چریک‌های فدائی‌ی خلق (طرفداران دیدگاه بیژن جزنی و طرفداران دیدگاه مسعود احمدزاده) شانه به شانه‌ی هر دو بخش سازمان مجاهدین خلق (مذهبی و مارکسیست)، با استفاده از تمامی‌ی تجربیات چریکی‌ی خود، فاز مقابله‌ی مسلحانه را، تا سقوط محمدرضا شاه پهلوی و رژیم پادشاهی، در خیابان‌های ایران هدایت کردند. و این همیاری در صورتی بود که مذاکرات سازمان چریک‌ها و مجاهدین خلق پیرامون «وحدت» این سازمان‌ها، هرگز به جائی نرسیده بود و بین دو شاخه‌ی هر سازمان و بین هر چهار شاخه‌ی یادشده، «وحدت» یا «ائتلاف»ی صورت نپذیرفته بود. اما هدف مشترک، همه‌ی آن‌ها – و همه‌ی حزب‌ها و سازمان‌های چپ و ملی/ مذهبی- را در کنار هم به کار سرنگونی‌ی رژیم شاه و سلطنت مشروطه واداشته بود.

***

رسیدگی به فرایندهای عینی و ذهنی‌ای که پس از انقلاب در «سازمان چریک‌های فدائی‌ی خلق ایران» و «سازمان مجاهدین خلق ایران» رخ داد، به کلی از قلمرو این مبحث بیرون است. اما در مقایسه‌ای کمی و کیفی بین «سازمان چریک‌های فدائی‌ی خلقِ» اولیه و «سازمان مجاهدین خلقِ» اولیه (پیش از حکومت اسلامی)- صرف نظر از تفاوت‌ها- نکات مشترکی به دید می‌آید که تأملی **چندین و چند وجهی** بر مجموعه‌ای از آن‌ها، ما را در شناختِ ذهنیت مبارزانِ آن‌زمانی‌ی این دو سازمان، و گوشه‌هائی از شرایط سیاسی/ فرهنگی‌ی جاری در این دو سازمان یاری می‌دهد:

یک) شجاعت، اعتماد به نفس، ایمان بی‌چون و چرا به حقانیت مبارزه، و فداکاری در هر دو سازمان، در راه هدفی مردمی. مهدی اخوان ثالث، در سپهر ساکنِ پس از کودتای ۱۳۳۲ سروده بود: «طمع شعله نمی‌بندم/ خُردک شرری هست

---

[۶۱۹] مسعود رجوی (متولد ۱۳۲۷) و موسی خیابانی (۱۳۲۲- ۱۳٦۰) در سال ۵۰ دستگیر شدند و همراه با دیگر اعضاء مرکزیت سازمان به اعدام محکوم شدند. اما حکم اعدام آن‌ها به حبس ابد کاهش یافت. بنا بر اظهار محسن نجات‌حسینی، برادر مسعود رجوی که در سوئیس اقامت داشت، به سازمان‌های حقوق بشر مراجعه کرده بود، و از آن رو که نقض حقوق بشر در ایران در آن زمان مورد توجه و انتقاد سازمان‌های بین‌المللی قرار داشت، شاه به کاهش محکومیت مسعود رجوی تن داده بود. البته، در منابعی که مخالفان رجوی نوشته‌اند، چنین می‌خوانیم که ابراز ندامت، همکاری با ساواک، و دادن اطلاعات مربوط به سازمان، در تخفیف مجازات مسعود رجوی مؤثر بوده است. و این در حالی است که پیرامون کاهش مجازات موسی خیابانی- که او هم شامل کاهش مجازات شده بود- چنین تردیدهائی برانگیخته نشده است. مخالفانِ مجاهدین خلق، و مخالفان بخش مارکسیست/ لنینیستی‌ی آن، همین برچسب را به تقی شهرام زده‌اند. تقی شهرام، از جمله دستگیرشدگان سال ۵۰، پس از چندی به زندان ساری تبعید شد. اما در آغاز سال ۵۲ با همکاری‌ی افسر نگهبان زندان و همراه با او و همه‌ی تسلیحات زندان ساری، از زندان گریخت. در هر حال، مسعود رجوی و موسی خیابانی، پس از تحمل هفت سال زندان (و به شهادت آیت‌الله طالقانی: تحمل شکنجه)، روز ۳۰ دی ماه ۱۳۵۷ از زندان آزاد شدند.

هنوز؟» و اعضاء این دو سازمان- در هیئت «شیرآهنکوه»های احمد شاملو، سوار بر «اسب سفید خشمگینِ» منوچهر آتشی- با گیراندن شعله‌هائی از تن و روان جوان خود، به او پاسخ دادند: «آری، هست»؛ چرا که هوش و گوش به فروغ فرخزاد سپرده بودند که: «پرواز را به خاطر بسپار، پرنده مردنی‌ست.» صرف نظر از اعضائی که به دلایل مختلف از نیمه راه مبارزه برگشتند، انبوهی از پیکارگرانِ زن و مرد در هر دو سازمان، به معنای اخص کلمه، تجسم «شعله» و «شیرآهنکوه»، «اسب خشمگین»، و نمود «پرنده»ای بودند که می‌دانست «پرواز»اش اهمیت دارد و میانگین عمرِ چریکی‌اش بیش از شش ماه نیست. گذشتن از لذت‌های معمول زندگی، ترک خانه و خانواده و تحصیل، تحمل مقررات توان‌فرسا در خانه‌های تیمی، هراس مداوم از خطر دستگیری، رویاروئی با انبوهِ مأموران سراپا مسلح رژیم، وارد کردن اسلحه و مهمات به ایران از مرزهای زمینی- و گاه با هواپیما و زیر چشم مأموران فرودگاه‌های مبداء و مقصد- ساختن بمب‌های دستی با حداقل امکانات، زندگی و مرگ با کپسول سیانور، پاره‌شدن زیر شلاقِ شکنجه‌گران، سوختن و آب شدن بر شعله‌ی بخاری و فندک و آتش سیگارِ بازجویان، و دم برنیاوردن یا تسلیم نشدن در برابر آن‌ها، خمیرمایه‌ای جز شهامت، ایمان به حقانیت مبارزه و ازخودگذشتگی نمی‌تواند داشته باشد؛ که حتا خواندن شرح بزنگاه‌های آن، هراس و شگفتی و ستایش خواننده را یکجا برمی‌انگیزد. به عنوان مثال، خواننده‌ام را به فرازی از کتاب «حمید اشرف: آمیزه‌ی سرود و فلز»، نوشته‌ی تیمور پیروانی، رجوع می‌دهم:

> [...] خانه‌ی تیمی‌ی خیابان سلیمانیه مورد محاصره قرار می‌گیرد. محمد صفاری آشتیانی که در حال رفتن به این خانه بود، با مأمورین در خیابان درگیر می‌شود. صدای تیراندازی، حمید [اشرف] و رفیقِ جان‌باخته شیرین معاضد [فضیلت‌کلام] را که در خانه مستقر بودند، هوشیار می‌سازد. آن‌ها برخی اسناد و مدارک موجود را آتش می‌زنند و بعد در حین درگیری فرار می‌کنند. در حین جنگ و گریز، گلوله‌ای به پای رفیق شیرین اصابت می‌کند. خودِ او در [«بولتن درونی‌ی سچفخا»] در این مورد می‌نویسد: «از آن جائی که تجربه‌ای از تیرخوردن نداشتم، تصور کردم که دیگر قادر به راه رفتن نیستم. در این هنگام، رفیقِ مجروح، حمید اشرف هم خودش را به من رساند و به تصور این که دیگر نمی‌توانم حرکت کنم، در حالی که گلنگدن مسلسل را می‌کشید، خود را آماده می‌کرد که در صورت لزوم، وظیفه‌ی چریکی‌اش را انجام دهد، و نگذارد زنده به دست دشمن اسیر شوم. گرچه خود نیز مسلح بودم و در صورتی که قادر به فرار نبودم، چنین وظیفه‌ای را انجام می‌دادم. در این موقع، رفیق از من پرسید: با مسلسل بزنمت یا می‌توانی فرار کنی؟ سریعاً این فکر از ذهنم گذشت که باید فرار کنم. به رفیق گفتم می‌توانم فرار کنم.»[۶۲۰] (قلاب‌ها از من است.)

شیرین معاضد، به سلامت از آن مهلکه گریخت؛ تا جائی دیگر، و در حمله‌ای دیگر، جان خود را به پیشگاه هدفش تقدیم کند. مازیار بهروز (استاد دانشگاه و پژوهشگر این دوره از تاریخ چپ ایران)، در یک سخنرانی، با اشاره به متن نوارهای منتشرشده از نشست سران دو سازمان «چریک‌های فدائی‌ی خلق» و بخش «مارکسیست‌شده‌ی سازمان مجاهدین خلق» که در سال ۵۴ انجام شده، هم ترس ساواک از این پیکارگران را، هم شرایط مخفی‌کاری‌ی چریکی را، و هم ایمان و اعتقاد و اعتماد به نفس در چریک‌های آن دوره را در چند جمله‌ی زیر به زیبائی ترسیم کرده است:

> آن‌هایی که گفت‌وگوهای حمید اشرف و تقی شهرام را نشنیده‌اند، حتماً در سایت‌ها بشنوند و یا متن پیاده‌شده را بخوانند: چهار جوان زیر سی سال در آپارتمانی در تهران نشسته‌اند در دو سوی پرده (که همدیگر را نبینند). این‌ها رهبران دو سازمان چریکی‌اند که ساواک برای کشتن‌شان حاضر است میلیون‌ها تومان پول بدهد. یک سازمان مجاهدینِ مارکسیست لنینیست آمده افراد مسلمان خودش را تصفیه کرده و حالا به چریک‌ها می‌گوید بیایید با هم جبهه درست کنیم. حمید اشرف [از سازمان چریک‌ها] می گوید بگذارید ببینیم شما کی هستید و چی هستید؛ و جبهه نداریم؛ شما می‌توانید حل شوید در ما.

---

[۶۲۰] تیمور پیروانی، ***حمید اشرف: آمیزه‌ی سرود و فلز***، نشر الکترونیکی‌ی «آلترناتیو»، مرداد ۱۳۹۰، ص ۲۵.
http://www.fwhi.org/maqale/ashraf%20Alternative.pdf

این‌ها دارند با هم صحبت می‌کنند که نکات اشتراک و اختلاف برای هم روشن شود. [...] اعتماد به نفس این‌ها نجومیه. یک چیز عجیب غریب است. چهار نفر نشسته‌اند تو تهران، ساواک داره با مسلسل دنبال اینا می‌گرده تا بگیردشون؛ و این‌ها نشسته‌اند از چین، از ویتنام، از مسائل ایران، از جبهه‌ی مشترک، از نابودی رژیم، از فردای ایران و از همه چی صحبت می‌کنند، ولی پرده و سطشونه. این موضوع یک فیلم یا یک رمان جالب است. این اتکاء به نفس که این نسل داشت، به نظر من یک وجه بسیار مهم نقش چپ است. این احساس که هر کاری می‌توانند بکنند. این در تاریخ ایران که نگاه کنید کم‌تر دیده می‌شود. کاری که می‌خواستند انجام دهند رفتند دنبالش و انجام دادند و موفق هم نشدند، اما ارزش کارشان فقط در موفقیت و یا عدم موفقیت‌شان نیست؛ در شناخت و ارزش‌گذاری‌ی کارشان است.[۶۲۱]

همین جا به عنوان معترضه‌ای کوتاه بگویم که بر سر این گزاره‌ی مطلق که «موفق هم نشدند»، با مازیار بهروز هم‌نظر نیستم. چرا که این سلحشوران در نخستین مرحله‌ی هدف خود- که لرزاندن پایه‌های دیکتاتوری‌ی شاه و کشاندن مردم به مبارزه با آن بود- موفق شدند.

البته حالا با چشم بستن بر مجموعه‌ی شرایط حاکم بر ایران و جهان، که جنبش چریکی را در آن بزنگاه تاریخی در ایران پدید آورد، می‌توان- مانند حزب توده در تبعید- جمله به جمله‌ی لنین را نقل قول کرد و نشان داد که عمل چریکی خلاف «مارکسیسم/ لنینیسم» است؛ یا می‌توان بر «اراده‌گرائی»ی پیشتازان مشی‌ی مسلحانه، و حتا بر استبداد فکری‌ی آن‌ها خرده گرفت؛ یا می‌توان نشست و متن‌ها را خواند و دقایق را ملاحظه کرد، و در خوش‌بینانه‌ترین داوری گفت که این پیکارگران در این جا و آن جای نظر یا عمل خود «اشتباه» کردند. اما- گذشته از انکارِ سندسازانِ حرفه‌ای- تردید دارم که حتا در بدبینانه‌ترین داوری‌های پژوهشگرانه، بتوان هدف مردمی‌ی این پیکارگران، و از جان‌گذشتگی‌ی آن‌ها در راه این هدف را نفی کرد. کما این که پژوهندگانِ منتقد مشی‌ی چریکی، مانند مازیار بهروز و پیمان و هابزاده، نیز بر این ویژگی‌ها صحه گذاشته‌اند. این هدف، در جای جای متن‌های مختلف این دو سازمان، و با بیان‌های مختلف یادآوری شده است. به عنوان نمونه، بیژن جزنی در متن «آخرین دفاع خود در دادگاهِ ۲۲/ ۱۰/ ۱۳۴۷» می‌گوید:

[...] ایران در نظر من فقط نقشه‌ی جغرافیائی‌ی آن نیست. ضمن این که تمامیت ارضی‌ی ایران را محترم و مقدس می‌شمارم، بیش از هر چیز به مردمی که روی این خاک زندگی می‌کنند توجه دارم. آن چه متضمن منافع این مردم است، هدف و مقصد زندگی‌ی من است. آن چه برای این مردم عزیز است برای من محترم است. [...] من به عنوان یک انسان، انسانی که به قیمت رنج و محرومیت مردم ستم‌کش ایران توانسته است از نعمت تحصیلات عالی بهره‌مند شود، نتوانسته‌ام نسبت به سرنوشت و منافع مردم این سرزمین که همه گونه حق به گردن من دارد، بی‌اعتناء بمانم. وجدان آگاه بشری و مسئولیت‌های یک روشنفکر در کشوری که در جهان امروز، توسعه نیافته به حساب می‌آید، به من حکم کرده است که فقط متوجه دفع زیان و جلب منافع فردی نباشم. پس به هر صورت، من خود این سرنوشت را انتخاب کرده‌ام. [...][۶۲۲]

و حسن ضیاء ظریفی در «رد صلاحیت دادگاهِ بدوی» می‌گوید:

[...] چه اکنون و چه بعد از این، یک امر به عنوان نیت من و به عنوان نیت مقدسم، و به عنوان راهنمای من در کارهای سیاسی و اجتماعی مطرح بوده و خواهد بود؛ و آن، آزادی و سعادت وطنم، سرافرازی و خوشبختی‌ی مردم زحمت‌کش و رنجدیده‌ای است، که به نام ملت ایران خوانده می‌شود. من به عنوان یک ایرانی و به عنوان یک روشنفکر ایرانی، به خود

---

[۶۲۱] فرح طاهری، ***چپ ایران در میانه‌ی دو تحول تاریخی: سخنرانی‌ی نویسنده‌ی شورشیان آرمانخواه در کانون کتاب تورنتو***، تارنمای هفته‌نامه‌ی «شهروند»، ۱۶ ژوئن ۲۰۱۱:
http://www.shahrvand.com/?p=15108

[۶۲۲] متن دفاعیه‌های بیژن جزنی و حسن ضیاء ظریفی، پس از چهل و چهار سال برای نخستین بار به همت پرویز قلیچ‌خانی در نشریه‌ی «آرش»، چاپ پاریس، شماره‌ی ۱۰۸، تیر ۱۳۹۱/ ژوئیه ۲۰۱۲ منتشر شد. بازگفت از دفاعیه‌ی بیژن جزنی را از صفحات ۱۱ و ۱۴ این نشریه برگرفته‌ام.

حق می‌دهم و خود را موظف می‌دانم که با علاقمندی و دلسوزی و با احساس مسئولیت عمیق نسبت به سرنوشت ملتم و نسبت به حیات سیاسی و اجتماعیِ میهنم رفتار کنم؛ و در این راه، تمام ملاحظات و منافع حقیر شخصی را کنار گذاشته‌ام. زیرا می‌کوشم شایسته‌ی آن باشم که ملتم مرا فرزند وفادار و خدمتگزار خود بداند. [...] (پیشین، ص ۲۱)

یا مهدی رضائی (۱۳۳۱- ۱۳۵۱) از سازمان مجاهدین خلق، در حضور خبرنگاران داخلی و خارجی در دادگاه نظامی چنین از خود دفاع می‌کند:

من در این جا به اتهام عشق به خلق و پیکار در راه خلق محاکمه می‌شوم. هدف ما فراهم آوردن چنان شرایطی است که همه‌ی انسان‌ها تحت آن شرایط به آخرین حد کمال و انسانیت برسند[۶۲۳].

شاید بتوان نقشه‌ای از جهان آرمانیِ این پیکارگران را در تصویری مشاهده کرد که در شاکله‌های شناختیِ اشرف دهقانی شکل بسته است. اشرف دهقانی، به قول خودش: «بدون آن که لازم باشد از جامعه‌ای که کمونیست‌ها خواهان برپائیِ آن می‌باشند، تصویر دقیق و همه‌جانبه ارائه شود»، جهان آرمانیِ خود و هموندانش را به شرح زیر ترسیم می‌کند:

جامعه‌ای را مجسم کنیم که در آن دیگر گرسنگی مفهوم ندارد و فقر و فلاکت از آن رخت بربسته است. در آن جا از اعتیاد، از زنانی که برای گذران زندگی مجبور به تن‌فروشی می‌شوند، از دختران نوجوانِ فراری، که در معرض هرگونه سوءاستفاده و جنایت قرار دارند، از کودکانِ خیابانی و کارتُن‌خواب‌ها و غیره خبری نیست. در آن جا زندان نیست؛ شکنجه نیست؛ اعدام نیست؛ انسان‌ها همدیگر را نمی‌دَرَند؛ جنگ نیست؛ برعکس، دوستی‌ها و روابط توأم با صلح و صفا بین انسان‌ها، مشخصه‌ی آن جامعه است؛ جامعه‌ای که مردم درهای خانه‌شان را نمی‌بندند؛ قفل، افسانه‌ای است؛ و قلب، برای زندگی بس است؛ جامعه‌ای که مهربانی دست زیبائی را گرفته است؛ و خلاصه در آن جامعه عشق است که حکم می‌راند.[۶۲۴]

اشرف دهقانی در دنباله‌ی ترسیم تصویر بالا می‌پرسد: «آیا کسی هست که حتا از تصور چنین دنیائی لذت نبرد؟ چه کسی می‌گوید که از بین رفتن کینه و نفرت و خشم و عداوت در روابط انسان‌ها با یکدیگر، آرزو و ایده‌آل هر انسان شرافتمندی نیست.» منتها، چنان که اشرف دهقانی در دنباله‌ی سخن می‌گوید و چنان که از تاریخ جنبش چریکی برمی‌آید، برای دست‌یابی به آن جهان آرمانی، کینه و خشم و نفرت، بایسته‌ی مبارزه است؛ که در کوران آن- افزون بر «امپریالیسم» و «سگ زنجیری‌اش در ایران»- کارگزاران خُرده پای رژیم را نیز در برمی‌گیرد. کما این که، هم سازمان چریک‌های فدائیِ خلق و هم سازمان مجاهدین خلق، افرادی چون «نگهبانِ بانک» یا «ژاندارم پاسگاه» یا «سرباز»، یا «پاسبان» را به عنوان «مزدور رژیم»، از «مردم»- یا به قول خودشان از «خلق»- جدا پنداشتند.

با این همه، شاید این جداپنداری، در فهرست «خطا»های استراتژیک آن‌ها (و یا در بررسیِ ذهنیت و معرفت‌شناسیِ ایده‌آلیستیِ آن‌ها)، قابل انتقاد باشد، اما ذات باورِ این پیکارگران به «مردم» (با تعریفی که از آن داشتند) را نفی نمی‌کند. مهم‌ترین نشانه‌ای که ما را به «هدفِ» غیرشخصیِ سرانِ هر دو سازمان هدایت می‌کند، تأکیدِ مکرری است که هر دو بر «طولانی بودنِ» پروسه‌ی مبارزه‌ی مسلحانه داشتند. این تأکید، همراه با شیوه‌ی تصمیم‌گیریِ آن‌ها در بزنگاه‌های مرگ و زندگی، به تاریخ گزارش می‌دهد که این پیکارگران، نه تنها شخصاً به امید دستیابی به «قدرت سیاسی» نبودند، بلکه- با این یقین که پرچم مبارزه‌شان بر زمین نخواهد ماند- در هر لحظه‌ای از حیات چریکی، برای مرگ آمادگی داشتند؛ و یکی از مهم‌ترین انگیزه‌هائی که جان و روان و استقامت این جنگاوران را زیر شکنجه در زندان شاه از خطر وادادگی

---

۶۲۳ مهدی رضائی روز ۱۸ اردیبهشت ۱۳۵۱- در حالی که برای اجرای یک قرار سازمانی می‌رفت- مورد تعقیب اکیپی از کمیته‌ی مشترک ساواک، به سرپرستیِ ستوان «جاویدمند»، قرار گرفت. او در حال فرار به سوی مأموران تیراندازی کرد. ستوان جاویدمند مورد اصابت گلوله‌ی او قرار گرفت و کشته شد. خود مهدی رضائی نیز توسط بقیه‌ی مأموران دستگیر شد. جمله‌های دفاعیه‌ی او را در مأخذ زیر بخوانید:

❖ ***سازمان مجاهدین خلق: از پیدائی تا فرجام***، تهران: مؤسسه‌ی مطالعات و پژوهش‌های سیاسی، جلد اول، ص ۵۲۹.

۶۲۴ اشرف دهقانی، ***بذرهای ماندگار***، لندن: چریک‌های فدائیِ خلق ایران، آوریل ۲۰۰۵، ص ۲۰۰.

حفظ می‌کرد، اندیشیدن به هدف، و به «مردم»ی بود، که برخواهند خاست و مبارزه‌ی آن‌ها را ادامه خواهند داد.[۶۲۵] یا مثلاً، صفائی فراهانی (فرمانده‌ی عملیات سیاهکل)، با این که می‌داند چندی از هموندان تیم‌های کوه و شهر دستگیر شده‌اند، و در حالی که گروه کوه با برف و سرما و کمبود نیروی انسانی و مشکل دسترسی به انبارک‌های غذا و دارو مواجه است، حمله به پاسگاه ژاندارمری‌ی سیاهکل را اجراء می‌کند. چرا که می‌داند در صورت تأخیر در اجراء آن، به زودی دستگیر یا کشته خواهند شد؛ پس بهتر است ضربه‌ای را که حدود ۵ ماه برای آن تدارک دیده‌اند، پیش از مرگ یا دستگیری (که برای آن‌ها بدتر از مرگ بود)، به رژیم وارد کنند؛ و اگر قرار به مرگ باشد، بهتر است در حین عملیات یا پس از آن به سراغشان بیاید. یا، آن سه تن پیکارگر مجاهدی که زیر چشم پلیس بین‌المللی به هواپیماربائی دست زدند، با این امید خطر کرده بودند که نه تنها یاران کارآزموده‌ی خود را (به عنوان سرمایه‌های سازمان) از چنگال ساواک برهانند، بلکه اسرار یک سازمانِ «خلقی» را از خطر افشاء در امان دارند.

همین جا باید یادآور شد که ویژگی‌ی «مردمی»بودن در دستگاه نظری‌ی این دو سازمان، خط فاصل پررنگی رسم می‌کند که آن‌ها را از «فدائیان اسلام» یا از ذوب‌شدگانِ «حمله‌های انتحاری» جدا می‌کند. گرچه هدفِ فدائیان اسلام نیز مانند هدف نهائی‌ی این دو سازمان، تحقق نوع معیّنی از حکومت در ایران بود. اما درونه‌ی این «نوعِ معین»، نجات «اسلام»ی بود که توسط روحانیت سنتی نمایندگی می‌شد. به بیان دیگر، هدف فدائیان اسلام، مشخصاً، بازتولید نفوذ روحانیت شیعه بود که در تصادم با فکرت‌های «مدرن» در ایران، به مخاطره افتاده بود. (نفوذی که، دسترسی به کانون‌های قدرت در پیکره‌ی جامعه و در هرم قدرت سیاسی را در درازنای تاریخ برای این لایه‌ی اجتماعی میسر کرده بود.) در نتیجه، «فداکاری»ی فدائی‌ی اسلام یا آن افسون‌شده‌ای که با هدف ضربه زدن به «دشمن» خود را به بمب می‌بندد، قرار است که در بهشتِ موعودِ روحانیت پاداش گیرد. اما «فداکاری»ی چریک‌های این دو سازمان، نه تنها در انتظار پاداش نیست، بلکه، اگر هم انتظار «پاداش» در میان باشد، قرار است با تحقق عدالت اجتماعی و رفاه «مردم»، بر همین زمین تحقق یابد. حتا سازمان مجاهدین خلق- که «اسلام» عنصرِ اصلی‌ی سازنده‌ی ایدئولوژی‌ی آن‌ها بود- قرآن را «نه به مثابه کلام خدا»، بلکه به عنوان «یک مدرک تاریخی»، پویا، و الهام‌بخشِ حرکت به سوی «تغییرات دینامیک و عمل انقلابی» برانداز می‌کردند؛ و بر این باور بودند که پیام پیامبر اسلام، «نه مذهب توحیدی، بلکه نظام توحیدی، یعنی جامعه‌ی بی‌طبقه و رها از فقر و فساد و جنگ و بی‌عدالتی و نابرابری و سرکوب است»[۶۲۶]. از این تفاوت نظری گذشته، فدائیان اسلام که از درون لایه‌ی روحانی برآمدند، طبیعتاً از حمایتِ مادی و معنوی‌ی روحانیتِ رسمی و با نفوذِ آن زمان (در ایران و در نجف) برخوردار بودند. در حالی که چریک‌های فدائی از سوی هیچ قدرتی در ایران حمایت نمی‌شدند. مجاهدین خلق نیز مانند چریک‌های فدائی مورد نفرت روحانیت رسمی بودند، و معدودی از شخصیت‌های روحانی که- به سبب اعتقادات مشابه- از مجاهدین حمایت می‌کردند، اکثراً در مقام اپوزیسیون رژیم در زندان به سر می‌بردند. به بیانی دیگر، این دو سازمان، برخلاف فدائیان اسلام، از مغز و اندیشه و دانشی ایرانی و انگیزه‌ای سنت‌شکن برمی‌آمد که رو در روی سنتِ «نجف»ی فدائیان اسلام و حامیان آن هم ایستاده بود. همین جا اشاره کنم که مفاهیم نظری در ساختار ایدئولوژی‌ی مجاهدین در شکل‌بندی‌ی دستگاه نظری‌ی علی شریعتی و «اسلامِ بدون روحانیت»اش نقش اساسی داشت.

---

[۶۲۵] پس از انقلاب و در تبعید، خاطرات زندانیان سیاسی‌ی متعددی از زندان‌های ساواک منتشر شد، که بسیاری از آن‌ها به علت‌های استقامت خود زیر شکنجه اشاره کرده‌اند. اما، اشرف دهقانی در خاطرات خود از زندان‌های شهربانی و ساواک، این گوهر را در بند بند لحظه‌های اسارت خود بازنمائی کرده است. این کتاب، تا جائی که من می‌دانم، تنها کتابی بود که در همان دوره (۱۳۵۲)، با عنوان «حماسه‌ی مقاومت»، توسط سازمان چریک‌های فدائی‌ی خلق (با مقدمه‌ی حمید اشرف) منتشر شد. این کتاب، به شرح زیر در تبعید تجدید چاپ شده است:

- اشرف دهقانی، ***حماسه‌ی مقاومت***، چاپ دوم، لندن: انتشارات چریک‌های فدائی‌ی خلق ایران، ۱۳۸۳.

[۶۲۶] فشرده‌ی پرواند آبراهامیان از کتاب «چه‌گونه قرآن بیاموزیم»- یکی از متن‌های ایدئولوژیک/ آموزشی‌ی مجاهدین خلق- برگرفته از صفحات ۹۳ تا ۹۶ کتاب «The Iranian Mojahedin»، ۱۹۸۹.

دو) این پرسش که چرا این بزنگاهِ پرخروش از تاریخ ایران به حضور هیچ «زن»ی به عنوان «پایه‌گذارِ مستقل» یک «سازمان سیاسی» شهادت نمی‌دهد،[۶۲۷] گفتمان درازدامن و پُر پُرس‌وُجوی جداگانه‌ای است که باز کردنِ آن در این مجال نمی‌گنجد. اما در ارتباط با مبحث حاضر، تأکید بر این نکته‌ی بدیهی را بایسته می‌دانم که شخصیت‌های هسته‌ی نخستین و لایه‌های آغازینِ هر دو سازمان، مرد بودند. و این در حالی بود که در زمان شکل‌گیری‌ی این دو سازمان، افزون بر حضور زنانِ فعال در حزب توده، زنان پرشماری از لایه‌های دانشجو، کارمند، پرستار، پزشک و معلم، در حزب‌ها و سازمان‌های جبهه‌ی ملی، در نهضت آزادی، و در اتحادیه‌ی معلمان (در «باشگاه مهرگان») حضوری فعال داشتند؛ که اگر مردانِ پایه‌گذارِ این دو سازمان- از ابتدای کار- در صدد جذب آن‌ها بودند، بی‌تردید دست خالی برنمی‌گشتند. کما این که وقتی- به لحاظ تاکتیکی- حضور زن در این سازمان‌ها الزامی شد، زنان بی‌شماری از لایه‌های مختلف اجتماعی و با موقعیت‌های مختلف شغلی و تحصیلی به هر دو سازمان پیوستند. این خطکشی به قدری پررنگ بود و هنوز هم هست، که مثلاً، از اشرف دهقانی و روح‌انگیز دهقانی (سعادتی) در فهرست بنیادگذاران هسته‌ی تبریز یاد نمی‌شود (یا من ندیده‌ام). در حالی که از نوشته‌های اشرف دهقانی چنین برمی‌آید که، دست کم، او در نظر و عملِ تشکیل این هسته، گام به گام، با بهروز دهقانی و کاظم سعادتی و صمد بهرنگی و مردان دیگر همراه بوده است. از امر «پایه‌گذاری» گذشته، به جز اشرف دهقانی، که «عضو رهبری»ی خارج از کشورِ سازمان چریک‌های فدائی خلق بود، و به جز صبا بیژن‌زاده (سیمین) که در یک موردِ صد در صد اجباری و در مدتی کوتاه، «رهبری»ی سازمان چریک‌ها را به عهده داشت، هیچ یک از زنان فعال در این دو سازمان در آن دوره، به مقام رهبری نرسید. و این در حالی بود که برخی از آن‌ها- مانند مهرنوش ابراهیمی، نسترن آل‌آقا، مرضیه احمدی اسکوئی، نزهت روحی آهنگران در سازمان چریک‌ها، و اشرف ربیعی، که خود را تا حد «فرماندهی»ی عملیات چریکی، و تا عضویت در «مرکزیت» سازمانِ مجاهدین بالا کشیده بودند. گرچه جمع‌بندی‌ی حاضر به دوره‌ی پیش از انقلاب مربوط است، اما ناگزیرم که به ادامه‌ی همین سنت در سازمان چریک‌های بعد از انقلاب (پیش از انشعاب بزرگ) نیز اشاره کنم؛ یعنی به عدم حضور زنان در مرکزیتی که بعد از «پیروزی‌ی انقلاب» در سازمان چریک‌های فدائی‌ی خلق ایران تشکیل شد. مهدی فتاپور- یکی از اعضاء کمیته‌ی مرکزی‌ی این سازمان در سال ۵۸- در یک مصاحبه در تبعید، پیرامون انتخاباتِ کمیته‌ی مرکزی‌ی این سازمان در بهار ۵۸ می‌گوید:

> [پس از انتخابات] از مریم سطوت، مستوره احمدزاده، رقیه دانشگری و ویدا حاجبی نام برده شد. در جلسه، تنها در مورد مریم سطوت به دلیل تأکید مجید عبدالرحیم‌پور بر توانائی‌های وی در دوره‌ی چریکی بحث صورت گرفت، و با یک استدلال عمومی مورد پذیرش قرار نگرفت. و راجع به دیگران اصلاً بحثی صورت نگرفت. [...استدلال این بود که]

---

[۶۲۷] البته پس از انقلاب ۵۷، زنان مذهبی‌ی متعددی گفته‌اند که پیش از انقلاب، «سازمان» یا «جمعیت» یا «هسته»ای را پایه‌گذاری کرده بودند. اما واقعیت این است که ، پیش از «فضای باز سیاسی»، محتوای هسته‌های زنان مذهبی را مراسمی مانند قرآن‌خوانی و دعای کمیل تشکیل می‌داد. منتها، گروهی از همین‌ها بودند که در سال‌های ۵۵ تا ۵۷ با هدایت مردان روحانی وارد صحنه‌ی مبارزه‌ی سیاسی شدند . به عنوان نمونه، یکی از این موارد را در این جا ثبت می‌کنم: مریم بهروزی، «دبیر کل جامعه‌ی زینب، مشاور حقوقی و امور مجلس در نهاد ریاست جمهوری (دوره‌ی محمود احمدی‌نژاد)، رئیس بنیاد شهید و ایثارگران، استاد دانشگاه در درس‌های حوزوی»، در مصاحبه‌ای می‌گوید: «قبل از انقلاب از سال ۱۳۴۲ مقلد حضرت امام بودم. تا سال‌های ۱۳۵۲- ۱۳۵۳ که رسماً وارد صحنه‌ی سیاست شدم. گروهی از زنان را به نام «هسته های مقاومت» در تهران تشکیل دادم که این گروه‌ها در ده منطقه‌ی تهران فعال بودند. در کلاس‌های قرآن و احکام، جلسات را اداره می‌کردم و درس می‌دادم و سخنرانی‌های مذهبی- سیاسی داشتیم. از بین این کلاس‌ها و جلسات سخنرانی، خانم‌هائی که دارای شم سیاسی بودند، اطلاعاتی داشتند، اطلاعاتی می‌خواستند، شجاع بودند و می‌توانستند فعالیت سیاسی داشته باشند، وارد این هسته‌های مقاومت (البته آن موقع اسم نداشت و اواخر با آقای دکتر مفتح چنین اسمی را برای آن انتخاب کردیم) می‌شدند. در این گروه، اطلاعیه‌ها و بیانیه‌های حضرت امام را بین هم رد و بدل و تکثیر و توزیع می‌کردند. [...] ما از مساجد، تکایا، حسینیه‌ها و منازل استفاده می‌کردیم. جلسات در همان مکان‌ها تشکیل می‌شد. در سال‌های ۵۵- ۵۶ ممنوع‌المنبر شدم. وقتی سال ۵۷ آقای دکتر مفتح از من دعوت کردند که در مسجد قباد سخنرانی کنم، گفتم آقای دکتر من ممنوع‌المنبر هستم. ایشان گفتند: "اولاً، ما برای شما منبر نمی‌گذاریم. ثانیاً، اطلاعیه‌ی اخیر حضرت امام هم مبنی بر این است که بر کلیه‌ی خطبا و سخنرانان فرض است مفاسد رژیم را افشا کنند. هر اتفاقی هم که می‌خواهد بیافتد، بیافتد." به این ترتیب، برای سخنرانی‌ی مسجد قباد رفتم و روز ششم دستگیر شدم. مدتی هم در زندان بودم. از زندان که آزاد شدم، فاجعه‌ی هفده شهریور اتفاق افتاد. بعد از هفده شهریور هم وارد اوج نهضت شدیم تا انقلاب پیروز شد.»
به مأخذ زیر نگاه کنید:

❖ مریم محمدی، ***نقش زنان در انقلاب: گفت‌وگو با مریم سطوت، چریک فدایی خلق و مریم بهروزی، دبیر «جامعه ی زنان زینب»***، خاطرات انقلابی‌ی دو زن از دو پایگاه متفاوت فکری، برگرفته از تارنمای «مهدی فتاپور»، تاریخ بازدید: ۱۲ مه ۲۰۱۲:
http://www.fatapour.de/Maryam/bahman.htm

> «اضافه شدن یک یا دو زن به ترکیبِ [کمیته‌ی مرکزی]، با توجه به رأیِ پائین همه‌ی آنان،[هر یک سه رأی] ما را در مقابل این سئوال قرار می‌دهد که چرا در میان زنان، فلانی انتخاب شده و دیگری برگزیده نشده، که ما با توجه به این که با آنان کار مشترک نکرده‌ایم، قادر به پاسخ‌گوئی نیستیم. و این امر، رابطه‌ی ما و فرد انتخاب‌شده را با سایر کادرهای زن تیره می‌کند. به همین دلیل بهتر است انتخاب زنان را به ترمیم‌های بعد موکول کنیم.» [...] عدم انتخاب زن در جمع اعضای کمیته‌ی مرکزی و مشاوران، در شرایطی که نزدیک به سی در صد از کادرهای سازمان زن بودند، یک عقب‌گرد بزرگ بود که متأسفانه در دوره‌های بعد هم تداوم داشت.[۶۲۸] (تمام قلاب‌ها از من است، با فشرده‌ای از سخنان مهدی فتاپور.)

می‌پذیریم که هر یک از زنان یادشده- در متن بالا- فقط «سه رأی» آورده بودند. اما اگر قرارِ مردان به حذف زنان از مرکزیت نبود، می‌شد با انتخابات مجدد یا با قرعه‌کشی، مسئله‌ی «چرا فلانی انتخاب شد» را حل کرد.

تفسیرِ این «استدلالِ» مغشوش را به خواننده‌ام وامی‌نهم، و به عقب برمی‌گردم؛ یعنی به زمانی که، حضور زن- به عنوان «عضو»- در این دو سازمان وجهی الزامی یافت. صرف نظر از این که گزینش عضو از میان اعضاء خانواده‌ی خودِ چریک‌ها- از جمله زنان خانواده- مطمئن‌ترین و امن‌ترین نوع گزینش بود، خمیرمایه‌های عمده‌ی این الزام- به عریان‌ترین کلام- عبارت بودند از: رفع نیاز جنسیِ مردانِ سازمان، و ایجاد پوشش امنیتی برای سازمان. درباره‌ی «رفع نیاز جنسی»، حجتِ کلام را از خاطراتِ محسن نجات‌حسینی می‌گیرم. او، پیرامون سال‌های نخستِ سازمان مجاهدین خلق می‌نویسد:

> در بین اعضای سازمان، تعداد کسانی که ازدواج کرده بودند، بسیار اندک بود. برخورد با غریزه‌ی جنسی، یکی از دشوارترین مسائل فردی بود که [در هسته‌های آموزشی] روی آن بحث و تبادل نظر می‌شد. برای حل این مسئله که نزد افراد مختلف شدت و ضعف داشت، راهی جز ازدواج نبود. ازدواج نیز مانع بزرگی برای فعالیت مخفی بشمار می‌آمد. [...] شاهد بودم که یک یارِ تشکیلاتی برای برخورد خصمانه با غریزه‌ی جنسی‌اش، هرگاه فکری «شیطانی» به سرش می‌زد، سرش را به دیوار می‌کوبید، و خود را سرزنش می‌کرد. از آن جا که ازدواجی سازگار با کار تشکیلاتی برای او میسر نشد، سازمان او را کنار گذاشت و وی به زندگی‌ی عادی بازگشت. بعدها با حضور رزمندگان زن در سازمان‌های انقلابی، ازدواج‌های درون‌تشکیلاتی رایج شد.[۶۲۹] (گیومه در متن اصلی هست.)

افزون بر این انگیزه، حضور زن در خانه‌های تیمی، نوعی پوشش امنیتی نیز بود. چرا که خانه، باید به نام «خانواده» اجاره می‌شد و در چشم همسایگانِ محلّه همه‌ی وجوه آن باید عادی جلوه می‌کرد. مریم سطوت، عضو آن زمانی‌ی سازمان چریک‌های فدائی‌ی خلق، در تبعید می‌گوید:

> [...] این درست است که مسئولیت توجیه خانه‌های تیمی با زنان بود، ولی کسانی که این نقش را نقشی فرعی می‌نامند از مکانیسم مبارزه‌ی مخفی بی‌اطلاع‌اند. توجیه خانه‌ی مخفی و ارتباط با همسایگان نقشی تعیین کننده در بقای این تشکل‌ها داشت. این مسئولیت یکی از وظایف پراهمیت در آن دوران است. زنان در آن دوره نقشی به مراتب پراهمیت‌تر از دوره‌های بعد دارند. زنان در مبارزه‌ی مخفی توانایی داشتند. زنان ریزبین‌تر بوده و موارد مشکوک را زودتر تشخیص می‌دادند. زنان در کارشان منظم‌تر و دقیق‌تر بودند و در آن دوران بی‌نظمی و بی‌دقتی می‌توانست به قیمت جان فرد و دیگران منجر شود و علاوه بر آن حرکت زیر چادر امکان استتار بهتری برای آنان به وجود می‌آورد. این توانائی‌ها در حفظ یک تیم در آن دوران تعیین کننده بود. [...][۶۳۰]

---

۶۲۸ گفت‌وگو با مهدی فتاپور، ***روند شکل‌گیری‌ی رهبری‌ی سازمان چریک‌های فدائی‌ی خلق ایران پس از انقلاب و شکل‌گیری‌ی اولین کمیته‌ی مرکزی‌ی آن***، تارنمای «فتاپور»، ۲۴ اکتبر ۲۰۱۰:
http://fatapour.blogspot.com/2010/11/blog-post.html

۶۲۹ محسن نجات‌حسینی، ***بر فراز خلیج فارس***، پیشین، ص ۵۷.

۶۳۰ گفت‌وگوی شیرین فامیلی (سایت تهیه) و مریم سطوت، ***نقش زنان در سازمان‌های سیاسی***، برگرفته از تارنمای «مهدی فتاپور»، ۲۲ آوریل ۲۰۰۹:

با این که ازدواج‌های درون‌سازمانی در سازمان چریک‌های فدائی خلق نیز امری محرز است، اما من پیرامون چه‌گونگی آن به متن متقنی دست نیافتم. منتها، به برکت خاطرات اعضاء سازمان مجاهدین خلق، می‌دانم که ازدواج‌ها در این سازمان با رضایت سرشاخه، و موافقت مرکزیت سازمان، و البته، با اجازه‌ی آیت‌الله طالقانی و آیت‌الله ربانی انجام می‌شد.[۶۳۱] با این که یرواند آبراهامیان در کتاب «مجاهدین ایرانی» پیرامون جایگاه معتبر زن در این سازمان سخن گفته است، اما گزارشِ مستقیم زنان مجاهد (البته تا جائی که منتشر شده و تا جائی که من خوانده‌ام) نشان می‌دهد که زیربنای ساختارهای ذهنی در این سازمان نیز از ذهنیت مردسالارانه‌ی جامعه جدا نبوده است. منتها، زمانی که از «سازمان مجاهدین خلق» در این زمینه سخن می‌گوئیم بایسته است به دوره‌های مختلف در تاریخ این سازمان توجه کنیم: در دوره‌ی نخست، مبنای ایدئولوژی‌ی مجاهدین خلق، یکسره «اسلامی» بود؛ از سوی «نهضت آزادی» پشتیبانی می‌شد؛ و «نهضت آزادی» (به رهبری‌ی مهدی بازرگان و یدالله سحابی و آیت‌الله‌ها طالقانی و ربانی و ...) نیز پس از اعلام مواد «انقلاب سفید»، «با علماء مخالف با حق رأی‌ی زنان به توافق کامل رسیده بود.»[۶۳۲] پس می‌توان شرایط اجتماعی/ حقوقی‌ی زن در این دوره از سازمان را گمانه زد. پس از «تغییر مواضع ایدئولوژیک» و مارکسیست شدنِ بخشی از اعضاء، دوره‌ای شکل گرفت که کلیت این سازمان هنوز در هاشوری از «اسلام»/ «مارکسیسم» سرگردان بود. از این دوره، گزارش لیلا زمردیان را داریم که هم خود قربانی‌ی این سرگردانی‌ی ذهنی شد و هم در نوشته‌ای با عنوان «به داستان زندگی‌ی من گوش کنید»، گوشه‌هائی از رسوب ذهنیت مردسالارانه و نمودهای عملی‌ی آن در مناسبات این سازمان را ثبت کرد.[۶۳۳] از دوره‌ی بعدی (سال ۱۳۵۶)- که مارکسیست‌های این سازمان با «رهبر سکتاریست» خود تسویه حساب کردند- گزارش توران بازرگان را در دست داریم که ضمن یک نگاه سراسری به همه‌ی این دوره‌ها، به استقلال نسبی‌ی زن در این دوره گواهی داده است. (البته در درازنای این دوره، نام و عنوان سازمان نیز از نام و عنوان «مجاهدین» کاملاً متمایز شده بود، و با نام «سازمان پیکار در راه آزادی‌ی طبقه‌ی کارگر» شناسائی می‌شد.) دوره‌ی بعدی‌ی «سازمان مجاهدین خلق ایران»، پس از انقلاب و در تبعید است، که نادره افشاری (عضو سابق این سازمان)، تصویر هولناکی از برخورد کادر رهبری و «رهبر مجاهدین خلق» با زنان عضو سازمان را در کتاب «زن در دولت خیال» به تاریخ سپرده است.[۶۳۴]

اما داستان دردناک لیلا زمردیان (همسر سازمانی‌ی مجید شریف واقفی)، که به همت تراب حق‌شناس و «آرشیو سازمان پیکار» در تبعید بر تارنمای «اندیشه و پیکار» نشست، به عنوان «انتقاد از خود» و اعتراف به گناه، در دوره‌ی طوفانی‌ی «تغییر مواضع ایدئولوژیک» و خطاب به کادر رهبری‌ی وقت بخش مارکسیست این سازمان (تقی شهرام و بهرام آرام) نوشته شده است. در صفحه‌ی آغازین این جزوه‌ی ۵۰ صفحه‌ای می‌خوانیم:

> [...] نوشتن این مطالب برایم دشوارترین کار است. ابتدا فکر می‌کردم که فرار کنم ولی بعد از تأمل زیاد به این فکر افتادم که باید بمانم و هر تصمیمی که در مورد من می‌گیرند، ولو کشتن من، با جان و دل بپذیرم. در هر صورت من می‌دانم که جز انتقام و نفرین و دشنام شما و خلق چیز دیگری نخواهم شنفت. ولی با این وجود آماده‌ی آنم.

و در صفحه‌ی پایانی می‌نویسد:

---

http://www.fatapour.de/Maryam/naghshe_zanan.htm

[۶۳۱] لطف‌الله میثمی در جلد دوم خاطرات خود («آن‌ها که رفتند»، ص ۳۳۶) می‌نویسد: «وقتی سرشاخه و مرکزیت موافقت می‌کرد ازدواج بین جوانان صورت می‌گرفت. بقیه‌ی اعضاء گواهی می‌کردند که این دو نفر با هم ازدواج کرده‌اند، سپس طبق احکام رساله، آن دو با هم محرم می‌شدند.»

[۶۳۲] یرواند آبراهامیان، ***ایران بین دو انقلاب***، پیشین، ص ۴۲۳.

[۶۳۳] لیلا زمردیان، ***به داستان زندگی‌ی من گوش کنید***، برگرفته از «آرشیو سازمان پیکار در راه آزادی‌ی طبقه‌ی کارگر»، تارنمای «اندیشه و پیکار»:

http://www.peykarandeesh.org/PeykarArchive/Mojahedin-ML/pdf/be-dastane-zendegiye-man-leyla-zomorodian.pdf

[۶۳۴] نادره افشاری، ***زن در دولت خیال (نگاهی به نقش زن در سازمان مجاهدین)***، ناشر: نویسنده، مکان نشر: ندارد، ۱۳۷۹/ ۲۰۰۰.

> من می‌دانم که جای من جز در زیر خاک نیست. حاضرم آن‌ها که مرا می‌شناسند دعوت کنید و به دست همه‌ی شما اعدام شوم. همان طور که A گفته و خودم به خوبی می‌دانم، من دیگر جائی در هیچ کجا ندارم. آن وقت که صرفاً مسائل فردی و ضعف فردی داشتم، بار زیادی‌ی سازمان بودم و حالا که علاوه بر آن، یک سری بدبینی و اسمش را بگذاریم شناخت و یک سری رضالت هستم. [این واژه در متن ناخوانا است و اگر من آن را درست خوانده‌باشم، بایستی «رذالت» نوشته می‌شد.] در این مرحله و مراحل بعد می‌دانم که صرف سازمان نیست که مسائل مرا وقت بگذارد که حل کند. باید مرا به قتل برساند. این حق من است و این خواست خلق است. من از این که هرگز نتوانستم خدمتی به خلق کنم متأسفم.

لیلا چه کرده بود؟ و «ضعف فردی»ی او چه بود؟ چه‌گونه و با چه ابزاری شست‌وشوی مغزی شده بود که خود را مستحق اعدام می‌دانست؟ جزوه، متأسفانه تاریخ ندارد، و در آن از نام و نشانی‌ی افراد، با اشاره و با نام‌های مستعار سخن رفته است. (مانند: «مسئول»، «A»، «B»، «اصغر»، «علی»، «خواهر»، «حسن»، که با او در تماس بوده‌اند.) آرشیو سازمان پیکار نیز پیرامون این جزوه هیچ اظهار نظری نکرده اســـت. اما از متن- به کمک قرائن تاریخی- چنین به نظر می‌آید که پس از «تغییر مواضع ایدئولوژیک»، رهبری‌ی بخش مارکسیست سازمان (تقی شهرام و بهرام آرام)، لیلا را- که گویا بین دو ایدئولوژی مردد بوده- «کنار» گذاشـــته بود و او را در «خانه‌ای جداگانه» در اختیار «A» گذاشـــته بود تا به عنوان «مسئول»، هم او را «حفظ» کند و هم تردیدهای «خرده بورژوازی»ی او را نسبت به ایدئولوژی‌ی مارکسیسم بزداید. (از ص ۱۸ متن چنین به نظر می‌آید که خود «A» نیز از سوی رهبری به عنوان یک عنصر مردد شناخته شده بود و او را از «مسئولیت»ی که در هدایت چند تن از کادرها داشت، معزول کرده بودند.) در هر حال، لیلا در میانه‌ی راه متوجه می‌شود که «A» نسبت به رهبری‌ی مارکسیست‌های سازمان معترض است؛ با اسلامی‌های این سازمان به طور مخفیانه مراوده دارد؛ و از آن‌ها طرفداری می‌کند. لیلا از او می‌خواهد که واقعیت را به رهبری‌ی بخش مارکسیســـت ســـازمان خبر دهد. «A» «عصـبانی» می‌شـود، به او «سـیلی می‌زند»، به او تلقین می‌کند که انگیزه‌ی او در این اطلاع‌رسـانی حفظ «منافع فردی» اسـت. و ضـمن این که آموزه‌های اسـلام انقلابی را به گوش او می‌خواند، از هیچ تحقیری در خرد کردن فردیت و اعتماد به نفس این زن ابا نمی‌کند. لیلا هم در زیر این آوار و کشـــمکش با خود، متقاعد می‌شـــود و تصـــمیم می‌گیرد که موضوع وابستگی‌ی «A» به بخش اسلامی را با مرکزیت مارکسیستِ سازمان «مطرح» نکند:

> او راست می‌گوید. او از من به سـازمان نزدیک‌تر است و صـداقتش را در اعمال گذشته‌اش نشـان داده و این من هستم که بی‌صـداقت بودم. من آن قدر خودکم‌بین شـده بودم که به این احسـاس واقعی و درسـت در خودم- که باید به سـازمان اطلاع بدهم- هم شک کردم و گفتم شاید همین‌طور که او می‌گوید به خاطر منافع فردی‌ی من باشد. (ص ۱۳)

لیلا زمردیان مسئله‌ی «عصبانیتِ A» و «سیلی» خوردن از او را در صفحه‌ی ۱۱ جزوه آورده است، و باران تحقیرهای این «مسئول» و البته «کادر رهبری» را (و شگفتا که بی هیچ گلایه‌ای و حتا با پذیرش کامل) در سراسر متن تکرار کرده اســت. اما درنگ من بر پیامدهای دردناک روان‌شـــناختی‌ی این رفتار در «لیلا زمردیان»ی اســت که چند ســال پیش از نگارش این جزوه، با پیوستن به یک سازمان زیرزمینی/ چریکی، شخصاً «تصمیم» گرفته بود؛ و اکنون، به خاطر این که نمی‌داند چه راهی درسـت اسـت و چه راهی غلط، خود را نادان و بی‌عرضـه و «بدبخت» و «متلاشـی» و مسـتحق اعدام می‌بیند. منتها صـرف نظر از عوامل بیرونی، پیش‌زمینه‌ی پذیرشِ تحقیر، در بنیاد ذهنیت خود لیلا هم قابل بررسـی اسـت؛ که با دانش اندکی که از اسلام و مارکسیسم دارد، مدام نسبت «به اسـلام، و به خلق، و به خدا» احسـاس «گناه» می‌کند. او در جائی از این جزوه می‌نویسد:

> [...] این بود که واقعاً من مسئله‌ی ایدئولوژیک را اصل قرار دادم و حرف‌های A برای من احساس مسئولیت در برابر خدا و ایدئولوژی‌ی گذشته‌ی سازمان ایجاد کرد. من که حالا دین درستی نداشتم؛ نه مسلمان بودم و نه مارکسیست. اسلام قبلم را

> از دست داده بودم ولی چیزی هم جایشان ننشانده بودم. صرفاً مسئله‌ی طبقات و مبارزه با خصلت‌های بورژوازی برایم اصل قرار گرفته بود. قبول کرده بودم که اسلامی که قبلاً داشتم یک اسلام خرده بورژوازی بود. ولی در این که اصلاً اسلام روبنای طبقه‌ی متوسط و خرده بورژوازی است یا این که آیا اسلام می‌تواند ایدئولوژی‌ی طبقه‌ی کارگر باشد یا نه؛ و آیا ایدئولوژی‌ی طبقه‌ی کارگر فقط مارکسیست است و ایدئولوژی‌ی مارکسیست از زیربنای طبقه‌ی پرولتاریا زاده شده و ... هنوز مفهوم درستی نداشتم و حتا حالا هم ندارم. و از نوشته‌هایم می‌توانید بفهمید. با مطالعه‌ی فقط کتاب سیر تحولات فلسفه‌ی مارکسیسم، تقریباً قبول کرده بودم که ماده بر فکر تقدم داشته؛ ولی مسئله‌ی تکامل و جهت‌دار بودن آن و مسئله‌ی وحی و قیامت و یا این که ماده چه طور نیروئی است و ... شک داشتم و این‌ها مسائلی بود که برایم سئوال بود و حل نشده بود. هنوز مسئله‌ی قیامت و خدا در اعماق ذهنم بود. لازم است بگویم که مسئول من در جواب به این سئوالاتِ سیر تحولات و سئوالات مطروحه‌ی من و حل آن‌ها قادر نبود. (ج) زیرا خودش هم برایش این مسائل وجود داشت. به هر جهت در برخورد با مسائلی که A مطرح می‌کرد احساس مسئولیتم به خدا و قران و ترس از خیانت به اسلام و ... رشد می‌کرد و رنجم می‌داد. به همان اندازه که صداقتم به سازمان در نگفتن مسئله رنجم می‌داد. [...] من تصمیم گرفتم که به خاطر این که صلاحیت تشخیص این که کدام دو طرف حق دارند را ندارم، از A خواستم تا دیگر کوچک‌ترین اطلاعی از کارش و فعالیتش به من ندهد و اگر چنانچه من هم کنجکاوی کردم مرا تنبیه کند. [...] (صص ۱۴ تا ۱۷) (نقطه‌چین‌های بدون قلاب و حرف «ج» درون پرانتز از لیلا زمردیان هستند.)

لیلا زمردیان در چنین شرایط روانی‌ای بود که اندکی پس از نوشتن این متن، به آسانی آلت دست مرکزیت بخش مارکسیست شده‌ی سازمان مجاهدین (گروه اولِ رهبری) قرار گرفت؛ و بدون آن که بداند این «مرکزیت» قصد کشتن همسر سازمانی‌اش- مجید شریف واقفی- را دارد، او را به میعادگاه مرگ فراخواند. و سپس، به خاطر پی‌گیری در پرس‌وجو پیرامون قتل همسرش، تأیید نیم‌بندِ رهبری‌ی مارکسیست سازمان را از دست داد؛ خلع سلاح شد؛ در یک درگیری‌ی خیابانی بدون سلاح ماند؛ و با قرص سیانور خودکشی کرد.[۶۳۵] (من نمی‌دانم منظور لیلا زمردیان از «A» در متن یادشده، همانا «مجید شریف واقفی» بوده، یا کس دیگری. اما لیلا در صفحه‌ی ۴ از متن یادشده نوشته است: «بالأخره شناسنامه‌ها را جور کردیم و بعد از آن شب همراه «A» به مسافرخانه می‌رفتیم.» با توجه به مناسبات موجود در جامعه و با توجه به تاکتیک‌های رایج در سازمان‌های چریکی، می‌توان گمانه زد که این «A» همان «همسر سازمانی»ی لیلا، یعنی مجید شریف واقفی بوده است. از گمانه‌زنی گذشته، یرواند آبراهامیان در کتاب «مجاهدین ایرانی- انگلیسی- صص ۱۶۲-۱۶۴» اشاره کرده که اطلاعات مربوط به فعالیت‌های مخفیانه‌ی شریف واقفی را همسرش، لیلا زمردیان، به بهرام آرام و تقی شهرام رسانده بود.)

سخنان پوران بازرگان پیرامون برخورد سازمان مجاهدین خلق به زنان عضو، نیز شهادتی دست اول است. منتها برخلاف گزارش لیلا زمردیان که در شرایط بحرانی‌ی این سازمان نوشته شده بود، پوران بازرگان، در شرایطی نسبتاً امن، فرصت داشته که ضمن نشان دادن برخی از نمونه‌های رفتار مردسالارانه در این سازمان، ریشه‌های فرهنگی‌ی بزنگاه‌های تبعیض جنسی در جامعه را نیز واکاود. پوران بازرگان- که قدمت حضورش در «انجمن اسلامی‌ی بانوان»، به پیش از تشکیل «سازمان مجاهدین خلق ایران» می‌رسد- اینک در تبعید، «احساسِ تبعیض» جنسی در خانواده و اجتماع، و «محرومیتِ ناشی از آن» را، «عاملی برای تلاش و پشتکار و فعالیت» خود، «حتا در زمینه‌ی سیاسی» می‌داند. «ژانت بوئر» (پژوهشگر امریکائی) در گفت‌وگوئی که با او داشت، از او می‌پرسد: «آیا در سازمان مجاهدین به نقش مستقل زنان فکر می‌کردید؟» و پوران بازرگان پاسخ می‌دهد:

> در هیچ یك از سازمان‌های چریکی به نقش مستقل زنان فکر نمی‌کردند؛ زیرا دست کم از نظر تئوریك و به طور رسمی، با نداشتنِ نقش مستقل و با مشارکت در همه‌ی کارها بود که زنان خود را با مردان برابر می‌دانستند. زن اگر به اصطلاح

---

[۶۳۵] ***ازدواج درون‌سازمانی***، تارنمای «شهید مهندس سیدمجید شریف واقفی»، بازدید: ۱۲ فوریه ۲۰۱۱:
http://www.msharifvaghefi.blogfa.com/post-34.aspx

«کار مردانه» می‌کرد، مثلاً سلاح به کمر می‌بست، در عملیات نظامی شرکت می‌جست، فرماندهی‌ی عملیات یا مسئولیت سیاسی و تشکیلاتی‌ی گروه را به عهده می‌گرفت، خود را ارتقاء یافته می‌دید. اما اگر منظور حقوق ویژه‌ی زنان در برابر مردان است، باید بگویم که این، بین ما در سازمان مطرح نبود. گمان ما بر این بود که هر یك از ما بر اساس صلاحیت‌هایش وظایفی را به عهده می‌گیرد و فرقی بین زن یا مرد بودن نیست، هرچند در عمل همیشه این ایده‌آل رعایت نمی‌شد. ما هم جزئی از جامعه بودیم و روحیه‌ی مردسالاری در مردان و خودکم بینی و پذیرش فرهنگ مردسالاری در زنان وجود داشت. همان طور که گفتم سازمان از نظر تئوریك امتیازی برای مردان قائل نبود و لذا وقتی می‌دیدم که در قرآن (که ما همه بدان معتقد بودیم و آن را پایه‌ی ایدئولوژی خود می‌دانستیم) بین زن و مرد تبعیض آشکار قائل شده، برایم سئوال ایجاد می‌شد. در کلاس‌های ایدئولوژی به قرآن استناد می‌کردیم و مفهوم‌هائی از آن را که برای ما مهم بود- مثل مبارزه با ظلم، و جهاد در راه آزادی و عدالت- مثال می‌زدیم و در تأیید اهداف مبارزاتی‌مان آیه‌ها را به زبان روز تفسیر می‌کردیم. اما از جمله، از کنار آیاتی که بین زن و مرد تبعیض قائل شده رد می‌شدیم و سئوالاتی نظیر آن چه برای من مطرح بود بی‌جواب می‌ماند. نمی‌دانستم چرا در سوره‌ی ۳ (آل عمران) آیه‌ی ۱۴ وقتی از هوس‌های مردان سخن می‌گوید، زنان را در ردیف پول و اسب و رمه ذکر می‌کند و یا چه‌طور در سوره‌ی ۲۳ (مؤمنون) آیه‌ی ۶، همخوابگی با کنیز (یعنی زنی که در بازار بردگان خریده شده و یا در جنگ به غنیمت گرفته شده) و یا درست‌تر بگوئیم تجاوز به او، مجاز تلقی شده است. خب، توجه به این تناقض‌ها از زن بودن من ناشی می‌شد و البته در چهارچوب آن ایدئولوژی و اعتقادات بی‌جواب می‌ماند. ما توجه نمی‌کردیم که قرآن و احکام آن زاده‌ی شرایط تاریخی‌ی زمان خود بوده و اشکال نه از آن، بلکه از ما بود که می‌خواستیم آن کتاب را دستورالعمل امروز و فردای خود بسازیم. یك نکته هم به اختصار اشاره کنم که هرچند توجه به حقوق ویژه‌ی زن در برابر مرد و به اصطلاح مبارزه با مردسالاری موکول به پیروزی‌ی مبارزه‌ی انقلابی و ضد امپریالیستی و نیل به آزادی‌ی عمومی می‌شد ولی به جرأت می‌توانم بگویم که بخشی از انگیزه‌ی زنان در پیوستن به مبارزه‌ی انقلابی، اثبات برابری‌ی زن و مرد در مبارزه‌ی انقلابی و نشان دادن حیثیت انسانی‌ی برابر بود. خانمی را در دوره‌ی مجاهدین می‌شناختم که با داشتن دو فرزند از دست کتك‌ها و تحقیر شوهرش خانواده را رها کرده و به سازمان پیوسته بود. یك بار به من می‌گفت من با مبارزه و بعد با شهادتم به او (یعنی به شوهر سابقش) نشان خواهم داد که آن طور که او فکر می‌کرده بی‌لیاقت نیستم. این رفیق در سال ۵۵ در تهران با رگبار مأموران ساواك به شهادت رسید. در همان سال‌ها خانمی دیگر در گفت‌وگو از دشواری‌های مبارزه‌ی مخفی و تلفات بسیار آن، می‌گفت اگر این مبارزات نه به سقوط رژیم و کسب آزادی، بلکه اندکی از حقوق زنان را تحقق بخشد من راضی خواهم بود.[۶۳۶]

همچنین، می‌دانیم که در زمان انقلاب، و پیش از اجباری شدنِ حجاب توسط جمهوری‌ی اسلامی، زنان «سازمان مجاهدین خلق ایران» و زنان هوادار این سازمان، موظف به استفاده از «حجاب اسلامی» بودند، و در سال‌های ۵۷ تا ۶۰ (که این سازمان فعالیت علنی داشت)، یونیفرم آن‌ها را روسری و روپوش و شلوار گشاد و سرمه‌ای رنگ تشکیل می‌داد. و نیز، باز به برکت پژوهش پرواند آبراهامیان، و البته به یاری‌ی حافظه‌ی شخصی، می‌دانم که پس از «پیروزی‌ی انقلاب» و تا زمانی که سازمان مجاهدین خلق (حالا به رهبری‌ی مسعود رجوی) در جمهوری‌ی اسلامی هنوز فعال بود، «انجمن زنان مسلمان»، «انجمن مادران مسلمان»، و «انجمن خوهران مسلمان»، نقش بازوهای تبلیغاتی‌ی این سازمان را بازی می‌کردند.

از سازمان چریک‌های فدائی، اما این را نیز می‌دانیم که روابط شخصی/ عشقی بین هموندان ممنوع بود؛ و تخطی از این قانون نیز پیامدهائی تنبیهی داشت. حتا زن و شوهری که به سازمان می‌پیوستند، هر یک در خانه‌ی تیمی‌ی جداگانه زندگی می‌کردند. البته، گزارش محمد قراگوزلو- با تعریف متفاوتی از «عشق»-حکایت دیگری را روایت می‌کند. او در تفسیر رمان «پرستو در باد» (نوشته‌ی خودش) می‌گوید:

---

۶۳۶ ***در گفت‌وگو با پوران بازرگان***، مصاحبه کننده: پژوهشگر امریکائی خانم ژانت بوئر، ۱۹۹۹ (۱۳۷۸)، تارنمای «پیکار اندیشه»: http://www.peykarandeesh.org/PouranBazargan/Pouran-Bazargan-Janet.html

> [...] زنان و مردان رزمنده‌ی چپ، در عین پیشبرد وظایف سیاسی و تشکیلاتی‌ی خود و مشارکت در مبارزه‌ی مسلحانه، عاشق می‌شدند و معشوق را در تلفیقی سوسیالیستی از عشق فردی و اجتماعی‌ی منطبق با آرمان‌های انسانی و برابری دوست می‌داشتند. رمان پرستو در باد نشان می‌دهد که مناسبات عاشقانه میان چریک‌ها تا چه حد بر پایه‌ی روابط انسانی استوار بوده، و تا کجا از ابتذال رایج در فرقه‌های چپِ معاصرِ بی‌ربط شده با طبقه‌ی کارگر فاصله دارد.[۶۳۷]

اما «اعدام انقلابی»ی عبدالله پنجه‌شاهی در سازمان چریک‌های فدائی‌ی خلق نیز، داستان دیگری می‌گوید. در بسیاری از متن‌ها آمده است که اعدام این هموند به سبب رابطه‌ی عاشقانه‌ای بود که بین او و ادنا ثابت (هموند سازمانی و همخانه‌ی تیمی‌ی او) ایجاد شده بود. منتها، به رغم گفت‌وگوهای بسیار در زمینه‌ی این قتل، چرائی‌های آن هنوز در ابری از ابهام فرو رفته است.[۶۳۸] (همین «ابر»، در داستان «رودخانه‌ی تمبی» نوشته‌ی خسرو دوامی به زیبائی تصویر شده است.) در هر حال، افزون بر پژوهش‌های متعددی که در زمینه‌ی تبعیض جنسیتی در سازمان‌های چپِ ایران انجام شده، برخی از زنان چریک نیز (در تبعید) به وجود تبعیض جنسی در سازمان چریک‌های فدائی‌ی خلقِ آن‌زمانی شهادت داده‌اند.[۶۳۹] اگر از ناسزاهائی مانند «زوزه‌های خشم‌آگینِ تئوریسین‌های سلطه و ستم»، یا «فمینیسم توهم‌زده و لیبرال وطنی»- که از سوی برخی از شخصیت‌های وفادار به چریک‌ها، نثار منتقدان چپ می‌شود[۶۴۰] - نهراسیم، نمی‌توانیم بر شهادت برخی از اعضاء و کادرهای آن‌زمانی‌ی سازمان چریک‌ها مبنی بر وجود رفتار تبعیض‌آمیزِ مردان با زنانِ این سازمان تأکید نکنیم؛ یا دست کم، نمی‌توانیم بر واقعیتِ جنسیت‌زُدائی از «زن» در این سازمان (و کلاً سازمان‌های چپ) که خود شاهد برخی از نمودهایش بوده‌ایم، دیده‌پوشی کنیم. از بلوز و شلوارهای گل و گشاد، و پرهیز از آرایش مو و صورت گذشته، رفتار و حتا

---

۶۳۷ محمد قراگوزلو، ***تبار خونین تاریخ بی‌قراری‌ی ما: سند تاریخی از قطعه‌ی ۳۳ تا خاوران***، نشریه‌ی «آرش»، چاپ پاریس، شماره‌ی ۱۰۸، تیر ۱۳۹۱/ ژوئیه ۲۰۱۲، ص ۱۰۶.

توضیح: محمد قراگوزلو، که بنا به توضیح خودش در متن بالا، «تاریخ جنبش فدائی را به دقت نخوانده» و «با عناصر تشکیلاتی‌ی آن هرگز ارتباط مستقیم نداشته»، رمانِ «پرستو در باد» را «در چارچوب داستانی واقعی»، در بازتاب به رمان «ایمپالای سرخ» (بنفشه حجازی) و با استفاده از «تجربیات فردی»ی خودش نوشته است. این کتاب در سال ۱۳۹۰/ ۲۰۱۱ توسط نشر آلفایت ماکسیما در سوئد منتشر شد.

۶۳۸ گرچه در برخی از متن‌ها، سازمان چریک‌های فدائی‌ی خلق متهم شده است که قتل عبدالله پنجه شاهی انگیزه‌ی سیاسی داشته، اما شخصیت‌های معتبری از این سازمان (مانند حیدر تبریزی) شهادت داده‌اند که انگیزه‌ی این قتل رابطه‌ی عاشقانه‌ای بوده که بین او و ادنا ثابت ایجاد شده بود. من در جلد چهارم مجموعه‌ی حاضر با تفصیل بیش‌تری پیرامون این رویداد سخن گفته‌ام. اما همین جا یادآوری می‌کنم که عباس توکل، یکی از اعضاء مرکزیتِ آن‌زمانی‌ی سازمان، در دوران تبعید، قتل عبدالله پنجه‌شاهی به دست «رفیق هادی (احمد غلامی لنگرودی) را یک «تهمت بی‌اساس» می‌داند، و آن را شایعه‌ای بر اساس «شنیده‌ام، شنیده‌ام، شنیده‌ام»ها برآورد می‌کند. تا این جای سخن، به نظر می‌آید که تلاش توکل بر این است که «رفیق هادی» را از این قتل تبرئه کند. منتها، در ادامه می‌گوید: «در این سازمان اولین بار نبود که دو رفیق زن و مرد به هم علاقمند می‌شوند. ضوابطی که وجود داشت، برای همه یکسان بود. چرا چنین مسئله‌ای برای دیگران پیش نیامد؟» اما نمی‌گوید که به هر حال علت این قتل چه بود. و بدین ترتیب، باز، علت قتل پنجه‌شاهی در پرده‌ای از ابهام فرو می‌رود. به مأخذ زیر نگاه کنید:

- ***گفت‌وگو با رفیق توکل***، (نشریه‌ی کار)، تاریخ بازدید ۲۲ مه ۲۰۱۲:

http://www.ghatipati.net/akhbar-iran/tavakol-mosahebeh.htm

۶۳۹ به عنوان مثال، در سال ۲۰۰۲ متنی به قلم مریم سطوت در رسانه‌های اینترنتی منتشر شد که تأثیر تبعیض جنسیتی در سازمان چریک‌ها را بر روی زندگی‌ی «سه زن» چریک توضیح داده بود. من با کمال تأسف نتوانستم این متن در لابه‌لای یادداشت‌های خود، یا از طریق اینترنت، پیدا کنم. اما نمونه‌های دیگری از شهادت زنان سازمان چریک‌های فدائی‌ی خلق آن‌زمانی در دسترس است که در دو جلد کتاب «داد بی‌داد»، به همت ویدا حاجبی تبریزی گردآوری و منتشر شده است. در این مقاله‌ها، بیش‌تر، بر عدم آزادی‌های فردی و سرکوب فردیت تأکید شده است تا صرفاً «تبعیض جنسی». از آن رو که این دو کتاب را در جلد چهارم مجموعه‌ی حاضر باز کرده‌ام، در این جا پیرامون آن سکوت می‌کنم.

۶۴۰ بنفشه حجازی، در کتاب «ایمپالای سرخ» (۱۳۸۹)، مناسبات جاری در سازمان چریک‌های فدائی‌ی خلق و کلاً مشی‌ی چریکی را در قالب رمانی عاشقانه، از دیدگاه خود به نقد کشیده است. از دو متنی که در معرفی‌ی این کتاب خوانده‌ام چنین برمی‌آید که «نقد» او یکسره «منفی» است. محمد قراگوزلو آن را «نقد تخریبی»، از جمله «تخریب احمدزاده و پویان و حمید مؤمنی و حمید اشرف» تلقی کرده و آن را برآمده از «تصور فمینیسم توهم‌زده و لیبرال وطنی» شناسائی کرده است. متن دوم را نیز گروهی با عنوان «زنان دیگر» نوشتند، و کل رمان را «زوزه‌ی خشم‌آگین تئوریسین‌های سلطه و ستم» نامیدند، که نوشته شده تا بگوید: «آرمان چپ مرده است.» از آن جا که من رمان «ایمپالای سرخ» را نخوانده‌ام، نمی‌توانم پیرامون آن و نظرات ابرازشده پیرامون آن سخن بگویم. اما با پشتوانه‌ی موارد مشابه در ادبیات سیاسی‌ی تبعید، در این جا منظورم از یادکردِ این کتاب و دو معرفی‌ی آن، تنها، ثبتِ برخی از عنوان‌ها و برچسب‌هائی است که از سوی نویسندگان وفادار به چریک‌ها، به منتقدان جنبش چریکی و مناسبات جاری در سازمان چریک‌های فدائی‌ی خلق اعطا می‌شود. به عنوان نمونه به دو مأخذ زیر نگاه کنید:

- محمد قراگوزلو، ***تبار خونین تاریخ بی‌قراری‌ی ما***، پیشین، صص ۱۰۲ تا ۱۰۷.
- زنانی دیگر، ***فرمان ایمپالای سرخ به وسیله چه کسانی و به کدام سمت رانده می‌شود؟*** تارنمای «اخبار روز»، ۲۵ اسفند ۱۳۹۰/ ۱۵ مارس ۲۰۱۲:

http://www.akhbar-rooz.com/article.jsp?essayId=44360

نظام گفتاریِ زنانِ سازمان‌های خرد و کلانِ «چپ» چنان هنجارهای مردانه داشت که در روزهای انقلاب ۵۷ و تا چندی پس از «پیروزی»یِ آن (تا زمانی که حجاب اجباری نشده بود، و تا زمانی که گفت‌وگو و مناظره‌های خیابانی در کنار میزهای کتاب و نشریه، ممکن بود)، گرایش سیاسیِ آن‌ها، از زبان/ اخلاق/ رفتارِشان قابل گمانه‌زنی بود. شاید مسئله‌ی جنسیت‌زدائی در طیف چپِ مبارزان را بتوان از زبان عضو مرکزیتِ یکی از این سازمان‌ها در این عبارت خلاصه کرد که: «همه‌ی مبارزان برابرند؛ نه زن داریم نه مرد؛ ما فقط رفیق داریم.»[۶۴۱] کما این که اشرف دهقانی در سال ۱۳۵۲ در کتاب «حماسه‌ی مقاومت» نوشته بود:

> [...] هنگامی که زن آگاهیِ طبقاتیِ خود را بازمی‌یابد و همراه مردی که آگاهیِ طبقاتیِ خود را بازیافته است- آن چنان آگاهی و شناختی که او را به درهم کوبیدن نظام فاسد طبقاتی وامی‌دارد- دیگر او یک «زن» با معیارهای ارتجاعی نیست. بلکه «انسانی» است آگاه؛ و به ساختن نظامی می‌پردازد که در آن «انسان» مقام راستین و شکوه شایسته‌ی خود را بازیابد. [...][۶۴۲]

قدسی قاضی‌نور، نویسنده، شاعر، و نقاشِ چپ‌گرای آن‌زمانی نیز، در همان روزهای نخستِ جمهوریِ اسلامی و در کوران جنبش زنان در اعتراض به حجاب اجباری، در کیهان روز ۲۱ اسفند ۵۷ نوشت: «به امید روزی که روز زن، حقوق زن، و مسئله‌ی زن نباشد.»[۶۴۳] یا، هما ناطق، پژوهشگر تاریخ دوران مشروطه، در سال ۱۳۵۹ در معرفیِ نشریه‌ی زنانه‌ی «فصلی در گلسرخ» (ارگان «اتحاد ملی زنان» و «انجمن رهائیِ زن») ابتدا به وجه «مبارزات دموکراتیک و ضدامپریالیستی»یِ این نشریه اشاره می‌کند و بعد به «گام‌های ارزنده در ربط به مسئله‌ی زنان».[۶۴۴] و از آن رو که برخی از نویسندگان این نشریه زیر نفوذ سازمان چریک‌های فدائیِ خلق بودند (یا به قولی: این سازمان می‌کوشید که از این تشکل زنان به عنوان حلقه‌ی وابسته به خود سود جوید)، در ویژه‌نامه‌ی روز جهانیِ زن، اسفند ۵۹، نوشتند: «من برای دنیائی مبارزه می‌کنم که مسئله‌ای به نام زن و مرد در آن وجود ندارد.»[۶۴۵] به بیانی دیگر، این نوع از «برابری»، بر این اصلِ مارکسیستی استوار است که «آزادی»یِ همگان، از جمله آزادیِ زنان، با تحقق جامعه‌ی سوسیالیستی و بی‌طبقه، یا جامعه‌ی ایده‌آل مجاهدین (با نظم توحیدی)، خود به خود متحقق خواهد شد؛ یعنی همان جهان آرمانی‌ای که نمونه‌اش را اشرف دهقانی ترسیم کرده است. اما در این جهان زیبا، نه تنها «زن» مسئله نیست، بلکه فردانیت و مفهومِ «خود» هم نمی‌تواند مسئله باشد؛ یعنی، در راه مبارزه برای تحقق این جهان آرمانی، و حتا در زمان وقوع آن، نه تنها «جنسیت» مطرح نیست، بلکه اندیشیدن به «فردیت» نیز از گناهان کبیره است؛ چرا که «مفاهیم خرده بورژوائی»- یعنی مفاهیم دشمن جامعه‌ی بی‌طبقه- را با خود حمل می‌کند. به عنوان نمونه‌ای از این جهان‌بینی- که در لابه‌لای متون چریک‌های آن دوره نمونه‌های فراوان دارد - باز به اشرف دهقانی رجوع می‌کنم. او در خاطرات زندان ساواک می‌نویسد:

---

۶۴۱ حامد شهیدیان، استاد دانشگاه و پژوهشگر فمینیست، در زیرنویس مربوط به این جمله می‌نویسد: «این بازگفت از مصاحبه‌ام با یکی از اعضاء کادر مرکزیِ یکی از سازمان‌های چپ است (اروپا، تابستان ۱۹۹۴)». به مأخذ زیر نگاه کنید:
- ❖ دکتر حامد شهیدیان، ***نقشی از یک دوست ، نقشی از یک دوستی*** (مجموعه مقالات)، لس‌انجلس: نشر نارنجستان، تاریخ نشر ندارد، ص ۶۳.

۶۴۲ اشرف دهقانی، ***حماسه‌ی مقاومت***، چاپ دوم، لندن: بهار ۱۳۸۳، ص ۸۵.

۶۴۳ روزنامه‌ی کیهان، ۲۱ اسفند ۱۳۵۷، ص ٦. برگرفته از: دکتر حامد شهیدیان، ***نقشی از یک دوست، نقشی از یک دوستی***، پیشین، ص ٦٢.

۶۴۴ عین جمله‌ی هما ناطق به قرار زیر است: «این نشریه همواره در جهت مبارزات دموکراتیک و ضدامپریالیستیِ میهن ما گام‌های ارزنده برداشته است و در ربط به مسئله‌ی زنان نیز سخت‌کوش بوده است.» این متن در نشریه‌ی «فصلی در گلسرخ»، شماره‌ی ۶، ویژه‌نامه‌ی ۱۷ اسفند، (۸ مارس) روز جهانیِ زن، اسفند ۱۳۵۹، انتشارات کاوش منتشر شده است. به مأخذ زیر که این متن را به همت عاطفه‌ی گرگین، در تبعید بازچاپ کرده است، نگاه کنید:
- ❖ مهناز متین (گردآورنده و ویراستار)، ***بازبینیِ تجربه‌ی «اتحاد ملیِ زنان»***، امریکا: نشر نقطه، ۱۳۷۸، ص ۳۷۳.

۶۴۵ مأخذ پیشین، ص ۳۷۲.

> [...] کلمه‌ی «خود» در ذهنم جا نمی‌گرفت. این خود «کی» بود؟ دلم از این مفاهیم خرده بورژوائی به هم می‌خورد؛ به نفع خود؛ برای خود؛ من ... من ... من ... [...] (حماسه‌ی مقاومت، ۱۳۸۳، ص ۱۳۰. گیومه‌ها از اشرف دهقانی هستند.)

منتها، زمانی که «هدفِ» این مبارزان را در نظر داشته باشیم، «دل به هم خوردنِ» اشرف دهقانی جای شگفتی و اعتراض ندارد، چرا که انزجار از مفهوم «خود» و نفی‌ی «فردیت»، از ویژگی‌های بنیادین در تئوری‌های مارکسیستی و جهان «سوسیالیستی» است. من، بدون آن که از جهان آرمانی‌ی چریک‌های فدائی‌ی خلق و نوع «برابری» در آن جهان، نقشه‌ی ممکن و ملموسی در ذهن داشته باشم، بدون آن که (بنا بر مشاهده و برداشت‌های خود) وجود پرهیبی از «سنت‌های دینی» در سازمان‌های چپ‌گرا را نفی کنم، و بدون آن که از تلاش‌های این سازمان‌ها در مهار کردنِ جنبش‌های صرفاً زنانه دفاع کنم، و با توجه به این واقعیت که زنان عضو این سازمان، و کلاً سازمان‌های مارکسیستی، از **هدف** و آرمان مبارزه‌ی این سازمان‌ها با خبر بودند، این پرسش را مطرح می‌کنم که این زنانِ حالا معترض به روند جاری در سازمان‌های چپِ آن‌زمانی، چرا در آن زمان به این سازمان‌ها پیوستند؟ چرا به محض دریافت این تبعیض‌ها (یا به محض دریافت این که مردان سازمان جنسیت زیست‌شناختی یا جامعه‌شناختی‌ی آن‌ها را درک و رعایت نمی‌کنند)، از سازمان خود جدا نشدند؟ نه تنها جدا نشدند، بلکه به تأییدِ مریم سطوت- عضو آن‌زمانی‌ی سازمان چریک‌های فدائی‌ی خلق ایران:

> قبل از انقلاب تعداد زنان در سازمان چریک‌های فدائی‌ی خلق و در حلقه‌های وابسته به این سازمان قابل توجه بود. در زمان انقلاب بخش بزرگی از فعالان این سازمان را زنان تشکیل می‌دادند. در سازمان جوانانِ «پیشگام» نزدیک به ۵۰ در صد فعالین را دختران تشکیل می‌دادند.[۶۴۶]

ناهید قاجار، که به گفته‌ی خودش، سال ۱۳۵۰ با گروه احمدزاده در ارتباط بوده و از سال ۱۳۵۴ رسماً از «کادرهای سازمان چریک‌های فدائی‌ی خلق» برشمرده می‌شده، با این که بعدها از این سازمان جدا شده، در متن کوتاه خود، در تبعید، «هدفِ» زنان فدائی را به روشنی ترسیم کرده است:

> [...] پیوستن زنان به جنبش مسلحانه، **نه با هدف تأمین حقوق زنان، بلکه با هدف تحقق یک مجموعه‌ی به‌هم‌پیوسته‌ی نظرات ایدئولوژیکی و اهداف سیاسی و مبارزاتی بود.** [...] ما در سازمان از حقوق برابر برخوردار بودیم. هیچ زنی در سازمان با تبعیض جنسیتی روبه‌رو نبود. همه‌ی اعضاء با افکار و ایدئولوژی‌ی سازمان، به مسائل جامعه و نابرابری‌های سیاسی و اجتماعی برخورد می‌کردند. [...] در چنین شرایطی، زنان نقش کلیدی برای حفظ و تطبیق شرایط، تأمین ایمنی، و جابه‌جائی و ... داشتند. گرچه مردان و زنان همه‌ی وظائف محوله را به یکسان برعهده داشتند، اما **نوع مبارزه به زنان فرصت نمی‌داد که با توانائی‌های فکری و نظری و سیاسی نقش بیش‌تری برعهده بگیرند.** واقعیت این بود که **مردان** از آزادی بیش‌تری در جامعه برخوردار بودند و در نتیجه **با تجربه‌ی بیش‌تر و توانائی‌های سیاسی- عملی‌ی بالاتری می‌توانستند** مسئولیت‌های سازمان را در دست داشته باشند. با این همه در بیش از هفت سال مبارزه‌ی چریکی، زنانی مانند نسترن آل آقا و نزهت روحی آهنگران در مسئولیت‌های بالائی انجام وظیفه می‌کردند و یا در مرکزیت سازمان قرار داشتند. با توجه به تعداد کم‌تر زنان در زندگی مخفی‌ی چریکی، نمی‌توان این مسئله را به منزله‌ی نوعی تبعیض تلقی کرد؛ چرا که کیفیت‌ها وشایستگی‌ها از درون جامعه و از شرایط اقتصادی و اجتماعی و فرهنگی‌ی جامعه برمی‌خاست. ما در آن زمان هرگز چنین احساسی نداشتیم و رفقای مرد سازمان نیز هرگز تمایلات تبعیض‌آمیزی از خود نشان ندادند.[۶۴۷] (تأکیدها از من است.)

---

[۶۴۶] گفت‌وگوی شیرین فامیلی (سایت تهیه) و مریم سطوت، ***نقش زنان در سازمان‌های سیاسی***، برگرفته از تارنمای «مهدی فتاپور»، ۲۲ آوریل ۲۰۰۹:

http://www.fatapour.de/Maryam/naghshe_zanan.htm

[۶۴۷] در زندگی‌نامه‌ی کوتاه ناهید قاجار می‌خوانیم: ناهید قاجار از دوره‌ی دبیرستان، از طریق دائی‌ی خود رحیم کریمیان، با گروه مفتاحی- پویان- احمدزاده در ارتباط قرار گرفت. در نیمه‌ی اول سال ۱۳۵۰، ارتباط او با گروه قطع شد. او سپس به خدمت سپاهی‌ی دانش رفت و در روستا معلم شد. در سال ۱۳۵۳ از طریق زندانیان آزاد شده با سازمان چریک‌های فدائی خلق تماس بر قرار کرد، و در نهایت از سال ۵۴ تا انقلاب بهمن

از این عبارتِ تأسف‌برانگیز، که ناهید قاجار پیرامون کاستیِ «توانائی»های زنان (نسبت به مردان) ابراز کرده است، در این جا می‌گذرم. همچنین، یادآوری می‌کنم که به شهادت زنانی که- مثلاً در دو جلد کتاب «داد بی‌داد» نوشته‌ی ویدا حاجبی تبریزی- به تبعیض جنسی و سرکوب فردیت در این سازمان گواهی داده‌اند، این «ما»ئی که ناهید قاجار در سخنش به کار برده، «ما»ی چندان فراگیری به نظر نمی‌رسد. اما نکته در این جا، «هدف»ی است که ناهید قاجار به درستی بر آن انگشت گذاشته است. می‌توان به فروکاستنِ همه‌ی مناسبات انسانی در چارچوب «مناسبات تولید»، انتقاد داشت؛ می‌توان با ذات آزادی و حقوق زن، که در دستگاه نظریِ مارکسیسم به آینده‌ای نامعلوم محول شده، چون و چرا کرد؛ می‌توان بر سر هر یک از عناصر درونیِ این هدف، با سازمان‌های چپ وارد دیالوگ شد؛ اما به باور من، نمی‌توان از یک سو به عنوان «عضوِ» یک سازمان، «هدفِ» آن سازمان را پذیرفت، و از سوی دیگر وظایف و بازتاب‌های عملیِ آن هدف را رَدّ کرد. و این نکته‌ای است که کند وُ کاو و یافتن پاسخ پیرامون آن به عهده‌ی زنان معترضی مانند ویدا حاجبی تبریزی و یارانِ کتاب «داد بی‌داد» است که پیش از انقلاب، مدتی عضو یا هوادارِ سازمان چریک‌های فدائیِ خلق ایران بوده‌اند؛ بعد از انقلاب نیز، تا زمانی که سرکوب حکومتی سازمان را از هم بپاشد، به عضویت و فعالیت خود در این سازمان ادامه داده‌اند؛ و اینک- در تبعید- نه تنها به لحاظ تبعیض جنسیتی، بلکه به لحاظ سرکوب آزادی‌های فردی، کلیت این سازمان را زیر ضرب می‌گیرند. (در جلد هفتم مجموعه‌ی حاضر به کتاب ویدا حاجبی تبریزی پرداخته‌ام.)

با این همه، مواردی که در زمینه‌ی تحمیل و تبعیض نسبت به زنان در سازمان‌های چپ از سوی منتقدان مطرح شده است، از مرز جنسیتِ جامعه‌شناختی (gender) فراتر رفته، و تا دامنه‌ی جنسیت زیست‌شناختی (sex)- مانند عدم توجه به وضع روحی و جسمیِ زنان سازمان، از جمله، در دوره‌های عادت ماهانه- هم گسترده بوده است؛ که در این جا، مسئله، از «هدفِ سازمان» جدا می‌شود، و به بازتولید چرخه‌ی پدر/ مردسالاری شهادت می‌دهد.

پیمان وهاب‌زاده (استاد دانشگاه و پژوهشگر تاریخِ سازمان چریک‌های فدائیِ خلق)، با پشتوانه‌ی گواهی‌های زنان چریک فدائی، و یافته‌های پژوهشگرانی که به وجود تبعیض جنسی در سازمان چریک‌های فدائیِ خلق، گواهی داده‌اند، به مسئله‌ی بی‌توجهیِ مردان به مسئله‌ی «عادت ماهانه»ی زنان در این سازمان نیز اشاره می‌کند، و نتیجه می‌گیرد که: «[از این یافته‌ها و شهادت‌ها] درمی‌یابیم که چه‌گونه سنت‌های دینی در سازمانی که به سبب چپ بودنش باید سکولار هم می‌بود، نفوذ و عمل می‌کرد.»[٦٤٨]

سهیلا دهماسی، از چریک‌های فدائیِ خلق در تبعید، در یک مقاله، با ادبیاتی آکنده از ناسزا نسبت به نظرات وهاب‌زاده و شخصیت او، سوژه‌ی عدم توجه مردان سازمان چریک‌ها به «عادت ماهانه»ی زنان هموند را نیز به چالش می‌گیرد، اما خود نمی‌تواند این ادعا را (که ادعای شخص وهاب زاده نیست، و او آن را از قول زنان فدائی یا پژوهشگرانِ فمینیست بازگو کرده است) به گونه‌ای مستدل رد کند:

> [...] وهاب‌زاده [...] تلاش می‌کند که زنان آگاه و انقلابیِ چریک فدائیِ خلق را به عنوان زنانی معرفی کند که حتا قادر نبودند تلنگری به دنیای مردسالارانه و خشونت‌طلب رفقای مرد خود بزنند؛ «فدائیانِ مردمحوری»ی که از ترس آن‌ها، «زنان باید تمام جنبه‌های زنانه‌ی خود را نزد آن‌ها پنهان می‌کردند. موهای کوتاه، لباس‌های گشاد با رنگ‌های تیره.» یکی دیگر از گناهان نابخشودنیِ چریک‌ها از نظر وهاب‌زاده و هم‌فکرهای او این است که «در تمرینات ورزشی مسئله‌ی

---

۵۷ به صورت یک کادر چریک فدائی، در این سازمان فعالیت کرد. در جریان انشعاب‌های پس از انقلاب، او با سازمان فدائیان خلق (اکثریت) بود. در تابستان سال ۱۳۶۹ از این سازمان استعفاء داد و از آن پس از هر گونه فعالیت تشکیلاتی در خارج از کشور خودداری کرد. به مأخذ زیر نگاه کنید:

❖ ناهید قاجار، ***زنان و چریک‌های فدائیِ خلق***، تارنمای «بی بی سی»، ۰۶ فوریه ۲۰۱۱ - ۱۷ بهمن ۱۳۸۹:
http://www.bbc.co.uk/persian/iran/2011/02/110204_l13_siahkal_nahid_qajar.shtml

٦٤٨ فرح طاهری، ***چهلمین سالگرد جنبش سیاهکل و حماسه‌ی چریک‌های فدائی: سخنرانیِ دکتر پیمان وهاب‌زاده در تورنتو***، تارنمای نشریه‌ی «شهروند»، چاپ کانادا، ۲۵ نوامبر ۲۰۱۰:
http://www.shahrvand.com/archives/10613

> عادت ماهانه‌ی زنان در نظر گرفته نمی‌شد. و برخی مردها اصلاً نسبت به آن آگاهی نداشتند»!! [...] اما واقعیت، کاملاً برخلاف این دروغ‌ها و تحریف‌های وهابزاده‌هاست. واقعیتی که در حافظه‌ی زحمتکشان آگاه و مبارز ایران حفظ شده و خواهد شد این است که زنان و مردان مبارز چریک فدائی‌ی خلق (و بسیاری دیگر از مبارزین انقلابی‌ی کل جنبش ما در آن سال‌ها) فرزندان برحق زحمتکشان ایران بودند. [...] زنان چریک فدائی‌ی خلق شیرزنانی بودند که با تفکرات ارتجاعی‌ی طبقه‌ی حاکم به مبارزه برخاستند و چهره‌ی نوینی از زن مبارز آگاه و مترقی را به جامعه‌ی ایران معرفی کردند. [...][۶۴۹]

وقتی به این جای سخن دهماسی می‌رسیم که: « اما واقعیت، کاملاً برخلاف این دروغ‌ها و تحریف‌های وهابزاده‌هاست»، امیدوار می‌شویم که او در دنباله‌ی سخن، «واقعیتِ» این قضیه‌ی مشخص را برای مخاطب خود مستدل می‌کند. اما ناگهان با جائی پرتاب می‌شویم که ربطی به این «قضیه‌ی مشخص» ندارد. من، بدون آن که با همه‌ی نظرهای سیاسی/ جامعه‌شناختی/ تاریخی‌ی پیمان و هابزاده پیرامون سازمان چریک‌های فدائی‌ی خلق موافق باشم؛ و بدون پروا از دشنام‌های سهیلا دهماسی و «همفکرانش»، بر این باورم که «شیرزنانِ» چریک در هر دو سازمانِ فدائیان و مجاهدین، به نسبت زمان خود «چهره‌ی نوینی از زن مبارز آگاه و مترقی را به جامعه‌ی ایران معرفی کردند.» و بر این باورم که اکثر آن‌ها، «فرزندان برحق زحمتکشان ایران بودند.» اما هیچ کدام از این گزاره‌ها، گزاره‌های مشخصِ عدم رعایت وضع جسمی/ روانی‌ی زنان فدائی توسط مردان این سازمان- به عنوان نمودی از نمودهای مردسالاری در این سازمان- را نفی نمی‌کند.

صرف نظر از همه‌ی تفسیرها و گزارش‌های پژوهشی یا تجربی، که به بازتولید سامانه‌ی پدر/ مردسالاری در سازمان‌های چریک‌های فدائی‌ی خلق و مجاهدین خلق شهادت داده‌اند، این «بازتولید»، نمود بارز خود را در روزهای پایانی‌ی اسفند ۱۳۵۷ زیر چشم همه‌ی زنان ایران به سینه‌ی تاریخ ایران سنجاق کرده است. و شگفتا که در این «مراسم آئینی»، برخی از زنانِ عضو یا هوادار سازمان چریک‌های فدائی‌ی خلق نیز- به رغم فعالیت در نهاد «اتحاد ملی‌ی زنان»- به عنوان بازوی مردانِ این سازمان عمل کردند. من در جای دیگر مجموعه‌ی حاضر به جنس این «سنجاقِ سینه» به تفصیل پرداخته‌ام. اما همین جا اشاره‌وار می‌گویم که جنبش خودجوش زنان، که فتوای شخص آیت‌الله خمینی («زنان می‌توانند سرِ کار بروند، اما با حجاب») را در ابتدای این نظام به چالش گرفت (۱۷ تا ۲۱ اسفند ۵۷)، از سوی کمیته‌ی مرکزی‌ی سازمان چریک‌های فدائی‌ی خلق ایران، نه تنها به گونه‌ای رسمی حمایت نشد، بلکه به شکل‌های ظریف، سرکوب هم شد. این جنبش، که در اعتراض به فتوای اجباری شدن حجاب و حذف زنان از جایگاه قضاوت صورت گرفت، از دید اکثریت اعضاء مرکزیتِ این سازمان، «اعتراضِ عده‌ای از زنان خرده‌بورژوا» تلقی شد؛ که «تفرقه‌انداز» است، و «موجب سردشدن رابطه [ی سازمان ما] با نیروهای ضدامپریالیست و دولت می‌شود.» علی کشتگر، عضو کمیته‌ی مرکزی‌ی آن زمانِ سازمان (که در انشعاب بزرگ به «اقلیت» پیوست، و بعد هم از «اقلیت» جدا شد) در تبعید می‌گوید: «مثلاً می‌گفتند: مگر چند تا زن قاضی هستند؟ ۲۰، ۳۰ تا. هیچ اتفاقی نمی‌افتد اگر این چند نفر از کانون وکلا کنار گذاشته شوند.»[۶۵۰] و این در حالی بود که خود آیت‌الله و کارگزارانش (از جمله دولت بازرگان)، که هنوز در مسند قدرت مستقر نشده بودند، در برابر اعتراض گسترده‌ی زنان- تا استقرار کامل اهرم‌های سرکوب- کوتاه آمدند. اما «چپِ ضدامپریالیستِ» ما این فرصت طلائی را از دست داد و کوتاه نیامد، تا رژیم اسلامی مستقر شد، و فتواهای آیت‌الله، نه تنها حجاب را به اجبار بر زن

---

۶۴۹ سهیلا دهماسی، ***پیمان وهابزاده و وظیفه‌ی «بازنگری‌ی تاریخی»ی جنبش فدائی در سمینار آمستردام***، تارنمای «گولالک- شقایق»، ۱۱ ژانویه ۲۰۱۱:
http://gulalek.blogspot.com/2011/01/blog-post_11.html

۶۵۰ هایده مغیثی، ***«اتحاد ملی‌ی زنان»، یک تجربه‌ی سوسیال- فمینیستی‌ی ناکام***، در کتاب:
❖ مهناز متین (گردآورنده و ویراستار)، بازبینی‌ی تجربه‌ی «اتحاد ملی‌ی زنان» ۱۳۵۷- ۱۳۶۰، امریکا: نشر نقطه، ۱۳۷۸، ص ۱۹۱.

ایرانی تحمیل کرد، بلکه هر چه حرکتِ «ضدامپریالیستی» بود، با چماق و زندان و شکنجه و اعدام شست و با خود برد. در این جا دیگر مسئله، مسئله‌ی «زن» به تنهائی مطرح نیست. چرا که به باور من، حمایت سازمان‌های چپ، به ویژه سازمان چریک‌های فدائی‌ی خلق (که در آن زمان نیروی عظیمی از مردم سکولار را پشت سر داشت) از این جنبش، می‌توانست سرنوشت بهتری را برای سازمان‌های چپ و مخالف در این رژیم رقم بزند. در این خوانش است که من، در ژرفنای این وادادگی‌ی سرنوشت‌ساز، چیزی جز رسوبِ «سنت‌های دینی» و فرهنگِ پدر/ مردسالار (حتا در زنان فدائی) نمی‌بینم. و تردید دارم که اعضاء یا سمپات‌های آن‌زمانی‌ی این سازمان- که دستور و سیاستِ مرکزیتِ آن را در برخورد با تظاهرات زنان اعمال کردند- در حال حاضر به آن اشتباه بزرگ معترف نباشند. مهناز متین در کتاب «بازبینی‌ی تجربه‌ی اتحاد ملی‌ی زنان، نظر شخصیت‌های فراوانی را پیرامون این رویداد گردآوری کرده است، که اکثر آن‌ها، به عدم حمایت سازمان چریک‌های فدائی‌ی خلق و سازمان مجاهدین خلق نسبت به این خیزش (و کلاً، نسبت به نهادهای دموکراتیک زنان) گواهی داده‌اند، بدون آن که از سهم خود در این کوتاهی سخنی گفته باشند. من به جای خود پیرامون این کتاب سخن گفته‌ام. اما در این جا پاسخ دلیرانه‌ی هما ناطق به پرسش منصوره شجاعی را به عنوان نمونه‌ی آشکار و مستقیم این اعتراف ثبت می‌کنم. با این توضیح که هما ناطق- یکی از اعضای نهاد «اتحاد ملی‌ی زنان»- در هم‌سوئی با سیاست سازمان چریک‌ها علیه تظاهرات زنان مطلب نوشته بود و سخنرانی کرده بود.

> **منصوره شجاعی:** خبر را در آن روزها اما از روزنامه‌ی «کیهان» گرفتیم که در تاریخ ۱۹ اسفند ۱۳۵۷ پس از راهپیمائی‌ی زنان در اعتراض به حجاب اجباری از قول سیمین دانشور نوشته بود که او مسئله‌ی حجاب را فرعی می‌داند و حل این مسئله را منوط به حل مسائل مهم‌تر در میهن دانسته است. آری خبر را آن روزها از «کیهان» می‌گرفتیم که در تاریخ ۲۱ اسفند ۱۳۵۷ این بار از قول هما ناطق نوشته بود که گفته است اگر نظام شاهنشاهی برگردانده نشود **عیبی ندارد روسری هم سر می‌کنیم** فقط به نام ما توطئه نشود. [تأکید از من است.]
>
> **هما ناطق**: خانم شجاعی، من از شما خواهش می‌کنم بنویسید ما غلط کردیم این حرف را درباره‌ی زنان زدیم.
>
> **منصور شجاعی:** زبانم کوتاه استاد!
>
> **هما ناطق:** اصلاً بنویسید خاک بر سر من که این را گفتم.
>
> **منصوره شجاعی:** اختیار دارید استاد! این حرف‌ها را نزنید!
>
> **هما ناطق:** ...[...] شما این را بنویسد که من خیلی بی‌جا کردم که این حرف را زدم. اصلاً ما به زن‌ها خیانت کردیم، شما باید ما را محاکمه کنید؛ خواهش می‌کنم بنویسید که من خودم از شما می‌خواهم که مرا محاکمه کنید.[۶۵۱]

شاید پس از این اعتراف سخاوتمندانه، یادآوری‌ی نکته‌ی زیر از انصاف به دور باشد، اما تا نمونه‌ای از تمکین ایدئولوژیک، به رغم باورهای شخصی- حتا از سوی زنان دانش‌آموخته و فرهیخته‌ی ما- در این جا ثبت شود، بر فراز دیگری از سخنان هما ناطق درنگ می‌کنم، که نمودار بینش شخصی‌ی او نسبت به حجاب است. او، که به دستور سازمان سیاسی‌ی خود (سازمان چریک‌های فدائی‌ی خلق) در آن روزهای سرنوشت‌ساز از فتوای آیت‌الله خمینی دفاع کرده بود، در گفت‌وگوئی که در ژوئیه ۱۹۹۰ در تبعید با هایده مغیثی داشت، به تاریخ ما گزارش می‌دهد که از دیدن زنانِ چادری در راهپیمائی‌های اوایل انقلاب «مو بر تنش راست» می‌شد:

---

[۶۵۱] گفت‌وگوی منصوره شجاعی با هما ناطق، ***سیمین دانشور «عیال فاضله»ی عصر مردان فضل‌فروش***، تارنمای «ایران امروز»، ۲۵ آوریل ۲۰۱۱:
http://www.iran-emrooz.net/index.php?/fschool/more/28267

نقش زنان در این انقلاب، همچون انقلاب های دموکراتیک این قرن، بی‌نهایت ارتجاعی بوده است. رک بگوئیم؛ اولین راهپیمائی‌ها در مراحل اول انقلاب، موجب دهشت من شد. همه‌ی زن‌ها در چادر سیاه. وقتی شعارهای‌شان را شنیدم، مو بر تنم راست شد: «خمینی‌ی عزیزم، بگو تا خون بریزم».[۶۵۲]

به خود می‌لرزم که با چنان «دهشتی» از نشانه‌ی «ارتجاع»، دستور رهبری‌ی سازمان هما ناطق ما را وامی‌دارد که بدون هیچ «دهشتی»، پوشش «روسری» را به زنان ایران تجویز کند. ونمونه‌ی زیر نیز، به باور من، نشانه‌ای از اعترافِ پوشیده و غیرمستقیم به آن اشتباه تاریخی است: شهین نوائی (سوسیالیست و کوشنده‌ی فمینیست و از جمله پایه‌گذاران نهاد «اتحاد ملی‌ی زنان») در ضمن سخنرانی‌ی روز ۱۵ سپتامبر ۲۰۱۱ در شهر کلن، به عدم حمایت سازمان‌های چپ- از جمله سازمان چریک‌های فدائی‌ی خلق ایران- از این حرکت خودجوش زنان، اشاره می‌کند، و می‌گوید:

فتوا[ی آیت‌الله خمینی] با عکس‌العمل شدید زنان مواجه شد. بلافاصله دانشجویان، دانش آموزان، زنان پرستار، زنان کارمند، شروع به اعتراض به فتوای خمینی نمودند، و به خیابان ها ریختند که به تظاهرات عظیمی تبدیل شد. متأسفانه هیچ کدام از سازمان‌های سیاسی‌ی چپ آن دوره از این حرکت وسیع زنان حمایت نکردند. چند روزی این تظاهرات ادامه داشت که حتا شعار مرگ بر خمینی نیز در آن دوره داده شد. زنان به طرف ستاد فدائیان رفتند و خواهان سخنرانی‌ی اشرف دهقانی در این زمینه بودند که متأسفانه اشرف دهقانی در جمع تظاهرکنندگان حاضر نشد. [...] چپ‌های آن دوران مرتب به زنان سیاسی‌ی خود می‌گفتند به این تظاهرات نروید، زیرا این زنان همانند زنان قابلمه به دست شیلی می‌باشند که در سرنگونی‌ی سالوادر آلنده شرکت داشتند.[۶۵۳]

سهیلا دهماسی‌ی ما، در بازتاب به این گزارش نیز متنی می‌نویسد و ضمن ردّ همه‌ی گزاره‌ها و داوری‌های شهین نوائی، می‌گوید:

[...] هر فردی که کوچکترین آشنایی با مسائل سیاسی‌ی ایران داشته باشد، به خوبی می‌داند که این اتهامی که نوائی می‌زند، به هیچ‌وجه به رفیق اشرف دهقانی نمی‌چسبد؛ به رفیقی که به مثابه یک زن کمونیست، مبارزه برای تحقق خواست‌های برحق زنان را به طور پیگیر دنبال نموده و همواره با تواضع کامل با زنان مبارز و همه‌ی توده‌های رزمنده‌ی ایران گفت‌وگو و برخورد داشته است. امروز، پس از ۳۳ سال، هر فرد تازه وارد به مسائل سیاسی‌ی چپ هم فهمیده است که رفیق اشرف اساساً با آن سازمانی که ستادی به اسم ستاد فدائی در خیابان میکده دایر کرده بودند، همراه و هم‌فکر نبوده و اساساً با آن سازمان همکاری نداشت که از آن ستاد با تظاهرکنندگان صحبت بکند. [...در آن زمان] رفیق اشرف معتقد بود که در رأس «سازمان چریک‌های فدائی‌ی خلق»ی که در خیابان میکده ستاد زده بود، «ماران خوش و خط و خالی» قرار دارند که آن سازمان را به انحراف و به راهی علیه فدائی می‌برند. [...] آیا واقعاً نوائی پس از گذشت ۳۳ سال هنوز هم از چنین واقعیتی مطلع نیست؟[۶۵۴]

---

۶۵۲ مهناز متین (گردآورنده و ویراستار)، ***بازبینی‌ی تجربه‌ی اتحاد ملی‌ی زنان***، امریکا: انتشارات نقطه، ۱۳۷۸، ص ۱۸۷.

۶۵۳ اکرم موسوی، ***رابطه‌ی جنبش چپ با جنبش زنان در سی و سه سال گذشته: گزارش سخنرانی‌ی شهین نوائی در کلن***، تارنمای «همبستگی‌ی زنان ایران»، ۲۹ سپتامبر ۲۰۱۱:

http://www.iran-women-solidarity.net/spip.php?article2212

۶۵۴ سهیلا دهماسی، ***باز هم درباره‌ی جنبش زنان! (نگاهی به سخنان نادرست و تحریف آمیز شهین نوائی)***، تارنمای «سیاهکل»، بازدید ۲۵ دسامبر ۲۰۱۱:

http://www.siahkal.com/index/right-col/zanan-Koln-2011.htm

البته جدا شدنِ رسمی‌ی اشرف دهقانی و هم‌فکرانش از سازمان چریک‌ها یک «واقعیت» است. منتها، همگان می‌دانند که این واقعیت در خرداد ۱۳۵۸ (یعنی چند ماه پس از جنبش خودجوش زنان در اسفند ۱۳۵۷) روی داد. اما یادآوری‌ی این تاریخ بدان معنا نیست که روز رجوعِ شهین نوائی (و همراهانش) به ستاد فدائیان، اشرف دهقانی الزاماً در «ستاد خیابان میکده» حضور داشته بوده است. زیرا می‌دانیم که مشکل اشرف دهقانی با تصمیم‌گیری‌های کمیته‌ی مرکزی‌ی «سازمان چریک‌های فدائی‌ی خلق ایران»، به مدتی پیش از اعلام رسمی‌ی جدائی‌ی او برمی‌گردد. منتها، این واقعیت را هم همگان می‌دانند که «جریان اشرف دهقانی» نیز- در هر «ستاد»ی که بود- پیرامون مقاومت زنان در روزهای ۱۷ تا ۲۱ اسفند ۵۷ سکوت کرد. و اینک سهیلا دهماسی تلویحاً و به گونه‌ای پوشیده به آن سکوت اعتراف می‌کند. منتها، به درستی یادآور می‌شود که اشرف دهقانی «رفیقی است که به مثابه یک زن کمونیست، با خواست‌های برحق زنان برخورد می‌کند.» و این را هم باز همگان می‌دانند که از دید «زن کمونیست»ی با ذهنیت اشرف دهقانی- که مفاهیمی چون «خود» و «من» را «مفاهیم خرده بورژوائی» معنی می‌کند، و برای زنان «زحمت‌کش» الگوئی مشخصی در ذهن دارد- آزادی‌ی پوشش، از سوی لایه‌های معلم و پرستار و کارمند و دانشگاهی و وکیل و قاضی‌ی زن، نه تنها در این بزنگاه تاریخی نمی‌توانست «برحق» جلوه کند، بلکه به عنوان دفاع از حقوق زن، در گفتمان‌های جاری در سپهر ایدئولوژی‌ی چپ نیز نمی‌گنجید.

این فراز از سخن را با پرسش و پاسخی پایان می‌دهم که در ژوئیه ۲۰۱۲ به مناسبت «کمپین علیه حجاب اجباری»، بین بهزاد مهرانی و عبدی کلانتری در تبعید رد و بدل شد. یادآوری می‌کنم که عبدی کلانتری، نویسنده، جامعه‌شناس، و اندیشه‌ورز مارکسیست (مقیم نیویورک)، به عنوان کوشنده‌ی سیاسی‌ی چپ در کوران انقلاب و سال‌های آغازین حکومت اسلامی، شخصاً در متن و بطن شرایط و رویدادها حضور داشته است:

> **بهزاد مهرانی**: چه‌گونه است که پس از انقلاب اسلامی و اجباری‌شدن حجاب در آن برهه‌ی زمانی، صدای اعتراض چندانی از میان نیروهای سکولار و فعالین سیاسی و اندیشه‌ورزان غیردینی به گوش نمی‌رسد؟
> **عبدی کلانتری**: [...] در سازمان‌ها و احزابِ به اصطلاح پیشرو، خودشان نیز صدای زنان مستقل را جدی نمی‌گرفتند؛ چه برسد به این بخواهند به خاطر حقوق زنان با حاکمیت در بیافتند. آگاهی نسبت به فمینیسم و حقوق زنان در میان روشنفکران چیزی نزدیک به صفر بود. تازه اگر فمینیسم را مسخره نمی‌کردند! [...] اساساً در فرهنگ روشنفکری‌ی ما آگاهی نسبت به مسئله‌ی زن غایب بود. در این زمینه ما دچار ناآگاهی‌ی تئوریک بودیم. [...][۶۵۵]

سه) تعریفِ هر یک از مفهوم‌های «مردم»، «خلق»، «دشمن خلق»، «خلق زحمت‌کش»، «طبقه‌ی کارگر»، و ارزیابی‌ی « آگاهی/ ناآگاهی‌ی توده»، در تئوری و تحلیل و عملِ هر دو سازمان، به دور از معیارهای علمی و واقعیت‌های روان-جامعه‌شناختی، و آکنده از «رمانتیسیسم انقلابی» است. در متنی با عنوان «چریک‌های فدائی‌ی خلق برای خلق توضیح می‌دهند» (که بنا به گفته‌ی اشرف دهقانی: «در بهار سال ۵۰ به میان توده‌ها برده شد»)، می‌خوانیم:

> [...] برادران و خواهران ستمدیده! چرا ما به پاسگاه قلهک حمله کردیم؟ زیرا برای مبارزه‌ی مسلحانه‌ای که به خاطر نجاتِ هم‌میهنان‌مان از زیر حکومت بیگانه‌پرستِ شاه صورت می‌گیرد، به اسلحه احتیاج داریم. [...] چرا سرپاسبان پاسگاه قلهک کشته شد؟ زیرا در برابر خواست عادلانه‌ی ما مقاومت نمود، و به روی ما تیراندازی کرد. ما از مرگ او متأسفیم و تأکید می‌کنیم که اگر پاسبانان در برابر ما مقاومت نکنند، ما هم به آن‌ها آسیبی نخواهیم رساند. ولی پاسبانی که خود از حکومت شاه رنج می‌برد و در ازای یک دستمزد ناچیز مجبور است تن به خطر بدهد و بر خلاف میلش مردم را به خاطر منافع

---

۶۵۵ گفت‌وگوی بهزاد مهرانی با عبدی کلانتری، ***روشنفکران صدای زنان را جدی نمی‌گرفتند***، تارنمای «بامداد نیوز»، ۱ مرداد ۱۳۹۱: http://bamdadkhabar.com/2012/07/9794

> غارتگران دستگیر کند یا بکشد، در عین حال در برابر ما مقاومت می‌کند، در واقع خودش مرگ را انتخاب کرده است. (بذرهای ماندگار، ۲۰۰۵، ص ۱۷۵)

البته، هر «پاسبانِ ستم‌دیده»ای می‌داند که در صورت عدم مقاومت در برابر چریک‌ها نیز، «مرگ را انتخاب کرده است.» در این صورت، پیدا نیست که این پیکارگران از جان‌گذشته، چه‌گونه و در درازنای چه زمانی می‌خواستند این «ستمدیدگان» را «آگاه» کنند و آن‌ها را به راه خود بکشانند، تا در حمله‌های بعدی به سوی آنان شلیک نکنند؟ در این جا نیز باز به حمید اشرف رجوع می‌کنم. او در شرح چرائی‌های شکستِ سیاهکل، در جزوه‌ی «تحلیل یک سال ...» می‌نویسد:

> این واضح بود که بلافاصله پس از اولین عمل چریکی، روستائیان که **هنوز درک روشنی** از دسته‌ی چریکی ندارند، واکنش موافقی نشان نخواهند داد؛ بلکه تداوم در عملیات نظامی است که می‌تواند به تدریج روستائیان یک منطقه را تحت تأثیر قرار دهد، و آن‌ها را به حمایت معنوی و سپس به حمایت مادی وادار سازد. [...] در اوایل، ملایمت به حساب ضعف گذاشته می‌شود، **چریک باید قدرت تمام و خشونت کامل موجودیت خودش را اثبات کند. آن‌گاه با استفاده از این قدرت،** برنامه‌هائی به سود دهقانان و به زیان دشمنان آن‌ها انجام دهند. تنها به این صورت است که دهقانان به **قدرت** و **نیت** چریک پی می‌برند و از او حمایت می‌کنند. (تأکیدها از من است.)

گیرم که منظور از داشتنِ «درک روشن»، فهم و درکِ پدیده‌ی « تازه/ مدرن»ی است به نام عمل چریکی و پیامدهای نیک آن برای مردم. اما- با توجه به محدودیت تماس سازمان‌یافته‌ی چریک‌ها با مردم- «درک»ی که در طول تاریخ آکنده از «سنت» بوده، چه زمانی در فاهمه‌ی آن «پاسبان» یا این «روستائی»، «روشن» می‌شود؟ چه «تدریج»ی را طلب می‌کند؟ آن «قدرتِ تمام و خشونتِ کامل» چند قربانی خواهد گرفت تا این «درک روشن» محقق شود؟ اصولاً و بنا بر اصل دیالکتیک، آیا اِعمالِ «قدرت تمام و خشونت کامل» بر مخاطب، همنهادی به عنوان «درک روشن» می‌آفریند؟ «قدرت تمام و خشونت کاملِ» چریک‌ها، از دید «پاسبانی» که از «دسته‌ی چریکی درک روشنی ندارد»، با «قدرت تمام و خشونت کاملِ» شاه **در ذاتِ بروز**، چه تفاوتی می‌توانست داشته باشد؟ پرسش بنیادی تر این است که چرا نگوئیم مردمی که با چریک‌ها همکاری نکردند، با **روشی** مخالفت می‌کردند که از آن درک روشنی داشتند. به گواهی‌ی تاریخ، حافظه‌ی جمعی‌ی مردم ایران، به ویژه مردم خطه‌ی شمالی‌ی ایران، آکنده است از آسیب‌های موحشی که پس از سقوط میرزاکوچک‌خان و فرقه‌ی دموکرات آذربایجان (و حتا در اوج پیروزی‌ی این جنبش‌ها) از سوی نیروهای دولتی و آشوب‌طلبان فرصت‌طلبِ غیردولتی، بر مردم معمولی‌ی این سرزمین‌ها آوار شد. البته باید به یاد داشته باشیم که در زمان مشروطیت، همین «مردم» در شهر و روستا با «فدائیانِ» مسلح همراهی کردند، و بسیاری از آن‌ها نیز در این راه جان باختند. منتها، این را هم باید به یاد داشته باشیم که در آن زمان، مردم می‌دانستند برای چه و کدام «انقلاب» پا در راه نهاده‌اند؛ و با تعریفی که از آن پدیده‌ی «نو» داشتند، آن را با «سنت»های دیرینه‌ی خود در تضادی بنیادی نمی‌دیدند. اما این جا و در این برنگاه از تاریخ، در حالی که بیانیه‌ها و اطلاعیه‌های هر دو سازمان مداوماً از «انقلاب» سخن می‌گفت، و در حالی که رژیم شاه این مبارزان را «کمونیست»، و انقلابِ آرمانی‌ی آن‌ها را «انقلاب کمونیستی» می‌خواند، عدم همکاری‌ی مردم شهر و روستا با چریک‌ها، می‌تواند گویای عدم پذیرش آن‌ها نسبت به «دسته‌ی چریکی» و نمودِ «درک روشنِ» آن‌ها از عمل چریکی‌ای باشد، که این «انقلاب» را وعده می‌داد. مگر آن که بپذیریم، منظور از «درک روشن»، همانا «پذیراندن» یا «وادار کردن» باشد. و شگفتا که در سخن حمید اشرف، دو مفهوم «قدرت» و «نیت»، در کنار هم آمده‌اند. یعنی، «حمایتِ» مردم قرار است زمانی جلب شود، که آن‌ها، نه تنها به «نیتِ» چریک‌ها در انجام «برنامه‌هائی به سود دهقانان»، بلکه به «قدرتِ» چریک‌ها- که با ذاتِ «آگاهانیدن» بیگانگی می‌کند- نیز پی برده باشند. در این جا، اگر

علت شکست چریک‌های هر دو سازمان در «توده‌ای کردن مشیِ مسلحانه» و در همگام کردن مردم با آرمان‌هاشان را، نداشتنِ «درک روشن» خودِ آن‌ها از جامعه‌ی ایران برآورد نکنیم، به ناگزیر باید ژرف‌تر برویم و بگوئیم که «شکست» را آن ذهنیتی پدید آورد که این بررسی‌ها و پرس وُ جوها را در ابری از توهم نسبت به «آرمان» گم کرده بود.

چهار) با این که هر دو سازمان، مبارزات مردم ویتنام را ستایش کرده‌اند، و از متن‌ها پیداست که از آن الهام گرفته‌اند، اما هیچ یک، برای آموزش نظامی، یا کمک به مردم ویتنام، به ویتنام نرفت. در حالی که هر دو سازمان، عمدتاً، در اردوگاه‌های فلسطینی آموزش نظامی دیدند؛ از انقلابیون **مسلمان** (تا حد شرکت در جنگ و گریزهاشان) حمایت کردند؛ و از حمایت آن‌ها و چند کشور مسلمان دیگر برخوردار بودند. البته، باید بی‌درنگ یادآور شوم که در دوران انقلاب فرهنگی در اروپا (دهه‌ی ۱۹۶۰)، گروهی از انقلابیون آلمانی نیز در همین اردوگاه‌های فلسطینی آموزش نظامی دیدند، که گفته شده، بسیاری از مقررات سنتی/ دینیِ این اردوگاه‌ها- از جمله جدائیِ کمپ زنان و مردان- را رعایت نمی‌کردند.[۶۵۶] اما شگفتیِ بیش‌تر در این است که در همان دوران، دولت‌های عراق و سوریه و اردن (جایگاه بیش‌تر اردوگاه‌های فلسطینی)، به تصفیه و کشتار کردها و دفن آن‌ها در گورهای دسته‌جمعی مشغول بودند؛ اما نسبت به این نسل‌کشی، صدای اعتراضی از بیانیه‌های دو سازمانِ مورد بحث ما برنخاست. به بیانی دیگر- و البته از دیدگاه بحث حاضر- این احتمالِ روان- جامعه‌شناختی پیش می‌آید که شاید الگوی جنگِ «**مسلمان**» با «**یهود**» در پیشینه‌ی تاریخیِ پیامبر اسلام، در حافظه‌ی جمعیِ چریک‌های هر دو سازمان، در این گزینش، دستی توانا داشته است.

پنج) افزون بر استقلال در تصمیم‌گیری‌های عملی، گزینشِ مستقل در زمینه‌ی برداشت‌های نظری از الگوهای ایدئولوژیک، می‌تواند به عنوان وجه مشترک دیگری در این دو سازمان (حتا در حزب توده‌ی آغازین) تلقی شود. تزهای بیژن جزنی، امیرپرویز پویان، مسعود احمدزاده، و مجاهدینِ آغازین، در براوردِ شرایط عینی و ذهنیِ جامعه‌ی ایران و راه رهائی از آن- با تمام تفاوت‌هائی که با هم داشتند، و صرف نظر از کیفیت‌هائی که در عمل تجلی کرد- فرآورده‌ی خلاقیت و کشفِ خودِ این پیشاهنگان بود، در تحلیل از مجموعه‌ی مشاهده‌ها، شنیده‌ها و خوانده‌هاشان. به عنوان نمونه، می‌توان از چون و چرای مسعود احمدزاده با گزاره‌ها و تزهای رژی دبره (در کتاب «انقلاب در انقلاب؟»)، در رابطه با جامعه‌ی ایران، یاد کرد؛ که یک بخش کامل از کتاب «مبارزه‌ی مسلحانه، هم استراتژی هم تاکتیکِ» او را رقم زده است. نمونه‌ی مشابه این خلاقیت، در تدوین کلیت ایدئولوژی/ متدولوژیِ مجاهدینِ آغازین قابل مشاهده است. با این که در آن دوره، گرایش التقاطیِ مارکسیسم و الاهیات در جنبش‌های امریکای لاتین هم رواج یافته بود (حتا می‌توان گفت که خود فیدل کاسترو آن را رواج داده بود[۶۵۷])، اما، استقلالِ اندیشه‌ای که مجاهدین خلقِ اولیه در گزینش و تفسیر آموزه‌هائی از اسلام و مارکسیسم، و پیوند آن‌ها به یکدیگر، به خرج دادند، امری غیرقابل انکار است.

---

[۶۵۶] شیوا فرهمند راد، بر اساس فیلمِ آلمانیِ « Baader-Meinhof Complex » (عقده‌ی بادر ماینهوف)، که واقعیت‌های جنبش چریکی در آلمان را بازنمائی کرده، می‌نویسد: «شباهت‌ها بسیار است و شگفت‌انگیز. اما دست‌کم یک تفاوت بزرگ و آن نیز شگفت‌انگیز، میان رفتار و اخلاق چریک‌های آلمانی و چریک‌های ایرانی وجود دارد: جنبش چریکیِ آلمانی عناصری از هیپی‌گری، جنبش "عشق بورز، جنگ نکن"، و آزادیِ جنسی دهه‌ی هفتاد میلادی را در خود دارد. [...] اینان هیچ مرز و محدودیتی در عشق ورزیدن و همخوابگی نمی‌شناسند. در این راه حتا مقررات سخت اردوگاه‌های فلسطینی را به‌هم می‌ریزند. [...] در این دوران در پاره‌ای از محافل جوانان و دانشجویان ایران نیز هیپی‌گری رواج دارد و در "پارتی"ها حشیش می‌کشند. اما زندگی و اخلاق چریکیِ ایرانی ریاضت را و روزه‌ی عشق را تجویز می‌کند. [...]» به مأخذ زیر نگاه کنید:

- ش. فرهمند راد، ***چریک آلمانی و چریک ایرانی***، تارنمای «شیوا»، بازدید ۱۰ فوریه ۲۰۱۲:
http://web.comhem.se/shivaf/Cherik.htm

[۶۵۷] افزون بر برخی از مارکسیست‌های ایتالیائی و فرانسوی، که دین (مسیحیت) و مارکسیسم را مغایر یکدیگر نمی‌دیدند، فیدل کاسترو نیز این دو پدیده را مغایر هم برانداز نمی‌کرد. او با این که در ابتدای پیروزیِ انقلاب کوبا، گروهی از کشیشان بومی را دستگیر کرد و کشیشان غیر بومی را از کوبا اخراج کرد، اما انگیزه‌ی او در این پاکسازی، نه مخالفت با ذات دین، بلکه- چنان که خود اعلام کرد- همدلی و همنشینیِ کشیشان بود با مردم طبقات ثروتمند، و بی‌توجهیِ کلیسا به مردم فرودست؛ «در حالی که خواسته‌ی خود مسیح این بود که کشیشان هم کار کنند.» اما زمانی که عوامل کلیسا را در خدمت به فرودستان با خود همراه کرد، قدرت به کلیساها بازگشت، و در انجام پروژه‌های مارکسیستی به

منتها، از کنار این واقعیت هم نمی‌توان به سکوت گذشت که سقف این پرواز را سپهری آکنده از کهن‌الگوهای فرهنگی رقم زده بود، که دست در دستِ همه‌ی عناصر بازدارنده‌ی بیرونی، بلوغ سیاسی‌ی این پیشاهنگان و آینده‌هاشان را تا آن جا به تعویق انداخت، که انقلاب آرمانی‌ی آن‌ها از جائی سر برکرد، که این پیشاهنگان علیه آن برخاسته بودند. کما این که نمود الگوی «شهریار الاهی»، با تمام تبعات ممکنه‌ی آن، در نظر و عملِ هر دو سازمان قابل ردیابی است. البته، با توجه به تکیه‌ی پایه‌گذاران سازمان مجاهدین بر آموزه‌های اسلام شیعی- که قرار بود با عنوان «نظم توحیدی»، «سیاسی» هم بشود- حتا نیازمند «ردیابی»ی کهن‌الگوهای فرهنگی در فکرت‌های این سازمان نیستیم. چرا که به رغم تلاش برای سنت‌شکنی، این تکیه، خواسته یا ناخواسته گویای پذیرش آن فرهنگی است که تجویز سلسله مراتب مرید و مرادی، زن ستیزی، و ضدیت با انتخاب و استقلال اندیشه را با خود حمل می‌کند. با این که هر دو سازمان در بیانیه‌های خود از آرمانِ «آزادی» نیز دم می‌زدند، اما، به حکم ساختار نظری و بینش سیاسی‌ی خود، بارقه‌ی هر نمودی از «اندیشه‌ی مستقل» و فردی را- که گاه، این جا و آن جا، در حاشیه‌ی جَوّ حاکم بر سازمان بروز می‌کرد- با عنوان‌هائی مانند «فرصت‌طلبی»، «تکرَوی» و «تخطی» از قانون‌های سازمان، سرکوب کردند. تازه، همین «اندیشه»ی ظاهراً «مستقل»ی که از سوی سازمان خود سرکوب می‌شد، باز به دنبال الگوئی می‌گشت که از آن پیروی کند. مثال بارز این حکایت دردناک در سازمان مجاهدین خلق، در رویدادهای پس از «تغییر مواضع ایدئولوژیکِ» سازمان قابل مشاهده است. در این ماجرا، گروهی که تازه با راندن «اسلام» از ایدئولوژی‌ی خود به بلوغ نسبی هم دست یافته بودند، نه تنها مالکیت کل سازمان را ادعا کردند، بلکه عدم تبعیت (از سوی معتقدان به همان ایدئولوژی‌ی اسلامی/ مارکسیستی که تا چندی پیش شانه به شانه‌ی آن‌ها جنگیده بودند) را برنتابیدند و اندیشه‌ی مخالف را به خون و خاکستر تبدیل کردند. با توجه به این که تصمیم‌گیرندگان این حذف، در مقام رهبری‌ی یک سازمان سیاسی قرار داشتند، می‌توان گفت که حذف فیزیکی‌ی اندیشه‌ی مخالف، انگیزه‌ای نداشت به جز تبعیتِ خودِ تصمیم‌گیرندگان از تزِ نوشته وُ نانوشته‌ی «هدف، وسیله را توجیه می‌کند» بر فراز ایدئولوژی‌ی آن‌ها. حذف‌های فیزیکی و شخصیتی، نه تنها در اثر عدم اطاعت و ابراز مقاومت، بلکه در صورت تردید نسبت به وفاداری‌ی عضو نیز، در این سازمان تجربه شده است. مثلاً، جوانی به نام مرتضی هودشتیان (نام مستعار «حمید»)، از سوی مرکزیت سازمان مجاهدین، برای آموزش نظامی به بخش برون‌مرزی‌ی سازمان منتقل می‌شود؛ به خاطر «ضعف تشکیلاتی» مورد سوءظن اعضاء برون‌مرزی قرار می‌گیرد؛ از سوی محسن فاضل و محمد یقینی شکنجه می‌شود تا به «ساواکی بودن خود اعتراف کند»؛ و این شکنجه، تا مرگِ این جوان نوزده ساله ادامه می‌یابد. محسن نجات‌حسینی، پیرامون این فاجعه می‌نویسد:

> او، با نادیده گرفتن برخی از اصول و معیارهای زندگی‌ی سیاسی و تشکیلاتی، نوعی بیگانگی با تشکیلات و کار گروهی را به نمایش می‌گذارد. به عنوان مثال، وی رزمندگان خردسال فلسطینی را که به عربی آن‌ها را «شِبل» (بچه شیر) نام گذاشته بودند، با زبان طنز «پشکل» می‌نامد و یادآوری‌ی اطرافیانش نیز او را از این شوخی بازنمی‌دارد. [...] محسن فاضل که از یک سو با سختگیری‌های تشکیلات در داخل کشور خو گرفته بود، و از سوی دیگر فرصتی بدست آورده بود تا توان تشکیلاتی‌ی خود را به رقیبانش در خارج از کشور نشان دهد، وظیفه‌ی بررسی‌ی وضع حمید را به عهده می‌گیرد. [...] فاضل بدون این که در انتظار اطلاعات بیش‌تری از داخل بماند، با توافق حسین روحانی [...] برای اعتراف گرفتن از حمید، او را تحت فشار می‌گذارد و حتا به شکنجه نیز مبادرت می‌کند، و در این کار از محمد یقینی هم کمک می‌گیرد. [...]

استقرار رژیم کاسترو یاری داد. این انقلابِ کلیسائی، به زودی به کشورهای انقلابی‌ی سراسر امریکای جنوبی راه یافت. و طرفه این که، پذیرش فیدل کاسترو نسبت به مذهب، نه از روی «سیاست‌ورزی»، بلکه از روی باور و اعتقاد خود او به آموزه‌های مذهبی بوده است. پیرامون چه‌گونگی‌ی این فرایند و آراء مذهبی‌ی فیدل کاسترو در رابطه با مارکسیسم، به کتاب زیر نگاه کنید:
Fidel and Religion: Castro Talks on Revolution and Religion with Frei Betto, Translated by the Cuban Center for Translation and Interpretaion, New York: Simon & Schuster Inc.,1987.

> بعدها [یعنی پس از مرگ او در زیر شکنجه] معلوم شد که حمید کاملاً مورد شناخت و اعتماد تشکیلات در داخل کشور بوده است.[۶۵۸]

این پدیده‌ی شوم، شاید یکی از فراورده‌های زندگی و فعالیت مخفی باشد. کما این که حمید اشرف، در «تحلیل یک سال مبارزه‌ی چریکی در کوه و شهر»، پس از شرح چرائی‌های شکست در عملیات سیاهکل (به عنوان یک دستورالعمل عام برای عملیات چریکی) در بند ۸ دستورالعمل خود نوشته بود: «سه اصل طلائی‌ی چریکی، تحرک مطلق – عدم اطمینان مطلق – هوشیاری مطلق، را باید همیشه و همه جا رعایت کرد.» البته «سه اصل طلائی»ی یادشده، اصول ازلی و ابدی در هر «جَنگ»ی بوده و هست و خواهد بود. اما، در این جا، و به ویژه در یک گروه زیرزمینی، مرز «اطمینان مطلق» و «عدم اطمینان مطلق» را چه معیارهائی مشخص می‌کنند؟ کشتن، قطعه قطعه‌کردن و سوزاندنِ بدن عضو مخالف یا شکنجه تا سرحد قتلِ آن مجاهد جوان، در کجای این معیار قرار دارند، هیچ معلوم نیست. شاید لازم هم نیست، نبوده، که این معیارها چندان «معلوم» باشد. چرا که سرمشقِ «هدف، وسیله را توجیه می‌کند»، پاسخگوی این «نامعلومی» خواهد بود. حمید اشرف در متن یادشده، از «ملایمت و ملاطفت» چریک‌هائی که به روی روستائیان اسلحه نگشودند، انتقاد می‌کند، و در بند ۶ دستورالعمل خود می‌نویسد: «باید از هر وسیله‌ای برای وصول به هدف سود جست و از رمانتیسم انقلابی پرهیز کرد.»

و همین جاست که می‌توان شهادت داد: کهن‌الگوهای قدرت‌طلبی، مرید/ مرادی، و تبعیت‌خواهی از فرودست/ تابعیت از فرادست در ساختار ذهنی و نظام گفتمانی‌ی این دو سازمان چریکی کارکرد خود را نمادینه کرده‌اند؛ فرقی هم نمی‌کند که این «مراد/ فرادست»، «پیامبر اسلام» یا «امام علی» باشد، یا «مارکس»، یا «لنین»، یا «مائو»؛ مهم این است که در تار و پود اندیشه‌ی دینی- به ویژه در مذهب شیعه- سرشت «اراده‌ی معطوف به قدرت»، جانی همواره تپنده دارد.

ترور شخصیت و قتل‌های درون‌سازمانی- که میراث سیاهی از «سازمان اطلاعاتی‌ی حزب توده» است- در کارنامه‌ی سازمان چریک‌های فدائی‌ی خلق ایران هم نمونه‌هائی دارد. به عنوان مثال، برخورد حذفی با مصطفی شعاعیان و منوچهر هلیل رودی (به سبب اندیشه‌ی مخالف) و قتل عبدالله پنجه‌شاهی (به سبب رابطه‌ی عاشقانه با یک هموند زن)،[۶۵۹] در کارنامه‌ی این سازمان به ثبت رسیده است؛ و من در جاهای دیگر مجموعه‌ی حاضر بر این موارد و موارد مشابه درنگ کرده‌ام. اما این جا به نمونه‌ای می‌پردازم که به گونه‌ای خاموش و غیرمستقیم، از ذهنیت حاکم بر این سازمان (و کلاً، بر جنبش چپ ما در آن دوره) سخن می‌گوید: این حکایت دردناک را «گروه منشعب از سازمان چریک‌های فدائی‌ی خلق» (به رهبری‌ی تورج حیدری بیگوند)- البته به برکت «یادمانده‌ها»ی علی خدائی- به تاریخ فکر ما سپرده است. علی خدائی، که در جریان پیوستن «گروه منشعب» به «سازمان نوید» (وابسته به حزب توده) بوده، شرح مفصلی دارد از فرایندی که این پیوند طی کرده است. مهم‌ترین بخش از یادمانده‌های او، که به بحث حاضر مربوط است، پیرامون «سئوال»هائی دور می‌زند که افراد این گروه، توسط رابط خود برای رحمان هاتفی (رهبر سازمان نوید) می‌فرستادند، تا پس از گرفتنِ «پاسخ‌های قانع‌کننده»، مبارزه‌ی مسلحانه را کنار بگذارند و به خط مشی‌ی سیاسی‌ی سازمان نوید (حزب توده) بپیوندند؛ به طوری که فرزاد دادگر (رابط این گروه)، «به شوخی» گفته بود: «من که از بس با این موتور سئوال بردم و آوردم، خسته شدم.» علی خدائی، که این جمله‌ی فرزاد دادگر را نقل کرده است، در همان متن می‌گوید:

---

۶۵۸ محسن نجات‌حسینی، ***بر فراز خلیج فارس***، پیشین، صص ۳۶۳ تا ۳٦٤.

۶۵۹ عبدالله پنجه شاهی، عضو سازمان چریک‌های فدائی‌ی خلق، و از خانواده‌ای که همه‌ی افراد آن (برادر و خواهر و مادر و پدر) عضو این سازمان بودند، به دلیل رابطه‌ی عاشقانه‌ای که با «ادنا ثابت»، یکی از هموندان زن، برقرار کرده بود، توسط یکی از رهبران سازمان- که هنوز به روشنی معلوم نیست کدام یک از رهبران- به قتل می‌رسد. پیرامون این فاجعه، در جلد چهارم مجموعه‌ی حاضر سخن گفته‌ام.

آن‌ها سئوالاتی داشتند که تا گرفتن پاسخ آن‌ها و قانع‌شدن، حاضر نبودند مشیِ مسلحانه را به کلی کنار بگذارند و به حزب بپیوندند. از سوی این گروه، زنده یاد فرزاد دادگر به همراه سیامک (حسین قلمبر) با نوید در ارتباط قرار گرفتند. [...] یک سلسله سئوالات [...] باز می‌گشت به اتحاد شوروی [...] مثلاً چرا در شوروی ارث وجود دارد و یا چرا شوروی به رژیم شاه ذوب آهن داده؛ و از این قبیل. [...] ما بر سر آخرین سئوال گروه فرزاد درباره‌ی دلیل ارث در اتحاد شوروی گیر کرده بودیم. نمی‌دانستیم پاسخ آن را از کجا بدست بیاوریم و یا از چه کسی بگیریم و تحویل آن‌ها بدهیم. [...] بالأخره تصمیم گرفتیم نقب بزنیم به زنده یاد به آذین. [...] سیاوش کسرائی درجا تلفن کرد، و به آذین هم برای چند روز بعد ساعت ۳ بعد از ظهر وقت ملاقات داد. روز موعود من و هاتفی به همراه کسرائی رفتیم به خانه‌ی به آذین که در شهرآرا بود. [...] فضای اتاق و دیدار به گونه‌ای خشک بود که هاتفی خیلی زود حوصله‌اش سر رفت و بی‌مقدمه پرسید: ما می‌خواهیم بدانیم در اتحاد شوروی چرا «ارث» وجود دارد؟ به آذین یک نگاهی به کسرائی انداخت و بعد کمی به هاتفی نگاه کرد. هاتفی موهای خرمائیِ روشن داشت. مثل خیلی از مردم قزوین. به آذین ظاهراً با کنایه به همین موی روشنِ هاتفی پرسید: خانواده‌ی شما در روسیه ارثیه‌ای برای شما باقی گذاشته‌اند؟ هاتفی گفت: خیر! و به آذین هم اضافه کرد: پس به شما چه که در اتحاد شوروی ارث هست یا نیست؟ هاتفی گفت: بله. اما بعضی‌ها علاقه دارند این مسئله را بدانند. به آذین هم گفت: این بعضی‌ها بروند آن همه چیزی که درباره‌ی مملکت خودشان نمی‌دانند بدانند. دیدار تمام شده بود؛ و پیش از آن که چای و یا چیزی برای نوشیدن بیاورند، هاتفی بلند شد که برویم. با بدرقه‌ی نیمه‌کاره‌ی به آذین، خانه را ترک کردیم. تا رسیدیم به کوچه، کسرائی شروع کرد به دلجوئی، و به هاتفی گفت: این اخلاقش این طوری است، والا خیلی قلبش صاف و مهربان است. هاتفی هم گفت: حرف حساب زد! جلسه‌ی بعد که فرزاد برای گرفتن پاسخ آخرین سئوالش آمد، هاتفی همین پاسخِ به آذین را از قول خودش به او داد، و گفت از خانه‌ی تیمی بیائید بیرون و اول مملکت خودتان را بشناسید. نوبت به ارث در اتحاد شوروی هم می رسد. [...][۶۶۰]

پرسش این است که اگر به آذین- فرهنگورزِ کهنه‌کارِ حزب توده- پاسخ را نمی‌دانست، چرا نگفت «نمی دانم»؟ یا اگر می‌دانست، چرا آن را به این جوانانِ جویا منتقل نکرد؟ چرا لحن او تحقیرآمیز و رَماننده بود؟ اگر به جای این پرسش، پرسشی مطرح شده بود که پاسخ آن، «بهشتیّتِ» اتحاد شوروی را تأیید می‌کرد، آیا باز هم به آذینِ ما از همین پاسخ سربالا و لحن تحقیرآمیز سود می‌جست؟ به باور من، برنامه‌ها و دستورالعمل‌های حزب توده (که در دوره‌ی مورد بحث، سرپوش گذاشتن بر کاستی‌ها و انحراف از فکرت‌های مارکسیسم در شوروی را از اهمّ وظایف خود می‌دانست) در این فرارِ رو به جلو، و در این لحن تحقیرآمیز دستی توانا داشت. با این دریافت است که می‌بینیم، کیش شخصیت و سرشتِ «مراد/ مریدی»، در این جا به صورت یک هِرَم (از پایه به سوی تارک) عمل کرده است: «گروه منشعب»، «رحمان هاتفی» را در نقش دانای کل برانداز می‌کند؛ رحمان هاتفی، در نقش دانای کلِ گروه منشعب، «به آذین» را دانای کل می‌بیند؛ و به آذین- که جواب به این پرسش سرراست را با مشیِ حزب خود مغایر می‌داند- سیاست‌های «حزب» را دانای کل می‌بیند؛ و البته حزب نیز، مراد و قطبِ اعظمی دارد به نام «اتحاد شوروی».

شاید این چند نمونه (از انبوه موارد مشابه)، تکیه‌ی مصرانه‌ی من بر «سنت‌شکنی» و «خلاقیتِ» ایدئولوگ‌های این دو سازمان- و حتا حزب توده‌ی آغازین- را به زیر سئوال ببرد. همین جا اشاره کنم که به باور من، هیچ یک از عناصرِ «سنت‌شکنی» و «خلاقیت»، کیفیت فراورده را توضیح نمی‌دهد. پشتوانه‌ی این نظر نیز موارد مشابهی است که تاریخ ایران و جهان به آن شهادت می‌دهد. به عنوان مثال، جنبش‌های ضداستعماریِ مبارزان ایرانی در چند سده‌ی نخست

---

[۶۶۰] بخش دوم از یادمانده‌های علی خدائی در دیدار و گفت‌وگو با «ن. کیانی» و «ع. خیرخواه»، ***پیوستن گروه منشعب به نوید، روزگاری که آسان سپری نشد***، تارنمای «راه توده»، شماره‌ی ۱۷۴، ۲۸ آوریل ۲۰۰۸:
http://www.rahetudeh.com/rahetude/mataleb/nagofteha/html/nagofteha-2.html

اشغال ایران توسط تازیان (حتا جنبش‌های شیخیه و حروفیه و باب و مشروطیت، حتا جنبش‌های موسوم به «اصلاحات» و «سبز» در زمانه‌ی ما) و جنبش‌های منتهی به پروتستانیسم در غرب، که عمدتاً بر پایه‌ی سنت‌شکنی و خلاقیتِ ایدئولوگ‌های آن‌ها در قرائتِ متون مقدس و احکام مذهبی سبز شدند، از درون ذهنیت‌هائی برآمدند که شاکله‌های شناختی‌ی آن‌ها در همان فضا/ زمانِ سنت بسته شده بود. (به ویژه که در دوره‌ی مورد بحث ما، دیکتاتوری‌ی همه‌جانبه، امکان رشد ذهنی را به شدت محدود کرده بود.)

شش) بی‌توجهی به «تاریخ»: خلاء اطلاعاتی و بی‌اعتنائی به ریزه‌کاری‌های ظاهراً بی‌اهمیت در بیانیه‌ها و اسناد، که کم یا بیش در هر دو سازمان مشترک است. در هر دو سازمان، اعضاء و هوادارانی در مبارزه جان خود را از دست دادند، که ظاهراً به دلیل مخفی بودن این دو سازمان و رعایت ملاحظات امنیتی، نام و نشانی از آن‌ها در هیچ جا ثبت نشده است.[۶۶۱] کما این که تارنمای «۱۹ بهمن» در سال ۱۳۸۹ فهرستی از «به خون خفتگان چریک‌های فدائی‌ی خلق» منتشر کرد که در صدر آن می‌خوانیم:

> بازدید کننده‌ی گرامی، چنانچه در مورد هر یک از عزیزان، اطلاعاتی دارید که ما را در تصحیح و یا تکمیل زندگی‌نامه‌ی آنان یاری رساند، لطفاً به ما اطلاع دهید. اسامی و مطالبی را که در لیست با رنگ قرمز مشاهده می‌کنید، بیانگر اطلاعات نیمه‌موثق است.[۶۶۲]

افزون بر انبوه جان‌باختگانِ گمنام، عدم ثبت یا بازچاپ اساسنامه‌ها، برنامه‌ها، فهرست کادرهای «مرکزیت» در هر دوره، و فهرست اعضاء در هر دوره، وجود انبوهی از «اطلاعات نیمه‌موثق» را سبب شده، که تفاوت‌ها و تناقض‌ها را در «تاریخچه»‌های متعدد این دو سازمان رقم زده‌اند. البته، نباید فراموش کرد که در آن شرایط سیاسی، مخفی‌کاری و حتا نابود کردنِ عامدانه‌ی مدارک برای جلوگیری از افشاء، شرط بقاء این سازمان‌ها بود، و به دلایل امنیتی، کم‌تر عضوی در این سازمان‌ها بود که نام و نشان واقعی‌ی هموندان خود را بداند و گروه بزرگی از آن‌ها را حتا ملاقات کرده باشد. حمید اشرف، حتا پس از شکست پروژه‌ی سیاهکل، در «تحلیل یک سال ...»، از هموندی که پیش از عملیات برای همیشه «در جنگل گم شد»، نام نمی‌بَرد؛ چرا که نام او نیز می‌توانست سرنخی به ساواک بدهد. حتا مذاکره‌ی اعضاء ارشد سازمان‌های «چریک‌های فدائی‌ی خلق» و «بخش مارکسیست سازمان مجاهدین خلق» در سال ۵۴ (با هدف اتحاد این دو سازمان)- که نوار شنیداری‌ی آن سی و پنج سال بعد، به همت «گروه اندیشه و پیکار» منتشر شد- از پس پرده صورت گرفت.[۶۶۳] بدیهی است که در چنین جوّی از اختناق مضاعف، نه تنها «شناختِ» شبکه‌های پیچیده‌ای از مفاهیم تئوریک و راهبردهای عملی‌ی آن‌ها به مخاطره می‌افتد، بلکه نام و نشان و فهرست اعضاء و برنامه‌ها نیز نمی‌تواند در درون پایگاه‌های درون‌مرزی‌ی این سازمان‌ها ثبت شود.

---

[۶۶۱] به طوری که اکنون، پس از گذشت چهار دهه از شروع جنبش مسلحانه، و پس از سی و سه سال زندگی در تبعید، هنوز فهرست کاملی از جان‌باختگان این دو سازمان (حتا قربانیان کشتار سال ۱۳۶۷) در دست نیست. فهرست‌های متعدد و متباینی که از کشتار ۶۷ منتشر شده، تعداد جان‌باختگان این دو سازمان را بین ۵۰۰۰ تا ۱۲۰۰۰ تن ثبت کرده‌اند.

[۶۶۲] به مأخذ زیر- بازدید: ۱۲ دی ماه ۱۹۸۹- نگاه کنید:
http://19bahman.net/biography/list_e_shohada_e_sazman.htm

[۶۶۳] در سال ۱۳۸۹ یک سلسله نوار ضبط شده از گفت‌وگوهای حمید اشرف و بهروز ارمغانی از سازمان چریک‌های فدائی‌ی خلق، و تقی شهرام و جواد قائدی از شاخه‌ی مارکسیست شده‌ی سازمان مجاهدین خلق، که در سال ۱۳۵۴ و با هدف اتحاد بین دو سازمان انجام شده بود، توسط آرشیو سازمان «پیکار در راه آزادی‌ی طبقه‌ی کارگر» و با امضاء تراب حق شناس در تارنمای «اندیشه و پیکار» منتشر شد. تاریخ بازدید ۲۰ فوریه ۲۰۱۱:
http://www.peykarandeesh.org/PeykarArchive/Mojahedin-ML/mojahed_fadaii.html

اما به رغم این محدودیت‌ها، این واقعیت را نیز نباید فراموش کنیم که هر دو سازمان، «بخش خارج از کشور» داشتند، و اگر با نگاهی «مدرن»، به «تاریخ» و به حفظ اسناد سازمان خود می‌نگریستند، از امکانات آن برخوردار بودند. به باور من، در این جا واقعیتی پشت واقعیتِ ملاحظاتِ «امنیتی» نهفته است که ریشه در فرهنگ سنتی دارد. چرا که در گزارش‌ها و یادواره‌های پیکارگرانِ بازمانده از آن روزگار، که حالا در تبعید، «مشکل امنیتی» هم ندارند، به ثبت اطلاعات دقیق تاریخی اهمیت چندانی داده نمی‌شود. مثلاً، اشرف دهقانی متن‌های متعددی از آن دوره‌ی سازمان چریک‌های فدائی‌ی خلق را در کتابِ «بذرهای ماندگار، ۲۰۰۵» بازچاپ کرده است، که تاریخِ انتشار ندارند. او در حالی که از این امر اظهار «تأسف» می‌کند (ص ۱۷۴)، خودش نیز در جای جای کتاب، همان الگو را تکرار کرده است.[۶۶۴] یا، هنوز که هنوز است، ما نمی‌دانیم که اشرف دهقانی، به عنوان «نماینده/ رهبر سازمان چریک‌های فدائی در خارج از کشور»، در آن سال‌ها، در کجا یا در کجاهای «خارج از کشور» زندگی و فعالیت داشته است. چرا که خودش همواره از «منطقه‌ی خاورمیانه» یاد می‌کند. یا، عباس هاشمی، از بخش «اقلیتِ» سازمان چریک‌های فدائی‌ی خلق، فرمانده‌ی عملیات چریک‌ها در ترکمن صحرا؛ یعنی، تاریخ زنده‌ی دوره‌ای از این سازمان، در پاسخ به پرسش پرویز قلیچ‌خانی (مدیر نشریه‌ی آرش- پاریس)، در تبعید، می‌گوید:

> بعد از سال ۵۵ ما کمیته‌ی مرکزی نداشتیم. رفقای شاخه‌ی مشهد که ضربه نخورده بودند، عملاً مسئولیت کل تشکیلات را به عهده گرفتند و تازه در سال ۵۶ هم چند رفیق دیگر ضربه خوردند. که دو عضو اصلی از سه عضو جانشین کشته شدند؛ یعنی رفیق فرجودی (رحیم) و رفیق صبا بیژن‌زاده (سیمین)؛ که به طور نسبی از سایرین توانایی‌ی بیش‌تری داشتند. رحیم، سیاسی/ تئوریک‌تر، و صبا، تشکیلاتی‌تر بود. بعد از آن‌ها، هادی و مجید و منصور شدند «مرکزیت». از مجید بپرسید؛ می‌داند.[۶۶۵]

یادآوری می‌کنم که پرسش قلیچ‌خانی از عباس هاشمی، پیرامون قتل عبدالله پنجه‌شاهی، یکی از همونداِن، در درون سازمان بوده است؛ که هاشمی در جریان آن نبوده و بعداً هم به آن اعتراض کرده است. اما در این جا منظور من از بازگو کردن سخن هاشمی، نه مطرح کردنِ تصفیه‌های درون‌سازمانی، بلکه نشان دادنِ شیوه‌ی سهل‌انگارانه‌ای است که در انتقال اطلاعات تاریخی بکار می‌رود. البته، نسل من و هاشمی، از خلال متن‌های پراکنده، اکنون می‌داند که «مجید»، نام مستعار «قربانعلی عبدالرحیم‌پور» بوده است. اما در صورتی که هیچ سند مدون و مطمئنی از ساختار تشکیلاتی‌ی این سازمان- به ویژه در سال‌های سرنوشت‌ساز ۵۶ و ۵۷- در دست نیست، نسل‌های آینده، که به این همه متن پراکنده دسترسی ندارند، از کجا بدانند که نام و هویت واقعی‌ی «هادی» و «مجید» و «منصور» چه بوده است. بدین ترتیب، آیا این شخصیت‌های تاریخ‌ساز، جای «عمرو وُ زید» را در ضرب‌المثل‌های آینده نخواهند گرفت؟

در **جمع‌بندی‌ی گزاره‌های مربوط به این دو سازمان**، و در تأملی دقیق بر موارد شش‌گانه‌ی بالا، دو الگوی مرتبط و غیرقابل تفکیک از یکدیگر به دید می‌آید. الگوی نخست، به بُن‌ساخت سیاسی‌ی کشور - در آن برش مخصوص از تاریخ ایران و جهان- مربوط است؛ و الگوی دوم، به بافت فرهنگی‌ی جامعه‌ی ایران.

تا عناصر متشکله‌ی بُن‌ساخت سیاسی‌ی کشور را در این جمع‌بندی نشان دهم، از تکرار این گزاره‌ها ناگزیرم که: در آن دوره بن‌ساخت سیاسی‌ی ایران را، از یک سو، پیامدهای عینی و ذهنی‌ی کودتای ۲۸ مرداد، قرارداد کنسرسیوم،

---

[۶۶۴] به عنوان نمونه، منابعی که در زیرنویس‌های صفحه‌های ۱۷۸ و ۱۷۹ آورده، تاریخ انتشار ندارند.

[۶۶۵] ***گفت‌وگو با عباس هاشمی (هاشم)***، نشریه‌ی «آرش»، چاپ پاریس، شماره‌ی ۷۹، آبان ۱۳۸۰/ نوامبر ۲۰۰۱، ص ۴۳.

وابستگی‌ی روزافزون سیاسی/ اقتصادی/ نظامی‌ی شاه به امریکا رقم می‌زد، و از سوی دیگر، پیامدهای عینی و ذهنی‌ی سیاست‌های شاه در مدرنیزه کردن ایران- که سیل‌آسا نیک و بد جامعه‌ی سنتی را با خود می‌برد- و از سوی سوم، خودکامگی‌های او- که تا پیش از رسیدن جامعه به فازِ اسلحه و شعار «مرگ بر شاهِ دزد و...»- مجال هر نوع سازش با پیکارگرانی را که در چارچوب قانون اساسی و سلطنت مشروطه مبارزه می‌کردند، از او گرفته بود. این مجموعه- در حالی که با انبوه مخالفانِ سازمانی یا غیرسازمانی رویارو بود- برای استقرار و حفظ حاکمیت خود، به ناگزیر، وسیله‌ای نداشت به جز ایجاد خفقانِ روزافزون و نابودی‌ی مخالفانی که اینک او را به عنوان «دشمن» شناسائی می‌کردند. عناصرِ پارادوکسیکالِ ناچاری و بن‌بست شاه، از یک سو رسالتی بود که در نوسازی و «مدرنیزه» کردن ایران برای خود قائل بود، از سوی دیگر، حفظ منافع اقتصادی‌ی غرب و عمدتاً امریکا در ایران بود، و از سوی دیگر، حفظ قدرت بلامنازعی بود که می‌خواست و بدست آورده بود. البته شاه ایران- با این مجموعه از شرایط- در جهانِ آن روز تنها نبود. منتها، رویاروئی مخالفان با دیکتاتورهای وابسته در بسیاری از کشورهای دیگر جهان، حالا، از «تظاهرات» و «راهپیمائی»ها و «بیانیه»های برتراند راسل و ژان پل سارتر و مانندههای آن‌ها برگذشته بود، و به رویاروئی‌ی مسلحانه جا سپرده بود، و در بسیاری از کشورهای جهان، مکانِ فعالیت نیز، از «خیابان» و «میدان» به زیرزمین یا جنگل‌ها منتقل شده بود؛ و در برخی از کشورها، از زیرزمین‌ها و جنگل‌های آغشته به خونِ مبارزان، به بارگاه استبداد نقب نیز زده بود. این واقعیت‌ها، هم به هراس پادشاه ایران و تراکم خفقان می‌افزود، و هم به جسارت و امید مخالفانِ براندازِ او دامن می‌زد.

اما الگوی دوم، در حالی که به برشی از تاریخ ایران و جهانِ «مدرن» مربوط است، در فرهنگی ریشه دارد که تا بن دندان به مایه‌های متراکم و شبکه‌وارِ شهریار الاهی، تک‌قدرتی، مرد/ پدرسالاری، بینش اسطوره‌ای: سیاووشی، حسینی، و مهم‌ترین تبعاتِ آن‌ها، یعنی: نه«اندیشیدنی از آنِ خود»، مجهز است. به بیانی دیگر، اگر تعریف ایمانوئل کانت از مفاهیم «خود» و «اندیشیدن»- یعنی فردیتِ قائم به ذات- را به عنوان ملاکی برای رسیدن به مرحله‌ی تاریخی‌ی «مدرنیسم» (نه «مدرنیته») و آغاز فکرت سکولاریسم بپذیریم، باید بپذیریم که از یکان ملت ایران گرفته تا پیشاهنگ مبارزه، تا پیشاهنگ «مدرنیزه» کردن ایران، کم یا بیش به بن‌مایه‌های فرهنگِ «پیش‌مدرن» مجهز بودند. با این خوانش است که می‌بینیم تحولات ناشی از «مدرنیزاسیون» شاه، همان‌قدر خوابِ ناخودآگاهی‌ی ملت ایران- از جمله پیکارگران ما- را آشفته بود، که تحولات چریکی، خواب ناخودآگاهی‌ی ملت ایران و البته پادشاهِ ظاهراً «مدرن» آن را. چرا که این مجموعه، پدیده‌های عینی و ذهنی‌ی «مدرنیسم» را – که هیچ پروتوتایپِ درستی از آن‌ها در فاهمه‌ی خود ندارد- از دریچه‌ی آمیزه‌ای از بن‌مایه‌های «پیش‌مدرن» درک و معنی می‌کرد.

گروهی از پژوهشگران/ دانشمندان، با دست‌مایه‌ای از دانش‌های «ریاضی، فیزیک ذره‌ای، شیمی‌ی زیستی، عصب‌شناسی، جامعه‌شناسی، و روان‌شناسی»، پس از دهه‌ها آزمایش و تجربه، این تئوری را تأیید کرده‌اند که: تا تصویر پروتوتایپِ یک جسم، با نگاه‌های تکراری و در طول زمان، در مراکز بینائی‌ی مغز انسان تثبیت نشده باشد، آن جسم، در نخستین نگاه‌ها، به صورت توده‌ای ابری و بی‌شکل به دید می‌آید؛ چرا که در خلاء تجربی، ابعاد و خطوط هندسی‌ی آن جسم برای مغزِ مشاهده‌گر قابل شناسائی و تفکیک از یکدیگر نیستند. این تئوری، البته با فرایندهای بسیار پیچیده‌تر، از سوی همین دانشمندان و بسیاری از جامعه‌شناسان و دانشمندان علوم انسانی، به پدیده‌های ذهنی نیز اطلاق شده است.[۶۶۶] کما این که ردّ پای این فرایندهای ذهنی، در تک تک موارد شش‌گانه‌ی بالا، و در تعریفی که این دو سازمان از مفهوم‌های «آگاهی‌ی توده» «خلق زحمت‌کش» داشتند، قابل مشاهده است.

---

۶۶۶ به عنوان نمونه‌ای از این گونه پژوهش‌ها، به مأخذ زیر- که با شرکت ۱۴ دانشمند اجراء شده و روی کامپکت دیسک ضبط شده است- نگاه کنید:

❖ ***What the Bleep Do We (K)now!?***, 2004, 108 minutes.

در حالی که انبوهِ جوان‌های دانش‌آموخته و اهل مطالعه‌ی ما در این دو سازمان، دچار این کاستی‌ها بود، می‌توان موقعیت و فضای ذهنی‌ی گروه‌های چریکی‌ی کوچک‌تر و ناآزموده‌تر را در آن زمان مجسم کرد. به عنوان نمونه، یکی از پرشمار گروه‌های کوچک مارکسیستی‌ای که به مشی‌ی مبارزه‌ی مسلحانه رسیده بودند، «گروه فلسطین» بود، که در سال ۱۳۴۸ از سوی ساواک کاملاً سرکوب شد.[۶۶۷] «رفیق پولاد»، از گروه «چریک‌های فدائی‌ی خلق ایران» در تبعید، گوشه‌ای از فضای ذهنی/ عینی‌ی حاکم بر این سازمان کوچک را به شکل زیر ترسیم کرده است:

> یکی از مسئولین این گروه [فلسطین]، فردی بود به نام احمد صبوری، که به «احمد مائو» معروف شده بود. معروف بود که او ضمن رونویسی از آثار مائو، به جای کلمه‌ی «چین» کلمه‌ی «ایران» را می‌نوشته و ضمن برخی تغییرات لازم و البته قابل فهم، این به اصطلاح تحلیل‌های «زنده و عینی» را به نام خودش در اختیار رفقایش قرارمی‌داده! جدا از همه‌ی مسائلی که این روش‌های ناسالم و شناخته شده با خود دارد، اما این نمونه، خود از این واقعیت نیز پرده برمی‌دارد که به واقع در آن زمان خیلی از روشنفکران برای پیدا کردن راه مبارزه در ایران، مرجعی جز صرفاً متون مارکسیستی و مطالعه‌ی تئوریک نمی‌شناختند.[۶۶۸] (تأکید از «رفیق پولاد» است.)

منتها، «متون مارکسیستی»، فقط به نوشته‌های شخص «مارکس» منحصر نبود، و خوانش‌ها و برداشت‌های متعددِ مارکسیست‌های سرشناس جهان از پیشنهادهای نظری و عملی‌ی مارکس، حالا «مرجع»های متعددی پدید آورده بود. این سخن را نیز تکرار می‌کنم که پایه‌گذارانِ «سازمان چریک‌های فدائی‌ی خلق» و «سازمان مجاهدین خلق»، هر یک بر مبنای دریافتی که از «مرجع» انتخابی‌ی خود داشتند، برای تدوین متن‌های تئوریک و یافتن استراتژی‌ها و تاکتیک‌های مبارزه‌ای درخور با جامعه‌ی ایران، از خلاقیت‌های خود نیز مایه گذاشتند. همچنین، شخصیت‌هائی در هر دو سازمان بودند که پیرامون خوانشی از این یا آن «مرجع»، با مرکزیتِ سازمان خود به چون و چرا نیز پرداختند. اما این واقعیت‌ها، حضور تأثیرپذیری از «الگو»های رایج زمانه در ذهنیت نخبگان این سازمان‌ها را منتفی نمی‌کنند؛ و درست همین نقطه است که به زیرساختِ فرهنگِ «پیش‌مدرن» در ذهنیتِ نه تنها سازمان‌های چپ، نه تنها «خاص و عام» ملت ایران، بلکه محمدرضا شاه پهلوی و کل اپوزیسیون او، گواهی می‌دهد: تأثیرپذیری‌ی نیاندیشیده از منتقدان غربی (مانند هانری کربن و فرانس فانون و هایدگر)؛ تأثیرپذیری‌ی نیاندیشیده و حتا «نفهمیده» از تئوری‌های ثابت‌شده و نشده‌ی علمی،[۶۶۹] و ضدیت با علم و فن‌آوری توسط «نواندیشان دینی»ی ما؛ تأثیرپذیری‌ی نیاندیشیده از الگوهای پیشنهادی‌ی «نواندیشان دینی» توسط پیکارگران سیاسی‌ی ما؛ تأثیرپذیری‌ی نیاندیشیده، از «مارکسیسم»- که در همان زادگاهِ خود و در همان زمانه‌ی موسوم به «مدرنیته» ده‌ها شاخه شده بود- توسط پیکارگران سیاسی‌ی ما؛ تأثیرپذیری از پیشنهادهای تاکتیکی/ استراتژیکی‌ی رژی دبره و «موتور»های «کوچک و بزرگ»اش؛ تأثیرپذیری‌ی نیاندیشیده به پیامدها از عمل چریک‌هائی مانند فیدل کاسترو و ارنستو چه گوارا؛ تأثیرپذیری‌ی پادشاه ایران فقط از **مظاهر** «مدرنیسم»، که خود او با زیربنائی‌ترین **عنصر** آن (یعنی اندیشیدنی از آنِ خود) بیگانه بود.

---

۶۶۷ شکرالله پاک‌نژاد از بنیادگذاران گروه فلسطین، زندان شاه را تجربه کرد، در جریان انقلاب از زندان آزاد شد، اما در آذر ماه ۱۳۶۰ در زندان اوین تیرباران شد.

۶۶۸ رفیق پولاد، ***نکاتی درباره‌ی تاریخ سازمان چریک‌های فدائی‌ی خلق ایران***، نشریه‌ی « پیام فدائی»، ارگان چریک‌های فدائی‌ی خلق ایران، شماره‌ی۵۹، فروردین ۱۳۸۳ :

http://www.siahkal.com/history/ipfg-history-speech.htm

۶۶۹ کافی است که فقط به کتاب «انسان، اسلام و مکتب‌های مغرب زمین» نوشته‌ی علی شریعتی نگاه کنیم تا نمونه‌های بدفهمی، سطحی‌نگری، یا وارونه‌نمائی را ببینیم. به عنوان مثال، مفهوم «از خود بیگانگی»ی کارگر، که مارکس آن را در رابطه با محصول کارِ کارگر در نظام سرمایه‌داری تعریف می‌کند، در دستگاه نظری‌ی علی شریعتی به کاهش گرایش انسان به «معنویات و اخلاق سنتی و مذهب» معنی شده است. به بیانی دیگر، علی شریعتی دورشدن انسان از اخلاق سنتی را به معنای «از خود بیگانگی» می‌گیرد و آن را برآمده از علم و تکنولوژی برآورد می‌کند. یا تعریف و تشریحی که علی شریعتی، از «مادگرائی» بدست می‌دهد، هیچ شباهتی به تعریف علمی/ فلسفی‌ی این مفهوم ندارد.

منتها، تاریخ آینده‌ی آن سال‌های جهان نشان داد که نه تنها کارکردِ عناصر فرهنگ سنتی در خودآگاه و ناخودگاه ما، بلکه حضور عناصر پیش‌مدرن در خودِ «الگو»های ما، در شدنِ این فرایندها و فراورده‌های متوهمی که به بار آوردند دستی توانا داشت. در درجه‌ی نخست، «مدرنیسمِ» پیشنهادی‌ی پروژه‌ی روشنگری- زمانی که خبرش به ما رسید- در التقاطی از «اثبات‌گرائی‌ی منطقی» و «پروژه‌ی توسعه» و «مناسبات سرمایه» در همان زادگاه خود در نطفه خفه شده بود. من در جلد دوم مجموعه‌ی حاضر پیرامون این پدیده سخن گفته‌ام. اما همین جا یادآوری‌ی چند نکته را بایسته می‌دانم: در دو دهه‌ی گذشته، منتقدان بسیاری در تحلیل و شناختِ انگیزه‌های فرهنگی‌ی افول فکرت «مدرنیسم» در «مدرنیته» قلم زده‌اند. مثلا رژی دبره، در اوج خیزش کشورهای عربی- سال ۲۰۰۸- (که به «بهار عربی» معروف شد)، از پیامدهای عینی‌ی این خیزش‌ها، به زیرساختِ ذهنی‌ی کل ارزیابی‌های علمی در سده‌ی گذشته نقب (نقبی البته نیمه‌کاره) می‌زند، و «اشتباهِ» محاسبه را (البته، نیمه‌کاره) نشان دهد:

> در قاهره، تونس و دیگر حواشی‌ی مدیترانه، اولین نشانه‌های اسلام‌گرایی در میان دانشجویان دانشکده‌های فنی و عاقبت در دانشکده‌های علوم اتفاق افتاد. یعنی در قشرهائی از جامعه، که تجددگرا و بیش از همه در معرض جهان خارج بودند. اما مگر این جامعه‌شناسان ما نبودند که می‌گفتند هر آن چه مذهبی است، از خاک، از تاریخ، و از سنت نشأت گرفته است؟ مگر یک قرن پیش، مورخان ما، فیلسوفان ما، نمی‌گفتند که پیشرفت علم، صنعتی‌شدن و توسعه‌ی ارتباطات، بدون تردید، مذهب و ناسیونالیسم را برخواهد انداخت؟ چه‌گونه است که [اکنون] مباحث روزانه‌ی ما، همه بر سر «تضادها»ی میراث قرن نوزدهم (مقدس در برابر نامقدس، غیرعقلانی در مقابل عقلانی، «سنت‌گرایی» در برابر مدرنیته، ملی‌گرایی در مقابل جهانی‌شدن) دور می‌زند؟ ظاهراً ما [در همه چیز] اشتباه کردیم. معلوم شد این تصور تجددگرای ما از مدرنیته، چیزی بیش از «سنت‌گرائی»ی عصر صنعتی نبوده است. «نابهنگامی» و «سنت‌گرایی» در سیاست جهان مدرن جای خاصی دارند؛ چرا که «مدرن» جائی خاص در زمان را مشخص نمی‌کند؛ مقامی است که از آن بر تاثیرات و مقاصد (نه آن‌هائی که از مد افتاده‌اند، بلکه آن‌هایی که بنیادین‌اند؛ نه آن‌هائی که عتیقه شده‌اند، بلکه آن‌هائی که عمقی دارند؛ و نه آن‌هائی که با گذشته سپری شده‌اند، بلکه آن‌هائی که سرکوب شده‌اند)، ناظر است. تصادفی نیست که شمار بزرگی از رازهای فرهنگ معاصر تنها با پرتونگاری **جوامع ابتدایی** قابل درک‌اند. در این میان آشکار شد شرایطی که در فکر جامعه‌شناسی‌ی مدرن متضاد به نظر می‌آمد، در حقیقت با هم در ارتباط بود. هرگونه بی‌توازنی که در اثر پیشرفت صنعتی پدید آمد، از سوی جامعه، با حرکت اخلاقی‌ی تعادل‌بخشی مواجه شد که حاصل آن پریشانی میان همسان کردن جهان و تاکید بر تفاوت‌ها، آگاهی روشنفکرانه و احساسات ریشه‌دار، میان ضرورت‌های اقتصادی و بلندپروازی‌های معنوی شد. هنگامی که زادگاه انسان جائی مبهم شد، تهدید مرگ بزرگ‌تر به نظر می‌رسد. ما دیگر نمی‌دانیم «کجا هستیم»، چرا که دیگر نمی‌دانیم از کجا آمده‌ایم. آدم‌ها پی می‌برند که گم شده‌اند و به همین سبب **صف مؤمنان** طولانی‌تر می‌شود. رابطه‌ای درونی میان **ناپدید شدن نقاط آشنای ذهن و اوج‌گیری‌ی اسطوره‌ی «خاستگاه»** وجود دارد. صنعتی شدن امری ضد مذهبی است، چرا که سبب حرکت مردم از روستاها، دگرگونی امر اشتغال، مهاجرت، حضور کارگران خارجی، فزونی تحرک اجتماعی و در نتیجه از میان رفتن قوانین اخلاقی‌ی اجتماعات بسته می‌شود. اما درست به دلیل همین جابه‌جایی است که در ممالک صنعتی از طریق جنبش‌هایی که در پی‌ی «منطقه‌گرایی» یا «قوم‌گرایی» هستند، علاقه به «محلی»کردن آن خیال و آرزو به شدت دنبال می‌شود. تا آن جا که رهنمود «محیطزیستی»ی عصر ما «جهانی فکر کن، منطقه‌ای عمل کن!» است. در کشورهائی با زیربنای اقتصاد کشاورزی که «صنعتی‌شدن» بدان‌ها یورش برده، بازگشت به سرچشمه‌های هویت‌های فرضی‌ای با هیجان دنبال می‌شود که در اثر «یکسان‌سازی»ی صنعتی ویران شده‌اند. این موضوع، ایران شاهنشاهی و آزادشده به دست خمینی را به یاد می‌آورد. مدرنیزاسیون ساختار اقتصادی به جای آن که اسباب زوال افکار سنتی شود، به رشد آن‌ها

می‌انجامد. [...][۶۷۰] (قلاب‌ها را، من در رهگذر تطبیق متن انگلیسی با فارسی به این بازگفت افزوده‌ام؛ برخی از گیومه‌ها و پرانتزها در متن انگلیسی وجود دارند، و بسیاری را نیز مترجم فارسی- احتمالاً، برای کمک به درک متن- به آن افزوده است.)

حال مجسم کنیم موقعیتی را که این «اشتباه»، یا توهمِ شناخت‌شناسیِ روشنفکران و پیکارگران جهانی، (یعنی الگوهای ما)، با نگاه سنتی به زن، اطاعت‌خواهی، قدرت‌طلبی، و آکنده از ریشه‌های زنده و کارآمدِ کهن‌الگوهای سیاووشی/ حسینیِ ما همراه باشد. در انتهای تصویر این موقعیت است که هزاران جزنی و احمدزاده و حنیف‌نژادِ ما، یا در خاک خونین ایران خفته‌اند، یا با جوانیِ از دست‌رفته در زندان و زیر شکنجه، اکنون در اقصا نقاط دنیا سرگردان‌اند. اینان، البته، با میراندن مرگ، در گام نخستِ هدفِ نهائیِ خود پیروز شدند. منتها، به حکم دو حاکم بیرونی و درونی، «پیروزی» را به دسته‌ی «مذهبی/ سنتی» باختند. حاکم بیرونی، همانا خفقان و استبدادی بود که مطالعه‌ی آزاد و بحث و جست‌وجو و مبادله‌ی اندیشه را با زندان و شکنجه و مرگ پاسخ می‌داد؛ و حاکم درونی نیز همانا خمیرمایه‌ی معرفت‌شناختیِ مشترک در ذهنیتِ پایه‌گذارانِ «ایران نوین» بود: از پیشاهنگان جنبش مشروطیت- که «سلطنت را ودیعه‌ای الاهی» می‌دانستند- گرفته تا پادشاهان پهلوی- که این ودیعه‌ی الاهی را همان «شهریار الاهی» تعبیر کردند- تا پیکارگرانِ مذهبی و مارکسیست، که- به فرمان ذهنیتِ این «شهریاران» فرصت رشد نیافتند و با حمل زائده‌های زیان‌بارِ همان «شهریار الاهی»- با این دو «شهریار» جنگیدند.

اگر رویداد شومِ «کودتای ۲۸ مرداد ۱۳۳۲» و پیامدهای آن را نشانه‌هائی از کارکردِ همین ذهنیت در فاهمه‌ی محمدرضا شاه پهلوی بدانیم، و اگر در نظر داشته باشیم که مردم ایران و پیشاهنگان مبارزه هرگز فرآورده‌ی آن ذهنیت را بر شاه ایران نبخشیدند، آیا باید یا نباید بپذیریم که مردم ایران و پیشاهنگان مبارزه (آن‌ها که از همان دوران مانده‌اند و آن‌ها که در دنبال خواهند آمد)، همین ذهنیت در سپهر معرفت‌شناسیِ پیکارگران و پیشاهنگان مبارزه با شاه را- که در پیدایش پدیده‌ی شومِ «جمهوریِ اسلامی» دستی توانا داشت- نخواهند بخشید؟

البته، همین جا بایسته است این یادآوری را مکرر کنم که داوریِ بالا، به معنای نفیِ آرزوی ایرانی برای ساختن ایرانی بهتر و هوش و توان بالقوه‌ی او برای یادگیری و رشد نیست. کما این که تفاوت‌های مثبتِ چشمگیری که در مقایسه‌ی ایرانِ عصر مشروطیت با ایرانِ زمانِ انقلاب ۵۷ به دید می‌آیند، نشانه‌های عینیت‌یافتنِ آن آرزو، و نشانه‌های هوش و توانِ به فعل‌رسیده‌ی «شهریارانِ» پهلوی هستند؛ و تفاوت‌های مثبتِ چشمگیر در کردارها و گفتارهای پیکارگران ادبی و فرهنگی و سیاسیِ ما از آن انقلاب تا این انقلاب، نشانه‌ی هوش و توان به فعل‌رسیده‌ی آن‌ها. افزون بر این، درخششِ هزاران ایرانیِ مهاجر یا خودتبعیدی در قلمروهای مختلف علم و تکنولوژی و هنر در کشورهای میزبان (از ناسا گرفته تا هالیوود) - که در فضای دموکراتیک و انتقال آزادِ اطلاعات، از مرز «یادگیری» گذشته و به مرزهای کشف و خلاقیت و نوآوری هم رسیده- این ویژگی‌های ایرانی را تأیید می‌کند. در این جا سخن من بر سر عنصری در زیرین‌ترین لایه‌ی ناخودآگاهیِ جمعی است که بر بزنگاه‌های تحلیل‌ها و داوری‌های ما (از جمله داوری‌های من) سایه می‌اندازد. می‌دانم که با آوردن نمونه‌ی زیر از موضوع سخن پرت می‌شوم. اما برای حجت کلام ناگزیرم که از آن یاد کنم. پیشاپیش بگویم که این نمونه را از آن رو برگزیده‌ام که زبان در نوشته‌های نویسنده‌ی آن، پرهیخته، و به دور از اصطلاحات رایج در نظام

---

[۶۷۰] رژی دبره، ***دین و سیاست در عصر ما***، ترجمه‌ی کیوان مهجور، تارنمای «سکولاریسم نو»، اردی‌بهشت ۱۳۸۸/ آوریل ۲۰۰۹:
https://newsecul.ipower.com/2009/04/23.Thursday/042309-Regis-Debre-Religion-and-Politics.htm
برای اصل این مقاله به مأخذ زیر مراجعه کنید:

- Regis Debray, ***God and the Political Planet***, New Perspective Quarterly, vol. 25, No. 4, Fall 2008, pp.33-35; Abstract also available online, 13 Oct. 2008:

http://onlinelibrary.wiley.com/doi/10.1111/j.1540-5842.2008.01019.x/abstract

گفتاری‌ی بسیاری از منتقدانِ سیاسی‌ی ناسزاگو است: محمد امینی، ژورنالیست، تحلیل‌گر، و فعال سیاسی در تبعید، سی و چهار سال پس از انقلاب ۵۷، در انتقاد به سخنانِ شاهزاده رضا پهلوی[۶۷۱] متن مستدلی می‌نویسد؛ و در میانه‌ی آن می‌گوید:

> هرآینه شاه، هنگامی که از میزان بیماری‌ی خویش آگاهی یافته بود- که می‌دانیم سالیانی پیش از انقلاب است- پادشاهی را به سود پسرش رها می‌کرد، و به راستی داوطلبانه کناره می‌گرفت؛ و هرآینه، دولت‌مردان و آزادزنانِ رژیم پادشاهی، پیش از آن که کار به تنگناهای ماه‌های پایانی برسد، «صدای انقلاب» و نارضایتی مردم را از فساد و خودکامگی شنیده بودند، **عوام‌فریبانی** مانند آیت‌الله خمینی و دیگر رهبران انقلاب اسلامی نمی‌توانستند جامه از تن **مردم هشیار** بربایند. [...][۶۷۲]

محمد امینی در بخش شرط این جمله‌ی بلند، به واقعیتی انکارناپذیر اشاره کرده است. اما، از همنشینی‌ی واژگانِ «عوام‌فریب»، «جامه» و عبارتِ «مردم هشیار»- در بخش جزای این جمله- مفهومی بسیار تأمل‌برانگیز برآمده است. بخش جزای این جمله چنین متبادر می‌کند که «آیت‌الله خمینی و رهبران انقلاب اسلامی، با عوام‌فریبی، جامه از تن مردم هشیار ربودند». یا: « این عوام‌فریبان، اول عوام را فریب دادند، و این عوام بودند که جامه از تن مردم هشیار ربودند». در هر دو صورت- با توجه به واقعیت انکارناپذیرِ پذیرشِ انبوهانی، از «مردم هشیار» نسبت به آیت‌الله خمینی‌ی دوران انقلاب و رهنمودهای کمپ او- اصولاً ذات هشیاری‌ی «مردم هشیار» به زیر سئوال می‌رود. تأیید، یا شرکت در فریاد «الله اکبر» بر بام‌ها، تأییدِ شعار «استقلال، آزادی، جمهوری‌ی اسلامی»، صدها شعر و مقاله و بیانیه در ستایش آیت‌الله به عنوان «رهبر انقلاب» را چه‌گونه می‌توان با مفهوم «هشیاری» جمع‌بندی کرد؟ و این جاست که واژه‌ی «جامه» در این عبارت، جای پرسش دیگری را باز می‌کند: آیا هم‌صداشدن با عوام و شرکت‌کردن در رهنمودهائی که «فریب‌کاران» به «عوام» می‌دادند، همه «جامه»‌ای بود بر «تنِ هشیاران»، که قرار بود هدف واقعی‌ی آن‌ها را بپوشاند؟ در این صورت، آیا «فریب‌دهندگان» از «مردم هشیار» هشیارتر نبودند که «جامه» را دیدند و برای رسیدن به هدف خود آن را به دست «عوام» ربودند؟ آیا در این تقابل مفهومی، این واقعیت گویا نمی‌شود که «مردم هشیارِ» ما نه تنها در آن دوره، بلکه هم‌اکنون نیز، زیر بار سنگین کهن‌الگوهای فرهنگی چنان کمر خم کرده است که به خودفریبی دست می‌زند؟

اما آیا این «خودفریبی»‌ی اکنونی، خاص فرهنگ و ذهنیت ایرانی است، یا در رفتار و گفتار اندیشه‌ورزان فرهنگ‌های دیگر نیز رد پا دارد؟ همین جا، دوباره به رژی دبره- یکی از «الگو»های پیشاهنگان سیاسی‌مان- برمی‌گردم. رژی دبره- که کتاب «انقلاب در انقلاب» (۱۹۶۷) او در درازنای چند دهه، کتاب بالینی‌ی پیکارگران رادیکال جهان بود، با هدف پیاده کردن مارکسیسم (از نوع کوبائی‌ی آن) در بُلیوی، مدتی در کنار چه گوارا جنگید؛ چند ماه پیش از اعدام چه گوارا (۹ اکتبر ۱۹۶۷)، دستگیر شد و سی سال محکومیت زندان گرفت؛ با فشار کمپین‌های بین‌المللی و با حمایت شخصیت‌هائی مانند ژان پل سارتر، سیمون دبوار، شارل دوگل، و حتا پاپ (پل ششم)، پس از سه سال از زندان آزاد شد؛ پس از آزادی، فکر مبارزه‌ی مسلحانه را کنار گذاشت؛ و در زمان ریاست جمهوری‌ی فرانسوا میتران (سوسیالیست)، مشاور سیاسی‌ی او شد. به شهادت بازگفتی که پیش از این از او آوردم، او اکنون، در عین حال که به «اشتباهِ» خود (البته در قالب «ما») اعتراف می‌کند، و در عین حال که با کاربرد واژه‌ی «ما»، سرگشتگی را به نوع انسان کنونی تعمیم می‌دهد، به خاطر

---

۶۷۱ شاهزاده رضا پهلوی در گفت‌وگوی زیر، نه در مقام یک فعال سیاسی، بلکه در مقام «پادشاه ایران»، سخنانی ایراد کرد که انتقاد محافل سیاسی‌ی در تبعید را برانگیخت. به محتوای این «گفت‌وگو» به جای خود پرداخته‌ام. گفت‌وگوی رضا پهلوی با Andrea-Claudia Hoffmann با نام „werde, hängt vom Willen des Volkes ab Ob ich die Krone tragen" در تارنمای هفته‌نامه‌ی آلمانی‌ی «فوکوس آنلاین» در روز هفتم ژوئن ۲۰۱۲ منتشر شد. برگردان فارسی‌ی آن نیز در تارنمای «ایران در جهان»، که دربرگیرنده‌ی برگردان فارسی‌ی نوشتارهای آلمانی است، در تاریخ ۱۰ ژوئن ۲۰۱۲ منتشر شد.

۶۷۲ محمد امینی، ***آرزوهای محمدعلی شاهی***، تارنمای «اخبار روز»، ۳ تیر ۱۳۹۱/ ۲۳ ژوئن ۲۰۱۲:
http://www.akhbar-rooz.com/article.jsp?essayId=46304

طولانی شدن «صف مؤمنان»، و به خاطر خیزش بینش‌های «اسطوره‌ای» در زمان حال، «جوامع ابتدائی» را نشانه می‌گیرد، و به گونه‌ای متبادر می‌کند که این جوامع، ظرفیت «صنعتی‌شدن» ندارند. رژی دبره‌ی اکنونی، در اوج خودفریبی، رشدِ روزافزونِ اسلام‌گرائی، پوشش اسلامی، و ساختن مسجد و مدرسه‌ی اسلامی از سوی شهروندان کشورهای اروپائی، از جمله کشور خودش (لابد «غیرابتدائی») را نمی‌بیند. رژی دبره‌ی اکنونی در بازگفت بالا، به این نکته توجه ندارد، یا توجه نمی‌کند که «ناپدیدشدنِ نقاط آشنای ذهن» و ناپدیدشدن «اسطوره‌ی خاستگاه» و خشکیدن «سرچشمه‌های هویت‌های فرضی» در فاهمه‌ی انسان- از جمله خودش و ماننده‌های خودش و اروپای خودش- زمان می‌خواست؛ و مناسبات قدرت (سرمایه) بود که «زمان» را از نهادینه‌شدنِ فکرت مدرنیسم در جهان گرفت؛ آرزوهای عصر روشنگری را خاموش کرد؛ با پروژه‌های «توسعه» و «سرعت در پیشرفت»، و به ضرب «اثبات‌گرائی‌ی منطقی»، پدیده‌ی خودخواسته‌ای به نام «مدرنیته» آفرید؛ از قانونِ «جهان‌شمولی‌ی انسان»، به «اندازه‌گیری‌ی مغز انسان»ها رسید؛ در جنگ‌های اول و دوم جهانی میلیون‌ها انسان را میراند، سوزاند، یا آواره کرد؛ تا از مرحله‌های «استعمار» و «امپریالیسم» عبور کند و قانون «مدرنیزاسیون ساختار اقتصادی» را به سود خود بنویسد؛ و به ضرب آن، بر زندگی‌ی تمام «جوامع» انسانی محاط شود. در حالی که اگر پروژه‌ی روشنگری و فکرت بنیادی‌ی مدرنیسم- بدون مانع عظیمِ یادشده و «ایسم»های رنگارنگی که در کنار این «مانع»، یا در تقابلی کم‌رنگ با آن، روئید- به راه خود می‌رفت، «نقاط آشنای ذهن» و «سرچشمه‌ی هویت‌های فرضی» در تمام جوامع- از زادگاه مدرنیسم گرفته تا «جوامع ابتدائی»- دیر یا زود «ناپدید» می‌شد. از این گذشته، رژی دبره‌ی کنونی، «یکسان‌سازی‌ی صنعتی» را، نه به عنوان زائده و ضایعه‌ای ناشی از همین «مدرنیزاسیونِ ساختار اقتصادی»، بلکه به عنوان پدیده‌ای مستقل (که «بازگشت به سرچشمه‌های هویت‌های فرضی» در ایران، یا حالا در تونس و مصر و ... را سبب شد) برانداز می‌کند. در حالی که اگر پروژه‌ی روشنگری و فکرت پیشنهادی آن، مجال رشد و اشاعه در جهان را می‌یافت، یعنی، اگر مردم جهان- در هر کشور و فرهنگ و تمدن- فرصت ارتقاء به مرحله‌ی «خوداندیشی» را می‌یافتند، بدون حضور «یکسان‌سازان»، و بدون آویختنِ خونبار به هیچ ایسمِ «نجات‌دهنده»ای، قادر بودند که مراحل دستیابی به «صنعت» را نیز به عنوان حق خود، و بنا بر مصالح و نیازهای خود، خود برگزینند، و آن را با سرمایه‌های مادی و فرهنگی‌ی خود به پیش بَرند؛ گیرم که در این جا و آن جای جهان دیر و زود داشت، اما سوخت و سوز نداشت. همین جا- و به عنوان معترضه- بگویم که رژی دبره‌ی کنونی- به درستی- دیگر از «امپریالیسم» سخن نمی‌گوید. چرا که در سایه‌ی کارکردهای تز «جهانی‌سازی»، واژه‌ی «امپریالیسم» ساختار و مناسبات جهان سرمایه‌داری‌ی کنونی را توضیح نمی‌دهد؛ این ترکیب و مناسبتش اکنون، همانی است که رژی دبره آن را با زیرکی، «مدرنیزاسیون ساختار اقتصادی» می‌نامد.

***

اما برگردم به گذشته و به رهگذرِ آن چه که شد: جنبش مسلحانه- با همان اندیشه‌ای که پیش رفت و با همان کیفیتی که داشت- و نمودهای آن در کوچه و خیابان‌های ایران، و خبر کشتار و شکنجه‌ی پیکارگران در زندان‌های ایران، هر دو «مطلقِ» پیشنهادی‌ی امیرپرویز پویان را هم تأیید کرد و هم شکست: یعنی، هم اعتراض‌های سرکوب‌شده را از دل و جان و اندیشه‌ی بسیاری از مردم ناراضی‌ی ایران بیرون کشید، و هم پیکر آسیب‌پذیر رژیم شاه را لرزاند. (و البته، کلان‌نهادهای سیاسی/ اقتصادی را نسبت به توانائی‌ی شاه در حفظ منافع آن‌ها دچار تردید کرد.) با برایند این نیروها بود که اختناق روزافزونِ سیاسی، تبلیغات گسترده، کوشش دستگاه عریض و طویل ساواک، اعدام‌ها و شکنجه‌ها نیز نتوانست جوشش مداوم و مؤثر پیکارگران را خاموش کند؛ امروز ساواک به تیمی از آنان دست می‌یافت و آن را یکسره نابود می‌کرد، فردا بود که جوجه‌ققنوس‌ها در این جا و آن جای ایران از خاکستر آنان برمی‌خاستند. همین جا بود که جامعه‌ی روحانیت و بازار خود را در مبارزه عقب‌تر دید. آیت‌الله خمینی از تبعیدگاه

خود (عراق) به کوشندگان روحانی در ایران پیام فرستاد: «**از این جوانان یاد بگیرید**»؛ و تاریخ نشان داد که اپوزیسیون روحانی/ بازاری، که حالا موقعیت را مناسب می‌دید، از همین «جوانان» یاد گرفت.

آیت‌الله خمینی، البته از شأنِ محوریت خود به دور می‌دانست که رهنمودهای «جوانان» را به کلام بپذیرد. اما تاریخ نشان می‌دهد که خود، از آن‌ها «یاد» گرفت، و به پیروانش هم آموخت. تراب حق‌شناس (از اعضاء اولیه‌ی سازمان مجاهدین خلق، و سپس عضو سازمان «پیکار») در مصاحبه‌ای که روز ۲۱ مهر ۱۳۵۹ در نشریه‌ی «پیکار»، ارگانِ «سازمان پیکار در راه رهائی‌ی طبقه‌ی کارگر»، منتشر شد، می‌گوید:

> یک بار پس از خرداد ۱۳۴۲ با تعداد قابل توجهی از دانشجویان انجمن اسلامی یک راهپیمایی در قم ترتیب دادیم و به منزل آیت الله خمینی، که تازه از زندان چند ماهه آزاد شده بود، رفتیم. در آن جا طی یک سخنرانی و نشست، نظرات همفکران‌مان را برای آیت‌الله گفتیم. در آن زمان با وجود آن که اندیشه‌ی مبارزاتی‌ی ما شکل ابتدایی‌ی خود را می‌گذراند و از حدود طبقاتی و ایدئولوژیک خود البته نمی‌توانست فراتر برود، روی این مسائل تأکید می‌ورزیدیم؛ مسائلی که نشان‌دهنده‌ی نوع برخورد و سمت‌گیری‌ی فکری و مبارزاتی‌ی ما در آن سال‌هاست: ۱- لبه‌ی تیز حمله باید متوجه امریکا و اسرائیل و عمال آن‌ها در ایران باشد و مسائل جزئی، نظیر انجمن‌های ایالتی و ولایتی قابل طرح نیستند. ۲- «روحانیت مبارز» و «جنبش اسلامی» باید از حالت خودبه‌خودی بیرون بیاید و ضروری است که تشکیلات داشته باشد. ۳- در برابر «دشمنان مردم» باید برخوردی انقلابی داشت نه اصلاح طلبانه. [...] ۴- ایدئولوژی و برنامه‌ی اسلامی، به خصوص در زمینه‌های اقتصادی و اجتماعی مدون نشده است. و در این باره ما از آیت‌الله چاره‌جوئی می‌کردیم. ما پس از ذکر تلاشی که خودمان به کمک کسانی امثال آیت‌الله طالقانی، علی گلزاده غفوری و مطهری انجام داده بودیم، به آیت‌الله گفتیم که برنامه‌ی «جوانان مسلمان» در مقایسه با برنامه‌های سایر مکاتب فکری (به تعبیر آن روزمان) دارای نقص فراوان است؛ و آیت‌الله در جواب ما گفت که «نه، اصلاً چنین نیست، اسلام برای همه چیز برنامه دارد.»[۶۷۳] (پرانتز و گیومه‌ها در متن اصلی هستند.)

و البته، این مربوط به سال‌های دور از انقلاب ۵۷ است، که هر چه به آن نزدیک‌تر شدیم، الگوهای مبارزاتی‌ی بیش‌تری از «جوانانِ» پیکارگر در اختیار آیت‌الله خمینی قرار گرفت. کما این که آیت‌الله، در تمام دوران زندگی‌ی خود تا میانه‌های سال ۵۷، با نظام پادشاهی مشکلی ابراز نمی‌کرد، و حتا پس از تبعید، تنها به دلیل «نقض قانون اساسی»‌ی مشروطه در کاهش اختیارات روحانیت، و کوتاه کردن دست این لایه‌ی اجتماعی از کانون‌های قدرت، با شاه مخالفت می‌کرد. کما این که موافقت او با «دولت» و «حکومت» در چند جای کتاب «کشف‌الاسرار» تأکید شده است؛ و مشکلِ او «سلب نفوذ روحانیت» است، و توصیه می‌کند که روحانیت و دولت باید «پشتیبان» یکدیگر باشند.[۶۷۴] سیداحمد خمینی، فرزند آیت‌الله خمینی نیز، بعد از انقلاب ۵۷ گفت.

---

[۶۷۳] آیت‌الله خمینی، پس از آن که راه را از «جوانان» آموخت، و پس از آن که بر دوش آن‌ها پا گذاشت و بر مرکب قدرت سوار شد، و پس از این که مجاهدین و مجاهدین مارکسیست لنینیست، همگام با برخی دیگر از سازمان‌های سیاسی، با اصل ولایت فقیه و با دیگر سیاست‌های او به مخالفت برخاستند، مجاهدین خلق را «منافق»، «بدتر از کفار»، «دروغگو»، «فریبکار»، «غارتگر»، «خرمن‌سوز»، «عامل امریکا»، و «دزد» نامید، و گفت: «اگر یک دزدی را کشتند و از طایفه‌ی شما بود، آن وقت شما می‌شوید انقلابی؟» (مندرج در روزنامه‌های ۵ تیر ۱۳۵۹). تراب حق‌شناس (قبلاً مجاهد، و سپس مجاهد مارکسیست لنینیست و از سازمان «پیکار»)، ضمن حمله‌ی دلاورانه به سخنان آیت‌الله و اعوان و انصارش در ده شماره‌ی نشریه‌ی «پیکار» ارگان «سازمان پیکار در راه طبقه‌ی کارگر»، این خاطره را در شماره‌ی ۷۶، ۲۱ مهر ۱۳۵۹ همین نشریه بیان کرد. به مأخذ زیر، که بازچاپ همان شماره‌های نشریه‌ی «پیکار» است، نگاه کنید:

- ***مصاحبه با روحانی و حق‌شناس: تماس با خمینی در نجف***، تارنمای «پیکار اندیشه»، ۱۰ آبان ۱۳۹۰/ ۲۳ اکتبر ۲۰۱۱:
http://peykarandeesh.org/articles/642-pepykarkhomeini.html?showall=1

[۶۷۴] روح‌الله موسوی خمینی، ***کشف‌الاسرار***، ۱۳۲۳، صص ۱۸۶، ۱۸۷، ۲۰۵، ۲۰۸.

> اکثریت عظیم روحانیون تا اواسط دهه‌ی ۵۰ به سیاست کاری نداشتند، نه مخالف شاه و نه علناً حامی‌ی او بودند؛ اما مآلاً به جنبش انقلابی پیوستند؛ بیش‌تر به آن سبب که رژیم نتوانسته بود جلو انحطاط اخلاقی را بگیرد و خیابان‌ها را از لوث وجود مفاسد قبیح اجتماعی پاک کند.[۶۷۵]

تاریخ نشان می‌دهد که «پاک کردن خیابان‌ها از لوث وجود مفاسد قبیح اجتماعی»، تنها انگیزه‌ی «روحانیت» در ورود به مبارزه نبود؛ بلکه، همان گونه که آیت‌الله خمینی در کشف‌الاسرار (ص ۱۸۶) گفته بود، «تا نظام بهتری نشود تأسیس کرد»، «مجتهدین»، همین نظام را «محترم می‌شمارند و لغو نمی‌کنند.» و بعد، همان گونه که خودش در آستانه‌ی ۱۵ خرداد ۴۲ به شاه پیام داده بود، در تمام راه پنجاه ساله، در «کمینِ تأسیس نظام بهتر» و بدست آوردن قدرت مطلق، منتظر پیکارگرانی «ایستاده» بود، که راه را برای او هموار کنند. البته رضا شاه پهلوی «کمینِ مجتهدین» را دیده بود و جدی گرفته بود. اما ذهنیت متوهم و خودبین محمدرضا شاه پهلوی یا آن را دید و جدی نگرفت؛ یا اصلاً ندید؛ یا دید و کوشید که با انواع و اقسام رشوه آنان را با خود همراه کند. در آبر این ذهنیت بود که شاه ایران، از کوشندگان روحانی نگرانی‌ی چندانی نداشت؛[۶۷۶] البته، از خرداد ۴۲ به بعد، افزون بر آن چه که در مواد «انقلاب سفید» گنجانده بود، پروژه‌هائی- مانند اجباری کردن خدمت نظام وظیفه برای طلاب- را در محدود کردن اختیارات و قدرت این جامعه به اجرا گذاشت؛ برخی از شخصیت‌های این لایه‌ی اجتماعی زندانی هم می‌شدند؛ منتها، حتا یک تن از خرد یا کلان آن‌ها - به جز نواب صفوی- اعدام نشد. (تازه، با پادرمیانی‌ی غیرمستقیم «حجت‌الاسلام خمینی» و سفارش آیت‌الله بروجردی، نواب صفوی را بدون لباس روحانیت اعدام کردند، تا «عمامه» اعدام نشود.)[۶۷۷] شاه، حتا روحانیان زندانی را گاه به گاه در همان زندان به «کبابِ» ساواک دعوت می‌کرد، تا ضمن «صرف نهار» با سرشکنجه‌گران و بازجویان، علیه کمونیست‌های برون و درون زندان توطئه کنند؛ و البته «روحانیانِ زندانی» هم، با شکنجه‌گرانی چون «عضدی» هم‌نشین می‌شدند و به قول آیت‌الله منتظری (یکی از همان روحانیانِ زندانی)، غذای «چرب‌تر» را نوش جان می‌کردند.[۶۷۸] در میان اسناد منتشرشده‌ی ساواک، اسناد فراوانی به چشم می‌خورند، که نه از ترس یا مدارای سیاستمدارانه، بلکه از اعتقاد مذهبی‌ی سران ساواک و دولتمردان کشور (که طبیعتاً از اعتقاد مذهبی‌ی شاه، یا دست کم از سیاست‌های جانبدارانه‌ی او نسبت به «طبقه‌ی روحانی»، پیروی می‌کردند)، حکایت می‌کنند. به عنوان نمونه، یکی از این گونه سندهای ساواک را در این جا ثبت می‌کنم:

> گزارش: به طوری که مجله‌ی تهران مصور مورخه‌ی ۲۸ مهر [۱۳۴۰] در صفحه‌ی پنجم خود نقل کرده است، شعبه‌ی ۹ دادگاه جنحه‌ی مرکز، به ریاست آقای دکتر ناصر وثوقی، کلیه‌ی نشریات و کتاب‌های مرحوم کسروی را برای پخش و فروش، آزاد اعلام داشته و دادگاه نظر داده است که کتاب‌های کسروی علیه اسلام نیست. با توجه به این که دکتر ناصر وثوقی، رئیس محکمه‌ی مزبور، یکی از سوسیالیست‌های پر و پا قرص می‌باشد، و مدتی نیز در حزب منحله‌ی توده عضویت داشته، و اصولاً چون سوسیالیست‌ها پای‌بند مذهب و خداپرستی نیستند، ارجاع این پرونده به دادگاه مزبور اشتباه

---

۶۷۵ یرواند آبراهامیان، ***ایران بین دو انقلاب: از مشروطه تا انقلاب اسلامی***، ترجمه به فارسی از: کاظم فیروزمند، حسن شمس‌آوری، محسن مدیر شانه‌چی ، چاپ هشتم، ۱۳۸۳، ص ۴۳۶.

۶۷۶ مهدی بازرگان در این زمینه به گونه‌ی دیگری شهادت داده است؛ اما کشتارگسترده‌ی کمونیست‌ها توسط ساواک، شهادت او را نقض می‌کند. بازرگان می‌نویسد: «ساواک و سیاست‌های استیلاگر حامی‌ی شاه متوجه شده بودند که خطر این دسته از مخالفین، یعنی ملیّون مسلمان و روشنفکران مذهبی که پایه‌ی اعتقادی و پایگاه مردمی‌ی دینی در جامعه دارند، به مراتب بیش‌تر از چپی‌های کمونیست و احزاب سیاسی غیردینی است.» به بخش مقدمه‌ی مأخذ زیر نگاه کنید:

- جعفر سعیدی، ***شخصیت و اندیشه‌ی دکتر علی شریعتی***، تهران: انتشارات چاپخش، ۱۳۷۲.

۶۷۷ به نقل از تراب حق‌شناس در مأخذ زیر:

- ***مصاحبه با روحانی و حق‌شناس: تماس با خمینی در نجف***، پیشین.

۶۷۸ ***خاطرات آیت‌الله حسینعلی منتظری، به انضمام کلیه‌ی پیوست‌ها***، لس‌انجلس: انتشارات شرکت کتاب، ۱۳۷۹/ ۲۰۰۱، ص ۲۱۶.

> بوده است. ضمناً با حکمی که دادگاه صادر کرده، دیگر جلوگیری از انتشار کتاب‌های کسروی- که اکثر آن‌ها مخالف دین اسلام و رَدّ مهدویت و شیعه‌گری است (مانند کتاب‌های شیعی‌گری، بخوانند و داوری کنند)، مقدور نبوده و البته بر اثر انتشار این کتاب‌ها عصبانیت طبقه‌ی روحانی برانگیخته خواهد شد. همچنین به عرض می‌رساند که اربابزاده، مدیر انتشارات کسروی، چندی پیش تعهد سپرده است که از انتشار کتاب‌های کسروی خودداری نماید. اکنون، با صدور حکم دادگاه، این تعهد خود به خود ملغا می‌شود.[۶۷۹]

در حاشیه‌ی این سندِ تایپ‌شده بر سر برگِ «نخست وزیری: سازمان اطلاعات و امنیت کشور»- که در مأخذ من عیناً کلیشه شده- با دست نوشته شده است:

> به عرض جناب آقای نخست وزیر رسید؛ با آقای وزیر دادگستری مذاکره فرمودند؛ قرار شد پرونده‌ی وثوقی به دادگاه انتظامی‌ی قضات داده شود؛ به پرونده‌ی کسروی استیناف دهند و در آن جا حکم لغو شود. کتاب‌ها را اجازه ندهید آزاد کنند و تجدید چاپ نمایند و فعالیت کنند. ۳۰/ ۷/ ۴۰. بایگانی شود. برابر امر تیمسار قائم مقام رفتار گردید. در پرونده‌ی چاپاک و اربابزاده بایگانی گردد. ۳۰/ ۷/ ۴۰ بایگانی. (مأخذ پیشین. علامت‌های سجاوندی از من است.)

وحشت و تنفر شاه (و دستگاهش) نسبت به گسترش هر سوژه‌ی پرسش‌برانگیز و آگاهی‌دهنده، و نسبت به هر مطالبه‌ای که سر نخش به عدالت اجتماعی می‌رسید، به میزانی بالا بود که نه تنها پیکارگران آشتی‌ناپذیرِ چپ، بلکه همه‌ی منتقدان دموکرات/ سکولار خود را نیز با عنوان «توده‌ای» و «مارکسیست» و «بی‌وطن» شناسائی می‌کرد. (گزارش‌ها نشان می‌دهند که شاه، حتا در واپسین روزهای سلطنت خود، یعنی زمانی که انقلاب مردم ایران به نام «اسلامی» شناسائی شده بود و آیت‌الله، بنا به موقعیت، از «کمین»گاه خود بیرون جسته بود، باز، از «کمونیست‌ها» بیش‌تر می‌ترسید تا از «روحانیون».)

***

شاه، در همان حال که پیر و جوان منتقد و معترض را با شکنجه و توابسازی و اعدام پَر پَر می‌کرد، در همان حال که هزاران استعداد درخشان برای رشد فرهنگی و برای نوسازی‌ی ایران را از ایران می‌راند، از یک سو، رسیدن به «تمدن بزرگ» را به ایرانیان وعده می‌داد، و از سوی دیگر، با تأسیس «حزب رستاخیز ملی» (۱۱ اسفند ۱۳۵۳)، عقب‌مانده‌ترین ساختار سیاسی/ مدنی، یعنی سیستم تک‌حزبی را به ایرانیان تحمیل کرد، و گفت: هر کس در این حزب عضو نشود، یا باید از ایران برود، یا جایش در زندان است. از همین جمله پیداست که او تعداد مخالفان خود را اندک می‌پنداشت. و اصلاً به روی خود نمی‌آورد که جوجه‌ققنوس‌ها در این جا و آن جای خاک سوخته‌ی ایران، علیه او، از خاکستر یکدیگر برمی‌خیزند؛ یا، دانشجویان کنفدراسیون در این کشور و آن کشورِ اروپائی پی در پی به سفارت‌خانه‌های «کشور شاهنشاهی» حمله می‌کنند، و خبرهایش از رسانه‌های خارجی تا گوش مردم ایران نیز می‌رسد. با این توهم بود که او انبوه مخالفانِ غیرسازمانی و پیکارگران سازمانی را «تعدادی خرابکار» و «اقلیتی ناچیز» برآورد می‌کرد، و طبیعتاً باور نداشت که در میان ملت خود پایگاه استواری ندارد. چرا که از دیدن تصویر بزرگ ناتوان بود؛ نمی‌دید: در حالی که بسیارانی از مردم معمولی در «جشن‌ها»ی سالانه‌ی چهارم آبان- سالروز تولد او، و سپس، نهم آبان به مناسبت سالروز تولد پسرش- به اجبار و از روی ترس شرکت می‌کنند؛ یا وقتی که خون دانشجویان ساحت دانشگاه‌های ایران را فرش می‌کند؛ یا زمانی که امیران ارتش و شخصیت‌های مهم دولتی، در هر ملاقات رسمی باید تا کمر در برابر او خم شوند و

---

۶۷۹ مرکز بررسی‌ی اسناد تاریخی، ***مطبوعات عصر پهلوی به روایت اسناد ساواک، کتاب اول: مجله‌ی تهران مصور***، تهران: انتشارات مرکز بررسی‌ی اسناد تاریخی‌ی وزارت اطلاعات، ۱۳۷۹، ص ۲۶.

دست او را ببوسند؛ یا وقتی مردم ایران پیش از تماشای یک فیلم در سینما باید تا پایان پخش «سرود شاهنشاهی» در برابر تصویر او بایستند؛ یا زمانی که در نمایشِ «جشن‌های دو هزار و پانصد سال شاهنشاهی»، دو اسب‌سوار، از مجلس شورای ملی‌ی فرمایشی تا تخت جمشیدِ شیراز را با اسب می‌پیمایند تا «نامه‌ای از سوی ملت» را در تأیید شاه و دستگاهش، به شاه و سرانِ ۶۹ کشور جهان برسانند؛ یا وقتی که فرش‌های دست‌بافت کارگران محروم ایران را به سرانِ این یا آن کشور هدیه می‌دهد، وقتی که شهبانویش دسترنج دختران محروم بلوچ را جلو دوربین رسانه‌ها می‌پوشد؛ زمانی که روزنامه‌های رسمی‌ی کشور مرتب از اعدام جوان‌های ایران خبر می‌دهند؛ یا زمانی که خبر شکنجه در زندان‌ها، جسته و گریخته، دهان به دهان می‌گردد؛ بهمنی از جنس خشم و نفرت و کینه نسبت به او را در سپهر همگانی‌ی ایران روان می‌کند، که هیچ تناسبی با «اقلیت ناچیز» ندارد. البته بخشی از سبب‌های این توهم- غیر از گزارش‌های سراسر دروغی که (به شهادت خاطرات سیاسی‌ی منتشرشده) کارگزانش به او می‌دادند و غیر از لبخند «دوستانه»‌ای که دولتمردان امریکا به او نشان می‌دادند و غیر از «دکترای افتخاری»‌ای که دانشگاه‌های امریکا به او اهدا می‌کردند (سه دانشگاه، در سال ۱۳۴۴)- تا میزان زیادی در همان «انقلاب سفید» نهفته بود. شاه، بارها در مصاحبه‌ها و سخنرانی‌های خود می‌بالید که به زنان ایران حق رأی و قضاوت داده است؛ به دورافتاده‌ترین روستاهای ایران «سپاه دانش و سپاه بهداشت» فرستاده است؛ با اصلاحات ارضی، رژیم ارباب و رعیتی را برچیده است و انبوهی از کشاورزان ایران را صاحب زمین کرده است؛ با هدف بی‌نیاز کردن ایران از مشاوران و کارشناسان خارجی، رشته‌ی «حرفه و فن» را در دبیرستان‌ها مقرر داشته است؛ آموزشگاه‌ها و هنرستان‌های حرفه‌ای تأسیس کرده است؛ برای تربیت کارشناس و کادرهای حرفه‌ای، گروه گروه دانشجویان را با هزینه‌ی دولت به خارج می‌فرستد؛ ایران، رو به «صنعتی شدن» می‌رود، و در آستانه‌ی «تمدن بزرگ» قرار دارد؛ وضع اقتصادی‌ی مردم «به نسبت دهه‌ی پیش بهتر است»، و «حتا یک کارگر می‌تواند روزی یک مرغ سر سفره‌ی خانواده‌اش بگذارد.» (نقل از حافظه) البته هیچ یک از این ادعاها هم دروغ نبود. در اوج گرانی‌ی قیمت نفت در سطح جهانی، بهره‌ای از درآمد هنگفت نفت، به سازندگی، کارآفرینی، آموزش، بهداشت، بیمه، و سفره‌ی مردم ایران هم می‌رسید؛ و حتا طبقه‌ی متوسط شهری را- که از میانه‌های دهه‌ی چهل خورشیدی رشدی روزافزون داشت- برای تعطیلات نوروز به اروپا هم می‌فرستاد؛ آخرین مدهای اروپائی را به بوتیک‌های تهران می‌رساند؛ دختران فلیپینی را در خانه‌ی به دوران‌رسیده‌ها به خدمتکاری هم استخدام می‌کرد؛ برای تأسیس مدرسه‌های عالی‌ی صنعتی، مانند «دانشگاه صنعتی‌ی آریامهر»، و مدرسه‌ها و کارگاه‌های فنی و هنری، یا وارد کردن ابزار تکنولوژی‌ی آموزشی و کاربردی، بودجه‌های سنگینی صرف می‌شد، و بخشی از این بودجه‌ها که از لُفت و لیس مجریان باقی می‌ماند، چهره‌ی ایران را به نفع «توسعه و پیشرفت» دگرگون کرده بود. همچنین، پروژه‌ی اصلاحات ارضی- اگر از فساد سلسه‌مراتبی در امان می‌ماند- قابلیت داشت که به رونق کشاورزی‌ی ایران بیافزاید. اما ناآگاهی‌ی شاه در این بود که نمی‌دید هیچ یک از این‌ها، دردهای مزمنِ خفقان سیاسی، نادیده گرفتن حق مردم در تعیین سرنوشت خود، وابستگی‌ی او و اقتصاد ایران به امریکا، شکاف فزاینده‌ی طبقاتی، به ویژه شکاف فزاینده‌ی فرهنگی، هجوم بی‌رویه‌ی روستائیان به شهرها را درمان نمی‌کند. محمد رضا شاه پهلوی که در برج عاج توهم خود نشسته بود، رشد فزاینده‌ی «حلبی‌آباد»ها و زاغه‌نشین‌های حاشیه‌ی شهرهای بزرگ را در کنار ساختمان‌های بلند و مجلل- به ویژه در تهران- نمی‌دید؛ یا می‌دید، اما بنا بر بینش اقتصادی‌ی خود، آن را «طبیعی» می‌پنداشت؛ نمی‌دید که کل اصلاحات او- به قول یرواند آبراهامیان- بارآور «توسعه‌ی ناموزون» است؛ نمی‌دید وقتی در اثر فساد در سطوح بالای اداری، بسیاری از روستاهای دورافتاده‌ی ایران، نه تنها از ساختمانی به نام «مدرسه»، بلکه از امکاناتی مانند آب آشامیدنی و برق و سوخت کافی- محروم هستند، و برخی از این «سپاهیان دانش» کلاس درس خود را در بیابان‌ها یا ساختمان‌های ویرانه تشکیل می‌دهند، وعده‌ی «تمدن بزرگ»، توهینی بزرگ به شعور مردم است؛ نمی‌دید وقتی در یک مصاحبه، به ایران و جهان اعلام می‌کند که: «هوشمندی و درایت در زن امری استثنائی است»، نه تنها «حق رأی»، «حق قضاوت»، «حق طلاق و حضانت فرزند» (در «قانون حمایت از خانواده») را از زن ایرانی پس گرفته است؛ نه تنها، کرامت انسانی‌ی زن را به هیچ گرفته است، بلکه، درست در آستانه‌ی «تمدن بزرگ»اش، با سوره‌ی

«نساء» قرآن بیعتی مجدد کرده است؛ نمی دید وقتی کشاورزان، به سبب نداشتن ابزار تولید، زمین‌های «اهدائی» یا خریداری‌کرده از بانک کشاورزی را به ثمن بخس به مالکان و سرمایه‌داران کلان می‌فروشند و با دست خالی در شهرهای ایران سرگردان می‌شوند، از سوئی، زرق و برق‌های شهر همان هوش و اتکاء به نفس روستائی را از سرشان می‌پراند، از سوی دیگر، به اعاده‌ی نان و عزت‌نفسِ از دست‌رفته‌ی خود می‌اندیشند، و از سوی سوم، به مثابه انسان‌هائی بی‌چهره، به آسانی به هر سمت و سو گرایش می‌یابند؛ نمی‌دید که وقتی زنِ «باحجاب» یا تیپ‌های سنتی را در اداره‌های دولتی و نهادهای وابسته به آن تحقیر می‌کنند، و امکان اجرای طرح «بی‌حجابی‌ی اجباری» از سوی خواهرش، شاهزاده اشرف پهلوی، بر سر زبان‌هاست؛ وقتی واردات یا صادرات بسیاری از اقلام تجاری در انحصار خانواده‌ی دربار است و اجناس وارادتی‌ی دولت در گمرک‌ها می‌پوسد؛ وقتی بی‌مسئولیتی‌های اقتصادی و فسادِ مالی در خاندان خودش و دستگاه‌های دولتی و نخبگان حکومتی به صورت سلسله‌مراتبی با پائین هرم هم می‌رسد؛[۶۸۰] وقتی که شهردار تهران و سناتور انتصابی‌ی او (غلامرضا نیک پی) با چمدانی پر از ارز و پول و چکِ قاچاق، قصد خروج از ایران را دارد و رسانه‌های داخلی و خارجی از این دزدی‌ی آشکار پرده برمی‌دارند؛ زمانی که ۴۵۰ میلیون دلار از بودجه‌ی کشور (که برای خرید وسائل تکنولوژیک در اختیار دکتر شیخ‌الاسلامی، وزیر بهداری‌ی وقت بود) ناپدید می‌شود، و خبرش به رسانه‌ها درز می‌کند؛ وقتی که حتا از «تغذیه‌ی رایگان»ی که او برای کودکستان‌ها، دبستان‌ها، و دبیرستان‌ها مقرر کرده بود و زیر نظر فریده دیبا (مادر شهبانو فرح) اداره می‌شد، آشکارا دزدیده می‌شود؛[۶۸۱] وقتی که شاه ایران، در صدر استادیوم‌های تهران می‌نشیند و مانند انسانی نابالغ مراسم «جشن تولد» خود را (که با صرف هزینه‌های سنگین توسط کودکان و نوجوانان و جوانانِ لایه‌های مختلف اجتماعی- راضی و ناراضی- اجرا می‌شد) تماشا می‌کند؛ وقتی که ساواک مخالفان و منتقدان حکومت را در زیر شکنجه می‌کشد، یا زندانیان سیاسی‌ی محاکمه شده را بر تپه‌های اوین به گلوله می‌بندد؛ وقتی یک پیام روشنگر در شعر یا داستان یا نمایش‌نامه، نویسندگانی چون غلامحسین ساعدی و رضا براهنی و احمد شاملو و ده‌ها تن دیگر از نخبگان فرهنگی را به بازجوئی و زندان و شکنجه و تحقیر می‌سپارد؛ وقتی که تدوین یک جزوه‌ی علمی/ گزارشی از وضع اسفبارِ آب آشامیدنی در شهرهای جنوبی‌ی ایران، پژوهشگری چون دکتر مرتضی محیط، در مقام متخصص آسیب‌شناسی و استاد دانشگاه را به شکنجه و زندان انفرادی محکوم می‌کند؛ وقتی اجرای نمایشنامه‌هائی مانند «انگل‌ها» (نوشته‌ی ماکسیم گورکی)، یا «آموزگاران»، نویسنده و مترجم و کارگردانانی چون ناصر رحمانی‌نژاد و محسن یلفانی، در مقام هنرمندان «انجمن تئاتر ایران» را به شکنجه و زندان محکوم می‌کند، خبر به گوش مردم ایران، از جمله به گوش «سپاهیان دانش و بهداشت»، هم می‌رسد؛ و این جوانان به تنگ آمده از ستمِ نابرابری و از خفقان سیاسی، پیش و بیش از هر «دانش و بهداشت»ی، این خبرها را و استنتاج خود از علل آن‌ها را (حتا اگر شده به ضربِ سرود رزمی/ انقلابی‌ی «بهاران خجسته باد»- به جای «سرود شاهنشاهی») به دانش‌آموزان روستاهای کشور و خانواده‌هاشان منتقل می‌کنند،[۶۸۲] و یا در گفته‌ها و نوشته‌های خود، با هر تمهیدی که به عقلشان می‌رسد، خبر روستاهای محروم را به عرض

---

[۶۸۰] اسدالله علم، مدتی وزیر دربار، و شخصیت همواره مورد اعتماد شاه، در یادداشت‌های روزانه‌اش، به ویژه در سال‌های دهه‌ی ۵۰، بارها نشانه‌های تصمیم‌های غلط و نامسئولانه، و فساد مالی را در سازمان برنامه‌ریزی و بودجه‌ی کشور گزارش داده است. و این در حالی است که زبده‌ترین نیروهای کارشناس و انبوهی از چهره‌های خوشنام و دلسوزِ آن روزگار نیز در این سازمان کار می‌کردند.

[۶۸۱] «تغذیه‌ی رایگان» عنوان پروژه‌ای بود که در سال‌های ابتدای دهه‌ی ۵۰ به اجرا گذاشته شد. به این ترتیب که در طول سال تحصیلی هر روز صبح به تعداد دانش‌آموزان هر مدرسه، صبحانه‌ای که معمولاً عبارت بود از شیر و میوه، یا شیر و بیسکوئیت، به همه‌ی مدرسه‌های سراسر کشور فرستاده می‌شد. روزنامه‌های همان زمان، بارها گزارش می‌دادند که کامیون‌های حمل این مواد غذائی در مناطق مختلف شهرها به فروش محصولات مشغول بوده‌اند. ناصر امینی، روزنامه‌نگار و دیپلمات در رژیم پیشین در کتاب «روزها در پی سال‌ها»، صفحه‌ی ۲۳۹ می‌نویسد: «به دستور شاه قرار شد امر توزیع غذای رایگان بین دانش‌آموزان، تحت نظر سرکار خانم فریده دیبا مادر ملکه به اجرا درآید، آن چنان سوءاستفاده‌هائی صورت می‌گرفت که یکی از دوستانم می‌گفت در یکی از شهرهای ساحلی‌ی دریای خزر به چشم خود دیده که کامیون‌های حاوی مواد غذائی (شیر و موز) برای مدارس آن شهر، محصولات خود را در بازار می‌فروخته‌اند.»

[۶۸۲] در «***تاریخچه‌ی سرود بهاران خجسته باد***» می‌خوانیم: این شعر را دکتر عبدالله بهزادی (از اعضای حزب توده‌ی ایران) در اسفند ۱۳۳۹ و در سوگ پاتریس لومومبا، رهبر انقلاب ملی‌ی کنگو، و خطاب به همسر سوگوار او سروده بود. سال‌ها بعد، کرامت دانشیان، که در سپاه دانش خدمت می‌کرد، به روی چند بیت از آن آهنگ گذاشت؛ آن را به شاگردانش در روستای «سلیران» هم آموخت؛ و دانش‌آموزان او، صبح‌ها این سرود را به جای سرود شاهنشاهی می‌خواندند. برگرفته از تارنمای «با چراغ ترانه در کوچه باغ خاطره»، بازدید ۱۲ شهریور ۱۳۸۹:

ملت ایران می‌رسانند.

در ذهنیت دوپاره‌ی محمدرضا شاه پهلوی همین بس، که از سوئی، مفهوم پیش‌اسلامی‌ی «آریا مهر» را به خود می‌بندد؛ سپس، در سخنرانی‌ی رسمی‌ی خود در «جشن‌های دو هزار و پانصد سال شاهنشاهی» (۲۰ تا ۲۴ مهر ۱۳۵۰ برابر با ۱۲ تا ۱۶ اکتبر ۱۹۷۱)، کوروش هخامنشی را به عنوان نماد عظمت ایران باستان می‌ستاید و با جمله‌ی: «کوروش! آسوده بخواب، زیرا که ما بیداریم»، خود را به این شخصیت باستانی پیوند می‌زند؛[۶۸۳] و سپس‌تر، تقویم «اسلامی/ هجری» را به تقویم «شاهنشاهی» (با مبداء پادشاهی‌ی هخامنشیان) تغییر می‌دهد؛ و از سوی دیگر، مرتب تکرار می‌کند که این امام و آن امام را در خواب و بیداری به چشم دیده است، یا با امام زمان رابطه‌ی معنوی دارد، یا «نظر کرده» است؛ به «زیارت امام رضا» می‌رود؛ به سفر «حج» می‌رود و مناسک آن را به جا می‌آورد؛ با تمکین به فتواهای آیت‌الله بروجردی (از جمله منع حمل مشعل المپیک در ایران) از این آیت‌الله لقب «حافظ بیضه‌ی اسلام» می‌گیرد؛ با وجود همسری که «نایب‌السلطنه»ی ایران است،[۶۸۴] و لابد با پشتوانه‌ی قانون «تعدد زوجات» در اسلام، با زن دیگری ازدواج می‌کند؛[۶۸۵] روزنامه‌ها تصویر او را بر سجاده‌ی نماز، و تصویر ولیعهد نوجوان او را در حال بوسیدنِ «ضریح امام هشتم شیعیان» منتشر می‌کنند؛ در مسجد سپهسالار تهران، بر روی آن تک‌صندلی‌ی سلطنتی روبه‌روی «عزادارانِ حسینی» می‌نشیند و سوگواری‌ی عاشورا را تماشا می‌کند؛ مواد «انقلاب سفید» را «مطابق با دستورات اسلام» برآورد می‌کند و می‌گوید: «اسلام! اسلام روز اول! مکتب اسلامی که پیغمبر آورد! نه این چیزهائی که به آن اضافه کرده‌اند و برای منافع خود از آن استفاده می‌کنند.» (۱۳۵۱) انگار نه انگار که همین «اسلام» و همین «حسین» بود که «شاهنشاهی»ی ایران را زایل کرد. شاه ایران چنان درگیر توهم است که نمی‌بیند با این دوگانگی‌ها، هم حافظه‌ی تاریخی‌ی مردم ایران را مغشوش می‌کند، و هم به باورهای مذهبی‌ی مردم حقانیت و ژرفا می‌بخشد. البته همواره هم این زمزمه می‌پیچید- و هنوز پیچیده است- که رفتار و گفتار مذهبی‌ی شاه برای حفظ ظاهر و با هدف جلب نظر دین‌یاران و فریب مردم مذهبی بوده است. اما باید به یاد داشته باشیم که شاه، پیکر پدرش را پیش از دفن در آرامگاهِ ساخته‌شده در حاشیه‌ی تهران، به «طوافِ حَرَمِ مطهرِ حضرت معصومه در قم» فرستاده بود و خواسته بود که مجتهدی سرشناس بر آن نماز بگزارد. که البته «مجتهدان» نیز به انواع ترفندهای کلامی از این کار طفره رفته بودند.[۶۸۶]

---

http://www.parand.se/t-baharan-khojasteh-bad.htm

[۶۸۳] برنامه‌ریزی‌ی جشن‌های دو هزار و پانصد سال شاهنشاهی‌ی ایران، پروژه‌ای ده ساله بود، که زیر نظر مستقیم شاه و گروهی از برگزیدگان او طراحی شد، و در روزهای ۲۰ تا ۲۴ مهر ۱۳۵۰ با حضور سران و پادشاهان ۶۹ کشور جهان در تخت جمشید (پارسه) و در پاسارگاد (کنار آرامگاه کورش هخامنشی) به اجرا گذاشته شد. در این مراسم باشکوه- که در عین حال، مضحکه‌ی بسیاری از خبرنگاران و گزارشگران خارجی قرار گرفت- ۱۶ رئیس جمهور، ۳ نخست وزیر، ٤ معاون رئیس جمهور، و ٦۹ وزیر خارجه شرکت داشتند و مدت سه روز را- پس از برنامه‌های روزانه‌ی جشن- در چادرهای مجلل و باشکوهی که در جوار دشت تخت جمشید برپا شده بود، زندگی کردند. میزان دقیق هزینه‌ی این جشن‌ها به درستی پیدا نیست. تا جائی که من خوانده‌ام، این هزینه، در متن‌های پرده‌پوشانه‌ی کارگزاران این جشن‌ها حدود ۲۲ میلیون دلار، و در متن‌های غلوآمیز مخالفان، بین ۲۰۰ تا ۳۰۰ میلیون دلار ثبت شده است.

[۶۸٤] شاه، پیش از تاجگذاری، تجدید نظر در قانون اساسی را از مجلس خواست. در این تجدید نظر، مقرر شد که در صورت درگذشت شاه، تا رسیدن ولیعهد به سن قانونی (۲۰ سالگی)، اداره‌ی کشور به عهده‌ی نایب‌السطنه باشد. شاه در ٤ آبان ۱۳٤٦ در کاخ گلستان (تهران) تاجگذاری کرد، و تاج باشکوهی نیز با عنوان نایب‌السلطنه‌ی ایران، بر سر شهبانو فرح پهلوی گذاشت.

[٦٨٥] مارگارت لینگ، ژورنالیست و پژوهشگر انگلیسی، که با هدف نوشتن کتابی درباره‌ی شاه، به مدت یک ماه با خانواده‌ی دربار زندگی کرد، در کتابش از «هر دو زن شاه» سخن گفته است. در متن‌های مربوطه آمده است که نام اصلی‌ی این زن، گیلدا آزاد، دختر سرلشگر آزاد، امیر نیروی هوائی بود که شاه به خاطر موهای طلائی‌اش او را «طلا» صدا می‌کرد. تاج‌الملوک ملکه‌ی پهلوی (مادر محمد رضا شاه) در خاطرات شفاهی‌ی خود گفته است: «حالا ازدواج بود یا نه، من درست نمی‌دانم، البته ازدواج به این معنی نبود که محمدرضا او را با تشریفات به عقد رسمی خود در آورده باشد.» به مآخذ زیر نگاه کنید:

- ❖ Margaret Laing, ***The Shah***, London: Sidgwick & Jackson, 1977, p. 108.
- ❖ ***خاطرات ملکه‌ی پهلوی، تاج‌الملوک آیرملو***، تهیه‌کننده: تورج انصاری، محمودعلی باتمانقلیچ، و ملیحه خسروداد، تهران: نشر به آفرین، ۱۳۸۰، ص ۳۶۳.

[٦٨٦] حسین کاوشی، ***تلاش شاه برای زدودن چهره‌ی ضدمذهبی پدرش***، تارنمای «مرکز اسناد انقلاب اسلامی»، ۲۷ اردی‌بهشت ۱۳۸۸:

شاه ایران، با بالا گرفتن جنبش چریکی و گرایش و پیوستن جوانان به سازمان‌های مخفی، «سازمان مجاهدین خلق ایران» را با اصطلاحِ «مارکسیست‌های اسلامی» شناسائی کرد؛ مخالفان کمونیست را «ارتجاع سرخ»، و مخالفان لایه‌ی روحانیت را «ارتجاع سیاه» نامید. اما در همان حال بود که از یک سو، خود را «سوسیالیست» خواند، و از سوی دیگر کازینوها، ویلاها، پلاژها و گردشگاه‌های مجلل را در جزیره‌ی کیش ساخت، و به مثابه یک دلال معاملات ملکی، در تبلیغِ آن برای ثروتمندان، «عموم» مردم را تحقیر کرد و گفت: «پلاژهای شمال دیگه خیلی عمومی شده!» (به نقل از حافظه. و این، البته، تا قیامِ «عموم» فاصله‌ی چندانی نداشت.) در همان حال بود که از سوئی، «جشن هنر شیراز»، «مدرن»ترین برنامه‌های هنرِ غربی را در کوی و بازار شیراز- شهری که در حاشیه‌ی جنوبی‌ی آن گروهی از مردم در قبرستانی متروک و در میان قبرها زندگی می‌کردند- به نمایش می‌گذاشت،[۶۸۷] و نشریه‌های ایران، از ازدواج دو تن از مردان همجنس‌گرا (از کارمندان دفتر مخصوص شهبانو) خبر می‌دادند، و از سوی دیگر، آیت‌الله مرتضی مطهری (همان شخصیتی که «استشمام عطر زنانه» و «شنیدن صدای پای زن، اگر به اصطلاح مهیج باشد» را «حرام» اعلام می‌کند)،[۶۸۸] به توصیه‌ی شهبانو فرح پهلوی به عضویت «شورای سلطنتی‌ی فلسفه» و به دریافت دکترای افتخاری نائل شد. در حالی که پیکارگران آزادی‌خواه و برابری‌طلبِ ما زیر شکنجه جان می‌دادند، یا تیرباران می‌شدند، احمد فردید و رضا داوری و همتایانش در تلویزیون ایران یا در کلاس‌های دانشگاهی یا در حسینه‌ی ارشاد، آزادانه مشغول دفاع از تز غرب‌زدگی، و سَم‌پاشی بر «خُردک شررِ» مدرنیسم ایرانی- یا به قول شهلا شفیق: «مدرنیت مثله‌شده»- بودند.

و باز در همان حال بود که شاه ایران با تکیه بر توسعه‌ای که از یک سو پیامد بالارفتِ بهاء نفت بود و از سوی دیگر برآیشِ اجراء مواد «انقلاب سفید»، با شگفتی پرسید: «ما به ملت ایران تمدن بزرگ را وعده داده‌ایم، و آن‌ها به دنبال وحشت بزرگ می‌روند؟» (به نقل از حافظه.) اما گوئی در پی‌ی یافتن پاسخ و ریشه‌یابی‌ی مشکل نبود؛ مشکلی که، عمدتاً در دیکتاتوری‌ی خود و پدرش ریشه داشت. از قول شهلا شفیق، جامعه‌شناس مقیم فرانسه، می‌گویم:

> اصلاحات دوره‌ی پهلوی بی‌شک در نوسازی‌ی اجتماعی، از جمله در حیطه‌ی آموزش و ارتباطات و دستگاه‌های اجرائی و قضائی نقش مهمی داشت؛ اما حفظ و تقویت استبداد، روند دگرگونی ارزش‌های سنتی و تحول جایگاه فرد از «بنده‌ی خدا»، «رعیت» و «تحت امر سلطان» به «شهروند» را مختل کرد و جامعه را از ساز و کار شهروندی‌ی دمکراتیک (که امکان حل کشمکش‌ها و تنش‌های اجتناب‌ناپذیر روند تحول از سنت به تجدد را با تکیه بر قانون فراهم می‌کند) محروم کرد.[۶۸۹]

زمانی هم که حلقه‌ی محاصره تنگ‌تر شد، پادشاه ایران به جای انتشار کتاب‌های «کشف‌الاسرار» و «حکومت اسلامی»، نوشته‌های آیت‌الله خمینی، و به جای اجازه‌ی بحث و مناظره درباره‌ی آن‌ها (که می‌توانست جهان‌بینی و آرمان این آیت‌الله را به مردم ایران بشناساند)، مقاله‌ای از سوی دربار به روزنامه‌ی اطلاعات دیکته کرد، که سراسر ناسزا به روحانیت بود و آیت‌الله خمینی را «سید هندی» و تلویحاً، دست‌پرورده‌ی بریتانیا نامیده بود. این متن، که با عنوانِ «ایران و استعمار سرخ و سیاه» و با نام مستعارِ احمد رشیدی مطلق، روز ۱۷ دی ۱۳۵۶ منتشر شد، چونان بوم رنگ، به سوی خودِ شاه کمانه کرد، سند مشروعیت آیت‌الله خمینی را در دل و جان زخمی‌ی مردم به امضاء رساند، و به منزله‌ی تیر خلاص، به

---

http://www.irdc.ir/fa/content/6931/default.aspx

۶۸۷ رضا اغنمی، ***یادواره‌ای از غلامحسین ساعدی***، نامه‌ی کانون نویسندگان ایران در تبعید، دفتر هفتم، سوئد: نشر آموزش، زمستان ۱۳۷۵/ ۱۹۹۶، صص ۱۲۶- ۱۳۴.

۶۸۸ مرتضی مطهری، ***مجموعه‌ی آثار***، تهران: انتشارات صدرا، ۱۳۷۱، جلد ۱۷، ص ۴۰۰.

۶۸۹ شهلا شفیق، ***چرا بخت با شاپور بختیار یار نشد؟*** تارنمای «بی بی سی»، ۶ اوت ۲۰۱۱/ ۱۵ مرداد ۱۳۹۰:
http://www.bbc.co.uk/persian/iran/2011/08/110802_l78_bakhtiar_20th_anniv_shahla_shafigh.shtml

موجودیت شاه و نظام مشروطه‌ی ایران شلیک شد.[۶۹۰] دو روز پس از انتشار این متن بود که طرفداران آیت‌الله خمینی در قم قیام کردند؛ کشته دادند؛ برگزاری‌ی «هفتم» و «چلهم» کشته‌شدگانِ قم، در تبریز کشته داد؛ برگزاری‌ی هفتم و چهلم کشته‌شدگان تبریز، در یزد کشته داد؛ و حلقه‌های این زنجیره، تا سقوط حکومت «مشروطه» و آغاز حکومت «مشروعه» گسترده شد.

***

محمد رضا شاه پهلوی در مورد سیاست خارجی‌ی خود نیز دچار همین توهم بود. او نمی‌دید که با گام نخستِ وابستگی‌ی رسمی- که در مرداد ۱۳۳۲ برداشته بود- یا باید تا به آخر و مو به مو، گوش به فرمان حامیان خارجی‌ی خود باقی بماند، یا ملت ایران را به عنوان پشتوانه‌ی بریدنش از وابستگی، پشت سر داشته باشد. در واقع، و چون نیک بنگریم، محمدرضا شاه پهلوی، حتا به توصیه‌های حامیان خارجی‌ی خود پیرامون لزوم رفاه مردم و جلب رضایت و حمایت ملت ایران نیز اهمیت نداد. از رؤسای جمهوری گرفته تا آکادمسین‌ها و تحلیل‌گران سیاسی، از سفیران گرفته تا خبرنگاران معتبر امریکائی، انفجار قریب‌الوقوع ملت ایران را به او هشدار داده بودند- و البته برای حفظ منافع خود در ایران- راه‌هائی را برای جلوگیری از آن به شاه پیشنهاد کرده بودند. در مروری گذرا بر سیاست‌های کلی‌ی ایالات متحده امریکا در ایرانِ دوره‌ی محمدرضا شاه پهلوی، این هشدارها، به شکل‌های مختلف به دید می‌آیند.

سیاست فقرزدائی در کشورهائی که از نظر ژئوپولیتیک در معرض «نفوذ کمونیسم» و شوروی قرار داشتند، اصل مهمی از دکترین هری ترومن (نخستین رئیس جمهور امریکا پس از پایان جنگ دوم جهانی، از حزب دموکرات، از سال ۱۹۴۵ تا ۱۹۵۳) بود، و بر اساس آن، ایران وام‌های کلان (البته با بهره‌های کلان) و کمک‌های اقتصادی و نظامی‌ی فراوانی از ایالات متحده دریافت کرد. با این که «سازمان برنامه و بودجه» و «کمیسیون مشترک ایران و آمریکا برای بهبود امور روستائی» با وام ۲۵۰ میلیون دلاری‌ی «اصل چهار ترومن» در ایران پدید آمدند، و در تغییر سیمای فقیر و عقب‌مانده‌ی روستاهای ایران بی‌تأثیر نبودند، اما «سیاست فقرزدائی»، و لزوم آن برای رفاه و پیشرفت مردم ایران، در ذهنیت شاه ایران نهادینه نشد. سیاست کمک مالی به ایران، در زمان ریاست جمهوری‌ی دوایت آیزنهاور (از حزب جمهوری‌خواه، از ۱۹۵۳ تا ۱۹۶۱) به گونه‌ای دیگر و در قالب دکترین متفاوتی ادامه یافت. در دکترین آیزنهاور، گرچه هر کشوری در هر نقطه‌ی جهان که منافع و هدف‌های آمریکا را تهدید می‌کرد، باید با هر وسیله‌ی ممکن (از جمله نیروهای مسلح) سرکوب می‌شد. اما بر حفظ استقلال و تمامیت ارضی‌ی کشورهای خاورمیانه و امریکای لاتین تأکید داشت. کودتا علیه دولت دکتر مصدق، ورود ایران به پیمان بغداد (سنتو)، امضای قراردادهای نظامی میان آمریکا و ایران- که ورود مستشاران نظامی آمریکائی و نفوذ آن‌ها در ارتش ایران را به همراه داشت- و تشکیل ساواک، که با کمک و همکاری سازمان سیا صورت گرفت، همه از پیامدهای این دکترین بودند. منتها، آیزنهاور پس از پیام تبریکی که به محمد رضا شاه پهلوی فرستاد، به سرعت به تقویت نظامی، سیاسی و اقتصادی دولت کودتا پرداخت. در این جا نیز توجه شاه ایران، نه بر رفاه و رضایت مردم ایران، بلکه بر بخش «نظامی»ی این «کمک»ها متمرکز بود و اهم کمک‌های اقتصادی، به اضافه‌ی سهم بزرگی از درآمد نفت ایران را نیز با خرید اسلحه، به امریکا بازمی‌گرداند. جان کندی (رئیس جمهور بعدی، از حزب دموکرات امریکا، از ژانویه‌ی ۱۹۶۱ تا نوامبر ۱۹۶۳) نیز، گرچه با پیروزی انقلاب کوبا و استقرار حکومت کمونیستی در این

---

۶۹۰ این متن با عنوان «***ایران و استعمار سرخ و سیاه***»، به نویسندگی‌ی احمد رشیدی مطلق، در روزنامه‌ی اطلاعات، ۱۷ دی ۱۳۵۶ منتشر شد. در ابتدای امر، گمان اکثر مردم بر این بود که داریوش همایون، وزیر اطلاعات وقت آن را نوشته است. اما بعدها در منابع مختلف، «فرهاد نیکخواه»، رئیس دفتر مطبوعاتی‌ی امیرعباس هویدا (وزیر دربار)، به عنوان نویسنده‌ی متن شناسائی شد. بنا بر روایت مرکز اسناد انقلاب اسلامی، این متن، بازتاب شاه بود نسبت به پاسخ آیت‌الله خمینی به تلگراف تسلیت یاسر عرفات (برای درگذشت مصطفی خمینی) که: «درد و محنت من روزی پایان می‌گیرد که ملت ایران از شر این آدم جابر فارغ شود»:

❖ اسماعیل حسن‌زاده، ***تحلیلی بر واقعه‌ی ۱۹ دی ۱۳۵۶ قم***، تارنمای «مرکز اسناد انقلاب اسلامی»، ۱۷ دی ۱۳۹۰:
http://www.irdc.ir/fa/content/4887/default.aspx

کشـور، و ناآرامی‌های گسترده‌ی مردم در کشـورهای دیگرِ امریکای لاتین، حالت تهاجمی‌ی بیش‌تری نسبت به کمونیسـم اعلام و اعمال کرد، اما کمک برای توسعه و پیشرفت اقتصادی به کشورهای «جهان سوم» و زیر سلطه‌ی حکومت‌های اسـتبدادی را یکی از مهم‌ترین راه‌های جلوگیری از نفوذ کمونیسـم برآورد کرد. کندی در اجرای این دکترین، در دوره‌ی کوتاه ریاست جمهوری‌ی خود، بارها بر لزوم اصلاحات سیاسی/ اجتماعی/ اقتصادی در ایران انگشت گذاشت، و اجرای آن را بارها به شـاه ایران نیز توصـیه کرد؛ به ویژه پس از انتشـار گفت‌وگوی «والتر لیپمن» (روزنامه‌نگار امریکائی) با خروشـچف (رهبر شـوروی)، در ۱۰ آوریل ۱۹۶۱. خروشـجف در آن مصـاحبه گفته بود: «رژیم ایران مثل یک سـیب رسیده است و ما منتظر افتادن آن در دامان خود هستیم.»[۶۹۱] جان کندی، با گزارش‌هائی که از شرایط سیاسی/ اقتصادی‌ی حاکم بر ایران از تحلیل‌گران سیاسی‌ی خود دریافت می‌کرد، این «سیب رسیده» را دید، و به خاطر نقض حقوق شهروندان ایران و نادیده گرفتن نارضایتی‌ی آن‌ها، شاه ایران را دیکتاتور خواند و رژیم او را فاسد نامید.[۶۹۲] گوش شاه ایران، اما، بر این هشدارها بسته بود. او پس از دوران کندی، و تحکیم دوباره‌ی روابطش با واشنگتن، در سال ۱۹۶۹ در مصاحبه‌ای به خبرنگار امریکائی گفت:

> بدترین دوران شما، سال‌های ۱۹۶۱- ۱۹۶۲ بود. حتا پیش از آن زمان هم سران لیبرال شما می‌خواستند دموکراسی‌ی خود را به دیگران تحمیل کنند.[۶۹۳]

اما رئیس جمهور محبوب شـاه ایران، لیندن جانسـون بود، که تا در مقام معاون جان کندی خدمت می‌کرد، از «آزادی، دموکراسـی، و عدالت اجتماعی» سـخن می‌گفت، اما به محض رسـیدن به ریاسـت جمهوری (پس از ترور جان کندی)، فاجعه‌ی جنگ ویتنام را به ملت‌های ویتنام و امریکا تحمیل کرد. «ریچارد نیکسـون» (از حزب جمهوری‌خواه، از سـال ۱۹۶۹ تا ۱۹۷٤)، به سبب درگیری در جنگ ویتنام و اوج‌گیری‌ی نارضایتی مردم آمریکا از شرکت آمریکا در آن جنگ، پیروزی‌ی نهضت‌های رهائی‌بخش در آسیا و آفریقا و آمریکای لاتین، دستیابی‌ی شوروی به بمب اتم، و تصمیم بریتانیا به خروج از شرق سوئز تا ۱۹۷۱، تنها رئیس جمهوری بود که با شرایط اجتماعی/ سیاسی/ اقتصادی‌ی کشورهای «جهان سوم»، و از جمله ایران کاری نداشت؛ حل و فصل مسائل این کشورها را به عهده‌ی دیکتاتورهای بومی گذاشت؛ و با هدف جلوگیری از نفوذ کمونیسم، هر گونه کمک ایالات متحده را به تجهیز نظامی‌ی آن کشورها منحصر کرد.[۶۹٤] از پیامدهای این دکترین، که محمدرضـا شـاه پهلوی را هم خوش می‌آمد، این بود که ایران به بزرگـترین خریدار اسـلحه‌ی امریکائی تبدیل شـد، و سـرمایه‌گذاری‌های سـودآور امریکائیان در ایران اوج گرفت. دوره‌ی ریاسـت جمهوری‌ی جرالد فورد، (از حزب جمهوری‌خواه، از ۱۹۷٤ تا ۱۹۷۷، پس از استعفای ریچارد نیکسون به دنبال رسوائی‌ی «واترگیت») نیز همزمان

---

[۶۹۱] جیمز بیل، ***شیر و عقاب***، ترجمه‌ی مهوش غلامی، تهران: انتشارات کوبه، ۱۳۷۱، صص ۱۸۵ تا ۱۸۹.

[۶۹۲] برگرفته از: سرهنگ غلامرضا نجاتی، ***تاریخ سیاسی‌ی بیست و پنج ساله‌ی ایران: از کودتا تا انقلاب***، پیشین، ص ۲۹۵. **توضیح**: مأخذ غلامرضا نجاتی برای این نقل قول به قرار زیر است:
William O.Douglas, ***The Court Years: 1939-1975***, New York: Random House, 1980, p. 304.

[۶۹۳] برگرفته از: سرهنگ غلامرضا نجاتی، تاریخ سیاسی‌ی بیست و پنج ساله‌ی ایران: از کودتا تا انقلاب، پیشین، ص ۲۹۵. **توضیح**: مأخذ غلامرضا نجاتی برای این نقل قول- که من برای برابری‌ی ترجمه‌ی غلامرضا نجاتی با متن اصلی به آن دست نیافتم- به قرار زیر است:
News and Word Report, June 27, 1969, p. 49.

[۶۹٤] ریچارد نیکسون در ۲۲ ژوئیه ۱۹۶۹ در راه سفر به فیلیپین در جزیره‌ی گوام، دکترین خود را به شرح زیر اعلام کرد: « گمان می کنم وقت آن رسیده باشد که ایالات متحده در زمینه‌ی مناسباتش با کشورهای آسیائی به دو نکته توجه کند: اولاً، ما به همه‌ی تعهدات قراردادی‌ی خود احترام خواهیم گذاشت؛ ثانیاً، تا جائی که مربوط به مسـائل امنیت داخلی و مسـائل دفاع نظامی باشـد- صـرف نظر از تهدید از جانب یک دولت بزرگ، که مسلماً منجر به توسل به سلاح هسته‌ای خواهد شد- دولت آمریکا ملل آسیائی را تشویق می‌کند که مسائل امنیت داخلی و دفاعی را بین خودشان حل و فصل کنند و انتظار دارد خودشـان این مسئولیت را به عهده بگیرند.» (هنری کیسینجر، سیاست خارجی‌ی امریکا، ترجمه‌ی حسن محمدی‌نژاد، تهران: انتشارات دانشگاه تهران، ۱۳۵۵، ص ۵-۷) برگرفته از:
❖ دکتر مصطفی ملکوتیان، ***ایران و امنیت ملی‌ی امریکا (۱۳۲٤-۱۳۵۷)***، تهران: مجله‌ی علوم سیاسی، شماره‌ی ۱۶، صفحه ۹.

بود با اوج درگیری‌ی امریکا در ویتنام- که نهایتاً به پایان این جنگ جهنمی انجامید. از این رو، دغدغه‌ی فورد و دولتمردان کابینه‌اش، نه شرایط سیاسی/ اقتصادی/ اجتماعی‌ی مردم خاورمیانه و ایران، بلکه از یک سو قیمت نفت بود، که با پیشنهاد شاه ایران رو به افزایشی تصاعدی می‌رفت، و از سوی دیگر، حجم سنگین سلاح‌های پیشرفته‌ای بود که شاه ایران سفارش می‌داد، و امریکا- شاید به علت بلندپروازی‌های شاه- با برخی از اقلام آن مخالف بود. «جیمی کارتر» (از حزب دموکرات، ۱۹۷۷- ۱۹۸۱) آخرین رئیس جمهور آمریکا تا پیش از «پیروزی‌ی انقلاب» ایران بود. سرلوحه‌ی سیاست خارجی‌ی جیمی کارتر در کشورهای جهان سوم- که او در سخنرانی‌های انتخاباتی‌ی خود، بر آن پافشاری داشت- دکترین «حقوق بشر»، و البته برای حفظ منافع درازمدتِ امریکا بود. تکیه‌ی جمیی کارتر در مورد ایران، بیش از همه بر نقض حقوق بشر و تحدید فروش سلاح‌های سنگین بود.[۶۹۵] جیمی کارتر در واپسین دیدارِ خصوصی‌ی خود با محمدرضا شاه پهلوی در کاخ سفید (۱۵ نوامبر ۱۹۷۷)، شاه را به صحبتی «بی‌رودربایستی/ رو- راست frankly» فرامی‌خواند، و به او می‌گوید:

> من با پیشرفت‌های مهمی که در کشور شما انجام شده آشنا هستم. اما از مشکلاتی هم که در ایران وجود دارند، خبر دارم. شما بیانیه‌ی حقوق بشر من را شنیده‌اید. تعداد فزاینده‌ای از شهروندان شما ادعا می‌کنند که حقوق آن‌ها همیشه رعایت نمی‌شود. تا جائی که من خبر دارم، بیش‌ترین ناآرامی‌ها از میان ملاها و رهبران دیگر مذهبی و طبقه‌ی متوسط جدید- که در جست‌وجوی مشارکت در امور سیاسی هستند- و دانشجویان داخل و خارج ایران، برخاسته است. نارضایتی و شکایت این گروه‌ها به اعتبار سیاسی‌ی ایران در انظار جهانی آسیب زده است. آیا می‌توان از راه مشورت با مخالفان و آسان‌گیری‌ی سیاست پلیسی، از بار این مشکل کاست؟[۶۹۶]

پاسخ شاه ایران به این پرسشِ هشداردهنده- آن هم درست در روزی که پلیس امریکا اعضا و هواداران کنفدراسیون دانشجویان و مخالفان شاه را با گاز اشک‌آور از اطراف کاخ سفید تارانده است، آن هم درست در زمانی که شاعران و نویسندگان ایران در باغ «انستیتو گوته»، فریاد مخالفت خود را به گوش هزاران ایرانی‌ی مشتاق رسانده‌اند- تنها و تنها ذهنیت مستبد و متوهم او را نمایندگی می‌کند. جیمی کارتر می‌نویسد:

> شاه با دقت به حرف‌های من گوش داد، اندکی مکث کرد، و سپس با حالتی اندوهگین گفت: «نه، کاری از دست من برنمی‌آید. من باید قوانین ایران را- که برای نبرد با کمونیسم طراحی شده- اعمال کنم. این [کمونیسم]، برای ایران، و در واقع، برای کشورهای دیگر منطقه و جهان غرب، مشکلی واقعی و خطرناک است. ممکن است زمانی که این خطر از بین برود، قوانین هم تغییر کنند. اما این به زودی اتفاق نمی‌افتد. در هر حال، این شکایت‌های اخیر از اخلال‌گرانی سرچشمه می‌گیرد که قانون علیه آن‌ها و برای حمایت از کشورمان، طراحی شده است؛ این‌ها در واقع اقلیت کوچکی هستند که از سوی اکثریت گسترده‌ی مردم ایران حمایت نمی‌شوند. (مأخذ پیشین)

این هشدار، البته خاص رئیس جمهور امریکا نبود. در واقع از اوایل دهه‌ی هفتاد میلادی/ پنجاه خورشیدی، مشابه این

---

۶۹۵ در تنظیم اطلاعات مربوط به سیاست خارجی‌ی رئیس‌جمهورهای امریکا، افزون بر منابعی که در این مقوله بدست داده‌ام، از مآخذ زیر نیز سود جسته‌ام:

- James A. Bill, ***The Eagle and the Lion: The Tragedy of American-Iranian Relations***, Yale University Press, 1989.
- مارک ج. گازیوروسکی، ***سیاست خارجی‌ی امریکا و شاه***، ترجمه‌ی فریدون کاظمی، تهران: نشر مرکز، ۱۳۷۱.
- هنری کیسینجر، ***سیاست خارجی‌ی امریکا***، ترجمه‌ی حسن محمدی‌نژاد، تهران: انتشارات دانشگاه تهران، ۱۳۵۵.
- عبدالرضا هوشنگ مهدوی، ***سیاست خارجی‌ی ایران در دوران پهلوی ۱۳۰۰- ۱۳۵۷***، تهران: نشر البرز، ۱۳۷٤.

696 Jimmy Carter, ***Keeping Faith: Memoirs of a President***, Bantam Books, 1982, pp. 436- 437.

هشدارها از سوی بسیاری از دیپلمات‌ها، استادان برجسته و خبرنگاران معتبر امریکائی و اروپائی، و نمایندگان سازمان ملل و حقوق بشر، به شاه داده شده بود. کویلر یانگ (استاد دانشگاه پرینستون)، ماروین زونیس (استاد دانشگاه شیکاگو)، ریچارد کاتم (استاد دانشگاه پیتسبورگ و کارشناس مسائل ایران)، جان بولینگ (تحلیل‌گر سیاسیِ وزارت خارجه‌ی امریکا)، والتر لیپمن (خبرنگار امریکائی)، اریک رولو (خبرنگار لوموند)، از جمله شخصیت‌هائی بودند که با اشاره به نارضایتی‌های گسترده‌ی مردم ایران، برای بهبود وضع اقتصادیِ مردم و کاهش اختلاف طبقاتی و رفع فساد در هرم قدرت ایران، پیشنهادهائی هم ارائه داده بودند. بدیهی است که هدف دولت امریکا (و تحلیل‌گران و مشاوران سیاسیِ آن) از این توصیه‌ها، حفظ منافع و منابعی بود که امریکا در ایران داشت؛ به ویژه در زمانی که دیپلمات‌ها و مستشاران نظامیِ امریکائی در ایران در معرض ترور چریک‌های فدائی و مجاهد قرار داشتند. با این وصف، در نظر گرفتن و رعایت آن پیشنهادها، شاید می‌توانست در جلب رضایت لایه‌هائی از مردم ایران کارساز باشد، و مسیر تاریخ را به نفع سلطنت محمدرضا شاه و خاندانش و رژیم مشروطه‌ی ایران تغییر دهد. اما ذهن شاه ایران- انگار بیش از پیکارگران امریکائی در «جنگ سرد»- دچار بختکی بود به نام «کمونیسم»، بدون آن که ریشه‌های خیزش این فکرت را در جوانان ایران به درستی شناسائی کند. به نظر می‌آید که در سال‌های دهه‌ی پنجاه گسترش دانش و آگاهی، به عنوان سبب‌سازِ این خیزش در فاهمه‌ی شاه ایران نشسته بود. چرا که در اسفند ۱۳۵۱ فرمان نوشت که تمام مدرسه‌های ملی باید دولتی شوند؛ و شدند، تا شاید نخبه‌پروری موقوف شود؛ چون دریافته بود که پادگانی کردن دانشگاه‌ها- به ویژه پلی‌تکنیک و آریا مهر- در خروش و خیزش دانشجویان اثری معکوس داشته، قرار بر این گذاشته بود که این دانشگاه‌ها را تعطیل کند یا به شهرهای دیگر ایران منتقل کند.

محمدرضا شاه پهلوی، که چنین می‌پنداشت یا چنین وانمود می‌کرد که کل جنبش چپ ایران «خائن»، «بی‌وطن»، «وابسته به بیگانه»، و انگیخته‌ی شوروی است، با استفاده‌ی تمثیلی از نام جمهوری‌های اتحاد جماهیر شوروی، به مردم ایران اعلام کرد: «تا وطن‌پرستانی چون من هستند، ایران ایرانستان نخواهد شد.» (به نقل از حافظه) اما خود، دقیقاً به خاطر «وابستگی به بیگانه»، در مطالبه‌ی حق حاکمیت ایران بر جزایر بحرین، به ناگزیر، کوتاه آمد: در ژانویه ۱۹۶۸ (زمستان ۱۳۴۶) انگلستان اعلام کرد که تا سال ۱۹۷۱ نیروهای خود را از شرق سوئز (و از جمله از بحرین) خارج خواهد کرد، و پیشنهاد داد که فدراسیونی از نُه شیخ‌نشین خلیج فارس (از جمله بحرین) به نام «امارات خلیج فارس» تشکیل شود. محمدرضا شاه پهلوی در برابر این پیشنهاد موضع مخالف گرفت، آن را «ورود استعمار از درب پشتیِ منطقه» خواند، و اعلام کرد که در برابر جدائیِ بحرین از ایران مقاومت خواهد کرد (تیر ماه ۱۳۴۷). بلافاصله نیز، بحرین را به عنوان «استان چهاردهم ایران» در ساختار کشوریِ ایران گنجاند. اما زمانی که توافق‌های پنهانی بین قدرت‌های غربی و عربی انجام شد و به اطلاع شاه رسید،[۶۹۷] او در سفرش به هندوستان، روز ۴ ژانویه ۱۹۶۹/ دی ۱۳۴۸ در دهلی نو در یک کنفرانس مطبوعاتی، ضمن اشاره به این که «بحرین ۱۵۰ سال پیش به وسیله‌ی انگلستان اشغال شد»، و ضمن اشاره به این که «حالا که انگلستان در حال ترک خلیج فارس است، نمی‌تواند آن چه را که از ایران گرفته، بدون رضایت این کشور به طرف دیگری بدهد»، و ضمن ابراز مخالفت با استفاده از «زور» و «اشغال» برای حل مسئله‌ی ارضیِ بحرین، بر «خواست مردم بحرین» تکیه کرد و گفت: «اگر مردم بحرین خواهان پیوستن به کشورم نباشند»، ایران از ادعاهای مالکیت بحرین صرف نظر خواهد کرد. و با این ژشت دموکراتیک، جدائیِ بحرین از ایران را به رفراندم و به رأی مردم بحرین (زیر نظر شورای امنیت سازمان ملل) واگذاشت. انگار نه انگار که این «کشورم» نیز، «مردم» دارد؛ انگار نه انگار که این «مردم» نیز «خواسته»هائی دارند؛ انگار نه انگار که این «کشورم»، مجلس قانون‌گذاری دارد. و

---

[۶۹۷] به روایت محمد قائد، سبب‌ساز این تغییر روش، «زیرمیزی»ای بود که «ظاهراً» به شاه داده شد. به مأخذ زیر نگاه کنید:

❖ محمد قائد، ***درباره‌ی محمدرضا پهلوی***، ص ۱، تارنمای «محمد قائد»، بازدید ۱۰ ژوئیه ۲۰۱۲:

http://www.mghaed.com/ay/shah.pdf

این چنین شد که شاه ایران، این «رئیس قوای سه گانه‌ی مملکت»، پس از زد و بندهای پنهانی و پس از اخذ تصمیم نهائی، لایحه‌ی جدائی‌ی بحرین از ایران را به مجلس شورای ملی سپرد. پژواک فریادهای التماس‌آمیز محسن پزشکپور، نماینده‌ی وقتِ مجلس شورای ملی نیز- که تبلور صدای مردم ایران بود- فقط زیر سقف مجلس فرمایشی پیچید، و البته، در سپهر تاریخ معاصر ایران باقی ماند. بدین ترتیب بود که شاه ایران رسماً از حق مالکیت ایران بر بحرین گذشت. (۱۴ اوت ۱۹۷۱) و «استقلال» آن را به رسمیت شناخت.[۶۹۸] در همین دوران بود که رسانه‌های رسمی، پیرامون موضوع بحرین تا حد ممکن سکوت کردند، و در عوض، هلهله سر دادند که ایران حق حاکمیت بر جزایر «تنب کوچک»، «تنب بزرگ» و «ابوموسی» را (که آن‌ها هم از دیرباز ملک طلق ایران بوده‌اند) پس گرفته است. اما پس از «استرداد» نیز، این جزایر به همان حال نیمه مسکونی‌ای که داشتند باقی ماندند، و شاه و دستگاه‌های قانون‌گذاری و اجرائی‌ی او از انجام هرگونه بازسازی- که می‌توانست به سود لایه‌های فرودست و بی‌خانمان ملت ایران باشد، و در عین حال حق مالکیت ایران بر این جزایر را در جامعه‌ی بین‌المللی تثبیت کند- در این جزایر خودداری کردند؛ تا تاریخ دوری بزند و روزی برسد که حکومت‌های عربی‌ی حاشیه‌ی خلیج فارس، حق مالکیت این جزایر را طلب کنند (۲۰۱۲).

البته- با توجه به فشار دویست ساله‌ی استعمار بر توش ُ توان ایران، و با توجه به وزن و جایگاه سیاسی‌ی ایران در سیاست‌های بین‌المللی‌ی آن زمان- شاید تنها راهِ ناگزیر برای حل مسئله‌ی بحرین، راه حل دیپلماتیک بود. همچنین- اگر ناسیونالیست دوآتشه نباشیم- اعلام عدم توسل به «زور» در پس گرفتن بحرین، از دیدگاه انسانی می‌تواند قابل ستایش باشد. اما اندکی بعد دیدیم که اعلام عدم توسل به «زور» از سوی شاه، تنها ژستی دموکراتیک، و برای پرده‌پوشی‌ی ناچاری و وابستگی‌ی خودش، و یا شاید «زیرمیزی»‌ای بود که به بهای این واگذاری به دستش رسیده بود. چرا که این ژست، در مورد «مردم» آزادی‌خواه کشور عمان- که سال‌ها علیه استعمار بریتانیا، و علیه «سلطان»‌های دست‌ساز،[۶۹۹] و علیه فقر و بی‌سوادی مبارزه کرده بودند- جهتی معکوس یافت. هسته‌های مختلف پیکارگران این کشور، که در طول زمان (از سال ۱۹۶۴) در ایالت ظفار مجتمع شده بودند، پس از تشکیل کنگره‌های متعدد، به گرایش «سوسیالیسم علمی»، ایدئولوژی‌ی مارکسیست/ لنینیسم، و به مشی‌ی مبارزه‌ی مسلحانه رأی دادند، و با عنوان «جبهه‌ی ملی برای آزادسازی‌ی عمان و خلیج اشغال‌شده‌ی عربی» رسماً اعلام حضور کردند، و در جنگ و گریزهای چریکی، به پیروزی‌های قابل ملاحظه‌ای هم دست

---

[۶۹۸] محمدرضا شاه پهلوی، پس از قرار و مدارهای محرمانه با دولت‌های امریکا و انگلستان، مجلس شورای ملی را در برابر کار انجام شده قرار داد و لایحه را توسط اردشیر زاهدی (وزیر خارجه‌ی وقت) برای «تصویب» به مجلس شورای ملی برد. تنها چهار تن از ۱۸۷ تن نمایندگان مجلس با این لایحه مخالفت کردند. در حالی که، در طول سخنرانی‌ی دلسوخته‌ی محسن پزشکپور، صدای «صحیح است، صحیح است»، بر فضای مجلس فرمایشی پیچیده بود. درد مردم ایران و فریاد پزشکپور از آن رو بود که جزایر بحرین از زمان هخامنشیان، از متعلقات امپراتوری‌ی ایران بود. در زمان ساسانیان، که بحرین توسط قبیله‌ای از اعراب اشغال شد، شاپور ساسانی آن را پس گرفت. شاه عباس صفوی نیز این مجمع‌الجزایر را از استعمار پرتقال رهاند، و از آن پس نیز- تا اواخر قاجاریه- بحرین جزئی از استان فارس شناسائی می‌شد. در تمام نقشه‌ها و اسناد سیاسی‌ی مربوط به ایران و خلیج فارس، که در سده‌های هجدهم و نوزدهم میلادی توسط کارشناسان و دولتمردان بریتانیا ثبت شده، و مورد تأیید این کشور بوده، بحرین، جزء خاک ایران برشمرده شده است. افزون بر ذخایر نفتی در بحرین، و امکاناتی که در صید مروارید دارد، اهمیت بحرین در نقش سوق‌الجیشی‌ی آن است که حق مالکیت ایران بر آن، یکپارچگی‌ی تملک ایران بر تمامی‌ی خلیج فارس را تضمین می‌کرد، و عبارت مجعول «خلیج عربی» را ورد زبان «اتحادیه‌ی عرب» نمی‌کرد.

برای آگاهی از این تاریخچه، و از وابستگی‌ی شاه به امریکا، و عواملی که او را به جدائی‌ی بحرین از ایران ناگزیر کرد، به مآخذ زیر نگاه کنید:

- ❖ عبدالرضا هوشنگ مهدوی، ***تاریخ روابط خارجی‌ی ایران از پایان جنگ دوم تا سقوط رژیم پهلوی: ۱۳۲۴ تا ۱۳۵۷***، جلد دوم، تهران: نشر نو، ۱۳۶۸.
- ❖ عبدالرضا هوشنگ مهدوی، ***سیاست خارجی‌ی ایران در دوران پهلوی: ۱۳۰۰- ۱۳۵۷***، تهران: انتشارات پیکان، ۱۳۸۹.
- ❖ مارک گازیوروسکی، ***سیاست خارجی‌ی امریکا و شاه: بنای دولتی دست‌نشانده در ایران***، ترجمه‌ی فریدون فاطمی، تهران: نشر مرکز، ۱۳۷۱.

[۶۹۹] چه‌گونگی‌ها و چرائی‌های «کشورسازی» و یافتن و گماشتن افرادی با عنوان «سلطان» یا «شاه» برای اداره‌ی این «کشور»‌ها در سراسر منطقه‌ی خاورمیانه، توسط دستگاه‌های اطلاعاتی‌ی بریتانیا و امریکا، به گونه‌ای مستند در بخش‌های کتاب زیر پراکنده است. بخش‌های ۱ تا ۹ این کتاب، عمدتاً به کشورهای عربی اختصاص دارند:

- ❖ Karl E. Meyer & Shareen Blair Brysac, ***Kingmakers: The invention of the Modern Middle East***, New York, London: W. W. Norton & Company, 2008

یافتند. سلطان قابوس، از شاه ایران کمک خواست، و در مارس ۱۹۷۲/ بهار ۱۳۵۱ پیمان محرمانه‌ای بین مشاور نظامی‌ی سلطان قابوس و مقامات ایرانی به امضاء رسید که تا مدتی از مردم ایران پنهان ماند. حدود یک ماه پس از امضاء قرارداد بود که امیر عباس هویدا، نخست وزیر وقت، در فشرده‌ترین کلام اعلام کرد: «ایران به درخواست سلطان قابوس برای دریافت کمک از ایران، پاسخ مثبت داده است.» و این چنین بود که پیشرفته‌ترین سلاح‌ها و تجهیزات نظامی (که شاه خریده بود و باید آزمایش می‌شد) و نیروهای ویژه‌ی هوابرد و تفنگداران دریائی‌ی ارتش ایران (که برای مصرف داخلی، باید با جنگ‌های پارتیزانی و ضدحمله‌های چریکی آشنا می‌شدند)، در حوالی‌ی منطقه‌ی ظفار پیاده شد. (۲۹ آذر ۱۳۵۲/ ۲۰ دسامبر ۱۹۷۳) این ارتش، در درازنای کم‌تر از دو سال بخش‌هائی از منطقه‌ی پیکارگران را بمباران کرد؛ با کشیدن «خط دماوند» به گرداگرد منطقه‌ی انقلابیون، راه‌های دریافت کمک (از یمن جنوبی و چین) را بر آن‌ها بست؛ و با یاری‌ی سلطان قابوس و نیروهای انگلیسی، بخش مهمی از بلندی‌های استراتژیک آنان را تصرف کرد. خبر این «پیروزی»، روز ۲۰ اکتبر ۱۹۷۵ در رسانه‌های خارجی منعکس شد. البته باید این نکته را هم یادآوری کنم که انقلابیون ظفار پس از کنگره‌ی سوم (اوت ۱۹۷۱)، خود را با عنوان «جبهه‌ی ملی‌ی دموکراتیک برای آزادسازی‌ی عمان و **خلیج اشغال‌شده‌ی عربی**» معرفی کرده بودند، و در کنگره‌ی چهارم بود که به خاطر دخالت ارتش ایران و شکست‌های کمرشکنی که بر آن‌ها وارد شده بود، در هدف خود تجدید نظر کردند و عنوان «جبهه‌ی آزادی‌بخش خلق عمان» را برای خود برگزیدند. بنابراین، افزون بر ضدیتی که شاه با مرام کمونیستی داشت، تغییر نام خلیج فارس و تهدید برای تمامیت ارضی‌ی ایران نیز می‌توانست/ می‌تواند به عنوان انگیزه‌ی او (با گرایش‌های ناسیونالیستی‌ای که ابراز می‌کرد) برای این دخالت نظامی برشمرده شود. این بود که روزنامه‌ی کیهان، «کمک‌های ایران به عمان» و «پیروزی‌ی نیروهای ایران در عمان» را با افتخار گزارش کرد. (۲۲ بهمن ۱۳۵۲)[۷۰۰] در هر حال، شرکت ایران در سرکوب شورشیان ظفار از دیدگاه مردمِ هر روز انقلابی‌ترشده‌ی ایران، به اعتراض و مخالفت داخلی علیه شاه دامن زد؛ و از سوی دیگر، ذات دخالت پیروزمندانه‌ی ایران در عمان، از دیدگاه کشورهای عرب- که همواره نگران تسلط ایران بر منطقه بوده‌اند- «توسعه‌طلبی» تلقی شد، و مخالفت «اتحادیه‌ی عرب» را نسبت به ایران و شاه ایران برانگیخت؛ مخالفتی که، دو سه سال بعد نتایج خود را در تضعیف محمدرضا شاه (در اُپک و مسئله‌ی قیمت نفت) و عدم حمایت از او (در زد و بندهای بین‌المللی‌ی دوران انقلاب) به عرض تاریخ رساند.[۷۰۱]

محمدرضا شاه پهلوی، در حالی که بخش مهمی از ذخایر ارزی‌ی کشور را صرف خرید اسلحه از امریکا و اسرائیل می‌کرد، و در حالی که پشتیبانی‌ی اکثریت قاطع مردم – حتا دولتمردان و کارگزاران دو روی خودش- را از دست داده بود، در چانه‌زنی بر سر بهاء نفت با دولت‌های غربی، از «منافع ملی» سخن می‌گفت؛ برای بالابردن بهاء نفت در سازمان اُپک پیش‌قدم می‌شد؛ و در یک سخنرانی، به حق پایمال شده‌ی ایران در قرارداد کنسرسیومِ سال ۱۳۳۲ اشاره کرد و گفت:

> [...] شاید آن موقع ما بیش‌تر از این هم نمی‌توانستیم به دست بیاوریم، اما آن شرایط - که ما دلایل کافی داریم که در مورد منافع ایران به طور کامل هم اجرا نشده- ادامه نخواهد داشت. ما قراردادمان را در سال ۱۹۷۹، یعنی ۶ شش سال دیگر، به هیچ وجه تمدید نخواهیم کرد. (۱۳۵۱).

---

۷۰۰ برگرفته از: غلامرضا نجاتی، ***تاریخ سیاسی‌ی بیست و پنج ساله‌ی ایران: از کودتا تا انقلاب***، جلد اول، پیشین، ص ۳۶۵.

۷۰۱ افزون بر کتاب غلامرضا نجاتی، برای تدوین این بخش از گفتار از مآخذ زیر سود جسته‌ام:
- عبدالرضا هوشنگ مهدوی، ***سیاست خارجی‌ی ایران در دوران پهلوی***، پیشین.
- ***Dhofar Rebellion in Oman 1964 - 1975***, Walden University online, Dec. 16, 2000: http://www.onwar.com/aced/data/oscar/oman1964.htm

و «۶ سال دیگر»، یعنی سال ۱۹۷۸/۱۳۵۷. گرچه هستند مورخان و پژوهشگرانی که با تکیه بر برخی از مدارک، چنین دریافت کرده‌اند که این گونه نافرمانی هم- با هدف بدست آوردن اعتماد مردم ایران و کاهش از موج نارضایتی- از سوی امریکا به شاه دیکته می‌شد. البته، ماده‌ی دهم از پیشنهاد چهارده ماده‌ای «جان بولینگ»- تحلیل‌گر مسائل ایران در وزارت خارجه‌ی امریکا- که او با هدفِ نشان دادن راه‌هائی برای دوام سلطنت شاه در ۲۰ مارس ۱۳۶۱ (اسفند ۱۳۳۹) به عنوان گزارش به وزارت متبوع خود عرضه کرده است،[۷۰۲] چنین متبادر می‌شود که یکی از راه‌های پیشنهادی برای جلوگیری از روند نارضایتی مردم ایران، همانا تظاهر شاه به مخالفت با کنسرسیوم نفت است.[۷۰۳] با این وصف، مدارک فراوانی نیز در دست داریم که هم از نارضایتی‌ی شاه نسبت به امریکا و اسرائیل و رسانه‌های امریکائی در سال‌های واپسین سلطنتش خبر می‌دهند، و هم از مقاومت او در برابر آن‌ها. افزون بر نافرمانی‌ی شاه در قلمرو نفت و سازمان «اپک»، که در عمل واقع شد، مثال‌های فراوانی از تصمیم‌گیری‌های مستقل و موضع‌گیری‌های مخالف او، در منابع مختلف ثبت شده است. مثلاً، جیمی کارتر در دفتر روزانه‌ی خود- به تاریخ ۳۱ ژوئیه‌ی ۱۹۷۷- به «پیام خشمگین شاه به» خودش، «به خاطر تأخیر در ارسال هواپیماهای آواکس به ایران»، اشاره کرده است.[۷۰۴] یا، زمانی که شاه به مایک والاس، خبرنگار امریکائی، می‌گوید: «اسرائیل روزنامه‌ها و رسانه، و بانک‌ها و معاملات مالی‌ی امریکا را کنترل می‌کند»، خبرنگار، به عنوان پرسش، از نشریه‌های متعددی (مانند نیویورک تایمز، واشنگتن پست، و چند نشریه‌ی معتبر دیگر) نام می‌برد، و شاه یک به یک تأیید می‌کند که «بله، این هم زیر نفوذ اسرائیل است.» و در پایان، با اطمینانی حیرت‌انگیز می‌افزاید: «و من این را متوقف خواهم کرد.»[۷۰۵]

گرچه در آن زمان، اعتماد اکثریت دانش‌آموختگان و دانشجویان و پیکارگران سیاسی/ مدنی/ فرهنگی‌ی ایران نسبت به شاه به کلی از بین رفته بود، و پس از انقلاب ایران نیز برخی از نویسندگان و مورخان ایرانی‌ی مخالف شاه- مانند سرهنگ غلامرضا نجاتی- همه‌ی مخالفت‌های شاه با امریکا و اسرائیل و کشورهای غربی را به عنوان همان «ژست تبلیغاتی» برآورد کردند، اما اکنون، با آگاهی از برخوردهای سرسختانه‌ی شاه با «حامیانِ» خود، می‌توان دید که بیانیه‌ی او پیرامون عدم تمدید قرارداد کنسرسیوم، در چشم دولتمردان این کشورها بسی بیش‌تر از یک «ژستِ تبلیغاتی» برآورد شده بود. با این دریافت بود که طرف‌های قراردادی که قرار بود «به هیچ وحه تمدید» نشود، با استفاده از مخالفت کشورهای عربی (به ویژه عربستان سعودی) نسبت به ایران و شخص محمدرضا شاه، به چاره‌جوئی افتادند. از جمله ده‌ها گزارشی که در زمینه‌ی این چاره‌جوئی منتشر شده، متن زیر است که در اکتبر ۱۹۷۷ به عنوان گزارش، در نهاد «امور خارجی foreign affairs» امریکا تهیه شده است:

> در چشم محمدرضا شاه پهلوی، ایران یک امپراتوری‌ی بزرگ بوده و در آینده هم امپراتوری‌ی بزرگ‌تری خواهد شد. در چند سال آینده، در منطقه‌ی خلیج فارس و حوالی‌ی اقیانوس هند نقش انحصاری خواهد داشت. تا سال ۱۹۹۹ در سلسله مراتب قدرت جهانی، به موقعیت بریتانیا و فرانسه خواهد رسید. شاه با دیدن چنین رؤیائی از آینده، چنان عمل می‌کند که انگار همه‌ی این‌ها واقعیت دارد. در حالی که عربستان سعودی، همسایه‌ی او در آن سوی خلیج، کم‌تر از امپراتوری سخن

---

702 Yonah Alexander and Allen Nanes (eds.). ***The United States and Iran: A Documentary History***. Frederick, Md: Alethia Books, 1980. PP. 315- 322.

۷۰۳ ماده‌ی دهم از این پیشنهادِ ۱٤ ماده‌ای را غلامرضا نجاتی به شرح زیر ترجمه کرده است: «شاه باید علیه کنسرسیوم نفت ژشت تهدید برای دریافت امتیازات بیش‌تری بگیرد و این طور وانمود کند که کنسرسیوم نسبت به اقتدار و تصمیات او تمکین نمی‌کند.» به مأخذ زیر نگاه کنید:

❖ سرهنگ غلامرضا نجاتی، ***تاریخ سیاسی‌ی بیست و پنج ساله‌ی ایران: از کودتا تا انقلاب***، تهران: مؤسسه‌ی خدمات فرهنگی رسا، چاپ هفتم، ۱۳۸٤، صص ۱۳۷ تا ۱۳۸.

704 Jimmy Carter, ***Keeping Faith: Memoirs of a President***, Bantam Books, 1982, pp. ٤۳٤.

۷۰۵ به مأخذ زیر، که من آخرین بار آن را در تاریخ ۱۸ دسامبر ۲۰۱۱ مشاهده کرده‌ام، نگاه کنید:
http://www.youtube.com/watch?v=s_u0Hqzf_DU

می‌گوید ولی به تدریج نفوذ خود را به جهان عرب توسعه می‌دهد. شیخ احمد زکی یمانی، وزیر نفت عربستان سعودی، تا زمانی که از سوی پادشاه خود سخن می‌گوید، عملاً می‌تواند بهاء جهانی‌ی نفت را دیکته کند. او می‌تواند اُپک را رهبری کند یا آن را بشکند. او می‌تواند با «معتدل» نگاه داشتن بهاء نفت، امریکائیان را خشنود کند، و در همان حال به آن‌ها یادآوری کند که اسرائیل را به قراری پس برانند که مورد پذیرش جهان عرب باشد. ایالات متحده از میزان بالای وارادت نفت، که به آسیب‌پذیری‌ی آن در برابر تصمیم‌های اوپک می‌افزاید، نگران است، اما از این واقعیت احساس آسودگی می‌کند که دوستی در ریاض دارد.[۷۰۶] (گیومه در متن انگلیسی وجود دارد.)

البته خبرنگارانِ غیرایرانی می‌توانستند با شاه ایران مصاحبه کنند، یا در کنفرانس‌های مطبوعاتی پیرامون برنامه‌های آینده‌ی او، یا خرید جنگ‌افزار و هواپیماهای کنکورد، او را به باد پرسش‌های اعتراضی بگیرند؛ مثلاً بپرسند: چرا این همه پول صرف خرید جنگ‌افزار می‌کنی؟ چرا اصلاً اسلحه می‌خری؟ برای مقابله با کدام دشمن می‌خری؟ و شاه هم، در حالی که بیش‌ترِ این خبرنگاران را با نام کوچک صدا می‌کرد، گرچه گاه با لحنی تند، اما در کمال بردباری، به آن‌ها پاسخ می‌داد.[۷۰۷] در برابر، نه تنها خبرنگاران ما جرأت چنین پرسش‌هائی با چنان لحنی را نداشتند، بلکه خود شاه هم در مورد قراردادهای اقتصادی/ نظامی با شرکت‌های خارجی، یا خریدهای هنگفت جنگ‌افزار با مردم ایران سخن نمی‌گفت، و سرفصل مذاکرات خود را با سران کشورهائی که از آن‌ها دیدار می‌کرد، با ملت ایران و با رسانه‌های ایرانی، و حتا با مجلس قانون‌گذاری‌ی کشورش در میان نمی‌گذاشت. منتها اکنون با انتشار سندهای سری و نیمه‌سری‌ی آرشیوهای دولت‌های غربی، و به برکت جست‌وجوهای پژوهشگران ایرانی، به این استنتاج می‌رسیم که برخی از «رؤیاها»ی شاه با رسیدن به واقعیت چندان فاصله‌ای نداشت. مثلاً زمانی که مذاکره بر سر تشکیل «اتحادیه‌ی اروپا» در کش و قوس‌های نخستین بود، محمدرضا شاه پهلوی برای ایجاد «موازنه» در سطح جهانی، از اتحاد کشورهای در حال توسعه در منطقه‌ی اقیانوس هند (ایران، هند، پاکستان، بنگلادش، برمه، تایلند، مالزی، و سنگاپور) سخن گفته بود، و در این زمینه با سران برخی از این کشورها، از جمله هند، گفت‌وگو کرده بود.[۷۰۸] بنابراین، جای شگفتی نیست که در حوالی‌ی انقلاب ۵۷، افزون بر تکیه‌ی مکرر بر «دیکتاتوری»ی شاه و «نقض حقوق بشر در ایران»، عبارتِ «بلندپروازی‌های شاه» (به عنوان یکی از علل انقلاب ایران) ورد زبان سخنگویان دولت‌های غربی و رسانه‌هاشان بود.

افزون بر اقدام پیرامون این «رؤیاها»، و افزون بر چانه‌زنی بر سر بهاء نفت و تهدید رگ حیاتی‌ی دولت‌های غربی از سوی ایران، زمانی که عراق در یک حمله‌ی هوائی‌ی برق‌آسا به شهرهای مرزی‌ی خسروی و قصر شیرین، امکان جنگ دو کشور ایران و عراق را پدید آورد (۱۹۷۵/ ۱۳۵۴)، محمدرضا شاه پهلوی، با وجود غنای ارتش و جنگ‌افزار، به جنگ تن نداد[۷۰۹] و در مذاکره‌ای با نماینده‌ی عراق (در حاشیه‌ی کنفرانس اوپک در الجزایر)، و بعد، با فرستادن

---

[706] John C. Campbell, ***On Power: Oil Power in the Middle East***, Oct. 1977, visited on Jan. 4th. 199۹ at "Foreign Affairs" site:
http://www.foreignaffairs.com/articles/41947/john-c-campbell/mission-to-tehran

[۷۰۷] مجله‌ی «اشپیگل»، ژانویه ۱۹۷٤، برگرفته از:
- Ardavan Bahrami, ***H.I.M. Mohammad Reza Pahlavi, The Late Shah of Iran***, Free Republic, August 13, 2004:

www.freerepublic.com/focus/f-news/1190947/posts

[۷۰۸] مایکل هورنسبی (Michael Hornsby) مجله‌ی تایمز، ۳ اکتبر ۱۹۷۳، برگرفته از:
- Ardavan Bahrami, ***H.I.M. Mohammad Reza Pahlavi, The Late Shah of Iran***, Free Republic, August 13, 2004:

www.freerepublic.com/focus/f-news/1190947/posts

[۷۰۹] مرتضی کاخی، نماینده‌ی تام‌الاختیار دولت ایران برای تعیین مرزهای آبی‌ی ایران و عراق (در سال ۱۹۷۵)، در مصاحبه‌ای که در سال ۱۳۸۹ با روزنامه‌ی «اعتماد» چاپ تهران انجام داد، با این که اعتراف می‌کند در مذاکرات «نظامی»ی ایران و عراق شرکت نداشته و از

کارشناسان متعدد برای گفت‌وگو با مسئولان عراقی، در کوتاه‌ترین زمان ممکن و بدون هیچ آسیبی به ارتش، و بدون هیچ آسیبی به تمامیت ارضیِ ایران، به بحران خط مرزیِ بین دو کشور پایان داد. پروژه‌ی اتمیِ شاه، و برنامه‌ها مخفیِ او پیرامون خرید ابزار هسته‌ای از کشورهائی مانند استرالیا و افریقای جنوبی نیز از چشم سازمان اطلاعاتیِ امریکا پنهان نماند. افزون بر موارد مخفی، شاه، ضمن گفت‌وگو با مقامات امریکائی در زمینه‌ی پروژه‌ی اتمیِ ایران، و دریافت ابزار لازم از امریکا، از سال ۱۳۵۳ تا زمان سقوط، با برقراریِ رابطه با هند، آرژانتین، آلمان، فرانسه، اتریش، و دانمارک در زمینه‌های مختلف مربوط به تکنولوژیِ هسته‌ای، انحصار امریکا بر خود و ایران را شکست. او در سال ۱۳۵۳ از دست‌یابیِ ایران به سلاح هسته‌ای، «زودتر از آن چه فکر کنید»، خبر داد. گرچه در برابر تذکر انحصارطلبان هسته‌ایِ دنیا از این سخن عقب‌نشینی کرد؛ اما یک سال بعد گفت: «ایران تمایلی به ساخت سلاح‌های هسته‌ای ندارد. اما اگر کشورهای کوچک ساخت این سلاح را شروع کنند، ایران نیز ممکن است در این سیاست خود تجدید نظر کند.»[۷۱۰] و جهان می‌دانست که سه سال پیش از این سخن، «کشور کوچک»یِ چون پاکستان، ساخت جنگ‌افزار هسته‌ای را «شروع» کرده بود. و کشورهای غربی هم می‌دانستند که «سازمان انرژیِ اتمیِ ایران»، در همان سال ۱۳۵۴، تعداد ۱۵۰ کارشناس فیزیک هسته‌ای دارد، و صدها تن دانشجو نیز در «مرکز پژوهش‌های هسته‌ایِ دانشگاه» تحصیل کرده‌اند و در حال تحصیل هستند، که به زودی نیاز ایران به کارشناسان آن‌ها را منتفی خواهند کرد.[۷۱۱] به بیانی دیگر، شاه ایران در سال‌های پایانیِ سلطنت، هم رویاروی «هفت خواهران» قدیم نفتی ایستاد و هم در برابر کارتل‌های اسلحه‌سازیِ امریکا، و هم در برابر هژمونیِ امریکا در ایران.[۷۱۲] و شاید عدم موافقت کشورهای غربی با آرزوی اتمیِ شاه (که

مفاد قرار و مدارهای نظامی بی‌خبر بوده است، بدون هیچ اشاره‌ای به حمله‌ی چندساعتیِ عراق به مرزهای ایران، و بدون اشاره به امکان عدم تمایل شاه به شروع یک جنگ تمام عیار با عراق، تمام ماجرا را یک «مانور» تعبیر می‌کند. (در حالی که من، ملیحه تیره گل، در آن زمان در شهر کرمانشاه زندگی می‌کردم و خبر بمباران شهرهای مرزیِ خسروی و قصر شیرین را همان روز هم از رادیو و هم از مردم این شهرها شنیدم.) تا نمونه‌ای از تحریف تاریخ توسط دولتمردان مورد اعتماد «شاه» و بعداً ماندگار در جمهوریِ اسلامی در این جا به ثبت رسد، بخشی از این مصاحبه را عیناً درج می‌کنم:

- پیش از ملاقات صدام و شاه در الجزایر گویا یک درگیریِ چند ساعته هم بین دو کشور به وجود می‌آید؟

مرتضی کاخی: جنگ نشد. ایران قوای خودش را به خوزستان برده و فرمانده ارتش ایران گفته بود اگر اجازه دهند ما ناهار را در بغداد می‌خوریم. یعنی صبح حرکت کنیم، ظهر بغداد را می‌گیریم.

- خب علت لشکرکشیِ ایران به خوزستان چه بود؟

مرتضی کاخی: همین روابط نامناسب مرزی و بدرفتاری عراقی ها با ایرانی‌ها. دولت عراق اموال ایرانیانی را که سه نسل در عراق بودند ضبط می‌کرد و آن‌ها را به ایران می‌فرستاد، علاوه بر این، چون این‌ها شیعه بودند همواره مورد اذیت و آزار قرار می‌گرفتند. البته در عوضش ایران هم به کردهایی که در شمال عراق درگیر بودند کمک می‌کرد.

- یعنی بعد از این لشکرکشی بود که دولت الجزایر پادرمیانی کرد تا دو طرف با هم مذاکره کنند؟

مرتضی کاخی: خیر این تهدید به جایی نرسید چون کشورهای دیگر دخالت کردند و بعدها متوجه شدند این فقط یک مانور بوده. بعدها همه متوجه شدیم که شاه اسلحه به قوای ایران نداده بود. یعنی گلوله به اندازه کافی به قوای ایران نداده بود. چون هراس داشت. شاه می‌ترسید که قوای مسلح یک دفعه به طرف تهران حرکت کنند و خودش را ساقط کنند. به هر حال دیکتاتورها همیشه این گرفتاری‌ها را دارند.

برای مطالعه‌ی گفت‌وگوی یادشده به مأخذ زیر مراجعه کنید:

- ***ناگفته‌های قرارداد ۱۹۷۵ الجزایر: گفت‌وگوی روزنامه‌ی اعتماد با دکتر مرتضی کاخی- دیپلمات سابق***، تارنمای «دیپلماسیِ ایرانی»، بازدید ۲۳ مرداد ۱۳۸۹:

http://www.irdiplomacy.ir/index.php?Lang=fa&Page=24&TypeId=11&ArticleId=1307&Action=ArticleBodyView

[710] ***Timeline: The U.s., Iran And The Nuclear Question***, National Public Radio (online), August 25, 2009: http://www.unz.org/Pub/NPR-2009aug-01005
Sources: James Martin Center for Nonproliferation Studies at the Monterey Institute of International Studies/ NTI, Council on Foreign Relations, Stratfor.com, Globalsecurity.org

[۷۱۱] ***سال‌شمار هسته‌ایِ ایران***، دانشنامه‌ی «ویکی‌پدیا».

[۷۱۲] عباس امیرانتظام، معاون مهندس مهدی بازرگان در دولت موقت جمهوریِ اسلامی، معتقد است که افزایش بهاء نفت به پیشنهاد خود امریکائیان بود، تا ضمن آفریدن «بحران مصنوعی» پیرامون نفت، کشورهای نفت‌خیز نیز با پول فراوانی که به دست می‌آورند، بتوانند کالاهای غرب را خریداری کنند. امیرانتظام، پیرامون خرید اسلحه از امریکا نیز معتقد است که تمام ابزار نظامی‌ای که شاه از امریکا خریداری کرد، به پیشنهاد خود امریکا بود، تا به شاه چنین القاء کنند که سرآمد و نگهبان منطقه است؛ ودر عین حال، کشورهای منطقه را برانگیزند تا برای مسابقه با ایران، به خرید سلاح اقدام کنند. به مأخذ زیر نگاه کنید:

خود آن را «تبعیض» می‌نامید) نیز در نارضایتی و دلسردی‌ی او نسبت به حامیان امریکائی‌اش مؤثر بود. از همان دوران بود که طرح سقوط شاه در دستور کار امریکا و متحدانش قرار گرفت؛ و چنان که عباس میلانی در تحقیق خود نشان می‌دهد، گردهم‌آئی‌ی سران کشورها در «گوادولوپ» (ژانویه‌ی ۱۹۷۹) از یک «تأییدیه» بر تصمیم پیشین فراتر نبود.[۷۱۳]

دکتر سیروس بینا (استاد اقتصاد سیاسی در دانشگاه مینه‌سوتا) در کلیه‌ی نوشته‌ها و گفتارهای سی سال گذشته‌ی خود (از ۱۹۸۵ تا مارس ۲۰۱۴)، از چشم‌اندازی گسترده‌تر، سقوط شاه را یکی از پیامدهای دگردیسی‌ی دوران و افول هژمونی‌ی امریکا در سیاست جهانی برآورد کرده است. سیروس بینا در یکی از مصاحبه‌های خود، با اشاره به فرسودگی‌ی امریکا در اثر شکست در ویتنام و فروپاشی‌ی سیستم «برتون وودز»[۷۱٤] (نظام پولی‌ی بین‌المللی) در سال ۱۹۷۱، می‌گوید:

> هم‌زمانی‌ی افول رژیم شاه و فروپاشی‌ی دوران پاکس امریکانا (یعنی نظام بین‌المللی‌ی پس از جنگ جهانی‌ی دوم در لوای هژمونی‌ی امریکا) از رویدادهای یگانه‌ی تاریخ است، که به ندرت برای کشوری اتفاق می‌افتد؛ گو این که در این مورد نیکاراگوئه نیز با ما (ایران) هم‌داستان است. باید توجه داشت که فروپاشی‌ی پاکس امریکانا از فروریختن یک **کل** در جهان آن روز حکایت می‌کرد، که رژیم شاه خود **جزئی** از آن به شمار می‌رفت. بنابراین، با توجه به مناسبات ارگانیک اجزای این نظام بین‌المللی، افول رژیم شاه لزوماً از شکستن ستون فقرات تمامی‌ی رژیم‌هائی خبر می‌داد که خود پاره‌ای عظیم (کشورهائی که تحت هژمونی‌ی امریکا بودند و به «جهان سوم» تعلق داشتند) از پیکر فرسوده‌ی پاکس امریکانا به شمار می‌آمدند. [...][۷۱٥] (تأکیدها از سیروس بینا هستند.)

مجید تفرشی (پژوهشگر این دوره از تاریخ ایران)، با استفاده از آرشیو ملی‌ی بریتانیا (که در سال ۲۰۰۷ در اختیار شمار معدودی از پژوهشگران و روزنامه‌نگاران داخلی و خارجی قرار گرفت)، گزارش‌های سِر آنتونی پارسونز، سفیر وقت بریتانیا در تهران، در سال ۱۹۷۶ (۱۳۵۵)، و پیش‌بینی‌های او برای سال ۱۹۷۷ (۱۳۵۶) را به شرح زیر مرور کرده است:

> [...] سر آنتونی پارسونز سفیر کبیر وقت بریتانیا در تهران در گزارش محرمانه‌ی اول ژانویه‌ی خود در مرور سال ۱۹۷۶، تحولات ایران در طول این سال را «در برخی موارد آغاز شکل گیری‌ی فضای بی‌ثباتی، اندکی اضطراب‌آلود و آغاز بیماری که به عنوان واکنش از ابتدای رشد بالای اقتصادی‌ی جمع شده» توصیف می‌کند. پارسونز تأکید می‌کند: «اوج‌گیری‌ی مالی و اقتصادی شاید کاهش یافته باشد، ولی بلندپروازی‌های شاه برای کشورش کاهش نیافته است. او از هر زمان دیگری بیش‌تر برای رسیدن به تمدن بزرگ مصمم است، ولی اکنون توجه خاص باید بر نیاز به کار سخت‌تر در جهت افزایش تولید در جهت جلوگیری از اتلاف و افزایش هزینه‌ها باشد.» بر اساس این گزارش، تغییر سیاست‌های

❖ ***ناگفته‌های انقلاب ۵۷، در گفت‌وگوی روزبه میرابراهیمی با عباس امیرانتظام***، پاریس: انتشارات خاوران، ۱۳۸۷/ ۲۰۰۸، صص ۱۱۸ تا ۱۱۹.

713 Abbas Milani, ***The Shah***, New York: Palgrave macmillan, 2011, p. 405.

۷۱٤ پیرامون مفهوم «برتون وودز» در جلد چهارم مجموعه‌ی حاضر توضیح داده‌ام.

۷۱٥ از جمله آثار متعددی که سیروس بینا در آن‌ها به این تشخیص پرداخته است، به مآخذ زیر نگاه کنید:

❖ گفت‌وگوی «نگاه» با سیروس بینا: ***دگرگونی‌ی دورانی‌ی جهان، مناسبات و مذاکرات جمهوری‌ی اسلامی با امریکا و چشم‌انداز آینده***، نشریه‌ی «نگاه»، مارس ۲۰۱۴، صص ۳۰ تا ۳۶.

❖ Syrus Bina, ***Oil: A Time Machine- Journey Beyond Fanciful Economies and Frightful Politics***, New York: Linus Publiction, 2011.

❖ Syrus Bina & Hamid Zangeneh, ***Modern Capitalism and Islamic Idiology in Iran***, St. Martin's Press, 1991.

> اقتصادی و آغاز کاهش درآمدهای نفتی، دولت وقت ایران را مجبور کرده بود تا از بیشتر برنامه‌های گسترش سرمایه گذاری‌های بین‌المللی خود چشم پوشیده و بر خلاف سال‌های قبل، به جز مشارکت مالی در کمپانی‌ی کروپس آلمان، در هیچ پروژه‌ی جدید خارجی‌ی دیگری سرمایه‌گذاری نکند. [...] پارسونز مناسبات دوجانبه را با وجود حل اغلب مشکلات شرکت‌های بریتانیایی، از نظر تجاری چندان شکوفا ندانسته و عنوان کرده که در سال ۱۹۷۶، از شدت هجوم گسترده‌ی شرکت های بریتانیایی به ایران در دوران اوجگیری‌ی رشد اقتصادی کاسته شده بود و «**به طور خلاصه، بریتانیا و دیگر کشورها و شرکت‌های غربی دریافته‌اند که به دست آوردن طلاهایی که خیابان‌های تهران با آن سنگفرش شده به مراتب سخت‌تر از آنی بوده که قبلاً تصور می‌کرده‌اند.**»[۷۱۶] (تأکید از من است.)

اسناد محرمانه/ آزادشده‌ی وزات امور خارجه و کتابخانه‌های رئیس جمهورهای امریکا نیز از بازتاب واشنگتن در مورد کوتاه شدن دست این کشور و کارتل‌های آن از «طلاهایی» که فکر می‌کردند «خیابان‌های تهران با آن سنگفرش شده» حکایت می‌کنند. اندرو اسکات کوپر، پژوهشگر امریکائی، با دو سال کار پژوهشی عمدتاً روی اسناد بایگانی شده در کتابخانه‌ی ریاست جمهوری جرالد فورد، در اکتبر ۲۰۰۸ گزارشی در نشریه‌ی «میدل ایست ژورنال»- مؤسسه‌ی مطالعاتی‌ی «انستیتوی خاورمیانه»- منتشر کرد. به روایت تارنمای بی‌بی‌سی در این گزارش می‌خوانیم: «دولت‌های نیکسون و فورد شرایطی را پدید آوردند که به تزلزل حکومت پهلوی در اواخر دهه ۱۹۷۰ و وقوع انقلاب اسلامی در ایران دامن زد.» پس از انتشار این گزارش، برزو درآگاهی، متنی درباره‌ی آن نوشت که در نشریه‌ی لس‌انجلس تایمز منتشر شد. در متن برزو درآگاهی می‌خوانیم:

> گنجینه‌ای از یادداشت‌ها، متون مکالمات و سایر مناظرات نشان می دهد که در اواسط دهه ۱۹۷۰ اختلافات شدیدی میان دولت‌های جمهوری خواه امریکا و محمد رضا شاه پهلوی بر سر قیمت نفت بروز کرد. گزارش آقای کوپر در «میدل ایست ژورنال» بر نقش سیاستگذاران کاخ سفید - از جمله دونالد رامسفلد دستیار ارشد پرزیدنت فورد - تمرکز دارد که امیدوار بودند بهای نفت را پائین ببرند و بلندپروازی‌های شاه را مهار کنند. [...] تحلیل‌گران و مورخان اغلب بر این باورند که این جیمی کارتر، رئیس جمهور دموکرات بود که در مورد ایران خرابکاری کرد و اجازه داد این کشور به یکی از مخالفان امریکا در منطقه بدل شود. اما این گزارش (میدل ایست ژورنال) حاکی است که پیشینیان جمهوری‌خواه وی، نه تنها به سقوط شاه کمک کردند بلکه درحال حرکت به سوی عربستان سعودی به عنوان متحد کلیدی امریکا در منطقه‌ی خلیج فارس بودند. [...] این اسناد حاکی است که با نمایان شدن آثار شدیداً منفی‌ی بهای سنگین نفت در اوایل دهه‌ی ۱۹۷۰، واشنگتن به تدریج به ایران ترشرویی نشان داد. [...] پس از پایان تحریم نفتی به خاطر حمایت امریکا از اسرائیل در مارس ۱۹۷٤، مقام های امریکایی شاه را عامل اصلی‌ی بالا ماندن قیمت نفت می‌دانستند و خواهان دست برداشتن وی از تندروی بودند. در یک مقطع، دونالد رامسفلد، که بعداً به عنوان وزیر دفاع جورج بوش [در زمان اشغال عراق] خدمت کرد، به یک مقام ارشد ایرانی که مسئول خریداری‌ی تسلیحات بود هشدار داد که تهران در حال از دست دادن دوستانش در واشنگتن است. [...] ویلیام سایمون وزیر خزانه داری و انرژی در دولت های نیکسون و فورد، از جمله کسانی بود که طرفدار فشار بر ایران بودند. وی شاه را به خاطر بهای بالای نفت مقصر می‌شناخت و می‌خواست امریکا از معاملات تسلیحاتی به عنوان اهرم فشار استفاده کند. وی در ژوئیه‌ی ۱۹۷٤ در اشاره به شاه ایران به پرزیدنت نیکسون گفت: «او، به همراه ونزوئلا، سرکرده‌ی کسانی است که مسئول

---

[۷۱۶] مجید تفرشی، پژوهشگر تاریخ معاصر، ***تحولات داخلی‌ی ایران: «انقلاب محتمل» یا «شاه همچنان با اقتدار»***، تارنمای بی‌بی‌سی، ۲۹ دسامبر ۲۰۰۷/ ۸ دی ماه ۱۳۸٦، به نشانی‌ی زیر:
http://www.bbc.co.uk/persian/iran/story/2007/12/071226_bd-mt-archive1.shtml

> قیمت نفت هستند. آیا می شود بر شاه فشار وارد کرد؟» [...] سعودی ها در اجلاس ماه دسامبر [۱۹۷۶] در دوحه، قطر، با اعلام این که تولید نفت را سه میلیون بشکه در روز افزایش خواهند داد (از ۸ میلیون و ۶۰۰ هزار به ۱۱ میلیون و ۶۰۰ هزار) اوپک را شگفت زده کردند. آن حرکت باعث افت قیمت نفت شد. کیسینجر به فورد گفت: «ما باید به خاطر آن چه در اوپک اتفاق افتاد به خود تبریک بگوییم. من همواره گفته‌ام که سعودی‌ها نقش کلیدی دارند... دیپلماسی‌ی عالی‌ی ماست که باعث این وضع شد.» اما این یک پیروزی بود که ضررهای زیادی به دنبال داشت. ایران که همه‌ی ذخایر خود را صرف خریداری‌ی سلاح‌های امریکایی و برنامه‌ی تمدن بزرگ شاه کرده بود - برنامه ای که با تزریق حجم عظیمی پول به کشور باعث تورم شد - با کمبود شدید مالی روبه‌رو شد. شاه ورشکسته شده بود. افت بهای نفت همراه با تورم او را وادار به ترک طرح های بلندپروازانه برای مدرن سازی کشورش کرد. کوپر در گزارش خود می‌نویسد: « اجلاس دوحه، و تصمیم عربستان سعودی برای تضعیف بهای نفت خام و افزایش تولید برای اشباع بازار، اقتصاد ایران را به سوی پرتگاه سوق داد.» دولت شاه که به دلیل افت شدید درآمد نفتی به لرزه درآمده بود، یک بودجه ریاضتی را اعمال کرد که باعث بیکاری هزاران نفر و از بین رفتن اعتماد سرمایه‌گذاران شد و طبقه‌ی متوسط ایران را وحشتزده کرد. هرج و مرج اقتصادی و بیکاری به سرعت گسترش یافت. ظرف یک سال پس از اجلاس دوحه، اولین تظاهرات انبوه در خیابان‌های پایتخت ایران شکل گرفت؛ تظاهراتی که انقلاب را به دنبال داشت.[۷۱۷]

عباس امیرانتظام در کتاب «در جستوجوی حقیقت» و هم در «گفت‌وگو با روزبه میرابراهیمی»، بالا بردن بهاء نفت و حتا تأسیس «اوپک» را فرایندی آگاهانه و برنامه‌ریزی‌شده از سوی خود امریکا می‌داند. او با ارائه‌ی دلیل، معتقد است که امریکائی‌ها برای ایجاد نارضایتی در مردم ایران و به ویژه قشر روحانیت، تز اصلاحات ارضی و قانون کاپیتولاسیون (مصونیت نظامیان امریکائی) و حق رأی برای زنان را به طور غیرمستقیم به شاه القاء و تحمیل کردند.[۷۱۸] در گفته‌های عباس امیرانتظام، حتا با این جمله برمی‌خوریم که:

> من با مطالعات خودم به این نتیجه رسیدم که امریکا اصرار داشت در فاصله‌ی بین سال‌های ۳۲ تا ۵۷ تنفر ملت ایران را نسبت به خودش (امریکا) و نسبت به سلطنت تشدید کند.[۷۱۹]

بسیاری از این گزاره‌های عباس امیرانتظام، در کتاب «تاریخ سیاسی‌ی بیست و پنج ساله‌ی ایران: از کودتا تا انقلاب» تألیف سرهنگ غلامرضا نجاتی نیز تأیید شده است.[۷۲۰]

در هر حال، چنین به نظر می‌رسد که آخرین اتمام حجت‌های امریکا در سفر «جرج بوش» (پدر)، رئیس وقتِ سازمان سیا، به ایران (اردی‌بهشت ۱۳۵۶) با شاه در میان گذاشته شد. شاه، اما- به گونه‌ای همگانی و غیرمستقیم در یک مصاحبه- پاسخ داد که: «ایران بازیچه‌ی هیچ کشوری نیست؛ از جمله ایالات متحده!» و در جای دیگر گفت: «ما از چشم آبی‌ها

---

[۷۱۷] برزو درآگاهی، ***نقش نیکسون و فورد در تضعیف شاه***، تجدید چاپ شده در تارنمای بی‌بی‌سی، ۱۹ اکتبر ۲۰۰۸/ ۲۸ مهر ۱۳۸۷، به نشانی‌ی زیر:
http://www.bbc.co.uk/persian/iran/story/2008/10/081019_si-nixon-shah.shtml

[۷۱۸] عباس امیرانتظام در گفت‌وگو با روزبه میرابراهیمی، ***ناگفته‌های انقلاب ۵۷***، پاریس: نشر خاوران، ۱۳۸۷/ ۲۰۰۸، صص ۱۱۶ تا ۱۳۹.

[۷۱۹] عباس امیرانتظام در گفت‌وگو با روزبه میرابراهیمی، ***ناگفته‌های انقلاب ۵۷***، پاریس: نشر خاوران، ۱۳۸۷/ ۲۰۰۸، ص ۱۱۷.

[۷۲۰] سرهنگ غلامرضا نجاتی، ***تاریخ سیاسی‌ی بیست و پنج ساله‌ی ایران: از کودتا تا انقلاب***، تهران: انتشارات خدمات فرهنگی‌ی رسا، چاپ هفتم، ۱۳۸۴، جلد اول، صص ۳۰۳ تا ۳۶۱.

دستور نمی‌گیریم». «چشم آبی‌ها»ی جرّار نیز از سوئی، با تبانی با عربستان سعودی در بالابردن تولید روزانه‌ی نفت، از بهاء نفت در سطح جهانی کاستند و به این وسیله با افزایش تورم اقتصادی در ایران، به قول خودشان با «بلندپروازی‌ها»ی او مقابله کردند،[۷۲۱] و از سوی دیگر، به شخصی که سال‌ها «در کمین ایستاده بود»- اما خودش هم احتمالاً فکر نمی‌کرد روزی بدیلی برای شاه باشد- آماده باش دادند، و از سوی سوم، با باز کردن پرونده‌ی تاریک شاه در «حقوق بشر»، به او پاسخ دادند. پیامد آن «تبانی» و این «پاسخ»، بازشدن فضای تنفس بود برای پیکارگران فرهنگی و سیاسی‌ی ایران، که حالا دیگر هیچ گوشی برای شنیدن و **هیچ خِردی** برای تجزیه و تحلیل برایشان باقی نمانده بود.[۷۲۲]

***

اما پیش از رسیدن به این بن‌بست، هشدارهای اندیشه‌ورزان و خبرگان سیاسی‌ی ایران به شاه نیز، از سوی او پاسخ مثبت دریافت نکرد. اندکی پیش از آن که فضای سیاسی به اجبار «باز» شود و از هم بشکافد، علی‌اصغر حاج سیدجوادی، روزنامه‌نگار و کوشنده‌ی سیاسی (از طیف ملی/ مذهبی)، در دی ماه ۱۳۵۴ نامه‌ای به دربار نوشت، و طی‌ی آن، انتصاب امیرعباس هویدا (نخست وزیر وقت) به سرپرستی‌ی پروژه‌ی مبارزه با فساد اداری (بازرسی‌ی شاهنشاهی) را، نشانه‌ی فساد و ورشکستگی‌ی کل رژیم برآورد کرد. حاج سیدجوادی، در خرداد ۱۳۵۵ نامه‌ی دیگری به دربار نوشت و در آن شخص شاه را به خاطر نقض قانون اساسی به پرسش گرفت. من متن این نامه را در زمان انتشار آن خوانده بودم، اما در زمان نگارش این مبحث، آن را میان مآخذ خود نیافتم؛ منتها خود حاج سیدجوادی سی سال بعد، در مصاحبه‌ای در تبعید، پیرامون آن نامه می‌گوید:

> [در آن نامه ...] خطرات و ضایعات بعد از فروپاشی را برشمردم و آخر گفتم من صدای شکستن سقف رژیم را با تمام هوش و حواسم احساس می‌کنم و بعد از آن معلوم نیست که نظام دچار چه حوادث هولناکی در رابطه با مناسبات خارجی و آشفتگی‌ی نتایج استبداد و فساد شود. [...] اما من با جامعه‌ام قهر نکردم و قلم می‌زدم تا چشم‌های نسل جوان را نسبت به حقایق باز کنم؛ با توجه به این که مسئله‌ی براندازی‌ی شاهنشاهی مد نظر ما نبود.[۷۲۳]

البته محمدرضا شاه پهلوی، که برخلاف پدرش، دروغ‌های سفلگانِ تملق‌گو و دسیسه‌کاران تحقیرشده‌ی اطرافش را خوش‌تر داشت تا نظر اندیشمندان دلسوز ایران را، به این دو نامه ترتیب اثر نداد، اما انتشار گسترده‌ی این دو نامه، به ویژه نامه‌ی دوم- که برای نخستین بار از سوی یک ژورنالیست مستقل به شخص شاه نوشته شده بود، بر امید و جسارت پیکارگران داخل و خارج از ایران افزود. عبدالکریم لاهیجی، حقوق‌دان، گفته است: «این نامه، جدای از نقد مفصل و جان‌دارش، هیبت رژیم و شاه را شکست و روحیه‌ی بزرگی به مبارزان با رژیم پهلوی داد.»[۷۲۴] در بهمن ماه ۱۳۵۵ بود که به دنبال افشاگری‌های نشریه‌های غربی، عمدتاً، «ساندی تایمز» لندن، روزنامه‌های ایران برای نخستین بار پس از کودتای سال

---

[۷۲۱] از جمله متن‌هائی که پیرامون توطئه‌ی امریکا جهت تضعیف محمدرضا شاه و نهایتاً سقوط سلطنت او نوشته شده، خواننده‌ام را به متن کوتاه اما گویای زیر رجوع می‌دهم:

❖ برزو درگاهی، ***اقدامات نیکسون و فورد برای تضعیف محمدرضا شاه***، لس‌انجلس تایمز، ۱۶ اکتبر ۲۰۰۸، ترجمه از انگلیسی: احسان نوروزی، تارنمای «پشتیبانان»، بازدید مه ۲۰۱۰ (اردیبهشت ۱۳۸۹):

http://poshtibanan.org/index.php?option=com_content&task=view&id=302&Itemid=42

[۷۲۲] من در این جا واژه‌ی «خرد» را دقیقاً با معنای فلسفی/ روان‌شناختی‌ی آن به کار برده‌ام: اریک فروم، با ترجمه‌ی بهرام محیی می‌نویسد: «خرد، آن فعالیت ذهنی است که تلاش می‌کند از سطح اشیاء به عمق و هستی‌ی آن‌ها نفوذ کند، تا دریابد که واقعاً در ورای اشیاء چه چیزی نهفته است، چه نیروها و کشش‌هائی هستند که خود قابل رؤیت نیستند اما پدیدارهای ظاهری را متأثر و متعیّن می‌سازند».

[۷۲۳] ***حاج سید جوادی: این بار هم سقف رژیم شکسته است***، گفت‌وگوی فرزانه بذرپور از نشریه‌ی «جرس» با علی‌اصغر حاج سید جوادی، تیر ماه ۱۳۸۹:

http://09oct09.rapidshare-uae.com/index.php?url=nlgq6AxEkQLrS8FlZuO6MimFmJF2SYWTvvYHKZInOijGO1E0kXn6

[۷۲۴] ***حاج سیدجوادی: این بار هم سقف رژیم شکسته است***، پیشین.

۳۲، از «ممنوعیت شکنجه» سخن گفتند، و از امکان بازدید زندان‌ها توسط گروه‌های حقوق بشر خبر دادند.[۷۲۵] با ورود این گروه‌ها به زندان‌های ایران و گزارش‌هائی که تهیه کردند، «در سال ۱۳۵۶، تعداد ۵۶۱ زندانی‌ی سیاسی آزاد شدند، و گزارش برخی از فعالیت‌های مخالفان سیاسی نیز در روزنامه‌ها درج می‌شد.»[۷۲۶] در اردی‌بهشت ۱۳۵۶، تعداد ۵۳ تن از حقوق‌دان‌های دادگستری در نامه‌ی سرگشاده‌ای که به شاه نوشتند، نسبت به دادگاه‌های سیاسی و بی‌حقوقی‌ی زندانیان سیاسی اعتراض کردند. در خرداد ۱۳۵۶ شاپور بختیار، داریوش فروهر، و کریم سنجابی (از اعضاء شورای عالی‌ی جبهه‌ی ملی‌ی ایران) نیز نامه‌ی سرگشاده‌ای با عنوان «اعتراض به نقض قانون اساسی‌ی مشروطیت» به شاه نوشتند، و بر اساس مطالبات آن نامه، تظاهرات عظیمی در تهران برگزار کردند. به گفته‌ی دکتر شاپور بختیار، صد و پنجاه هزار نفر در آن تظاهرات شرکت داشتند. البته مفاد آن نامه و فریادِ تأییدکنندگان آن به گوش و هوش شاه ایران راه نیافت؛ در عوض، نویسندگان نامه را روانه‌ی زندان کرد. در تیر ۱۳۵۶ چهل تن از شخصیت‌های ادبی و فرهنگی، نامه‌ای به امیرعباس هویدا نوشتند و نسبت به دخالت ساواک در فعالیت‌های ادبی و فرهنگی و سانسورِ بیان اندیشه اعتراض کردند.

اما یکی از مهم‌ترین پیامدهای فضای باز سیاسی، زمزمه‌ی تجدید حیات «کانون نویسندگان ایران» و رویدادِ بزرگ و مؤثر «ده شب شعر گوته» بود. در «ده شب شعر گوته» (۱۸ تا ۲۷ مهر ماه ۱۳۵۶)، پس از چند دهه خفقان، ۶۰ شاعر و نویسنده و پژوهشگر و مترجم و هنرمند، در حالی که در محاصره‌ی نیروهای انتظامی و امنیتی بودند، صدای اعتراض خود را نسبت به سانسور و نبود آزادی به گوش هزارها شنونده‌ای رساندند که در درون و بیرون «انستیتو گوته»‌ی تهران به مدت ده شب- و گاه زیر باران - به گوش ایستاده بودند. قرارِ دکتر بِکِر (رئیس انستیتو گوته، یا کانون فرهنگی‌ی ایران و آلمان) با دکتر باقر پرهام (نماینده‌ی «کانون نویسندگان ایران») این بود که در سخنرانی‌ها و شعرخوانی‌ها از ورود به مسائل سیاسی خودداری شود. اما پیمانه‌ها آن‌چنان لبریز، و فرصت آن‌چنان کمیاب و غنیمت بود که هر یک از شاعران و نویسندگان و هنرمندانی که پشت تریبون قرار گرفت، مستقیم یا غیر مستقیم، کم یا بیش، به سانسور و خفقان فرهنگی و سیاسی اشاره کرد. برخی از نویسندگان شرکت‌کننده در این شعرخوانی/ سخنرانی- هم در آن زمان و هم بعداً- گناه سیاسی‌شدن آن نشست‌ها را به گردن شعرخوانی‌ی سعید سلطان‌پور گذاشته‌اند. گرچه حمله به رژیم شاه و نمادهای ایدئولوژیک برای انقلاب و حکومت آینده در شعرهای سعید سلطان‌پور و برخی از جمله‌هائی که در میانه‌ی شعرخوانی بیان کرد، به گونه‌ای مستقیم و آشکار بیان شد، اما با مرور متن سخنرانی‌ها و شعرهای این ده شب، در می‌یابیم که اعتراض و افشاگری (به گونه‌های مختلف) وجه اشتراک در سخن همه‌ی نویسندگان شرکت‌کننده بوده است. کما این که اسماعیل خوئی (یکی از شرکت‌کنندگان)، سی و پنج سال بعد در فیلم مستندی که شمیم دوستدار تهیه کرد، می‌گوید: «اگر قرار بود این ده شبِ ما، پانزده شب باشد، فاجعه‌ای حتماً پیش می‌آمد.»[۷۲۷] حتا اگر سخنان هیچ یک از سخنرانانِ آن ده شب را نشنیده باشیم، از همین سخن پیداست که مسئله‌ی اعتراض و افشاگری، به سعید سلطان‌پور منحصر نبود. دکتر بکر در فیلم یادشده به «اضطراب و هیجانی که در فضا بود» و به انبوه شنوندگان اشاره می‌کند و می‌گوید: «خیلی‌هاشان داشتند اشک می‌ریختند.» او در جای دیگری از این مستند می‌گوید: «من البته فارسی‌ام خیلی خوب نبود و خوب نمی‌فهمیدم. دستیارم در گوشم گفت آقای بکر، دارند ضد رژیم حرف می‌زنند. [...] من چنین چیزی را قبلاً تجربه نکرده بودم. من در آن ده شب، هشت کیلو وزن کم کردم.» از گزارش‌های مربوط به آن «ده شب» چنین برمی‌آید که با اوج‌گیری‌ی لحن اعتراض نسبت به خفقان و شرایط سیاسی حاکم بر ایران در سخنرانی‌ها و شعرها، تعداد شنوندگان و مخاطبان این «شب‌ها» فزونی گرفته بود. و این بدان معناست که افزون بر پیشاهنگان فرهنگی، مردم تحصیل‌کرده و طبقه‌ی متوسط

---

۷۲۵ صادق زیباکلام، ***مقدمه‌ای بر انقلاب اسلامی***، تهران: انتشارات روزنه، ۱۳۸۰، صص ۲۱۹ تا ۲۲۰.

۷۲۶ صادق زیبا کلام، پیشین، صص ۲۲۳ تا ۲۲٤.

۷۲۷ شمیم دوستدار، ***ده شب گوته، روایت یک رویداد فرهنگی‌ی مهم***، تارنمای «بی بی سی»، ۱۷ اوت ۲۰۱۲/ ۲۷ مرداد ۱۳۹۱: http://www.bbc.co.uk/persian/arts/2012/08/120817_10nights_tamasha.shtml

ایران تشنه‌ی مقابله با رژیم شاه بودند. در این جا نیز باید به یک استثناء اشاره کنم: با این که برخی از شخصیت‌های شرکت‌کننده در آن «ده شب»، با سیاسی کردن این جلسه‌ها موافق نبودند،و با این که باقر پرهام اعتراض کرده بود که «ما قرار نبود در این جا میتینگ راه بیاندازیم»، اما فقط بهرام بیضائی بود که در سخنرانی‌ی خود (با عنوان «نظارت نامرئی») به ریشه‌ی فرهنگی‌ی فاجعه نیز اشاره کرد؛ نویسندگان و هنرمندان ایرانی را «پروژه‌های ناتمام» نامید؛ و ضمن اشاره‌های مستقیم به «دستگاه نظارتِ» دولتی، ذهنیت فرهنگی‌ی مردم را نیز- که «چهره‌های مشخص ندارن و نمی‌دونیم با کی طرفیم»- در این ناتمامیت دخیل دانست؛ و گفت که ما در طول تاریخ «دسته دسته، همدیگر رو در برابر هم و در برابر مهاجمان تنها گذاشته‌ایم.» اما، هشدار تکان‌دهنده‌ی او در تپش تبدار سخنرانان و مخاطبان آن «شب‌ها» و شب‌ها و شب‌های دیگر تحلیل رفت، و در صحنه‌ی جنگِ خیر و شّر، «مردم» با «چهره‌های مشخص» و «نامشخص» ماندند و حاکمیت شاه.[۷۲۸]

هنوز فریاد سعید سلطانپور که: «سلام، شکستگان سال‌های سیاه! تشنگان آزادی!» و، «دیگر ببار، ببار ای خشم»، از باغ انستیتو گوته در سپهر سیاسی‌ی ایران جاری بود، که هزاران دانشجو و دانش‌آموخته‌ی کنفدراسیون و نویسندگان و هنرمندان تبعیدی، در واپسین سفر رسمی‌ی شاه و شهبانو به امریکا (۱۵ نوامبر ۱۹۷۷ برابر با آبان ۱۳۵۶)، در محوطه‌ی بیرونی‌ی کاخ سفید، جلو دوربین رسانه‌های جهان، با شعارهای خود از شاه ایران اعتبارزدائی کردند. پس از اوجگیری‌ی نافرمانی‌های شاه بود که پیگیری‌ی سازمان ملل در مورد نقض حقوق بشر در ایران، اوج گرفت، و سند بود که پشت سند در این زمینه منتشر شد، و رسانه‌های امریکائی یکی پس از دیگری نخبگان تبعیدی‌ی ما را به گفت‌وگو فراخواندند؛ و یکی پس از دیگری شاه را با عنوان «دیکتاتور فاسد» و «خون‌آشام قرن» شناسائی کردند (همان رسانه‌هائی که، زیر پوشش «تفاوت فرهنگ‌ها»ی پست مدرنیسم، سی و چهار سال است در برابر نقض آشکار «حقوق بشر» در جمهوری‌ی اسلامی سکوت کرده‌اند)؛ تا برسد به هلهله و هورای رسانه‌های غربی پیرامون آیت‌الله خمینی، که حالا از عراق به پاریس منتقل شده بود؛[۷۲۹] تا برسد به کنفرانس گوادولوپ، و رأیِ سران کشورهای غربی به حذف شاه و حمایت

---

[۷۲۸] برای آگاهی از متن سخنرانی‌ها و شعرها و شیوه‌ی برگزاری «ده شب شعر گوته» به منابع زیر رجوع کنید:

- ❖ کتاب ***ده شب: شب‌های شاعران و نویسندگان در انجمن فرهنگی‌ی ایران- آلمان،*** به همت ناصر مؤذن، تهران: انتشارات امیرکبیر، ۱۳۵۷. این کتاب شامل متن همه‌ی سخنرانی‌ها و شعرخوانی‌ها است.
- ❖ گیتی مهدوی، با استفاده از نوارهای ضبط شده‌ی آن شب‌ها- که از سوی مؤسسه‌ی نابینایان رودکی در اختیارش گذاشته شده بود- فایل شنیداری‌ی هشت شب از ده شب را با عنوان ***ده شب شعر در انستیتو گوته مهر ماه ۵٦*** در تارنمای «کتابخانه‌ی گویا» در اختیار همگان گذاشت:

http://ketabkhaneyegooya.blogspot.com/2010/02/blog-post.html

برای آگاهی از جزئیات برگزاری‌ی این شب‌ها به مأخذ زیر مراجعه کنید:

- ❖ مسعود نقره کار، **بخشی از تاریخ جنبش روشنفکری‌ی ایران: بررسی‌ی تاریخی- تحلیلی‌ی کانون نویسندگان ایران**، جلد دوم، سوئد: نشر باران، ۲۰۰۲ (۱۳۸۱).
- ❖ به عنوان نمونه از جستارهای تحلیلی/ جامعه‌شناختی‌ای که پیرامون متن‌های نویسندگان و شاعران ده شب نوشته شده، به جستار زیر مراجعه کنید:
- ❖ ناصر پاکدامن، ***ده شب شعر: بررسی و ارزیابی‌ی یک تجربه***، نشریه‌ی «کنکاش»، چاپ امریکا، دفتر ۱۲، پائیز ۱۳۷٤، صص ۱۲۵ تا ۱۷۰.

[۷۲۹] در اواخر تابستان سال ۱۳۵۷ با اوجگیری‌ی انقلاب، و به درخواست دولت شاه، رژیم عراق آیت‌الله خمینی را از عراق اخراج کرد. گزینه‌ی آیت‌الله خمینی این بود که ابتدا زمینی به کویت برود و از آن جا از طریق هوائی راهی‌ی سوریه شود. اما دولت کویت، با این که به او ویزا داده بود، از ورود او به خاک کویت جلوگیری کرد. این موضوع سبب شد که آیت‌الله خمینی به فرانسه برود. در آن زمان ایرانیان برای ورود به فرانسه نیاز به ویزای توریستی نداشتند. با این همه درخواست سفر آیت‌الله خمینی از قبل به دولت فرانسه اعلام شد و این درخواست تا سطح رئیس جمهور فرانسه بالا رفت. رئیس جمهور و دولت فرانسه از شاه و دولت ایران در این زمینه نظر خواستند. گفته می‌شود که رئیس جمهور فرانسه شخصاً سفیر فرانسه در ایران را برای ملاقات شاه به کاخ نیاوران فرستاد. درخواست سفر و اقامت آیت‌الله در فرانسه مورد موافقت شخص شاه ایران و نخست وزیر او (جعفر شریف امامی) قرار گرفت. با این مقدمه دولت فرانسه مجوز و امکانات برای ورود آیت‌الله خمینی را به فرانسه فراهم آورد. تصمیم شاه برای تقاضای اخراج آیت‌الله خمینی از عراق و در مرحله‌ی بعد موافقت شاه برای اقامت آیت‌الله خمینی در فرانسه را باید یکی بزرگترین اشتباه‌ها و گاف‌های سیاسی شاه در نظر گرفت. اقامت در فرانسه سبب شد که آیت‌الله خمینی از انزوای عراق خارج شده و در مرکز خبر دنیا ساکن شود. به این صورت او که قبلاً در عراق به قلعه رفته بود با حرکت سفر به فرانسه در قلبگاه شطرنج سیاسی ایران قرار گرفت. به این ترتیب از ۱۲ مهر سال ۱۳۵۷ (۸ اکتبر ۱۹۷۸) آیت‌الله خمینی از عراق به فرانسه رفت و چند روز بعد هم در شهرک نوفل‌لوشاتو در نزدیکی پاریس اقامت کرد. **توضیح:** این یاداشت، فشرده‌ای است از نوشته‌ی سحاب سپهری:

از آیت‌الله خمینی؛ تا برسد به ورود مخفیانه‌ی ژنرال هویزر امریکائی به ایران؛ تا برسد به تیتر درشت «شاه رفت» در روزنامه‌های ایران؛ تا برسد به تیتر درشت «امام آمد»؛ تا برسد به دیدار و بیعت همافران نیروی هوائی با آیت‌الله خمینی؛ تا برسد به قیام همافران (در مرکز آموزش‌های هوائی در پادگان دوشان تپه در شرق تهران) در برابر گارد شاهنشاهی؛ تا برسد به افتادن انبار اسلحه و تانک‌های گارد به دست همافران، سازمان‌های سیاسی، و مردم معمولی؛[۷۳۰] تا برسد به امضای بیانیه‌ی «بی‌طرفی‌ی ارتش» از سوی ژنرال‌های ارتش ایران؛ تا برسد به صدای گوینده‌ای از رادیو و تلویزیون دولتی‌ی ایران، که: «این صدای انقلاب ایران است»؛ تا برسد به تحققِ هشدارِ بهرام بیضائی، که: «ما، دسته دسته، همدیگر رو در برابر هم و در برابر مهاجمان تنها می‌گذاریم».

***

محمدرضا شاه پهلوی و شهبانو فرح پهلوی، روز ۲۶ دی ماه ۱۳۵۷ از ایران به مصر پرواز کردند. سرهنگ بهزاد معزی، خلبان اختصاصی‌ی شاه همراه با کارکنان هواپیما، با رضایت و به توصیه‌ی شاه به ایران بازگشتند، اما آوارگی‌ی شاه و شهبانویش که تازه آغاز شده بود، هجده ماه، تا زمان مرگ شاه، ادامه یافت. امریکا، بریتانیا، فرانسه، اتریش، و حتا اردن، او را نپذیرفتند. شاه و همسرش بعد از مصر، به مراکش رفتند (که پس از ده هفته عذرشان را از آن جا هم خواستند)؛ با پا در میانی‌ی دوستان امریکائی‌ی شاه، یازده هفته در باهاماس زندگی کردند، و هفده هفته در مکزیک. در مکزیک بود که بیماری‌ی سرطان شاه شدت گرفت، و پزشکان معالج او عمل جراحی را لازم دیدند، و به او توصیه کردند که به امریکا برود. رئیس جمهور امریکا، پس از مذاکرات پی در پی و طولانی با مشاورانش، با اکراه، و فقط برای معالجه به او اجازه‌ی ورود داد. به محض ورود شاه به امریکا، سفارت امریکا در «جمهوری‌ی اسلامی‌ی ایران» اشغال شد، و کارکنان و دیپلمات‌های این سفارتخانه به وسیله‌ی «دانشجویان خط امام» به گروگان گرفته شدند. شاه، به دستور رئیس جمهور امریکا (جیمی کارتر)، از بیمارستانی در نیویورک، به بیمارستان نیروی هوائی‌ی ایالات متحده در شهر «سن‌آنتونیو» در ایالت تگزاس، منتقل شد، و پس از دو هفته اقامت در آن مرکز (جمعاً ده هفته در امریکا)، به پاناما منتقل شد. خواستِ ناگزیر شاه این بود که به مکزیک مراجعت کند، اما مکزیک نیز این بار او را نپذیرفت. انور سادات، رئیس جمهور مصر، از او دعوت کرد که برای اقامت و معالجه به مصر برود. شاه روزهای پایانی‌ی عمرش را در مصر و در بستر بیماری گذراند؛ در تاریخ ۲۷ ژوئیه ۱۹۸۰/ ۵ مرداد ۱۳۵۹ در همان جا درگذشت؛ و در همان جا به خاک سپرده شد. فرح پهلوی ماجراهای این آوارگی‌ی عینی و ذهنی را در کتاب «کهن دیارا: خاطرات فرح پهلوی» به کمال بازنموده است؛ و شاه نیز پیش از مرگش کتاب «پاسخ به تاریخ» را به زبان فرانسه نوشت، که به زودی به زبان انگلیسی نیز ترجمه شد.[۷۳۱] او در این کتاب، به هیچ یک از خطاهای تاریخی‌ی خود در دوران سلطنت اشاره نکرد؛ منش و کنش خود را در سقوط خود دخیل ندانست؛ و هنوز باور داشت که «آن‌ها» (یعنی مردم) او را «دوست دارند»؛ منتها، با پشتوانه‌ی دلایلی که ارائه داد، دولت‌های غربی و به ویژه امریکا را مسبب سقوط خود شناسائی کرد. فرح پهلوی نیز افزون بر آن

❖ سحاب سپهری، ***سه روز تاریخ ساز، بیست تا بیست و دو بهمن ۵۷***، بخش ۱، تارنمای «رادیو زمانه»، ۱۱ مرداد ۱۳۸۹:
http://radiozamaneh.com/specials/revolution/2011/01/25/1178

۷۳۰ ***مصاحبه‌ی پیام فدائی با یکی از دانشجویان خلبانی در زمان قیام بهمن ۵۷ در تهران***، به نقل از نشریه‌ی «پیام فدائی»، ارگان چریک‌های فدائی‌ی خلق ایران، شماره‌ی ۱۱۶، بهمن ماه ۱۳۸۷، برگرفته از تارنمای «سیاهکل»:
http://www.siahkal.com/index/mid-col/PF116-Mosahebeh-ba-Morteza-Ansari-1.htm

۷۳۱ نخستین مترجم کتاب «پاسخ به تاریخ» به زبان فارسی، شناخته شده نیست. حسین ابوترابیان، مترجمی که این کتاب را در ایران به انتشار سپرد، در «پیش‌گفتار» آن نوشته است: «در خاطرات احمدعلی مسعود انصاری، با نام "من و خاندان پهلوی"، چنین آمده است: "وقتی شاه در مکزیک به سر می‌برد، دکتر سیدحسین نصر و دکتر هوشنگ نهاوندی برای ترجمه‌ی کتاب "پاسخ به تاریخ" به مکزیک فراخوانده شدند. بنا بود دکتر هوشنگ نهاوندی ترجمه‌ی فارسی‌ی کتاب، و دکتر حسین نصر آن را به انگلیسی ترجمه کند.» به مآخذ زیرنگاه کنید:

❖ محمد رضا پهلوی، ***پاسخ به تاریخ***، ترجمه‌ی حسین ابوترابیان، تهران: ناشر: مترجم، ۱۳۷۱، ص ١٤.

❖ احمدعلی مسعود انصاری، ***من و خاندان پهلوی***، کالیفرنیا: انتشارات توکا، ۱۹۹۲، ص ۱۳۹.

چه که در این زمینه در کتابش نوشته، در گفت‌وگوهای پرشماری که در سی و پنج سال گذشته با رسانه‌های ایرانی و غیرایرانی داشت، همواره این گزاره را تأیید کرد، و حتا مرگ شاه را در اثر بی‌توجهی‌های پزشکی، برآمده از فضای سیاسی‌ی علیه او برآورد کرد. این جاست که سخن دکتر محمد مصدق، در ذهن مخاطب این متن‌ها، بی‌اختیار، جان می‌گیرد که در دادگاه نظامی گفته بود:

> می‌خواستم هدف ملت ایران پیش برود و کشور ایران همان مقامی را که داشته، مجدداً به دست آورد؛ می‌خواستم شاه بر مملکتی سلطنت کند که در اعداد ملل مستقل و آزاد دنیا باشد؛ و اگر روزی به شاه گفتند برو، بگوید نمی‌روم.

چرا که دکتر محمد مصدق- به سبب درک انقلاب مشروطه، خدمت در استانداری‌های فارس و آذربایجان، شرکت در کابینه‌ی سیدضیاءالدین طباطبائی، در جریان «رفتنِ» قاجارها، آمدن و «رفتنِ» رضا شاه پهلوی- بسی بیش‌تر از محمدرضا شاه پهلوی به این واقعیت آگاه بود که گرچه ایران به ظاهر «مستعمره» نشد، اما تا بن دندان زیر نفوذ استعمارگرانی بود که به آسانی «به شاه» می‌گویند «برو»؛ و دستورشان هم برو/ برگرد نداشت؛ و خود در صدد بود تا جای ممکن به این نفوذ پایان دهد.

جمع‌بندی

دو پادشاه خاندان پهلوی، پیش از آن که «قدرت سیاسی» باشند، «ایرانی» بودند، و از زمره‌ی «بیدارشدگان»، و پیکارگران با عقب‌ماندگی‌ی ایران نیز برشمرده می‌شوند. رضا شاه پهلوی و جانشین او- محمدرضا شاه پهلوی- پس از دست‌یابی به قدرت سیاسی، با آرزوی تجدید عظمت و قدرت ایران، با پل زدن بین فرهنگ و تمدن ایران باستان و تمدن جهانِ «مدرن»، بر آن بودند که ایران را با هویتی که برای ایرانی‌ی زمان هخامنشیان می‌شناختند، به پای جهان امروز برسانند، و حتا آن را دوباره بر فراز جهان بنشانند. منتها به شرطی که خود و خاندانشان، با همان قدرتِ مطلق و ثروت افسانه‌ای شاهان هخامنشی، بر رأس این قله نشسته باشند. این شرط ناگفته، به رغم کوشش‌ها و کنش‌های مترقی‌ی آن‌ها در قلمرو نوسازی‌ی ساختارهای دولتی/ نظامی/ اجتماعی/ فرهنگی/ اقتصادی‌ی ایران، خط فاصلی پررنگ شد بین آن‌ها- به عنوان «قدرت سیاسی»- و «پیکارگران»؛ حتا با پیکارگرانی که با «هویت شناسی»ی ناسیونالیستی‌ی این دو پادشاه همسو بودند. نمودهای عملی‌ی همین شرطِ ناگفته و نیمه‌نوشته، یعنی، اعمال دیکتاتوری‌ی بلامنازع رضا شاه پهلوی، راه نفس را بر جنبش‌های اجتماعی‌ی حوالی‌ی مشروطیت بست، و آن همه جوشش و تمنای ایرانی برای رشد را متوقف کرد. این فرمان ایست سبب شد که شجاعانه‌ترین و نوترین دستاوردهای او - مثلاً «کشف حجابِ زن» (۱۷ دی ۱۳۱۴) - به گونه‌ای اجباری و به زور پلیس اجرا شود؛ همان شرط ناگفته و نیمه‌نوشته سبب شد که این دو پادشاه، نه تنها پیکارگرانِ بینش‌های متفاوت و حرکت‌های آزادی‌خواهانه و حق‌طلبانه‌ی روشنفکران مردمی و مدافعان لایه‌های تهی‌دستِ جامعه را سرکوب کنند، بلکه بسیاری از باستان‌گرایان را هم- به صِرف هر نوع مخالفتی با یکه تازی‌های خود- با اعدام و زندان از سر راه خود بردارند؛ مخصوصاً اگر شعور و درایتی بالاتر از خودشان در آن‌ها تشخیص می‌دادند. بدین ترتیب بود که این دو آرزومندِ «آبادانی و سربلندی‌ی ایران»، انبوه روشنفکران آزادی‌خواه و عدالت‌جو، و نیز، انبوه تهی‌دستان و محرومانِ مادی و معنوی‌ی جامعه‌ی عقب‌مانده‌ی ایران را از تصویر آرزوئی‌ی آن «آبادانی و سربلندی» بیرون گذاشتند؛ ۳۸۷
و بدین ترتیب بود که این دو پادشاه، نام خود را به عنوان دو مستبد، در تاریخ معاصر ایران به ثبت رسانیدند؛ و آن چنان ژرف به ثبت رسانیدند که پیش و بیش از آن که کوشش‌ها و کنش‌های انکارناپذیرشان برای نو کردن ایران و ساختن «ایران آباد و سربلند» به یاد آید، نام آن‌ها مفهوم «دیکتاتور» را به ذهن آزادی‌خواهان و آزاداندیشان ایران و جهان متبادر می‌کند. از چشم‌اندازی آسیب‌شناختی می‌توان دید که شناخت و بازتعریفی که این دو پادشاه از «هویت ایرانی»، از «جهان کنونی»، از «علل عقب ماندن ایران از جهان معاصر»، از «راهکار همپاشدن با جهان»، و از مفهوم‌های «آبادانی و سربلندی» داشتند، بر رسوبی از کهن‌ترین الگوهای فرهنگ ایرانی، یعنی همان «شهریار الاهی» روئیده بود. به بیانی دیگر- صرف نظر از سدّ سکندر «علمای دینی» که همواره در برابر پدیده‌های نو می‌ایستاد- هم ترازوی سنجشِ کهنه و نو، و هم زمینه‌ی رویش اندیشه‌های نو در ذهنیت خودِ این دو پادشاه، از ژرفترین لایه‌های فرهنگ «دین- مذهب- دولت» و تبعات آن آب می‌خورد. «رضا خان سردار سپه»، پیش از رسیدن به مقام پادشاهی، در روزهای تاسوعا و عاشورا، به رسم عزاداری، کاه به سر می‌ریخت و جلو صف سربازان ارتش به راه می‌افتاد. در ذهنیت مذهبی‌ی رضا شاه پهلوی همین بس که، در روز ۱۷ دی ۱۳۱۴، روز اعلام «کشف حجاب»، در حالی که همسر و دو دختر او - با

لباس‌های سراپا پوشیده و با کلاه- در کنارش نشسته‌اند، و آماده‌اند که همراه او برای نخستین بار بدون چادر و چاقچور و روبنده در میان مردم ظاهر شوند، می‌گوید: «مرگ برای من آسان‌تر و گواراتر است از این که دست زنم و دخترانم را در حالی که بی‌حجاب هستند بگیرم و با هم از میان جمعیت عبور کنیم.»[۷۳۲] محسن نجات حسینی، عضو سابق سازمان مجاهدین خلق ایران، فشرده‌ی هولناکی از همین حس ناگوار در مردانِ مذهبیِ آن زمان ایران را در خاطراتش تصویر کرده است. او در شرح حال و شخصیت «آقای حیدری»، ناظم دبستان خود، از قول مادربزرگش می‌نویسد:

> بی بی جان می‌گفت وقتی در زمان رضا شاه، کشف حجاب شده بود، پدر آقای حیدری ترکه‌ای در دست می‌گرفت و در کوچه و بازار، هر جائی زنی را بی‌حجاب یا با چادر و بی‌مقنعه می‌دید، با ترکه‌اش «حیدر حیدر»گویان، بر سر آن زن می‌کوبید و می‌گفت: «پرده‌ی خلا را بیانداز!» به همین خاطر، آن خانواده که به حیدری شهرت یافته بود، در مشهد بسیار معروف و در محافل مذهبی بسیار گرامی بود. پدرم در هاله‌ی شهرت این خانواده، به آقای حیدری‌ی ناظم ارادت پیدا کرده بود و تربیت من و برادرم را به او سپرد.[۷۳۳]

این «ناظم»، این ناظمِ «سه قطره خون»، این «ناظمِ» درونی/ بیرونی، ناظر بر ذهنیت رضا شاه پهلوی نیز بود، و افزون بر شرکت در «عزاداریِ عاشورا» و حس «ناگوارِ» دیدن زن و دخترانش بدون روبنده، نمود دیگر آن نیز بی‌اعتنائیِ او نسبت به حقی بود که در گوشه و کنار ایران به طور مداوم از «اقلیت‌های مذهبی» باطل می‌شد. به عنوان نمونه، پادشاهی که با نظم آهنین خود بر فرمانداران و مجریان سراسر کشور تسلطی بی‌چون و چرا داشت، نسبت به کشتاری که در سال‌های ۱۳۰۶ و ۱۳۰۸ از بهائیان شهرهای ایران شد، بی‌تفاوت ماند؛ و در سال ۱۳۱۷ آموزشگاه‌های ارمنی‌ها و آشوری‌ها را تعطیل کرد. (با این که ارمنی‌ها نیز مانند زرتشیان و یهودیان در مجلس شورای ملی نماینده داشتند.) رضا شاه پهلوی با همه‌ی شهرت به «آخوندستیزی»، به ساختار و منابع مالیِ روحانیت (از جمله، خمس و ذکاة) دست نبرد. و از آن رو که بازاریان مهم‌ترین نیروهای تأمین‌کننده‌ی منابع مالی برای روحانیت بودند، رابطه‌ی تنگاتنگ روحانیت و بازار را دست‌نخورده باقی گذاشت. در سال ۱۳۱۰ (یعنی همان سالی که مجلس شورای ملی قانون ممنوعیت فعالیت در جهت «مرام اشتراکی» را تصویب کرد)، مجلس چهارم، دو متمم نیز به قانون مطبوعات افزود، که در ماده‌ی اول آن می‌خوانیم:

> [...] عموم مدیران جراید و با مجلات و ارباب مطابع باید ملتزم شوند که هر وقت بخواهند در امور مربوط به دین اسلام و مذهب، اصولاً و فروعاً انشائاً و یا نقلاً ولو هزلاً چیزی طبع کنند، قبلاً به ناظر شرعیات که خبرویّت او توسط دو نفر مجتهد جامع‌الشرایط تصدیق و از طرف وزارت معارف در تهران و در هر یک از مراکز ایالات و ولایات معرفی شده باشد، مراجعه نمایند تا مداقه نماید؛ پس از آن که عدم مضربودنِ آن به دین اسلام و مذهب کتباً تصدیق شد، طبع و نشر کنند.[۷۳۴]

از این‌ها فراتر- به گزارش یرواند آبراهامیان- رضا شاه پهلوی، روحانیانی را که از عراقِ تحت سلطه‌ی انگلستان به ایران گریخته بودند، در قم پناه داد.(دهه‌ی نخستِ ۱۳۰۰ خورشیدی) همین روحانیان بودند که به تدریج، مکتب‌خانه‌ها و

---

[۷۳۲] جلال متینی این جمله را از «دکتر محمد باهری» نقل می‌کند، که او نیز این سخنان را از «ملکه پهلوی» (همسر رضا شاه) شنیده است. به مأخذ زیر نگاه کنید:

❖ جلال متینی، ***هفدهم دی ماه ۱۳۱۴***، فصل‌نامه‌ی «ایران‌شناسی»، سال دهم، شماره‌ی ٤، زمستان ۱۳۷۷، ص ٦٨١.

[۷۳۳] محسن نجات حسینی، ***بر فراز خلیج***، تهران: نشر نی، ۱۳۷۹، ص ۱۷.

[۷۳٤] ***مطبوعات عصر پهلوی به روایت اسناد ساواک؛ کتاب اول: مجله‌ی تهران مصور***، تهران: مرکز بررسی‌ی اسناد تاریخی‌ی وزارت اطلاعات، ۱۳۷۹، ص ده.

مدرسه‌های دینی را به حوزه‌ی علمیه‌ی قم تبدیل کردند، و با دریافت «سهم امام» از مردم و به ویژه بازاریان، مؤسسات خود را- «شاید برای نخستین بار، در سراسر ایران» ساختند و سلسله مراتب آموزشی‌ی خود را، اعم از «واعظ معمولی، حجت‌الاسلام، آیت‌الله، آیت‌الله عظما، و مجتهد» در ایرانِ «مدرن» بنا نهادند.[۷۳۵] به فرمان همین ذهنیت است که محمدرضا شاه پهلوی نیز از آیت‌الله بروجردی تقاضا کرد که در جلوگیری از نشر «نشریات مضرِ به اسلام» او را یاری دهد.

به شهادت تاریخ، رضا شاه پهلوی و فرزندش، که رسالت مدرنیزه کردن ایران و استقرار یک حکومت سکولار را پذیرفته بودند، نه تنها کارکرد کهن‌الگوهای فرهنگی را در بازشناسی‌های خود ندیدند، بلکه این واقعیت آشکار را هم ندیدند که برای پالایش ذهنیت مردم از بینش اسطوره‌ای و از باورهای پیش‌مدرن، به جای زندان و شکنجه و کشتار، نیازمند نهادهای مدنی، حزب‌های سیاسی، و روشنگران تاریخ فکر و فلسفه هستند. این ندیدن، یا دیدن وُ باور نکردن، با خودکامگی و قدرت‌طلبی‌ی این دو ایرانی‌ی به قدرت رسیده دست به دست هم دادند، و سیاست‌گذاری‌های آن دو را رقم زدند. بازتاب‌های عملی‌ی این پیوند نامبارک، انگیزه‌ای شد برای آشکارتر شدنِ بینشی که در کشاکش انقلاب مشروطیت زیر نام «قانون مشروعه» بروز کرده بود. با خیزش مجدد این بینش، که عمدتاً در زمان محمدرضا شاه پهلوی در میان پیکارگران مذهبی نمودهای عینی یافت، کلاف رویاروئی‌ها از آن چه بود شوریده‌تر شد. در فرایند این رویاروئی‌ها بود که تعریف هویت، تعریف هدف، و تعریف روش مبارزه، به تدریج رنگی دیگر گرفت. به گونه‌ای که، اگر ملت ایران در سال ۱۲۸۵ خورشیدی (۱۳۲۴ قمری/ ۱۹۰۶ میلادی) با به کرسی نشاندن «قانون مشروطه»‌ای نیم‌بند، نماینده‌ی «قانون مشروعه» (شیخ فضل‌الله نوری) را به «دار» آویخت، هفتاد و دو سال بعد- یعنی در انقلاب ۱۳۵۷- با اعتماد بر سنتی‌ترین نماد اسلام شیعی به عنوان «رهبر مبارزه»، دانسته یا نادانسته، بر «نعش آن بزرگوارِ بر فراز دار» نماز گزارد.[۷۳۶] تا جائی که تاریخ صد و پنجاه سال گذشته نشان می‌دهد، می‌توان دید که چند نیروی ذهنی و عینی- دست در دست هم- این فرایند را تحقق بخشیدند: نیروی ذهنی‌ی آن، باورهای ژرف مردم ایران و از جمله روشن‌ترین پیکارگران ما بود به آموزه‌های نهادینه‌شده‌ی مذهبی و مفهوم «شهریار الاهی». و نیروهای عینی‌ی آن، عمدتاً عبارت بودند از: ۱) خفقان سیاسی، و توقف جوششی که در حوالی‌ی مشروطیت، برای درک و فهم جهان تازه، جامعه‌ی ایران را فراگرفته بود. ۲) قانون اساسی‌ی «مشروطه»، که نطفه‌های «قانون مشروعه» یا «حکومت اسلامی» را هفتاد سال در نهفت خود، و در نهفت قوانین قضائی و جزائی پنهان داشت،[۷۳۷] و با دستِ گشوده‌ای که به مثلثِ روحانیت، دربار، و بازار داد، هفتاد سال

---

[735] Ervand Abrahamian, ***Radical Islam, The Iranian Mojahedin***, London: I.B. Tauris & Co Ltd., 1989, pp. 18-19.

[۷۳۶] «نعش آن بزرگوار»، عبارتی است از جلال آل احمد درباره‌ی شیخ فضل‌الله نوری. جلال آل احمد (۱۳۰۲- ۱۳۴۸)، نویسنده، مترجم، و پیکارگری بود که پس از بریدن از خانواده‌ی روحانی‌ی خود، عضو حزب توده (با بینش طبقاتی) شد، و از حزب توده، به «نیروی سوم»، یعنی به بینش «ایران اسلامی» پیوست، و از آن جا نیز به بینش «مکتب اسلام» روی آورد. کتاب «غربزدگی»‌ی او (۱۳۴۱)، مورد توجه آیت‌الله خمینی در تبعید قرار گرفت، از مریدان سرسخت آیت‌الله خمینی شد، و کتاب «در خدمت و خیانت روشنفکران» (۱۳۴۷) را به گفته‌ی خودش در مقدمه‌ی کتاب، «به انگیزه‌ی خونی که در ۱۵ خرداد ۱۳۴۲ از مردم تهران ریخته شد»- و البته پس از ملاقات با آیت‌الله خمینی- نوشت. شیخ فضل‌الله نوری است، که در مقابل مشروطه‌خواهان از «قانون مشروعه» دفاع می‌کرد، و از جمله طرفداران و حامیان محمدعلی‌شاه قاجار بود. محمدعلی‌شاه قاجار، مجلس قانونگذاری‌ی نوپای ایران را که به بهای خون صدها تن از ایرانیان آزادی‌خواه دایر شده بود، در تیرماه ۱۲۸۷ خورشیدی به توپ بست، و گروهی از مشروطه‌خواهان و آزادی‌خواهان، از جمله «میرزا جهانگیرخان صوراسرافیل» و «ملک‌المتکلمین» را اعدام کرد. شیخ فضل‌الله نوری، ۱۲ روز پس از «فتح تهران» و تجدید مشروطیت (۲۸ تیرماه ۱۲۸۸ خورشیدی) در دادگاهی به ریاست شیخ ابراهیم زنجانی، روحانی‌ی آزادی‌خواه و اصلاح‌طلب دینی، محکوم به اعدام شد، و روز ۱۰ مرداد ۱۲۸۸ برابر با ۱۳ رجب ۱۳۲۷ قمری (سالروز تولد امام اول شیعیان) در برابر مردم تهران به دار آویخته شد. برای آگاهی‌ی بیش‌تر از این موضوع، به کتاب زیر نگاه کنید:

- ❖ فریدون آدمیت، ***عقاید و آراء شیخ فضل‌الله نوری***، بازچاپ شده در نشریه‌ی مهرگان، امریکا، شماره‌ی ۴، سال دوم، زمستان ۱۳۷۲ (۱۹۹۴).

[۷۳۷] از میان متن‌های فراوانی که وجوه مختلف این فرایند را پژوهیده‌اند، خواننده‌ام را به متن‌های زیر که در تبعید نوشته شده رجوع می‌دهم:

- ❖ ماشاءالله آجودانی، ***مشروطه‌ی ایرانی و پیش‌زمینه‌های نظریه‌ی «ولایت فقیه»***، لندن: انتشارات فصل کتاب، ۱۳۷۶/ ۱۹۹۷ (**توضیح:** در شناسنامه‌ی این کتاب، تاریخ خورشیدی به اشتباه ۱۳۶۷ نوشته شده است.)

با باورهای سنتی و خرافی‌ رو به زوال مردم ایران- یعنی با رشد ذهنی‌ی مردم ایران- مقابله کرد، و به یاری‌ی روش‌شناسی‌ی همان «مثلث»، انقلاب دوم مردم ایران را نیز ناکام باقی گذاشت. فرآورده‌های دوگانه‌ی این ناکامی را در فصل‌ها و بخش‌های آینده‌ی مجموعه‌ی حاضر بررسی می‌کنم. اما همین جا باید یادآور شوم که در نظر گروه عظیمی از نیروهای چپ کنونی‌ی ایران که از چشم‌انداز خوانش ویژه‌ای از مارکسیسم به این دو انقلاب نگاه می‌کنند، ضمن این که هر دو این انقلاب‌ها «ناتمام» برآورد می‌شوند، هیچ یک از این دو انقلاب- به ویژه انقلاب ۵۷- «ناکام» نمانده‌اند. از این منظر، انقلاب مشروطه‌ی ایران خاستگاه «بورژوازی» داشت، و با همه‌ی کاستی‌هایش، شروع دوره‌ی «سرمایه‌داری» (از نوع تجاری‌ی آن) را اعلام کرد، و انقلاب دوم نیز «راه رشد غیرسرمایه‌داری» را گشود، که نظام آن باید حمایت و حفظ شود تا نهایتاً مردم ایران را به انقلاب بعدی و به حکومت پرولتاریا برساند. از تُه توی این دریچه‌ی تنگ است که می‌بینیم، نه تنها پادشاهان پهلوی میراث‌داران به حق **رسوب** فرهنگ موروثی بودند، بلکه بخش عظیمی از پیکارگران ما- نه تنها «راست»هائی مانند علی شریعتی و مهدی بازرگان و عزت‌الله سحابی، بلکه «چپ» نیز- میراث‌دار به حق تز باستانی/ اسلامی‌ی «مذهب انتظار» بوده و هستند. با این ذهنیت، جای شگفتی نیست که مثلاً، نورالدین کیانوری، دبیر کل کمیته‌ی مرکزی‌ی حزب «طراز نوین توده»، خلیل ملکی و دیگر منتقدان این حزبِ «کمونیستی» را- که از آن انشعاب کردند- با اصطلاح مذهبی‌ی «مرتد» شناسائی می‌کند.[۷۳۸] و باز جای شگفتی نیست که احسان طبری، ایدئولوگ حزب توده، ضمن ستایشی شیفته‌وار از استالین، چونان عابدی که معبود خود را «زیارت» کرده باشد، می‌نویسد: «ما استالین پیرشده را می‌دیدیم که در لباس نظامی دقیقه‌ای پیش از دیگران بالای آرامگاه لنین ظاهر می‌شد و ارتش و جمعیت برای او هورا می‌کشیدند و او با تکان دادن انگشتان، به احساس نیمه مذهبی‌ی آنان پاسخ می‌داد.»[۷۳۹]

پایان جلد اول

مارس ۲۰۱۴

اسفند ۱۳۹۲

- ❖ باقر مؤمنی، ***دین و دولت در عصر مشروطیت***، سوئد: نشر باران، چاپ اول: ۱۹۹۳ (۱۳۷۲)، چاپ دوم: ۱۹۹۸ (۱۳۷۷).
- ❖ احمد توکلی، ***مشروطه‌ای که نبود***، امریکا: انتشاراتِ کتابِ پر، ۱۳۷۲ (۱۹۹۳).
- ❖ حمید حمید، ***علما در اعلامیه‌ها***، پیشین.

[۷۳۸] نورالدین کیانوری، ***حزب توده و دکتر محمد مصدق***، تهران: ۱۳۵۷، صفحه‌ی ۱۱، برگرفته از تارنمای «رحمان هاتفی»، بازدید ۱۰ بهمن ۱۳۸۹:

www.rahman-hatefi.net/mossadegh-kia-230-86022.pdf

[۷۳۹] احسان طبری، ***از دیدار خویشتن (یادنامه‌ی زندگی، ۱۳٦۰ - پیش از زندان)***، به کوشش ف. شیوا، سوئد: نشر باران، چاپ دوم، ۱۳۷۹، ص ۱٤۵.

نامنامه

آ

آبراهام بن سولومون ۸۹
آبراهامیان، یرواند ۷۰، ۱۱۴، ۱۵۹،۱۶۴، ۱۸۲، ۱۸۵، ۴۰۸، ۴۰۹، ۴۱۳، ۴۱۴، ۴۱۷، ۴۲۹، ۴۳۶، ۴۳۸، ۴۳۹، ۴۴۱
آجودانی، ماشاءالله ۱۳۰، ۱۵۹، ۱۶۰، ۱۶۳، ۴۵۸
آخوندزاده، فتحعلی ۱۰۷، ۱۰۸، ۱۳۶، ۱۴۲، ۱۴۶، ۱۴۷، ۱۴۸، ۱۶۴، ۲۸۵
آدمیت، فریدون ۱۲۹، ۱۵۹، ۱۶۰، ۱۶۲، ۱۶۴، ۴۱۹، ۴۲۱، ۴۵۸
آذر، مهدی ۲۲۸، ۴۱۵
آذرنگ، عبدالحسین ۴۱۴
آذرنور، فریدون ۴۳۶
آذری، علی ۱۶۶
آرام، بهرام ۳۲۸، ۳۲۹، ۳۳۱، ۳۴۳، ۳۴۴، ۳۴۶، ۴۴۰
آریان، سعید ۱۱۰، ۴۳۱
آرین پور، یحیی ۸
آزاد، گیلدا ۴۴۷
آژنگ، بهمن ۴۳۱
آشوری، داریوش ۱۱۴، ۲۶۸، ۲۶۹، ۲۷۱، ۲۷۵، ۲۸۲، ۲۸۳، ۴۲۰، ۴۲۶، ۴۲۸
آفاری، ژانت ۱۵۹، ۱۶۳، ۱۶۴
آقائی، مسعود ۱۴۱، ۴۲۶
آل احمد، جلال ۲۶۱، ۴۲۱، ۴۲۲، ۴۲۷، ۴۵۷
آلتوسر، لوئی ۴۳۸
آملی، شمس الدین ۱۰۳
آموزگار، ژاله ۵۳، ۱۱۰، ۱۱۲
آوانسیان، آربی ۴۲۴
آیرملو، تاج الملوک ۴۰۲، ۴۴۷
آیرونساید، ادموند (ژنرال) ۱۷۱، ۱۷۷، ۱۷۹، ۱۸۱، ۱۸۶
آیزنهاور، دوایت ۲۰۸، ۳۸۴، ۴۱۱

ا

ابتهاج، هوشنگ ۴۲۰، ۴۲۱
ابراهیم زاده، سیروس ۲۲۲، ۴۱۲
ابن ابی اصیبعه، ۱۱۸
ابن حزم، ابو محمد علی بن احمد ۹۱
ابن سهل، ابو سعد العلاء ۵۷
ابن سینا، ۷۳، ۷۶، ۸۲، ۸۴، ۸۹، ۹۲، ۱۱۲، ۱۱۷، ۱۸۱، ۲۷۷
ابن مقفع، ۶۹
ابن ندیم ۵۴، ۶۹، ۱۱۳، ۱۱۴
ابوترابیان، حسین ۱۸۱، ۴۰۱، ۴۵۲
ابوحاتم رازی، ۹۲، ۱۱۸
ابوریحان بیرونی، ۸۲، ۸۳، ۸۴، ۸۷، ۸۸ ،۹۲، ۱۱۷
ابومسلم، ۷۷
ابومعشر بلخی، ۶۹، ۹۲، ۱۱۳
ابونصر فارابی، ۸۰، ۸۱
اتابکی، تورج ۱۵۹، ۱۷۵، ۱۸۲، ۱۸۵
اتحادیه، منصور ۱۱۵
احسانی، عنایت‌الله ۴۱۹
احمدزاده، مجید ۳۰۱، ۴۳۲
احمدزاده، مسعود ۲۹۱، ۲۹۵، ۲۹۶، ۲۹۷، ۲۹۸، ۲۹۹، ۳۰۰، ۳۰۱، ۳۰۹، ۳۱۰، ۳۴۱، ۳۵۱، ۳۶۰، ۴۳۱، ۴۳۲، ۴۳۴، ۴۳۸، ۴۴۲، ۴۴۳
احمدزاده، مسعود ۲۹۲، ۲۹۵، ۲۹۷، ۲۹۸، ۳۰۱، ۳۰۸، ۳۱۰، ۳۳۱، ۳۳۴، ۳۶۰، ۴۲۹، ۴۳۱، ۴۳۴، ۴۳۸
احمدی روحانی، حسین ۳۲۱، ۳۲۵، ۳۲۶، ۴۳۷، ۴۳۸، ۴۳۹
احمدی نژاد، محمود ۱۲۵، ۴۲۶
احمدی، حمید ۱۸۳
احمدی، رامین ۱۱۹
اخوان ثالث، مهدی ۲۵۵، ۳۳۴، ۴۲۰
اذکائی، پرویز ۸۸، ۱۱۸
ارانی، تقی ۱۷۴، ۱۸۳
اردشیر بابکان، ۵۹، ۱۱۰، ۱۱۲، ۱۱۴
ارسطو، ۱۴، ۲۲، ۴۲، ۴۵، ۷۶، ۸۰، ۸۱، ۸۲، ۸۴، ۸۶، ۸۷، ۹۲، ۱۱۱، ۱۱۶، ۱۱۷، ۲۶۶
ارگانی، عبدالله ۴۰۳
ارمغانی، بهروز ۴۴۵
اَزلی، سِر گُر ۱۶۱
استاذ سیس، ۷۷
استالین، یوسیف (ویساریونویچ جوگاشویلی) ۲۲، ۱۷۴، ۴۰۲، ۴۰۷، ۴۲۰
اسکندری، ایرج ۱۹۳، ۳۱۷، ۴۰۶، ۴۳۶، ۴۳۷
اسماعیل سامانی، ۷۸
افشانی، تقی ۴۳۱
الماسی، نسرین ۷
امانی، الهه ۷
امید، آرمان ۴۱۹
امیر خسروی، بابک ۴۲۰، ۴۳۶
انتظامی، عزت‌الله ۴۱۹

ب

بابک خرمدین ۵۷، ۷۷
بهاردوست، شهلا ۷، ۴۲۹، ۴۳۰، ۴۳۴
بهبهانی، سیمین ۲۵۵
بهرنگی، صمد ۲۵۲، ۲۶۱، ۲۹۲، ۳۴۰، ۴۲۲، ۴۳۱
بهنام، جمشید (دکتر) ۲۵۵
بیجاری، بیژن ۸، ۲۹

پ

پاکدامن، ناصر ۷، ۲۰۱، ۲۰۲، ۲۸۳، ۴۰۵، ۴۰۶، ۴۲۸، ۴۵۱

ت

تنزی، پَت ۸
توکل، عبدالله ۲۵۵

توکلی، حمید ۳۰۱، ۴۳۱
تیره گل، ملیحه ۱، ۳، ۴، ۵، ۹، ۳۲، ۳۵، ۴۰، ۱۱۱، ۱۸۹، ۲۵۹، ۴۲۳، ۴۴۹

ج

جهانگیری، گلرخ ۷

ح

حاج سید جوادی، علی‌اصغر ۲۵۵
حسن‌پور، غفور ۲۹۲

خ

خاکسار، منصور ۷، ۸
خسرو پرویز ساسانی، ۷۸
خلیلی، پیرایه ۷
خیابانی، محمد ۱۵۳، ۱۵۴، ۱۶۵، ۱۶۶، ۱۷۲، ۱۷۳، ۱۸۱، ۲۸۰، ۴۰۴

د

دوامی، خسرو ۷، ۸، ۳۴۸
دهقانی، اشرف ۲۹۱، ۲۹۲، ۲۹۳، ۲۹۴، ۲۹۹، ۳۰۲، ۳۰۵، ۳۰۶، ۳۰۷، ۳۱۱، ۳۱۶، ۳۳۸، ۳۴۰، ۳۴۹، ۳۵۰، ۳۵۶، ۳۵۸، ۳۶۶، ۴۲۲، ۴۲۹، ۴۳۰، ۴۳۱، ۴۳۲، ۴۳۳، ۴۳۴، ۴۳۵، ۴۳۶، ۴۳۹، ۴۴۰، ۴۴۱، ۴۴۳
دهقانی، بهروز ۲۹۲، ۳۴۰، ۴۳۱
دهقانی، روح انگیز ۳۴۰، ۴۳۱

ذ

ذوالانوار، کاظم ۳۲۶، ۳۲۸، ۳۲۹

ر

راسخ، شاپور ۲۵۵
رایت، آذین ۸
رضا شاه پهلوی، ۶، ۲۰، ۱۳۷، ۱۶۱، ۱۶۷، ۱۶۸، ۱۷۳، ۱۷۴، ۱۷۵، ۱۷۶، ۱۷۸، ۱۷۹، ۱۸۰، ۱۸۲، ۱۸۶، ۱۸۷، ۱۸۹، ۱۹۲، ۱۹۵، ۲۰۱، ۲۰۲، ۲۰۳، ۲۱۶، ۲۲۸، ۲۳۲، ۲۳۴، ۲۵۶، ۳۷۶، ۳۷۹، ۳۸۳، ۳۸۴، ۳۹۵، ۴۰۱، ۴۰۷، ۴۲۰، ۴۵۳، ۴۵۴، ۴۵۵
رضائی، رضا ۳۲۸، ۳۲۹، ۴۳۸
روشنگر، مجید ۷، ۸
رهبر، محمد ۴۱۹
رهنما، فریدون ۲۵۵

ز

زرهی، حسن ۷
زید بن علی ۷۷

س

سروش، علی‌اصغر ۲۵۵
سعادتی، کاظم ۳۴۰، ۴۳۱
سلحشور، کوروس ۴۱۹
سنباذ ۷۷
سوالونی، مهدی ۴۳۱

ش

شاملو، احمد ۱۵۱، ۲۵۵، ۳۳۴، ۳۸۰، ۴۲۱، ۴۲۳

ط

طباطبایی، سید جواد ۷۸، ۱۱۶

ص

صدیقی، غلامحسین ۷۷، ۲۱۹، ۲۲۹
صدیقیم، فریبا ۸
صفا، ذبیح الله ۸، ۶۵، ۸۰، ۸۱، ۸۵، ۱۰۲، ۱۰۳، ۱۰۹، ۱۱۲، ۱۱۳، ۱۱۵، ۱۱۶، ۱۱۷، ۱۲۰
صفریان، محمود ۷

ع

عاشورپور، محسن ۴۳۶
عسگری، میرزاآقا ۷

غ

غفاری، فرخ ۲۵۵

ف

فراهانی، بهزاد ۴۱۹
فرخزاد، فروغ ۲۵۵، ۲۶۰، ۲۶۳، ۳۳۴
فرهی، فرهنگ ۷، ۲۵۴، ۴۱۹
فلکی، مناف ۴۳۱

ق

قلیچ خانی، پرویز ۷، ۳۶۶، ۴۳۷، ۴۳۸، ۴۳۹، ۴۴۰
قهرمان، لاله ۷
قیطانچی، الهام ۷

ک

کاردان، علی‌محمد ۲۵۵
کاظمی، منیره ۷

گ

گرگین، ایرج ۲۵۴، ۲۵۵، ۴۱۹
گلوی، غلامرضا ۴۳۱
گوهرزاد، رضا ۷

ل

قهرمان، لاله ۷

م

محب، رباب ۷
محجوب، محمدجعفر ۲۵۵، ۴۱۹
محمدرضا شاه پهلوی، ۶، ۲۰، ۷۹، ۱۶۹، ۱۸۰، ۱۸۳، ۱۸۷، ۱۸۸، ۱۸۹، ۱۹۰، ۱۹۱، ۱۹۴، ۲۰۱، ۲۰۴، ۲۰۶، ۲۰۷، ۲۱۳، ۲۱۸، ۲۳۴، ۲۴۰، ۲۴۸، ۲۵۱، ۲۵۷، ۲۸۴، ۲۸۷، ۲۸۹، ۲۹۰، ۳۱۹، ۳۲۷، ۳۳۴، ۳۶۹، ۳۷۱، ۳۷۶، ۳۸۱، ۳۸۳، ۳۸۵، ۳۸۷، ۳۹۱، ۳۹۲، ۳۹۷، ۴۰۰، ۴۰۱، ۴۰۲، ۴۰۳، ۴۱۵، ۴۱۹، ۴۴۸، ۴۵۳، ۴۵۵، ۴۵۶
مختار، تقی ۷
مزارعی، مهرنوش ۷، ۸
مصدق، محمد (دکتر) ۱۰۷، ۱۷۷، ۱۷۹، ۲۰۷، ۲۰۸، ۲۰۹، ۲۱۱، ۲۱۴، ۲۱۶، ۲۱۸، ۲۱۹، ۲۲۰، ۲۲۲، ۲۲۳، ۲۲۶، ۲۲۷، ۲۲۸، ۲۲۹، ۲۳۰، ۲۳۱، ۲۳۲، ۲۳۳، ۲۳۴، ۲۳۶، ۲۳۷، ۲۳۸، ۲۴۲، ۲۶۹، ۳۸۴، ۴۰۳، ۴۰۷، ۴۰۸، ۴۰۹، ۴۱۰، ۴۱۱، ۴۱۲
مفتاحی، اسدالله ۳۰۱، ۴۳۱
مکی، حسین ۱۶۳، ۱۸۲، ۱۸۴، ۱۸۶، ۲۱۸، ۴۱۳، ۴۱۹
منز، رالی ۸
موسوی، نجمه ۷
مِی، اَلکس ۷
میرافشار، ژیلا ۷
میرآفتابی، مرتضا ۷
میرفطروس، علی ۷۷، ۹۵، ۱۰۱، ۱۰۲، ۱۱۶، ۱۱۹، ۱۲۰، ۱۵۹، ۲۱۸، ۲۱۹، ۴۰۹، ۴۱۰، ۴۱۲

ن

نابدل، علیرضا ۳۰۱، ۴۳۱
ناجی، سهیلا ۷، ۴۲۸
ناجی، ن. ۷
نادرپور، نادر ۲۵۴، ۲۵۵، ۴۱۹، ۴۲۱
نرودا، پابلو ۸
نصر، سیدحسین ۸۸
نعمت، حمید ۴۱۹
نفیسی، مجید ۸
نهاوندی، هوشنگ ۲۵۵، ۴۵۲
نیمایر، کریستوفر ۸

و

وجدی، شاداب ۷

ه

هافکر، باربارا ۷
هنرمندی، حسن ۲۵۵

ی

یعقوب لیث، ۷۶، ۷۸

نشر آفتاب منتشر کرده است:

گذار زنان از سایه به نور / ترجمه: عصمت صوفیه / عباس شکری
روشنایی / شعر / ریتوا لوکانن / برگردان: کیامرث باغبانی
واحه‌ی حیران / شعر: حسن مهدوی‌منش
از این‌سوی جهان / *نامه‌های منصور کوشان*
جادوی کلام / *سخنرانی برندگان نوبل ادبیات: ترجمه: عباس شکری*
حریر، مخمل، بابونه / *رمان: مرجان ریاحی*
سبک‌تر از هوا / *شعر: فارسی، روسی و اوکراینی / آزیتا قهرمان*
در جاده‌های بهار / *شعر / مرجان ریاحی*
همنشین باد و سایه / *شعر / سهراب رحیمی/ برگردان: آزیتا قهرمان*
شهر مرقدی / داستان کوتاه: حسین رحمت
سپنتا / رمان / کوشیار پارسی
Alive and Kiching / مجموعه داستان / ترجمه: امیر مرعشی
سوگ‌رنج‌نامه‌ی شهادت حضرت باب / نمایشنامه / علی رفیعی
داستان‌های غریبِ غربت / مجموعه داستان / محمود فلکی
یک شب بارانی / داستان بلند / م. ب. پگاه
ما ساده‌ایم / شعر / انوشیروان سرحدی
زرافه / رمان / برگردان: زین‌العابدین آذرخش
نامه / داستان کوتاه / مرجان ریاحی
چهل‌تکه / مجموعه داستان / قدسی قاضی‌نور
مرداب عشق و تنفر / رمان / برگردان: مریم علیزاده
ضمیر اول شخص مفرد / شعر / کتایون آذرلی
کادیش برای یک کُس / رمان / برگردان: کوشیار پارسی
Tehran Stories / مجموعه داستان انگلیسی / امیر مرعشی
تو کوچه‌های تهرون / مجموعه شعر / اکبر ذوالقرنین
دندان بی عقل / رمان / مرجان ریاحی
سقفِ بلندِ تنهایی / رمان / حسین رادبوی
دال و مدلول / گفتگو / برگردان: عباس شکری
رنگ و کلمه / شعر و نقشی / قدسی قاضی‌نور
گاهی از سکوت شروع می‌شود / شعر / محمود معتقدی
40 short letters to my wife، نادر ابراهیمی، برگردان: امیر مرعشی
نه سنگی، نه گوری / مجموعه داستان: عشرت رحمان‌پور
کمی پیش از شروع / داستان بلند: مرجان ریاحی
رُهام / رمان: م. ب. پگاه
سفر شگفت‌انگیز مرتاض هندی / رمان: برگردان: کوشیار پارسی
مهلتی بایست تا خون شیر شد / مجموعه مقاله: شهروز رشید
چهل سالگی، Being Forty / رمان: میترا طباطبایی، برگردان: امیر مرعشی
در کوچه‌ی زندگی / رمان: سمیرا شیری‌پور
شعرهای سکوت / مجموعه شعر: منصوره اشرافی
ناسَرآندازان / رمان: ماه‌دوران معیری
نامه‌ها / نامه نگاری: یداله رؤیایی – پرویز اسلامپور
انتظار / مجموعه شعر: اکبر ذوالقرنین
موش و گربه Cats and Mice / شعر طنز / عبید زاکانی / برگردان: امیر مرعشی
سایه باد سکوت باران / گفتگو: عباس شکری
هتل پرابلمسکی / رمان / برگردان: کوشیار پارسی
نامه / رمان: م.ب. پگاه
در جستجوی سبک گمشده / مجموعه مقاله نقد ادبی: کاظم امیری

بیشماران / رمان: کوشیار پارسی
کوچه گلشن / رمان: مرجان ریاحی
کوچ چهارفصل / شعر: سارا زارع سریزدی
سیمپوزیوم / مجموعه داستان: آرش تهرانی
پاییز واژه در بهار / مجموعه مقاله: عباس شکری
دُم جنبانک / مجموعه داستان: علیرضا شاکر
پاییز واژه در کلام / مجموعه جستار: عباس شکری
سنگ‌ها و ستاره‌ها / رمان: م.ب. پگاه
ترانه‌های کوچک خورشید / شعر: زنده‌یاد حسین جوان
سنگ‌ها بسته، سگ‌ها باز / شعر: مصطفی توفیقی
در گستره‌ی زوال / مجموعه مقاله: احمد نوردآموز
چگونه دخترم را فراری دادم / رمان: مهرنوش خرسند
مرگ رنگ در غربت / گفتگو: عباس شکری
ایران خدا ندارد / شعر: فرهاد عزیزی
بر ارتفاع شب / شعر: حسین جوان
تمام جهان قدماگاه بهار بود / شعر-نثر: ایلدا هیوا
نیرنگ / مجموعه داستان: علیرضا شاکر
عروس نخل‌ها / مجموعه داستان: حسن زرهی
پارک جوان / شعر: پُل والری، برگردان: یداله رؤیایی
ماهی در بیابان / مجموعه داستان: حسن زرهی
برای Brain / رمان: م. ب. پگاه
ازدست‌رفته / مجموعه داستان: حسین نوش‌آذر
و سپس آفتاب / شعر: مهرانگیز رساپور (م. پگاه)
زیبایی شکوه حقیقت است / مجموعه نقد ادبی: عباس شکری
عبور گرم تابستان / رمان: محمد عقیلی
بشنو این نی... / پژوهش: محمود کویر
بوی شبدرهای سوخته / رمان: پوران موسوی
کالبد شکافی مرگ / برگردان: الف. رخساریان و ناصر زراعتی
دشت‌های سرد سوئد / شعر: سهراب رحیمی
پنجاه رمان برتر سده‌ی بیستم میلادی / معرفی ۵۰ رمان: یواخیم شول / برگردان: رحمت بنی‌اسدی
ستاره دنباله‌دار / مجموعه داستان: مهرنوش خُرسند
پیامک حوا / شعر: ندا مقدم (ویلا)
کتاب چاکرا / أشو/ ترجمه: شهروز رشید
برایم از آفتابگردان‌ها بگو / شعر: علیرضا شمس
راه و رسم کاسبی / رمان: مرجان ریاحی
داستان‌هایی برای باور نکردن / مجموعه داستان: یانا فوسن / برگردان: جواد طالعی
و من سردم است، من سردم است / شعر: فریده امیری
Talking to the mirror گفتگو با آینه / شعر (فارسی - انگلیسی): امیر مرعشی
این النگوها را کجا می‌برید / شعر: نرگس الیکایی
انتظار / نمایشنامه: علی گزرسز (م. رها)
شکوه کلام / مجموعه نقد و بررسی کتاب : عباس شکری
وابسته و گسسته / مجموعه داستان: شهیره شریف
گفتگو با رضا براهنی / حسن زرهی
کشمکش / داستان کوتاه: علیرضا شاکر
ماه در پیاله / پژوهش شعر حافظ: محمود کویر
شبِ جانان / رمان: کنت هاروف / برگردان: حسن زرهی — بهرام بهرامی
سکوت یک شعر است / شعر: ژاله چگنی
اینجا تنهایی تمام نمی‌شود / مجموعه داستان، فاطمه پوراحمد
روانی / رمان: رابرت بلاک / برگردان: ف. ایروانیان
ارنست همینگوی – سال های کوبا / پژوهش: نوربرتو فوئنتس / برگردان: مهدی مجتهدپور
شگفتی در سر / رمان: اورهان پاموک / برگردان: بهرام بهرامی و حسن زرهی
عصر بی‌شعوری: شعر: امید طوطیان
رُژ لب قرمز / رمان: احمد خلیلی

واژیسم / شعر: نانام
از ترس تا اعتماد / سفرنامه: کریستینا پالتن / دسیره وارن استا تبین / برگردان: س. س. اعتماد
از بی‌راهه به خانه و به خویش / مجموعه مقاله: علی نگهبان
پرده را کنار نزن / رمان: مهری رحمانی
و روزی همه خواهند دانست / نمایشنامه: عباس صفایی
فریادِ زیرِ خاکستر / شعر: حسین رادبوی
راه نرفته / رمان-خاطره: شه‌راز شاکری / پوراندخت امیرافسر
بار دیگر شهری که دوست می‌داشتم / رمان: نادر ابراهیمی / برگردان به انگلیسی: امیر مرعشی
آرش کمانگیر / شعر: سیاوش کسرایی / برگردان به انگلیسی: امیر مرعشی
تتابع اضافات / مجموعه داستان: وحید ضرابی نسب
خانه در ناخانگی / مجموعه مقاله: علی نگهبان
باززایی فرهنگی در ایران / مجموعه مقاله: محمود کویر
آقای ورلاک / رمان: ژوزف کُنراد / برگردان: ف. ایروانیان
عشق و مرگ در ادبیات فارسی / مجموعه مقاله: مجید نفیسی
یادآوری / رمان: پویا خدیش
حکایت‌های فی‌البداهه / مجموعه داستان: حسن نصیری

aftab.publication@gmail.com
info@aftab.pub
www.aftab.pub

Book Identity:

An Account of Persian Literature in Exile 1979-2014

First volume :**Who are we?**

Author**: Maliheh Tirehgol**

Genre: **Research on literature**

*Publisher/ **Aftab Publication, Norway***

*Publication Year / **2020***

*Layout / **Aziz Atai / Mahtab Mohammadi***

*Photo on cover: **Aziz Atai***

*Implementation of Cover / **Nadia Vyshnvska***

ISBN / **978-1-67814-924-6**